THE UNABRIDGED MARK TWAIN

THE UNABRIDGED

MARK TWAIN

Opening Remarks by
Kurt Vonnegut, Jr.

Edited by Lawrence Teacher

Running Press
Philadelphia, Pennsylvania

PRINTED IN THE UNITED STATES OF AMERICA

Canadian representatives: John Wiley & Sons Canada, Ltd.
22 Worcester Road, Rexdale, Ontario M9W 1L1
International representatives: Kaiman & Polon, Inc.
2175 Lemoine Avenue, Fort Lee, New Jersey 07024

20   19   18   17   16
Digit on the right indicates the number of this printing.

Library of Congress Cataloging in Publication Data

Clemens, Samuel Langhorne, 183531910
The Unabridged Mark Twain
I. Title
PZ3.C59Un3   PS1302   813 .4   76–43094
ISBN 0–914294–53–9 library binding
ISBN 0–914294–54–7 paperback

Art direction and cover design by Jim Wilson
Cover illustration by Charles Santore
Cover calligraphy by Peter Ruge
Editorial assistance by Andrew Hoffman

Typography: English Roman, by Type Design Innovations, Philadelphia,
Pennsylvania; composition direction by Joe Hammond
Printed and bound by Port City Press, Baltimore, Maryland

This book may be ordered directly from the publisher.
Please include 75 cents postage.
Try your bookstore first.
RUNNING PRESS
125 South Twenty-Second Street
Philadelphia, Pennsylvania 19103

THE WEATHER IN THIS BOOK

No weather will be found in this book. This is an attempt to pull a book through without weather. It being the first attempt of the kind in fictitious literature, it may prove a failure, but it seemed worth the while of some dare-devil person to try it, and the author was in just the mood.

Many a reader who wanted to read a tale through was not able to do it because of delays on account of the weather. Nothing breaks up an author's progress like having to stop every few pages to fuss-up the weather. Thus it is plain that persistent instrusions of weather are bad for both reader and author.

Of course weather is necessary to a narrative of human experience. That is conceded. But it ought to be put where it will not be in the way; where it will not interrupt the flow of the narrative. And it ought to be the ablest weather than can be had, not ignorant, poor-quality, amateur weather. Weather is a literary specialty, and no untrained hand can turn out a good article of it. The present author can do only a few trifling ordinary kinds of weather, and he cannot do those very good. So it has seemed wisest to borrow such weather as is necessary for the book from qualified and recognized experts—giving credit, of course. This weather will be found over in the back part of the book, out of the way. *See Appendix.* The reader is requested to turn over and help himself from time to time as he goes along.

—MARK TWAIN

CONTENTS

Erratum

Please note:

The first paragraph on page 331 through the first paragraph on page 333 are repeated unintentionally, starting from the second paragraph on page 333 through the first paragraph on page 335.

OPENING REMARKS

by Kurt Vonnegut, Jr.

Mark Twain (1835-1910) was an autodidact, of course. His schoolbooks were steamboats and mining camps and newspaper offices and so on. His eventual greatness might almost be taken as an insult to formal education in America. It begs this question: "What good is school?"

This is the best reply, I think: "School is for people who are not nearly as gifted as was Mark Twain, who need lessons in counterfeiting gifts they do not have." It is an unfair world. Twain was as unfairly endowed with literary talent at birth as descendents of John D. Rockefeller, his contemporary, would be endowed with mountains of money a little later on.

Yes, and Twain was as shrewd and puritanical in managing his literary talent as Rockefeller was in managing money, it seems to me. He squandered almost none of it. His collected works are, among other things, a monument to nineteenth century ambition, single-mindedness, and efficiency—like Standard Oil.

They are a good deal funnier than Standard Oil.

* * * * * *

Rockefeller was a devout Christian, given to supposing out loud that God must have wished him to be as rich as he was. Twain, on the other hand, had almost nothing to say about God and His possible intentions. God does not make an appearance even in the Garden of Eden, in "Eve's Diary," and not even in Paradise itself, in "Captain Stormfield's Visit to Heaven."

* * * * * *

Although he was raised in what has been called the country's "Bible Belt," Twain found church services, especially the praying, to be downright comical. Why? Because, in an age of steam engines and dynamos and the telegraph and so on, praying seemed so *impractical,* I think.

Twain himself had had tremendously satisfying adventures with the most glamorous conglomerations of machinery imaginable, which were riverboats. So praying, as opposed to inventing and engineering, was bound to seem to him, and to so many like him, as the silliest possible way to get things done.

He was what would later be called "a technocrat."

He wished to sweep away superstitions and romantic illusions with laughter—because they were so *useless.* Connecticut Yankees should run the world, because they kept up with scientific discoveries and they had no illusions. They knew what would *really* work. They knew what was *really* going on.

Hi ho.

* * * * * *

I have heard it said that the ending of *A Connecticut Yankee* was a prophecy of the World Wars Twain did not live to see. Superstitious knights fight technocrats, and both armies become parts of a pestilential mulch of corpses. This seems to me a better description of the war between the Confederacy and the Union than of the World Wars, which pitted technocrats against technocrats, and in which no one could have any illusions any more.

It is my belief that Twain was less interested in prophecy than ending his tale some way—almost any *which* way. So he did what Herman Melville did in *Moby Dick.* He killed everybody, except for one survivor to tell the tale.

It is such a clumsy ending, in my opinion, that it destroys the balance of the author himself. It causes him to suggest some things about himself which he would have preferred not to see the light of day.

For instance: Merlin, the personification of contemptible superstititions, is present at the end. All through the book, Merlin has been a transparent fraud. But then he casts a spell which is more astonishing than anything the Connecticut Yankee has done. Merlin puts the Yankee to sleep for thirteen centuries. He can work miracles after all.

Not only that, but Merlin comes on his wicked errand *disguised as a woman.*

Imagine that.

Is it possible that Twain, the clear-eyed technocrat, could not help believing in magic after all? I think maybe so.

Is it possible that he suspected that women and their praying, from whom Huck Finn fled in such a frenzy, had mysterious powers superior to those of scientists and engineers? I think maybe so.

* * * * * *

He was surely devoted to women, no matter how ambivalently he treated them in his writings. Of the fifteen volumes of his works issued by Harper and Brothers in 1897, only three carry dedications, all of them to females.

They are as follows:

The Innocents Abroad, Volume I.: "To my most patient reader and most charitable critic, my aged Mother, this volume is affectionately inscribed."

Tom Sawyer: "To my wife this book is affectionately dedicated."

And *The Prince and the Pauper:* "To those good-mannered and agreeable children Suzie and Clara Clemens this book is affectionately inscribed by their father."

* * * * * *

I do not mean to raise Freudian questions about Twain. I am not particularly respectful of the sorts of answers they can bring.

Sigmund Freud himself *did* write about Twain, incidentally—after Twain was dead. He set a refreshingly un-Freudian example by saying little about Twain's relationships to women, or any of that. He did what we should do, too, which was to celebrate how cunningly Twain's best jokes were made.

* * * * * *

Ernest Hemingway, another famous autodidact, once said, "All modern American literature comes from one book by Mark Twain called 'Huckleberry Finn.'" This is at least vaguely true, I suppose, of many modern books written by American men.

I am struck, though, by how little Hemingway's work resembles Twain's. He has no ear for dialects, he severely limits his vocabulary, he is enchanted by violence, he can't tell jokes. Perhaps he was inspired by Twain's writing so movingly without taking God into account, and by his demonstration that an American male could be a first-rate artist and a man's man, too. I don't know.

One thing I do know: A single modern American writer has seemed on occasion like a true son of Twain to me. He is the late Henry Louis Mencken (1880-1956), who, like Twain, grew up in a border state, had a technical background, was not a college graduate, and who was taught to write by newspaper men.

All these shared circumstances tended to make both men irreverent about so-called spiritual matters and conventional patriotism, I think. But their most admirable similarity was their genius for perceiving and exploiting the American language's peculiar powers to surprise and amuse. If a writer does not have such genius, and it is rare, then he cannot be a true follower of Mark Twain.

Mencken's masterpiece, incidentally, is a scholarly work entitled, simply enough, *The American Language*.

* * * * * *

So many of America's funniest writers have come up through newspapers—not only Twain and Mencken, but George Ade and Robert Benchley and Don Marquis and Kin Hubbard and Ring Lardner, and on and on—that it may be correct to think of them as editorial writers gone berserk.

It is as though they had written solemnly and respectfully about mankind's problems year after year after year. And then, one day, they couldn't stand it any more. Nothing would do but that they jeer at their readers for belonging to such a stupid and vain and unlucky and greedy species.

Hi ho.

* * * * * *

Mencken's reputation does not continue to bloom as Twain's does. Little about Twain's work seems dated now, save for his pre-Freudian innocence about sexual matters, which only makes him more beguiling. But a lot of Mencken seems narrowly and crankily political now.

And he wrote no fiction. Fiction just might have done for

Mencken what it did for Twain—just might have given his often outrageous prejudices the semblance of being universal.

Then again, Mencken never wished to be a man of the people. He was squeamish about his relations with the general population. Whereas Twain was almost Lincolnesque, and Quixotic, too, in his wish to please crowds without lying to them.

This he did, I think—and this he continues to do.

* * * * * *

Twain was so good with crowds that he became, in competition with singers and dancers and actors and acrobats, one of the most popular performers of his time. It is so unusual, and so psychologically unlikely for a great writer to be a great performer, too, that I can think of only two similar cases—Homer's, perhaps, and Molière's.

And I will guess now that the pessimism and religious skepticism and anti-patriotism of his writings would have been unacceptable to his contemporaries, if he had not dared to make public appearances as well.

True—within the body of his writings, he softened his harsh opinion of humanity with his adoration of the women in his life, and with his wide-eyed enchantment with the beauty of the planet itself, especially with its waters. Also, as I have already said, he was the most able lover the American language had so far had.

But it was the personal appearances, I am sure, that persuaded his fellow-citizens that the holder of often-monstrous opinions was not a monster after all. As Twain presented himself in lecture halls, in fact, he was an utterly winsome sort of teddy bear, in need of all the love he could get.

If I am right about this, then every present-day comedian who says after mocking something supposedly sacred, "But I'm only kidding, folks," is following in the footsteps of Samuel Clemens, of the uxorious, Victorian American gentleman, diligent in business and often depressed, who became a world citizen while necessarily disguised as Mark Twain.

Kurt Vonnegut, Jr.
April 24, 1976

A SHORT NOTE
FROM THE EDITOR

Mark Twain was a literary cuckold, put upon, mistreated, and simultaneously loved by his American readers, with part of the population of England thrown in. Twain eventually had to go to England to protect his American copyrights, and even that did not solve his problems well. "Publishers," Twain said, "are not accountable to the laws of Heaven and earth in any country, as I understand it." Mark Twain's understanding was, unfortunately, true.

This accumulation of his work has been made as if he were alive, sitting near my desk and eyeing me. Because so many typesetters, writers, editors, and publishers mucked around with his words, I have attempted to go back and set stories and novels from his first editions. These were the only works that came close to being approved by him.

It seems that every particle of man's thought, given enough time, will eventually attract a group of scholars who lay claim to it. Mark Twain's group has become legion. I am not a Twain scholar. I read his works for pleasure, sorted them out, and put together those that I felt you would most enjoy.

All the selections are arranged in chronological order—it made the most sense. Each piece is preceded by a little note containing a brief chronology of its publication. This information, sometimes including historical insights, was often culled from interpretations of reviews contemporary to the piece. Publication dates were taken, in the most part, from Twain's wizard-like bibliographer, Merle Johnson.

The Unabridged Mark Twain was originally conceived as a 1248-page book. Without going into the technicalities of publishing, I will simply tell you that it was nearly impossible to predict the precise amount of Twain that could be included. Happily, at the last moment, I was able to slip in an extra sixty-four pages. There were a lot of last minute judgments to be made: is *A Connecticut Yankee* worth 38 cents? can I spend an additional 8 cents and include *The Man That Corrupted Hadleyburg*? etc. Well, I spent the money, used the pages, and, hopefully, have given you three pounds' worth of the best one-third of Mark Twain's writings.

Lawrence Teacher

THE UNABRIDGED

MARK TWAIN

"AFTER" JENKINS

" 'After' Jenkins" *is a tidy, early sketch that was published under the title* "The Pioneer Ball" *in both* The Territorial Enterprise *and* The Californian *in November, 1865. It then appeared in Mark Twain's first volume,* The Celebrated Jumping Frog of Calaveras County and Other Sketches, *published in 1867 by C.H. Webb, New York, as* " 'After' Jenkins." *No one seems to know why the title changed.*

"AFTER" JENKINS

A grand affair of a ball—the Pioneers'—came off at the Occidental some time ago. The following notes of the costumes worn by the belles of the occasion may not be uninteresting to the general reader, and Jenkins may get an idea therefrom:

Mrs. W. M. was attired in an elegant *paté de foie gras,* made especially for her, and was greatly admired. Miss S. had her hair done up. She was the center of attraction for the gentlemen and the envy of all the ladies. Mrs. G. W. was tastefully dressed in a *tout ensemble,* and was greeted with deafening applause wherever she went. Mrs. C. N. was superbly arrayed in white kid gloves. Her modest and engaging manner accorded well with the unpretending simplicity of her costume and caused her to be regarded with absorbing interest by every one.

The charming Miss M. M. B. appeared in a thrilling waterfall, whose exceeding grace and volume compelled the homage of pioneers and emigrants alike. How beautiful she was!

The queenly Mrs. L. R. was attractively attired in her new and beautiful false teeth, and the *bon jour* effect they naturally produced was heightened by her enchanting and well-sustained smile.

Miss R. P., with that repugnance to ostentation in dress which is so peculiar to her, was attired in a simple white lace collar, fastened with a neat pearl-button solitaire. The fine contrast between the sparkling vivacity of her natural optic, and the steadfast attentiveness of her placid glass eye, was the subject of general and enthusiastic remark.

Miss C. L. B. had her fine nose elegantly enameled, and the easy grace with which she blew it from time to time marked her as a cultivated and accomplished woman of the world; its exquisitely modulated tone excited the admiration of all who had the happiness to hear it.

*"The Celebrated Jumping Frog of Calaveras County"
was set down by Twain at the request of Artemus Ward.
Ward's publisher did not care for the piece and gave it
as a gift to Henry Clapp for his faltering journal,* The
Saturday Press. *It appeared there under the title, "Jim
Smiley and His Frog," November, 1865. In 1867 the
story became the title of Twain's first book,* The
Celebrated Jumping Frog of Calaveras County and
Other Sketches, *published by C.H. Webb, New York.*

THE CELEBRATED JUMPING FROG OF CALAVERAS COUNTY

In compliance with the request of a friend of mine, who wrote me from the East, I called on good-natured, garrulous old Simon Wheeler, and inquired after my friend's friend, Leonidas W. Smiley, as requested to do, and I hereunto append the result. I have a lurking suspicion that *Leonidas W.* Smiley is a myth; that my friend never knew such a personage; and that he only conjectured that if I asked old Wheeler about him, it would remind him of his infamous *Jim* Smiley, and he would go to work and bore me to death with some exasperating reminiscence of him as long and as tedious as it should be useless to me. If that was the design, it succeeded.

I found Simon Wheeler dozing comfortably by the barroom stove of the dilapidated tavern in the decayed mining camp of Angel's, and I noticed that he was fat and bald-headed, and had an expression of winning gentleness and simplicity upon his tranquil countenance. He roused up, and gave me good-day. I told him a friend of mine had commissioned me to make some inquiries about a cherished companion of his boyhood named *Leonïdas W.* Smiley— *Rev. Leonïdas W.* Smiley, a young minister of the Gospel, who he had heard was at one time a resident of Angel's Camp. I added that if Mr. Wheeler could tell me anything about this Rev. Leonidas W. Smiley, I would feel under many obligations to him.

Simon Wheeler backed me into a corner and blockaded me there with his chair, and then sat down and reeled off the monotonous narrative which follows this paragraph. He never smiled, he never frowned, he never changed his voice from the gentle-flowing key to which he turned his initial sentence, he never betrayed the slightest suspicion of enthusiasm; but all through the interminable narrative there ran a vein of impressive earnestness and sincerity, which showed me plainly that, so far from his imagining that there was anything ridiculous or funny about his story, he regarded it as a really important matter, and admired its two heroes as men of transcendent genius in *finesse.* I let him go on in his own way, and never interrupted him once.

"Rev. Leonidas W. H'm, Reverend Le—well, there was a feller here once by the name of *Jim* Smiley, in the winter of '49—or may be it was the spring of '50—I don't recollect exactly, somehow, though what makes me think it was one or the other is because I remember the big flume warn't finished when he first come to the camp; but any way, he was the curiosest man about always betting on anything that turned up you ever see, if he could get anybody to bet on the other side; and if he couldn't he'd change sides. Any way that suited the other man would suit *him*—any way just so's he got a bet, *he* was satisfied. But still he was lucky, uncommon lucky; he most always come out winner. He was always ready and laying for a chance; there couldn't be no solit'ry thing mentioned but that feller'd offer to bet on it, and take any side you please, as I was just telling you. If there was a horse-race, you'd find him flush or you'd find him busted at the end of it; if there was a dog-fight, he'd bet on it; if there was a cat-fight, he'd bet on it; if there was a chicken-fight, he'd bet on it; why, if there was two birds setting on a fence, he would bet you which one would fly first; or if there was a camp-meeting, he would be there reg'lar to bet on Parson Walker, which he judged to be the best exhorter about here, and so he was too, and a good man. If he even see a straddle-bug start to go anywheres, he would bet you how long it would take him to get to—to wherever he was going to, and if you took him up, he would foller that straddle-bug to Mexico but what he would find out where he was bound for and how long he was on the road. Lots of the boys here has seen that Smiley, and can tell you about him. Why, it never made no difference to *him*—he'd bet on *any* thing—the dangdest feller. Parson Walker's wife laid very sick once, for a good while, and it seemed as if they warn't going to save her; but one morning he come in, and Smiley up and asked him how she was, and he said she was considable better—thank the Lord for his inf'nite mercy—and coming on so smart that with the blessing of Prov'dence she'd get well yet; and Smiley, before he thought, says, "Well, I'll resk two-and-a-half she don't anyway."

Thish-yer Smiley had a mare—the boys called her the fifteen-minute nag, but that was only in fun, you know, because of course she was faster than that—and he used to win money on that horse, for all she was so slow and always had the asthma, or the distemper, or the consumption, or something of that kind. They used to give her two or three hundred yards start, and then pass her under way; but always at the fag end of the race she'd get excited and desperate like, and come cavorting and straddling up, and scattering her legs around limber, sometimes in the air, and sometimes out to one side among the fences, and kicking up m-o-r-e dust and raising m-o-r-e racket with her coughing and sneezing and blowing her nose—and *always* fetch up at the stand just about a neck ahead, as near as you could cipher it down.

And he had a little small bull-pup, that to look at him you'd think he warn't worth a cent but to set around and look ornery and lay for a chance to steal something. But as soon as money was up on him he was a different dog; his under-jaw'd begin to stick out like the fo'castle of a steamboat, and his teeth would uncover and shine like the furnaces. And a dog might tackle him and bully-rag him, and bite him, and throw him over his shoulder two or three times, and Andrew Jackson—which was the name of the pup—Andrew Jackson would never let on but what *he* was satisfied, and hadn't expected nothing else—and the bets being doubled and doubled on the other side all the time, till the money was all up; and then all of a sudden he would grab that other dog jest by the j'int of his hind leg and freeze to it—not chaw, you understand, but only just grip and hang on till they throwed up the sponge, if it was a year. Smiley always come out winner on that pup, till he harnessed a dog once that didn't have no hind legs, because they'd been sawed off in a circular saw, and when the thing had gone along far enough, and the money was all up, and he come to make a snatch for his pet holt, he see in a minute how he'd been imposed on, and how the other dog had him in the door, so to speak, and he 'peared surprised, and then he looked sorter discouraged-like, and didn't try no more to win the fight, and so he got shucked out bad. He give Smiley a look, as much as to say his heart was broke, and it was *his* fault, for putting up a dog that hadn't no hind legs for him to **take** holt of, which was his main dependence in a fight, and then he limped off a piece and laid down and died. It was a good pup, was that Andrew Jackson, and would have made a name for hisself if he'd lived, for the stuff was in him and he had genius—I know it, because he hadn't no opportunities to speak of, and it don't stand to reason that a dog could make such a fight as he could under them circumstances if he hadn't no talent. It always makes me feel sorry when I think of that last fight of his'n, and the way it turned out.

Well, thish-yer Smiley had rat-tarriers, and chicken cocks, and tomcats and all them kind of things, till you couldn't rest, and you couldn't fetch nothing for him to bet on but he'd match you. He ketched a frog one day, and took him home, and said he cal'lated to educate him; and so he never done nothing for three months but set in his back yard and learn that frog to jump. And you bet you he *did* learn him, too. He'd give him a little punch behind, and the next minute you'd see that frog whirling in the air like a doughnut—see him turn one summerset, or may be a couple, if he got a good start, and come down flat-footed and all right, like a cat. He got him up so in the matter of ketching flies, and kep' him in practice so constant, that he'd nail a fly every time as fur as he could see him. Smiley said all a frog wanted was education, and he could do 'most anything—and I believe him. Why, I've seen him set Dan'l Webster down here on this floor—Dan'l, Webster was the name of the frog—and sing out, "Flies, Dan'l, flies!" and quicker'n you could wink he'd spring straight up and snake a fly off'n the counter there, and flop down on the floor ag'in as solid as a gob of mud, and fall to scratching the side of his head with his hind foot as indifferent as if he hadn't no idea he'd been doin' any more'n any frog might do. You never see a frog so modest and straightfor'ard as he was, for all he was so gifted. And when it come to fair and square jumping on a dead level, he could get over more ground at one straddle than any animal of his breed you ever see. Jumping on a dead level was his strong suit, you understand; and when it come to that, Smiley would ante up money on him as long as he had a red. Smiley was monstrous proud of his frog, and well he might be, for fellers that had traveled and been everywheres all said he laid over any frog that ever *they* see.

Well, Smiley kep' the beast in a little lattice box, and he used to fetch him down town sometimes and lay for a bet. One day a feller—a stranger in the camp, he was—come acrost him with his box, and says:

"What might it be that you've got in the box?"

And Smiley says, sorter indifferent-like, "It might be a parrot, or it might be a canary, maybe, but it ain't—its only just a frog."

And the feller took it, and looked at it careful, and turned it round this way and that, and says, "H'm—so 'tis. Well, what's *he* good for?"

"Well," Smiley says, easy and careless, "he's good enough for *one* thing, I should judge—he can outjump any frog in Calaveras county."

The feller took the box again, and took another long, particular look, and give it back to Smiley, and says, very deliberate, "Well," he says, "I don't see no p'ints about that frog that's any better'n any other frog."

"Maybe you don't," Smiley says. "Maybe you understand frogs and maybe you don't understand 'em; maybe you've had experience, and maybe you ain't only a amature, as it were. Anyways, I've got *my* opinion, and I'll resk forty dollars that he can outjump any frog in Calaveras county."

And the feller studied a minute, and then says, kinder sad like, "Well, I'm only a stranger here, and I ain't got no frog; but if I had a frog, I'd bet you."

And then Smiley says, "That's all right—that's all right—if you'll hold my box a minute, I'll go and get you a frog." And so the feller took the box, and put up his forty dollars along with

Smiley's, and set down to wait.

So he set there a good while thinking and thinking to hisself, and then he got the frog out and prized his mouth open and took a teaspoon and filled him full of quail shot—filled him pretty near up to his chin—and set him on the floor. Smiley he went to the swamp and slopped around in the mud for a long time, and finally he ketched a frog, and fetched him in, and give him to this feller, and says:

"Now, if you're ready, set him alongside of Dan'l, with his fore-paws just even with Dan'l's, and I'll give the word." Then he says, "One—two—three—*git!*" and him and the feller touched up the frogs from behind, and the new frog hopped off lively, but Dan'l give a heave, and hysted up his shoulders—so—like a Frenchman, but it warn't no use—he couldn't budge: he was planted as solid as a church, and he couldn't no more stir than if he was anchored out. Smiley was a good deal surprised, and he was disgusted too, but he didn't have no idea what the matter was, of course.

The feller took the money and started away; and when he was going out at the door, he sorter jerked his thumb over his shoulder—so—at Dan'l, and says again, very deliberate, "Well," he says, "*I* don't see no p'ints about that frog that's any better'n any other frog."

Smiley he stood scratching his head and looking down at Dan'l a long time, and at last he says, "I do wonder what in the nation that frog throw'd off for—I wonder if there ain't something the matter with him—he 'pears to look mighty baggy, somehow." And he ketched Dan'l by the nap of the neck, and hefted him, and says, "Why blame my cats if he don't weigh five pound!" and turned him upside down and he belched out a double handful of shot. And then he see how it was, and he was the maddest man— he set the frog down and took out after that feller, but he never ketched him. And——".

[Here Simon Wheeler heard his name called from the front yard, and got up to see what was wanted.] And turning to me as he moved away, he said: "Just set where you are, stranger, and rest easy—I ain't going to be gone a second."

But, by your leave, I did not think that a continuation of the history of the enterprising vagabond *Jim* Smiley would be likely to afford me much information concerning the Rev. *Leonidas W.* Smiley, and so I started away.

At the door I met the sociable Wheeler returning, and he button-holed me and re-commenced:

"Well, thish-yer Smiley had a yaller one-eyed cow that didn't have no tail, only just a short stump like a bannanner, and——"

However, lacking both time and inclination, I did not wait to hear about the afflicted cow, but took my leave.

The substance of The Innocents Abroad *was extracted primarily from letters written to* The Alta California *of San Francisco, and from several letters to the* New York Tribune, *between 1867 and 1868. This material was first published in book form by The American Publishing Company of Hartford, Connecticut, in 1869. Unavailable through bookstores, the book was sold by subscription only, primarily through door-to-door salesmen. This nonfiction classic, documenting Twain's travels to Europe aboard the Steamship Quaker City, catapulted the author to international fame.*

THE INNOCENTS ABROAD
VOLUME I

PREFACE
TO
THE UNIFORM EDITION

So far as I remember, I have never seen an Author's Preface which had any purpose but one—to furnish reasons for the publication of the Book. Prefaces wear many disguises, call themselves by various names, and pretend to come on various businesses, but I think that upon examination we are quite sure to find that their errand is always the same: they are there to apologize for the book; in other words, furnish reasons for its publication. This often insures brevity.

Upon these terms, if there is nothing to explain or nothing worth the explanation, there is no occasion for a Preface; there is nothing for it to do—except to explain its own presence, apologize for its intrusion. That is what this present Preface does.

When the books in this collection appeared in print originally, most of them had Prefaces which furnished reasons for publication. Those Introductions will be found in their places, and need not be repeated here. The jurisdiction of the present Preface is restricted to furnishing reasons for the publication of the Collection as a whole. This is not easy to do. Aside from the ordinary commercial reasons I find none that I can offer with dignity. I cannot say without immodesty that the books have merit; I cannot say without immodesty that the public want a Uniform Edition; I cannot say without immodesty that a Uniform Edition will turn the nation toward high ideals and elevated thought; I cannot say without immodesty that a Uniform Edition will eradicate crime. Though I think it will. I find no reason which I can offer without immodesty except the rather poor one that I should like to see a Uniform Edition myself. It is nothing; a cat could say it about her kittens. Still, I believe I will stand upon that. I have to have a Preface and a reason, by law of custom, and the reason which I am putting forward is at least without offense.

MARK TWAIN.

Vienna, January, 1899.

PREFACE

This book is a record of a pleasure trip. If it were a record of a solemn scientific expedition, it would have about it that gravity, that profundity, and that impressive incomprehensibility which are so proper to works of that kind, and withal so attractive. Yet notwithstanding it is only a record of a picnic, it has a purpose, which is, to suggest to the reader how *he* would be likely to see Europe and the East if he looked at them with his own eyes instead of the eyes of those who traveled in those countries before him. I make small pretence of showing any one how he *ought* to look at objects of interest beyond the sea—other books do that, and therefore, even if I were competent to do it, there is no need.

I offer no apologies for any departures from the usual style of travel-writing that may be charged against me—for I think I have seen with impartial eyes, and I am sure I have written at least honestly, whether wisely or not.

In this volume I have used portions of letters which I wrote for the *Daily Alta California,* of San Francisco, the proprietors of that journal having waived their rights and given me the necessary permission.

I have also inserted portions of several letters written for the New York *Tribune* and the New York *Herald.*

THE AUTHOR.

SAN FRANCISCO.

CHAPTER I

For months the great Pleasure Excursion to Europe and the Holy Land was chatted about in the newspapers everywhere in America, and discussed at countless firesides. It was a novelty in the way of excursions—its like had not been thought of before, and it compelled that interest which attractive novelties always command. It was to be a picnic on a gigantic scale. The participants in it, instead of freighting an ungainly steam ferry-boat with youth and beauty and pies and doughnuts, and paddling up some obscure creek to disembark upon a grassy lawn and wear themselves out with a long summer day's laborious frolicking under the impression that it was fun, were to sail away in a great steamship with flags flying and cannon pealing, and take a royal holiday beyond the broad ocean, in many a strange clime and in many a land renowned in history! They were to sail for months over the breezy Atlantic and the sunny Mediterranean; they were to scamper about the decks by day, filling the ship with shouts and laughter—or read novels and poetry in the shade of the smoke-stacks, or watch for the jelly-fish and the nautilus, over the side, and the shark, the whale, and other strange monsters of the deep; and at night they were to dance in the open air, on the upper deck, in the midst of a ballroom that stretched from horizon to horizon, and was domed by the bending heavens and lighted by no meaner lamps than the stars and the magnificent moon— dance, and promenade, and smoke, and sing, and make love, and search the skies for constellations that never associate with the "Big Dipper" they were so tired of: and they were to see the ships of twenty navies—the customs and costumes of twenty curious peoples—the great cities of half a world—they were to hobnob with nobility and hold friendly converse with kings and princes, Grand Moguls, and the anointed lords of mighty empires!

It was a brave conception; it was the offspring of a most ingenious brain. It was well advertised, but it hardly needed it: the bold originality, the extraordinary character, the seductive nature, and the vastness of the enterprise provoked comment everywhere and advertised it in every household in the land. Who could read the program of the excursion without longing to make one of the party? I will insert it here. It is almost as good as a map. As a text for this book, nothing could be better:

EXCURSION TO THE HOLY LAND, EGYPT, THE CRIMEA, GREECE, AND INTERMEDIATE POINTS OF INTEREST.

BROOKLYN, *February 1st, 1867.*

The undersigned will make an excursion as above during the coming season, and begs to submit to you the following programme:

A first-class steamer, to be under his own command, and capable of accommodating at least one hundred and fifty cabin passengers, will be selected, in which will be taken a select company, numbering not more than three-fourths of the ship's capacity. There is good reason to believe that this company can be easily made up in this immediate vicinity, of mutual friends and acquaintances.

The steamer will be provided with every necessary comfort, including library and musical instruments.

An experienced physician will be on board.

Leaving New York about June 1st, a middle and pleasant route will be taken across the Atlantic, and, passing through the group of Azores, St. Michael will be reached in about ten days. A day or two will be spent here, enjoying the fruit and wild scenery of these islands, and the voyage continued, and Gibraltar reached in three or four days.

A day or two will be spent here in looking over the wonderful subterraneous fortifications, permission to visit these galleries being readily obtained.

From Gibraltar, running along the coasts of Spain and France, Marseilles will be reached in three days. Here ample time will be given not only to look over the city, which was founded six hundred years before the Christian era, and its artificial port, the finest of the kind in the Mediterranean, but to visit Paris during the Great Exhibition; and the beautiful city of Lyons, lying intermediate, from the heights of which, on a clear day, Mont Blanc and the Alps can be distinctly seen. Passengers who may wish to extend the time at Paris can do so, and, passing down through Switzerland, rejoin the steamer at Genoa.

From Marseilles to Genoa is a run of one night. The excursionists will have an opportunity to look over this, the "magnificent city of palaces," and visit the birthplace of Columbus, twelve miles off, over a beautiful road built by Napoleon I. From this point, excursions may be made to Milan, Lakes Como and Maggiore, or to Milan, Verona (famous for its extraordinary fortifications), Padua, and Venice. Or, if passengers desire to visit Palma (famous for Correggio's frescoes) and Bologna, they can by rail go on to Florence, and rejoin the steamer at Leghorn, thus spending about three weeks amid the cities most famous for art in Italy.

From Genoa the run to Leghorn will be made along the coast in one night, and time appropriated to this point in which to visit Florence, its palaces and galleries; Pisa, its Cathedral and "Leaning Tower," and Lucca and its baths and Roman amphitheater; Florence, the most remote, being distant by rail about sixty miles.

From Leghorn to Naples (calling at Civita Vecchia to land any who may prefer to go to Rome from that point) the distance will be made in about thirty-six hours; the route will lay along the coast of Italy, close by Caprera, Elba, and Corsica. Arrangements have been made to take on board at Leghorn a pilot for Caprera, and, if practicable, a call will be made there to visit the home of Garibaldi.

Rome (by rail), Herculaneum, Pompeii, Vesuvius, Virgil's tomb, and possibly, the ruins of Paestum, can be visited, as well as the beautiful surroundings of Naples and its charming bay.

The next point of interest will be Palermo, the most beautiful city of Sicily, which will be reached in one night from Naples. A day will be spent here, and, leaving in the evening, the course will be taken towards Athens.

Skirting along the north coast of Sicily, passing through the group of Aeolian Isles, in sight of Stromboli and Vulcania, both active volcanoes, through the Straits of Messina, with "Scylla" on the one hand and "Charybdis" on the other, along the east coast of Sicily, and in sight of Mount Aetna, along the south coast of Italy, the west and south coast of Greece, in sight of ancient Crete, up Athens Gulf, and into the Piraeus, Athens will be reached in two and a half or three days. After tarrying here awhile, the Bay of Salamis will be crossed, and a day given to Corinth, whence the voyage will be continued to Constantinople, passing on the way through the Grecian Archipelago, the Dardanelles, the Sea of Marmora, and the mouth of the Golden Horn, and arriving in about forty-eight hours from Athens.

After leaving Constantinople, the way will be taken out through the beautiful Bosphorus, across the Black Sea to Sebastopol and Balaklava, a run of about twenty-four hours. Here it is proposed to remain two days, visiting the harbors, fortifications, and battlefields of the Crimea; thence back through the Bosphorus, touching at Constantinople to take in any who may have preferred to remain there; down through the Sea of Marmora and the Dardanelles, along the coasts of ancient Troy and Lydia in Asia, to Smyrna, which will be reached in two or two and a half days from Constantinople. A sufficient stay will be made here to give opportunity of visiting Ephesus, fifty miles distant by rail.

From Smyrna towards the Holy Land the course will lay through the Grecian Archipelago, close by the Isle of Patmos, along the coast of Asia, ancient Pamphylia, and the Isle of Cyprus. Beirout will be reached in three days. At Beirout time will be given to visit Damascus; after which the steamer will proceed to Joppa.

From Joppa, Jerusalem, the River Jordan, the Sea of Tiberias, Nazareth, Bethany, Bethlehem, and other points of interest in the Holy Land can be visited, and here those who may have preferred to make the journey from Beirout *through* the country, passing through Damascus, Galilee, Capernaum, Samaria, and by the River Jordan and Sea of Tiberias, can rejoin the steamer.

Leaving Joppa, the next point of interest to visit will be Alexandria, which will be reached in twenty-four hours. The ruins of Caesar's Palace, Pompey's Pillar, Cleopatra's Needle, the Catacombs, and ruins of ancient Alexandria, will be found worth the visit. The journey to Cairo, one hundred and thirty miles by rail, can be made in a few hours, and from which can be visited the site of ancient Memphis, Joseph's Granaries, and the Pyramids.

From Alexandria the route will be taken homeward, calling at Malta, Cagliari (in Sardinia), and Palma (in Majorca), all magnificent harbors, with charming scenery, and abounding in fruits.

A day or two will be spent at each place, and leaving Palma in the evening, Valencia in Spain will be reached the next morning. A few days will be spent in this, the finest city of Spain.

From Valencia, the homeward course will be continued, skirting along the coast of Spain, Alicante, Carthagena, Palos, and Malaga will be passed but a mile or two distant, and Gibraltar reached in about twenty-four hours.

A stay of one day will be made here, and the voyage continued to Madeira, which will be reached in about three days. Captain Marryatt writes: "I do not know a spot on the globe which so much astonishes and delights upon first arrival as Madeira." A stay of one or two days will be made here, which, if time permits, may be extended, and passing on through the islands, and probably in sight of the Peak of Teneriffe, a southern track will be taken, and the Atlantic crossed within the latitudes of the Northeast trade winds, where mild and pleasant weather and a smooth sea can always be expected.

A call will be made at Bermuda, which lies directly in this route homeward, and will be reached in about ten days from Madeira, and after spending a short time with our friends the Bermudians, the final departure will be made for home, which will be reached in about three days.

Already, applications have been received from parties in Europe wishing to join the Excursion there.

The ship will at all times be a home, where the excursionists, if sick, will be surrounded by kind friends, and have all possible comfort and sympathy.

Should contagious sickness exist in any of the ports named in the programme, such ports will be passed, and others of interest substituted.

The price of passage is fixed at $1,250, currency, for each adult passenger. Choice of rooms and of seats at the tables apportioned in the order in which passages are engaged, and no passage considered engaged until ten per cent. of the passage money is deposited with the treasurer.

Passengers can remain on board of the steamer at all ports, if they desire, without additional expense, and all boating at the expense of the ship.

All passages must be paid for when taken, in order that the most perfect arrangements be made for starting at the appointed time.

Applications for passage must be approved by the committee before tickets are issued, and can be made to the undersigned.

Articles of interest or curiosity, procured by the passengers during the voyage, may be brought home in the steamer free of charge.

Five dollars per day, in gold, it is believed, will be a fair calculation to make for *all* traveling expenses on shore, and at the various points where passengers may wish to leave the steamer for days at a time.

The trip can be extended, and the route changed, by *unanimous* vote of the passengers.

CHAS. C. DUNCAN,
117 WALL STREET, NEW YORK.

R. R. G******, Treasurer.

COMMITTEE ON APPLICATIONS.

J. T. H******, ESQ.,   R. R. G******, ESQ.,   C. C. DUNCAN.

COMMITTEE ON SELECTING STEAMER.

CAPT. W. W. S******, *Surveyor for Board of Underwriters.*
C. W. C******, *Consulting Engineer for U.S. and Canada.*
J. T. H******, ESQ.
C. C. DUNCAN.

P.S.—The very beautiful and substantial side-wheel steamship *"Quaker City"* has been chartered for the occasion, and will leave New York, June 8th. Letters have been issued by the government commending the party to courtesies abroad.

What was there lacking about that program, to make it perfectly irresistible? Nothing, that any finite mind could discover. Paris, England, Scotland, Switzerland, Italy—Garibaldi! The Grecian archipelago! Vesuvius! Constantinople! Smyrna! The Holy Land! Egypt and "our friends the Bermudians"! People in Europe desiring to join the Excursion—contagious sickness to be avoided—boating at the expense of the ship—physician on board—the circuit of the globe to be made if the passengers unanimously desired it—the company to be rigidly selected by a pitiless "Committee on Applications"—the vessel to be as rigidly selected by as pitiless a "Committee on Selecting Steamer." Human nature could not withstand these bewildering temptations. I hurried to the Treasurer's office and deposited my ten per cent. I rejoiced to know that a few vacant staterooms were still left. I *did* avoid a critical personal examination into my character, by that bowelless committee, but I referred to all the people of high standing I could think of in the community who would be least likely to know anything about me.

Shortly a supplementary program was issued which set forth that the Plymouth Collection of Hymns would be used on board the ship. I then paid the balance of my passage money.

I was provided with a receipt, and duly and officially accepted as an excursionist. There was happiness in that, but it was tame compared to the novelty of being "select."

This supplementary program also instructed the excursionists to provide themselves with light musical instruments for amusement in the ship; with saddles for Syrian travel; green spectacles and umbrellas; veils for Egypt; and substantial clothing to use in rough pilgrimizing in the Holy Land. Furthermore, it was suggested that although the ship's library would afford a fair amount of reading matter, it would still be well if each passenger would provide himself with a few guide-books, a Bible, and some standard works of travel. A list was appended, which consisted cheifly of books relating to the Holy Land, since the Holy Land was part of the excursion and seemed to be its main feature.

Rev. Henry Ward Beecher was to have accompanied the expedition, but urgent duties obliged him to give up the idea. There were other passengers who could have been spared better, and would have been spared more willingly. Lieutenant-General Sherman was to have been of the party, also, but the Indian war compelled his presence on the plains. A popular actress had entered her name on the ship's books, but something interfered, and *she* couldn't go. The "Drummer Boy of the Potomac" deserted, and lo, we had never a celebrity left!

However, we were to have a "battery of guns" from the Navy Department (as per advertisement), to be used in answering royal salutes; and the document furnished by the Secretary of the Navy, which was to make "General Sherman and party" welcome guests in the courts and camps of the old world, was still left to us, though both document and battery, I think, were shorn of somewhat of their original august proportions. However, had not we the seductive program, still, with its Paris, its Constantinople, Smyrna, Jerusalem, Jericho, and "our friends the Bermudians"? What did we care?

CHAPTER II

Occasionally, during the following month, I dropped in at 117 Wall Street to inquire how the repairing and refurnishing of the vessel was coming on; how additions to the passenger list were averaging; how many people the committee were decreeing not "select," every day, and banishing in sorrow and tribulation. I was glad to know that we were to have a little printing-press on board and issue a daily newspaper of our own. I was glad to learn that our piano, our parlor organ, and our melodeon were to be the best instruments of the kind that could be had in the market. I was proud to observe that among our excursionists were three ministers of the gospel, eight doctors, sixteen or eighteen ladies, several military and naval chieftains with sounding titles, an ample crop of "Professors" of various kinds, and a gentleman who had "COMMISSIONER OF THE UNITED STATES OF AMERICA TO EUROPE, ASIA, AND AFRICA" thundering after his name in one awful blast! I had carefully prepared myself to take rather a back seat in that ship, because of the uncommonly select material that would alone be permitted to pass through the camel's eye of that committee on credentials; I had schooled my-

self to expect an imposing array of military and naval heroes, and to
have to set that back seat still further back in consequence of it, may
be; but I state frankly that I was all unprepared for *this* crusher.

I fell under that titular avalanche a torn and blighted thing. I said
that if that potentate *must* go over in our ship, why, I supposed he
must—but that to my thinking, when the United States considered
it necessary to send a dignitary of that tonnage across the ocean, it
would be in better taste, and safer, to take him apart and cart him
over in sections, in several ships.

Ah, if I had only known, then, that he was only a common mortal,
and that his mission had nothing more overpowering about it than
the collecting of seeds, and uncommon yams and extraordinary
cabbages and peculiar bullfrogs for that poor, useless, innocent, mildewed old fossil, the Smithsonian Institute, I would have felt *so*
much relieved.

During that memorable month I basked in the happiness of being
for once in my life drifting with the tide of a great popular movement. Everybody was going to Europe—I, too, was going to Europe.
Everybody was going to the famous Paris Exposition—I, too, was going to the Paris Exposition. The steamship lines were carrying
Americans out of the various ports of the country at the rate of four
or five thousand a week, in the aggregate. If I met a dozen individuals, during that month, who were not going to Europe shortly, I have
no distinct remembrance of it now. I walked about the city a good
deal with a young Mr. Blucher, who was booked for the excursion.
He was confiding, good-natured, unsophisticated, companionable;
but he was not a man to set the river on fire. He had the most extraordinary notions about this European exodus, and came at last to
consider the whole nation as packing up for emigration to France.
We stepped into a store in Broadway, one day, where he bought a
handkerchief, and when the man could not make change, Mr. B.
said:

"Never mind, I'll hand it to you in Paris."

"But I am not going to Paris."

"How is—what did I understand you to say?"

"I said I am not going to Paris."

"Not going to *Paris!* Not g— well then, where in the nation *are* you
going to?"

"Nowhere at all."

"Not anywhere whatsoever?—not any place on earth but this?"

"Not any place at all but just this—stay here all summer."

My comrade took his purchase and walked out of the store without a word—walked out with an injured look upon his countenance.
Up the street apiece he broke silence and said impressively: "It was
a lie—that is my opinion of it!"

In the fullness of time the ship was ready to receive her passengers. I was introduced to the young gentleman who was to be my

room-mate, and found him to be intelligent, cheerful of spirit, unselfish, full of generous impulses, patient, considerate, and wonderfully good-natured. Not any passenger that sailed in the *Quaker
City* will withhold his endorsement of what I have just said. We selected a stateroom forward of the wheel, on the starboard side, "below decks." It had two berths in it, a dismal dead-light, a sink with a
wash-bowl in it, and a long sumptuously cushioned locker, which
was to do service as a sofa—partly, and partly as a hiding place for
our things. Notwithstanding all this furniture, there was still room
to turn around in, but not to swing a cat in, at least with entire security to the cat. However, the room was large, for a ship's stateroom,
and was in every way satisfactory.

The vessel was appointed to sail on a certain Saturday early in
June.

A little after noon, on the distinguished Saturday, I reached the
ship and went on board. All was bustle and confusion. [I have seen
that remark before, somewhere.] The pier was crowded with carriages and men; passengers were arriving and hurrying on board;
the vessel's decks were encumbered with trunks and valises; groups
of excursionists, arrayed in unattractive traveling costumes, were
moping about in a drizzling rain and looking as droopy and woe-
begone as so many molting chickens. The gallant flag was up, but
it was under the spell, too, and hung limp and disheartened by the
mast. Altogether, it was the bluest, bluest spectacle! It was a pleasure excursion—there was no gainsaying that, because the program
said so—it was so nominated in the bond—but it surely hadn't the
general aspect of one.

Finally, above the banging, and rumbling, and shouting and hissing of steam, rang the order to "cast off!"—a sudden rush to the
gangways—a scampering ashore of visitors—a revolution of the
wheels, and we were off—the picnic was begun! Two very mild
cheers went up from the dripping crowd on the pier; we answered
them gently from the slippery decks; the flag made an effort to wave,
and failed; the "battery of guns" spake not—the ammunition was
out.

We steamed down to the foot of the harbor and came to anchor.
It was still raining. And not only raining, but storming. "Outside"
we could see, ourselves, that there was a tremendous sea on. We
must lie still, in the calm harbor, till the storm should abate. Our
passengers hailed from fifteen states; only a few of them had ever
been to sea before; manifestly it would not do to pit them against a
full-blown tempest until they had got their sea-legs on. Towards
evening the two steam tugs that had accompanied us with a rollicking champagne party of young New Yorkers on board who wished to
bid farewell to one of our number in due and ancient form, departed, and we were alone on the deep. On deep five fathoms,
and anchored fast to the bottom. And out in the solemn rain, at

that. This was pleasuring with a vengeance.

It was an appropriate relief when the gong sounded for prayer-meeting. The first Saturday night of any other pleasure excursion might have been devoted to whist and dancing; but I submit it to the unprejudiced mind if it would have been in good taste for *us* to engage in such frivolities, considering what we had gone through and the frame of mind we were in. We would have shone at a wake, but not at anything more festive.

However, there is always a cheering influence about the sea; and in my berth, that night, rocked by the measured swell of the waves, and lulled by the murmur of the distant surf, I soon passed tranquilly out of all consciousness of the dreary experiences of the day and damaging premonitions of the future.

CHAPTER III

All day Sunday at anchor. The storm had gone down a great deal, but the sea had not. It was still piling its frothy hills high in air "outside," as we could plainly see with the glasses. We could not properly begin a pleasure excursion on Sunday; we could not offer untried stomachs to so pitiless a sea as that. We must lie still till Monday. And we did. But we had repetitions of church and prayer-meetings; and so, of course, we were just as eligibly situated as we could have been anywhere.

I was up early that Sabbath morning, and was early to breakfast. I felt a perfectly natural desire to have a good, long, unprejudiced look at the passengers, at a time when they should be free from self-consciousness—which is at breakfast, when such a moment occurs in the lives of human beings at all.

I was greatly surprised to see so many elderly people—I might almost say, so many venerable people. A glance at the long lines of heads was apt to make one think it was *all* gray. But it was not. There was a tolerably fair sprinkling of young folks, and another fair sprinkling of gentlemen and ladies who were non-committal as to age, being neither actually old or absolutely young.

The next morning, we weighed anchor and went to sea. It was a great happiness to get away, after this dragging, dispiriting delay. I thought there never was such gladness in the air before, such brightness in the sun, such beauty in the sea. I was satisfied with the picnic, then, and with all its belongings. All my malicious instincts were dead within me; and as America faded out of sight, I think a spirit of charity rose up in their place that was as boundless, for the time being, as the broad ocean that was heaving its billows about us. I wished to express my feelings—I wished to lift up my voice and sing, but I did not know anything to sing, and so I was obliged to give up the idea. It was no loss to the ship though, perhaps.

It was breezy and pleasant, but the sea was still very rough. One could not promenade without risking his neck; at one moment the bowsprit was taking a deadly aim at the sun in mid-heaven, and at the next it was trying to harpoon a shark in the bottom of the ocean. What a weird sensation it is to feel the stern of a ship sinking swiftly from under you and see the bow climbing high away among the clouds! One's safest course, that day, was to clasp a railing and hang on; walking was too precarious a pastime.

By some happy fortune I was not seasick. That was a thing to be proud of. I had not always escaped before. If there is one thing in the world that will make a man peculiarly and insufferably self-conceited, it is to have his stomach behave itself, the first day at sea, when nearly all his comrades are seasick. Soon, a venerable fossil, shawled to the chin and bandaged like a mummy, appeared at the door of the after deck-house, and the next lurch of the ship shot him into my arms. I said:

"Good morning, sir. It is a fine day."

He put his hand on his stomach and said, "*Oh*, my!" and then staggered away and fell over the coop of a skylight.

Presently another old gentleman was projected from the same door, with great violence. I said:

"Calm yourself, sir—There is no hurry. It is a fine day, sir."

He, also, put his hand on his stomach and said "*Oh*, my!" and reeled away.

In a little while another veteran was discharged abruptly from the same door, clawing at the air for a saving support. I said:

"Good morning, sir. It is a fine day for pleasuring. You were about to say—"

"*Oh*, my!"

I thought so. I anticipated *him*, anyhow. I stayed there and was bombarded with old gentlemen for an hour, perhaps; and all I got out of any of them was "*Oh*, my!"

I went away, then, in a thoughtful mood. I said, this is a good pleasure excursion. I like it. The passengers are not garrulous, but still they are sociable. I like those old people, but somehow they all seem to have the "Oh, my" rather bad.

I knew what was the matter with them. They were seasick. And I was glad of it. We all like to see people seasick when we are not, ourselves. Playing whist by the cabin lamps, when it is storming outside, is pleasant; walking the quarter-deck in the moonlight is pleasant; smoking in the breezy foretop is pleasant, when one is not afraid to go up there; but these are all feeble and commonplace compared with the joy of seeing people suffering the miseries of seasickness.

I picked up a good deal of information during the afternoon. At one time I was climbing up the quarter-deck when the vessel's stern was in the sky; I was smoking a cigar and feeling passably comfortable. Somebody ejaculated:

"Come, now, *that* won't answer. Read the sign up there—No SMOKING ABAFT THE WHEEL!"

It was Captain Duncan, chief of the expedition. I went forward, of course. I saw a long spyglass lying on a desk in one of the upper-deck staterooms back of the pilot-house, and reached after it—there was a ship in the distance:

"Ah, ah—hands off! Come out of that!"

I came out of that. I said to a deck-sweep—but in a low voice:

"Who is that overgrown pirate with the whiskers and the discordant voice?"

"It's Captain Bursley—executive officer—sailing master."

I loitered about awhile, and then, for want of something better to do, fell to carving a railing with my knife. Somebody said, in an insinuating, admonitory voice:

"Now, *say*—my friend—don't you know any better than to be whittling the ship all to pieces that way? *You* ought to know better than that."

I went back and found the deck-sweep:

"Who is that smooth-faced animated outrage yonder in the fine clothes?"

"That's Captain L****, the owner of the ship—he's one of the main bosses."

In the course of time I brought up on the starboard side of the pilot-house, and found a sextant lying on a bench. Now, I said, they "take the sun" through this thing; I should think I might see that vessel through it. I had hardly got it to my eye when some one touched me on the shoulder and said, deprecatingly:

"I'll have to get you to give that to me, sir. If there's anything you'd like to know about taking the sun, I'd as soon tell you as not—but I don't like to trust anybody with that instrument. If you want any figuring done— Aye-aye, sir!"

He was gone, to answer a call from the other side. I sought the deck-sweep:

"Who is that spider-legged gorilla yonder with the sactimonious countenance?"

"It's Captain Jones, sir—the chief mate."

"Well. This goes clear away ahead of anything I ever heard of before. Do you—now I ask you as a man and a brother—*do* you think I could venture to throw a rock here in any given direction without hitting a captain of this ship?"

"Well, sir, I don't know—I think likely you'd fetch the captain of the watch, maybe, because he's a-standing right yonder in the way."

I went below—meditating, and a little downhearted. I thought, if five cooks can spoil a broth, what may not five captains do with a pleasure excursion.

CHAPTER IV

We plowed along bravely for a week or more, and without any conflict of jurisdiction among the captains worth mentioning. The passengers soon learned to accommodate themselves to their new circumstances, and life in the ship became nearly as systematically monotonous as the routine of a barrack. I do not mean that it was dull, for it was not entirely so by any means—but there was a good deal of sameness about it. As is always the fashion at sea, the passengers shortly began to pick up sailor terms—a sign that they were beginning to feel at home. Half-past six was no longer half-past six to these pilgrims from New England, the South, and the Mississippi Valley, it was "seven bells"; eight, twelve, and four o'clock were "eight bells"; the captain did not take the longitude at nine o'clock, but at "two bells." They spoke glibly of the "after cabin," the "for'rard cabin," "port and starboard" and the "fo'castle."

At seven bells the first gong rang; at eight there was breakfast, for such as were not too seasick to eat it. After that all the well people walked arm-in-arm up and down the long promenade deck, enjoying the fine summer mornings, and the seasick ones crawled out and propped themselves up in the lee of the paddle-boxes and ate their dismal tea and toast, and looked wretched. From eleven o'clock until luncheon, and from luncheon until dinner at six in the evening, the employments and amusements were various. Some reading was done; and much smoking and sewing, though not by the same parties; there were the monsters of the deep to be looked after and wondered at; strange ships had to be scrutinized through opera-glasses, and sage decisions arrived at concerning them; and more than that, everybody took a personal interest in seeing that the flag was run up and politely dipped three times in response to the salutes of those strangers; in the smoking-room there were always parties of gentlemen playing euchre, draughts, and dominoes, especially dominoes, that delightfully harmless game; and down on the main deck, "for'rard"—for'rard of the chicken coops and the cattle—we had what was called "horse-billiards." Horse-billiards is a fine game. It affords good, active exercise, hilarity, and consuming excitement. It is a mixture of "hop-scotch" and shuffle-board played with a crutch. A large hop-scotch diagram is marked out on the deck with chalk, and each compartment numbered. You stand off three or four steps, with some broad wooden disks before you on the deck, and these you send forward with a vigorous thrust of a long crutch. If a disk stops on a chalk line, it does not count anything. If it stops in division No. 7, it counts 7; in 5, it counts 5, and so on. The game is 100, and four can play at a time. That game would be very simple, played on a stationary floor, but with us, to play it well required science. We had to allow for the reeling of the ship to the right or the left. Very often one made calculations for a heel to the right and the ship did not go that way. The consequence was that that disk missed the whole hop-scotch plan a yard or two, and then there was humiliation on one side and laughter on the other.

When it rained, the passengers had to stay in the house, of course—or at least the cabins—and amuse themselves with games, reading, looking out of the windows at the very familiar billows, and talking gossip.

By 7 o'clock in the evening, dinner was about over; an hour's promenade on the upper deck followed; then the gong sounded and a large majority of the party repaired to the after cabin (upper) a handsome saloon fifty or sixty feet long, for prayers. The unregenerated called this saloon the "Synagogue." The devotions consisted only of two hymns from the "Plymouth Collection," and a short prayer, and seldom occupied more than fifteen minutes. The hymns were accompanied by parlor organ music when the sea was smooth enough to allow a performer to sit at the instrument without being lashed to his chair.

After prayers the Synagogue shortly took the semblance of a writing-school. The like of that picture was never seen in a ship before. Behind the long dining-tables on either side of the saloon, and scattered from one end to the other of the latter, some twenty or thirty gentlemen and ladies sat them down under the swaying lamps, and for two or three hours wrote diligently in their journals. Alas! that journals so voluminously begun should come to so lame and impotent a conclusion as most of them did! I doubt if there is a single pilgrim of all that host but can show a hundred fair pages of journal concerning the first twenty days' voyaging in the *Quaker City;* and I am morally certain that not ten of the party can show twenty pages of journal for the succeeding twenty thousand miles of voyaging! At certain periods it becomes the dearest ambition of a man to keep a faithful record of his performances in a book; and he dashes at this work with an enthusiasm that imposes on him the notion that keeping a journal is the veriest pastime in the world, and the pleasantest. But if he only lives twenty-one days, he will find out that only those rare natures that are made up of pluck, endurance, devotion to duty for duty's sake, and invincible determination, may hope to venture upon so tremendous an enterprise as the keeping of a journal and not sustain a shameful defeat.

One of our favorite youths, Jack, a splendid young fellow with a head full of good sense, and a pair of legs that were a wonder to look upon in the way of length and straightness and slimness, used to report progress every morning in the most glowing and spirited way, and say:

"Oh, I'm coming along bully!" (he was a little given to slang, in his happier moods) "I wrote ten pages in my journal last night—and you know I wrote nine the night before, and twelve the night before that. Why, it's only fun!"

"What do you find to put in it, Jack?"

"Oh, everything. Latitude and longitude, noon every day; and how many miles we made last twenty-four hours; and all the domino games I beat, and horse-billiards; and whales and sharks and porpoises; and the text of the sermon, Sundays (because that'll tell at home, you know); and the ships we saluted and what nation they were; and which way the wind was, and whether there was a heavy sea, and what sail we carried, though we don't ever carry *any*, principally, going against a head wind always—wonder what is the reason of that?—and how many lies Moult has told—Oh, everything! I've got everything down. My father told me to keep that journal. Father wouldn't take a thousand dollars for it when I get it done."

"No, Jack; it will be worth more than a thousand dollars—when you get it done."

"Do you?—no, but do you think it will, though?"

"Yes, it will be worth at least as much as a thousand dollars—when you get it done. Maybe, more."

"Well, I about half think so, myself. It ain't no slouch of a journal."

But it shortly became a most lamentable "slouch of a journal." One night in Paris, after a hard day's toil in sight-seeing, I said:

"Now I'll go and stroll around the cafés awhile, Jack, and give you a chance to write up your journal, old fellow."

His countenance lost its fire. He said:

"Well, no, you needn't mind. I think I won't run that journal any more. It is awful tedious. Do you know—I reckon I'm as much as four thousand pages behindhand. I haven't got any France in it at all. First I thought I'd leave France out and start fresh. But that wouldn't do, *would* it? The governor would say, 'Hello, here—didn't see anything in France?' *That* cat wouldn't fight, you know. First I thought I'd copy France out of the guidebook, like old Badger in the for'rard cabin who's writing a book, but there's more than three hundred pages of it. Oh, *I* don't think a journal's any use—do you? They're only a bother, *ain't* they?"

"Yes, a journal that is incomplete isn't of much use, but a journal properly kept is worth a thousand dollars,—when you've got it done."

"A thousand!—well, I should think so. *I* wouldn't finish it for a million."

His experience was only the experience of the majority of that industrious night-school in the cabin. If you wish to inflect a heartless and malignant punishment upon a young person, pledge him to keep a journal a year.

A good many expedients were resorted to keep the excursionists amused and satisfied. A club was formed, of all the passengers, which met in the writing-school after prayers and read aloud about the countries we were approaching, and discussed the information so obtained.

Several times the photographer of the expedition brought out his tranparent pictures and gave us a handsome magic lantern exhibition. His views were nearly all of foreign scenes, but there were one or two home pictures among them. He advertised that he would "open his performance in the after cabin at 'two bells' (9 p.m.), and show the passengers where they shall eventually arrive"—which was all very well, but by a funny accident the first picture that flamed out upon the canvas was a view of Greenwood Cemetery!

On several starlight nights we danced on the upper deck, under the awnings, and made something of a ball-room display of brilliancy by hanging a number of ship's lanterns to the stanchions. Our music consisted of the well-mixed strains of a melodeon which was a little asthmatic and apt to catch its breath where it ought to come out strong; a clarinet which was a little unreliable on the high keys and rather melancholy on the low ones; and a disreputable accordion that had a leak somewhere and breathed louder than it squawked—a more elegant term does not occur to me just now. However, the dancing was infinitely worse than the music. When the ship rolled to starboard the whole platoon of dancers came charging down to starboard with it, and brought up in mass at the rail; and when it rolled to port, they went floundering down to port with the same unanimity of sentiment. Waltzers spun around precariously for a matter of fifteen seconds and then went skurrying down to the rail as if they meant to go overboard. The Virginia reel, as performed on board the *Quaker City*, had more genuine reel about it than any reel I ever saw before, and was as full of interest to the spectator as it was full of desperate chances and hairbreadth escapes to the participant. We gave up dancing, finally.

We celebrated a lady's birthday anniversary, with toasts, speeches, a poem, and so forth. We also had a mock trial. No ship ever went to sea that hadn't a mock trial on board. The purser was accused of stealing an overcoat from stateroom No. 10. A judge was appointed; also clerks, a crier of the court, constables, sheriffs; counsel for the state and for the defendant; witnesses were subpoenaed, and a jury empaneled after much challenging. The witnesses were stupid and unreliable and contradictory, as witnesses always are. The counsel were eloquent, argumentative, and vindictively abusive of each other, as was characteristic and proper. The case was at last submitted, and duly finished by the judge with an absurd decision and a ridiculous sentence.

The acting of charades was tried, on several evenings, by the young gentlemen and ladies, in the cabins, and proved the most distinguished success of all the amusement experiments.

An attempt was made to organize a debating club, but it was a failure. There was no oratorical talent in the ship.

We all enjoyed ourselves—I think I can safely say that, but it was in a rather quiet way. We very, very seldom played the piano; we played the flute and the clarinet together, and made good music, too, what there was of it, but we always played the same old tune; it was a very pretty tune—how well I remember it—I wonder when I shall ever get rid of it. We never played either the melodeon or the organ, except at devotions—but I am too fast; young Albert *did* know part of a tune—something about "O Something-Or-Other How Sweet it is to Know that he's his What's-his-Name" (I do not remember the exact title of it, but it was very plaintive, and full of sentiment), Albert played that pretty much all the time, until we contracted with him to restrain himself. But nobody ever sang by moonlight on the upper deck, and the congregational singing at church and prayers was not of a superior order of architecture. I put up with it as long as I could, and then joined in and tried to improve it, but this encouraged young George to join in, too, and that made a failure of it; because George's voice was just "turning," and when he was singing a dismal sort of bass, it was apt to fly off the handle and startle everybody with a most discordant cackle on the upper notes. George didn't know the tunes, either, which was also a drawback to his performances. I said:

"Come, now, George, *don't* improvise. It looks too egotistical. It will provoke remark. Just stick to 'Coronation,' like the others. It is a good tune—*you* can't improve it any, just off-hand, in this way."

"Why, I'm not trying to improve it—and I *am* singing like the others—just as it is in the notes."

And he honestly thought he was, too; and so he had no one to blame but himself when his voice caught on the center occasionally and gave him the lockjaw.

There were those among the unregenerated who attributed the unceasing head winds to our distressing choir music. There were those who said openly that it was taking chances enough to have such ghastly music going on, even when it was at its best; and that to exaggerate the crime by letting George help, was simply flying in the face of Providence. These said that the choir would keep up their lacerating attempts at melody until they would bring down a storm some day that would sink the ship.

There were even grumblers at the prayers. The executive officer said the Pilgrims had no charity.

"There they are, down there every night at eight bells, praying for fair winds—when they know as well as I do that this is the only ship going east this time of the year, but there's a thousand coming west—what's a fair wind for us is a *head* wind to them—the Almighty's blowing a fair wind for a thousand vessels, and this tribe wants him to turn it clear around so as to accommodate *one*,—and she a steamship at that! It ain't good sense, it ain't good reason, it ain't good Christianity, it ain't common human charity. Avast with such nonsense!"

CHAPTER V

Taking it "by and large," as the sailors say, we had a pleasant ten days' run from New York to the Azores islands—not a fast run, for the distance is only twenty-four hundred miles—but a right pleasant one, in the main. True, we had head winds *all* the time, and several stormy experiences which sent fifty per cent of the passengers to bed, sick, and made the ship look dismal and deserted—stormy experiences that all will remember who weathered them on the tumbling deck, and caught the vast sheets of spray that every now and then sprang high in air from the weather bow and swept the ship like a thunder shower; but for the most part we had balmy summer weather, and nights that were even finer than the days. We had the phenomenon of a full moon located just in the same spot in the heavens at the same hour every night. The reason of this singular conduct on the part of the moon did not occur to us at first, but it did afterward when we reflected that we were gaining about twenty minutes every day, because we were going east so fast—we gained just about enough every day to keep along with the moon. It was becoming an old moon to the friends we had left behind us, but to us Joshuas it stood still in the same place, and remained always the same.

Young Mr. Blucher, who is from the Far West, and is on his first voyage, was a good-deal worried by the constantly changing "ship time." He was proud of his new watch at first, and used to drag it out promptly when eight bells struck at noon, but he came to look after a while as if he were losing confidence in it. Seven days out from New York he came on deck, and said with great decision:

"This thing's a swindle!"

"What's a swindle?"

"Why, this watch. I bought her out in Illinois—gave $150 for her—and I thought she was good. And, by George, she *is* good on shore, but somehow she don't keep up her lick here on the water—gets seasick, maybe. She skips; she runs along regular enough till half-past eleven, and then, all of a sudden, she lets down. I've set that old regulator up faster and faster, till I've shoved it clear around, but it don't do any good; she just distances every watch in the ship, and clatters along in a way that's astonishing till it is noon, but them eight bells always gets in about ten minutes ahead of her, anyway. I don't know what to do with her now. She's doing all she can—she's going her best gait, but it won't save her. Now, don't you know, there ain't a watch in the ship that's making better time than she is; but what does it signify? When you hear them eight bells you'll find her just about ten minutes short of her score, sure."

The ship was gaining a full hour every three days, and this fellow was trying to make his watch go fast enough to keep up to her. But, as he had said, he had pushed the regulator up as far as it would go, and the watch was "on its best gait," and so nothing was left him but to fold his hands and see the ship beat the race. We sent him to the captain, and he explained to him the mystery of "ship time," and set his troubled mind at rest. This young man asked a great many questions about seasickness before we left, and wanted to know what its characteristics were, and how he was to tell when he had it. He found out.

We saw the usual sharks, blackfish, porpoises, etc., of course, and by and by large schools of Portuguese men-of-war were added to the regular list of sea wonders. Some of them were white and some of a brilliant carmine color. The nautilus is nothing but a transparent web of jelly, that spreads itself to catch the wind, and has fleshy-looking strings a foot or two long dangling from it to keep it steady in the water. It is an accomplished sailor, and has good sailor judgment. It reefs its sail when a storm threatens or the wind blows pretty hard, and furls it entirely and goes down when a gale blows. Ordinarily it keeps its sail wet and in good sailing order by turning over and dipping it in the water for a moment. Seamen say the nautilus is only found in these waters between the 35th and 45th parallels of latitude.

At three o'clock on the morning of the 21st of June we were awakened and notified that the Azores islands were in sight. I said I did not take any interest in islands at three o'clock in the morning. But another persecutor came, and then another and another, and finally believing that the general enthusiasm would permit no one to slumber in peace, I got up and went sleepily on deck. It was five and a half o'clock now, and a raw, blustering morning. The passengers were huddled about the smoke stacks and fortified behind ventilators, and all were wrapped in wintry costumes, and looking sleepy and unhappy in the pitiless gale and the drenching spray.

The island in sight was Flores. It seemed only a mountain of mud standing up out of the dull mists of the sea. But as we bore down upon it, the sun came out and made it a beautiful picture—a mass of green farms and meadows that swelled up to a height of fifteen hundred feet, and mingled its upper outlines with the clouds. It was ribbed with sharp, steep ridges, and cloven with narrow cañons, and here and there on the heights, rocky upheavals shaped themselves into mimic battlements and castles; and out of rifted clouds came broad shafts of sunlight, that painted summit and slope and glen with bands of fire, and left belts of somber shade between. It was the aurora borealis of the frozen pole exiled to a summer land!

We skirted around two-thirds of the island, four miles from shore, and all the opera-glasses in the ship were called into requisition to settle disputes as to whether mossy spots on the uplands were groves of trees or groves of weeds, or whether the white villages down by the sea were really villages or only the clustering tombstones of cemeteries. Finally, we stood to sea and bore away for San Miguel, and

Flores shortly became a dome of mud again, and sank down among the mists and disappeared. But to many a seasick passenger it was good to see the green hills again, and all were more cheerful after this episode than anybody could have expected them to be, considering how sinfully early they had gotten up.

But we had to change our purpose about San Miguel, for a storm came up about noon that so tossed and pitched the vessel that common sense dictated a run for shelter. Therefore we steered for the nearest island of the group—Fayal (the people there pronounce it Fy-all, and put the accent on the first syllable). We anchored in the open roadstead of Horta, half a mile from the shore. The town has eight thousand to ten thousand inhabitants. Its snow-white houses nestle cosily in a sea of fresh green vegetation, and no village could look prettier or more attractive. It sits in the lap of an amphitheater of hills which are three hundred to seven hundred feet high, and carefully cultivated clear to their summits—not a foot of soil left idle. Every farm and every acre is cut up into little square inclosures by stone walls, whose duty it is to protect the growing products from the destructive gales that blow there. These hundreds of green squares, marked by their black lava walls, make the hills look like vast checker-boards.

The islands belong to Portugal, and everything in Fayal has Portuguese characteristics about it. But more of that anon. A swarm of swarthy, noisy, lying, shoulder-shrugging, gesticulating Portuguese boatmen, with brass rings in their ears, and fraud in their hearts, climbed the ship's sides, and various parties of us contracted with them to take us ashore at so much a head, silver coin of any country. We landed under the walls of a little fort, armed with batteries of twelve and thirty-two pounders, which Horta considered a most formidable institution, but if we were ever to get after it with one of our turreted monitors, they would have to move it out in the country if they wanted it where they could go and find it again when they needed it. The group on the pier was a rusty one—men and women, and boys and girls, all ragged and barefoot, uncombed and unclean, and by instinct, education, and profession, beggars. They trooped after us, and never more, while we tarried in Fayal, did we get rid of them. We walked up the middle of the principal street, and these vermin surrounded us on all sides, and glared upon us; and every moment excited couples shot ahead of the procession to get a good look back, just as village boys do when they accompany the elephant on his advertising trip from street to street. It was very flattering to me to be part of the material for such a sensation. Here and there in the doorways we saw women, with fashionable Portuguese hoods on. This hood is of thick blue cloth, attached to a cloak of the same stuff, and is a marvel of ugliness. It stands up high, and spreads far abroad, and is unfathomably deep. It fits like a circus tent, and a woman's head is hidden away in it like the man's who prompts the

singers from his tin shed in the stage of an opera. There is no particle of trimming about this monstrous *capote,* as they call it—it is
just a plain, ugly dead-blue mass of sail, and a woman can't go within eight points of the wind with one of them on; she has to go before
the wind or not at all. The general style of the capote is the same in
all the islands, and will remain so for the next ten thousand years,
but each island shapes its capotes just enough differently from the
others to enable an observer to tell at a glance what particular island
a lady hails from.

The Portuguese pennies or *reis* (pronounced rays) are prodigious.
It takes one thousand reis to make a dollar, and all financial esti-
mates are made in reis. We did not know this until after we had
found it out through Blucher. Blucher said he was so happy and so
grateful to be on solid land once more, that he wanted to give a
feast—said he had heard it was a cheap land, and he was bound to
have a grand banquet. He invited nine of us, and we ate an excellent
dinner at the principal hotel. In the midst of the jollity produced by
good cigars, good wine, and passable anecdotes, the landlord presented his bill. Blucher glanced at it and his countenance fell. He
took another look to assure himself that his senses had not deceived
him, and then read the items aloud, in a faltering voice, while the
roses in his cheecks turned to ashes:

" 'Ten dinners, at 600 reis, 6,000 reis!' Ruin and desolation!"

" 'Twenty-five cigars, at 100 reis, 2,500 reis!' Oh, my sainted
mother!"

" 'Eleven bottles of wine, at 1,200 reis, 13,200 reis!' Be with us
all!"

" 'TOTAL, TWENTY-ONE THOUSAND SEVEN HUNDRED REIS!' The
suffering Moses!—there ain't money enough in the ship to pay that
bill! Go—leave me to my misery, boys, I am a ruined community."

I think it was the blankest looking party I ever saw. Nobody could
say a word. It was as if every soul had been stricken dumb. Wine
glasses descended slowly to the table, their contents untasted.
Cigars dropped unnoticed from nerveless fingers. Each man sought
his neighbor's eye, but found in it no ray of hope, no encouragement.
At last the fearful silence was broken. The shadow of a desperate
resolve settled upon Blucher's countenance like a cloud, and he rose
up and said:

"Landlord, this is a low, mean swindle, and I'll never, never stand
it. Here's a hundred and fifty dollars, sir, and it's all you'll get—I'll
swim in blood, before I'll pay a cent more."

Our spirits rose and the landlord's fell—at least we thought so; he
was confused at any rate, notwithstanding he had not understood a
word that had been said. He glanced from the little pile of gold
pieces to Blucher several times, and then went out. He must have
visited an American, for, when he returned, he brought back his bill
translated into a language that a Christian could understand—thus:

10 dinners, 6,000 reis, or	$ 6.00
25 cigars, 2,500 reis, or	2.50
11 bottles wine, 13,200 reis, or	13.20
Total 21,700 reis, or	$21.70

Happiness reigned once more in Blucher's dinner party. More refreshments were ordered.

CHAPTER VI

I think the Azores must be very little known in America. Out of our whole ship's company there was not a solitary individual who knew anything whatever about them. Some of the party, well read concerning most other lands, had no other information about the Azores than that they were a group of nine or ten small islands far out in the Atlantic, something more than half way between New York and Gibraltar. That was all. These considerations move me to put in a paragraph of dry facts just here.

The community is eminently Portuguese—that is to say, it is slow, poor, shiftless, sleepy, and lazy. There is a civil governor, appointed by the King of Portugal; and also a military governor, who can assume supreme control and suspend the civil government at his pleasure. The islands contain a population of about 200,000, almost entirely Portuguese. Everything is staid and settled, for the country was one hundred years old when Columbus discovered America. The principal crop is corn, and they raise it and grind it just as their great-great-great-grandfathers did. They plow with a board slightly shod with iron; their trifling little harrows are drawn by men and women; small windmills grind the corn, ten bushels a day, and there is one assistant superintendent to feed the mill and a general superintendent to stand by and keep him from going to sleep. When the wind changes they hitch on some donkeys, and actually turn the whole upper half of the mill around until the sails are in proper position, instead of fixing the concern so that the sails could be moved instead of the mill. Oxen tread the wheat from the ear, after the fashion prevalent in the time of Methuselah. There is not a wheelbarrow in the land—they carry everything on their heads or on donkeys, or in a wicker-bodied cart, whose wheels are solid blocks of wood and whose axles turn with the wheel. There is not a modern plow in the islands, or a threshing-machine. All attempts to introduce them have failed. The good Catholic Portuguese crossed himself and prayed God to shield him from all blasphemous desire to know more than his father did before him. The climate is mild; they never have snow or ice, and I saw no chimneys in the town. The donkeys and the men, women, and children of a family, all eat and sleep in the same room, and are unclean, are ravaged by vermin, and are truly happy. The people lie, and cheat the stranger, and are desperately ignorant, and have hardly any reverence for their dead. The latter trait shows how little better they are than the donkeys they eat and sleep with. The only well-dressed Portuguese in the camp are the half a dozen well-to-do families, the Jesuit priests, and the soldiers of the little garrison. The wages of a laborer are twenty to twenty-four cents a day, and those of a good mechanic about twice as much. They count it in reis at a thousand to the dollar, and this makes them rich and contented. Fine grapes used to grow in the islands, and an excellent wine was made and exported. But a disease killed all the vines fifteen years ago, and since that time no wine has been made. The islands being wholly of volcanic origin, the soil is necessarily very rich. Nearly every foot of ground is under cultivation, and two or three crops a year of each article are produced, but nothing is exported save a few oranges—chiefly to England. Nobody comes here, and nobody goes away. News is a thing unknown in Fayal. A thirst for it is a passion equally unknown. A Portuguese of average intelligence inquired if our civil war was over? because, he said, somebody had told him it was—or at least, it ran in his mind, that somebody had told him something like that! And when a passenger gave an officer of the garrison copies of the *Tribune*, the *Herald*, and *Times*, he was surprised to find later news in them from Lisbon than he had just received by the little monthly steamer. He was told that it came by cable. He said he knew they had tried to lay a cable ten years ago, but it had been in his mind, somehow, that they hadn't succeeded!

It is in communities like this that Jesuit humbuggery flourishes. We visited a Jesuit cathedral nearly two hundred years old, and found in it a piece of the veritable cross upon which our Saviour was crucified. It was polished and hard, and in as excellent a state of preservation as if the dread tragedy on Calvary had occurred yesterday instead of eighteen centuries ago. But these confiding people believe in that piece of wood unhesitatingly.

In a chapel of the cathedral is an altar with facings of solid Silver—at least, they call it so, and I think myself it would go a couple of hundred to the ton (to speak after the fashion of the silver miners), and before it is kept forever burning a small lamp. A devout lady who died, left money and contracted for unlimited masses for the repose of her soul, and also stipulated that this lamp should be kept lighted always, day and night. She did all this before she died, you understand. It is a very small lamp, and a very dim one, and it could not work her much damage, I think, if it went out altogether.

The great altar of the cathedral, and also three or four minor ones, are a perfect mass of gilt gimcracks and gingerbread. And they have a swarm of rusty, dusty, battered apostles standing around the filigree work, some on one leg and some with one eye out but a gamey look in the other, and some with two or three fingers gone, and some with not enough nose left to blow—all of them crippled and discouraged, and fitter subjects for the hospital than the cathedral.

The walls of the chancel are of porcelain, all pictured over with figures of almost life size, very elegantly wrought, and dressed in the fanciful costumes of two centuries ago. The design was a history of something or somebody, but none of us were learned enough to read the story. The old father, reposing under a stone close by, dated 1686, might have told us if he could have risen. But he didn't.

As we came down through the town, we encountered a squad of little donkeys ready saddled for use. The saddles were peculiar, to say the least. They consisted of a sort of saw-buck, with a small mattress on it, and this furniture covered about half the donkey. There were no stirrups, but really such supports were not needed—to use such a saddle was the next thing to riding a dinner table—there was ample support clear out to one's knee joints. A pack of ragged Portuguese muleteers crowded around us, offering their beasts at half a dollar an hour—more rascality to the stranger, for the market price is sixteen cents. Half a dozen of us mounted the ungainly affairs, and submitted to the indignity of making a ridiculous spectacle of ourselves through the principal streets of a town of 10,000 inhabitants.

We started. It was not a trot, a gallop, or a canter, but a stampede, and made up of all possible or conceivable gaits. No spurs were necessary. There was a muleteer to every donkey and a dozen volunteers beside, and they banged the donkeys with their goad-sticks, and pricked them with their spikes, and shouted something that sounded like "*Sekki-yah!*" and kept up a din and a racket that was worse than Bedlam itself. These rascals were all on foot, but no matter, they were always up to time—they can outrun and outlast a donkey. Altogether ours was a lively and picturesque procession, and drew crowded audiences to the balconies wherever we went.

Blucher could do nothing at all with his donkey. The beast scampered zigzag across the road and the others ran into him; he scraped Blucher against carts and the corners of houses; the road was fenced in with high stone walls, and the donkey gave him a polishing first on one side and then on the other, but never once took the middle; he finally came to the house he was born in and darted into the parlor, scraping Blucher off at the doorway. After remounting, Blucher said to the muleteer, "Now, that's enough, you know; you go slow hereafter." But the fellow knew no English and did not understand, so he simply said, "*Sekki-yah!*" and the donkey was off again like a shot. He turned a corner suddenly, and Blucher went over his head. And, to speak truly, every mule stumbled over the two, and the whole cavalcade was piled up in a heap. No harm done. A fall from one of those donkeys is of little more consequence than rolling off a sofa. The donkeys all stood still after the catastrophe, and waited for their dismembered saddles to be patched up and put on by the noisy muleteers. Blucher was pretty angry, and wanted to swear, but every time he opened his mouth his animal did so also, and let off a series of brays that drowned all other sounds.

It was fun, skurrying around the breezy hills and through the beautiful cañons. There was that rare thing, novelty, about it; it was a fresh, new, exhilarating sensation, this donkey riding, and worth a hundred worn and threadbare home pleasures.

The roads were a wonder, and well they might be. Here was an island with only a handful of people in it—25,000—and yet such fine roads do not exist in the United States outside of Central Park. Everywhere you go, in any direction, you find either a hard, smooth, level thoroughfare, just sprinkled with black lava sand, and bordered with little gutters neatly paved with small smooth pebbles, or compactly paved ones like Broadway. They talk much of the Russ pavement in New York, and call it a new invention—yet here they have been using it in this remote little isle of the sea for two hundred years! Every street in Horta is handsomely paved with the heavy Russ blocks, and the surface is neat and true as a floor—not marred by holes like Broadway. And every road is fenced in by tall, solid lava walls, which will last a thousand years in this land where frost is unknown. They are very thick, and are often plastered and whitewashed, and capped with projecting slabs of cut stone. Trees from gardens above hang their swaying tendrils down, and contrast their bright green with the whitewash or the black lava of the walls, and make them beautiful. The trees and vines stretch across these narrow roadways sometimes, and so shut out the sun that you seem to be riding through a tunnel. The pavements, the roads, and the bridges are all government work.

The bridges are of a single span—a single arch—of cut stone, without a support, and paved on top with flags of lava and ornamental pebble work. Everywhere are walls, walls, walls,—and all of them tasteful and handsome—and eternally substantial; and everywhere are those marvelous pavements, so neat, so smooth, and so indestructible. And if ever roads and streets, and the outsides of houses, were perfectly free from any sign or semblance of dirt or dust or mud, or uncleanliness of any kind, it is Horta, it is Fayal. The lower classes of the people, in their persons and their domiciles, are not clean—but there it stops—the town and the island are miracles of cleanliness.

We arrived home again finally, after a ten-mile excursion, and the irrepressible muleteers scampered at our heels through the main street, goading the donkeys, shouting the everlasting *"Sekki-yah,"* and singing "John Brown's Body" in ruinous English.

When we were dismounted and it came to settling, the shouting and jawing and swearing and quarreling among the muleteers and with us, was nearly deafening. One fellow would demand a dollar an hour for the use of his donkey; another claimed half a dollar for pricking him up, another a quarter for helping in that service, and about fourteen guides presented bills for showing us the way through the town and its environs; and every vagrant of them was more vociferous, and more vehement, and more frantic in gesture than his neighbor. We paid one guide, and paid for one muleteer to each donkey.

The mountains on some of the islands are very high. We sailed along the shore of the Island of Pico, under a stately green pyramid that rose up with one unbroken sweep from our very feet to an altitude of 7,613 feet, and thrust its summit above the white clouds like an island adrift in a fog!

We got plenty of fresh oranges, lemons, figs, apricots, etc., in these Azores, of course. But I will desist. I am not here to write patent office reports.

We are on our way to Gibraltar, and shall reach there five or six days out from the Azores.

CHAPTER VII

A week of buffeting a tempestuous and relentless sea; a week of seasickness and deserted cabins; of lonely quarter-decks drenched with spray—spray so ambitious that it even coated the smoke stacks thick with a white crust of salt to their very tops; a week of shivering in the shelter of the lifeboats and deck-houses by day, and blowing suffocating "clouds" and boisterously performing at dominoes in the smoking-room at night.

And the last night of the seven was the stormiest of all. There was no thunder, no noise but the pounding bows of the ship, the keen whistling of the gale through the cordage, and the rush of the seething waters. But the vessel climbed aloft as if she would climb to heaven—then paused an instant that seemed a century, and plunged headlong down again, as from a precipice. The sheeted sprays drenched the decks like rain. The blackness of darkness was everywhere. At long intervals a flash of lightning clove it with a quivering line of fire, that revealed a heaving world of water where was nothing before, kindled the dusky cordage to glittering silver, and lit up the faces of the men with a ghastly luster!

Fear drove many on deck that were used to avoiding the night winds and the spray. Some thought the vessel could not live through the night, and it seemed less dreadful to stand out in the midst of the wild tempest and *see* the peril that threatened than to be shut up in the sepulchral cabins, under the dim lamps, and imagine the horrors that were abroad on the ocean. And once out—once where they could see the ship struggling in the strong grasp of the storm—once where they could hear the shriek of the winds, and face the driving spray and look out upon the majestic picture the lightnings disclosed, they were prisoners to a fierce fascination they could not resist, and so remained. It was a wild night—and a very, very long one.

Everybody was sent scampering to the deck at seven o'clock this lovely morning of the 30th of June with the glad news that land was in sight! It was a rare thing and a joyful, to see *all* the ship's family abroad once more, albeit the happiness that sat upon every countenance could only partly conceal the ravages which that long siege of storms had wrought there. But dull eyes soon sparkled with pleasure, pallid cheeks flushed again, and frames weakened by sickness gathered new life from the quickening influences of the bright, fresh morning. Yea, and from a still more potent influence: the worn castaways were to see the blessed land again!—and to see it was to bring back that mother-land that was in all their thoughts.

Within the hour we were fairly within the Straits of Gibraltar, the tall yellow-splotched hills of Africa on our right, with their bases veiled in a blue haze and their summits swathed in clouds—the same being according to Scripture, which says that "clouds and darkness are over the land." The words were spoken of this particular portion of Africa, I believe. On our left were the granite-ribbed domes of old Spain. The Strait is only thirteen miles wide in its narrowest part.

At short intervals, along the Spanish shore, were quaint-looking old stone towers—Moorish, we thought—but learned better afterward. In former times the Morocco rascals used to coast along the Spanish Main in their boats till a safe opportunity seemed to present itself, and then dart in and capture a Spanish village, and carry off all the pretty women they could find. It was a pleasant business, and was very popular. The Spaniards built these watch towers on the hills to enable them to keep a sharper lookout on the Moroccan speculators.

The picture, on the other hand, was very beautiful to eyes weary of the changeless sea, and by and by the ship's company grew wonderfully cheerful. But while we stood admiring the cloud-capped peaks and the lowlands robed in misty gloom, a finer picture burst upon us and chained every eye like a magnet—a stately ship, with canvas piled on canvas till she was one towering mass of bellying sail! She came speeding over the sea like a great bird. Africa and Spain were forgotten. All homage was for the beautiful stranger. While everybody gazed, she swept superbly by and flung the Stars and Stripes to the breeze! Quicker than thought, hats and handkerchiefs flashed in the air, and a cheer went up! She was beautiful before—she was radiant now. Many a one on our decks knew then for the first time how tame a sight his country's flag is at home compared to what it is in a foreign land. To see it is to see a vision of home itself and all its idols, and feel a thrill that would stir a very river of sluggish blood!

We were approaching the famed Pillars of Hercules, and already the African one, "Ape's Hill," a grand old mountain with summit streaked with granite ledges, was in sight. The other, the great Rock of Gibraltar, was yet to come. The ancients considered the Pillars of Hercules the head of navigation and the end of the world. The information the ancients didn't have was very voluminous. Even the prophets wrote book after book and epistle after epistle, yet never once hinted at the existence of a great continent on our side of the water; yet they must have known it was there, I should think.

In a few moments a lonely and enormous mass of rock, standing seemingly in the center of the wide strait and apparently washed on all sides by the sea, swung magnificently into view, and we needed no tedious traveled parrot to tell us it was Gibraltar. There could not be two rocks like that in one kingdom.

The Rock of Gibraltar is about a mile and a half long, I should say, by 1,400 to 1,500 feet high, and a quarter of a mile wide at its base. One side and one end of it come about as straight up out of the sea as the side of a house, the other end is irregular and the other side is a steep slant which an army would find very difficult to climb. At the foot of this slant is the walled town of Gibraltar—or rather the town occupies part of the slant. Everywhere—on hillside, in the precipice, by the sea, on the heights,—everywhere you choose to look, Gibraltar is clad with masonry and bristling with guns. It makes a striking and lively picture, from whatsoever point you contemplate it. It is pushed out into the sea on the end of a flat, narrow strip of land, and is suggestive of a "gob" of mud on the end of a shingle. A few hundred yards of this flat ground at its base belongs to the English, and then, extending across the strip from the Atlantic to the Mediterranean, a distance of a quarter of a mile, comes the "Neutral Ground," a space two or three hundred yards wide, which is free to both parties.

"Are you going through Spain to Paris?" That question was bandied about the ship day and night from Fayal to Gibraltar, and I thought I never could get so tired of hearing any one combination of words again, or more tired of answering, "I don't know."

At the last moment six or seven had sufficient decision of character to make up their minds to go, and did go, and I felt a sense of relief at once—it was forever too late, now, and I could make up my mind at my leisure, not to go. I must have a prodigious quantity of mind; it takes me as much as a week, sometimes, to make it up.

But behold how annoyances repeat themselves. We had no sooner gotten rid of the Spain distress than the Gibraltar guides started another—a tiresome repetition of a legend that had nothing very astonishing about it, even in the first place: "That high hill yonder is called the Queen's Chair; it is because one of the queens of Spain placed her chair there when the French and Spanish troops were besieging Gibraltar, and said she would never move from the spot till the English flag was lowered from the fortresses. If the English hadn't been gallant enough to lower the flag for a few hours one day, she'd have had to break her oath or die up there."

We rode on asses and mules up the steep, narrow streets and

entered the subterranean galleries the English have blasted out in the rock. These galleries are like spacious railway tunnels, and at short intervals in them great guns frown out upon sea and town through portholes five or six hundred feet above the ocean. There is a mile or so of this subterranean work, and it must have cost a vast deal of money and labor. The gallery guns command the peninsula and the harbors of both oceans, but they might as well not be there, I should think, for an army could hardly climb the perpendicular wall of the rock anyhow. Those lofty portholes afford superb views of the sea, though. At one place, where a jutting crag was hollowed out into a great chamber whose furniture was huge cannon and whose windows were portholes, a glimpse was caught of a hill not far away, and a soldier said:

"That high hill yonder is called the Queen's Chair; it is because a queen of Spain placed her chair there once, when the French and Spanish troops were besieging Gibraltar, and said she would never move from the spot till the English flag was lowered from the fortresses. If the English hadn't been gallant enough to lower the flag for a few hours, one day, she'd have had to break her oath or die up there."

On the topmost pinnacle of Gibraltar we halted a good while, and no doubt the mules were tired. They had a right to be. The military road was good, but rather steep, and there was a good deal of it. The view from the narrow ledge was magnificent; from it vessels seeming like the tiniest little toy boats, were turned into noble ships by the telescopes; and other vessels that were fifty miles away, and even sixty, they said, and invisible to the naked eye, could be clearly distinguished through those same telescopes. Below, on one side, we looked down upon an endless mass of batteries, and on the other straight down to the sea.

While I was resting ever so comfortably on a rampart, and cooling my baking head in the delicious breeze, an officious guide belonging to another party came up and said:

"Senor, that high hill yonder is called the Queen's Chair—"

"Sir, I am a helpless orphan in a foreign land. Have pity on me. Don't—now *don't* inflict that most in-FERNAL old legend on me any more today!"

There—I had used strong language, after promising I would never do so again; but the provocation was more than human nature could bear. If you had been bored so, when you had the noble panorama of Spain and Africa and the blue Mediterranean spread abroad at your feet, and wanted to gaze, and enjoy, and surfeit yourself with its beauty in silence, you might have even burst into stronger language than I did.

Gibraltar has stood several protracted sieges, one of them of nearly four years' duration (it failed), and the English only captured it by stratagem. The wonder is that anybody should ever dream of trying so impossible a project as the taking it by assault—and yet it has been tried more than once.

The Moors held the place twelve hundred years ago, and a staunch old castle of theirs of that date still frowns from the middle of the town, with moss-grown battlements and sides well scarred by shots fired in battles and sieges that are forgotten now. A secret chamber, in the rock behind it, was discovered some time ago, which contained a sword of exquisite workmanship, and some quaint old armor of a fashion that antiquaries are not acquainted with, though it is supposed to be Roman. Roman armor and Roman relics, of various kinds, have been found in a cave in the sea extremity of Gibraltar; history says Rome held this part of the country about the Christian era, and these things seem to confirm the statement.

In that cave, also, are found human bones, crusted with a very thick, stony coating, and wise men have ventured to say that those men not only lived before the flood, but as much as ten thousand years before it. It may be true—it looks reasonable enough—but as long as those parties can't vote any more, the matter can be of no great public interest. In this cave, likewise, are found skeletons and fossils of animals that exist in every part of Africa, yet within memory and tradition have never existed in any portion of Spain save this lone peak of Gibraltar! So the theory is that the channel between Gibraltar and Africa was once dry land, and that the low, neutral neck between Gibraltar and the Spanish hills behind it was once ocean, and, of course, that these African animals, being over at Gibraltar (after rock, perhaps—there is plenty there), got closed out when the great change occurred. The hills in Africa, across the channel, are full of apes, and there are now, and always have been, apes on the rock of Gibraltar—but not elsewhere in Spain! The subject is an interesting one.

There is an English garrison at Gibraltar of 6,000 or 7,000 men, and so uniforms of flaming red are plenty; and red and blue, and undress costumes of snowy white, and also the queer uniform of the bare-kneed Highlander; and one sees soft-eyed Spanish girls from San Roque, and veiled Moorish beauties (I suppose they are beauties) from Tarifa, and turbaned, sashed, and trowsered Moorish merchants from Fez, and long-robed, bare-legged, ragged Mohammedan vagabonds from Tetouan and Tangier, some brown, some yellow, and some as black as virgin ink—and Jews from all around, in gaberdine, skull-cap, and slippers, just as they are in pictures and theaters, and just as they were three thousand years ago, no doubt. You can easily understand that a tribe (somehow our pilgrims suggest that expression, because they march in a straggling procession through these foreign places with such an Indian-like air of complacency and independence about them) like ours, made up from fifteen or sixteen states of the Union, found enough to stare at in this shifting panorama of fashion to-day.

Speaking of our pilgrims reminds me that we have one or two people among us who are sometimes an annoyance. However, I do not count the Oracle in that list. I will explain that the Oracle is an innocent old ass who eats for four and looks wiser than the whole Academy of France would have any right to look, and never uses a one-syllable word when he can think of a longer one, and never by any possible chance knows the meaning of any long word he uses, or ever gets it in the right place; yet he will serenely venture an opinion on the most abstruse subject, and back it up complacently with quotations from authors who never existed, and finally when cornered will slide to the other side of the question, say he has been there all the time, and come back at you with your own spoken arguments, only with the big words all tangled, and play them in your very teeth as original with himself. He reads a chapter in the guide books, mixes the facts all up, with his bad memory, and then goes off to inflict the whole mess on somebody as wisdom which has been festering in his brain for years, and which he gathered in college from erudite authors who are dead now and out of print. This morning at breakfast he pointed out of the window, and said:

"Do you see that there hill out there on that African coast? It's one of them Pillows of Herkewls, I should say—and there's the ultimate one alongside of it."

"The ultimate one—that is a good word—but the Pillars are not both on the same side of the strait." (I saw he had been deceived by a carelessly written sentence in the Guide Book.)

"Well, it ain't for you to say, nor for me. Some authors states it that way, and some states it different. Old Gibbons don't say nothing about it,—just shirks it complete—Gibbons always done that when he got stuck—but there is Rolampton, what does *he* say? Why, he says that they was both on the same side, and Trinculian, and Sobaster, and Syraccus, and Langomarganbl—"

"Oh, that will do—that's enough. If you have got your hand in for inventing authors and testimony, I have nothing more to say—let them *be* on the same side."

We don't mind the Oracle. We rather like him. We can tolerate the Oracle very easily; but we have a poet and a good-natured, enterprising idiot on board, and they *do* distress the company. The one gives copies of his verses to consuls, commanders, hotel keepers, Arabs, Dutch,—to anybody, in fact, who will submit to a grievous infliction most kindly meant. His poetry is all very well on shipboard, notwithstanding when he wrote an "Ode to the Ocean in a Storm" in one half-hour, and an "Apostrophe to the Rooster in the Waist of the Ship" in the next, the transition was considered to be rather abrupt; but when he sends an invoice of rhymes to the governor of Fayal and another to the commander-in-chief and other dignitaries in Gibraltar, with the compliments of the Laureate of the Ship, it is not popular with the passengers.

The other personage I have mentioned is young and green, and not bright, not learned, and not wise. He will be, though, some day, if he recollects the answers to all his questions. He is known about the ship as the "Interrogation Point," and this by constant use has become shortened to "Interrogation." He has distinguished himself twice already. In Fayal they pointed out a hill and told him it was eight hundred feet high and eleven hundred feet long. And they told him there was a tunnel two thousand feet long and one thousand feet high running through the hill, from end to end. He believed it. He repeated it to everybody, discussed it, and read it from his notes. Finally, he took a useful hint from this remark which a thoughtful old pilgrim made:

"Well, yes, it *is* a little remarkable—singūlar tunnel altogether—stands up out of the top of the hill about two hundred feet, and one end of it sticks out of the hill about nine hundred!"

Here in Gibraltar he corners these educated British officers and badgers them with braggadocio about America and the wonders she can perform. He told one of them a couple of our gunboats could come here and knock Gibraltar into the Mediterranean sea!

At this present moment, half a dozen of us are taking a private pleasure excursion of our own devising. We form rather more than half the list of white passengers on board a small steamer bound for the venerable Moorish town of Tangier, Africa. Nothing could be more absolutely certain than that we are enjoying ourselves. One cannot do otherwise who speeds over these sparkling waters, and breathes the soft atmosphere of this sunny land. Care cannot assail us here. We are out of its jurisdiction.

We even steamed recklessly by the frowning fortress of Malabat (a stronghold of the Emperor of Morocco), without a twinge of fear. The whole garrison turned out under arms, and assumed a threatening attitude—yet still we did not fear. The entire garrison marched and counter-marched, within the rampart, in full view—yet notwithstanding even this, we never flinched.

I suppose we really do not know what fear is. I inquired the name of the garrison of the fortress of Malabat, and they said it was Mehemet Ali Ben Sancom. I said it would be a good idea to get some more garrisons to help him; but they said no; he had nothing to do but hold the place, and he was competent to do that; had done it two years already. That was evidence which one could not well refute. There is nothing like reputation.

Every now and then, my glove purchase in Gibraltar last night intrudes itself upon me. Dan and the ship's surgeon and I had been up to the great square, listening to the music of the fine military bands, and contemplating English and Spanish female loveliness and fashion and, at 9 o'clock, were on our way to the theater, when we met the General, the Judge, the Commodore, the Colonel, and the Commissioner of the United States of America to Europe, Asia, and Africa, who had been to the Club House, to register their several titles and impoverish the bill of fare; and they told us to go over to the little variety store, near the Hall of Justice, and buy some kid gloves. They said they were elegant, and very moderate in price. It seemed a stylish thing to go to the theater in kid gloves, and we acted upon the hint. A very handsome young lady in the store offered me a pair of blue gloves. I did not want blue, but she said they would look very pretty on a hand like mine. The remark touched me tenderly. I glanced furtively at my hand, and somehow it did seem rather a comely member. I tried a glove on my left, and blushed a little. Manifestly the size was too small for me. But I felt gratified when she said:

"Oh, it is just right!"—yet I knew it was no such thing.

I tugged at it diligently, but it was discouraging work. She said:

"Ah! I see *you* are accustomed to wearing kid gloves—but some gentlemen are *so* awkward about putting them on."

It was the last compliment I had expected. I only understand putting on the buckskin article perfectly. I made another effort, and tore the glove from the base of the thumb into the palm of the hand—and tried to hide the rent. She kept up her compliments, and I kept up my determination to deserve them or die:

"Ah, you have had experience!" [A rip down the back of the hand.] "They are just right for you—your hand is very small—if they tear you need not pay for them." [A rent across the middle.] "I can always tell when a gentleman understands putting on kid gloves. There is a grace about it that only comes with long practice." [The whole after guard of the glove "fetched away," as the sailors say, the fabric parted across the knuckles, and nothing was left but a melancholy ruin.]

I was too much flattered to make an exposure, and throw the merchandise on the angel's hands. I was hot, vexed, confused, but still happy; but I hated the other boys for taking such an absorbing interest in the proceedings. I wished they were in Jericho. I felt exquisitely mean when I said cheerfully:

"This one does very well; it fits elegantly. I like a glove that fits. No, never mind, ma'am, never mind; I'll put the other on in the street. It is warm here."

It *was* warm. It was the warmest place I ever was in. I paid the bill, and as I passed out with a fascinating bow, I thought I detected a light in the woman's eye that was gently ironical; and when I looked back from the street, and she was laughing all to herself about something or other, I said to myself, with withering sarcasm, "Oh, certainly; *you* know how to put on kid gloves, don't you?—a self-complacent ass, ready to be flattered out of your senses by every petticoat that chooses to take the trouble to do it!"

The silence of the boys annoyed me. Finally, Dan said, musingly:

"Some gentlemen don't know how to put on kid gloves at all;

but some do."

And the doctor said (to the moon, I thought):

"But it is always easy to tell when a gentleman is used to putting on kid gloves."

Dan soliloquized, after a pause:

"Ah, yes; there is a grace about it that only comes with long, very long practice."

"Yes, indeed, I've noticed that when a man hauls on a kid glove like he was dragging a cat out of an ash-hole by the tail, *he* understands putting on kid gloves; *he's* had ex—"

"Boys, enough of a thing's enough! You think you are very smart, I suppose, but I don't. And if you go and tell any of those old gossips in the ship about this thing, I'll never forgive you for it; that's all."

They let me alone then, for the time being. We always let each other alone in time to prevent ill feeling from spoiling a joke. But they had bought gloves, too, as I did. We threw all the purchases away together this morning. They were coarse, unsubstantial, freckled all over with broad yellow splotches, and could neither stand wear nor public exhibition. We had entertained an angel unawares, but we did not take her in. She did that for us.

Tangier! A tribe of stalwart Moors are wading into the sea to carry us ashore on their backs from the small boats.

CHAPTER VIII

This is royal! Let those who went up through Spain make the best of it—these dominions of the Emperor of Morocco suit our little party well enough. We have had enough of Spain at Gibraltar for the present. Tangier is the spot we have been longing for all the time. Elsewhere we have found foreign-looking things and foreign-looking people, but always with things and people intermixed that we were familiar with before, and so the novelty of the situation lost a deal of its force. We wanted something thoroughly and uncompromisingly foreign—foreign from top to bottom—foreign from center to circumference—foreign inside and outside and all around—nothing anywhere about it to dilute its foreignness—nothing to remind us of any other people or any other land under the sun. And lo! in Tangier we have found it. Here is not the slightest thing that ever we have seen save in pictures—and we always mistrusted the pictures before. We can not any more. The pictures used to seem exaggerations—they seemed too weird and fanciful for reality. But behold, they were not wild enough—they were not fanciful enough—they have not told half the story. Tangier is a foreign land if ever there was one; and the true spirit of it can never be found in any book save the Arabian Nights. Here are no white men visible, yet swarms of humanity are all about us. Here is a packed and jammed city inclosed in a massive stone wall which is more than a thousand years old. All the houses nearly are one and two story; made of thick walls of stone; plastered outside; square as a dry-goods box; flat as a floor on top; no cornices; white-washed all over—a crowded city of snowy tombs! And the doors are arched with a peculiar arch we see in Moorish pictures; the floors are laid in vari-colored diamond flags; in tessellated many-colored porcelain squares wrought in the furnaces of Fez; in red tiles and broad bricks that time cannot wear; there is no furniture in the rooms (of Jewish dwellings) save divans—what there is in Moorish ones no man may know; within their sacred walls no Christian dog can enter. And the streets are oriental—some of them three feet wide, some six, but only two that are over a dozen; a man can blockade the most of them by extending his body across them. Isn't it an oriental picture?

There are stalwart Bedouins of the desert here, and stately Moors, proud of a history that goes back to the night of time; and Jews, whose fathers fled hither centuries upon centuries ago; and swarthy Riffians from the mountains—born cutthroats—and original, genuine negroes, as black as Moses; and howling dervishes, and a hundred breeds of Arabs—all sorts and descriptions of people that are foreign and curious to look upon.

And their dresses are strange beyond all description. Here is a bronzed Moor in a prodigious white turban, curiously embroidered jacket, gold and crimson sash of many folds, wrapped round and round his waist, trowsers that only come a little below his knee, and yet have twenty yards of stuff in them, ornamented scimetar, bare shins, stockingless feet, yellow slippers, and gun of preposterous length—a mere soldier!—I thought he was the Emperor at least. And here are aged Moors with flowing white beards, and long white robes with vast cowls; and Bedouins with long, cowled, striped cloaks, and negroes and Riffians with heads clean-shaven, except a kinky scalp-lock back of the ear, or rather up on the after corner of the skull, and all sorts of barbarians in all sorts of weird costumes, and all more or less ragged. And here are Moorish women who are enveloped from head to foot in coarse white robes and whose sex can only be determined by the fact that they only leave one eye visible, and never look at men of their own race, or are looked at by them in public. Here are five thousand Jews in blue gaberdines, sashes about their waists, slippers upon their feet, little skull-caps upon the backs of their heads, hair combed down on the forehead, and cut straight across the middle of it from side to side—the self-same fashion their Tangier ancestors have worn for I don't know how many bewildering centuries. Their feet and ankles are bare. Their noses are all hooked, and hooked alike. They all resemble each other so much that one could almost believe they were of one family. Their women are plump and pretty, and do smile upon a Christian in a way which is in the last degree comforting.

What a funny old town it is! It seems like profanation to laugh and jest and bandy the frivolous chat of our day amid its hoary relics. Only the stately phraseology and the measured speech of the sons of the Prophet are suited to a venerable antiquity like this. Here is a crumbling wall that was old when Columbus discovered America; was old when Peter the Hermit roused the knightly men of the Middle Ages to arm for the first Crusade; was old when Charlemagne and his paladins beleaguered enchanted castles and battled with giants and genii in the fabled days of the olden time; was old when Christ and his disciples walked the earth; stood where it stands to-day when the lips of Memnon were vocal, and men bought and sold in the streets of ancient Thebes!

The Phoenicians, the Carthaginians, the English, Moors, Romans, all have battled for Tangier—all have won it and lost it. Here is a ragged, oriental-looking negro from some desert place in interior Africa, filling his goat-skin with water from a stained and battered fountain built by the Romans twelve hundred years ago. Yonder is a ruined arch of a bridge built by Julius Caesar nineteen hundred years ago. Men who had seen the infant Saviour in the Virgin's arms have stood upon it, may be.

Near it are the ruins of a dockyard where Caesar repaired his ships and loaded them with grain when he invaded Britain, fifty years before the Christian era.

Here, under the quiet stars, these old streets seemed thronged with the phantoms of forgotten ages. My eyes are resting upon a spot where stood a monument which was seen and described by Roman historians less than two thousand years ago, whereon was inscribed:

"WE ARE THE CANAANITES. WE ARE THEY THAT HAVE BEEN DRIVEN OUT OF THE LAND OF CANAAN BY THE JEWISH ROBBER, JOSHUA."

Joshua drove them out, and they came here. Not many leagues from here is a tribe of Jews whose ancestors fled thither after an unsuccessful revolt against King David, and these their descendants are still under a ban and keep to themselves.

Tangier has been mentioned in history for three thousand years. And it was a town, though a queer one, when Hercules, clad in his lion-skin, landed here, four thousand years ago. In these streets he met Anytus, the king of the country, and brained him with his club, which was the fashion among gentlemen in those days. The people of Tangier (called Tingis, then) lived in the rudest possible huts, and dressed in skins and carried clubs, and were as savage as the wild beasts they were constantly obliged to war with. But they were a gentlemanly race, and did no work. They lived on the natural products of the land. Their king's country residence was at the famous Garden of Hesperides, seventy miles down the coast from here. The garden, with its golden apples (oranges), is gone now—no vestige of it remains. Antiquarians concede that such a personage as Hercules did exist in ancient times, and agree that he was an enterprising and energetic man, but decline to believe him a good, bona fide god, because that would be unconstitutional.

Down here at Cape Spartel is the celebrated cave of Hercules, where that hero took refuge when he was vanquished and driven out of the Tangier country. It is full of inscriptions in the dead languages, which fact makes me think Hercules could not have traveled much, else he would not have kept a journal.

Five days' journey from here—say two hundred miles—are the ruins of an ancient city, of whose history there is neither record nor tradition. And yet its arches, its columns, and its statues, proclaim it to have been built by an enlightened race.

The general size of a store in Tangier is about that of an ordinary shower-bath in a civilized land. The Mohammedan merchant, tinman, shoemaker, or vender of trifles, sits cross-legged on the floor, and reaches after any article you may want to buy. You can rent a whole block of these pigeon-holes for fifty dollars a month. The market people crowd the market-place with their baskets of figs, dates, melons, apricots, etc., and among them file trains of laden asses, not much larger, if any, than a Newfoundland dog. The scene is lively, is picturesque, and smells like a police court. The Jewish money-changers have their dens close at hand; and all day long are counting bronze coins and transferring them from one bushel basket to another. They don't coin much money now-a-days, I think. I saw none but what was dated four or five hundred years back, and was badly worn and battered. These coins are not very valuable. Jack went out to get a napoleon changed, so as to have money suited to the general cheapness of things, and came back and said he had "swamped the bank; had bought eleven quarts of coin, and the head of the firm had gone on the street to negotiate for the balance of the change." I bought nearly half a pint of their money for a shilling myself. I am not proud on account of having so much money, though. I care nothing for wealth. The Moors have some small silver coins, and also some silver slugs worth a dollar each. the latter are exceedingly scarce—so much so that when poor ragged Arabs see one they beg to be allowed to kiss it.

They have also a small gold coin worth two dollars. And that reminds me of something. When Morocco is in a state of war, Arab couriers carry letters through the country, and charge a liberal postage. Every now and then they fall into the hands of marauding bands and get robbed. Therefore, warned by experience, as soon as they have collected two dollars' worth of money they exchange it for one of those little gold pieces, and when robbers come upon them, swallow it. The stratagem was good while it was unsuspected, but after that the marauders simply gave the sagacious United States mail an emetic and sat down to wait.

The Emperor of Morocco is a soulless despot, and the great officers under him are despots on a smaller scale. There is no regular system of taxation, but when the Emperor or the Bashaw want money, they levy on some rich man, and he has to furnish the cash or go to prison. Therefore, few men in Morocco dare to be rich. It is too dangerous a luxury. Vanity occasionally leads a man to display wealth, but sooner or later the Emperor trumps up a charge against him—any sort of one will do—and confiscates his property. Of course, there are many rich men in the empire, but their money is buried, and they dress in rags and counterfeit poverty. Every now and then the Emperor imprisons a man who is suspected of the crime of being rich, and makes things so uncomfortable for him that he is forced to discover where he has hidden his money.

Moors and Jews sometimes place themselves under the protection of the foreign consuls, and then they can flout their riches in the Emperor's face with impunity.

CHAPTER IX

About the first adventure we had yesterday afternoon, after landing here, came near finishing that heedless Blucher. We had just mounted some mules and asses, and started out under the guardianship of the stately, the princely, the magnificent Hadji Mohammed Lamarty (may his tribe increase!), when we came upon a fine Moorish mosque, with tall tower, rich with checker-work of many-colored porcelain, and every part and portion of the edifice adorned with the quaint architecture of the Alhambra, and Blucher started to ride into the open doorway. A startling "Hi-hi!" from our camp followers, and a loud "Halt!" from an English gentlemen in the party, checked the adventurer, and then we were informed that so dire a profanation is it for a Christian dog to set foot upon the sacred threshold of a Moorish mosque, that no amount of purification can ever make it fit for the faithful to pray in again. Had Blucher succeeded in entering the place, he would no doubt have been chased through the town and stoned; and the time has been, and not many years ago either, when a Christian would have been most ruthlessly slaughtered, if captured in a mosque. We caught a glimpse of the handsome tessellated pavements within, and of the devotees performing their ablutions at the fountains; but even that we took that glimpse was a thing not relished by the Moorish bystanders.

Some years ago the clock in the tower of the mosque got out of order. The Moors of Tangier have so degenerated that it has been long since there was an artificer among them capable of curing so delicate a patient as a debilitated clock. The great men of the city met in solemn conclave to consider how the difficulty was to be met. They discussed the matter thoroughly but arrived at no solution. Finally, a patriarch arose and said:

"Oh, children of the Prophet, it is known unto you that a Portuguese dog of a Christian clockmender pollutes the city of Tangier with his presence. Ye know, also, that when mosques are builded, asses bear the stones and the cement, and cross the sacred threshold. Now, therefore, send the Christian dog on all fours, and barefoot, into the holy place to mend the clock, and let him go as an ass!"

And in that way it was done. Therefore, if Blucher ever sees the inside of a mosque, he will have to cast aside his humanity and go in his natural character. We visited the jail, and found Moorish prisoners making mats and baskets. (This thing of utilizing crime savors of civilization.) Murder is punished with death. A short time ago three murderers were taken beyond the city walls and shot. Moorish guns are not good, and neither are Moorish marksmen. In this instance, they set up the poor criminals at long range, like so many targets, and practiced on them—kept them hopping about and dodging bullets for half an hour before they managed to drive the center.

When a man steals cattle, they cut off his right hand and left leg, and nail them up in the market-place as a warning to everybody. Their surgery is not artistic. They slice around the bone a little; then break off the limb. Sometimes the patient gets well; but, as a general thing, he don't. However, the Moorish heart is stout. The Moors were always brave. These criminals undergo the fearful operation without a wince, without a tremor of any kind, without a groan! No amount of suffering can bring down the pride of a Moor, or make him shame his dignity with a cry.

Here, marriage is contracted by the parents of the parties to it. There are no valentines, no stolen interviews, no riding out, no courting in dim parlors, no lovers' quarrels and reconciliations—no nothing that is proper to approaching matrimony. The young man takes the girl his father selects for him, marries her, and after that she is unveiled, and he sees her for the first time. If after due acquaintance, she suits him, he retains her; but if he suspects her purity, he bundles her back to her father; if he finds her diseased, the same; or if, after just and reasonable time is allowed her, she neglects to bear children, back she goes to the home of her childhood.

Mohammedans here, who can afford it, keep a good many wives on hand. They are called wives, though I believe the Koran only allows four genuine wives—the rest are concubines. The Emperor of Morocco don't know how many wives he has, but thinks he has five hundred. However, that is near enough—a dozen or so, one way or the other, don't matter.

Even the Jews in the interior have a plurality of wives.

I have caught a glimpse of the faces of several Moorish women (for they are only human, and will expose their faces for the admiration of a Christian dog when no male Moor is by), and I am full of veneration for the wisdom that leads them to cover up such atrocious ugliness.

They carry their children at their backs, in a sack, like other savages the world over.

Many of the negroes are held in slavery by the Moors. But the moment a female slave becomes her master's concubine her bonds are broken, and as soon as a male slave can read the first chapter of the Koran (which contains the creed) he can no longer be held in bondage.

They have three Sundays a week in Tangier. The Mohammedan's comes on Friday, the Jew's on Saturday, and that of the Christian Consuls on Sunday. The Jews are the most radical. The Moor goes to his mosque about noon on his Sabbath, as on any other day, removes his shoes at the door, performs his ablutions, makes his salaams, pressing his forehead to the pavement time and again, says his prayers, and goes back to his work.

But the Jew shuts up shop; will not touch copper or bronze money at all; soils his fingers with nothing meaner than silver and gold; attends the synagogue devoutly; will not cook or have anything to do with fire; and religiously refrains from embarking in any enterprise.

The Moor who has made a pilgrimage to Mecca is entitled to high distinction. Men call him Hadji, and he is thenceforward a great personage. Hundreds of Moors come to Tangier every year, and embark for Mecca. They go part of the way in English steamers; and the ten or twelve dollars they pay for passage is about all the trip costs. They take with them a quantity of food, and when the commissary department fails they "skirmish," as Jack terms it in his sinful, slangy way. From the time they leave till they get home again, they never wash, either on land or sea. They are usually gone from five to seven months, and as they do not change their clothes during all that time, they are totally unfit for the drawing-room when they get back.

Many of them have to rake and scrape a long time to gather together the ten dollars their steamer passage costs; and when one of them gets back he is a bankrupt forever after. Few Moors can ever build up their fortunes again in one short lifetime, after so reckless an outlay. In order to confine the dignity of Hadji to gentlemen of patrician blood and possessions, the Emperor decreed that no man should make the pilgrimage save bloated aristocrats who were worth a hundred dollars in specie. But behold how iniquity can circumvent the law! For a consideration, the Jewish money-changer lends the pilgrim one hundred dollars long enough for him to swear himself through, and then receives it back before the ship sails out of the harbor!

Spain is the only nation the Moors fear. The reason is, that Spain sends her heaviest ships of war and her loudest guns to astonish these Moslems; while America, and other nations, send only a little contemptible tub of a gunboat occasionally. The Moors, like other savages, learn by what they see; not what they hear or read. We have great fleets in the Mediterranean, but they seldom touch at African ports. The Moors have a small opinion of England, France, and America, and put their representatives to a deal of red-tape circumlocution before they grant them their common rights, let alone a favor. But the moment the Spanish minister makes a demand, it is acceded to at once, whether it be just or not.

Spain chastised the Moors five or six years ago, about a disputed piece of property opposite Gibraltar, and captured the city of Tetouan. She compromised on an augmentation of her territory; twenty million dollars indemnity in money; and peace. And then she gave up the city. But she never gave it up until the Spanish soldiers had eaten up all the cats. They would not compromise as long as the cats held out. Spaniards are very fond of cats. On the contrary, the Moors reverence cats as something sacred. So the Spaniards touched them on a tender point that time. Their unfeline conduct in eating up all the Tetouan cats aroused a hatred toward them in the breasts of the Moors, to which even the driving them out of Spain was tame and passionless. Moors and Spaniards are foes forever now. France had a minister here once who embittered the nation against him in the most innocent way. He killed a couple of battalions of cats (Tangier is full of them) and made a parlor carpet out of their hides. He made his carpet in circles—first a circle of old gray tom-cats, with their tails all pointing toward the center; then a circle of yellow cats; next a circle of black cats and a circle of white ones; then a circle of all sorts of cats; and finally, a centerpiece of assorted kittens. It was very beautiful; but the Moors curse his memory to this day.

When we went to call on our American Consul-general, to-day, I noticed that all possible games for parlor amusement seemed to be represented on his center-tables. I thought that hinted at lonesomeness. The idea was correct. His is the only American family in Tangier. There are many foreign Consuls in this place; but much visiting is not indulged in. Tangier is clear out of the world, and what is the use of visiting when people have nothing on earth to talk about? There is none. So each consul's family stays at home chiefly, and amuses itself as best it can. Tangier is full of interest for one day, but after that it is a weary prison. The consul-general has been here five years, and has got enough of it to do him for a century, and is going home shortly. His family seize upon their letters and papers when the mail arrives, read them over and over again for two days or three, talk them over and over again for two or three more, till they wear them out, and after that, for days together, they eat and drink and sleep, and ride out over the same old road, and see the same old tiresome things that even decades of centuries have scarcely changed, and say never a single word! They have literally nothing whatever to talk about. The arrival of an American man-of-war is a godsend to them. "Oh, solitude, where are the charms which sages have seen in thy face?" It is the completest exile that I can conceive of. I would seriously recommend to the government of the United States that when a man commits a crime so heinous that the law provides no adequate punishment for it, they make him consul-general to Tangier.

I am glad to have seen Tangier—the second oldest town in the world. But I am ready to bid it good-bye, I believe.

We shall go hence to Gibraltar this evening or in the morning; and doubtless the *Quaker City* will sail from that port within the next forty-eight hours.

CHAPTER X

We passed the Fourth of July on board the *Quaker City*, in mid-ocean. It was in all respects a characteristic Mediterranean day—faultlessly beautiful. A cloudless sky; a refreshing summer wind; a radiant sunshine that glinted cheerily from dancing wavelets instead of crested mountains of water; a sea beneath us that was so wonderfully blue, so richly, brilliantly blue, that it overcame the dullest sensibilities with the spell of its fascination.

They even have fine sunsets on the Mediterranean—a thing that is certainly rare in most quarters of the globe. The evening we sailed away from Gibraltar, that hard-featured rock was swimming in a creamy mist so rich, so soft, so enchantingly vague and dreamy, that even the Oracle, that serene, that inspired, that overpowering humbug, scorned the dinner-gong and tarried to worship!

He said: "Well, that's gorgis, ain't it! They don't have none of them things in our parts, *do* they? I consider that them effects is on account of the superior refragability, as you may say, of the sun's diramic combination with the lymphatic forces of the perihelion of Jubiter. What should you think?"

"Oh, *go* to bed!" Dan said that, and went away.

"Oh, yes, it's all very well to say go to bed when a man makes an argument which another man can't answer. Dan don't never stand any chance in an argument with me. And he knows it, too. What should you say, Jack?"

"Now, doctor, don't you come bothering around me with that dictionary bosh. I don't do you any harm, do I? Then you let *me* alone."

"He's gone, too. Well, them fellows have all tackled the old Oracle, as they say, but the old man's most too many for 'em. Maybe the Poet Lariat ain't satisfied with them deductions?"

The poet replied with a barbarous rhyme, and went below.

"'Pears that *he* can't qualify, neither. Well, I didn't expect nothing out of *him*. I never see one of them poets yet that knowed anything. He'll go down, now, and grind out about four reams of the awfullest slush about that old rock, and give it to a consul or a pilot or a nigger, or anybody he comes across first which he can impose on. Pity but somebody'd take that poor old lunatic and dig all that poetry rubbage out of him. Why can't a man put his intellect onto things that's some value? Gibbons and Hippocratus and Sarcophagus, and all them old ancient philosophers, was down on poets—"

"Doctor," I said, "you are going to invent authorities now, and I'll leave you, too. I always enjoy your conversation, notwithstanding the luxuriance of your syllables, when the philosophy you offer rests on your own responsibility; but when you begin to soar—when you begin to support it with the evidence of authorities who are the creations of your own fancy, I lose confidence."

That was the way to flatter the doctor. He considered it a sort of acknowledgment on my part of a fear to argue with him. He was always persecuting the passengers with abstruse propositions framed in language that no man could understand, and they endured the exquisite torture a minute or two and then abandoned the field. A triumph like this, over half a dozen antagonists, was sufficient for one day; from that time forward he would patrol the decks beaming blandly upon all comers, and so tranquilly, blissfully happy!

But I digress. The thunder of our two brave cannon announced the Fourth of July, at daylight, to all who were awake. But many of us got our information at a later hour, from the almanac. All the flags were sent aloft, except half a dozen that were needed to decorate portions of the ship below, and in a short time the vessel assumed a holiday appearance. During the morning, meetings were held and all manner of committees set to work on the celebration ceremonies. In the afternoon the ship's company assembled aft, on deck, under the awnings; the flute, the asthmatic melodeon, and the consumptive clarinet, crippled the Star Spangled Banner, the choir chased it to cover, and George came in with a peculiarly lacerating screech on the final note and slaughtered it. Nobody mourned.

We carried out the corpse on three cheers (that joke was not intentional and I do not indorse it), and then the President, throned behind a cable-locker with a national flag spread over it, announced the "Reader," who rose up and read that same old Declaration of Independence which we have all listened to so often without paying any attention to what it said; and after that the President piped the Orator of the Day to quarters and he made that same old speech about our national greatness which we so religiously believe and so fervently applaud. Now came the choir into court again, with the complaining instruments, and assaulted Hail Columbia; and when victory hung wavering in the scale, George returned with his dreadful wild-goose stop turned on, and the choir won, of course. A minister pronounced the benediction, and the patriotic little gathering disbanded. The Fourth of July was safe, as far as the Mediterranean was concerned.

At dinner in the evening, a well-written original poem was recited with spirit by one of the ship's captains, and thirteen regular toasts were washed down with several baskets of champagne. The speeches were bad—execrable, almost without exception. In fact, without *any* exception, but one. Captain Duncan made a good speech; he made the only good speech of the evening. He said:

"LADIES AND GENTLEMEN:—May we all live to a green old age, and be prosperous and happy. Steward, bring up another basket of champagne."

It was regarded as a very able effort.

The festivities, so to speak, closed with another of those miraculous balls on the promenade deck. We were not used to dancing on an even keel, though, and it was only a questionable success. But take it altogether, it was a bright, cheerful, pleasant Fourth.

Toward nightfall, the next evening, we steamed into the great artificial harbor of this noble city of Marseilles, and saw the dying sunlight gild its clustering spires and ramparts, and flood its leagues of environing verdure with a mellow radiance that touched with an added charm the white villas that flecked the landscape far and near. [Copyright secured according to law.]

There were no stages out, and we could not get on the pier from the ship. It was annoying. We were full of enthusiasm—we wanted to see France! Just at nightfall our party of three contracted with a waterman for the privilege of using his boat as a bridge—its stern was at our companion ladder and its bow touched the pier. We got in and the fellow backed out into the harbor. I told him in French that all we wanted was to walk over his thwarts and step ashore, and asked him what he went away out there for? He said he could not understand me. I repeated. Still, he could not understand. He appeared to be very ignorant of French. The doctor tried him, but he could not understand the doctor. I asked this boatman to explain his conduct, which he did; and then I couldn't understand *him*. Dan said:

"Oh, go to the pier, you old fool—that's where we want to go!"

We reasoned calmly with Dan that it was useless to speak to this foreigner in English—that he had better let us conduct this business in the French language and not let the stranger see how uncultivated he was.

"Well, go on, go on," he said, "don't mind me. I don't wish to interfere. Only, if you go on telling him in your kind of French he never will find out where we want to go to. That is what I think about it."

We rebuked him severely for this remark, and said we never knew an ignorant person yet but was prejudiced. The Frenchman spoke again, and the doctor said:

"There, now, Dan, he says he is going to *allez* to the *douain*. Means he is going to the hotel. Oh, certainly—*we* don't know the French language."

This was a crusher, as Jack would say. It silenced further criticism from the disaffected member. We coasted past the sharp bows of a navy of great steamships, and stopped at last at a government building on a stone pier. It was easy to remember then that the *douain* was the custom-house, and not the hotel. We did not mention it, however. With winning French politeness, the officers merely opened and closed our satchels, declined to examine our passports, and sent us on our way. We stopped at the first café we came to, and entered. An old woman seated us at a table and waited for orders. The doctor said:

"Avez-vous du vin?"

The dame looked perplexed. The doctor said again, with elaborate distinctness of articulation:

"Avez-vous du—vin!"

The dame looked more perplexed than before. I said:

"Doctor, there is a flaw in your pronunciation somewhere. Let me try her. Madame, avez-vous du vin? It isn't any use, doctor—take the witness."

"Madame, avez-vous do vin—ou fromage—pain—pickled pigs' feet—beurre—des oefs—du beuf—horseradish, sour-crout, hog and hominy—anything, *anything* in the world that can stay a Christian stomach!"

She said:

"Bless you, why didn't you speak English before?—I don't know anything about your plagued French!"

The humiliating taunts of the disaffected member spoiled the supper, and we dispatched it in angry silence and got away as soon as we could. Here we were in beautiful France—in a vast stone house of quaint architecture—surrounded by all manner of curiously worded French signs—stared at by strangely-habited, bearded French people—everything gradually and surely forcing upon us the coveted consciousness that at last, and beyond all question, we *were* in beautiful France and absorbing its nature to the forgetfulness of everything else, and coming to feel the happy romance of the thing in all its enchanting delightfulness—and to think of this skinny veteran intruding with her vile English, at such a moment, to blow the fair vision to the winds! It was exasperating.

We set out to find the center of the city, inquiring the direction every now and then. We never did succeed in making anybody understand just exactly what we wanted, and neither did we ever succeed in comprehending just exactly what they said in reply—but then they always pointed—they always did that, and we bowed politely and said "Merci, Monsieur," and so it was a blighting triumph over the disaffected member, anyway. He was restive under these victories and often asked:

"What did that pirate say?"

"Why, he told us which way to go, to find the Grand Casino."

"Yes, but what did he *say?*"

"Oh, it don't matter what he said—*we* understood him. These are educated people—not like that absurd boatman."

"Well, I wish they were educated enough to tell a man a direction that goes *some*where—for we've been going around in a circle for an hour—I've passed this same old drug store seven times."

We said it was a low, disreputable falsehood (but we knew it was not). It was plain that it would not do to pass that drug store again, though—we might go on asking directions, but we must cease from following finger pointings if we hoped to check the suspicions of the disaffected member.

A long walk through smooth, asphaltum-paved streets, bordered by blocks of vast new mercantile houses of cream-colored stone,—every house and every block precisely like all the other houses and all the other blocks for a mile, and all brilliantly lighted,—brought us at last to the principal thoroughfare. On every hand were bright colors, flashing constellations of gas-burners, gaily-dressed men and women thronging the sidewalks—hurry, life, activity, cheerfulness, conversation, and laughter everywhere! We found the Grand Hotel du Louvre et de la Paix, and wrote down who we were, where we were born, what our occupations were, the place we came from last, whether we were married or single, how we liked it, how old we were, where we were bound for and when we expected to get there, and a great deal of information of similar importance—all for the benefit of the landlord and the secret police. We hired a guide and began the business of sight-seeing immediately. That first night on French soil was a stirring one. I cannot think of half the places we went to, or what we particularly saw; we had no disposition to examine carefully into anything at all—we only wanted to glance and go—to move, keep moving! The spirit of the country was upon us. We sat down, finally, at a late hour, in the great Casino, and called for unstinted champagne. It is so easy to be bloated aristocrats where it costs nothing of consequence! There were about five hundred people in that dazzling place, I suppose, though the walls being papered entirely with mirrors, so to speak, one could not really tell but that there were a hundred thousand. Young, daintily-dressed exquisites and young, stylishly-dressed women, and also old gentlemen and old ladies, sat in couples and groups about innumerable marble-topped tables, and ate fancy suppers, drank wine, and kept up a chattering din of conversation that was dazing to the senses. There was a stage at the far end, and a large orchestra; and every now and then actors and actresses in preposterous comic dresses came out and sang the most extravagantly funny songs, to judge by their absurd actions; but that audience merely suspended its chatter, stared cynically, and never once smiled, never once applauded! I had always thought that Frenchmen were ready to laugh at anything.

CHAPTER XI

We are getting foreignized rapidly, and with facility. We are getting reconciled to halls and bed-chambers with unhomelike stone floors, and no carpets—floors that ring to the tread of one's heels with a sharpness that is death to sentimental musing. We are getting used to tidy, noiseless waiters, who glide hither and thither, and hover about your back and your elbows like butterflies, quick to comprehend orders, quick to fill them; thankful for a gratuity without regard to the amount; and always polite—never otherwise than polite. That is the strangest curiosity yet—a really polite hotel waiter who isn't an idiot. We are getting used to driving right into the central court of the hotel, in the midst of a fragrant circle of vines and flowers, and in the midst, also, of parties of gentlemen sitting quietly reading the paper and smoking. We are getting used to ice frozen by artificial process in ordinary bottles—the only kind of ice they have here. We are getting used to all these things; but we are *not* getting used to carrying our own soap. We are sufficiently civilized to carry our own combs and tooth-brushes; but this thing of having to ring for soap every time we wash is new to us, and not pleasant at all. We think of it just after we get our heads and faces thoroughly wet, or just when we think we have been in the bath-tub long enough, and then, of course, an annoying delay follows. These Marseillaise make Marseillaise hymns, and Marseilles vests, and Marseilles soap for all the world; but they never sing their hymns, or wear their vests, or wash with their soap themselves.

We have learned to go through the lingering routine of the table d'hote with patience, with serenity, with satisfaction. We take soup; then wait a few minutes for the fish; a few minutes more and the plates are changed, and the roast beef comes; another change and we take peas; change again and take lentils; change and take snail patties (I prefer grasshoppers); change and take roast chicken and salad; then strawberry pie and ice cream; then green figs, pears, oranges, green almonds, etc., finally coffee. Wine with every course, of course, being in France. With such a cargo on board, digestion is a slow process, and we must sit long in the cool chambers and smoke—and read French newspapers, which have a strange fashion of telling a perfectly straight story till you get to the "nub" of it, and then a word drops in that no man can translate, and that story is ruined. An embankment fell on some Frenchmen yesterday, and the papers are full of it to-day—but whether those sufferers were killed, or crippled, or bruised, or only scared, is more than I can possibly make out, and yet I would just give anything to know.

We were troubled a little at dinner to-day, by the conduct of an

American, who talked very loudly and coarsely, and laughed boisterously where all others were so quiet and well-behaved. He ordered
wine with a royal flourish, and said: "I never dine without wine,
sir" (which was a pitiful falsehood), and looked around upon the
company to bask in the admiration he expected to find in their faces.
All these airs in a land where they would as soon expect to leave the
soup out of the bill of fare as the wine!—in a land where wine is
nearly as common among all ranks as water! This fellow said: 'I am
a free-born sovereign, sir, an American, sir, and I want everybody to
know it!" He did not mention that he was a lineal descendant of
Balaam's ass; but everybody knew that without his telling it.

We have driven in the Prado—that superb avenue bordered with
patrician mansions and noble shade trees—and have visited the
Chateau Borély and its curious museum. They showed us a miniature cemetery there—a copy of the first graveyard that was ever in
Marseilles, no doubt. The delicate little skeletons were lying in
broken vaults, and had their household gods and kitchen utensils
with them. The original of this cemetery was dug up in the principal
street of the city a few years ago. It had remained there, only twelve
feet underground, for a matter of twenty-five hundred years, or
thereabouts. Romulus was here before he built Rome, and thought
something of founding a city on this spot, but gave up the idea. He
may have been personally acquainted with some of these Phoenicians whose skeletons we have been examining.

In the great Zoölogical Gardens we found specimens of all the
animals the world produces, I think, including a dromedary, a monkey ornamented with tufts of brilliant blue and carmine hair—a very
gorgeous monkey he was—a hippopotamus from the Nile, and a sort
of tall, long-legged bird with a beak like a powder-horn, and close-
fitting wings like the tails of a dress-coat. This fellow stood up with
his eyes shut and his shoulders stooped forward a little, and looked
as if he had his hands under his coat-tails. Such tranquil stupidity,
such supernatural gravity, such self-righteousness, and such ineffable self-complacency as were in the countenance and attitude of
that gray-bodied, dark-winged, bald-headed, and preposterously
uncomely bird! He was so ungainly, so pimply about the head, so
scaly about the legs; yet so serene, so unspeakably satisfied! He was
the most comical-looking creature that can be imagined. It was
good to hear Dan and the doctor laugh—such natural and such enjoyable laughter had not been heard among our excursionists since
our ship sailed away from America. This bird was a godsend to us,
and I should be an ingrate if I forgot to make honorable mention of
him in these pages. Ours was a pleasure excursion; therefore we
stayed with that bird an hour, and made the most of him. We stirred
him up occasionally, but he only unclosed an eye and slowly closed
it again, abating no jot of his stately piety of demeanor or his tremendous seriousness. He only seemed to say, "Defile not Heaven's

anointed with unsanctified hands." We did not know his name, and so we called him "The Pilgrim." Dan said:

"All he wants now is a Plymouth Collection."

The boon companion of the colossal elephant was a common cat! This cat had a fashion of climbing up the elephant's hind legs, and roosting on his back. She would sit up there, with her paws curved under her breast, and sleep in the sun half the afternoon. It used to annoy the elephant at first, and he would reach up and take her down, but she would go aft and climb up again. She persisted until she finally conquered the elephant's prejudices, and now they are inseparable friends. The cat plays about her comrade's forefeet or his trunk often, until dogs approach, and then she goes aloft out of danger. The elephant has annihilated several dogs lately, that pressed his companion too closely.

We hired a sailboat and a guide and made an excursion to one of the small islands in the harbor to visit the Castle d'If. This ancient fortress has a melancholy history. It has been used as a prison for political offenders for two or three hundred years, and its dungeon walls are scarred with the rudely-carved names of many and many a captive who fretted his life away here, and left no record of himself but these sad epitaphs wrought with his own hands. How thick the names were! And their long-departed owners seemed to throng the gloomy cells and corridors with their phantom shapes. We loitered through dungeon after dungeon, away down into the living rock below the level of the sea, it seemed. Names everywhere!—some plebeian, some noble, some even princely. Plebeian, prince, and noble, had one solicitude in common—they would not be forgotten! They could suffer solitude, inactivity, and the horrors of a silence that no sound ever disturbed; but they could not bear the thought of being utterly forgotten by the world. Hence the carved names. In one cell, where a little light penetrated, a man had lived twenty-seven years without seeing the face of a human being—lived in filth and wretchedness, with no companionship but his own thoughts, and they were sorrowful enough, and hopeless enough, no doubt. Whatever his jailers considered that he needed was conveyed to his cell by night, through a wicket. This man carved the walls of his prison-house from floor to roof with all manner of figures of men and animals, grouped in intricate designs. He had toiled there year after year, at his self-appointed task, while infants grew to boyhood—to vigorous youth—idled through school and college—acquired a profession—claimed man's mature estate—married and looked back to infancy as to a thing of some vague, ancient time, almost. But who shall tell how many ages it seemed to this prisoner? With the one, time flew sometimes; with the other, never—it crawled always. To the one, nights spent in dancing had seemed made of minutes instead of hours; to the other, those self-same nights had been like all other nights of dungeon life, and seemed made of slow, dragging weeks, instead of hours and minutes.

One prisoner of fifteen years had scratched verses upon his walls, and brief prose sentences—brief, but full of pathos. These spoke not of himself and his hard estate; but only of the shrine where his spirit fled the prison to worship—of home and the idols that were templed there. He never lived to see them.

The walls of these dungeons are as thick as some bed-chambers at home are wide—fifteen feet. We saw the damp, dismal cells in which two of Dumas' heroes passed their confinement—heroes of "Monte Cristo." It was here that the brave Abbé wrote a book with his own blood; with a pen made of a piece of iron hoop, and by the light of a lamp made out of shreds of cloth soaked in grease obtained from his food; and then dug through the thick wall with some trifling instrument which he wrought himself out of a stray piece of iron or table cutlery, and freed Dantés from his chains. It was a pity that so many weeks of dreary labor should have come to naught at last.

They showed us the noisome cell where the celebrated "Iron Mask"—that ill-starred brother of a hard-hearted king of France—was confined for a season, before he was sent to hide the strange mystery of his life from the curious in the dungeons of St. Marguerite. The place had a far greater interest for us than it could have had if we had known beyond all question who the Iron Mask was, and what his history had been, and why this most unusual punishment had been meted out to him. Mystery! That was the charm. That speechless tongue, those prisoned features, that heart so freighted with unspoken troubles, and that breast so oppressed with its piteous secret, had been here. These dank walls had known the man whose dolorous story is a sealed book forever! There was fascination in the spot.

CHAPTER XII

We have come five hundred miles by rail through the heart of France. What a bewitching land it is! What a garden! Surely the leagues of bright green lawns are swept and brushed and watered every day and their grasses trimmed by the barber. Surely the hedges are shaped and measured and their symmetry preserved by the most architectural of gardeners. Surely the long, straight rows of stately poplars that divide the beautiful landscape like the squares of a checker-board are set with line and plummet, and their uniform height determined with a spirit level. Surely the straight, smooth, pure white turnpikes are jack-planed and sand-papered every day. How else are these marvels of symmetry, cleanliness, and order attained? It is wonderful. There are no unsightly stone walls, and never a fence of any kind. There is no dirt, no decay, no rubbish anywhere—nothing that even hints at untidiness—nothing that ever suggests neglect. All is orderly and beautiful—everything is charming to the eye.

We had such glimpses of the Rhone gliding along between its grassy banks; of cosy cottages buried in flowers and shrubbery; of quaint old red-tiled villages with mossy mediaeval cathedrals looming out of their midst; of wooded hills with ivy-grown towers and turrets of feudal castles projecting above the foliage; such glimpses of Paradise, it seemed to us, such visions of fabled fairy-land!

We knew, then, what the poet meant, when he sang of—

> "—thy cornfields green, and sunny vines,
> O pleasant land of France!"

And it *is* a pleasant land. No word described it so felicitously as that one. They say there is no word for "home" in the French language. Well, considering that they have the article itself in such an attractive aspect, they ought to manage to get along without the word. Let us not waste too much pity on "homeless" France. I have observed that Frenchmen abroad seldom wholly give up the idea of going back to France some time or other. I am not surprised at it now.

We are not infatuated with these French railway cars, though. We took first-class passage, not because we wished to attract attention by doing a thing which is uncommon in Europe, but because we could make our journey quicker by so doing. It is hard to make railroading pleasant, in any country. It is too tedious. Stage-coaching is infinitely more delightful. Once I crossed the plains and deserts and mountains of the West, in a stage-coach, from the Missouri line to California, and since then all my pleasure-trips must be measured to that rare holiday frolic. Two thousand miles of ceaseless rush and rattle and clatter, by night and by day, and never a weary moment, never a lapse of interest! The first seven hundred miles a level continent, its grassy carpet greener and softer and smoother than any sea, and figured with designs fitted to its magnitude—the shadows of the clouds. Here were no scenes but summer scenes, and no disposition inspired by them but to lie at full length on the mail sacks, in the grateful breeze, and dreamily smoke the pipe of peace—what other, where all was repose and contentment? In cool mornings, before the sun was fairly up, it was worth a lifetime of city toiling and moiling, to perch in the foretop with the driver and see the six mustangs scamper under the sharp snapping of a whip that never touched them; to scan the blue distances of a world that knew no lords but us; to cleave the wind with uncovered head and feel the sluggish pulses rousing to the spirit of a speed that pretended to the resistless rush of a typhoon! Then thirteen hundred miles of desert solitudes; of limitless panoramas of bewildering perspective; of mimic cities, of pinnacled cathedrals, of massive fortresses, counterfeited in the eternal rocks and splendid with the crimson and gold of the setting sun; of dizzy altitudes among fog-wreathed peaks and never-melting snows, where thunders and lightnings and tempests warred magnificently at our feet and the storm-clouds above swung their shredded banners in our very faces!

But I forgot. I am in elegant France, now, and not skurrying through the great South Pass and the Wind River Mountains, among antelopes and buffaloes, and painted Indians on the war-path. It is not meet that I should make too disparaging comparisons between humdrum travel on a railway and that royal summer flight across a continent in a stage-coach. I meant, in the beginning, to say that railway journeying is tedious and tiresome, and so it is—though at the time, I was thinking particularly of a dismal fifty-hour pilgrimage between New York and St. Louis. Of course our trip through France was not really tedious, because all its scenes and experiences were new and strange; but as Dan says, it had its "discrepancies."

The cars are built in compartments that hold eight persons each. Each compartment is partially subdivided, and so there are two tolerably distinct parties of four in it. Four face the other four. The seats and backs are thickly padded and cushioned, and are very comfortable; you can smoke, if you wish; there are no bothersome peddlers; you are saved the infliction of a multitude of disagreeable fellow-passengers. So far, so well. But then the conductor locks you in when the train starts; there is no water to drink in the car; there is no heating apparatus for night travel; if a drunken rowdy should get in, you could not remove a matter of twenty seats from him, or enter another car; but, above all, if you are worn out and must sleep, you must sit up and do it in naps, with cramped legs and in a torturing misery that leaves you withered and lifeless the next day—for behold, they have not that culmination of all charity and human kindness, a sleeping car, in all France. I prefer the American system. It has not so many grievous "discrepancies."

In France, all is clockwork, all is order. They make no mistakes. Every third man wears a uniform, and whether he be a marshal of the empire or a brakeman, he is ready and perfectly willing to answer all your questions with tireless politeness, ready to tell you which car to take, yea, and ready to go and put you into it to make sure that you shall not go astray. You cannot pass into the waiting-room of the depot till you have secured your ticket, and you cannot pass from its only exit till the train is at its threshold to receive you. Once on board, the train will not start till your ticket has been examined—till every passenger's ticket has been inspected. This is chiefly for your own good. If by any possibility you have managed to take the wrong train, you will be handed over to a polite official who will take you whither you belong, and bestow you with many an affable bow. Your ticket will be inspected every now and then along the route, and when it is time to change cars you will know it. You are in the hands of officials who zealously study your welfare and your interest, instead of turning their talents to the invention of new methods of discommoding and snubbing you, as is very often the main employment of that exceedingly self-satisfied monarch, the railroad conductor of America.

But the happiest regulation in French railway government, is—thirty minutes to dinner! No five-minute boltings of flabby rolls, muddy coffee, questionable eggs, gutta-percha beef, and pies whose conception and execution are a dark and bloody mystery to all save the cook who created them! No; we sat calmly down—it was in old Dijon, which is so easy to spell and so impossible to pronounce, except when you civilize it and call it Demijohn—and poured out rich Burgundian wines and munched calmly through a long table d'hote bill of fare, snail patties, delicious fruits and all, then paid the trifle it cost and stepped happily aboard the train again, without once cursing the railroad company. A rare experience, and one to be treasured forever.

They say they do not have accidents on these French roads, and I think it must be true. If I remember rightly, we passed high above wagon roads, or through tunnels under them, but never crossed them on their own level. About every quarter of a mile, it seemed to me, a man came out and held up a club till the train went by, to signify that everything was safe ahead. Switches were changed a mile in advance, by pulling a wire rope that passed along the ground by the rail, from station to station. Signals for the day and signals for the night gave constant and timely notice of the position of switches.

No, they have no railroad accidents to speak of in France. But why? Because when one occurs, *somebody* has to hang for it!* Not hang, maybe, but be punsihed at least with such vigor of emphasis as to make negligence a thing to be shuddered at by railroad officials for many a day thereafter. "No blame attached to the officers"—that lying and disaster-breeding verdict so common to our soft-hearted juries, is seldom rendered in France. If the trouble occurred in the conductor's department, that officer must suffer if his subordinate cannot be proven guilty; if in the engineer's department, and the case be similar, the engineer must answer.

The Old Travelers—those delightful parrots who have "been here before," and know more about the country than Louis Napoleon knows now or ever will know,—tell us these things, and we believe them because they are pleasant things to believe, and because they are plausible and savor of the rigid subjection to law and order which we behold about us everywhere.

But we love the Old Travelers. We love to hear them prate and drivel and lie. We can tell them the moment we see them. They

---

*They go on the principle that it is better that one innocent man should suffer than five hundred.

always throw out a few feelers: they never cast themselves adrift till
they have sounded every individual and know that he has not traveled. Then they open their throttle-valves, and how they do brag,
and sneer, and swell, and soar, and blaspheme the sacred name of
Truth! Their central idea, their grand aim, is to subjugate you, keep
you down, make you feel insignificant and humble in the blaze of
their cosmopolitan glory! They will not let you know anything.
They sneer at your most inoffensive suggestions; they laugh unfeel-
ingly at your treasured dreams of foreign lands; they brand the statements of your traveled aunts and uncles as the stupidest absurdities;
they deride your most trusted authors and demolish the fair images
they have set up for your willing worship with the pitiless ferocity of
the fanatic iconoclast! But still I love the Old Travelers. I love
them for their witless platitudes; for their supernatural ability to
bore; for their delightful asinine vanity; for their luxuriant fertility
of imagination; for their startling, their brilliant, their overwhelming
mendacity!

By Lyons and the Saône (where we saw the Lady of Lyons and
thought little of her comeliness); by Villa Franca, Tonnerre, venerable Sens, Melun, Fontainebleau, and scores of other beautiful cities, we swept, always noting the absence of hog-wallows, broken
fences, cowlots, unpainted houses, and mud, and always noting, as
well, the presence of cleanliness, grace, taste in adorning and beauti-
fying, even to the disposition of a tree or the turning of a hedge, the
marvel of roads in perfect repair, void of ruts and guiltless of even an
inequality of surface—we bowled along, hour after hour, that brilliant summer day, and as nightfall approached we entered a wilderness of odorous flowers and shrubbery, sped through it, and then,
excited, delighted, and half persuaded that we were only the sport of
a beautiful dream, lo, we stood in magnificent Paris!

What excellent order they kept about that vast depot! There was
no frantic crowding and jostling, no shouting and swearing, and no
swaggering intrusion of services by rowdy hackmen. These latter
gentry stood outside—stood quietly by their long line of vehicles and
said never a word. A kind of hackman-general seemed to have the
whole matter of transportation in his hands. He politely received the
passengers and ushered them to the kind of conveyance they wanted,
and told the driver where to deliver them. There was no "talking
back," no dissatisfaction about overcharging, no grumbling about
anything. In a little while we were speeding through the streets of
Paris, and delightfully recognizing certain names and places with
which books had long ago made us familiar. It was like meeting an
old friend when we read "*Rue de Rivoli*" on the street corner; we
knew the genuine vast palace of the Louvre as well as we knew its
picture; when we passed by the Column of July we needed no one to
tell us what it was, or to remind us that on its site once stood the
grim Bastile, that grave of human hopes and happiness, that dismal

prison-house within whose dungeons so many young faces put on the wrinkles of age, so many proud spirits grew humble, so many brave hearts broke.

We secured rooms at the hotel, or rather, we had three beds put into one room, so that we might be together, and then we went out to a restaurant, just after lamp-lighting, and ate a comfortable, satisfactory, lingering dinner. It was a pleasure to eat where everything was so tidy, the food so well cooked, the waiters so polite, and the coming and departing company so moustached, so frisky, so affable, so fearfully and wonderfully Frenchy! All the surroundings were gay and enlivening. Two hundred people sat at little tables on the sidewalk, sipping wine and coffee; the streets were thronged with light vehicles and with joyous pleasure-seekers; there was music in the air, life and action all about us, and a conflagration of gaslight everywhere!

After dinner we felt like seeing such Parisian specialties as we might see without distressing exertion, and so we sauntered through the brilliant streets and looked at the dainty trifles in variety stores and jewelry shops. Occasionally, merely for the pleasure of being cruel, we put unoffending Frenchmen on the rack with questions framed in the incomprehensible jargon of their native language, and while they writhed, we impaled them, we peppered them, we scarified them, with their own vile verbs and participles.

We noticed that in the jewelry stores they had some of the articles marked "gold," and some labeled "imitation." We wondered at this extravagance of honesty, and inquired into the matter. We were informed that inasmuch as most people are not able to tell false gold from the genuine article, the government compels jewelers to have their gold work assayed and stamped officially according to its fineness, and their imitation work duly labeled with the sign of its falsity. They told us the jewelers would not dare to violate this law, and that whatever a stranger bought in one of their stores might be depended upon as being strictly what it was represented to be. Verily, a wonderful land is France!

Then we hunted for a barber-shop. From earliest infancy it had been a cherished ambition of mine to be shaved some day in a palatial barber-shop of Paris. I wished to recline at full length in a cushioned invalid-chair, with pictures about me, and sumptuous furniture; with frescoed walls and gilded arches above me, and vistas of Corinthian columns stretching far before me; with perfumes of Araby to intoxicate my senses, and the slumbrous drone of distant noises to soothe me to sleep. At the end of an hour I would wake up regretfully and find my face as smooth and as soft as an infant's. Departing, I would lift my hands above that barber's head and say, "Heaven bless you, my son!"

So we searched high and low, for a matter of two hours, but never a barber-shop could we see. We saw only wig-making establishments, with shocks of dead and repulsive hair bound upon the heads of painted waxen brigands who stared out from glass boxes upon the passer-by, with their stony eyes, and scared him with the ghostly white of their countenances. We shunned these signs for a time, but finally we concluded that the wig-makers must of necessity be the barbers as well, since we could find no single legitimate representative of the fraternity. We entered and asked, and found that it was even so.

I said I wanted to be shaved. The barber inquired where my room was. I said, never mind where my room was, I wanted to be shaved—there, on the spot. The doctor said he would be shaved also. Then there was an excitement among those two barbers! There was a wild consultation, and afterward a hurrying to and fro and a feverish gathering up of razors from obscure places and a ransacking for soap. Next they took us into a little mean, shabby back room; they got two ordinary sitting-room chairs and placed us in them, with our coats on. My old, old dream of bliss vanished into thin air!

I sat bolt upright, silent, sad, and solemn. One of the wig-making villains lathered my face for ten terrible minutes and finished by plastering a mass of suds into my mouth. I expelled the nasty stuff with a strong English expletive and said, "Foreigner, beware!" Then this outlaw strapped his razor on his boot, hovered over me ominously for six fearful seconds, and then swooped down upon me like the genious of destruction. The first rake of his razor loosened the very hide from my face and lifted me out of the chair. I stormed and raved, and the other boys enjoyed it. Their beards are not strong and thick. Let us draw the curtain over this harrowing scene. Suffice it that I submitted, and went through with the cruel infliction of a shave by a French barber; tears of exquisite agony coursed down my cheecks, now and then, but I survived. Then the incipient assassin held a basin of water under my chin and slopped its contents over my face, and into my bosom, and down the back of my neck, with a mean pretense of washing away the soap and blood. He dried my features with a towel, and was going to comb my hair; but I asked to be excused. I said, with withering irony, that it was sufficient to be skinned—I declined to be scalped.

I went away from there with my handkerchief about my face, and never, never, never desired to dream of palatial Parisian barber-shops any more. The truth is, as I believe I have since found out, that they have no barber-shops worthy of the name in Paris—and no barbers, either, for that matter. The impostor who does duty as a barber brings his pans and napkins and implements of torture to your residence and deliberately skins you in your private apartments. Ah, I have suffered, suffered, suffered, here in Paris, but never mind—the time is coming when I shall have a dark and bloody revenge. Some day a Parisian barber will come to my room to skin me, and from that day forth that barber will never be heard of more.

At eleven o'clock we alighted upon a sign which manifestly referred to billiards. Joy! We had played billiards in the Azores with balls that were not round, and on an ancient table that was very little smoother than a brick pavement—one of those wretched old things with dead cushions, and with patches in the faded cloth and invisible obstructions that made the balls describe the most astonishing and unsuspected angles, and perform feats in the way of unlooked-for and almost impossible "scratches," that were perfectly bewildering. We had played at Gibraltar with balls the size of a walnut, on a table like a public square—and in both instances we achieved far more aggravation than amusement. We expected to fare better here, but we were mistaken. The cushions were a good deal higher than the balls, and as the balls had a fashion of always stopping under the cushions, we accomplished very little in the way of caroms. The cushions were hard and unelastic, and the cues were so crooked that in making a shot you had to allow for the curve or you would infallibly put the "English" on the wrong side of the ball. Dan was to mark while the doctor and I played. At the end of an hour neither of us had made a count, and so Dan was tired of keeping tally with nothing to tally, and we were heated and angry and disgusted. We paid the heavy bill—about six cents—and said we would call around some time when we had a week to spend, and finish the game.

We adjourned to one of those pretty cafés and took supper and tested the wines of the country, as we had been instructed to do, and found them harmless and unexciting. They might have been exciting, however, if we had chosen to drink a sufficiency of them.

To close our first day in Paris cheerfully and pleasantly, we now sought our grand room in the Grand Hotel du Louvre and climbed into our sumptuous bed, to read and smoke—but alas!

> It was pitiful,
> In a whole city-full,
> Gas, we had none.

No gas to read by—nothing but dismal candles. It was a shame. We tried to map out excursions for the morrow; we puzzled over French "Guides to Paris"; we talked disjointedly, in a vain endeavor to make head or tail of the wild chaos of the day's sights and experiences; we subsided to indolent smoking; we gaped and yawned, and stretched—then feebly wondered if we were really and truly in renowned Paris, and drifted drowsily away into that vast mysterious void which men call sleep.

CHAPTER XIII

The next morning we were up and dressed at ten o'clock. We went to the *commissionaire* of the hotel—I don't know what a *commissionaire* is, but that is the man we went to—and told him we wanted a guide. He said the great International Exposition had drawn such multitudes of Englishmen and Americans to Paris that it would be next to impossible to find a good guide unemployed. He said he usually kept a dozen or two on hand, but he only had three now. He called them. One looked so like a very pirate that we let him go at once. The next one spoke with a simpering precision of pronunciation that was irritating, and said:

"If ze zhentlemans will to me make ze grande honneur to me rattain in hees serveece, I shall show to him everysing zat is magnifique to look upon in ze beautiful Paree. I speaky ze Angleesh pairfaitemaw."

He would have done well to have stopped there, because he had that much by heart and said it right off without making a mistake. But his self-complacency seduced him into attempting a flight into regions of unexplored English, and the reckless experiment was his ruin. Within ten seconds he was so tangled up in a maze of mutilated verbs and torn and bleeding forms of speech that no human ingenuity could ever have gotten him out of it with credit. It was plain enough that he could not "speaky" the English quite as "pairfaitemaw" as he had pretended he could.

The third man captured us. He was plainly dressed, but he had a noticeable air of neatness about him. He wore a high silk hat which was a little old, but had been carefully brushed. He wore secondhand kid gloves, in good repair, and carried a small rattan cane with a curved handle—a female leg, of ivory. He stepped as gently and as daintily as a cat crossing a muddy street; and oh, he was urbanity; he was quiet, unobtrusive self-possession; he was deference itself! He spoke softly and guardedly; and when he was about to make a statement on his sole responsibility, or offer a suggestion, he weighed it by drachms and scruples first, with the crook of his little stick placed meditatively to his teeth. His opening speech was perfect. It was perfect in construction, in phraseology, in grammar, in emphasis, in pronunciation—everything. He spoke little and guardedly, after that. We were charmed. We were more than charmed—we were overjoyed. We hired him at once. We never even asked him his price. This man—our lackey, our servant, our unquestioning slave though he was, was still a gentleman—we could see that—while of the other two one was course and awkward, and the other was a born pirate. We asked our man Friday's name. He drew from his pocketbook a snowy little card, and passed it to us with a profound bow:

A. BILLFINGER,
Guide to Paris, France, Germany, Spain, &c., &c.,
Grande Hotel du Louvre.

"Billfinger! Oh, carry me home to die!"

That was an "aside" from Dan. The atrocious name grated harshly on my ear, too. The most of us can learn to forgive, and even to like, a countenance that strikes us unpleasantly at first, but few of us, I fancy, become reconciled to a jarring name so easily. I was almost sorry we had hired this man, his name was so unbearable. However, no matter. We were impatient to start. Billfinger stepped to the door to call a carriage, and then the doctor said:

"Well, the guide goes with the barber-shop, with the billiard table, with the gasless room, and maybe with many another pretty romance of Paris. I expected to have a guide named Henri de Montmorency, or Armand de la Chartreuse, or something that would sound grand in letters to the villagers at home; but to think of a Frenchman by the name of Billfinger! Oh! this is absurd, you know. This will never do. We can't say Billfinger; it is nauseating. Name him over again; what had we better call him? Alexis du Caulaincourt?"

"Alphonse Henri Gustave de Hauteville," I suggested.

"Call him Ferguson," said Dan.

That was practical, unromantic good sense. Without debate, we expunged Billfinger *as* Billfinger, and called him Ferguson.

The carriage—an open barouche—was ready. Ferguson mounted beside the driver, and we whirled away to breakfast. As was proper, Mr. Ferguson stood by to transmit our orders and answer questions. By and by, he mentioned casually—the artful adventurer—that he would go and get his breakfast as soon as we had finished ours. He knew we could not get along without him, and that we would not want to loiter about and wait for him. We asked him to sit down and eat with us. He begged, with many a bow, to be excused. It was not proper, he said; he would sit at another table. We ordered him peremptorily to sit down with us.

Here endeth the first lesson. It was a mistake.

As long as we had the fellow after that, he was always hungry; he was always thirsty. He came early; he stayed late; he could not pass a restaurant; he looked with a lecherous eye upon every wine-shop. Suggestions to stop, excuses to eat and to drink were forever on his lips. We tried all we could to fill him so full that he would have no room to spare for a fortnight; but it was a failure. He did not hold enough to smother the cravings of his superhuman appetite.

He had another "discrepancy" about him. He was always wanting us to buy things. On the shallowest pretenses, he would inveigle us into shirt-stores, boot-stores, tailor-shops, glove-shops—anywhere under the broad sweep of the heavens that there seemed a chance of our buying anything. Any one could have guessed that the shopkeepers paid him a percentage on the sales; but in our blessed innocence we didn't, until this feature of his conduct grew unbearably prominent. One day, Dan happened to mention that he thought of buying three or four silk dress-patterns for presents. Ferguson's hungry eye was upon him in an instant. In the couse of twenty minutes, the carriage stopped.

"What's this?"

"Zis is ze finest silk magazin in Paris—ze most celebrate."

"What did you come here for? We told you to take us to the palace of the Louvre."

"I suppose ze gentleman say he wish to buy some silk."

"You are not required to 'suppose' things for the party, Ferguson. We do not wish to tax your energies too much. We will bear some of the burden and heat of the day ourselves. We will endeavor to do such 'supposing' as is really necessary to be done. Drive on." So spake the doctor.

Within fifteen minutes the carriage halted again, and before another silk-store. The doctor said:

"Ah, the palace of the Louvre; beautiful, beautiful edifice! Does the Emperor Napoleon live here now, Ferguson?"

"Ah, doctor! you do jest; zis is no ze palace; we come there directly. But since we pass right by zis store, where is such beautiful silk—"

"Ah! I see, I see. I meant to have told you that we did not wish to purchase any silks to-day; but in my absentmindedness I forgot it. I also meant to tell you we wished to go directly to the Louvre; but I forgot that also. However, we will go there now. Pardon my seeming carelessness, Ferguson. Drive on."

Within the half-hour, we stopped again—in front of another silk-store. We were angry; but the doctor was always serene, always smooth-voiced. He said.

"At last! How imposing the Louvre is, and yet how small! how exquisitely fashioned! how charmingly situated! Venerable, venerable pile—"

"Pairdon, doctor, zis is not ze Louvre—it is—"

"*What* is it?"

"I have ze idea—it come to me in a moment—zat ze silk in zis magazin—"

"Ferguson, how heedless I am! I fully intended to tell you that we did not wish to buy any silks to-day, and I also intended to tell you that we yearned to go immediately to the palace of the Louvre, but enjoying the happiness of seeing you devour four breakfasts this morning has so filled me with pleasurable emotions that I neglect the commonest interests of the time. However, we will proceed now to the Louvre, Ferguson."

"But, doctor" (excitedly), "it will take not a minute—not but one small minute! Ze gentleman need not to buy if he not wish to—but only *look* at ze silk—*look* at ze beautiful fabric." [Then pleadingly.] "*Sair*—just only one *leetle* moment!"

Dan said, "Confound the idiot! I don't want to see any silks to-day, and I *won't* look at them. Drive on."

And the doctor: "We need no silks now, Ferguson. Our hearts yearn for the Louvre. Let us journey on—let us journey on."

"But, *doctor!* it is only one moment—one leetle moment. And ze time will be save—entirely save! Because zere is nothing to see, now—it is too late. It want ten minute to four and ze Louvre close at four—*only* one leetle moment, doctor!"

The treacherous miscreant! After four breakfasts and a gallon of champagne, to serve us such a scurvy trick. We got no sight of the countless treasures of art in the Louvre galleries that day, and our only poor little satisfaction was in the reflection that Ferguson sold not a solitary silk dress-pattern.

I am writing this chapter partly for the satisfaction of abusing that accomplished knave, Billfinger, and partly to show whosoever shall read this how Americans fare at the hands of the Paris guides, and what sort of people Paris guides are. It need not be supposed that we were a stupider or an easier prey than our countrymen generally are, for we were not. The guides deceive and defraud every American who goes to Paris for the first time and sees its sights alone or in company with others as little experienced as himself. I shall visit Paris again some day, and then let the guides beware! I shall go in my war-paint—I shall carry my tomahawk along.

I think we have lost but little time in Paris. We have gone to bed every night tired out. Of course, we visited the renowned International Exposition. All the world did that. We went there on our third day in Paris—and we stayed there *nearly two hours.* That was our first and last visit. To tell the truth, we saw at a glance that one would have to spend weeks—yea, even months—in that monstrous establishment, to get an intelligible idea of it. It was a wonderful show, but the moving masses of people of all nations we saw there were a still more wonderful show. I discovered that if I were to stay there a month, I should still find myself looking at the people instead of the inanimate objects on exhibition. I got a little interested in some curious old tapestries of the thirteenth century, but a party of Arabs came by, and their dusky faces and quaint costumes called my attention away at once. I watched a silver swan, which had a living grace about his movements, and a living intelligence in his eyes— watched him swimming about as comfortably and as unconcernedly as if he had been born in a morass instead of a jeweler's shop— watched him seize a silver fish from under the water and hold up his head and go through all the customary and elaborate motions of swallowing it—but the moment it disappeared down his throat some tattooed South Sea Islanders approached and I yielded to their at- tractions. Presently I found a revolving pistol several hundred years old which looked strangely like a modern Colt, but just then I heard that the Empress of the French was in another part of the building, and hastened away to see what she might look like. We heard

martial music—we saw an unusual number of soldiers walking hurriedly about—there was a general movement among the people.
We inquired what it was all about, and learned that the Emperor of
the French and the Sultan of Turkey were about to review twenty-
five thousand troops at the *Arc de l'Étoile*. We immediately departed. I had a greater anxiety to see these men than I could have
had to see twenty expositions.

We drove away and took up a position in an open space opposite
the American minister's house. A speculator bridged a couple of
barrels with a board and we hired standing places on it. Presently
there was a sound of distant music; in another minute a pillar of
dust came moving slowly toward us; a moment more, and then, with
colors flying and a grand crash of military music, a gallant array of
cavalrymen emerged from the dust and came down the street on a
gentle trot. After them came a long line of artillery; then more cavalry, in splendid uniforms; and then their Imperial Majesties, Napoleon III and Abdul Aziz. The vast concourse of people swung their
hats and shouted—the windows and housetops in the wide vicinity
burst into a snow-storm of waving handkerchiefs, and the wavers
of the same mingled their cheers with those of the masses below. It
was a stirring spectacle.

But the two central figures claimed all my attention. Was ever
such a contrast set up before a multitude till then? Napoleon, in
military uniform—a long-bodied, short-legged man, fiercely mus-
tached, old, wrinkled, with eyes half closed, and *such* a deep, crafty,
scheming expression about them! Napoleon, bowing ever so gently
to the loud plaudits, and watching everything and everybody with his
cat-eyes from under his depressed hat-brim, as if to discover any sign
that those cheers were not heartfelt and cordial.

Abdul Aziz, absolute lord of the Ottoman Empire,—clad in dark
green European clothes, almost without ornament or insignia of
rank; a red Turkish fez on his head—a short, stout, dark man,
black-bearded, black-eyed, stupid, unprepossessing—a man whose
whole appearance somehow suggested that if he only had a cleaver
in his hand and a white apron on, one would not be at all surprised
to hear him say: "A mutton roast to-day, or will you have a nice
porterhouse steak?"

Napoleon III, the representative of the highest modern civilization, progress, and refinement; Abdul Aziz, the representative of a
people by nature and training filthy, brutish, ignorant, unprogres-
sive, superstitious—and a government whose Three Graces are Tyranny, Rapacity, Blood. Here in brilliant Paris, under this majestic
Arch of Triumph, the First Century greets the Nineteenth!

NAPOLEON III, Emperor of France! Surrounded by shouting
thousands, by military pomp, by the splendors of his capital city,
and companioned by kings and princes—this is the man who was
sneered at, and reviled, and called Bastard—yet who was dreaming

of a crown and an empire all the while; who was driven into exile—but carried his dreams with him; who associated with the common herd in America, and ran foot-races for a wager—but still sat upon a throne, in fancy; who braved every danger to go to his dying mother —and grieved that she could not be spared to see him cast aside his plebeian vestments for the purple of royalty; who kept his faithful watch and walked his weary beat a common policeman of London—but dreamed the while of a coming night when he should tread the long-drawn corridors of the Tuileries; who made the miserable *fiasco* of Strasbourg; saw his poor, shabby eagle, forgetful of its lesson, refuse to perch upon his shoulder; delivered his carefully prepared, sententious burst of eloquence upon unsympathetic ears; found himself a prisoner, the butt of small wits, a mark for the pitiless ridicule of all the world—yet went on dreaming of coronations and splendid pageants as before; who lay a forgotten captive in the dungeons of Ham—and still schemed and planned and pondered over future glory and future power; President of France at last! a *coup d'état* and surrounded by applauding armies, welcomed by the thunders of cannon, he mounts a throne and waves before an astounded world the scepter of a mighty empire! Who talks of the marvels of fiction? Who speaks of the wonders of romance? Who prates of the tame achievements of Aladdin and the Magi of Arabia?

ABDUL AZIZ, Sultan of Turkey, Lord of the Ottoman Empire! Born to a throne; weak, stupid, ignorant, almost, as his meanest slave; chief of a vast royalty, yet the puppet of his premier and the obedient child of a tyrannical mother; a man who sits upon a throne —the beck of whose finger moves navies and armies—who holds in his hands the power of life and death over millions—yet who sleeps, sleeps, eats, eats, idles with his eight hundred concubines, and when he is surfeited with eating and sleeping and idling, and would rouse up and take the reins of government and threaten to *be* a Sultan, is charmed from his purpose by wary Fuad Pacha with a pretty plan for a new palace or a new ship—charmed away with a new toy, like any other restless child; a man who sees his people robbed and oppressed by soulless tax-gatherers, but speaks no word to save them; who believes in gnomes and genii and the wild fables of the Arabian Nights, but has small regard for the mighty magicians of to-day, and is nervous in the presence of their mysterious railroads and steamboats and telegraphs; who would see undone in Egypt all that great Mehemet Ali achieved, and would prefer rather to forget than emulate him; a man who found his great empire a blot upon the earth—a degraded, poverty-stricken, miserable, infamous agglomeration of ignorance, crime, and brutality, and will idle away the allotted days of his trivial life, and then pass to the dust and the worms and leave it so!

Napoleon has augmented the commercial prosperity of France, in ten years, to such a degree that figures can hardly compute it. He has rebuilt Paris, and has partly rebuilt every city in the state. He condemns a whole street at a time, assesses the damages, pays them, and rebuilds superbly. Then speculators buy up the ground and sell, but the original owner is given the first choice by the government at a stated price before the speculator is permitted to purchase. But above all things, he has taken the sole control of the empire of France into his hands, and made it a tolerably free land—for people who will not attempt to go too far in meddling with government affairs. No country offers greater security to life and property than France, and one has all the freedom he wants, but no license—no license to interfere with anybody, or make any one uncomfortable.

As for the Sultan, one could set a trap anywhere and catch a dozen abler men in a night.

The bands struck up, and the brilliant adventurer, Napoleon III, the genius of Energy, Persistence, Enterprise; and the feeble Abdul Aziz, the genius of Ignorance, Bigotry, and Indolence, prepared for the Forward—March!

We saw the splendid review, we saw the white-moustached old Crimean soldier, Canrobert, Marshal of France, we saw—well, we saw everything, and then we went home satisfied.

CHAPTER XIV

We went to see the Cathedral of Notre Dame. We had heard of it before. It surprises me, sometimes, to think how much we *do* know, and how intelligent we are. We recognized the brown old Gothic pile in a moment; it was like the pictures. We stood at a little distance and changed from one point of observation to another, and gazed long at its lofty square towers and its rich front, clustered thick with stony, mutilated saints who had been looking calmly down from their perches for ages. The Patriarch of Jerusalem stood under them in the old days of chivalry and romance, and preached the third Crusade, more than six hundred years ago; and since that day they have stood there and looked quietly down upon the most thrilling scenes, the grandest pageants, the most extraordinary spectacles that have grieved or delighted Paris. These battered and broken-nosed old fellows saw many and many a cavalcade of mail-clad knights come marching home from Holy Land; they heard the bells above them toll the signal for the St. Bartholomew's Massacre, and they saw the slaughter that followed; later, they saw the Reign of Terror, the carnage of the Revolution, the overthrow of a king, the coronation of two Napoleons, the christening of the young prince that lords it over a regiment of servants in the Tuileries to-day—and they may possibly continue to stand there until they see the Napoleon dynasty swept away and the banners of a great Republic floating above its ruins. I wish these old parties could speak. They could tell a tale worth the listening to.

They say that a pagan temple stood where Notre Dame now stands, in the old Roman days, eighteen or twenty centuries ago— remains of it are still preserved in Paris; and that a Christian church took its place about A.D. 300; another took the place of that in A.D. 500; and that the foundations of the present cathedral were laid about A.D. 1100. The ground ought to be measurably sacred by this time, one would think. One portion of this noble old edifice is suggestive of the quaint fashions of ancient times. It was built by Jean Sans-Peur, Duke of Burgundy, to set his conscience at rest—he had assassinated the Duke of Orleans. Alas! those good old times are gone, when a murderer could wipe the stain from his name and soothe his troubles to sleep simply by getting out his bricks and mortar and building an addition to a church.

The portals of the great western front are bisected by square pillars. They took the central one away, in 1852, on the occasion of thanksgivings for the reinstitution of the Presidential power—but precious soon they had occasion to reconsider that motion and put it back again! And they did.

We loitered through the grand aisles for an hour or two, staring up at the rich stained-glass windows embellished with blue and yellow and crimson saints and martyrs, and trying to admire the numberless great pictures in the chapels, and then we were admitted to the sacristy and shown the magnificent robes which the Pope wore when he crowned Napoleon I; a wagon-load of solid gold and silver utensils used in the great public processions and ceremonies of the church; some nails of the true cross, a fragment of the cross itself, a part of the crown of thorns. We had already seen a large piece of the true cross in a church in the Azores, but no nails. They showed us likewise the bloody robe which that Archbishop of Paris wore who exposed his sacred person and braved the wrath of the insurgents of 1848, to mount the barricades and hold aloft the olive branch of peace in the hope of stopping the slaughter. His noble effort cost him his life. He was shot dead. They showed us a cast of his face, taken after death, the bullet that killed him, and the two vertebrae in which it lodged. These people have a somewhat singular taste in the matter of relics. Ferguson told us that the silver cross which the good archbishop wore at his girdle was seized and thrown into the Seine, where it lay embedded in the mud for fifteen years, and then an angel appeared to a priest and told him where to dive for it; he *did* dive for it and got it, and now it is there on exhibition at Notre Dame, to be inspected by anybody who feels an interest in inanimate objects of miraculous intervention.

Next we went to visit the Morgue, that horrible receptacle for the dead who die mysteriously and leave the manner of their taking off a dismal secret. We stood before a grating and looked through into a room which was hung all about with the clothing of dead men; coarse blouses, water-soaked; the delicate garments of women and children; patrician vestments, flecked and stabbed and stained with red; a hat that was crushed and bloody. On a slanting stone lay a drowned man, naked, swollen, purple; clasping the fragment of a broken bush with a grip which death had so petrified that human strength could not unloose it—mute witness of the last despairing effort to save the life that was doomed beyond all help. A stream of water trickled ceaselessly over the hideous face. We knew that the body and the clothing were there for identification by friends, but still we wondered if anybody could love that repulsive object or grieve for its loss. We grew meditative and wondered if, some forty years ago, when the mother of that ghastly thing was dandling it upon her knee, and kissing it and petting it and displaying it with satisfied pride to the passers-by, a prophetic vision of this dread ending ever flitted through her brain. I half feared that the mother, or the wife or a brother of the dead man might come while we stood there, but nothing of the kind occurred. Men and women came, and some looked eagerly in, and pressed their faces against the bars; others glanced carelessly at the body, and turned away with a disappointed look—people, I thought, who live upon strong excitements, and who attend the exhibitions of the Morgue regularly, just as other people go to see theatrical spectacles every night. When one of these looked in and passed on, I could not help thinking—

"Now this don't afford you any satisfaction—a party with his head shot off is what *you* need."

One night we went to the celebrated *Jardin Mabille*, but only stayed a little while. We wanted to see some of this kind of Paris life, however, and therefore the next night we went to a similar place of entertainment in a great garden in the suburb of Asniéres. We went to the railroad depot, toward evening, and Ferguson got tickets for a second-class carriage. Such a perfect jam of people I have not often seen—but there was no noise, no disorder, no rowdyism. Some of the women and young girls that entered the train we knew to be of the *demi-monde,* but others we were not at all sure about.

The girls and women in our carriage behaved themselves modestly and becomingly all the way out, except that they smoked. When we arrived at the garden in Asniéres, we paid a franc or two admission, and entered a place which had flower-beds in it, and grass-plats, and long, curving rows of ornamental shrubbery, with here and there a secluded bower convenient for eating ice-cream in. We moved along the sinuous gravel walks, with the great concourse of girls and young men, and suddenly a domed and filigreed white temple, starred over and over and over again with brilliant gas jets, burst upon us like a fallen sun. Near by was a large, handsome house with its ample front illuminated in the same way, and above its roof floated the Star Spangled Banner of America.

"Well!" I said. "How is this?" It nearly took my breath away. Ferguson said an American—a New Yorker—kept the place, and was carrying on quite a stirring opposition to the *Jardin Mabille*.

Crowds, composed of both sexes and nearly all ages, were frisking about the garden or sitting in the open air in front of the flagstaff and the temple, drinking wine and coffee, or smoking. The dancing had not begun yet. Ferguson said there was to be an exhibition. The famous Blondin was going to perform on a tight rope in another part of the garden. We went thither. Here the light was dim, and the masses of people were pretty closely packed together. And now I made a mistake which any donkey might make, but a sensible man never. I committed an error which I find myself repeating every day of my life. Standing right before a young lady, I said:

"Dan, just look at this girl, how beautiful she is!"

"I thank you more for the evident sincerity of the compliment, sir, than for the extraordinary publicity you have given to it!" This in good, pure English.

We took a walk, but my spirits were very, very sadly dampened. I did not feel right comfortable for some time afterward. Why *will* people be so stupid as to suppose themselves the only foreigners among a crowd of ten thousand persons?

But Blondin came out shortly. He appeared on a stretched cable, far away above the sea of tossing hats and handkerchiefs, and in the glare of the hundreds of rockets that whizzed heavenward by him he looked like a wee insect. He balanced his pole and walked the length of his rope—two or three hundred feet; he came back and got a man and carried him across; he returned to the center and danced a jig; next he performed some gymnastic and balancing feats too perilous to afford a pleasant spectacle; and he finished by fastening to his person a thousand Roman candles, Catherine wheels, serpents and rockets of all manner of brilliant colors, setting them on fire all at once and walking and waltzing across his rope again in a blinding blaze of glory that lit up the garden and people's faces like a great conflagration at midnight.

The dance had begun, and we adjourned to the temple. Within it was a drinking-saloon; and all around it was a broad circular platform for the dancers. I backed up against the wall of the temple, and waited. Twenty sets formed, the music struck up, and then—I placed my hands before my face for very shame. But I looked through my fingers. They were dancing the renowned "*Can-can*." A handsome girl in the set before me tripped forward lightly to meet the opposite gentleman—tripped back again, grasped her dresses vigorously on both sides with her hands, raised them pretty high, danced an extraordinary jig that had more activity and exposure about it than any jig I ever saw before, and then, drawing her clothes still higher, she advanced gaily to the center and launched a viscious kick full at her *vis-a-vis* that must infallibly have removed his nose if he had been seven feet high. It was a mercy he was only six.

That is the *can-can*. The idea of it is to dance as wildly, as noisily, as furiously as you can; expose yourself as much as possible if you are a woman; and kick as high as you can, no matter which sex you belong to. There is no word of exaggeration in this. Any of the staid, respectable, aged people who were there that night can testify to the truth of that statement. There were a good many such people present. I suppose French morality is not of that strait-laced description which is shocked at trifles.

I moved aside and took a general view of the *can-can*. Shouts, laughter, furious music, a bewildering chaos of darting and intermingling forms, stormy jerking and snatching of gay dresses, bobbing heads, flying arms, lightning flashes of white-stockinged calves and dainty slippers in the air, and then a grand final rush, riot, a terrific hubbub, and a wild stampede! Heavens! Nothing like it has been seen on earth since trembling Tam O'Shanter saw the devil and the witches at their orgies that stormy night in "Alloway's auld haunted kirk."

We visited the Louvre, at a time when we had no silk purchases in view, and looked at its miles of paintings by the old masters. Some of them were beautiful, but at the same time they carried such evidences about them of the cringing spirit of those great men that we found small pleasure in examining them. Their nauseous adulation of princely patrons was more prominent to me and chained by attention more surely than the charms of color and expression which are claimed to be in the pictures. Gratitude for kindnesses is well, but it seems to me that some of those artists carried it so far that it ceased to be gratitude, and became worship. If there is a plausible excuse for the worship of men, then by all means let us forgive Rubens and his brethren.

But I will drop the subject, lest I say something about the old masters that might as well be left unsaid.

Of course we drove in the *Bois de Boulogne*, that limitless park, with its forests, its lakes, its cascades, and its broad avenues. There were thousands upon thousands of vehicles abroad, and the scene was full of life and gayety. There were very common hacks, with father and mother and all the children in them; conspicuous little open carriages with celebrated ladies of questionable reputation in them; there were Dukes and Duchesses abroad, with gorgeous footmen perched behind, and equally gorgeous outriders perched on each of the six horses; there were blue and silver, and green and gold, and pink and black, and all sorts and descriptions of stunning and startling liveries out, and I almost yearned to be a flunkey myself, for the sake of the fine clothes.

But presently the Emperor came along and he outshone them all. He was preceded by a bodyguard of gentlemen on horseback in showy uniforms, his carriage horses (there appeared to be somewhere in the remote neighborhood of a thousand of them) were bestridden by gallant looking fellows, also in stylish uniforms, and after the carriage followed another detachment of body-guards. Everybody got out of the way; everybody bowed to the Emperor and his friend the Sultan, and they went by on a swinging trot and disappeared.

I will not describe the *Bois de Boulogne.* I cannot do it. It is simply a beautiful, cultivated, endless, wonderful wilderness. It is an enchanting place. It is in Paris, now, one may say, but a crumbling old cross in one portion of it reminds one that it was not always so. The cross marks the spot where a celebrated troubadour was waylaid and murdered in the fourteenth century. It was in this park that that fellow with an unpronounceable name made the attempt upon the Russian Czar's life last spring with a pistol. The bullet struck a tree. Ferguson showed us the place. Now in America that interesting tree would be chopped down or forgotten within the next five years, but it will be treasured here. The guides will point it out to visitors for the next eight hundred years, and when it decays and falls down they will put up another there and go on with the same old story just the same

CHAPTER XV

One of our pleasantest visits was to Père la Chaise, the national burying-ground of France, the honored resting-place of some of her greatest and best children, the last home of scores of illustrious men and women who were born to no titles, but achieved fame by their own energy and their own genius. It is a solemn city of winding streets, and of miniature marble temples and mansions of the dead gleaming white from out a wilderness of foliage and fresh flowers. Not every city is so well peopled as this, or has so ample an area within its walls. Few palaces exist in any city that are so exquisite in design, so rich in art, so costly in material, so graceful, so beautiful.

We had stood in the ancient church of St. Denis, where the marble effigies of thirty generations of kings and queens lay stretched at length upon the tombs, and the sensations invoked were startling and novel; the curious armor, the obsolete costumes, the placid faces, the hands placed palm to palm in eloquent supplication—it was a vision of gray antiquity. It seemed curious enough to be standing face to face, as it were, with old Dagobert I, and Clovis and Charlemagne, those vague, colossal heroes, those shadows, those myths of a thousand years ago! I touched their dust-covered faces with my finger, but Dagobert was deader than the sixteen centuries that have passed over him, Clovis slept well after his labor for Christ, and old Charlemagne went on dreaming of his paladins, of bloody Roncesvalles, and gave no heed to me.

The great names of Père la Chaise impress one, too, but differently. There the suggestion brought constantly to his mind is, that this place is sacred to a nobler royalty—the royalty of heart and brain.

Every faculty of mind, every noble trait of human nature, every high occupation which men engage in, seems represented by a famous name. The effect is a curious medley. Davoust and Massena, who wrought in many a battle-tragedy, are here, and so also is Rachel, of equal renown in mimic tragedy on the stage. The Abbé Sicard sleeps here—the first great teacher of the deaf and dumb—a man whose heart went out to every unfortunate, and whose life was given to kindly offices in their service; and not far off, in repose and peace at last, lies Marshal Ney, whose stormy spirit knew no music like the bugle call to arms. The man who originated public gas lighting, and that other benefactor who introduced the cultivation of the potato and thus blessed millions of his starving countrymen, lie with the Prince of Masserano, and with exiled queens and princes of Further India. Gay-Lussac, the chemist; Laplace, the astronomer; Larrey, the surgeon; de Sèze, the advocate, are here, and with them are Talma, Bellini, Rubini; de Balzac, Beaumarchais, Béranger; Molière and Lafontaine, and scores of other men whose names and whose worthy labors are as familiar in the remote byplaces of civilization as are the historic deeds of the kings and princes that sleep in the marble vaults of St. Denis.

But among the thousands and thousands of tombs in Père la Chaise, there is one that no man, no woman, no youth of either sex, ever passes by without stopping to examine. Every visitor has a sort of indistinct idea of the history of its dead, and comprehends that homage is due there, but not one in twenty thousand clearly remembers the story of that tomb and its romantic occupants. This is the grave of Abelard and Heloise—a grave which has been more revered, more widely known, more written and sung about and wept over, for seven hundred years, than any other in Christendom, save only that of the Saviour. All visitors linger pensively about it; all young people capture and carry away keepsakes and mementoes of it; all Parisian youths and maidens who are disappointed in love come there to bail out when they are full of tears; yea, many stricken lovers make pilgrimages to this shrine from distant provinces to weep and wail and "grit" their teeth over their heavy sorrows, and to purchase the sympathies of the chastened spirits of that tomb with offerings of immortelles and budding flowers.

Go when you will, you find somebody snuffling over that tomb. Go when you will, you find it furnished with those bouquets and immortelles. Go when you will, you find a gravel train from Marseilles arriving to supply the deficiencies caused by memento-cabbaging vandals whose affections have miscarried.

Yet who really knows the story of Abelard and Heloise? Precious few people. The names are perfectly familiar to everybody, and that is about all. With infinite pains I have acquired a knowledge of that history, and I propose to narrate it here, partly for the honest information of the public and partly to show that public that they have been wasting a good deal of marketable sentiment very unnecessarily.

STORY OF ABELARD AND HELOISE.

Heloise was born seven hundred and sixty-six years ago. She may have had parents. There is no telling. She lived with her uncle Fulbert, a canon of the cathedral of Paris. I do not know what a canon of a cathedral is, but that is what he was. He was nothing more than a sort of a mountain howitzer, likely, because they had no heavy artillery in those days. Suffice it, then, that Heloise lived with her uncle the howitzer, and was happy. She spent the most of her childhood in the convent of Argenteuil—never heard of Argenteuil before, but suppose there was really such a place. She then returned to her uncle, the old gun, or son of a gun, as the case may be, and he taught her to write and speak Latin, which was the language of literature and polite society at that period.

Just at this time, Pierre Abelard, who had already made himself widely famous as a rhetorician, came to found a school of rhetoric in Paris. The originality of is principles, his eloquence, and his great physical strength and beauty created a profound sensation. He saw Heloise, and was captivated by her blooming youth, her beauty, and her charming disposition. He wrote to her; she answered. He wrote again, she answered again. He was now in love. He longed to know her—to speak to her face to face.

His school was near Fulbert's house. He asked Fulbert to allow him to call. The good old swivel saw here a rare opportunity; his niece, whom he so much loved, would absorb knowledge from this man, and it would not cost him a cent. Such was Fulbert—penurious.

Fulbert's first name is not mentioned by any author, which is unfortunate. However, George W. Fulbert will answer for him as well as any other. We will let him go at that. He asked Abelard to teach her.

Abelard was glad enough of the opportunity. He came often and stayed long. A letter of his shows in its very first sentence that he came under that friendly roof, like a cold-hearted villain as he was, with the deliberate intention of debauching a confiding, innocent girl. This is the letter:

"I cannot cease to be astonished at the simplicity of Fulbert; I was as much surprised as if he had placed a lamb in the power of a hungry wolf. Heloise and I, under pretext of study, gave ourselves up wholly to love, and the solitude that love seeks our studies procured for us. Books were open before us, but we spoke oftener of love than philosophy, and kisses came more readily from our lips than words."

And so, exulting over an honorable confidence which to his degraded instinct was a ludicrous "simplicity," this unmanly Abelard seduced the niece of the man whose guest he was. Paris found it out. Fulbert was told of it—told often—but refused to believe it. He could not comprehend how a man could be so depraved as to use the sacred protection and security of hospitality as a means for the commission of such a crime as that. But when he heard the rowdies in the streets singing the love-songs of Abelard to Heloise, the case was too plain—love-songs come not properly within the teachings of rhetoric and philosophy.

He drove Abelard from his house. Abelard returned secretly and carried Heloise away to Palais, in Brittany, his native country. Here, shortly afterward, she bore a son, who, from his rare beauty, was surnamed Astrolabe—William G. The girl's flight enraged Fulbert, and he longed for vengeance, but feared to strike lest retaliation visit Heloise—for he still loved her tenderly. At length Abelard offered to marry Heloise—but on a shameful condition: that the marriage should be kept secret from the world, to the end that (while her good name remained a wreck, as before) his priestly reputation might be kept untarnished. It was like that miscreant. Fulbert saw his opportunity and consented. He would see the parties married, and then violate the confidence of the man who had taught him that trick; he would divulge the secret and so remove somewhat of the obloquy that attached to his niece's fame. But the niece suspected his scheme. She refused the marriage at first, she said Fulbert would betray the secret to save her, and besides, she did not wish to drag down a lover who was so gifted, so honored by the world, and who had such a splendid career before him. It was noble, self-sacrificing love, and characteristic of the pure-souled Heloise, but it was not good sense.

But she was overruled, and the private marriage took place. Now for Fulbert! The heart so wounded should be healed at last; the proud spirit so tortured should find rest again; the humbled head should be lifted up once more. He proclaimed the marriage in the high places of the city, and rejoiced that dishonor had departed from his house. But lo! Abelard denied the marriage! Heloise denied it! The people, knowing the former circumstances, might have believed Fulbert, had only Abelard denied it, but when the person chiefly interested—the girl herself—denied it, they laughed despairing Fulbert to scorn.

The poor canon of the cathedral of Paris was spiked again. The last hope of repairing the wrong that had been done his house was gone. What next? Human nature suggested revenge. He compassed it. The historian says:

"Ruffians, hired by Fulbert, fell upon Abelard by night, and inflicted upon him a terrible and nameless mutilation."

I am seeking the last resting-place of those "ruffians." When I find it I shall shed some tears on it, and stack up some bouquets and immortelles, and cart away from it some gravel whereby to remember that howsoever blotted by crime their lives may have been, these ruffians did one just deed, at any rate, albeit it was not warranted by the strict letter of the law.

Heloise entered a convent and gave good-bye to the world and its pleasures for all time. For twelve years she never heard of Abelard—never even heard his name mentioned. She had become prioress of Argenteuil, and led a life of complete seclusion. She happened one day to see a letter written by him, in which he narrated his own history. She cried over it, and wrote him. He answered, addressing her as his "sister in Christ." They continued to correspond, she in the unweighed language of unwavering affection, he in the chilly phraseology of the polished rhetorician. She poured out her heart in passionate, disjointed sentences; he replied with finished essays, divided deliberately into heads and sub-heads, premises and argument. She showered upon him the tenderest epithets that love could devise, he addressed her from the North Pole of his frozen heart as the "Spouse of Christ!" The abandoned villain!

On account of her too easy government of her nuns, some disreputable irregularities were discovered among them, and the Abbot of St. Denis broke up her establishment. Abelard was the official head of the monastery of St. Gildas de Ruys, at that time, and when he heard of her homeless condition a sentiment of pity was aroused in his breast (it is a wonder the unfamiliar emotion did not blow his head off), and he placed her and her troop in the little oratory of the Paraclete, a religious establishment which he had founded. She had many privations and sufferings to undergo at first, but her worth and her gentle disposition won influential friends for her, and she built up a wealthy and flourishing nunnery. She became a great favorite with the heads of the church, and also the people, though she seldom appeared in public. She rapidly advanced in esteem, in good report and in usefulness, and Abelard as rapidly lost ground. The Pope so honored her that he made her the head of her order. Abelard, a man of splendid talents, and ranking as the first debater of his time, became timid, irresolute, and distrustful of his powers. He only needed a great misfortune to topple him from the high position he held in the world of intellectual excellence, and it came. Urged by kings and princes to meet the subtle St. Bernard in debate and crush him, he stood up in the presence of a royal and illustrious assemblage, and when his antagonist had finished he looked about him, and stammered a commencement; but his courage failed him, the cunning of his tongue was gone; with his speech unspoken, he trembled and sat down, a disgraced and vanquished champion.

He died a nobody, and was buried at Cluny, A.D. 1144. They removed his body to the Paraclete afterward, and when Heloise died, twenty years later, they buried her with him in accordance with her last wish. He died at the ripe age of 64, and she at 63. After the bodies had remained entombed three hundred years, they were removed once more. They were removed again in 1800, and finally, seventeen years afterward, they were taken up and transferred to Père la Chaise, where they will remain in peace and quiet until it comes time for them to get up and move again.

History is silent concerning the last acts of the mountain howitzer. Let the world say what it will about him, *I*, at least, shall always respect the memory and sorrow for the abused trust, and the broken heart, and the troubled spirit of the old smooth-bore. Rest and repose be his!

Such is the story of Abelard and Heloise. Such is the history that Lamartine has shed such cataracts of tears over. But that man never could come within the influence of a subject in the least pathetic without overflowing his banks. He ought to be dammed—or leveed, I should more properly say. Such is the history—not as it is usually told, but as it is when stripped of the nauseous sentimentality that would enshrine for our loving worship a dastardly seducer like Pierre Abelard. I have not a word to say against the misused, faithful girl, and would not withhold from her grave a single one of those simple tributes which blighted youths and maidens offer to her memory, but I am sorry enough that I have not time and opportunity to write four or five volumes of my opinion of her friend the founder of the Parachute, or the Paraclete, or whatever it was.

The tons of sentiment I have wasted on that unprincipled humbug, in my ignorance! I shall throttle down my emotions hereafter, about this sort of people, until I have read them up and know whether they are entitled to any tearful attentions or not. I wish I had my immortelles back, now, and that bunch of radishes.

In Paris we often saw in shop windows the sign, *"English Spoken Here,"* just as one sees in the windows at home the sign, *"Ici on parle française."* We always invaded these places at once—and invariably received the information, framed in faultless French, that the clerk who did the English for the establishment had just gone to dinner and would be back in an hour—would Monsieur buy something? We wondered why those parties happened to take their dinners at such erratic and extraordinary hours, for we never called at a time when an exemplary Christian would be in the least likely to be abroad on such an errand. The truth was, it was a base fraud—a snare to trap the unwary—chaff to catch fledglings with. They had no English-murdering clerk. They trusted to the sign to inveigle foreigners into their lairs, and trusted to their own blandishments to keep them there till they bought something.

We ferreted out another French imposition—a frequent sign to this effect: "ALL MANNER OF AMERICAN DRINKS ARTISTICALLY PREPARED HERE." We procured the services of a gentleman experienced in the nomenclature of the American bar, and moved upon the works of one of these impostors. A bowing, aproned Frenchman skipped forward and said:

"Que voulez les messieurs?" I do not know what "Que voulez les messieurs" means, but such was his remark.

Our General said, "We will take a whisky straight."

[A stare from the Frenchman.]

"Well, if you don't know what that is, give us a champagne cocktail."

[A stare and a shrug.]

"Well, then, give us a sherry cobbler."

The Frenchman was checkmated. This was all Greek to him.

"Give us a brandy smash!"

The Frenchman began to back away, suspicious of the ominous vigor of the last order—began to back away, shrugging his shoulders and spreading his hands apologetically.

The General followed him up and gained a complete victory. The uneducated foreigner could not even furnish a Santa Cruz Punch, an Eye-Opener, a Stone-Fence, or an Earthquake. It was plain that he was a wicked impostor.

An acquaintance of mine said, the other day, that he was doubtless the only American visitor to the Exposition who had had the high honor of being escorted by the Emperor's body-guard. I said with unobtrusive frankness that I was astonished that such a long-legged, lantern-jawed, unprepossessing looking specter as he should be singled out for a distinction like that, and asked how it came about. He said he had attended a great military review in the *Champ de Mars*, some time ago, and while the multitude about him was growing thicker and thicker every moment, he observed an open space inside the railing. He left his carriage and went into it. He was the only person there, and so he had plenty of room, and the situation being central, he could see all the preparations going on about the field. By and by there was a sound of music, and soon the Emperor of the French and the Emperor of Austria, escorted by the famous *Cent Gardes*, entered the inclosure. They seemed not to observe him, but directly, in response to a sign from the commander of the Guard, a young lieutenant came toward him with a file of his men following, halted, raised his hand and gave the military salute, and then said in a low voice that he was sorry to have to disturb a stranger and a gentleman, but the place was sacred to royalty. Then this New Jersey phantom rose up and bowed and begged pardon, then with the officer beside him, the file of men marching behind him, and with every mark of respect, he was escorted to his carriage by the imperial *Cent Gardes!* The officer saluted again and fell back, the New Jersey sprite bowed in return and had presence of mind enough to pretend that he had simply called on a matter of private business with those emperors, and so waved them an adieu, and drove from the field!

Imagine a poor Frenchman ignorantly intruding upon a public rostrum sacred to some sixpenny dignitary in America. The police would scare him to death, first, with a storm of their elegant blasphemy, and then pull him to pieces getting him away from there. We are measurably superior to the French in some things, but they are immeasurably our betters in others.

Enough of Paris for the present. We have done our whole duty by it. We have seen the Tuileries, the Napoleon Column, the Madeleine, that wonder of wonders the tomb of Napoleon, all the great churches and museums, libraries, imperial palaces, and sculpture and picture galleries, the Pantheon, *Jardin des Plantes*, the opera, the circus, the legislative body, the billiard-rooms, the barbers, the *grisettes*—

Ah, the *grisettes!* I had almost forgotten. They are another romantic fraud. They were (if you let the books of travel tell it) always so beautiful—so neat and trim, so graceful—so naive and trusting—so gentle, so winning—so faithful to their shop duties, so irresistible to buyers in their prattling importunity—so devoted to their poverty-stricken students of the Latin Quarter—so light hearted and happy on their Sunday picnics in the suburbs—and oh, so charmingly, so delightfully immoral!

Stuff! For three or four days I was constantly saying:

"Quick, Ferguson! is that a *grisette?*"

And he always said "No."

He comprehended, at last, that I wanted to see a grisette. Then he showed me dozens of them. They were like nearly all the Frenchwomen I ever saw—homely. They had large hands, large feet, large mouths; they had pug noses as a general thing, and moustaches that not even good breeding could overlook; they combed their hair straight back without parting; they were ill-shaped, they were not winning, they were not graceful; I knew by their looks that they ate garlic and onions; and lastly and finally, to my thinking it would be base flattery to call them immoral.

Aroint thee, wench! I sorrow for the vagabond student of the Latin Quarter now, even more than formerly I envied him. Thus topples to earth another idol of my infancy.

We have seen everything, and to-morrow we go to Versailles. We shall see Paris only for a little while as we come back to take up our line of march for the ship, and so I may as well bid the beautiful city a regretful farewell. We shall travel many thousands of miles after we leave here, and visit many great cities, but we shall find none so enchanting as this.

Some of our party have gone to England, intending to take a roundabout course and rejoin the vessel at Leghorn or Naples, several weeks hence. We came near going to Geneva, but have concluded to return to Marseilles and go up through Italy from Genoa.

I will conclude this chapter with a remark that I am sincerely proud to be able to make—and glad, as well, that my comrades cordially indorse it, to wit: by far the handsomest women we have seen in France were born and reared in America.

I feel, now, like a man who has redeemed a failing reputation and shed luster upon a dimmed escutcheon, by a single just deed done at the eleventh hour.

Let the curtain fall, to slow music.

CHAPTER XVI

Versailles! It is wonderfully beautiful! You gaze, and stare, and try to understand that it is real, that it is on the earth, that it is not the Garden of Eden—but your brain grows giddy, stupefied by the world of beauty around you, and you half believe you are the dupe of an exquisite dream. The scene thrills one like military music! A noble palace, stretching its ornamented front block upon block away, till it seemed that it would never end; a grand promenade before it, whereon the armies of an empire might parade; all about it rainbows of flowers, and colossal statues that were almost numberless, and yet seemed only scattered over the ample space; broad flights of stone steps leading down from the promenade to lower grounds of the Park—stairways that whole regiments might stand to arms upon and have room to spare; vast fountains whose great bronze effigies discharged rivers of sparkling water into the air and mingled a hundred curving jets together in forms of matchless beauty; wide grass-carpeted avenues that branched hither and thither in every direction and wandered to seemingly interminable distances, walled all the way on either side with compact ranks of leafy trees whose branches met above and formed arches as faultless and as symmetrical as ever were carved in stone; and here and there were glimpses of sylvan lakes with miniature ships glassed in their surfaces. And everywhere—on the palace steps, and the great promenade, around the fountains, among the trees, and far under the arches of the endless avenues, hundreds and hundreds of people in gay costumes walked or ran or danced, and gave to the fairy picture the life and animation which was all of perfection it could have lacked.

It was worth a pilgrimage to see. Everything is on so gigantic a scale. Nothing is small—nothing is cheap. The statues are all large; the palace is grand; the park covers a fair-sized county; the avenues are interminable. All the distances and all the dimensions about Versailles are vast. I used to think the pictures exaggerated these distances and these dimensions beyond all reason, and that they made Versailles more beautiful than it was possible for any place in the world to be. I know now that the pictures never came up to the subject in any respect, and that no painter could represent Versailles on canvas as beautiful as it is in reality. I used to abuse Louis XIV for spending two hundred millions of dollars in creating this marvelous park, when bread was so scarce with some of his subjects; but I have forgiven him now. He took a tract of land sixty miles in circumference and set to work to make this park and build this palace and a road to it from Paris. He kept 36,000 men employed daily on it, and the labor was so unhealthy that they used to die and be hauled off by cart-loads every night. The wife of a nobleman of the time speaks of this as an "*inconvenience*," but naively remarks that "it does not seem worthy of attention in the happy state of tranquillity we now enjoy."

I always thought ill of people at home, who trimmed their shrubbery into pyramids and squares and spires and all manner of unnatural shapes, and when I saw the same thing being practiced in this great park I began to feel dissatisfied. But I soon saw the idea of the thing and the wisdom of it. They seek the *general* effect. We distort a dozen sickly trees into unaccustomed shapes in a little yard no bigger than a dining-room, and then surely they look absurd enough. But here they take two hundred thousand tall forest trees and set them in a double row; allow no sign of leaf or branch to grow on the trunk lower down than six feet above the ground; from that point the boughs begin to project, and very gradually they extend outward further and further till they meet overhead, and a faultless tunnel of foliage is formed. The arch is mathematically precise. The effect is then very fine. They make trees take fifty different shapes, and so these quaint effects are infinitely varied and picturesque. The trees in no two avenues are shaped alike, and consequently the eye is not fatigued with anything in the nature of monotonous uniformity. I will drop this subject now, leaving it to others to determine how these people manage to make endless ranks of lofty forest trees grow to just a certain thickness of trunk (say a foot and two-thirds); how they make them spring to precisely the same height for miles; how they make them grow so close together; how they compel one huge limb to spring from the same identical spot on each tree and form the main sweep of the arch; and how all these things are kept exactly in the same condition, and in the same exquisite shapeliness and symmetry month after month and year after year— for I have tried to reason out the problem, and have failed.

We walked through the great hall of sculpture and the one hundred and fifty galleries of paintings in the palace of Versailles, and felt that to be in such a place was useless unless one had a whole year at his disposal. These pictures are all battle-scenes, and only one solitary little canvas among them all treats of anything but great French victories. We wandered, also, through the Grand Trianon and the Petit Trianon, those monuments of royal prodigality, and with histories so mournful—filled, as it is, with souvenirs of Napoleon the First, and three dead kings and as many queens. In one sumptuous bed they had all slept in succession, but no one occupies it now. In a large dining-room stood the table at which Louis XIV and his mistress, Madame Maintenon, and after them Louis XV, and Pompadour, had sat at their meals naked and unattended—for the table stood upon a trap-door, which descended with it to regions below when it was necessary to replenish its dishes. In a room of the Petit Trianon stood the furniture, just as poor Marie Antoinette left it when the mob came and dragged her and the King to Paris, never to return. Near at hand, in the stables, were prodigious carriages that showed no color but gold—carriages used by former kings of France on state occasions, and never used now save when a kingly head is to be crowned, or an imperial infant christened. And with them were some curious sleighs, whose bodies were shaped like lions, swans, tigers, etc.—vehicles that had once been handsome with pictured designs and fine workmanship, but were dusty and decaying now. They had their history. When Louis XIV had finished the Grand Trianon, he told Maintenon he had created a Paradise for her, and asked if she could think of anything now to wish for. He said he wished the Trianon to be perfection—nothing less. She said she could think of but one thing—it was summer, and it was balmy France—yet she would like well to sleigh-ride in the leafy avenues of Versailles! The next morning found miles and miles of grassy avenues spread thick with snowy salt and sugar, and a procession of those quaint sleighs waiting to receive the chief concubine of the gayest and most unprincipled court that France has ever seen!

From sumptuous Versailles, with its palaces, its statues, its gardens and its fountains, we journeyed back to Paris and sought its antipodes—the Faubourg St. Antoine. Little, narrow streets; dirty children blockading them; greasy, slovenly women capturing and spanking them; filthy dens on first floors, with rag stores in them (the heaviest business in the Faubourg is the chiffonier's); other filthy dens where whole suits of second and third-hand clothing are sold at prices that would ruin any proprietor who did not steal his stock; still other filthy dens where they sold groceries—sold them by the half-pennyworth—five dollars would buy the man out, good-will and all. Up these little crooked streets they will murder a man for seven dollars and dump the body in the Seine. And up some other of these streets—most of them, I should say—live lorettes.

All through this Faubourg St. Antoine, misery, poverty, vice, and crime go hand in hand, and the evidences of it stare one in the face from every side. Here the people live who begin the revolutions. Whenever there is anything of that kind to be done, they are always ready. They take as much genuine pleasure in building a barricade as they do in cutting a throat or shoving a friend into the Seine. It is these savage-looking ruffians who storm the splendid halls of the Tuileries, occasionally, and swarm into Versailles when a king is to be called to account.

But they will build no more barricades, they will break no more soldiers' heads with paving-stones. Louis Napoleon has taken care of all that. He is annihilating the crooked streets, and building in their stead noble boulevards as straight as an arrow—avenues which a cannon-ball could traverse from end to end without meeting an obstruction more irresistible than the flesh and bones of men— boulevards whose stately edifices will never afford refuges and plot- ting-places for starving, discontented revolution-breeders. Five of these great thoroughfares radiate from one ample center—a center which is exceedingly well adapted to the accommodation of heavy artillery. The mobs used to riot there, but they must seek another rallying-place in future. And this ingenious Napoleon paves the streets of his great cities with a smooth, compact composition of as- phaltum and sand. No more barricades of flagstones—no more as- saulting his Majesty's troops with cobbles. I cannot feel friendly toward my quondam fellow-American, Napoleon III, especially at this time,* when in fancy I see his credulous victim, Maximilian, ly- ing stark and stiff in Mexico, and his maniac widow watching eager- ly from her French asylum for the form that will never come—but I do admire his nerve, his calm self-reliance, his shrewd good sense.

CHAPTER XVII

We had a pleasant journey of it seaward again. We found that for the three past nights our ship had been in a state of war. The first night the sailors of the British ship, being happy with grog, came down on the pier and challenged our sailors to a free fight. They ac- cepted with alacrity, repaired to the pier and gained—their share of a drawn battle. Several bruised and bloody members of both parites were carried off by the police, and imprisoned until the following morning. The next night the British boys came again to renew the fight, but our men had had strict orders to remain on board and out of sight. They did so, and the besieging party grew noisy, and more and more abusive as the fact became apparent (to them) that our men were afraid to come out. They went away, finally, with a closing burst of ridicule and offensive epithets. The third night they came again, and were more obstreperous than ever. They swaggered up and down the almost deserted pier, and hurled curses, obscenity, and stinging sarcasms at our crew. It was more than human nature could bear. The executive officer ordered our men ashore—with in- structions not to fight. They charged the British and gained a bril- liant victory. I probably would not have mentioned this war had it ended differently. But I travel to learn, and I still remember that they picture no French defeats in the battle-galleries of Versailles.

It was like home to us to step on board the comfortable ship again, and smoke and lounge about her breezy decks. And yet it was not

*July, 1867.

altogether like home, either, because so many members of the family were away. We missed some pleasant faces which we would rather have found at dinner, and at night there were gaps in the euchre-parties which could not be satisfactorily filled. "Moult." was in England, Jack in Switzerland, Charley in Spain. Blucher was gone, none could tell where. But we were at sea again, and we had the stars and the ocean to look at, and plenty of room to meditate in.

In due time the shores of Italy were sighted, and as we stood gazing from the decks early in the bright summer morning, the stately city of Genoa rose up out of the sea and flung back the sunlight from her hundred palaces.

Here we rest, for the present—or rather, here we have been trying to rest, for some little time, but we run about too much to accomplish a great deal in that line.

I would like to remain here. I had rather not go any further. There may be prettier women in Europe, but I doubt it. The population of Genoa is 120,000; two-thirds of these are women, I think and at least two-thirds of the women are beautiful. They are as dressy and as tasteful and as graceful as they could possibly be without being angels. However, angels are not very dressy, I believe. At least the angels in pictures are not—they wear nothing but wings. But these Genoese women do look so charming. Most of the young demoiselles are robed in a cloud of white from head to foot, though many trick themselves out more elaborately. Nine-tenths of them wear nothing on their heads but a filmy sort of veil, which falls down their backs like a white mist. They are very fair, and many of them have blue eyes, but black and dreamy dark brown ones are met with oftenest.

The ladies and gentlemen of Genoa have a pleasant fashion of promenading in a large park on the top of a hill in the center of the city, from six till nine in the evening, and then eating ices in a neighboring garden an hour or two longer. We went to the park on Sunday evening. Two thousand persons were present, chiefly young ladies and gentlemen. The gentlemen were dressed in the very latest Paris fashions, and the robes of the ladies glinted among the trees like so many snow-flakes. The multitude moved round and round the park in a great procession. The bands played, and so did the fountains; the moon and the gas-lamps lit up the scene, and altogether it was a brilliant and an animated picture. I scanned every female face that passed, and it seemed to me that all were handsome. I never saw such a freshet of loveliness before. I do not see how a man of only ordinary decision of character could marry here, because, before he could get his mind made up he would fall in love with somebody else.

Never smoke any Italian tobacco. Never do it on any account. It makes me shudder to think what it must be made of. You cannot throw an old cigar "stub" down anywhere, but some vagabond will pounce upon it on the instant. I like to smoke a good deal, but it wounds my sensibilities to see one of these stub-hunters watching me out of the corners of his hungry eyes and calculating how long my cigar will be likely to last. It reminded me too painfully of that San Francisco undertaker who used to go to sick beds with his watch in his hand and time the corpse. One of these stub-hunters followed us all over the park last night, and we never had a smoke that was worth anything. We were always moved to appease him with the stub before the cigar was half gone, because he looked so viciously anxious. He regarded us as his own legitimate prey, by right of discovery, I think, because he drove off several other professionals who wanted to take stock in us.

Now, they surely must chew up those old stubs, and dry and sell them for smoking tobacco. Therefore, give your custom to other than Italian brands of the article.

"The Superb" and the "City of Palaces" are names which Genoa has held for centuries. She is full of palaces, certainly, and the palaces are sumptuous inside, but they are very rusty without, and make no pretensions to architectural magnificence. "Genoa, the Superb," would be a felicitous title if it referred to the women.

We have visited several of the palaces—immense thick-walled piles, with great stone staircases, tessellated marble pavements on the floors (sometimes they make a mosaic work, of intricate designs, wrought in pebbles, or little fragments of marble laid in cement), and grand *salons* hung with pictures by Rubens, Guido, Titian, Paul Veronese, and so on, and portraits of heads of the family, in plumed helmets and gallant coats of mail, and patrician ladies, in stunning costumes of centuries ago. But, of course, the folks were all out in the country for the summer, and might not have known enough to ask us to dinner if they had been at home, and so all the grand empty *salons*, with their resounding pavements, their grim pictures of dead ancestors, and tattered banners with the dust of bygone centuries upon them, seemed to brood solemnly of death and the grave, and our spirits ebbed away, and our cheerfulness passed from us. We never went up to the eleventh story. We always began to suspect ghosts. There was always an undertaker-looking servant along, too, who handed us a programme, pointed to the picture that began the list of the *salon* he was in, and then stood stiff and stark and unsmiling in his petrified livery till we were ready to move on to the next chamber, whereupon he marched sadly ahead and took up another malignantly respectful position as before. I wasted so much time praying that the roof would fall in on these dispiriting flunkeys that I had but little left to bestow upon palace and pictures.

And besides, as in Paris, we had a guide. Perdition catch all the guides. This one said he was the most gifted linguist in Genoa, as far as English was concerned, and that only two persons in the city beside himself could talk the language at all. He showed us the birthplace of Christopher Columbus, and after we had reflected in silent awe before it for fifteen minutes, he said it was not the birthplace of Columbus, but of Columbus's grandmother! When we demanded an explanation of his conduct he only shrugged his shoulders and answered in barbarous Italian. I shall speak further of this guide in a future chapter. All the information we got out of him we shall be able to carry along with us, I think.

I have not been to church so often in a long time as I have in the last few weeks. The people in these old lands seem to make churches their specialty. Especially does this seem to be the case with the citizens of Genoa. I think there is a church every three or four hundred yards all over town. The streets are sprinkled from end to end with shovel-hatted, long-robed, well-fed priests, and the church bells by dozens are pealing all the day long, nearly. Every now and then one comes across a friar of orders gray, with shaven head, long, coarse robe, rope girdle and beads, and with feet cased in sandals or entirely bare. These worthies suffer in the flesh, and do penance all their lives, I suppose, but they look like consummate famine-breeders. They are all fat and serene.

The old Cathedral of San Lorenzo is about as notable a building as we have found in Genoa. It is vast, and has colonnades of noble pillars, and a great organ, and the customary pomp of gilded moldings, pictures, frescoed ceilings, and so forth. I cannot describe it, of course—it would require a good many pages to do that. But it is a curious place. They said that half of it—from the front door half way down to the altar—was a Jewish Synagogue before the Saviour was born, and that no alteration had been made in it since that time. We doubted the statement, but did it reluctantly. We would much rather have believed it. The place looked in too perfect repair to be so ancient.

The main point of interest about the cathedral is the little Chapel of St. John the Baptist. They only allow women to enter it on one day in the year, on account of the animosity they still cherish against the sex because of the murder of the Saint to gratify a caprice of Herodias. In this chapel is a marble chest, in which, they told us, were the ashes of St. John; and around it was wound a chain, which, they said, had confined him when he was in prison. We did not desire to disbelieve these statements, and yet we could not feel certain that they were correct—partly because we could have broken that chain, and so could St. John, and partly because we had seen St. John's ashes before, in another church. We could not bring ourselves to think St. John had two sets of ashes.

They also showed us a portrait of the Madonna which was painted by St. Luke, and it did not look half as old and smoky as some of the pictures by Rubens. We could not help admiring the Apostle's modesty in never once mentioning in his writings that he could paint.

But isn't this relic matter a little overdone? We find a piece of the true cross in every old church we go into, and some of the nails that held it together. I would not like to be positive, but I think we have seen as much as a keg of these nails. Then there is the crown of thorns; they have part of one in Sainte Chapelle, in Paris, and part of one, also, in Notre Dame. And as for bones of St. Denis, I feel certain we have seen enough of them to duplicate him, if necessary.

I only meant to write about the churches, but I keep wandering from the subject. I could say that the Church of the Annunciation is a wilderness of beautiful columns, of statues, gilded moldings, and pictures almost countless, but that would give no one an entirely perfect idea of the thing, and so where is the use? One family built the whole edifice, and have got money left. There is where the mystery lies. We had an idea at first that only a mint could have survived the expense.

These people here live in the heaviest, highest, broadest, darkest, solidest houses one can imagine. Each one might "laugh a siege to scorn." A hundred feet front and a hundred high is about the style, and you go up three flights of stairs before you begin t come upon signs of occupancy. Everything is stone, and stone of the heaviest— floors, stairways, mantels, benches—everything. The walls are four to five feet thick. The streets generally are four or five to eight feet wide and as crooked as a corkscrew. You go along one of these gloomy cracks, and look up and behold the sky like a mere ribbon of light, far above your head, where the tops of the tall houses on either side of the street bend almost together. You feel as if you were at the bottom of some tremendous abyss, with all the world far above you. You wind in and out and here and there, in the most mysterious way, and have no more idea of the points of the compass than if you were a blind man. You can never persuade yourself that these are actually streets, and the frowning, dingy, monstrous houses dwellings, till you see one of these beautiful, prettily-dressed women emerge from them—see her emerge from a dark, dreary-looking den that looks dungeon all over, from the ground away half-way up to heaven. And then you wonder that such a charming moth could come from such a forbidding shell as that. The streets are wisely made narrow and the houses heavy and thick and stony, in order that the people may be cool in this roasting climate. And they are cool, and stay so. And while I think of it—the men wear hats and have very dark complexions, but the women wear no headgear but a flimsy veil like a gossamer's web, and yet are exceedingly fair as a general thing. Singular, isn't it?

The huge palaces of Genoa are each supposed to be occupied by one family, but they could accommodate a hundred, I should think. They are relics of the grandeur of Genoa's palmy days—the days when she was a great commercial and maritime power several centuries ago. These houses, solid marble palaces though they be, are, in many cases, of a dull pinkish color, outside, and from pavement to eaves are pictured with Genoese battle-scenes, with monstrous Jupiters and Cupids and with familiar illustrations from Grecian mythology. Where the paint has yielded to age and exposure and is peeling off in flakes and patches, the effect is not happy. A noseless Cupid, or a Jupiter with an eye out, or a Venus with a fly-blister on her breast, are not attractive features in a picture. Some of these painted walls reminded me somewhat of the tall van, plastered with fanciful bills and posters, that follows the band wagon of a circus about a country village. I have not read or heard that the outsides of the houses of any other European city are frescoed in this way.

I cannot conceive of such a thing as Genoa in ruins. Such massive arches, such ponderous substructions as support these towering broad-winged edifices, we have seldom seen before; and surely the great blocks of stone of which these edifices are built can never decay; walls that are as thick as an ordinary American doorway is high, cannot crumble.

The Republics of Genoa and Pisa were very powerful in the Middle Ages. Their ships filled the Mediterranean, and they carried on an extensive commerce with Constantinople and Syria. Their warehouses were the great distributing depots from whence the costly merchandise of the East was sent abroad over Europe. They were warlike little nations, and defied, in those days, governments that overshadow them now as mountains overshadow molehills. The Saracens captured and pillaged Genoa nine hundred years ago, but during the following century Genoa and Pisa entered into an offensive and defensive alliance and besieged the Saracen colonies in Sardinia and the Balearic Isles with an obstinacy that maintained its pristine vigor and held to its purpose for forty long years. They were victorious at last, and divided their conquests equally among their great patrician families. Descendants of some of those proud families still inhabit the palaces of Genoa, and trace in their own features a resemblance to the grim knights whose portraits hang in their stately halls, and to pictured beauties with pouting lips and merry eyes whose originals have been dust and ashes for many a dead and forgotten century.

The hotel we live in belonged to one of those great orders of Knights of the Cross in the times of the Crusades, and its mailed sentinels once kept watch and ward in its massive turrets and woke the echoes of these halls and corridors with their iron heels.

But Genoa's greatness has degenerated into an unostentatious commerce in velvets and silver filigree work. They say that each European town has its specialty. These filigree things are Genoa's specialty. Her smiths take silver ingots and work them up into all manner of graceful and beautiful forms. They make bunches of flowers, from flakes and wires of silver, that counterfeit the delicate creations the frost weaves upon a window pane; and we were shown a miniature silver temple whose fluted columns, whose Corinthian capitals and rich entablatures, whose spire, statues, bells, and ornate lavishness of sculpture were wrought in polished silver, and with such matchless art that every detail was a fascinating study, and the finished edifice a wonder of beauty.

We are ready to move again, though we are not really tired, yet, of the narrow passages of this old marble cave. Cave is a good word— when speaking of Genoa under the stars. When we have been prowling at midnight through the gloomy crevices they call streets, where no footfalls but ours were echoing, where only ourselves were abroad, and lights appeared only at long intervals and at a distance, and mysteriously disappeared again, and the houses at our elbows seemed to stretch upward farther than ever toward heavens, the memory of a cave I used to know at home was always in my mind, with its lofty passages, its silence and solitude, its shrouding gloom, its sepulchral echoes, its flitting lights, and more than all, its sudden revelations of branching crevices and corridors where we least expected them.

We are not tired of the endless processions of cheerful, chattering gossipers that throng these courts and streets all day long, either; nor of the coarse-robed monks; nor of the "Asti" wines, which that old doctor (whom we call the Oracle) with customary felicity in the matter of getting everything wrong, misterms "nasty." But we must go, nevertheless.

Our last sight was the cemetery (a burial place intended to accommodate 60,000 bodies), and we shall continue to remember it after we shall have forgotten the palaces. It is a vast marble colonnaded corridor extending around a great unoccupied square of ground; its broad floor is marble, and on every slab is an inscription—for every slab covers a corpse. On either side, as one walks down the middle of the passage, are monuments, tombs, and sculptured figures that are exquisitely wrought and are full of grace and beauty. They are new and snowy; every outline is perfect, every feature guiltless of mutilation, flaw, or blemish; and, therefore, to us these far-reaching ranks of bewitching forms are a hundredfold more lovely than the damaged and dingy statuary they have saved from the wreck of ancient art and set up in the galleries of Paris for the worship of the world.

Well provided with cigars and other necessaries of life, we are now ready to take the cars for Milan.

CHAPTER XVIII

All day long we sped through a mountainous country whose peaks were bright with sunshine, whose hillsides were dotted with pretty villas sitting in the midst of gardens and shrubbery, and whose deep ravines were cool and shady, and looked ever so inviting from where we and the birds were winging our flight through the sultry upper air.

We had plenty of chilly tunnels wherein to check our perspiration, though. We timed one of them. We were twenty minutes passing through it, going at the rate of thirty to thirty-five miles an hour.

Beyond Alessandria we passed the battlefield of Marengo.

Toward dusk we drew near Milan, and caught glimpses of the city and the blue mountain-peaks beyond. But we were not caring for these things—they did not interest us in the least. We were in a fever of impatience; we were dying to see the renowned cathedral! We watched—in this direction and that—all around—everywhere. We needed no one to point it out—we did not wish any one to point it out—we would recognize it, even in the desert of the great Sahara.

At last, a forest of graceful needles, shimmering in the amber sunlight, rose slowly above the pigmy housetops, as one sometimes sees, in the far horizon, a gilded and pinnacled mass of cloud lift itself above the waste of waves, at sea,—the cathedral! We knew it in a moment.

Half of that night, and all of the next day, this architectural autocrat was our sole object of interest.

What a wonder it is! So grand, so solemn, so vast! And yet so delicate, so airy, so graceful! A very world of solid weight, and yet it seems in the soft moonlight only a fairy delusion of frostwork that might vanish with a breath! How sharply its pinnacled angles and its wilderness of spires were cut against the sky, and how richly their shadows fell upon its snowy roof! It was a vision!—a miracle!—an anthem sung in stone, a poem wrought in marble!

Howsoever you look at the great cathedral, it is noble, it is beautiful! Wherever you stand in Milan, or within seven miles of Milan, it is visible—and when it is visible, no other object can chain your whole attention. Leave your eyes unfettered by your will but a single instant and they will surely turn to seek it. It is the first thing you look for when you rise in the morning, and the last your lingering gaze rests upon at night. Surely, it must be the princeliest creation that ever brain of man conceived.

At nine o'clock in the morning we went and stood before this marble colossus. The central one of its five great doors is bordered with a bas-relief of birds and fruits and beasts and insects, which have been so ingeniously carved out of the marble that they seem like living creatures—and the figures are so numerous and the design so complex, that one might study it a week without exhausting its interest. On the great steeple—surmounting the myriad of spires—inside of the spires—over the doors, the windows—in nooks and corners—everywhere that a niche or a perch can be found about the enormous building, from summit to base, there is a marble statue, and every statue is a study in itself! Raphael, Angelo, Canova—giants like these gave birth to the designs, and their own pupils carved them. Every face is eloquent with expression, and every attitude is full of grace. Away above, on the lofty roof, rank on rank of carved and fretted spires spring high in the air, and through their rich tracery one sees the sky beyond. In their midst the central steeple towers prowdly up like the mainmast of some great Indiaman among a fleet of coasters.

We wished to go aloft. The sacristan showed us a marble stairway (of course it was marble, and of the purest and whitest—there is no other stone, no brick, no wood, among its building materials), and told us to go up one hundred and eighty-two steps and stop till he came. It was not necessary to say stop—we should have done that anyhow. We were tired by the time we got there. This was the roof. Here, springing from its broad marble flagstones, were the long files of spires, looking very tall close at hand, but diminishing in the distance like the pipes of an organ. We could see, now, that the statue on the top of each was the size of a large man, though they all looked like dolls from the street. We could see, also, that from the inside of each and every one of these hollow spires, from sixteen to thirty-one beautiful marble statues looked out upon the world below.

From the eaves to the comb of the roof stretched in endless succession great curved marble beams, like the fore-and-aft braces of a steamboat, and along each beam from end to end stood up a row of richly carved flowers and fruits—each separate and distinct in kind, and over 15,000 species represented. At a little distance these rows seem to close together like the ties of a railroad track, and then the mingling together of the buds and blossoms of this marble garden forms a picture that is very charming to the eye.

We descended and entered. Within the church, long rows of fluted columns, like huge monuments, divided the building into broad aisles, and on the figured pavement fell many a soft blush from the painted windows above. I knew the church was very large, but I could not fully appreciate its great size until I noticed that the men standing far down by the altar looked like boys, and seemed to glide, rather than walk. We loitered about gazing aloft at the monster windows all aglow with brilliantly colored scenes in the lives of the Saviour and his followers. Some of these pictures are mosaics, and so artistically are their thousand particles of tinted glass or stone put together that the work has all the smoothness and finish of a painting. We counted sixty panes of glass in one window, and each pane was adorned with one of these master achievements of genius and patience.

The guide showed us a coffee-colored piece of sculpture which he said was considered to have come from the hand of Phidias, since it was not possible that any other artist, of any epoch, could have copied nature with such faultless accuracy. The figure was that of a man without a skin; with every vein, artery, muscle, every fibre and tendon and tissue of the human frame, represented in minute detail. It looked natural, because somehow it looked as if it were in pain. A skinned man would be likely to look that way, unless his attention were occupied with some other matter. It was a hideous thing, and yet there was a fascination about it somewhere. I am very sorry I saw it, because I shall always see it, now. I shall dream of it, sometimes. I shall dream that it is resting its corded arms on the bed's head and looking down on me with its dead eyes; I shall dream that it is stretched between the sheets with me and touching me with its exposed muscles and its stringy cold legs.

It is hard to forget repulsive things. I remember yet how I ran off from school once, when I was a boy, and then, pretty late at night, concluded to climb into the window of my father's office and sleep on a lounge, because I had a delicacy about going home and getting thrashed. As I lay on the lounge and my eyes grew accustomed to the darkness, I fancied I could see a long, dusky, shapeless thing stretched upon the floor. A cold shiver went through me. I turned my face to the wall. That did not answer. I was afraid that that thing would creep over and seize me in the dark. I turned back and stared at it for minutes and minutes—they seemed hours. It appeared to me that the lagging moonlight never, never would get to it. I turned to the wall and counted twenty, to pass the feverish time away. I looked—the pale square was nearer. I turned again and counted fifty—it was almost touching it. With desperate will I turned again and counted one hundred, and faced about, all in a tremble. A white human hand lay in the moonlight! Such an awful sinking at the heart—such a sudden gasp for breath! I felt—I cannot tell *what* I felt. When I recovered strength enough, I faced the wall again. But no boy could have remained so, with that mysterious hand behind him. I counted again, and looked—the most of a naked arm was exposed. I put my hands over my eyes and counted till I could stand it no longer, and then—the pallid face of a man was there, with the corners of the mouth drawn down, and the eyes fixed and glassy in death! I raised to a sitting posutre and glowered on that corpse till the light crept down the bare breast,—line by line— inch by inch—past the nipple,—and then it disclosed a ghastly stab!

I went away from there. I do not say that I went away in any sort of a hurry, but I simply went—that is sufficient. I went out at the window, and I carried the sash along with me. I did not need the sash, but it was handier to take it than it was to leave it, and so I took it. I was not scared, but I was considerably agitated.

When I reached home, they whipped me, but I enjoyed it. It seemed perfectly delightful. That man had been stabbed near the office that afternoon, and they carried him in there to doctor him, but he only lived an hour. I have slept in the same room with him often, since then—in my dreams.

Now we will descend into the crypt, under the grand altar of Milan cathedral, and receive an impressive sermon from lips that have been silent and hands that have been gestureless for three hundred years.

The priest stopped in a small dungeon and held up his candle. This was the last resting-place of a good man, a warm-hearted, unselfish man; a man whose whole life was given to succoring the poor, encouraging the faint-hearted, visiting the sick; in relieving distress, whenever and wherever he found it. His heart, his hand, and his purse were always open. With his story in one's mind he can almost see his benignant countenance moving calmly among the haggard faces of Milan in the days when the plague swept the ciy, brave where all others were cowards, full of compassion where pity had been crushed out of all other breasts by the instinct of self-preservation gone mad with terror, cheering all, praying with all, helping all, with hand and brain and purse, at a time when parents forsook their children, the friend deserted the friend, and the brother turned away from the sister while her pleadings were still wailing in his ears.

This was good St. Charles Borromeo, Bishop of Milan. The people idolized him; princes lavished uncounted treasures upon him. We stood in his tomb. Near by was the sarcophagus, lighted by the dripping candles. The walls were faced with bas-reliefs representing scenes in his life done in massive silver. The priest put on a short white lace garment over his black robe, crossed himself, bowed reverently, and began to turn a windlass slowly. The sarcophagus separated in two parts, lengthwise, and the lower part sank down and disclosed a coffin of rock crystal as clear as the atmosphere. Within lay the body, robed in costly habiliments covered with gold embroidery and starred with scintillating gems. The decaying head was black with age, the dry skin was drawn tight to the bones, the eyes were gone, there was a hole in the temple and another in the cheek, and the skinny lips were parted as in a ghastly smile! Over this dreadful face, its dust and decay, and its mocking grin, hung a crown sown thick with flashing brilliants; and upon the breast lay crosses and croziers of solid gold that were splendid with emeralds and diamonds.

How poor, and cheap, and trivial these gewgaws seemed in presence of the solemnity, the grandeur, the awful majesty of Death! Think of Milton, Shakespeare, Washington, standing before a reverent world tricked out in the glass beads, the brass earrings, and tin trumpery of the savages of the plains!

Dead Borromeo preached his pregnant sermon, and its burden was: You that worship the vanities of earth—you that long for worldly honor, worldly wealth, worldly fame—behold their worth!

To us it seemed that so good a man, so kind a heart, so simple a nature, deserved rest and peace in a grave sacred from the intrusion of prying eyes, and believed that he himself would have preferred to have it so, but peradventure our wisdom was at fault in this regard.

As we came out upon the floor of the church again, another priest volunteered to show us the treasures of the church. What, more? The furniture of the narrow chamber of death we had just visited, weighed six millions of francs in ounces and carats alone, without a penny thrown into the account for the costly workmanship bestowed upon them! But we followed into a large room filled with tall wooden presses like wardrobes. He threw them open, and behold, the cargoes of "crude bullion" of the assay offices of Nevada faded out of my memory. There were Virgins and bishops there, above their natural size, made of solid silver, each worth, by weight, from eight hundred thousand to two millions of francs, and bearing gemmed books in their hands worth eighty thousand; there were bas-reliefs that weighed six hundred pounds, carved in solid silver; croziers and crosses, and candlesticks six and eight feet high, all of virgin gold, and brilliant with precious stones; and beside these were all manner of cups and vases, and such things, rich in proportion. It was an Aladdin's palace. The treasures here, by simple weight, without counting workmanship, were valued at fifty millions of francs! If I could get the custody of them for a while, I fear me the market price of silver bishops would advance shortly, on account of their exceeding scarcity in the Cathedral of Milan.

The priests showed us two of St. Paul's fingers, and one of St. Peter's; a bone of Judas Iscariot (it was black), and also bones of all the other disciples; a handkerchief in which the Saviour had left the impression of his face. Among the most precious of the relics were, a stone from the Holy Sepulchre, part of the crown of thorns (they have a whole one at Notre Dame), a fragment of the purple robe worn by the Saviour, a nail from the Cross, and a picture of the Virgin and Child painted by the veritable hand of St. Luke. This is the second of St. Luke's Virgins we have seen. Once a year all these holy relics are carried in procession through the streets of Milan.

I like to revel in the dryest details of the great cathedral. The building is five hundred feet long by one hundred and eighty wide, and the principal steeple is in the neighborhood of four hundred feet high. It has 7,148 marble statues, and will have upward of three thousand more when it is finished. In addition, it has one thousand five hundred bas-reliefs. It has one hundred and thirty-six spires—twenty-one more are to be added. Each spire is surmounted by a statue six and a half feet high. Everything about the church is marble, and all from the same quarry; it was bequeathed to the Archbishopric for this purpose centuries ago. So nothing but the mere workmanship costs; still that is expensive—the bill foots up six hundred and eighty-four millions of francs, thus far (considerably over a hundred millions of dollars), and it is estimated that it will take a hundred and twenty years yet to finish the cathedral. It looks complete, but is far from being so. We saw a new statue put in its niche yesterday, alongside of one which had been standing these four hundred years, they said. There are four staircases leading up to the main steeple, each of which cost a hundred thousand dollars, with the four hundred and eight statues which adorn them. Marcoda

Campione was the architect who designed the wonderful structure more than five hundred years ago, and it took him forty-six years to work out the plan and get it ready to hand over to the builders. He is dead now. The building was begun a little less than five hundred years ago, and the third generation hence will not see it completed.

The building looks best by moonlight, because the older portions of it being stained with age, contrast unpleasantly with the newer and whiter portions. It seems somewhat too broad for its height, but may be familiarity with it might dissipate this impression.

They say that the Cathedral of Milan is second only to St. Peter's at Rome. I cannot understand how it can be second to anything made by human hands.

We bid it good-bye now—possibly for all time. How surely, in some future day, when the memory of it shall have lost its vividness, shall we half believe we have seen it in a wonderful dream, but never with waking eyes!

CHAPTER XIX

"Do you wis zo haut can be?"

That was what the guide asked, when we were looking up at the bronze horses on the Arch of Peace. It meant, Do you wish to go up there? I give it as a specimen of guide-English. These are the people that make life a burthen to the tourist. Their tongues are never still. They talk forever and forever, and that is the kind of billingsgate they use. Inspiration itself could hardly comprehend them. If they would only show you a masterpiece of art, or a venerable tomb, or a prison-house, or a battlefield, hallowed by touching memories, or historical reminiscences, or grand traditions, and then step aside and hold still for ten minutes and let you think, it would not be so bad. But they interrupt every dream, every pleasant train of thought, with their tiresome cackling. Sometimes when I have been standing before some cherished old idol of mine that I remembered years and years ago in pictures in the geography at school, I have thought I would give a whole world if the human parrot at my side would suddenly perish where he stood and leave me to gaze, and ponder, and worship.

No, we did not "wis zo haut can be." We wished to go to La Scala, the largest theater in the world, I think they call it. We did so. It was a large place. Seven separate and distinct masses of humanity—six great circles and a monster parquette.

We wished to go to the Ambrosian Library, and we did that also. We saw a manuscript of Virgil, with annotations in the handwriting of Petrarch, the gentleman who loved another man's Laura, and lavished upon her all through life a love which was a clear waste of the raw material. It was sound sentiment, but bad judgment. It brought both parties fame, and created a fountain of commiseration for them in sentimental breasts that is running yet. But who says a word in behalf of poor Mr. Laura? (I do not know his other name.) Who glorifies him? Who bedews him with tears? Who writes poetry about him? Nobody. How do you suppose *he* liked the state of things that has given the world so much pleasure? How did he enjoy having another man following his wife everywhere and making her name a familiar word in every garlic-exterminating mouth in Italy with his sonnets to her pre-empted eyebrows? *They* got fame and sympathy—he got neither. This is a peculiarly felicitous instance of what is called poetical justice. It is all very fine; but it does not chime with my notions of right. It is too one-sided—too ungenerous. Let the world go on fretting about Laura and Petrarch if it will; but as for me, my tears and my lamentations shall be lavished upon the unsung defendant.

We saw also an autograph letter of Lucrezia Borgia, a lady for whom I have always entertained the highest respect, on account of her rare histrionic capabilities, her opulence in solid gold goblets made of gilded wood, her high distinction as an operatic screamer, and the facility with which she could order a sextuple funeral and get the corpses ready for it. We saw one single coarse yellow hair from Lucrezia's head, likewise. It awoke emotions, but we still live. In this same library we saw some drawings by Michael Angelo (these Italians call him Mickel Angelo), and Leonardo da Vinci. (They spell it Vinci and pronounce it Vinchy; foreigners always spell better than they pronounce.) We reserve our opinion of these sketches.

In another building they showed us a fresco representing some lions and other beasts drawing chariots; and they seemed to project so far from the wall that we took them to be sculptures. The artist had shrewdly heightened the delusion by painting dust on the creatures' backs, as if it had fallen there naturally and properly. Smart fellow—if it be smart to deceive strangers.

Elsewhere we saw a huge Roman amphitheater, with its stone seats still in good preservation. Modernized, it is now the scene of more peaceful recreations than the exhibition of a party of wild beasts with Christians for dinner. Part of the time, the Milanese use it for a race track, and at other seasons they flood it with water and have spirited yachting regattas there. The guide told us these things, and he would hardly try so hazardous an experiment as the telling of a falsehood, when it is all he can do to speak the truth in English without getting the lockjaw.

In another place we were shown a sort of summer arbor, with a fence before it. We said that was nothing. We looked again, and saw, through the arbor, an endless stretch of garden, and shrubbery, and grassy lawn. We were perfectly willing to go in there and rest, but it could not be done. It was only another delusion—a painting by some ingenious artist with little charity in his heart for tired folk. The deception was perfect. No one could have imagined the park was not real. We even thought we smelled the flowers at first.

We got a carriage at twilight and drove in the shaded avenues with the other nobility, and after dinner we took wine and ices in a fine garden with the great public. The music was excellent, the flowers and shrubbery were pleasant to the eye, the scene was vivacious, everybody was genteel and well-behaved, and the ladies were slightly moustached, and handsomely dressed, but very homely.

We adjourned to the café and played billiards an hour, and I made six or seven points by the doctor pocketing his ball, and he made as many by my pocketing my ball. We came near making a carom sometimes, but not the one we were trying to make. The table was of the usual European style—cushions dead and twice as high as the balls; the cues in bad repair. The natives play only a sort of pool on them. We have never seen anybody playing the French three-ball game yet, and I doubt if there is any such game known in France, or that there lives any man mad enough to try to play it on one of these European tables. We had to stop playing, finally, because Dan got to sleeping fifteen minutes between the counts and paying no attention to his marking.

Afterward we walked up and down one of the most popular streets for some time, enjoying other people's comfort and wishing we could export some of it to our restless, driving, vitality-consuming marts at home. Just in this one matter lies the main charm of life in Europe—comfort. In America, we hurry—which is well; but when the day's work is done, we go on thinking of losses and gains, we plan for the morrow, we even carry our business cares to bed with us, and toss and worry over them when we ought to be restoring our racked bodies and brains with sleep. We burn up our energies with these excitements, and either die early or drop into a lean and mean old age at a time of life which they call a man's prime in Europe. When an acre of ground has produced long and well, we let it lie fallow and rest for a season; we take no man clear across the continent in the same coach he started in—the coach is stabled somewhere on the plains and its heated machinery allowed to cool for a few days; when a razor has seen long service and refuses to hold an edge, the barber lays it away for a few weeks, and the edge comes back of its own accord. We bestow thoughtful care upon inanimate objects, but none upon ourselves. What a robust people, what a nation of thinkers we might be, if we would only lay ourselves on the shelf occasionally and renew our edges!

I do envy these Europeans the comfort they take. When the work of the day is done, they forget it. Some of them go, with wife and children, to a beer hall, and sit quietly and genteelly drinking a mug or two of ale and listening to music; others walk the streets, others drive in the avenues; others assemble in the great ornamental squares in the early evening to enjoy the sight and the fragrance of flowers and to hear the military bands play—no European city being

without its fine military music at eventide; and yet others of the populace sit in the open air in front of the refreshment houses and eat
ices and drink mild beverages that could not harm a child. They go
to bed moderately early, and sleep well. They are always quiet, always orderly, always cheerful, comfortable, and appreciative of life
and its manifold blessings. One never sees a drunken man among
them. The change that has come over our little party is surprising.
Day by day we lose some of our restlessness and absorb some of the
spirit of quietude and ease that is in the tranquil atmosphere about
us and in the demeanor of the people. We grow wise apace. We begin to comprehend what life is for.

We have had a bath in Milan, in a public bath-house. They were
going to put all three of us in one bathtub, but we objected. Each of
us had an Italian farm on his back. We could have felt affluent if we
had been officially surveyed and fenced in. We chose to have three
bathtubs, and large ones—tubs suited to the dignity of aristocrats
who had real estate, and brought it with them. After we were
stripped and had taken the first chilly dash, we discovered that
haunting atrocity that has embittered our lives in so many cities and
villages of Italy and France—there was no soap. I called. A woman
answered, and I barely had time to throw myself against the door—
she would have been in, in another second. I said:

"Beware, woman! Go away from here—go away, now, or it will be
the worse for you. I am an unprotected male, but I will preserve my
honor at the peril of my life!"

These words must have frightened her, for she skurried away very
fast.

Dan's voice rose on the air:

"Oh, bring some soap, why don't you!"

The reply was Italian. Dan resumed:

"Soap, you know—soap. That is what I want—soap. S-o-a-p,
soap; s-o-p-e, soap; s-o-u-p, soap. Hurry up! I don't know how you
Irish spell it, but I want it. Spell it to suit yourself, but fetch it. I'm
freezing."

I heard the doctor say, impressively:

"Dan, how often have we told you that these foreigners cannot
understand English? Why will you not depend upon us? Why will
you not tell *us* what you want, and let us ask for it in the language of
the country? It would save us a great deal of the humiliation your
reprehensible ignorance causes us. I will address this person in his
mother tongue: 'Here, cospetto! corpo di Bacco! Sacramento! Sol-
ferino!—Soap, you son of a gun!' Dan, if you would let *us* talk for
you, you would never expose your ignorant vulgarity."

Even this fluent dischage of Italian did not bring the soap at once,
but there was a good reason for it. There was not such an article
about the establishment. It is my belief that there never had been.
They had to send far up town, and to several different places before

they finally got it, so they said. We had to wait twenty or thirty minutes. The same thing had occurred the evening before, at the hotel. I think I have divined the reason for this state of things at last. The English know how to travel comfortably, and they carry soap with them; other foreigners do not use the article.

At every hotel we stop at we always have to send out for soap, at the last moment, when we are grooming ourselves for dinner, and they put it in the bill along with the candles and other nonsense. In Marseilles they make half the fancy toilet soap we consume in America, but the Marseillaise only have a vague theoretical idea of its use, which they have obtained from books of travel, just as they have acquired an uncertain notion of clean shirts, and the peculiarities of the gorilla, and other curious matters. This reminds me of poor Blucher's note to the landlord in Paris:

"PARIS, le 7 Juillet.

"Monsieur le Landlord—Sir: Pourquoi don't you mettez some savon in your bedchambers? Est-ce que vous pensez I will steal it? La nuit passée you charged me pour deux chandelles when I only had one; hier vous avez charged me avec glace when I had none at all; tout les jours you are coming some fresh game or other on me, mais vous ne pouvez pas play this savon dodge on me twice. Savon is a necessary de la vie to anybody but a Frenchman, et je l'aurai hors de cet hôtel or make trouble. You hear me. Allons.   BLUCHER."

I remonstrated against the sending of this note, because it was so mixed up that the landlord would never be able to make head or tail of it; but Blucher said he guessed the old man could read the French of it and average the rest.

Blucher's French is bad enough, but it is not much worse than the English one finds in advertisements all over Italy every day. For instance, observe the printed card of the hotel we shall probably stop at on the shores of Lake Como:

"NOTISH."

"This hotel which the best it is in Italy and most superb, is handsome locate on the best situation of the lake, with the most splendid view near the Villas Melzy, to the King of Belgian, and Serbelloni. This hotel have recently enlarge, do offer all commodities on moderate price, at the strangers gentlemen who whish spend the seasons on the Lake Come."

How is that for a specimen? In the hotel is a handsome little chapel where an English clergyman is employed to preach to such of the guests of the house as hail from England and America, and this fact is also set forth in barbarous English in the same advertisement. Wouldn't you have supposed that the adventurous linguist who framed the card would have known enough to submit it to that clergyman before he sent it to the printer?

Here, in Milan, in an ancient tumble-down ruin of a church, is the mournful wreck of the most celebrated painting in the world—"The

Last Supper," by Leonardo da Vinci. We are not infallible judges of pictures, but of course, we went there to see this wonderful painting, once so beautiful, always so worshiped by masters in art, and forever to be famous in song and story. And the first thing that occurred was the infliction on us of a placard fairly reeking with wretched English. Take a morsel of it:

"Bartholomew (that is the first figure on the left hand side at the spectator), uncertain and doubtful about what he thinks to have heard, and upon which he wants to be assured by himself at Christ and by no others."

Good, isn't it? And then Peter is described as "argumenting in a threatening and angrily condition at Judas Iscariot."

This paragraph recalls the picture. "The Last Supper" is painted on the dilapidated wall of what was a little chapel attached to the main church in ancient times, I suppose. It is battered and scarred in every direction, and stained and discolored by time, and Napoleon's horses kicked the legs off most the disciples when they (the horses, not the disciples) were stabled there more than half a century ago.

I recognized the old picture in a moment—the Saviour with bowed head seated at the center of a long, rough table with scattering fruits and dishes upon it, and six disciples on either side in their long robes, talking to each other—the picture from which all engravings and all copies have been made for three centuries. Perhaps no living man has ever known an attempt to paint the Lord's Supper differently. The world seems to have become settled in the belief, long ago, that it is not possible for human genious to outdo this creation of Da Vinci's. I suppose painters will go on copying it as long as any of the original is left visible to the eye. There were a dozen easels in the room, and as many artists transferring the great picture to their canvases. Fifty proofs of steel engravings and lithographs were scattered around, too. And as usual, I could not help noticing how superior the copies were to the original, that is, to my inexperienced eye. Wherever you find a Raphael, a Rubens, a Michael Angelo, a Caracci, or a Da Vinci (and we see them every day) you find artists copying them, and the copies are always the handsomest. Maybe the originals were handsome when they were new, but they are not now.

This picture is about thirty feet long, and ten or twelve high, I should think, and the figures are at least life size. It is one of the largest paintings in Europe.

The colors are dimmed with age; the countenances are scaled and marred, and nearly all expression is gone from them; the hair is a dead blur upon the wall, and there is no life in the eyes. Only the attitudes are certain.

People come here from all parts of the world, and glorify this masterpiece. They stand entranced before it with bated breath and parted lips, and when they speak, it is only in the catchy ejaculations of rapture:

"Oh, wonderful!"

"Such expression!"

"Such grace of attitude!"

"Such dignity!"

"Such faultless drawing!"

"Such matchless coloring!"

"Such feeling!"

"What delicacy of touch!"

"What sublimity of conception!"

"A vision! a vision!"

I only envy these people; I envy them their honest admiration, if it be honest—their delight, if they feel delight. I harbor no animosity toward any of them. But at the same time the thought *will* intrude itself upon me, How can they see what is not visible? What would you think of a man who looked at some decayed, blind, toothless, pock-marked Cleopatra, and said: "What matchless beauty! What soul! What expression!" What would you think of a man who gazed upon a dingy, foggy sunset, and said: "What sublimity! what feeling! what richness of coloring!" What would you think of a man who stared in ecstasy upon a desert of stumps and said: "Oh, my soul, my beating heart, what a noble forest is here!"

You would think that those men had an astonishing talent for seeing things that had already passed away. It was what I thought when I stood before the Last Supper and heard men apostrophizing wonders and beauties and perfections which had faded out of the picture and gone, a hundred years before they were born. We can imagine the beauty that was once in an aged face; we can imagine the forest if we see the stumps; but we cannot absolutely *see* these things when they are not there. I am willing to believe that the eye of the practiced artist can rest upon the Last Supper and renew a lustre where only a hint of it is left, supply a tint that has faded away, restore an expression that is gone; patch, and color, and add to the dull canvas until at last its figures shall stand before him aglow with the life, the feeling, the freshness, yea, with all the noble beauty that was theirs when first they came from the hand of the master. But *I* cannot work this miracle. Can those other uninspired visitors do it, or do they only happily imagine they do?

After reading so much about it, I am satisfied that the Last Supper was a very miracle of art once. But it was three hundred years ago.

It vexes me to hear people talk so glibly of "feeling," "expression," "tone," and those other easily-acquired and inexpensive technicalities of art that make such a fine show in conversations concerning pictures. There is not one man in seventy-five hundred that can tell *what* a pictured face is intended to express. There is not one man in five hundred that can go into a court-room and be sure that he will not mistake some harmless innocent of a jury-man for the black-hearted assassin on trial. Yet such people talk of "character" and presume to interpret "expression" in pictures. There is an old story that Matthews, the actor, was once lauding the ability of the human face to express the passions and emotions hidden in the breast. He said the countenance could disclose what was passing in the heart plainer than the tongue could.

"Now," he said, "observe my face—what does it express?"

"Despair!"

"Bah, it expresses peaceful resignation! What does *this* express?"

"Rage!"

"Stuff! it means terror! *This!*"

"Imbecility!"

"Fool! It is smothered ferocity! Now *this!*"

"Joy!"

"Oh, perdition! *Any* ass can see it means insanity!"

Expression! People coolly pretend to read it who would think themselves presumptuous if they pretended to interpret the hieroglyphics on the obelisk of Luxor—yet they are fully as competent to do the one thing as the other. I have heard two very intelligent critics speak of Murillo's Immaculate Conception (now in the museum at Seville) within the past few days. One said:

"Oh, the Virgin's face is full of the ecstasy of a joy that is complete—that leaves nothing more to be desired on earth!"

The other said:

"Ah, that wonderful face is so humble, so pleading—it says as plainly as words could say it: 'I fear; I tremble; I am unworthy. But Thy will be done; sustain Thou Thy servant!' "

The reader can see the picture in any drawing-room; it can be easily recognized; the Virgin (the only young and really beautiful Virgin that was ever painted by one of the old masters, some of us think) stands in the crescent of the new moon, with a multitude of cherubs hovering about her, and more coming; her hands are crossed upon her breast, and upon her uplifted countenance falls a glory out of the heavens. The reader may amuse himself, if he chooses, in trying to determine which of these gentlemen read the Virgin's "expression" aright, or if either of them did it.

Any one who is acquainted with the old masters will comprehend how much the Last Supper is damaged when I say that the spectator cannot really tell, now, whether the disciples are Hebrews or Italians. These ancient painters never succeeded in denationalizing themselves. The Italian artists painted Italian Virgins, the Dutch painted Dutch Virgins, the Virgins of the French painters were Frenchwomen—none of them ever put into the face of the Madonna that indescribable something which proclaims the Jewess, whether you find her in New York, in Constantinople, in Paris, Jerusalem, or in the Empire of Morocco. I saw in the Sandwich Islands, once, a picture, copied by a talented German artist from an engraving in one of the American illustrated papers. It was an allegory, representing Mr. Davis in the act of signing a secession act or some such document. Over him hovered the ghost of Washington in warning attitude, and in the background a troop of shadowy soldiers in Continental uniform were limping with shoeless, bandaged feet through a driving snowstorm. Valley Forge was suggested, of course. The copy seemed accurate, and yet there was a discrepancy somewhere. After a long examination I discovered what it was—the shadowy soldiers were all Germans! Jeff. Davis was a German! even the hovering ghost was a German ghost! The artist had unconsciously worked his nationality into the picture. To tell the truth, I am getting a little perplexed about John the Baptist and his portraits. In France I finally grew reconciled to him as a Frenchman; here he is unquestionably an Italian. What next? Can it be possible that the painters make John the Baptist a Spaniard in Madrid and an Irishman in Dublin?

We took an open barouche and drove two miles out of Milan to "see ze echo," as the guide expressed it. The road was smooth, it was bordered by trees, fields, and grassy meadows, and the soft air was filled with the odor of flowers. Troops of picturesque peasant girls, coming from work, hooted at us, shouted at us, made all manner of game of us, and entirely delighted me. My long-cherished judgment was confirmed. I always did think those frowsy, romantic, unwashed peasant girls I had read so much about in poetry were a glaring fraud.

We enjoyed our jaunt. It was an exhilarating relief from tiresome sightseeing.

We distressed ourselves very little about the astonishing echo the guide talked so much about. We were growing accustomed to encomiums on wonders that too often proved no wonders at all. And so we were most happily disappointed to find in the sequel that the guide had even failed to rise to the magnitude of his subject.

We arrived at a tumble-down old rookery called the Palazzo Simonetti—a massive hewn-stone affair occupied by a family of ragged Italians. A good-looking young girl conducted us to a window on the second floor which looked out on a court walled on three sides by tall buildings. She put her head out at the window and shouted. The echo answered more times than we could count. She took a speaking-trumpet and through it she shouted, sharp and quick, a single

"Ha!" The echo answered:

"Ha———ha!!——ha!——ha!—ha!—ha! ha! h-a-a-a-a-a!" and finally went off into a rollicking convulsion of the jolliest laughter that could be imagined. It was so joyful, so long-continued, so perfectly cordial and hearty, that everybody was forced to join in. There was no resisting it.

Then the girl took a gun and fired it. We stood ready to count the astonishing clatter of reverberations. We could not say one, two, three, fast enough, but we could dot our note-books with our pencil-points almost rapidly enough to take down a sort of shorthand report of the result. My page revealed the following account. I could not keep up, but I did as well as I could.

I set down fifty-two distinct repetitions, and then the echo got the advantage of me. The doctor set down sixty-four, and thenceforth the echo moved too fast for him, also. After the separate concusions could no longer be noted, the reverberations dwindled to a wild, long-sustained clatter of sounds such as a watchman's rattle produces. It is likely that this is the most remarkable echo in the world.

The doctor, in jest, offered to kiss the young girl, and was taken a little aback when she said he might for a franc! The commonest gallantry compelled him to stand by his offer, and so he paid the franc and took the kiss. She was a philosopher. She said a franc was a good thing to have, and she did not care anything for one paltry kiss, because she had a million left. Then our comrade, always a shrewd business man, offered to take the whole cargo at thirty days, but that little financial scheme was a failure.

CHAPTER XX

We left Milan by rail. The cathedral six or seven miles behind us—vast, dreamy, bluish, snow-clad mountains twenty miles in front of us,—these were the accented points in the scenery. The more immediate scenery consisted of fields and farmhouses outside the car and a monster-headed dwarf and a moustached woman inside it. These latter were not show-people. Alas, deformity and female beards are too common in Italy to attract attention.

We passed through a range of wild, picturesque hills, steep, wooded, cone-shaped, with rugged crags projecting here and there, and with dwellings and ruinous castles perched away up toward the drifting clouds. We lunched at the curious old town of Como, at the foot of the lake, and then took the small steamer and had an after-noon's pleasure excursion to this place,—Bellagio.

When we walked ashore, a party of policemen (people whose cocked hats and showy uniforms would shame the finest uniform in the military service of the United States) put us into a little stone cell and locked us in. We had the whole passenger list for company, but their room would have been preferable, for there was no light, there were no windows, no ventilation. It was close and hot. We were much crowded. It was the Black Hole of Calcutta on a small scale. Presently a smoke rose about our feet—a smoke that smelt of all the dead things of earth, of all the putrefaction and corruption imaginable.

We were there five minutes, and when we got out it was hard to tell which of us carried the vilest fragrance.

These miserable outcasts called that "fumigating" us, and the term was a tame one, indeed. They fumigated us to guard themselves against the cholera, though we hailed from no infected port. We had left the cholera far behind us all the time. However, they must keep epidemics away somehow or other, and fumigation is cheaper than soap. They must either wash themselves or fumigate other people. Some of the lower classes had rather die than wash, but the fumigation of strangers causes them no pangs. They need no fumigation themselves. Their habits make it unnecessary. They carry their preventive with them; they sweat and fumigate all the day long. I trust I am a humble and a consistent Christian. I try to do what is right. I know it is my duty to "pray for them that despitefully use me"; and therefore, hard as it is, I shall still try to pray for these fumigating, macaroni-stuffing organ-grinders.

Our hotel sits at the water's edge—at least its front garden does—and we walk among the shrubbery and smoke at twilight; we look afar off at Switzerland and the Alps, and feel an indolent willingness to look no closer; we go down the steps and swim in the lake; we take a shapely little boat and sail abroad among the reflections of the stars; lie on the thwarts and listen to the distant laughter, the singing, the soft melody of flutes and guitars that comes floating across the water from pleasuring gondolas; we close the evening with exasperating billiards on one of those same old execrable tables. A midnight luncheon in our ample bed-chamber; a final smoke in its contracted veranda facing the water, the gardens, and the mountains; a summing up of the day's events. Then to bed, with drowsy brains harassed with a mad panorama that mixes up pictures of France, of Italy, of the ship, of the ocean, of home, in grotesque and bewildering disorder. Then a melting away of familiar faces, of cities and of tossing waves, into a great calm of forgetfulness and peace.

After which, the nightmare.

Breakfast in the morning, and then the lake.

I did not like it yesterday. I thought Lake Tahoe was *much* finer. I have to confess now, however, that my judgment erred somewhat, though not extravagantly. I always had an idea that Como was a vast basin of water, like Tahoe, shut in by great mountains. Well, the border of huge mountains is here, but the lake itself is not a basin. It is as crooked as any brook, and only from one-quarter to two-thirds as wide as the Mississippi. There is not a yard of low ground on either side of it—nothing but endless chains of mountains that spring abruptly from the water's edge, and tower to altitudes varying from a thousand to two thousand feet. Their craggy sides are clothed with vegetation, and white specks of houses peep out from the luxuriant foliage everywhere; they are even perched upon jutting and picturesque pinnacles a thousand feet above your head.

Again, for miles along the shores, handsome country seats,

surrounded by gardens and groves, sit fairly in the water, sometimes in nooks carved by Nature out of the vine-hung precipices, and with no ingress or egress save by boats. Some have great broad stone staircases leading down to the water, with heavy stone balustrades ornamented with statuary and fancifully adorned with creeping vines and bright-colored flowers—for all the world like a drop-curtain in a theater, and lacking nothing but long-waisted, high-heeled women and plumed gallants in silken tights coming down to go serenading in the splendid gondola in waiting.

A great feature of Como's attractiveness is the multitude of pretty houses and gardens that cluster upon its shores and on its mountain sides. They look so snug and so homelike, and at eventide when everything seems to slumber, and the music of the vesper bells comes stealing over the water, one almost believes that nowhere else than on the Lake of Como can there be found such a paradise of tranquil repose.

Fom my window here in Bellagio, I have a view of the other side of the lake now, which is as beautiful as a picture. A scarred and wrinkled precipice rises to a height of eighteen hundred feet; on a tiny bench half way up its vast wall, sits a little snow-flake of a church, no bigger than a martin-box, apparently; skirting the base of the cliff are a hundred orange groves and gardens, flecked with glimpses of the white dwellings that are buried in them; in front, three or four gondolas lie idle upon the water—and in the burnished mirror of the lake, mountain, chapel, houses, groves, and boats are counterfeited so brightly and so clearly that one scarce knows where the reality leaves off and the reflection begins!

The surroundings of this picture are fine. A mile away, a grove-plumed promontory juts far into the lake and glasses its palace in the blue depths; in midstream a boat is cutting the shining surface and leaving a long track behind, like a ray of light; the mountains beyond are veiled in a dreamy purple haze; far in the opposite direction a tumbled mass of domes and verdant slopes and valleys bars the lake, and here, indeed, does distance lend enchantment to the view—for on this broad canvas, sun and clouds and the richest of atmospheres have blended a thousand tints together, and over its surface the filmy lights and shadows drift, hour after hour, and glorify it with a beauty that seems reflected out of Heaven itself. Beyond all question, this is the most voluptuous scene we have yet looked upon.

Last night the scenery was striking and picturesque. On the other side crags and trees and snowy houses were reflected in the lake with a wonderful distinctness, and streams of light from many a distant window shot far abroad over the still waters. On this side, near at hand, great mansions, white with moonlight, glared out from the midst of masses of foliage that lay black and shapeless in the shadows that fell from the cliff above—and down in the margin of the lake every feature of the weird vision was faithfully repeated.

To-day we have idled through a wonder of a garden attached to a ducal estate—but enough of description is enough, I judge. I suspect that this was the same place the gardener's son deceived the Lady of Lyons with, but I do not know. You may have heard of the passage somewhere:

> "A deep vale,
> Shut out by Alpine hills from the rude world,
> Near a clear lake margined by fruits of gold
> And whispering myrtles:
> Glassing softest skies, cloudless,
> Save with rare and roseate shadows;
> A palace, lifting to eternal heaven its marbled walls,
> From out a glossy bower of coolest foliage musical
> with birds."

That is all very well, except the "clear" part of the lake. It certainly is clearer than a great many lakes, but how dull its waters are compared with the wonderful transparence of Lake Tahoe! I speak of the north shore of Tahoe, where one can count the scales on a trout at a depth of a hundred and eighty feet. I have tried to get this statement off at par here, but with no success; so I have been obliged to negotiate it at fifty per cent. discount. At this rate I find some takers; perhaps the reader will receive it on the same terms—ninety feet instead of one hundred and eighty. But let it be remembered that those are forced terms—sheriff's-sale prices. As far as I am privately concerned, I abate not a jot of the original assertion that in those strangely-magnifying waters one may count the scales on a trout (a trout of the large kind) at a depth of a hundred and eighty feet—may see every pebble on the bottom—might even count a paper of dray-pins. People talk of the transparent waters of the Mexican Bay of Acapulco, but in my own experience I know they cannot compare with those I am speaking of. I have fished for trout in Tahoe, and at a measured depth of eighty-four feet I have seen them put their noses to the bait and I could see their gills open and shut. I could hardly have seen the trout themselves at that distance in the open air.

As I go back in spirit and recall that noble sea, reposing among the snow-peaks six thousand feet above the ocean, the conviction comes strong upon me again that Como would only seem a bedizened little courtier in that august presence.

Sorrow and misfortune overtake the legislature that still from year to year permits Tahoe to retain its unmusical cognomen! Tahoe! It suggests no crystal waters, no picturesque shores, no sublimity. Tahoe for a sea in the clouds; a sea that has character, and asserts it in solemn calms, at times, at times in savage storms; a sea, whose royal seclusion is guarded by a cordon of sentinel peaks that lift their frosty fronts nine thousand feet above the level world; a sea whose every aspect is impressive, whose belongings are all beautiful, whose lonely majesty types the Deity!

Tahoe means grasshoppers. It means grasshopper soup. It is Indian, and suggestive of Indians. They say it is Pi-ute—possibly it is Digger. I am satisfied it was named by the Diggers—those degraded savages who roast their dead relatives, then mix the human grease and ashes of bones with tar, and "gaum" it thick all over their heads and foreheads and ears, and go caterwauling about the hills and call it *mourning*. *These* are the gentry that named the lake.

People say that Tahoe means "Silver Lake"—"Limpid Water"— "Falling Leaf." Bosh! It means grasshopper soup, the favorite dish of the Digger tribe—and of the Pi-utes as well. It isn't worth while, in these practical times, for people to talk about Indian poetry— there never was any in them—except in the Fenimore Cooper Indians. But *they* are an extinct tribe that never existed. I know the Noble Red Man. I have camped with the Indians; I have been on the warpath with them, taken part in the chase with them—for grasshoppers; helped them steal cattle; I have roamed with them, scalped them, had them for breakfast. I would gladly eat the whole race if I had a chance.

But I am growing unreliable. I will return to my comparison of the lakes. Como is a little deeper than Tahoe, if people here tell the truth. They say it is eighteen hundred feet deep at this point, but it does not look a dead enough blue for that. Tahoe is one thousand five hundred and twenty-five feet deep in the center, by the State Geologist's measurement. They say the great peak opposite this town is five thousand feet high; but I feel sure that three thousand feet of that statement is a good, honest lie. The lake is a mile wide here, and maintains about that width from this point to its northern extremity—which is distant sixteen miles; from here to its southern extremity—say fifteen miles—it is not over half a mile wide in any place, I should think. Its snow-clad mountains one hears so much about are only seen occasionally, and then in the distance, the Alps. Tahoe is from ten to eighteen miles wide, and its mountains shut it in like a wall. Their summits are never free from snow the year round. One thing about it is very strange: it never has even a skim of ice upon its surface, although lakes in the same range of mountains, lying in a lower and warmer temperature, freeze over in winter.

It is cheerful to meet a shipmate in these out-of-the-way places and compare notes with him. We have found one of ours here—an old soldier of the war, who is seeking bloodless adventures and rest from his campaigns, in these sunny lands.*

---

*Col. J. HERON FOSTER, editor of a Pittsburgh journal, and a most estimable gentleman. As these sheets are being prepared for the press, I am pained to learn of his decease shortly after his return home.—M.T.

CHAPTER XXI

We voyaged by steamer down the Lago di Lecco, through wild mountain scenery, and by hamlets and villas, and disembarked at the town of Lecco. They said it was two hours, by carriage, to the ancient city of Bergamo, and that we would arrive there in good season for the railway train. We got an open barouche and a wild, boisterous driver, and set out. It was delightful. We had a fast team and a perfectly smooth road. There were towering cliffs on our left, and the pretty Lago di Lecco on our right, and every now and then it rained on us. Just before starting, the driver picked up, in the street, a stump of a cigar an inch long, and put it in his mouth. When he had carried it thus about an hour, I thought it would be only Christian charity to give him a light. I handed him my cigar, which I had just lit, and he put it in his mouth and returned his stump to his pocket! I never saw a more sociable man. At least I never saw a man who was more sociable on a short acquaintance.

We saw interior Italy now. The houses were of solid stone, and not often in good repair. The peasants and their children were idle, as a general thing, and the donkeys and chickens made themselves at home in drawing-room and bed-chamber and were not molested. The drivers of each and every one of the slow-moving market-carts we met were stretched in the sun upon their merchandise, sound asleep. Every three or four hundred yards, it seemed to me, we came upon the shrine of some saint or other—a rude picture of him built into a huge cross or a stone pillar by the roadside. Some of the pictures of the Saviour were curiosities in their way. They represented him stretched upon the cross, his countenance distorted with agony. From the wounds of the crown of thorns; from the pierced side; from the mutilated hands and feet; from the scourged body—from every hand-breadth of his person, streams of blood were flowing! Such a gory, ghastly spectacle would frighten the children out of their senses, I should think. There were some unique auxiliaries to the painting which added to its spirited effect. These were genuine wooden and iron implements, and were prominently disposed round about the figure: a bundle of nails; the hammer to drive them; the sponge; the reed that supported it; the cup of vinegar; the ladder for the ascent of the cross; the spear that pierced the Saviour's side. The crown of thorns was made of real thorns, and was nailed to the sacred head. In some Italian church paintings, even by the old masters, the Saviour and the Virgin wear silver or gilded crowns that are fastened to the pictured head with nails. The effect is as grotesque as it is incongruous.

Here and there, on the fronts of roadside inns, we found huge, coarse frescoes of suffering martyrs like those in the shrines. It could not have diminished their sufferings any to be so uncouthly represented. We were in the heart and home of priest-craft—of a happy, cheerful, contented ignorance, superstition, degradation, poverty, indolence, and everlasting unaspiring worthlessness. And we said fervently, It suits these people precisely; let them enjoy it, along with the other animals, and Heaven forbid that they be molested. *We* feel no malice toward these fumigators.

We passed through the strangest, funniest, un-dreamt-of old towns, wedded to the customs and steeped in the dreams of the elder ages, and perfectly unaware that the world turns round! And perfectly indifferent, too, as to whether it turns around or stands still. *They* have nothing to do but eat and sleep and sleep and eat, and toil a little when they can get a friend to stand by and keep them awake. *They* are not paid for thinking—*they* are not paid to fret about the world's concerns. They were not respectable people—they were not worthy people—they were not learned and wise and brilliant people—but in their breasts, all their stupid lives long, resteth a peace that passeth understanding! How can men, calling themselves men, consent to be so degraded and happy.

We whisked by many a gray old medieval castle, clad thick with ivy that swung its green banners down from towers and turrets where once some old Crusader's flag had floated. The driver pointed to one of these ancient fortresses, and said (I translate):

"Do you see that great iron hook that projects from the wall just under the highest window in the ruined tower?"

We said we could not see it at such a distance, but had no doubt it was there.

"Well," he said, "there is a legend connected with that iron hook. Nearly seven hundred years ago, that castle was the property of the noble Count Luigi Gennaro Guido Alphonso di Genova——"

"What was his other name?" said Dan.

"He had no other name. The name I have spoken was all the name he had. He was the son of——"

"Poor but honest parents—that is all right—never mind the particulars—go on with the legend."

THE LEGEND.

Well, then, all the world, at that time, was in a wild excitement about the Holy Sepulchre. All the great feudal lords in Europe were pledging their lands and pawning their plate to fit out men-at-arms so that they might join the grand armies of Christendom and win renown in the Holy Wars. The Count Luigi raised money, like the rest, and one mild September morning, armed with battle-axe, portcullis and thundering culverin, he rode through the greaves and bucklers of his donjon-keep with as gallant a troop of Christian bandits as ever stepped in Italy. He had his sword, Excalibur, with him. His beautiful countess and her young daughter waved him a tearful adieu from the battering-rams and buttresses of the fortress, and he galloped away with a happy heart.

He made a raid on a neighboring baron and completed his outfit with the booty secured. He then razed the castle to the ground, massacred the family, and moved on. They were hardy fellows in the grand old days of chivalry. Alas! those days will never come again.

Count Luigi grew high in fame in Holy Land. He plunged into the carnage of a hundred battles, but his good Excalibur always brought him out alive, albeit often sorely wounded. His face became browned by exposure to the Syrian sun in long marches; he suffered hunger and thirst; he pined in prisons, he languished in loathsome plague-hospitals. And many and many a time he thought of his loved ones at home, and wondered if all was well with them. But his heart said, Peace, is not thy brother watching over thy household?

.   .   .   .   .   .

Forty-two years waxed and waned; the good fight was won; Godfrey reigned in Jerusalem—the Christian hosts reared the banner of the cross above the Holy Sepulchre!

Twilight was approaching. Fifty harlequins, in flowing robes, approached this castle wearily, for they were on foot, and the dust upon their garments betokened that they had traveled far. They overtook a peasant, and asked him if it were likely they could get food and a hospitable bed there, for love of Christian charity, and if, perchance, a moral parlor entertainment might meet with generous countenance—"for," said they, "this exhibition hath no feature that could offend the most fastidious taste."

"Marry," quoth the peasant, "an' it please your worships, ye had better journey many a good rood hence with your juggling circus than trust your bones in yonder castle."

"How now, sirrah!" exclaimed the chief monk, "explain thy ribald speech, or by'r Lady it shall go hard with thee."

"Peace, good mountebank, I did but utter the truth that was in my heart. San Paolo be my witness that did ye but find the stout Count Leonardo in his cups, sheer from the castle's top-most battlements would he hurl ye all! Alack-a-day! the good Lord Luigi reigns not here in these sad times."

"The good Lord Luigi?"

"Aye, none other, please your worship. In his day, the poor rejoiced in plenty and the rich he did oppress; taxes were not known, the fathers of the church waxed fat upon his bounty; travelers went and came, with none to interfere; and whosoever would, might tarry in his halls in cordial welcome, and eat his bread and drink his wine, withal. But woe is me! some two and forty years agone the good count rode hence to fight for Holy Cross, and many a year hath flown since word or token have we had of him. Men say his bones lie bleaching in the fields of Palestine."

"And now?"

"*Now!* God 'a mercy, the cruel Leonardo lords it in the castle. He wrings taxes from the poor; he robs all travelers that journey by his gates; he spends his days in feuds and murders, and his nights in revel and debauch; he roasts the fathers of the church upon his kitchen spits, and enjoyeth the same, calling it pastime. These thirty years Luigi's countess hath not been seen by any he in all this land, and many whisper that she pines in the dungeons of the castle for that she will not wed with Leonardo, saying her dear lord still liveth and that she will die ere she prove false to him. They whisper likewise that her daughter is a prisoner as well. Nay, good jugglers, seek ye refreshment otherwheres. 'Twere better that ye perished in a Christian way than that ye plunged from off yon dizzy tower. Give ye good-day."

"God keep ye, gentle knave—farewell."

But heedless of the peasant's warning, the players moved straightway toward the castle.

Word was brought to Count Leonardo that a company of mountebanks besought his hospitality.

" 'Tis well. Dispose of them in the customary manner. Yet stay! I have need of them. Let them come hither. Later, cast them from the battlements—or—how many priests have ye on hand?"

"The day's results are meager, good my lord. An abbot and a dozen beggarly friars is all we have."

"Hell and furies! Is the estate going to seed? Send hither the mountebanks. Afterward, broil them with the priests."

The robed and close-cowled harlequins entered. The grim Leonardo sat in state at the head of his council board. Ranged up and down the hall on either hand stood near a hundred men-at-arms.

"Ha, villains!" quoth the count, "What can ye do to earn the hospitality ye crave?"

"Dread lord and mighty, crowded audiences have greeted our humble efforts with rapturous applause. Among our body count we the versatile and talented Ugolino; the justly celebated Rodolpho; the gifted and accomplished Roderigo; the management have spared neither pains nor expense——"

"S'death! what can ye *do?* Curb thy prating tongue."

"Good my lord, in acrobatic feats, in practice with the dumbbells, in balancing and ground and lofty tumbling are we versed—and sith your highness asketh me, I venture here to publish that in the truly marvelous and entertaining Zampillaerostation——"

"Gag him! throttle him! Body of Bacchus! am I a dog that I am to be assailed with polysyllabled blasphemy like to this? But hold! Lucretia, Isabel, stand forth! Sirrah, behold this dame, this weeping wench. The first I marry, within the hour; the other shall dry her tears or feed the vultures. Thou and thy vagabonds shall crown the wedding with thy merry-makings. Fetch hither the priest!"

The dame sprang toward the chief player.

"Oh, save me!" she cried; "save me from a fate far worse than death! Behold these sad eyes, these sunken cheeks, this withered frame! See thou the wreck this fiend hath made, and let thy heart be moved with pity! Look upon this damosel; note her wasted form, her halting step, her bloomless cheeks where youth should blush and happiness exult in smiles! Hear us, and have compassion. This monster was my husband's brother. He who should have been our shield against all harm, hath kept us shut within the noisome caverns of his donjon-keep for, lo, these thirty years. And for what crime? None other than that I would not belie my troth, root out my strong love for him who marches with the legions of the cross in Holy Land (for oh, he is not dead), and wed with him! Save us, oh, save thy persecuted suppliants!"

She flung herself at his feet and clasped his knees.

"Ha!-ha!-ha!" shouted the brutal Leonardo. "Priest, to thy work!" and he dragged the weeping dame from her refuge. "Say, once for all, *will* you be mine?—for by my halidome, that breath that uttereth thy refusal shall be thy last on earth!"

"NE-VER!" and the sword leaped from its scabbard.

Quicker than thought, quicker than the lightning's flash, fifty monkish habits disappeared, and fifty knights in splendid armor stood revealed! fifty falchions gleamed in air above the men-at-arms, and brighter, fiercer than them all, flamed Excalibur aloft, and cleaving downward struck the brutal Leonardo's weapon from his grasp!

"A Luigi to the rescue! Whoop!"

"A Leonardo! tare an ouns!"

"Oh, God, oh, God, my husband!"

"Oh, God, oh, God, my wife!"

"My father!"

"My precious!" [Tableau.]

Count Luigi bound his usurping brother hand and foot. The practiced knights from Palestine made holiday sport of carving the awkward men-at-arms into chops and steaks. The victory was complete. Happiness reigned. The knights all married the daughter. Joy! wassail! finis!

"But what did they do with the wicked brother?"

"Oh, nothing—only hanged him on that iron hook I was speaking of. By the chin."

"As how?"

"Passed it up through his gills into his mouth."

"Leave him there?"

"Couple of years."

"Ah—is—is he dead?"

"Six hundred and fifty years ago, or such a matter."

"Splendid legend—splendid lie—drive on."

We reached the quaint old fortified ciy of Bergamo, the renowed in history, some three-quarters of an hour before the train was ready to start. The place has thirty or forty thousand inhabitants and is remarkable for being the birthplace of harlequin. When we discovered that, that legend of our driver took to itself a new interest in our eyes.

Rested and refreshed, we took the rail happy and contented. I shall not tarry to speak of the handsome Lago di Garda; its stately castle that holds in its stony bosom the secrets of an age so remote that even tradition goeth not back to it; the imposing mountain scenery that ennobles the landscape thereabouts; nor yet of ancient Padua or haughty Verona; nor of their Montagues and Capulets, their famous balconies and tombs of Juliet and Romeo *et al.*, but hurry straight to the ancient city of the sea, the widowed bride of the Adriatic. It was a long, long ride. But toward evening, as we sat silent and hardly conscious of where we were—subdued into that meditative calm that comes so surely after a conversational storm—some one shouted:

"VENICE!"

And sure enough, afloat on the placid sea a league away, lay a great city, with its towers and domes and steeples drowsing in a golden mist of sunset.

CHAPTER XXII

This Venice, which was a haughty, invincible, magnificent Republic for nearly fourteen hundred years; whose armies compelled the world's applause whenever and wherever they battled; whose navies well nigh held dominion of the seas, and whose merchant fleets whitened the remotest oceans with their sails and loaded these piers with the products of every clime, is fallen a prey to poverty, neglect and melancholy decay. Six hundred years ago, Venice was the Autocrat of Commerce; her mart was the great commercial center, the distributing house from whence the enormous trade of the Orient was spread abroad over the Western world. To-day her piers are deserted, her warehouses are empty, her merchant fleets are vanished, her armies and her navies are but memories. Her glory is departed, and with her crumbling grandeur of wharves and palaces about her she sits among her stagnant lagoons, forlorn and beggared, forgotten of the world. She, that in her palmy days commanded the commerce of a hemisphere and made the weal or woe of nations with a beck of her puissant finger, is become the humblest among the peoples of the earth,—a peddler of glass beads for women, and trifling toys and trinkets for school-girls and children.

The venerable Mother of the Republics is scarce a fit subject for flippant speech or the idle gossiping of tourists. It seems a sort of sacrilege to disturb the glamour of old romance that pictures her to us softly from afar off as through a tinted mist, and curtains her ruin and her desolation from our view. One ought, indeed, to turn away from her rags, her poverty, and her humiliation, and think of her only as she was when she sunk the fleets of Charlemagne; when she humbled Frederick Barbarossa or waved her victorious banners above the battlements of Constantinople.

We reached Venice at eight in the evening, and entered a hearse belonging to the Grand Hotel d'Europe. At any rate, it was more like a hearse than anything else, though, to speak by the card, it was a gondola. And this was the storied gondola of Venice!—the fairy boat in which the princely cavaliers of the olden time were wont to cleave the waters of the moonlit canals and look the eloquence of love into the soft eyes of patrician beauties, while the gay gondolier in silken doublet touched his guitar and sang as only gondoliers can sing! This the famed gondola and this the gorgeous gondolier!—the one an inky, rusty old canoe with a sable hearse-body clapped on to the middle of it, and the other a mangy, barefooted gutter-snipe with a portion of his raiment on exhibition which should have been sacred from public scrutiny. Presently, as he turned a corner and shot his hearse into a dismal ditch between two long rows of towering, untenanted buildings, the gay gondolier began to sing, true to the traditions of his race. I stood it a little while. Then I said:

"Now, here, Roderigo Gonzales Michael Angelo, I'm a pilgrim, and I'm a stranger, but I am not going to have my feelings lacerated by any such caterwauling as that. If that goes on, one of us has got to take water. It is enough that my cherished dreams of Venice have been blighted forever as to the romantic gondola and the gorgeous gondolier; this system of destruction shall go no farther; I will accept the hearse, under protest, and you may fly your flag of truce in peace, but here I register a dark and bloody oath that you shan't sing. Another yelp, and overboard you go."

I began to feel that the old Venice of song and story had departed forever. But I was too hasty. In a few minutes we swept gracefully out into the Grand Canal, and under the mellow moonlight the Venice of poetry and romance stood revealed. Right from the water's edge rose long lines of stately palaces of marble; gondolas were gliding swiftly hither and thither and disappearing suddenly through unsuspected gates and alleys; ponderous stone bridges threw their shadows athwart the glittering waves. There was life and motion everywhere, and yet everywhere there was a hush, a stealthy sort of stillness, that was suggestive of secret enterprises of bravoes and of lovers; and, clad half in moonbeams and half in mysterious shadows, the grim old mansions of the Republic seemed to have an expression about them of having an eye out for just such enterprises as these at that same moment. Music came floating over the waters—Venice was complete.

It was a beautiful picture—very soft and dreamy and beautiful. But what was this Venice to compare with the Venice of midnight?

Nothing. There was a fête—a grand fête in honor of some saint who had been instrumental in checking the cholera three hundred years ago, and all Venice was abroad on the water. It was no common affair, for the Venetians did not know how soon they might need the saint's services again, now that the cholera was spreading everywhere. So in one vast space—say a third of a mile wide and two miles long—were collected two thousand gondolas, and every one of them had from two to ten, twenty, and even thirty colored lanterns suspended about it, and from four to a dozen occupants. Just as far as the eye could reach, these painted lights were massed together—like a vast garden of many-colored flowers, except that these blossoms were never still; they were ceaselessly gliding in and out, and mingling together, and seducing you into bewildering attempts to follow their mazy evolutions. Here and there a strong red, green, or blue glare from a rocket that was struggling to get away splendidly illuminated all the boats around it. Every gondola that swam by us, with its crescents and pyramids and circles of colored lamps hung aloft, and lighting up the faces of the young and the sweet-scented and lovely below, was a picture; and the reflections of those lights, so long, so slender, so numberless, so many-colored and so distorted and wrinkled by the waves, was a picture likewise, and one that was enchantingly beautiful. Many and many a party of young ladies and gentlemen had their state gondolas handsomely decorated, and ate supper on board, bringing their swallow-tailed, white-cravated varlets to wait upon them, and having their tables tricked out as if for a bridal supper. They had brought along the costly globe lamps from their drawing-rooms, and the lace and silken curtains from the same places, I suppose. And they had also brought pianos and guitars, and they played and sang operas, while the plebeian paper-lanterned gondolas from the suburbs and the back alleys crowded around to stare and listen.

There was music everywhere—choruses, string bands, brass bands, flutes, everything. I was so surrounded, walled in with music, magnificence, and loveliness, that I became inspired with the spirit of the scene, and sang one tune myself. However, when I observed that the other gondolas had sailed away, and my gondolier was preparing to go overboard, I stopped.

The fete was magnificent. They kept it up the whole night long, and I never enjoyed myself better than I did while it lasted.

What a funny old city this Queen of the Adriatic is! Narrow streets, vast, gloomy marble palaces, black with the corroding damps of centuries, and all partly submerged; no dry land visible anywhere, and no sidewalks worth mentioning; if you want to go to church, to the theater, or to the restaurant, you must call a gondola. It must be a paradise for cripples, for verily a man has no use for legs here.

For a day or two the place looked so like an overflowed Arkansas town, because of its currentless waters laving the very doorsteps of all the houses, and the cluster of boats made fast under the windows, or skimming in and out of the alleys and by-ways, that I could not get rid of the impression that there was nothing the matter here but a spring freshet, and that the river would fall in a few weeks and leave a dirty high-water mark on the houses, and the streets full of mud and rubbish.

In the glare of day, there is little poetry about Venice, but under the charitable moon her stained palaces are white again, their battered sculptures are hidden in shadows, and the old city seems crowned once more with the grandeur that was hers five hundred years ago. It is easy, then, in fancy, to people these silent canals with plumed gallants and fair ladies—with Shylocks in gaberdine and sandals, venturing loans upon the rich argosies of Venetian commerce—with Othellos and Desdemonas, with Iagos and Roderigos—with noble fleets and victorious legions returning from the wars. In the treacherous sunlight we see Venice decayed, forlorn, poverty-stricken, and commerceless—forgotten and utterly insignificant. But in the moonlight, her fourteen centuries of greatness fling their glories about her, and once more is she the princeliest among the nations of the earth.

> "There is a glorious city in the sea;
> The sea is in the broad, the narrow streets,
> Ebbing and flowing; and the salt sea-weed
> Clings to the marble of her palaces.
> No track of men, no footsteps to and fro,
> Lead to her gates! The path lies o'er the sea,
> Invisible: and from the land we went,
> As to a floating city—steering in,
> And gliding up her streets, as in a dream,
> So smoothly, silently—by many a dome,
> Mosque-like, and many a stately portico,
> The statues ranged along an azure sky;
> By many a pile, in more than Eastern pride,
> Of old the residence of merchant kings;
> The fronts of some, tho' time had shatter'd them,
> Still glowing with the richest hues of art,
> As tho' the wealth within them had run o'er."

What would one naturally wish to see first in Venice? The Bridge of Sighs, of course—and next the Church and the Great Square of St. Mark, the Bronze Horses, and the famous Lion of St. Mark.

We intended to go to the Bridge of Sighs, but happened into the Ducal Palace first—a building which necessarily figures largely in Venetian poetry and tradition. In the Senate Chamber of the ancient Republic we wearied our eyes with staring at acres of historical paintings by Tintoretto and Paul Veronese, but nothing struck us forcibly except the one thing that strikes *all* strangers forcibly—a black square in the midst of a gallery of portraits. In one long row, around the great hall, were painted the portraits of the doges of Venice (venerable fellows, with flowing white beards, for of the three hundred Senators eligible to the office, the oldest was usually chosen doge), and each had its complimentary inscription attached—till you came to the place that should have had Marino Faliero's picture in it, and that was blank and black—blank, except that it bore a terse inscription, saying that the conspirator had died for his crime. It seemed cruel to keep that pitiless inscription still staring from the walls after the unhappy wretch had been in his grave five hundred years.

At the head of the Giant's Staircase, where Marino Faliero was beheaded, and where the doges were crowned in ancient times, two small slits in the stone wall were pointed out—two harmless, insignificant orifices that would never attract a stranger's attention—yet these were the terrible Lions' Mouths! The heads were gone (knocked off by the French during their occupation of Venice), but these were the throats, down which went the anonymous accusation, thrust in secretly at dead of night by an enemy, that doomed many an innocent man to walk the Bridge of Sighs and descend into the dungeon which none entered and hoped to see the sun again. This was in the old days when the Patricians alone governed Venice—the common herd had no vote and no voice. There were one thousand five hundred Patricians; from these, three hundred Senators were chosen; from the Senators a Doge and a Council of Ten were selected, and by secret ballot the Ten chose from their own number a Council of Three. All these were government spies, then, and every spy was under surveillance himself—men spoke in whispers in Venice, and no man trusted his neighbor—not always his own brother. No man knew who the Council of Three were—not even the Senate, not even the Doge; the members of that dread tribunal met at night in a chamber to themselves, masked, and robed from head to foot in scarlet cloaks, and did not even know each other, unless by voice. It was their duty to judge heinous political crimes, and from their sentence there was no appeal. A nod to the executioner was sufficient. The doomed man was marched down a hall and out at a doorway into the covered Bridge of Sighs, through it and into the dungeon and unto his death. At no time in his transit was he visible to any save his conductor. If a man had an enemy in those old days, the cleverest thing he could do was to slip a note for the Council of Three into the Lion's mouth, saying "This man is plotting against the government." If the awful Three found no proof, ten to one they would drown him anyhow, because he was a deep rascal, since his plots were unsolvable. Masked judges and masked executioners, with unlimited power, and no appeal from their judgments, in that hard, cruel age, were not likely to be lenient with men they suspected yet could not convict.

We walked through the hall of the Council of Ten, and presently entered the infernal den of the Council of Three.

The table around which they had sat was there still, and likewise the stations where the masked inquisitors and executioners formerly stood, frozen, upright and silent, till they received a bloody order, and then, without a word, moved off, like the inexorable machines they were, to carry it out. The frescoes on the walls were startlingly suited to the place. In all the other saloons, the halls, the great state chambers of the palace, the walls and ceilings were bright with gilding, rich with elaborate carving, and resplendent with gallant pictures of Venetian victories in war, and Venetian display in foreign courts, and hallowed with portraits of the Virgin, the Saviour of men, and the holy saints that preached the Gospel of Peace upon earth—but here, in dismal contrast, were none but pictures of death and dreadful suffering!—not a living figure but was writhing in torture, not a dead one but was smeared with blood, gashed with wounds, and distorted with the agonies that had taken away its life!

From the palace to the gloomy prison is but a step—one might almost jump across the narrow canal that intervenes. The ponderous stone Bridge of Sighs crosses it at the second story—a bridge that is a covered tunnel—you cannot be seen when you walk in it. It is partitioned lengthwise, and through one compartment walked such as bore light sentences in ancient times, and through the other marched sadly the wretches whom the Three had doomed to lingering misery and utter oblivion in the dungeons, or to sudden and mysterious death. Down below the level of the water, by the light of smoking torches, we were shown the damp, thick-walled cells where many a proud patrician's life was eaten away by the long-drawn miseries of solitary imprisonment—without light, air, books; naked, unshaven, uncombed, covered with vermin; his useless tongue forgetting its office, with none to speak to; the days and nights of his life no longer marked, but merged into one eternal eventless night; far away from all cheerful sounds, buried in the silence of a tomb; forgotten by his helpless friends, and his fate a dark mystery to them forever; losing his own memory at last, and knowing no more who he was or how he came there; devouring the loaf of bread and drinking the water that were thrust into the cell by unseen hands, and troubling his worn spirit no more with hopes and fears and doubts and longings to be free; ceasing to scratch vain prayers and complainings on walls where none, not even himself, could see them, and resigning himself to hopeless apathy, driveling childishness, lunacy! Many and many a sorrowful story like this these stony walls could tell if they could but speak.

In a little narrow corridor, near by, they showed us where many a prisoner, after lying in the dungeons until he was forgotten by all save his persecutors, was brought by masked executioners and garroted, or sewed up in a sack, passed through a little window to a boat, at dead of night, and taken to some remote spot and drowned.

They used to show to visitors the implements of torture wherewith the Three were wont to worm secrets out of the accused—villainous machines for crushing thumbs; the stocks where a prisoner sat immovable while water fell drop by drop upon his head till the torture was more than humanity could bear; and a devilish contrivance of steel, which inclosed a prisoner's head like a shell, and crushed it slowly by means of a screw. It bore the stains of blood that had trickled through its joints long ago, and on one side it had a projection whereon the torturer rested his elbow comfortably and bent down his ear to catch the moanings of the sufferer perishing within.

Of course, we went to see the venerable relic of the ancient glory of Venice, with its pavements worn and broken by the passing feet of a thousand years of plebeians and patricians—The Cathedral of St. Mark. It is built entirely of precious marbles, brought from the Orient—nothing in its composition is domestic. Its hoary traditions make it an object of absorbing interest to even the most careless stranger, and thus far it had interest for me; but no further. I could not go into ecstasies over its coarse mosaics, its unlovely Byzantine architecture, or its five hundred curious interior columns from as many distant quarries. Everything was worn out—every block of stone was smooth and almost shapeless with the polishing hands and shoulders of loungers who devoutly idled here in bygone centuries and have died and gone to the dev—no, simply died, I mean.

Under the altar repose the ashes of St. Mark—and Matthew, Luke, and John, too, for all I know. Venice reveres those relics above all things earthly. For fourteen hundred years St. Mark has been her patron saint. Everything about the city seems to be named after him or so named as to refer to him in some way—so named, or some purchase rigged in some way to scrape a sort of hurrahing acquaintance with him. That seems to be the idea. To be on good terms with St. Mark seems to be the very summit of Venetian ambition. They say St. Mark had a tame lion, and used to travel with him—and everywhere that St. Mark went, the lion was sure to go. It was his protector, his friend, his librarian. And so the Winged Lion of St. Mark, with the open Bible under his paw, is a favorite emblem in the grand old city. It casts its shadow from the most ancient pillar in Venice, in the Grand Square of St. Mark, upon the throngs of free citizens below, and has so done for many a long century. The winged lion is found everywhere—and doubtless here, where the winged lion is, no harm can come.

St. Mark died at Alexandria, in Egypt. He was martyred, I think. However, that has nothing to do with my legend. About the founding of the city of Venice—say four hundred and fifty years after Christ (for Venice is much younger than any other Italian city)—a priest dreamed that an angel told him that until the remains of St. Mark were brought to Venice, the city could never rise to high distinction among the nations; that the body must be captured, brought to the city, and a magnificent church built over it; and that if ever the Venetians allowed the Saint to be removed from his new resting place, in that day Venice would perish from off the face of the earth. The priest proclaimed his dream, and forthwith Venice set about procuring the corpse of St. Mark. One expedition after another tried and failed, but the project was never abondoned during four hundred years. At last it was secured by stratagem, in the year eight hundred and something. The commander of a Venetian expedition disguised himself, stole the bones, separated them, and packed them in vessels filled with lard. The religion of Mahomet causes its devotees to abhor anything that is in the nature of pork, and so when the Christian was stopped by the officers at the gates of the city, they only glanced once into his precious baskets, then turned up their noses at the unholy lard, and let him go. The bones were buried in the vaults of the grand cathedral, which had been waiting long years to receive them, and thus the safety and the greatness of Venice were secured. And to this day there be those in Venice who believe that if those holy ashes were stolen away, the ancient city would vanish like a dream, and its foundations be buried forever in the unremembering sea.

CHAPTER XXIII

The Venetian gondola is as free and graceful, in its gliding movement, as a serpent. It is twenty or thirty feet long, and is narrow and deep, like a canoe; its sharp bow and stern sweep upward from the water like the horns of a crescent with the abruptness of the curve slightly modified.

The bow is ornamented with a steel comb with a battle-axe attachment which threatens to cut passing boats in two occasionally, but never does. The gondola is painted black because in the zenith of Venetian magnificence the gondolas became too gorgeous altogether, and the Senate decreed that all such display must cease, and a solemn, unembellished black be substituted. If the truth were known, it would doubtless appear that rich plebeians grew too prominent in their affectation of patrician show on the Grand Canal, and required a wholesome snubbing. Reverence for the hallowed Past and its traditions keeps the dismal fashion in force now that the compulsion exists no longer. So let it remain. It is the color of mourning. Venice mourns. The stern of the boat is decked over and the gondolier stands there. He uses a single oar—a long blade, of course, for he stands nearly erect. A wooden peg, a foot and a half high, with two slight crooks or curves in one side of it and one in the other, projects above the starboard gunwale. Against that peg the gondolier takes a purchase with his oar, changing it at intervals to the other side of the peg or dropping it into another of the crooks, as the steering of the craft may demand—and how in the world he can back and fill, shoot straight ahead, or flirt suddenly around a corner, and make the oar stay in those insignificant notches, is a problem to me and a never-diminishing matter of interest. I am afraid I study the gondolier's marvelous skill more than I do the sculptured palaces we glide among. He cuts a corner so closely, now and then, or misses another gondola by such an imperceptible hair-breadth, that I feel myself "scrooching," as the children say, just as one does when a buggy wheel grazes his elbow. But he makes all his calculations with the nicest precision, and goes darting in and out among a Broadway confusion of busy craft with the easy confidence of the educated hackman. He never makes a mistake.

Sometimes we go flying down the great canals at such a gait that we can get only the merest glimpses into front doors, and again, in obscure alleys in the suburbs, we put on a solemnity suited to the silence, the mildew, the stagnant waters, the clinging weeds, the deserted houses, and the general lifelessness of the place, and move to the spirit of grave meditation.

The gondolier *is* a picturesque rascal for all he wears no satin harness, no plumed bonnet, no silken tights. His attitude is stately; he is lithe and supple; all his movements are full of grace. When his long canoe, and his fine figure, towering from its high perch on the stern, are cut against the evening sky, they make a picture that is very novel and striking to a foreign eye.

We sit in the cushioned carriage-body of a cabin, with the curtains drawn, and smoke, or read, or look out upon the passing boats, the houses, the bridges, the people, and enjoy ourselves much more than we could in a buggy jolting over our cobblestone pavements at home. This is the gentlest, pleasantest locomotion we have ever known.

But it seems queer—ever so queer—to see a boat doing duty as a private carriage. We see business men come to the front door, step into a gondola, instead of a street car, and go off down town to the counting-room.

We see visiting young ladies stand on the stoop, and laugh, and kiss good-bye, and flirt their fans and say "Come soon—now *do*— you've been just as mean as ever you can be—mother's dying to see you—and we've moved into the new house, oh, such a love of a place!—so convenient to the post-office and the church, and the Young Men's Christian Association; and we do have such fishing, and such carrying on, and *such* swimming-matches in the back yard—Oh, you *must* come—no distance at all, and if you go down through by St. Mark's and the Bridge of Sighs, and cut through the alley and come up by the church of Santa Maria dei Frari, and into the Grand Canal, there isn't a *bit* of current—now *do* come, Sally Maria—by-bye!" and then the little humbug trips down the steps, jumps into the gondola, says, under her breath, "Disagreeable old thing, I hope she *won't!*" goes skimming away, round the corner; and the other girl slams the street door and says, "Well, *that* infliction's over, anyway,—but I suppose I've got to go and see her—tiresome, stuck-up thing!" Human nature appears to be just the same, all over the world. We see the diffident young man, mild of moustache, affluent of hair, indigent of brain, elegant of costume, drive up to *her* father's mansion, tell his hackman to bail out and wait, start fearfully up the steps and meet "the old gentleman" right on the threshold!—hear him ask what street the new British Bank is in—as if *that* were what he came for—and then bounce into his boat and skurry away with his coward heart in his boots!—see him come sneaking around the corner again, directly, with a crack of the curtain open toward the old gentleman's disappearing gondola, and out scampers his Susan with a flock of little Italian endearments fluttering from her lips, and goes to drive with him in the watery avenues down toward the Rialto.

We see the ladies go out shopping, in the most natural way, and flit from street to street and from store to store, just in the good old fashion, except that they leave the gondola, instead of a private carriage, waiting at the curbstone a couple of hours for them,—waiting while they make the nice young clerks pull down tons and tons of silks and velvets and moire antiques and those things; and then they buy a paper of pins and go paddling away to confer the rest of their disastrous patronage on some other firm. And they always have their purchases sent home just in the good old way. Human nature is *very* much the same all over the world; and it is *so* like my dear native home to see a Venetian lady go into a store and buy ten cents' worth of blue ribbon and have it sent home in a scow. Ah, it is these little touches of nature that move one to tears in these far-off foreign lands.

We see little girls and boys go out in gondolas with their nurses, for an airing. We see staid families, with prayer book and beads, enter the gondola dressed in their Sunday best, and float away to church. And at midnight we see the theater break up and discharge its swarm of hilarious youth and beauty; we hear the cries of the hackman-gondoliers, and behold the struggling crowd jump aboard, and the black multitude of boats go skimming down the moonlit avenues; we see them separate here and there, and disappear up divergent streets; we hear the faint sounds of laughter and of shouted farewells floating up out of the distance; and then, the strange pageant being gone, we have lonely stretches of glittering water—of stately buildings—of blotting shadows—of weird stone faces creeping into the moonlight—of deserted bridges—of motionless boats at anchor. And over all broods that mysterious stillness, that stealthy quiet, that befits so well this old dreaming Venice.

We have been pretty much everywhere in our gondola. We have bought beads and photographs in the stores, and wax matches in the Great Square of St. Mark. The last remark suggests a digression. Everybody goes to this vast square in the evening. The military bands play in the center of it and countless couples of ladies and gentlemen promenade up and down on either side, and platoons of them are constantly drifting away toward the old cathedral, and by the venerable column with the Winged Lion of St. Mark on its top, and out to where the boats lie moored; and other platoons are as constantly arriving from the gondolas and joining the great throng. Between the promenaders and the sidewalks are seated hundreds and hundreds of people at small tables, smoking and taking *granita* (a first cousin to ice-cream); on the sidewalks are more employing themselves in the same way. The shops in the first floor of the tall rows of buildings that wall in three sides of the square are brilliantly lighted, the air is filled with music and merry voices, and altogether the scene is as bright and spirited and full of cheerfulness as any man could desire. We enjoy it thoroughly. Very many of the young women are exceedingly pretty and dress with rare good taste. We are gradually and laboriously learning the ill-manners of staring them unflinchingly in the face—not because such conduct is agreeable to us, but because it is the custom of the country and they say the girls like it. We wish to learn all the curious, outlandish ways of all the different countries, so that we can "show off" and astonish people when we get home. We wish to excite the envy of our untraveled friends with our strange foreign fashions which we can't shake off. All our passengers are paying strict attention to this thing, with the end in view which I have mentioned. The gentle reader will never, never know what a consummate ass he can become until he goes abroad. I speak now, of course, in the supposition that the gentle reader has not been abroad, and therefore is not already a consummate ass. If the case be otherwise, I beg his pardon and extend to him the cordial hand of fellowship and call him brother. I shall always delight to meet an ass after my own heart when I shall have finished my travels.

On this subject let me remark that there are Americans abroad in Italy who have actually forgotten their mother tongue in three months—forgot it in France. They cannot even write their address in English in a hotel register. I append these evidences, which I copied *verbatim* from the register of a hotel in a certain Italian city:

"John P. Whitcomb, *États Unis.*
"William L. Ainsworth, *travailleur* (he meant traveler, I suppose), *États Unis.*
"George P. Morton *et fils, d'Amerique.*
"Lloyd B. Williams, *et trois amis, ville de* Boston, *Amerique.*
"J. Ellsworth Baker, *tout de suite de France, place de naissance Amerique, destination la Grande Bretagne.*"

I love this sort of people. A lady passenger of our tells of a fellow-citizen of hers who spent eight weeks in Paris and then returned home and addressed his dearest old bosom friend Herbert as Mr. "Er-bare!" He apologized, though, and said, " 'Pon my soul it is aggravating, but I cahn't help it—I have got so used to speaking no-thing but French, my dear Erbare—damme there it goes again!—got so used to French pronunciation that I cahn't get rid of it—it is positively annoying, I assure you." This entertaining idiot, whose name was Gordon, allowed himself to be hailed three times in the street before he paid any attention, and then begged a thousand par-dons and said he had grown so accustomed to hearing himself ad-dressed as M'sieu Gor-r-*dong*," with a roll to the r, that he had for-gotten the legitimate sound of his name! He wore a rose in his but-tonhole; he gave the French salutation—two flips of the hand in front of the face; he called Paris *Pairree* in ordinary English conver-sation; he carried envelopes bearing foreign postmarks protruding from his breast pocket; he cultivated a moustache and imperial, and did what else he could to suggest to the beholder his pet fancy that he resembled Louis Napoleon—and in a spirit of thankfulness which is entirely unaccountable, considering the slim foundation there was for it, he praised his Maker that he was *as* he was, and went on en-joying his little life just the same as if he really *had* been deliberate-ly designed and erected by the great Architect of the Universe.

Think of our Whitcombs and our Ainsworths and our Williamses writing themselves down in dilapidated French in a foreign hotel register! We laugh at Englishmen, when we are at home, for stick-ing so sturdily to their national ways and customs, but we look back upon it from abroad very forgivingly. It is not pleasant to see an American thrusting his nationality forward *obtrusively* in a foreign land, but oh, it is pitiable to see him making of himself a thing that is neither male nor female, neither fish, flesh, nor fowl—a poor, miserable, hermaphrodite Frenchman!

Among a long list of churches, art galleries, and such things, vis-ited by us in Venice, I shall mention only one—the Church of Santa Maria dei Frari. It is about five hundred years old, I believe, and stands on twelve hundred thousand piles. In it lie the body of Canova and the heart of Titian, under magnificent monuments. Titian died at the age of almost one hundred years. A plague which swept away fifty thousand lives was raging at the time, and there is notable evidence of the reverence in which the great painter was held, in the fact that to him alone the state permitted a public funer-al in all that season of terror and death.

In this church, also, is a monument to the doge Foscari, whose name a once resident of Venice, Lord Byron, has made permanently famous.

The monument to the doge Giovanni Pesaro, in this church, is a curiosity in the way of mortuary adornment. It is eighty feet high and is fronted like some fantastic pagan temple. Against it stand four colossal Nubians, as black as night, dressed in white marble garments. The black legs are bare, and through rents in sleeves and breeches, the skin, of shiny black marble, shows. The artist was as ingenious as his funeral designs were absurd. There are two bronze skeletons bearing scrolls, and two great dragons uphold the sarcophagus. On high, amid all this grotesqueness, sits the departed doge.

In the conventual buildings attached to this church are the state archives of Venice. We did not see them, but they are said to number millions of documents. "They are the records of centuries of the most watchful, observant, and suspicious government that ever existed—in which everything was written down and nothing spoken out." They fill nearly three hundred rooms. Among them are manuscripts from the archives of nearly two thousand families, monasteries, and convents. The secret history of Venice for a thousand years is here—its plots, its hidden trials, its assassinations, its commissions of hireling spies and masked bravoes—food, ready to hand, for a world of dark and mysterious romances.

Yes, I think we have seen all of Venice. We have seen, in these old churches, a profusion of costly and elaborate sepulchre ornamentation such as we never dreamt of before. We have stood in the dim religious light of these hoary sanctuaries, in the midst of long ranks of dusty monuments and effigies of the great dead of Venice, until we seemed drifting back, back, back, into the solemn past, and looking upon the scenes and mingling with the peoples of a remote antiquity. We have been in a half-waking sort of dream all the time. I do not know how else to describe the feeling. A part of our being has remained still in the nineteenth century, while another part of it has seemed in some unaccountable way walking among the phantoms of the tenth.

We have seen famous pictures until our eyes are weary with looking at them and refuse to find interest in them any longer. And what wonder, when there are twelve hundred pictures by Palma the Younger in Venice and fifteen hundred by Tintoretto? And behold, there are Titians and the works of other artists in proportion. We have seen Titian's celebrated Cain and Abel, his David and Goliah, his Abraham's Sacrifice. We have seen Tintoretto's monster picture, which is seventy-four feet long and I do not know how many feet high, and thought it a very commodious picture. We have seen pictures of martyrs enough, and saints enough, to regenerate the world. I ought not to confess it, but still, since one has no opportunity in America to acquire a critical judgment in art, and since I could not hope to become educated in it in Europe in a few short weeks, I may therefore as well acknowledge with such apologies as may be due, that to me it seemed that when I had seen one of these martyrs I had seen them all. They all have a marked family resemblance to each other, they dress alike, in coarse monkish robes and sandals, they are all bald-headed, they all stand in about the same attitude, and without exception they are gazing heavenward with countenances which the Ainsworths, the Mortons, and the Williamses, et fils, inform me are full of "expression." To me there is nothing tangible about these imaginary portraits, nothing that I can grasp and take a living interest in. If great Titian had only been gifted with prophecy, and had skipped a martyr, and gone over to England and painted a portrait of Shakespeare, even as a youth, which we could all have confidence in now, the world down to the latest generations would have forgiven him the lost martyr in the rescued seer. I think posterity could have spared one more martyr for the sake of a great historical picture of Titian's time and painted by his brush—such as Columbus returning in chains from the discovery of a world, for instance. The old masters did paint some Venetian historical pictures, and these we did not tire of looking at, notwithstanding representations of the formal introduction of defunct Doges to the Virgin Mary in regions beyond the clouds clashed rather harshly with the proprieties, it seemed to us.

But, humble as we are, and unpretending, in the matter of art, our researches among the painted monks and martyrs have not been wholly in vain. We have striven hard to learn. We have had some success. We have mastered some things, possibly of trifling import in the eyes of the learned, but to us they give pleasure, and we take as much pride in our little acquirements as do others who have learned far more, and we love to display them full as well. When we see a monk going about with a lion and looking tranquilly up to heaven, we know that that is St. Mark. When we see a monk with a book and a pen, looking tranquilly up to heaven, trying to think of a word, we know that that is St. Matthew. When we see a monk sitting on a rock, looking tranquilly up to heaven, with a human skull beside him, and without other baggage, we know that that is St. Jerome. Because we know that he always went flying light in the matter of baggage. When we see a party looking tranquilly up to heaven, unconscious that his body is shot through and through with arrows, we know that that is St. Sebastian. When we see other monks looking tranquilly up to heaven, but having no trademark, we always ask who those parties are. We do this because we humbly wish to learn. We have seen thirteen thousand St. Jeromes, and twenty-two thousand St. Marks, and sixteen thousand St. Matthews, and sixty thousand St. Sebastians, and four millions of assorted monks, undesignated, and we feel encouraged to believe that when we have seen some more of these various pictures, and had a larger experience, we shall begin to take an absorbing interest in them like our cultivated countrymen from *Amerique*.

Now it does give me real pain to speak in this almost unappreciative way of the old masters and their martyrs, because good friends of mine in the ship—friends who do thoroughly and conscientiously appreciate them and are in every way competent to discriminate between good pictures and inferior ones—have urged me for my own sake not to make public the fact that I lack this appreciation and this critical discrimination myself. I believe that what I have written and may still write about pictures will give them pain, and I am honestly sorry for it. I even promised that I would hide my uncouth sentiments in my own breast. But alas! I never could keep a promise. I do not blame myself for this weakness, because the fault must lie in my physical organization. It is likely that such a very liberal amount of space was given to the organ which enables me to *make* promises, that the organ which should enable me to keep them was crowded out. But I grieve not. I like no half-way things. I had rather have one faculty nobly developed than two faculties of mere ordinary capacity. I certainly meant to keep that promise, but I find I cannot do it. It is impossible to travel through Italy without speaking of pictures, and can I see them through others' eyes?

If I did not so delight in the grand pictures that are spread before me every day of my life by that monarch of all the old masters, Nature, I should come to believe, sometimes, that I had in me no appreciation of the beautiful, whatsoever.

It seems to me that whenever I glory to think that for once I have discovered an ancient painting that is beautiful and worthy of all praise, the pleasure it gives me is an infallible proof that it is *not* a beautiful picture and not in any wise worthy of commendation. This very thing has occurred more times than I can mention, in Venice. In every single instance the guide has crushed out my swelling enthusiasm with the remark:

"It is nothing—it is of the *Renaissance.*"

I did not know what in the mischief the Renaissance was, and so always I had to simply say:

"Ah! so it is—I had not observed it before."

I could not bear to be ignorant before a cultivated negro, the offspring of a South Carolina slave. But it occurred too often for even my self-complacency, did that exasperating "It is nothing—it is of the *Renaissance.*" I said at last:

"*Who* is this Renaissance? Where did he come from? Who gave him permission to cram the Republic with his execrable daubs?"

We learned, then that Renaissance was not a man; that *renaissance* was a term used to signify what was at best but an imperfect rejuvenation of art. The guide said that after Titian's time and the time of the other great names we had grown so familiar with, high art declined; then it partially rose again—an inferior sort of painters sprang up, and these shabby pictures were the work of their hands. Then I said, in my heat, that I "wished to goodness high art had declined five hundred years sooner." The Renaissance pictures suit me very well, though sooth to say its school were too much given to painting real men and did not indulge enough in martyrs.

The guide I have spoken of is the only one we have had yet who knew anything. He was born in South Carolina, of slave parents. They came to Venice while he was an infant. He has grown up here. He is well educated. He reads, writes, and speaks English, Italian,

Spanish, and French, with perfect facility; is a worshiper of art and thoroughly conversant with it; knows the history of Venice by heart and never tires of talking of her illustrious career. He dresses better than any of us, I think, and is daintily polite. Negroes are deemed as good as white people, in Venice, and so this man feels no desire to go back to his native land. His judgment is correct.

I have had another shave. I was writing in our front room this afternoon and trying hard to keep my attention on my work and refrain from looking out upon the canal. I was resisting the soft influences of the climate as well as I could, and endeavoring to overcome the desire to be indolent and happy. The boys sent for a barber. They asked me if I would be shaved. I reminded them of my tortures in Genoa, Milan, Como; of my declaration that I would suffer no more on Italian soil. I said: "Not any for me, if you please."

I wrote on. The barber began on the doctor. I heard him say:

"Dan, this is the easiest shave I have had since we left the ship."

He said again, presently:

"Why, Dan, a man could go to sleep with this man shaving him."

Dan took the chair. Then he said:

"Why, this is Titian. This is one of the old masters."

I wrote on. Directly Dan said:

"Doctor, it is perfect luxury. The ship's barber isn't anything to him."

My rough beard was distressing me beyond measure. The barber was rolling up his apparatus. The temptation was too strong. I said:

"Hold on, please. Shave me also."

I sat down in the chair and closed my eyes. The barber soaped my face, and then took his razor and gave me a rake that well nigh threw me into convulsions. I jumped out of the chair: Dan and the doctor were both wiping blood off their faces and laughing.

I said it was a mean, disgraceful fraud.

They said that the misery of this shave had gone so far beyond anything they had ever experienced before, that they could not bear the idea of losing such a chance of hearing a cordial opinion from me on the subject.

It was shameful. But there was no help for it. The skinning was begun and had to be finished. The tears flowed with every rake, and so did the fervent execrations. The barber grew confused, and brought blood every time. I think the boys enjoyed it better than anything they have seen or heard since they left home.

We have seen the Campanile, and Byron's house, and Balbi's the geographer, and the palaces of all the ancient dukes and doges of Venice, and we have seen their effeminate descendants airing their nobility in fashionable French attire in the Grand Square of St. Mark, and eating ices and drinking cheap wines, instead of wearing gallant coats of mail and destroying fleets and armies as their great ancestors did in the days of Venetian glory. We have seen no bravoes with poisoned stilettoes, no masks, no wild carnival; but we have seen the ancient pride of Venice, the grim Bronze Horses that figure in a thousand legends. Venice may well cherish them, for they are the only horses she ever had. It is said there are hundreds of people in this curious city who never have seen a living horse in their lives. It is entirely true, no doubt.

And so, having satisfied ourselves, we depart tomorrow, and leave the venerable Queen of the Republics to summon her vanished ships, and marshal her shadowy armies, and know again in dreams the pride of her old renown.

CHAPTER XXIV

Some of the *Quaker City's* passengers had arrived in Venice from Switzerland and other lands before we left there, and others were expected every day. We heard of no casualties among them, and no sickness.

We were a little fatigued with sightseeing, and so we rattled through a good deal of country by rail without caring to stop. I took few notes. I find no mention of Bologna in my memorandum book, except that we arrived there in good season, but saw none of the sausages for which the place is so justly celebrated.

Pistoia awoke but a passing interest.

Florence pleased us for a while. I think we appreciated the great figure of David in the grand square, and the sculptured group they call the Rape of the Sabines. We wandered through the endless collections of paintings and statues of the Pitti and Uffizzi galleries, of course. I make that statement in self-defense; there let it stop. I could not rest under the imputation that I visited Florence and did not traverse its weary miles of picture galleries. We tried indolently to recollect something about the Guelphs and Ghibelines and the other historical cut-throats whose quarrels and assassinations make up so large a share of Florentine history, but the subject was not attractive. We had been robbed of all the fine mountain scenery on our little journey by a system of railroading that had three miles of tunnel to a hundred yards of daylight, and we were not inclined to be sociable with Florence. We had seen the spot, outside the city somewhere, where these people had allowed the bones of Galileo to rest in unconsecrated ground for an age because his great discovery that the world turned around was regarded as a damning heresy by the church; and we know that long after the world had accepted his theory and raised his name high in the list of its great men, they had still let him rot there. That we had lived to see his dust in honored sepulture in the Church of Santa Croce we owed to a society of *literati,* and not to Florence or her rulers. We saw Dante's tomb in that church, also, but we were glad to know that his body was not in it; that the ungrateful city that had exiled him and persecuted him would give much to have it there, but need not hope to ever secure that high honor to herself. Medicis are good enough for Florence. Let her plant Medicis and build grand monuments over them to testify how gratefully she was wont to lick the hand that scourged her.

Magnanimous Florence! Her jewelry marts are filled with artists in mosaic. Florentine mosaics are the choicest in all the world. Florence loves to have that said. Florence is proud of it. Florence would foster this specialty of hers. She is grateful to the artists that bring to her this high credit and fill her coffers with foreign money, and so she encourages them with pensions. With pensions! Think of the lavishness of it. She knows that people who piece together the beautiful trifles die early, because the labor is so confining, and so exhausting to hand and brain, and so she has decreed that all these people who reach the age of sixty shall have a pension after that! I have not heard that any of them have called for their dividends yet. One man did fight along till he was sixty, and started after his pension, but it appeared that there had been a mistake of a year in his family record, and so he gave it up and died. These artists will take particles of stone or glass no larger than a mustard seed, and piece them together on a sleeve-button or a shirt-stud, so smoothly and with such nice adjustment of the delicate shades of color the pieces bear, as to form a pigmy rose with stem, thorn, leaves, petals complete, and all as softly and as truthfully tinted as though Nature had builded it herself. They will counterfeit a fly, or a high-toned bug, or the ruined Coliseum, within the cramped circle of a breastpin, and do it so deftly and so neatly that any man might think a master painted it.

I saw a little table in the great mosaic school in Florence—a little trifle of a center-table—whose top was made of some sort of precious polished stone, and in the stone was inlaid the figure of a flute, with bell-mouth and a mazy complication of keys. No painting in the world could have been softer or richer; no shading out of one tint into another could have been more perfect; no work of art of any kind could have been more faultless than this flute, and yet to count the multitude of little fragments of stone of which they swore it was formed would bankrupt any man's arithmetic! I do not think one could have seen where two particles joined each other with eyes of ordinary shrewdness. Certainly *we* could detect no such blemish. This table top cost the labor of one man for ten long years, so they said, and it was for sale for thirty-five thousand dollars.

We went to the Church of Santa Croce, from time to time, in Florence, to weep over the tombs of Michael Angelo, Raphael, and Machiavelli (I suppose they are buried there, but it may be that they reside elsewhere and rent their tombs to other parties—such being the fashion in Italy), and between times we used to go and stand on the bridges and admire the Arno. It is popular to admire the Arno.

It is a great historical creek with four feet in the channel and some scows floating around. It would be a very plausible river if they would pump some water into it. They all call it a river, and they honestly think it *is* a river, do these dark and bloody Florentines. They even help out the delusion by building bridges over it. I do not see why they are too good to wade.

How the fatigues and annoyances of travel fill one with bitter prejudices sometimes! I might enter Florence under happier auspices a month hence and find it all beautiful, all attractive. But I do not care to think of it now, at all, nor of its roomy shops filled to the ceiling with snowy marble and alabaster copies of all the celebrated sculptures in Europe—copies so enchanting to the eye that I wonder how they can really be shaped like the dingy petrified nightmares they are the portraits of. I got lost in Florence at nine o'clock, one night, and stayed lost in that labyrinth of narrow streets and long rows of vast buildings that look all alike, until toward three o'clock in the morning. It was a pleasant night and at first there were a good many people abroad, and there were cheerful lights about. Later, I grew accustomed to prowling about mysterious drifts and tunnels and astonishing and interesting myself with coming around corners expecting to find the hotel staring me in the face, and not finding it doing anything of the kind. Later still, I felt tired. I soon felt remarkably tired. But there was no one abroad, now—not even a policeman. I walked till I was out of all patience, and very hot and thirsty. At last, somewhere after one o'clock, I came unexpectedly to one of the city gates. I knew then that I was very far from the hotel. The soldiers thought I wanted to leave the city, and they sprang up and barred the way with their muskets. I said:

"Hotel d'Europe!"

It was all the Italian I knew, and I was not certain whether that was Italian or French. The soldiers looked stupidly at each other and at me, and shook their heads and took me into custody. I said I wanted to go home. They did not understand me. They took me into the guard-house and searched me, but they found no sedition on me. They found a small piece of soap (we carry soap with us now), and I made them a present of it, seeing that they regarded it as a curiosity. I continued to say Hotel d'Europe, and they continued to shake their heads, until at last a young soldier nodding in the corner roused up and said something. He said he knew where the hotel was, I suppose, for the officer of the guard sent him away with me. We walked a hundred or a hundred and fifty miles, it appeared to me, and then *he* got lost. He turned this way and that, and finally gave it up and signified that he was going to spend the remainder of the morning trying to find the city gate again. At that moment it struck me that there was something familiar about the house over the way. It was the hotel!

It was a happy thing for me that there happened to be a soldier there that knew even as much as he did; for they say that the policy of the government is to change the soldiery from one place to another constantly and from country to city, so that they cannot become acquainted with the people and grow lax in their duties and enter into plots and conspiracies with friends. My experiences of Florence were chiefly unpleasant. I will change the subject.

At Pisa we climbed up to the top of the strangest structure the world has any knowledge of—the Leaning Tower. As every one knows, it is in the neighborhood of one hundred and eighty feet high—and I beg to observe that one hundred and eighty feet reach to about the height of four ordinary three-story buildings piled one on top of the other, and is a very considerable altitude for a tower of uniform thickness to aspire to, even when it stands upright—yet this one leans more than thirteen feet out of the perpendicular. It is seven hundred years old, but neither history nor tradition say whether it was built as it is, purposely, or whether one of its sides has settled. There is no record that it ever stood straight up. It is built of marble. It is an airy and a beautiful structure, and each of its eight stories is encircled by fluted columns, some of marble and some of granite, with Corinthian capitals that were handsome when they were new. It is a bell tower, and in its top hangs a chime of ancient bells. The winding staircase within is dark, but one always knows which side of the tower he is on because of his naturally gravitating from one side to the other of the staircase with the rise or dip of the tower. Some of the stone steps are foot-worn only on one end; others only on the other end; others only in the middle. To look down into the tower from the top is like looking down into a tilted well. A rope that hangs from the center of the top touches the wall before it reaches the bottom. Standing on the summit, one does not feel altogether comfortable when he looks down from the high side; but to crawl on your breast to the verge on the lower side and try to stretch your neck out far enough to see the base of the tower, makes your flesh creep, and convinces you for a single moment, in spite of all your philosophy, that the building is falling. You handle yourself very carefully, all the time, under the silly impression that if it is *not* falling your trifling weight will start it unless you are particular not to "bear down" on it.

The Duomo, close at hand, is one of the finest cathedrals in Europe. It is eight hundred years old. Its grandeur has outlived the high commercial prosperity and the political importance that made it a necessity, or rather a possibility. Surrounded by poverty, decay, and ruin, it conveys to us a more tangible impression of the former greatness of Pisa than books could give us.

The Baptistery, which is a few years older than the Leaning Tower, is a stately rotunda of huge dimensions, and was a costly structure. In it hangs the lamp whose measured swing suggested to Galileo the pendulum. It looked an insignificant thing to have conferred upon the world of science and mechanics such a mighty extension of their dominions as it has. Pondering, in its suggestive presence, I seemed to see a crazy universe of swinging disks, the toiling children of this sedate parent. He appeared to have an intelligent expression about him of knowing that he was not a lamp at all; that he was a Pendulum; a pendulum disguised, for prodigious and inscrutable purposes of his own deep devising, and not a common pendulum either, but the old original patriarchal Pendulum—the Abraham Pendulum of the world.

This Baptistery is endowed with the most pleasing echo of all the echoes we have read of. The guide sounded two sonorous notes, about half an octave apart; the echo answered with the most enchanting, the most melodious, the richest blending of sweet sounds that one can imagine. It was like a long-drawn chord of a church organ, infinitely softened by distance. I may be extravagant in this matter, but if this be the case my ear is to blame—not my pen. I am describing a memory—and one that will remain long with me.

The peculiar devotional spirit of the olden time, which placed a higher confidence in outward forms of worship than in the watchful guarding of the heart against sinful thoughts and the hands against sinful deeds, and which believed in the protecting virtues of inanimate objects made holy by contact with holy things, is illustrated in a striking manner in one of the cemeteries of Pisa. The tombs are set in soil brought in ships from the Holy Land ages ago. To be buried in such ground was regarded by the ancient Pisans as being more potent for salvation than many masses purchased of the church and the vowing of many candles to the Virgin.

Pisa is believed to be about three thousand years old. It was one of the twelve great cities of ancient Etruria, that commonwealth which has left so many monuments in testimony of its extraordinary advancement, and so little history of itself that is tangible and comprehensible. A Pisan antiquarian gave me an ancient tear-jug which he averred was full four thousand years old. It was found among the ruins of one of the oldest of the Etruscan cities. He said it came from a tomb, and was used by some bereaved family in that remote age when even the Pyramids of Egypt were young, Damascus a village, Abraham a prattling infant and ancient Troy not yet dreamt of, to receive the tears wept for some lost idol of a household. It spoke to us in a language of its own; and with a pathos more tender than any words might bring, its mute eloquence swept down the long roll of the centuries with its tale of a vacant chair, a familiar footstep missed from the threshold, a pleasant voice gone from the chorus, a vanished form!—a tale which is always so new to us, so startling, so terrible, so benumbing to the senses, and behold how threadbare and old it is! No shrewdly-worded history could have brought the myths and shadows of that old dreamy age before us clothed with human flesh and warmed with human sympathies so vividly as did this poor little unsentient vessel of pottery.

Pisa was a republic in the Middle Ages, with a government of her own, armies and navies of her own, and a great commerce. She was a warlike power, and inscribed upon her banners many a brilliant fight with Genoese and Turks. It is said that the city once numbered a population of four hundred thousand; but her scepter has passed from her grasp now, her ships and her armies are gone, her commerce is dead. Her battle-flags bear the mold and the dust of centuries, her marts are deserted, she has shrunken far within her crumbling walls, and her great population has diminished to twenty thousand souls. She has but one thing left to boast of, and that is not much; viz., she is the second city of Tuscany.

We reached Leghorn in time to see all we wished to see of it long before the city gates were closed for the evening, and then came on board the ship.

We felt as though we had been away from home an age. We never entirely appreciated, before, what a very pleasant den our state-room is: nor how jolly it is to sit at dinner in one's own seat in one's own cabin, and hold familiar conversation with friends in one's own language. Oh, the rare happiness of comprehending every single word that is said, and knowing that every word one says in return will be understood as well! We would talk ourselves to death now, only there are only about ten passengers out of the sixty-five to talk to. The others are wandering, we hardly know where. We shall not go ashore in Leghorn. We are surfeited with Italian cities for the present, and much prefer to walk the familiar quarter-deck and view this one from a distance.

The stupid magnates of this Leghorn government cannot understand that so large a steamer as ours could cross the broad Atlantic with no other purpose than to indulge a party of ladies and gentlemen in a pleasure excursion. It looks too improbable. It is suspicious, they think. Something more important must be hidden behind it all. They cannot understand it, and they scorn the evidence of the ship's papers. They have decided at last that we are a battalion of incendiary, blood-thirsty Garibaldians in disguise! And in all seriousness they have set a gunboat to watch the vessel night and day, with orders to close down on any revolutionary movement in a twinkling! Police-boats are on patrol duty about us all the time, and it is as much as a sailor's liberty is worth to show himself in a red shirt. These policemen follow the executive officer's boat from shore to ship and from ship to shore, and watch his dark maneuvers with a vigilant eye. They will arrest him yet unless he assumes an expression of countenance that shall have less of carnage, insurrection, and sedition in it. A visit paid in a friendly way to General Garibaldi yesterday (by cordial invitation) by some of our passengers, has gone far to confirm the dread suspicions the government harbors toward us. It is thought the friendly visit was only the cloak of a bloody conspiracy. These people draw near and watch us when we bathe in the sea from the ship's side. Do they think we are communing with a reserve force of rascals at the bottom?

It is said that we shall probably be quarantined at Naples. Two or three of us prefer not to run this risk. Therefore, when we are rested, we propose to go in a French steamer to Civita Vecchia, and from thence to Rome, and by rail to Naples. They do not quarantine the cars, no matter where they got their passengers from.

CHAPTER XXV

There are a good many things about this Italy which I do not understand—and more especially I cannot understand how a bankrupt government can have such palatial railroad depots and such marvels of turnpikes. Why, these latter are as hard as adamant, as straight as a line, as smooth as a floor, and as white as snow. When it is too dark to see any other object, one can still see the white turnpikes of France and Italy; and they are clean enough to eat from, without a table-cloth. And yet no tolls are charged.

As for the railways—we have none like them. The cars slide as smoothly along as if they were on runners. The depots are vast palaces of cut marble, with stately colonnades of the same royal stone traversing them from end to end, and with ample walls and ceilings richly decorated with frescoes. The lofty gateways are graced with statues, and the broad floors are all laid in polished flags of marble.

These things win me more than Italy's hundred galleries of priceless art treasures, because I can understand the one and am not competent to appreciate the other. In the turnpikes, the railways, the depots, and the new boulevards of uniform houses in Florence and other cities here, I see the genius of Louis Napoleon, or rather, I see the works of that statesman imitated. But Louis has taken care that in France there shall be a foundation for these improvements—money. He has always the where-withal to back up his projects; they strengthen France and never weaken her. Her material prosperity is genuine. But here the case is different. This country is bankrupt. There is no real foundation for these great works. The prosperity they would seem to indicate is a pretense. There is no money in the treasury, and so they enfeeble her instead of strengthening. Italy has achieved the dearest wish of her heart and become an independent state—and in so doing she has drawn an elephant in the political lottery. She has nothing to feed it on. Inexperienced in government, she plunged into all manner of useless expenditure, and swamped her treasury almost in a day. She squandered millions of francs on a navy which she did not need, and the first time she took her new toy into action she got it knocked higher than Gilderoy's kite—to use the language of the Pilgrims.

But it is an ill-wind that blows nobody good. A year ago, when

Italy saw utter ruin staring her in the face and her greenbacks hardly worth the paper they were printed on, her Parliament ventured upon a *coup de main* that would have appalled the stoutest of her statesmen under less desperate circumstances. They, in a manner, confiscated the domains of the Church! This in priest-ridden Italy! This in a land which has groped in the midnight of priestly superstition for sixteen hundred years! It was a rare good fortune for Italy, the stress of weather that drove her to break from this prison-house.

They do not call it *confiscating* the church property. That would sound too harshly yet. But it amounts to that. There are thousands of churches in Italy, each with untold millions of treasures stored away in its closets, and each with its battalion of priests to be supported. And then there are the estates of the Church—league on league of the richest lands and the noblest forests in all Italy—all yielding immense revenues to the Church, and none paying a cent in taxes to the state. In some great districts the Church owns *all* the property—lands, water-courses, woods, mills and factories. They buy, they sell, they manufacture, and since they pay no taxes, who can hope to compete with them!

Well, the government has seized all this in effect, and will yet seize it in rigid and unpoetical reality, no doubt. Something must be done to feed a starving treasury, and there is no other resource in all Italy—none but the riches of the Church. So the government intends to take to itself a great portion of the revenues arising from priestly farms, factories, etc., and also intends to take possession of the churches and carry them on, after its own fashion and upon its own responsibility. In a few instances it will leave the establishments of great pet churches undisturbed, but in all others only a handful of priests will be retained to preach and pray, a few will be pensioned, and the balance turned adrift.

Pray glance at some of these churches and their embellishments, and see whether the government is doing a righteous thing or not. In Venice, to-day, a city of a hundred thousand inhabitants, there are twelve hundred priests. Heaven only knows how many there were before the Parliament reduced their numbers. There was the great Jesuit Church. Under the old régime it required sixty priests to engineer it—the government does it with five now, and the others are discharged from service. All about that church wretchedness and poverty abound. At its door a dozen hats and bonnets were doffed to us, as many heads were humbly bowed, and as many hands extended, appealing for pennies—appealing with foreign words we could not understand, but appealing mutely, with sad eyes, and sunken cheeks, and ragged raiment, that no words were needed to translate. Then we passed within the great doors, and it seemed that the riches of the world were before us! Huge columns carved out of single masses of marble, and inlaid from top to bottom with a hundred intricate figures wrought in costly verde antique; pulpits of the same rich materials, whose draperies hung down in many a pictured fold, the stony fabric counterfeiting the delicate work of the loom; the grand altar brilliant with polished facings and balustrades of oriental agate, jasper, verde antique, and other precious stones, whose names, even, we seldom hear—and slabs of priceless lapis lazuli lavished everywhere as recklessly as if the church had owned a quarry of it. In the midst of all this magnificence, the solid gold and silver furniture of the altar seemed cheap and trivial. Even the floors and ceilings cost a princely fortune.

Now, where is the use of allowing all those riches to lie idle, while half of that community hardly know, from day to day, how they are going to keep body and soul together? And, where is the wisdom in permitting hundreds upon hundreds of millions of francs to be locked up in the useless trumpery of churches all over Italy, and the people ground to death with taxation to uphold a perishing government?

As far as I can see, Italy, for fifteen hundred years, has turned all her energies, all her finances, and all her industry to the building up of a vast array of wonderful church edifices, and starving half her citizens to accomplish it. She is to-day one vast museum of magnificence and misery. All the churches in an ordinary American city put together could hardly buy the jeweled frippery in one of her hundred cathedrals. And for every beggar in America, Italy can show a hundred—and rags and vermin to match. It is the wretchedest, princeliest land on earth.

Look at the grand Duomo of Florence—a vast pile that has been sapping the purses of her citizens for five hundred years, and is not nearly finished yet. Like all other men, I fell down and worshiped it, but when the filthy beggars swarmed around me the conrast was too striking, too suggestive, and I said, "Oh, sons of classic Italy, *is* the spirit of enterprise, of self-reliance, of noble endeavor, utterly dead within ye? Curse your indolent worthlessness, why don't you rob your church?"

Three hundred happy, comfortable priests are employed in that cathedral.

And now that my temper is up, I may as well go on and abuse everybody I can think of. They have a grand mausoleum in Florence, which they built to bury our Lord and Saviour and the Medici family in. It sounds blasphemous, but it is true, and here they *act* blasphemy. The dead and damned Medicis who cruelly tyrannized over Florence and were her curse for over two hundred years, are salted away in a circle of costly vaults, and in their midst the Holy Sepulchre was to have been set up. The expedition sent to Jerusalem to seize it got into trouble and could not accomplish the burglary, and so the center of the mausoleum is vacant now. They say the entire mausoleum was intended for the Holy Sepulchre, and was only turned into a family burying place after the Jerusalem expedition failed—but you will excuse me. Some of those Medicis would have smuggled themselves in sure. What *they* had not the effrontery to do, was not worth doing. Why, they had their trivial, forgotten exploits on land and sea pictured out in grand frescoes (as did also the ancient doges of Venice) with the Saviour and the Virgin throwing bouquets to them out of the clouds, and the Deity himself applauding from his throne in Heaven! And who painted these things? Why, Titian, Tintoretto, Paul Veronese, Raphael—none other than the world's idols, the "old masters."

Andrea del Sarto glorified his princes in pictures that must save them forever from the oblivion they merited, and they let him starve. Served him right. Raphael pictured such infernal villains as Catherine and Marie de Medici seated in heaven and conversing familiarly with the Virgin Mary and the angels (to say nothing of higher personages), and yet my friends abuse me because I am a little prejudiced against the old masters—because I fail sometimes to see the beauty that is in their productions. I cannot help but see it, now and then, but I keep on protesting against the groveling spirit that could persuade those masters to prostitute their noble talents to the adulation of such monsters as the French, Venetian, and Florentine princes of two and three hundred years ago, all the same.

I am told that the old masters had to do these shameful things for bread, the princes and potentates being the only patrons of art. If a grandly gifted man may drag his pride and his manhood in the dirt for bread rather than starve with the nobility that is in him untainted, the excuse is a valid one. It would excuse theft in Washingtons and Wellingtons, and unchastity in women as well.

But, somehow, I cannot keep that Medici mausoleum out of my memory. It is as large as a church; its pavement is rich enough for the pavement of a king's palace; its great dome is gorgeous with frescoes; its walls are made of—what? Marble?—plaster?— wood?—paper?—No. Red porphyry—verde antique—jasper—oriental agate—alabaster—mother-of-pearl—chalcedony—red coral— lapis lazuli! All the vast walls are made wholly of these precious stones, worked in and in and in together in elaborate patterns and figures, and polished till they glow like great mirrors with the pictured splendors reflected from the dome overhead. And before a statue of one of those dead Medicis reposes a crown that blazes with diamonds and emeralds enough to buy a ship-of-the-line, almost. These are the things the government has its evil eye upon, and a happy thing it will be for Italy when they melt away in the public treasury.

And now—. However, another beggar approaches. I will go out and destroy him, and then come back and write another chapter of vituperation.

Having eaten the friendless orphan—having driven away his comrades—having grown calm and reflective at length—I now feel in a kindlier mood. I feel that after talking so freely about the priests and the churches, justice demands that if I know anything good about either I ought to say it. I *have* heard of many things that redound to the credit of the priesthood, but the most notable matter that occurs to me now is the devotion one of the mendicant orders showed during the prevalence of the cholera last year. I speak of the Dominican friars—men who wear a coarse, heavy brown robe and a cowl, in this hot climate, and go barefoot. They live on alms altogether, I believe. They must unquestionably love their religion, to suffer so much for it. When the cholera was raging in Naples; when the people were dying by hundreds and hundreds every day; when every concern for the public welfare was swallowed up in selfish private interest, and every citizen made the taking care of himself his sole object, these men banded themselves together and went about nursing the sick and burying the dead. Their noble efforts cost many of them their lives. They laid them down cheerfully, and well they might. Creeds mathematically precise, and hair-splitting niceties of doctrine, are absolutely necessary for the salvation of some kinds of souls, but surely the charity, the purity, the unselfishness that are in the hearts of men like these would save their souls though they were bankrupt in the true religion—which is ours.

One of these fat barefooted rascals came here to Civita Vecchia with us in the little French steamer. There were only half a dozen of us in the cabin. He belonged in the steerage. He was the life of the ship, the bloody-minded son of the Inquisition! He and the leader of the marine band of a French man-of-war played on the piano and sang opera turn about; they sang duets together; they rigged impromptu theatrical costumes and gave us extravagant farces and pantomimes. We got along first-rate with the friar, and were excessively conversational, albeit he could not understand what we said, and certainly he never uttered a word that we could guess the meaning of.

This Civita Vecchia is the finest nest of dirt, vermin, and ignorance we have found yet, except that African perdition they call Tangier, which is just like it. The people here live in alleys two yards wide, which have a smell about them which is peculiar but not entertaining. It is well the alleys are not wider, because they hold as much smell now as a person can stand, and, of course, if they were wider they would hold more, and then the people would die. These alleys are paved with stone, and carpeted with deceased cats, and decayed rags, and decomposed vegetable tops, and remnants of old boots, all soaked with dish-water, and the people sit around on stools and enjoy it. They are indolent, as a general thing, and yet have few pastimes. They work two or three hours at a time, but not hard, and then they knock off and catch flies. This does not require any talent, because they only have to grab—if they do not get the one they are after, they get another. It is all the same to them. They have no partialities. Whichever one they get is the one they want.

They have other kinds of insects, but it does not make them arrogant. They are very quiet, unpretending people. They have more of these kind of things than other communities, but they do not boast.

They are very uncleanly—these people—in face, in person, and dress. When they see anybody with a clean shirt on, it arouses their scorn. The women wash clothes, half the day, at the public tanks in the streets, but they are probably somebody else's. Or may be they keep one set to wear and another to wash; because they never put on any that have ever been washed. When they get done washing, they sit in the alleys and nurse their cubs. They nurse one ash-cat at a time, and the others scratch their backs against the door-post and are happy.

All this country belongs to the Papal states. They do not appear to have any schools here, and only one billiard table. Their education is at a very low stage. One portion of the men go into the military, another into the priesthood, and the rest into the shoemaking business.

They keep up the passport system here, but so they do in Turkey. This shows that the Papal states are as far advanced as Turkey. This fact will be alone sufficient to silence the tongues of malignant calumniators. I had to get my passport *viséd* for Rome in Florence, and then they would not let me come ashore here until a policeman had examined it on the wharf and sent me a permit. They did not even dare to let me take my passport in my hands for twelve hours, I looked so formidable. They judged it best to let me cool down. They thought I wanted to take the town, likely. Little did they know me. I wouldn't have it. They examined my baggage at the depot. They took one of my ablest jokes and read it over carefully twice and then read it backwards. But it was too deep for them. They passed it around, and everybody speculated on it awhile, but it mastered them all.

It was no common joke. At length a veteran officer spelled it over deliberately and shook his head three or four times and said that, in his opinion, it was seditious. That was the first time I felt alarmed. I immediately said I would explain the document, and they crowded around. And so I explained and explained and explained, and they took notes of all I said, but the more I explained the more they could not understand it, and when they desisted at last, I could not even understand it myself. They said they believed it was an incendiary document, leveled at the government. I declared solemnly that it was not, but they only shook their heads and would not be satisfied. Then they consulted a good while; and finally they confiscated it. I was very sorry for this, because I had worked a long time on that joke, and took a good deal of pride in it, and now I suppose I shall never see it any more. I suppose it will be sent up and filed away among the criminal archives of Rome, and will always be regarded as a mysterious infernal machine which would have blown up like a mine and scattered the good Pope all around, but for a miraculous providential interference. And I suppose that all the time I am in Rome the police will dog me about from place to place because they think I am a dangerous character.

It is fearfully hot in Civita Vecchia. The streets are made very narrow and the houses built very solid and heavy and high, as a protection against the heat. This is the first Italian town I have seen which does not appear to have a patron saint. I suppose no saint but the one that went up in the chariot of fire could stand the climate.

There is nothing here to see. They have not even a cathedral, with eleven tons of solid silver archbishops in the back room; and they do not show you any moldy buildings that are seven thousand years old; nor any smoke-dried old fire-screens which are *chef d'oeuvres* of Rubens and Simpson, or Titian or Ferguson, or any of those parties; and they haven't any bottled fragments of saints, and not even a nail from the true cross. We are going to Rome. There is nothing to see here.

CHAPTER XXVI

What is it that confers the noblest delight? What is that which swells a man's breast with pride above that which any other experience can bring to him? Discovery! To know that you are walking where none others have walked; that you are beholding what human eye has not seen before; that you are breathing a virgin atmosphere. To give birth to an idea—to discover a great thought—an intellectual nugget, right under the dust of a field that many a brain-plow had gone over before. To find a new planet, to invent a new hinge, to find the way to make the lightnings carry your messages. To be the *first*—that is the idea. To do something, say something, see something, before *anybody* else—these are the things that confer a pleasure compared with which other pleasures are tame and commonplace, other ecstasies cheap and trivial. Morse, with his first message, brought by his servant, the lightning; Fulton, in that long-drawn century of suspense, when he placed his hand upon the throttle-valve, and lo, the steamboat moved; Jenner, when his patient with the cow's virus in his blood, walked through the small-pox hospitals unscathed; Howe, when the idea shot through his brain that for a hundred and twenty generations the eye had been bored through the wrong end of the needle; the nameless lord of art who laid down his chisel in some old age that is forgotten now, and gloated upon the finished Laocoön; Daguerre, when he commanded the sun, riding in the zenith, to print the landscape upon his insignificant silvered plate, and he obeyed; Columbus, in the Pinta's shrouds, when he swung his hat above a fabled sea and gazed abroad

upon an unknown world! These are the men who have really *lived*—
who have actually comprehended what pleasure is—who have
crowded long lifetimes of ecstasy into a single moment.

What is there in Rome for me to see that others have not seen before me? What is there for me to touch that others have not touched?
What is there for me to feel, to learn, to hear, to know, that shall
thrill me before it pass to others? What can I discover? Nothing.
Nothing whatsoever. One charm of travel dies here. But if I were
only a Roman! If, added to my own I could be gifted with modern
Roman sloth, modern Roman superstition, and modern Roman
boundlessness of ignorance, what bewildering worlds of unsuspected
wonders I would discover! Ah, if I were only a habitant of the Campagna five and twenty miles from Rome! *Then* I would travel.

I would go to America, and see, and learn, and return to the Campagna and stand before my countrymen an illustrious discoverer. I
would say:

"I saw there a country which has no overshadowing Mother
Church, and yet the people survive. I saw a government which never
was protected by foreign soldiers at a cost greater than that required
to carry on the government itself. I saw common men and common
women who could read; I even saw small children of common country people reading from books; if I dared think you would believe it,
I would say they could write, also. In the cities I saw people drinking
a delicious beverage made of chalk and water, but never once saw
goats driven through their Broadway or their Pennsylvania avenue or
their Montgomery street and milked at the doors of the houses. I
saw real glass windows in the houses of even the commonest people.
Some of the houses are not of stone, nor yet of bricks; I solemnly
swear they are made of wood. Houses there will take fire and burn,
sometimes—actually burn entirely down, and not leave a single vestige behind. I could state that for a truth, upon my death-bed. And
as a proof that the circumstance is not rare, I aver that they have a
thing which they call a fire-engine, which vomits forth great streams
of water, and is kept always in readiness, by night and by day, to
rush to houses that are burning. You would think one engine would
be sufficient, but some great cities have a hundred; they keep men
hired, and pay them by the month to do nothing but put out fires.
For a certain sum of money other men will insure that your house
shall not burn down; and if it burns they will pay you for it. There
are hundreds and thousands of schools, and anybody may go and
learn to be wise, like a priest. In that singular country, if a rich man
dies a sinner, he is damned; he cannot buy salvation with money for
masses. There is really not much use in being rich, there. Not much
use as far as the other world is concerned, but much, very much use,
as concerns this; because there, if a man be rich, he is very greatly
honored, and can become a legislator, a governor, a general, a senator, no matter how ignorant an ass he is—just as in our beloved Italy

the nobles hold all the great places, even though sometimes they are born noble idiots. There, if a man be rich, they give him costly presents, they ask him to feasts, they invite him to drink complicated beverages; but if he be poor and in debt, they require him to do that which they term to 'settle.' The women put on a different dress almost every day; the dress is usually fine, but absurd in shape; the very shape and fashion of it changes twice in a hundred years; and did I but covet to be called an extravagant falsifier, I would say it changed even oftener. Hair does not grow upon the American women's heads; it is made for them by cunning workmen in the shops, and is curled and frizzled into scandalous and ungodly forms. Some persons wear eyes of glass which they see through with facility perhaps, else they would not use them; and in the mouths of some are teeth made by the sacrilegious hand of man. The dress of the men is laughably grotesque. They carry no musket in ordinary life, nor no long-pointed pole; they wear no wide green-lined cloak; they wear no peaked black felt hat, no leathern gaiters reaching to the knee, no goatskin breeches with the hair side out, no hob-nailed shoes, no prodigious spurs. They wear a conical hat termed a 'nail-kag'; a coat of saddest black; a shirt which shows dirt so easily that it has to be changed every month, and is very troublesome; things called pantaloons, which are held up by shoulderstraps, and on their feet they wear boots which are ridiculous in pattern and can stand no wear. Yet dressed in this fantastic garb, these people laughed at *my* costume. In that country, books are so common that it is really no curiosity to see one. Newspapers also. They have a great machine which prints such things by thousands every hour.

"I saw common men there—men who were neither priests nor princes—who yet absolutely owned the land they tilled. It was not rented from the church, nor from the nobles. I am ready to take my oath of this. In that country you might fall from a third-story window three several times, and not mash either a soldier or a priest. The scarcity of such people is astonishing. In the cities you will see a dozen civilians for every soldier, and as many for every priest or preacher. Jews, there, are treated just like human beings, instead of dogs. They can work at any business they please; they can sell brand new goods if they want to; they can keep drugstores; they can practice medicine among Christians; they can even shake hands with Christians if they choose; they can associate with them, just the same as one human being does with another human being; they don't have to stay shut up in one corner of the towns; they can live in any part of a town they like best; it is said they even have the privilege of buying land and houses, and owning them themselves, though I doubt that myself; they never have had to run races naked through the public streets, against jackasses, to please the people in carnival time; there they never have been driven by the soldiers into a church every Sunday for hundreds of years to hear themselves and their religion especially and particularly cursed; at this very day, in that curious country, a Jew is allowed to vote, hold office, yea, get up on a rostrum in the public street and express his opinion of the government if the government don't suit him! Ah, it is wonderful. The common people there know a great deal; they even have the effrontery to complain if they are not properly governed, and to take hold and help conduct the government themselves; if they had laws like ours, which give one dollar of every three a crop produces to the government for taxes, they would have that law altered; instead of paying thirty-three dollars in taxes, out of every one hundred they receive, they complain if they have to pay seven. They are curious people. They do not know when they are well off. Mendicant priests do not prowl among them with baskets begging for the church and eating up their substance. One hardly ever sees a minister of the Gospel going around there in his bare feet, with a basket, begging for subsistence. In that country the preachers are not like our mendicant orders of friars—they have two or three suits of clothing, and they wash sometimes. In that land are mountains far higher than the Alban mountains; the vast Roman Campagna, a hundred miles long and full forty broad, is really small compared to the United States of America; the Tiber, that celebrated river of ours, which stretches its mighty course almost two hundred miles, and which a lad can scarcely throw a stone across at Rome, is not so long, nor yet so wide, as the American Mississippi—nor yet the Ohio, nor even the Hudson. In America the people are absolutely wiser and know much more than their grandfathers did. *They* do not plow with a sharpened stick, nor yet with a three-cornered block of wood that merely scratches the top of the ground. We do that because our fathers did, three thousand years ago, I suppose. But those people have no holy reverence for their ancestors. They plow with a plow that is a sharp, curved blade of iron, and it cuts into the earth full five inches. And this is not all. They cut their grain with a horrid machine that mows down whole fields in a day. If I dared, I would say that sometimes they use a blasphemous plow that works by fire and vapor and tears up an acre of ground in a single hour—but—but—I see by your looks that you do not believe the things I am telling you. Alas, my character is ruined, and I am a branded speaker of untruths."

Of course we have been to the monster Church of St. Peter, frequently. I knew its dimensions. I knew it was a prodigious structure. I knew it was just about the length of the capitol at Washington—say seven hundred and thirty feet. I knew it was three hundred and sixty-four feet wide, and consequently wider than the capitol. I knew that the cross on the top of the dome of the church was four hundred and thirty-eight feet above the ground, and therefore about a hundred or may be a hundred and twenty-five feet higher than the dome of the capitol. Thus I had one gauge. I wished to come as near forming a correct idea of how it was going to look as possible; I had a curiosity to see how much I would err. I erred considerably. St. Peter's did not look nearly so large as the capitol, and certainly not a twentieth part as beautiful, from the outside.

When we reached the door, and stood fairly within the church, it was impossible to comprehend that it was a *very* large building. I had to *cipher* a comprehension of it. I had to ransack my memory for some more similes. St. Peter's is bulky. Its height and size would represent two of the Washington capitol set one on top of the other— if the capitol were wider; or two blocks or two blocks and a half of ordinary buildings set one on top of the other. St. Peter's *was* that large, but it could and would not look so. The trouble was that everything in it and about it was on such a scale of uniform vastness that there were no contrasts to judge by—none but the people, and I had not noticed them. They were insects. The statues of children holding vases of holy water were immense, according to the tables of figures, but so was everything else around them. The mosaic pictures in the dome were huge, and were made of thousands and thousands of cubes of glass as large as the end of my little finger, but those pictures looked smooth, and gaudy of color, and in good proportion to the dome. Evidently they would not answer to measure by. Away down toward the far end of the church (I thought it was really clear at the far end, but discovered afterward that it was in the center, under the dome) stood the thing they call the *baldacchino*— a great bronze pyramidal frame-work like that which upholds a mosquito-bar. It only looked like a considerably magnified bedstead— nothing more. Yet I knew it was a good deal more than half as high as Niagara Falls. It was overshadowed by a dome so mighty that its own height was snubbed. The four great square piers or pillars that stand equidistant from each other in the church, and support the roof, I could not work up to their real dimensions by any method of comparison. I knew that the faces of each were about the width of a very large dwelling-house front (fifty or sixty feet), and that they were twice as high as an ordinary three-story dwelling, but still they looked small. I tried all the different ways I could think of to compel myself to understand how large St. Peter's was, but with small success. The mosaic portrait of an Apostle who was writing with a pen six feet long seemed only an ordinary Apostle.

But the people attracted my attention after a while. To stand in the door of St. Peter's and look at men down toward its further extremity, two blocks away, has a diminishing effect on them; surrounded by the prodigious pictures and statues, and lost in the vast spaces, they look very much smaller than they would if they stood two blocks away in the open air. I "averaged" a man as he passed me and watched him as he drifted far down by the *baldacchino* and beyond—watched him dwindle to an insignificant school-boy, and then, in the midst of the silent throng of human pigmies gliding about him, I lost him. The church had lately been decorated, on the occasion of a great ceremony in honor of St. Peter, and men were engaged now in removing the flowers and gilt paper from the walls and pillars. As no ladders could reach the great heights, the men swung themselves down from balustrades and the capitals of pilasters by ropes, to do this work. The upper gallery which encircles the inner sweep of the dome is two hundred and forty feet above the floor of the church—very few steeples in America could reach up to it. Visitors always go up there to look down into the church because one gets the best idea of some of the heights and distances from that point. While we stood on the floor one of the workmen swung loose from that gallery at the end of a long rope. I had not supposed, before, that a man *could* look so much like a spider. He was insignificant in size, and his rope seemed only a thread. Seeing that he took up so little space, I could believe the story, then, that ten thousand troops went to St. Peter's once to hear mass, and their commanding officer came afterward, and not finding them, supposed they had not yet arrived. But they were in the church, nevertheless—they were in one of the transepts. Nearly fifty thousand persons assembled in St. Peter's to hear the publishing of the dogma of the Immaculate Conception. It is estimated that the floor of the church affords standing room for—for a large number of people; I have forgotten the exact figures. But it is no matter—it is near enough.

They have twelve small pillars, in St. Peter's, which came from Solomon's Temple. They have, also—which was far more interesting to me—a piece of the true cross, and some nails, and a part of the crown of thorns.

Of course, we ascended to the summit of the dome, and, of course, we also went up into the gilt copper ball which is above it. There was room there for a dozen persons, with a little crowding, and it was as close and hot as an oven. Some of those people who are so fond of writing their names in prominent places had been there before us—a million or two, I should think. From the dome of St. Peter's one can see every notable object in Rome, from the Castle of St. Angelo to the Coliseum. He can discern the seven hills upon which Rome is built. He can see the Tiber, and the locality of the bridge which Horatius kept "in the brave days of old" when Lars Porsena attempted to cross it with his invading host. He can see the spot where the Horatii and the Curiatii fought their famous battle. He can see the broad green Campagna, stretching away toward the mountains, with its scattered arches and broken aqueducts of the olden time, so picturesque in their gray ruin, and so daintily festooned with vines. He can see the Alban Mountains, the Apennines, the Sabine Hills, and the blue Mediterranean. He can see a panorama that is varied, extensive, beautiful to the eye, and more illustrious in history than any other in Europe. About his feet is spread the remnant of a city that once had a population of four million souls; and among its massed edifices stand the ruins of temples, columns, and triumphal arches that knew the Caesars, and the noonday of Roman splendor; and close by them, in unimpaired strength, is a drain of arched and heavy masonry that belonged to that older city which stood here before Romulus and Remus were born or Rome thought of. The Appian Way is here yet, and looking much as it did, perhaps, when the triumphal processions of the emperors moved over it in other days bringing fettered princes from the confines of the earth. We cannot see the long array of chariots and mail-clad men laden with the spoils of conquest, but we can imagine the pageant, after a fashion. We look out upon many objects of interest from the dome of St. Peter's; and last of all, almost at our feet, our eyes rest upon the building which was once the Inquisition. How times changed, between the older ages and the new! Some seventeen or eighteen centuries ago, the ignorant men of Rome were wont to put Christians in the arena and turn the wild beasts in upon them for a show. It was for a lesson as well. It was to teach the people to abhor and fear the new doctrine the followers of Christ were teaching. The beasts tore the victims limb from limb and made poor mangled corpses of them in the twinkling of an eye. But when the Christians came into power, when the holy Mother Church became mistress of the barbarians, she taught them the error of their ways by no such means. No, she put them in this pleasant Inquisition and pointed to the Blessed Redeemer, who was so gentle and so merciful toward all men, and they urged the barbarians to love him; and they did all they could to persuade them to love and honor him—first by twisting their thumbs out of joint with a screw; then by nipping their flesh with pincers—red-hot ones, because they are the most comfortable in cold weather; then by skinning them alive a little, and finally by roasting them in public. They always convinced those barbarians. The true religion, properly administered, as the good Mother Church used to administer it, is very, very soothing. It is wonderfully persuasive, also. There is a great difference between feeding parties to wild beasts and stirring up their finer feelings in an Inquisition. One is the system of degraded barbarians, the other of enlightened, civilized people. It is a great pity the playful Inquisition is no more.

I prefer not to describe St. Peter's. It has been done before. The ashes of Peter, the disciple of the Saviour, repose in a crypt under the *baldacchino*. We stood reverently in that place; so did we also in the Mamertine Prison, where he was confined, where he converted the soldiers, and where tradition says he caused a spring of water to flow in order that he might baptize them. But when they showed us the print of Peter's face in the hard stone of the prison wall and said he made that by falling up against it, we doubted. And when, also, the monk at the Church of San Sebastian showed us a paving stone with two great footprints in it and said that Peter's feet made those, we lacked confidence again. Such things do not impress one. The monk said that angels came and liberated Peter from prison by night, and he started away from Rome by the Appian Way. The Saviour met him and told him to go back, which he did. Peter left those footprints in the stone upon which he stood at the time. It was not stated how it was ever discovered whose footprints they were, seeing the interview occurred secretly and at night. The print of the face in the prison was that of a man of common size; the footprints were those of a man ten or twelve feet high. The discrepancy confirmed our unbelief.

We necessarily visited the Forum, where Caesar was assassinated, and also the Tarpeian Rock. We saw the Dying Gladiator at the Capitol, and I think that even we appreciated that wonder of art; as much, perhaps, as we did that fearful story wrought in marble, in the Vatican—the Laocoön. And then the Coliseum.

Everybody knows the picture of the Coliseum; everybody recognizes at once that "looped and windowed" band-box with a side bitten out. Being rather isolated, it shows to better advantage than any other of the monuments of ancient Rome. Even the beautiful Pantheon, whose pagan altars uphold the cross now, and whose Venus, tricked out in consecrated gimcracks, does reluctant duty as a Virgin Mary to-day, is built about with shabby houses and its stateliness sadly marred. But the monarch of all European ruins, the Coliseum, maintains that reserve and that royal seclusion which is proper to majesty. Weeds and flowers spring from its massy arches and its circling seats, and vines hang their fringes from its lofty walls. An impressive silence broods over the monstrous structure where such multitudes of men and women were wont to assemble in other days. The butterflies have taken the places of the queens of fashion and beauty of eighteen centuries ago, and the lizards sun themselves in the sacred seat of the emperor. More vividly than all the written histories, the Coliseum tells the story of Rome's grandeur and Rome's decay. It is the worthiest type of both that exists. Moving about the Rome of to-day, we might find it hard to believe in her old magnificence and her millions of population; but with this stubborn evidence before us that she was obliged to have a theater with sitting room for twenty thousand more, to accommodate such of her citizens as required amusement, we find belief less difficult. The Coliseum is over one thousand six hundred feet long, seven hundred and fifty wide, and one hundred and sixty-five high. Its shape is oval.

In America we make convicts useful at the same time that we punish them for their crimes. We farm them out and compel them to earn money for the state by making barrels and building roads. Thus we combine business with retribution, and all things are lovely. But in ancient Rome they combined religious duty with pleasure. Since it was necessary that the new sect called Christians should be exterminated, the people judged it wise to make this work profitable to the state at the same time, and entertaining to the public. In addition to the gladiatorial combats and other shows, they sometimes threw members of the hated sect into the arena of the Coliseum and turned wild beasts in upon them. It is estimated that seventy thousand Christians suffered martyrdom in this place. This has made the Coliseum holy ground, in the eyes of the followers of the Saviour. And well it might; for if the chain that bound a saint, and the footprints a saint has left upon a stone he chanced to stand upon, be holy, surely the spot where a man gave up his life for his faith is holy.

Seventeen or eighteen centuries ago this Coliseum was *the* theater of Rome, and Rome was mistress of the world. Splendid pageants were exhibited here, in presence of the emperor, the great ministers of state, the nobles, and vast audiences of citizens of smaller consequence. Gladiators fought with gladiators and at times with warrior prisoners from many a distant land. It was *the* theater of Rome—of the world—and the man of fashion who could not let fall in a casual and unintentional manner something about "my private box at the Coliseum" could not move in the first circles. When the clothing-store merchant wished to consume the corner-grocery man with envy, he bought secured seats in the front row and let the thing be known. When the irresistible drygoods clerk wished to blight and destroy, according to his native instinct, he got himself up regardless of expense and took some other fellow's young lady to the Coliseum, and then accented the affront by cramming her with ice-cream between the acts, or by approaching the cage and stirring up the martyrs with his whalebone cane for her edification. The Roman swell was in his true element only when he stood up against a pillar and fingered his moustache unconscious of the ladies; when he viewed the bloody combats through an opera-glass two inches long; when he excited the envy of provincials by criticisms which showed that he had been to the Coliseum many and many a time and was long ago over the novelty of it; when he turned away with a yawn at last and said:

"*He* a star! handles his sword like an apprentice brigand! he'll do for the country, maybe, but he don't answer for the metropolis!"

Glad was the contraband that had a seat in the pit at the Saturday matinee, and happy the Roman street boy who ate his peanuts and guyed the gladiators from the dizzy gallery.

For me was reserved the high honor of discovering among the rubbish of the ruined Coliseum the only playbill of that establishment now extant. There was a suggestive smell of mint drops about it still, a corner of it had evidently been chewed, and on the margin, in choice Latin, these words were written in a delicate female hand:

"*Meet me on the Tarpeian Rock to-morrow evening, dear, at sharp seven. Mother will be absent on a visit to her friends in the Sabine Hills.* CLAUDIA."

Ah, where is that lucky youth to-day, and where the little hand that wrote those dainty lines? Dust and ashes these seventeen hundred years!

Thus reads the bill:

ROMAN COLISEUM.

UNPARALLELED ATTRACTION!

NEW PROPERTIES! NEW LIONS! NEW GLADIATORS!

Engagement of the renowned

MARCUS MARCELLUS VALERIAN!

FOR SIX NIGHTS ONLY!

The management beg leave to offer to the public an entertainment surpassing in magnificence anything that has heretofore been attempted on any stage. No expense has been spared to make the opening season one which shall be worthy the generous patronage which the management feel sure will crown their efforts. The management beg leave to state that they have succeeded in securing the services of a

GALAXY OF TALENT!

such as has not been beheld in Rome before.

The performance will commence this evening with a

GRAND BROADSWORD COMBAT!

between two young and promising amateurs and a celebrated Parthian gladiator who has just arrived a prisoner from the Camp of Verus.

This will be followed by a grand moral

BATTLE-AX ENGAGEMENT!

between the renowned Valerian (with one hand tied behind him) and two gigantic savages from Britain.

After which the renowned Valerian (if he survive) will fight with the broadsword,

LEFT HANDED!

against six Sophomores and a Freshman from the Gladiatorial College!

A long series of brilliant engagements will follow, in which the finest talent of the Empire will take part.

After which the celebrated Infant Prodigy known as

"THE YOUNG ACHILLES,"

will engage four tiger whelps in combat, armed with no other weapon than his little spear!

The whole to conclude with a chaste and elegant

GENERAL SLAUGHTER!

In which thirteen African Lions and twenty-two Barbarian Prisoners will war with each other until all are exterminated.

BOX OFFICE NOW OPEN.

Dress Circle One Dollar; Children and Servants half price.

An efficient police force will be on hand to preserve order and keep the wild beasts from leaping the railings and discommoding the audience.

Doors open at 7; performance begins at 8.

POSITIVELY NO FREE LIST.

Diodorus Job Press.

It was as singular as it was gratifying that I was also so fortunate as to find among the rubbish of the arena a stained and mutilated copy of the *Roman Daily Battle-Axe*, containing a critique upon this very performance. It comes to hand too late by many centuries to rank as news, and therefore I translate and publish it simply to show how very little the general style and phraseology of dramatic criticism has altered in the ages that have dragged their slow length along since the carriers laid this one damp and fresh before their Roman patrons:

"THE OPENING SEASON.—COLISEUM.—Notwithstanding the inclemency of the weather, quite a respectable number of the rank and fashion of the city assembled last night to witness the debut upon metropolitan boards of the young tragedian who has of late been winning such golden opinions in the amphitheaters of the provinces. Some sixty thousand persons were present, and but for the fact that the streets were almost impassable, it is fair to presume that the house would have been full. His august Majesty, the Emperor Aurelius, occupied the imperial box, and was the cynosure of all eyes. Many illustrious nobles and generals of the Empire graced the occasion with their presence, and not the least among them was the young patrician lieutenant whose laurels, won in the ranks of the 'Thundering Legion,' are still so green upon his brow. The cheer which greeted his entrance was heard beyond the Tiber!

"The late repairs and decorations add both to the comeliness and the comfort of the Coliseum. The new cushions are a great improvement upon the hard marble seats we have been so long accustomed to. The present management deserve well of the public. They have restored to the Coliseum the gilding, the rich upholstery, and the uniform magnificence which old Coliseum frequenters tell us Rome was so proud of fifty years ago.

"The opening scene last night—the broadsword combat between two young amateurs and a famous Parthian gladiator who was sent here a prisoner—was very fine. The elder of the two young gentlemen handled his weapon with a grace that marked the possession of extraordinary talent. His feint of thrusting, followed instantly by a happily delivered blow which unhelmeted the Parthian, was received with hearty applause. He was not thoroughly up in the backhanded stroke, but it was very gratifying to his numerous friends to know that, in time, practice would have overcome this defect. However, he was killed. His sisters, who were present, expressed considerable regret. His mother left the Coliseum. The other youth maintained the contest with such spirit as to call forth enthusiastic bursts of applause. When at last he fell a corpse, his aged mother ran screaming, with hair disheveled and tears streaming from her eyes, and swooned away just as her hands were clutching at the railings of the arena. She was promptly removed by the police. Under the circumstances the woman's conduct was pardonable, perhaps, but we suggest that such exhibitions interfere with the decorum which should be preserved during the performances, and are highly improper in the presence of the Emperor. The Parthian prisoner fought bravely and well; and well he might, for he was fighting for both life and liberty. His wife and children were there to nerve his arm with their love, and to remind him of the old home he should see again if he conquered. When his second assailant fell, the woman clasped her children to her breast and wept for joy. But it was only a transient happiness. The captive staggered toward her and she saw that the liberty he had earned was earned too late. He was wounded unto death. Thus the first act closed in a manner which was entirely satisfactory. The manager was called before the curtain and returned his thanks for the honor done him, in a speech which was replete with wit and humor, and closed by hoping that his humble efforts to afford cheerful and instructive entertainment would continue to meet with the approbation of the Roman public.

"The star now appeared, and was received with vociferous applause and the simultaneous waving of sixty thousand handkerchiefs. Marcus Marcellus Valerian (stage name—his real name is Smith) is a splendid specimen of physical development, and an artist of rare merit. His management of the battle-axe is wonderful. His gayety and his playfulness are irresistible, in his comic parts, and yet they are inferior to his sublime conceptions in the grave realm of tragedy. When his axe was describing fiery circles about the heads of the bewildered barbarians, in exact time with his springing body and his prancing legs, the audience gave way to uncontrollable bursts of laughter; but when the back of his weapon broke the skull of one and almost in the same instant its edge clove the other's body in twain, the howl of enthusiastic applause that shook the building was the acknowledgment of a critical assemblage that he was a master of the noblest department of his profession. If he has a fault (and we are sorry to even intimate that he has), it is that of glancing at the audience, in the midst of the most exciting moments of the performance, as if seeking admiration. The pausing in a fight to bow when bouquets are thrown to him is also in bad taste. In the great left-handed combat he appeared to be looking at the audience half the time, instead of carving his adversaries; and when he had slain all the sophomores and was dallying with the freshmen, he stooped and snatched a bouquet as it fell, and offered it to his adversary at a time when a blow was descending which promised favorably to be his death-warrant. Such levity is proper enough in the provinces, we make no doubt, but it ill suits the dignity of the metropolis. We trust our young friend will take these remarks in good part, for we mean them solely for his benefit. All who know us are aware that although we are at times justly severe upon tigers and martyrs, we never intentionally offend gladiators.

"The Infant Prodigy performed wonders. He overcame his four tiger whelps with ease, and with no other hurt than the loss of a portion of his scalp. The General Slaughter was rendered with a faithfulness to details which reflects the highest credit upon the late participants in it.

"Upon the whole, last night's performances shed honor not only upon the management but upon the city that encourages and sustains such wholesome and instructive entertainments. We would simply suggest that the practice of vulgar young boys in the gallery of shying peanuts and paper pellets at the tigers, and saying 'Hi-yi!' and manifesting approbation or dissatisfaction by such observations as 'Bully for the lion!' 'Go it, Gladdy!' 'Boots!' 'Speech!' 'Take a walk round the block!' and so on, are extremely reprehensible, when the Emperor is present, and ought to be stopped by the police. Several times last night, when the supernumeraries entered the arena to drag out the bodies, the young ruffians in the gallery shouted, 'Supe! supe!' and also, 'Oh, what a coat!' and 'Why don't you pad them shanks?' and made use of various other remarks expressive of derision. These things are very annoying to the audience.

"A matinée for the little folks is promised for this afternoon, on which occasion several martyrs will be eaten by the tigers. The regular performance will continue every night till further notice. Material change of programme every evening. Benefit of Valerian, Tuesday, 29th, if he lives."

I have been a dramatic critic myself, in my time, and I was often surprised to notice how much more I knew about Hamlet than Forrest did; and it gratifies me to observe, now, how much better my brethren of ancient times knew how a broadsword battle ought to be fought than the gladiators.

CHAPTER XXVII

So far, good. If any man has a right to feel proud of himself, and satisfied, surely it is I. For I have written about the Coliseum and the gladiators, the martyrs and the lions, and yet have never once used the phrase "butchered to make a Roman holiday." I am the only free white man of mature age who has accomplished this since Byron originated the expression.

Butchered to make a Roman holiday sounds well for the first
seventeen or eighteen hundred thousand times one sees it in print,
but after that it begins to grow tiresome. I find it in all the books
concerning Rome—and here latterly it reminds me of Judge Oliver.
Oliver was a young lawyer, fresh from the schools, who had gone out
to the deserts of Nevada to begin life. He found that country, and
our ways of life there, in those early days, different from life in New
England or Paris. But he put on a woolen shirt and strapped a navy
revolver to his person, took to the bacon and beans of the country,
and determined to do in Nevada as Nevada did. Oliver accepted the
situation so completely that, although he must have sorrowed over
many of his trials, he never complained—that is, he never complained but once. He, two others, and myself, started to the new silver mines in the Humboldt mountains—he to be Probate Judge of
Humboldt county, and we to mine. The distance was two hundred
miles. It was dead of winter. We bought a two-horse wagon and put
eighteen hundred pounds of bacon, flour, beans, blasting powder,
picks, and shovels in it; we bought two sorry-looking Mexican
"plugs," with the hair turned the wrong way and more corners on
their bodies than there are on the mosque of Omar; we hitched up
and started. It was a dreadful trip. But Oliver did not complain.
The horses dragged the wagon two miles from town and then gave
out. Then we three pushed the wagon seven miles, and Oliver moved
ahead and pulled the horses after him by the bits. We complained,
but Oliver did not. The ground was frozen, and it froze our backs
while we slept; the wind swept across our faces and froze our noses.
Oliver did not complain. Five days of pushing the wagon by day and
freezing by night brought us to the bad part of the journey—the
Forty Mile Desert, or the Great American Desert, if you please.
Still, this mildest-mannered man that ever was had not complained.
We started across at eight in the morning, pushing through sand
that had no bottom: toiling all day long by the wrecks of a thousand
wagons, the skeletons of ten thousand oxen; by wagon-tires enough
to hoop the Washington Monument to the top, and ox-chains
enough to girdle Long Island; by human graves; with our throats
parched always with thirst; lips bleeding from the alkali dust; hungry, perspiring, and very, very weary—so weary that when we
dropped in the sand every fifty yards to rest the horses, we could
hardly keep from going to sleep—no complaints from Oliver; none
the next morning at three o'clock, when we got across, tired to death.
Awakened two or three nights afterward at midnight, in a narrow
cañon, by the snow falling on our faces, and appalled at the imminent danger of being "snowed in," we harnessed up and pushed on
till eight in the morning, passed the "Divide" and knew we were
saved. No complaints. Fifteen days of hardship and fatigue brought
us to the end of the two hundred miles, and the judge had not complained. We wondered if anything *could* exasperate him. We built a

Humboldt house. It is done in this way. You dig a square in the
steep base of the mountain, and set up two uprights and top them
with two joists. Then you stretch a great sheet of "cotton domestic"
from the point where the joists join the hillside down over the joists
to the ground; this makes the roof and the front of the mansion;
the sides and back are the dirt walls your digging has left. A chimney is easily made by turning up one corner of the roof. Oliver was
sitting alone in this dismal den, one night, by a sage-brush fire, writing poetry; he was very fond of digging poetry out of himself—or
blasting it out when it came hard. He heard an animal's footsteps
close to the roof; a stone or two and some dirt came through and fell
by him. He grew uneasy and said: "Hi!—clear out from there, can't
you!"—from time to time. But by and by he fell asleep where he sat,
and pretty soon a mule fell down the chimney! The fire flew in every
direction, and Oliver went over backwards. About ten nights after
that he recovered confidence enough to go to writing poetry again.
Again he dozed off to sleep, and again a mule fell down the chimney.
This time, about half of that side of the house came in with the mule.
Struggling to get up, the mule kicked the candle out and smashed
most of the kitchen furniture, and raised considerable dust. These
violent awakenings must have been annoying to Oliver, but he never
complained. He moved to a mansion on the opposite side of the
cañon, because he had noticed the mules did not go there. One
night about eight o'clock he was endeavoring to finish his poem,
when a stone rolled in—then a hoof appeared below the canvas—
then part of a cow—the after part. He leaned back in dread, and
shouted "Hooy! hooy! get out of this!" and the cow struggled manfully—lost ground steadily—dirt and dust streamed down, and before Oliver could get well away, the entire cow crashed through on to
the table and made a shapeless wreck of everything!

Then, for the first time in his life, I think, Oliver complained. He
said:

"This thing is growing monotonous!"

Then he resigned his judgeship and left Humboldt county.
"Butchered to make a Roman holiday" has grown monotonous to me.

In this connection I wish to say one word about Michael Angelo
Buonarotti. I used to worship the mighty genius of Michael Angelo—
that man who was great in poetry, painting, sculpture, architecture—great in everything he undertook. But I do not want Michael
Angelo for breakfast—for luncheon—for dinner—for tea—for supper—for between meals. I like a change, occasionally. In Genoa, he
designed everything; in Milan he or his pupils designed everything;
he designed the Lake of Como; in Padua, Verona, Venice, Bologna,
who did we ever hear of, from guides, but Michael Angelo? In Florence, he painted everything, designed everything, nearly, and what
he did not design he used to sit on a favorite stone and look at, and
they showed us the stone. In Pisa he designed everything but the old

shot-tower, and they would have attributed that to him if it had not been so awfully out of the perpendicular. He designed the piers of Leghorn and the custom-house regulations of Civita Vecchia. But, here—here it is frightful. He designed St. Peter's; he designed the Pope; he designed the Pantheon, the uniform of the Pope's soldiers, the Tiber, the Vatican, the Coliseum, the Capitol, the Tarpeian Rock, the Barberini Palace, St. John Lateran, the Campagna, the Appian Way, the Seven Hills, the Baths of Caracalla, the Claudian Aqueduct, the Cloaca Maxima—the eternal bore designed the Eternal City, and unless all men and books do lie, he painted everything in it! Dan said the other day to the guide, "Enough, enough, enough! Say no more! Lump the whole thing! say that the Creator made Italy from designs by Michael Angelo!"

I never felt so fervently thankful, so soothed, so tranquil, so filled with a blessed peace, as I did yesterday when I learned that Michael Angelo was dead.

But we have taken it out of this guide. He has marched us through miles of pictures and sculpture in the vast corridors of the Vatican; and through miles of pictures and sculpture in twenty other palaces; he has shown us the great picture in the Sistine Chapel, and frescoes enough to fresco the heavens—pretty much all done by Michael Angelo. So with him we have played that game which has vanquished so many guides for us—imbecility and idiotic questions. These creatures never suspect—they have no idea of a sarcasm.

He shows us a figure and says: "Statoo brunzo." (Bronze statue.)

We look at it indifferently and the doctor asks: "By Michael Angelo?"

"No—not know who."

Then he shows us the ancient Roman Forum. The doctor asks: "Michael Angelo?"

A stare from the guide. "No—a thousan' year before he is born."

Then an Egyptian obelisk. Again: "Michael Angelo?"

"Oh, *mon dieu*, genteelmen! Zis is *two* thousan' year before he is born!"

He grows so tired of that unceasing question sometimes, that he dreads to show us anything at all. The wretch has tried all the ways he can think of to make us comprehend that Michael Angelo is only responsible for the creation of a *part* of the world, but somehow he has not succeeded yet. Relief for overtasked eyes and brain from study and sightseeing is necessary, or we shall become idiotic sure enough. Therefore this guide must continue to suffer. If he does not enjoy it, so much the worse for him. We do.

In this place I may as well jot down a chapter concerning those necessary nuisances, European guides. Many a man has wished in his heart he could do without his guide; but knowing he could not, has wished he could get some amusement out of him as a remuneration for the affliction of his society. We accomplished this latter matter, and if our experience can be made useful to others they are welcome to it.

Guides know about enough English to tangle everything up so that a man can make neither head nor tail of it. They know their story by heart—the history of every statue, painting, cathedral, or other wonder they show you. They know it and tell it as a parrot would—and if you interrupt, and throw them off the track, they have to go back and begin over again. All their lives long, they are employed in showing strange things to foreigners and listening to their bursts of admiration. It is human nature to take delight in exciting admiration. It is what prompts children to say "smart" things, and do absurd ones, and in other ways "show off" when company is present. It is what makes gossips turn out in rain and storm to go and be the first to tell a startling bit of news. Think, then, what a passion it becomes with a guide, whose privilege it is, every day, to show to strangers wonders that throw them into perfect ecstasies of admiration! He gets so that he could not by any possibility live in a soberer atmosphere. After we discovered this, we *never* went into ecstasies any more—we never admired anything—we never showed any but impassible faces and stupid indifference in the presence of the sublimest wonders a guide had to display. We had found their weak point. We have made good use of it ever since. We have made some of those people savage, at times, but we have never lost our own serenity.

The doctor asks the questions, generally, because he can keep his countenance, and look more like an inspired idiot, and throw more imbecility into the tone of his voice than any man that lives. It comes natural to him.

The guides in Genoa are delighted to secure an American party, because Americans so much wonder, and deal so much in sentiment and emotion before any relic of Columbus. Our guide there fidgeted about as if he had swallowed a spring mattress. He was full of animation—full of impatience. He said:

"Come wis me, genteelmen!—come! I show you ze letter writing by Christopher Colombo!—write it himself!—write it wis his own hand!—come!"

He took us to the municipal palace. After much impressive fumbling of keys and opening of locks, the stained and aged document was spread before us. The guide's eyes sparkled. He danced about us and tapped the parchment with his finger:

"What I tell you, genteelmen! Is it not so? See! handwriting Christopher Colombo!—write it himself!"

We looked indifferent—unconcerned. The doctor examined the document very deliberately, during a painful pause. Then he said, without any show of interest:

"Ah—Ferguson—what—what did you say was the name of the party who wrote this?"

"Christopher Colombo! ze great Christopher Colombo!"
Another deliberate examination.

"Ah—did he write it himself, or—or how?"

"He write it himself!—Christopher Colombo! he's own handwriting, write by himself!"

Then the doctor laid the document down and said:

"Why, I have seen boys in America only fourteen years old that could write better than that."

"But zis is ze great Christo——"

"I don't care who it is! It's the worst writing I ever saw. Now you mustn't think you can impose on us because we are strangers. We are not fools, by a good deal. If you have got any specimens of penmanship of real merit, trot them out!—and if you haven't, drive on!"

We drove on. The guide was considerably shaken up, but he made one more venture. He had something which he thought would overcome us. He said:

"Ah, genteelmen, you come wis me! I show you beautiful, oh, magnificent bust Christopher Colombo!—splendid, grand, magnificent!"

He brought us before the beautiful bust—for it *was* beautiful—and sprang back and struck an attitude:

"Ah, look, genteelmen!—beautiful, grand,—bust Christopher Colombo!—beautiful bust, beautiful pedestal!"

The doctor put up his eyeglass—procured for such occasions:

"Ah—what did you say this gentleman's name was?"

"Christopher Colombo!—ze great Christopher Colombo!"

"Christopher Colombo—the great Christopher Colombo. Well, what did *he* do?"

"Discover America!—discover America, oh, ze devil!"

"Discover America. No—that statement will hardly wash. We are just from America ourselves. We heard nothing about it. Christopher Colombo—pleasant name—is—is he dead?"

"Oh, corpo di Baccho!—three hundred year!"

"What did he die of?"

"I do not know!—I cannot tell."

"Small-pox, think?"

"I do not know, genteelmen!—I do not know *what* he die of!"

"Measles, likely?"

"May be—may be—I do *not* know—I think he die of somethings."

"Parents living?"

"Im-posseeble!"

"Ah—which is the bust and which is the pedestal?"

"Santa Maria!—*zis* ze bust!—*zis* ze pedestal!"

"Ah, I see, I see—happy combination—very happy combination, indeed. Is—is this the first time this gentleman was ever on a bust?"

That joke was lost on the foreigner—guides cannot master the subtleties of the American joke.

We have made it interesting for this Roman guide. Yesterday we spent three or four hours in the Vatican again, that wonderful world of curiosities. We came very near expressing interest, sometimes— even admiration—it was very hard to keep from it. We succeeded though. Nobody else ever did, in the Vatican museums. The guide was bewildered—nonplussed. He walked his legs off, nearly, hunting up extraordinary things, and exhausted all his ingenuity on us, but it was a failure; we never showed any interest in anything. He had reserved what he considered to be his greatest wonder till the last—a royal Egyptian mummy, the best-preserved in the world, perhaps. He took us there. He felt so sure, this time, that some of his old enthusiasm came back to him:

"See, genteelmen!—Mummy! Mummy!"

The eyeglass came up as calmly, as deliberately as ever.

"Ah,—Ferguson—what did I understand you to say the gentleman's name was?"

"Name?—he got no name!—Mummy!—'Gyptian mummy!"

"Yes, yes. Born here?"

"No! 'Gyptian mummy!"

"Ah, just so. Frenchman, I presume?"

"No!—not Frenchman, not Roman!—born in Egypta!"

"Born in Egypta. Never heard of Egypta before. Foreign locality, likely. Mummy—mummy. How calm he is—how self-possessed. Is, ah—is he dead?"

"Oh, sacré bleu, been dead three thousan' year!"

The doctor turned on him savagely:

"Here, now, what do you mean by such conduct as this! Playing us for Chinamen because we are strangers and trying to learn! Trying to impose your vile second-hand carcasses on us!—thunder and lightning, I've a notion to—to—if you've got a nice fresh corpse, fetch him out!—or, by George, we'll brain you!"

We make it exceedingly interesting for this Frenchman. However, he has paid us back, partly, without knowing it. He came to the hotel this morning to ask if we were up, and he endeavored as well as he could to describe us, so that the landlord would know which persons he meant. He finished with the casual remark that we were lunatics. The observation was so innocent and so honest that it amounted to a very good thing for a guide to say.

There is one remark (already mentioned) which never yet has failed to disgust these guides. We use it always, when we can think of nothing else to say. After they have exhausted their enthusiasm pointing out to us and praising the beauties of some ancient bronze image or broken-legged statue, we look at it stupidly and in silence for five, ten, fifteen minutes—as long as we can hold out, in fact— and then ask:

"Is—is he dead?"

That conquers the serenest of them. It is not what they are

looking for—especially a new guide. Our Roman Ferguson is the most patient, unsuspecting, long-suffering subject we have had yet. We shall be sorry to part with him. We have enjoyed his society very much. We trust he has enjoyed ours, but we are harassed with doubts.

We have been in the catacombs. It was like going down into a very deep cellar, only it was a cellar which had no end to it. The narrow passages are roughly hewn in the rock, and on each hand, as you pass along, the hollowed shelves are carved out, from three to fourteen deep; each held a corpse once. There are names, and Christian symbols, and prayers, or sentences expressive of Christian hopes, carved upon nearly every sarcophagus. The dates belong away back in the dawn of the Christian era, of course. Here, in these holes in the ground, the first Christians sometimes burrowed to escape persecution. They crawled out at night to get food, but remained under cover in the daytime. The priest told us that St. Sebastian lived under ground for some time while he was being hunted; he went out one day, and the soldiery discovered and shot him to death with arrows. Five or six of the early Popes—those who reigned about sixteen hundred years ago—held their papal courts and advised with their clergy in the bowels of the earth. During seventeen years—from A.D. 235 to A.D. 252—the Popes did not appear above ground. Four were raised to the great office during that period. Four years apiece, or thereabouts. It is very suggestive of the unhealthiness of underground graveyards as places of residence. One Pope afterward spent his entire pontificate in the catacombs—eight years. Another was discovered in them and murdered in the episcopal chair. There was no satisfaction in being a Pope in those days. There were too many annoyances. There are one hundred and sixty catacombs under Rome, each with its maze of narrow passages crossing and recrossing each other and each passage walled to the top with scooped graves its entire length. A careful estimate makes the length of the passages of all the catacombs combined foot up nine hundred miles, and their graves number seven millions. We did not go through all the passages of all the catacombs. We were very anxious to do it, and made the necessary arrangements, but our too limited time obliged us to give up the idea. So we only groped through the dismal labyrinth of St. Calixtus, under the Church of St. Sebastian. In the various catacombs are small chapels rudely hewn in the stones, and here the early Christians often held their religious services by dim, ghostly lights. Think of mass and a sermon away down in those tangled caverns under ground!

In the catacombs were buried St. Cecilia, St. Agnes, and several other of the most celebrated of the saints. In the catacomb of St. Calixtus, St. Bridget used to remain long hours in holy contemplation, and St. Charles Borromeo was wont to spend whole nights in prayer there. It was also the scene of a very marvelous thing.

"Here the heart of St. Philip Neri was so inflamed with divine love as to burst his ribs."

I find that grave statement in a book published in New York in 1858, and written by "Rev. William H. Neligan, LL.D., M.A., Trinity College, Dublin; Member of the Archaeological Society of Great Britain." Therefore, I believe it. Otherwise, I could not. Under other circumstances I should have felt a curiosity to know what Philip had for dinner.

This author puts my credulity on its mettle every now and then. He tells of one St. Joseph Calasanctius whose house in Rome he visited; he visited only the house—the priest has been dead two hundred years. He says the Virgin Mary appeared to this saint. Then he continues:

"His tongue and his heart, which were found after nearly a century to be whole, when the body was disinterred before his canonization, are still preserved in a glass case, and after two centuries the heart is still whole. When the French troops came to Rome, and when Pius VII was carried away prisoner, blood dropped from it."

To read that in a book written by a monk far back in the Middle Ages, would surprise no one; it would sound natural and proper; but when it is seriously stated in the middle of the nineteenth century, by a man of finished education, an LL.D., M.A., and an archaeological magnate, it sounds strangely enough. Still, I would gladly change my unbelief for Neligan's faith, and let him make the conditions as hard as he pleased.

The old gentleman's undoubting, unquestioning simplicity has a rare freshness about it in these matter-of-fact railroading and telegraphing days. Hear him, concerning the Church of Ara Coeli:

"In the roof of the church, directly above the high altar, is engraved, 'Regina Coeli laetare Alleluia.' In the sixth century Rome was visited by a fearful pestilence. Gregory the Great urged the people to do penance, and a general procession was formed. It was to proceed from Ara Coeli to St. Peter's. As it passed before the mole of Adrian, now the Castle of St. Angelo, the sound of heavenly voices was heard singing (it was Easter morn)—'Regina Coeli, laetare! alleluia! quia quem meruisti portare, alleluia! resurrexit sicut dixit; alleluia!' The Pontiff, carrying in his hands the portrait of the Virgin (which is over the high altar and is said to have been painted by St. Luke), answered, with the astonished people, 'Ora pro nobis Deum, alleluia!' At the same time an angel was seen to put up a sword in a scabbard, and the pestilence ceased on the same day. There are four circumstances which confirm* this miracle: the annual procession which takes place in the western church on the feast of St. Mark: the statue of St. Michael, placed on the mole of Adrian, which has since that time been called the Castle of St. Angelo; the antiphon Regina Coeli, which the Catholic church sings during paschal time; and the inscription in the church."

---

*The italics are mine—M.T.

THE INNOCENTS ABROAD
VOLUME II

THE INNOCENTS ABROAD
VOLUME II

CHAPTER I

From the sanguinary sports of the Holy Inquisition; the slaughter of the Coliseum; and the dismal tombs of the Catacombs, I naturally pass to the picturesque horrors of the Capuchin Convent. We stopped a moment in a small chapel in the church to admire a picture of St. Michael vanquishing Satan — a picture which is so beautiful that I cannot but think it belongs to the reviled *"Renaissance,"* notwithstanding I believe they told us one of the ancient masters painted it — and then we descended into the vast vault underneath.

Here was a spectacle for sensitive nerves! Evidently the old masters had been at work in this place. There were six divisions in the apartment, and each division was ornamented with a style of decoration peculiar to itself — and these decorations were in every instance formed of human bones! There were shapely arches, built wholly of thigh bones; there were startling pyramids, built wholly of grinning skulls; there were quaint architectural structures of various kinds, built of shin bones and the bones of the arm; on the wall were elaborate frescoes, whose curving vines were made of knotted human vertebrae; whose delicate tendrils were formed of knee-caps and toe nails. Every lasting portion of the human frame was represented in these intricate designs (they were by Michael Angelo, I think), and there was a careful finish about the work, and an attention to details that betrayed the artist's love of his labors as well as his schooled ability. I asked the good-natured monk who accompanied us, who did this? And he said, *"We* did it" — meaning himself and his brethren up stairs. I could see that the old friar took a high pride in his curious show. We made him talkative by exhibiting an interest we never betrayed to guides.

"Who were these people?"

"We — up stairs — Monks of the Capuchin order — my brethren."

"How many departed monks were required to upholster these six parlors?"

These are the bones of four thousand."

"It took a long time to get enough?"

"Many, many centuries."

"Their different parts are well separated — skulls in one room, legs in another, ribs in another — there would be stirring times here for a while if the last trump should blow. Some of the brethren might get hold of the wrong leg, in the confusion, and the wrong skull, and find themselves limping, and looking through eyes that were wider apart or closer together than they were used to. You cannot tell any of these parties apart, I suppose?"

"Oh, yes, I know many of them."

He put his finger on a skull. "This was Brother Anselmo — dead three hundred years — a good man."

He touched another. "This was Brother Alexander — dead two hundred and eighty years. This was Brother Carlo — dead about as long."

Then he took a skull and held it in his hand, and looked reflectively upon it, after the manner of the grave-digger when he discourses of Yorick.

"This," he said, "was Brother Thomas. He was a young prince, the scion of a proud house that traced its lineage back to the grand old days of Rome well nigh two thousand years ago. He loved beneath his estate. His family persecuted him; persecuted the girl, as well. They drove her from Rome; he followed; he sought her far and wide; he found no trace of her. He came back and offered his broken heart at our altar and his weary life to the service of God. But look you. Shortly his father died, and likewise his mother. The girl returned, rejoicing. She sought everywhere for him whose eyes had used to look tenderly into hers out of this poor skull, but she could not find him. At last, in this coarse garb we wear, she recognized him in the street. He knew her. It was too late. He fell where he stood. They took him up and brought him here. He never spoke afterward. Within the week he died. You can see the color of his hair — faded, somewhat — by this thin shred that clings still to the temple. This (taking up a thigh bone) was his. The veins of this leaf in the decorations over your head, were his finger-joints, a hundred and fifty years ago."

This business-like way of illustrating a touching story of the heart by laying the several fragments of the lover before us and naming them, was as grotesque a performance, and as ghastly, as any I ever witnessed. I hardly knew whether to smile or shudder. There are nerves and muscles in our frames whose functions and whose methods of working it seems a sort of sacrilege to describe by cold physiological names and surgical technicalities, and the monk's talk suggested to me something of this kind. Fancy a surgeon, with his nippers lifting tendons, muscles, and such things into view, out of the complex machinery of a corpse, and observing, "Now this little nerve quivers — the vibration is imparted to this muscle — from here it is passed to this fibrous substance, here its ingredients are separated by the chemcial action of the blood — one part goes to the heart and thrills it with what is popularly termed emotion, another part follows this nerve to the brain and communicates intelligence of a startling character — the third part glides along this passage and touches the spring connected with the fluid receptacles that lie in the rear of the eye. Thus, by this simple and beautiful process, the party is informed that his mother is dead, and he weeps." Horrible!

I asked the monk if all the brethren up stairs expected to be put in this place when they died. He answered quietly:

"We must all lie here at last."

See what one can accustom himself to. The reflection that he must some day be taken apart like an engine or a clock, or like a house whose owner is gone, and worked up into arches and pyramids and hideous frescoes, did not distress this monk in the least. I thought he even looked as if he were thinking, with complacent vanity, that his own skull would look well on top of the heap and his own ribs add a charm to the frescoes which possibly they lacked at present.

Here and there, in ornamental alcoves, stretched upon beds of bones, lay dead and dried-up monks, with lank frames dressed in the black robes one sees ordinarily upon priests. We examined one closely. The skinny hands were clasped upon the breast; two lusterless tufts of hair stuck to the skull; the skin was brown and shrunken; it stretched tightly over the cheek bones and made them stand out sharply; the crisp dead eyes were deep in the sockets; the nostrils were painfully prominent, the end of the nose being gone; the lips had shriveled away from the yellow teeth; and brought down to us through the circling years, and petrified there, was a weird laugh a full century old!

It was the jolliest laugh, but yet the most dreadful, that one can imagine. Surely, I thought, it must have been a most extraordinary joke this veteran produced with his latest breath, that he has not got done laughing at it yet. At this moment I saw that the old instinct was strong upon the boys, and I said we had better hurry to St. Peter's. They were trying to keep from asking, "Is — is he dead?"

It makes me dizzy to think of the Vatican — of its wilderness

of statues, paintings, and curiosities of every description and
every age. The "old masters" (especially in sculpture) fairly
swarm, there. I cannot write about the Vatican. I think I shall
never remember anything I saw there distinctly but the mummies, and the Transfiguration, by Raphael, and some other
things it is not necessary to mention now. I shall remember the
Transfiguration partly because it was placed in a room almost by
itself; partly because it is acknowledged by all to be the first oil-
painting in the world; and partly because it was wonderfully
beautiful. The colors are fresh and rich, the "expression," I am
told, is fine, the "feeling" is lively, the "tone" is good, the
"depth" is profound, and the width is about four and a half
feet, I should judge. It is a picture that really holds one's attention; its beauty is fascinating. It is fine enough to be a
Renaissance. A remark I made a while ago suggests a thought —
and a hope. Is it not possible that the reason I find such charms
in this picture is because it is out of the crazy chaos of the
galleries? If some of the others were set apart, might not they be
beautiful? If this were set in the midst of the tempest of pictures
one finds in the vast galleries of the Roman palaces, would I
think it so handsome? If, up to this time, I had seen only one
"old master" in each palace, instead of acres and acres of walls
and ceilings fairly papered with them, might I not have a more
civilized opinion of the old masters than I have now? I think so.
When I was a schoolboy and was to have a new knife, I could
make up my mind as to which was the prettiest in the showcase,
and I did not think any of them were particularly pretty; and so
I chose with a heavy heart. But when I looked at my purchase,
at home, where no glittering blades came into competition with
it, It was astonished to see how handsome it was. To this day my
new hats look better out of the shop than they did in it with
other new hats. It begins to dawn upon me, now, that possibly,
what I have been taking for uniform ugliness in the galleries may
be uniform beauty after all. I honestly hope it is, to others, but
certainly it is not to me. Perhaps the reasons I used to enjoy
going to the Academy of Fine Arts in New York was because
there were but a few hundred paintings in it, and it did not surfeit me to go through the list. I suppose the Academy was bacon
and beans in the Forty-Mile Desert, and a European gallery is a
state dinner of thirteen courses. One leaves no sign after him of
the one dish, but the thirteen frighten away his appetite and give
him no satisfaction.

There is one thing I am certain of, though. With all the
Michael Angelos, the Raphaels, the Guidos, and the other old
masters, the sublime history of Rome remains unpainted! They
painted Virgins enough, and Popes enough, and saintly scarecrows enough, to people Paradise, almost, and these things are

all they did paint. "Nero fiddling o'er burning Rome," the assassination of Caesar, the stirring spectacle of a hundred thousand people bending forward with rapt interest, in the Coliseum, to see two skillful gladiators hacking away each others' lives, a tiger springing upon a kneeling martyr — these and a thousand other matters which we read of with a living interest, must be sought for only in books — not among the rubbish left by the old masters — who are no more, I have the satisfaction of informing the public.

They did paint, and they did carve in marble, one historical scene, and one only (of any great hsitorical consequence). And what was it and why did they choose it, particularly? It was the Rape of the Sabines, and they chose it for the legs and busts.

I like to look at statues, however, and I like to look at pictures, also — even of monks looking up in sacred ecstasy, and monks looking down in meditation, and monks skirmishing for something to eat — and therefore I drop ill-nature to thank the papal government for so jealously guarding and so industriously gathering up these things; and for permitting me, a stranger and not an entirely friendly one, to roam at will and unmolested among them, charging me nothing, and only requiring that I shall behave myself simply as well as I ought to behave in any other man's house. I thank the Holy Father right heartily, and I wish him long life and plenty of happiness.

The Popes have long been the patrons and preservers of art, just as our new practical Republic is the encourager and upholder of mechanics. In their Vatican is stored up all that is curious and beautiful in art; in our Patent Office is hoarded all that is curious or useful in mechanics. When a man invents a new style of horse-collar or discovers a new and superior method of telegraphing, our government issues a patent to him that is worth a fortune; when a man digs up an ancient statue in the Campagna, the Pope gives him a fortune in gold coin. We can make something of a guess at a man's character by the style of nose he carries on his face. The Vatican and the Patent Office are governmental noses, and they bear a deal of character about them.

The guide showed us a colossal statue of Jupiter, in the Vatican, which he said looked so damaged and rusty — so like the God of the Vagabonds — because it had but recently been dug up in the Campagna. He asked how much we supposed this Jupiter was worth. I replied, with intelligent promptness, that he was probably worth about four dollars — may be four and a half. "A hundred thousand dollars!" Ferguson said. Ferguson said, further, that the Pope permits no ancient work of this kind to leave his dominions. He appoints a commission to examine discoveries like this and report upon the value; then the Pope pays the discoverer one-half of that assessed value and takes the statue. He said this Jupiter was dug from a field which had just been bought for thirty-six thousand dollars, so the first crop was a good one for the new farmer. I do not know whether Ferguson always tells the truth or not, but I suppose he does. I know that an exorbitant export duty is exacted upon all pictures painted by the old masters, in order to discourage the sale of those in the private collections. I am satisfied, also, that genuine old masters hardly exist at all, in America, because the cheapest and most insignificant of them are valued at the price of a fine farm. I proposed to buy a small trifle of a Raphael, myself, but the price of it was eighty thousand dollars, the export duty would have made it considerably over a hundred, and so I studied on it awhile and concluded not to take it.

I wish here to mention an inscription I have seen, before I forget it:

"Glory to God in the highest, peace on earth TO MEN OF GOOD WILL!" It is not good scripture, but it is sound Catholic and human nature.

This is in letters of gold around the apsis of a mosaic group at the side of the *scala santa*, church of St. John Lateran, the Mother and Mistress of all the Catholic churches of the world. The group represents the Saviour, St. Peter, Pope Leo, St. Silvester, Constantine, and Charlemagne. Peter is giving the *pallium* to the Pope, and a standard to Charlemagne. The Saviour is giving the keys to St. Silvester, and a standard to Constantine. No prayer is offered to the Saviour, who seems to be of little importance anywhere in Rome; but an inscription says, "*Blessed Peter, give life to Pope Leo and victory to King Charles.*" It does not say, "*Intercede for us*, through the Saviour, with the Father, for this boon," but "Blessed Peter, *give it* us."

In all seriousness — without meaning to be frivolous — without meaning to be irreverent, and more than all, without meaning to be blasphemous, — I state as my simple deduction from the things I have seen and the things I have heard, that the Holy Personages rank thus in Rome:

First — "The Mother of God" — otherwise the Virgin Mary.

Second — The Deity.

Third — Peter.

Fourth — Some twelve or fifteen canonized Popes and martyrs.

Fifth — Jesus Christ the Saviour — (but always as an infant in arms).

I may be wrong in this — my judgment errs often, just as is the case with other men's — but it *is* my judgment, be it good or bad.

Just here I will mention something that seems curious to me. There are no "Christ's Churches" in Rome, and no "Churches of the Holy Ghost," that I can discover. There are some four hundred churches, but about a fourth of them seem to be named for the Madonna and St. Peter. There are so many named for Mary that they have to be distinguished by all sorts of affixes, if I understand the matter rightly. Then we have churches of St. Louis; St. Augustine; St. Agnes; St. Calixtus; St. Lorenzo in Lucina; St. Lorenzo in Damaso; St. Cecilia; St. Athanasius; St. Philip Neri; St. Catherine; St. Domenico, and a multitude of lesser saints whose names are not familiar in the world — and away down, clear out of the list of the churches, comes a couple of hospitals: one of them is named for the Saviour and the other for the Holy Ghost!

Day after day and night after night we have wandered among the crumbling wonders of Rome; day after day and night after night we have fed upon the dust and decay of five-and-twenty centuries — have brooded over them by day and dreamt of them by night till sometimes we seemed moldering away ourselves, and growing defaced and cornerless, and liable at any moment to fall a prey to some antiquary and be patched in the legs, and "restored" with an unseemly nose, and labeled wrong and dated wrong, and set up in the Vatican for poets to drivel about and vandals to scribble their names on forever and forevermore.

But the surest way to stop writing about Rome is to stop. I wished to write a real "guide-book" chapter on this fascinating city, but I could not do it, because I have felt all the time like a boy in a candy-shop — there was everything to choose from, and yet no choice. I have drifted along hopelessly for a hundred pages of manuscript without knowing where to commence. I will not commence at all. Our passports have been examined. We will go to Naples.

CHAPTER II

The ship is lying here in the harbor of Naples — quarantined. She has been here several days and will remain several more. We that came by rail from Rome have escaped this misfortune. Of course no one is allowed to go on board the ship, or come ashore from her. She is a prison, now. The passengers probably spend the long, blazing days looking out from under the awnings at Vesuvius and the beautiful city — and in swearing. Think of ten days of this sort of pastime! — We go out every day in a boat and request them to come ashore. It soothes them. We lie ten steps from the ship and tell them how splendid the city is; and how much better the hotel fare is here than anywhere else in Europe; and how cool it is; and what frozen continents of ice-cream there are; and what a time we are having cavorting about the country and sailing to the islands in the Bay. This tranquilizes them.

ASCENT OF VESUVIUS.

I shall remember our trip to Vesuvius for many a day — partly because of its sight-seeing experiences, but chiefly on account of the fatigue of the journey. Two or three of us had been resting ourselves among the tranquil and beautiful scenery of the island of Ischia, eighteen miles out in the harbor, for two days; we called it "resting," but I do not remember now what the resting consisted of, for when we got back to Naples we had not slept for forty-eight hours. We were just about to go to bed early in the evening, and catch up on some of the sleep we had lost, when we heard of this Vesuvius expedition. There were to be eight of us in the party, and we were to leave Naples at midnight. We laid in some provisions for the trip, engaged carriages to take us to Annunciation, and then moved about the city, to keep awake, till twelve. We got away punctually, and in the course of an hour and a half arrived at the town of Annunication. Annunciation is the very last place under the sun. In other towns in Italy, the people lie around quietly and wait for you to ask them a question or do some overt act that can be charged for — but in Annunication they have lost even that fragment of delicacy; they seize a lady's shawl from a chair and hand it to her and charge a penny; they open a carriage door, and charge for it — shut it when you get out, and charge for it; they help you take off a duster — two cents; brush your clothes and make them worse than they were before — two cents; smile upon you — two cents; bow, with a lickspittle smirk, hat in hand — two cents; they volunteer all information, such as that the mules will arrive presently — two cents — warm day, sir — two cents — take you four hours to make the ascent — two cents. And so they go. They crowd you — infest you — swarm about you, and sweat and smell offensively, and look sneaking and mean, and obsequious. There is no office too degrading for them to perform, for money. I have had no opportunity to find out anything about the upper classes by my own observation, but from what I hear said about them I judge that what they lack in one or two of the bad traits the *canaille* have, they make up in one or two others that are worse. How the people beg! — many of them very well dressed, too.

I said I knew nothing against the upper classes by personal observation. I must recall it! I had forgotten. What I saw their bravest and their fairest do last night, the lowest multitude that could be scraped up out of the purlieus of Christendom would blush to do, I think. They assembled by hundreds, and even thousands, in the great Theater of San Carlo, to do — what? Why, simply, to make fun of an old woman — to deride, to hiss, to jeer at an actress they once worshipped, but whose beauty is faded now and whose voice has lost its former richness. Everybody spoke of the rare sport there was to be. They said the theater would be crammed, because Frezzolini was going to sing. It was said she could not sing well, now, but then the people liked to see her, anyhow. And we went. And every time the woman sang they hissed and laughed — the whole magnificent house — and as soon as she left the stage they called her on again with applause. Once or twice she was encored five and six times in succession, and received with hisses and when she appeared, and discharged with hisses and laughter when she had finished — then instantly encored and insulted again! And how the high-born knaves enjoyed it! White-kidded gentlemen and ladies laughed till the tears came, and clapped their hands in very ecstasy when that unhappy old woman would come meekly out for the sixth time, with uncomplaining patience, to meet a storm of hisses! It was the cruelest exhibition — the most wanton, the most unfeeling. The singer would have conquered an audience of American rowdies by her brave, unflinching tranquility (for she answered encore after encore, and smiled and bowed pleasantly, and sang the best she possibly could, and went bowing off, through all the jeers and hisses, without ever losing countenance or temper); and surely in any other land than Italy her sex and her helplessness must have been an ample protection to her — she could have needed no other. Think what a multitude of small souls were crowded into that theater last night. If the manager could have filled his theater with Neapolitan souls alone, without the bodies, he could not have cleared less than ninety millions of dollars. What traits of character must a man have to enable him to help three thousand miscreants to hiss, and jeer, and laugh at one friendless old woman, and shamefully humiliate her? He must have *all* the vile, mean traits there are. My observation persuades me (I do not like to venture beyond my own personal observation) that the upper classes of Naples possess those traits of character. Otherwise they may be very good people; I cannot say.

ASCENT OF VESUVIUS—CONTINUED.

In this city of Naples, they believe in and support one of the wretchedest of all the religious impostures one can find in Italy — the miraculous liquefaction of the blood of St. Januarius. Twice a year the priests assemble all the people at the Cathedral, and get out this vial of clotted blood and let them see it slowly dissolve and become liquid — and every day for eight days this dismal farce is repeated, while the priests go among the crowd and collect money for the exhibition. The first day, the blood liquefies in forty-seven minutes — the church is crammed, then, and time must be allowed the collectors to get around: after that it liquefies a little quicker and a little quicker, every day, as the houses grow smaller, till on the eighth day, with only a few dozen present to see the miracle, it liquefies in four minutes.

And here, also, they used to have a grand procession, of priests, citizens, soldiers, sailors, and the high dignitaries of the City Government, once a year, to shave the head of a made up Madonna — a stuffed and painted image, like a milliner's dummy — whose hair miraculously grew and restored itself every twelve months. They still kept up this shaving procession as late as four or five years ago. It was a source of great profit to the church that possessed the remarkable effigy, and the ceremony of the public barbering of her was always carried out with the greatest possible eclat and display — the more the better, because the more excitement there was about it the larger the crowds it drew and the heavier the revenues it produced — but at last a day came when the Pope and his servants were unpopular in Naples, and the City Government stopped the Madonna's annual show.

There we have two specimens of these Neapolitans — two of the silliest possible frauds, which half the population religiously and faithfully believed, and the other half either believed also or else said nothing about, and thus lent themselves to the support of the imposture. I am very well satisfied to think the whole population believed in those poor, cheap, miracles — a people who want two cents every time they bow to you, and who abuse a woman, are capable of it, I think.

ASCENT OF VESUVIUS — CONTINUED.

These Neapolitans always ask four times as much money as they intend to take, but if you give them what they first demand, they feel ashamed of themselves for aiming so low, and immediately ask more. When money is to be paid and received, there is always some vehement jawing and gesticulating about it. One cannot buy and pay for two cents' worth of clams without trouble and a quarrel. One "course," in a two-horse carriage, costs a franc — that is law — but the hackman always demands more, on some pretense or other, and if he gets it he makes a new demand. It is said that a stranger took a one-horse carriage for a course — tariff, half a franc. He gave the man five francs, by the way of experiment. He demanded more, received

another franc. Again he demanded more, and got a franc —
demanded more, and it was refused. He grew vehement — was
again refused, and became noisy. The stranger said, "Well, give
me the seven francs again, and I will see what I can do" — and
when he got them, he handed the hackman half a franc, and he
immediately asked for two cents to buy a drink with. It may be
thought that I am prejudiced. Perhaps I am. I would be ashamed
of myself if I were not.

ASCENT OF VESUVIUS—CONTINUED.

Well, as I was saying, we got our mules and horses, after an
hour and a half of bargaining with the population of Annunciation, and started sleepily up the mountain, with a vagrant
at each mule's tail who pretended to be driving the brute along,
but was really holding on and getting himself dragged up instead. I made slow headway at first, but I began to get
dissatisfied at the idea of paying my minion five francs to hold
my mule back by the tail and keep him from going up the hill,
and so I discharged him. I got along faster then.

We had one magnificent picture of Naples from a high point
on the mountian side. We saw nothing but the gas lamps, of
course — two-thirds of a circle, skirting the great Bay — a
necklace of diamonds glinting up through the darkness from the
remote distance — less brilliant than the stars overhead, but
more softly, richly beautiful — and over all the great city the
lights crossed and recrossed each other in many and many a
sparkling line and curve. And back of the town, far around and
abroad over the miles of level campagna, were scattered rows,
and circles, and clusters of lights, all glowing like so many gems,
and marking where a score of villages were sleeping. About this
time, the fellow who was hanging on to the tail of the horse in
front of me and practicing all sorts of unnecessary cruelty upon
the animal, got kicked some fourteen rods, and this incident,
together with the fairy spectacle of the lights far in the distance,
made me serenely happy, and I was glad I started to Vesuvius.

ASCENT OF VESUVIUS—CONTINUED.

This subject will be excellent matter for a chapter, and to-
morrow or next day I will write it.

CHAPTER III

ASCENT OF VESUVIUS—CONTINUED.

"See Naples and die." Well, I do not know that one would
necessarily die after merely seeing it, but to attempt to live there

might turn out a little differently. To see Naples as we saw it in
the early dawn from far up on the side of Vesuvius, is to see a
picture of wonderful beauty. At that distance its dingy buildings
looked white — and so, rank on rank of balconies, windows,
and roofs, they piled themselves up from the blue ocean till the
colossal castle of St. Elmo topped the grand white pyramid and
gave the picture symmetry, emphasis, and completeness. And
when its lilies turned to roses — when it blushed under the sun's
first kiss — it was beautiful beyond all description. One might
well say, then, "See Naples and die." The frame of the picture
was charming, itself. In front, the smooth sea — a vast mosaic
of many colors; the lofty islands swimming in a dreamy haze in
the distance; at our end of the city the stately double peak of
Vesuvius, and its strong black ribs and seams of lava stretching
down to the limitless level campagna — a green carpet that en-
chants the eye and leads it on and on, past clusters of trees, and
isolated houses, and snowy villages, until it shreds out in a fringe
of mist and general vagueness far away. It is from the Hermitage, there on the side of Vesuvius, that one should "see
Naples and die."

But do not go within the walls and look at it in detail. That
takes away some of the romance of the thing. The people are
filthy in their habits, and this makes filthy streets and breeds
disagreeable sights and smells. There never was a community so
prejudiced against the cholera as these Neapolitans are. But they
have good reason to be. The cholera generally vanquishes a
Neapolitan when it seizes him, because, you understand, before
the doctor can dig through the dirt and get at the disease the
man dies. The upper classes take a sea-bath every day, and are
pretty decent.

The streets are generally about wide enough for one wagon,
and how they do swarm with people! It is Broadway repeated in
every street, in every court, in every alley! Such masses, such
throngs, such multitudes of hurrying, bustling, struggling
humanity! We never saw the like of it, hardly even in New York,
I think. There are seldom any sidewalks, and when there are,
they are not often wide enough to pass a man on without
caroming on him. So everybody walks in the street — and where
the street is wide enough, carriages are forever dashing along.
Why a thousand people are not run over and crippled every day
is a mystery that no man can solve.

But if there is an eighth wonder in the world, it must be the
dwelling-houses of Naples. I honestly believe a good majority of
them are a hundred feet high! And the solid brick walls are
seven feet through. You go up nine flights of stairs before you
get to the "first" floor. No, not nine, but there or thereabouts.
There is a little bird-cage of an iron railing in front of every win-

dow clear away up, up, up, among the eternal clouds, where the
roof is, and there is always somebody looking out of every window — people of ordinary size looking out from the first floor,
people a shade smaller from the second, people that look a little
smaller yet from the third — and from thence upward they grow
smaller and smaller by a regularly graduated diminution, till the
folks in the topmost windows seem more like birds in the uncommonly tall martin-box than anything else. The perspective of
one of these narrow cracks of streets, with its rows of tall houses
stretching away till they come together in the distance like
railway tracks; its clothes-lines crossing over at all altitudes and
waving their bannered raggedness over the swarms of people
below; and the white-dressed women perched in balcony railings
all the way from the pavement up to the heavens — a perspective
like that is really worth going into Neapolitan details to see.

Naples, with its immediate suburbs, contains six hundred and
twenty-five thousand inhabitants, but I am satisfied it covers no
more ground than an American city of one hundred and fifty
thousand. It reaches up into the air infinitely higher than three
American cities, though, and there is where the secret of it lies. I
will observe here, in passing, that the contrasts between opulence
and poverty, and magnificence and misery, are more frequent
and more striking in Naple than in Paris even. One must go to
the Bois de Boulogne to see fashionable dressing, splendid
equipages, and stunning liveries, and to the Faubourg St. Antoine to see vice, misery, hunger, rags, dirt — but in the
thoroughfares of Naples these things are all mixed together.
Naked boys of nine years and the fancy-dressed children of
luxury; shreds and tatters, and brilliant uniforms; jackass carts
and state carriages; beggars, princes, and bishops, jostle each
other in every street. At six o'clock every evening, all Naples
turns out to drive on the *Riviera di Chiaja* (whatever that may
mean); and for two hours one may stand there and see the
motliest and the worst-mixed procession go by that ever eyes
beheld. Princes (there are more princes than policemen in Naples
— the city is infested with them) — princes who live up seven
flights of stairs and don't own any principalities, will keep a
carriage and go hungry; and clerks, mechanics, milliners, and
strumpets will go without their dinners and squander the money
on a hack-ride in the Chiaja; the rag-tag and rubbish of the city
stack themselves up, to the number of twenty or thirty, on a
rickety little go-cart hauled by a donkey not much bigger than a
cat, and *they* drive in the Chiaja; dukes and bankers, in sumptuous carriages and with gorgeous drivers and footmen, turn out,
also, and so the furious procession goes. For two hours rank and
wealth, and obscurity and poverty, clatter along side by side in
the wild procession, and then go home serene, happy, covered

with glory!

I was looking at a magnificent marble staircase in the King's palace, the other day, which, it was said, cost five million francs, and I suppose it did cost half a million, may be. I felt as if it must be a fine thing to live in a country where there was such comfort and such luxury as this. And then I stepped out musing, and almost walked over a vagabond who was eating his dinner on the curbstone — a piece of bread and a bunch of grapes. When I found that this mustang was clerking in a fruit establishment (he had the establishment along with him in a basket), at two cents a day, and that he had no palace at home where he lived, I lost some of my enthusiasm concerning the happiness of living in Italy.

This naturally suggests to me a thought about wages there. Lieutenants in the army get about a dollar a day, and common soldiers a couple of cents. I only know one clerk — he gets four dollars a month. Printers get six dollars and a half a month, but I have heard of a foreman who gets thirteen. To be growing suddenly and violently rich, as this man is, naturally makes him a bloated aristocrat. The airs he puts on are insufferable.

And, speaking of wages, reminds me of prices of merchandise. In Paris you pay twelve dollars a dozen for Jouvin's best kid gloves; gloves of about as good quality sell here at three or four dollars a dozen. You pay five and six dollars apiece for fine linen shirts in Paris; here and in Leghorn you pay two and a half. In Marseilles you pay forty dollars for a first-class dress coat made by a good tailor, but in Leghorn you can get a full dress suit for the same money. Here you get handsome business suits at from ten to twenty dollars, and in Leghorn you can get an overocat for fifteen dollars that would cost you seventy in New York. Fine kid boots are worth eight dollars in Marseilles and four dollars here. Lyons velvets rank higher in America than those of Genoa. Yet the bulk of Lyons velvets you buy in the States are made in Genoa and imported into Lyons, where they receive the Lyons stamp and are then exported to America. You can buy enough velvet in Genoa for twenty-five dollars to make a five hundred dollar cloak in New York — so the ladies tell me. Of course, these things bring me back, by a natural and easy transition, to the

ASCENT OF VESUVIUS—CONTINUED.

And thus the wonderful Blue Grotto is suggested to me. It is situated on the island of Capri, twenty-two miles from Naples. We chartered a little steamer and went out there. Of course, the police boarded us and put us through a health examination, and inquired into our politics, before they would let us land. The airs these little insect governments put on are in the last degree ridiculous. They even put a policeman on board of our boat to keep an eye on us as long as we were in the Capri dominions. They thought we wanted to steal the grotto, I suppose. It was worth stealing. The entrance to the cave is four feet high and four feet wide, and is in the face of a lofty perpendicular cliff — the sea wall. You enter in small boats — and a tight squeeze it is, too. You cannot go in at all when the tide is up. Once within, you find yourself in an arched cavern about one hundred and sixty feet long, one hundred and twenty wide, and about seventy high. How deep it is no man knows. It goes down to the bottom of the ocean. The waters of this placid subterranean lake are the brightest, loveliest blue that can be imagined. They are as transparent as plate glas, and their coloring would shame the richest sky that ever bent over Italy. No tint could be more ravishing, no luster more superb. Throw a stone into the water, and the myriad of tiny bubbles that are created flash out a brilliant glare like blue theatrical fires. Dip an oar, and its blade turns to splendid frosted silver, tinted with blue. Let a man jump in, and instantly he is cased in an armor more gorgeous than ever kingly Crusader wore.

Then we went to Ischia, but I had already been to that island and tired myself to death "resting" a couple of days and studying human villainy, with the landlord of the Grande Sentinelle for a model. So we went to Procida, and from thence to Pozzuoi, where St. Paul landed after he sailed from Samos. I landed at precisely the same spot where St. Paul landed, and so did Dan and the others. It was a remarkable coincidence. St. Paul preached to these people seven days before he started to Rome.

Nero's Baths, the ruins of Baiae, the Temple of Serapis; Cumae, where the Cumaean Sibyl interpreted the oracles, the Lake Agnano, with its ancient submerged city still visible far down in tis depths — these and a hundred other points of interest we examined with critical imbecility, but the Grotto of the Dog claimed our chief attention, because we had heard and read so much about it. Everybody has written about the Grotto del Cane and its poisonous vapors, from Pliny down to Smith, and every tourist has held a dog over its floor by the legs to test the capabilities of the place. The dog dies in a minute and a half — a chicken instantly. As a general thing, strangers who crawl in there to sleep do not get up until they are called. And then they don't, either. The stranger that ventures to sleep there takes a permanent contract. I longed to see this grotto. I resolved to take a dog and hold him myself; suffocate him a little, and time him; suffocate him some more, and then finish him. We reached the grotto about three in the afternoon, and proceeded at once to make the experiments. But now, an important difficulty presented itself. We had no dog.

ASCENT OF VESUVIUS—CONTINUED.

At the Hermitage we were about fifteen or eighteen hundred feet above the sea, and thus far a portion of the ascent had been pretty abrupt. For the next two miles the road was a mixture — sometimes the ascent was abrupt and sometimes it was not; but one characteristic it possessed all the time, without failure — without modification — it was all uncompromisingly and unspeakably infamous. It was a rough, narrow trail, and led over an old lava-flow — a black ocean which was tumbled into a thousand fantastic shapes — a wild chaos of ruin, desolation, and barrenness — a wilderness of billowy upheavals, of furious whirpools, of miniature mountains rent asunder — of gnarled and knotted, wrinkled and twisted masses of blackness that mimicked branching roots, great vines, trunks of trees, all interlaced and mingled together; and all these weird shapes, all this turbulent panorama, all this stormy, far-stretching waste of blackness, with its thrilling suggestiveness of life, of action, of boiling, surging, furious motion, was petrified! — all stricken dead and cold in the instant of its maddest rioting! — fettered, paralyzed, and left to glower at heaven in impotent rage forevermore!

Finally we stood in a level, narrow valley (a valley that had been created by the terrific march of some old-time eruption) and on either hand towered the two steep peaks of Vesuvius. The one we had to climb — the one that contains the active volcano — seemed about eight hundred or one thousand feet high, and looked almost too straight-up-and-down for any man to climb, and certainly no mule could climb it with a man on his back. Four of these native pirates will carry you to the top in a sedan chair, if you wish it, but suppose they were to slip and let you fall, — is it likely that you would ever stop rolling? Not this side of eternity, perhaps. We left the mules, sharpened our finger nails, and began the ascent I have been writing about so long, at twenty minutes to six in the morning. The path led straight up a rugged sweep of loose chunks of pumice-stone, and for about every two steps forward we took, we slid back one. It was so excessively steep that we had to stop, every fifty or sixty steps, and rest a moment. To see our comrades, we had to look very nearly straight up at those above us, and very nearly straight down at those below. We stood on the summit at last — it had taken an hour and fifteen minutes to make the trip.

What we saw there was simply a circular crater — a circular ditch, if you please — about two hundred feet deep, and four or five hundred feet wide, whose inner wall was about half a mile in circumference. In the center of the great circus-ring thus formed was a torn and ragged upheaval a hundred feet high, all snowed over with a sulphur crust of many and many brilliant and beautiful color, and the ditch inclosed this like the moat of a castle, or surrounded it as a little river does a little island, if the simile is better. The sulphur coating of that island was gaudy in the extreme — all mingled together in the richest confusion were red, blue, brown, black, yellow, white — I do not know that there was a color, or shade of a color, or combination of colors, unrepresented — and when the sun burst through the morning mists and fired this tinted magnificence, it topped imperial Vesuvius like a jeweled crown!

The crater itself — the ditch — was not so variegated in coloring, but yet, in its softness, richness, and unpretentious elegance, it was more charming, more fascinating to the eye. There was nothing "loud" about its well-bred and well-dressed look. Beautiful? One could stand and look down upon it for a week without getting tired of it. It had the semblance of a pleasant meadow, whose slender grasses and whose velvety mosses were frosted with a shining dust, and tinted with palest green that deepened gradually to the darkest hue of the orange leaf, and deepened yet again into gravest brown, then faded into orange, then into brightest gold, and culminated in the delicate pink of a new-blown rose. Where portions of the meadow had sunk, and where other portions had been broken up like an ice-floe, the cavernous openings of the one, and the ragged upturned edges exposed by the other, were hung with a lacework of soft-tinted crystals of sulphur that changed their deformities into quaint shapes and figures that were full of grace and beauty.

The walls of the ditch were brilliant with yellow banks of sulphur and with lava and pumice-stone of many colors. No fire was visible anywhere, but gusts of sulphorus steam issued silently and invisibly from a thousand little cracks and fissures in the crater, and were wafted to our noses with every breeze. But so long as we kept our nostrils buried in our handkerchiefs, there was small danger of suffocation.

Some of the boys thrust long slips of paper down into holes and set them on fire, and so achieved the glory of lighting their cigars by the flames of Vesuvius, and others cooked eggs over fissures in the rocks and were happy.

The view from the summit would have been superb but for the fact that the sun could only pierce the mists at long intervals. Thus the glimpses we had of the grand panorama below were only fitful and unsatisfactory.

THE DESCENT.

The descent of the mountain was a labor of only four minutes. Instead of stalking down the rugged path we ascended, we chose one which was bedded knee-deep in loose ashes, and plowed our way with prodigious strides that would almost have shamed the performance of him of the seven-league boots.

The Vesuvius of to-day is a very poor affair compared to the mighty volcano of Kilauea, in the Sandwich Islands, but I am glad I visited it. It was well worth it.

It is said that during one of the grand eruptions of Vesuvius it discharged massy rocks weighing many tons a thousand feet into the air, its vast jets of smoke and steam ascended thirty miles toward the firmament, and clouds of its ashes were wafted abroad and fell upon the decks of ships seven hundred and fifty miles at sea! I will take the ashes at a moderate discount, if any one will take the thirty miles of smoke, but I do not feel able to take a commanding interest in the whole story by myself.

CHAPTER IV
THE BURIED CITY OF POMPEII.

They pronounce it Pom-*pay*-e. I always had an idea that you went down into Pompeii with torches, by the way of damp, dark stairways, just as you do in silver mines, and traversed gloomy tunnels with lava overhead and something on either hand like dilapidated prisons gouged out of the solid earth, that faintly resembled houses. But you do nothing of the kind. Fully one-half of the buried city, perhaps, is completely exhumed and thrown open freely to the light of day; and there stand the long rows of solidly-built brick houses (roofless) just as they stood eighteen hundred years ago, hot with the flaming sun; and there lie their floors, clean-swept, and not a bright fragment tarnished or wanting of the labored mosaics that pictured them with the beasts and birds and flowers which we copy in perishable carpets to-day; and there are the Venuses and Bacchuses and Adonises, making love and getting drunk in many-hued frescoes on the walls of saloon and bedchamber; and there are the narrow streets and narrower sidewalks, paved with flags of good hard lava, the one deeply rutted with the chariot-wheels, and the other with the passing feet of the Pompeiians of by-gone centuries; and there are the bake-shops, the temples, the halls of justice, the baths, the theaters — all clean-scraped and neat, and suggesting nothing of the nature of a silver mine away down in the bowels of the earth. The broken pillars lying about, the doorless doorways, and the crumbled tops of the wilderness of walls, were wonderfully suggestive of the "burnt district" in one of our cities, and if there had been any charred timbers, shattered windows, heaps of debris, and general blackness and smokiness about the place, the resemblance would have been perfect. But no — the sun

shines as brightly down on old Pompeii to-day as it did when
Christ was born in Bethlehem, and its streets are cleaner a hundred times than ever Pompeiian saw them in her prime. I know
whereof I speak — for in the great, chief thoroughfares (Merchant Street and the Street of Fortune) have I not seen with my
own eyes how for two hundred years at least the pavements were
not repaired! — how ruts five and even ten inches deep were
worn into the thick flagstones by the chariot-wheels of
generations of swindled taxpayers? And do I not know by these
signs that street commissioners of Pompeii never attended to
their business, and that if they never mended the pavements they
never cleaned them? And, besides, is it not the inborn nature of
street commissioners to avoid their duty whenever they get a
chance? I wish I knew the name of the last one that held office
in Pompeii so that I could give him a blast. I speak with feeling
on this subject, because I caught my foot in one of those ruts,
and the sadness that came over me when I saw the first poor
skeleton, with ashes and lava sticking to it, was tempered by the
reflection that may be that party was the street commissioner.

No — Pompeii is no longer a buried city. It is a city of hundreds and hundreds of roofless houses, and a tangled maze of
streets where one could easily get lost, without a guide, and have
to sleep in some ghostly palace that had known no living tenant
since that awful November night of eighteen centuries ago.

We passed through the gate which faces the Mediterranean
(called the "Marine Gate"), and by the rusty, broken image of
Minerva, still keeping tireless watch and ward over the
possessions it was powerless to save, and went up a long street
and stood in the broad court of the Forum of Justice. The floor
was level and clean, and up and down either side was a noble
colonnade of broken pillars, with their beautiful Ionic and
Corinthian columns scattered about them. At the upper end were
the vacant seats of the judges, and behind them we descended into a dungeon where the ashes and cinders had found two
prisoners chained on that memorable November night, and tortured them to death. How they must have tugged at the pitiless
fetters as the fierce fires surged around them!

Then we lounged through many and many a sumptuous
private mansion which we could not have entered without a formal invitation in incomprehensible Latin, in the olden time,
when the owners lived there — and we probably wouldn't have
got it. These people built their houses a good deal alike. The
floors were laid in fanciful figures wrought in mosaics of many-
colored marbles. At the threshold your eyes fall upon a Latin
sentence of welcome, sometimes, or a picture of a dog, with the
legend, "Beware of the Dog," and sometimes a picture of a bear
or a faun with no inscription at all. Then you enter a sort of

vestibule, where they used to keep the hat-rack, I suppose; next a
room with a large marble basin in the midst and the pipes of a
fountain; on either side are bedrooms; beyond the fountain is a
reception-room, then a little garden, dining-room, and so forth
and so on. The floors were all mosaic, the walls were stuccoed,
or frescoed, or ornamented with bas-reliefs, and here and there
were statues, large and small, and little fish-pools, and cascades
of sparkling water that sprang from secret places in the colonnade of handsome pillars that surrounded the court, and kept
the flower beds fresh and the air cool. Those Pompeiians were
very luxurious in their tastes and habits. The most exquisite
bronzes we have seen in Europe came from the exhumed cities of
Herculaneum and Pompeii, and also the finest cameos and the
most delicate engravings on precious stones; their pictures, the
leader of the orchestra beating time, and the "versatile" So-and-
So (who had "just returned from a most successful tour in the
provinces to play his last and farewell engagement of positively
six nights only, in Pompeii, previous to his departure for Herculaneum") charging around the stage and piling the agony
mountains high — but I could not do it with such a "house" as
that; those empty benches tied my fancy down to dull reality. I
said, these people that ought to be here have been dead, and
still, and moldering to dust for ages and ages, and will never
care for the trifles and follies of life any more forever —
"Owing to circumstances, etc., etc., there will not be any performance to-night." Close down the curtain. Put out the lights.

And so I turned away and went through shop after shop and
store after store, far down the long street of the merchants, and
called for the wares of Rome and the East, but the tradesmen
were gone, the marts were silent, and nothing was left but the
broken jars all set in cement of cinders and ashes; the wine and
the oil that once had filled them were gone with their owners.

In a bake-shop was a mill for grinding the grain, and the furnaces for baking the bread; and they say that here, in the same
furnaces, the exhumers of Pompeii found nice, well-baked loaves
which the baker had not found time to remove from the ovens
the last time he left his shop, because circumstances compelled
him to leave in such a hurry.

In one house (the only building in Pompeii which no woman is
now allowed to enter) were the small rooms and short beds of
solid masonry, just as they were in the old times, and on the
walls were pictures which looked almost as fresh as if they were
painted yesterday, but which no pen could have the hardihood to
describe; and here and there were Latin inscriptions — obscene
scintillations of wit, scratched by hands that possibly were uplifted to Heaven for succor in the midst of a driving storm of
fire before the night was done.

In one of the principal streets was a ponderous stone tank, and a waterspout that supplied it, and where the tired, heated toilers from the Campagna used to rest their right hands when they bent over to put their lips to the spout, the thick stone was worn down to a broad groove an inch or two deep. Think of the countless thousands of hands that had pressed that spot in the ages that are gone, to so reduce a stone that is as hard as iron!

They had a great public bulletin-board in Pompeii — a place where announcements for gladiatorial combats, elections, and such things, were posted — not on perishable paper, but carved in enduring stone. One lady, who, I take it, was rich and well brought up, advertised a dwelling or so to rent, with baths and all the modern improvements, and several hundred shops, stipulating that the dwellings should not be put to immoral purposes. You can find out who lived in many a house in Pompeii by the carved stone door-plates affixed to them: and in the same way you can tell who they were that occupy the tombs. Everywhere around are things that reveal to you something of the customs and history of this forgotten people. But what would a volcano leave of an American city, if it once rained its cinders on it? Hardly a sign or a symbol to tell its story.

In one of these long Pompeiian halls the skeleton of a man was found, with ten pieces of gold in one hand and a large key in the other. He had seized his money and started toward the door, but the fiery tempest caught him at the very threshold, and he sank down and died. One more minute of precious time would have saved him. I saw the skeletons of a man, a woman, and two young girls. The woman had her hands spread wide apart, as if in mortal terror, and I imagined I could still trace upon her shapeless face something of the expression of wild despair that distorted it when the heavens rained fire in these streets, so many ages ago. The girls and the man lay with their faces upon their arms, as if they had tried to shield them from the enveloping cinders. In one apartment eighteen skeletons were found, all in sitting postures, and blackened places on the walls still mark their shapes and show their attitudes, like shadows. One of them, a woman, still wore upon her skeleton throat a necklace, with her name engraved upon it — JULIE DI DIOMEDE.

But perhaps the most poetical thing Pompeii has yielded to modern research, was that grand figure of a Roman soldier, clad in complete armor; who, true to his duty, true to his proud name of a soldier of Rome, and full of the stern courage which had given to that name its glory, stood to his post by the city gate, erect and unflinching, till the hell that raged around him *burned out* the dauntless spirit it could not conquer.

We never read of Pompeii but we think of that soldier; we cannot write of Pompeii without the natural impulse to grant to

him the mention he so well deserves. Let us remember that he
was a soldier — not a policeman — and so, priase him. Being a
soldier, he stayed, — because the warrior instinct forbade him to
fly. Had he been a policeman he would have stayed, also —
because he would have been asleep.

There are not half a dozen flights of stairs in Pompeii, and no
other evidences that the houses were more than one story high.
The people did not live in the clouds, as do the Venetians, the
Genovese and Neapolitans of to-day.

We came out from under the solemn mysteries of this city of
the Venerable Past — this city which perished, with all its old
ways and its quaint old fashions about it, remote centuries ago,
when the Disciples were preaching the new religion, which is as
old as the hills to us now — and went dreaming among the trees
that grow over acres and acres of its still buried streets and
squares, till a shrill whistle and the cry of *"All aboard — last
train for Naples!"* woke me up and reminded me that I belonged
in the nineteenth century, and was not a dusty mummy, caked
with ashes and cinders, eighteen hundred years old. The transition was startling. The idea of a railroad train actually running
to old dead Pompeii, and whistling irreverently, and calling for
passengers in the most bustling and business-like way, was as
strange a thing as one could imagine, and as unpoetical and
disagreeable as it was strange.

Compare the cheerful life and the sunshine of this day with
the horrors the younger Pliny saw here, the 9th of November,
A.D. 79, when he was so bravely striving to remove his mother
out of reach of harm, while she begged him, with all a mother's
unselfishness, to leave her to perish and save himself.

"By this time the murky darkness had so increased that one might have
believed himself abroad in a black and moonless night, or in a chamber where all
the lights had been extinguished. On every hand was heard the complaints of
women, the wailing of children, and the cries of men. One called his father,
another his son, and another his wife, and only by their voices could they know
each other. Many in their despair begged that death would come and end their
distress.

"Some implored the gods to succor them, and some believed that the night was
the last, the eternal night which should engulf the universe!

"Even so it seemed to me — and I consoled myself for the coming death with
the reflection: BEHOLD! THE WORLD IS PASSING AWAY!"

.   .   .   .

After browsing among the stately ruins of Rome, of Baiae, of
Pompeii, and after glancing down the long marble ranks of battered and nameless imperial heads that stretch down the
corridors of the Vatican, one thing strikes me with a force it
never had before: the unsubstantial, unlasting character of fame.
Men lived long lives, in the olden time, and struggled feverishly
through them, toiling like slaves, in oratory, in generalship, or in
literature, and then laid them down and died, happy in the

possession of an enduring history and a deathless name. Well, twenty little centuries flutter away, and what is left of these things? A crazy inscription on a block of stone, which snuffy antiquaries bother over and tangle up and make nothing out of but a bare name (which they spell wrong) — no history, no tradition, no poetry — nothing that can give it even a passing interest. What may be left to General Grant's great name forty centuries hence? This — in the Encyclopedia for A.D. 5868, possibly.

"URIAH S. (or Z.) GRAUNT — popular poet of ancient times in the Aztec provinces of the United States of British America. Some authors say flourished about A.D. 742; but the learned Ah-ah Foo-foo states that he was a contemporary of Scharkspyre, the English poet, and flourished about A.D. 1328, some three centuries *after* the Trojan war instead of before it. He wrote 'Rock me to Sleep, Mother.' "

These thoughts sadden me. I will to bed.

CHAPTER V

Home again! For the first time, in many weeks, the ship's entire family met and shook hands on the quarter-deck. They had gathered from many points of the compass and from many lands, but not one was missing; there was no tale of sickness or death among the flock to dampen the pleasure of the reunion. Once more there was a full audience on deck to listen to the sailors' chorus as they got the anchor up, and to wave an adieu to the land as we sped away from Naples.

The seats were full at dinner again, the domino parties were complete, and the life and bustle on the upper deck in the fine moonlight at night was like old times — old times that had been gone weeks only, but yet they were weeks so crowded with incident, adventure, and excitement, that they seemed almost like years. There was no lack of cheerfulness on board the *Quaker City*. For once, her title was a misnomer.

At seven in the evening, with the western horizon all golden from the sunken sun, and specked with distant ships, the full moon sailing high over head, the dark blue of the sea under foot, and a strange sort of twilight affected by all these different lights and colors around us and about us, we sighted superb Stromboli. With what majesty the monarch held his lonely state above the level sea! Distance clothed him in a purple gloom, and added a veil of shimmering mist that so softened his rugged features that we seemed to see him through a web of silver gauze. His torch was out; his fires were smoldering; a tall column of smoke that rose up and lost itself in the growing moonlight was all the sign he gave that he was a living Autocrat of the Sea and not the specter of a dead one.

At two in the morning we swept through the Straits of

Messina, and so bright was the moonlight that Italy on the one
hand and Sicily on the other seemed almost as distinctly visible
as though we looked at them from the middle of a street we were
traversing. The city of Messina, milk-white, and starred and
spangled all over with gaslights, was a fairy spectacle. A great
party of us were on deck smoking and making a noise, and
waiting to see famous Scylla and Charybdis. And presently the
Oracle stepped out with his eternal spy-glass and squared himself
on the deck like another Colossus of Rhodes. It was a surprise to
see him abroad at such an hour. Nobody supposed he cared
anything about an old fable like that of Scylla and Charybdis.
One of the boys said:

"Hello, doctor, what are you doing up here at this time of
night? — What do you want to see this place for?"

"What do *I* want to see this place for? Young man, little do
you know me, or you wouldn't ask such a question. I wish to see
all the places that's mentioned in the Bible."

"Stuff! This place isn't mentioned in the Bible."

"It ain't mentioned in the Bible! — *this* place ain't — well
now, what place *is* this, since you know so much about it?"

"Why it's Scylla and Charybdis."

"Scylla and Cha — confound it, I thought it was Sodom and
Gomorrah!"

And he closed up his glass and went below. The above is the
ship story. Its plausibility is marred a little by the fact that the
Oracle was not a biblical student, and did not spend much of his
time instructing himself about Scriptural localities. — They say
the Oracle complains, in this hot weather, lately, that the only
beverage in the ship that is passable, is the butter. He did not
mean butter, of course, but inasmuch as that article remains in a
melted state now since we are out of ice, it is fair to give him the
credit of getting one long word in the right place, anyhow, for
once in his life. He said, in Rome, that the Pope was a noble-
looking old man, but he never *did* think much of his Iliad.

We spent one pleasant day skirting along the Isles of Greece.
They are very mountainous. Their prevailing tints are gray and
brown, approaching to red. Little white villages, surrounded by
trees, nestle in the valleys or roost upon the lofty perpendicular
sea-walls.

We had one fine sunset — a rich carmine flush that suffused
the western sky and cast a ruddy glow far over the sea. Fine sunsets seem to be rare in this part of the world — or at least,
striking ones. They are soft, sensuous, lovely — they are
exquisite, refined, effeminate, but we have seen no sunsets here
yet like the gorgeous conflagrations that flame in the track of the
sinking sun in our high northern latitudes.

But what were sunsets to us, with the wild excitement upon us

of approaching the most renowned of cities! What cared we for
outward visions, when Agamemnon, Achilles, and a thousand
other heroes of the great Past were marching in ghostly
procession through our fancies? What were sunsets to us, who
were about to live and breathe and walk in actual Athens; yea,
and go far down into the dead centuries and bid in person for
the slaves, Diogenes and Plato, in the public market-place, or
gossip with the neighbors about the siege of Troy or the splendid
deeds of Marathon? We scorned to consider sunsets.

We arrived, and entered the ancient harbor of the Piraeus at
last. We dropped anchor within half a mile of the village. Away
off, across the undulating Plain of Attica, could be seen a little
square-topped hill with a something on it, which our glasses soon
discovered to be the ruined edifices of the citadel of the
Athenians, and most prominent among them loomed the
venerable Parthenon. So exquisitely clear and pure is this wonderful atmosphere that every column of the noble structure was
discernible through the telescope, and even the smaller ruins
about it assumed some semblance of shape. This at a distance of
five or six miles. In the valley, near the Acropolis (the square-
tipped hill before spoken of), Athens itself could be vaguely
made out with an ordinary lorgnette. Everybody was anxious to
get ashore and visit these classic localities as quickly as possible.
No land we had yet seen had aroused such universal interest
among the passengers.

But bad news came. The commandant of the Piraeus came in
his boat, and said we must either depart or else get outside the
harbor and remain imprisoned in our ship, under rigid quarantine, for eleven days! So we took up the anchor and moved outside, to lie a dozen hours or so, taking in supplies, and then sail
for Constantinople. It was the bitterest disappointment we had
yet experienced. To lie a whole day in sight of the Acropolis,
and yet be obliged to go away without visiting Athens! Disappointment was hardly a strong enough word to describe the circumstances.

All hands were on deck, all the afternoon, with books and
maps and glasses, trying to determine which "narrow rocky
ridge" was the Areopagus, which sloping hill the Pnyx, which
elevation the Museum Hill, and so on. And we got things confused. Discussion became heated, and party spirit ran high.
Church members were gazing with emotion upon a hill which
they said was the one St. Paul preached from, and another fac-
tion claimed that that hill was Hymettus, and another that it was
Pentelicon! After all the trouble, we could be certain of only one
thing — the square-topped hill was the Acropolis, and the grand
ruin that crowned it was the Parthenon, whose picture we knew
in infancy in the schoolbooks.

We inquired of everybody who came near the ship, whether there were guards in the Piraeus, whether they were strict, what the chances were of capture should any of us slip ashore, and in case any of us made the venture and were caught, what would be probably done to us? The answers were discouraging: There was a strong guard or police force; the Piraeus was a small town, and any stranger seen in it would surely attract attention — capture would be certain. The commandant said the punishment would be "heavy"; when asked "How heavy?" he said it would be "very severe" — that was all we could get out of him.

At eleven o'clock at night, when most of the ship's company were abed, four of us stole softly ashore in a small boat, a clouded moon favoring the enterprise, and started two and two, and far apart, over a low hill, intending to go clear around the Piraeus, out of the range of its police. Picking our way so stealthily over that rocky, nettle-grown eminence, made me feel a good deal as if I were on my way somewhere to steal something. My immediate comrade and I talked in an undertone about quarantine laws and their penalties, but we found nothing cheering in the subject. I was posted. Only a few days before, I was talking with our captain, and he mentioned the case of a man who swam ashore from a quarantined ship somewhere, and got imprisoned six months for it; and when he was in Genoa a few years ago, a captain of a quarantined ship went in his boat to a departing ship, which was already outside of the harbor, and put a letter on board to be taken to his family, and the authorities imprisoned him three months for it, and then conducted him and his ship fairly to sea, and warned him never to show himself in that port again while he lived. This kind of conversation did no good, further than to give a sort of dismal interest to our quarantine-breaking expedition, and so we dropped it. We made the entire circuit of the town without seeing anybody but one man, who stared at us curiously, but said nothing, and a dozen persons asleep on the ground before their doors, whom we walked among and never woke — but we woke up dogs enough, in all conscience — we always had one or two barking at our heels, and several times we had as many as ten and twelve at once. They made such a preposterous din that persons aboard our ship said they could tell how we were progressing for a long time, and where we were, by the barking of the dogs. The clouded moon still favored us. When we had made the whole circuit, and were passing among the houses on the further side of the town, the moon came out splendidly, but we no longer feared the light. As we approached a well, near a house, to get a drink, the owner merely glanced at us and went within. He left the quiet, slumbering town at our mercy. I record it here proudly, that we didn't do anything to it.

Seeing no road, we took a tall hill to the left of the distant
Acropolis for a mark, and steered straight for it over all obstructions, and over a little rougher piece of country than exists
anywhere else outside of the State of Nevada, perhaps. Part of
the way it was covered with small, loose stones — we trod on six
at a time, and they all rolled. Another part of it was dry, loose,
newly-plowed ground. Still another part of it was a long stretch
of low grapevines, which were tanglesome and troublesome, and
which we took to be brambles. The Attic Plain, barring the
grapevines, was a barren, desolate, unpoetical waste — I wonder
what it was in Greece's Age of Glory, five hundred years before
Christ?

In the neighborhood of one o'clock in the morning, when we
were heated with fast walking and parched with thirst, Denny exclaimed, "Why, these weeds are grapevines!" and in five
minutes we had a score of bunches of large, white, delicious
grapes, and were reaching down for more when a dark shape
rose mysteriously up out of the shadows beside us and said
"Ho!" And so we left.

In ten minutes more we struck into a beautiful road, and
unlike some others we had stumbled upon at intervals, it led in
the right direction. We followed it. It was broad and smooth and
white — handsome and in perfect repair, and shaded on both
sides for a mile or so with single ranks of trees, and also with
luxuriant vineyards. Twice we entered and stole grapes, and the
second time somebody shouted at us from some invisible place.
Whereupon we left again. We speculated in grapes no more on
that side of Athens.

Shortly we came upon an ancient stone aqueduct, built upon
arches, and from that time forth we had ruins all about us — we
were approaching our journey's end. We could not see the
Acropolis now or the high hill, either, and I wanted to follow
the road till we were abreast of them, but the others overruled
me, and we toiled laboriously up the stony hill immediately in
our front — and from its summit saw another — climbed it and
saw another! It was an hour of exhausting work. Soon we came
upon a row of open graves, cut in the solid rock — (for a while
one of them served Socrates for a prison) — we passed around
the shoulder of the hill, and the citadel, in all its ruined
magnificence, burst upon us! We hurried across the ravine and
up a winding road, and stood on the old Acropolis, with the
prodigious walls of the citadel towering above our heads. We did
not stop to inspect their massive blocks of marble, or measure
their height, or guess at their extraordinary thickness, but passed
at once through a great arched passage like a railway tunnel, and
went straight to the gate that leads to the ancient temples. It was
locked! So, after all, it seemed that we were not to see the great

Parthenon face to face. We sat down and held a council of war. Result: The gate was only a flimsy structure of wood — we would break it down. It seemed like desecration, but then we had traveled far, and our necessities were urgent. We could not hunt up guides and keepers — we must be on the ship before daylight. So we argued. This was all very fine, but when we came to break the gate, we could not do it. We moved around an angle of the wall and found a low bastion — eight feet high without — ten or twelve within. Denny prepared to scale it, and we got ready to follow. By dint of hard scrambling he finally straddled the top, but some loose stones crumbled away and fell with a crash into the court within. There was instantly a banging of doors and a shout. Denny dropped from the wall in a twinkling, and we retreated in disorder to the gate. Xerxes took that mighty citadel four hundred and eighty years before Christ, when his five millions of soldiers and camp-followers followed him to Greece, and if we four Americans could have remained unmolested five minutes longer, we would have taken it too.

The garrison had turned out — four Greeks. We clamored at the gate, and they admitted us. [Bribery and corruption.]

We crossed a large court, entered a great door, and stood upon a pavement of purest white marble, deeply worn by footprints. Before us, in the flooding moonlight, rose the noblest ruins we had ever looked upon — the Propylaea; a small temple of Minerva; the Temple of Hercules, and the grand Parthenon. [We got these names from the Greek guide, who didn't seem to know more than seven men ought to know.] These edifices were all built of the whitest Pentelic marble, but have a pinkish stain upon them now. Where any part is broken, however, the fracture looks like fine loaf sugar. Six caryatides, or marble women, clad in flowing robes, support the portico of the Temple of Hercules, but the porticoes and colonnades of the other structures are formed of massive Doric and Ionic pillars, whose flutings and capitals are still measurably perfect, notwithstanding the centuries that have gone over them and the sieges they have suffered. The Parthenon, originally, was two hundred and twenty-six feet long, one hundred wide, and seventy high, and had two rows of great columns, eight in each, at either end, and single rows of seventeen each down the sides, and was one of the most graceful and beautiful edifices ever erected.

Most of the Parthenon's imposing columns are still standing, but the roof is gone. It was a perfect building two hundred and fifty years ago, when a shell dropped into the Venetian magazine stored here, and the explosion which followed wrecked and unroofed it. I remember but little about the Parthenon, and I have put in one or two facts and figures for the use of other people with short memories. Got them from the guide-book.

As we wandered thoughtfully down the marble-paved length of this stately temple, the scene about us was strangely impressive. Here and there, in lavish profusion, were gleaming white statues of men and women, propped against blocks of marble, some of them armless, some without legs, others headless — but all looking mournful in the moonlight, and startlingly human! They rose up and confronted the midnight intruder on every side — they stared at him with stony eyes from unlooked-for nooks and recesses; they peered at him over fragmentary heaps far down the desolate corridors; they barred his way in the midst of the broad forum, and solemnly pointed with handless arms the way from the sacred fane; and through the roofless temple the moon looked down, and banded the floor and darkened the scattered fragments and broken statues with the slanting shadows of the columns.

What a world of ruined sculpture was about us! Set up in rows — stacked up in piles — scattered broadcast over the wide area of the Acropolis — were hundreds of crippled statues of all sizes and of the most exquisite workmanship; and vast fragments of marble that once belonged to the entablatures, covered with bas-reliefs representing battles and sieges, ships of war with three and four tiers of oars, pageants and processions — everything one could think of. History says that the temples of the Acropolis were filled with the noblest works of Praxiteles and Phidias, and of many a great master in sculpture besides — and surely these elegant fragments attest it.

We walked out into the grass-grown, fragment-strewn court beyond the Parthenon. It startled us, every now and then, to see a stony white face stare suddenly up at us out of the grass with its dead eyes. The place seemed alive with ghosts. I half expected to see the Athenian heroes of twenty centuries ago glide out of the shadows and steal into the old temple they knew so well and regarded with such boundless pride.

The full moon was riding high in the cloudless heavens now. We sauntered carelessly and unthinkingly to the edge of the lofty battlements of the citadel, and looked down — a vision! And such a vision! Athens by moonlight! The prophet that thought the splendors of the New Jerusalem were revealed to him, surely saw this instead! It lay in the level plain right under our feet — all spread abroad like a picture — and we looked down upon it as we might have looked from a balloon. We saw no semblance of a street, but every house, every window, every clinging vine, every projection, was as distinct and sharply marked as if the time were noonday; and yet there was no glare, no glitter, nothing harsh or repulsive — the noiseless city was flooded with the mellowest light that ever streamed from the moon, and seemed like some living creature wrapped in peaceful slumber.

On its further side was a little temple, whose delicate pillars and ornate front glowed with a rich luster that chained the eye like a spell; and nearer by, the palace of the king reared its creamy walls out of the midst of a great garden of shrubbery that was flecked all over with a random shower of amber lights — a spray of golden sparks that lost their brightness in the glory of the moon, and glinted softly upon the sea of dark foliage like the pallid stars of the milky-way. Overhead the stately columns, majestic still in their ruin — under foot the dreaming city — in the distance the silver sea — not on the broad earth is there another picture half so beautiful!

As we turned and moved again through the temple, I wished that the illustrious men who had sat in it in the remote ages could visit it again and reveal themselves to our curious eyes — Plato, Aristotle, Demosthenes, Socrates, Phocion, Pythagoras, Euclid, Pindar, Xenophon, Herodotus, Praxiteles and Phidias, Zeuxis the painter. What a constellation of celebrated names! But more than all, I wished that old Diogenes, groping so patiently with his lantern, searching so zealously for one solitary honest man in all the world, might meander along and stumble on our party. I ought not to say it, may be, but still I suppose he would have put out his light.

We left the Parthenon to keep its watch over old Athens, as it had kept it for twenty-three hundred years, and went and stood outside the walls of the citadel. In the distance was the ancient, but still almost perfect, Temple of Theseus, and close by, looking to the West, was the Bema, from whence Demosthenes thundered his philippics and fired the wavering patriotism of his countrymen. To the right was Mars Hill, where the Areopagus sat in ancient times, and where St. Paul defined his position, and below was the market-place where he "disputed daily" with the gossip-loving Athenians. We climbed the stone steps St. Paul ascended, and stood in the square-cut place he stood in, and tried to recollect the Bible account of the matter — but for certain reasons, I could not recall the words. I have found them since:

"Now while Paul waited for them at Athens, his spirit was stirred in him, when he saw the city wholly given up to idolatry.

"Therefore disputed he in the synagogue with the Jews, and with the devout persons, and in the market daily with them that met with him.

. . . .

"And they took him and brought him unto Areopagus, saying, May we know what this new doctrine whereof thou speakest is?

. . . .

"Then Paul stood in the midst of Mars hill, and said, Ye men of Athens, I perceive that in all things ye are too superstitious;

"For as I passed by and beheld your devotions, I found an altar with this inscription: TO THE UNKNOWN GOD. Whom, therefore, ye ignorantly worship, him declare I unto you." — *Acts*, ch. xvii.

It occured to us, after a while, that if we wanted to get home before daylight betrayed us, we had better be moving. So we hurried away. When far on our road, we had a parting view of the Parthenon, with the moonlight streaming through its open colonnades and touching its capitals with silver. As it looked then, solemn, grand, and beautiful, it will always remain in our memories.

As we marched along, we began to get over our fears, and ceased to care much about quarantine scouts or anybody else. We grew bold and reckless; and once, in a sudden burst of courage, I even threw a stone at a dog. It was a pleasant reflection, though, that I did not hit him, because his master might just possibly have been a policeman. Inspired by this happy failure, my valor became utterly uncontrollable, and at intervals I absolutely whistled, though on a moderate key. But boldness breeds boldness, and shortly I plunged into a vineyard, in the full light of the moon, and captured a gallon of superb grapes, not even minding the presence of a peasant who rode by on a mule. Denny and Birch followed my example. Now I had grapes enough for a dozen, but then Jackson was all swollen up with courage, too, and he was obliged to enter a vineyard presently. The first bunch he seized brought trouble. A frowsy, bearded brigand sprang into the road with a shout, and flourished a musket in the light of the moon! We sidled toward the Piraeus — not running, you understand, but only advancing with celerity. The brigand shouted again, but still we advanced. It was getting late, and we had no time to fool away on every ass that wanted to drivel Greek platitudes to us. We would just as soon have talked with him as not if we had not been in a hurry. Presently Denny said, "Those fellows are following us!"

We turned, and, sure enough, there they were — three fantastic pirates armed with guns. We slackened our pace to let them come up, and in the meantime I got out my cargo of grapes and dropped them firmly but reluctantly into the shadows by the wayside. But I was not afraid. I only felt that it was not right to steal grapes. And all the more so when the owner was around — and not only around, but with his friends around also. The villains came up and searched a bundle Dr. Birch had in his hand, and scowled upon him when they found it had nothing in it but some holy rocks from Mars Hill, and these were not contraband. They evidently suspected him of playing some wretched fraud upon them, and seemed half inclined to scalp the party. But finally they dismissed us with a warning, couched in excellent Greek, I suppose, and dropped tranquilly in our wake. When they had gone three hundred yards they stopped, and we went on rejoiced. But behold, another armed rascal came out of the shadows and took their place, and followed us two hundred yards. Then he delivered us over to another miscreant, who emerged from some mysterious place, and he in turn to another! For a mile and a half our rear was guarded all the while by armed men. I never traveled in so much state before in all my life.

It was a good while after that before we ventured to steal any more grapes, and when we did we stirred up another troublesome brigand, and then we ceased all further speculation in that line. I suppose that fellow that rode by on the mule posted all the sentinels, from Athens to the Piraeus, about us.

Every field on that long route was watched by an armed sentinel, some of whom had fallen asleep, no doubt, but were on hand, nevertheless. This shows what sort of a country modern Attica is — a community of questionable characters. These men were not there to guard their possessions against strangers, but against each other; for strangers seldom visit Athens and the Piraeus, and when they do, they go in daylight, and can buy all the grapes they want for a trifle. The modern inhabitants are confiscators and falsifiers of high repute, if gossip speaks truly concerning them, and I freely believe it does.

Just as the earliest tinges of the dawn flushed the eastern sky and turned the pillared Parthenon to a broken harp hung in the pearly horizon, we closed our thirteenth mile of weary, round-about marching, and emerged upon the seashore abreast the ships, with our usual escort of fifteen hundred Piraean dogs howling at our heels. We hailed a boat that was two or three hundred yards from shore, and discovered in a moment that it was a police-boat on the lookout for any quarantine breakers that might chance to be abroad. So we dodged — we were used to that by this time — and when the scouts reached the spot we had so lately occupied, we were absent. They cruised along the shore, but in the wrong direction, and shortly our own boat issued from the gloom and took us aboard. They had heard our signal on the ship. We rowed noiselessly away, and before the police-boat came in sight again, we were safe at home once more.

Four more of our passengers were anxious to visit Athens, and started half an hour after we returned; but they had not been ashore five minutes till the police discovered and chased them so hotly that they barely escaped to their boat again, and that was all. They pursued the enterprise no further.

We set sail for Constantinople to-day, but some of us little care for that. We have seen all there was to see in the old city that had its birth sixteen hundred years before Christ was born, and was an old town before the foundations of Troy were laid — and saw it in its most attractive aspect. Wherefore, why should *we* worry?

Two other passengers ran the blockade successfully last night. So we learned this morning. They slipped away so quietly that they were not missed from the ship for several hours. They had the hardihood to march into the Piraeus in the early dusk and hire a carriage. They ran some danger of adding two or three months' imprisonment to the other novelties of their Holy Land Pleasure Excurion. I admire "cheek."* But they went and came safely, and never walked a step.

CHAPTER VI

From Athens all through the islands of the Grecian Archipelago, we saw little but forbidding sea-walls and barren hills, sometimes surmounted by three or four graceful columns of some ancient temple, lonely and deserted—a fitting symbol of the desolation that has come upon all Greece in these latter ages. We saw no plowed fields, very few villages, no trees or grass or vegetation of any kind, scarcely, and hardly ever an isolated house. Greece is a bleak, unsmiling desert, without agriculture, manufactures, or commerce, apparently. What supports its provety-stricken people or its government, is a mystery.

I suppose that ancient Greece and modern Greece compared, furnish the most extravagant contrast to be found in history. George I, an infant of eighteen, and a scraggy nest of foreign office-holders, sit in the places of Themistocles, Pericles, and the illustrious scholars and generals of the Golden Age of Greece. The fleets that were the wonder of the world when the Parthenon was new, are a beggarly handful of fishing-smacks now, and the manly people that performed such miracles of valor at Marathon are only a tribe of unconsidered slaves to-day. The classic Ilissus has gone dry, and so have all the sources of Grecian wealth and greatness. The nation numbers only eight hundred thousand souls, and there is poverty and misery and mendacity enough among them to furnish forty millions and be liberal about it. Under King Otho the revenues of the state were five millions of dollars—raised from a tax of *one-tenth* of all the agricultural products of the land (which tenth the farmer had to bring to the royal granaries on pack-mules any distance not exceeding six leagues) and from extravagant taxes on trade and commerce. Out of that five millions the small tyrant tried to keep an army of ten thousand men, pay all the hundreds of useless Grand Equerries in Waiting, First Grooms of the Bedchamber, Lord High Chancellors of the Exploded Exchequer, and all the other absurdities which these puppy-kingdoms indulge in, in imitation of the great monarchies; and in addition he set

*Quotation from the Pilgrims.

about building a white marble palace to cost about five millions itself. The result was, simply: Ten into five goes no times and none over. All these things could not be done with five millions, and Otho fell into trouble.

The Greek throne, with its unpromising adjuncts of a ragged population of ingenious rascals who were out of employment eight months in the year because there was little for them to borrow and less to confiscate, and a waste of barren hills and weed-grown deserts, went begging for a good while. It was offered to one of Victoria's sons, and afterward to various other younger sons of royalty who had no thrones and were out of business, but they all had the charity to decline the dreary honor, and veneration enough for Greece's ancient greatness to refuse to mock her sorrowful rags and dirt with a tinsel throne in this day of her humiliation—till they came to this young Danish George, and he took it. He had finished the splendid palace I saw in the radiant moonlight the other night, and is doing many other things for the salvation of Greece, they say.

We sailed through the barren Archipelago, and into the narrow channel they sometimes call the Dardanelles and sometimes the Hellespont. This part of the country is rich in historic reminiscences, and poor as Sahara in everything else. For instance, as we approached the Dardanelles, we coasted along the Plains of Troy and past the mouth of the Scamander; we saw where Troy had stood (in the distance), and where it does not stand now—a city that perished when the world was young. The poor Trojans are all dead now. They were born too late to see Noah's ark, and died too soon to see our menagerie. We saw where Agamemnon's fleets rendezvoused, and away inland a mountain which the map said was Mount Ida. Within the Hellespont we saw where the original first shoddy contract mentioned in history was carried out, and the "parties of the second part" gently rebuked by Xerxes. I speak of the famous bridge of boats which Xerxes ordered to be built over the narrowest part of the Hellespont (where it is only two or three miles wide). A moderate gale destroyed the flimsy structure, and the King, thinking that to publicly rebuke the contractors might have a good effect on the next set, called them out before the army and had them beheaded. In the next ten minutes he let a new contract for the bridge. It has been observed by ancient writers that the second bridge was a very good bridge. Xerxes crossed his host of five millions of men on it, and if it had not been purposely destroyed, it would probably have been there yet. If our government would rebuke some of our shoddy contractors occasionally, it might work much good. In the Hellespont we saw where Leander and Lord Byron swam across, the one to see her upon whom his soul's affections were fixed with a devotion that

only death could impair, and the other merely for a flyer, as
Jack says. We had two noted tombs near us, too. On one shore
slept Ajax, and on the other Hecuba.

We had water batteries and forts on both sides of the
Hellespont, flying the crimson flag of Turkey, with its white
crescent, and occasionally a village, and sometimes a train of
camels; we had all these to look at till we entered the broad sea
of Marmora, and then the land soon fading from view, we
resumed euchre and whist once more.

We dropped anchor in the mouth of the Golden Horn at
daylight in the morning. Only three or four of us were up to see
the great Ottoman capital. The passengers do not turn out at un-
seasonable hours, as they used to, to get the earliest possible
glimpse of strange foreign cities. They are well over that. If we
were lying in sight of the Pyramids of Egypt, they would not
come on deck until after breakfast, nowadays.

The Golden Horn is a narrow arm of the sea, which branches
from the Bosporus (a sort of broad river which connects the
Marmora and Black Seas), and, curving around, divides the city
in the middle. Galata and Pera are on one side of the Bosporus,
and the Golden Horn; Stamboul (ancient Byzantium) is upon the
other. On the other bank of the Bosporus is Scutari and other
suburbs of Constantinople. This great city contains a million
inhabitants, but so narrow are its streets, and so crowded
together are its houses, that it does not cover much more than
half as much ground as New York city. Seen from the anchorage
or from a mile or so up the Bosporus, it is by far the handsomest city we have seen. Its dense array of houses swells upward from the water's edge, and spreads over the domes of
many hills; and the gardens that peep out here and there, the
great globes of the mosques, and the countless minarets that
meet the eye everywhere, invest the metropolis with the quaint
Oriental aspect one dreams of when he reads books of Eastern
travel. Constantinople makes a noble picture.

But its attractiveness begins and ends with its picturesqueness.
From the time one starts ashore till he gets back again, he
execrates it. The boat he goes in is admirably miscalculated for
the service it is built for. It is handsomely and neatly fitted up,
but no man could handle it well in the turbulent currents that
sweep down the Bosporus from the Black Sea, and few men
could row it satisfactorily even in still water. It is a long, light
canoe (caique), large at one end and tapering to a knife blade at
the other. They make that long sharp end the bow, and you can
imagine how these boiling currents spin it about. It has two oars,
and sometimes four, and no rudder. You start to go to a given
point and you run in fifty different directions before you get
there. First one oar is backing water, and then the other; it is

seldom that both are going ahead at once. This kind of boating is calculated to drive an impatient man mad in a week. The boatmen are the awkwardest, the stupidest, and the most unscientific on earth, without question.

Ashore, it was—well, it was an eternal circus. People were thicker than bees, in those narrow streets, and the men were dressed in all the outrageous, outlandish, idolatrous, extravagant, thunder-and-lightning costumes that every a tailor with the delirium tremens and seven devils could conceive of. There was no freak in dress too crazy to be indulged in; no absurdity too absurd to be tolerated; no frenzy in ragged diabolism too fantastic to be attempted. No two men were dressed alike. It was a wild masquerade of all imaginable costumes—every struggling throng in every street was a dissolving view of stunning contrasts. Some patriarchs wore awful turbans, but the grand mass of the infidel horde wore the fiery red skull-cap they call a fez. All the remainder of the raiment they indulged in was utterly indescribable.

The shops here are mere coops, mere boxes, bathrooms, closets—anything you please to call them—on the first floor. The Turks sit cross-legged in them, and work and trade and smoke long pipes, and smell like—like Turks. That covers the ground. Crowding the narrow streets in front of them are beggars, who beg forever, yet never collect anything; and wonderful cripples, distorted out of all semblance of humanity, almost; vagabonds driving laden asses; porters carrying drygoods boxes as large as cottages on their backs; peddlers of grapes, hot corn, pumpkin seeds, and a hundred other things, yelling like fiends; and sleeping happily, comfortably, serenely, among the hurrying feet, are the famed dogs of Constantinople; drifting noiselessly about are squads of Turkish women, draped from chin to feet in flowing robes, and with snowy veils bound about their heads, that disclose only the eyes and a vague, shadowy notion of their features. Seen moving about, far away in the dim, arched aisles of the Great Bazaar, they look as the shrouded dead must have looked when they walked forth from their graves amid the storms and thunders and earthquakes that burst upon Calvary that awful night of the Crucifixion. A street in Constantinople is a picture which one ought to see once — not oftener.

And then there was the goose-rancher — a fellow who drove a hundred geese before him about the city, and tried to sell them. He had a pole ten feet long, with a crook in the end of it, and occasionally a goose would branch out from the flock and make a lively break around the corner, with wings half lifted and neck stretched to its utmost. Did the goose-merchant get excited? No. He took his pole and reached after that goose with unspeakable *sang froid* — took a hitch round his neck, and "yanked" him back to his place in the flock without an effort. He steered his geese with that stick as easily as another man would steer a yawl. A few hours afterward we saw him sitting on a stone at a corner, in the midst of the turmoil, sound asleep in the sun, with his geese squatting around him, or dodging out of the way of asses and men. We came by again, within the hour, and he was taking account of stock, to see whether any of his flock had strayed or been stolen. The way he did it was unique. He put the end of his stick within six or eight inches of a stone wall, and made the geese march in single file between it and the wall. He counted them as they went by. There was no dodging that arrangement.

If you want dwarfs — I mean just a few dwarfs for a curiosity — go to Genoa. If you wish to buy them by the gross, for retail, go to Milan. There are plenty of dwarfs all over Italy, but it did seem to me that in Milan the crop was luxuriant. If you would see a fair average style of assorted cripples, go to Naples, or travel through the Roman states. But if you would see the very heart and home of cripples and human monsters, both, go straight to Constantinople. A beggar in Naples who can show a foot which has all run into one horrible toe, with one shapeless nail on it, has a fortune — but such an exhibition as that would not provoke any notice in Constantinople. The man would starve. Who would pay any attention to attractions like his among the rare monsters that throng the bridges of the Golden Horn and display their deformities in the gutters of Stamboul? Oh, wretched impostor! How could he stand against the three-legged woman, and the man with his eye in his cheek? How would he blush in presence of the man with fingers on his elbow? Where would he hide himself when the dwarf with seven fingers on each hand, no upper lip, and his under-jaw gone, came down in his majesty? Bismillah! The cripples of Europe are a delusion and a fraud. The truly gifted flourish only in the by-ways of Pera and Stamboul.

That three-legged woman lay on the bridge, with her stock in trade so disposed as to command the most striking effect — one natural leg, and two long, slender, twisted ones with feet on them like somebody else's forearm. Then there was a man further along who had no eyes, and whose face was the color of a fly-blown beefsteak, and wrinkled and twisted like a lava-flow — and verily so tumbled and distorted were his features that no man could tell the wart that served him for a nose from his cheekbones. In Stamboul was a man with a prodigious head, an uncommonly long body, legs eight inches long, and feet like snow-shoes. He traveled on those feet and his hands, and was as sway-backed as if the Colossus of Rhodes had been riding him. Ah, a beggar has to have exceedingly good points to make a living in Constantinople. A blue-faced man, who had nothing to offer except that he had been blown up in a mine, would be regarded as a rank impostor, and a mere damaged soldier on crutches would never make a cent. It would pay him to get a piece of his head taken off, and cultivate a wen like a carpet sack.

The Mosque of St. Sophia is the chief lion of Constantinople. You must get a firman and hurry there the first thing. We did that. We did not get a firman, but we took along four or five francs apiece, which is much the same thing.

I do not think much of the Mosque of St. Sophia. I suppose I lack appreciation. We will let it go at that. It is the rustiest old barn in heathendom. I believe all the interest that attaches to it comes from the fact that it was built for a Christian church and then turned into a mosque, without much alterations, by the Mohammedan conquerors of the land. They made me take off my boots and walk into the place in my stocking feet. I caught cold, and got myself so stuck up with a complication of gums, slime, and general corruption, that I wore out more than two thousand pair of boot-jacks getting my boots off that night, and even then some Christian hide peeled off with them. I abate not a single boot-jack.

St. Sophia is a colossal church, thirteen or fourteen hundred years old, and unsightly enough to be very, very much older. Its immense dome is said to be more wonderful than St. Peter's, but its dirt is much more wonderful than its dome, though they never mention it. The church has a hundred and seventy pillars in it, each a single piece, and all of costly marbles of various kinds, but they came from ancient temples at Baalbec, Heliopolis, Athens, and Ephesus, and are battered, ugly, and repulsive. They were a thousand years old when this church was new, and then the contrast must have been ghastly — if Justinian's architects did not trim them any. The inside of the dome is figured all over with a monstrous inscription in Turkish characters, wrought in gold mosaic, that looks as glaring as a circus bill; the pavements and the marble balustrades are all battered and dirty; the perspective is marred everywhere by a web of ropes that depend from the dizzy height of the dome, and suspend countless dingy, coarse oil lamps, and ostrich-eggs, six or seven feet above the floor. Squatting and sitting in groups, here and there and far and near, were ragged Turks reading books, hearing sermons, or receiving lessons like children, and in fifty places were more of the same sort bowing and straightening up, bowing again and getting down to kiss the earth, muttering prayers the while, and keeping up their gymnastics till they ought to have been tired, if they were not.

Everywhere was dirt and dust and dinginess and gloom; everywhere were signs of a hoary antiquity, but with nothing touching or beautiful about it; everywhere were those groups of fantastic pagans; overhead the gaudy mosaics and the web of lampropes — nowhere was there anything to win one's love or challenge his admiration.

The people who go into ecstasies over St. Sophia must surely get them out of the guide-book (where every church is spoken of as being "considered by good judges to be the most marvelous structure, in many respects, that the world has ever seen"). Or else they are those old connoisseurs from the wilds of New Jersey who laboriously learn the difference between a fresco and a fire-plug, and from that day forward feel privileged to void their critical bathos on painting, sculpture, and architecture forevermore.

We visited the Dancing Dervishes. There were twenty-one of them. They wore a long, light-colored loose robe that hung to their heels. Each in his turn went up to the priest (they were all within a large circular railing) and bowed profoundly and then went spinning away deliriously and took his appointed place in the circle, and continued to spin. When all had spun themselves to their places, they were about five or six feet apart — and so situated, the entire circle of spinning pagans spun itself three separate times around the room. It took twenty-five minutes to do it. They spun on the left foot, and kept themselves going by passing the right rapidly before it and digging it against the waxed floor. Some of them made incredible "time." Most of them spun around forty times in a minute, and one artist averaged about sixty-one times a minute, and kept it up during the whole twenty-five. His robe filled with air and stood out all around him like a balloon.

They made no noise of any kind, and most of them tilted their heads back and closed their eyes, entranced with a sort of devotional ecstasy. There was a rude kind of music, part of the time, but the musicians were not visible. None but spinners were allowed within the circle. A man had to either spin or stay outside. It was about as barbarous an exhibition as we have witnessed yet. Then sick persons came and lay down, and beside them women laid their sick children (one a babe at the breast), and the patriarch of the Dervishes walked upon their bodies. He was supposed to cure their diseases by trampling upon their breasts or backs or standing on the back of their necks. This is well enough for a people who think all their affairs are made or marred by viewless spirits of the air — by giants, gnomes, and genii — and who still believe, to this day, all the wild tales in the Arabian Nights. Even so an intelligent missionary tells me.

We visited the Thousand and One Columns. I do not know what it was originally intended for, but they said it was built for a reservoir. It is situated in the center of Constantinople. You go down a flight of stone steps in the middle of a barren place, and there you are. You are forty feet underground, and in the midst of a perfect wilderness of tall, slender, granite columns, of Byzantine architecture. Stand where you would, or change your position as often as you pleased, you were always a center from which radiated a dozen long archways and colonnades that lost themselves in distance and the somber twilight of the place. This old dried-up reservoir is occupied by a few ghostly silk-spinners now, and one of them showed me a cross cut high up in one of the pillars. I suppose he meant me to understand that the institution was there before the Turkish occupation, and I thought he made a remark to that effect; but he must have had an impediment in his speech, for I did not understand him.

We took off our shoes and went into the marble mausoleum of the Sultan Mahmoud, the neatest piece of architecture, inside, that I have seen lately. Mahmoud's tomb was covered with a black velvet pall, which was elaborately embroidered with silver railing; at the sides and corners were silver candlesticks that would weigh more than a hundred pounds, and they supported candles as large as a man's leg; on the top of the sarcophagus was a fez, with a handsome diamond ornament upon it, which an attendant said cost a hundred thousand pounds, and lied like a Turk when he said it. Mahmoud's whole family were comfortably planted around him.

We went to the Great Bazaar in Stamboul, of course, and I shall not describe it further than to say it is a monstrous hive of little shops — thousands, I should say — all under one roof, and cut up into innumerable little blocks by narrow streets which are arched overhead. One street is devoted to a particular kind of merchandise, another to another, and so on. When you wish to buy a pair of shoes you have the swing of the whole street — you do not have to walk yourself down hunting stores in different localities. It is the same with silks, antiquities, shawls, etc. The place is crowded with people all the time, and as the gay-colored Eastern fabrics are lavishly displayed before every shop, the Great Bazaar of Stamboul is one of the sights that are worth seeing. It is full of life, and stir, and business, dirt, beggars, asses, yelling peddlers, porters, dervishes, high-born Turkish female shoppers, Greeks, and weird-looking and weirdly-dressed Mohammedans from the mountains and the far provinces — and the only solitary thing one does not smell when he is in the Great Bazaar, is something which smells good.

CHAPTER VII

Mosques are plenty, churches are plenty, graveyards are plenty, but morals and whisky are scarce. The Koran does not permit

Mohammedans to drink. Their natural instincts do not permit them to be moral. They say the Sultan has eight hundred wives. This almost amounts to bigamy. It makes our cheeks burn with shame to see such a thing permitted here in Turkey. We do not mind it so much in Salt Lake, however.

Circassian and Georgian girls are still sold in Constantinople by their parents, but not publicly. The great slave marts we have all read so much about — where tender young girls were stripped for inspection, and criticised and discussed just as if they were horses at an agricultural fair — no longer exist. The exhibition and the sales are private now. Stocks are up, just at present, partly because of a brisk demand created by the recent return of the Sultan's suite from the courts of Europe; partly on account of an unusual abundance of breadstuffs, which leaves holders untortured by hunger and enables them to hold back for high prices; and partly because buyers are too weak to bear the market, while sellers are amply prepared to bull it. Under these circumstances, if the American metropolitan newspapers were published here in Constantinople, their next commercial report would read about as follows, I suppose:

SLAVE GIRL MARKET REPORT

"Best brands Circassian, crop of 1850, £200; 1852, £250; 1854, £300. Best brands Georgian, none in market; second quality, 1851, £180. Nineteen fair to middling Wallachian girls offered at £130 @ 150, but no takers; sixteen prime A1 sold in small lots to close out — terms private.

"Sales of one lot Circassians, prime to good, 1852 to 1854, at £240 @ 24½, buyer 30; one forty-niner — damaged at £23, seller ten, no deposit. Several Georgians, fancy brands, 1852, changed hands to fill orders. The Georgians now on hand are mostly last year's crop, which was usually poor. The new crop is a little backward, but will be coming shortly. As regards its quantity and quality, the accounts are most encouraging. In this connection we can safely say, also, that the new crop of Circassians is looking extremely well. His Majesty the Sultan has already sent in large orders for his new harem, which will be finished within a fortnight, and this has naturally strengthened the market and given Circassian stock a strong upward tendency. Taking advantage of the inflated market, many of our shrewdest operators are selling short. There are hints of a 'corner' on Wallachians.

"There is nothing new in Nubians. Slow sale.

"Eunuchs — none offering; however, large cargoes are expected from Egypt to-day."

I think the above would be about the style of the commercial report. Prices are pretty high now, and holders firm; but, two or three years ago, parents in a starving condition brought their young daughters down here and sold them for even twenty and thirty dollars, when they could do no better, simply to save themselves and the girls from dying of want. It is sad to think of so distressing a thing as this, and I for one am sincerely glad the prices are up again.

Commercial morals, especially, are bad. There is no gainsaying that. Greek, Turkish, and Armenian morals consist only in attending church regularly on the appointed Sabbaths, and in breaking the ten commandments all the balance of the week. It comes natural to them to lie and cheat in the first place, and then they go on and improve on nature until they arrive at perfection. In recommending his son to a merchant as a valuable salesman, a father does not say he is a nice, moral, upright boy, and goes to Sunday-School and is honest, but he says, "This boy is worth his weight in broad pieces of a hundred — for behold, he will cheat whomsoever hath dealings with him, and from the Euxine to the waters of Marmora there abideth not so gifted a liar!" How is that for a recommendation? The missionaries tell me that they hear encomiums like that passed upon people every day. They say of a person they admire, "Ah, he is a charming swindler. and a most exquisite liar!"

Everybody lies and cheats — everybody who is in business, at any rate. Even foreigners soon have to come down to the custom of the country, and they do not buy and sell long in Constantinople till they lie and cheat like a Greek. I say like a Greek, because the Greeks are called the worst transgressors in this line. Several Americans, long resident in Constantinople, contend that most Turks are pretty trustworthy, but few claim that the Greeks have any virtues that a man can discover — at least without a fire assay.

I am half willing to believe that the celebrated dogs of Constantinople have been misrepresented — slandered. I have always been led to suppose that they were so thick in the streets that they blocked the way; that they moved about in organized companies, platoons, and regiments, and took what they wanted by determined and ferocious assault; and that at night they drowned all other sounds with their terrible howlings. The dogs I see here cannot be those I have read of.

I find them everywhere, but not in strong force. The most I have found together has been about ten or twenty. And night or day a fair proportion of them were asleep. Those that were not asleep always looked as if they wanted to be. I never saw such utterly wretched, starved, sad-visaged, broken-hearted looking curs in my life. It seemed a grim satire to accuse such brutes as these of taking things by force of arms. They hardly seemed to have strength enough or ambition enough to walk across the street — I do not know that I have seen one walk that far yet. They are mangy and bruised and multilated, and often you see one with the hair singed off him in such wide and well-defined tracts that he looks like a map of the new Territories. They are the sorriest beasts that breathe — the most abject — the most pitiful. In their faces is a settled expression of melancholy, an air of hopeless despondency. The hairless patches on a scalded dog are preferred by the fleas of Constantinople to a wider range on a healthier dog; and the exposed places suit the fleas exactly. I saw a dog of this kind start to nibble at a flea — a fly attracted his attention, and he made a snatch at him; the flea called for him once more, and that forever unsettled him; he looked sadly at his flea-pasture, then sadly looked at his bald spot. Then he heaved a sigh and dropped his head resignedly upon his paws. He was not equal to the situation.

The dogs sleep in the streets, all over the city. From one end of the street to the other, I suppose they will average about eight or ten to a block. Sometimes, of course, there are fifteen or twenty to a block. They do not belong to anybody, and they seem to have no close personal friendships among each other. But they district the city themselves, and the dogs of each district, whether it be half a block in extent, or ten blocks, have to remain within its bounds. Woe to a dog if he crosses the line! His neighbors would snatch the balance of his hair off in a second. So it is said. But they don't look it.

They sleep in the streets these days. They are my compass — my guide. When I see the dogs sleep placidly on, while men, sheep, geese, and all moving things turn out and go around them, I know I am not in the great street where the hotel is, and must go further. In the Grand Rue the dogs have a sort of air of being on the lookout — an air born of being obliged to get out of the way of many carriages every day — and that expression one recognizes in a moment. It does not exist upon the face of any dog without the confines of that street. All others sleep placidly and keep no watch. They could not move, though the Sultan himself passed by.

In one narrow street (but none of them are wide) I saw three dogs lying coiled up, about a foot or two apart. End to end they lay, and so they just bridged the street neatly, from gutter to gutter. A drove of a hundred sheep came along. They stepped right over the dogs, the rear crowding the front, impatient to get on. The dogs looked lazily up, flinched a little when the impatient feet of the sheep touched their raw backs — sighed, and lay peacefully down again. No talk could be plainer than that. So some of the sheep jumped over them and others scrambled between, occasionally chipping a leg with their sharp hoofs, and when the whole flock had made the trip, the dogs sneezed a little, in the cloud of dust, but never budged their bodies an inch. I though I was lazy, but I am a steam engine compared to a Constantinople dog. But was not that a singular scene for a city of a million inhabitants?

These dogs are the scavengers of the city. That is their official position, and a hard one it is. However, it is their protection. But for their usefulness in partially cleansing these terrible streets, they would not be tolerated long. They eat anything and everything that comes in their way, from melon rinds and spoiled grapes up through all the grades and species of dirt and refuse to their own dead friends and relatives — and yet they are always lean, always hungry, always despondent. The people are loth to kill them — do not kill them, in fact. The Turks have innate antipathy to taking the life of any dumb animal, it is said. But they do worse. They hang and kick and stone and scald these wretched creatures to the very verge of death, and then leave them to live and suffer.

Once a Sultan proposed to kill off all the dogs here, and did begin the work — but the populace raised such a howl of horror about it that the massacre was stayed. After a while, he proposed to remove them all to an island in the Sea of Marmora. No objection was offered, and a ship-load or so was taken away. But when it came to be known that somehow or other the dogs never got to the island, but always fell overboard in the night and perished, another howl was raised and the transportation scheme was dropped.

So the dogs remain in peaceable possession of the streets. I do not say that they do not howl at night, nor that they do not attack people who have not a red fez on their heads. I only say that it would be mean for *me* to accuse them of these unseemly things who have not seen them do them with my own eyes or heard them with my own ears.

I was a little surprised to see Turks and Greeks playing newsboy right here in the mysterious land where the giants and genii of the Arabian Nights once dwelt — where winged horses and hydra-headed dragons guarded enchanted castles — where Princes and Princesses flew through the air on carpets that obeyed a mystic talisman — where cities whose houses were made of precious stones sprang up in a night under the hand of the magician, and where busy marts were suddenly stricken with a spell and each citizen lay or sat, or stood with weapon raised or foot advanced, just as he was speechless and motionless, till time had told a hundred years!

The newspaper business has its inconveniences in Constantinople. Two Greek papers and one French one were suppressed here within a few days of each other. No victories of the Cretans are allowed to be printed. From time to time the Grand Vizier sends a notice to the various editors that the Cretan insurrection is entirely suppressed, and although that editor knows better, he still has to print the notice. The *Levant Herald* is too fond of speaking praisefully of Americans to be popular with the Sultan, who does not relish our sympathy with the Cretans, and therefore that paper has to be particularly circumspect in order to keep out of trouble. Once the editor, forgetting the official notice in his paper that the Cretans were crushed out, printed a letter of a very different tenor, from the American Consul in Crete, and was fined two hundred and fifty dollars for it. Shortly he printed another from the same source and was imprisoned three months for his pains. I think I could get the assistant editorship of the *Levant Herald*, but I am going to try to worry along without it.

To suppress a paper here involves the ruin of the publisher, almost. But in Naples I think they speculate on misfortunes of that kind. Papers are suppressed there every day, and spring up the next day under a new name. During the ten days or a fortnight we stayed there one paper was murdered and resurrected twice. The newsboys are smart there, just as they are elsewhere. They take advantage of popular weaknesses. When they find they are not likely to sell out, they approach a citizen mysteriously, and say in a low voice — "Last copy, sir: double price; paper just been suppressed!" The man buys it, of course, and finds nothing in it. They do say — I do not vouch for it — but they do say that men sometimes print a vast edition of a paper, with a ferociously seditious article in it, distribute it quickly among the newsboys, and clear out till the Government's indignation cools. It pays well. Confiscation don't amount to anything. The type and presses are not worth taking care of.

There is only one English newspaper in Naples. It has seventy subscribers. The publisher is getting rich very deliberately — very deliberately indeed.

I shall never want another Turkish lunch. The cooking apparatus was in a little lunch-room, near the bazaar, and it was all open to the street. The cook was slovenly, and so was the table, and it had no cloth on it. The fellow took a mass of sausage-meat and coated it round a wire and laid it on a charcoal fire to cook. When it was done, he laid it aside and a dog walked sadly in and nipped it. He smelt it first, and probably recognized the remains of a friend. The cook took it away from him and laid it before us. Jack said, "I pass" — he plays euchre sometimes — and we all passed in turn. Then the cook baked a broad, flat, wheaten cake, greased it well with the sausage, and started towards us with it. It dropped in the dirt, and he picked it up and polished it on his breeches, and laid it before us. Jack said, "I pass." We all passed. He put some eggs in a frying-pan, and stood pensively prying slabs of meat from his teeth with a fork. Then he used the fork to turn the eggs with — and brought them along. Jack said "Pass again." All follwed suit. We did not know what to do, and so we ordered a new ration of sausage. The cook got out his wire, apportioned a proper amount of sausage-meat, spat on his hands, and fell to work! This time, with one accord, we all passed out. We paid and left.

That is all I learned about Turkish lunches. A Turkish lunch is good, no doubt, but it has its little drawbacks.

When I think how I have been swindled by books of Oriental travel, I want a tourist for breakfast. For years and years I have dreamed of the wonders of the Turkish bath; for years and years I have promised myself that I would yet enjoy one. Many and many a time, in fancy, I have lain in the marble bath, and breathed the slumbrous fragrance of Eastern spices that filled the air; then passed through a weird and complicated system of pulling and hauling and drenching and scrubbing, by a gang of naked savages who loomed vast and vaguely through the steaming mists, like demons; then rested for a while on a divan fit for a king; then passed through another complex ordeal, and one more fearful than the first; and, finally, swathed in soft fabrics, been conveyed to a princely saloon and laid on a bed of eiderdown, where eunuchs, gorgeous of costume, fanned me while I drowsed and dreamed, or contently gazed at the rich hangings of the apartment, the soft carpets, the sumptuous furniture, the pictures, and drank delicious coffee, smoked the soothing narghili, and dropped, at the last, into tranquil repose, lulled by sensuous odors from unseen censers, by the gentle influence of the narghili's Persian tobacco, and by the music of fountains that counterfeited the pattering of summer rain.

That was the picture, just as I got it from incendiary books of travel. It was a poor, miserable imposture. The reality is no more like it than the Five Points are like the Garden of Eden. They received me in a great court, paved with marble slabs; around it were broad galleries, one above another, carpeted with seedy matting, railed with unpainted balustrades, and furnished with huge rickety chairs, cushioned with rusty old mattresses, indented with impressions left by the forms of nine successive generations of men who had reposed upon them. The place was vast, naked, dreary; its court a barn, its galleries stalls for human horses. The cadaverous, half-nude varlets that served in the establishment had nothing of poetry in their appearance, nothing of romance, nothing of Orietnal splendor. They shed no entrancing odors — just the contrary. Their hungry eyes and their lank forms continually suggested one glaring, unsentimental fact — they wanted what they term in California "a square meal."

I went into one of the racks and undressed. An unclean starveling wrapped a gaudy tablecloth about his loins, and hung a white rag over my shoulders. If I had a tub then, it would have come natural to me to take in washing. I was then conducted down stairs into the wet, slippery court, and the first things that attracted my attention were my heels. My fall excited no comment. They expected it, no doubt. It belonged in the list of softening, sensuous influences peculiar to this home of Eastern luxury. It was softening enough, certainly, but its application was not happy. They now gave me a pair of wooden clogs — benches in miniature, with leather straps over them to confine my feet (which they would have done, only I do not wear No. 13s). These things dangled uncomfortably by the straps when I lifted my feet, and came down in awkward and unexpected places when I put them on the floor again, and sometimes turned sideways and wrenched my ankles out of joint. However, it was all Oriental luxury, and I did what I could to enjoy it.

They put me in another part of the barn and laid me on a stuffy sort of pallet, which was not made of cloth of gold, or Persian shawls, but was merely the unpretending sort of thing I have seen in the negro quarters of Arkansas. There was nothing whatever in this dim marble prison but five more of these biers. It was a very solemn place. I expected that the spiced odors of Araby were going to steal over my senses now, but they did not. A copper-colored skeleton, with a rag around him, brought me a glass decanter of water, with a lighted tobacco pipe in the top of it, and a pliant stem a yard long, with a brass mouth-piece to it.

It was the famous "narghili" of the East — the thing the Grand Turk smokes in the pictures. This began to look like luxury. I took one blast at it, and it was sufficient; the smoke went in a great volume down into my stomach, my lungs, even into the uttermost parts of my frame. I exploded one mighty cough, and it was as if Vesuvius had let go. For the next five minutes I smoked at every pore, like a frame house that is on fire on the inside. Not any more narghili for me. The smoke had a vile taste, and the taste of a thousand infidel tongues that remained on that brass mouthpiece was viler still. I was getting discouraged. Whenever, hereafter, I see the cross-legged Grand Turk smoking his narghili, in pretended bliss, on the outside of a paper of Connecticut tabacco, I shall know him for the shameless humbug he is.

This prison was filled with hot air. When I had got warmed up sufficiently to prepare me for a still warmer temperature, they took me where it was — into a marble room, wet, slippery, and steamy, and laid me out on a raised platform in the center. It was very warm. Presently my man sat me down by a tank of hot water, drenched me well, gloved his hand with a coarse mitten, and began to polish me all over with it. I began to smell disagreeably. The more he polished the worse I smelt. It was alarming. I said to him:

"I perceive that I am pretty far gone. It is plain that I ought to be buried without any unnecessary delay. Perhaps you had better go after my friends at once, because the weather is warm, and I cannot 'keep' long."

He went on scrubbing, and paid no attention. I soon saw that he was reducing my size. He bore hard on his mitten, and from under it rolled little cylinders, like macaroni. It could not be dirt, for it was too white. He pared me down in this way for a long time. Finally I said:

"It is a tedious process. It will take hours to trim me to the size you want me; I will wait; go and borrow a jack-plane."

He paid no attention at all.

After a while be brought a basin, some soap, and something that seemed to be the tail of a horse. He made up a prodigious quantity of soapsuds, deluged me with them from head to foot, without warning me to shut my eyes, and then swabbed me viciously with the horse-tail. Then he left me there, a snowy statue of lather, and went away. When I got tired of waiting I went and hunted him up. He was propped against the wall, in another room asleep. I woke him. He was not disconcerted. He took me back and flooded me with hot water, then turbaned my head, swathed my with dry tablecloths, and conducted me to a latticed chicken-coop in one of the galleries, and pointed to one of those Arkansas beds. I mounted it, and vaguely expected the odors of Araby again. They did not come.

The blank, unornamented coop had nothing about if of that oriental voluptuousness one reads of so much. It was more suggestive of the county hospital than anything else. The skinny servitor brought a narghili, and I got him to take it out again without wasting any time about it. Then he brought the world-renowned Turkish coffee that poets have sung so rapturously for many generations, and I seized upon it as the last hope that was left of my old dreams of Eastern luxury. It was another fraud. Of all the unchristian beverages that ever passed my lips, Turkish coffee is the worst. The cup is small, it is smeared with grounds; the coffee is black, thick, unsavory of smell, and execrable in taste. The bottom of the cup has a muddy sediment in it half an inch deep. This goes down your throat, and portions of it lodge by the way, and produce a tickling aggravation that keeps you barking and coughing for an hour.

Here endeth my experience of the celebrated Turkish bath, and here also endeth my dream of the bliss the mortal revels in who passes through it. It is a malignant swindle. The man who enjoys it is qualified to enjoy anything that is repulsive to sight or sense, and he that can invest it with a charm of poetry is able to do the same with anything else in the world that is tedious, and wretched, and dismal, and nasty.

CHAPTER VIII

We left a dozen passengers in Constantinople, and sailed

through the beautiful Bosporus and far up into the Black Sea. We left them in the clutches of the celebrated Turkish guide, "FAR-AWAY MOSES," who will seduce them into buying a shipload of ottar of roses, splendid Turkish vestments, and all manner of curious things they can never have any use for. Murray's invaluable guidebooks have mentioned Far-away Moses' name, and he is a made man. He rejoices daily in the fact that he is a recognized celebrity. However, we cannot alter our established customs to please the whims of guides; we cannot show partialities this late in the day. Therefore, ignoring this fellow's brilliant fame, and ignoring the fanciful name he takes such pride in, we called him Ferguson, just as we had done with all other guides. It has kept him in a state of smothered exasperation all the time. Yet we meant him no harm. After he has gotten himself up regardless of expense, in showy, baggy trowsers, yellow, pointed slippers, fiery fez, silken jacket of blue, voluminous waist-sash of fancy Persian stuff filled with a battery of silver-mounted horse-pistols, and has strapped on his terrible scimeter, he considers it an unspeakable humiliation to be called Ferguson. It cannot be helped. All guides are Ferguson to us. We cannot master their dreadful foreign names.

Sebastopol is probably the worst battered town in Russia or anywhere else. But we ought to be pleased with it, nevertheless, for we have been in no country yet where we have been so kindly received, and where we felt that to be Americans was a sufficient *visé* for our passports. The moment the anchor was down, the Governor of the town immediately dispatched an officer on board to inquire if he could be of any assistance to us, and to invite us to make ourselves at home in Sebastopol! If you know Russia, you know that this was a wild stretch of hospitality. They are usually so suspicious of strangers that they worry them excessively with the delays and aggravations incident to a complicated passport system. Had we come from any other country we could not have had permission to enter Sebastopol and leave again under three days — but as it was, we were at liberty to go and come when and where we pleased. Everybody in Constantinople warned us to be very careful about our passports, see that they were strictly *en regle,* and never to mislay them for a moment: and they told us of numerous instances of Englishmen and others who were delayed days, weeks, and even months, in Sebastopol, on account of trifling informalities in their passports, and for which they were not to blame. I had lost my passport, and was traveling under my room-mate's, who stayed behind in Constantinople to await our return. To read the description of him in that passport and then look at me, any man could see that I was no more like him than I am like Hercules. So I went into the harbor of Sebastopol with fear and trembling

— full of a vague, horrible apprehension that I was going to be found out and hanged. But all that time my true passport had been floating gallantly overhead — and behold it was only our flag. They never asked us for any other.

We have had a great many Russian and English gentlemen and ladies on board to-day, and the time has passed cheerfully away. They were all happy-spirited people, and I never heard our mother tongue sound so pleasantly as it did when it fell from those English lips in this far-off land. I talked to the Russians a good deal, just to be friendly, and they talked to me from the same motive; I am sure that both enjoyed the conversation, but never a word of it either of us understood. I did most of my talking to those English people though, and I am sorry we cannot carry some of them along with us.

We have gone whithersoever we chose, to-day, and have met with nothing but the kindest attentions. Nobody inquired whether we had any passports or not.

Several of the offers of the government have suggested that we take the ship to a little water place thirty miles from here, and pay the Emperor of Russia a visit. He is rusticating there. These officers said they would take it upon themselves to insure us a cordial reception. They said if we would go, they would not only telegraph the Emperor, but send a special courier overland to announce our coming. Our time is so short, though, and more especially our coal is so nearly out, that we judged it best to forego the rare pleasure of holding social intercourse with an Emperor.

Ruined Pompeii is in good condition compared to Sebastopol. Here, you may look in whatsoever direction you please, and your eye encounters scarcely anything but ruin, ruin, ruin! — fragments of houses, crumbled walls, torn and ragged hills, devastation everywhere! It is as if a mighty earhquake had spent all its terrible forces upon this one little spot. For eighteen long months the storm of war beat upon the helpless town, and left it at last the saddest wreck that ever the sun has looked upon. Not one solitary house escaped unscathed — not one remained habitable, even. Such utter and complete ruin one could hardly conceive of. The houses had all been solid, dressed-stone structures; most of them were plowed through and through by cannon-balls — unroofed and sliced down from eaves to foundation — and now a row of them, half a mile long, looks merely like an endless procession of battered chimneys. No semblance of a house remains in such as these. Some of the larger buildings had corners knocked off; pillars cut in two; cornices smashed; holes driven straight through the walls. Many of these holes are as round and as cleanly cut as if they had been made with an auger. Others are half pierced through, and the clean impression is there in the rock, as smooth and as shapely as if it were done in putty. Here and there a ball still sticks in a wall, and from it iron tears trickle down and discolor the stone.

The battle-fields were pretty close together. The Malakoff tower is on a hill which is right in the edge of the town. The Redan was within rifle-shot of the Malakoff; Inkerman was a mile away; and Balaklava removed but an hour's ride. The French trenches, by which they approached and invested the Malakoff, were carried so close under its sloping sides that one might have stood by the Russian guns and tossed a stone into them. Repeatedly, during three terrible days, they swarmed up the little Malakoff hill, and were beaten back with terrible slaughter. Finally, they captured the place, and drove the Russians out, who then tried to retreat into the town, but the English had taken the Redan, and shut them off with a wall of flame; there was nothing for them to do but go back and retake the Malakoff or die under its guns. They did go back; they took the Malakoff and retook it two or three times, but their desperate valor could not avail, and they had to give up at last.

These fearful fields, where such tempests of death used to rage, are peaceful enough now; no sound is heard, hardly a living thing moves about them, they are lonely and silent — their desolation is complete.

There was nothing else to do, and so everybody went to hunting relics. They have stocked the ship with them. They brought them from the Malakoff, from the Redan, Inkerman, Balaklava — everywhere. They have brought cannon-balls, broken ramrods, fragments of shell — iron enough to freight a sloop. Some have even brought bones — brought them laboriously from great distances, and were grieved to hear the surgeon pronounce them only bones of mules and oxen. I knew Blucher would not lose an opportunity like this. He brought a sack full on board and was going for another. I prevailed upon him not to go. He has already turned his stateroom into a museum of worthless trumpery, which he has gathered up in his travels. He is labeling his trophies, now. I picked up one a while ago, and found it marked "Fragment of a Russian General." I carried it out to get a better light upon it — it was nothing but a couple of teeth and part of the jawbone of a horse. I said with some asperity:

"Fragment of a Russian General! This is absurb. Are you never going to learn any sense?"

He only said: "Go slow — the old woman won't know any different." [His aunt.]

This person gathers mementoes with a perfect recklessness, nowadays; mixes them all up together and then serenely lables them without any regard to truth, propriety, or even plausibility.

I have found him breaking a stone in two, and labeling half of it "Chunk busted from the pulpit of Demosthenes," and the other half "Darnick from the Tomb of Abelard and Heloise." I have known him to gather up a handful of pebbles by the roadside, and bring them on board ship and label them as coming from twenty celebrated localities five hundred miles apart. I remonstrate against these outrages upon reason and truth, of course, but it does no good. I get the same tranquil, unanswerable reply every time:

"It don't signify — the old woman won't know any different."

Ever since we three or four fortunate ones made the midnight trip to Athens, it has afforded him genuine satisfaction to give everybody in the ship a pebble from the Mars Hill where St. Paul preached. He got all those pebbles on the seashore, abreast the ship, but professes to have gathered them from one of our party. However, it is not of any use for me to expose the deception — if affords him pleasure, and does no harm to anybody. He says he never expects to run out of mementoes of St. Paul as long as he is in reach of a sand bank. Well, he is no worse than others. I notice that all travelers supply deficiencies in their collections in the same way. I shall never have any confidence in such things again while I live.

CHAPTER IX

We have got so far East now—a hundred and fifty-five degrees of longitude from San Francisco — that my watch cannot "keep the hang" of the time any more. It has grown discouraged, and stopped. I think it did a wise thing. The difference in time between Sebastopol and the Pacific coast is enormous. When it is six o'clock in the morning here, it is somewhere about week before last in California. We are excusable for getting a little tangled as to time. These distractions and distresses about the time have worried me so much that I was afraid my mind was so much affected that I never would have any appreciation of time again; but when I noticed how handy I was yet about comprehending when it was dinner-time, a blessed tranquillity settled down upon me, and I am tortured with doubts and fears no more.

Odessa is about twenty hours' run from Sebastopol, and is the most northerly port in the Black Sea. We came here to get coal, principally. The city has a population of one hundred and thirty-three thousand, and is growing faster than any other small city out of America. It is a free port, and is the great grain mart of this particular part of the world. Its roadstead is full of ships. Engineers are at work, now, turning the open roadstead into a spacious artificial harbor. It is to be almost inclosed by massive stone piers, one of which will extend into the sea over three thousand feet in a straight line.

I have not felt so much at home for a long time as I did when I "raised the hill" and stood in Odessa for the first time. It looked just like an American city; fine, broad streets, and straight as well; low houses (two or three stories), wide, neat, and free from any quaintness of architectural ornamentation; locust trees bordering the sidewalks (they call them acacias); a stirring, business-look about the streets and the stores; fast walkers; a familiar *new* look about the houses and everything; yea, and a driving and smothering cloud of dust that was so like a message from our own dear native land that we could hardly refrain from shedding a few grateful tears and execrations in the old time-honored American way. Look up the street or down the street, this way or that way, we saw only America! There was not one thing to remind us that we were in Russia. We walked for some little distance, reveling in this home vision, and then we came upon a church and a hack-driver, and presto! the illusion vanished! The church had a slender-spired dome that rounded inward at its base, and looked like a turnip turned upside down, and the hackman seemed to be dressed in a long petticoat without any hoops. These things were essentially foreign, and so were the carriages — but everybody knows about these things, and there is no occasion for my describing them.

We were only to stay here a day and a night and take in coal; we consulted the guide-books and were rejoiced to know that there were no sights in Odessa to see; and so we had one good, untrammeled holiday on our hands, with nothing to do but idle about the city and enjoy ourselves. We sauntered through the markets and criticised the fearful and wonderful costumes from the back country; examined the populace as far as eyes could do it; and closed the entertainment with an ice-cream debauch. We do not get ice-cream everywhere, and so, when we do, we are apt to dissipate to excess. We never cared anything about ice-cream at home, but we look upon it with a sort of idolatry now that it is so scarce in these red-hot climates of the East.

We only found two pieces of statuary, and this was another blessing. One was a bronze image of the Duc de Richelieu, grandnephew of the splendid Cardinal. It stood in a spacious, handsome promenade, overlooking the sea, and from its base a vast flight of stone steps led down to the harbor — two hundred of them, fifty feet long, and a wide landing at the bottom of every twenty. It is a noble staircase, and from a distance the people toiling up it looked like insects. I mention this statue and this stairway because they have their story. Richelieu founded Odessa — watched over it with paternal care — labored with a

fertile brain and a wise understanding for its best interests —
spent his fortune freely to the same end — endowed it with a
sound prosperity, and one which will yet make it one of the
great cities of the Old World — built this noble stairway with
money from his own private purse — and —— Well, the people
for whom he had done so much let him walk down these same
steps, one day, unattended, old, poor, without a second coat to
his back; and when, years afterward, he died in Sebastopol in
poverty and neglect, they called a meeting, subscribed liberally,
and immediately erected this tasteful monument to his memory,
and named a great street after him. It reminds me of what
Robert Burns' mother said when they erected a stately
monument to his memory: "Ah, Robbie, ye asked them for
bread and they hae gi'en ye a stane."

The people of Odessa have warmly recommended us to go and
call on the Emperor, as did the Sebastopolians. They have
telegraphed his Majesty, and he had signified his willingness to
grant us an audience. So we are getting up the anchors and
preparing to sail to his watering-place. What a scratching around
there will be now! what a holding of important meetings and appointing of solemn committees! — and what a furbishing up of
claw-hammer coats and white silk neckties! As this fearful ordeal
we are about to pass through pictures itself to my fancy in all its
dread sublimity, I begin to fell my fierce desire to converse with
a genuine Emperor cooling down and passing away. What am I
to do with my hands? What am I to do with my feet? What in
the world an I to do with myself?

CHAPTER X

We anchored here at Yalta, Russia, two or three days ago. To
me the place was a vision of the Sierras. The tall, gray mountains that back it, their sides bristling with pines — cloven with
ravines — here and there a hoary rock towering into view —
long, straight streaks sweeping down from the summit to the sea,
marking the passage of some avalanche of former times — all
these were as like what one sees in the Sierras as if the one were
a portrait of the other. The little village of Yalta nestles at the
foot of an amphitheater which slopes backward and upward to
the wall of hills, and looks as if it might have sunk quietly down
to its present position from a higher elevation. This depression is
covered with the great parks and gardens of noblemen, and
through the mass of green foliage the bright colors of their
palaces bud out here and there like flowers. It is a beautiful
spot.

We had the United States consul on board — the Odessa consul. We assembled in the cabin and commanded him to tell us

what we must do to be saved, and tell us quickly. He made a speech. The first thing he said fell like a blight on every hopeful spirit; he had never seen a court reception. (Three groans for the consul.) But he said he had seen receptions at the Governor-General's in Odessa, and had often listened to people's experiences of receptions at the Russian and other courts, and believed he knew very well what sort of ordeal we were about to essay. (Hope budded again.) He said we were many; the summer-palace was small — a mere mansion; doubtless we should be received in summer fashion — in the garden; we would stand in a row, all the gentlemen in swallow-tail coats, white kids, and white neckties, and the ladies in light-colored silks, or something of that kind; at the proper moment — 12 meridian — the Emperor, attended by his suite arrayed in splendid uniforms, would appear and walk slowly along the line, bowing to some, and saying two or three words to others. At the moment his Majesty appeared, a universal, delighted, enthusiastic smile ought to break out like a rash among the passengers — a smile of love, of gratification, of admiration — and with one accord, the party must begin to bow — not obsequiously, but respectfully, and with dignity; at the end of fifteen minutes the Emperor would go in the house, and we could run along home again. We felt immensely relieved. It seemed, in a manner, easy. There was not a man in the party but believed that with a little practice he could stand in a row, especially if there were others along; there was not a man but believed he could bow without tripping on his coat-tail and breaking his neck; in a word, we came to believe we were equal to any item in the performance except that complicated smile. The consul also said we ought to draft a little address to the Emperor, and present it to one of his aids-de-camp, who would forward it to him at the proper time. Therefore, five gentlemen were appointed to prepare the document, and the fifty others went sadly smiling about the ship — practicing. During the next twelve hours we had the general appearance, somehow, of being at a funeral, where everybody was sorry the death had occurred, but glad it was over — where everybody was smiling, and yet broken-hearted.

A committee went ashore to wait on his Excellency, the Governor-General, and learn our fate. At the end of three hours of boding suspense, they came back and said the Emperor would receive us at noon the next day — would send carriages for us — would hear the address in person. The Grand Duke Michael had sent to invite us to his palace also. Any man could see that there was an intention here to show that Russia's friendship for America was so genuine as to render even her private citizens objects worthy of kindly attentions.

At the appointed hour we drove out three miles, and assembled in the handsome garden in front of the Emperor's palace.

We formed a circle under the trees before the door, for there was no one room in the house able to accommodate our threescore persons comfortably, and in a few minutes the imperial family came out bowing and smiling, and stood in our midst. A number of great dignitaries of the empire, in undress uniforms, came with them. With every bow, His Majesty said a word of welcome. I copy these speeches. There is character in them — Russian character — which is politeness itself, and the genuine article. The French are polite, but it is often mere ceremonious politeness. A Russian imbues his polite things with a heartiness, both of phrase and expression, that compels belief in their sincerity. As I was saying, the Czar punctuated his speeches with bows:

"Good morning — I am glad to see you — I am gratified — I am delighted — I am happy to receive you!"

All took off their hats, and the consul inflicted the address on him. He bore it with unflinching fortitude; then took the rusty-looking document and handed it to some great officer or other, to be filed away among the archives of Russia — in the stove. He thanked us for the address, and said he was very much pleased to see us, especially as such friendly relations existed between Russia and the United States. The Empress said the Americans were favorites in Russia, and she hoped the Russians were similarly regarded in America. These were all the speeches that were made, and I recommend them to parties who present policemen with gold watches, as models of brevity and point. After this the Empress went and talked sociably (for an Empress) with various ladies around the circle; several gentlemen entered into a disjointed general conversation with the Emperor; the Dukes and Princes, Admirals and Maids of Honor dropped into free-and-easy chat with first one and then another of our party, and whoever chose stepped forward and spoke with the modest little Grand Duchess Marie, the Czar's daughter. She is fourteen years old, light-haired, blue-eyed, unassuming, and pretty. Everybody talks English.

The Emperor wore a cap, frock-coat, and pantaloons, all of some kind of plain white drilling—cotton or linen—and sported no jewelry or any insignia whatever of rank. No costume could be less ostentatious. He is very tall and spare, and a determined-looking man, though a very pleasant-looking one, nevertheless. It is easy to see that he is kind and affectionate. There is something very noble in his expression when his cap is off. There is none of that cunning in his eye that all of us noticed in Louis Napoleon's.

The Empress and the little Grand Duchess wore simple suits of foulard (or foulard silk, I don't know which is proper), with a small blue spot in it; the dresses were trimmed with blue; both ladies wore broad blue sashes about their waists; linen collars and clerical ties of muslin; low-crowned straw-hats trimmed with blue velvet; parasols and flesh-colored gloves. The Grand Duchess had no heels on her shoes. I do not know this of my own knowledge, but one of our ladies told me so. I was not looking at her shoes. I was glad to observe that she wore her own hair, plaited in thick braids against the back of her head, instead of the uncomely thing they call a waterfall, which is about as much like a waterfall as a canvas-covered ham is like a cataract. Taking the kind expression that is in the Emperor's face and the gentleness that is in his young daughter's into consideration, I wondered if it would not tax the Czar's firmness to the utmost to condemn a supplicating wretch to misery in the wastes of Siberia if she pleaded for him. Every time their eyes met, I saw more and more what a tremendous power that weak, diffident schoolgirl could wield if she chose to do it. Many and many a time she might rule the Autocrat of Russia, whose lightest word is law to seventy millions of human beings! She was only a girl, and she looked like a thousand others I have seen, but never a girl provoked such a novel and peculiar interest in me before. A strange, new sensation is a rare thing in this humdrum life, and I had it here. There was nothing stale or worn out about the thoughts and feelings the situation and the circumstances created. It seemed strange — stranger than I can tell — to think that the central figure in the cluster of men and women, chatting here under the trees like the most ordinary individual in the land, was a man who could open his lips and ships would fly through the waves, locomotives would speed over the plains, couriers would hurry from village to village, a hundred telegraphs would flash the word to the four corners of an empire that stretches its vast proportions over a seventh part of the habitable globe, and a countless multitude of men would spring to do his bidding. I had a sort of vague desire to examine his hands and see if they were of flesh and blood, like other men's. Here was a man who could do this wonderful thing, and yet if I chose I could knock him down. The case was plain, but it seemed preposterous, nevertheless — as preposterous as trying to knock down a mountain or wipe out a continent. If this man sprained his ankle, a million miles of telegraph would carry the news over mountains — valleys — uninhabited deserts — under the trackless sea — and ten thousand newspapers would prate of it; if he were grievously ill, all the nations would know it before the sun rose again; if he dropped lifeless where he stood, his fall might shake the thrones of half a world! If I could have stolen his coat, I would have done it. When I meet a man like that, I want something to remember him by.

As a general thing, we have been shown through palaces by some plush-legged, filigreed flunkey or other, who charged a franc for it; but after talking with the company half an hour, the Emperor of Russia and his family conducted us all through their mansion themselves. They made no charge. They seemed to take a real pleasure in it.

We spent half an hour idling through the palace, admiring the cosy apartments and the rich but eminently home-like appointments of the place, and then the imperial family bade our party a kind goodbye, and proceeded to count the spoons.

An invitation was extended to us to visit the palace of the eldest son, the Crown Prince of Russia, which was near at hand. The young man was absent, but the Dukes and Countesses and Princes went over the premises with us as leisurely as was the case at the Emperor's, and conversation continued as lively as ever.

It was a little after one o'clock now. We drove to the Grand Duke Michael's, a mile away, in response to his invitation, previously given.

We arrived in twenty minutes from the Emperor's. It is a lovely place. The beautiful palace nestles among the grand old groves of the park, the park sits in the lap of the picturesque crags and hills, and both look out upon the breezy ocean. In the park are rustic seats, here and there, in secluded nooks that are dark with shade; there are rivulets of crystal water; there are glimpses of sparkling cascades through openings in the wilderness of foliage; there are streams of clear water gushing from mimic knots on the trunks of forest trees; there are miniature marble temples perched upon gray old crags; there are airy lookouts whence one may gaze upon a broad expanse of landscape and ocean. The palace is modeled after the choicest forms of Grecian architecture, and its wide colonnades surround a central court that is banked with rare flowers that fill the place with their fragrance, and in their midst springs a fountain that cools the summer air, and may possibly breed mosquitoes, but I do not think it does.

The Grand Duke and his Duchess came out, and the presentation ceremonies were as simple as they had been at the Emperor's. In a few minutes, conversation was under way, as before. The Empress appeared in the veranda, and the little Grand Duchess came out into the crowd. They had beaten us there. In a few minutes, the Emperor came himself on horseback. It was very pleasant. You can appreciate it if you have ever visited royalty and felt occasionally that possibly you might be wearing out your welcome — though as a general thing, I believe, royalty is not scrupulous about discharging you when it is done with you.

The Grand Duke is the third brother of the Emperor, is about thirty-seven years old, perhaps, and is the princeliest figure in Russia. He is even taller than the Czar, as straight as an Indian, and bears himself like one of those gorgeous knights we read about in romances of the Crusades. He looks like a great-hearted fellow who would pitch an enemy into the river in a moment, and then jump in and risk his life fishing him out again. The stories they tell of him show him to be of a brave and generous nature. He must have been desirous of proving that Americans were welcome guests in the imperial palaces of Russia, because he rode all the way to Yalta and escorted our procession to the Emperor's himself, and kept his aids scurrying about, clearing the road and offering assistance wherever it could be needed. We were rather familiar with him then, because we did not know who he was. We recognized him now, and appreciated the friendly spirit that prompted him to do us a favor that any other Grand Duke in the world would have doubtless declined to do. He had plenty of servitors whom he could have sent, but he chose to attend to the matter himself.

The Grand Duke was dressed in the handsome and showy uniform of a Cossack officer. The Grand Duchess had on a white alpaca robe, with the seams and gores trimmed with black barb lace, and a little gray hat with a feather of the same color. She is young, rather pretty, modest and unpretending, and full of winning politeness.

Our party walked all through the house, and then the nobility escorted them all over the grounds, and finally brought them back to the palace about half-past two o'clock to breakfast. They called it breakfast, but we would have called it luncheon. It consisted of two kinds of wine; tea, bread, cheese, and cold meats, and was served on the center-tables in the reception-room and the verandas — anywhere that was convenient; there was no ceremony. It was a sort of picnic. I had heard before that we were to breakfast there, but Blucher said he believed Baker's boy had suggested it to his Imperial Highness. I think not — though it would be like him. Baker's boy is the famine-breeder of the ship. He is always hungry. They say he goes about the staterooms when the passengers are out, and eats up all the soap. And they say he eats oakum. They say he will eat anything he can get between meals, but he prefers oakum. He does not like oakum for dinner, but he likes it for a lunch, at odd hours, or anything that way. It makes him very disagreeable, because it makes his breath bad, and keeps his teeth all stuck up with tar. Baker's boy may have suggested the breakfast, but I hope he did not. It went off well, anyhow. The illustrious host moved about from place to place, and helped to destroy the provisions and keep the conversation lively, and the Grand Duchess talked with the veranda parties and such as had satisfied their appetites and straggled out from the reception-room.

The Grand Duke's tea was delicious. They give one a lemon to squeeze into it, or iced milk, if he prefer it. The former is best. This tea is brought overland from China. It injures the article to transport it by sea.

When it was time to go, we bade our distinguished hosts good-bye, and they retired happy and contented to their apartments to count *their* spoons.

We had spent the best part of a day in the home of royalty, and had been as cheerful and comfortable all the time as we could have been in the ship. I would as soon have thought of being cheerful in Abraham's bosom as in the palace of an Emperor. I supposed that Emperors were terrible people. I thought they never did anything but wear magnificent crowns and red velvet dressing-gowns with dabs of wool sewed on them in spots, and sit on thrones and scowl at the flunkies and the people in the parquette, and order Dukes and Duchesses off to execution. I find, however, that when one is so fortunate as to get behind the scenes and see them at home and in the privacy of their firesides, they are strangely like common mortals. They are pleasanter to look upon then than they are in their theatrical aspect. It seems to come as natural to them to dress and act like other people as it is to put a friend's cedar pencil in your pocket when you are done using it. But I can never have any confidence in the tinsel kings of the theater after this. It will be a great loss. I used to take such a thrilling pleasure in them. But, hereafter, I will turn me sadly away and say:

"This does not answer — this isn't the style of king the *I* am acquainted with."

When they swagger around the stage in jeweled crowns and splendid robes, I shall feel bound to observe that all the Emperors that every *I* was personally acquainted with wore the commonest sort of clothes, and did not swagger. And when they come on the stage attended by a vast body-guard of supes in helmets and tin breastplates, it will be my duty as well as my pleasure to inform the ignorant that no crowned head of my acquaintance has a soldier anywhere about his house or his person.

Possibly it may be thought that our party tarried too long, or did other improper things, but such was not the case. The company felt that they were occupying an unusually responsible position — they were representing the people of America, not the government — and therefore they were careful to do their best to perform their high mission with credit.

On the other hand, the Imperial families, no doubt, considered that in entertaining us they were more especially entertaining the people of America than they could by showering attentions on a whole platoon of ministers plenipotentiary; and therefore they gave to the event its fullest significance, as an expression of good will and friendly feeling toward the entire country. We took the kindnesses we received as attentions thus directed, of course, and not to ourselves as a party. That we felt a personal pride in being received as the representatives of a nation, we do not deny; that we felt a national pride in the warm cordiality of that reception, cannot be doubted.

Our poet has been rigidly suppressed, from the time we let go the anchor. When it was announced that we were going to visit the Emperor of Russia, the fountains of his great deep were broken up, and he rained ineffable bosh for four-and-twenty hours. Our original anxiety as to what we were going to do with ourselves, was suddenly transformed into anxiety about what we were going to do with our poet. The problem was solved at last. Two alternatives were offered him — he must either swear a dreadful oath that he would not issue a line of his poetry while he was in the Czar's dominions, or else remain under guard on board the ship until we were safe at Constantinople again. He fought the dilemma long, but yielded at last. It was a great deliverance. Perhaps the savage reader would like a specimen of his style. I do not mean this term to be offensive. I only use it because "the gentle reader" has been used so often that any change from it cannot but be refreshing:

> "Save us and sanctify us, and finally, then,
> See good provisions we enjoy while we journey to
>   Jerusa*lem*.
> For so man proposes, which it is most true,
> And time will wait for none, nor for us too."

The sea has been unusually rough all day. However, we have had a lively time of it, anyhow. We have had quite a run of visitors. The Governor-General came, and we received him with a salute of nine guns. He brought his family with him. I observed that carpets were spread from the pier-head to his carriage for him to walk on, though I have seen him walk there without any carpet when he was not on business. I thought may be he had what the accidental insurance people might call an extra-hazardous polish ("policy" — joke, but not above mediocrity) on his boots, and wished to protect them, but I examined and could not see that they were blacked any better than usual. It may have been that he had forgotten his carpet before, but he did not have it with him, anyhow. He was an exceedingly pleasant old gentleman; we all liked him, especially Blucher. When he went away, Blucher invited him to come again and fetch his carpet along.

Prince Dolgorouki and a Grand Admiral or two whom we had seen yesterday at the reception, came on board also. I was a little distant with these parties, at first, because when I have been visiting Emperors I do not like to be too familiar with people I only know by reputation, and whose moral characters and standing in society I cannot be thoroughly acquainted with. I judged it best to be a little offish, at first. I said to myself, Princes and Counts and Grand Admirals are very well, but they are not Emperors, and one cannot be too particular about whom he associates with.

Baron Wrangel came, also. He used to be a Russian Ambassador at Washington. I told him I had an uncle who fell down a shaft and broke himself in two, as much as a year before that. That was a falsehood, but then I was not going to let any man eclipse me on surprising adventures, merely for the want of a little invention. The Baron is a fine man, and is said to stand high in the Emperor's confidence and esteem.

Baron Ungern-Sternberg, a boisterous, whole-souled old nobleman, came with the rest. He is a man of progress and enterprise — a representative man of the age. He is the Chief Director of the railway system of Russia — a sort of railroad king. In his line he is making things move along in this country. He has traveled extensively in America. He says he has tried convict labor on his railroads, and with perfect success. He says the convicts work well, and are quiet and peaceable. He observed that he employs nearly ten thousand of them now. This appeared to be another call on my resources. I was equal to the emergency. I said we had eighty thousand convicts employed on the railways in America — all of them under sentence of death for murder in the first degree. That closed *him* out. We had General Todleben (the famous defender of Sebastopol, during the siege), and many inferior army and also navy officers, and a number of unofficial Russian ladies and gentlemen. Naturally, a champagne luncheon was in order, and was accomplished without loss of life. Toasts and jokes were discharged freely, but no speeches were made save one thanking the Emperor and the Grand Duke, through the Governor-General, for our hospitable reception, and one by the Governor-General in reply, in which he returned the Emperor's thanks for the speech, etc.

CHAPTER XI

We returned to Constantinople, and after a day or two spent in exhausting marches about the city and voyages up the Golden Horn in *caiques*, we steamed away again. We passed through the Sea of Mamora and the Dardanelles, and steered for a new land — a new one to us, at least — Asia. We had as yet only acquired a bowing acquaintance with it, through pleasure excursions to Scutari and the regions round about.

We passed between Lemnos and Mytilene, and saw them as we had seen Elba and the Balearic Isles — mere bulky shapes, with the softening mists of distance upon them — whales in a fog, as it were. The we held our course southward, and began to "read up" celebrated Smyrna.

At all hours of the day and night the sailors in the forecastle amused themselves and aggravated us by burlesquing our visit to royalty. The opening paragraph of our Address to the Emperor was framed as follows:

"We are a handful of private citizens of America, traveling simply for recreation — and unostentatiously, as becomes our unofficial state — and, therefore, we have no excuse to tender for presenting ourselves before Your Majesty, save the desire of offering out grateful acknowledgments to the lord of a realm, which, through good and through evil report, has been the steadfast friend of the land we love so well."

The third cook, crowned with a resplendent tin basin and wrapped royally in a tablecloth mottled with grease-spots and coffee-stains, and bearing a scepter that looked strangely like a belaying pin, walked upon a dilapidated carpet and perched himself on the capstan, careless of the flying spray; his tarred and weather-beaten Chamberlains, Dukes, and Lord High Admirals surrounded him, arrayed in all the pomp that spare tarpaulins and remnants of old sails could furnish. Then the visiting "watch below," transformed into graceless ladies and uncouth pilgrims, by rude travesties upon waterfalls, hoop-skirts, white kid gloves, and swallow-tail coats, moved solemnly up the campanion-way, and bowing low, began a system of complicated and extraordinary smiling which few monarchs could look upon and live. Then the mock consul, a slush-plastered deck-sweep, drew out a soiled fragment of paper and proceeded to read, laboriously:

"To His Imperial Majesty, Alexander II., Emperor of Russia:

"We are a handful of private citizens of America, traveling simply for recreation — and unostentatiously, as becomes our unofficial state — and therefore, we have no excuse to tender for presenting ourselves before your Majesty —"

The Emperor — "Then what the devil did you come for?

— "Save the desire of offering our grateful acknowledgments to the lord of a realm which —"

The Emperor — "Oh, d—n the Address! — read it to the police. Chamberlain, take these people over to my brother, the Grand Duke's, and give them a square meal. Adieu! I am happy — I am gratified — I am delighted — I am bored. Adieu, adieu — vamose the ranch! The First Groom of the Palace will proceed to count the portable articles of value belonging to the premises."

234 THE UNABRIDGED MARK TWAIN

The farce then closed, to be repeated again with every change of the watches, and embellished with new and still more extravagant inventions of pomp and conversation.

At all times of the day and night the phraseology of that tiresome address fell upon our ears. Grimy sailors came down out of the foretop placidly announcing themselves as "a handful of private citizens of America, *traveling simply for recreation and unostentatiously,*" etc.; the coal-passers moved to their duties in the profound depths of the ship, explaining the blackness of their faces and their uncouthness of dress, with the reminder that *they* were "a handful of private citizens, traveling simply for recreation," etc., and when the cry rang through the vessel at midnight: "EIGHT BELLS! — LAR-BOARD WATCH, TURN OUT!" the larboard watch came gaping and stretching out of their den, with the everlasting formula: "Aye, aye, sir! We are a handful of private citizens of America, traveling simply for recreation, and unostentatiously, as becomes our unofficial state!"

As I was a member of the committee, and helped to frame the Address, these sarcasms came home to me. I never heard a sailor proclaiming himself as a handful of American citizens traveling for recreation, but I wished he might trip and fall overboard, and so reduce his handful by one individual, at least. I never was so tired of any one phrase as the sailors made me of the opening sentence of the Address to the Emperor of Russia.

This seaport of Smyrna, our first notable acquaintance in Asia, is a closely-packed city of one hundred and thirty thousand inhabitants, and, like Constantinople, it has no outskirts. It is as closely packed at its outer edges as it is in the center, and then the habitations leave suddenly off and the plain beyond seems houseless. It is just like any other Oriental city. That is to say, its Moslem houses are heavy and dark, and as comfortless as so many tombs; its streets are crooked, rudely and roughly paved, and as narrow as an ordinary staircase; the streets uniformly carry a man to any other place than the one he wants to go to, and surprise him by landing him in the most unexpected localities; business is chiefly carried on in great covered bazaars, celled like a honeycomb with innumerable shops no larger than a common closet, and the whole hive cut up into a maze of alleys about wide enough to accommodate a laden camel, and well calculated to confuse a stranger and eventually lose him; everywhere there is dirt, everywhere there are fleas, everywhere there are lean, broken-hearted dogs; every alley is thronged with people; wherever you look, your eye rests upon a wild masquerade of extravagant costumes; the workshops are all open to the streets, and the workmen visible; all manner of sounds assail the ear, and over them all rings out the muezzin's cry from some tall minaret, calling the faithful vagabonds to prayer; and superior to the call to prayer, the noises in the streets, the interest of the costumes — superior to everything, and claiming the bulk of attention first, last, and all the time — is a combination of Mohammedan stenches, to which the smell of even a Chinese quarter would be as pleasant as the roasting odors of the fatted calf to the nostrils of the returning Prodigal. Such is Oriental luxury — such is Oriental splendor! We read about it all our days, but we comprehend it not until we see it. Symrna is a very old city. Its name occurs several times in the Bible, one or two of the disciples of Christ visited it, and here was located one of the original seven apocalyptic churches spoken of in Revelations. These churches were symbolized in the Scriptures as candlesticks, and on certain conditions there was a sort of implied promise that Smyrna should be endowed with a "crown of life." She was to "be faithful unto death" — those were the terms. She has not kept up her faith straight along, but the pilgrims that wander hither consider that she has come near enough to it to save her, and so they point to the fact that Smyrna to-day wears her crown of life, and is a great city, with a great commerce and full of energy, while the cities wherein were located the other six churches, and to which no crown of life was promised, have vanished from the earth. So Smyrna really still possesses her crown of life, in a business point of view. Her career, for eighteen centuries, has been a chequered one, and she has been under the rule of princes of many creeds, yet there has been no season during all that time, as far as we know (and during such seasons as she was inhabited at all, that she has been without her little community of Christians "faithful unto death." Hers was the only church against which no threats were implied in the Revelation, and the only one which survived.

With Ephesus, forty miles from here, where was located another of the seven churches, the case was different. The "candlestick" has been removed from Ephesus. Her light has been put out. Pilgrims, always prone to find prohecies in the Bible, and often where none exist, speak cheerfully and complacently of poor, ruined Ephesus as the victim of prophecy. And yet there is no sentence that promises, without due qualification, the destruction of the city. The words are:

"Remember, therefore, from whence thou art fallen, and repent, and do the first works; or else I will come unto thee quickly, and will remove thy candlestick out of his place, except thou repent."

That is all; the other verses are singularly *complimentary* to Ephesus. The threat is qualified. There is no history to show that she did not repent. But the cruelest habit the modern prophecy-savans have, is that one of coolly and arbitrarily fitting the prophetic shirt on to the wrong man. They do it without regard to rhyme or reason. But the cases I have just mentioned are instances in point. Those "prophecies" are distinctly leveled at the "*churches* of Ephesus, Smyrna," etc., and yet the pilgrims invariably make them refer to the *cities* instead. No crown of life is promised to the town of Smyrna and its commerce, but to the handful of Christians who formed its "church." If *they* were "faithful unto death," they have their crown now — but no amount of faithfulness and legal shrewdness combined could legitimately drag the *city* into a participation in the promises of the prophecy. The stately language of the Bible refers to a crown of life whose luster will reflect the day-beams of the endless ages of eternity, not the butterfly existence of a city built by men's hands, which must pass to dust with the builders and be forgotten even in the mere handful of centuries vouchsafed to the solid world itself between its cradle and its grave.

The fashion of delving out fulfillments of prophecy where that prophecy consists of mere "ifs," trenches upon the absurd. Suppose, a thousand years from now, a malarious swamp builds itself up in the shallow harbor of Smyrna, or something else kills the town; and suppose, also, that within that time the swamp that has filled the renowned harbor of Ephesus and rendered her ancient site deadly and uninhabitable to-day, becomes hard and healthy ground; suppose the natural consequence ensues, to wit: that Smyrna becomes a melancholy ruin, and Ephesus is rebuilt. What would the prophecy savans say? They would coolly skip over our age of the world, and say: "Smyrna was not faithful unto death, and so her crown of life was denied her; Ephesus repented, and lo! her candlestick was not removed. Behold these evidences! How wonderful is propechy!"

Smyrna has been utterly destroyed six times. If her crown of life had been an insurance policy, she would have had an opportunity to collect on it the first time she fell. But she holds it on sufferance and by a complimentary construction of language which does not refer to her. Six different times, however, I suppose some infatuated prophecy-enthusiast blundered along and said, to the infinite disgust of Smyrna and the Smyrniotes: "In sooth, here is astounding fulfillment of prophecy! Smyrna hath not been faithful unto death, and behold her crown of life is vanished from her head. Verily, these things be astonishing!"

Such things have a bad influence. They provoke worldly men into using light conversation concerning sacred subjects. Thick-headed commentators upon the Bible, and stupid preachers and teachers, work more damage to religion than sensible, cool-brained clergymen can fight away again, toil as they may. It is not good judgment to fit a crown of life upon a city which has been destroyed six times. That other class of wiseacres who twist prophecy in such a manner as to make it promise the destruction and desolation of the same city, use judgment just as bad, since the city is in a very flourishing condition now, unhappily for them. These things put arguments into the mouth of infidelity.

A portion of the city is pretty exclusively Turkish; the Jews have a quarter to themselves; the Franks another quarter; so also, with the Armenians. The Armenians, of course, are Christians. Their houses are large, clean, airy, handsomely paved with black and white squares of marble, and in the center of many of them is a square court, which has in it a luxuriant flower-garden and a sparkling fountain; the doors of all the rooms open on this. A very wide hall leads to the street door, and in this women sit, the most of the day. In the cool of the evening they dress up in their best raiment and show themselves at the door. They are all comely of countenance, and exceedingly neat and cleanly; they look as if they were just out of a band-box. Some of the young ladies — many of them, I may say — are even very beautiful; they average a shade better than American girls — which treasonable words I pray may be forgiven me. They are very sociable, and will smile back when a stranger smiles at them, bow back when he bows, and talk back if he speaks to them. No introduction is required. An hour's chat at the door with a pretty girl one never saw before, is easily obtained and is very pleasant. I have tried it. I could not talk anything but English, and the girl knew nothing but Greek, or Armenian, or some such barbarous tongue, but we got along very well. I find that in cases like these, the fact that you cannot comprehend each other isn't much of a drawback. In that Russian town of Yalta I danced an astonishing sort of dance an hour long, and one I had not heard of before, with a very pretty girl, and we talked incessantly, and laughed exhaustingly, and neither one ever knew what the other was driving at. But it was splendid. There were twenty people in the set, and the dance was very lively and complicated. It was complicated enough without me — with me it was more so. I threw in a figure now and then that surprised those Russians. But I have never ceased to think of that girl. I have written to her, but I cannot direct the epistle because her name is one of those nine-jointed Russian affairs, and there are not letters enough in our alphabet to hold out. I am not reckless enough to try to pronounce it when I am awake, but I make a stagger at it in my dreams, and get up with the lockjaw in the morning. I am fading. I do not take my meals now, with any sort or regularity. Her dear name haunts me still in my dreams. It is awful on teeth. It never comes out of my mouth but it fetches an old snag along with it. And then the lockjaw closes down and nips off a couple of the last syllables — but they taste good.

Coming through the Dardanelles, we saw camel trains on shore with the glasses, but we were never close to one till we got to Smyrna. These camels are very much larger than the scrawny specimens one sees in the menagerie. They stride along these streets, in single file, a dozen in a train, with heavy loads on their backs, and a fancy-looking negro in Turkish costume, or an Arab, preceding them on a little donkey and completely over-shadowed and rendered insignificant by the huge beasts. To see a camel train laden with the spices of Arabia and the rare fabrics of Persia come marching through the narrow alleys of the bazaar, among porters with their burdens, money-changers, lamp merchants, Alnaschars in the glassware business, portly cross-legged Turks smoking the famous narghili, and the crowds drift-ing to and fro in the fanciful costumes of the East, is a genuine revelation of the Orient. The picture lacks nothing. It casts you back at once into your forgotten boyhood, and again you dream over the wonders of the Arabian Nights; again your companions are princes, your lord is the Caliph Haroun Al Raschid, and your servants are terrific giants and genii that come with smoke and lightning and thunder, and go as a storm goes when they depart!

CHAPTER XII

We inquired, and learned that the lions of Smyrna consisted of the ruins of the ancient citadel, whose broken and prodigious battlements frown upon the city from a lofty hill just in the edge of the town — the Mount Pagus of Scripture, they call it; the site of that one of the seven apocalyptic churches of Asia which was located here in the first century of the Christian era; and the grave and the place of martyrdom of the venerable Polycarp, who suffered in Smyrna for his religion some eighteen hundred years ago.

We took little donkeys and started. We saw Polycarp's tomb, and then hurried on.

The "Seven Churches" — thus they abbreviate it — came next on the list. We rode there — about a mile and a half in the sweltering sun — and visited a little Greek church which they said was built upon the ancient site; and we paid a small fee, and the holy attendant gave each of us a little wax candle as a remembrancer of the place, and I put mine in my hat and the sun melted it and the grease all ran down the back of my neck; and so now I have not anything but the wick, and it is a sorry and wilted-looking wick at that.

Several of us argued as well as we could that the "church" mentioned in the Bible meant a party of Christians, and not a building; that the Bible spoke of them as being very poor —

poor, I thought, and so subject to persecution (as per Polycarp's martyrdom) that in the first place they probably could not have afforded a church edifice, and in the second would not have dared to build it in the open light of day if they could; and finally, that if they had had the prvilege of building it, common judgment would have suggested that they build it somewhere near the town. But the elders of the ship's family ruled us down and scouted our evidences. However, retribution came to them afterward. They found that they had been led astray and had gone to the wrong place; they discovered that the accepted site is in the city.

Riding through the town, we could see marks of the six Smyrnas that have existed here and been burned up by fire or knocked down by earthquakes. The hills and the rocks are rent asunder in places, excavations expose great blocks of building-stone that have lain buried for ages, and all the mean houses and walls of modern Smyrna along the way are spotted white with broken pillars, capitals, and fragments of sculptured marble that once adorned the lordly palaces that were the glory of the city in the olden times.

The ascent of the hill of the citadel is very steep, and we proceeded rather slowly. But there were matters of interest about us. In one place, five hundred feet above the sea, the perpendicular bank on the upper side of the road was ten or fifteen feet high, and the cut exposed three veins of oyster-shells, just as we have seen quartz veins exposed in the cutting of a road in Nevada or Montana. The veins were about eighteen inches thick and two or three feet apart, and they slanted along downward for a distance of thirty feet or more, and then disappeared where the cut joined the road. Heaven only knows how far a man might trace them by "stripping." They were clean, nice oyster-shells, large, and just like any other oyster-shells. They were thickly massed together, and none were scattered or below the veins. Each one was a well-defined lead by itself, and without a spur. My first instinct was to set up the usual —

NOTICE:

"We, the undersigned, claim five claims of two hundred feet each (and one for discovery) on this ledge or lode of oyster-shells with all its dips, spurs, angles, variations, and sinuosities, and fifty feet on each side of the same, to work it, etc., etc., according to the mining laws of Smyrna."

They were such perfectly natural-looking leads that I could hardly keep from "taking them up." Among the oyster-shells were mixed many fragments of ancient, broken crockeryware. Now how did those masses of oyster-shells get there? I cannot determine. Broken crockery and oyster-shells are suggestive of restaurants — but then they could have had no such places away up there on that mountain-side in our time, because nobody has lived up there. A restaurant would not pay in such a stony, forbidding, desolate place. And besides, there were no champagne corks among the shells. If there ever was a restaurant there, it must have been in Smyrna's palmy days, when the hills were covered with palaces. I could believe in one restaurant, on those terms; but then how about the three? Did they have restaurants there at three different periods of the world? — because there are two or three feet of solid earth between the oyster leads. Evidently, the restaurant solution will not answer.

The hill might have been the bottom of the sea, once, and been lifted up, with oyster-beds, by an eathquake — but, then, how about the crockery? And, moreover, how about *three* oyster-beds, one above another, and thick strata of good honest earth between?

That theory will not do. It is just possible that this hill is Mount Ararat, and that Noah's Ark rested here, and he ate oysters and threw the shells overboard. But that will not do, either. There are the three layers again and the solid earth between — and, besides, there were only eight in Noah's family, and they could not have eaten all these oysters in the two or three months they stayed on top of that mountain. The beasts — however, it is simply absurd to suppose he did not know any more than to feed the beasts on oyster suppers.

It is painful — it is even humiliating — but I am reduced at last to one slender theory: that the oysters climbed up there of their own accord. But what object could that have had in view? — what did they want up there? What could any oyster want to climb a hill for? To climb a hill must necessarily be fatiguing and annoying exercise for an oyster. The most natural conclusion would be that the oysters climbed up there to look at the scenery. Yet when one comes to reflect upon the nature of an oysters, it seems plain that he does not care for scenery. An oyster has no taste for such things; he cares nothing for the beautiful. An oyster is of a retiring disposition, and not lively — not even cheerful above the average, and never enterprising. But, above all, an oyster does not take any interest in scenery — he scorns it. What have I arrived at now? Simply at the point I started from, namely, *those oyster shells are there,* in regular layers, five hundred feet above the sea, and no man knows how they got there. I have hunted up the guide-books, and the gist of what they say is this: "They are there, but how they got there is a mystery."

Twenty-five years ago, a multitude of people in America put on their ascension robes, took a tearful leave of their friends, and made ready to fly up into heaven at the first blast of the trumpet. But the angel did not blow it. Miller's resurrection day

was a failure. The Millerites were disgusted. I did not suspect
that there were Millers in Asia Minor, but a gentleman tells me
that they had it all set for the world to come to an end in Smyrna one day about three years ago. There was much buzzing and
preparation for a long time previously, and it culminated in a
wild excitement at the appointed time. A vast number of the
populace ascended the citadel hill early in the morning, to get
out of the way of the general destruction, and many of the infatuated closed up their shops and retired from all earthly
business. But the strange part of it was that about three in the
afternoon, while this gentleman and his friends were at dinner in
the hotel, a terrific storm of rain, accompanied by thunder and
lightning, broke forth and continued with dire fury for two or
three hours. It was a thing unprecedented in Smyrna at that time
of the year, and scared some of the most skeptical. The streets
ran rivers and the hotel floor was flooded with water. The dinner
had to be suspended. When the storm finished and left
everybody drenched through and through, and melancholy and
half-drowned, the ascensionists came down from the mountain
as dry as so many charity-sermons! They had been looking down
upon the fearful storm going on below, and really believed that
their proposed destruction of the world was proving a grand success.

A railway here in Asia — in the dreamy realm of the Orient —
in the fabled land of the Arabian Nights — is a strange thing to
think of. And yet they have one already, and are building
another. The present one is well built and well conducted, by an
English Company, but is not doing an immense amount of
business. The first year it carried a good many passengers, but
its freight list only comprised eight hundred pounds of figs!

It runs almost to the very gates of Ephesus — a town great in
all ages of the world — a city familiar to readers of the Bible,
and one which was as old as the very hills when the disciples of
Christ preached in its streets. It dates back to the shadowy ages
of tradition, and was the birthplace of gods renowned in Grecian
mythology. The idea of a locomotive tearing through such a
place as this, and waking the phantoms of its old days of romance out of their dreams of dead and gone centuries, is curious
enough.

We journey thither to-morrow to see the celebrated ruins.

CHAPTER XIII

This has been a stirring day. The superintendent of the railway
put a train at our disposal, and did us the further kindness of accompanying us to Ephesus and giving to us his watchful care.
We brought sixty scarcely perceptible donkeys in the freight cars,

for we had much ground to go over. We have seen some of the
most grotesque costumes, along the line of the railroad, that can
be imagined. I am glad that no possible combination of words
could describe them, for I might then be foolish enough to attempt it.

At ancient Ayassalook, in the midst of a forbidding desert, we
came upon long lines of ruined aqueducts, and other remnants
of architectural grandeur, that told us plainly enough we were
nearing what had been a metropolis once. We left the train and
mounted the donkeys, along with our invited guests — pleasant
young gentlemen from the officers' list of an American man-of-
war.

The little donkeys had saddles upon them which were made
very high in order that the rider's feet might not drag the
ground. The preventative did not work well in the cases of our
tallest pilgrims, however. There were no bridles — nothing but a
single rope, tied to the bit. It was purely ornamental, for the
donkey cared nothing for it. If he were drifting to starboard,
you might put your helm down hard the other way, if it were
any satisfaction to you to do it, but he would continue to drift
to starboard all the same. There was only one process which
could be depended on, and that was to get down and lift his rear
around until his head pointed in the right direction, or take him
under your arm and carry him to a part of the road which he
could not get out of without climbing. The sun flamed down as
hot as a furnace, and neck-scarfs, veils and umbrellas seemed
hardly any protection; they served only to make the long
procession look more than ever fantastic — for be it known the
ladies were all riding astride because they could not stay on the
shapeless saddles sidewise, the men were perspiring and out of
temper, their feet were banging against the rocks, the donkeys
were capering in every direction but the right one and being
belabored with clubs for it, and every now and then a broad umbrella would suddenly go down out of the cavalcade, announcing
to all that one more pilgrim had bitten the dust. It was a wilder
picture than those solitudes had seen for many a day. No
donkeys ever existed that were as hard to navigate as these, I
think, or that had so many vile, exasperating instincts. Occasionally, we grew so tired and breathless with fighting them
that we had to desist, — and immediately the donkey would
come down to a deliberate walk. This, with the fatigue, and the
sun, would put a man asleep; and as soon as the man was
asleep, the donkey would lie down. My donkey shall never see
his boyhood's home again. He has lain down once too often. He
must die.

We all stood in the vast theater of ancient Ephesus, — the
stone-benched amphitheater, I mean — and had our picture

taken. We looked as proper there as we would look anywhere, I suppose. We do not embellish the general desolation of a desert much. We add what dignity we can to a stately ruin with our green umbrellas and jackasses, but it is little. However, we mean well.

I wish to say a brief word of the aspect of Ephesus.

On a high, steep hill, toward the sea, is a gray ruin of ponderous blocks of marble, wherein, tradition says, St. Paul was imprisoned eighteen centuries ago. From these old walls you have the finest view of the desolate scene where once stood Ephesus, the proudest city of ancient times, and whose Temple of Diana was so noble in disign and so exquisite of workmanship, that it ranked high in the list of the Seven Wonders of the World.

Behind you is the sea; in front is a level green valley (a marsh, in fact), extending far away among the mountains; to the right of the front view is the old citadel of Ayassalook, on a high hill; the ruined mosque of the Sultan Selim stands near it in the plain (this is built over the grave of St. John, and was formerly a Christian church); further toward you is the hill of Prion, around whose front is clustered all that remains of the ruins of Ephesus that still stand; divided from it by a narrow valley is the long, rocky, rugged mountain of Coressus. The scene is a pretty one, and yet desolate — for in that wide plain no man can live, and in it is no human habitation. But for the crumbling arches and monstrous piers and broken walls that rise from the foot of the hill of Prion, one could not believe that in this place once stood a city whose renown is older than tradition itself. It is incredible to reflect that things as familiar all over the world today as household words belong in the history and in the shadowy legends of this silent, mournful solitude. We speak of Apollo and of Diana — they were born here; of the metamorphosis of Syrinx into a reed — it was done here; of the great god Pan — he dwelt in the caves of this hill of Coressus; of the Amazons — this was their best-prized home; of Bacchus and Hercules — both fought the warlike women here; of the Cyclops — they laid the ponderous marble blocks of some of the ruins yonder; of Homer — this was one of his many birthplaces; of Cimon of Athens; of Alcibiades, Lysander, Agesilaus — they visited here; so did Alexander the Great; so did Hannibal and Antiochus, Scipio, Lucullus, and Sylla; Brutus, Cassius, Pompey, Cicero, and Augustus; Antony was a judge in this place, and left his seat in the open court, while the advocates were speaking, to run after Cleopatra, who passed the door; from this city these two sailed on pleasure excursions, in galleys with silver oars and perfumed sails, and with companies of beautiful girls to serve them, and actors and musicians to amuse them; in days that seem

almost modern, so remote are they from the early history of this
city, Paul the Apostle preached the new religion here, and so did
John, and here it is supposed the former was pitted against wild
beasts, for in I Corinthians, XV. 32, he says:

"If after the manner of men I have fought with beasts at Ephesus," etc.

when many men still lived who had seen the Christ; here Mary
Magdalen died, and here the Virgin Mary ended her days with
John, albeit Rome has since judged it best to locate her grave
elsewhere; six or seven hundred years ago — almost yesterday, as
it were — troops of mail-clad Crusaders thronged the streets;
and to come down to trifles, we speak of meandering streams,
and find a new interest in a common word when we discover
that the crooked river Meander, in yonder valley, gave it to our
dictionary. It makes me feel as old as these dreary hills to look
down upon these moss-hung ruins, this historic desolation. One
may read the Scriptures and believe, but he cannot go and stand
yonder in the ruined theater and in imagination people it again
with the vanished multitudes who mobbed Paul's comrades there
and shouted, with one voice, "Great is Diana of the Ephesians!"
The idea of a shout in such a solitude as this almost makes one
shudder.

It was a wonderful city, this Ephesus. Go where you will
about these broad plains, you find the most exquisitely-
sculptured marble fragments scattered thick among the dust and
weeds; and protruding from the ground, or lying prone upon it,
are beautiful fluted columns of porphyry and all precious marbles; and at every step you find elegantly-carved capitals and
massive bases, and polished tablets engraved with Greek inscriptions. It is a world of precious relics, a wilderness of marred
and mutilated gems. And yet what are these things to the wonders that lie buried here under the ground? At Constantinople, at
Pisa, in the cities of Spain, are great mosques and cathedrals,
whose grandest columns came from the temples and palaces of
Ephesus, and yet one has only to scratch the ground here to
match them. We shall never know what magnificence is, until
this imperial city is laid bare to the sun.

The finest piece of sculpture we have yet seen and the one that
impressed us most (for we do not know much about art and cannot easily work up ourselves into ecstasies over it), is one that
lies in this old theater of Ephesus which St. Paul's riot has made
so celebrated. It is only the headless body of a man, clad in a
coat of mail, with a Medusa head upon the breast-plate, but we
feel persuaded that such dignity and such majesty were never
thrown into a form of stone before.

What builders they were, these men of antiquity! The massive
arches of some of these ruins rest upon piers that are fifteen feet

square and built entirely of solid blocks of marble, some of which are as large as a Saratoga trunk, and some the size of a boardinghouse sofa. They are not shells or shafts of stone filled inside with rubbish, but the whole pier is a mass of solid masonry. Vast arches, that may have been the gates of the city, are built in the same way. They have braved the storms and sieges of three thousand years, and have been shaken by many an earthquake, but still they stand. When they dig alongside of them, they find ranges of ponderous masonry that are as perfect in every detail as they were the day those old Cyclopian giants finished them. An English company is going to excavate Ephesus—and then!

And now am I reminded of —

THE LEGEND OF THE SEVEN SLEEPERS.

In the Mount of Prion, yonder, is the Cave of the Seven Sleepers. Once upon a time, about fifteen hundred years ago, seven young men lived near each other in Ephesus, who belonged to the despised sect of the Christians. It came to pass that the good King Maximilianus (I am telling this story for nice little boys and girls), it came to pass, I say, that the good King Maximilianus fell to persecuting the Christians, and as time rolled on he made it very warm for them. So the seven young men said one to the other, Let us get up and travel. And they got up and traveled. They tarried not to bid their fathers and mothers good-bye, or any friend they knew. They only took certain moneys which their parents had, and garments that belonged unto their friends, whereby they might remember them when far away; and they took also the dog Ketmehr, which was the property of their neighbor Malchus, because the beast did run his head into a noose which one of the young men was carrying carelessly, and they had not time to release him; and they took also certain chickens that seemed lonely in the neighboring coops, and likewise some bottles of curious liquors that stood near the grocer's window; and then they departed from the city. By-and-by they came to a marvelous cave in the Hill of Prion and entered into it and feasted, and presently they hurried on again. But they forgot the bottles of curious liquors, and left them behind. They traveled in many lands, and had many strange adventures. They were virtuous young men, and lost no opportunity that fell in their way to make their livelihood. Their motto was in these words, namely, "Procrastination is the thief of time." And so, whenever they did come upon a man who was alone, they said, Behold, this person hath the where withal — let us go through him. And they went through him. At the end of five years they had waxed tired of travel and adventure, and

longed to revisit their old home again and hear the voices and
see the faces that were dear unto their youth. Therefore they
went through such parties as fell in their way where they sojourned at that time, and journeyed back toward Ephesus
again. For the good King Maximilianus was become converted
unto the new faith, and the Christians rejoiced because they
were no longer persecuted. One day as the sun went down,
they came to the cave in the Mount of Prion, and they said,
each to his fellow, Let us sleep here, and go and feast and
make merry with our friends when the morning cometh. And
each of the seven lifted up his voice and said, It is a whiz. So
they went in, and lo, where they had put them, there lay the
bottles of strange liquors, and they judged that age had not
impaired their excellence. Wherein the wanderers were right,
and the heads of the same were level. So each of the young
men drank six bottles, and behold they felt very tired, then,
and lay down and slept soundly.

When they awoke, one of them, Johannes — surnamed
Smithianus — said, We are naked. And it was so. Their raiment
was all gone, and the money which they had gotten from a
stranger whom they had proceeded through as they approached
the city, was lying upon the ground, corroded and rusted and
defaced. Likewise the dog Ketmehr was gone, and nothing save
the brass that was upon his collar remained. They wondered
much at these things. But they took the money, and they wrapped about their bodies some leaves, and came up to the top of
the hill. Then were they perplexed. The wonderful temple of
Diana was gone; many grand edifices they had never seen before
stood in the city; men in strange garbs moved about the streets,
and every thing was changed.

Johannes said, It hardly seems like Ephesus. Yet here is the
great gymnasium; here is the mighty theater, wherein I have seen
seventy thousand men assembled; here is the Agora; there is the
font where the sainted John the Baptist immersed the converts;
yonder is the prison of the good St. Paul, where we all did use
to go to touch the ancient chains that bound him and be cured
of our distempers; I see the tomb of the disciple Luke, and afar
off is the church wherein repose the ashes of the holy John,
where the Christians of Ephesus go twice a year to gather the
dust from the tomb, which is able to make bodies whole again
that are corrupted by disease, and cleanse the soul from sin; but
see how the wharves encroach upon the sea, and what multitudes
of ships are anchored in the bay; see, also, how the city hath
stretched abroad, far over the valley behind Prion, and even unto the walls of Ayassalook; and lo, all the hills are white with
palaces and ribbed with colonnades of marble. How mighty is
Ephesus become!

And wondering at what their eyes had seen, they went down into the city and purchased garments and clothed themselves. And when they would have passed on, the merchant bit the coins which they had given him, with his teeth, and turned them about and looked curiously upon them, and cast them upon his counter, and listened if they rang; and then he said, These be bogus. And they said, Depart thou to Hades, and went their way. When they were come to their houses, they recognized them, albeit they seemed old and mean; and they rejoiced, and were glad. They ran to the doors, and knocked, and strangers opened, and looked inquiringly upon them. And they said, with great excitement, while their hearts beat high, and the color in their faces came and went, Where is my father? Where is my mother? Where are Dionysius and Serapion, and Pericles, and Decius? And the strangers that opened said, We know not these. The Seven said, How, you know them not? How long have ye dwelt here, and whither are they gone that dwelt here before ye? And the strangers said, Ye play upon us with a jest, young men; we and our fathers have sojourned under these roofs these six generations; the names ye utter rot upon the tombs, and they that bore them have run their brief race, have laughed and sung, have borne the sorrow and the weariness that were allotted them, and are at rest; for nine-score years and summers have come and gone, and the autumn leaves have fallen, since the roses faded out of their cheeks and they laid them to sleep with the dead.

Then the seven young men turned them away from their homes, and the strangers shut the doors upon them. The wanderers marveled greatly, and looked into the faces of all they met, as hoping to find one that they knew; but all were strange, and passed them by and spake no friendly word. They were sore distressed and sad. Presently they spake unto a citizen and said, Who is King in Ephesus? And the citizen answered and said, Whence come ye that ye know not that great Laertius reigns in Ephesus? They looked one at the other, greatly perplexed, and presently asked again, Where, then, is the good King Maximilianus? The citizen moved him apart, as one who is afraid, and said, Verily these men be mad, and dream dreams, else would they know that the King whereof they speak is dead above two hundred years agone.

Then the scales fell from the eyes of the Seven, and one said, Alas, that we drank of the curious liquors. They have made us weary, and in dreamless sleep these two long centuries have we lain. Our homes are desolate, our friends are dead. Behold, the jig is up — let us die. And that same day went they forth and laid them down and died. And in the selfsame day, likewise, the Seven-up did cease in Ephesus, for that the Seven that were up were down again, and departed and dead withal. And the names that be upon their tombs, even unto this time, are Johannes Smithianus, Trumps, Gift, High, and Low, Jack, and The Game. And with the sleepers lie also the bottles wherein were once the curious liquors; and upon them is writ, in ancient letters, such words as these — names of heathen gods of olden time, perchance; Rumpunch, Jinsling, Eggnog.

Such is the story of the Seven Sleepers (with slight variations), and I know it is true, because I have seen the cave myself.

Really, so firm a faith had the ancients in this legend, that as late as eight or nine hundred years ago, learned travelers held it in superstitious fear.

Two of them record that they ventured into it, but ran quickly out again, not daring to tarry lest they should fall asleep and outlive their great-grandchildren a century or so. Even at this day the ignorant denizens of the neighboring country prefer not to sleep in it.

CHAPTER XIV

When I last made a memorandum, we were at Ephesus. We are in Syria, now, encamped in the mountains of Lebanon. The interregnum has been long, both as to time and distance. We brought not a relic from Ephesus! After gathering up fragments of sculptured marbles and breaking ornaments from the interior work of the mosques; and after bringing them, at a cost of infinite trouble and fatigue, five miles on muleback to the railway depot, a government officer compelled all who had such things to disgorge! He had an order from Constantinople to *look out for our party,* and see that we carried nothing off. It was a wise, a just, and a well-deserved rebuke, but it created a sensation. I never resist a temptation to plunder a stranger's premises without feeling insufferably vain about it. This time I felt proud beyond expression. I was serene in the midst of the scoldings that were heaped upon the Ottoman government for its affront offered to a pleasuring party of entirely respectable gentlemen and ladies. I said, "We that have free souls, it touches us not." The shoe not only pinched our party, but it pinched hard; a principal sufferer discovered that the imperial order was inclosed in an envelope bearing the seal of the British Embassy at Constantinople, and therefore must have been inspired by the representative of the Queen. This was bad — very bad. Coming solely from the Ottomans, it might have signified only Ottoman hatred of Christians, and a vulgar ignorance as to genteel methods of expressing it; but coming from the Christianized, educated, polite British legation, it simply intimated that we were a sort of gentlemen and ladies who would bear watching! So the party regarded it, and were incensed accordingly. The truth doubtless was,

that the same precautions would have been taken against *any*
travelers, because the English Company who have acquired the
right to excavate Ephesus, and have paid a great sum for that
right, need to be protected, and deserve to be. They cannot afford to run the risk of having their hospitality abused by
travelers, especially since travelers are such notorious scorners of
honest behavior.

We sailed from Smyrna, in the wildest spirit of expectancy, for
the chief feature, the grand goal of the expedition, was near at
hand — we were approaching the Holy Land! Such a burrowing
into the hold for trunks that had lain buried for weeks, yes, for
months; such a hurrying to and fro above decks and below; such
a riotous system of packing and unpacking; such a littering up of
the cabins with shirts and skirts, and indescribable and un-
classable odds and ends; such a making up of bundles, and setting apart of umbrellas, green spectacles, and thick veils; such a
critical inspection of saddles and bridles that had never yet
touched horses; such a cleaning and loading of revolvers and
examining of bowie-knives; such a half-soling of the seats of
pantaloons with serviceable buckskin; then such a poring over
ancient maps; such a reading up of Bibles and Palestine travels;
such a marking out of routes; such exasperating efforts to divide
up the company into little bands of congenial spirits who might
make the long and arduous journey without quarreling; and
morning, noon, and night, such mass-meetings in the cabins,
such speech-making, such sage suggesting, such worrying and
quarreling, and such a general raising of the very mischief, was
never seen in the ship before!

But it is all over now. We are cut up into parties of six or
eight, and by this time are scattered far and wide. Ours is the
only one, however, that is venturing on what is called "the long
trip" — that is, out into Syria, by Baalbec to Damascus, and
thence down through the full length of Palestine. It would be a
tedious, and also a too risky journey, at this hot season of the
year, for any but strong, healthy men, accustomed somewhat to
fatigue and rough life in the open air. The other parties will take
shorter journeys.

For the last two months we have been in a worry about one
portion of this Holy Land pilgrimage. I refer to transportation
service. We knew very well that Palestine was a country which
did not do a large passenger business, and every man we came
across who knew anything about it gave us to understand that
not half of our party would be able to get dragomen and
animals. At Constantinople everybody fell to telegraphing the
American consuls at Alexandria and Beirout to give notice that
we wanted dragomen and transportation. We were desperate —
would take horses, jackasses, camelopards, kangaroos —

anything. At Smyrna, more telegraphing was done, to the same end. Also, fearing for the worst, we telegraphed for a large number of seats in the diligence for Damascus, and horses for the ruins of Baalbec.

As might have been expected, a notion got abroad in Syria and Egypt that the whole population of the Province of America (the Turks consider us a trifling little province in some unvisited corner of the world) were coming to the Holy Land — and so, when we got to Beirout yesterday, we found the place full of dragomen and their outfits. We had all intended to go by diligence to Damascus, and switch off to Baalbec as we went along — because we expected to rejoin the ship, go to Mount Carmel, and take to the woods from there. However, when our own private party of eight found that it was possible, and proper enough, to make the "long trip," we adopted that program. We have never been much trouble to a consul before, but we have been a fearful nuisance to our consul at Beirout. I mention this because I cannot help admiring his patience, his industry, and his accommodating spirit. I mention it, also, because I think some of our ship's company did not give him as full credit for his excellent services as he deserved.

Well, out of our eight, three were selected to attend to all business connected with the expedition. The rest of us had nothing to do but look at the beautiful city of Beirout, with its bright, new houses nestled among a wilderness of green shrubbery spread abroad over an upland that sloped gently down to the sea; and also at the mountains of Lebanon that environ it; and likewise to bathe in the transparent blue water that rolled its billows about the ship (we did not know there were sharks there). We had also to range up and down through the town and look at the costumes. These are picturesque and fanciful, but not so varied as at Constantinople and Smyrna; the women of Beirout add an agony — in the two former cities the sex wear a thin veil which one can see through (and they often expose their ankles), but at Beirout they cover their entire faces with dark-colored or black veils, so that they look like mummies, and then expose their breasts to the public. A young gentleman (I believe he was a Greek) volunteered to show us around the city, and said it would afford him great pleasure, because he was studying English and wanted practice in that language. When we had finished the rounds, however, he called for remuneration — said he hoped the gentlemen would give him a trifle in the way of a few piasters (equivalent to a few five-cent pieces). We did so. The consul was surprised when he heard it, and said he knew the young fellow's family very well, and that they were an old and highly respectable family and worth a hundred and fifty thousand dollars! Some people, so situated, would have been ashamed of the berth he had with us and his manner of crawling into it.

At the appointed time our business committee reported, and said all things were in readiness — that we were to start to-day, with horses, pack animals, and tents, and go to Baalbec, Damascus, the Sea of Tiberias, and thence southward by the way of the scene of Jacob's Dream and other notable Bible localities to Jerusalem — from thence probably to the Dead Sea, but possibly not — and then strike for the ocean and rejoin the ship three or four weeks hence at Joppa; terms, five dollars a day apiece, in gold, and everything to be furnished by the dragoman. They said we would live as well as at a hotel. I had read something like that before, and did not shame my judgment by believing a word of it. I said nothing, however, but packed up a blanket and a shawl to sleep in, pipes and tobacco, two or three woolen shirts, a portfolio, a guide-book, and a Bible. I also took along a towel and a cake of soap, to inspire respect in the Arabs, who would take me for a king in disguise.

We were to select our horses at 3 P.M. At that hour Abraham, the dragoman, marshaled them before us. With all solemnity I set it down here, that those horses were the hardest lot I ever did come across, and their accoutrements were in exquisite keeping with their style. One brute had an eye out; another had his tail sawed off close, like a rabbit, and was proud of it; another had a bony ridge running from his neck to his tail, like one of those ruined aqueducts one sees about Rome, and had a neck on him like a bowsprit; they all limped, and had sore backs, and likewise raw places and old scales scattered about their persons like brass nails in a hair trunk; their gaits were marvelous to contemplate, and replete with variety — under way the procession looked like a fleet in a storm. It was fearful. Blucher shook his head and said:

"That dragon is going to get himself into trouble fetching these old crates out of the hospital the way they are, unless he has got a permit."

I said nothing. The display was exactly according to the guide-book, and were we not traveling by the guide-book? I selected a certain horse because I thought I saw him shy, and I thought that a horse that had spirit enough to shy was not to be despised.

At 6 o'clock P.M. we came to a halt here on the breezy summit of a shapely mountain overlooking the sea, and the handsome valley where dwelt some of those enterprising Phoenicians of ancient times we read so much about; all around us are what were once the dominions of Hiram, King of Tyre, who furnished timber from the cedars of these Lebanon hills to build portions of King Solomon's Temple with.

Shortly after six, our pack-train arrived. I had not seen it before, and a good right I had to be astonished. We had nineteen serving men and twenty-six pack mules! It was a perfect caravan. It looked like one, too, as it wound among the rocks. I wondered what in the very mischief we wanted with such a vast turnout as that, for eight men. I wondered awhile, but soon I began to long for a tin plate, and some bacon and beans. I had camped out many and many a time before, and knew just what was coming. I went off, without waiting for serving men, and unsaddled my horse, and washed such portions of his ribs and his spine as projected through his hide, and when I came back, behold five stately circus-tents were up — tents that were brilliant, within, with blue and gold and crimson, and all manner of splendid adornment! I was speechless. Then they brought eight little iron bedsteads, and set them up in the tents; they put a soft mattress and pillows and good blankets and two snow-white sheets on each bed. Next, they rigged a table about the center-pole, and on it placed pewter pitchers, basins, soap, and the whitest of towels — one set for each man; they pointed to pockets in the tent, and said we could put our small trifles in them for convenience, and if we needed pins or such things, they were sticking everywhere. Then came the finishing touch — they spread carpets on the floor! I simply said, "If you call this camping out, all right — but it isn't the style *I* am used to; my little baggage that I brought along is at a discount."

It grew dark, and they put candles on the tables — candles set in bright, new, brazen candlesticks. And soon the bell — a genuine, simon-pure bell — rang, and we were invited to "the saloon." I had thought before that we had a tent or so too many, but now here was one, at least, provided for; it was to be used for nothing but an eating saloon. Like the others, it was high enough for a family of giraffes to live in, and was very handsome and clean and bright-colored within. It was a gem of a place. A table for eight, and eight canvas chairs; a tablecloth and napkins whose whiteness and whose fineness laughed to scorn the things we were used to in the great excursion steamer; knives and forks, soup-plates, dinner-plates — everything, in the handsomest kind of style. It was wonderful! And they call *this* camping out. Those stately fellows in baggy trowsers and turbaned fezes brought in a dinner which consisted of roast mutton, roast chicken, roast goose, potatoes, bread, tea, pudding, apples, and delicious grapes; the viands were better cooked than any we had eaten for weeks, and the table made a finer appearance, with its large German silver candlesticks and other finery, than any table we had sat down to for a good while, and yet that polite dragoman, Abraham, came bowing in and apologizing for the whole affair, on account of the unavoidable confusion of getting under way for a very long trip, and promising to do a great deal better in future!

It is midnight now, and we break camp at six in the morning. They call this camping out. At this rate it is a glorious privilege to be a pilgrim to the Holy Land.

CHAPTER XV

We are camped near *Temnin-el-Foka* — a name which the boys have simplified a good deal, for the sake of convenience in spelling. They call it Jacksonville. It sounds a little strangely, here in the Valley of Lebanon, but it has the merit of being easier to remember than the Arabic name.

> "COME LIKE SPIRITS, SO DEPART."
> "The night shall be filled with music,
>   And the cares that infest the day
> Shall fold their tents like the Arabs,
>   And as silently steal away."

I slept very soundly last night, yet when the dragoman's bell rang at half-past five this morning and the cry went abroad of "Ten minutes to dress for breakfast!" I heard both. It surprised me, because I have not heard the breakfast gong in the ship for a month, and whenever we have had occasion to fire a salute at daylight, I have only found it out in the course of conversation afterward. However, camping out, even though it be in a gorgeous tent, makes one fresh and lively in the morning — especially if the air you are breathing is the cool, fresh air of the mountains.

I was dressed within the ten minutes, and came out. The saloon tent had been stripped of its sides, and had nothing left but its roof; so when we sat down to table we could look out over a noble panorama of mountain, sea, and hazy valley. And sitting thus, the sun rose slowly up and suffused the picture with a world of rich coloring.

Hot mutton-chops, fried chicken, omelettes, fried potatoes, and coffee — all excellent. This was the bill of fare. It was sauced with a savage appetite purchased by hard riding the day before, and refreshing sleep in a pure atmosphere. As I called for a second cup of coffee, I glanced over my shoulder, and behold, our white village was gone — the splendid tents had vanished like magic! It was wonderful how quickly those Arabs had "folded their tents"; and it was wonderful, also, how quickly they had gathered the thousand odds and ends of the camp together and disappeared with them.

By half-past six we were under way, and all the Syrian world seemed to be under way also. The road was filled with mule trains and long processions of camels. This reminds me that we have been trying for some time to think what a camel looks like, and now we have made it out. When he is down on all his knees, flat on his breast to receive his load, he looks something like a goose swimming; and when he is upright he looks like an ostrich with an extra set of legs. Camels are not beautiful, and their long under lip gives them an exceedingly "gallus"* expression. They have immense flat, forked cushions of feet, that make a track in the dust like a pie with a slice cut out of it. They are not particular about their diet. They would eat a tombstone if they could bite it. A thistle grows about here which has needles on it that would pierce through leather, I think; if one touches you, you can find relief in nothing but profanity. The camels eat these. They show by their actions that they enjoy them. I suppose it would be a real treat to a camel to have a keg of nails for supper.

While I am speaking of animals, I will mention that I have a horse now by the name of "Jericho." He is a mare. I have seen remarkable horses before, but none so remarkable as this. I wanted a horse that could shy, and this one fills the bill. I had an idea that shying indicated spirit. If I was correct, I have got the most spirited horse on earth. He shies at everything he comes across, with the utmost impartiality. He appears to have a mortal dread of telegraph poles, especially; and it is fortunate that these are on both sides of the road, because as it is now, I never fall off twice in succession on the same side. If I fell on the same side always, it would get to be monotonous after a while. This creature has scared at everything he has seen today, except a haystack. He walked up to that with an intrepidity and a recklessness that were astonishing. And it would fill any one with admiration to see how he preserves his self-possession in the presence of a barley-sack. This dare-devil bravery will be the death of this horse some day.

He is not particularly fast, but I think he will get me through the Holy Land. He has only one fault. His tail has been chopped off or else he has sat down on it too hard, some time or other, and he has to fight the flies with his heels. This is all very well, but when he tries to kick a fly off the top of his head with his hind foot, it is too much variety. He is going to get himself into trouble that way some day. He reaches around and bites my legs, too. I do not care particularly about that, only I do not like to see a horse too sociable.

I think the owner of this prize had a wrong opinion about him. He had an idea that he was one of those fiery, untamed steeds, but he is not of that character. I know the Arab had this idea, because when he brought the horse out for inspection in Beirout; he kept jerking at the bridle and shouting in Arabic, "Whoa! will you? Do you want to run away, you ferocious beast, and break your neck?" when all the time the horse was not doing anything in the world, and only looked like he wanted to lean up against something and think. Whenever he is not shying at things, or reaching after a fly, he wants to do that yet. How it would surprise his owner to know this.

We have been in a historical section of country all day. At noon we camped three hours and took luncheon at Mekseh, near the junction of the Lebanon Mountains and the Jebel el Kuneiyiseh, and looked down into the immense, level, garden-like Valley of Lebanon. To-night we are camping near the same valley, and have a very wide sweep of it in view. We can see the long, whale-backed ridge of Mount Hermon projecting above the eastern hills. The "dews of Hermon" are falling upon us now, and the tents are almost soaked with them.

Over the way from us, and higher up the valley we can discern, through the glasses, the faint outlines of the wonderful ruins of Baalbec, the supposed Baal-Gad of Scripture. Joshua and another person were the two spies who were sent into this land of Canaan by the children of Israel to report upon its character — I mean they were the spies who reported favorably. They took back with them some specimens of the grapes of this country, and in the children's picture-books they are always represented as bearing one monstrous bunch swung to a pole between them, a respectable load for a pack-train. The Sunday-school books exaggerated it a little. The grapes are most excellent to this day, but the bunches are not as large as those in the pictures. I was surprised and hurt when I saw them, because those colossal bunches of grapes were one of my most cherished juvenile traditions.

Joshua reported favorably, and the children of Israel journeyed on, with Moses at the head of the general government, and Joshua in command of the army of six hundred thousand fighting men. Of women and children and civilians there was a countless swarm. Of all that mighty host, none but the two faithful spies ever lived to set their feet in the Promised Land. They and their descendants wandered forty years in the desert, and then Moses, the gifted warrior, poet, statesman, and philosopher, went up into Pisgah and met his mysterious fate. Where he was buried no man knows — for

> ". . . no man dug that sepulchre,
>   And no man saw it e'er —
> For the sons of God upturned the sod
>   And laid the dead man there!"

Then Joshua began his terrible raid, and from Jericho clear to this Baal-Gad, he swept the land like the Genius of Destruction. He slaughtered the people, laid waste their soil, and razed their cities to the ground. He wasted thirty-one kings also. One may call it that, though really it can hardly be called wasting them, because there were always plenty of kings in those days, and to spare. At any rate, he destroyed thirty-one kings, and divided up their realms among his Israelites. He divided up this valley stretched out here

before us, and so it was once Jewish territory. The Jews have long
since disappeared from it, however.

Back yonder, an hour's journey from here, we passed through an
Arab village of stone dry-goods boxes (they look like that), where
Noah's tomb lies under lock and key. [Noah built the ark.] Over
these old hills and valleys the ark that contained all that was left
of a vanished world once floated.

I make no apology for detailing the above information. It will be
news to some of my readers, at any rate.

Noah's tomb is built of stone, and is covered with a long stone
building. Bucksheesh let us in. The building had to be long, because
the grave of the honored old navigator is two hundred and ten feet
long itself! It is only about four feet high, though. He must have
cast a shadow like a lightning-rod. The proof that this is the
genuine spot where Noah was buried can only be doubted by uncommonly incredulous people. The evidence is pretty straight.
Shem, the son of Noah, was present at the burial, and showed the
place to his descendants, who transmitted the knowledge to their
descendants, and the lineal descendants of these introduced themselves to us to-day. It was pleasant to make the acquaintance of
members of so respectable a family. It was a thing to be proud of.
It was the next thing to being acquainted with Noah himself.

Noah's memorable voyage will always possess a living interest
for me, henceforward.

If ever an oppressed race existed, it is this one we see fettered
around us under the inhuman tyranny of the Ottoman empire. I
wish Europe would let Russia annihilate Turkey a little — not
much, but enough to make it difficult to find the place again
without a divining-rod or a diving-bell. The Syrians are very poor,
and yet they are ground down by a system of taxation that would
drive any other nation frantic. Last year their taxes were heavy
enough, in all conscience — but this year they have been increased
by the addition of taxes that were forgiven them in times of famine
in former years. On top of this the government has levied a tax of
one-tenth of the whole proceeds of the land. This is only half the
story. The Pacha of a Pachalic does not trouble himself with appointing tax-collectors. He figures up what all these taxes ought to
amount to in a certain district. Then he farms the collection out. He
calls the rich men together, the highest bidder gets the speculation,
pays the Pacha on the spot, and then sells out to smaller fry, who
sell in turn to a piratical horde of still smaller fry. These latter compel the peasant to bring his little trifle of grain to the village, at his
own cost. It must be weighed, the various taxes set apart, and the
remainder returned to the producer. But the collector delays this
duty day after day, while the producer's family are perishing for
bread; at last the poor wretch, who cannot but understand the
game, says, "Take a quarter — take half — take two-thirds if you

will, and let me go!'' It is a most outrageous state of things.

These people are naturally good-hearted and intelligent, and, with education and liberty, would be a happy and contented race. They often appeal to the stranger to know if the great world will not some day come to their relief and save them. The Sultan has been lavishing money like water in England and Paris, but his subjects are suffering for it now.

This fashion of camping out bewilders me. We have bootjacks and a bathtub now, and yet all the mysteries the pack-mules carry are not revealed. What next?

CHAPTER XVI

We had a tedious ride of about five hours, in the sun, across the Valley of Lebanon. It proved to be not quite so much of a garden as it had seemed from the hillsides. It was a desert, weed-grown waste, littered thickly with stones the size of a man's fist. Here and there the natives had scratched the ground and reared a sickly crop of grain, but for the most part the valley was given up to a handful of shepherds, whose flocks were doing what they honestly could to get a living, but the chances were against them. We saw rude piles of stones standing near the roadside, at intervals, and recognized the custom of marking boundaries which obtained in Jacob's time. There were no walls, no fences, no hedges — nothing to secure a man's possessions but these random heaps of stones. The Israelites held them sacred in the old patriarchial times, and these other Arabs, their lineal descendants, do so likewise. An American, of ordinary intelligence, would soon widely extend his property, at an outlay of mere manual labor, performed at night, under so loose a system of fencing as this.

The plows these people use are simply a sharpened stick, such as Abraham plowed with, and they still winnow their wheat as he did — they pile it on the house top, and then toss it by shovelfuls into the air until the wind has blown all the chaff away. They never invent anything, never learn anything.

We had a fine race, of a mile, with an Arab perched on a camel. Some of the horses were fast, and made very good time, but the camel scampered by them without any very great effort. The yelling and shouting, and whipping and galloping, of all parties interested, made it an exhilarating, exciting, and particularly boisterous race.

At eleven o'clock, our eyes fell upon the walls and columns of Baalbec, a noble ruin whose history is a sealed book. It has stood there for thousands of years, the wonder and admiration of travelers; but who built it, or when it was built, are questions that may never be answered. One thing is very sure, though.

Such grandeur of design, and such grace of execution, as one sees in the temples of Baalbec, have not been equaled or even approached in any work of men's hands that has been built within twenty centuries past.

The great Temple of the Sun, the Temple of Jupiter, and several smaller temples, are clustered together in the midst of one of these miserable Syrian villages, and look strangely enough in such plebeian company. These temples are built upon massive substructions that might support a world, almost; the materials used are blocks of stone as large as an omnibus — very few, if any, of them are smaller than a carpenter's tool chest — and these substructions are traversed by tunnels of masonry through which a train of cars might pass. With such foundations as these, it is little wonder that Baalbec has lasted so long. The Temple of the Sun is nearly three hundred feet long and one hundred and sixty feet wide. It had fifty-four columns around it, but only six are standing now — the others lie broken at its base, a confused and picturesque heap. The six columns are perfect, as also are their bases, Corinthian capitals and entablature — and six more shapely columns do not exist. The columns and the entablature together are ninety feet high — a prodigious altitude for shafts of stone to reach, truly — and yet one only thinks of their beauty and symmetry when looking at them; the pillars look slender and delicate, the entablature, with its elaborate sculpture, looks like rich stucco-work. But when you have gazed aloft till your eyes are weary, you glance at the great fragments of pillars among which you are standing, and find that they are eight feet through; and with them lie beautiful capitals apparently as large as a small cottage; and also single slabs of stone, superbly sculptured, that are four or five feet thick, and would completely cover the floor of any ordinary parlor. You wonder where these monstrous things came from, and it takes some little time to satisfy yourself that the airy and graceful fabric that towers above your head is made up of their mates. It seems too preposterous.

The Temple of Jupiter is a smaller ruin than the one I have been speaking of, and yet is immense. It is in a tolerable state of preservation. One row of nine columns stands almost uninjured. They are sixty-five feet high and support a sort of porch or roof, which connects them with the roof of the building. This porch-roof is composed of tremendous slabs of stone, which are so finely sculptured on the under side that the work looks like a fresco from below. One or two of these slabs had fallen, and again I wondered if the gigantic masses of carved stone that lay about me were no larger than those above my head. Within the temple, the ornamentation was elaborate and colossal. What a wonder of architectural beauty and grandeur this edifice must

have been when it was new! And what a noble picture it and its
statelier companion, with the chaos of mighty fragments scattered about them, yet makes in the moonlight!

I cannot conceive how those immense blocks of stone were
ever hauled from the quarries, or how they were ever raised to
the dizzy heights they occupy in the temples. And yet these
sculptured blocks are trifles in size compared with the rough-
hewn blocks that form the wide veranda or platform which
surrounds the Great Temple. One stretch of that platform, two
hundred feet long, is composed of blocks of stone as large and
some of them larger, than a street-car. They surmount a wall
about ten or twelve feet high. I thought those were large rocks,
but they sank into insignificance compared with those which
formed another section of the platform. These were three in
number, and I thought that each of them was about as long as
three street cars placed end to end, though, of course, they are a
third wider and a third higher than a street car. Perhaps two
railway freight cars of the largest pattern, placed end to end,
might better represent their size. In combined length these three
stones stretch nearly two hundred feet; they are thirteen feet
square; two of them are sixty-four feet long each, and the third
is sixty-nine. They are built into the massive wall some twenty
feet above the ground. They are there, but how they got there is
the question. I have seen the hull of a steamboat that was
smaller than one of those stones. All these great walls are as
exact and shapely as the flimsy things we build of bricks in these
days. A race of gods or of giants must have inhabited Baalbec
many a century ago. Men like the men of our day could hardly
rear such temples as these.

We went to the quarry from whence the stones of Baalbec
were taken. It was about a quarter of a mile off, and down hill.
In a great pit lay the mate of the largest stone in the ruins. It lay
there just as the giants of that old forgotten time had left it
when they were called hence — just as they had left it, to remain
for thousands of years, an eloquent rebuke unto such as are
prone to think slightingly of the men who lived before them.
This enormous block lies there, squared and ready for the
builders' hands — a solid mass fourteen feet by seventeen, and
but a few inches less than seventy feet long! Two buggies could
be driven abreast of each other, on its surface, from one end of
it to the other, and leave room enough for a man or two to walk
on either side.

One might swear that all the John Smiths and George Wilkin-
sons, and all the other pitiful nobodies between Kingdom Come
and Baalbec would inscribe their poor little names upon the walls
of Baalbec's magnificent ruins, and would add the town, the
county, and the state they came from — and, swearing thus, be

infallibly correct. It is a pity some great ruin does not fall in and flatten out some of these reptiles, and scare their kind out of ever giving their names to fame upon any walls or monuments again, forever.

Properly, with the sorry relics we bestrode, it was a three-days journey to Damascus. It was necessary that we should do it in less than two. It was necessary because our three pilgrims would not travel on the Sabbath day. We were all perfectly willing to keep the Sabbath day, but there are times when to keep the *letter* of a sacred law whose spirit is righteous, becomes a sin, and this was a case in point. We pleaded for the tired, ill-treated horses, and tried to show that their faithful service deserved kindness in return, and their hard lot compassion. But when did ever self-righteousness know the sentiment of pity? What were a few long hours added to the hardships of some overtaxed brutes when weighed against the peril of those human souls? It was not the most promising party to travel with and hope to gain a higher veneration for religion through the example of its devotees. We said the Saviour, who pitied dumb beasts and taught that the ox must be rescued from the mire even on the Sabbath day, would not have counseled a forced march like this. We said the "long trip" was exhausting and therefore dangerous in the blistering heats of summer, even when the ordinary days' stages were traversed, and if we persisted in this hard march, some of us might be stricken down with the fevers of the country in consequence of it. Nothing could move the pilgrims. They *must* press on. Men might die, horses might die, but they must enter upon holy soil next week, with no Sabbath-breaking stain upon them. Thus they were willing to commit a sin against the spirit of religious law, in order that they might preserve the letter of it. It was not worth while to tell them "the letter kills." I am talking now about personal friends; men whom I like; men who are good citizens; who are honorable, upright, conscientious: but whose idea of the Saviour's religion seems to me distorted. They lecture our shortcomings unsparingly, and every night they call us together and read to us chapters from the Testament that are full of gentleness, of charity, and of tender mercy; and then all the next day they stick to their saddles clear up to the summits of these rugged mountains, and clear down again. Apply the Testament's gentleness, and charity, and tender mercy to a toiling, worn, and weary horse? Nonsense — these are for God's human creatures, not His dumb ones. What the pilgrims choose to do, respect for their almost sacred character demands that I should allow to pass — but I would so like to catch any other member of the party riding his horse up one of these exhausting hills once!

We have given the pilgrims a good many examples that might

benefit them, but it is virtue thrown away. They have never heard a cross word out of our lips toward each other — but *they* have quarreled once or twice. We love to hear them at it, after they have been lecturing us. The very first thing they did, coming ashore at Beirout, was to quarrel in the boat. I have said I like them, and I do like them — but every time they read me a scorcher of a lecture I mean to talk back in print.

Not content with doubling the legitimate stages, they switched off the main road and went away out of the way to visit an absurd fountain called Figia, because Balaam's ass had drank there once. So we journeyed on, through the terrible hills and deserts and the roasting sun, and then far into the night, seeking the honored pool of Balaam's ass, the patron saint of all pilgrims like us. I find no entry but this in my note-book:

"Rode to-day, altogether, thirteen hours, through deserts, partly, and partly over barren, unsightly hills, and latterly through wild, rocky scenery, and camped at about eleven o'clock at night on the banks of a limpid stream, near a Syrian village. Do not know its name — do not wish to know it — want to go to bed. Two horses lame (mine and Jack's) and the others worn out. Jack and I walked three or four miles, over the hills, and led the horses. Fun — but of a mild type."

Twelve or thirteen hours in the saddle, even in a Christian land and a Christian climate, and on a good horse, is a tiresome journey; but in an oven like Syria, in a ragged spoon of a saddle that slips fore-and-aft, and "thort-ships," and every way, and on a horse that is tired and lame, and yet must be whipped and spurred with hardly a moment's cessation all day long, till the blood comes from his side, and your conscience hurts you every time you strike, if you are half a man, — it is a journey to be remembered in bitterness of spirit and execrated with emphasis for a liberal division of a man's lifetime.

CHAPTER XVII

The next day was an outrage upon men and horses both. It was another thirteen-hour stretch (including an hour's "nooning"). It was over the barrenest chalk-hills and through the baldest canons that even Syria can show. The heat quivered in the air everywhere. In the canons we almost smothered in the baking atmosphere. On high ground, the reflection from the chalk-hills was blinding. It was cruel to urge the crippled horses, but it had to be done in order to make Damascus Saturday night. We saw ancient tombs and temples of fanciful architecture carved out of the solid rock high up in the face of precipices above our heads, but we had neither time nor strength to climb up there and examine them. The terse language of my note-book will answer for the rest of this day's experiences:

Broke camp at 7 A.M., and made a ghastly trip through the Zeb Dana valley and the rough mountains — horses limping and that Arab screech-owl that does most of the singing and carries the water-skins, always a thousand miles ahead of course, and no water to drink — will he *never* die? Beautiful stream in a chasm, lined thick with pomegranate, fig, olive, and quince orchards, and nooned an hour at the celebrated Balaam's Ass Fountain of Figia, second in size in Syria, and the coldest water out of Siberia — guide-books do not say Balaam's ass ever drank there — somebody been imposing on the pilgrims, may be. Bathed in it — Jack and I. Only a second — ice water. It is the principal source of the Abana river — only one-half mile down to where it joins. Beautiful place — giant trees all around — *so* shady and cool, if one could keep awake — vast stream gushes straight out from under the mountain in a torrent. Over it is a very ancient ruin, with no known history — supposed to have been for the worship of the deity of the fountain or Balaam's ass or somebody. Wretched nest of human vermin about the fountain — rags, dirt, sunken cheeks, pallor of sickness, sores, projecting bones, dull, aching misery in their eyes and ravenous hunger speaking from every eloquent fiber and muscle from head to foot. How they sprang upon a bone, how they crunched the bread we gave them! Such as these to swarm about one and watch every bite he takes with greedy looks, and swallow unconsciously every time he swallows, as if they half fancied the precious morsel went down their own throats — hurry up the caravan! — I never shall enjoy a meal in this distressful country. To think of eating three times every day under *such* circumstances for three weeks yet — it is worse punishment than riding all day in the sun. There are sixteen starving babies from one to six years old in the party, and their legs are no larger than broom handles. Left the fountain at 1 P.M. (the fountain took us at least two hours out of our way), and reached Mahomet's lookout perch, over Damascus, in time to get a good long look before it was necessary to move on. Tired? Ask of the winds that far away with fragments strewed the sea.

As the glare of day mellowed into twilight, we looked down upon a picture which is celebrated all over the world. I think I have read about four hundred times that when Mahomet was a simple camel-driver he reached this point and looked down upon Damascus for the first time, and then made a certain renowned remark. He said man could enter only one paradise; he preferred to go to the one above. So he sat down there and feasted his eyes upon the earthly paradise of Damascus, and then went away without entering its gates. They have erected a tower on the hill to mark the spot where he stood.

Damascus *is* beautiful from the mountain. It is beautiful even to foreigners accustomed to luxuriant vegetation, and I can easily understand how unspeakably beautiful it must be to eyes that are only used to the God-forsaken barrenness and desolation of Syria. I should think a Syrian would go wild with ecstasy when such a picture bursts upon him for the first time.

From his high perch, one sees before him and below him a wall of dreary mountains, shorn of vegetation, glaring fiercely in the sun; it fences in a level desert of yellow sand, smooth as velvet and threaded far away with fine lines that stand for roads, and dotted with creeping mites we know are camel trains and journeying men; right in the midst of the desert is spread a billowy expanse of green foliage; and nestling in its heart sits the great white city, like an island of pearls and opals gleaming out of a sea of emeralds. This is the picture you see spread far below you, with distance to soften it, the sun to glorify it, strong contrasts to heighten the effects, and over it and about it a drowsing air of repose to spiritualize it and make it seem rather a beautiful estray from the mysterious worlds we visit in dreams than a substantial tenant of our coarse, dull globe. And when you think of the leagues of blighted, blasted, sandy, rocky, sunburnt, ugly, dreary, infamous country you have ridden over to get here, you think it is the most beautiful, beautiful picture that ever human eyes rested upon in all the broad universe! If I were to go to Damascus again, I would camp on Mahomet's hill about a week, and then go away. There is no need to go inside the walls. The Prophet was wise without knowing it when he decided not to go down into the paradise of Damascus.

There is an honored old tradition that the immense garden which Damascus stands in was the Garden of Eden, and modern writers have gathered up many chapters of evidence tending to show that it really was the Garden of Eden, and that the rivers Pharpar and Abana are the "two rivers" that watered Adam's Paradise. It may be so, but it is not paradise now, and one would be as happy outside of it as he would be likely to be within. It is so crooked and cramped and dirty that one cannot realize that he is in the splendid city he saw from the hilltop. The gardens are hidden by high mud-walls, and the paradise is become a very sink of pollution and uncomeliness. Damascus has plenty of clear, pure water in it, though, and this is enough, of itself, to make an Arab think it beautiful and blessed. Water is scarce in blistered Syria. We run railways by our large cities in America; in Syria they curve the roads so as to make them run by the meager little puddles they call "fountains," and which are not found oftener on a journey than every four hours. But the "rivers" of Pharpar and Abana of Scripture (mere creeks) run through Damascus, and so every house and every garden have their sparkling fountains and rivulets of water. With her forest of foliage and her abaundance of water, Damascus must be a wonder of wonders to the Bedouin from the deserts. Damascus is simply an oasis — that is what it is. For four thousand years its waters have not gone dry or its fertility failed. Now we can understand why the city has existed so long. It could not die. So long as its waters remain to it away out there in the midst of that howling desert, so long will Damascus live to bless the sight of the tired and thirsty wayfarer.

"Though old as history itself, thou art fresh as the breath of spring, blooming as thine own rose-bud, and fragrant as thine own orange flower, O Damascus, pearl of the East!"

Damascus dates back anterior to the days of Abraham, and is the oldest city in the world. It was founded by Uz, the grandson of Noah. "The early history of Damascus is shrouded in the mists of a hoary antiquity." Leave the matters written of in the first eleven chapters of the Old Testament out, and no recorded event has occurred in the world but Damascus was in existence to receive the news of it. Go back as far as you will into the vague past, there was always a Damascus. In the writings of every century for more than four thousand years, its name has been mentioned and its praises sung. To Damascus, years are only moments, decades are only flitting trifles of time. She measures time, not by days and months and years, but by the empires she has seen rise and prosper and crumble to ruin. She is a type of immortality. She saw the foundations of Baalbec, and Thebes, and Ephesus laid; she saw these villages grow into mighty cities, and amaze the world with their grandeur — and she has lived to see them desolate, deserted, and given over to the owls and the bats. She saw the Israelitish empire exalted, and she saw it annihilated. She saw Greece rise, and flourish two thousand years, and die. In her old age she saw Rome built; she saw it overshadow the world with its power; she saw it perish. The few hundreds of years of Genoese and Venetian might and splendor were, to grave old Damascus, only a trifling scintillation hardly worth remembering. Damascus has seen all that has ever occurred on earth, and still she lives. She has looked upon the dry bones of a thousand empires, and will see the tombs of a thousand more before she dies. Though another claims the name, old Damascus is by right the Eernal City.

We reached the city gates just at sundown. They do say that one can get into any walled city of Syria, after night, for bucksheesh, except Damascus. But Damascus, with its four thousand years of respectability in the world, has many old fogy notions. There are no street lamps there, and the law compels all who go abroad at night to carry lanterns, just as was the case in old days, when heroes and heroines of the Arabian Nights walked the streets of Damascus, or flew away toward Bagdad on enchanted carpets.

It was fairly dark a few minutes after we got within the wall, and we rode long distances through wonderfully crooked streets, eight to ten feet wide, and shut in on either side by the high mud walls of the gardens. At last we got to where lanterns could be seen flitting about here and there, and knew we were in the midst of the curious old city. In a little narrow street, crowded with our packmules and with a swarm of uncouth Arabs, we alighted, and through a kind of a hole in the wall entered the hotel. We stood in a great flagged court, with flowers and citron trees about us, and a huge tank in the center that was receiving the waters of many pipes. We crossed the court and entered the rooms prepared to receive four of us. In a large marble-paved recess between the two rooms was a tank of clear, cool water, which was kept running over all the time by the streams that were pouring into it from half a dozen pipes. Nothing, in this scorching, desolate land could look so refreshing as this pure water flashing in the lamplight; nothing could look so beautiful, nothing could sound so delicious as this mimic rain to ears long unaccustomed to sounds of such a nature. Our rooms were large, comfortably furnished, and even had their floors clothed with soft, cheerful-tinted carpets. It was a pleasant thing to see a carpet again, for if there is anything drearier than the tomb-like, stone-paved parlors and bedrooms of Europe and Asia, I do not know what it is. They make one think of the grave all the time. A very broad, gaily caparisoned divan, some twelve or fourteen feet long, extended across one side of each room, and opposite were single beds with spring mattresses. There were great looking-glasses and marble-top tables. All this luxury was as grateful to systems and senses worn out with an exhausting day's travel, as it was unexpected — for one cannot tell what to expect in a Turkish city of even a quarter of a million inhabitants.

I do not know, but I think they used that tank between the rooms to draw drinking water from; that did not occur to me, however, until I had dipped my baking head far down into its cool depths. I thought of it then, and, superb as the bath was, I was sorry I had taken it, and was about to go and explain to the landlord. But a finely curled and scented poodle dog frisked up and nipped the calf of my leg just then, and before I had time to think I had soused him to the bottom of the tank, and when I saw a servant coming with a pitcher I went off and left the pup trying to climb out and not succeeding very well. Satisfied revenge was all I needed to make me perfectly happy, and when I walked in to supper that first night in Damascus I was in that condition. We lay on those divans a long time, after supper, smoking narghilis and long-stemmed chibouks, and talking about the dreadful ride of the day, and I knew then what I had sometimes known before — that it is worth while to get tired out, because one so enjoys resting afterward.

In the morning we sent for donkeys. It is worthy of note that we had to *send* for these things. I said Damascus was an old fossil, and she is. Anywhere else we would have been assailed by a clamorous army of donkey-drivers, guides, peddlers, and beggars — but in Damascus they so hate the very sight of a foreign Christian that they want no intercourse whatever with him; only a year or two ago, his person was not always safe in Damascus streets. It is the most fanatical Mohammedan purgatory out of Arabia. Where you see one green turban of a

Hadji elsewhere (the honored sign that my lord has made the pilgrimage to Mecca), I think you will see a dozen in Damascus. The Damascenes are the ugliest, wickedest looking villains we have seen. All the veiled women we had seen yet, nearly, left their eyes exposed, but numbers of these in Damascus completely hid the face under a close-drawn black veil that made the woman look like a mummy. If ever we caught an eye exposed it was quickly hidden from our contaminating Christian vision; the beggars actually passed us by without demanding bucksheesh; the merchants in the bazaars did not hold up their goods and cry out eagerly, "Hey, John!" or "Look this, Howajji!" On the contrary, they only scowled at us and said never a word.

The narrow streets swarmed like a hive with men and women in strange Oriental costumes, and our small donkeys knocked them right and left as we plowed through them, urged on by the merciless donkey-boys. These persecutors run after the animals, shouting and goading them for hours together; they keep the donkey in a gallop always, yet never get tired themselves or fall behind. The donkeys fell down and split us over their heads occasionally, but there was nothing for it but to mount and hurry on again. We were banged against sharp corners, loaded porters, camels, and citizens generally; and we were so taken up with looking out for collisions and casualties that we had no chance to look about us at all. We rode half through the city and through the famous "street which is called Straight" without seeing anything, hardly. Our bones were nearly knocked out of joint, we were wild with excitement, and our sides ached with the jolting we had suffered. I do not like riding in the Damascus street cars.

We were on our way to the reputed houses of Judas and Ananias. About eighteen or nineteen hundred years ago, Saul, a native of Tarsus, was particularly bitter against the new sect called Christians, and he left Jerusalem and started across the country on a furious crusade against them. He went forth "breathing threatenings and slaughter against the disciples of the Lord."

"And as he journeyed, he came near Damascus, and suddenly there shined round about him a light from heaven:

"And he fell to the earth and heard a voice saying unto him, 'Saul, Saul, why persecutest thou me?'

"And when he knew that it was Jesus that spoke to him he trembled, and was astonished, and said, 'Lord, what wilt thou have me to do?' "

He was told to arise and go into the ancient city and one would tell him what to do. In the meantime his soldiers stood speechless and awe-stricken, for they heard the mysterious voice but saw no man. Saul rose up and found that that fierce supernatural light had destroyed his sight, and he was blind, so "they led him by the hand and brought him to Damascus." He was converted.

Paul lay three days blind, in the house of Judas, and during that time he neither ate nor drank.

There came a voice to a citizen of Damascus, named Ananias, saying, "Arise, and go into the street which is called Straight, and inquire at the house of Judas, for one called Saul, of Tarsus; for behold, he prayeth."

Ananias did not wish to go at first, for he had heard of Saul before, and he had his doubts about that style of a "chosen vessel" to preach the gospel of peace. However, in obedience to orders, he went into the "street called Straight" (how he ever found his way into it, and after he did, how he ever found his way out of it again, are mysteries only to be accounted for by the fact that he was acting under Divine inspiration). He found Paul and restored him, and ordained him a preacher; and from this old house we had hunted up in the street which is miscalled Straight, he had started out on that bold missionary career which he prosecuted till his death.

It was not the house of the disciple who sold the Master for thirty pieces of silver. I make this explanation in justice to Judas, who was a far different sort of man from the person just referred to. A very different style of man, and lived in a very good house. It is a pity we do not know more about him.

I have given, in the above paragraphs, some more information for people who will not read Bible history until they are defrauded into it by some such method as this. I hope that no friend of progress and education will obstruct or interfere with my peculiar mission.

The street called Straight is straighter than a corkscrew, but not as straight as a rainbow. St. Luke is careful not to commit himself; he does not say it is the street which *is* straight, but the "street which is *called* Straight." It is a fine piece of irony; it is the only facetious remark in the Bible, I believe. We traversed the street called Straight a good way, and then turned off and called at the reputed house of Ananias. There is small question that a part of the original house is there still; it is an old room twelve or fifteen feet under ground, and its masonry is evidently ancient. If Ananias did not live there in St. Paul's time, somebody else did, which is just as well. I took a drink out of Ananias' well, and, singularly enough, the water was just as fresh as if the well had been dug yesterday.

We went out toward the north end of the city to see the place where the disciples let Paul down over the Damascus wall at dead of night — for he preached Christ so fearlessly in Damascus that the people sought to kill him, just as they would to-day for the same offense, and he had to escape and flee to Jerusalem.

Then we called at the tomb of Mahomet's children and at a tomb which purported to be that of St. George who killed the dragon, and so on out to the hollow place under a rock where Paul hid during his flight till his pursuers gave him up; and to the mausoleum of the five thousand Christians who were massacred in Damascus in 1861 by the Turks. They say those narrow streets ran blood for several days, and that men, women, and children were butchered indiscriminately and left to rot by hundreds all through the Christian quarter; they say, further, that the stench was dreadful. All the Christians who could get away fled from the city, and the Mohammedans would not defile their hands by burying the "infidel dogs." The thirst for blood extended to the high lands of Hermon and Anti-Lebanon, and in a short time twenty-five thousand more Christians were massacred and their possessions laid waste. How they hate a Christian in Damascus! — and pretty much all over Turkeydom as well. And how they will pay for it when Russia turns her guns upon them again!

It is soothing to the heart to abuse England and France for interposing to save the Ottoman Empire from the destruction it has so richly deserved for a thousand years. It hurts my vanity to see these pagans refuse to eat of food that has been cooked for us; or to eat from a dish we have eaten from; or to drink from a goatskin which we have polluted with our Christian lips, except by filtering the water through a rag which they put over the mouth of it or through a sponge! I never disliked a Chinaman as I do these degraded Turks and Arabs, and, when Russia is ready to war with them again, I hope England and France will not find it good breeding or good judgment to interfere.

In Damascus they think there are no such rivers in all the world as their little Abana and Pharpar. The Damascenes have always thought that way. In 2 Kings, chapter v, Naaman boasts extravagantly about them. That was three thousand years ago. He says: "Are not Abana and Pharpar, rivers of Damascus, better than all the waters of Israel? May I not wash in them and be clean?" But some of my readers have forgotten who Naaman was, long ago. Naaman was the commander of the Syrian armies. He was the favorite of the king and lived in great state. "He was a mighty man of valor, but he was a leper." Strangely enough, the house they point out to you now as his has been turned into a leper hospital, and the inmates expose their horrid deformities and hold up their hands and beg for bucksheesh when a stranger enters.

One cannot appreciate the horror of this disease until he looks upon it in all its ghastliness, in Naaman's ancient dwelling in

Damascus. Bones all twisted out of shape, great knots
protruding from face and body, joints decaying and dropping
away — horrible!

CHAPTER XVIII

The last twenty-four hours we stayed in Damascus I lay
prostrate with a violent attack of cholera, or cholera morbus,
and therefore had a good chance and a good excuse to lie there
on that wide divan and take an honest rest. I had nothing to do
but listen to the pattering of the fountains and take medicine and
throw it up again. It was dangerous recreation, but it was
pleasanter than traveling in Syria. I had plenty of snow from
Mount Hermon, and, as it would not stay on my stomach, there
was nothing to interfere with my eating it — there was always
room for more. I enjoyed myself very well. Syrian travel has its
interesting features, like travel in any other part of the world,
and yet to break your leg or have the cholera adds a welcome
variety to it.

We left Damascus at noon and rode across the plain a couple
of hours, and then the party stopped a while in the shade of
some fig-trees to give me a chance to rest. It was the hottest day
we had seen yet — the sun-flames shot down like the shafts of
fire that stream out before a blowpipe; the rays seemed to fall in
a steady deluge on the head and pass downward like rain from a
roof. I imagined I could distinguish between the floods of rays
— I thought I could tell when each flood struck my head, when
it reached my shoulders, and when the next one came. It was
terrible. All the desert glared so fiercely that my eyes were swimming in tears all the time. The boys had white umbrellas heavily
lined with dark green. They were a priceless blessing. I thanked
fortune that I had one, too, notwithstanding it was packed up
with the baggage and was ten miles ahead. It is madness to
travel in Syria without an umbrella. They told me in Beirout
(these people who always gorge you with advice) that it was
madness to travel in Syria without an umbrella. It was on this
account that I got one.

But, honestly, I think an umbrella is a nuisance anywhere
when its business is to keep the sun off. No Arab wears a brim
to his fez, or uses an umbrella, or anything to shade his eyes or
his face, and he always looks comfortable and proper in the sun.
But of all the ridiculous sights I ever have seen, our party of
eight is the most so — they do cut such an outlandish figure.
They travel single file; they all wear the endless white rag of
Constantinople round their hats and dangling down their backs;
they all wear thick green spectacles, with side-glasses to them;

they all hold white umbrellas, lined with green, over their heads; without exception their stirrups are too short — they are the very worst gang of horsemen on earth; their animals to a horse trot fearfully hard — and when they get strung out one after the other, glaring straight ahead and breathless; bouncing high and out of turn, all along the line; knees well up and stiff, elbows flapping like a rooster's that is going to crow, and the long file of umbrellas popping convulsively up and down — when one sees this outrageous picture exposed to the light of day, he is amazed that the gods don't get out their thunderbolts and destroy them off the face of the earth! I do — I wonder at it. I wouldn't let any such caravan go through a country of mine.

And when the sun drops below the horizon and the boys close their umbrellas and put them under their arms, it is only a variation of the picture, not a modification of its absurdity.

But maybe you cannot see the wild extravagance of my panorama. You could if you were here. Here, you feel all the time just as if you were living about the year 1200 before Christ — or back to the patriarchs — or forward to the New Era. The scenery of the Bible is about you — the customs of the patriarchs are around you — the same people, in the same flowing robes, and in sandals, cross your path — the same long trains of stately camels go and come — the same impressive religious solemnity and silence rest upon the desert and the mountains that were upon them in the remote ages of antiquity, and behold, intruding upon a scene like this, comes this fantastic mob of green-spectacled Yanks, with their flapping elbows and bobbing umbrellas! It is Daniel in the lion's den with a green cotton umbrella under his arm, all over again.

My umbrella is with the baggage, and so are my green spectacles — and there they shall stay. I will not use them. I will show some respect for the eternal fitness of things. It will be bad enough to get sunstruck, without looking ridiculous into the bargain. If I fall, let me fall bearing about me the semblance of a Christian, at least.

Three or four hours out from Damascus we passed the spot where Saul was so abruptly converted, and from this place we looked back over the scorching desert, and had our last glimpse of beautiful Damascus, decked in its robes of shining green. After nightfall we reached our tents, just outside of the nasty Arab village of Jonesborough. Of course the real name of the place is El something or other, but the boys still refuse to recognize the Arab names or try to pronounce them. When I say that that village is of the usual style, I mean to insinuate that all Syrian villages within fifty miles of Damascus are alike — so much alike that it would require more than human intelligence to tell wherein one differed from another. A Syrian village is a hive of

huts one story high (the height of a man), and as square as a
drygoods box; it is mud-plastered all over, flat roof and all, and
generally whitewashed after a fashion. The same roof often extends over half the town, covering many of the *streets,* which are
generally about a yard wide. When you ride through one of these
villages at noonday, you first meet a melancholy dog, that looks
up at you and silently begs that you won't run over him, but he
does not offer to get out of the way; next you meet a young boy
without any clothes on, and he holds out his hand and says
"Bucksheesh!" — he don't really expect a cent, but then he
learned to say that before he learned to say mother, and now he
cannot break himself of it; next you meet a woman with a black
veil drawn closely over her face, and her bust exposed; finally,
you come to several sore-eyed children and children in all stages
of mutilation and decay; and sitting humbly in the dust, and all
fringed with filthy rags, is a poor devil whose arms and legs are
gnarled and twisted like grapevines. These are all the people you
are likely to see. The balance of the population are asleep within
doors, or abroad tending goats in the plains and on the hillsides.
The village is built on some consumptive little water-course, and
about it is a little fresh-looking vegetation. Beyond this charmed
circle, for miles on every side, stretches a weary desert of sand
and gravel, which produces a gray bunchy shrub like sage brush.
A Syrian village is the sorriest sight in the world, and its
surroundings are eminently in keeping with it.

I would not have gone into this dissertation upon Syrian
villages but for the fact that Nimrod, the Mighty Hunter of
Scriptural notoriety, is buried in Jonesborough, and I wished the
public to know about how he is located. Like Homer, he is said
to be buried in many other places, but this is the only true and
genuine place his ashes inhabit.

When the original tribes were dispersed, more than four
thousand years ago, Nimrod and a large party traveled three or
four hundred miles, and settled where the great city of Babylon
afterwards stood. Nimrod built that city. He also began to build
the famous Tower of Babel, but circumstances over which he
had no control put it out of his power to finish it. He ran it up
eight stories high, however, and two of them still stand at this
day, a colossal mass of brickwork, rent down the center by
earthquakes,and seared and vitrified by the lightnings of an
angry God. But the vast ruin will still stand for ages, to shame
the puny labors of these modern generations of men. Its huge
compartments are tenanted by owls and lions, and old Nimrod
lies neglected in this wretched village, far from the scene of his
grand enterprise.

We left Jonesborough very early in the morning, and rode
forever and forever and forever, it seemed to me, over parched

deserts and rocky hills, hungry, and with no water to drink. We had drained the goat-skins dry in a little while. At noon we halted before the wretched Arab town of El Yuba Dam, perched on the side of a mountain, but the dragoman said if we applied there for water we would be attacked by the whole tribe, for they did not love Christians. We had to journey on. Two hours later we reached the foot of a tall isolated mountain, which is crowned by the crumbling castle of Banias, the stateliest ruin of that kind on earth, no doubt. It is a thousand feet long and two hundred wide, all of the most symmetrical, and at the same time the most ponderous, masonry. The massive towers and bastions are more than thirty feet high, and have been sixty. From the mountain's peak its broken turrets rise above the groves of ancient oaks and olives, and look wonderfully picturesque. It is of such high antiquity that no man knows who built it or when it was built. It is utterly inaccessible, except in one place, where a bridle-path winds upward among the solid rocks to the old portcullis. The horses' hoofs have bored holes in these rocks to the depth of six inches during the hundreds and hundreds of years that the castle was garrisoned. We wandered for three hours among the chambers and crypts and dungeons of the fortress, and trod where the mailed heels of many a knightly Crusader had rang, and where Phoenician heroes had walked ages before them.

We wondered how such a solid mass of masonry could be affected even by an earthquake, and could not understand what agency had made Banias a ruin; but we found the destroyer, after a while, and then our wonder was increased tenfold. Seeds had fallen in crevices in the vast walls; the seeds had sprouted; the tender, insignificant sprouts had hardened; they grew larger and larger, and by a steady, imperceptible pressure forced the great stones apart, and now are bringing sure destruction upon a giant work that has even mocked the earthquakes to scorn! Gnarled and twisted trees spring from the old walls everywhere, and beautify and overshadow the gray battlements with a wild luxuriance of foliage.

From these old towers we looked down upon a broad, far-reaching green plain, glittering with the pools and rivulets which are the sources of the sacred river Jordan. It was a grateful vision, after so much desert.

And as the evening drew near, we clambered down the mountain, through groves of the Biblical oaks of Bashan (for we were just stepping over the border and entering the long-sought Holy Land), and at its extreme foot, toward the wide valley, we entered this little execrable village of Banias and camped in a great grove of olive trees near a torrent of sparkling water whose banks are arrayed in fig-trees, pomegranates, and oleanders in full leaf. Barring the proximity of the village, it is a sort of paradise.

The very first thing one feels like doing when he gets into camp, all burning up and dusty, is to hunt up a bath. We followed the stream up to where it gushes out of the mountain side, three hundred yards from the tents, and took a bath that was so icy that if I did not know this was the main source of the sacred river, I would expect harm to come of it. It was bathing at noonday in the chilly source of the Abana, "River of Damascus," that gave me the cholera, so Dr. B. said. However, it generally does give me the cholera to take a bath.

The incorrigible pilgrims have come in with their pockets full of specimens broken from the ruins. I wish this vandalism could be stopped. They broke off fragments from Noah's tomb; from the exquisite sculptures of the temples of Baalbec; from the houses of Judas and Ananias, in Damascus; from the tomb of Nimrod the Mighty Hunter in Jonesborough; from the worn Greek and Roman inscriptions set in the hoary walls of the castle of Banias; and now they have been hacking and chipping these old arches here that Jesus looked upon in the flesh. Heaven protect the Sepulchre when this tribe invades Jerusalem!

The ruins here are not very interesting. There are the massive walls of a great square building that was once the citadel; there are many ponderous old arches that are so smothered with debris that they barely project above the ground; there are heavy walled sewers through which the crystal brook of which Jordan is born still runs; in the hillside are the substructions of a costly marble temple that Herod the Great built here — patches of its handsome mosaic floor still remain; there is a quaint old stone bridge that was here before Herod's time, may be; scattered everywhere, in the paths and in the woods, are Corinthian capitals, broken porphyry pillars, and little fragments of sculpture; and up yonder in the precipice where the fountain gushes out, are well-worn Greek inscriptions over niches in the rock where in ancient times the Greeks, and after them the Romans, worshiped the sylvan god Pan. But trees and bushes grow above many of these ruins now; the miserable huts of a little crew of filthy Arabs are perched upon the broken masonry of antiquity, the whole place has a sleepy, stupid, rural look about it, and one can hardly bring himself to believe that a busy, substantially built city once existed here, even two thousand years ago. The place was nevertheless the scene of an event whose effects have added page after page and volume after volume to the world's history. For in this place Christ stood when He said to Peter:

"Thou art Peter; and upon this rock will I build my church, and the gates of hell shall not prevail against it. And I will give unto thee the keys of the

Kingdom of Heaven; and whatsoever thou shalt bind on earth shall be bound in heaven, and whatsoever thou shalt loose on earth shall be loosed in heaven.''

On these little sentences have been built up the mighty edifice of the Church of Rome; in them lie the authority for the imperial power of the Popes over temporal affairs, and their godlike power to curse a soul or wash it white from sin. To sustain the position of "the only true Church," which Rome claims was thus conferred upon her, she has fought and labored and struggled for many a century, and will continue to keep herself busy in the same work to the end of time. The memorable words I have quoted give to this ruined city about all the interest it possesses to people of the present day.

It seems curious enough to us to be standing on ground that was once actually pressed by the feet of the Saviour. The situation is suggestive of a reality and a tangibility that seem at variance with the vagueness and mystery and ghostliness that one naturally attaches to the character of a god. I cannot comprehend yet that I am sitting where a god has stood, and looking upon the brook and the mountains which that god looked upon, and am surrounded by dusky men and women whose ancestors saw him, and even talked with him, face to face, and carelessly, just as they would have done with any other stranger. I cannot comprehend this; the gods of my understanding have been always hidden in clouds and very far away.

This morning, during breakfast, the usual assemblage of squalid humanity sat patiently without the charmed circle of the camp and waited for such crumbs as pity might bestow upon their misery. There were old and young, brown-skinned and yellow. Some of the men were tall and stalwart (for one hardly sees anywhere such splendid looking men as here in the East), but all the women and children looked worn and sad, and distressed with hunger. They reminded me much of Indians, did these people. They had but little clothing, but such as they had was fanciful in character and fantastic in its arrangement. Any little absurd gewgaw or gimcrack they had they disposed in such a way as to make it attract attention most readily. They sat in silence, and with tireless patience watched our every motion with that vile, uncomplaining impoliteness which is so truly Indian, and which makes a white man so nervous and uncomfortable and savage that he wants to exterminate the whole tribe.

These people about us had other peculiarities, which I have noticed in the noble red man, too: they were infested with vermin, and the dirt had caked on them till it amounted to bark.

The little children were in a pitiable condition — they all had sore eyes, and were otherwise afflicted in various ways. They say that hardly a native child in all the East is free from sore eyes, and that thousands of them go blind of one eye or both every year. I think this must be so, for I see plenty of blind people every day, and I do not remember seeing any children that hadn't sore eyes. And, would you suppose that an American mother could sit for an hour, with her child in her arms, and let a hundred flies roost upon its eyes all that time undisturbed? I see that every day. It makes my flesh creep. Yesterday we met a woman riding on a little jackass, and she had a little child in her arms; honestly, I thought the child had goggles on as we approached, and I wondered how its mother could afford so much style. But when we drew near, we saw that the goggles were nothing but a camp meeting of flies assembled around each of the child's eyes, and at the same time there was a detachment prospecting its nose. The flies were happy, the child was contented, and so the mother did not interfere.

As soon as the tribe found out that we had a doctor in our party, they began to flock in from all quarters. Dr. B., in the charity of his nature, had taken a child from a woman who sat near by, and put some sort of a wash upon its diseased eyes. That woman went off and started the whole nation, and it was a sight to see them swarm! The lame, the halt, the blind, the leprous — all the distempers that are bred of indolence, dirt, and iniquity — were represented in the congress in ten minutes, and still they came! Every woman that had a sick baby brought it along, and every woman that hadn't, borrowed one. What reverent and what worshiping looks they bent upon that dread, mysterious power, the Doctor! They watched him take his phials out; they watched him measure the particles of white powder; they watched him add drops of one precious liquid, and drops of another; they lost not the slightest movement; their eyes were riveted upon him with a fascination that nothing could distract. I believe they thought he was gifted like a god. When each individual got his portion of medicine, his eyes were radiant with joy — notwithstanding by nature they are a thankless and impassive race — and upon his face was written the unquestioning fath that nothing on earth could prevent the patient from getting well now.

Christ knew how to preach to these simple, superstitious, disease-tortured creatures: He healed the sick. They flocked to our poor human doctor this morning when the fame of what he had done to the sick child went abroad in the land, and they worshiped him with their eyes while they did not know as yet whether there was virtue in his simples or not. The ancestors of these — people precisely like them in color, dress, manners, customs, simplicity — flocked in vast multitudes after Christ, and when they saw Him make the afflicted whole with a word, it is no wonder they worshiped Him. No wonder His deeds were the talk of the nation. No wonder the multitude that followed

Him was so great that at one time — thirty miles from here — they had to let a sick man down through the roof because no approach could be made to the door; no wonder His audiences were so great at Galilee that He had to preach from a ship removed a little distance from the shore; no wonder that even in the desert places about Bethsaida, five thousand invaded His solitude, and He had to feed them by a miracle or else see them suffer for their confiding faith and devotion; no wonder when there was a great commotion in a city in those days, one neighbor explained it to another in words to this effect: "They say that Jesus of Nazareth is come!"

Well, as I was saying, the doctor distributed medicine as long as he had any to distribute, and his reputation is mighty in Galilee this day. Among his patients was the child of the Sheik's daughter — for even this poor, ragged handful of sores and sin has its royal Sheik — a poor old mummy that looked as if he would be more at home in a poor-house than in the Chief Magistracy of this tribe of hopeless, shirtless savages. The princess — I mean the Sheik's daughter — was only thirteen or fourteen years old, and had a very sweet face and a pretty one. She was the only Syrian female we have seen yet who was not so sinfully ugly that she couldn't smile after ten o'clock Saturday night without breaking the Sabbath. Her child was a hard specimen, though — there wasn't enough of it to make a pie, and the poor little thing looked so pleadingly up at all who came near it (as if it had an idea that now was its chance or never) that we were filled with compassion which was genuine and not put on.

But this last new horse I have got is trying to break his neck over the tent-ropes, and I shall have to go out and anchor him. Jericho and I have parted company. The new horse is not much to boast of, I think. One of his hind legs bends the wrong way, and the other one is as straight and stiff as a tent-pole. Most of his teeth are gone, and he is as blind as a bat. His nose has been broken at some time or other, and is arched like a culvert now. His under lip hangs down like a camel's, and his ears are chopped off close to his head. I had some trouble at first to find a name for him, but I finally concluded to call him Baalbec, because he is such a magnificent ruin. I cannot keep from talking about my horses, because I have a very long and tedious journey before me, and they naturally occupy my thoughts about as much as matters of apparently much greater importance.

We satisfied our pilgrims by making those hard rides from Baalbec to Damascus, but Dan's horse and Jack's were so crippled we had to leave them behind and get fresh animals for them. The dragoman says Jack's horse died. I swapped horses with Mohammed, the kingly-looking Egyptian who is our Ferguson's lieutenant. By Ferguson I mean our dragoman

Abraham, of course. I did not take this horse on account of his personal appearance, but because I have not seen his back. I do not wish to see it. I have seen the backs of all the other horses, and found most of them covered with dreadful saddle-boils which I know have not been washed or doctored for years. The idea of riding all day long over such ghastly inquisitions of torture is sickening. My horse must be like the others, but I have at least the consolation of not knowing it to be so.

I hope that in future I may be spared any more sentimental praises of the Arab's idolatry of his horse. In boyhood I longed to be an Arab of the desert and have a beautiful mare, and call her Selim or Benjamin or Mohammed, and feed her with my own hands, and let her come into the tent, and teach her to caress me and look fondly upon me with her great tender eyes; and I wished that a stranger might come at such a time and offer me a hundred thousand dollars for her, so that I could do like the other Arabs — hesitate, yearn for the money, but, overcome by my love for my mare, at last say, "Part with thee, my beautiful one! Never with my life! Away, tempter, I scorn thy gold!" and then bound into the saddle and speed over the desert like the wind!

But I recall those aspirations. If these Arabs be like the other Arabs, their love for their beautiful mares is a fraud. These of my acquaintance have no love for their horses, no sentiment of pity for them, and no knowledge of how to treat them or care for them. The Syrian saddle-blanket is a quilted mattress two or three inches thick. It is never removed from the horse, day or night. It gets full of dirt and hair, and becomes soaked with sweat. It is bound to breed sores. These pirates never think of washing a horse's back. They do not shelter the horses in the tents, either; they must stay out and take the weather as it comes. Look at poor cropped and dilapidated "Baalbec," and weep for the sentiment that has been wasted upon the Selims of romance.

CHAPTER XIX

About an hour's ride over a rough, rocky road, half flooded with water, and through a forest of oaks of Bashan, brought us to Dan.

From a little mound here in the plain issues a broad stream of limpid water and forms a large shallow pool, and then rushes furiously onward, augmented in volume. This puddle is an important source of the Jordan. Its banks, and those of the brook, are respectably adorned with blooming oleanders, but the unutterable beauty of the spot will not throw a well-balanced man into convulsions, as the Syrian books of travel would lead one to suppose.

From the spot I am speaking of, a cannon-ball would carry beyond the confines of Holy Land and light upon profane ground three miles away. We were only one little hour's travel within the borders of Holy Land — we had hardly begun to appreciate yet that we were standing upon any different sort of earth than that we had always been used to, and yet see how the historic names began already to cluster! Dan — Bashan — Lake Huleh — the Sources of Jordan — the Sea of Galilee. They were all in sight but the last, and it was not far away. The little township of Bashan was once the kingdom so famous in Scripture for its bulls and its oaks. Lake Huleh is the Biblical "Waters of Merom." Dan was the northern and Beersheba the southern limit of Palestine — hence the expression "from Dan to Beersheba." It is equivalent to our phrases "from Maine to Texas" — "from Baltimore to San Francisco." Our expression and that of the Israelites both mean the same — great distance. With their slow camels and asses, it was about a seven-days journey from Dan to Beersheba — say a hundred and fifty or sixty miles — it was the entire length of their country, and was not to be undertaken without great preparation and much ceremony. When the prodigal traveled to "a far country," it is not likely that he went more than eighty or ninety miles. Palestine is only from forty to sixty miles wide. The state of Missouri could be split into three Palestines, and there would then be enough material left for part of another — possibly a whole one. From Baltimore to San Francisco is several thousand miles, but it will be only a seven-days journey in the cars when I am two or three years older.* If I live I shall necessarily have to go across the continent every now and then in those cars, but one journey from Dan to Beersheba will be sufficient, no doubt. It must be the most trying of the two. Therefore, if we chance to discover that from Dan to Beersheba seemed a mighty stretch of country to the Israelites, let us not be airy with them, but reflect that it *was* and *is* a mighty stretch when one cannot traverse it by rail.

The small mound I have mentioned a while ago was once occupied by the Phoenician city of Laish. A party of filibusters from Zorah and Eshcol captured the place, and lived there in a free and easy way, worshiping gods of their own manufacture and stealing idols from their neighbors whenever they wore their own out. Jeroboam set up a golden calf here to fascinate his people and keep them from making dangerous trips to Jerusalem to worship, which might result in a return to their rightful allegiance. With all respect for those ancient Israelities, I cannot overlook the fact that they were not always virtuous enough to withstand the seductions of a golden calf. Human nature has not

*The railroad has been completed since the above was written.

changed much since then.

Some forty centuries ago the city of Sodom was pillaged by the Arab princes of Mesopotamia, and among other prisoners they seized upon the patriarch Lot and brought him here on their way to their own possessions. They brought him to Dan, and father Abraham, who was pursuing them, crept softly in at dead of night, among the whispering oleanders and under the shadows of the stately oaks, and fell upon the slumbering victors and startled them from their dreams with the clash of steel. He recaptured Lot and all the other plunder.

We moved on. We were now in a green valley, five or six miles wide and fifteen long. The streams which are called the sources of the Jordan flow through it to Lake Huleh, a shallow pond three miles in diameter, and from the southern extremity of the lake the concentrated Jordan flows out. The lake is surrounded by a broad marsh, grown with reeds. Between the marsh and the mountains which wall the valley is a respectable strip of fertile land; at the end of the valley, toward Dan, as much as half the land is solid and fertiloe, and watered by Jordan's sources. There is enough of it to make a farm. It almost warrants the enthusiasm of the spies of that rabble of adventurers who captured Dan. They said: "We have seen the land, and behold it is very good. . . . A place where there is no want of anything that is in the earth."

Their enthusiasm was at least warranted by the fact that they had never seen a country as good as this. There was enough of it for the ample support of their six hundred men and their families, too.

When we got fairly down on the level part of the Danite farm, we came to places where we could actually run our horses. It was a notable circumstance.

We had been painfully clambering over interminable hills and rocks for days together, and when we suddenly came upon this astonishing piece of rockless plain, every man drove the spurs into his horse and sped away with a velocity he could surely enjoy to the utmost, but could never hope to comprehend in Syria.

Here were evidences of cultivation — a rare sight in this country — an acre or two of rich soil studded with last season's dead cornstalks of the thickness of your thumb and very wide apart. But in such a land it was a thrilling spectacle. Close to it was a stream, and on its banks a great herd of curious-looking Syrian goats and sheep were gratefully eating gravel. I do not state this as a petrified fact — I only *suppose* they were eating gravel, because there did not appear to be anything else for them to eat. The shepherds that tended them were the very pictures of Joseph and his brethren, I have no doubt in the world. They were tall, muscular, and very dark-skinned Bedouins, with inky black beards. They had firm lips, unquailing eyes, and a kingly stateliness of bearing. They wore the parti-colored half bonnet, half hood, with fringed ends falling upon their shoulders, and the full, flowing robe barred with broad black stripes — the dress one sees in all pictures of the swarthy sons of the desert. These chaps would sell their younger brothers if they had a chance, I think. They have the manners, the customs, the dress, the occupation, and the loose principles of the ancient stock. [They attacked our camp last night, and I bear them no good will.] They had with them the pigmy jackasses one sees all over Syria and remembers in all pictures of the "Flight into Egypt," where Mary and the Young Child are riding and Joseph is walking alongside, towering high above the little donkey's shoulders.

But, really, here the man rides and carries the child, as a general thing, and the woman walks. The customs have not changed since Joseph's time. We would not have in our houses a picture representing Joseph riding and Mary walking; we would see profanation in it, but a Syrian Christian would not. I know that hereafter the picture I first spoke of will look odd to me.

We could not stop to rest two or three hours out from our camp, of course, albeit the brook was beside us. So we went on an hour longer. We saw water then, but nowhere in all the waste around was there a foot of shade, and we were scorching to death. "Like unto the shadow of a great rock in a weary land." Nothing in the Bible is more beautiful than that, and surely there is no place we have wandered to that is able to give it such touching expression as this blistering, naked, treeless land.

Here you do not stop just when you please, but when you can. We found water, but no shade. We traveled on and found a tree at last, but no water. We rested and lunched, and came on to this place, Ain Mellahah (the boys call it Baldwinsville). It was a very short day's run, but the dragoman does not want to go further, and has invented a plausible lie about the country beyond this being infested by ferocious Arabs, who would make sleeping in their midst a dangerous pastime. Well, they ought to be dangerous. They carry a rusty old weather-beaten flintlock gun, with a barrel that is longer than themselves; it has no sights on it; it will not carry farther than a brickbat, and is not half so certain. And the great sash they wear in many a fold around their waists has two or three absurd old horse pistols in it that are rusty from eternal disuse — weapons that would hang fire just about long enough for you to walk out of range, and then burst and blow the Arab's head off. Exceedingly dangerous these sons of the desert are.

It used to make my blood run cold to read Wm. C. Grimes' hairbreadth escapes from Bedouins, but I think I could read them now without a tremor. He never said he was attacked by

Bedouins, I believe, or was ever treated uncivilly, but then in about every other chapter he discovered them approaching, anyhow, and he had a blood-curdling fashion of working up the peril; and of wondering how his relations far away would feel could they see their poor wandering boy, with his weary feet and his dim eyes, in such fearful danger; and of thinking for the last time of the old homestead, and the dear old church, and the cow, and those things; and of finally straightening his form to its utmost height in the saddle, drawing his trusty revolver, and then dashing the spurs into "Mohammed" and sweeping down upon the ferocious enemy determined to sell his life as dearly as possible. True, the Bedouins never did anything to him when he arrived, and never had any intention of doing anything to him in the first place, and wondered what in the mischief he was making all that to-do about; but still I could not divest myself of the idea, somehow, that a frightful peril had been escaped through that man's dare-devil bravery, and so I never could read about Wm. C. Grimes' Bedouins and sleep comfortably afterward. But I believe the Bedouins to be a fraud, now. I have seen the monster, and I can outrun him. I shall never be afraid of his daring to stand behind his own gun and discharge it.

About fifteen hundred years before Christ, this campground of ours by the Waters of Merom was the scene of one of Joshua's exterminating battles. Jabin, King of Hazor (up yonder above Dan), called all the sheiks about him together, with their hosts, to make ready for Israel's terrible General who was approaching.

"And when all these Kings were met together, they came and pitched together by the Waters of Merom, to fight against Israel.

"And they went out, they and all their hosts with them, much people, even as the sand that is upon the seashore for multitude," etc.

But Joshua fell upon them and utterly destroyed them, root and branch. That was his usual policy in war. He never left any chance for newspaper controversies about who won the battle. He made this valley, so quiet now, a reeking slaughter-pen.

Somewhere in this part of the country — I do not know exactly where — Israel fought another bloody battle a hundred years later. Deborah, the prophetess, told Barak to take ten thousand men and sally forth against another King Jabin who had been doing something. Barak came down from Mount Tabor, twenty or twenty-five miles from here, and gave battle to Jabin's forces, who were in command of Sisera. Barak won the fight, and while he was making the victory complete by the usual method of exterminating the remnant of the defeated host, Sisera fled away on foot, and when he was nearly exhausted by fatigue and thirst, one Jael, a woman he seems to have been acquainted

with, invited him to come into her tent and rest himself. The
weary soldier acceded readily enough, and Jael put him to bed.
He said he was very thirsty, and asked his generous preserver to
get him a cup of water. She brought him some milk, and he
drank of it gratefully and lay down again, to forget in pleasant
dreams his lost battle and his humbled pride. Presently when he
was asleep she came softly in with a hammer and drove a
hideous tent-pin down through his brain!

"For he was fast asleep and weary. So he died." Such is the
touching language of the Bible. "The Song of Deborah and
Barak" praises Jael for the memorable service she had rendered,
in an exultant strain:

"Blessed above women shall Jael the wife of Heber the Kenite be, blessed shall
she be above women in the tent.

"He asked for water, and she gave him milk; she brought forth butter in a
lordly dish.

"She put her hand to the nail, and her right hand to the workman's hammer;
and with the hammer she smote Sisera, she smote off his head when she had
pierced and stricken through his temples.

"At her feet he bowed, he fell, he lay down: at her feet he bowed, he fell;
where he bowed, there he fell down dead."

Stirring scenes like these occur in this valley no more. There is
not a solitary village throughout its whole extent — not for thirty miles in either direction. There are two or three small clusters
of Bedouin tents, but not a single permanent habitation. One
may ride ten miles, hereabouts, and not see ten human beings.

To this region one of the prophecies is applied:

"I will bring the land into desolation; and your enemies which dwell therein
shall be astonished at it. And I will scatter you among the heathen, and I will
draw out a sword after you; and your land shall be desolate and your cities
waste."

No man can stand here by deserted Ain Mellahah and say the
prophecy has not been fulfilled.

In a verse from the Bible which I have quoted above, occurs
the phrase "all these kings." It attracted my attention in a
moment, because it carries to my mind such a vastly different
significance from what it always did at home. I can see easily
enough that if I wish to profit by this tour and come to a correct
understanding of the matters of interest connected with it, I must
studiously and faithfully unlearn a great many things I have
somehow absorbed concerning Palestine. I must begin a system
of reduction. Like my grapes which the spies bore out of the
Promised Land, I have got everything in Palestine on too large a
scale. Some of my ideas were wild enough. The word Palestine
always brought to my mind a vague suggestion of a country as
large as the United States. I do not know why, but such was the

case. I suppose it was because I could not conceive of a small country having so large a history. I think I was a little surprised to find that the grand Sultan of Turkey was a man of only ordinary size. I must try to reduce my ideas of Palestine to a more reasonable shape. One gets large impressions in boyhood, sometimes, which he has to fight against all his life. "All these kings." When I used to read that in Sunday-school, it suggested to me the several kings of such countries as England, France, Spain, Germany, Russia, etc., arrayed in splendid robes ablaze with jewels, marching in grave procession, with scepters of gold in their hands and flashing crowns upon their heads. But here in Ain Mellahah, after coming through Syria, and after giving serious study to the character and customs of the country, the phrase "all these kings" loses its grandeur. It suggests only a parcel of petty chiefs — ill-clad and ill-conditioned savages much like our Indians, who lived in full sight of each other and whose "kingdoms" were large when they were five miles square and contained two thousand souls. The combined monarchies of the thirty "kings" destroyed by Joshua on one of his famous campaigns, only covered an area about equal to four of our counties of ordinary size. The poor old sheik we saw at Cesarea Philippi, with his ragged band of a hundred followers, would have been called a "king" in those ancient times.

It is seven in the morning, and as we are in the country, the grass ought to be sparkling with dew, the flowers enriching the air with their fragrance, and the birds singing in the trees. But, alas! there is no dew here, nor flowers, nor birds, nor trees. There is a plain and an unshaded lake, and beyond them some barren mountains. The tents are tumbling, the Arabs are quarreling like dogs and cats, as usual, the campground is strewn with packages and bundles, the labor of packing them upon the backs of the mules is progressing with great activity, the horses are saddled, the umbrellas are out, and in ten minutes we shall mount and the long procession will move again. The white city of the Mellahah, resurrected for a moment out of the dead centuries, will have disappeared again and left no sign.

CHAPTER XX

We traversed some miles of desolate country whose soil is rich enough, but is given over wholly to weeds — a silent, mournful expanse, wherein we saw only three persons — Arabs, with nothing on but a long coarse shirt like the "towlinen" shirts which used to form the only summer garment of little negro boys on Southern plantations. Shepherds they were, and they charmed their flocks with the traditional shepherd's pipe — a reed instrument that made music as exquisitely infernal as these same

Arabs create when they sing.

In their pipes lingered no echo of the wonderful music the shepherd forefathers heard in the Plains of Bethlehem what time the angels sang "Peace on earth, good will to men."

Part of the ground we came over was not ground at all, but rocks — cream-colored rocks, worn smooth, as if by water; with seldom an edge or a corner on them, but scooped out, honey-combed, bored out with eye-holes, and thus wrought into all manner of quaint shapes, among which the uncouth imitation of skulls was frequent. Over this part of the route were occasional remains of an old Roman road like the Appian Way, whose paving stones still clung to their places with Roman tenacity.

Gray lizards, those heirs of ruin, of sepulchres and desolation, glided in and out among the rocks or lay still and sunned themselves. Where prosperity has reigned, and fallen; where glory has flamed, and gone out; where beauty has dwelt, and passed away; where gladness was, and sorrow is; where the pomp of life has been, and silence and death brood in its high places, there this reptile makes his home, and mocks at human vanity. His coat is the color of ashes; and ashes are the symbol of hopes that have perished, of aspirations that came to naught, of loves that are buried. If he could speak, he would say, Build temples: I will lord it in their ruins; build palaces: I will inhabit them; erect empires: I will inherit them; bury your beautiful: I will watch the worms at their work; and you, who stand here and moralize over me: I will crawl over *your* corpse at the last.

A few ants were in this desert place, but merely to spend the summer. They brought their provisions from Ain Mellahah — eleven miles.

Jack is not very well to-day, it is easy to see; but, boy as he is, he is too much of a man to speak of it. He exposed himself to the sun too much yesterday, but since it came of his earnest desire to learn, and to make this journey as useful as the opportunities will allow, no one seeks to discourage him by fault-finding. We missed him an hour from the camp, and then found him some distance away, by the edge of a brook, and with no umbrella to protect him from the fierce sun. If he had been used to going without his umbrella, it would have been well enough, of course; but he was not. He was just in the act of throwing a clod at a mud-turtle which was sunning itself on a small log in the brook. We said:

"Don't do that, Jack. What do you want to harm him for? What has he done?"

"Well, then, I won't kill him, but I ought to, because he is a fraud."

We asked him why, but he said it was no matter. We asked him why, once or twice, as we walked back to the camp, but he still said it was no matter. But late at night, when he was sitting in a thoughtful mood on the bed, we asked him again and he said:

"Well, it don't matter; I don't mind it now, but I did not like it to-day, you know, because *I* don't tell anything that isn't so, and I don't think the Colonel ought to, either. But he did; he told us at prayers in the Pilgrims' tent, last night, and he seemed as if he was reading it out of the Bible, too, about this country flowing with milk and honey, and about the voice of the turtle being heard in the land. I thought that was drawing it a little strong, about the turtles, anyhow, but I asked Mr. Church if it was so, and he said it was, and what Mr. Chruch tells me, I believe. But I sat there and watched that turtle nearly and hour to-day, and I almost burned up in the sun; but I never heard him sing. I believe I sweated a double handful of sweat—I *know* I did — because it got in my eyes, and it was running down over my nose all the time; and you know my pants are tighter than anybody else's — Paris foolishness — and the buckskin seat of them got wet with sweat, and then got dry again and began to draw up and pinch and tear loose — it was awful — but I never heard him sing. Finally I said, This is a fraud — that is what it is, it is a fraud — and if I had had any sense I might have known a cursed mud-turtle couldn't sing. And then I said, I don't wish to be hard on this fellow, and I will just give him ten minutes to commence; ten minutes — and then if he don't, down goes his building. But he *didn't* commence, you know. I had stayed there all that time, thinking maybe he might, pretty soon, because he kept on raising his head up and letting it down, and drawing the skin over his eyes for a minute and then opening them out again, as if he was trying to study up something to sing, but just as the ten minutes were up and I was all beat out and blistered, he laid his blamed head down on a knot and went fast asleep."

"It *was* a little hard, after you had waited so long."

"I should think so. I said, Well, if you won't sing, you shan't sleep, anyway; and if you fellows had let me alone I would have made him shin out of Galilee quicker than any turtle ever did yet. But it isn't any matter now — let it go. The skin is all off the back of my neck."

About ten in the morning we halted at Joseph's Pit. This is a ruined Khan of the Middle Ages, in one of whose side courts is a great walled and arched pit with water in it, and this pit, one tradition says, is the one Joseph's brethren cast him into. A more authentic tradition, aided by the geography of the country, places the pit in Dothan, some two days journey from here. However, since there are many who believe in this present pit as the true one, it has its interest.

It is hard to make a choice of the most beautiful passage in a book which is so gemmed with beautiful passages as the Bible; but it is certain that not many things within its lids may take rank above the exquisite story of Joseph. Who taught those ancient writers their simplicity of language, their felicity of expression, their pathos, and, above all, their faculty of sinking themselves entirely out of sight of the reader and making the narrative stand out alone and seem to tell itself? Shakespeare is always present when one reads his book; Macaulay is present when we follow the march of his stately sentences; but the Old Testament writers are hidden from view.

If the pit I have been speaking of is the right one, a scene transpired there, long ages ago, which is familiar to us all in pictures. The sons of Jacob had been pasturing their flocks near there. Their father grew uneasy at their long absence, and sent Joseph, his favorite, to see if anything had gone wrong with them. He traveled six or seven days' journey; he was only seventeen years old, and, boy like, he toiled through that long stretch of the vilest, rockiest, dustiest country in Asia, arrayed in the pride of his heart, his beautiful claw-hammer coat of many colors. Joseph was the favorite, and that was once crime in the eyes of his brethren; he had dreamed dreams, and interpreted them to foreshadow his elevation far above all his family in the far future, and that was another; he was dressed well and had doubtless displayed the harmless vanity of youth in keeping the fact prominently before his brothers. These were crimes his elders fretted over among themselves and proposed to punish when the opportunity should offer. When they saw him coming up from the Sea of Galilee, they recognized him and were glad. They said, "Lo, here is this dreamer — let us kill him." But Reuben pleaded for his life, and they spared it. But they seized the boy, and stripped the hated coat from his back and pushed him into the pit. *They* intended to let him die there, but Reuben intended to liberate him secretly. However, while Reuben was away for a little while, the brethren sold Joseph to some Ishmaelitish merchants who were journeying toward Egypt. Such is the history of the pit. And the self-same pit is there in that place, even to this day; and there it will remain until the next detachment of image-breakers and tomb-desecrators arrives from the *Quaker City* excursion, and they will infallibly dig it up and carry it away with them. For behold in them is no reverence for the solemn monuments of the past, and whithersoever they go they destroy and spare not.

Joseph became rich, distinguished, powerful — as the Bible expresses it, "lord over all the land of Egypt." Joseph was the real king, the strength, the brain of the monarchy, though Pharaoh held the title. Joseph is one of the truly great men of the Old Testament. And he was the noblest and the manliest, save Esau. Why shall we not say a good word for the princely Bedouin? The only crime that can be brought against him is that he was unfortunate. Why must everybody praise Joseph's great-hearted generosity to his cruel brethren, without stint of fervent language, and fling only a reluctant bone of praise of Esau for his still sublimer generosity to the brother who had wronged him? Jacob took advantage of Esau's consuming hunger to rob him of his birthright and the great honor and consideration that belonged to the position; by treachery and falsehood he robbed him of his father's blessing; he made of him a stranger in his home, and a wanderer. Yet after twenty years had passed away and Jacob met Esau and fell at his feet quaking with fear and begging piteously to be spared the punishment he knew he deserved, what did the magnificent savage do? He fell upon his neck and embraced him! When Jacob — who was incapable of comprehending nobility of character — still doubting, still fearing, insisted upon "finding grace with my lord" by the bribe of a present of cattle, what did the gorgeous son of the desert say?

"Nay, I have enough, my brother; keep that thou hast unto thyself!"

Esau found Jacob rich, beloved by wives and children, and traveling in state, with servants, herds of cattle and trains of camels — but he himself was still the uncourted outcast this brother had made him. After thirteen years of romantic mystery, the brethren who had wronged Joseph, came, strangers in a strange land, hungry and humble, to buy "a little food"; and being summoned to a palace, charged with crime, they beheld in its owner their wronged brother; they were trembling beggars — he, the lord of a mighty empire! What Joseph that ever lived would have thrown away such a chance to "show off"? Who stands first — outcast Esau forgiving Jacob in prosperity, or Joseph on a king's throne forgiving the ragged tremblers whose happy rascality placed him there?

Just before we came to Joseph's Pit, we have "raised" a hill, and there, a few miles before us, with not a tree or a shrub to interrupt the view, lay a vision which millions of worshipers in the far lands of the earth would give half their possessions to see — the sacred Sea of Galilee!

Therefore we tarried only a short time at the pit. We rested the horses and ourselves, and felt for a few minutes the blessed shade of the ancient buildings. We were out of water, but the two or three scowling Arabs, with their long guns, who were idling about the place, said they had none and that there was none in the vicinity. They knew there was a little brackish water in the pit, but they venerated a place made sacred by their ancestor's imprisonment too much to be willing to see Christian dogs drink from it. But Ferguson tied rags and handkerchiefs together till he made a rope long enough to lower a vessel to the bottom, and we drank and then rode on; and in a short time we dismounted on those shores which the feet of the Saviour have made holy ground.

At noon we took a swim in the Sea of Galilee — a blessed privilege in this roasting climate — and then lunched under a neglected old fig tree at the fountain they call Ain-et-Tin, a hundred yards from ruined Capernaum. Every rivulet that gurgles out of the rocks and sands of this part of the world is dubbed with the title of "fountain," and people familiar with the Hudson, the Great Lakes, and the Mississippi fall into transports of admiration over them, and exhaust their powers of compositon in writing their praises. If all the poetry and nonsense that have been discharged upon the fountains and the bland scenery of this region were collected in a book, it would make a most valuable volume to burn.

During luncheon, the pilgrim enthusiasts of our party, who had been so light-hearted and happy ever since they touched holy ground that they did little but mutter incoherent rhapsodies, could scarcely eat, so anxious were they to "take shipping" and sail in very person upon the waters that had borne the vessels of the Apostles. Their anxiety grew and their excitement augmented with every fleeting moment, until my fears were aroused and I began to have misgivings that in their present condition they might break recklessly loose from all considerations of prudence and buy a whole fleet of ships to sail in instead of hiring a single one for an hour, as quiet folk are wont to do. I trembled to think of the ruined purses this day's performances might result in. I could not help reflecting bodingly upon the intemperate zeal with which middle-aged men are apt to surfeit themselves upon a seductive folly which they have tasted for the first time. And yet I did not feel that I had a right to be surprised at the state of things which was giving me so much concern. These men had been taught from infancy to revere, almost to worship, the holy places whereon their happy eyes were resting now. For many and many a year this very picture had visited their thoughts by day and floated through their dreams by night. To stand before it in the flesh — to see it as they saw it now — to sail upon the hallowed sea, and kiss the holy soil that compassed it about; these were aspirations they cherished while a generation dragged its lagging seasons by and left its furrows in their faces and its frosts upon their hair. To look upon this picture, and sail upon this sea, they had forsaken home and its idols and journeyed thousands and thousands of miles, in weariness and tribulation. What wonder that the sordid lights of work-day prudence should pale before the glory of a hope like theirs in the full splendor of its fruition? Let them squander millions! I said — who speaks of money at a time like this?

In this frame of mind I followed, as fast as I could, the eager footsteps of the pilgrims, and stood upon the shore of the lake, and swelled, with hat and voice, the frantic hail they sent after the "ship" that was speeding by. It was a success. The toilers of the sea ran in and beached their bark. Joy sat upon every countenance.

"How much? — ask him how much, Ferguson! — how much to take us all — eight of us, and you — to Bethsaida, yonder, and to the mouth of Jordan, and to the place where the swine ran down into the sea — quick! — and we want to coast around everywhere — everywhere! — all day long! — *I* could sail a year in these waters! — and tell him we'll stop at Magdala and finish at Tiberias! — ask him how much! — anything — anything whatever! — tell him we don't care what the expense is!" [I said to myself, I knew how it would be.]

Ferguson — (interpreting) — "He says two napoleons — eight dollars."

One or two countenances fell. Then a pause.

"Too much! — we'll give him one!"

I never shall know how it was — I shudder yet when I think how the place is given to miracles — but in a single instant of time, as it seemed to me, that ship was twenty paces from the shore, and speeding away like a frightened thing! Eight crest-fallen creatures stood upon the shore, and oh, to think of it! this — this — after all that overmastering ecstasy! Oh, shameful, shameful ending, after such unseemly boasting! It was too much like "Ho! let me at him!" followed by a prudent "Two of you hold him — one can hold me!"

Instantly there was wailing and gnashing of teeth in the camp. The two napoleons were offered — more if necessary — and pilgrims and dragoman shouted themselves hoarse with pleadings to the retreating boatmen to come back. But they sailed serenely away and paid no further heed to pilgrims who had dreamed all their lives of some day skimming over the sacred waters of Galilee and listening to its hallowed story in the whispering of its waves, and had journeyed countless leagues to do it, and — and then concluded that the fare was too high. Impertinent Mohammedan Arabs, to think such things of gentlemen of another faith.

Well, there was nothing to do but just submit and forego the privilege of voyaging on Gennesaret, after coming half around the globe to taste that pleasure. There was a time, when the Saviour taught here, that boats were plenty among the fishermen of the coasts — but boats and fishermen both are gone now; and old Josephus had a fleet of men-of-war in these waters eighteen centuries ago — a hundred and thirty bold canoes — but they, also, have passed away and left no sign. They battle here no more by sea, and the commercial marine of Galilee numbers only two small ships, just of a pattern with the little skiffs the disciples knew. One was lost to us for good — the other was miles away and far out of hail. So we mounted the horses and rode grimly on toward Magdala, cantering along in the edge of the water for want of the means of passing over it.

How the pilgrims abused each other! Each said it was the other's fault, and each in turn denied it. No word was spoken by the sinners — even the mildest sarcasm might have been dangerous at such a time. Sinners that have been kept down and had examples held up to them, and suffered frequent lectures, and been so put upon in a moral way and in the matter of going slow and being serious and bottling up slang, and so crowded in regard to the matter of being proper and always and forever behaving, that their lives have become a burden to them, would not lag behind pilgrims at such a time as this, and wink furtively, and be joyful, and commit other such crimes — because it would not occur to them to do it. Otherwise they would. But they did it, though — and it did them a world of good to hear the pilgrims abuse each other, too. We took an unworthy satisfaction in seeing them fall out, now and then, because it showed that they were only poor human people like us, after all.

So we all rode down to Magdala, while the gnashing of teeth waxed and waned by turns, and harsh words troubled the holy calm of Galilee.

Lest any man think I mean to be ill-natured when I talked about our pilgrims as I have been talking, I wish to say in all sincerity that I do not. I would not listen to lectures from men I did not like and could not respect; and none of these can say I ever took their lectures unkindly, or was restive under the infliction, or failed to try to profit by what they said to me. They are better men than I am; I can say that honestly; they are good friends of mine, too — and besides, if they did not wish to be stirred up occasionally in print, why in the mischief did they travel with me? They knew me. They knew my liberal way — that I like to give and take — when it is for me to give and other people to take. When one of them threatened to leave me in Damascus when I had the cholera, he had no real idea of doing it — I know his passionate nature and the good impulses that underlie it. And did I not overhear Church, another pilgrim, say he did not care who went or who stayed, *he* would stand by me till I walked out of Damascus on my own feet or was carried out in a coffin, if it was a year? And do I not include Church every time I abuse the pilgrims — and would I be likely to speak ill-naturedly of him? I wish to stir them up and make them healthy; that is all.

We had left Capernaum behind us. It was only a shapeless ruin. It bore no semblance to a town, and had nothing about it to suggest that it had ever been a town. But all desolate and un-peopled as it was, it was illustrious ground. From it sprang that tree of Christianity whose broad arms overshadow so many distant lands to-day. After Christ was tempted of the devil in the desert, he came here and began his teachings; and during the three or four years he lived afterward, this place was his home almost altogether. He began to heal the sick, and his fame soon spread so widely that sufferers came from Syria and beyond Jor-dan, and even from Jerusalem, several days journey away, to be cured of their diseases. Here he healed the centurion's servant and Peter's mother-in-law, and multitudes of the lame and the blind and persons possessed of devils; and here, also, he raised Jairus' daughter from the dead. He went into a ship with his disciples, and when they roused him from sleep in the midst of a storm, he quieted the winds and lulled the troubled sea to rest with his voice. He passed over to the other side, a few miles away, and relieved two men of devils, which passed into some swine. After his return he called Matthew from the the receipt of customs, performed some cures, and created scandal by eating with publicans and sinners. Then he went healing and teaching through Galilee, and even journeyed to Tyre Sidon. He chose the twelve disciples, and sent them abroad to preach the new gospel. He worked miracles in Bethsaida and Chorazin — villages two or three miles from Capernaum. It was near one of them that the miraculous draft of fishes is supposed to have been taken, and it was in the desert places near the other that he fed the thousands by the miracles of the loaves and fishes. He cursed them both, and Capernaum also, for not repenting, after all the great works he had done in their midst, and prophesied against them. They are all in ruins now — which is gratifying to the pilgrims, for, as usual, they fit the eternal words of gods to the evanescent things of this earth; Christ, it is more probable, referred to the *people,* not their shabby villages of wigwams; he said it would be sad for them at "the Day of Judgment" — and what business have mud-hovels at the Day of Judgment? it would not affect the prophecy in the least — it would neither prove it nor disprove it — if these towns were splendid cities now instead of the almost vanished ruins they are. Christ visited Magdala, which is near by Capernaum, and he also visited Cesarea Philippi. He went up to his old home at Nazareth, and saw his brothers Joses, and Judas, and James, and Simon — those persons who, being own brothers to Jesus Christ, one would expect to hear mentioned sometimes, yet who ever saw their names in a newspaper or

heard them from a pulpit? Who ever inquires what manner of
youths they were; and whether they slept with Jesus, played with
him and romped about him; quarreled with him concerning toys
and trifles; struck him in anger, not suspecting what he was?
Who ever wonders what they thought when they saw him come
back to Nazareth a celebrity, and looking long at this unfamiliar
face to make sure, and then said, "It *is* Jesus?" Who wonders
what passed in their minds when they saw this brother (who was
only a brother to them, however much he might be to others a
mysterious stranger who was a god and had stood face to face
with God above the clouds) doing strange miracles with crowds
of astonished people for witnesses? Who wonders if the brothers
of Jesus asked him to come home with them, and said his
mother and his sister were grieved at his long absence, and
would be wild with delight to see his face again? Who ever gives
a thought to the sisters of Jesus at all? — yet he had sisters; and
memories of them must have stolen into his mind often when he
was ill-treated among strangers; when he was homeless and said
he had not where to lay his head; when all deserted him, even
Peter, and he stood alone among his enemies.

Christ did few miracles in Nazareth, and stayed but a little
while. The people said, "*This* the Son of God! Why, his father
is nothing but a carpenter. We know the family. We see them
every day. Are not his brothers named so and so, and his sisters
so and so, and is not his mother the person they call Mary? This
is absurd." He did not curse his home, but he shook its dust
from his feet and went away.

Capernaum lies close to the edge of the little sea, in a small
plain some five miles long and a mile or two wide, which is
mildly adorned with oleanders which look all the better contrasted with the bald hills and the howling deserts which
surround them, but they are not as deliriously beautiful as the
books paint them. If one be calm and resolute he can look upon
their comeliness and live.

One of the most astonishing things that have yet fallen under
our observation is the exceedingly small portion of the earth
from which sprang the now flourishing plant of Christianity. The
longest journey our Saviour ever performed was from here to
Jerusalem — about one hundred to one hundred and twenty
miles. The next longest was from here to Sidon — say about sixty or seventy miles. Instead of being wide apart — as American
appreciation of distances would naturally suggest — the places
made most particularly celebrated by the presence of Christ are
nearly all right here in full view, and within cannon-shot of
Capernaum. Leaving out two or three short journeys of the
Saviour, he spent his life, preached his gospel, and performed his
miracles within a compass no larger than an ordinary county in

the United States. It is as much as I can do to comprehend this stupefying fact. How it wears a man out to have to read up a hundred pages of history every two or three miles — for verily the celebrated localities of Palestine occur that close together. How wearily, how bewilderingly they swarm about your path!

In due time we reached the ancient village of Magdala.

CHAPTER XXI

Madgala is not a beautiful place. It is thoroughly Syrian, and that is to say that it is thoroughly ugly, and cramped, squalid, uncomfortable, and filthy — just the style of cities that have adorned the country since Adam's time, as all writers have labored hard to prove, and have succeeded. The streets of Magdala are anywhere from three to six feet wide, and reeking with uncleanliness. The houses are from five to seven feet high, and all built upon one arbitrary plan — the ungraceful form of a drygoods box. The sides are daubed with a smooth white plaster, and tastefully frescoed aloft and alow with disks of camel-dung placed there to dry. This gives the edifice the romantic appearance of having been riddled with cannon-balls, and imparts to it a very warlike aspect. When the artist has arranged his materials with an eye to just proportion — the small and the large flakes in alternate rows, and separated by carefully-considered intervals — I know of nothing more cheerful to look upon than a spirited Syrian fresco. The flat, plastered roof is garnished by picturesque stacks of fresco materials, which, having become thoroughly dried and cured, are placed there where it will be convenient. It is used for fuel. There is no timber of any consequence in Palestine — none at all to waste upon fires — and neither are there any mines of coal. If my description has been intelligible, you will perceive, now, that a square, flat-roofed hovel, neatly frescoed, with its wall-tops gallantly bastioned and turreted with dried camel-refuse, gives to a landscape a feature that is exceedingly festive and picturesque, especially if one is careful to remember to stick in a cat wherever, about the premises, there is room for a cat to sit. There are no windows to a Syrian hut, and no chimneys. When I used to read that they let a bedridden man down through the roof of a house in Capernaum to get him into the presence of the Saviour, I generally had a three-story brick in my mind, and marveled that they did not break his neck with the strange experiment. I perceive now, however, that they might have taken him by the heels and thrown him clear over the house without discommoding him very much. Palestine is not changed any since those days, in manners, customs, architecture, or people.

As we rode into Magdala not a soul was visible. But the ring of the horses' hoofs roused the stupid population, and they all came trooping out — old men and old women, boys and girls, the blind, the crazy, and the crippled, all in ragged, soiled, and scanty raiment, and all abject beggars by nature, instinct, and education. How the vermin-tortured vagabonds did swarm! How they showed their scars and sores, and piteously pointed to their maimed and crooked limbs, and begged with their pleading eyes for charity! We had invoked a spirit we could not lay. They hung to the horses' tails, clung to their manes and the stirrups, closed in on every side in scorn of dangerous hoofs — and out of their infidel throats, with one accord, burst an agonizing and most infernal chorus: "Howajji, bucksheesh! howajji, bucksheesh! howajji, bucksheesh! bucksheesh! bucksheesh!" I never was in a storm like that before.

As we paid the bucksheesh out to sore-eyed children and brown, buxom girls with repulsively tattooed lips and chins, we filed through the town and by many an exquisite fresco, till we came to a bramble-infested inclosure and a Roman looking ruin which had been the veritable dwelling of St. Mary Magdalene, the friend and follower of Jesus. The guide believed it, and so did I. I could not well do otherwise, with the house right there before my eyes as plain as day. The pilgrims took down portions of the front wall for specimens, as is their honored custom, and then we departed.

We are camped in this place, now, just within the city walls of Tiberias. We went into the town before nightfall and looked at its people — we cared nothing about its houses. Its people are best examined at a distance. They are particularly uncomely Jews, Arabs, and negroes. Squalor and poverty are the pride of Tiberias. The young women wear their dower strung upon a strong wire that curves downward from the top of the head to the jaw — Turkish silver coins which they have raked together or inherited. Most of these maidens were not wealthy, but some few had been very kindly dealt with by fortune. I saw heiresses there worth, in their own right — worth, well, I suppose I might venture to say, as much as nine dollars and a half. But such cases are rare. When you come across one of these, she naturally puts on airs. She will not ask for bucksheesh. She will not even permit of undue familiarity. She assumes a crushing dignity and goes on serenely practicing with her fine-tooth comb and quoting poetry just the same as if you were not present at all. Some people cannot stand prosperity.

They say that the long-nosed, lanky, dyspeptic-looking body-snatchers, with the indescribable hats on, and a long curl dangling down in front of each ear, are the old, familiar, self-righteous Pharisees we read of in the Scriptures. Verily, they look it. Judging merely by their general style, and without other evidence, one might easily suspect that selfrighteousness was their specialty.

From various authorities I have culled information concerning Tiberias. It was built by Herod Antipas, the murderer of John the Baptist, and named after the Emperor Tiberius. It is believed that it stands upon the site of what must have been, ages ago, a city of considerable architectural pretensions, judging by the fine porphyry pillars that are scattered through Tiberias and down the lake shore southward. These were fluted once, and yet, although the stone is about as hard as iron, the flutings are almost worn away. These pillars are small, and doubtless the edifices they adorned were distinguished more for elegance than grandeur. This modern town — Tiberias — is only mentioned in the New Testament; never in the Old.

The Sanhedrim met here last, and for three hundred years Tiberias was the metropolis of the Jews in Palestine. It is one of the four holy cities of the Israelites, and is to them what Mecca is to the Mohammedan and Jerusalem to the Christian. It has been the abiding place of many learned and famous Jewish rabbins. They lie buried here, and near them lie also twenty-five thousand of their faith who traveled far to be near them while they lived and lie with them when they died. The great Rabbi Ben Israel spent three years here in the early part of the third century. He is dead, now.

The celebrated Sea of Galilee is not so large a sea as Lake Tahoe* by a good deal — it is just about two-thirds as large. And when we come to speak of beauty, this sea is no more to be compared to Tahoe than a meridian of longitude is to a rainbow. The dim waters of this pool cannot suggest the limpid brilliancy of Tahoe; these low, shaven, yellow hillocks of rocks and sand, so devoid of perspective, cannot suggest the grand peaks that compass Tahoe like a wall, and whose ribbed and chasmed fronts are clad with stately pines that seem to grow small and smaller as they climb, till one might fancy them reduced to weeds and shrubs far upward, where they join the everlasting snows. Silence and solitude brood over Tahoe; and silence and solitude brood also over this lake of Gennesaret. But the solitude of the one is as cheerful and fascinating as the solitude of the other is dismal and repellent.

In the early morning one watches the silent battle of dawn and darkness upon the waters of Tahoe with a placid interest; but

---

*I measure all lakes by Tahoe, partly because I am far more familiar with it than with any other, and partly because I have such a high admiration for it and such a world of pleasant recollections of it, that it is very nearly impossible for me to speak of lakes and not mention it.

when the shadows sulk away and one by one the hidden beauties of the shore unfold themselves in the full splendor of noon; when the still surface is belted like a rainbow with broad bars of blue and green and white, half the distance from circumference to center; when, in the lazy summer afternoon, he lies in a boat, far out to where the dead blue of the deep water begins, and smokes the pipe of peace and idly winks at the distant crags and patches of snow from under his cap-brim; when the boat drifts shoreward to the white water, and he lolls over the gunwale and gazes by the hour down through the crystal depths and notes the colors of the pebbles and reviews the finny armies gliding in procession a hundred feet below; when at night he sees moon and stars, mountain ridges feathered with pines, jutting white capes, bold promontories, grand sweeps of rugged scenery topped with bald, glimmering peaks, all magnificently pictured in the polished mirror of the lake, in richest, softest detail, the tranquil interest that was born with the morning deepens and deepens, by sure degrees, till it culminates at last in resistless fascination!

It is solitude, for birds and squirrels on the shore and fishes in the water are all the creatures that are near to make it otherwise, but it is not the sort of solitude to make one dreary. Come to Galilee for that. If these unpeopled deserts, these rusty mounds of barrenness, that never, never, never do shake the glare from their harsh outlines, and fade and faint into vague perspective; that melancholy ruin of Capernaum; this stupid village of Tiberias, slumbering under its six funereal plumes of palms; yonder desolate declivity where the swine of the miracle ran down into the sea, and doubtless thought it was better to swallow a devil or two and get drowned into the bargain than have to live longer in such a place; this cloudless, blistering sky; this solemn, sailless, tintless lake, reposing within its rim of yellow hills and low, steep banks, and looking just as expressionless and unpoetical (when we leave its sublime history out of the question), as any metropolitan reservoir in Christendom — if these things are not food for rock me to sleep, mother, none exist, I think.

"We had taken ship to go over to the other side. The sea was not more than six miles wide. Of the beauty of the scene, however, I can not say enough, nor can I imagine where those travelers carried their eyes who have described the scenery of the lake as tame or uninteresting. The first great characteristic of it is the deep basin in which it lies. This is from three to four hundred feet deep on all sides except at the lower end, and the sharp slope of the banks, which are all of the richest green, is broken and diversified by the wadys and water-courses which work their way down through the sides of the basin, forming dark chasms or light sunny valleys. Near Tiberias these banks are rocky, and ancient sepulchres open in them, with their doors toward the water. They selected grand spots, as did the Egyptians of old, for burial places, as if they designed that when the voice of God should reach the sleepers they should walk forth and open their eyes on scenes of glorious beauty. On the east, the wild and desolate mountains contrast finely with the deep blue lake; and toward the north, sublime and majestic, Hermon looks down on the sea, lifting his white crown to heaven with the pride of a hill that has seen the departing footsteps of a hundred generations. On the northeast shore of the sea was a single tree, and this is the only tree of any size visible from the water of the lake, except a few lonely palms in the city of Tiberias, and by its solitary position attracts more attention than would a forest. The whole appearance of the scene is precisely what we would expect and desire the scenery of Gennesaret to be, grand beauty, but quiet calm. The very mountains are calm."

It is an ingeniously written description, and well calculated to deceive. But if the paint and the ribbons and the flowers be stripped from it, a skeleton will be found beneath.

So stripped, there remains a lake six miles wide and neutral in color; with steep green banks, unrelieved by shrubbery; at one end bare, unsightly rocks, with (almost invisible) holes in them of no consequence to the picture; eastward, "wild and desolate mountains" (low, desolate hills, he should have said); in the north, a mountain called Hermon, with snow on it; peculiarity of the picture, "calmness"; its prominent feature, one tree.

No ingenuity could make such a picture beautiful — to one's actual vision.

I claim the right to correct misstatements, and have so corrected the color of the water in the above recapitulation. The waters of Gennesaret are of an exceedingly mild blue, even from a high elevation and a distance of five miles. Close at hand (the witness was sailing on the lake), it is hardly proper to call them blue at all, much less "deep" blue. I wish to state, also, not as a correction, but as a matter of opinion, that Mount Hermon is not a striking or picturesque mountain, by any means, being too near the height of its immediate neighbors to be so. That is all. I do not object to the witness dragging a mountain forty-five miles to help the scenery under consideration, because it is entirely proper to do it, and, besides, the picture needs it.

"C. W. E." (of "Life in the Holy Land"), deposes as follows:

"A beautiful sea lies unbosomed among the Galilean hills, in the midst of that land once possessed by Zebulon and Naphtali, Asher and Dan. The azure of the sky penetrates the depths of the lake, and the waters are sweet and cool. On the west, stretch broad fertile plains; on the north the rocky shores rise step by step until in the far distance tower the snowy heights of Hermon; on the east through a mistry veil are seen the high plains of Perea, which stretch away in rugged mountains leading the mind by varied paths toward Jerusalem the Holy. Flowers bloom in this terrestrial paradise, once beautiful and verdant with waving trees; singing birds enchant the ear; the turtle-dove soothes with its soft note; the crested lark sends up its song toward heaven, and the grave and stately stork inspires the mind with thought, and leads it on to meditation and repose. Life here was once idyllic, charming; here were once no rich, no poor, no high, no low. It was a world of ease, simplicity, and beauty; now it is a scene of desolation and misery."

This is not an ingenious picture. It is the worst I ever saw. It describes in elaborate detail what it terms a "terrestrial paradise," and closes with the startling information that this paradise is "a scene of *desolation and misery*."

I have given two fair, average specimens of the character of the testimony offered by the majority of the writers who visit this region. One says, "Of the beauty of the scene I cannot say enough," and then proceeds to cover up with a woof of glittering sentences a thing which, when stripped for inspection, proves to be only an unobtrusive basin of water, some mountainous desolation, and one tree. The other, after a conscientious effort to build a terrestrial paradise out of the same materials, with the addition of a "grave and stately stork," spoils it all by blundering upon the ghastly truth at the last.

Nearly every book concerning Galilee and its lake describes the scenery as beautiful. No — not always so straightforward as that. Sometimes the *impression* intentionally conveyed is that it is beautiful, at the same time that the author is careful not to *say* that it is, in plain Saxon. But a careful analysis of these descriptions will show that the materials of which they are formed are not individually beautiful and cannot be wrought into combinations that are beautiful. The veneration and the affection which some of these men felt for the scenes they were speaking of heated their fancies and biased their judgment; but the pleasant falsities they wrote were full of honest sincerity, at any rate. Others wrote as they did, because they feared it would be unpopular to write otherwise. Others were hypocrites and deliberately meant to deceive. Any of them would say in a moment, if asked, that it was *always* right and always *best* to tell the truth. They would say that, at any rate, if they did not perceive the drift of the question.

But why should not the truth be spoken of this region? Is the truth harmful? Has it ever needed to hide its face? God made the Sea of Galilee and its surroundings as they are. Is it the province of Mr. Grimes to improve upon the work?

I am sure, from the tenor of books I have read, that many who have visited this land in years gone by, were Presbyterians, and came seeking evidences in support of their particular creed; they found a Presbyterian Palestine, and they had already made up their minds to find no other, though possibly they did not know it, being blinded by their zeal. Others were Baptists, seeking Baptist evidences and a Baptist Palestine. Others were Catholics, Methodists, Episcopalians, seeking evidences indorsing their several creeds, and a Catholic, a Methodist, an Episcopalian Palestine. Honest as these men's intentions may have been, they were full of partialities and prejudices, they entered the country with their verdicts already prepared, and they could no more write dispassionately and impartially about it than they could about their own wives and children. Our pilgrims have brought *their* verdicts with them. They have shown it in their conversation ever since we left Beirout. I can almost tell, in set phrase, what they will say when they see Tabor, Nazareth, Jericho, and Jerusalem — *because I have the books they will "smouch" their ideas from.* These authors write pictures and frame rhapsodies, and lesser men follow and see with the author's eyes instead of their own, and speak with his tongue. What the pilgrims said at Cesarea Philippi surprised me with its wisdom. I found it afterwards in Robinson. What they said when Gennesaret burst upon their vision charmed me with its grace. I find it in Mr. Thompson's "Land and the Book." They have spoken often, in happily-worded language which never varied, of how they mean to lay their weary heads upon a stone at Bethel, as Jacob did, and close their dim eyes, and dream, perchance, of angels descending out of heaven on a ladder. It was very pretty. But I have recognized the weary head and the dim eyes, finally. They borrowed the idea — and the words — and the construction — and the punctuation — from Grimes. The pilgrims will tell of Palestine, when they get home, not as it appeared to *them,* but as it appeared to Thompson and Robinson and Grimes — with the tints varied to suit each pilgrim's creed.

Pilgrims, sinners, and Arabs are all abed, now, and the camp is still. Labor in loneliness is irksome. Since I made my last few notes, I have been sitting outside the tent for half an hour. Night is the time to see Galilee. Gennesaret under these lustrous stars has nothing repulsive about it. Gennesaret with the glittering reflections of the constellations flecking its surface, almost makes me regret that I ever saw the rude glare of the day upon it. Its history and its associations are its chiefest charm, in any eyes, and the spells they weave are feeble in the searching light of the sun. *Then,* we scarcely feel the fetters. Our thoughts wander constantly to the practical concerns of life, and refuse to dwell upon things that seem vague and unreal. But when the day is done, even the most unimpressible must yield to the dreamy influences of this tranquil starlight. The old traditions of the place steal upon his memory and haunt his reveries, and then his fancy clothes all sights and sounds with the supernatural. In the lapping of the waves upon the beach, he hears the dip of ghostly oars; in the secret noises of the night he hears spirit voices; in the soft sweep of the breeze, the rush of invisible wings. Phantom ships are on the sea, the dead of twenty centuries come forth from the tombs, and in the dirges of the night wind the songs of old forgotten ages find utterance again.

In the starlight, Galilee has no boundaries but the broad compass of the heavens, and is a theater meet for great events; meet for the birth of a religion able to save a world; and meet for the stately Figure appointed to stand upon its stage and proclaim its high decrees. But in the sunlight, one says: Is it for the deeds which were done and the words which were spoken in this little acre of rocks and sand eighteen centuries gone, that the bells are ringing to-day in the remote islands of the sea and far and wide over continents that clasp the circumference of the huge globe?

One can comprehend it only when night has hidden all incongruities and created a theater proper for so grand a drama.

CHAPTER XXII

We took another swim in the Sea of Galilee at twilight yesterday, and another at sunrise this morning. We have not sailed, but three swims are equal to a sail, are they not? There were plenty of fish visible in the water, but we have no outside aids in this pilgrimage but "Tent Life in the Holy Land," "The Land and the Book," and other literature of like description — no fishing tackle. There were no fish to be had in the village of Tiberias. True, we saw two or three vagabonds mending their nets, but never trying to catch anything with them.

We did not go to the ancient warm baths two miles below Tiberias. I had no desire in the world to go there. This seemed a little strange, and prompted me to try to discover what the cause of this unreasonable indifference was. It turned out to be simply because Pliny mentions them. I have conceived a sort of unwarrantable unfriendliness toward Pliny and St. Paul, because it seems as if I can never ferret out a place that I can have to myself. It always and eternally transpires that St. Paul has been to that place, and Pliny has "mentioned" it.

In the early morning we mounted and started. And then a weird apparition marched forth at the head of the procession — a pirate, I thought, if ever a pirate dwelt upon land. It was a tall Arab, as swarthy as an Indian, young — say thiry years of age. On his head he had closely bound a gorgeous yellow and red striped silk scarf, whose ends, lavishly fringed with tassels, hung down between his shoulders and dallied with the wind. From his neck to his knees, in ample folds, a robe swept down that was a very star-spangled banner of curved and sinuous bars of black and white. Out of his back, somewhere, apparently, the long stem of a chilbouk projected, and reached far above his right shoulder. Athwart his back, diagonally, and extending high above his left shoulder, was an Arab gun of Saladin's time, that was splendid with silver plating from stock clear up to the end of its measureless stretch of barrel. About his waist was bound many and many a yard of elaborately figured but sadly tarnished stuff that came from sumptuous Persia, and among the baggy folds in front the sunbeams glinted from a formidable battery of old brass-mounted horse pistols and the gilded hilts of blood-thirsty knives. There were holsters for more pistols appended to the wonderful stack of long-haired goat-skins and Persian car-pets, which the man had been taught to regard in the light of a saddle; and down among the pendulous rank of vast tassels that swung from that saddle, and clanging against the iron shovel of a stirrup that propped the warrior's knees up toward his chin, was a crooked, silver-clad scimetar of such awful dimensions and such implacable expression that no man might hope to look upon it and not shudder. The fringed and bedizened prince whose privilege it is to ride the pony and lead the elephant into a country village is poor and naked compared to this chaos of paraphernalia, and the happy vanity of the one is the very pover-ty of satisfaction compared to the majestic serentiy, the over-whelming complacency of the other.

"*Who* is this? *What* is this?" That was the trembling inquiry all down the line.

"Our guard! From Galilee to the birthplace of the Saviour, the country is infested with fierce Bedouins, whose sole hap-piness it is, in this life, to cut and stab and mangle and murder unoffending Christians. Allah be with us!"

"Then hire a regiment! Would you send us out among these desperate hordes, with no salvation in our utmost need but this old turret?"

The dragoman laughed — not at the facetiousness of the simile, for verily, that guide or that courier or that dragoman never yet lived upon earth who had in him the faintest ap-preciation of a joke, even though that joke were so broad and so ponderous that if it fell on him it would flatten him out like a postage-stamp — the dragoman laughed, and then, emboldened by some thought that was in his brain, no doubt, proceeded to extremities and winked.

In straits like these, when a man laughs, it is encouraging; when he winks, it is positively reassuring. He finally intimated that one guard would be sufficient to protect us, but that that one was an absolute necessity. It was because of the moral weight his awful panoply would have with the Bedouins. Then I said we didn't want any guard at all. If one fantastic vagabond could protect eight armed Christians and a pack of Arab ser-vants from all harm, surely that detachment could protect them-selves. He shook his head doubtfully. Then I said, just think of how it looks — think of how it would read, to self-reliant Americans, that we went sneaking through this deserted wilder-ness under the protection of this masquerading Arab, who would break his neck getting out of the country if a man that *was* a man ever started after him. It was a mean, low, degrading position. Why were we ever told to bring navy revolvers with us if we had to be protected at last by this infamous star-spangled scum of the desert? These appeals were vain — the dragoman only smiled and shook his head.

I rode to the front and struck up an acquaintance with King Solomon-in-all-his-glory, and got him to show me his lingering eternity of a gun. It had a rusty flint lock; it was ringed and barred and plated with silver from end to end, but it was as desperately out of the perpendicular as are the billiard cues of '49 that one finds yet in service in the ancient mining camps of California. The muzzle was eaten by the rust of centuries into a ragged filigree-work, like the end of a burnt-out stovepipe. I shut one eye and peered within — it was flaked with iron rust like and old steamboat boiler. I borrowed the ponderous pistols and snapped them. They were rusty inside, too — had not been loaded for a generation. I went back, full of encouragement, and reported to the guide, and asked him to discharge this disman-tled fortress. It came out, then. This fellow was a retainer of the Sheik of Tiberias. He was a source of Government revenue. He was to the Empire of Tiberias what the customs are to America. The Sheik imposed guards upon travelers and charged them for it. It is a lucrative source of emolument, and sometimes brings into the national treasury as much as thirty-five or forty dollars a year.

I knew the warrior's secret now; I knew the hollow vanity of his rusty trumpery, and despised his asinine complacency. I told on him, and with reckless daring the cavalcade rode straight ahead into the perilous solitudes of the desert, and scorned his frantic warnings of the mutilation and death that hovered about them on every side.

Arrived at an elevation of twelve hundred feet above the lake (I ought to mention that the lake lies six hundred feet below the level of the Mediterranean — no traveler ever neglects to flourish that fragment of news in his letters), as bald and unthrilling a panorama as any land can afford, perhaps, was spread out before us. Yet it was so crowded with historical interest, that if all the pages that have been written about it were spread upon its surface, they would flag it from horizon to horizon like a pavement. Among the localities comprised in this view, were Mount Hermon; the hills that border Cesarea Philippi, Dan, the Sources of the Jordan and the Waters of Merom; Tiberias; the Sea of Galilee; Joseph's Pit; Capernaum; Bethsaida; the sup-posed scenes of the Sermon on the Mount, the feeding of the multitudes and the miraculous draught of fishes; the declivity down which the swine ran to the sea; the entrance and the exit of the Jordan; Safed, "the city set upon a hill," one of the four

holy cities of the Jews, and the place where they believe the real
Messiah will appear when he comes to redeem the world; part of
the battlefield of Hattin, where the knightly Crusaders fought
their last fight, and in a blaze of glory passed from the stage and
ended their splendid career forever; Mount Tabor, the traditional
scene of the Lord's Transfiguration. And down toward the
southeast lay a landscape that suggested to my mind a quotation
(imperfectly remembered, no doubt):

"The Ephraimites, not being called upon to share in the rich spoils of the Am-
monitish war, assembled a mighty host to fight against Jeptha, Judge of Israel;
who being apprised of their approach, gathered together the men of Israel and
gave them battle and put them to flight. To make his victory the more secure, he
stationed guards at the different fords and passages of the Jordan, with instructions to let none pass who could not say Shibboleth. The Ephraimites, being
of a different tribe, could not frame to pronounce the word aright, but called it
Sibboleth, which proved them enemies and cost them their lives; wherefore forty
and two thousand fell at the different fords and passages of the Jordan that
day."

We jogged along peacefully over the great caravan route from
Damascus to Jerusalem and Egypt, past Lubia and other Syrian
hamlets, perched, in the unvarying style, upon the summit of
steep mounds and hills, and fenced round about with giant cac-
tuses (the sign of worthless land), with prickly pears upon them
like harms, and came at last to the battlefield of Hattin.

It is a grand, irregular plateau, and looks as if it might have
been created for a battlefield. Here the peerless Saladin met the
Christian host some seven hundred years ago, and broke their
power in Palestine for all time to come. There had long been a
truce between the opposing forces, but according to the Guide-
Book, Raynauld of Chatillon, Lord of Kerak, broke it by plun-
dering a Damascus caravan, and refusing to give up either the
merchants or their goods when Saladin demanded them. This
conduct of an insolent petty chieftain stung the Sultan to the
quick, and he swore that he would slaughter Raynauld with his
own hand, no matter how, or when, or where he found him.
Both armies prepared for war. Under the weak King of
Jerusalem was the very flower of the Christian chivalry. He
foolishly compelled them to undergo a long, exhausting march,
in the scorching sun, and then, without water or other refreshment, ordered them to encamp in this open plain. The splendidly
mounted masses of Moslem soldiers swept round the north end
of Gennesaret, burning and destroying as they came, and pitched
their camp in front of the opposing lines. At dawn the terrific
fight began. Surrounded on all sides by the Sultan's swarming
battalions, the Christian Knights fought on without a hope for
their lives. They fought with desperate valor, but to no purpose;
the odds of heat and numbers and consuming thirst were too

great against them. Toward the middle of the day the bravest of their band cut their way through the Moslem ranks and gained the summit of a little hill, and there, hour after hour, they closed around the banner of the Cross, and beat back the charging squadrons of the enemy.

But the doom of the Christian power was sealed. Sunset found Saladin Lord of Palestine, the Christian chivalry strewn in heaps upon the field, and the King of Jerusalem, the Grand Master of the Templars, and Raynauld of Chatillon, captives in the Sultan's tent. Saladin treated two of the prisoners with princely courtesy, and ordered refreshments to be set before them. When the King handed an iced Sherbet to Chatillon, the Sultan said, "It is thou that givest it to him, not I." He remembered his oath, and slaughtered the hapless Knight of Chatillon with his own hand.

It was hard to realize that this silent plain had once resounded with martial music and trembled to the tramp of armed men. It was hard to people this solitude with rushing columns of cavalry, and stir its torpid pulses with the shouts of victors, the shrieks of the wounded, and the flash of banner and steel above the surging billows of war. A desolation is here that not even imagination can grace with the pomp of life and action.

We reached Tabor safely, and considerably in advance of that old iron-clad swindle of a guard. We never saw a human being on the whole route, much less lawless hordes of Bedouins. Tabor stands solitary and alone, a giant sentinel above the Plain of Esdraelon. It rises some fourteen hundred feet above the surrounding level, a green, wooded cone, symmetrical and full of grace — a prominent landmark, and one that is exceedingly pleasant to eyes surfeited with the replusive monotony of desert Syria. We climbed the steep path to its summit, through breezy glades of thorn and oak. The view presented from its highest peak was almost beautiful. Below, was the broad, level plain of Esdraelon, checkered with fields like a chessboard, and full as smooth and level, seemingly; dotted about its borders with white, compact villages, and faintly penciled, far and near, with the curving lines of roads and trails. When it is robed in the fresh verdure of spring, it must form a charming picture, even by itself. Skirting its southern border rises "Little Hermon," over whose summit a glimpse of Gilboa is caught. Nain, famous for the raising of the widow's son, and Endor, as famous for the performances of her witch, are in view. To the eastward lies the Valley of the Jordan and beyond it the mountains of Gilead. Westward is Mount Carmel. Hermon in the north — the tablelands of Bashan — Safed, the holy city, gleaming white upon a tall spur of the mountains of Lebanon — a steel-blue corner of the Sea of Galilee — saddle-peaked Hattin, traditional "Mount

of Beatitudes" and mute witness of the last brave fight of the
Crusading host for Holy Cross — these fill up the picture.

To glance at the salient features of this landscape through the
picturesque framework of a ragged and ruined stone window-
arch of the time of Christ, thus hiding from sight all that is
unattractive, is to secure to yourself a pleasure worth climbing
the mountain to enjoy. One must stand on his head to get the
best effect in a fine sunset, and set a landscape in a bold, strong
framewrok that is very close at hand, to bring out all its beauty.
One learns this latter truth never more to forget it, in this mimic
land of enchantment, the wonderful garden of my lord the
Count Pallavicini, near Genoa. You go wandering for hours
among hills and wooded glens, artfully contrived to leave the impression that Nature shaped them and not man; following winding paths and coming suddenly upon leaping cascades and rustic
bridges; finding sylvan lakes where you expected them not;
loitering through battered medieval castles in miniature that seem
hoary with age and yet were built a dozen years ago; meditating
over ancient crumbling tombs, whose marble columns were
marred and broken purposely by the modern artist that made
them; stumbling unawares upon toy palaces, wrought of rare and
costly materials, and again upon a peasant's hut, whose
dilapidated furniture would never suggest that it was made so to
order; sweeping round and round in the midst of a forest on an
enchanted wooden horse that is moved by some invisible agency;
traversing Roman roads and passing under majestic triumphal
arches; resting in quaint bowers where unseen spirits discharge,
and where even the flowers you touch assail you with a shower;
boating on a subterranean lake among caverns and arches royally
draped with clustering stalactites, and passing out into open day
upon another lake, which is bordered with sloping banks of grass
and gay with patrician barges that swim at anchor in the shadow
of a miniature marble temple that rises out of the clear water
and glasses its white statues, its rich capitals and fluted columns
in the tranquil depths. So, from marvel to marvel you have drifted on, thinking all the time that the one last seen must be the
chiefest. And, verily, the chiefest wonder *is* reserved until the
last, but you do not see it until you step ashore, and passing
through a wilderness of rare flowers, collected from every corner
of the earth, you stand at the door of one more mimic temple.
Right in this place the artist taxed his genius to the utmost, and
fairly opened the gates of fairy land. You look through an unpretending pane of glass, stained yellow; the first thing you see is
a mass of quivering foliage, ten short steps before you, in the
midst of which is a ragged opening like a gateway — a thing that
is common enough in nature, and not apt to excite suspicions of
a deep human design — and above the bottom of the gateway,

project, in the most careless way, a few broad tropic leaves and brilliant flowers. All of a sudden, through this bright, bold gateway, you catch a glimpse of the faintest, softest, richest picture that ever graced the dream of a dying Saint, since John saw the New Jerusalem glimmering above the clouds of Heaven. A broad sweep of sea, flecked with careening sails; a sharp, jutting cape, and a lofty lighthouse on it; a sloping lawn behind it; beyond, a portion of the old "city of palaces," with its parks and hills and stately mansions; beyond these, a prodigious mountain, with its strong outlines sharply cut against ocean and sky; and, over all, vagrant shreds and flakes of clouds, floating in a sea of gold. The ocean is gold, the city is gold, the meadow, the mountain, the sky — everything is golden — rich, and mellow, and dreamy as a vision of Paradise. No artist could put upon canvas its entrancing beauty, and yet, without the yellow glass, and the carefully contrived accident of a framework that case it into enchanted distance and shut out from it all unattractive features, it was not a picture to fall into ecstasies over. Such is life, and the trail of the serpent is over us all.

There is nothing for it now but to come back to old Tabor, though the subject is tiresome enough, and I cannot stick to it for wandering off to scenes that are pleasanter to remember. I think I will skip, anyhow. There is nothing about Tabor (except we concede that it was the scene of the Transfiguration), but some gray old ruins, stacked up there in all ages of the world from the days of stout Gideon and parties that flourished thirty centuries ago to the fresh yesterday of Crusading times. It has its Greek Convent, and the coffee there is good, but never a splinter of the true cross or bone of a hallowed saint to arrest the idle thoughts of worldlings and turn them into graver channels. A Catholic church is nothing to me that has no relics.

The plain of Esdraelon — "the battlefield of the nations" — only sets one to dreaming of Joshua, and Benhadad, and Saul, and Gideon; Tamerlane, Tancred, Coeur de Lion, and Saladin, the warrior Kings of Persia, Egypt's heroes, and Napoleon — for they all fought here. If the magic of the moonlight could summon from the graves of forgotten centuries and many lands the countless myriads that have battled on this wide, far-reaching floor, and array them in the thousands strange costumes of their hundred nationalities, and send the vast host sweeping down the plain, splendid with plumes and banners and glittering lances, I could stay here an age to see the phantom pageant. But the magic of the moonlight is a vanity and a fraud; and whoso putteth his trust in it shall suffer sorrow and disappointment.

Down at the foot of Tabor, and just at the edge of the storied Plain of Esdraelon, is the insignificant village of Deburieh, where Deborah, prophetess of Israel, lived. It is just like Magdala.

CHAPTER XXIII

We descended from Mount Tabor, crossed a deep ravine, and followed a hilly, rocky road to Nazareth — distant two hours. All distances in the East are measured by hours, not miles. A good horse will walk three miles an hour over nearly any kind of a road; therefore, an hour here always stands for three miles. This method of computation is bothersome and annoying; and until one gets thoroughly accustomed to it, it carries no intelligence to his mind until he has stopped and translated the pagan hours into Christian miles, just as people do with the spoken words of a foreign language they are acquainted with, but not familiarly enough to catch the meaning in a moment. Distances traveled by human feet are also estimated by hours and minutes, though I do not know what the base of the calculation is. In Constantinople you ask, "How far is it to the Consulate?" and they answer, "About ten minutes." "How far is it to the Lloyds' Agency?" "Quarter of an hour." "How far is it to the lower bridge?" "Four minutes." I cannot be positive about it, but I think that there, when a man orders a pair of pantaloons, he says he wants them a quarter of a minute in the legs and nine seconds around the waist.

Two hours from Tabor to Nazareth — and as it was an uncommonly narrow, crooked trail, we necessarily met all the camel trains and jackass caravans between Jericho and Jacksonville in that particular place and nowhere else. The donkeys do not matter so much, because they are so small that you can jump your horse over them if he is an animal of spirit, but a camel is not jumpable. A camel is as tall as any ordinary dwelling-house in Syria — which is to say a camel is from one to two, and sometimes nearly three feet taller than a good-sized man. In this part of the country his load is oftenest in the shape of colossal sacks — one on each side. He and his cargo take up as much room as a carriage. Think of meeting this style of obstruction in a narrow trail. The camel would not turn out for a king. He stalks serenely along, bringing his cushioned stilts forward with the long, regular swing of a pendulum, and whatever is in the way must get out of the way peaceably, or be wiped out forcibly by the bulky sacks. It was a tiresome ride to us, and perfectly exhausting to the horses. We were compelled to jump over upward of eighteen hundred donkeys, and only one person in the party was unseated less than sixty times by the camels. This seems like a powerful statement, but the poet has said, "Things are not what they seem." I cannot think of anything now more certain to make one shudder, than to have a soft-footed camel sneak up behind him and touch him on the ear with its cold, flabby under lip. A camel did this for one of the boys, who was drooping over his saddle in a brown study. He glanced up and saw the majestic apparition hovering above him, and made frantic efforts to get out of the way, but the camel reached out and bit him on the shoulder before he accomplished it. This was the only pleasant incident of the journey.

At Nazareth we camped in an olive grove near the Virgin Mary's fountain, and that wonderful Arab "guard" came to collect some bucksheesh for his "services" in following us from Tiberias and warding off invisible dangers with the terrors of his armament. The dragoman had paid his master, but that counted as nothing — if you hire a man to sneeze for you here, and another man chooses to help him, you have got to pay both. They do nothing whatever without pay. How it must have surprised these people to hear the way of salvation offered to them *"without money and without price."* If the manners, the people, or the customs of this country have changed since the Saviour's time, the figures and metaphors of the Bible are not the evidences to prove it by.

We entered the great Latin Convent which is built over the traditional dwelling-place of the Holy Family. We went down a flight of fifteen steps below the ground level, and stood in a small chapel tricked out with tapestry hangings, silver lamps, and oil paintings. A spot marked by a cross, in the marble floor, under the altar, was exhibited as the place made forever holy by the feet of the Virgin when she stood up to receive the message of the angel. So simple, so unpretending a locality, to be the scene of so mighty an event! The very scene of the Annunciation — an event which has been commemorated by splendid shrines and august temples all over the civilized world, and one which the princes of art have made it their loftiest ambition to picture worthily on their canvas; a spot whose history is familiar to the very children of every house, and city, and obscure hamlet of the furthest lands of Christendom; a spot which myriads of men would toil across the breadth of a world to see, would consider it a priceless privilege to look upon. It was easy to think these thoughts. But it was not easy to bring myself up to the magnitude of the situation. I could sit off several thousand miles and imagine the angel appearing, with shadowy wings and lustrous countenance, and note the glory that streamed downward upon the Virgin's head while the message from the Throne of God fell upon her ears — any one can do that, beyond the ocean, but few can do it here. I saw the little recess from which the angel stepped, but could not fill its void. The angels that I know are creatures of unstable fancy — they will not fit in

niches of substantial stone. Imagination labors best in distant
fields. I doubt if any man can stand in the Grotto of the Annunciation and people with the phantom images of his mind its
too tangible walls of stone.

They showed us a broken granite pillar, depending from the
roof, which they said was hacked in two by the Moslem
conquerors of Nazareth, in the vain hope of pulling down the
sanctuary. But the pillar remained miraculously suspended in the
air, and, unsupported itself, supported then and still supports the
roof. By dividing this statement up among eight, it was found
not difficult to believe it.

These gifted Latin monks never do anything by halves. If they
were to show you the Brazen Serpent that was elevated in the
wilderness, you could depend upon it that they had on hand the
pole it was elevated on also, and even the hole it stood in. They
have got the "Grotto" of the Annunciation here; and just as
convenient to it as one's throat is to his mouth, they have also
the Virgin's Kitchen, and even her sitting-room, where she and
Joseph watched the infant Saviour play with Hebrew toys
eighteen hundred years ago. All under one roof, and all clean,
spacious, comfortable "grottoes." It seems curious that personages intimately connected with the Holy Family always lived
in grottoes — in Nazareth, in Bethlehem, in imperial Ephesus —
and yet nobody else in their day and generation thought of doing
anything of the kind. If they ever did, their grottoes are all gone,
and I suppose we ought to wonder at the peculiar marvel of the
preservation of these I speak of. When the Virgin fled from
Herod's wrath, she hid in a grotto in Bethlehem, and the same is
there to this day. The slaughter of the innocents in Bethlehem
was done in a grotto; the Saviour was born in a grotto — both
are shown to pilgrims yet. It is exceedingly strange that these
tremendous events all happened in grottoes — and exceedingly
fortunate, likewise, because the strongest houses must crumble to
ruin in time, but a grotto in the living rock will last forever. It is
an imposture — this grotto stuff — but it is one that all men
ought to thank the Catholics for. Wherever they ferret out a lost
locality made holy by some Scriptural event, they straightway
build a massive — almost imperishable — church there, and
preserve the memory of that locality for the gratification of
future generations. If it had been left to Protestants to do this
most worthy work, we would not even know where Jerusalem is
to-day, and the man who could go and put his finger on
Nazareth would be too wise for this world. The world owes the
Catholics its good will even for the happy rascality of hewing out
these bogus grottoes in the rock; for it is infinitely more satisfactory to look at a grotto, where people have faithfully believed
for centuries that the Virgin once lived, than a have to imagine a

dwelling-place for her somewhere, anywhere, nowhere, loose and at large all over this town of Nazareth. There is too large a scope of country. The imagination cannot work. There is no one particular spot to chain your eye, rivet your interest, and make you think. The memory of the Pilgrims cannot perish while Plymouth Rock remains to us. The old monks are wise. They know how to drive a stake through a pleasant tradition that will hold it to its place forever.

We visited the places where Jesus worked for fifteen years as a carpenter, and where he attempted to teach in the synagogue and was driven out by a mob. Catholic chapels stand upon these sites and protect the little fragments of the ancient walls which remain. Our pilgrims broke off specimens. We visited, also, a new chapel, in the midst of the town, which is built around a bowlder some twelve feet long by four feet thick; the priests discovered, a few years ago, that the disciples had sat upon this rock to rest once, when they had walked up from Capernaum. They hastened to preserve the relic. Relics are very good property. Travelers are expected to pay for seeing them, and they do it cheerfully. We like the idea. One's conscience can never be the worse for the knowledge that he has paid his way like a man. Our pilgrims would have liked very well to get out their lampblack and stencil-plates and paint their names on that rock, together with the names of the villages they hail from in America, but the priests permit nothing of that kind. To speak the strict truth, however, our party seldom offend in that way, though we have men in the ship who never lose an opportunity to do it. Our pilgrims' chief sin is their lust for "specimens." I suppose that by this time they know the dimensions of that rock to an inch, and its weight to a ton; and I do not hesitate to charge that they will go back there to-night and try to carry it off.

This "Fountain of the Virgin" is the one which tradition says Mary used to get water from, twenty times a day, when she was a girl, and bear it away in a jar upon her head. The water streams through faucets in the face of a wall of ancient masonry which stands removed from the houses of the village. The young girls of Nazareth still collect about it by the dozen and keep up a riotous laughter and skylarking. The Nazarene girls are homely. Some of them have large, lustrous eyes, but none of them have pretty faces. These girls wear a single garment, usually, and it is loose, shapeless, of undecided color; it is generally out of repair, too. They wear, from crown to jaw, curious strings of old coins, after the manner of the belles of Tiberias, and brass jewelry upon their wrists and in their ears. They wear no shoes and stockings. They are the most human girls we have found in the country yet, and the best natured. But there is no question that these picturesque maidens sadly lack comeliness.

A pilgrim — the "Enthusiast" — said: "See that tall, graceful girl! look at the Madonna-like beauty of her countenance!"

Another pilgrim came along presently and said: "Observe that tall, graceful girl; what queenly Madonna-like gracefulness of beauty is in her countenance."

I said: "She is not tall, she is short, she is not beautiful, she is homely; she is graceful enough, I grant, but she is rather boisterous."

The third and last pilgrim moved by, before long, and he said: "Ah, what a tall, graceful girl! what Madonna-like gracefulness of queenly beauty!"

The verdicts were all in. It was time, now, to look up the authorities for all these opinions. I found this paragraph, which follows. Written by whom? Wm. C. Grimes:

"After we were in the saddle, we rode down to the spring to have a last look at the women of Nazareth, who were, as a class, much the prettiest that we had seen in the East. As we approached the crowd a tall girl of nineteen advanced toward Miriam and offered her a cup of water. Her movement was graceful and queenly. We exclaimed on the spot at the Madonna-like beauty of her countenance. Whitely was suddenly thirsty, and begged for water, and drank it slowly, with his eyes over the top of the cup, fixed on her large black eyes, which gazed on him quite as curiously as he on her. Then Moreright wanted water. She gave it to him and he managed to spill it so as to ask for another cup, and by the time she came to me she saw through the operation; her eyes were full of fun as she looked at me. I laughed outright, and she joined me in as gay a shout as ever country maiden in old Orange county. I wished for a picture of her. A Madonna, whose face was a portrait of that beautiful Nazareth girl, would be a 'thing of beauty' and 'a joy forever.' "

That is the kind of gruel which been served out from Palestine for ages. Commend me to Fenimore Cooper to find beauty in the Indians, and to Grimes to find it in the Arabs. Arab men are often fine looking, but Arab women are not. We can all believe that the Virgin Mary was beautiful; it is not natural to think otherwise; but does it follow that it is our duty to find beauty in these present women of Nazareth?

I love to quote from Grimes, because he is so dramatic. And because he is so romantic. And because he seems to care but little whether he tells the truth or not, so he scares the reader or excites his envy or his admiration.

He went through this peaceful land with one hand forever on his revolver, and the other on his pocket-handkerchief. Always, when he was not on the point of crying over a holy place, he was on the point of killing an Arab. More surprising things happened to him in Palestine than ever happened to any traveler here or elsewhere since Munchausen died.

At Beit Jin, where nobody had interfered with him, he crept out of his tent at dead of night and shot at what he took to be

an Arab lying on the rock, some distance away, planning evil.
The ball killed a wolf. Just before he fired, he makes a dramatic
picture of himself — as usual, to scare the reader:

> "Was it imagination, or did I see a moving object on the surface of the rock?
> If it were a man, why did he not now drop me? He had a beautiful shot as I
> stood out in my black boornoose against the white tent. I had the sensation of an
> entering bullet in my throat, breast, brain."

Reckless creature!
Riding toward Gennesaret, they saw two Bedouins, and "we
looked to our pistols and loosened them quietly in our shawls,"
etc. Always cool.
In Samaria, he charged up a hill, in the face of a volley of
stones; he fired into the crowd of men who threw them. He says:

> "*I never lost an opportunity* of impressing the Arabs with the perfection of
> American and English weapons, and the danger of attacking any one of the
> armed Franks. I think the lesson of that ball not lost."

At Beitin he gave his while band of Arab muleteers a piece of
his mind, and then —

> "I contented myself with a solemn assurance that if there occurred another in-
> stance of disobedience to orders, I would thrash the responsible party as he never
> dreamed of being thrashed, and if I could not find who was responsible, I would
> whip them all, from first to last, whether there was a governor at hand to do it
> or I had to do it myself."

Perfectly fearless, this man.
He rode down the perpendicular path in the rocks, from the
Castle of Banias to the oak grove, at a flying gallop, his horse
striding "thirty feet" at every bound. I stand prepared to bring
thirty reliable witnesses to prove that Putnam's famous feat at
Horseneck was insignificant compared to this.
Behold him — always theatrical — looking at Jerusalem —
this time, by an oversight, with his hand off his pistol for once.

> "I stood in the road, my hand on my horse's neck, and with my dim eyes
> sought to trace the outlines of the holy places which I had long before fixed in
> my mind, but the fast-flowing tears forbade my succeeding. There were our
> Mohammedan servants, a Latin monk, two Armenians, and a Jew in our cortege,
> and all alike gazed with overflowing eyes."

If Latin monks and Arabs cried, I know to a moral certainty
that the horses cried also, and so the picture is complete.
But when necessity demanded he could be firm as adamant. In
the Lebanon Valley an Arab youth — a Christian; he is particular to explain that Mohammedans do not steal — robbed him
of a paltry ten dollars' worth of powder and shot. He convicted
him before a sheik and looked on while he was punished by the

terrible bastinado. Hear him:

"He (Mousa) was on his back in a twinkling, howling, shouting, screaming, but he was carried out to the piazza before the door, where we could see the operation, and laid face down. One man sat on his back and one on his legs, the latter holding up his feet, while a third laid on the bare soles a rhinoceros-hide koorbash* that whizzed through the air at every stroke. Poor Moreright was in agony, and Nama and Nama the Second (mother and sister of Mousa) were on their faces begging and wailing, now embracing my knees and now Whitely's, while the brother, outside, made the air ring with cries louder than Mousa's. Even Yusef came and asked me on his knees to relent, and last of all, Betuni — the rascal had lost a feed-bag in their house and had been loudest in his denunciations that morning — besought the Howajji to have mercy on the fellow."

But not he! The punishment was "suspended," at the *fifteenth blow*, to hear the confession. Then Grimes and his party rode away, and left the entire Christian family to be fined and as severely punished as the *Mohammedan sheik* should deem proper.

"As I mounted, Yusef once more begged me to interfere and have mercy on them, but I looked around at the dark faces of the crowd, and I couldn't find one drop of pity in my heart for them."

He closes his picture with a rollicking burst of humor which contrasts finely with the grief of the mother and her children. One more paragraph:

"Then once more I bowed my head. It is no shame to have wept in Palestine. I wept when I saw Jerusalem, I wept when I lay in the starlight at Bethlehem, I wept on the blessed shores of Galilee. My hand was no less firm on the rein, my finger did not tremble on the trigger of my pistol when I rode with it in my right hand along the shore of the blue sea" (weeping.) "My eye was not dimmed by those tears nor my heart in aught weakened. Let him who would sneer at my emotion close this volume here, for he will find little to his taste in my journeyings through Holy Land."

He never bored but he struck water.

I am aware that this is a pretty voluminous notice of Mr. Grimes' book. However, it is proper and legitimate to speak of it, for "Nomadic Life in Palestine" is a representative book — the representative of a *class* of Palestine books — and a criticism upon it will serve for a criticism upon them all. And since I am treating it in the comprehensive capacity of a representative book, I have taken the liberty of giving to both book and author fictitious names. Perhaps it is in better taste, anyhow, to do this.

---

*"A koorbash is Arabic for cowhide, the cow being a rhinoceros. It is the most cruel whip known to fame. Heavy as lead and flexible as Indian-rubber, usually about forty inches long and tapering gradually from an inch in diameter to a point, it administers a blow which *leaves its mark for time*." — Scow Life in Egypt, by the same author.

CHAPTER XXIV

Nazareth is wonderfully interesting because the town has an air about it of being precisely as Jesus left it, and one finds himself saying, all the time, "The boy Jesus has stood in this doorway — has played in that street — has touched these stones with this hands — has rambled over these chalky hills." Whoever shall write the Boyhood of Jesus ingeniously, will make a book which will possess a vivid interest for young and old alike. I judge so from the greater interest we found in Nazareth than any of our speculations upon Capernaum and the Sea of Galilee gave rise to. It was not possible, standing by the Sea of Galilee, to frame more than vague, far-away idea of the majestic Personage who walked upon the crested waves as if they had been solid earth, and who touched the dead and they rose up and spoke. I read among my notes, now, with a new interest, some sentences from an edition of 1621 of the Apocryphal New Testament. [Extract.]

"Christ, kissed by a bride made dumb by sorcerers, cures her. A leprous girl cured by the water in which the infant Christ was washed, and becomes the servant of Joseph and Mary. The leprous son of a Prince cured in like manner.

"A young man who had been bewitched and turned into a mule, miraculously cured by the infant Saviour being put on his back, and is married to the girl who had been cured of leprosy. Whereupon the bystanders praise God.

"Chapter 16. Christ miraculously widens or contracts gates, milk-pails, sieves, or boxes not properly made by Joseph, he not being skillful at his carpenter's trade. The King of Jerusalem gives Joseph an order for a throne. Joseph works on it for two years and makes it two spans too short. The King being angry with him, Jesus comforts him — commands him to pull one side of the throne while he pulls the other, and brings it to its proper dimensions.

"Chapter 19. Jesus, charged with throwing a boy from the roof of a house, miraculously caused the dead boy to speak and acquit him; fetches water for his mother, breaks the pitcher and miraculously gathers the water in his mantle and brings it home.

"Sent to a schoolmaster, refuses to tell his letters, and the schoolmaster going to whip him, his hand withers."

Further on in this quaint volume of rejected gospels is an epistle of St. Clement to the Corinthians, which was used in the churchs and considered genuine fourteen or fifteen hundred years ago. In it this account of the fabled phoenix occurs:

"1. Let us consider that wonderful type of the resurrection, which is seen in the Eastern countries, that is to say, in Arabia.

"2. There is a certain bird called a phoenix. Of this there is never but one at a time, and that lives five hundred years. And when the time of its dissolution draws near, that it must die, it makes itself a nest of frankincense and myrrh, and other spices, into which, when its time is fulfilled, it enters and dies.

"3. But its flesh, putrefying, breeds a certain worm, which being nourished by the juice of the dead bird, brings forth feathers; and when it is grown to a per-

fect state, it takes up the nest in which the bones of its parent lie, and carries it
from Arabia into Egypt, to a city called Heliopolis:

"4. And flying in open day in the sight of all men, lays it upon the altar of the
sun, and so returns from whence it came.

"5. The priests then search into the records of the time, and find that it returned precisely at the end of five hundred years."

Business is business, and there is nothing like punctuality,
especially in a phoenix.

The few chapters relating to the infancy of the Saviour contain
many things which seem frivolous and not worth preserving. A
large part of the remaining portions of the book read like good
Scripture, however. There is one verse that ought not to have
been rejected, because it so evidently prophetically refers to the
general run of Congresses of the United States:

"199. They carry themselves high, and as prudent men; and though they are
fools, yet would seem to be teachers."

I have set these extracts down, as I found them. Everywhere,
among the cathedrals of France and Italy, one finds traditions of
personages that do not figure in the Bible, and of miracles that
are not mentioned in its pages. But they are all in this
Apocryphal New Testament, and though they have been ruled
out of our modern Bible, it is claimed that they were accepted
gospel twelve or fifteen centuries ago, and ranked as high in
credit as any. One needs to read this book before he visits those
venerable cathedrals, with their treasures of tabooed and forgotten tradition.

They imposed another pirate upon us at Nazareth — another
invincible Arab guard. We took our last look at the city, clinging
like a whitewashed wasp's nest to the hillside, and at eight
o'clock in the morning, departed. We dismounted and drove the
horses down a bridle-path which I think was fully as crooked as
a corkscrew; which I know to be as steep as the downward sweep
of a rainbow, and which I believe to be the worst piece of road
in the geography, except one in the Sandwich Islands, which I
remember painfully, and possible one or two mountain trails in
the Sierra Nevadas. Often, in this narrow path, the horse had to
poise himself nicely on a rude stone step and then drop his
forefeet over the edge and down something more than half his
own height. This brought his nose near the ground, while his tail
pointed up toward the sky somewhere, and gave him the appearance of preparing to stand on his head. A horse cannot look
dignified in this position. We accomplished the long descent at
last, and trotted across the great Plain of Esdraelon.

Some of us will be shot before we finish this pilgrimage. The
pilgrims read "Nomadic Life" and keep themselves in a constant
state of Quixotic heroism. They have their hands on their pistols

all the time, and every now and then, when you least expect it,
they snatch them out and take aim at Bedouins who are not
visible, and draw their knives and make savage passes at other
Bedouins who do not exist. I am in deadly peril always, for these
spasms are sudden and irregular, and, of course, I cannot tell
when to be getting out of the way. If I am accidentally murdered, some time, during one of these romantic frenzies of the
pilgrims, Mr. Grimes must be rigidly held to answer as an ac-
cessory before the fact. If the pilgrims would take deliberate aim
and shoot at a man, it would be all right and proper — because
that man would not be in any danger; but these random assaults
are what I object to. I do not wish to see any more places like
Esdraelon, where the ground is level and people can gallop. It
puts melodramatic nonsense into the pilgrims' heads. All at
once, when one is jogging along stupidly in the sun, and thinking
about something ever so far away, here they come, at a stormy
gallop, spurring and whooping at those ridgy old sore-backed
plugs till their heels fly higher than their heads, and, as they
whiz by, out comes a little potato gun of a revolver, there is a
startling little pop, and a small pellet goes singing through the
air. Now that I have begun this pilgrimage, I intend to go
through with it, though, sooth to say, nothing but the most
desperate valor has kept me to my purpose up to the present
time. I do not mind Bedouins, — I am not afraid of them;
because neither Bedouins nor ordinary Arabs have shown any
disposition to harm us, but I *do* feel afraid of my own
comrades.

Arriving at the furthest verge of the Plain, we rode a little way
up a hill and found ourselves at Endor, famous for its witch.
Her descendants are there yet. They were the wildest horde of
half-naked savages we have found thus far. They swarmed out
of mud beehives; out of hovels of the drygoods box pattern; out
of gaping caves under shelving rocks; out of crevices in the
earth. In five minutes the dead solitude and silence of the place
were no more, and a begging, screeching, shouting mob were
struggling about the horses' feet and blocking the way.
"Bucksheesh! bucksheesh! buchsheesh! howajji, bucksheesh!" It
was Magdala over again, only here the glare from the infidel
eyes was fierce and full of hate. The population numbers two
hundred and fifty, and more than half the citizens live in caves
in the rock. Dirt, degradation, and savagery are Endor's
specialty. We say no more about Magdala and Deburieh now.
Endor heads the list. It is worse than any Indian *campoodie*. The
hill is barren, rocky, and forbidding. No sprig of grass is visible,
and only one tree. This is a fig tree, which maintains a
precarious footing among the rocks at the mouth of the dismal
cavern once occupied by the veritable Witch of Endor. In this

cavern, tradition says, Saul, the King, sat at midnight, and
stared and trembled, while the earth shook, the thunders crashed
among the hills, and out of the midst of fire and smoke the
spirit of the dead prophet rose up and confronted him. Saul had
crept to this place in the darkness, while his army slept, to learn
what fate awaited him in the morrow's battle. He went away a
sad man, to meet disgrace and death.

A spring trickles out of the rock in the gloomy recesses of the
cavern, and we were thirsty. The citizens of Endor objected to
our going in there. They do not mind dirt; they do not mind
rags; they do not mind vermin; they do not mind barbarous
ignorance and savagery; they do not mind a reasonable degree of
starvation, but they *do* like to be pure and holy before their god,
whoever he may be, and therefore they shudder and grow almost
pale at the idea of Christian lips polluting a spring whose waters
must descend into their sanctified gullets. We had no wanton
desire to wound even *their* feelings or trample upon their
prejudices, but we were out of water, thus early in the day, and
were burning up with thirst. It was at this time and under these
circumstances that I framed an aphorism which has already
become celebrated. I said: "Necessity knows no law." We went
in and drank.

We got away from the noisy wretches, finally, dropping them
in squads and couples as we filed over the hills — the aged first,
the infants next, the young girls further on; the strong men ran
beside us a mile, and only left when they had secured the last
possible piastre in the way of bucksheesh.

In an hour, we reached Nain, where Christ raised the widow's
son to life. Nain is Magdala on a small scale. It has no
population of any consequence. Within a hundred yards of it is
the original graveyard, for aught I know; the tombstones lie flat
on the ground, which is Jewish fashion in Syria. I believe the
Moslems do not allow them to have upright tombstones. A
Moslem grave is usually roughly plastered over and whitewashed,
and has at one end an upright projection which is shaped into
exceedingly rude attempts at ornamentation. In the cities, there is
often no appearance of a grave at all; a tall, slender marble
tombstone, elaborately lettered, gilded and painted, marks the
burial place, and this is surmounted by a turban, so carved and
shaped as to signify the dead man's rank in life.

They showed a fragment of ancient wall which they said was
one side of the gate out of which the widow's dead son was
being brought so many centuries ago when Jesus met the
procession:

"Now when he came nigh to the gate of the city, behold there was a dead man
carried out, the only son of his mother, and she was a widow; and much people
of the city was with her.

"And when the Lord saw her, he had compassion on her, and said, Weep not.

"And he came and touched the bier: and they that bare him stood still. And he said, Young man, I say unto thee, arise.

"And he that was dead sat up, and began to speak. And he delivered him to his mother.

"And there came a fear on all. And they glorified God, saying, That a great prophet is risen up among us; and That God hath visited his people."

A little mosque stands upon the spot which tradition says was occupied by the widow's dwelling. Two or three aged Arabs sat about its door. We entered, and the pilgrims broke specimens from the foundation walls, though they had to touch, and even step, upon the "praying carpets" to do it. It was almost the same as breaking pieces from the hearts of those old Arabs. To step rudely upon the sacred praying mats, with booted feet — a thing not done by any Arab — was to inflict pain upon men who had not offended us in any way. Suppose a party of armed foreigners were to enter a village church in America and break ornaments from the altar railings for curiosities, and climb up and walk upon the Bible and the pulpit cushions? However, the cases are different. One is the profanation of a temple of our faith — the other only the profanation of a pagan one.

We descended to the Plain again, and halted a moment at a well — of Abraham's time, no doubt. It was in a desert place. It was walled three feet above ground with squared and heavy blocks of stone, after the manner of Bible pictures. Around it some camels stood, and others knelt. There was a group of sober little donkeys with naked, dusky children clambering about them, or sitting astride their rumps, or pulling their tails. Tawny, black-eyed, barefooted maids, arrayed in rags and adorned with brazen armlets and pinchbeck earrings, were poising water-jars upon their heads, or drawing water from the well. A flock of sheet stood by, waiting for the shepherd to fill the hollowed stones with water, so that they might drink — stones which, like those that walled the well, were worn smooth and deeply creased by the chafing chins of a hundred generations of thirsty animals. Picturesque Arabs sat upon the ground, in groups, and solemnly smoked their long-stemmed chilbouks. Other Arabs were filling black hog-skins with water — skins which, well filled, and distended with water till the short legs projected painfully out of the proper line, looked like the corpses of hogs bloated by drowning. Here was a grand Oriental picture which I had worshiped a thousand times in soft, rich steel engravings! But in the engraving there was no desolation; no dirt; no rags; no fleas; no ugly features; no sore eyes; no feasting flies; no besotted ignorance in the countenances; no raw places on the donkeys' backs; no disagreeable jabbering in unknown tongues; no stench of camels; no suggestion that a couple of tons of powder placed under the party and touched off would heighten the effect and give to the scene a genuine interest and a charm which it would always be pleasant to recall, even though a man lived a thousand years.

Oriental scenes look best in steel engravings. I cannot be imposed upon any more by that picture of the Queen of Sheba visiting Solomon. I shall say to myself, You look fine, madam, but your feet are not clean, and you smell like a camel.

Presently, a wild Arab in charge of a camel train recognized an old friend in Ferguson, and they ran and fell upon each other's necks and kissed each other's grimy, bearded faces upon both cheeks. It explained instantly, a something which had always seemed to me only a far-fetched Oriental figure of speech. I refer to the circumstance of Christ's rebuking a Pharisee, or some such character, and reminding him that from him he had received no "kiss of welcome." It did not seem reasonable to me that men should kiss each other, but I am aware, now, that they did. There was reason in it, too. The custom was natural and proper; because people must kiss, and a man would not be likely to kiss one of the women of this country of his own free will and accord. One must travel, to learn. Every day, now, old Scriptural phrases that never possessed any significance for me before take to themselves a meaning.

We journeyed around the base of the mountain — "Little Hermon," — past the old Crusaders' castle of El Fuleh, and arrived at Shunem. This was another Magdala, to a fraction, frescoes and all. Here, tradition says, the prophet Samuel was born, and here the Shunamite woman built a little house upon the city wall for the accommodation of the prophet Elisha. Elisha asks her what she expected in return. It was a perfectly natural question, for these people are and were in the habit of proffering favors and services and then expecting and begging for pay. Elisha knew them well. He could not comprehend that anybody should build for him that humble little chamber for the mere sake of old friendship, and with no selfish motive whatever. It used to seem a very impolite, not to say a rude question, for Elisha to ask the woman, but it does not seem so to me now. The woman said she expected nothing. Then, for her goodness and her unselfishness, he rejoiced her heart with the news that she should bear a son. It was a high reward — but she would not have thanked him for a daughter — daughters have always been unpopular here. The son was born, grew, waxed strong, died. Elisha restored him to life in Shunem.

We found here a grove of lemon trees — cool, shady, hung with fruit. One is apt to overestimate beauty when it is rare, but to me this grove seemed very beautiful. It *was* beautiful. I do not overestimate it. I must always remember Shunem gratefully, as a place which gave to us this leafy shelter after our long, hot ride. We lunched, rested, chatted, smoked our pipes an hour, and then mounted and moved on.

As we trotted across the Plain of Jezreel, we met half a dozen Digger Indians (Bedouins) with very long spears in their hands, cavorting around an old crowbait horses, and spearing imaginary enemies; whooping, and fluttering their rags in the wind, and carrying on in every respect like a pact of hopeless lunatics. At last, here were the "wild, free sons of the desert, speeding over the plain like the wind, on their beautiful Arabian mares" we had read so much about and longed so much to see! Here were the "picturesque costumes"! This was the "gallant spectacle"! Tatterdemalion vagrants — cheap braggadocio — "Arabian mares" spined and necked like the ichthyosaurus in the museum, and humped and cornered like a dromedary! To glance at the genuine son of the desert is to take the romance out of him forever — to behold his steed is to long in charity to strip his harness off and let him fall to pieces.

Presently we came to a ruinous old town on a hill, the same being the ancient Jezreel.

Ahab, King of Samaria (this was a very vast kingdom, for those days, and was very nearly half as large as Rhode Island) dwelt in the city of Jezreel, which was his capital. Near him lived a man by the name of Naboth, who had a vineyard. The King asked him for it, and when he would not give it, offered to buy it. But Naboth refused to sell it. In those days it was considered a sort of crime to part with one's inheritance at any price — and even if a man did part with it, it reverted to himself or his heirs again at the next jubilee year. So this spoiled child of a King went and lay down on the bed with his face to the wall, and grieved sorely. The Queen, a notorious character in those days, and whose name is a byword and a reproach even in these, came in and asked him wherefore he sorrowed, and he told her. Jezebel said she could secure the vineyard; and she went forth and forged letters to the nobles and wise men, in the King's name, and ordered them to proclaim a fast and set Naboth on high before the people, and suborn two witnesses to swear that he had blasphemed. They did it, and the people stoned the accused by the city wall, and he died. Then Jezebel came and told the King, and said, Behold, Naboth is no more — rise up and seize the vineyard. So Ahab seized the vineyard, and went into it to possess it. But the Prophet Elijah came to him there and read his fate to him, and the fate of Jezebel; and said that in the place where dogs licked the blood of Naboth, dogs should also lick his blood — and he said, likewise, the dogs should eat Jezebel by the wall of Jezreel. In the course of time, the King was killed in battle, and when his chariot wheels were washed in the pool of Samaria, the dogs licked the blood. In after years, Jehu, who was King of Israel, marched down against Jezreel, by order of the one of the Prophets, and administered one of those convincing rebukes so common among the people of those days: he killed many kings and their subjects, and as he came along he saw Jezebel, painted and finely dressed, looking out of a window, and ordered that she be thrown down to him. A servant did it, and Jehu's horse trampled her under foot. Then Jehu went in and sat down to dinner; and presently he said, Go and bury this cursed woman, for she is a King's daughter. The spirit of charity came upon him too late, however, for the prophecy had already been fulfilled — the dogs had eaten her, and they "found no more of her than the skull, and the feet, and the palms of her hands."

Ahab, the late King, had left a helpless family behind him, and Jehu killed seventy of the orphan sons. Then he killed all the relatives, and teachers, and servants and friends of the family, and rested from his labors, until he was come near to Samaria, where he met forty-two persons and asked them who they were; they said they were brothers of the King of Judah. He killed them. When he got to Samaria, he said he would show his zeal for the Lord; so he gathered all the priests and people together that worshiped Baal, pretending that he was going to adopt that worship and offer up a great sacrifice; and when they were all shut up where they could not defend themselves, he caused every person of them to be killed. Then Jehu, the good missionary, rested from his labors once more.

We went back to the valley, and rode to the Fountain of Ain Jelüd. They call it the Fountain of Jezeel, usually. It is a pond about one hundred feet square and four feet deep, with a stream of water trickling into it from under an overhanging ledge of rocks. It is in the midst of a great solitude. Here Gideon pitched his camp in the old times; behind Shunem lay the "Midianites, the Amalekites, and the Children of the East," who were "as grasshoppers for multitude; both they and their camels were without number, as the sand by the seaside for multitude." Which means that there were one hundred and thirty-five thousand men, and that they had transportation service accordingly.

Gideon, with only three hundred men, surprised them in the night, and stood by and looked on while they butchered each other until a hundred and twenty thousand lay dead on the field.

We camped at Jenin before night, and got up and started again at one o'clock in the morning. Somewhere towards daylight we passed the locality where the best authenticated tradition locates the pit into which Joseph's brethren threw him, and about noon, after passing over a succession of mountain tops, clad with groves of fig and olive trees, with the Mediterranean in sight some forty miles away, and going by many ancient Biblical cities whose inhabitants glowered savagely upon our Christian procession, and were seemingly inclined to practice on it with stones, we came to the singularly terraced and unlovely hills that betrayed that we were out of Galilee and into Samaria at last.

We climbed a high hill to visit the city of Samaria, where the woman may have hailed from who conversed with Christ at Jacob's Well, and from whence, no doubt, came also the celebrated Good Samaritan. Herod the Great is said to have made a magnificent city of this place, and a great number of coarse limestone columns, twenty feet high and two feet through, that are almost guiltless of architectural grace of shape and ornament, are pointed out by many authors as evidence of the fact. They would not have been considered handsome in ancient Greece, however.

The inhabitants of this camp are particularly vicious, and stoned two parties of our pilgrims a day or two ago who brought about the difficulty by showing their revolvers when they did not intend to use them — a thing which is deemed bad judgment in the Far West, and ought certainly to be so considered anywhere. In the new Territories, when a man puts his hand on a weapon, he knows that he must use it; he must use it instantly or expect to be shot down where he stands. Those pilgrims had been reading Grimes.

There was nothing for us to do in Samaria but buy handfuls of old Roman coins at a franc a dozen, and look at a dilapidated church of the Crusaders and a vault in it which once contained the body of John the Baptist. This relic was long ago carried away to Genoa.

Samaria stood a disastrous siege, once, in the days of Elisha, at the hands of the King of Syria. Provisions reached such a figure that "an ass's head was sold for eighty pieces of silver and the fourth part of a cab of dove's dung for five pieces of silver."

An incident recorded of that heavy time will give one a very good idea of the distress that prevailed within these crumbling walls. As the King was walking upon the battlements one day, "a woman cried out, saying, Help, my lord, O King! And the King said, What aileth thee? and she answered, This woman said unto me, Give thy son, that we may eat him to-day, and we will eat my son to-morrow. So we boiled my son, and did eat him; and I said unto her on the next day, Give thy son that we may eat him; and she hath hid her son."

The prophet Elisha declared that within four and twenty hours the prices of food should go down to nothing almost, and it was so. The Syrian army broke camp and fled, for some cause or other, the famine was relieved from without, and many a shoddy speculator in dove's dung and ass's meat was ruined.

We were glad to leave this hot and dusty old village and hurry on. At two o'clock we stopped to lunch and rest at ancient Shechem, between the historic Mounts of Gerizim and Ebal where in the old times the books of the law, the curses and the blessings, were read from the heights to the Jewish multitudes below.

CHAPTER XXV

The narrow canyon in which Nablous, or Shechem, is situated, is under high cultivation, and the soil is exceedingly black and fertile. It is well watered, and its affluent vegetation gains effect by contrast with the barren hills that tower on either side. One of these hills is the ancient Mount of Blessings and the other the Mount of Curses; and wise men who seek for fulfillments of prophecy think they find here a wonder of this kind — to wit, that the Mount of Blessings is strangely fertile and its mate as strangely unproductive. We could not see that there was really much difference between them in this respect, however.

Shechem is distinguished as one of the residences of the patriarch Jacob, and as the seat of those tribes that cut themselves loose from their brethren of Israel and propagated doctrines not in conformity with those of the original Jewish creed. For thousands of years this clan have dwelt in Shechem under strict *tabu,* and having little commerce or fellowship with their fellow-men of any religion or nationality. For generations they have not numbered more than one or two hundred, but they still adhere to their ancient faith and maintain their ancient rites and ceremonies. Talk of family and old descent! Princes and nobles pride themselves upon lineages they can trace back some hundreds of years. What is this trifle to this handful of old first families of Shechem, who can name their fathers straight back without a flaw for thousands — straight back to a period so remote that men reared in a country where the days of two hundred years ago are called "ancient" times grow dazed and bewildered when they try to comprehend it! Here is respectability for you — here is "family" — here is high descent worth talking about. This sad, proud remnant of a once mighty community still hold themselves aloof from all the world; they still live as their fathers lived, labor as their fathers labored, think as they did, feel as they did, worship in the same place, in sight of the same landmarks, and in the same quaint, patriarchal way their ancestors did more than thirty centuries ago. I found myself gazing at any straggling scion of this strange race with a riveted fascination, just as one would stare at a living mastodon, or a megatherium that had moved in the gray dawn of creation and seen the wonders of the mysterious world that was before the flood.

Carefully preserved among the sacred archives of this curious community is a MS. copy of the ancient Jewish law, which is said to be the oldest document on earth. It is written on vellum, and is some four or five thousand years old. Nothing but bucksheesh can purchase a sight. Its fame is somewhat dimmed in these latter days, because of the doubts so many authors of Palestine travels have felt themselves privileged to cast upon it. Speaking of this MS. reminds me that I procured from the high priest of this ancient Samaritan community, at great expense, a secret document of still higher antiquity and far more extraordinary interest, which I propose to publish as soon as I have finished translating it.

Joshua gave his dying injunction to the children of Israel at Shechem, and buried a valuable treasure secretly under an oak tree there about the same time. The superstitious Samaritans have always been afraid to hunt for it. They believe it is guarded by fierce spirits invisible to men.

About a mile and a half from Shechem we halted at the base of Mount Ebal, before a little square area, inclosed by a high stone wall, neatly whitewashed. Across one end of this enclosure is a tomb built after the manner of the Moslems. It is the tomb of Joseph. No truth is better authenticated than this.

When Joseph was dying he prophesied that exodus of the Israelites from Egypt which occured four hundred years afterwards. At the same time he exacted of his people an oath that when they journeyed to the land of Canaan, they would bear his bones with them and bury them in the ancient inheritance of his fathers. The oath was kept.

"And the bones of Joseph, which the children of Israel brought up out of Egypt, buried they in Shechem, in a parcel of ground which Jacob bought of the sons of Hamor the father of Shechem, for a hundred pieces of silver."

Few tombs on earth command the veneration of so many races and men of divers creeds as this of Joseph. "Samaritan and Jew, Moslem and Christian alike, revere it, and honor it with their visits. The tomb of Joseph, the dutiful son, the affectionate, forgiving brother, the virtuous man, the wise Prince and ruler. Egypt felt his influence — the world knows his history."

In this same "parcel of ground" which Jacob bought of the sons of Hamor for a hundred pieces of silver, is Jacob's celebrated well. It is cut in the solid rock, and is nine feet square and ninety feet deep. The name of this unpretending hole in the ground, which one might pass by and take no notice of, is as familiar as household words to even the children and the peasants of many a far-off country.

It is more famous than the Parthenon; it is older than the Pyramids.

It was by this well that Jesus sat and talked with a woman of that strange, antiquated Samaritan community I have been speaking of, and told her of the mysterious water of life. As descendants of old English nobles still cherish in the traditions of their houses how that this king or that king tarried a day with some favored ancestor three hundred years ago, no doubt the descendants of the woman of Samaria, living there in Shechem, still refer with pardonable vanity to this conversation of their ancestor, held some little time gone by, with the Messiah of the Christians. It is not likely that they undervalue a distinction such as this. Samaritan nature is human nature, and human nature remembers contact with the illustrious, always.

For an offense done to the family honor, the sons of Jacob exterminated all Shechem once.

We left Jacob's Well and traveled till eight in the evening, but rather slowly, for we had been in the saddle nineteen hours, and the horses were cruelly tired. We got so far ahead of the tents that we had to camp in an Arab village, and sleep on the ground. We could have slept in the largest of the houses; but there were some little drawbacks; it was populous with vermin, it had a dirt floor, it was in no respect cleanly, and there was a family of goats in the only bedroom, and two donkeys in the parlor. Outside there were no inconveniences, except that the dusky, ragged, earnest-eyed villagers of both sexes and all ages grouped themselves on their haunches all around us, and discussed us and criticised us with noisy tongues till midnight. We did not mind the noise, being tired, but, doubtless, the reader is aware that it is almost an impossible thing to go to sleep when you know that people are looking at you. We went to bed at ten, and got up again at two and started once more. Thus are people persecuted by dragomen, whose sole ambition in life is to get ahead of each other.

About daylight we passed Shiloh, where the Ark of the Covenant rested three hundred years, and at whose gates good old Eli fell down and "brake his neck" when the messenger, riding hard from the battle, told him of the defeat of his people, the death of his sons, and, more than all, the capture of Israel's pride, her hope, her refuge, the ancient Ark her forefathers brought with them out of Egypt. It is little wonder that under circumstances like these he fell down and brake his neck. But Shiloh had no charms for us. We were so cold that there was no comfort but in motion, and so drowsy we could hardly sit upon the horses.

After a while we came to a shapeless mass of ruins, which still bears the name of Beth-el. It was here that Jacob lay down and had that superb vision of angels flitting up and down a ladder that reached from the clouds to earth, and caught glimpses of their blessed home through the open gates of Heaven.

The pilgrims took what was left of the hallowed ruin, and we pressed on toward the goal of our crusade, renowned Jerusalem.

The further we went the hotter the sun got, and the more rocky and bare, repulsive and dreary the landscape became. There could not have been more fragments of stone strewn broadcast over this part of the world, if every ten square feet of the land had been occupied by a separate and distinct stonecutter's establishment for an age. There was hardly a tree or a shrub anywhere. Even the olive and the cactus, those fast friends of a worthless soil, had almost deserted the country. No landscape exists that is more tiresome to the eye that which bounds the approaches to Jerusalem. The only difference between the roads and the surrounding country, perhaps, is that there are rather more rocks in the roads than in the surrounding country.

We passed Ramah and Beroth, and on the right saw the tomb of the prophet Samuel, perched high upon a commanding eminence. Still no Jerusalem came in sight. We hurried on impatiently. We halted a moment at the ancient Fountain of Beira, but its stones, worn deeply by the chins of thirsty animals that are dead and gone centuries ago, had no interest for us — we longed to see Jerusalem. We spurred up hill after hill, and usually began to stretch our necks minutes before we got to the top — but disappointment always followed — more stupid hills beyond — more unsightly landscape — no Holy City.

At last, away in the middle of the day, ancient bits of wall and crumbling arches began to line the way — we toiled up one more hill, and every pilgrim and every sinner swung his hat on high! Jerusalem!

Perched on its eternal hills, white and domed and solid, massed together and hooped with high gray walls, the venerable city gleamed in the sun. So small! Why, it was not larger than an American village of four thousand inhabitants, and no larger than an ordinary Syrian city of thirty thousand. Jerusalem numbers only fourteen thousand people.

We dismounted and looked, without speaking a dozen sentences, across the wide intervening valley for an hour or more; and noted those prominent features of the city that pictures make familiar to all men from their school days till their death. We could recognize the Tower of Hippicus, the Mosque of Omar, the Damascus Gate, the Mount of Olives, the Valley of Jehoshaphat, the Tower of David, and the Garden of Gethsemane — and dating from these landmarks could tell very nearly the localities of many others we were not able to distinguish.

I record it here as a notable but not discreditable fact that not even our pilgrims wept. I think there was not an individual in the party whose brain was not teeming with thoughts and images and memories invoked by the grand history of the venerable city that lay before us, but still among them all was no "voice of them that wept."

There was no call for tears. Tears would have been out of place. The thoughts Jerusalem suggests are full of poetry, sublimity, and more than all, dignity. Such thoughts do not find their appropriate expression in the emotions of the nursery.

Just after noon we entered these narrow, crooked streets, by the ancient and the famed Damascus Gate, and now for several hours I have been trying to comprehend that I am actually in the illustrious old city where Solomon dwelt, where Abraham held converse with the Deity, and where walls still stand that witnessed the spectacle of the Crucifixion.

CHAPTER XXVI

A fast walker could go outside the walls of Jerusalem and walk entirely around the city in an hour. I do not know how else to make one understand how small it is. The appearance of the city is peculiar. It is as knobby with countless little domes as a prison door is with bolt-heads. Every house has from one to half a dozen of these white plastered domes of stone, broad and low, sitting in the center of, or in a cluster upon, the flat roof. Wherefore, when one looks down from an eminence, upon the compact mass of houses (so closely crowded together, in fact, that there is no appearance of streets at all, and so the city looks solid) he sees the knobbiest town in the world, except Constantinople. It looks as if it might be roofed, from center to circumference, with inverted saucers. The monotony of the view is interupted only by the great Mosque of Omar, the Tower of Hippicus, and one or two other buildings that rise into commanding prominence.

The houses are generally two stories high, built strongly of masonry, whitewashed or plastered outside, and have a cage of wooden lattice-work projecting in front of every window. To reproduce a Jerusalem street, it would only be necessary to upend a chicken-coop and hang it before each window in an alley of American houses.

The streets are roughly and badly paved with stone, and are tolerably crooked — enough so to make each street appear to close together constantly and come to an end about a hundred yards ahead of a pilgrim as long as he chooses to walk in it.

Projecting from the top of the lower story of many of the houses
is a very narrow porch-roof or shed, without supports from
below; and I have several times seen cats jump across the street
from one shed to the other when they were out calling. The cats
could have jumped double the distance without extraordinary
exertion. I mention these things to give an idea of how narrow
the streets are. Since a cat can jump across them without the
least inconvenience, it is hardly necessary to state that such
streets are too narrow for carriages. These vehicles cannot
navigate the Holy City.

The population of Jerusalem is composed of Moslems, Jews,
Greeks, Latins, Armenians, Syrians, Copts, Abyssinians, Greek
Catholics, and a handful of Protestants. One hundred of the latter sect are all that dwell now in this birthplace of Christianity.
The nice shades of nationality comprised in the above list, and
the languages spoken by them, are altogether too numerous to
mention. It seems to me that all the races and colors and tongues
of the earth must be represented among the fourteen thousand
souls that dwell in Jerusalem. Rags, wretchedness, poverty, and
dirt, those signs and symbols that indicate the presence of
Moslem rule more surely than the crescent-flag itself, abound.
Lepers, cripples, the blind, and the idiotic, assail you on every
hand, and they know but one word of but one language apparently — the eternal "bucksheesh." To see the numbers that
throng the holy places and obstruct the gates, one might suppose
that the ancient days had come again, and that the angel of the
Lord was expected to descend at any moment to stir the waters
of Bethesda. Jerusalem is mournful and dreary, and lifeless. I
would not desire to live here.

One naturally goes first to the Holy Sepulchre. It is right in
the city, near the western gate; it and the place of the
Crucifixion, and, in fact, every other place intimately connected
with that tremendous event, are ingeniously massed together and
covered by one roof — the dome of the Church of the Holy
Sepulchre.

Entering the building, through the midst of the usual assemblage of beggars, one sees on his left a few Turkish guards —
for Christians of different sects will not only quarrel, but fight,
also, in this sacred place, if allowed to do it. Before you is a
marble slab, which covers the Stone of Unction, whereon the
Saviour's body was laid to prepare it for burial. It was found
necessary to conceal the real stone in this way in order to save it
from destruction. Pilgrims were too much given to chipping off
pieces of it to carry home. Near by is a circular railing which
marks the spot where the Virgin stood when the Lord's body was
anointed.

Entering the great Rotunda, we stand before the most sacred

locality in Christendom — the grave of Jesus. It is in the center of the church, and immediately under the great dome. It is inclosed in a sort of little temple of yellow and white stone, of fanciful design. Within the little temple is a portion of the very stone which was rolled away from the door of the Sepulchre, and on which the angel was sitting when Mary came thither "at early dawn." Stooping low, we enter the vault — the Sepulchre itself. It is only about six feet by seven, and the stone couch on which the dead Saviour lay extends from end to end of the apartment and occupies half its width. It is covered with a marble slab which has been much worn by the lips of pilgrims. This slab serves as an altar now. Over it hang some fifty gold and silver lamps, which are kept always burning, and the place is otherwise scandalized by trumpery gewgaws and tawdry ornamentation.

All sects of Christian (except Protestants) have chapels under the roof of the Church of the Holy Sepulchre, and each must keep to itself and not venture upon another's ground. It has been proven conclusively that they cannot worship together around the grave of the Saviour of the World in peace. The chapel of the Syrians is not handsome; that of the Copts is the humblest of them all. It is nothing but a dismal cavern, roughly hewn in the living rock of the Hill of Calvary. In one side of it two ancient tombs are hewn, which are claimed to be those in which Nicodemus and Joseph of Arimathea were buried.

As we moved among the great piers and pillars of another part of the church, we came upon a party of black-robed, animal-looking Italian monks, with candles in their hands, who were chanting something in Latin, and going through some kind of religious performance around a disk of white marble let into the floor. It was there that the risen Saviour appeared to Mary Magdalen in the likeness of a gardener. Near by was a similar stone, shaped like a star — here the Magdalen herself stood, at the same time. Monks were performing in this place also. They perform everywhere — all over the vast building, and at all hours. Their candles are always flitting about in the gloom, and making the dim old church more dismal than there is any necessity that it should be, even though it is a tomb.

We were shown the place where our Lord appeared to His mother after the Resurrection. Here, also, a marble slab marks the place where St. Helena, the mother of the Emperor Constantine, found the crosses about three hundred years after the Crucifixion. According to the legend, this great discovery elicited extravagant demonstrations of joy. But they were of short duration. The question intruded itself: "Which bore the blessed Saviour, and which the thieves?" To be in doubt, in so mighty a matter as this — to be uncertain which one to adore — was a grievous misfortune. It turned the public joy to sorrow. But when lived there a holy priest who could not set so simple a trouble as this at rest? One of these soon hit upon a plan that would be a certain test. A noble lady lay very ill in Jerusalem. The wise priests ordered that the three crosses be taken to her bedside one at a time. It was done. When her eyes fell upon the first one, she uttered a scream that was heard beyond the Damascus Gate, and even upon the Mount of Olives, it was said, and then fell back in a deadly swoon. They recovered her and brought the second cross. Instantly she went into fearful convulsions, and it was with the greatest difficulty that six strong men could hold her. They were afraid, now, to bring in the third cross. They began to fear that possibly they had fallen upon the wrong crosses, and that the true cross was not with this number at all. However, as the woman seemed likely to die with the convulsions that were tearing her, they concluded that the third could do no more than put her out of her misery with a happy dispatch. So they brought it, and behold, a miracle! The woman sprang from her bed, smiling and joyful, and perfectly restored to health. When we listen to evidence like this, we cannot but believe. We would be ashamed to doubt, and properly, too. Even the very part of Jerusalem where this all occurred is there yet. So there is really no room for doubt.

The priest tried to show us, through a small screen, a fragment of the genuine Pillar of Flagellation, to which Christ was bound when they scourged him. But we could not see it, because it was dark inside the screen. However, a baton is kept here, which the pilgrim thrusts through a hole in the screen, and then he no longer doubts that the true Pillar of Flagellation is in there. He cannot have any excuse to doubt it, for he can feel it with the stick. He can feel it as distinctly as he could feel anything.

Not far from here was a niche where they used to preserve a piece of the True Cross, but it is gone now. This piece of the cross was discovered in the sixteenth century. The Latin priests say it was stolen away, long ago, by priests of another sect. That seems like a hard statement to make, but we know very well that it *was* stolen, because we have seen it ourselves in several of the cathedrals of Italy and France.

But the relic that touched us most was the plain old sword of that stout Crusader, Godfrey of Bouillon — King Godfrey of Jerusalem. No blade in Christendom wields such enchantment as this — no blade of all that rust in the ancestral halls of Europe is able to invoke such visions of romance in the brain of him who looks upon it — none that can prate of such chivalric deeds or tell such brave tales of the warrior days of old. It stirs within a man every memory of the Holy Wars that has been sleeping in his brain for years, and peoples his thoughts with mail-clad images, with marching armies, with battles and with sieges. It speaks to him of Baldwin, and Tancred, the princely Saladin, and great Richard of the Lion Heart. It was with just such blades as these that these splendid heroes of romance used to segregate a man, so to speak, and leave the half of him to fall one way and the other half the other. This very sword has cloven hundreds of Saracen Knights from crown to chin in those old times when Godfrey wielded it. It was enchanted, then, by a genius that was under the command of King Solomon. When danger approached its master's tent it always struck the shield and clanged out a fierce alarm upon the startled ear of night. In times of doubt, or in fog or darkness, if it were drawn from its sheath it would point instantly toward the foe, and thus reveal the way — and it would also attempt to start after them of its own accord. A Christian could not be so disguised that it would not know him and refuse to hurt him — nor a Moslem so disguised that it would not leap from its scabbard and take his life. These statements are all well authenticated in many legends that are among the most trustworthy legends the good old Catholic monks preserve. I can never forget old Godfrey's sword now. I tried it on a Moslem, and clove him in twain like a doughnut. The spirit of Grimes was upon me, and if I had had a graveyard I would have destroyed all the infidels in Jerusalem. I wiped the blood off the old sword and handed it back to the priest — I did not want the fresh gore to obliterate those sacred spots that crimsoned its brightness one day six hundred years ago and thus gave Godfrey warning that before the sun went down his journey of life would end.

Still moving through the gloom of the Church of the Holy Sepulchre we came to a small chapel, hewn out of the rock — a place which has been known as "The Prison of Our Lord" for many centuries. Tradition says that here the Saviour was confined just previously to the crucifixion. Under an altar by the door was a pair of stone stocks for human legs. These things are called the "Bonds of Christ," and the use they were once put to has given them the name they now bear.

The Greek Chapel is the most roomy, the richest and the showiest chapel in the Church of the Holy Sepulchre. Its altar, like that of all the Greek churches, is a lofty screen that extends clear across the chapel, and is gorgeous with gilding and pictures. The numerous lamps that hung before it are of gold and silver, and cost great sums.

But the feature of the place is a short column that rises from the middle of the marble pavement of the chapel, and marks the exact *center of the earth*. The most reliable traditions tell us that this was known to be the earth's center, ages ago, and that when Christ was upon earth he set all doubts upon the subject at rest forever, by stating with his own lips that the tradition was

correct. Remember He said that that particular column stood
upon the center of the world. If the center of the world changes,
the column changes its position accordingly. This column has
moved three different times, of its own accord. This is because,
in great convulsions of nature, at three different times, masses of
the earth — whole ranges of mountains, probably — have flown
off into space, thus lessening the diameter of the earth, and
changing the exact locality of its center by a point or two. This is
a very curious and interesting circumstance, and is a withering
rebuke to those philosophers who would make us believe that it
is not possible for any portion of the earth to fly off into space.

To satisfy himself that this spot was really the center of the
earth, a skeptic once paid well for the privilege of ascending to
the dome of the church to see if the sun gave him a shadow at
noon. He came down perfectly convinced. The day was very
cloudy and the sun threw no shadows at all; but the man was
satisfied that if the sun had come out and made shadows it could
not have made any for him. Proofs like these are not to be set
aside by the idle tongues of cavilers. To such as are not bigoted,
and are willing to be convinced, they carry a conviction that
nothing can ever shake.

If even greater proofs than those I have mentioned are wanted, to satisfy the headstrong and the foolish that this is the
genuine center of the earth, they are here. The greatest of them
lies in the fact that from under this very column was taken the
dust from which Adam was made. This can surely be regarded in
the light of a settler. It is not likely that the original first man
would have been made from an inferior quality of earth when it
was entirely convenient to get first quality from the world's center. This will strike any reflecting mind forcibly. That Adam was
formed of dirt procured in this very spot is amply proven by the
fact that in six thousand years no man has ever been able to
prove that the dirt was *not* procured here whereof he was made.

It is a singular circumstance that right under the roof of this
great church, and not far away from that illustrious column,
Adam himself, the father of the human race, lies buried. There
is no question that he is actually buried in the grave which is
pointed out as his — there can be none — because it has never
yet been proven that that grave is not the grave in which he is
buried.

The tomb of Adam! How touching it was, here in a land of
strangers, far away from home, and friends, and all who cared
for me, thus to discover the grave of a blood relation. True, a
distant one, but still a relation. The unerring instinct of nature
thrilled its recognition. The fountain of my filial affection was
stirred to its profoundest depths, and I gave way to tumultuous
emotion. I leaned upon a pillar and burst into tears. I deem it no

shame to have wept over the grave of my poor dead relative. Let him who would sneer at my emotion close this volume here, for he will find little to his taste in my journeyings through Hold Land. Noble old man — he did not live to see me — he did not live to see his child. And I — I — alas, I did not live to see *him*. Weighed down by sorrow and disappointment, he died before I was born — six thousand brief summers before I was born. But let us try to bear it with fortitude. Let us trust that he is better off where he is. Let us take comfort in the thought that his loss is our eternal gain.

The next place the guide took us to in the holy church was an altar dedicated to the Roman soldier who was of the military guard that attended at the Crucifixion to keep order, and who — when the vail of the Temple was rent in the awful darkness that followed; when the rock of Golgotha was split asunder by an earthquake; when the artillery of heaven thundered, and in the baleful glare of the lightnings the shrouded dead flitted about the streets of Jerusalem — shook with fear and said, "Surely this was the Son of God!" Where this altar stands now, that Roman soldier stood then, in full view of the crucified Saviour — in full sight and hearing of all the marvels that were transpiring far and wide about the circumference of the Hill of Calvary. And in this self-same spot the priests of the Temple beheaded him for those blasphemous words he had spoken.

Still moving through the gloom of the Church of the Holy Sepulchre we came to a small chapel, hewn out of the rock — a place which has been known as "The Prison of Our Lord" for many centuries. Tradition says that here the Saviour was confined just previously to the crucifixion. Under an altar by the door was a pair of stone stocks for human legs. These things are called the "Bonds of Christ," and the use they were once put to has given them the name they now bear.

The Greek Chapel is the most roomy, the richest and the showiest chapel in the Church of the Holy Sepulchre. Its altar, like that of all the Greek churches, is a lofty screen that extends clear across the chapel, and is gorgeous with gilding and pictures. The numerous lamps that hung before it are of gold and silver, and cost great sums.

But the feature of the place is a short column that rises from the middle of the marble pavement of the chapel, and marks the exact *center of the earth*. The most reliable traditions tell us that this was known to be the earth's center, ages ago, and that when Christ was upon earth he set all doubts upon the subject at rest forever, by stating with his own lips that the tradition was correct. Remember He said that that particular column stood upon the center of the world. If the center of the world changes, the column changes its position accordingly. This column has moved three different times, of its own accord. This is because, in great convulsions of nature, at three different times, masses of the earth — whole ranges of mountains, probably — have flown off into space, thus lessening the diameter of the earth, and changing the exact locality of its center by a point or two. This is a very curious and interesting circumstance, and is a withering rebuke to those philosophers who would make us believe that it is not possible for any portion of the earth to fly off into space.

To satisfy himself that this spot was really the center of the earth, a skeptic once paid well for the privilege of ascending to the dome of the church to see if the sun gave him a shadow at noon. He came down perfectly convinced. The day was very cloudy and the sun threw no shadows at all; but the man was satisfied that if the sun had come out and made shadows it could not have made any for him. Proofs like these are not to be set aside by the idle tongues of cavilers. To such as are not bigoted, and are willing to be convinced, they carry a conviction that nothing can ever shake.

If even greater proofs than those I have mentioned are wanted, to satisfy the headstrong and the foolish that this is the genuine center of the earth, they are here. The greatest of them lies in the fact that from under this very column was taken the *dust from which Adam was made*. This can surely be regarded in the light of a settler. It is not likely that the original first man would have been made from an inferior quality of earth when it was entirely convenient to get first quality from the world's center. This will strike any reflecting mind forcibly. That Adam was formed of dirt procured in this very spot is amply proven by the fact that in six thousand years no man has ever been able to prove that the dirt was *not* procured here whereof he was made.

It is a singular circumstance that right under the roof of this great church, and not far away from that illustrious column, Adam himself, the father of the human race, lies buried. There is no question that he is actually buried in the grave which is pointed out as his — there can be none — because it has never yet been proven that that grave is not the grave in which he is buried.

The tomb of Adam! How touching it was, here in a land of strangers, far away from home, and friends, and all who cared for me, thus to discover the grave of a blood relation. True, a distant one, but still a relation. The unerring instinct of nature thrilled its recognition. The fountain of my filial affection was stirred to its profoundest depths, and I gave way to tumultuous emotion. I leaned upon a pillar and burst into tears. I deem it no shame to have wept over the grave of my poor dead relative. Let him who would sneer at my emotion close this volume here, for he will find little to his taste in my journeyings through Hold

Land. Noble old man — he did not live to see me — he did not live to see his child. And I — I — alas, I did not live to see *him*. Weighed down by sorrow and disappointment, he died before I was born — six thousand brief summers before I was born. But let us try to bear it with fortitude. Let us trust that he is better off where he is. Let us take comfort in the thought that his loss is our eternal gain.

The next place the guide took us to in the holy church was an altar dedicated to the Roman soldier who was of the military guard that attended at the Crucifixion to keep order, and who — when the vail of the Temple was rent in the awful darkness that followed; when the rock of Golgotha was split asunder by an earthquake; when the artillery of heaven thundered, and in the baleful glare of the lightnings the shrouded dead flitted about the streets of Jerusalem — shook with fear and said, "Surely this was the Son of God!" Where this altar stands now, that Roman soldier stood then, in full view of the crucified Saviour — in full sight and hearing of all the marvels that were transpiring far and wide about the circumference of the Hill of Calvary. And in this self-same spot the priests of the Temple beheaded him for those blasphemous words he had spoken.

In this altar they used to keep one of the most curious relics that human eyes ever looked upon — a thing that had power to fascinate the beholder in some mysterious way and keep him gazing for hours together. It was nothing less than the copper plate Pilate put upon the Saviour's cross, and upon which he wrote, "THIS IS THE KING OF THE JEWS." I think St. Helena, the mother of Constantine, found this wonderful memento when she was here in the third century. She traveled all over Palestine, and was always fortunate. Whenever the good old enthusiast found a thing mentioned in her Bible, Old or New, she would go and search for that thing, and never stop until she found it. If it was Adam, she would find Adam; if it was the Ark, she would find the Ark; if it was Goliah, or Joshua, she would find *them*. She found the inscription here that I was speaking of, I think. She found it in this very spot, close to where the martyred Roman soldier stood. That copper plate is in one of the churches in Rome now. Any one can see it there. The inscription is very distinct.

We passed along a few steps and saw the altar built over the very spot where the good Catholic priests say the soldiers divided the raiment of the Saviour.

Then we went down into a cavern which cavilers say was once a cistern. It is a chapel now, however — the Chapel of St. Helena. It is fifty-one feet long by forty-three wide. In it is a marble chair which Helena used to sit in while she superintended her workmen when they were digging and delving for the True

Cross. In this place is an altar dedicated to St. Dimas, the penitent thief. A new bronze statue is here — a statue of St. Helena. It reminded us of poor Maximilian, so lately shot. He presented it to this chapel when he was about to leave for his throne in Mexico.

From the cistern we descended twelve steps into a large roughly-shaped grotto, carved wholly out of the living rock. Helena blasted it out when she was searching for the true cross. She had a laborious piece of work here, but it was richly rewarded. Out of this place she got the crown of thorns, the nails of the cross, the true cross itself, and the cross of the penitent thief. When she thought she had found everything and was about to stop, she was told in a dream to continue a day longer. It was very fortunate. She did so, and found the cross of the other thief.

The walls and roof of this grotto still weep bitter tears in memory of the event that transpired on Calvary, and devout pilgrims groan and sob when these sad tears fall upon them from the dripping rock. The monks call this apartment the "Chapel of the Invention of the Cross" — a name which is unfortunate, because it leads the ignorant to imagine that a tacit acknowledgment is thus made that the tradition that Helena found the true cross here is a fiction — an invention. It is a happiness to know, however, that intelligent people do not doubt the story in any of its particulars.

Priests of any of the chapels and denominations in the Church of the Holy Sepulchre can visit this sacred grotto to weep and pray and worship the gently Redeemer. Two different congregations are not allowed to enter at the same time, however, because they always fight.

Still marching through the venerable Church of the Holy Sepulchre, among chanting priests in coarse long robes and sandals; pilgrims of all colors and many nationalities, in all sorts of strange costumes; under dusky arches and by dingy piers and columns; through a somber cathedral gloom, freighted with smoke and incense, and faintly starred with scores of candles that appeared suddenly and as suddenly disappeared, or drifted mysteriously hither and thither about the distant aisles like ghostly jack-o'-lanterns — we came at last to a small chapel which is called the "Chapel of the Mocking." Under the altar was a fragment of a marble column; this was the seat Christ sat on when he was reviled, and mockingly made King, crowned with a crown of thorns and sceptered with a reed. It was here that they blindfolded him and struck him, and said in derision, "Prophesy who it is that smote thee." The tradition that this is the identical spot of the mocking is a very ancient one. The guide said that Saewulf was the first to mention it. I do not

know Saewulf, but still, I cannot well refuse to receive his
evidence — none of us can.

They showed us where the great Godfrey and his brother Baldwin, the first Christian Kings of Jerusalem, once lay buried by
that sacred sepulchre they had fought so long and so valiantly to
wrest from the hands of the infidel. But the niches that had contained the ashes of these renowned crusaders were empty. Even
the coverings of their tombs were gone — destroyed by devout
members of the Greek church, because Godfrey and Baldwin
were Latin princes, and had been reared in a Christian faith
whose creed differed in some unimportant respects from theirs.

We passed on, and halted before the tomb of Melchisedek!
You will remember Melchisedek, no doubt; he was the King who
came out and levied a tribute on Abraham the time that he pursued Lot's captors to Dan, and took all their property from
them. That was about four thousand years ago, and Melchisedek
died shortly afterward. However, his tomb is in a good state of
preservation.

When one enters the Church of the Holy Sepulchre, the
Sepulchre itself is the first thing he desires to see, and really is
almost the first thing he does see. The next thing he has a strong
yearning to see is the spot where the Saviour was crucified. But
this they exhibit last. It is the crowning glory of the place. One is
grave and thoughtful when he stands in the little Tomb of the
Saviour — he could not well be otherwise in such a place — but
he has not the slightest possible belief that ever the Lord lay
there, and so the interest he feels in the spot is very, very greatly
marred by that reflection. He looks at the place where Mary
stood, in another part of the church, and where John stood, and
Mary Magdalen; where the mob derided the Lord; where the
angel sat; where the crown of thorns was found, and the true
cross; where the risen Saviour appeared — he looks at all these
places with interest, but with the same conviction he felt in the
case of the Sepulchre, that there is nothing genuine about them,
and that they are imaginary holy places created by the monks.
But the place of the Crucifixion affects him differently. He fully
believes that he is looking upon the very spot where the Saviour
gave up his life. He remembers that Christ was very celebrated,
long before he came to Jerusalem; he knows that his fame was
so great that crowds followed him all the time; he is aware that
his entry into the city produced a stirring sensation, and that his
reception was a kind of ovation; he cannot overlook the fact that
when he was crucified there were very many in Jerusalem who
believed that he was the true Son of God. To publicly execute
such a personage was sufficient in itself to make the locality of
the execution a memorable place for ages; added to this, the
storm, the darkness, the earthquake, the rending of the vail of

the Temple, and the untimely waking of the dead, were events
calculated to fix the execution and the scene of it in the memory
of even the most thoughtless witness. Fathers would tell their
sons about the strange affair, and point out the spot; the sons
would transmit the story to their children, and thus a period of
three hundred years would easily be spanned* — at which time
Helena came and built a church upon Calvary to commemorate
the death and burial of the Lord and preserve the sacred place in
the memories of men; since that time there has always been a
church there. It is not possible that there can be any mistake
about the locality of the Crucifixion. Not half a dozen knew
where they buried the Saviour, perhaps, and a burial is not a
startling event, anyhow; therefore, we can be pardoned for unbelief in the Sepulchre, but not in the place of the Crucifixion.
Five hundred years hence there will be no vestige of Bunker Hill
Monument left, but America will still know where the battle was
fought and where Warren fell. The crucifixion of Christ was too
notable an event in Jerusalem, and the Hill of Calvary made too
celebrated by it, to be forgotten in the short space of three hundred years. I climbed the stairway in the church which brings one
to the top of the small inclosed pinnacle of rock, and looked
upon the place where the true cross once stood, with a far more
absorbing interest than I had ever felt in anything earthly before.
I could not believe that the three holes in the top of the rock
were the actual ones the crosses stood in, but I felt satisfied that
those crosses had stood so near the place now occupied by them,
that the few feet of possible difference were a matter of no consequence.

When one stands where the Saviour was crucified, he finds it
all he can do to keep it strictly before his mind that Christ was
not crucified in a Catholic church. He must remind himself every
now and then that the great event transpired in the open air, and
not in a gloomy, candle-lighted cell in a little corner of a vast
church, up stairs — a small cell all bejeweled and bespangled
with flashy ornamentation, in execrable taste.

Under a marble altar like a table, is a circular hole in the marble floor, corresponding with the one just under it in which the
true cross stood. The first thing every one does is to kneel
known and take a candle and examine this hole. He does this
strange prospecting with an amount of gravity that can never be
estimated or appreciated by a man who has not seen the
operation. Then he holds his candle before a richly engraved picture of the Saviour, done on a massy slab of gold, and wonderfully rayed and starred with diamonds, which hangs above the
hole within the altar, and his solemnity changes to lively admiration. He rises and faces the finely wrought figures of the
Saviour and the malefactors uplifted upon their crosses behind

the altar, and bright with a metallic luster of many colors. He turns next to the figures close to them of the Virgin and Mary Magdalen; next to the rift in the living rock made by the earthquake at the time of the crucifixion, and an extension of which he had seen before in the wall of one of the grottoes below; he looks next at the show-case with a figure of the Virgin in it, and is amazed at the princely fortune in precious gems and jewelry that hangs so thickly about the form as to hide it like a garment almost. All about the apartment the gaudy trappings of the Greek church offend the eye and keep the mind on the rack to remember that this is the Place of the Crucifixion — Golgotha — the Mount of Calvary. And the last thing he looks at is that which was also the first — the place where the true cross stood. That will chain him to the spot and compel him to look once more, and once again, after he has satisfied all curiosity and lost all interest concerning the other matters pertaining to the locality.

And so I close my chapter on the Church of the Holy Sepulchre — the most sacred locality on earth to millions and millions of men, and women, and children, the noble and the humble, bond and free. In its history from the first, and in its tremendous associations, it is the most illustrious edifice in Christendom. With all its clap-trap side-shows and unseemly impostures of every kind, it is still grand, reverend, venerable — for a god died there; for fifteen hundred years its shrines have been wet with the tears of pilgrims from the earth's remotest confines; for more than two hundred, the most gallant knights that every wielded sword wasted their lives away in a struggle to seize it and hold it sacred from infidel pollution. Even in our own day a war, that cost millions of treasure and rivers of blood, was fought because two rival nations claimed the sole right to put a new dome upon it. History is full of this old Church of the Holy Sepulchre — full of blood that was shed because of the respect and the veneration in which men held the last resting-place of the meek and lowly, the mild and gentle Prince of Peace!

CHAPTER XXVII

We were standing in a narrow street, by the Tower of Antonio. "On these stones that are crumbling away," the guide said, "the Saviour sat and rested before taking up the cross. This is the beginning of the Sorrowful Way, or the Way of Grief." The party took note of the sacred spot, and moved on. We passed under the "Ecce Homo Arch," and saw the very window from which Pilate's wife warned her husband to have nothing to do with the persecution of the Just Man. This window is in an

excellent state of preservation, considering its great age. They
showed us where Jesus rested the second time, and where the
mob refused to give him up, and said, "Let his blood be upon
our heads, and upon our children's children forever." The
French Catholics are building a church on this spot, and with
their usual veneration for historical relics, are incorporating into
the new such scraps of ancient walls as they have found there.
Further on, we saw the spot where the fainting Saviour fell under the weight of his cross. A great granite column of some ancient temple lay there at the time, and the heavy cross struck it
such a blow that it broke in two in the middle. Such was the
guide's story when he halted us before the broken column.

We crossed a street, and came presently to the former residence of St. Veronica. When the Saviour passed there, she came
out, full of womanly compassion, and spoke pitying words to
him, undaunted by the hootings and the threatenings of the
mob, and wiped the perspiration from his face with her handkerchief. We had heard so much of St. Veronica, and seen her
picture by so many masters, that it was like meeting an old
friend unexpectedly to come upon her ancient home in
Jerusalem. The strangest thing about the incident that has made
her name so famous, is, that when she wiped the perspiration
away, the print of the Saviour's face remained upon the handkerchief, a perfect portrait, and so remains unto this day. We
knew this, because we saw this handkerchief in a cathedral in
Paris, in another in Spain, and in two others in Italy. In the
Milan cathedral it cost five francs to see it, and at St. Peter's, at
Rome, it is amost impossible to see it at any price. No tradition
is so amply verified as this of St. Veronica and her handkerchief.

At the next corner we saw a deep indentation in the hard stone
masonry of the corner of a house, but might have gone
heedlessly by it but the guide said it was made by the elbow of
the Saviour, who stumbled here and fell. Presently we came to
just such another indentation in a stone wall. The guide said the
Saviour fell here, and made this depression with his elbow.

There were other places where the Lord fell, and others where
he rested; but one of the most curious landmarks of ancient
history we found on this morning walk through the crooked
lanes that lead toward Calvary, was a certain stone built into a
house — a stone that was so seamed and scarred that it bore a
sort of grotesque resemblance to the human face. The projections that answered for cheeks were worn smooth by the
passionate kisses of generations of pilgrims from distant lands.
We asked "Why?" The guide said it was because this was one of
"the very stones of Jerusalem" that Christ mentioned when he
was reproved for permitting the people to cry "Hosannah!"
when he made memorable entry into the city upon an ass. One

of the pilgrims said, "But there is no evidence that the stones *did* cry out — Christ said that if the people stopped from shouting Hosannah, the very stones *would* do it." The guide was perfectly serene. He said, calmly, "This is one of the stones that *would* have cried out." It was of little use to try to shake this fellow's simple faith — it was easy to see that.

And so we came at last to another wonder, of deep and abiding interest — the veritable house where the unhappy wretch once lived who has been celebrated in song and story for more than eighteen hundred years as the Wandering Jew. On the memorable day of the Crucifixion he stood in this old doorway with his arms akimbo, looking upon the struggling mob that was approaching, and when the weary Saviour would have sat down and rested him a moment, push him rudely away and said, "Move on!" The Lord said, "Move on, thou, likewise," and the command has never been revoked from that day to this. All men know how that the miscreant upon whose head that just curse fell has roamed up and down the wide world, for ages and ages, seeking rest and never finding it — courting death but always in vain — longing to stop, in city, in wilderness, in desert solitudes, yet hearing always that relentless warning to march — march on! They say — do these hoary traditions — that when Titus sacked Jerusalem and slaughtered eleven hundred thousand Jews in her streets and byways, the Wandering Jew was seen always in the thickest of the fight, and that when battle-axes gleamed in the air, he bowed his head beneath them; when swords flashed their deadly lightnings, he sprang in their way; he bared his breast to whizzing javelins, to hissing arrows, to any and to every weapon that promised death and forgetfulness, and rest. But it was useless — he walked forth out of the carnage without a wound. And it is said that five hundred years afterward he followed Mahomet when he carried destruction to the cities of Arabia, and then turned against him, hoping in this way to win the death of a traitor. His calculations were wrong again. No quarter was given to any living creature but one, and that was the only one of all the host that did not want it. He sought death five hundred years later, in the wars of the Crusades and offered himself to famine and pestilence at Ascalon. He escaped again — he could not die. These repeated annoyances could have at last but one effect — they shook his confidence. Since then the Wandering Jew has carried on a kind of desultory toying with the most promising of the aids and implements of destruction, but with small hope, as a general thing. He has speculated some in cholera and railroads, and has taken almost a lively interest in infernal machines and patent medicines. He is old, now, and grave, as becomes an age like his; he indulges in no light amusements save that he goes sometimes to executions, and is fond of funerals.

There is one thing he cannot avoid; go where he will about the world, he must never fail to report in Jerusalem every fiftieth year. Only a year or two ago he was here for the thirty-seventh time since Jesus was crucified on Calvary. They say that many old people, who are here now, saw him then, and had seen him before. He looks always the same — old, and withered, and hollow-eyed, and listless, save that there is about him something which seems to suggest that he is looking for some one, expecting some one — the friends of his youth, perhaps. But the most of them are dead, now. He always pokes about the old streets looking lonesome, making his mark on a wall here and there, and eying the oldest buildings with a sort of friendly half interest; and he sheds a few tears at the threshold of his ancient dwelling, and bitter, bitter tears they are. He has been seen standing near the Church of the Holy Sepulchre on many a star-lit night, for he has cherished an idea for many centuries that if he could only enter there, he could rest. But when he approaches, the doors slam to with a crash, the earth trembles, and all the lights in Jerusalem burn a ghastly blue! He does this every fifty years, just the same. It is hopeless, but then it is hard to break habits one has been eighteen hundred years accustomed to. The old tourist is far away on his wanderings, now. How he must smile to see a pack of blockheads like us, galloping about the world, and looking wise, and imagining we are finding out a good deal about it! He must have a consuming contempt for the ignorant, complacent asses that go skurrying about the world in these railroading days and call it traveling.

When the guide pointed out where the Wandering Jew had left his familiar mark upon the wall, I was filled with astonishment. It read:

"S. T. — 1860 — X."

All I have revealed about the Wandering Jew can be amply proven by reference to our guide.

The mighty Mosque of Omar, and the paved court around it, occupy *a fourth part* of Jerusalem. They are upon Mount Moriah, where King Solomon's Temple stood. This Mosque is the holiest place the Mohammedan knows, outside of Mecca. Up to within a year or two past, no Christian could gain admission to it or its court for love or money. But the prohibition has been removed, and we entered freely for bucksheesh.

I need not speak of the wonderful beauty and the exquisite grace and symmetry that have made this Mosque so celebrated — because I did not see them. One cannot see such things at an instant glance — one frequently only finds out how really beautiful a really beautiful woman is after considerable acquaintance with her; and the rule applies to Niagara Falls, to majestic mountains, and to mosques — especially to mosques.

The great feature of the Mosque of Omar is the prodigious rock in the center of its rotunda. It was upon this rock that Abraham came so near offering up his son Isaac — this, at least, is authentic — it is very much more to be relied on than most of the traditions, at any rate. On this rock also, the angel stood and threatened Jerusalem, and David persuaded him to spare the city. Mahomet was well acquainted with this stone. From it he ascended to heaven. The stone tried to follow him, and if the angel Gabriel had not happened by the merest good luck to be there to seize it, it would have done it. Very few people have a grip like Gabriel — the prints of his monstrous fingers, two inches deep, are to be seen in that rock to-day.

This rock, large as it is, is suspended in the air. It does not touch anything at all. The guide said so. This is very wonderful. In the place on it where Mahomet stood, he left his footprints in the solid stone. I should judge that he wore about eighteens. But what I was going to say, when I spoke of the rock being suspended, was, that in the floor of the cavern under it they showed us a slab which they said covered a hole which was a thing of extraordinary interest to all Mohammedans, because that hole leads down to perdition, and every soul that is transferred from thence to Heaven must pass up through this orifice. Mahomet stands there and lifts them out by the hair. All Mohammedans shave their heads, but they are careful to leave a lock of hair for the Prophet to take hold of. Our guide observed that a good Mohammedan would consider himself doomed to stay with the damned forever if he were to lose his scalp-lock and die before it grew again. The most of them that I have seen ought to stay with the damned, anyhow, without reference to how they were barbered.

For several ages no woman has been allowed to enter the cavern where that important hole is. The reason is that one of the sex was once caught there blabbing everything she knew about what was going on above the ground, to the rapscallions in the infernal regions down below. She carried her gossiping to such an extreme that nothing could be kept private — nothing could be done or said on earth but everybody in perdition knew all about it before the sun went down. It was about time to suppress this woman's telegraph, and it was promptly done. Her breath subsided about the same time.

The inside of the great mosque is very showy with variegated marble walls and with windows and inscriptions of elaborate mosaic. The Turks have their sacred relics, like the Catholics. The guide showed us the veritable armor worn by the great son-in-law and successor of Mahomet, and also the buckler of

Mahomet's uncle. The great iron railing which surrounds the rock was ornamented in one place with a thousand rags tied to its open work. These are to remind Mahomet not to forget the worshipers who placed them there. It is considered the next best thing to tying threads around his fingers by way of reminders.

Just outside the mosque is a miniature temple, which marks the spot where David and Goliah used to sit and judge the people.*

Everywhere about the Mosque of Omar are portions of pillars, curiously wrought altars, and fragments of elegantly carved marble — precious remains of Solomon's Temple. These have been dug from all depths in the soil and rubbish of Mount Moriah, and the Moslems have always shown a disposition to preserve them with the utmost care. At that portion of the ancient wall of Solomon's Temple which is called the Jews Place of Wailing, and where the Hebrews assemble every Friday to kiss the venerated stones and weep over the fallen greatness of Zion, anyone can see a part of the unquestioned and undisputed Temple of Solomon, the same consisting of three or four stones lying one upon the other, each of which is about twice as long as a seven-octave piano, and about as thick as such a piano is high. But, as I have remarked before, it is only a year or two ago that the ancient edict prohibiting Christian rubbish like ourselves to *enter* the Mosque of Omar and see the costly marbles that once adorned the inner Temple was annulled. The designs wrought upon these fragments are all quaint and peculiar, and so the charm of novelty is added to the deep interest they naturally inspire. One meets with these venerable scraps at every turn, especially in the neighboring Mosque el Aksa, into whose inner walls a very large number of them are carefully built for preservation. These pieces of stone, stained and dusty with age, dimly hint at a grandeur we have all been taught to regard as the princeliest ever seen on earth; and they call up pictures of a pageant that is familiar to all imaginations — camels laden with spices and treasure — beautiful slaves, presents for Solomon's harem — a long cavalcade of richly caparisoned beasts and warriors — and Sheba's Queen in the van of this vision of "Oriental magnificence." These elegant fragments bear a richer interest than the solemn vastness of the stones the Jews kiss in the Place of Wailing can ever have for the heedless sinner.

Down in the hollow ground, underneath the olives and the orange trees that flourish in the court of the great Mosque, is a wilderness of pillars — remains of the ancient Temple; they sup-

---

*A pilgrim informs me that it was not David and Goliah, but David and Saul. I stick to my own statement — the guide told me, and he ought to know.

ported it. There are ponderous archways down there, also, over which the destroying "plough" of prophecy passed harmless. It is pleasant to know we are disappointed, in that we never dreamed we might see portions of the actual Temple of Solomon, and yet experience no shadow of suspicion that they were a monkish humbug and a fraud.

We are surfeited with sights. Nothing has any fascination for us, now, but the Church of the Holy Sepulchre. We have been there every day, and have not grown tired of it; but we are weary of everything else. The sights are too many. They swarm about you at every step; no single foot of ground in all Jerusalem or within its neighborhood seems to be without a stirring and important history of its own. It is a very relief to steal a walk of a hundred yards without a guide along to talk unceasingly about every stone you step upon and drag you back ages and ages to the day when it achieved celebrity.

It seems hardly real when I find myself leaning for a moment on a ruined wall and looking *listlessly* down into the historic pool of Bethesda. I did not think such things *could* be so crowded together as to diminish their interest. But, in serious truth, we have been drifting about, for several days, using our eyes and our ears from a sense of duty than any higher and worthier reason. And too often we have been glad when it was time to go home and be distressed no more about illustrious localities.

Our pilgrims compress too much into one day. One can gorge sights to repletion as well as sweet-meats. Since we breakfasted, this morning, we have seen enough to have furnished us food for a year's reflection if we could have seen the various objects in comfort and looked upon them deliberately. We visited the pool of Hezekiah, where David saw Uriah's wife coming from the bath and fell in love with her.

We went out of the city by the Jaffa gate, and of course were told many things about its Tower of Hippicus.

We rode across the Valley of Hinnom, between two of the Pools of Gihon, and by an aqueduct built by Solomon, which still conveys water to the city. We ascended the Hill of Evil Counsel, where Judas received his thirty pieces of silver, and we also lingered a moment under the tree a venerable tradition says he hanged himself on.

We descended to the canyon again, and then the guide began to give name and history to every bank and boulder we came to: "This was the Field of Blood; these cuttings in the rocks were shrines and Temples of Moloch; here they sacrificed children; yonder is the Zion Gate; the Tyropean Valley; the Hill of Ophel; here is the junction of the Valley of Jehoshaphat — on your right is the Well of Job." We turned up Jehoshaphat. The recital went on.

"This is the Mount of Olives; this is the Hill of Offense; the nest of huts is the Village of Siloam; here, yonder, everywhere, is the King's Garden; under this great tree Zacharias, the high priest, was murdered; yonder is Mount Moriah and the Temple wall; the tomb of Absalom; the tomb of St. James; the tomb of Zacharias; beyond, are the Garden of Gethsemane and the tomb of the Virgin Mary; here is the Pool of Siloam, and —"

We said we would dismount, and quench our thirst and rest. We were burning up with the heat. We were failing under the accumulated fatigue of days and days of ceaseless marching. All were willing.

The Pool is a deep, walled ditch, through which a clear stream of water runs, that comes from under Jerusalem somewhere, and passing through the Fountain of the Virgin, or being supplied from it, reaches this place by way of a tunnel of heavy masonry. The famous pool looked exactly as it looked in Solomon's time, no doubt, and the same dusky, Oriental women, came down in their old Oriental way and carried off jars of the water on their heads, just as they did three thousand years ago, and just as they will do fifty thousand years hence if any of them are still left on earth.

We went away from there and stopped at the Fountain of the Virgin. But the water was not good, and there was no comfort or peace anywhere, on account of the regiment of boys and girls and beggars that persecuted us all the time for bucksheesh. The guide wanted us to give them some money, and we did it; but when he went on to say that they were starving to death we could not but feel that we had done a great sin in throwing obstacles in the way of such a desirable consummation, and so we tried to collect it back, but it could not be done.

We entered the Garden of Gethsemane, and we visited the Tomb of the Virgin, both of which we had seen before. It is not meet that I should speak of them now. A more fitting time will come.

I cannot speak now of the Mount of Olives or its view of Jerusalem, the Dead Sea, and the mountains of Moab; nor of the Damascus Gate or the tree that was planted by King Godfrey of Jerusalem. One ought to feel pleasantly when he talks of these things. I cannot say anything about the stone column that projects over Jehoshaphat from the Temple wall like a cannon, except that the Moslems believe Mahomet will sit astride of it when he comes to judge the world. It is a pity he could not judge it from some roost of his own in Mecca, without trespassing on *our* holy ground. Close by is the Golden Gate, in the Temple wall — a gate that was an elegant piece of sculpture in the time of the Temple, and is even so yet. From it, in ancient times, the Jewish High Priest turned loose the scapegoat and let

him flee to the wilderness and bear away his twelvemonth load
of the sins of the people. If they were to turn one loose now, he
would not get as far as the Garden of Gethsemane, till these
miserable vagabonds here would gobble him up,* sins and all.
They wouldn't care. Mutton-chops and sin is good enough living
for them. The Moslems watch the Golden Gate with a jealous
eye, and an anxious one, for they have an honored tradition that
when it falls, Islamism will fall, and with it the Ottoman Empire.
It did not grieve me any to notice that the old gate was getting a
little shaky.

We are at home again. We are exhausted. The sun has roasted
us, almost.

We have full comfort in one reflection, however. Our experiences in Europe have taught us that in time this fatigue will
be forgotten; the heat will be forgotten; the thirst, the tiresome
volubility of the guide, the persecutions of the beggars — and
then, all that will be left will be pleasant memories of Jerusalem,
memories we shall call up with always increasing interest as the
years go by, memories which some day will become all beautiful
when the last annoyance that incumbers them shall have faded
out our of minds never again to return. Schoolboy days are no
happier than the days of after life, but we look back upon them
regretfully because we have forgotten our punishments at school,
and how we grieved when our marbles were lost and our kites
destroyed — because we have forgotten all the sorrows and
privations of that canonized epoch and remember only its or-
chard robberies, it wooden sword pageants, and its fishing
holidays. We are satisfied. We can wait. Our reward will come.
To us, Jerusalem and to-day's experiences will be an enchanted
memory a year hence — a memory which money could not buy
from us.

CHAPTER XXVIII

We cast up the account. It footed up pretty fairly. There was
nothing more at Jerusalem to be seen, except the traditional
houses of Dives and Lazarus of the parable, the Tombs of the
Kings, and those of the Judges; the spot where they stoned one
of the disciples to death, and beheaded another; the room and
the table made celebrated by the Last Supper; the fig-tree that
Jesus withered; a number of historical places about Gethsemane
and the Mount of Olives, and fifteen or twenty others in different portions of the city itself.

We were approaching the end. Human nature asserted itself,

*Favorite pilgrim expression.

now. Overwork and consequent exhaustion began to have their natural effect. They began to master the energies and dull the ardor of the party. Perfectly secure now against failing to accomplish any detail of the pilgrimage, they felt like drawing in advance upon the holiday soon to be placed to their credit. They grew a little lazy. They were late to breakfast and sat long at dinner. Thirty or forty pilgrims had arrived from the ship, by the short routes, and much swapping of gossip had to be indulged in. And in hot afternoons, they showed a strong disposition to lie on the cool divans in the hotel and smoke and talk about pleasant experiences of a month or so gone by — for even thus early do episodes of travel which were sometimes annoying, sometimes exasperating, and full as often of no consequence at all when they transpired, begin to rise above the dead level of monotonous reminiscences and become shapely landmarks in one's memory. The fog-whistle, smothered among a million of trifling sounds, is not noticed a block away, in the city, but the sailor hears it far at sea, whither none of those thousands of trifling sounds can reach. When one is in Rome, all the domes are alike; but when he has gone away twelve miles, the city fades utterly from sight and leaves St. Peter's swelling above the level plain like an anchored balloon. When one is traveling in Europe, the daily incidents seem all alike; but when he has placed them all two months and two thousand miles behind him, those that were worthy of being remembered are prominent, and those that were really insignificant have vanished. This disposition to smoke and idle and talk was not well. It was plain that it must not be allowed to gain ground. A diversion must be tried, or demoralization would ensure. The Jordan, Jericho, and the Dead Sea were suggested. The remainder of Jerusalem must be left unvisited, for a little while. The journey was approved at once. New life stirred in every pulse. In the saddle — abroad on the plains — sleeping in beds bounded only by the horizon: fancy was at work with these things in a moment. It was painful to note how readily these town-bred men had taken to the free life of the camp and the desert. The nomadic instinct is a human instinct; it was born with Adam and transmitted through the patriarchs, and after thirty centuries of steady effort, civilization has not educated it entirely out of us yet. It has a charm which, once tasted, a man will yearn to taste again. The Nomadic instinct cannot be educated out of an Indian at all.

The Jordan journey being approved, our dragoman was notified.

At nine in the morning the caravan was before the hotel door and we were at breakfast. There was a commotion about the place. Rumors of war and bloodshed were flying everywhere. The lawless Bedouins in the Valley of the Jordan and the deserts down by the Dead Sea were up in arms, and were going to destroy all comers. They had had a battle with a troop of Turkish cavalry and defeated them; several men killed. They had shut up the inhabitants of a village and a Turkish garrison in an old fort near Jericho, and were besieging them. They had marched upon a camp of our excursionists by the Jordan, and the pilgrims only saved their lives by stealing away and flying to Jerusalem under whip and spur in the darkness of the night. Another of our parties had been fired on from an ambush and then attacked in the open day. Shots were fired on both sides. Fortunately, there was no bloodshed. We spoke with the very pilgrim who had fired one of the shots, and learned from his own lips how, in this imminent deadly peril, only the cool courage of the pilgrims, their strength of numbers and imposing display of war material, had saved them from utter destruction. It was reported that the Consul had requested that no more of our pilgrims should go to the Jordan while this state of things lasted; and further, that he was unwilling that any more should go, at least without an unusually strong military guard. Here was trouble. But with the horses at the door and everybody aware of what they were there for, what would *you* have done? Acknowledged that you were afraid, and backed shamefully out? Hardly. It would not be human nature, where there were so many women. You would have done as we did: said you were not afraid of a million Bedouins — and make your will and proposed quietly to yourself to take up an unostentatious position in the rear of the procession.

I think we must all have determined upon the same line of tactics, for it did seem as if we never would get to Jericho. I had a notoriously slow horse, but somehow I could not keep him in the rear, to save my neck. He was forever turning up in the lead. In such cases I trembled a little, and got down to fix my saddle. But it was not of any use. The others all got down to fix their saddles, too. I never saw such a time with saddles. It was the first time any of them had got out of order in three weeks, and now they had all broken down at once. I tried walking, for exercise—I had not had enough in Jerusalem searching for holy places. But it was a failure. The whole mob were suffering for exercise, and it was not fifteen minutes till they were all on foot and I had the lead again. It was very discouraging.

This was all after we got beyond Bethany. We stopped at the village of Bethany, an hour out from Jerusalem. They showed us the tomb of Lazarus. I had rather live in it than in any house in the town. And they showed us also a large "Fountain of Lazarus," and in the center of the village the ancient dwelling of Lazarus. Lazarus appears to have been a man of property. The legends of the Sunday-schools do him great injustice; they give one the impression that he was poor. It is because they get him confused with that Lazarus who had no merit but his virtue, and virtue never has been as respectable as money. The house of Lazarus is a three-story edifice, of stone masonry, but the accumulated rubbish of ages has buried all of it but the upper story. We took candles and decended to the dismal cell-like chambers where Jesus sat at meat with Martha and Mary, and conversed with them about their brother. We could not but look upon these old dingy apartments with a more than common interest.

We had had a glimpse, from a mountain top, of the Dead Sea, lying like a blue shield in the plain of the Jordan, and now we were marching down a close, flaming, rugged, desolate defile, where no living creature could enjoy life, except, perhaps, a salamander. It was such a dreary, repulsive, horrible solitude. It was the "wilderness" where John preached, with camel's hair about his loins — raiment enough — but he never could have got his locusts and wild honey here. We were moping along down through this dreadful place, every man in the rear. Our guards — two gorgeous young Arab sheiks, with cargoes of swords, guns, pistols, and daggers on board — were loafing ahead.

"Bedouins!"

Every man shrunk up and disappeared in his clothes like a mud-turtle. My first impulse was to dash forward and destroy the Bedouins. My second was to dash to the rear to see if there were any coming in that direction. I acted on the latter impulse. So did all the others. If any Bedouins had approached us, then, from that point of the compass, they would have paid dearly for their rashness. We all remarked that, afterwards. There would have been scenes of riot and bloodshed there that no pen could describe. I know that, because each man told what he would have done, individually; and such a medley of strange and unheard-of inventions of cruelty you could not conceive of. One man said he had calmly made up his mind to perish where he stood, if need be, but never yield an inch; he was going to wait, with deadly patience, till he could count the stripes upon the first Bedouin's jacket, and then count them and let him have it. Another was going to sit till the first lance reached within an inch of his breast, and then dodge it and seize it. I forbear to tell what he was going to do to that Bedouin that owned it. It makes my blood run cold to think of it. Another was going to scalp such Bedouins as fell to his share, and take his bald-headed sons of the desert home with him alive for trophies. But the wild-eyed pilgrim rhapsodist was silent. His orbs gleamed with a deadly light, but his lips moved not. Anxiety grew, and he was questioned. If he had got a Bedouin, what would he have done with him — shot him? He smiled a smile of grim contempt and shook his head. Would he have stabbed him? Another shake. Would he have quartered him — flayed him? More shakes. Oh horror, what *would* he have done?

"Eat him!"

Such was the awful sentence that thundered from his lips. What was grammar to a desperado like that? I was glad in my heart that I had been spared these scenes of malignant carnage. No Bedouins attacked our terrible rear. And none attacked the front. The newcomers were only a re-enforcement of cadaverous Arabs, in shirts and bare legs, sent far ahead of us to brandish rusty guns, and shout and brag, and carry on like lunatics, and thus scare away all bands of marauding Bedouins that might lurk about our path. What a shame it is that armed white Christians must travel under guard of vermin like this as a protection against the prowling vagabonds of the desert — those sanguinary outlaws who are always going to do something desperate, but never do it. I may as well mention here that on our whole trip we saw no Bedouins, and had no more use for an Arab guard than we could have had for patent-leather boots and white kid gloves. The Bedouins that attacked the other parties of pilgrims so fiercely were provided for the occasion by the Arab guards of those parties, and shipped from Jerusalem for temporary service as Bedouins. They met together in full view of the pilgrims, after the battle, and took lunch, divided the bucksheesh extorted in the season of danger, and then accompanied the cavalcade home to the city! The nuisance of an Arab guard is one which is created by the Sheiks and the Bedouins together, for mutual profit, it is said, and no doubt there is a good deal of truth in it.

We visited the fountain the prophet Elisha sweetened (it is sweet yet); where he remained some time and was fed by the ravens.

Ancient Jericho is not very picturesque as a ruin. When Joshua marched around it seven times, some three thousand years ago, and blew it down with his trumpet, he did the work so well and so completely that he hardly left enough of the city to cast a shadow. The curse pronounced against the rebuilding of it has never been removed. One king, holding the curse in light estimation, made the attempt, but was stricken sorely for his presumption. Its site will always remain unoccupied; and yet it is one of the very best locations for a town we have seen in all Palestine.

At two in the morning they routed us out of bed — another piece of unwarranted cruelty, another stupid effort of our dragoman to get ahead of a rival. It was not two hours to the Jordan. However, we were dressed and under way before any one thought of looking to see what time it was, and so we drowsed on through the chill night air and dreamed of camp fires, warm beds, and other comfortable things.

There was no conversation. People do not talk when they are cold, and wretched, and sleepy. We nodded in the saddle, at times, and woke up with a start to find that the procession had disappeared in the gloom. Then there was energy and attention to business until its dusky outlines came in sight again. Occasionally the order was passed in a low voice down the line: "Close up — close up! Bedouins lurk here, everywhere!" What an exquisite shudder it sent shivering along one's spine!

We reached the famous river before four o'clock, and the night was so black that we could have ridden into it without seeing it. Some of us were in an unhappy frame of mind. We waited and waited for daylight, but it did not come. Finally we went away in the dark and slept an hour on the ground, in the bushes, and caught cold. It was a costly nap, on that account, but otherwise it was a paying investment because it brought unconsciousness of the dreary minutes and put us in a somewhat fitter mood for a first glimpse of the sacred river.

With the first suspicion of dawn, every pilgrim took off his clothes and waded into the dark torrent, singing:

> "On Jordan's stormy banks I stand,
> And cast a wistful eye
> To Canaan's fair and happy land,
> Where my possessions lie."

But they did not sing long. The water was so fearfully cold that they were obliged to stop singing and scamper out again. Then they stood on the bank shivering, and so chagrined and so grieved, that they merited honest compassion. Because another dream, another cherished hope, had failed. They had promised themselves all along that they would cross the Jordan where the Israelites crossed it when they entered Canaan from their long pilgrimage in the desert. They would cross where the twelve stones were placed in memory of that great event. While they did it they would picture to themselves that vast army of pilgrims marching through the cloven waters, bearing the hallowed ark of the covenant and shouting hosannahs, and singing songs of thanksgiving and praise. Each had promised himself that he would be the first to cross. They were at the goal of their hopes at last, but the current was too swift, the water was too cold!

It was then that Jack did them a service. With that engaging recklessness of consequences which is natural to youth, and so proper and so seemly, as well, he went and led the way across the Jordan, and all was happiness again. Every individual waded over, then, and stood upon the further bank. The water was not quite breast deep, anywhere. If it had been more, we could hardly have accomplished the feat, for the strong current would have swept us down the stream, and we would have been exhausted and drowned before reaching a place where we could make a landing. The main object compassed, the drooping, miserable party sat down to wait for the sun again, for all wanted to see the water as well as feel it. But it was too cold a pastime. Some cans were filled from the holy river, some canes cut from its banks, and then we mounted and rode reluctantly away to keep from freezing to death. So we saw the Jordan very dimly. The thickets of bushes that bordered its banks threw their shadows across its shallow, turbulent waters ("stormy," the hymn makes them, which is rather a complimentary stretch of fancy), and we could not judge of the width of the stream by the eye. We knew by our wading experience, however, that many streets in America are double as wide as the Jordan.

Daylight came, soon after we got under way, and in the course of an hour or two we reached the Dead Sea. Nothing grows in the flat, burning desert around it but weeds and the Dead Sea apple the poets say is beautiful to the eye, but crumbles to ashes and dust when you break it. Such as we found were not handsome, but they were bitter to the taste. They yielded no dust. It was because they were not ripe, perhaps.

The desert and the barren hills gleam painfully in the sun, around the Dead Sea, and there is no pleasant thing or living creature upon it or about its borders to cheer the eye. It is a scorching, arid, repulsive solitude. A silence broods over the scene that is depressing to the spirits. It makes one think of funerals and death.

The Dead Sea is small. Its waters are very clear, and it has a pebbly bottom and is shallow for some distance out from the shores. It yields quantities of asphaltum; fragments of it lie all about its banks; this stuff gives the place something of an unpleasant smell.

All our reading had taught us to expect that the first plunge into the Dead Sea would be attended with distressing results — our bodies would feel as if they were suddenly pierced by millions of red-hot needles; the dreadful smarting would continue for hours; we might even look to be blistered from head to foot, and suffer miserably for many days. We were disappointed. Our eight sprang in at the same time that another party of pilgrims did, and nobody screamed once. None of them ever did complain of anything more than a slight pricking sensation in places where their skin was abraded, and then only for a short time. My face smarted for a couple of hours, but it was partly because I got it badly sun-burned while I was bathing, and stayed in so long that it became plastered over with salt.

No, the water did not blister us; it did not cover us with a slimy ooze and confer upon us an atrocious fragrance; it was not very slimy; and I could not discover that we smelt really any worse than we have always smelt since we have been in Palestine. It was only a different kind of smell, but not conspicuous on that account, because we have a great deal of variety in that respect. We didn't smell, there on the Jordan, the same as we do in Jerusalem; and we don't smell in Jerusalem just as we did in Nazareth, or Tiberias, or Cesarea Phillippi, or any of those other ruinous ancient towns in Galilee. No, we change all the time, and generally for the worse. We do our own washing.

It was a funny bath. We could not sink. One could stretch himself at full length on his back, with his arms on his breast, and all of his body above a line drawn from the corner of his jaw past the middle of his side, the middle of his leg and through his ankle bone, would remain out of water. He could lift his head clear out if he chose. No position can be retained long; you lose your balance and whirl over, first on your back and then on your face, and so on. You can lie comfortably, on your back, with your head out, and your legs out from your knees down, by steadying yourself with your hands. You can sit, with your knees drawn up to your chin and your arms clasped around them, but you are bound to turn over presently, because you are topheavy in that position. You can stand up straight in water that is over your head, and from the middle of your breast upward you will not be wet. But you cannot remain so. The water will soon float your feet to the surface. You cannot swim on your back and make any progress of any consequence, because your feet stick away above the surface, and there is nothing to propel yourself with but your heels. If you swim on your face, you kick up the water like a stern-wheel boat. You make no headway. A horse is so topheavy that he can neither swim nor stand up in the Dead Sea. He turns over on his side at once. Some of us bathed for more than an hour, and then came out coated with salt till we shone like icicles. We scrubbed it off with a coarse towel and rode off with a splendid brand-new-smell, though it was one which was not any more disagreeable than those we have been for several weeks enjoying. It was the variegated villainy and novelty of it that charmed us. Salt crystals glitter in the sun about the shores of the lake. In places they coat the ground like a brilliant crust of ice.

When I was a boy I somehow got the impression that the river Jordan was four thousand miles long and thirty-five miles wide. It is only ninety miles long, and so crooked that a man does not know which side of it he is on half the time. In going ninety miles it does not get over more than fifty miles of ground. It is not any wider than Broadway in New York. There is the Sea of Galilee and this Dead Sea — neither of them twenty miles long or thirteen wide. And yet when I was in Sunday-school I thought they were sixty thousand miles in diameter.

Travel and experience mar the grandest pictures and rob us of the most cherished traditions of our boyhood. Well, let them go. I have already seen the Empire of King Solomon diminish to the State of Pennsylvania; I suppose I can bear the reduction of the seas and the river.

We looked everywhere, as we passed along, but never saw grain or crystal of Lot's wife. It was a great disappointment. For many and many a year we had known her sad story, and taken that interest in her which misfortune always inspires. But she was gone. Her picturesque form no longer looms above the desert of the Dead Sea to remind the tourist of the doom that fell upon the lost cities.

I cannot describe the hideous afternoon's ride from the Dead Sea to Mars Saba. It oppresses me yet, to think of it. The sun so pelted us that the tears ran down our cheeks once or twice. The ghastly, treeless, grassless, breathless canyons smothered us as if we had been in an oven. The sun had positive *weight* to it, I think. Not a man could sit erect under it. All drooped low in the saddles. John preached in this "Wilderness"! It must have been exhausting work. What a very heaven the massy towers and ramparts of vast Mars Saba looked to us when we caught a first glimpse of them!

We stayed at this great convent all night, guests of the hospitable priests. Mars Saba, perched upon a crag, a human nest stuck high up against a perpendicular mountain wall, is a world of grand masonry that rises, terrace upon terrace, away above your head, like the terraced and retreating colonnades one sees in fanciful pictures of Belshazzar's Feast and the palaces of the ancient Pharaohs. No other human dwelling is near. It was founded many ages ago by a holy recluse who lived at first in a cave in the rock — a cave which is inclosed in the convent walls now, and was reverently shown to us by the priests. This recluse, by his rigorous torturing of his flesh, his diet of bread and water, his utter withdrawal from all society and from the vanities of the world, and his constant prayer and saintly contemplation of a skull, inspired an emulation that brought about him many disciples. The precipice on the opposite side of the canyon is well perforated with the small holes they dug in the rock to live in. The present occupants of Mars Saba, about seventy in number, are all hermits. They wear a coarse robe, an ugly, brimless stovepipe of a hat, and go without shoes. They eat nothing whatever but bread and salt; they drink nothing but water. As long as they live they can never go outside the walls, or look upon a woman — for no woman is permitted to enter Mars Saba, upon any pretext whatsoever.

Some of those men have been shut up there for thirty years. In all that dreary time they have not heard the laughter of a child or the blessed voice of a woman; they have seen no human tears, no human smiles; they have known no human joys, no wholesome human sorrows. In their hearts are no memories of the past, in their brains no dreams of the future. All that is lovable, beautiful, worthy, they have put far away from them; against all things that are pleasant to look upon, and all sounds that are music to the ear, they have barred their massive doors and reared their relentless walls of stone forever. They have banished the tender grace of life and left only the sapped and skinny mockery. Their lips are lips that never kiss and never sing; their hearts are hearts that never hate and never love; their breasts are breasts that never swell with the sentiment, "I have a country and a flag." They are dead men who walk.

I set down these first thoughts because they are natural — not because they are just or because it is right to set them down. It is easy for bookmakers to say "I thought so and so as I looked upon such and such a scene" — when the truth is, they thought all those fine things afterward. One's first thought is not likely to be strictly accurate, yet it is no crime to think it and none to write it down, subject to modification by later experience. These hermits *are* dead men, in several respects, but not in all; and it is not proper that, thinking ill of them at first, I should go on doing so, or, speaking ill of them, I should reiterate the words and stick to them. No, they treated us too kindly for that. There is something human about them somewhere. They knew we were foreigners and Protestants, and not likely to feel admiration or much friendliness toward them. But their large charity was above considering such things. They simply saw in us men who were hungry, and thirsty, and tired, and that was sufficient. They opened their doors and gave us welcome. They asked no questions, and they made no self-righteous display of their hospitality. They fished for no compliments. They moved quietly about, setting the table for us, making the beds, and bringing water to wash in, and paid no heed when we said it was wrong for them to do that when we had men whose business it was to perform such offices. We fared most comfortably, and sat late at dinner. We walked all over the building with the hermits afterward, and then sat on the lofty battlements and smoked while we enjoyed the cool air, the wild scenery, and the sunset. One or two chose cosy bedrooms to sleep in, but the nomadic instinct prompted the rest to sleep on the broad divan that extended around the great hall, because it seemed like sleeping out of doors, and so was more cheery and inviting. It was a royal rest we had.

When we got up to breakfast in the morning, we were new men. For all this hospitality no strict charge was made. We could

give something if we chose; we need give nothing, if we were
poor or if we were stingy. The pauper and the miser are as free
as any in the Catholic convents of Palestine. I have been
educated to enmity toward everything that is Catholic, and
sometimes, in consequence of this, I find it much easier to
discover Catholic faults than Catholic merits. But there is one
thing I feel no disposition to overlook, and no disposition to
forget; and that is, the honest gratitude I and all pilgrims owe to
the Convent Fathers in Palestine. Their doors are always open,
and there is always a welcome for any worthy man who comes,
whether he comes in rags or clad in purple. The Catholic convents are a priceless blessing to the poor. A pilgrim without
money, whether he be a Protestant or a Catholic, can travel the
length and breadth of Palestine, and in the midst of her desert
wastes find wholesome food and a clean bed every night, in these
buildings. Pilgrims in better circumstances are often stricken
down by the sun and the fevers of the country, and then their
saving refuge is the convent. Without these hospitable retreats,
travel in Palestine would be a pleasure which none but the
strongest men could dare to undertake. Our party, pilgrims and
all, will always be ready and always willing to touch glasses and
drink health, prosperity, and long life to the Convent Fathers of
Palestine.

So, rested and refreshed, we fell into line and filed away over
the barren mountains of Judea, and along rocky ridges and
through sterile gorges, where eternal silence and solitude reigned.
Even the scattering groups of armed shepherds we met the afternoon before, tending their flocks of long-haired goats, were
wanting here. We saw but two living creatures. They were
gazelles of "soft-eyed" notoriety. They looked like very young
kids, but they annihilated distance like an express train. I have
not seen animals that moved faster, unless I might say it of the
antelopes of our own great plains.

At nine or ten in the morning we reached the Plain of the
Shepherds, and stood in a walled garden of olives where the
shepherds were watching their flocks by night, eighteen centuries
ago, when the multitude of angels brought them the tidings that
the Saviour was born. A quarter of a mile away was Bethlehem
of Judea, and the pilgrims took some of the stone and hurried
on.

The Plain of the Shepherds is a desert, paved with loose
stones, void of vegetation, glaring in the fierce sun. Only the
music of the angels it knew once could charm its shrubs and
flowers to life again and restore its vanished beauty. No less
potent enchantment could avail to work this miracle.

In the huge Church of the Nativity, in Bethlehem, built fifteen
hundred years ago by the inveterate St. Helena, they took us

below ground, and into a grotto cut in the living rock. This was
the "manger" where Christ was born. A silver star set in the
floor bears a Latin inscription to that effect. It is polished iwth
the kisses of many generations of worshiping pilgrims. The grotto was tricked out in the usual tasteless style observable in all the
holy places of Palestine. As in the Church of the Holy
Sepulchre, envy and uncharitableness were apparent here. The
priests and the members of the Greek and Latin churches cannot
come by the same corridor to kneel in the sacred birthplace of
the Redeemer, but are compelled to approach and retire by different avenues, lest they quarrel and fight on this holiest ground
on earth.

I have no "meditations," suggested by this spot where the
very first "Merry Christmas" was uttered in all the world, and
from whence the friend of my childhood, Santa Claus, departed
on his first journey to gladden and continue to gladden roaring
firesides on wintry mornings in many a distant land forever and
forever. I touch, with reverent finger, the actual spot where the
infant Jesus lay, but I think — nothing.

You *cannot* think in this place any more than you can in any
other in Palestine that would be likely to inspire reflection.
Beggars, cripples, and monks compass you about, and make you
think only of bucksheesh when you would rather think of
somethimg more in keeping with the character of the spot.

I was glad to get away, and glad when we had walked through
the grottoes where Eusebius wrote, and Jerome fasted, and
Joseph prepared for the flight into Egypt, and the dozen other
distinguished grottoes, and knew we were done. The Church of
the Nativity is almost as well packed with exceeding holy places
as the Church of the Holy Sepulchre itself. They even have in it
a grotto wherein twenty thousand children were slaughtered by
Herod when he was seeking the life of the infant Saviour.

We went to the Milk Grotto, of course — a cavern where
Mary hid herself for a while before the flight into Egypt. Its
walls were black before she entered, but in suckling the Child, a
drop of her milk fell upon the floor and instantly changed the
darkness of the walls to its own snowy hue. We took many little
fragments of stone from here, because it is well known in all the
East that a barren woman hath need only to touch her lips to
one of these and her failing will depart from her. We took many
specimens, to the end that we might confer happiness upon certain households that we wot of.

We got away from Bethlehem and its troops of beggars and
relic-peddlers in the afternoon, and after spending some little
time at Rachel's tomb, hurried to Jerusalem as fast as possible. I
never was *so* glad to get home again before. I never had enjoyed
rest as I have enjoyed it during these last few hours. The journey

to the Dead Sea, the Jordan, and Bethlehem was short, but it was an exhausting one. Such roasting heat, such oppressive solitude, and such dismal desolation cannot surely exist elsewhere on earth. And *such* fatigue!

The commonest sagacity warns me that I ought to tell the customary pleasant lie, and say I tore myself reluctantly from every noted place in Palestine. Everybody tells that, but with as little ostentation as I may, I doubt the word of every he who tells it. I could take a dreadful oath that I have never heard any one of our forty pilgrims say anything of the sort, and they are as worthy and as sincerely devout as any that come here. They will say it when they get home, fast enough, but why should they not? They do not wish to array themselves against all the Lamartines and Grimeses in the world. It does not stand to reason that men are reluctant to leave places where the very life is almost badgered out of them by importunate swarms of beggars and peddlers who hang in strings to one's sleeves and coat-tails and shriek and shout in his ears and horrify his vision with the ghastly sores and malformations they exhibit. One is *glad* to get away. I have heard shameless people say they were glad to get away from Ladies' Festivals where they were importuned to buy by bevies of lovely young ladies. Transform those houris into dusky hags and ragged savages, and replace their rounded form. with shrunken and knotted distortions, their soft hands with scarred and hideous deformities, and the persuasive music of their voices with the discordant din of a hated language, and *then* see how much lingering reluctance to leave could be mustered. No, it is the neat thing to say you were reluctant, and then append the profound thought that "struggled for utterance" in your brain; but it is the true thing to say you were not reluctant, and found it impossible to think at all—though in good sooth it is not respectable to say it, and not poetical, either.

We do not think, in the holy places; we think in bed, afterward, when the glare, and the noise, and the confusion are gone, and in fancy we revisit alone the solemn monuments of the past, and summon the phantom pageants of an age that has passed away.

CHAPTER XXIX

We visited all the holy places about Jerusalem which we had left unvisited when we journeyed to the Jordan, and then, about three o'clock one afternoon, we fell into procession and marched out at the stately Damascus gate, and the walls of Jerusalem shut us out forever. We paused on the summit of a distant hill and took a final look and made a final farewell to the venerable city which had been such a good home to us.

For about four hours we traveled down hill constantly. We followed a narrow bridle-path which traversed the beds of the mountain gorges, and when we could we got out of the way of the long trains of laden camels and asses, and when we could not we suffered the misery of being mashed up against perpendicular walls of rock and having our legs bruised by the passing freight. Jack was caught two or three times, and Dan and Moult as often. One horse had a heavy fall on the slippery rocks, and the others had narrow escapes. However, this was as good a road as we had found in Palestine, and possibly even the best, and so there was not much grumbling.

Sometimes, in the glens, we came upon luxuriant orchards of figs, apricots, pomegranates, and such things, but oftener the scenery was rugged, mountainous, verdureless, and forbidding. Here and there, towers were perched high up on acclivities which seemed almost inaccessible. This fashion is as old as Palestine itself, and was adopted in ancient times for security against enemies.

We crossed the brook which furnished David the stone that killed Goliath, and, no doubt, we looked upon the very ground whereon that noted battle was fought. We passed by a picturesque old gothic ruin whose stone pavements had rung to the armed heels of many a valorous Crusader, and we rode through a piece of country which we were told once knew Samson as a citizen.

We stayed all night with the good monks at the convent of Ramleh, and in the morning got up and galloped the horses a good part of the distance from there to Jaffa, or Joppa, for the plain was as level as a floor and free from stones, and besides this was our last march in Holy Land. These two or three hours finished, we and the tired horses could have rest and sleep as long as we wanted it. This was the plain of which Joshua spoke when he said, "Sun, stand thou still on Gibeon, and thou moon in the valley of Ajalon." As we drew near to Jaffa, the boys spurred up the horses and indulged in the excitement of an actual race — an experience we had hardly had since we raced on donkeys in the Azores islands.

We came finally to the noble grove of orange trees in which the Oriental city of Jaffa lies buried; we passed through the walls, and rode again down narrow streets and among swarms of animated rags, and saw other sights and had other experiences we had long been familiar with. We dismounted, for the last time, and out in the offing, riding at anchor, we saw the ship! I put an exclamation point there because we felt one when we saw the vessel. The long pilgrimage was ended, and somehow we seemed to feel glad of it.

For description of Jaffa, see Universal Gazetteer. Simon the Tanner formerly lived here. We went to his house. All the pilgrims visit Simon the Tanner's house. Peter saw the vision of the beasts let down in a sheet when he lay upon the roof of Simon the Tanner's house. It was from Jaffa that Jonah sailed when he was told to go and prophesy against Nineveh, and, no doubt, it was not far from the town that the whale threw him up when he discovered that he had no ticket. Jonah was disobedient, and of a fault-finding, complaining disposition, and deserves to be lightly spoken of, almost. The timbers used in the construction of Solomon's temple were floated to Jaffa in rafts, and the narrow opening in the reef through which they passed to the shore is not an inch wider or a shade less dangerous to nagitate than it was then. Such is the sleepy nature of the population Palestine's only good seaport has now and always had. Jaffa has a history and a stirring one. It will not be discovered anywhere in this book. If the reader will call at the circulating library and mention my name, he will be furnished with books which will afford him the fullest informaiton concerning Jaffa.

So ends the pilgrimage. We ought to be glad that we did not make it for the purpose of feasting our eyes upon fascinating aspects of nature, for we should have been disappointed — at least at this season of the year. A writer in "Life in the Holy Land" observes:

"Monotonous and uninviting as much of the Holy Land will appear to persons accustomed to the almost constant verdure of flowers, ample streams, and varied surface of our own country, we must remember that its aspect to the Israelites after the weary march of forty years through desert must have been very different.

Which all of us will freely grant. But it truly *is* "monotonous and uninviting," and there is no sufficient reason for describing it as being otherwise.

Of all the lands there are for dismal scenery, I think Palestine must be the prince. The hills are barren, they are dull of color, they are unpicturesque in shape. The valleys are unsightly deserts fringed with a feeble vegetation that has an expression about it of being sorrowful and despondent. The Dead Sea and the Sea of Galilee sleep in the midst of a vast stretch of hill and plain wherein the eye rests upon no pleasant tint, no striking object, no soft picture dreaming in a purple haze or mottled with the shadows of the clouds. Every outline is harsh, every feature is distinct, there is no perspective — distance works no enchantment here. It is a hopeless, dreary, heart-broken land.

Small shreds and patches of it must be very beautiful in the full flush of spring, however, and all the more beautiful by contrast with the far-reaching desolation that surrounds them on every side. I would like much to see the fringes of the Jordan in spring time, and Shechem, Esdraelon, Ajalon, and the borders of Galilee — but even then these spots would seem mere toy gardens set at wide intervals in the waste of a limitless desolation.

Palestine sits in sackcloth and ashes. Over it broods the spell of a curse that has withered its fields and fettered its energies. Where Sodom and Gomorrah reared their domes and towers, that solemn sea now floods the plain, in whose bitter waters no living thing exists—over whose waveless surface the blistering air hangs motionless and dead — about whose borders nothing grows but weeds, and scattering tufts of cane, and that treacherous fruit that promises refreshment to parching lips, but turns to ashes at the touch. Nazareth is forlorn; about that ford of Jordan where the hosts of Israel entered the Promised Land with songs of rejoicing, one finds only a squalid camp of fantastic Bedouins of the desert; Jericho the accursed lies a moldering ruin to-day, even as Joshua's miracle left it more than three thousand years ago; Bethlehem and Bethany, in their poverty and their humiliation, have nothing about them now to remind one that they once knew the high honor of the Saviour's presence; the hallowed spot where the shepherds watched their flocks by night, and where the angels sang Peace on earth, good will to men, is untenanted by any living creature, and unblessed by any feature that is pleasant to the eye. Renowned Jerusalem itself, the statliest name in history, has lost all its ancient grandeur, and is become a pauper village; the riches of Solomon are no longer there to compel the admiration of visiting Oriental queens; the wonderful temple which was the pride and the glory of Israel is gone, and the Ottoman crescent is lifted above the spot where, on that most memorable day in the annals of the world, they reared the Holy Cross. The noted Sea of Galilee, where Roman fleets once rode at anchor and the disciples of the Saviour sailed in their ships, was long ago deserted by the devotees of war and commerce, and its borders are a silent wilderness; Capernaum is a shapeless ruin; Magdala is the home of beggared Arabs; Bethsaida and Chorazin have vanished from the earth, and the "desert places" round about them where thousands of men once listened to the Saviour's voice and ate the miraculous bread sleep in the hush of a solitude that is inhabited only by birds of prey and skulking foxes.

Palestine is desolate and unlovely. And why should it be otherwise? Can the *curse* of the Deity beautify a land?

Palestine is no more of this work-day world. It is sacred to poetry and tradition — it is dream-land.

CHAPTER XXX

It was worth a kingdom to be at sea again. It was a relief to drop all anxiety whatsoever — all questions as to where we should go; how long we should stay; whether we should go; how long we should stay; whether it were worth while to go or not; all anxieties about the condition of the horses; all such question as "Shall we *ever* get to water?" "Shall we *ever* lunch?" "Ferguson, how many *more* million miles have we got to creep under this awful sun before we camp?" It was a relief to cast all these torturuing little anxieties far away — ropes of steel they were, and every one with a separate and distinct strain on it — and feel the temporary contentment that is born of the banishment of all care and responsiblility. We did not look at the compass; we did not care, now, where the ship went to, so that she went out of sight of land as quickly as possible. When I travel again, I wish to go in a pleasure ship. No amount of money could have purchased for us, in a strange vessel and among unfamiliar faces, the perfect satisfaction and the sense of being *at home* again which we experienced when we stopped on board the *Quaker City, — our own ship* — after this wearisome pilgrimage. It is a something we have felt always when we returned to her, and a something we had no desire to sell.

We took off our blue woolen shirts, our spurs and heavy boots, our sanguinary revolvers and our buckskin-seated pantaloons, and got shaved, and came out in Christian costume once more. All but Jack, who changed all other articles of his dress, but clung to his traveling pantaloons. They still preserved their ample buckskin seat intact; and so his short pea-jacket and his long, thin legs assisted to make him a picturesque object whenever he stood on the forecastle looking abroad upon the ocean over the bows. At such times his father's last injunction suggested itself to me. He said:

"Jack, my boy, you are about to go among a brilliant company of gentlemen and ladies, who are refined and cultivated, and thoroughly accomplished in the manners and customs of good society. Listen to their conversation, study their habits of life, and learn. Be polite and obliging to all, and considerate towards every one's opinions, failings, and prejudices. Command the just respect of all your fellow-voyagers, even though you fail to win their friendly regard. And Jack — don't you ever dare, while you live, appear in public on those decks in fair weather, in a costume unbecoming your mother's drawing-room!"

It would have been worth any price if the father of this hopeful youth could have stepped on board some time, and seen him standing high on the forecastle, pea-jacket, tasseled red fez, buckskin patch and all, — placidly contemplating the ocean — a rare spectacle for anybody's drawing-room.

After a pleasant voyage and a good rest, we drew near to Egypt, and out of the mellowest of sunsets we saw the domes and minarets of Alexandria rise into view. As soon as the anchor was down, Jack and I got a boat and went ashore. It was night by this time, and the other passengers were content to remain at home and visit ancient Egypt after breakfast. It was the way they did at Constantinople. They took a lively interest in new countries, but their schoolboy impatience had worn off, and they had learned that it was wisdom to take things easy and go along comfortably — these old countries do not go away in the night; they stay till after breakfast.

When we reached the pier we found an army of Egyptian boys with donkeys no larger than themselves, waiting for passengers — for donkeys are the omnibuses of Egypt. We preferred to walk, but we could not have our own way. The boys crowded about us, clamored around us, and slewed their donkeys exactly across our path, no matter which way we turned. They were good-natured rascals, and so were the donkeys. We mounted, and the boys ran behind us and kept the donkeys in a furious gallop, as is the fashion at Damascus. I believe I would rather ride a donkey than any beast in the world. He goes briskly, he puts on no airs, he is docile, though opinionated. Satan himself could not scare him, and he is convenient — very convenient. When you are tired riding you can rest your feet on the ground and let him gallop from under you.

We found the hotel and secured rooms, and were happy to know that the Prince of Wales had stopped there once. They had it everywhere on signs. No other princes had stopped there since, till Jack and I came. We went abroad through the town, then, and found it a city of huge commercial buildings, and broad, handsome streets brilliant with gaslight. By night it was a sort of reminiscence of Paris. But finally Jack found an ice-cream saloon, and that closed investigations for that evening. The weather was very hot, it had been many a day since Jack had seen ice-cream, and so it was useless to talk of leaving the saloon till it shut up.

In the morning the lost tribes of America came ashore and infested the hotels and took possession of all the donkeys and other open barouches that offered. They went in picturesque procession to the American Consul's; to the great gardens; to Cleopatra's Needles; to Pompey's Pillar; to the palace of the Viceroy of Egypt; to the Nile; to the superb groves of date-palms. One of our most inveterate relic-hunters had his hammer with him, and tried to break a fragment off the upright Needle and could not do it; he tried the prostrate one and failed; he borrowed a heavy sledge-hammer from a mason and failed again. He tried Pompey's Pillar, and this baffled him. Scattered all about the mighty monolith were sphinxes of noble countenance, carved out of Egyptian granite as hard as blue steel, and whose shapely features the wear of five thousand years had failed to mark or mar. The relic-hunter battered at these persistently, and sweated profusely over his work. He might as well have attempted to deface the moon. They regarded him serenely with the stately smile they had worn so long, and which seemed to say, "Peck away, poor insect; we were not made to fear such as you; in tenscore dragging ages we have seen more of your kind than there are sands at your feet; have they left a blemish upon us?"

But I am forgetting the Jaffa Colonists. At Jaffa we have taken on board some forty members of a very celebrated community. They were male and female; babies, young boys and young girls; young married people, and some who had passed a shade beyond the prime of life. I refer to the "Adams Jaffa Colony." Others had deserted before. We left in Jaffa Mr. Adams, his wife, and fifteen unfortunates who not only had no money but did not know where to turn or whither to go. Such was the statement made to us. Our forty were miserable enough in the first place, and they lay about the decks seasick all the voyage, which about completed their misery, I take it. However, one or two young men remained upright, and by constant persecution we wormed out of them some little information. They gave it reluctantly and in a very fragmentary condition, for, having been shamefully humbugged by their prophet, they felt humiliated and unhappy. In such circumstances people do not like to talk.

The colony was a complete *fiasco*. I have already said that such as could get away did so, from time to time. The prophet Adams — once an actor, then several other things, afterward a Mormon and a missionary, always an adventurer — remains at Jaffa with his handful of sorrowful subjects. The forty we brought away with us were chiefly destitute, though not all of them. They wished to get to Egypt. What might become of them then they did not know and probably did not care — anything to get away from hated Jaffa. They had little to hope for; because after many appeals to the sympathies of New England, made by strangers of Boston, through the newspapers, and after the establishment of an office there for the reception of moneyed contributions for the Jaffa colonists, one dollar was subscribed. The consul-general for Egypt showed me the newspaper paragraph which mentioned the circumstance, and mentioned also the discontinuance of the effort and the closing of the office. It was evident that practical New England was not sorry to be rid of such visionaries and was not in the least inclined to hire anybody to bring them back to her. Still, to get to Egypt was something, in the eyes of the unfortunate colonists, hopeless as the prospect seemed of ever getting further.

Thus circumstanced, they landed at Alexandria from our ship. One of our passengers, Mr. Moses S. Beach, of the New York *Sun,* inquired of the consul-general what it would cost to send these people to their home in Maine by the way of Liverpool, and he said fifteen hundred dollars in gold would do it. Mr. Beach gave his check for the money, and so the troubles of the Jaffa colonists were at an end.*

Alexandria was too much like a European city to be novel, and we soon tired of it. We took the cars and came up here to ancient Cairo, which *is* an Oriental city and of the completest pattern. There is little about it to disabuse one's mind of the error if he should take it into his head that he was in the heart of Arabia. Stately camels and dromedaries, swarthy Egyptians, and likewise Turks and black Ethiopians, turbaned, sashed, and blazing in a rich variety of Oriental costumes of all shades of flashy colors, are what one sees on every hand crowding the narrow streets and the honeycombed bazaars. We are stopping at Shepherd's Hotel, which is the worst on earth except the one I stopped at once in a small town in the United States. It is pleasant to read this sketch in my note-book, now, and know that I can stand Shepherd's Hotel, sure, because I have been in one just like it in America and survived:

> I stopped at the Benton House. It used to be a good hotel, but that proves nothing — I used to be a good boy, for that matter. Both of us have lost character of late years. The Benton is not a good hotel.
>
> The Benton lacks a very great deal of being a good hotel. Perdition is full of better hotels than the Benton.
>
> It was late at night when I got there, and I told the clerk I would like plenty of lights, because I wanted to read an hour or two. When I reached No. 15 with the porter (we came along a dim hall that was clad in ancient carpeting, faded, worn out in many places, and patched with old scraps of oil cloth — a hall that sank under one's feet, and creaked dismally to every footstep) he struck a light — two inches of sallow, sorrowful, consumptive tallow candle, that burned blue, and sputtered, and got discouraged and went out. The porter lit it again, and I asked if that was all the light the clerk sent. He said, "Oh no, I've got another one here," and he produced another couple of inches of tallow candle. I said, "Light them both — I'll have to have one to see the other by." He did it, but the result was drearier than darkness itself. He was a cheery, accommodating rascal. He said he would go "somewheres" and steal a lamp. I abetted and encouraged him in his criminal design. I heard the landlord get after him in the hall ten minutes afterward.

*It was an unselfish act of benevolence; it was done without any ostentation, and has never been mentioned in any newspaper, I think. Therefore it is refreshing to learn now, several months after the above narrative was written, that another man received all the credit of this rescue of the colonists. Such is life.

"Where are you going with that lamp?"

"Fifteen wants it, sir"

"Fifteen! why he's got a double lot of candles — does the man want to illuminate the house? — does he want to get up a torchlight procession? — what *is* he up to, any how?"

"He don't like them candles — says he wants a lamp."

"Why, what in the nation does — why I never heard of such a thing? What on earth can he want with that lamp?"

"Well, he only wants to read — that's what he says."

"Wants to read, does he? — ain't satisfied with a thousand candles, but has to have a lamp! — I do wonder what the devil that fellow wants that lamp for? Take him another candle, and then if —"

"But he wants the lamp — says he'll burn the d—d old house down if he don't get a lamp!" A remark which I never made.]

"I'd like to see him at it once. Well, you take it along — but I swear it beats *my* time, though — and see if you can't find out what in the very nation he *wants* with that lamp."

And he went off growling to himself and still wondering and wondering over the unaccountable conduct of No. 15. The lamp was a good one, but it revealed some disagreeable things — a bed in the suburbs of a desert of room — a bed that had hills and valleys in it, and you'd have to accommodate your body to the impression left in it by the man that slept there last, before you could lie comfortably; a carpet that had seen better days; a melancholy washstand in a remote corner, and a dejected pitcher on it sorrowing over a broken nose; a looking-glass split across the center, which chopped your head off at the chin and made you look like some dreadful unfinished monster or other; the paper peeling in shreds from the walls.

I sighed and said: "This is charming; and now don't you think you could get me something to read?"

The porter said, "Oh, certainly; the old man's got dead loads of books;" and he was gone before I could tell him what sort of literature I would rather have. And yet his countenance expressed the utmost confidence in his ability to execute the commission with credit to himself. The old man made a descent on him.

"What are you going to do with that pile of books?"

"Fifteen wants 'em, sir."

"Fifteen, is it? He'll want a warming-pan, next — he'll want a nurse! Take him everything there is in the house — take him the barkeeper — take him the baggage-wagon — take him a chambermaid! Confound me, I never saw anything like it. What did he say he wants with those books?"

"Wants to read 'em, like enough; it ain't likely he wants to eat 'em, I don't reckon."

"Wants to read 'em — wants to read 'em this time of night, the infernal lunatic! Well he can't have them."

"But he says he's mor'ly bound to have 'em: he says he'll just go a-rairin' and a-chargin' through this house and raise more — well, there's no tellin' what he won't do if he don't get 'em; because he's drunk and crazy and desperate, and nothing'll soothe him down but them cussed books." [I had not made any threats and was not in the condition ascribed to me by the porter.]

"Well, go on; but I will be around when he goes to rairing and charging, and the first rair he makes I'll make him rair out of the window." And then the old gentleman went off growling as before.

The genius of that porter was something wonderful. He put an armful of books on the bed and said "Good night" as confidently as if he knew perfectly well that those books were exactly my style of reading matter. And well he might. His selection covered the whole range of legitimate literature. It comprised "The Great Consummation," by Rev. Dr. Cummings — theology; "Revised Statutes of the State of Missouri" — law; "The Complete Horse-Doctor" —

medicine; "The Toilers of the Sea," by Victor Hugo — romance; "The works of William Shakespeare" — poetry. I shall never cease to admire the tact and the intelligence of that gifted porter.

But all the donkeys in Christendom, the most of the Egyptian boys, I think, are at the door, and there is some noise going on, not to put it in stronger language. We are about starting to the illustrious Pyramids of Egypt, and the donkeys for the voyage are under inspection. I will go and select one before the choice animals are all taken.

CHAPTER XXXI

The donkeys were all good, all handsome, all strong and in good condition, all fast and all willing to prove it. They were the best we had found anywhere, the most *recherche*. I do not know what *recherche* is, but that is what these donkeys were, anyhow. Some were of a soft mouse-color, and the others were white, black, and vari-colored. Some were close-shaven, all over, except that a tuft like a paint-brush was left on the end of the tail. Others were so shaven in fanciful landscape garden patterns, as to mark their bodies with curving lines, which were bounded on one side by hair and on the other by the close plush left by the shears. They had all been newly barbered, and were exceedingly stylish. Several of the white ones were barred like zebras with rainbow stripes of blue and red and yellow paint. These were indescribably gorgeous. Dan and Jack selected from this lot because they brought back Italian reminiscenes of the "old masters." The saddles were the high, stuffy, frog-shaped things we had known in Ephesus and Smyrna. The donkey-boys were lively young Egyptian rascals who could follow a donkey and keep him in a canter half a day without tiring. We had plenty of spectators when we mounted, for the hotel was full of English people bound overland to India and officers getting ready for the African campaign against the Abyssinian King Theodorus. We were not a very large party, but as we charged through the streets of the great metropolis, we made noise for five hundred, and displayed activity and created excitement in proportion. Nobody can steer a donkey, and some collided with camels, dervishes, effendis, asses, beggars, and everything else that offered to the donkeys a reasonable chance for a collision. When we turned into the broad avenue that leads out of the city toward Old Cairo, there was plenty of room. The walls of stately date-palms that fenced the gardens and bordered the way, threw their shadows down and made the air cool and bracing. We rose to the spirit of the time and the race became a wild rout, a stampede, a terrific panic. I wish to live to enjoy it again.

Somewhere along this route we had a few startling exhibitions of Oriental simplicity. A girl apparently thriteen years of age came along the great thoroughfare dressed like Eve before the fall. We would have called her thirteen at home; but here girls who look thriteen are often not more than nine, in reality.

Occasionally we saw stark-naked men of superb build, bathing, and making no attempt at concealment. However, an hour's acquaintance with this cheerful custom reconciled the pilgrims to it, and then it ceased to occasion remark. Thus easily do even the most startling novelties grow tame and spiritless to these sight-surfeited wanderers.

Arrived at Old Cairo, the camp-followers took up the donkeys and tumbled them bodily aboard a small boat with a lateen sail, and we followed and got under way. The deck was closely packed with donkeys and men; the two sailors had to climb over and under and trhough the wedged mass to work the sails, and the steersman had to crowd four or five donkeys out of the way when he wished to swing his tiller and put his helm hard down. But what were their troubles to us? We had nothing to do; nothing to do but enjoy the trip; nothing to do but shove the donkeys off our corns and look at the charming scenery of the Nile.

On the island at our right was the machine they call the Nilometer, a stone column whose business it is to mark the rise of the river and prophesy whether it will reach only thirty-two feet and produce a famine, or whether it will properly flood the land at forty and produce plenty, or whether it will rise to forty-three and bring death and destruction to flocks and crops — but how it does all this they could not explain to us so that we could understand. On the same island is still shown the spot where Pharaoh's daughter found Moses, in the bulrushes. Near the spot we sailed from, the Holy Family dwelt when they sojourned in Egypt till Herod should complete his slaughter of the in-nocents. The same tree they rested under when they first arrived was there a short time ago, bu the Viceroy of Egypt sent it to the Empress Eugenie lately. He was just in time, otherwise our pilgrims would have had it.

The Nile at this point is muddy, swift, and turbid, and does not lack a great deal of being as wide as the Mississippi.

We scrambled up the steep bank at the shabby town of Ghizeh, mounted the donkeys again, and scampered away. For four or five miles the route lay along a high embankment which they say is to be the bed of a railway the Sultan means to build for no other reason than that when the Empress of the French comes to visit him she can go to the Pyramids in comfort. This is true Oriental hospitality. I am very glad it is our privilege to have donkeys instead of cars.

At the distance of a few miles the Pyramids, rising above the palms, looked very clean-cut, very grand and imposing, and very soft and filmy, as well. They swam in a rich haze that took from them all suggestions of unfeeling stone, and made them seem only the airy nothings of a dream — structures which might blossom into tiers of vague arches, or ornate colonnades, maybe, and change and change again into all graceful forms of architecture while we looked, and then melt deliciously away and blend with the tremulous atmosphere.

At the end of the levee we left the mules and went in a sailboat across an arm of the Nile or an overflow, and landed where the sands of the Great Sahara left their embankment, as straight as a wall, along the verge of the alluvial plain of the river. A laborious walk in the flaming sun brought us to the foot of the great Pyramid of Cheops. It was a fairy vision no longer. It was a courrugated, unsightly mountain of stone. Each of its monstrous sides was a wide stairway which rose uprward, step above step, narrowing as it went, till it tapered to a point far aloft in the air. Insect men and women — pilgrims from the *Quaker City* — were creeping about its dizzy perches, and one little black swarm were waving postage stamps from the airy summit — handerkerchiefs will be understood.

Of course we were beseiged by a rabble of muscular Egyptians and Arabs who wanted the contract of dragging us to the top — all tourists are. O course you could not hear your own voice for the din that was around you. Of course the Shieks said *they* were the only responsible parties; that all contracts must be made with them, all moneys paid over to them, and none exacted from us by any but themselves alone. Of course they contracted that the varlets who dragged us up should not mention bucksheesh once. For such is the usual routine. Of course we contracted with them, paid them, were delivered into the hands of the draggers, dragged up the Pyramids, and harried and bedeviled for bucksheesh from the foundation clear to the summit. We paid it, too, for we were purposely spread very far apart over the vast side of the Pyramid. There was no help near if we called, and the Herculeses who dragged us had a way of asking sweetly and flatteringly for bucksheesh, which was seductive, and of looking fierce and threatening to throw us down the precipice, which was persuasive, and convincing.

Each step being full as high as a dinner table; there being very, very many of the steps; an Arab having hold of each of our arms and springing upward from step to step and snatching us with them, forcing us to lift our feet as high as our breasts every time, and do it rapidly and keep it up till we were ready to faint, — who shall say it is not lively, exhilarating, lacerating, muscle-straining, bone-wrenching, and perfectly excruciating and

exhausting pastime, climbing the Pyramids? I beseeched the
varlets not to twist *all* my joints asunder; I iterated, reiterated,
even *swore* to them that I did not wish to beat anybody to the
top; did all I could to convince them that if I got there the last
of all I would feel blessed above men and grateful to them
forever; I begged them, prayed them, pleaded with them to let
me stop and rest a moment — only one little moment: and they
only answered with some more frightful springs, and an
unenlisted volunteer behind opened a bombardment of determined boosts with his head which threatened to batter my whole
political economy to wreck and ruin.

Twice, for one minute, they let me rest while they extorted
bucksheesh, and then continued their maniac flight up the
Pyramid. They wished to beat the other parites. It was nothing
to them that *I*, a stranger, must be sacrificed upon the altar of
their unholy ambition. But in the midst of sorrow joy blooms.
Even in this dark hour I had a sweet consolation. For I knew
that except these Mohammedans repented they would go straight
to perdition some day. And *they* never repent — they never forsake their paganism. This thought calmed me, cheered me, and I
sank down, limp and exhausted, upon the summit, but happy, *so*
happy and serene within.

On the one hand, a mighty-sea of yellow sand stretched away
towards the ends of the earth, solemn, silent, shorn of
vegetation, its solitude uncheered by any forms of creature life;
on the other, the Eden of Egypt was spread below us — a broad
green floor, cloven by the sinuous river, dotted with villages, its
vast distance measured and marked by the dimishing stature of
receding clusters of palms. It lay asleep in an enchanted atmosphere. There was no sound, no motion. Above the date-
plumes in the middle distance, swelled a domed and pinnacled
mass, glimmering through a tinted, exquisite mist; away toward
the horizon a dozen shapely pyramids watched over ruined Memphis; and at our feet the bland impassible Sphinx looked out
upon the picture from her throne in the sands as placidly and
pensively as she had looked upon its like full fifty lagging centuries ago.

We suffered torture no pen can describe from the hungry appeals for bucksheesh that gleamed from Arab eyes and poured
incessantly from Arab lips. Why try to call up the traditions of
vanished Egyptian grandeur; why try to fancy Egypt following
dead Rameses to his tomb in the Pyramid, or the long multitude
of Israel departing over the desert yonder? Why try to think at
all? The thing was impossible. One must bring his meditations
cut and dried, or else cut and dry them afterward.

The traditional Arab proposed, in the traditional way, to run
down Cheops, cross the eighth of a mile of sand intervening be-

tween it and the tall pyramid of Cephren, ascent to Cephren's
summit and return to us on the top of Cheops — all in nine
minutes by the watch, and the whole service to be rendered for a
single dollar. In the first flush of irritation, I said left the Arab
and his exploits go to the mischief. But stay. The upper third of
Cephren was coated with dressed marble, smooth as glass. A
blessed thought entered my brain. He must infallibly break his
neck. Close the contract with dispatch, I said, and left him go.
He started. We watched. He went bounding down the vast
broadside, spring after spring, like an ibex. He grew smaller and
smaller till he became a bobbing pigmy, away down toward the
bottom — then disappeared. We turned and peered over the
other side — forty seconds — eighty seconds — a hundred —
happiness, he is dead already? — two minutes — and a quarter
— "There he goes!" Too true. He was very small, now.
Gradually, but surely, he overcame the level ground. He began
to spring and climb again. Up, up, up — at last he reached the
smooth coating — now for it. But he clung to it with toes and
fingers, like a fly. He crawled this way and that — away to the
right, slanting upward — away to the left, still slanting upward
— and stood at last, a black peg on the summit, and waved his
pigmy scarf! Then he crept downward to the raw steps again,
then picked up his agile heels and flew. We lost him presently.
But presently again we saw him under us, mounting with undiminished energy. Shortly he bounded into our midst with a
gallant war-whoop. Time, eight minutes, forty-one seconds. He
had won. His bones were intact. It was a failure. I reflected. I
said to myself, he is tired, and must grow dizzy. I will risk
another dollar on him.

He started again. Made the trip again. Slipped on the smooth
coating — I almost had him. But an infamous crevice saved him.
He was with us once more — perfectly sound. Time, eight
minutes, forty-six seconds.

I said to Dan, "Lend me a dollar — I can beat this game,
yet."

Worse and worse. He won again. Time, eight minutes, forty-
eight seconds. I was out of all patience, now. I was deperate.
Money was no longer of any consequence. I said, "Sirrah, I will
give you a hundred dollars to jump off this pyramid head first.
If you do not like the terms, name your bet. I scorn to stand on
expenses now. I will stay right here and risk money on you as
long as Dan has got a cent."

I was in a fair way to win, now, for it was a dazzling opportunity for an Arab. He pondered a moment, and would have
done it, I think, but his mother arrived then, and interfered. Her
tears moved me — I never can look upon the tears of woman
with indifference — and I said I would give her a hundred to

jump off, too.

But it was a failure. The Arabs are high-priced in Egypt. They put on airs unbecoming to such savages.

We descended, hot and out of humor. The dragoman lit candles, and we all entered a hole near the base of the pyramid, attended by a crazy rabble of Arabs who trust their services upon us uninvited. They dragged us up a long inclined chute, and dripped candle-grease all over us. This chute was not more than twice as wide and high as a Saratoga trunk, and was walled, roofed, and floored with solid blocks of Egyptian granite as wide as a wardrobe, twice as thick, and three times as long. We kept on climbing, through the oppressive gloom, till I thought we ought to be nearing the top of the pyramid again, and then came to the "Queen's Chamber," and shortly to the Chamber of the King. These large apartments were tombs. The walls were built of monstrous masses of smoothed granite, neatly joined together. Some of them were nearly as large square as an ordinary parlor. A great stone sarcophagus like a bathtub stood in the center of the King's Chamber. Around it were gathered a picturesque group of Arab savages and soiled and tattered pilgrims, who held their candles aloft in the gloom while they chattered, and the winking blurs of light shed a dim glory down upon one of the irrepressible memento-seekers who was pecking at the venerable sarcophagus with his sacrilegious hammer. We struggled out to the open air and the bright sunshine, and for the space of thirty minutes received ragged Arabs by couples, dozens, and platoons, and paid them bucksheesh for services they swore and proved by each other that they had rendered, but which we had not been aware of before — and as each party was paid, they dropped into the rear of the procession and in due time arrived again with a newly-invented delinquent list for liquidation.

We lunched in the shade of the pyramid, and in the midst of this encroaching and unwelcome company, and then Dan and Jack and I started away for a walk. A howling swarm of beggars followed us — surrounded us — almost headed us off. A shiek, in flowing white bournous and gaudy headgear, was with them. He wanted more bucksheesh. But we had adopted a new code — it was millions for defense, but not a cent for bucksheesh. I asked him if could persuade the others to depart if we paid him. He said yes — for ten francs. We accepted the contract, and said. —

"Now persuade your vassals to fallback."

He swung his long staff round his head and three Arabs bit the dust. He capered among the mob like a very maniac. His blows fell like hail, and wherever one fell a subject went down. We had to hurry to the rescue and tell him it was only necessary to damage them a little, he need not kill them. In two minutes we were alone with the sheik, and remained so. The persuasive powers of this illiterate savage were remarkable.

Each side of the Pyramid of Cheops is about as long as the Capitol at Washington, or the Sultan's new palace on the Bosporus, and is longer than the greatest depth of St. Peter's at Rome — which is to say that each side of Cheops extends seven hundred and some odd feet. It is about seventy-five feet higher than the cross on St. Peter's. The first time I ever went down the Mississippi, I thought the highest bluff on the river between St. Louis and New Orleans — it was near Selma, Missouri — was probably the highest mountain in the world. It is four hundred and thirteen feet high. It still looms in my memory with undiminished grandeur. I can still see the trees and bushes growing smaller and smaller as I followed them up its huge slant with my eye, till they became a feathery fringer on the distant summit. This symmetrical pyramid of Cheops — this soild mountain of stone reared by the patient hands of men — this mighty tomb of a forgotten monarch — dwarfs my cherished mountain. For it is four hundred and eighty feet high. In still earlier years than those I have been recalling, Holiday's Hill, in our town, was to me the noblest work of God. It appeared to pierce the skies. It was nearly three hundred feet high. In those days I pondered the subject much, but I never could understand why it did not swathe its summit with never-failing clouds, and crown its majestic brow with everlasting snows. I had heard that such was the custom of great mountains in other parts of the world. I remembered how I worked with another boy, at odd afternoons stolen from study and paid for with stripes, to undermine and start from its bed an immense boulder that rested upon the edge of that hilltop; I remembered how, one Staruday afternoon, we gave three hours of honest effort to the task, and saw at last that our reward was at hand; I remembered how we sat down, then, and wiped the perspiration away, and waited to let a picnic party get out of the way in the road below — and then we started the boulder. It was splendid. It went crashing down the hillside, tearing up saplings, mowing bushes down like grass, ripping and crushing and smashing everything in its path — eternally splintered and scattered a woodpile at the foot of the hill, and then sprang from the high bank clear over a dray on the road — the negro glanced up once and dodged — and the next second it made infinitesimal mincemeat of a frame cooper-shop, and the coopers swarmed out like bees. Then we said it was perfectly magnificent, and left. Because the coopers were starting up the hill to inquire.

Still, that mountain, prodigious as it was, was nothing to the Pyramid of Cheops. I could conjure up no comparison that would convey to my mind a satisfactory comprehension of the magnitude of a pile of monstrous stones that covered thirteen acres of ground and stretched upward four hundred and eighty tiresome feet, and so I gave it up and walked down to the Sphinx.

After years of waiting, it was before me at last. The great face was so sad, so earnest, so longing, so patient. There was a dignity not of earth in its mien, and in its countenance a benignity such as never anything human wore. It was stone, but it seemed sentient. If ever image of stone thought, it was thinking. It was looking toward the verge of the landscape, yet looking *at* nothing — nothing but distance and vacancy. It was looking over and beyond everything of the present, and far into the past. It was gazing out over the ocean of Time — over lines of century-waves which, further and further receding, closed nearer and nearer together, and blended at last into one unbroken tide, away toward the horizon of remote antiquity. It was thinking of the wars of departed ages; of the empires it had seen created and destroyed; of the nations whose birth it had witnessed, whose progress it had watched, whose annihilation it had noted; of the joy and sorrow, the life and death, the grandeur and decay, of five thousand slow revolving years. It was the type of an attribute of man — of a faculty of his heart and brain. It was MEMORY – RETROSPECTION – wrought into visible, tangible form. All who know what pathos there is in memories of days that are accomplished and faces that have vanished — albeit only a trifling score of years gone by — will have some appreciation of the pathos that dwells in these grave eyes that look so steadfastly back upon the things they knew before History was born — before Tradition had being — things that were, and forms that moved, in a vague era which even Poetry and Romance scarce know of — and passed one by one away and left the stony dreamer solitary in the midst of a strange new age, and uncomprehended scenes.

The Sphinx is grand in its loneliness; it is imposing in its magnitude; it is impressive in the mystery that hangs over its story. And there is that in the overshadowing majesty of this eternal figure of stone, with its accusing memory of the deeds of all ages, which reveals to one something of what he shall feel when he shall stand at last in the awful presence of God.

There are some things which, for the credit of America, should be left unsaid, perhaps; but these very things happen sometimes to be the very things which, for the real benefit of Americans, ought to have prominent notice. While we stood looking, a wart, or an excrescence of some kind, appeared on the jaw of the Sphinx. We heard the familiar clink of a hammer, and understood the case at once. One of our well-meaning reptiles — I mean relic-hunters — had crawled up there and was trying to break a "Specimen" from the face of this the most majestic creation the hand of man has wrought. But the great image contemplated the dead ages as calmly as ever, unconscious of the small insect that was fretting at its jaw. Egyptian granite that has defied the storms and earthquakes of all time has nothing to fear from the tack hammers of ignorant excursionists — highwaymen like this specimen. He failed in his enterprise. We sent a sheik to arrest him if he had the authority, or to warn him, if he had not, that by the laws of Egypt the crime he was attempting to commit was punishable with imprisonment or the bastinado. Then he desisted and went away.

The Sphinx: a hundred and twenty-five feet long, sixty feet high, and a hundred and two feet around the head, if I remember rightly — carved out of one solid block of stone harder than any iron. The block must have been as large as the Fifth Avenue Hotel before the usual waste (by the necessities of sculpture) of a fourth or a half of the original mass was begun. I only set down these figures and these remarks to suggest the prodigious labor the carving of it so elegantly, so symmetrically, so faultlessly, must have cost. This species of stone is so hard that figures cut in it remain sharp and unmarred after exposure to the weather for two or three thousand years. Now did it take a hundred years of patient toil to carve the Sphinx? It seems probable.

Something interfered, and we did not visit the Red Sea and walk upon the sands of Arabia. I shall not describe the great mosque of Mehemet Ali, whose entire inner walls are built of polished and glistening alabaster; I shall not tell how the little birds have built their nests in the globes of the great chandeliers that hang in the mosque, and how they fill the whole place with their music and are not afraid of anybody because their audacity is pardoned, their rights are respected, and nobody is allowed to interfere with them, even though the mosque be thus doomed to go unlighted; I certainly shall not tell the hackneyed story of the massacre of the Mamelukes, because I am glad the lawless rascals were massacred, and I do not wish to get up any sympathy in their behalf; I shall not tell how that one solitary Mameluke jumped his horse a hundred feet down from the battlements of the citadel and escaped, because I do not think much of that — I could have done it myself; I shall not tell of Joseph's well which he dug in the solid rock of the citadel hill and which is still as good as new, nor how the same mules be brought to draw up the water (with an endless chain) are still at it yet and are getting tired of it, too; I shall not tell about Joseph's granaries which he built to store the grain in, what time the Egyptian brokers were "selling short," unwitting that there would be no corn in all the land when it should be time for them to deliver; I shall not tell anything about the strange, strange city of Cairo, because it is only a repetition, a good deal intensified and exaggerated, of the Oriental cities I have already spoken of; I shall not tell of the Great Caravan which leaves for Mecca every year, for I did not see it; nor of the fashion the people have of prostrating themselves and so forming a long human pavement to be ridden over by the chief of the expedition on its return, to the end that their salvation may be thus secured, for I did not see that either; I shall not speak of the railway, for it is like any other railway — I shall only say that the fuel they use for the locomotive is composed of mummies three thousand years old, purchased by the ton or by the graveyard for that purpose, and that sometimes one hears the profane engineer call out pettishly, "D —n these plebeians, they don't burn worth a cent — pass out a king;"* I shall not tell of the groups of mud cones stuck like wasps' nests upon a thousand mounds above high-water mark the length and breadth of Egypt — villages of the lower classes; I shall not speak of the boundless sweep of level plain, green with luxuriant grain, that gladdens the eye as far as it can pierce through the soft, rich atmosphere of Egypt; I shall not speak of the vision of the Pyramids seen at a distance of five and twenty miles, for the picture is too ethereal to be limned by an uninspired pen; I shall not tell of the crowds of dusky women who flocked to the cars when they stopped a moment at a station, to sell us a drink of water or a ruddy, juicy pomegranate; I shall not tell of the motley multitudes and wild costumes that graced a fair we found in full blast at another barbarous station; I shall not tell how we feasted on fresh dates and enjoyed the pleasant landscape all through the flying journey; now how we thundered into Alexandria, at last, swarmed out of the cars, rowed aboard the ship, left a comrade behind (who was to return to Europe, thence home), raised the anchor, and turned our bows homeward finally and forever from the long voyage; nor how, as the mellow sun went down upon the oldest land on earth, Jack and Moult assembled in solemn state in the smoking-room and mourned over the lost comrade the whole night long, and would not be comforted. I shall not speak a word of any of these things, or write a line. They shall be as sealed book. I do not know what a sealed book is, because I never saw one, but a sealed book is the expression to use in this connection, because it is popular.

We were glad to have seen the land which was the mother of civilization — which taught Greece her letters, and through Greece Rome, and through Rome and world, the land which

*Stated to me for a fact. I only tell it as I got it. I am willing to believe it. I can believe anything.

could have humanized and civilized the hapless children of
Israel, but allowed them to depart out of her borders little better
than savages. We were glad to have seen that land which had an
enlightened religion with future eternal rewards and punishment
in it, while even Israel's religion contained no promise of a
hereafter. We were glad to have seen that land which had glass
three thousand years before England had it, and could paint
upon it as none of us can paint now; that land which knew,
three thousand years ago, well nigh all of medicine and surgery
which science has *discovered* lately; which had all those curious
surgical instruments which science has *invented* recently; which
had in high excellence a thousand luxuries and necessities of an
advanced civilization which we have gradually contrived and accumulated in modern times and claimed as things that were new
under the sun; that had paper untold centuries before we dreamt
of it — and waterfalls before our women thought of them; that
had a perfect system of common schools so long before we
boasted of our achievements in that direction that it seems
forever and forever ago; that so embalmed the dead that flesh
was made almost immortal — which we cannot do; that built
temples which mock at destroying time and smile grimly upon
our lauded little prodigies of architecture; that old land that
knew all which we know now, perchance, and more; that walked
in the broad highway of civilization in the gray dawn of
creation, ages and ages before we were born; that left the impress of exalted, cultivated Mind upon the eternal front of the
Sphinx to confound all scoffers who, when all her other proofs
had passed away, might seek to persuade the world that imperial
Egypt, in the days of her high renown, had groped in darkness.

CHAPTER XXXII

We were at sea now, for a very long voyage — we were to
pass through the entire length of the Levant; through the entire
length of the Mediterranean proper, also, and then cross the full
width of the Atlantic — a voyage of several weeks. We naturally
settled down into a very slow, stay-at-home manner of life, and
resolved to be quiet, exemplary people, and roam no more for
twenty or thirty days. No more, at least, than from stem to stern
of the ship. It was a very comfortable prospect, though, for we
were tired and needed a long rest.

We were all lazy and satisfied, now, as the meager entries in
my note-book (that sure index, to me, of my condition) prove.
What a stupid thing a notebook gets to be at sea, any way.
Please observe the style:

"*Sunday* — Services, as usual, at four bells. Services at night, also. No cards.

"*Monday* — Beautiful day, but rained hard. The cattle purchased at Alexandria for beef ought to be shingled. Or else fattened. The water stands in deep puddles in the depressions forward of their after shoulders. Also here and there all over their backs. It is well they are not cows — it would soak in and ruin the milk. The poor devil eagle* from Syria looks miserable and droopy in the rain perched on the forward capstan. He appears to have his own opinion of a sea voyage, and if it were put into language and the language solidified, it would probably essentially dam the widest river in the world.

"*Tuesday* — Somewhere in the neighborhood of the island of Malta. Can not stop there. Cholera. Weather very stormy. Many passengers seasick and invisible.

"*Wednesday* — Weather still very savage. Storm blew two land birds to sea, and they came on board. A hawk was blown off, also. He circled round and round the ship, wanting to light, but afraid of the people. He was so tired, though, that he had to light, at last, or perish. He stopped in the foretop, repeatedly, and was as often blown away by the wind. At last Harry caught him. Sea full of flying-fish. They rise in flocks of three hundred and flash along above the tops of the waves a distance of two or three hundred feet, then fall and disappear.

"*Thursday* — Anchored off Algiers, Africa. Beautiful city, beautiful green hilly landscape behind it. Stayed half a day and left. Not permitted to land, though we showed a clean bill of health. They were afraid of Egyptian plague and cholera.

"*Friday* — Morning, dominoes. Afternoon, dominoes. Evening, promenading the deck. Afterwards, charades.

"*Saturday* — Morning, dominoes. Afternoon dominoes. Evening, promenading the decks. Afterwards, dominoes.

"*Sunday* — Morning service, four bells. Evening service, eight bells. Monotony till midnight. — Whereupon, dominoes.

"*Monday* — Morning, dominoes. Afternoon, dominoes. Evening, promenading the decks. Afterwards, charades and a lecture from Dr. C. Dominoes.

"*No date* — Anchored off the picturesque city of Cagliari, Sardinia. Stayed till midnight, but not permitted to land by these infamous foreigners. They smell inodorously — they do not wash — they dare not risk cholera.

"*Thursday* — Anchored off the beautiful cathedral city of Malaga, Spain. — Went ashore in the captain's boat — not ashore, either, for they would not let us land. Quarantine. Shipped my newspaper correspondence, which they took with tongs, dipped it in sea water, clipped it full of holes, and then fumigated it with villainous vapors till it smelt like a Spaniard. Inquired about chances to run the blockade and visit the Alhambra at Granada. Too risky — they might hang a body. Set sail — middle of afternoon.

"And so on, and so on, and so forth, for several days. Finally, anchored off Gibraltar, which looks familiar and home-like."

It reminds me of the journal I opened with the New Year, once, when I was a boy and a confiding and a willing prey to those impossible schemes of reform which well-meaning old maids and grandmothers set for the feet of unwary youths at that season of the year — setting oversized tasks for them, which, necessarily failing, as infallibly weaken the boy's strength of will, diminish his confidence in himself, and injure his chances of success in life. Please accept of an extract:

---

* Afterwards presented to the Central Park.

> "*Monday* — Got up, washed, went to bed.
> "*Tuesday* — Got up, washed, went to bed.
> "*Wednesday* — Got up, washed, went to bed.
> "*Thursday* — Got up, washed, went to bed.
> "*Friday* — Got up, washed, went to bed.
> "*Next Friday* — Got up, washed, went to bed.
> "*Friday fortnight* — Got up, washed, went to bed.
> "*Following month* — Got up, washed, went to bed."

I stopped, then, discouraged. Startling events appeared to be too rare, in my career, to render a diary necessary. I still reflect with pride, however, that even at that early age I washed when I got up. That journal finished me. I never have had the nerve to keep one since. My loss of confidence in myself in that line was permanent.

The ship had to stay a week or more at Gilbraltar to take in coal for the home voyage.

It would be very tiresome staying here, and so four of us ran the quarantine blockade and spent seven delightlful days in Seville, Cordova, Cadiz, and wandering through the pleasant rural scenery of Andalusia, the garden of Old Spain. The experiences of that cheery week were too varied and numerous for a short chapter, and I have not room for a long one. Therefore I shall leave them all out.

CHAPTER XXXIII

Ten or eleven o'clock found us coming down to breakfast one morning in Cadiz. They told us the ship had been lying at anchor in the harbor two or three hours. It was time for us to bestir ourselves. The ship could wait only a little while because of the quarantine. We were soon on board, and within the hour the white city and the pleasant shores of Spain sank down behind the waves and passed out of sight. We had seen no land fade from view so regretfully.

It had long ago been decided in a noisy public meeting in the main cabin that we could not go to Lisbon, because we must surely be quarantined there. We did everything by mass-meeting, in the good old national way, from swapping off one empire for another on the programme of the voyage down to complaining of the cookery and the scarcity of napkins. I am reminded, now, of these complaints of the cookery made by a passenger. The coffee had been steadily growing more and more execrable for the space of three weeks, till at last it had ceased to be coffee altogether and had assumed the nature of mere discolored water — so this person said. He said it was so weak that it was transparent an inch in depth around the edge of the cup. As he approached the table one morning he saw the transparent edge — by means of his extraordinary vision — long before he got to his seat. He went back and complained in a high-handed way to

Captain Duncan. He said the coffee was disgraceful. The captain showed his. It seemed tolerably good. The incipient mutineer was more outraged than ever, then, at what he denounced as the partiality shown the captain's table over the other tables in the ship. He flourished back and got his cup and set it down triumphantly, and said:

"Just try that mixture once, Captain Duncan."

He smelt it — tasted it — smiled benignantly — then said:

"It *is* inferior — for *coffee* — but it is pretty fair *tea*."

The humbled mutineer smelt it, tasted it, and returned to his seat. He had made an egregious ass of himself before the whole ship. He did it no more. After that he took things as they came. That was me.

The old-fashioned ship-life had returned, now that we were no longer in sight of land. For days and days it continued just the same, one day being exactly like another, and, to me, every one of them pleasant. At last we anchored in the open roadstead of Funchal, in the beautiful islands we call the Madeiras.

The mountains looked surpassingly lovely, clad as they were in living green; ribbed with lava ridges; flecked with white cottages; riven by deep chasms purple with shade; the great slopes dashed with sunshine and mottled with shadows flung from the drifting squadrons of the sky, and the superb picture fitly crowned by towering peaks whose fronts were swept by the trailing fringes of the clouds.

But we could not land. We stayed all day and looked, we abused the man who invented quarantine, we held half a dozen mass-meetings and crammed them full of interrupted speeches, motions that fell still-born, amendments that came to naught, and resolutions that died from sheer exhaustion in trying to get before the house. At night we set sail.

We averaged four mass-meetings a week for the voyage — we seemed always in labor in this way, and yet so often fallaciously that whenever at long intervals we were safely delivered of a resolution, it was cause for public rejoicing, and we hoisted the flag and fired a salute.

Days passed — and nights; and then the beautiful Bermudas rose out of the sea, we entered the tortuous channel, steamed hither and thither among the bright summer islands, and rested at last under the flag of England and were welcome. We were not a nightmare here, where were civilization and intelligence in place of Spanish and Italian superstition, dirt and dread of cholera. A few days among the breezy groves, the flower gardens, the coral caves, and the lovely vistas of blue water that went curving in and out, disappearing and anon again appearing through jungle walls of brilliant foliage, restored the energies dulled by long drowsing on the ocean, and fitted us for our final

cruise — our little run of a thousand miles to New York —
America — HOME.

We bade good-bye to "our friends the Bermudians," as our
programme hath it — the majority of those we were most intimate with were negroes — and courted the great deep again. I
said the majority. We knew more negroes than white people,
because we had a deal of washing to be done, but we made some
most excellent friends among the whites, whom it will be a
pleasant duty to hold long in grateful remembrance.

We sailed, and from that hour all idling ceased. Such another
system of overhauling, general littering of cabins and packing of
trunks we had not seen since we let go the anchor in the harbor
of Beirout. Everybody was busy. Lists of all purchases had to be
made out, and values attached, to facilitate matters at the
custom-house. Purchases bought by bulk in partnership had to
be equitably divided, outstanding debts canceled, accounts compared, and trunks, boxes, and packages labeled. All day long the
bustle and confusion continued.

And now came our first accident. A passenger was running
through a gangway, between decks, one stormy night, when he
caught his foot in the iron staple of a door that had been
heedlessly left off a hatchway, and the bones of his leg broke at
the ankle. It was our first serious misfortune. We had traveled
much more than twenty thousand miles, by land and sea, in
many trying climates, without a single hurt, without a single case
of sickness, and without a death among five and sixty
passengers. Our good fortune had been wonderful. A sailor
jumped overboard at Constantinople one night, and was seen no
more, but it was suspected that his object was to desert, and
there was a slim chance, at least, that he reached the shore. But
the passenger list was complete. There was no name missing
from the register.

At last, one pleasant morning, we steamed up the harbor of
New York, all on deck, all dressed in Christian garb — by
special order, for there was a latent disposition in some quarters
to come out as Turks — and, amid a waving of handkerchiefs
from welcoming friends, the glad pilgrims noted the shiver of the
decks that told that ship and pier had joined hands again, and
the long, strange cruise was over. Amen.

A NEWSPAPER VALEDICTORY

In this place I will print an article which I wrote for the New
York *Herald* the night we arrived. I do it partly because my contract with my publishers makes it compulsory; partly because it
is a proper, tolerably accurate, and exhaustive summing-up of

the cruise of the ship and the performances of the pilgrims in foreign lands; and partly because some of the passengers have abused me for writing it, and I wish the public to see how thankless a task it is to put one's self to trouble to glorify unappreciative people. I was charged with "rushing into print" with these compliments. I did not rush. I had written news letters to the *Herald* sometimes, but yet when I visited the office that day I did not say anything about writing a valedictory. I did go to the *Tribune* office to see if such an article was wanted, because I belonged on the regular staff of the paper and it was simply a duty to do it. The managing editor was absent, and so I thought no more about it. At night when the *Herald's* request came for an article, I did not "rush." In fact, I demurred for a while, because I did not feel like writing compliments then, and therefore was afraid to speak of the cruise lest I might be betrayed into using other than complimentary language. However, I reflected that it would be a just and righteous thing to go down and write a kind word for the Hadjis — because parties not interested could not do it so feelingly as I, a fellow-Hadji, and so I penned the valedictory. I have read it, and read it again; and if there is a sentence in it that is not fulsomely complimentary to captain, ship, and passengers, *I* cannot find it. If it is not a chapter that any company might be proud to have a body write about them, my judgment is fit for nothing. With these remarks I confidently submit it to the unprejudiced judgment of the reader:

RETURN OF THE HOLY LAND EXCURSIONISTS — THE STORY OF THE CRUISE

To The Editor of The Herald:

The steamer *Quaker City* has accomplished at last her extraordinary voyage and returned to her old pier at the foot of Wall street. The expedition was a success in some respects, in some it was not. Originally it was advertised as a "pleasure excursion." Well, perhaps it was a pleasure excursion, but certainly it did not look like one; certainly it did not act like one. Anybody's and everybody's notion of a pleasure excursion is that the parties to it will of a necessity be young and giddy and somewhat boisterous. They will dance a good deal, sing a good deal, make love, but sermonize very little. Anybody's and everybody's notion of a well-conducted funeral is that there must be a hearse and a corpse, and chief mourners and mourners by courtesy, many old people, much solemnity, no levity, and a prayer and a sermon withal. Three-fourths of the *Quaker City's* passengers were between forty and seventy years of age! There was a picnic crowd for you! It may be supposed that the other fourth was composed of young girls. But it was not. It was chiefly composed of rusty old bachelors and a child of six years. Let us average the ages of the *Quaker City's* pilgrims and set the figure down as fifty years. Is any man insane enough to imagine that his picnic of patriarchs sang, made love, danced, laughed, told anecdotes, dealt in ungodly levity? In my experience they sinned little in these matters. No doubt it was presumed here at home that these frolicsome veterans laughed and sang and romped all day, and day after day, and kept up a noisy excitement from one end of the ship to the other; and that they played blindman's buff or danced quadrilles and waltzes on moonlight evenings on the quarter-deck; and that at odd moments of unoccupied time they jotted a laconic item or two in the journals they opened on such an elaborate plan when they left home, and then skurried off to their whist and euchre labors under the cabin lamps. If these things were presumed, the presumption was at fault. The venerable excursionists were not gay and frisky. They played no blindman's buff; they dealt not in whist; they shirked not the irksome journal, for alas! most of them were even writing books. They never romped, they talked but little, they never sang, save in the nighly prayer-meeting. The pleasure ship was a synagogue, and the pleasure trip was a funeral excursion without a corpse. (There is nothing exhilarating about a funeral excursion without a corpse.) A free, hearty laugh was a sound that was not heard oftener than once in seven days about those decks or in those cabins, and when it was heard it met with precious little sympathy. The excursionists danced, on three separate evenings, long, long ago (it seems an age) quadrilles, of a single set, made up of three ladies and five gentlemen (the latter with handkerchiefs around their arms to signify their sex), who timed their feet to the solemn wheezing of a melodeon; but even this melancholy orgie was voted to be sinful, and dancing was discontinued.

The pilgrims played dominoes when too much Josephus or Robinson's Holy Land Researches, or book-writing, made recreation necessary — for dominoes is about as mild and sinless a game as any in the world, perhaps, excepting always the ineffably insipid diversion they call croquet, which is a game where you don't pocket any balls and don't carom on any thing of any consequence, and when you are done nobody has to pay, and there are no refreshments to saw off, and, consequently, there isn't any satisfaction whatever about it — they played dominoes till they were rested, and then they blackguarded each other privately till prayer-time. When they were not seasick they were uncommonly prompt when the dinner-gong sounded. Such was our daily life on board the ship — solemnity, decorum, dinner, dominoes, devotions, slander. It was not lively enough for a pleasure trip; but if we had only had a corpse it would have made a noble funeral excursion. It is all over now; but when I look back, the idea of these venerable fossils skipping forth on a six-months picnic, seems exquisitely refreshing. The advertised title of the expedition — "The Grand Holy Land Pleasure Excursion" — was a misnomer. "The Grand Holy Land Funeral Procession" would have been better — much better.

Wherever we went, in Europe, Asia, or Africa, we made a sensation, and, I suppose I may add, created a famine. None of us had ever been any where before; we all hailed from the interior; travel was a wild novelty to us, and we conducted ourselves in accordance with the natural instincts that were in us, and trammeled ourselves with no ceremonies, no conventionalities. We always took care to make it understood that we were Americans — Americans! When we found that a good many foreigners had hardly ever heard of America, and that a good many more knew it only as a barbarous province away off somewhere, that had lately been at war with somebody, we pitied the ignorance of the Old World, but abated no jot of our importance. Many and many a simple community in the Eastern hemisphere will remember for years the incursion of the strange horde in the year of our Lord 1867, that called themselves Americans, and seemed to imagine in some unaccountable way that they had a right to be proud of it. We generally created a famine, partly because the coffee on the *Quaker City* was unendurable, and sometimes the more substantial fare was not strictly first-class; and partly because one naturally tires of sitting long at the same board and eating from the same dishes.

The people of those foreign countries are very, very ignorant. They looked curiously at the costumes we had brought from the wilds of America. They observed that we talked loudly at table sometimes. They noticed that we looked out for expenses, and got what we conveniently could out of a franc, and wondered where in the mischief we came from. In Paris they just simply opened their eyes and stared when we spoke to them in French! We never did succeed in making those idiots understand their own language. One of our passengers said to a shopkeeper, in reference to a proposed return to buy a pair of gloves, *"Allong restay trankeel — may be ve coom Moonday;"* and would you believe it, that shopkeeper, a born Frenchman, had to ask what it was that had been said. Sometimes it seems to me, somehow, that there must be a difference between Parisian French and *Quaker City* French.

The people stared at us everywhere, and we stared at them. We generally made them feel rather small, too, before we got done with them, because we bore down on them with America's greatness until we crushed them. And yet we took kindly to the manners and customs, and especially to the fashions of the various people we visited. When we left the Azores, we wore awful capotes and used fine tooth combs — successfully. When we came back from Tangier, in Arica, we were topped with fezzes of the bloodiest hue, hung with tassels like an Indian's scalp-lock. In Italy they naturally took us for distempered Garibaldians, and set a gunboat to look for anything significant in our changes of uniform. We made Rome howl. We could have made any place howl when we had all our clothes on. We got no fresh raiment in Greece — they had but little there of any kind. But at Constantinople, how we turned out! Turbans, scimetars, fezzes, horse-pistols, tunics, sashes, baggy trowsers, yellow slippers — Oh, we were gorgeous! The illustrious dogs of Constantinople barked their under jaws off, and even then failed to do us justice. They are all dead by this time. They could not go through such a run of business as we gave them and survive.

And then we went to see the Emperor of Russia. We just called on him as comfortably as if we had known him a century or so, and when we had finished our visit we variegated ourselves with selections from Russian costumes and sailed away again more picturesque than ever. In Smyrna we picked up camel's hair shawls and other dressy things from Persia; but in Palestine — ah, in Palestine — our splendid career ended. They didn't wear any clothes there to speak of. We were satisfied, and stopped. We made no experiments. We did not try their costume. But we astonished the natives of that country. We antonished them with such eccentricities of dress as we could muster. We prowled through the Holy Land, from Cesarea Philippi to Jerusalem and the Dead Sea, a weird procession of pilgrims, gotten up regardless of expense, solemn, gorgeous, green-spectacled, drowsing under blue umbrellas, and astride of a sorrier lot of horses, camels, and asses than those that came out of Noah's ark, after eleven months of seasickness and short rations. If ever those of Israel in Palestine forget when Gideon's Band went through there from America, they ought to be cursed once more and finished. It was rarest spectacle that ever astounded mortal eyes, perhaps.

Well, we were at home in Palestine. It was easy to see that that was the grand feature of the expedition. We had cared nothing much about Europe. We galloped through the Louvre, the Pitti, the Uffizzi, the Vatican — all the galleries — and through the picture and frescoed churches of Venice, Naples, and the cathedrals of Spain; some of us said that certain of the great works of the old masters were glorious creations of genius (we found it out in the guide-book, though we got hold of the wrong picture sometimes), and the others said they were disgraceful old daubs. We examined modern and ancient statuary with a critical eye in Florence, Rome, or anywhere we found it, and praised it if we saw fit, and if we didn't we said we preferred the wooden Indians in front of the cigar stores of America. But the Holy Land brought out all the enthusiasm. We fell into raptures by the barren shores of Galilee; we pondered at Tabor and at Nazareth; we exploded into poetry over the questionable loveliness of Esdraelon; we meditated at Jezreel and Samaria over the missionary zeal of Jehu; we rioted — fairly rioted among the holy places of Jerusalem; we bathed in Jordan and the Dead Sea, reckless whether our accident-insurance policies were extra-hazardous or not, and brought away so many jugs of precious water from both places that all the country from Jericho to the mountains of Moab will suffer from drouth this year, I think. Yet, the pilgrimage part of the excursion was its pet feature — there is no question about that. After dismal, smileless Palestine, beautiful Egypt had few charms for us. We merely glanced at it and it were ready for home.

They wouldn't let us land at Malta — quarantine; they would not let us land in Sardinia; nor at Algiers, Africa; nor at Malaga, Spain, nor Cadiz, nor at the Madeira Islands. So we got offended at all foreigners and turned our backs upon them and came home. I suppose we only stopped at the Bermudas because they were in the programme. We did not care anything about any place at all. We wanted to go home. Homesickness was abroad in the ship — it was epidemic. If the authorities of New York had known how badly we had it, they would have quarantined us here.

The grand pilgrimage is over. Good-bye to it, and a pleasant memory to it, I am able to say in all kindness. I bear no malice, no ill-will toward any individual that was connected with it, either as passenger or officer. Things I did not like at all yesterday I like very well to-day, now that I am at home, and always hereafter I shall be able to poke fun at the whole gang if the spirt so moves me to do, without ever saying a malicious word. The expedition accomplished all that its programme promised that it should accomplish, and we ought all to be satisfied with the management of the matter, certainly. Bye-bye!

MARK TWAIN.

I call that complimentary. and yet I never have received a word of thanks for it from the Hadjis; on the contrary, I speak nothing but the serious truth when I say that many of them even took exceptions to the article. In endeavoring to please them I slaved over that sketch for two hours, and had my labor for my pains. I never will do a generous deed again.

CONCLUSION

Nearly one year has flown since this notable pilgrimage was ended; and as I sit here at home in San Francisco thinking, I am moved to confess that day by day the mass of my memories of excursion have grown more and pleasant as the disagreeable incidents of travel which encumbered them flitted one by one of out my mind — and now, if the *Quaker City* were weighing her anchor to sail away on the very same cruise again, nothing could gratify me more than to be a passenger. With the same captain and even the same pilgrims, the same sinners. I was on excellent terms with eight or nine of the excursionists (they are my staunch friends yet), and was even on speaking terms with the rest of the sixty-five. I have been at sea quite enough to know that that was a very good average. Because a long sea-voyage not only brings out all the mean traits one has, and exaggerates them, but raises up others which he never suspected he posessed, and even creates new ones. A twelve months' voyage at sea would make an ordinary man a very miracle of meanness. On the other hand, if a man has good qualities, the spirit seldom moves him to exhibit them on shipboard, at least with any sort of emphasis. Now I am satisfied that our pilgrims are pleasant old people on shore; I am also satisfied that at sea on a second voyage they would be pleasanter, somewhat, than they were on our grand excursion, and so I say without hesitation that I would be glad enough to sail with them again. I could at least enjoy life with my handful of old friends. They could enjoy life with *their* cliques as well — passengers invariably divide up into cliques, on *all* ships.

And I will say, here, that I would rather travel with an excursion party of Methuselahs than have to be changing ships and comrades constantly, as people do who travel in the ordinary way. Those latter are always grieving over some *other* ship they have known and lost, and over *other* comrades whom diverging routes have separated from them. They learn to love a ship just in time to change it for another, and they become attached to a pleasant traveling companion only to lose him. They have that most dismal experience of being in a strange vessel, among strange people, who care nothing about them, and of undergoing the customary bullying by strange officers and the insolence of strange servants, repeated over and over again within the compass of every month. Thye have also that other misery of packing and unpacking trunks — of running the distressing gauntlet of custom-houses — of the anxieties attendant upon getting a mass of baggage from point to point on land in safety. I had rather sail with a whole brigade of patriarchs than suffer so. We never packed our trunks but twice — when we sailed from New York, and when we returned to it. Whenever we made a land journey, we estimated how many days we should be gone and what amount of clothing we should need, figured it down to a mathematical nicety, packed a valise or two accordingly, and left the trunks on board. We chose our comrades from among our old, tried friends, and started. We were never dependent upon strangers for companionship. We often had occasion to pity Americans whom we found traveling drearily among strangers with no friends to exchange pains and pleasures with. Whenever we were coming back from a land journey, our eyes sought one thing in the distance first — the ship — and when we saw it riding at anchor withe flag apeak, we felt as a returning wanderer feels when he sees his home. When we stepped on board, our cares vanished, our troubles were at an end — for the ship was home to us. We always had the same familiar old stateroom to go to, and fel safe and at peace and comfrotable again.

I have no fault to find with the manner in which our excursion was conducted. Its programme was faithfully carried out — a thing which surprised me, for great enterprises usually promise vastly more than they perform. It would be well if such an excursion could be gotten up every year and the system regularly inaugurated. Travel is fatal to prejudice, bigotry, and narrow-mindedness, and many of our people need it sorely on these accounts. Broad, wholesome, charitable views of men and things cannot be acquired by vegetating on one little corner of the earth all one's lifetime.

The excursion is ended, and has passed to its place among the things that were. But its varied scenes and its manifold incidents will linger pleasantly in our memories for many a year to come. Always on the wing, as we were, and merely pausing a moment to catch fitful glimpses of the wonders of half a world, we could not hope to receive ot retain vivid impressions of all it was our fortune to see. Yet our holiday flight has not been in vain — for above the confusion of vague recollections, certain of its best prized pictures lift themselves and will still continue perfect in tint and outline after their surroundings shall have faded away.

We shall remember something of pleasant France; and something also of Paris, though it flashed upon us a splendid meteor, and was gone again, we hardly knew how or where. We shall remember, always, how we saw majestic Gibraltar glorified with the rich coloring of a spanish sunset and swimming in a sea of rainbows. In fancy we shall see Milan again, and her stately cathedral with its marble wilderness of graceful spires. And Padua — Verona — Como, jeweled with stars; and patrician Venice, afloat on her stagnant flood — silent, desolate, haughty — scornful of her humbled state — wrapping herself in memories of her lost fleets, of battle and triumph, and all the pageantry of a glory that is departed.

We cannot forget Florence — Naples — nor the foretaste of heaven that is in the delicious atmosphere of Greece — and surely not Athens and the broken temples of the Acropolis. Surely not venerable Rome — nor the green plain that compasses her round about, contrasting its brightness with her gray decay — nor the ruined arches that stand apart in the plain and clothe their looped and windowed raggedness with vines. We shall remember St. Peter's; not as one sees it when he walks the streets of Rome and fancies all her domes are just alike, but as he sees it leagues away, when every meaner edifice has faded out of sight and that one dome looms superbly up in the flush of sunset, full of dignity and grace, strongly outlined as a mountain.

We shall remember Constantinople and the Bosperus — the colossal magnificence of of Baalbec — the Pyramids of Egypt — the prodigious form, the benignant countenance of the Sphynx — Oriental Smyrna — sacred Jerusalem — Damascus, the "Pearl of the East," the pride of Syria, the fabled Garden of Eden, the home of princes and genii of the Arabian Nights, the oldest metropolis on earth, the one city in all the world that has kept its name and held its place and looked serenely on while the

Kingdoms and Empires of four thousand years have risen to life, enjoyed their little season of pride and pomp, and then vanished and been forgotten!

"The Undertaker's Chat" appeared in November, 1870, under the title "Reminiscences of a Back Settlement" in Mark Twain's column in Galaxy, *a magazine of literature and entertainment. It began its metamorphosis in 1874 into book form through a 25ᶜ pamphlet called "Sketches". Finally, it appeared in the volume* Sketches, New and Old, *published by The American Publishing Company, Hartford, Connecticut, in 1875.*

THE UNDERTAKER'S CHAT

"Now that corpse," said the undertaker, patting the folded hands of deceased approvingly, "was a brick—every way you took him he was a brick. He was so real accommodating, and so modest-like and simple in his last moments. Friends wanted metallic burial-case—nothing else would do. *I* couldn't get it. There warn't going to be time—anybody could see that.

"Corpse said never mind, shake him up some kind of a box he could stretch out in comfortable, *he* warn't particular 'bout the general style of it. Said he went more on room than style, anyway in a last final container.

"Friends wanted a silver doorplate on the coffin, signifying who he was and wher' he was from. Now *you* know a fellow couldn't roust out such a gaily thing as that in a little country town like this. What did corpse say?

"Corpse said, whitewash his old canoe and dob his address and general destination onto it with a blacking brush and a stencil plate, 'long with a verse from some likely hymn or other, and p'int him for the tomb, and mark him C. O. D., and just let him flicker. *He* warn't distressed any more than you be—on the contrary just as ca'm and collected as a hearse-horse; said he judged that wher' he was going to a body would find it considerable better to attract attention by a picturesque moral character than a natty burial case with a swell doorplate on it.

"Splendid man, he was. I'd druther do for a corpse like that 'n any I've tackled in seven year. There's some satisfaction in buryin' a man like that. You feel that what you're doing is appreciated. Lord bless you, so's he got planted before he sp'iled, he was perfectly satisfied; said his relations meant well, *per*fectly well, but all them preparations was bound to delay the thing more or less, and he didn't wish to be kept layin' around. You never see such a clear head

as what he had—and so ca'm and so cool. Just a hunk of brains—
that is what *he* was. Perfectly awful. It was a ripping distance from
one end of that man's head to t'other. Often and over again he's
had brain fever a-raging in one place, and the rest of the pile didn't
know anything about it—didn't affect it any more than an Injun
insurrection in Arizona affects the Atlantic States.

"Well, the relations they wanted a big funeral, but corpse said he
was down on flummery—didn't want any procession—fill the hearse
full of mourners, and get out a stern line and tow *him* behind. He
was the most down on style of any remains I ever struck. A beautiful
simple-minded creature—it was what he was, you can depend on
that. He was just set on having things the way he wanted them, and
he took a solid comfort in laying his little plans. He had me measure
him and take a whole raft of directions; then he had the minister
stand up behind a long box with a tablecloth over it, to represent the
coffin, and read his funeral sermon, saying 'Angcore, angcore!' at
the good places, and making him scratch out every bit of brag about
him, and all the hifalutin; and then he made them trot out the choir
so's he could help them pick out the tunes for the occasion, and he
got them to sing 'Pop Goes the Weasel,' because he'd always liked
that tune when he was down-hearted, and solemn music made him
sad; and when they sung that with tears in their eyes (because they
all loved him), and his relations grieving around, he just laid there as
happy as a bug, and trying to beat time and showing all over how
much he enjoyed it; and presently he got worked up and excited, and
tried to join in, for, mind you, he was pretty proud of his abilities in
the singing line; but the first time he opened his mouth and was just
going to spread himself his breath took a walk.

"I never see a man snuffed out so sudden. Ah, it was a great loss—
a powerful loss to this poor little one-horse town. Well, well, well, I
hain't got time to be palavering along here—got to nail on the lid
and mosey along with him; and if you'll just give me a lift we'll skeet
him into the hearse and meander along. Relations bound to have it
so—don't pay no attention to dying injunctions, minute a corpse's
gone; but, if I had *my* way, if I didn't respect his last wishes and tow
him behind the hearse *I*'ll be cuss'd. I consider that whatever a
corpse wants done for his comfort is little enough matter, and a man
hain't got no right to deceive him or take advantage of him; and
whatever a corpse trusts me to do I'm a-going to *do,* you know, even
if it's to stuff him and paint him yaller and keep him for a
keepsake—you hear *me!*"

He cracked his whip and went lumbering away with his ancient
ruin of a hearse, and I continued my walk with a valuable lesson
learned—that a healthy and wholesome cheerfulness is not
necessarily impossible to *any* occupation. The lesson is likely to be
lasting, for it will take many months to obliterate the memory of the
remarks and circumstances that impressed it.

THE DANGER OF LYING IN BED

"The Danger of Lying in Bed" appeared in the Buffalo Express *and almost simultaneously in Mark Twain's* Galaxy *column early in 1871. It was later placed in the book* The $30,000 Bequest and Other Stories, *published in 1906 by Harper and Brothers, New York and London.*

THE DANGER OF LYING IN BED

The man in the ticket office said:

"Have an accident insurance ticket, also?"

"No," I said, after studying the matter over a little. "No, I believe not; I am going to be travelling by rail all day to-day. However, to-morrow I don't travel. Give me one for to-morrow."

The man looked puzzled. He said:

"But it is for accident insurance, and if you are going to travel by rail——"

"If I am going to travel by rail, I shan't need it. Lying at home in bed is the thing *I* am afraid of."

I had been looking into this matter. Last year I travelled twenty thousand miles, almost entirely by rail; the year before, I travelled over twenty-five thousand miles, half by sea and half by rail; and the year before that I travelled in the neighborhood of ten thousand miles, exclusively by rail. I suppose if I put in all the little odd journeys here and there, I may say I have travelled sixty thousand miles during the three years I have mentioned. *And never an accident.*

For a good while I said to myself every morning: "Now I have escaped thus far, and so the chances are just that much increased that I shall catch it this time. I will be shrewd, and buy an accident ticket." And to a dead moral certainty I drew a blank, and went to bed that night without a joint started or a bone splintered. I got tired of that sort of daily bother, and fell to buying accident tickets that were good for a month. I said to myself, "A man *can't* buy thirty blanks in one bundle."

But I was mistaken. There was never a prize in the lot. I could read of railway accidents every day—the newspaper atmosphere was foggy with them; but somehow they never came my way. I found

I had spent a good deal of money in the accident business, and had nothing to show for it. My suspicions were aroused, and I began to hunt around for somebody that had won in this lottery. I found plenty of people who had invested, but not an individual that had ever had an accident or made a cent. I stopped buying accident tickets and went to ciphering. The result was astounding. THE PERIL LAY NOT IN TRAVELLING, BUT IN STAYING AT HOME.

I hunted up statistics, and was amazed to find that after all the glaring newspaper headings concerning railroad disasters, less than *three hundred* people had really lost their lives by those disasters in the preceding twelve months. The Erie road was set down as the most murderous in the list. It had killed forty-six—or twenty-six, I do not exactly remember which, but I know the number was double that of any other road. But the fact straightway suggested itself that the Erie was an immensely long road, and did more business than any other line in the country; so the double number of killed ceased to be matter for surprise.

By further figuring, it appeared that between New York and Rochester the Erie ran eight passenger trains each way every day— sixteen altogether; and carried a daily average of 6,000 persons. That is about a million in six months—the population of New York city. Well, the Erie kills from thirteen to twenty-three persons out of *its* million in six months; and in the same time 13,000 of New York's million die in their beds! My flesh crept, my hair stood on end. "This is appalling!" I said. "The danger isn't in travelling by rail, but in trusting to those deadly beds. I will never sleep in a bed again."

I had figured on considerably less than one-half the length of the Erie road. It was plain that the entire road must transport at least eleven or twelve thousand people every day. There are many short roads running out of Boston that do fully half as much; a great many such roads. There are many roads scattered about the Union that do a prodigious passenger business. Therefore it was fair to presume that an average of 2,500 passengers a day for each road in the country would be about correct. There are 846 railway lines in our country, and 846 times 2,500 are 2,115,000. So the railways of America move more than two millions of people every day; six hundred and fifty millions of people a year, without counting the Sundays. They do that, too—there is no question about it; though where they get the raw material is clear beyond the jurisdiction of arithmetic; for I have hunted the census through and through, and I find that there are not that many people in the United States, by a matter of six hundred and ten millions at the very least. They must use some of the same people over again, likely.

San Francisco is one-eighth as populous as New York; there are 60 deaths a week in the former and 500 a week in the latter—if they have luck. That is 3,120 deaths a year in San Francisco, and eight times as many in New York—say about 25,000 or 26,000. The health of the two places is the same. So we will let it stand as a fair presumption that this will hold good all over the country, and that consequently 25,000 out of every million of people we have must die every year. That amounts to one-fortieth of our total population. Out of this million ten or twelve thousand are stabbed, shot, drowned, hanged, poisoned, or meet a similarly violent death in some other popular way, such as perishing by kerosene lamp and hoop-skirt conflagrations, getting buried in coal mines, falling off housetops, breaking through church or lecture-room floors, taking patent medicines, or committing suicide in other forms. The Erie railroad kills from 23 to 46; the other 845 railroads kill an average of one-third of a man each; and the rest of that million, amounting in the aggregate to the appalling figure of nine hundred and eighty-seven thousand six hundred and thirty-one corpses, die naturally in their beds!

You will excuse me from taking any more chances on those beds. The railroads are good enough for me.

And my advice to all people is, Don't stay at home any more than you can help; but when you have *got* to stay at home a while, buy a package of those insurance tickets and sit up nights. You cannot be too cautious.

[One can see now why I answered that ticket agent in the manner recorded at the top of this sketch.]

The moral of this composition is, that thoughtless people grumble more than is fair about railroad management in the United States. When we consider that every day and night of the year full fourteen thousand railway trains of various kinds, freighted with life and armed with death, go thundering over the land, the marvel is, *not* that they kill three hundred human beings in a twelvemonth, but that they do not kill three hundred times three hundred!

"Lionizing Murderers" first surfaced in London in *1872. Three years later it was brought out by The American Publishing Company, Hartford, Connecticut, in Twain's volume* Sketches, New and Old.

LIONIZING MURDERERS

I had heard so much about the celebrated fortune-teller
Madame ———, that I went to see her yesterday. She has a
dark complexion naturally, and this effect is heightened by
artificial aids which cost her nothing. She wears curls—very black
ones, and I had an impression that she gave their native
attractiveness a lift with rancid butter. She wears a reddish check
handkerchief, cast loosely around her neck, and it was plain that
her other one is slow getting back from the wash. I presume she
takes snuff. At any rate, something resembling it had lodged
among the hairs sprouting from her upper lip. I know she likes
garlic—I knew that as soon as she sighed. She looked at me
searchingly for nearly a minute, with her black eyes, and then said:

"It is enough. Come!"

She started down a very dark and dismal corridor—I stepping
close after her. Presently she stopped, and said that, as the way
was so crooked and dark, perhaps she had better get a light. But
it seemed ungallant to allow a woman to put herself to so much
trouble for me, and so I said:

"It is not worth while, madam. If you will heave another sigh,
I think I can follow it."

So we got along all right. Arrived at her official and mysterious
den, she asked me to tell her the date of my birth, the exact hour
of that occurrence, and the color of my grandmother's hair. I
answered as accurately as I could. Then she said:

"Young man, summon your fortitude—do not tremble. I am
about to reveal the past."

"Information concerning the *future* would be in a general way,
more—"

"Silence! You have had much trouble, some joy, some good
fortune, some bad. Your great grandfather was hanged."

"That is a l—"

"Silence! Hanged sir. But it was not his fault. He could not help it."

"I am glad you do him justice."

"Ah—grieve, rather, that the jury did. He was hanged. His star crosses yours in the fourth division, fifth sphere. Consequently you will be hanged also."

"In view of this cheerful—"

"I *must* have silence. Yours was not, in the beginning, a criminal nature, but circumstances changed it. At the age of nine you stole sugar. At the age of fifteen you stole money. At twenty you stole horses. At twenty-five you committed arson. At thirty, hardened in crime, you became an editor. You are now a public lecturer. Worse things are in store for you. You will be sent to Congress. Next, to the penitentiary. Finally, happiness will come again—all will be well—you will be hanged."

I was now in tears. It seemed hard enough to go to Congress; but to be hanged—this was too sad, too dreadful. The woman seemed surprised at my grief. I told her the thoughts that were in my mind. Then she comforted me.

"Why, man,"* she said, "hold up your head—*you* have nothing to grieve about. Listen. You will live in New Hampshire. In your sharp need and distress the Brown family will succor you—such of them as Pike the assassin left alive. They will be benefactors to you. When you shall have grown fat upon their bounty, and are grateful and happy, you will desire to make some modest return for these things, and so you will go to the house some night and brain the whole family with an axe. You will rob the dead bodies of your benefactors, and disburse your gains in riotous living among the rowdies and courtesans of Boston. Then you will be arrested, tried, condemned to be hanged, thrown into prison. Now is your happy day. You will be converted—you will be converted just as soon as every effort to compass pardon, commutation, or reprieve has failed—and then! Why, then, every monring and every afternoon, the best and purest young ladies of the village will assemble in your cell and sing hymns. This will show that

*In this paragraph the fortune-teller details the exact history of the Pike-Brown assassination case in New Hampsire, from the succoring and saving of the stranger Pike by the Browns, to the subsequent hanging and coffining of that treacherous miscreant. She adds nothing, invents nothing, exaggerates nothing (see any New England paper for November, 1869). This Pike-Brown case is selected merely as a type, to illustrate a custom that prevails, not in New Hampshire alone, but in every State of the Union—I mean the sentimental custom of visiting, petting, glorifying, and snuffling over murderers like this Pike, from the day they enter the jail under sentence of death until they swing from the gallows. The following extract from the *Temple Bar* (1886) reveals the fact that this custom is not confined to the United States:—"On December 31, 1841, a man named John Johnes, a shoemaker, murdered his sweetheart, Mary Hallam, the daughter of a respectable laborer, at Mansfield, in the county of Nottingham. He was executed on March 23, 1842. He was a man of unsteady habits, and gave way to violent fits of passion. The girl declined his addresses, and he said if he did not have her no one else should. After he had inflicted the first wound, which was not immediately fatal, she begged for her life, but seeing him assassination is respectable. Then you will write a touching letter, in which you will forgive all those recent Browns. This will excite the public admiration. No public can withstand magnanimity. Next, they will take you to the scaffold, with great *éclat*, at the head of an imposing procession composed of clergymen, officials, citizens generally, and young ladies walking pensively two and two, and bearing bouquets and immortelles. You will mount the scaffold, and while the great concourse stand uncovered in your presence, you will read your sappy little speech which the minister has written for you. And then, in the midst of a grand and impressive silence, they will swing you into per—— Paradise, my son. There will not be a dry eye on the ground. You will be a hero! Not a rough there but will envy you. Not a rough there but will resolve to emulate you. And next, a great procession will follow you to the tomb—will weep over your remains—the young ladies will sing again the hymns made dear by sweet associations connected with the jail, and, as a last tribute of affection, respect, and appreciation of your many sterling qualities, they will walk two and two around your bier, and strew wreaths of flowers on it. And lo! you are canonized. Think of it, son—ingrate, assassin, robber of the dead, drunken brawler among thieves and harlots in the slums of Boston one month, and the pet of the pure and innocent daughters of the land the next! A bloody and hateful devil—a bewept, bewailed, and sainted martyr—all in a month! Fool!—so noble a fortune, and yet you sit here grieving!"

"No, madame," I said, "you do me wrong, you do, indeed. I am perfectly satisfied. I did not know before that my great-grandfather was hanged, but it is of no consequence. He has probably ceased to bother about it by this time—and I have not commenced yet. I confess, madame, that I do something in the way of editing and lecturing, but the other crimes you mention have escaped my memory. Yet I must have committed them—you would not deceive a stranger. But let the past be as it was, and let the future be as it may—these are nothing. I have only cared for one thing. I have always felt that I should be hanged some day, and somehow the thought has annoyed me considerably; but if you can only assure me that I shall be hanged in New Hampshire—"

resolved, asked for time to pray. He said that he would pray for both, and completed the crime. The wounds were inflicted by a shoemaker's knife, and her throat was cut barbarously. After this he dropped on his knees some time, and prayed God to have mercy on two unfortunate lovers. He made no attempt to escape, and confessed the crime. After his imprisonment he behaved in a most decorous manner; he won upon the good opinion of the jail chaplain, and he was visited by the Bishop of Lincoln. It does not appear that he expressed any contrition for the crime, but seemed to pass away with triumphant certainty that he was going to rejoin his victim in heaven. *He was visited by some pious and benevolent ladies of Nottingham, some of whom declared he was a child of God, if ever there was one. One of the ladies sent him a white camelia to wear at his execution.*

"Not a shadow of a doubt!"

"Bless you, my benefactress!—excuse this embrace—you have removed a great load from my breast. To be hanged in New Hampshire is happiness—it leaves an honored name behind a man, and introduces him at once into the best New Hampshire society in the other world."

I then took leave of the fortune-teller. But, seriously, is it well to glorify a murderous villain on the scaffold, as Pike was glorified in New Hampshire? Is it well to turn the penalty for a bloody crime into a reward? Is it just to do it? Is it safe?

A TRUE STORY
REPEATED WORD FOR WORD
AS I HEARD IT

"A True Story Repeated Word for Word as I Heard It" *was printed in* Atlantic Monthly *in November, 1874. As Mark Twain's first work to be published in that magazine, "A True Story" established a long and beneficial relationship between the author and the* Atlantic *editors. This work was collated into* Sketches, New and Old, *published in 1875 by The American Publishing Company, Hartford, Connecticut.*

A TRUE STORY
REPEATED WORD FOR WORD AS I HEARD IT

It was summer time, and twilight. We were sitting on the porch of the farmhouse, on the summit of the hill, and "Aunt Rachel" was sitting respectfully below our level, on the steps—for she was our servant, and colored. She was of mighty frame and stature; she was sixty years old, but her eye was undimmed and her strength unabated. She was a cheerful, hearty soul, and it was no more trouble for her to laugh than it is for a bird to sing. She was under fire now, as usual when the day was done. That is to say, she was being chaffed without mercy, and was enjoying it. She would let off peal after peal of laughter, and then sit with her face in her hands and shake with throes of enjoyment which she could no longer get breath enough to express. At such a moment as this a thought occurred to me, and I said:

"Aunt Rachel, how is it that you've lived sixty years and never had any trouble?"

She stopped quaking. She paused, and there was a moment of silence. She turned her face over her shoulder toward me, and said, without even a smile in her voice:

"Misto C——, is you in 'arnest?"

It surprised me a good deal; and it sobered my manner and my speech, too. I said:

"Why, I thought—that is, I meant—why, you *can't* have had any trouble. I've never heard you sigh, and never seen your eye when there wasn't a laugh in it."

She faced fairly around now, and was full of earnestness.

"Has I had any trouble? Misto C——, I's gwyne to tell you, den I leave it to you. I was bawn down 'mongst de slaves; I knows all 'bout slavery, 'case I ben one of 'em my own se'f. Well, sah, my ole man—dat's my husban'—he was lovin' an' kind to me, jist as kind as you is to yo' own wife. An' we had chil'en—seven chil'en

—an' we loved dem chil'en jist de same as you loves yo' chil'en. Dey was black, but de Lord can't make no chil'en so black but what dey mother loves 'em an' wouldn't give 'em up, no, not for anything dat's in dis whole world.

"Well, sah, I was raised in ole Fo'ginny, but my mother she was raised in Maryland; an' my *souls!* she was turrible when she'd git started! My *lan'!* but she'd make de fur fly! When she'd git into dem tantrums, she always had one word dat she said. She'd straighten herse'f up an' put her fists in her hips an' say, 'I want you to understan' dat I wa'nt bawn in the mash to be fool' by trash! I's one o' de ole Blue Hen's Chickens, *I* is!' 'Ca'se, you see, dat's what folks dat's bawn in Maryland calls deyselves, an' dey's proud of it. Well, dat was her word. I don't ever forgit it, beca'se she said it so much, an' beca'se she said it one day when my little Henry tore his wris' awful, and most busted his head, right up at de top of his forehead, an' de niggers didn't fly aroun' fas' enough to 'tend to him. An' when dey talk' back at her, she up an' she says, 'Look-a-heah!' she says, 'I want you niggers to understan' dat I wa'nt bawn in de mash to be fool' by trash! I's one o' de ole Blue Hen's Chickens, *I* is!' an' den she clar' dat kitchen an' bandage' up de chile herse'f. So I says dat word, too, when I's riled.

"Well, bymeby my ole mistis say she's broke, an' she got to sell all de niggers on de place. An' when I heah dat dey gwyne to sell us all off at oction in Richmon', oh, de good gracious! I know what dat mean!"

Aunt Rachel had gradually risen, while she warmed to her subject, and now she towered above us, black against the stars.

"Dey put chains on us an' put us on a stan' as high as dis po'ch —twenty foot high—an' all de people stood aroun', crowds an' crowds. An' dey'd come up dah an' look at us all roun', an' squeeze our arm, an' make us git up an' walk, an' den say, 'Dis one too ole,' or 'Dis one lame,' or 'Dis one don't 'mount to much.' An' dey sole my ole man, an' took him away, an' dey begin to sell my chil'en an' take *dem* away, an' I begin to cry; an' de man say, 'Shet up yo' dem blubberin',' an' hit me on de mouf wid his han'. An' when de las' one was gone but my little Henry, I grab' *him* clost up to my breas' so, an' I ris up an' says, 'You shan't take him away,' I says; 'I'll kill de man dat tetches him!' I says. But my little Henry whisper an' say, 'I gwyne to run away, an' den I work an' buy yo' freedom.' Oh, bless de chile, he always so good! But dey got him—dey got him, de men did; but I took and tear de clo'es mos' off of 'em an' beat 'em over de head wid my chain; an' *dey* give it to *me,* too, but I didn't mine dat.

"Well, dah was my ole man gone, an' all my chil'en, all my seven chil'en—an' six of 'em I hain't set eyes on ag'in to dis day, an' dat's twenty-two year ago las' Easter. De man dat bought me b'long' in Newbern, an' he took me dah. Well, bymeby de years roll on an' de waw come. My marster he was a Confedrit colonel, an' I was his family's cook. So when de Unions took dat town, dey all run away an' lef' me all by myse'f wid de other niggers in dat mons'us big house. So de big Union officers move in dah, an' dey ask me would I cook for *dem*. 'Lord bless you,' says I, 'dat's what I's *for*.'

"Dey wa'nt no small-fry officers, mine you, dey was de biggest dey *is;* an' de way dey made dem sojers mosey roun'! De Gen'l he tole me to boss dat kitchen; an' he say, 'If anybody come meddlin' wid you, you jist make 'em walk chalk; don't you be afeared,' he say; 'you's 'mong frens now.'

"Well, I thinks to myse'f, if my little Henry ever got a chance to run away, he'd make to de Norf, o' course. So one day I comes in dah whar de big officers was, in de parlor, an' I drops a kurtchy, so, an' I up an' tole 'em 'bout my Henry, dey a-listenin' to my troubles jist de same as if I was white folks; an' I says, 'What I come for is beca'se if he got away and got up Norf whar you gemmen comes from, you might 'a' seen him, maybe, an' could tell me so as I could fine him ag'in; he was very little, an' he had a sk-yar on his lef' wris' an' at de top of his forehead.' Den dey look mournful, an' de Gen'l says, 'How long sence you los' him?' an' I say, 'Thirteen year.' Den de Gen'l say, 'He wouldn't be little no mo' now—he's a man!'

"I never thought o' dat befo'! He was only dat little feller to *me* yit. I never thought 'bout him growin' up an' bein' big. But I see it den. None o' de gemmen had run acrost him, so dey couldn't do nothin' for me. But all dat time, do' *I* didn't know it, my Henry *was* run off to de Norf, years an' years, an' he was a barber, too, an' worked for hisse'f. An' bymeby, when de waw come he ups an' he says: 'I's done barberin',' he says, 'I's gwyne to fine my ole mammy, less'n she's dead.' So he sole out an' went to whar dey was recruitin', an' hired hisse'f out to de colonel for his servant; an' den he went all froo de battles everywhah, huntin' for his ole mammy; yes, indeedy, he'd hire to fust one officer an' den another, tell he'd ransacked de whole Souf; but you see *I* didn't know nuffin 'bout *dis*. How was *I* gwyne to know it?

"Well, one night we had a big sojer ball; de sojers dah at Newbern was always havin' balls an' carryin' on. Dey had 'em in my kitchen, heaps o' times, 'ca'se it was so big. Mine you, I was *down* on sich doin's; beca'se my place was wid de officers, an' it rasp me to have dem common sojers cavortin' roun' my kitchen like dat. But I alway' stood aroun' an' kep' things straight, I did; an' sometimes dey'd git my dander up, an' den I'd make 'em clar dat kitchen, mine I *tell* you!

"Well, one night—it was a Friday night—dey comes a whole plattoon f'm a *nigger* ridgment dat was on guard at de house—de

house was headquarters, you know—an' den I was jist a-*bilin'!*
Mad? I was jist a-*boomin'!* I swelled aroun', an' swelled aroun';
I jist was a-itchin' for 'em to do somefin for to start me. *An'* dey
was a-waltzin' an' a-dancin'! *my!* but dey was havin' a time! an'
I jist a-swellin' an' a-swellin' up! Pooty soon, 'long comes *sich* a
spruce young nigger a-sailin' down de room wid a yaller wench
roun' de wais'; an' roun' an' roun' an roun' dey went, enough to
make a body drunk to look at 'em; an' when dey got abreas' o' me,
dey went to kin' o' balacin' aroun' fust on one leg an' den on
t'other, an' smilin' at my big red turban, an' makin' fun, an' I
ups an' says *'Git* along wid you!—rubbage!'' De young man's face
kin' o' changed, all of a sudden, for 'bout a second, but den he
went to smilin' ag'in, same as he was befo'. Well, 'bout dis time, in
comes some niggers dat played music and b'long' to de ban', an'
dey *never* could git along widout puttin' on airs. An' de very fust
air dey put on dat night, I lit into 'em! Dey laughed, an' dat made
me wuss. De res' o' de niggers got to laughin', an' den my soul *alive*
but I was hot! My eye was jist a-blazin'! I jist straightened myself
up so—jist as I is now, plum to de ceilin', mos'—an' I digs my
fists into my hips, an' I says, 'Look-a-heah!'' I says, 'I want you
niggers to understan' dat I wa'nt bawn in de mash to be fool' by
trash! I's one o' de ole Blue Hen's Chickens, *I* is!' an' den I see dat
young man stan' a-starin' an' stiff, lookin' kin' o' up at de ceilin'
like he fo'got somefin, an' couldn't 'member it no mo'. Well, I jist
march' on dem niggers—so, lookin' like a gen'l—an' dey jist cave'
away befo' me an' out at de do'. An' as dis young man was a-goin'
out, I heah him say to another nigger, 'Jim,' he says, 'you go 'long
an' tell de cap'n I be on han' 'bout eight o'clock in de mawnin';
dey's somefin on my mine,' he says; 'I don't sleep no mo' dis night.
You go 'long,' he says, 'an' leave me by my own se'f.'

"Dis was 'bout one o'clock in de mawnin'. Well, 'bout seven, I
was up an' on han', gettin' de officers' breakfast. I was a-stoopin'
down by de stove—jist so, same as if yo' foot was de stove—an' I'd
opened de stove do' wid my right han'—so, pushin' it back, jist as
I pushes yo' foot—an' I'd jist got de pan o' hot biscuits in my han'
an' was 'bout to raise up, when I see a black face come aroun'
under mine, an' de eyes a-lookin' up into mine, jist as I's a-lookin'
up clost under yo' face now; an' I jist stopped *right dah,* an' never
budged! jist gazed an' gazed so; an' de pan begin to tremble, an'
all of a sudden I *knowed!* De pan drop' on de flo' an' I grab his
lef' han' an' shove back his sleeve—jist so, as I's doin' to you—an'
den I goes for his forehead an' push de hair back so, an' 'Boy!''
I says, 'if you an't my Henry, what is you doin' wid dis welt on yo'
wris' an' dat sk-yar on yo' forehead? De Lord God ob heaven be
praise', I got my own ag'in!'

"Oh, no Misto C——, *I* hain't had no trouble. An' no *joy!*''

AN ENCOUNTER WITH AN INTERVIEWER

"An Encounter With an Interviewer" appeared as a contribution to Lotos Leaves, *published in Boston in 1875. Then in 1878 it was incorporated by the author into* Punch, Brothers, Punch! and Other Sketches, *released by Slote, Woodman and Company of New York. From there it went into* The Stolen White Elephant, Etc., *published in Boston in 1882 by James R. Osgood and Company. In 1896 "An Encounter With an Interviewer" found its final home in* Tom Sawyer Abroad, Tom Sawyer, Detective, and Other Stories, Etc., Etc., *published by Harper and Brothers, New York.*

AN ENCOUNTER WITH AN INTERVIEWER

The nervous, dapper, "peart" young man took the chair I offered him, and said he was connected with the *Daily Thunderstorm,* and added—

"Hoping it's no harm, I've come to interview you."

"Come to what?"

"*Interview* you."

"Ah! I see. Yes—yes. Um! Yes—yes."

I was not feeling bright that morning. Indeed, my powers seemed a bit under a cloud. However, I went to the bookcase, and when I had been looking six or seven minutes, I found I was obliged to refer to the young man. I said—

"How do you spell it?"

"Spell what?"

"Interview."

"Oh my goodness! what do you want to spell it for?"

"I don't want to spell it; I want to see what it means."

"Well, this is astonishing, I must say. *I* can tell you what it means, if you—if you—"

"Oh, all right! That will answer, and much obliged to you, too."

"In, *in,* ter, *ter, in*ter—"

"Then you spell it with an *I?*"

"Why, certainly!"

"Oh, that is what took me so long."

"Why, my *dear* sir, what did *you* propose to spell it with?"

"Well, I—I—hardly know. I had the Unabridged, and I was ciphering around in the back end, hoping I might tree her among the pictures. But it's a very old edition."

"Why, my friend, they wouldn't have a *picture* of it in even the latest e— My dear sir, I beg your pardon, I mean no harm in the world, but you do not look as—as—intelligent as I had expected you would. No harm—I mean no harm at all."

"Oh, don't mention it! It has often been said, and by people who would not flatter and who could have no inducement to flatter, that I am quite remarkable in that way. Yes—yes; they always speak of it with rapture."

"I can easily imagine it. But about this interview. You know it is the custom, now, to interview any man who has become notorious."

"Indeed, I had not heard of it before. It must be very interesting. What do you do it with?"

"Ah, well—well—well—this is disheartening. It *ought* to be done with a club in some cases; but customarily it consists in the interviewer asking questions and the interviewed answering them. It is all the rage now. Will you let me ask you certain questions calculated to bring out the salient points of your public and private history?"

"Oh, with pleasure—with pleasure. I have a very bad memory, but I hope you will not mind that. That is to say, it is an irregular memory—singularly irregular. Sometimes it goes in a gallop, and then again it will be as much as a fortnight passing a given point. This is a great grief to me."

"Oh, it is no matter, so you will try to do the best you can."

"I will. I will put my whole mind on it."

"Thanks. Are you ready to begin?"

"Ready."

Q. How old are you?

A. Nineteen, in June.

Q. Indeed! I would have taken you to be thirty-five or six. Where were you born?

A. In Missouri.

Q. When did you begin to write?

A. In 1836.

Q. Why, how could that be, if you are only nineteen now?

A. I don't know. It does seem curious, somehow.

Q. It does, indeed. Whom do you consider the most remarkable man you ever met?

A. Aaron Burr.

Q. But you never could have met Aaron Burr, if you are only nineteen years—

A. Now, if you know more about me than I do, what do you ask me for?

Q. Well, it was only a suggestion; nothing more. How did you happen to meet Burr?

A. Well, I happened to be at his funeral one day, and he asked me to make less noise, and—

Q. But, good heavens! if you were at his funeral, he must have been dead; and if he was dead, how could he care whether you made a noise or not?

A. I don't know. He was always a particular kind of a man that way.

Q. Still, I don't understand it at all. You say he spoke to you, and that he was dead.

A. I didn't say he was dead.

Q. But wasn't he dead?

A. Well, some said he was, some said he wasn't.

Q. What did you think?

A. Oh, it was none of my business! It wasn't any of my funeral.

Q. Did you— However, we can never get this matter straight. Let me ask about something else. What was the date of your birth?

A. Monday, October 31st, 1693.

Q. What! Impossible! That would make you a hundred and eighty years old. How do you account for that?

A. I don't account for it at all.

Q. But you said at first you were only nineteen, and now you make yourself out to be one hundred and eighty. It is an awful discrepancy.

A. Why, have you noticed that? (Shaking hands.) Many a time it has seemed to me like a discrepancy, but somehow I couldn't make up my mind: How quick you notice a thing!

Q. Thank you for the compliment, as far as it goes. Had you, or have you, any brothers or sisters?

A. Eh! I—I—I think so—yes—but I don't remember.

Q. Well, that is the most extraordinary statement I ever heard!

A. Why, what makes you think that?

Q. How could I think otherwise? Why, look here! Who is this a picture of on the wall? Isn't that a brother of yours?

A. Oh! yes, yes, yes! Now you remind me of it; that *was* a brother of mine. That's William—*Bill* we called him. Poor old Bill!

Q. Why? Is he dead, then?

A. Ah! well, I suppose so. We never could tell. There was a great mystery about it.

Q. That is sad, very sad. He disappeared, then?

A. Well, yes, in a sort of general way. We buried him.

Q. Buried him! *Buried* him, without knowing whether he was dead or not?

A. Oh, no! Not that. He was dead enough.

Q. Well, I confess that I can't understand this. If you buried him, and you knew he was dead—

A. No! no! We only thought he was.

Q. Oh, I see! He came to life again?

A. I bet he didn't.

Q. Well, I never heard anything like this. *Somebody* was dead. *Somebody* was buried. Now, where was the mystery?

A. Ah! that's just it! That's it exactly. You see, we were twins— defunct and I—and we got mixed in the bath-tub when we were only two weeks old, and one of us was drowned. But we didn't know which. Some think it was Bill. Some think it was me.

Q. Well, that *is* remarkable. What do *you* think!

A. Goodness knows! I would give whole worlds to know. This solemn, this awful mystery has cast a gloom over my whole life. But I will tell you a secret now, which I never have revealed to any creature before. One of us had a peculiar mark—a large mole on the back of his left hand; that was *me. That child was the one that was drowned!*

Q. Very well, then, I don't see that there is any mystery about it, after all.

A. You don't? Well, *I* do. Anyway, I don't see how they could ever have been such a blundering lot as to go and bury the wrong child. But, 'sh!—don't mention it where the family can hear of it. Heaven knows they have heart-breaking troubles enough without adding this.

Q. Well, I believe I have got material enough for the present, and I am very much obliged to you for the pains you have taken. But I was a good deal interested in that account of Aaron Burr's funeral. Would you mind telling me what particular circumstance it was that made you think Burr was such a remarkable man?

A. Oh! it was a mere trifle! Not one man in fifty would have noticed it at all. When the sermon was over, and the procession all ready to start for the cemetery, and the body all arranged nice in the hearse, he said he wanted to take a last look at the scenery, and so he *got up and rode with the driver.*

Then the young man reverently withdrew. He was very pleasant company, and I was sorry to see him go.

ABOUT BARBERS

"About Barbers" *made its debut in 1871 in Mark Twain's column in* Galaxy. *It was subsequently placed in Mark Twain's* Sketches, New and Old, *published in 1875 by The American Publishing Company of Hartford, Connecticut. Like many of Twain's* Galaxy *articles, "About Barbers" underwent substantial revision when published in book form.*

ABOUT BARBERS

All things change except barbers, the ways of barbers, and the surroundings of barbers. These never change. What one experiences in a barber's shop the first time he enters one is what he always experiences in barbers' shops afterward till the end of his days. I got shaved this morning as usual. A man approached the door from Jones street as I approached it from Main—a thing that always happens. I hurried up, but it was of no use; he entered the door one little step ahead of me, and I followed in on his heels and saw him take the only vacant chair, the one presided over by the best barber. It always happens so. I sat down, hoping that I might fall heir to the chair belonging to the better of the remaining two barbers, for he had already begun combing his man's hair, while his comrade was not quite done rubbing up and oiling his customer's locks. I watched the probabilities with strong interest. When I saw that No. 2 was gaining on No. 1 my interest grew to solicitude. When No. 1 stopped a moment to make change on a bath ticket for a new comer, and lost ground in the race, my solicitude rose to anxiety. When No. 1 caught up again, and both he and his comrade were pulling the towels away and brushing the powder from their customer's cheeks, and it was about an even thing which one would say "Next!" first, my very breath stood still with the suspense. But when at the culminating moment No. 1 stopped to pass a comb a couple of times through his customer's eyebrows, I saw that he had lost the race by a single instant, and I rose indignant and quitted the shop, to keep from falling into the hands of No. 2; for I have none of that enviable firmness that enables a man to look calmly into the eyes of a waiting barber and tell him he will wait for his fellow-barber's chair.

I stayed out fifteen minutes, and then went back, hoping for better luck. Of course all the chairs were occupied now, and four men sat waiting, silent, unsociable, distraught, and looking bored, as men always do who are waiting their turn in a barber's shop. I sat down in one of the iron-armed compartments of an old sofa, and put in the time for a while reading the framed advertisements of all sorts of quack nostrums for dyeing and coloring the hair. Then I read the greasy names on the private bay-rum bottles; read the names and noted the numbers on the private shaving cups in the pigeon-holes; studied the stained and damaged cheap prints on the walls, of battles, early Presidents, and voluptuous recumbent sultanas, and the tiresome and everlasting young girl putting her grandfather's spectacles on; execrated in my heart the cheerful canary and the distracting parrot that few barbers' shops are without. Finally, I searched out the least dilapidated of last year's illustrated papers that littered the foul center-table, and conned their unjustifiable misrepresentations of old forgotten events.

At last my turn came. A voice said "Next!" and I surrendered to—No. 2, of course. It always happens so. I said meekly that I was in a hurry, and it affected him as strongly as if he had never heard it. He shoved up my head, and put a napkin under it. He plowed his fingers into my collar and fixed a towel there. He explored my hair with his claws and suggested that it needed trimming. I said I did not want it trimmed. He explored again and said it was pretty long for the present style—better have a little taken off; it needed it behind especially. I said I had had it cut only a week before. He yearned over it reflectively a moment, and then asked with a disparaging manner, who cut it? I came back at him promptly with a "You did!" I had him there. Then he fell to stirring up his lather and regarding himself in the glass, stopping now and then to get close and examine his chin critically or inspect a pimple. Then he lathered one side of my face thoroughly, and was about to lather the other, when a dog fight attracted his attention, and he ran to the window and stayed and saw it out, losing two shillings on the result in bets with the other barbers, a thing which gave me great satisfaction. He finished lathering, and then began to rub in the suds with his hand.

He now began to sharpen his razor on an old suspender, and was delayed a good deal on account of a controversy about a cheap masquerade ball he had figured at the night before, in red cambric and bogus ermine, as some kind of a king. He was so gratified with being chaffed about some damsel whom he had smitten with his charms that he used every means to continue the controversy by pretending to be annoyed at the chaffings of his fellows. This matter begot more surveyings of himself in the glass, and he put down his razor and brushed his hair with elaborate care, plastering an inverted arch of it down on his forehead, accomplishing an accurate "part" behind, and brushing the two wings forward over his ears with nice exactness. In the meantime the lather was drying on my face, and apparently eating into my vitals.

Now he began to shave, digging his fingers into my countenance to stretch the skin and bundling and tumbling my head this way and that as convenience in shaving demanded. As long as he was on the tough sides of my face I did not suffer; but when he began to rake, and rip, and tug at my chin, the tears came. He now made a handle of my nose, to assist him in shaving the corners of my upper lip, and it was by this bit of circumstantial evidence that I discovered that a part of his duties in the shop was to clean the kerosene lamps. I had often wondered in an indolent way whether the barbers did that, or whether it was the boss.

About this time I was amusing myself trying to guess where he would be most likely to cut me this time, but he got ahead of me, and sliced me on the end of the chin before I had got my mind made up. He immediately sharpened his razor—he might have done it before. I do not like a close shave, and would not let him go over me a second time. I tried to get him to put up his razor, dreading that he would make for the side of my chin, my pet tender spot, a place which a razor cannot touch twice without making trouble; but he said he only wanted to just smooth off one little roughness, and in the same moment he slipped his razor along the forbidden ground, and the dreaded pimple-signs of a close shave rose up smarting and answered to the call. Now he soaked his towel in bay rum, and slapped it all over my face nastily; slapped it over as if a human being ever yet washed his face in that way. Then he dried it by slapping with the dry part of the towel, as if a human being ever dried his face in such a fashion; but a barber seldom rubs you like a Christian. Next he poked bay rum into the cut place with his towel, then choked the wound with powdered starch, then soaked it with bay rum again, and would have gone on soaking and powdering it forevermore, no doubt, if I had not rebelled and begged off. He powdered my whole face now, straightened me up, and began to plow my hair thoughtfully with his hands. Then he suggested a shampoo, and said my hair needed it badly, very badly. I observed that I shampooed it myself very thoroughly in the bath yesterday. I "had him" again. He next recommended some of "Smith's Hair Glorifier," and offered to sell me a bottle. I declined. He praised the new perfume, "Jones's Delight of the Toilet," and proposed to sell me some of that. I declined again. He tendered me a toothwash atrocity of his own invention, and when I declined offered to trade knives with me.

He returned to business after the miscarriage of this last enterprise, sprinkled me all over, legs and all, greased my hair in defiance of my protest against it, rubbed and scrubbed a good deal of it out by the roots, and combed and brushed the rest, parting it behind, and plastering the eternal inverted arch of hair down on my forehead, and then, while combing my scant eyebrows and defiling them with pomade, strung out an account of the achievements of a six-ounce black and tan terrier of his till I heard the whistles blow for noon, and knew I was five minutes too late for the train. Then he snatched away the towel, brushed it lightly about my face, passed his comb through my eyebrows once more, and gaily sang out "Next!"

This barber fell down and died of apoplexy two hours later. I am waiting over a day for my revenge—I am going to attend his funeral.

THE FACTS CONCERNING THE
RECENT CARNIVAL OF CRIME
IN CONNECTICUT

"The Facts Concerning the Recent Carnival of Crime in Connecticut" was first published in Atlantic Monthly, *June 1876. It then appeared in the volume* A True Story and the Recent Carnival of Crime, *published in 1877 by James R. Osgood and Company, Boston. The story was transformed slightly between publications.*

THE FACTS CONCERNING THE RECENT CARNIVAL OF CRIME IN CONNECTICUT

I was feeling blithe, almost jocund. I put a match to my cigar, and just then the morning's mail was handed in. The first superscription I glanced at was in a handwriting that sent a thrill of pleasure through and through me. It was Aunt Mary's; and she was the person I loved and honored most in all the world, outside of my own household. She had been my boyhood's idol; maturity, which is fatal to so many enchantments, had not been able to dislodge her from her pedestal; no, it had only justified her right to be there, and placed her dethronement permanently among the impossibilities. To show how strong her influence over me was, I will observe that long after everybody else's "*do*-stop-smoking" had ceased to affect me in the slightest degree, Aunt Mary could still stir my torpid conscience into faint signs of life when she touched upon the matter. But all things have their limit, in this world. A happy day came at last, when even Aunt Mary's words could no longer move me. I was not merely glad to see that day arrive; I was more than glad—I was grateful; for when its sun had set, the one alloy that was able to mar my enjoyment of my aunt's society was gone. The remainder of her stay with us that winter was in every way a delight. Of course she pleaded with me just as earnestly as ever, after that blessed day, to quit my pernicious habit, but to no purpose whatever; the moment she opened the subject I at once became calmly, peacefully, contentedly indifferent—absolutely, adamantinely indifferent. Consequently the closing weeks of that memorable visit melted away as pleasantly as a dream, they were so freighted, for me, with tranquil satisfaction. I could not have enjoyed my pet vice more if my gentle tormentor had been a smoker herself, and an advocate of the practice. Well, the sight of her handwriting reminded me that I was getting very hungry to see her again. I easily

guessed what I should find in her letter. I opened it. Good! just as
I expected; she was coming! Coming this very day, too, and by the
morning train; I might expect her any moment.

I said to myself, "I am thoroughly happy and content, now. If my
most pitiless enemy could appear before me at this moment, I would
freely right any wrong I may have done him."

Straightway the door opened, and a shrivelled, shabby dwarf
entered. He was not more than two feet high. He seemed to be about
forty years old. Every feature and every inch of him was a trifle out
of shape; and so, while one could not put his finger upon any
particular part and say, "This is a conspicuous deformity," the
spectator perceived that this little person was a deformity as a
whole—a vague, general, evenly blended, nicely adjusted deformity.
There was a fox-like cunning in the face and the sharp little eyes,
and also alertness and malice. And yet, this vile bit of human
rubbish seemed to bear a sort of remote and ill-defined resemblance
to me! It was dully perceptible in the mean form, the countenance,
and even the clothes, gestures, manner, and attitudes of the creature.
He was a far-fetched, dim suggestion of a burlesque upon me, a
caricature of me in little. One thing about him struck me forcibly,
and most unpleasantly: he was covered all over with a fuzzy, greenish
mould, such as one sometimes sees upon mildewed bread. The sight
of it was nauseating.

He stepped along with a chipper air, and flung himself into a
doll's chair in a very free-and-easy way, without waiting to be asked.
He tossed his hat into the waste-basket. He picked up my old chalk
pipe from the floor, gave the stem a wipe or two on his knee, filled
the bowl from the tobacco-box at his side, and said to me in a tone of
pert command—

"Gimme a match!"

I blushed to the roots of my hair; partly with indignation, but
mainly because it somehow seemed to me that this whole
performance was very like an exaggeration of conduct which I
myself had sometimes been guilty of in my intercourse with familiar
friends—but never, never with strangers, I observed to myself.
I wanted to kick the pygmy into the fire, but some incomprehensible
sense of being legally and legitimately under his authority forced me
to obey his order. He applied the match to the pipe, took a
contemplative whiff or two, and remarked, in an irritatingly
familiar way—

"Seems to me it's devilish odd weather for this time of year."

I flushed again, and in anger and humiliation as before; for the
language was hardly an exaggeration of some that I have uttered in
my day, and moreover was delivered in a tone of voice and with an
exasperating drawl that had the seeming of a deliberate travesty of
my style. Now there is nothing I am quite so sensitive about as a
mocking imitation of my drawling infirmity of speech. I spoke up

sharply and said—

"Look here, you miserable ash-cat! you will have to give a little more attention to your manners, or I will throw you out of the window!"

The manikin smiled a smile of malicious content and security, puffed a whiff of smoke contemptuously toward me, and said, with a still more elaborate drawl—

"Come—go gently, now; don't put on *too* many airs with your betters."

This cool snub rasped me all over, but it seemed to subjugate me, too, for a moment. The pygmy contemplated me awhile with his weasel eyes, and then said, in a peculiarly sneering way—

"You turned a tramp away from your door this morning."

I said crustily—

"Perhaps I did, perhaps I didn't. How do *you* know?"

"Well, I know. It isn't any matter *how* I know."

"Very well. Suppose I *did* turn a tramp away from the door— what of it?"

"Oh, nothing; nothing in particular. Only you lied to him."

"I *didn't*! That is, I—"

"Yes, but you did; you lied to him."

I felt a guilty pang—in truth I had felt it forty times before that tramp had travelled a block from my door—but still I resolved to make a show of feeling slandered; so I said—

"That is a baseless impertinence. I said to the tramp—"

"There—wait. You were about to lie again. *I* know what you said to him. You said the cook was gone down town and there was nothing left behind the door, and plenty of provisions behind *her.*"

This astonishing accuracy silenced me; and it filled me with wondering speculations, too, as to how this cub could have got his information. Of course he could have culled the conversation from the tramp, but by what sort of magic had he contrived to find out about the concealed cook? Now the dwarf spoke again:—

"It was rather pitiful, rather small, in you to refuse to read that poor young woman's manuscript the other day, and give her an opinion as to its literary value; and she had come so far, too, and *so* hopefully. Now *wasn't* it?"

I felt like a cur! And I had felt so every time the thing had recurred to my mind, I may as well confess. I flushed hotly and said—

"Look here, have you nothing better to do than prowl around prying into other people's business? Did that girl tell you that?"

"Never mind whether she did or not. The main thing is, you did that contemptible thing. And you felt ashamed of it afterwards. Aha! you feel ashamed of it *now!*"

This with a sort of devilish glee. With fiery earnestness I responded—

"I told that girl, in the kindest, gentlest way, that I could not consent to deliver judgment upon *any* one's manuscript, because an individual's verdict was worthless. It might underrate a work of high merit and lose it to the world, or it might overrate a trashy production and so open the way for its infliction upon the world. I said that the great public was the only tribunal competent to sit in judgment upon a literary effort, and therefore it must be best to lay it before that tribunal in the outset, since in the end it must stand or fall by that mighty court's decision anyway."

"Yes, you said all that. So you did, you juggling, small-souled shuffler! And yet when the happy hopefulness faded out of that poor girl's face, when you saw her furtively slip beneath her shawl the scroll she had so patiently and honestly scribbled at—so ashamed of her darling now, so proud of it before—when you saw the gladness go out of her eyes and the tears come there, when she crept away so humbly who had come so—"

"Oh, peace! peace! peace! Blister your merciless tongue, haven't all these thoughts tortured me enough without *your* coming here to fetch them back again!"

Remorse! remorse! It seemed to me that it would eat the very heart out of me! And yet that small fiend only sat there leering at me with joy and contempt, and placidly chuckling. Presently he began to speak again. Every sentence was an accusation, and every accusation a truth. Every clause was freighted with sarcasm and derision, every slow-dropping word burned like vitriol. The dwarf reminded me of times when I had flown at my children in anger and punished them for faults which a little inquiry would have taught me that others, and not they, had committed. He reminded me of how I had disloyally allowed old friends to be traduced in my hearing, and been too craven to utter a word in their defence. He reminded me of many dishonest things which I had done; of many which I had procured to be done by children and other irresponsible persons; of some which I had planned, thought upon, and longed to do, and been kept from the performance by fear of consequences only. With exquisite cruelty he recalled to my mind, item by item, wrongs and unkindnesses I had inflicted and humiliations I had put upon friends since dead, "who died thinking of those injuries, maybe, and grieving over them," he added, by way of poison to the stab.

"For instance," said he, "take the case of your younger brother, when you two were boys together, many a long year ago. He always lovingly trusted in you with a fidelity that your manifold treacheries were not able to shake. He followed you about like a dog, content to suffer wrong and abuse if he might only be with you; patient under these injuries so long as it was your hand that inflicted them. The latest picture you have of him in health and strength must be such a comfort to you! You pledged your honor that if he would let you blindfold him no harm should come to him; and then, giggling and choking over the rare fun of the joke, you led him to a brook thinly glazed with ice, and pushed him in; and how you did laugh! Man, you will never forget the gentle, reproachful look he gave you as he struggled shivering out, if you live a thousand years! Oho! you see it now, you see it *now!*"

"Beast, I have seen it a million times, and shall see it a million more! and may you rot away piecemeal, and suffer till doomsday what I suffer now, for bringing it back to me again!"

The dwarf chuckled contentedly, and went on with his accusing history of my career. I dropped into a moody, vengeful state, and suffered in silence under the merciless lash. At last this remark of his gave me a sudden rouse:—

"Two months ago, on a Tuesday, you woke up, away in the night, and fell to thinking, with shame, about a peculiarly mean and pitiful act of yours toward a poor ignorant Indian in the wilds of the Rocky Mountains in the winter of eighteen hundred and—"

"Stop a moment, devil! Stop! Do you mean to tell me that even my very *thoughts* are not hidden from you?"

"It seems to look like that. Didn't you think the thoughts I have just mentioned?"

"If I didn't, I wish I may never breathe again! Look here, friend—look me in the eye. Who *are* you?"

"Well, who do you think?"

"I think you are Satan himself. I think you are the devil."

"No."

"No? Then who *can* you be?"

"Would you really like to know?"

"*Indeed* I would."

"Well, I am your *Conscience!*"

In an instant I was in a blaze of joy and exultation. I sprang at the creature, roaring—

"Curse you, I have wished a hundred million times that you were tangible, and that I could get my hands on your throat once! Oh, but I will wreak a deadly vengeance on—"

Folly! Lightning does not move more quickly than my Conscience did! He darted aloft so suddenly that in the moment my fingers clutched the empty air he was already perched on the top of the high bookcase, with his thumb at his nose in token of derision. I flung the poker at him, and missed. I fired the boot-jack. In a blind rage I flew from place to place, and snatched and hurled any missile that came handy; the storm of books, inkstands, and chunks of coal gloomed the air and beat about the manikin's perch relentlessly, but all to no purpose; the nimble figure dodged every shot; and not only that, but burst into a cackle of sarcastic and triumphant laughter as I sat down exhausted. While I puffed and gasped with fatigue and excitement, my Conscience talked to this effect:—

"My good slave, you are curiously witless—no, I mean characteristically so. In truth, you are always consistent, always yourself, always an ass. Otherwise it must have occurred to you that if you attempted this murder with a sad heart and a heavy conscience, I would droop under the burdening influence instantly. Fool, I should have weighed a ton, and could not have budged from the floor; but instead, you are so cheerfully anxious to kill me that your conscience is as light as a feather; hence I am away up here out of your reach. I can almost respect a mere ordinary sort of fool; but *you*—pah!"

I would have given anything, then, to be heavy-hearted, so that I could get this person down from there and take his life, but I could no more be heavy-hearted over such a desire than I could have sorrowed over its accomplishment. So I could only look longingly up at my master, and rave at the ill-luck that denied me a heavy conscience the one only time that I had ever wanted such a thing in my life. By-and-by I got to musing over the hour's strange adventure, and of course my human curiosity began to work. I set myself to framing in my mind some questions for this fiend to answer. Just then one of my boys entered, leaving the door open behind him, and exclaimed,—

"My! what *has* been going on, here? The bookcase is all one riddle of—"

I sprang up in consternation, and shouted—

"Out of this! Hurry! Jump! Fly! Shut the door! Quick, or my Conscience will get away!"

The door slammed to, and I locked it. I glanced up and was grateful, to the bottom of my heart, to see that my owner was still my prisoner. I said—

"Hang you, I might have lost you! Children are the heedlessest creatures. But look here, friend, the boy did not seem to notice you at all; how is that?"

"For a very good reason. I am invisible to all but you."

I made mental note of that piece of information with a good deal of satisfaction. I could kill this miscreant now, if I got a chance, and no one would know it. But this very reflection made me so light-hearted that my Conscience could hardly keep his seat, but was like to float aloft toward the ceiling like a toy balloon. I said, presently—

"Come, my Conscience, let us be friendly. Let us fly a flag of truce for a while. I am suffering to ask you some questions."

"Very well. Begin."

"Well, then, in the first place, why were you never visible to me before?"

"Because you never asked to see me before; that is, you never asked in the right spirit and the proper form before. You were just in the right spirit this time, and when you called for your most pitiless enemy I was that person by a very large majority, though you did not suspect it."

"Well, did that remark of mine turn you into flesh and blood?"

"No. It only made me visible to you. I am unsubstantial, just as other spirits are."

This remark prodded me with a sharp misgiving. If he was unsubstantial, how was I going to kill him? But I dissembled, and said persuasively—

"Conscience, it isn't sociable of you to keep at such a distance. Come down and take another smoke."

This was answered with a look that was full of derision, and with this observation added—

"Come where you can get at me and kill me? The invitation is declined with thanks."

"All right," said I to myself; "so it seems a spirit *can* be killed, after all; there will be one spirit lacking in this world, presently, or I lose my guess." Then I said aloud—

"Friend—"

"There; wait a bit. I am not your friend, I am your enemy; I am not your equal, I am your master. Call me 'my lord,' if you please. You are too familiar."

"I don't like such titles. I am willing to call you *sir*. That is as far as—"

"We will have no argument about this. Just obey; that is all. Go on with your chatter."

"Very well, my lord—since nothing but my lord will suit you—I was going to ask you how long you will be visible to me?"

"Always!"

I broke out with strong indignation: "This is simply an outrage. That is what I think of it. You have dogged, and dogged, and *dogged* me, all the days of my life, invisible. That was misery enough; now to have such a looking thing as you tagging after me like another shadow all the rest of my days is an intolerable prospect. You have my opinion, my lord; make the most of it."

"My lad, there was never so pleased a conscience in this world as I was when you made me visible. It gives me an inconceivable advantage. *Now,* I can look you straight in the eye, and call you names, and leer at your, jeer at you, sneer at you; and *you* know what eloquence there is in visible gesture and expression, more especially when the effect is heightened by audible speech. I shall always address you henceforth in your o-w-n s-n-i-v-e-l-l-in-g d-r-a-w-l— baby!"

I let fly with the coal-hod. No result. My lord said—

"Come, come! Remember the flag of truce!"

"Ah, I forgot that. I will try to be civil; and *you* try it, too, for a novelty. The idea of a *civil* conscience! It is a good joke; an excellent joke. All the consciences *I* have every heard of were nagging, badgering, fault-finding, execrable savages! Yes; and always in a sweat about some poor little insignificant trifle or other—destruction catch the lot of them, *I* say! I would trade mine for the small-pox and seven kinds of consumption, and be glad of the chance. Now tell me, why *is* it that a conscience can't haul a man over the coals once, for an offence, and then let him alone? Why is it that it wants to keep on pegging at him, day and night and night and day, week in and week out, forever and ever, about the same old thing? There is no sense in that, and no reason in it. I think a conscience that will act like that is meaner than the very dirt itself."

"Well, *we* like it; that suffices."

"Do you do it with the honest intent to improve a man?"

That question produced a sarcastic smile, and this reply:—

"No, sir. Excuse me. We do it simply because it is 'business.' It is our trade. The *purpose* of it *is* to improve the man, but *we* are merely disinterested agents. We are appointed by authority, and haven't anything to say in the matter. We obey orders and leave the consequences where they belong. But I am willing to admit this much: we *do* crowd the orders a trifle when we get a chance, which is most of the time. We enjoy it. We are instructed to remind a man a few times of any error; and I don't mind acknowledging that we try to give pretty good measure. And when we get hold of a man of a peculiarly sensitive nature, oh, but we do haze him! I have known consciences to come all the way from China and Russia to see a person of that kind put through his paces, on a special occasion. Why, I knew a man of that sort who had accidentally crippled a mulatto baby; the news went abroad, and I wish you may never commit another sin if the consciences didn't flock from all over the earth to enjoy the fun and help his master exercise him. That man walked the floor in torture for forty-eight hours, without eating or sleeping, and then blew his brains out. The child was perfectly well again in three weeks."

"Well, you are a precious crew, not to put it too strong. I think I begin to see, now, why you have always been a trifle inconsistent with me. In your anxiety to get all the juice you can out of a sin, you make a man repent of it in three or four different ways. For instance, you found fault with me for lying to that tramp, and I suffered over that. But it was only yesterday that I told a tramp the square truth, to wit, that, it being regarded as bad citizenship to encourage vagrancy, I would give him nothing. What did you do *then?* Why, you made me say to myself, 'Ah, it would have been so much kinder and more blameless to ease him off with a little white lie, and send him away feeling that if he could not have bread, the gentle treatment was at least something to be grateful for!' Well, I suffered all day about *that.* Three days before I had fed a tramp, and fed him freely, supposing it a virtuous act. Straight off you said, 'O false citizen, to have fed a tramp!' and I suffered as usual. I gave a tramp work; you objected to it—*after* the contract was made, of course; you never speak up beforehand. Next, I *refused* a tramp work; you objected to *that.* Next I proposed to kill a tramp; you kept me awake all night, oozing remorse at every pore. Sure I was going to be right *this* time, I sent the next tramp away with my benediction; and I wish you may live as long as I do, if you didn't make me smart all night again because I didn't kill him. Is there *any* way of satisfying that malignant invention which is called a conscience?"

"Ha, ha! this is luxury! Go on!"

"But come, now, answer me that question. *Is* there any way?"

"Well, none that I propose to tell *you,* my son. Ass! I don't care *what* act you may turn your hand to, I can straightway whisper a word in your ear and make you think you have committed a dreadful meanness. It is my *business*—and my joy—to make you repent of *every*thing you do. If I have fooled away any opportunities it was not intentional; I beg to assure you it was not intentional!"

"Don't worry; you haven't missed a trick that *I* know of. I never did a thing in all my life, virtuous or otherwise, that I didn't repent of in twenty-four hours. In church last Sunday I listened to a charity sermon. My first impulse was to give three hundred and fifty dollars; I repented of that and reduced it a hundred; repented of that and reduced it another hundred; repented of that and reduced it another hundred; repented of that and reduced the remaining fifty to twenty-five; repented of that and came down to fifteen; repented of that and dropped to two dollars and a half; when the plate came around at last, I repented once more and contributed ten cents. Well, when I got home, I did wish goodness I had that ten cents back again! You never *did* let me get through a charity sermon without having something to sweat about."

"Oh, and I never shall, I never shall. You can always depend on me."

"I think so. Many and many's the restless night I've wanted to take you by the neck. If I could only get hold of you now!"

"Yes, no doubt. But I am not an ass; I am only the saddle of an ass. But go on, go on. You entertain me more than I like to confess."

"I am glad of that. (You will not mind my lying a little, to keep in practice.) Look here; not to be too personal, I think you are about the shabbiest and most contemptible little shrivelled-up reptile that can be imagined. I am grateful enough that you are invisible to other people, for I should die with shame to be seen with such a mildewed monkey of a conscience as *you* are. Now if you were five or six feet high, and—"

"Oh, come! who is to blame?"

"*I* don't know."

"Why, you are; nobody else."

"Confound you, I wasn't consulted about your personal appearance."

"I don't care, you had a good deal to do with it, nevertheless. When you were eight or nine years old, I was seven feet high, and as pretty as a picture."

"I wish you had died young! So you have grown the wrong way, have you?"

"Some of us grow one way and some the other. You had a large conscience once; if you've a small conscience now, I reckon there are reasons for it. However, both of us are to blame, you and I. You see, you used to be conscientious about a great many things; morbidly so, I may say. It was a great many years ago. You probably do not remember it, now. Well, I took a great interest in my work, and I so enjoyed the anguish which certain pet sins of yours afflicted you with, that I kept pelting at you until I rather overdid the matter. You began to rebel. Of course I began to lose ground, then, and shrivel a little,—diminish in stature, get mouldy, and grow deformed. The more I weakened, the more stubbornly you fastened on to those particular sins; till at last the places on my person that represent those vices became as callous as shark skin. Take smoking, for instance. I played that card a little too long, and I lost. When people plead with you at this late day to quit that vice, that old callous place seems to enlarge and cover me all over, like a shirt of mail. It exerts a mysterious, smothering effect; and presently I, your faithful hater, your devoted Conscience, go sound asleep! Sound? It is no name for it. I couldn't hear it thunder at such a time. You have some few other vices—perhaps eighty, or maybe ninety—that affect me in much the same way."

"This is flattering; you must be asleep a good part of your time."

"Yes, of late years. I should be asleep *all* the time, but for the help I get."

"Who helps you?"

"Other consciences. Whenever a person whose conscience I am acquainted with tries to plead with you about the vices you are callous to, I get my friend to give his client a pang concerning some villany of his own, and that shuts off his meddling and starts him off to hunt personal consolation. My field of usefulness is about trimmed down to tramps, budding authoresses, and that line of goods, now; but don't you worry—I'll harry you on *them* while they last! Just you put your trust in me."

"I think I can. But if you had only been good enough to mention these facts some thirty years ago, I should have turned my particular attention to sin, and I think that by this time I should not only have had you pretty permanently asleep on the entire list of human vices, but reduced to the size of a homoeopathic pill, at that. That is about the style of conscience *I* am pining for. If I only had you shrunk down to a homoeopathic pill, and could get my hands on you, would I put you in a glass case for a keepsake? No, sir. I would give you to a yellow dog! That is where *you* ought to be—you and all your tribe. You are not fit to be in society, in my opinion. Now another question. Do you know a good many consciences in this section?"

"Plenty of them."

"I would give anything to see some of them! Could you bring them here? And would they be visible to me?"

"Certainly not."

"I suppose I ought to have known that, without asking. But no matter, you can describe them. Tell me about my neighbor Thompson's conscience, please."

"Very well. I know him intimately; have known him many years. I knew him when he was eleven feet high and of a faultless figure. But he is very rusty and tough and misshapen now, and hardly ever interests himself about anything. As to his present size—well, he sleeps in a cigar box."

"Likely enough. There are few smaller, meaner men in this region than Hugh Thompson. Do you know Robinson's conscience?"

"Yes. He is a shade under four and a half feet high; used to be a blonde; is a brunette, now, but still shapely and comely."

"Well, Robinson is a good fellow. Do you know Tom Smith's conscience?"

"I have known him from childhood. He was thirteen inches high, and rather sluggish, when he was two years old—as nearly all of us are, at that age. He is thirty-seven feet high, now, and the stateliest figure in America. His legs are still racked with growing-pains, but he has a good time, nevertheless. Never sleeps. He is the most active and energetic member of the New England Conscience Club; is president of it. Night and day you can find him pegging away at Smith, panting with his labor, sleeves rolled up, countenance all alive with enjoyment. He has got his victim splendidly dragooned, now. He can make poor Smith imagine that the most innocent little thing he does is an odious sin; and then he sets to work and almost tortures the soul out of him about it."

"Smith is the noblest man in all this section, and the purest; and yet is always breaking his heart because he cannot be good! Only a conscience *could* find pleasure in heaping agony upon a spirit like that. Do you know my aunt Mary's conscience?"

"I have seen her at a distance, but am not acquainted with her. She lives in the open air altogether, because no door is large enough to admit her."

"I can believe that. Let me see. Do you know the conscience of that publisher who once stole some sketches of mine for a 'series' of his, and then left me to pay the law expenses I had to incur in order to choke him off?"

"Yes. He has a wide fame. He was exhibited, a month ago, with some other antiquities, for the benefit of a recent Member of the Cabinet's conscience, that was starving in exile. Tickets and fares were high, but I travelled for nothing by pretending to be the conscience of an editor, and got in for half-price by representing myself to be the conscience of a clergyman. However, the publisher's conscience, which was to have been the main feature of the entertainment, was a failure—as an exhibition. He was there, but what of that? The management had provided a microscope with a magnifying power of only thirty thousand diameters, and so nobody got to see him, after all. There was great and general dissatisfaction, of course, but—''

Just here there was an eager footstep on the stair; I opened the door, and my aunt Mary burst into the room. It was a joyful meeting, and a cheery bombardment of questions and answers concerning family matters ensued. By-and-by my aunt said—

"But I am going to abuse you a little now. You promised me, the day I saw you last, that you would look after the needs of the poor family around the corner as faithfully as I had done it myself. Well, I found out by accident that you failed of your promise. *Was* that right?"

In simple truth, I never had thought of that family a second time! And now such a splintering pang of guilt shot through me! I glanced up at my Conscience. Plainly, my heavy heart was affecting him. His body was drooping forward; he seemed about to fall from the bookcase. My aunt continued:—

"And think how you have neglected my poor *protégée* at the almshouse, you dear, hard-hearted promise-breaker!"

I blushed scarlet, and my tongue was tied. As the sense of my guilty negligence waxed sharper and stronger, my Conscience began to sway heavily back and forth; and when my aunt, after a little pause, said in a grieved tone, "Since you never once went to see her, maybe it will distress you now to know that that poor child died, months ago, utterly friendless and forsaken!" my Conscience could no longer bear up under the weight of my sufferings, but tumbled headlong from his high perch and struck the floor with a dull, leaden thump. He lay there writhing with pain and quaking with apprehension, but straining every muscle in frantic efforts to get up. In a fever of expectancy I sprang to the door, locked it, placed my back against it, and bent a watchful gaze upon my struggling master. Already my fingers were itching to begin their murderous work.

"Oh, what *can* be the matter!" exclaimed my aunt, shrinking from me, and following with her frightened eyes the direction of mine. My breath was coming in short, quick gasps now, and my excitement was almost uncontrollable. My aunt cried out,—

"Oh, do not look so! You appall me! Oh, what can the matter be? What is it you see? Why do you stare so? Why do you work your fingers like that?"

"Peace, woman!" I said, in a hoarse whisper. "Look elsewhere; pay no attention to me; it is nothing—nothing. I am often this way. It will pass in a moment. It comes from smoking too much."

My injured lord was up, wild-eyed with terror, and trying to hobble toward the door. I could hardly breathe, I was so wrought up. My aunt wrung her hands, and said—

"Oh, I knew how it would be; I knew it would come to this at last! Oh, I implore you to crush out that fatal habit while it may yet be time! You must not, you shall not be deaf to my supplications longer!" My struggling Conscience showed sudden signs of weariness! "Oh, promise me you will throw off this hateful slavery of tobacco!" My Conscience began to reel drowsily, and grope with his hands—enchanting spectacle! "I beg you, I beseech you, I implore you! Your reason is deserting you! There is madness in your eye! It flames with frenzy! Oh, hear me, hear me, and be saved! See, I plead with you on my very knees!" As she sank before me my Conscience reeled again, and then drooped languidly to the floor, blinking toward me a last supplication for mercy, with heavy eyes. "Oh, promise, or you are lost! Promise, and be redeemed! Promise! Promise and live!" With a long-drawn sigh my conquered Conscience closed his eyes and fell fast asleep!

With an exultant shout I sprang past my aunt, and in an instant I had my life-long foe by the throat. After so many years of waiting and longing, he was mine at last. I tore him to shreds and fragments. I rent the fragments to bits. I cast the bleeding rubbish into the fire, and drew into my nostrils the grateful incense of my burnt-offering. At last, and forever, my Conscience was dead!

I was a free man! I turned upon my poor aunt, who was almost petrified with terror, and shouted—

"Out of this with your paupers, your charities, your reforms, your pestilent morals! You behold before you a man whose life-conflict is done, whose soul is at peace; a man whose heart is dead to sorrow, dead to suffering, dead to remorse; a man WITHOUT A CONSCIENCE! In my joy I spare you, though I could throttle you and never feel a pang! Fly!"

She fled. Since that day my life is all bliss. Bliss, unalloyed bliss. Nothing in all the world could persuade me to have a conscience again. I settled all my old outstanding scores, and began the world anew. I killed thirty-eight persons during the first two weeks—all of them on account of ancient grudges. I burned a dwelling that interrupted my view. I swindled a widow and some orphans out of their last cow, which is a very good one, though not thoroughbred, I believe. I have also committed scores of crimes, of various kinds, and have enjoyed my work exceedingly, whereas it would formerly have broken my heart and turned my hair gray, I have no doubt.

In conclusion I wish to state, by way of advertisement, that medical colleges desiring assorted tramps for scientific purposes, either by the gross, by cord measurement, or per ton, will do well to examine the lot in my cellar before purchasing elsewhere, as these were all selected and prepared by myself, and can be had at a low rate, because I wish to clear out my stock and get ready for the spring trade.

The Adventures of Tom Sawyer was published in our Centennial year and has frequently been credited with starting the literary regeneration of the South. The only pre-publication appearance was the whitewash scene, printed in the Philadelphia Sunday Republic *July 23, 1876. The novel was published by The American Publishing Company, Hartford, Connecticut. Although it was first printed on a good quality paper, the publishers quickly changed to a heavy bulking stock because the public complained that* Tom Sawyer *did not appear as thick as some of Twain's previous books which were the same price — a device still used by many book publishers today.*

THE ADVENTURES OF TOM SAWYER

PREFACE

Most of the adventures recorded in this book really occurred; one or two were experiences of my own, the rest those of boys who were schoolmates of mine. Huck Finn is drawn from life; Tom Sawyer also, but not from an individual—he is a combination of the characteristics of three boys whom I knew, and therefore belongs to the composite order of architecture.

The odd superstitions touched upon were all prevalent among children and slaves in the West at the period of this story—that is to say, thirty or forty years ago.

Although my book is intended mainly for the entertainment of boys and girls, I hope it will not be shunned by men and women on that account, for part of my plan has been to try to pleasantly remind adults of what they once were themselves, and of how they felt and thought and talked, and what queer enterprises they sometimes engaged in.

THE AUTHOR.

HARTFORD, 1876.

CHAPTER I

"Tom!"

No answer.

"TOM!"

No answer.

"What's gone with that boy, I wonder? You TOM!"

No answer.

The old lady pulled her spectacles down and looked over them about the room; then she put them up and looked out under them. She seldom or never looked *through* them for so small a thing as a boy; they were her state pair, the pride of her heart, and were built for "style," not service—she could have seen through a pair of stove lids just as well. She looked perplexed for a moment, and then said, not fiercely, but still loud enough for the furniture to hear:

"Well, I lay if I get hold of you I'll—"

She did not finish, for by this time she was bending down and punching under the bed with the broom, and so she needed breath to punctuate the punches with. She resurrected nothing but the cat.

"I never did see the beat of that boy!"

She went to the open door and stood in it and looked out among the tomato vines and "jimpson" weeds that constituted the garden. No Tom. So she lifted up her voice at an angle calculated for distance, and shouted:

"Y-o-u-u Tom!"

There was a slight noise behind her and she turned just in time to seize a small boy by the slack of his roundabout and arrest his flight.

"There! I might 'a' thought of that closet. What you been doing in there?"

"Nothing."

"Nothing! Look at your hands. And look at your mouth. What *is* that truck?"

"*I* don't know, aunt."

"Well, *I* know. It's jam—that's what it is. Forty times I've said if you didn't let that jam alone I'd skin you. Hand me that switch."

The switch hovered in the air—the peril was desperate—

"My! Look behind you, aunt!"

The old lady whirled round, and snatched her skirts out of danger. The lad fled, on the instant, scrambled up the high board-fence, and disappeared over it.

His aunt Polly stood surprised a moment, and then broke into a gentle laugh.

"Hang the boy, can't I never learn anything? Ain't he played me tricks enough like that for me to be looking out for him by this time? But old fools is the biggest fools there is. Can't learn an old dog new tricks, as the saying is. But my goodness, he never plays them alike, two days, and how is a body to know what's coming? He

'pears to know just how long he can torment me before I get my
dander up, and he knows if he can make out to put me off for a
minute or make me laugh, it's all down again and I can't hit him a
lick. I ain't doing my duty by that boy, and that's the Lord's truth,
goodness knows. Spare the rod and spile the child, as the Good Book
says. I'm a laying up sin and suffering for us both. *I* know. He's full
of the Old Scratch, but laws-a-me! he's my own dead sister's boy,
poor thing, and I ain't got the heart to lash him, somehow. Every
time I let him off, my conscience does hurt me so, and every time I
hit him my old heart most breaks. Well-a-well, man that is born
of woman is of few days and full of trouble, as the Scripture says,
and I reckon it's so. He'll play hookey this evening,* and I'll just be
obleeged to make him work, tomorrow, to punish him. It's
mighty hard to make him work Saturdays, when all the boys is
having holiday, but he hates work more than he hates anything else,
and I've *got* to do some of my duty by him, or I'll be the ruination
of the child."

Tom did play hookey, and he had a very good time. He got back
home barely in season to help Jim, the small colored boy, saw
next-day's wood and split the kindlings before supper—at least
he was there in time to tell his adventures to Jim while Jim did
three-fourths of the work. Tom's younger brother (or rather,
half-brother) Sid, was already through with his part of the work
(picking up chips) for he was a quiet boy, and had no adventurous,
troublesome ways.

While Tom was eating his supper, and stealing sugar as
opportunity offered, Aunt Polly asked him questions that were full
of guile, and very deep—for she wanted to trap him into damaging
revealments. Like many other simple-hearted souls, it was her pet
vanity to believe she was endowed with a talent for dark and
mysterious diplomacy, and she loved to contemplate her most
transparent devices as marvels of low cunning. Said she:

"Tom, it was middling warm in school, warn't it?"

"Yes'm."

"Powerful warm, warn't it?"

"Yes'm."

"Didn't you want to go in a-swimming, Tom?"

A bit of a scare shot through Tom—a touch of uncomfortable
suspicion. He searched Aunt Polly's face, but it told him nothing.
So he said:

"No'm—well, not very much."

The old lady reached out her hand and felt Tom's shirt, and said:

"But you ain't too warm now, though. And it flattered her to
reflect that she had discovered that the shirt was dry without
anybody knowing that that was what she had in her mind. But in
spite of her. Tom knew where the wind lay, now. So he forestalled
what might be the next move:

*South-western for "afternoon."

"Some of us pumped on our heads—mine's damp yet. See?"

Aunt Polly was vexed to think she had overlooked that bit of circumstantial evidence, and missed a trick. Then she had a new inspiration:

"Tom, you didn't have to undo your shirt collar where I sewed it, to pump on your head, did you? Unbutton your jacket!"

The trouble vanished out of Tom's face. He opened his jacket. His shirt collar was securely sewed.

"Bother! Well, go 'long with you. I'd made sure you'd played hookey and been a-swimming. But I forgive ye, Tom. I reckon you're a kind of a singed cat, as the saying is—better'n you look. *This* time."

She was half sorry her sagacity had miscarried, and half glad that Tom had stumbled into obedient conduct for once.

But Sidney said:

"Well, now, if I didn't think you sewed his collar with white thread, but it's black."

"Why, I did sew it with white! Tom!"

But Tom did not wait for the rest. As he went out at the door he said:

"Siddy, I'll lick you for that."

In a safe place Tom examined two large needles which were thrust into the lappels of his jacket, and had thread bound about them—one needle carried white thread and the other black. He said:

"She'd never noticed if it hadn't been for Sid. Confound it! sometimes she sews it with white, and sometimes she sews it with black. I wish to geeminy she'd stick to one or t'other—*I* can't keep the run of 'em. But I bet you I'll lam Sid for that. I'll learn him!"

He was not the Model Boy of the village. He knew the model boy very well though—and loathed him.

Within two minutes, or even less, he had forgotten all his troubles. Not because his troubles were one whit less heavy and bitter to him than a man's are to a man, but because a new and powerful interest bore them down and drove them out of his mind for the time—just as men's misfortunes are forgotten in the excitement of new enterprises. This new interest was a valued novelty in whistling, which he had just acquired from a negro, and he was suffering to practice it undisturbed. It consisted in a peculiar bird-like turn, a sort of liquid warble, produced by touching the tongue to the roof of the mouth at short intervals in the midst of the music—the reader probably remembers how to do it, if he has ever been a boy. Diligence and attention soon gave him the knack of it, and he strode down the street with his mouth full of harmony and his soul full of gratitude. He felt much as an astronomer feels who has discovered a new planet—no doubt, as far as strong, deep, unalloyed pleasure is concerned, the advantage was with the boy, not the astronomer.

The summer evenings were long. It was not dark, yet. Presently Tom checked his whistle. A stranger was before him—a boy a shade larger than himself. A new comer of any age or either sex was an impressive curiosity in the poor little shabby village of St. Petersburgh. This boy was well-dressed, too—well-dressed on a week-day. This was simply astounding. His cap was a dainty thing, his close-buttoned blue cloth roundabout was new and natty, and so were his pantaloons. He had shoes on—and it was only Friday. He even wore a necktie, a bright bit of ribbon. He had a citified air about him that ate into Tom's vitals. The more Tom stared at the splendid marvel, the higher he turned up his nose at his finery and the shabbier and shabbier his own outfit seemed to him to grow. Neither boy spoke. If one moved, the other moved—but only sidewise, in a circle; they kept face to face and eye to eye all the time. Finally Tom said:

"I can lick you!"

"I'd like to see you try it."

"Well, I can do it."

"No you can't, either."

"Yes I can."

"No you can't."

"I can."

"You can't."

"Can!"

"Can't!"

An uncomfortable pause. Then Tom said?

"What's your name?"

" 'Tisn't any of your business, maybe."

"Well I 'low I'll *make* it my business."

"Well why don't you?"

"If you say much I will."

"Much—much—*much.* There now."

"Oh, you think you're mighty smart, *don't* you? I could lick you with one hand tied behind me, if I wanted to."

"Well why don't you *do* it? You *say* you can do it."

"Well I *will,* if you fool with me."

"Oh yes—I've seen whole families in the same fix."

"Smarty! You think you're *some,* now, *don't* you? Oh what a hat!"

"You can lump that hat if you don't like it. I dare you to knock it off—and anybody that'll take a dare will suck eggs."

"You're a liar!"

"You're another."

"You're a fighting liar and dasn't take it up."

"Aw—take a walk!"

"Say—if you give me much more of your sass I'll take and bounce a rock off'n your head."

"Oh, of *course* you will."

"Well I *will.*"

"Well why don't you *do* it then? What do you keep *saying* you will for? Why don't you *do* it? It's because you're afraid."

"I *ain't* afraid."

"You are."

"I ain't."

"You are."

Another pause, and more eyeing and sidling around each other. Presently they were shoulder to shoulder. Tom said:

"Get away from here!"

"Go away yourself!"

"I won't."

"*I* won't either."

So they stood, each with a foot placed at an angle as a brace, and both shoving with might and main, and glowering at each other with hate. But neither could get an advantage. After struggling till both were hot and flushed, each relaxed his strain with watchful caution, and Tom said:

"You're a coward and a pup. I'll tell my big brother on you, and he can thrash you with his little finger, and I'll make him do it, too."

"What do I care for your big brother? I've got a brother that's bigger than he is—and what's more, he can throw him over that fence, too." [Both brothers were imaginary.]

"That's a lie."

"*Your* saying so don't make it so."

Tom drew a line in the dust with his big toe, and said:

"I dare you to step over that, and I'll lick you till you can't stand up. Anybody that'll take a dare will steal sheep."

The new boy stepped over promptly, and said:

"Now you said you'd do it, now let's see you do it."

"Don't you crowd me now; you better look out."

"Well, you *said* you'd do it—why don't you do it?"

"By jingo! for two cents I *will* do it."

The new boy took two broad coppers out of his pocket and held them out with derision. Tom struck them to the ground. In an instant both boys were rolling and tumbling in the dirt, gripped together like cats; and for the space of a minute they tugged and tore at each other's hair and clothes, punched and scratched each other's noses, and covered themselves with dust and glory. Presently the confusion took form and through the fog of battle Tom appeared, seated astride the new boy, and pounding him with his fists.

"Holler 'nuff!" said he.

The boy only struggled to free himself. He was crying,—mainly from rage.

"Holler 'nuff!"—and the pounding went on.

At last the stranger got out a smothered "Nuff!" and Tom let him up and said:

"Now that'll learn you. Better look out who you're fooling with next time."

The new boy went off brushing the dust from his clothes, sobbing, snuffling, and occasionally looking back and shaking his head and threatening what he would do to Tom the "next time he caught him out." To which Tom responded with jeers, and started off in high feather, and as soon as his back was turned the new boy snatched up a stone, threw it and hit him between the shoulders and then turned tail and ran like an antelope. Tom chased the traitor home, and thus found out where he lived. He then held a position at the gate for some time, daring the enemy to come outside, but the enemy only made faces at him through the window and declined. At last the enemy's mother appeared, and called Tom a bad, vicious, vulgar child, and ordered him away. So he went away; but he said he "'lowed" to "lay" for that boy.

He got home pretty late, that night, and when he climbed cautiously in at the window, he uncovered an ambuscade, in the person of his aunt; and when she saw the state his clothes were in her resolution to turn his Saturday holiday into captivity at hard labor became adamantine in its firmness.

CHAPTER II

Saturday morning was come, and all the summer world was bright and fresh, and brimming with life. There was a song in every heart; and if the heart was young the music issued at the lips. There was cheer in every face and a spring in every step. The locust trees were in bloom and the fragrance of the blossoms filled the air. Cardiff Hill, beyond the village and above it, was green with vegetation, and it lay just far enough away to seem a Delectable Land, dreamy, reposeful, and inviting.

Tom appeared on the sidewalk with a bucket of whitewash and a long-handled brush. He surveyed the fence, and all gladness left him and a deep melancholy settled down upon his spirit. Thirty yards of board fence nine feet high. Life to him seemed hollow, and existence but a burden. Sighing he dipped his brush and passed it along the topmost plank; repeated the operation; did it again; compared the insignificant whitewashed streak with the far-reaching continent of unwhitewashed fence, and sat down on a tree-box discouraged. Jim came skipping out at the gate with a tin pail, and singing "Buffalo Gals." Bringing water from the town pump had always been hateful work in Tom's eyes, before, but now it did not strike him so. He remembered that there was company at the pump. White, mulatto, and negro boys and girls were always there waiting their turns, resting, trading playthings, quarreling, fighting, skylarking. And he remembered that although the pump was only a hundred and fifty yards off, Jim never got back with a bucket of water under an hour—and even then somebody generally had to go after him. Tom said:

"Say, Jim, I'll fetch the water if you'll whitewash some."

Jim shook his head and said:

"Can't, Mars Tom. Ole missis, she tole me I got to go an' git dis water an' not stop foolin' roun' wid anybody. She say she spec' Mars Tom gwine to ax me to whitewash, an' so she tole me go 'long an' 'tend to my own business—she 'lowed *she'd* 'tend to de whitewashin'."

"Oh, never you mind what she said, Jim. That's the way she always talks. Gimme the bucket—I won't be gone only a minute. *She* won't ever know."

"Oh, I dasn't Mars Tom. Ole missis she'd take an' tar de head off'n me. 'Deed she would."

"*She!* She never licks anybody—whacks 'em over the head with her thimble—and who cares for that, I'd like to know. She talks awful, but talk don't hurt—anyways it don't if she don't cry. Jim, I'll give you a marvel. I'll give you a white alley!"

Jim began to waver.

"White alley, Jim! And it's a bully taw."

"My! Dat's a mighty gay marvel, *I* tell you! But Mars Tom I's powerful 'fraid ole missis—"

"And besides, if you will I'll show you my sore toe."

Jim was only human—this attraction was too much for him. He put down his pail, took the white alley, and bent over the toe with absorbing interest while the bandage was being unwound. In another moment he was flying down the street with his pail and a tingling rear, Tom was whitewashing with vigor, and Aunt Polly was retiring from the field with a slipper in her hand and triumph in her eye.

But Tom's energy did not last. He began to think of the fun he had planned for this day, and his sorrows multiplied. Soon the free boys would come tripping along on all sorts of delicious expeditions, and they would make a world of fun of him for having to work—the very thought of it burnt him like fire. He got out his worldly wealth and examined it—bits of toys, marbles, and trash; enough to buy an exchange of *work* maybe, but not half enough to buy so much as half an hour of pure freedom. So he returned his straightened means to his pocket, and gave up the idea of trying to buy the boys. At this dark and hopeless moment an inspiration burst upon him! Nothing less than a great, magnificent inspiration.

He took up his brush and went tranquilly to work. Ben Rogers hove in sight presently—the very boy, of all boys, whose ridicule he had been dreading. Ben's gait was the hop-skip-and-jump—proof enough that his heart was light and his anticipations high. He was eating an apple, and giving a long, melodious whoop, at intervals, followed by a deep-toned ding-dong-dong, ding-dong-dong, for he was personating a steamboat. As he drew near, he slackened speed, took the middle of the street, leaned far over to starboard and rounded to ponderously and with laborious pomp and circumstance —for he was personating the "Big Missouri," and considered himself to be drawing nine feet of water. He was boat, and captain, and engine-bells combined, so he had to imagine himself standing on his own hurricane-deck giving the orders and executing them:

"Stop her, sir! Ting-a-ling-ling!" The headway ran almost out and he drew up slowly toward the side-walk.

"Ship up to back! Ting-a-ling-ling!" His arms straightened and stiffened down his sides.

"Set her back on the stabboard! Ting-a-ling-ling! Chow! ch-chow-wow! Chow!" His right hand, meantime, describing stately circles,—for it was representing a forty-foot wheel.

"Let her go back on the labboard! Ting-a-ling-ling! Chow-ch-chow-chow!" The left hand began to describe circles.

"Stop the stabboard! Ting-a-ling-ling! Stop the labbord! Come ahead on the stabboard! Stop her! Let your outside turn over slow! Ting-a-ling-ling! Chow-ow-ow! Get out that head-line! *Lively* now! Come—out with your spring-line—what're you about there! Take a turn round that stump with the bight of it! Stand by that stage, now—let her go! Done with the engines, sir! Ting-a-ling-ling! *Sh't! s'h't! sh't!*" (trying the gauge-cocks.)

Tom went on whitewashing—paid no attention to the steamboat. Ben stared a moment and then said:

"Hi-*yi! You're* up a stump, ain't you!"

No answer. Tom surveyed his last touch with the eye of an artist; then he gave his brush another gentle sweep and surveyed the result, as before. Ben ranged up alongside of him. Tom's mouth watered for the apple, but he stuck to his work. Ben said:

"Hello, old chap, you got to work, hey?"

Tom wheeled suddenly and said:

"Why it's you Ben! I warn't noticing."

"Say—*I*'m going in a swimming, *I* am. Don't you wish you could? But of course you'd druther *work*—wouldn't you? Course you would!"

Tom contemplated the boy a bit, and said:

"What do you call work?"

"Why ain't *that* work?"

Tom resumed his whitewashing, and answered carelessly:

"Well, maybe it is, and maybe it ain't. All I know, is, it suits Tom Sawyer."

"Oh come, now, you don't mean to let on that you *like* it?"

The brush continued to move.

"Like it? Well I don't see why I oughtn't to like it. Does a boy get a chance to whitewash a fence every day?"

That put the thing in a new light. Ben stopped nibbling his apple. Tom swept his brush daintily back and forth—stepped back to note the effect—added a touch here and there—criticised the effect again—Ben watching every move and getting more and more interested, more and more absorbed. Presently he said:

"Say, Tom, let *me* whitewash a little."

Tom considered, was about to consent; but he altered his mind:

"No—no—I reckon it wouldn't hardly do, Ben. You see, Aunt Polly's awful particular about this fence—right here on the street, you know—but if it was the back fence I wouldn't mind and *she* wouldn't. Yes, she's awful particular about this fence; it's got to be done very careful; I reckon there ain't one boy in a thousand, maybe two thousand, that can do it the way it's got to be done."

"No—is that so? Oh come, now—lemme just try. Only just a little—I'd let *you*, if you was me, Tom."

"Ben, I'd like to, honest injun; but Aunt Polly—well Jim wanted to do it, but she wouldn't let him; Sid wanted to do it, and she wouldn't let Sid. Now don't you see how I'm fixed? If you was to tackle this fence and anything was to happen to it—"

"Oh, shucks, I'll be just as careful. Now lemme try. Say—I'll give you the core of my apple."

"Well, here—. No Ben, now don't. I'm afeard—"

"I'll give you *all* of it!"

Tom gave up the brush with reluctance in his face but alacrity in his heart. And while the late steamer "Big Missouri" worked and sweated in the sun, the retired artist sat on a barrel in the shade close by, dangled his legs, munched his apple, and planned the slaughter of more innocents. There was no lack of material; boys happened along every little while; they came to jeer, but remained to whitewash. By the time Ben was fagged out, Tom had traded the next chance to Billy Fisher for a kite, in good repair; and when *he* played out, Johnny Miller bought in for a dead rat and a string to swing it with—and so on, and so on, hour after hour. And when the middle of the afternoon came, from being a poor poverty-stricken boy in the morning, Tom was literally rolling in wealth. He had beside the things before mentioned, twelve marbles, part of a jews-harp, a piece of blue bottle-glass to look through, a spool cannon, a key that wouldn't unlock anything, a fragment of chalk, a glass stopper of a decanter, a tin soldier, a couple of tadpoles, six fire-crackers, a kitten with only one eye, a brass door-knob, a dog-collar—but no dog—the handle of a knife, four pieces of orange peel, and a dilapidated old window-sash.

He had had a nice, good, idle time all the while—plenty of company—and the fence had three coats of whitewash on it! If he hadn't run out of whitewash, he would have bankrupted every boy in the village.

Tom said to himself that it was not such a hollow world, after all. He had discovered a great law of human action, without knowing it —namely, that in order to make a man or a boy covet a thing, it is only necessary to make the thing difficult to attain. If he had been a great and wise philosopher, like the writer of this book, he would now have comprehended that Work consists of whatever a body is *obliged* to do, and that Play consists of whatever a body is not obliged to do. And this would help him to understand why constructing artificial flowers or performing on a treadmill is work, while rolling ten-pins or climbing Mont Blanc is only amusement. There are wealthy gentlemen in England who drive four-horse passenger-coaches twenty or thirty miles on a daily line, in the summer, because the privilege costs them considerable money; but if they were offered wages for the service, that would turn it into work and then they would resign.

The boy mused a while over the substantial change which had taken place in his worldly circumstances, and then wended toward head-quarters to report.

CHAPTER III

Tom presented himself before Aunt Polly, who was sitting by an open window in a pleasant rearward apartment, which was bed-room, breakfast-room, dining-room, and library, combined. The balmy summer air, the restful quiet, the odor of the flowers, and the drowsing murmur of the bees had had their effect, and she was nodding over her knitting—for she had no company but the cat, and it was asleep in her lap. Her spectacles were propped up on her gray head for safety. She had thought that of course Tom had deserted long ago, and she wondered at seeing him place himself in her power again in this intrepid way. He said: "Mayn't I go and play now, aunt?"

"What, a'ready? How much have you done?"

"It's all done, aunt."

"Tom, don't lie to me—I can't bear it."

"I ain't, aunt; it *is* all done."

Aunt Polly placed small trust in such evidence. She went out to see for herself; and she would have been content to find twenty per cent of Tom's statement true. When she found the entire fence whitewashed, and not only whitewashed but elaborately coated and recoated, and even a streak added to the ground, her astonishment was almost unspeakable. She said:

"Well, I never! There's no getting round it, you *can* work when your'e a mind to, Tom." And then she diluted the compliment by adding, "But it's powerful seldom you're a mind to, I'm bound to say. Well, go 'long and play; but mind you get back sometime in a week, or I'll tan you."

She was so overcome by the splendor of his achievement that she took him into the closet and selected a choice apple and delivered it to him, along with an improving lecture upon the added value and flavor a treat took to itself when it came without sin through virtuous effort. And while she closed with a happy scriptural flourish, he "hooked" a doughnut.

Then he skipped out, and saw Sid just starting up the outside stairway that led to the back rooms on the second floor. Clods were handy and the air was full of them in a twinkling. They raged around Sid like a hail-storm; and before Aunt Polly could collect her surprised faculties and sally to the rescue, six or seven clods had taken personal effect, and Tom was over the fence and gone. There was a gate, but as a general thing he was too crowded for time to make use of it. His soul was at peace, now that he had settled with Sid for calling attention to his black thread and getting him into trouble.

Tom skirted the block, and came round into a muddy alley that led by the back of his aunt's cow-stable. He presently got safely beyond the reach of capture and punishment, and hasted toward the public square of the village, where two "military" companies of boys had met for conflict, according to previous appointment. Tom was General of one of these armies, Joe Harper (a bosom friend,) General of the other. These two great commanders did not condescend to fight in person—that being better suited to the still smaller fry— but sat together on an eminence and conducted the field operations by orders delivered through aides-de-camp. Tom's army won a great victory, after a long and hard-fought battle. Then the dead were counted, prisoners exchanged, the terms of the next disagreement agreed upon and the day for the necessary battle appointed; after which the armies fell into line and marched away, and Tom turned homeward alone.

As he was passing by the house where Jeff Thatcher lived, he saw a new girl in the garden—a lovely little blue-eyed creature with yellow hair plaited into two long tails, white summer frock and embroidered pantalettes. The fresh-crowned hero fell without firing a shot. A certain Amy Lawrence vanished out of his heart and left not even a memory of herself behind. He had thought he loved her to distraction, he had regarded his passion as adoration; and behold it was only a poor little evanescent partiality. He had been months winning her; she had confessed hardly a week ago; he had been the happiest and the proudest boy in the world only seven short days, and here in one instant of time she had gone out of his heart like a casual stranger whose visit is done.

He worshiped this new angel with furtive eye, till he saw that she had discovered him; then he pretended he did not know she was present, and began to "show off" in all sorts of absurd boyish ways, in order to win her admiration. He kept up this grotesque foolishness for some time; but by and by, while he was in the midst of some dangerous gymnastic performances, he glanced aside and saw that the little girl was wending her way toward the house. Tom came up to the fence and leaned on it, grieving, and hoping she would tarry yet a while longer. She halted a moment on the steps and then moved toward the door. Tom heaved a great sigh as she put her foot on the threshold. But his face lit up, right away, for she tossed a pansy over the fence a moment before she disappeared.

The boy ran around and stopped within a foot or two of the flower, and then shaded his eyes with his hand and began to look down street as if he had discovered something of interest going on in that direction. Presently he picked up a straw and began trying to balance it on his nose, with his head tilted far back; and as he moved from side to side, in his efforts, he edged nearer and nearer toward the pansy; finally his bare foot rested upon it, his pliant toes closed upon it, and he hopped away with the treasure and disappeared round the corner. But only for a minute—only while he could button the flower inside his jacket, next his heart—or next his stomach, possibly, for he was not much posted in anatomy, and not hypercritical, anyway.

He returned, now, and hung about the fence till nightfall, "showing off," as before; but the girl never exhibited herself again, though Tom comforted himself a little with the hope that she had been near some window, meantime, and been aware of his attentions. Finally he rode home reluctantly, with his poor head full of visions.

All through supper his spirits were so high that his aunt wondered "what had got into the child." He took a good scolding about clodding Sid, and did not seem to mind it in the least. He tried to steal sugar under his aunt's very nose, and got his knuckles rapped for it. He said:

"Aunt, you don't whack Sid when he takes it."

"Well, Sid don't torment a body the way you do. You'd be always into that sugar if I warn't watching you."

Presently she stepped into the kitchen, and Sid, happy in his immunity, reached for the sugar-bowl—a sort of glorying over Tom which was well-nigh unbearable. But Sid's fingers slipped and the bowl dropped and broke. Tom was in ecstasies. In such ecstasies that he even controlled his tongue and was silent. He said to himself that he would not speak a word, even when his aunt came in, but would sit perfectly still till she asked who did the mischief; and then he would tell, and there would be nothing so good in the world as to see that pet model "catch it." He was so brim-full of exultation that he could hardly hold himself when the old lady came back and stood above the wreck discharging lightnings of wrath from over her spectacles. He said to himself, "Now it's coming!" And the next

instant he was sprawling on the floor! The potent palm was uplifted
to strike again when Tom cried out:

"Hold on, now, what 'er you belting *me* for?—Sid broke it!"

Aunt Polly paused, perplexed, and Tom looked for healing pity.
But when she got her tongue again, she only said:

"Umf! Well, you didn't get a lick amiss, I reckon. You been into
some other audacious mischief when I wasn't around, like enough."

Then her conscience reproached her, and she yearned to say
something kind and loving; but she judged that this would be
construed into a confession that she had been in the wrong, and
discipline forbade that. So she kept silence, and went about her
affairs with a troubled heart. Tom sulked in a corner and exalted
his woes. He knew that in her heart his aunt was on her knees to him,
and he was morosely gratified by the consciousness of it. He would
hang out no signals, he would take notice of none. He knew that a
yearning glance fell upon him, now and then, through a film of tears,
but he refused recognition of it. He pictured himself lying sick unto
death and his aunt bending over him beseeching one little forgiving
word, but he would turn his face to the wall, and die with that word
unsaid. Ah, how would she feel then? And he pictured himself
brought home from the river, dead, with his curls all wet, and his
sore heart at rest. How she would throw herself upon him, and how
her tears would fall like rain, and her lips pray God to give her back
her boy and she would never, never abuse him any more! But he
would lie there cold and white and make no sign—a poor little
sufferer, whose griefs were at an end. He so worked upon his feelings
with the pathos of these dreams, that he had to keep swallowing, he
was so like to choke; and his eyes swam in a blur of water, which
overflowed when he winked, and ran down and trickled from the end
of his nose. And such a luxury to him was this petting of his sorrows,
that he could not bear to have any worldly cheeriness or any grating
delight intrude upon it; it was too sacred for such contact; and so,
presently, when his cousin Mary danced in, all alive with the joy of
seeing home again after an age-long visit of one week to the country,
he got up and moved in clouds and darkness out at one door as she
brought song and sunshine in at the other.

He wandered far from the accustomed haunts of boys, and sought
desolate places that were in harmony with his spirit. A log raft in the
river invited him, and he seated himself on its outer edge and
contemplated the dreary vastness of the stream, wishing, the while,
that he could only be drowned, all at once and unconsciously,
without undergoing the uncomfortable routine devised by nature.
Then he thought of his flower. He got it out, rumpled and wilted,
and it mightily increased his dismal felicity. He wondered if *she*
would pity him if she knew? Would she cry, and wish that she had
a right to put her arms around his neck and comfort him? Or would
she turn coldly away like all the hollow world? This picture brought

such an agony of pleasureable suffering that he worked it over and
over again in his mind and set it up in new and varied lights, till he
wore it threadbare. At last he rose up sighing and departed in
the darkness.

About half past nine or ten o'clock he came along the deserted
street to where the Adored Unknown lived; he paused a moment;
no sound fell upon his listening ear; a candle was casting a dull glow
upon the curtain of a second-story window. Was the sacred presence
there? He climbed the fence, threaded his stealthy way through the
plants, till he stood under that window; he looked up at it long, and
with emotion; then he laid him down on the ground under it,
disposing himself upon his back, with his hands clasped upon his
breast and holding his poor wilted flower. And this he would die—
out in the cold world, with no shelter over his homeless head, no
friendly hand to wipe the death-damps from his brow, no loving face
to bend pityingly over him when the great agony came. And thus
she would see him when she looked out upon the glad morning,
and oh! would she drop one little tear upon his poor, lifeless form,
would she heave one little sigh to see a bright young life so rudely
blighted, so untimely cut down?

The window went up, a maid-servant's discordant voice profaned
the holy calm, and a deluge of water drenched the prone martyr's
remains!

The strangling hero sprang up with a relieving snort. There was a
whiz as of a missile in the air, mingled with the murmur of a curse,
a sound as of shivering glass followed, and a small, vague form went
over the fence and shot away in the gloom.

Not long after, as Tom, all undressed for bed, was surveying his
drenched garments by the light of a tallow dip, Sid woke up; but if
he had any dim idea of making any "references to allusions," he
thought better of it and held his peace, for there was danger in
Tom's eye.

Tom turned in without the added vexation of prayers, and Sid
made mental note of the omission.

CHAPTER IV

The sun rose upon a tranquil world, and beamed down upon the
peaceful village like a benediction. Breakfast over, Aunt Polly had
family worship; it began with a prayer built from the ground up of
solid courses of Scriptural quotations, welded together with a thin
mortar of originality; and from the summit of this she delivered a
grim chapter of the Mosaic Law, as from Sinai.

Then Tom girded up his loins, so to speak, and went to work to
"get his verses." Sid had learned his lesson days before. Tom bent
all his energies to the memorizing of five verses, and he chose part of
the Sermon on the Mount, because he could find no verses that were

shorter. At the end of half an hour Tom had a vague general idea of his lesson, but no more, for his mind was traversing the whole field of human thought, and his hands were busy with distracting recreations. Mary took his book to hear him recite, and he tried to find his way through the fog:

"Blessed are the—a—a—"

"Poor"—

"Yes—poor; blessed are the poor—a—a—"

"In spirit—"

"In spirit; blessed are the poor in spirit, for they—they—"

"*Theirs*—"

"For *theirs*. Blessed are the poor in spirit, for *theirs* is the kingdom of heaven. Blessed are they that mourn, for they—they—"

"Sh—"

"For they—a—"

"S, H, A—"

"For they S, H—Oh I don't know what it is!"

"*Shall!*"

"Oh, *shall!* for they shall—for they shall—a—a—shall mourn—a —a—blessed are they that shall—they that—a—they that shall mourn, for they shall—a—shall *what?* Why don't you tell me Mary? —what do you want to be so mean for?"

"Oh, Tom, you poor thick-headed thing, I'm not teasing you. I wouldn't do that. You must go and learn it again. Don't be so discouraged, Tom, you'll manage it—and if you do, I'll give you something ever so nice. There, now, that's a good boy."

"All right! What is it, Mary, tell me what it is."

"Never you mind, Tom. You know if I say it's nice, it *is* nice."

"You bet you that's so, Mary. All right, I'll tackle it again."

And he did "tackle it again"—and under the double pressure of curiosity and prospective gain, he did it with such spirit that he accomplished a shining success. Mary gave him a bran-new "Barlow" knife worth twelve and a half cents; and the convulsion of delight that swept his system shook him to his foundations. True, the knife would not cut anything, but it was a "sure-enough" Barlow, and there was inconceivable grandeur in that—though where the western boys ever got the idea that such a weapon could possibly be counterfeited to its injury, is an imposing mystery and will always remain so, perhaps. Tom contrived to scarify the cupboard with it, and was arranging to begin on the bureau, when he was called off to dress for Sunday-School.

Mary gave him a tin basin of water and a piece of soap, and he went outside the door and set the basin on a little bench there; then he dipped the soap in the water and laid it down; turned up his sleeves; poured out the water on the ground, gently, and then entered the kitchen and began to wipe his face diligently on the towel behind the door. But Mary removed the towel and said:

"Now ain't you ashamed, Tom. You musn't be so bad. Water won't hurt you."

Tom was a trifle disconcerted. The basin was refilled, and this time he stood over it a little while, gathering resolution; took in a big breath and began. When he entered the kitchen presently, with both eyes shut and groping for the towel with his hands, an honorable territory stopped short at his chin and his jaws, like a mask; below emerged from the towel, he was not yet satisfactory, for the clean territory stopped shirt of his chin and his jaws, like a mask; below and beyond this line there was a dark expanse of unirrigated soil that spread downward in front and backward around his neck. Mary took him in hand, and when she was done with him he was a man and a brother, without distinction of color, and his saturated hair was neatly brushed, and its short curls wrought into a dainty and symmetrical general effect. [He privately smoothed out the curls, with labor and difficulty, and plastered his hair down close to his head; for he held curls to be effeminate, and his own filled his life with bitterness.] Then Mary got out a suit of his clothing that had been used only on Sundays during two years—they were simply called his "other clothes"—and so by that we know the size of his wardrobe. The girl "put him to rights" after he had dressed himself; she buttoned his neat roundabout up to his chin, turned his vast shirt collar down over his shoulders, brushed him off and crowned him with his speckled straw hat. He now looked exceedingly improved and uncomfortable. He was fully as uncomfortable as he looked; for there was a restraint about whole clothes and cleanliness that galled him. He hoped that Mary would forget his shoes, but the hope was blighted; she coated them thoroughly with tallow, as was the custom, and brought them out. He lost his temper and said he was always being made to do everything he didn't want to do. But Mary said, persuasively:

"Please, Tom—that's a good boy."

So he got into the shoes snarling. Mary was soon ready, and the three children set out for Sunday-school—a place that Tom hated with his whole heart; but Sid and Mary were fond of it.

Sabbath-school hours were from nine to half past ten; and then church service. Two of the children always remained for the sermon voluntarily, and the other always remained too—for stronger reasons. The church's high-backed, uncushioned pews would seat about three hundred persons; the edifice was but a small, plain affair, with a sort of pine board tree-box on top of it for a steeple. At the door Tom dropped back a step and accosted a Sunday-dressed comrade:

"Say, Billy, got a yaller ticket?"

"Yes."

"What'll you take for her?"

"What'll you give?"

"Piece of lickrish and a fish-hook."

"Less see 'em."

Tom exhibited. They were satisfactory, and the property changed hands. Then Tom traded a couple of white alleys for three red tickets, and some small trifle or other for a couple of blue ones. He waylaid other boys as they came, and went on buying tickets of various colors ten or fifteen minutes longer. He entered the church, now, with a swarm of clean and noisy boys and girls, proceeded to his seat and started a quarrel with the first boy that came handy. The teacher, a grave, elderly man, interfered; then turned his back a moment and Tom pulled a boy's hair in the next bench, and was absorbed in his book when the boy turned around; stuck a pin in another boy, presently, in order to hear him say "Ouch!" and got a new reprimand from his teacher. Tom's whole class were of a pattern—restless, noisy, and troublesome. When they came to recite their lessons, not one of them knew his verses perfectly, but had to be prompted all along. However, they worried through, and each got his reward—in small blue tickets, each with a passage of Scripture on it; each blue ticket was pay for two verses of the recitation. Ten blue tickets equalled a red one, and could be exchanged for it; ten red tickets equalled a yellow one: for ten yellow tickets the Superintendent gave a very plainly bound Bible, (worth forty cents in those easy times,) to the pupil. How many of my readers would have the industry and application to memorize two thousand verses, even for a Dore Bible? And yet Mary had acquired two Bibles in this way—it was the patient work of two years—and a boy of German parentage had won four or five. He once recited three thousand verses without stopping; but the strain upon his mental faculties was too great, and he was little better than an idiot from that day forth—a grievous misfortune for the school, for on great occasions, before company, the Superintendent (as Tom expressed it) had always made this boy come out and "spread himself." Only the older pupils managed to keep their tickets and stick to their tedious work long enough to get a Bible, and so the delivery of one of these prizes was a rare and noteworthy circumstance; the successful pupil was so great and conspicuous for that day that on the spot every scholar's heart was fired with a fresh ambition that often lasted a couple of weeks. It is possible that Tom's mental stomach had never really hungered for one of those prizes, but unquestionably his entire being had for many a day longed for the glory and the eclat that came with it.

In due course the Superintendent stood up in front of the pulpit, with a closed hymn book in his hand and his forefinger inserted between its leaves, and commanded attention. When a Sunday-school Superintendent makes his customary little speech, a hymn-book in the hand is as necessary as the inevitable sheet of music in the hand of a singer who stands forward on the platform and sings a solo at a concert—though why, is a mystery: for neither the hymn-book nor the sheet of music is ever referred to by the sufferer. This Superintendent was a slim creature of thirty-five, with a sandy goatee and short sandy hair; he wore a stiff standing-collar whose upper edge almost reached his ears and whose sharp points curved forward abreast the corners of his mouth—a fence that compelled a straight lookout ahead, and a turning of the whole body when a side view was required; his chin was propped on a spreading cravat which was as broad and as long as a bank note, and had fringed ends; his boot toes were turned sharply up, in the fashion of the day, like sleigh-runners—an effect patiently and laboriously produced by the young men by sitting with their toes pressed against a wall for hours together. Mr. Walters was very earnest of mein, and very sincere and honest at heart; and he held sacred things and places in such reverence, and so separated them from worldly matters, that unconsciously to himself his Sunday-school voice had acquired a peculiar intonation which was wholly absent on week-days. He began after this fashion:

"Now children, I want you all to sit up just as straight and pretty as you can and give me all your attention for a minute or two. There —that is it. That is the way good little boys and girls should do. I see one little girl who is looking out of the window—I am afraid she thinks I am out there somewhere—perhaps up in one of the trees making a speech to the little birds. [Applausive titter.] I want to tell you how good it makes me feel to see so many bright, clean little faces assembled in a place like this, learning to do right and be good." And so forth and so on. It is not necessary to set down the rest of the oration. It was of a pattern which does not vary, and so it is familiar to us all.

The latter third of the speech was marred by the resumption of fights and other recreations among certain of the bad boys, and by fidgetings and whisperings that extended far and wide, washing even to the bases of isolated and incorruptible rocks like Sid and Mary. But now every sound ceased suddenly, with the subsidence of Mr. Walters' voice, and the conclusion of the speech was received with a burst of silent gratitude.

A good part of the whispering had been occasioned by an event which was more or less rare—the entrance of visitors; lawyer Thatcher, accompanied by a very feeble and aged man; a fine, portly, middle-aged gentleman with iron-gray hair; and a dignified lady who was doubtless the latter's wife. The lady was leading a child. Tom had been restless and full of chafings and repinings; conscience-smitten, too—he could not meet Amy Lawrence's eye, he could not brook her loving gaze. But when he saw this small new-comer his soul was all ablaze with bliss in a moment. The next moment he was "showing off" with all his might—cuffing boys, pulling hair, making faces—in a word, using every art that seemed likely to fascinate a girl and win her applause. His exaltation had but

one alloy—the memory of his humiliation in this angel's garden—
and that record in sand was fast washing out, under the waves of
happiness that were sweeping over it now.

The visitors were given the highest seat of honor, and as soon as
Mr. Walters' speech was finished, he introduced them to the school.
The middle-aged man turned out to be a prodigious personage—no
less a one than the county judge—altogether the most august
creation these children had ever looked upon—and they wondered
what kind of material he was made of—and they half wanted to hear
him roar, and were half afraid he might, too. He was from
Constantinople, twelve miles away—so he had traveled, and seen the
world—these very eyes had looked upon the county court house—
which was said to have a tin roof. The awe which these reflections
inspired was attested by the impressive silence and the ranks of
staring eyes. This was the great Judge Thatcher, brother of their own
lawyer. Jeff Thatcher immediately went forward, to be familiar with
the great man and be envied by the school. It would have been music
to his soul to hear the whisperings:

"Look at him, Jim! He's a going up there. Say—look! he's a going
to shake hands with him—he *is* shaking hands with him! By jings,
don't you wish you was Jeff?"

Mr. Walters fell to "showing off," with all sorts of official
bustlings and activities giving orders, delivering judgments,
discharging directions here, there, everywhere that he could find a
target. The librarian "showed off"—running hither and thither with
his arms full of books and making a deal of the splutter and fuss that
insect authority delights in. The young lady teachers "showed off"
—bending sweetly over pupils that were lately being boxed, lifting
pretty warning fingers at bad little boys and patting good ones
lovingly. The young gentlemen teachers "showed off" with small
scoldings and other little displays of authority and fine attention to
discipline—and most of the teachers, of both sexes, found business
up at the library, by the pulpit; and it was business that frequently
had to be done over again two or three times, (with much
seeming vexation.) The little girls "showed off" in various ways, and
the little boys "showed off" with such diligence that the air was thick
with paper wads and the murmur of scufflings. And above it all the
great man sat and beamed a majestic judicial smile upon all the
house, and warmed himself in the sun of his own grandeur—for he
was "showing off," too.

There was only one thing wanting, to make Mr. Walters' ecstacy
complete, and that was a chance to deliver a Bible-prize and exhibit
a prodigy. Several pupils had a few yellow tickets, but none had
enough—he had been around among the star pupils inquiring. He
would have given worlds, now, to have that German lad back again
with a sound mind.

And now at this moment, when hope was dead, Tom Sawyer came

forward with nine yellow tickets, nine red tickets, and ten blue ones, and demanded a Bible. This was a thunderbolt out of a clear sky. Walters was not expecting an application from this source for the next ten years. But there was no getting around it—here were the certified checks, and they were good for their face. Tom was therefore elevated to a place with the Judge and the other elect, and the great news was announced from head-quarters. It was the most stunning surprise of the decade, and so profound was the sensation that it lifted the new hero up to the judicial one's altitude, and the school had two marvels to gaze upon in place of one. The boys were all eaten up with envy—but those that suffered the bitterest pangs were those who perceived too late that they themselves had contributed to this hated splendor by trading tickets to Tom for the wealth he had amassed in selling whitewashing privileges. These despised themselves, as being the dupes of a wily fraud, a guileful snake in the grass.

The prize was delivered to Tom with as much effusion as the Superintendent could pump up under the circumstances; but it lacked somewhat of the true gush, for the poor fellow's instinct taught him that there was a mystery here that could not well bear the light, perhaps; it was simply preposterous that *this* boy had warehoused two thousand sheaves of Scriptural wisdom on his premises—a dozen would strain his capacity, without a doubt.

Amy Lawrence was proud and glad, and she tried to make Tom see it in her face—but he wouldn't look. She wondered; then she was just a grain troubled; next a dim suspicion came and went—came again; she watched; a furtive glance told her worlds—and then her heart broke, and she was jealous, and angry, and the tears came and she hated everybody. Tom most of all, (she thought.)

Tom was introduced to the Judge; but his tongue was tied, his breath would hardly come, his heart quaked—partly because of the awful greatness of the man, but mainly because he was *her* parent. He would have liked to fall down and worship him, if it were in the dark. The Judge put his hand on Tom's head and called him a fine little man, and asked him what his name was. The boy stammered, gasped, and got it out:

"Tom."

"Oh, no, not Tom—it is—"

"Thomas."

"Ah, that's it. I thought there was more to it, maybe. That's very well. But you've another one I daresay, and you'll tell it to me, won't you?"

"Tell the gentleman your other name, Thomas," said Walters, "and say *sir.*—You mustn't forget your manners."

"Thomas Sawyer—sir."

"That's it! That's a good boy. Fine boy. Fine, manly little fellow. Two thousand verses is a great many—very, very great many. And you never can be sorry for the trouble you took to learn them; for knowledge is worth more than anything there is in the world; it's what makes great men and good men; you'll be a great man and a good man yourself, some day, Thomas, and then you'll look back and say, It's all owing to the precious Sunday-school privileges of my boyhood—it's all owing to my dear teachers that taught me to learn —it's all owing to the good Superintendent, who encouraged me, and watched over me, and gave me a beautiful Bible—a splendid elegant Bible, to keep and have it all for my own, always—it's all owing to right bringing up! That is what you will say, Thomas—and you wouldn't take any money for those two thousand verses—no indeed you wouldn't. And now you wouldn't mind telling me and this lady some of the things you've learned—no, I know you wouldn't—for we are proud of little boys that learn. Now no doubt you know the names of all the twelve disciples. Won't you tell us the names of the first two that were appointed?"

Tom was tugging at a button hole and looking sheepish. He blushed, now, and his eyes fell. Mr. Walters' heart sank within him. He said to himself, it is not possible that the boy can answer the simplest question—why *did* the Judge ask him? Yet he felt obliged to speak up and say:

"Answer the gentleman, Thomas—don't be afraid."

Tom still hung fire.

"Now I know you'll tell *me*" said the lady. "The names of the first two disciples were—"

"DAVID AND GOLIATH!"

Let us draw the curtain of charity over the rest of the scene.

CHAPTER V

About half-past ten the cracked bell of the small church began to ring, and presently the people began to gather for the morning sermon. The Sunday-school children distributed themselves about the house and occupied pews with their parents, so as to be under supervision. Aunt Polly came, and Tom and Sid and Mary sat with her—Tom being placed next the aisle, in order that he might be as far away from the open window and the seductive outside summer scenes as possible. The crowd filed up the aisles: the aged and needy postmaster, who had seen better days; the mayor and his wife—for they had a mayor there, among other unnecessaries; the justice of the peace; the widow Douglass, fair, smart and forty, a generous, good-hearted soul and well-to-do, her hill mansion the only palace in the town, and the most hospitable and much the most lavish in the matter of festivities that St. Petersburg could boast; the bent and venerable Major and Mrs. Ward; lawyer Riverson, the new notable from a distance; next the belle of the village, followed by a troop of lawn-clad and ribbon-decked young heart-breakers; then all the young clerks in town in a body—for they had stood in the vestibule sucking their cane-heads, a circling wall of oiled and simpering admirers, till the last girl had run their gauntlet; and last of all came the Model Boy, Willie Mufferson, taking as heedful care of his mother as if she were cut glass. He always brought his mother to church, and was the pride of all the matrons. The boys all hated him, he was so good. And besides, he had been "thrown up to them" so much. His white handkerchief was hanging out of his pocket behind, as usual on Sundays— accidentally. Tom had no handkerchief, and he looked upon boys who had, as snobs.

The congregation being fully assembled, now, the bell rang once more, to warn laggards and stragglers, and then a solemn hush fell upon the church which was only broken by the tittering and whispering of the choir in the gallery. The choir always tittered and whispered all through service. There was once a church choir that was not ill-bred, but I have forgotten where it was, now. It was a great many years ago, and I can scarcely remember anything about it, but I think it was in some foreign country.

The minister gave out the hymn, and read it through with a relish, in a peculiar style which was much admired in that part of the country. His voice began on a medium key and climbed steadily up till it reached a certain point, where it bore with strong emphasis upon the topmost word and then plunged down as if from a spring-board:

Shall I be car-ri-ed toe the skies, on flow'ry *beds*
of ease,

Whilst others fight to win the prize, and sail thro' *blood-*
-y seas?

He was regarded as a wonderful reader. At church "sociables" he was always called upon to read poetry; and when he was through, the ladies would lift up their hands and let them fall helplessly in their laps, and "wall" their eyes, and shake their heads, as much as to say, "Words cannot express it; it is too beautiful, *too* beautiful for this mortal earth."

After the hymn had been sung, the Rev. Mr. Sprague turned himself into a bulletin board, and read off "notices" of meetings and societies and things till it seemed that the list would stretch out to the crack of doom—a queer custom which is still kept up in America, even in cities, away here in this age of abundant newspapers. Often, the less there is to justify a traditional custom, the harder it is to get rid of it.

And now the minister prayed. A good, generous prayer, it was, and went into details: it pleaded for the church, and the little children of the church; for the other churches of the village; for the village itself; for the county; for the State; for the State officers; for the United States; for the churches of the United States; for Congress; for the President; for the officers of the Government; for poor sailors, tossed by stormy seas; for the oppressed millions groaning under the heel of European monarchies and Oriental despotisms; for such as have the light and the good tidings, and yet have not eyes to see nor ears to hear withal; for the heathen in the far islands of the sea; and closed with a supplication that the words he was about to speak might find grace and favor, and be as seed sown in fertile ground, yielding in time a grateful harvest of good. Amen.

There was a rustling of dresses, and the standing congregation sat down. The boy whose history this book relates did not enjoy the prayer, he only endured it—if he even did that much. He was restive all through it; he kept tally of the details of the prayer, unconsciously—for he was not listening, but he knew the ground of old, and the clergyman's regular route over it—and when a little trifle of new matter was interlarded, his ear detected it and his whole nature resented it; he considered additions unfair, and scoundrelly. In the midst of the prayer a fly had lit on the back of the pew in front of him and tortured his spirit by calmly rubbing its hands together, embracing its head with its arms, and polishing it so vigorously that it seemed to almost part company with the body, and the slender thread of a neck was exposed to view; scraping its wings with its hind legs and smoothing them to its body as if they had been coat tails; going through its whole toilet as tranquilly as if it knew it was perfectly safe. As indeed it was; for as sorely as Tom's hands itched to grab for it they did not dare—he believed his soul would be instantly destroyed if he did such a thing while the prayer was going on. But with the closing sentence his hand began to curve and steal forward; and the instant the "Amen" was out the fly was a prisoner of war. His aunt detected the act and made him let it go.

The minister gave out his text and droned along monotonously through an argument that was so prosy that many a head by and by began to nod—and yet it was an argument that dealt in limitless fire and brimstone and thinned the predestined elect down to a company so small as to be hardly worth the saving. Tom counted the pages of the sermon; after church he always knew how many pages there had been, but he seldom knew anything else about the discourse. However, this time he was really interested for a little while. The minister made a grand and moving picture of the assembling together of the world's hosts at the millennium when the lion and the lamb should lie down together and a little child should lead them. But the pathos, the lesson, the moral of the great spectacle were lost upon the boy; he only thought of the conspicuousness of the principal character before the on-looking nations; his face lit with the thought, and he said to himself that he wished he could be that child, if it was a tame lion.

Now he lapsed into suffering again, as the dry argument was resumed. Presently he bethought him of a treasure he had and got it out. It was a large black beetle with formidable jaws—a "pinch-bug," he called it. It was in a percussion-cap box. The first thing the beetle did was to take him by the finger. A natural fillip followed, the beetle went floundering into the aisle and lit on its back, and the hurt finger went into the boy's mouth. The beetle lay there working its helpless legs, unable to turn over. Tom eyed it, and longed for it; but it was safe out of his reach. Other people uninterested in the sermon, found relief in the beetle, and they eyed it too. Presently a vagrant poodle dog came idling along, sad at heart, lazy with the summer softness and the quiet, weary of captivity, sighing for change. He spied the beetle; the drooping tail lifted and wagged. He surveyed the prize; walked around it; smelt at it from a safe distance; walked around it again; grew bolder, and took a closer smell; then lifted his lip and made a gingerly snatch at it, just missing it; made another, and another; began to enjoy the diversion; subsided to his stomach with the beetle between his paws, and continued his experiments; grew weary at last, and then indifferent and absent-minded. His head nodded, and little by little his chin descended and touched the enemy, who seized it. There was a sharp yelp, a flirt of the poodle's head, and the beetle fell a couple of yards away, and lit on its back once more. The neighboring spectators shook with a gentle inward joy, several faces went behind fans and handkerchiefs, and Tom was entirely happy. The dog looked foolish, and probably felt so; but there was resentment in his heart, too, and a craving for revenge. So he went to the beetle and began a wary attack on it again; jumping at it from every point of a circle, lighting with his fore paws within an inch of the creature, making even closer snatches at it with his teeth, and jerking his head till his ears flapped again. But he grew tired once more, after a while; tried to amuse himself with a fly but found no relief; followed an ant around, with his nose close to the floor, and quickly wearied of that; yawned, sighed, forgot the beetle entirely, and sat down on it! Then there was a wild yelp of agony and the poodle went sailing up the aisle; the yelps continued, and so did the dog; he crossed the house in front of the altar; he flew down the other aisle; he crossed before the doors; he clamored up the home-stretch; his anguish grew with his progress, till presently he was but a woolly comet moving in its orbit with the gleam and the speed of light. At last the frantic sufferer sheered from its course, and sprang into its master's lap; he flung it out of the window, and the voice of distress quickly thinned away and died in the distance.

By this time the whole church was red-faced and suffocating with suppressed laughter, and the sermon had come to a dead stand-still. The discourse was resumed presently, but it went lame and halting, all possibility of impressiveness being at an end; for even the gravest sentiments were constantly being received with a smothered burst of unholy mirth, under cover of some remote pew-back, as if the poor parson had said a rarely facetious thing. It was a genuine relief to the whole congregation when the ordeal was over and the benediction pronounced.

Tom Sawyer went home quite cheerful, thinking to himself that there was some satisfaction about divine service when there was a bit of variety in it. He had but one marring thought: he was willing that the dog should play with his pinch-bug, but he did not think it was upright in him to carry it off.

CHAPTER VI

Monday morning found Tom Sawyer miserable. Monday morning always found him so—because it began another week's slow suffering in school. He generally began that day with wishing he had had no intervening holiday, it made the going into captivity and fetters again so much more odious.

Tom lay thinking. Presently it occurred to him that he wished he was sick; then he could stay home from school. Here was a vague possibility. He canvassed his system. No ailment was found, and he investigated again. This time he thought he could detect colicky symptoms, and he began to encourage them with considerable hope. But they soon grew feeble, and presently died wholly away. He reflected further. Suddenly he discovered something. One of his upper front teeth was loose. This was lucky; he was about to begin to groan, as a "starter," as he called it, when it occurred to him that if he came into court with that argument, his aunt would pull it out, and that would hurt. So he thought he would hold the tooth in reserve for the present, and seek further. Nothing offered for some little time, and then he remembered hearing the doctor tell about a certain thing that laid up a patient for two or three weeks and threatened to make him lose a finger. So the boy eagerly drew his sore toe from under the sheet and held it up for inspection. But now he did not know the necessary symptoms. However, it seemed well worth while to chance it, so he fell to groaning with considerable spirit.

But Sid slept on unconscious.

Tom groaned louder, and fancied that he began to feel pain in the toe.

No result from Sid.

Tom was panting with his exertions by this time. He took a rest and then swelled himself up and fetched a succession of admirable groans.

Sid snored on.

Tom was aggravated. He said, "Sid, Sid!" and shook him. This course worked well, and Tom began to groan again. Sid yawned, stretched, then brought himself up on his elbow with a snort, and began to stare at Tom. Tom went on groaning. Sid said:

"Tom! Say, Tom!" [No response.] "Here Tom! *Tom!* What is the matter, Tom?" And he shook him and looked in his face anxiously.

Tom moaned out:

"O don't, Sid. Don't joggle me."

"Why what's the matter Tom? I must call auntie."

"No—never mind. It'll be over by and by, maybe. Don't call anybody."

"But I must! *Don't* groan so, Tom, it's awful. How long you been this way?"

"Hours. Ouch! O don't stir so, Sid, you'll kill me."

"Tom, why didn't you wake me sooner? O, Tom, *don't!* It makes my flesh crawl to hear you. Tom, what *is* the matter?"

"I forgive you everything, Sid. [Groan.] Everything you've ever done to me. When I'm gone—"

"O, Tom, you ain't dying, are you? Don't, Tom—O, don't. Maybe—"

"I forgive everybody, Sid. [Groan.] Tell 'em so, Sid. And Sid, you give my window-sash and my cat with one eye to that new girl that's come to town, and tell her—"

But Sid had snatched his clothes and gone. Tom was suffering in reality, now, so handsomely was his imagination working, and so his groans had gathered quite a genuine tone.

Sid flew down stairs and said:

"O, Aunt Polly, come! Tom's dying!"

"Dying!"

"Yes'm. Don't wait—come quick!"

"Rubbage! I don't believe it!"

But she fled up stairs, nevertheless, with Sid and Mary at her heels. And her face grew white, too, and her lip trembled. When she reached the bedside she gasped out:

"You Tom! Tom, what's the matter with you?"

"O, auntie, I'm—"

"What's the matter with you—what *is* the matter with you, child?"

"O auntie, my sore toe's mortified!"

The old lady sank down into a chair and laughed a little, then cried a little, then did both together. This restored her and she said:

"Tom, what a turn you did give me. Now you shut up that nonsense and climb out of this."

The groans ceased and the pain vanished from the toe. The boy felt a little foolish, and he said:

"Aunt Polly it *seemed* mortified, and it hurt so I never minded my tooth at all."

"Your tooth, indeed! What's the matter with your tooth?"

"One of them's loose, and it aches perfectly awful."

"There, there, now, don't begin that groaning again. Open your mouth. Well—your tooth *is* loose, but you're not going to die about that. Mary get me a silk thread, and a chunk of fire out of the kitchen."

Tom said:

"O, please auntie, don't pull it out. It don't hurt any more. I wish I may never stir if it does. Please don't, auntie. *I* don't want to stay home from school."

"Oh, you don't, don't you? So all this row was because you thought you'd get to stay home from school and go fishing? Tom, Tom, I love you so, and you seem to try every way you can to break my old heart with your outrageousness." By this time the dental instruments were ready. The old lady made one end of the silk thread fast to Tom's tooth with a loop and tied the other to the bed-post. Then she seized the chunk of fire and suddenly thrust it almost into the boy's face. The tooth hung dangling by the bed-post, now.

But all trials bring their compensations. As Tom wended to school after breakfast, he was the envy of every boy he met because the gap in his upper row of teeth enabled him to expectorate in a new and admirable way. He gathered quite a following of lads interested in the exhibition; and one that had cut his finger and had been a centre of fascination and homage up to this time, now found himself suddenly without an adherent, and shorn of his glory. His heart was heavy, and he said with a disdain which he did not feel, that it wasn't anything to spit like Tom Sawyer; but another boy said "Sour grapes!" and he wandered away a dismantled hero.

Shortly Tom came upon the juvenile pariah of the village, Huckleberry Finn, son of the town drunkard. Huckleberry was cordially hated and dreaded by all the mothers of the town, because he was idle, and lawless, and vulgar and bad—and because all their children admired him so, and delighted in his forbidden society, and wished they dared to be like him. Tom was like the rest of the respectable boys, in that he envied Huckleberry his gaudy outcast condition, and was under strict orders not to play with him. So he played with him every time he got a chance. Huckleberry was always dressed in the cast-off clothes of full-grown men, and they were in perennial bloom and fluttering with rags. His hat was a vast ruin with a wide crescent lopped out of its brim; his coat, when he wore one, hung nearly to his heels and had the rearward buttons far down the back; but one suspender supported his trousers; the seat of the trousers bagged low and contained nothing; the fringed legs dragged in the dirt when not rolled up.

Huckleberry came and went, at his own free will. He slept on door-steps in fine weather and in empty hogsheads in wet; he did not have to go to school or to church, or call any being master or obey anybody; he could go fishing or swimming when and where he chose, and stay as long as it suited him; nobody forbade him to fight; he could sit up as late as he pleased; he was always the first boy that went barefoot in the spring and the last to resume leather in the fall; he never had to wash, nor put on clean clothes; he could swear wonderfully. In a word, everything that goes to make life precious, that boy had. So thought every harassed, hampered, respectable boy in St. Petersburgh.

Tom hailed the romantic outcast:

"Hello, Huckleberry!"

"Hello yourself, and see how you like it."

"What's that you got?"

"Dead cat."

"Lemme see him Huck. My, he's pretty stiff. Where'd you get him?"

"Bought him off'n a boy."

"What did you give?"

"I give a blue ticket and a bladder that I got at the slaughter house."

"Where'd you get the blue ticket?"

"Bought it off'n Ben Rogers two weeks ago for a hoop-stick."

"Say—what is dead cats good for, Huck?"

"Good for? Cure warts with."

"No! Is that so? I know something that's better."

"I bet you don't. What is it?"

"Why, spunk-water."

"Spunk-water! I wouldn't give a dern for spunk-water."

"You wouldn't wouldn't you? D'you ever try it?"

"No, I hain't. But Bob Tanner did."

"Who told you so!"

"Why he told Jeff Thatcher, and Jeff told Johnny Baker, and Johnny told Jim Hollis, and Jim told Ben Rogers, and Ben told a nigger, and the nigger told me. There now!"

"Well, what of it? They'll all lie. Leastways all but the nigger. I don't know him. But I never see a nigger that *wouldn't* lie. Shucks! Now you tell me how Bob Tanner done it, Huck."

"Why he took and dipped his hand in a rotten stump where the rain water was."

"In the day time?"

"Certainly."

"With his face to the stump?"

"Yes. Least I reckon so."

"Did he *say* anything?"

"I don't reckon he did. I don't know."

"Aha! Talk about trying to cure warts with spunk-water such a blame fool way as that! Why that ain't a going to do any good. You got to go all by yourself, to the middle of the woods, where you know there's a spunk-water stump, and just as it's midnight you back up against the stump and jam your hand in and say:

"Barley-corn, Barley-corn, injun-meal shorts,
Spunk-water, spunk-water, swaller these warts."

and then walk away quick, eleven steps, with your eyes shut, and then turn around three times and walk home without speaking to anybody. Because if you speak the charm's busted."

"Well that sounds like a good way; but that ain't the way Bob Tanner done."

"No, sir, you can bet he didn't, becuz he's the wartiest boy in this town; and he wouldn't have a wart on him if he'd knowed how to work spunk-water. I've took off thousands of warts off of my hands that way Huck. I play with frogs so much that I've always got considerable many warts. Sometimes I take 'em off with a bean."

"Yes, bean's good. I've done that."

"Have you? What's your way?"

"You take and split the bean, and cut the wart so as to get some blood, and then you put the blood on one piece of the bean and take and dig a hole and bury it 'bout midnight at the cross-roads in the dark of the moon, and then you burn up the rest of the bean. You see that piece that's got the blood on it will keep drawing and drawing, trying to fetch the other piece to it, and so that helps the blood to draw the wart, and pretty soon off she comes."

"Yes that's it Huck—that's it; though when you're burying it if you say 'Down bean; off wart; come no more to bother me!' it's better. That's the way Joe Harper does, and he's been nearly to Coonville and most everywheres. But say—how do you cure 'em with dead cats?"

"Why you take your cat and go and get in the graveyard 'long about midnight when somebody that was wicked has been buried; and when it's midnight a devil will come, or maybe two or three, but you can't see 'em, you can only hear something like the wind, or maybe hear 'em talk; and when they're taking that feller away, you heave your cat after 'em and say 'Devil follow corpse, cat follow devil, warts follow cat, I'm done with ye!' That'll fetch any wart."

"Sounds right. D'you ever try it, Huck?"

"No, but old mother Hopkins told me."

"Well I reckon it's so, then. Becuz they say she's a witch."

"Say! Why Tom I know she is. She witched pap. Pap says so his own self. He come along one day, and he see she was witching him, so he took up a rock, and if she hadn't dodged, he'd a got her. Well that very night he rolled off'n a shed where' he was a layin drunk, and broke his arm."

"Why that's awful. How did he know she was a witching him."

"Lord, pap can tell, easy. Pap says when they keep looking at you right stiddy, they're a witching you. Specially if they mumble. Becuz when they mumble they're saying the Lord's Prayer back-ards."

"Say, Hucky, when you going to try the cat?"

"To-night. I reckon they'll come after old Hoss Williams to-night."

"But they buried him Saturday. Didn't they get him Saturday night?"

"Why how you talk! How could their charms work till midnight? —and *then* it's Sunday. Devils don't slosh around much of a Sunday, I don't reckon."

"I never thought of that. That's so. Lemme go with you?"

"Of course—if you ain't afeard."

"Afeard! 'Tain't likely. Will you meow?"

"Yes—and you meow back, if you get a chance. Last time, you kep' me a meowing around till old Hays went to throwing rocks at me and says 'Dern that cat!' and so I hove a brick through his window—but don't you tell."

"I won't. I couldn't meow that night, becuz auntie was watching me, but I'll meow this time. Say—what's that?"

"Nothing but a tick."

"Where'd you get him?"

"Out in the woods."

"What'll you take for him?"

"I don't know. I don't want to sell him."

"All right. It's a mighty small tick, anyway."

"O, anybody can run a tick down that don't belong to them. I'm satisfied with it. It's a good enough tick for me."

"Sho, there's ticks a plenty. I could have a thousand of 'em if I wanted to."

"Well why don't you? Becuz you know mighty well you can't. This is a pretty early tick, I reckon. It's the first one I've seen this year."

"Say Huck—I'll give you my tooth for him."

"Less see it."

Tom got out a bit of paper and carefully unrolled it. Huckleberry viewed it wistfully. The temptation was very strong. At last he said:

"Is it genuwyne?"

Tom lifted his lip and showed the vacancy.

"Well, all right," said Huckleberry, "it's a trade."

Tom enclosed the tick in the percussion-cap box that had lately been the pinch-bug's prison, and the boys separated, each feeling wealthier than before.

When Tom reached the little isolated frame School-house, he strode in briskly, with the manner of one who had come with all honest speed. He hung his hat on a peg and flung himself into his seat with business-like alacrity. The master, throned on high in his great splint-bottom arm-chair, was dozing, lulled by the drowsy hum of study. The interruption roused him.

"Thomas Sawyer!"

Tom knew that when his name was pronounced in full, it meant trouble.

"Sir!"

"Come up here. Now sir, why are you late again, as usual?"

Tom was about to take refuge in a lie, when he saw two long tails of yellow hair hanging down a back that he recognized by the electric sympathy of love; and by that form was *the only vacant place* on the girl's side of the school-house. He instantly said:

"I STOPPED TO TALK WITH HUCKLEBERRY FINN!"

The master's pulse stood still, and he stared helplessly. The buzz of study ceased. The pupils wondered if this fool-hardy boy had lost his mind. The master said:

"You—you did what?"

"Stopped to talk with Huckleberry Finn."

There was no mistaking the words.

"Thomas Sawyer, this is the most astounding confession I have ever listened to. No mere ferule will answer for this offence. Take off your jacket."

The master's arm performed until it was tired and the stock of switches notably diminished. Then the order followed:

"Now sir, go and sit with the *girls!* And let this be a warning to you."

The titter that rippled around the room appeared to abash the boy, but in reality that result was caused rather more by his worshipful awe of his unknown idol and the dread pleasure that lay in his high good fortune. He sat down upon the end of the pine bench and the girl hitched herself away from him with a toss of her head. Nudges and winks and whispers traversed the room, but Tom sat still, with his arms upon the long, low desk before him, and seemed to study his book.

By and by attention ceased from him, and the accustomed school murmur rose upon the dull air once more. Presently the boy began to steal furtive glances at the girl. She observed it, "made a mouth" at him and gave him the back of her head for the space of a minute. When she cautiously faced around again, a peach lay before her. She thrust it away. Tom gently put it back. She thrust it away, again, but with less animosity. Tom patiently returned it to its place. Then she let it remain. Tom scrawled on his slate, "Please take it— I got more." The girl glanced at the words, but made no sign. Now the boy began to draw something on the slate, hiding his work with his left hand. For a time the girl refused to notice; but her human curiosity presently began to manifest itself by hardly perceptible signs. The boy worked on, apparently unconcious. The girl made a sort of non-committal attempt to see, but the boy did not betray that he was aware of it. At last she gave in and hesitatingly whispered:

"Let me see it."

Tom partly uncovered a dismal caricature of a house with two gable ends to it and a cork-screw of smoke issuing from the chimney. Then the girl's interest began to fasten itself upon the work and she forgot everything else. When it was finished, she gazed a moment, then whispered:

"It's nice—make a man."

The artist erected a man in the front yard, that resembled a derrick. He could have stepped over the house; but the girl was not hypercritical; she was satisfied with the monster, and whispered:

"It's a beautiful man—now make me coming along."

Tom drew an hour-glass with a full moon and straw limbs to it and armed the spreading fingers with a portentous fan. The girl said:

"It's ever so nice—I wish I could draw."

"It's easy," whispered Tom, "I'll learn you."

"O, will you? When?"

"At noon. Do you go home to dinner?"

"I'll stay if you will."

"Good,—that's a whack. What's your name?"

"Becky Thatcher. What's yours? Oh, I know. It's Thomas Sawyer."

"That's the name they lick me by. I'm Tom when I'm good. You call me Tom, will you?"

"Yes."

Now Tom began to scrawl something on the slate, hiding the words from the girl. But she was not backward this time. She begged to see. Tom said:

"Oh it ain't anything."

"Yes it is."

"No it ain't. You don't want to see."

"Yes I do, indeed I do. Please let me."

"You'll tell."

"No I won't—deed and deed and double deed I won't."

"You won't tell anybody at all? Ever, as long as you live?"

"No I won't ever tell *anybody*. Now let me."

"Oh, *you* don't want to see!"

"Now that you treat me so, I *will* see." And she put her small hand upon his and a little scuffle ensued, Tom pretending to resist in earnest but letting his hand slip by degrees till these words were revealed: *"I love you."*

"O, you bad thing!" And she hit his hand a smart rap but reddened and looked pleased, nevertheless.

Just at this juncture the boy felt a low, fateful grip closing on his ear, and a steady lifting impulse. In that vise he was borne across the house and deposited in his own seat, under a peppering fire of giggles from the whole school. Then the master stood over him during a few awful moments, and finally moved away to his throne without saying a word. But although Tom's ear tingled, his heart was jubilant.

As the school quieted down Tom made an honest effort to study, but the turmoil within him was too great. In turn he took his place in the reading class and made a botch of it; then in the geography class and turned lakes into mountains, mountains into rivers, and rivers into continents, till chaos was come again; then in the spelling class, and got "turned down," by a succession of mere baby words till he brought up at the foot and yielded up the pewter medal which he had worn with ostentation for months.

CHAPTER VII

The harder Tom tried to fasten his mind on his book, the more his ideas wandered. So at last, with a sigh and a yawn, he gave it up. It seemed to him that the noon recess would never come. The air was utterly dead. There was not a breath stirring. It was the sleepiest of sleepy days. The drowsing murmur of the five and twenty studying scholars, soothed the soul like the spell that is in the murmur of bees. Away off in the flaming sunshine, Cardiff Hill lifted its soft green sides through a shimmering veil of heat, tinted with the purple of distance; a few birds floated on lazy wing high in the air; no other living thing was visible but some cows, and they were asleep. Tom's heart ached to be free, or else to have something of interest to do to pass the dreary time. His hand wandered into his pocket and his face lit up with a glow of gratitude that was prayer, though he did not know it. Then furtively the percussion-cap box came out. He released the tick and put him on the long flat desk. The creature probably glowed with a gratitude that amounted to prayer, too, at this moment, but it was premature: for when he started thankfully to travel off, Tom turned him aside with a pin and made him take a new direction.

Tom's bosom friend sat next him, suffering just as Tom had been, and now he was deeply and gratefully interested in this entertainment in an instant. This bosom friend was Joe Harper. The two boys were sworn friends all the week, and embattled enemies on Saturdays. Joe took a pin out of his lappel and began to assist in exercising the prisoner. The sport grew in interest momently. Soon Tom said that they were interfering with each other, and neither getting the fullest benefit of the tick. So he put Joe's slate on the desk and drew a line down the middle of it from top to bottom.

"Now," said he, "as long as he is on your side you can stir him up and I'll let him alone; but if you let him get away and get on my side, you're to leave him alone as long as I can keep him from crossing over."

"All right, go ahead; start him up."

The tick escaped from Tom, presently, and crossed the equator. Joe harassed him a while, and then he got away and crossed back

again. This change of base occurred often. While one boy was
worrying the tick with absorbing interest, the other would look on
with interest as strong, the two heads bowed together over the slate,
and the two souls dead to all things else. At last luck seemed to settle
and abide with Joe. The tick tried this, that, and the other course,
and got as excited and as anxious as the boys themselves, but time
and again just as he would have victory in his very grasp, so to speak,
and Tom's fingers would be twitching to begin, Joe's pin would
deftly head him off, and keep possession. At last Tom could stand
it no longer. The temptation was too strong. So he reached out and
lent a hand with his pin. Joe was angry in a moment. Said he:

"Tom, you let him alone."

"I only just want to stir him up a little, Joe."

"No, sir, it ain't fair; you just let him alone."

"Blame it, I ain't going to stir him much."

"Let him alone, I tell you!"

"I won't!"

"You shall—he's on my side of the line."

"Look here, Joe Harper, whose is that tick?"

"*I* don't care whose tick he is—he's on my side of the line, and
you shan't touch him."

"Well I'll just bet I will, though. He's my tick and I'll do what I
blame please with him or die!"

A tremendous whack came down on Tom's shoulders, and its
duplicate on Joe's; and for the space of two minutes the dust
continued to fly from the two jackets and the whole school to enjoy
it. The boys had been too absorbed to notice the hush that had stolen
upon the school a while before when the master came tip-toeing
down the room and stood over them. He had contemplated a good
part of the performance before he contributed his bit of variety to it.

When school broke up at noon, Tom flew to Becky Thatcher, and
whispered in her ear:

"Put on your bonnet and let on you're going home; and when you
get to the corner, give the rest of 'em the slip, and turn down through
the lane and come back. I'll go the other way and come it over 'em
the same way."

So the one went off with one group of scholars, and the other with
another: In a little while the two met at the bottom of the lane, and
when they reached the school they had it all to themselves. Then
they sat together, with a slate before them, and Tom gave Becky the
pencil and held her hand in his, guiding it, and so created another
surprising house. When the interest in art began to wane, the two fell
to talking. Tom was swimming in bliss. He said:

"Do you love rats?"

"No! I hate them!"

"Well, I do too—*live* ones. But I mean dead ones, to swing
round your head with a string."

"No, I don't care for rats much, anyway. What *I* like is chewing-gum."

"O, I should say so! I wish I had some now."

"Do you? I've got some. I'll let you chew it awhile, but you must give it back to me."

That was agreeable, so they chewed it turn about, and dangled their legs against the bench in excess of contentment.

"Was you ever at a circus?" said Tom.

"Yes, and my pa's going to take me again some time, if I'm good."

"I been to the circus three or four times—lots of times. Church ain't shucks to a circus. There's things going on at a circus all the time. I'm going to be a clown in a circus when I grow up."

"O, are you! That will be nice. They're so lovely, all spotted up."

"Yes, that's so. And they get slathers of money—most a dollar a day, Ben Rogers says. Say, Becky, was you ever engaged?"

"What's that?"

"Why, engaged to be married."

"No."

"Would you like to?"

"I reckon so. I don't know. What is it like?"

"Like? Why it ain't like anything. You only just tell a boy you won't ever have any body but him: ever ever *ever,* and then you kiss and that's all. Anybody can do it."

"Kiss? What do you kiss for?"

"Why that, you know, is to—well, they always do that."

"Everybody?"

"Why yes, everybody that's in love with each other. Do you remember what I wrote on the slate?"

"Ye—yes."

"What was it?"

"I shant tell you."

"Shall I tell *you?*"

"Ye-yes—but some other time."

"No, now."

"No, not now—to-morrow."

"O, no, *now.* Please Becky—I'll whisper it, I'll whisper it ever so easy."

Becky hesitating, Tom took silence for consent, and passed his arm about her waist and whispered the tale ever so softly, with his mouth close to her ear. And then he added:

"Now you whisper it to me—just the same."

She resisted, for a while, and then said:

"You turn your face away so you can't see, and then I will. But you mustn't ever tell anybody—*will* you, Tom? Now you won't, *will* you?"

"No, indeed indeed I won't. Now Becky."

He turned his face away. She bent timidly around till her breath stirred his curls and whispered, "I—love—you!"

Then she sprang away and ran around and around the desks and benches, with Tom after her, and took refuge in a corner at last, with her little white apron to her face. Tom clasped her about her neck and pleaded:

"Now Becky, it's all done—all over but the kiss. Don't you be afraid of that—it ain't anything at all. Please, Becky."—And he tugged at her apron and the hands.

By and by she gave up, and let her hands drop; her face, all glowing with the struggle, came up and submitted. Tom kissed the red lips and said:

"Now it's all done, Becky. And always after this, you know, you ain't ever to love anybody but me, and you ain't ever to marry anybody but me, never never and forever. Will you?"

"No, I'll never love anybody but you, Tom, and I'll never marry anybody but you—and you ain't to ever marry anybody but me, either."

"Certainly. Of course. That's *part* of it. And always coming to school or when we're going home, you're to walk with me, when there ain't anybody looking—and you choose me and I choose you at parties, because that's the way you do when you're engaged."

"It's so nice. I never heard of it before."

"O, its ever so gay! Why me and Amy Lawrence—"

The big eyes told Tom his blunder and he stopped, confused.

"O, Tom! Then I ain't the first you've been engaged to!"

The child began to cry. Tom said:

"O don't cry, Becky, I don't care for her any more."

"Yes you do, Tom,—you know you do."

Tom tried to put his arm about her neck, but she pushed him away and turned her face to the wall, and went on crying. Tom tried again, with soothing words in his mouth, and was repulsed again. Then his pride was up and he strode away and went outside. He stood about, restless and uneasy, for a while, glancing at the door, every now and then, hoping she would repent and come to find him. But she did not. Then he began to feel badly and fear that he was in the wrong. It was a hard struggle with him to make new advances, now, but he nerved himself to it and entered. She was still standing back there in the corner, sobbing, with her face to the wall. Tom's heart smote him. He went to her and stood a moment, not knowing exactly how to proceed. Then he said hesitatingly:

"Becky, I—I don't care for anybody but you."

No reply—but sobs.

"Becky,"—pleadingly. "Becky, won't you say something?"

More sobs.

Tom got out his chiefest jewel, a brass knob from the top of an andiron, and passed it around her so that she could see it, and said:

"Please, Becky, won't you take it?"

She struck it to the floor. Then Tom marched out of the house and over the hills and far away, to return to school no more that day. Presently Becky began to suspect. She ran to the door; he was not in sight; she flew around to the play-yard; he was not there. Then she called:

"Tom! Come back Tom!"

She listened intently, but there was no answer. She had no companions but silence and loneliness. So she sat down to cry again and upbraid herself; and by this time the scholars began to gather again, and she had to hide her griefs and still her broken heart and take up the cross of a long, dreary, aching afternoon, with none among the strangers about her to exchange sorrows with.

CHAPTER VIII

Tom dodged hither and thither through lanes until he was well out of the track of returning scholars, and then fell into a moody jog. He crossed a small "branch" two or three times, because of prevailing juvenile superstition that to cross water baffled pursuit. Half an hour later he was disappearing behind the Douglas mansion on the summit of Cardiff Hill, and the school-house was hardly distinguishable away off in the valley behind him. He entered a dense wood, picked his pathless way to the centre of it, and sat down on a mossy spot under a spreading oak. There was not even a zephyr stirring; the dead noonday heat had even stilled the songs of the birds; nature lay in a trance that was broken by no sound but the occasional far-off hammering of a woodpecker, and this seemed to render the pervading silence and sense of loneliness the more profound. The boy's soul was steeped in melancholy; his feelings were in happy accord with his surroundings. He sat long with his elbows on his knees and his chin in his hands, meditating. It seemed to him that life was but a trouble, at best, and he more than half envied Jimmy Hodges, so lately released; it must be very peaceful, he thought, to lie and slumber and dream forever and ever, with the wind whispering through the trees and caressing the grass and the flowers over the grave, and nothing to bother and grieve about, ever any more. If he only had a clean Sunday-school record he could be willing to go, and be done with it all. Now as to this girl. What had he done? Nothing. He had meant the best in the world, and been treated like a dog—like a very dog. She would be sorry some day—maybe when it was too late. Ah, if he could only die *temporarily!*

But the elastic heart of youth cannot be compressed into one constrained shape long at a time. Tom presently began to drift insensibly back into the concerns of this life again. What if he turned his back, now, and disappeared mysteriously? What if he went away—ever so far away, into unknown countries beyond the seas—and never come back any more! How would she feel then! The idea of being a clown recurred to him now, only to fill him with disgust. For frivolity and jokes and spotted tights were an offense, when they intruded themselves upon a spirit that was exalted into the vague august realm of the romantic. No, he would be a soldier, and return after long years, all war-worn and illustrious. No— better still, he would join the Indians, and hunt buffaloes and go on the warpath in the mountain ranges and the trackless great plains of the Far West, and away in the future come back a great chief, bristling with feathers, hideous with paint, and prance into Sunday-school, some drowsy summer morning, with a blood-curdling war-whoop, and sear the eye-balls of all his companions with unappeasable envy. But no, there was something gaudier even than this. He would be a pirate! That was it! *Now* his future lay plain before him, and glowing with unimaginable splendor. How his name would fill the world, and make people shudder! How gloriously he would go plowing the dancing seas, in his long, low, black-hulled racer, the "Spirit of the Storm," with his grisly flag flying at the fore! And at the zenith of his time, how he would suddenly appear at the old village and stalk into church, brown and weather-beaten, in his black velvet doublet and trunks, his great jack-boots, his crimson sash, his belt bristling with horse-pistols, his crime-rusted cutlass at his side, his slouch hat with waving plumes, his black flag unfurled, with the skull and cross-bones on it, and hear with swelling ecstasy the whisperings, "It's Tom Sawyer the Pirate!—the Black Avenger of the Spanish Main!"

Yes, it was settled; his career was determined. He would run away from home and enter upon it. He would start the very next morning. Therefore he must now begin to get ready. He would collect his resources together. He went to a rotten log near at hand and began to dig under one end of it with his Barlow knife. He soon struck wood that sounded hollow. He put his hand there and uttered this incantation impressively:

"What hasn't come here, *come!* What's here, *stay* here!"

Then he scraped away the dirt, and exposed a pine shingle. He took it up and disclosed a shapely little treasure-house whose bottom and sides were of shingles. In it lay a marble. Tom's astonishment was boundless! He scratched his head with a perplexed air, and said:

"Well, that beats anything?"

Then he tossed the marble away pettishly, and stood cogitating. The truth was, that a superstition of his had failed, here, which he and his comrades had always looked upon as infallible. If you buried a marble with certain necessary incantations, and left it alone a fortnight, and then opened the place with the incantation he had just used, you would find that all the marbles you had ever lost had gathered themselves together there, meantime, no matter how widely they had been separated. But now, this thing had actually and unquestionably failed. Tom's whole structure of faith was shaken to its foundations. He had many a time heard of this thing succeeding, but never of its failing before. It did not occur to him that he had tried it several times before, himself, but could never find the hiding places afterwards. He puzzled over the matter some time, and finally decided that some witch had interfered and broken the charm. He thought he would satisfy himself on that point; so he searched around till he found a small sandy spot with a little funnel-shaped depression in it. He laid himself down and put his mouth close to this depression and called:

"Doodle-bug, doodle-bug, tell me what I want to know! Doodle-bug, doodle-bug tell me what I want to know!"

The sand began to work, and presently a small black bug appeared for a second and then darted under again in a fright.

"He dasn't tell! So it *was* a witch that done it. I just knowed it."

He well knew the futility of trying to contend against witches, so he gave up discouraged. But it occurred to him that he might as well have the marble he had just thrown away, and therefore he went and made a patient search for it. But he could not find it. Now he went back to his treasure-house and carefully placed himself just as he had been standing when he tossed the marble away; then he took another marble from his pocket and tossed it in the same way, saying:

"Brother go find your brother!"

He watched where it stopped, and went there and looked. But it must have fallen short or gone too far; so he tried twice more. The last repetition was successful. The two marbles lay within a foot of each other.

Just here the blast of a toy tin trumpet came faintly down the green aisles of the forest. Tom flung off his jacket and trousers, turned a suspender into a belt, raked away some brush behind the rotten log, disclosing a rude bow and arrow, a lath sword and a tin trumpet, and in a moment had seized these things and bounded away, bare legged, with fluttering shirt. He presently halted under a great elm, blew an answering blast, and then began to tip-toe and look warily out, this way and that. He said cautiously—to an imaginary company:

"Hold, my merry men! Keep hid till I blow."

Now appeared Joe Harper, as airily clad and elaborately armed as Tom. Tom called:

"Hold! Who come here into Sherwood Forest without my pass?"

"Guy of Guisborne wants no man's pass. Who art thou that—that—"

"Dares to hold such language," said Tom, prompting—for they talked "by the book," from memory.

"Who art thou that dares to hold such language?"

"I, indeed! I am Robin Hood, as thy caitiff carcase soon shall know."

"Then art thou indeed that famous outlaw? Right gladly will I dispute with thee the passes of the merry wood. Have at thee!"

They took their lath swords, dumped their other traps on the ground, struck a fencing attitude, foot to foot, and began a grave, careful combat, "two up and two down." Presently Tom said:

"Now if you've got the hang, go it lively!"

So they "went it lively," panting and perspiring with the work. By and by Tom shouted:

"Fall! fall! Why don't you fall?"

"I shan't! Why don't you fall yourself? You're getting the worst of it."

"Why that ain't anything. *I* can't fall; that ain't the way it is in the book. The book says 'Then with one back-handed stroke he slew poor Guy of Guisborne.' You're to turn around and let me hit you in the back."

There was no getting around the authorities, so Joe turned, received the whack and fell.

"Now," said Joe, getting up, "You got to let me kill *you.* That's fair."

"Why I can't do that, it ain't in the book."

"Well it's blamed mean,—that's all."

"Well, say, Joe, you can be Friar Tuck or Much the miller's son and lam me with a quarter-staff; or I'll be the Sheriff of Nottingham and you be Robin Hood a little while and kill me."

This was satisfactory, and so these adventures were carried out. Then Tom became Robin Hood again, and was allowed by the treacherous nun to bleed his strength away through his neglected wound. And at last Joe, representing a whole tribe of weeping outlaws, dragged him sadly forth, gave his bow into his feeble hands, and Tom said, "Where this arrow falls, there bury poor Robin Hood under the greenwood tree." Then he shot the arrow and fell back and would have died but he lit on a nettle and sprang up too gaily for a corpse.

The boys dressed themselves, hid their accoutrements, and went off grieving that there were no outlaws any more, and wondering what modern civilization could claim to have done to compensate for their loss. They said they would rather be outlaws a year in Sherwood Forest than President of the United States forever.

CHAPTER IX

At half past nine, that night, Tom and Sid were sent to bed, as usual. They said their prayers, and Sid was soon asleep. Tom lay awake and waited, in restless impatience. When it seemed to him that it must be nearly daylight, he heard the clock strike ten! This was despair. He would have tossed and fidgeted, as his nerves demanded, but he was afraid he might wake Sid. So he lay still, and stared up into the dark. Everything was dismally still. By and by, out of the stillness, little, scarcely preceptible noises began to emphasize themselves. The ticking of the clock began to bring itself into notice. Old beams began to crack mysteriously. The stairs creaked faintly. Evidently spirits were abroad. A measured, muffled snore issued from Aunt Polly's chamber. And now the tiresome chirping of a cricket that no human ingenuity could locate, began. Next the ghastly ticking of a death-watch in the wall at the bed's head made Tom shudder—it meant that somebody's days were numbered. Then the howl of a far-off dog rose on the night air, and was answered by a fainter howl from a remoter distance. Tom was in an agony. At last he was satisfied that time had ceased and eternity begun; he began to doze, in spite of himself; the clock chimed eleven but he did not hear it. And then there came mingling with his half-formed dreams, a most melancholy caterwauling. The raising of a neighboring window disturbed him. A cry of "Scat! you devil!" and the crash of an empty bottle against the back of his aunt's woodshed brought him wide awake, and a single minute later he was dressed and out of the window and creeping along the roof of the "ell" on all fours. He "meow'd" with caution once or twice, as he went; then jumped to the roof of the woodshed and thence to the ground. Huckleberry Finn was there, with his dead cat. The boys moved off and disappeared in the gloom. At the end of half an hour they were wading through the tall grass of the graveyard.

It was a graveyard of the old-fashioned western kind. It was on a hill, about a mile and a half from the village. It had a crazy board fence around it, which leaned inward in places, and outward the rest of the time, but stood upright nowhere. Grass and weeds grew rank over the whole cemetery. All the old graves were sunken in, there was not a tombstone on the place; round-topped, worm-eaten boards staggered over the graves, leaning for support and finding none. "Sacred to the memory of" So-and-So had been painted on them once, but it could no longer have been read, on the most of them, now, even if there had been light.

A faint wind moaned through the trees, and Tom feared it might be the spirits of the dead, complaining at being disturbed. The boys talked little, and only under their breath, for the time and the place and the pervading solemnity and silence oppressed their spirits. They found the sharp new heap they were seeking, and ensconsced themselves within the protection of three great elms that grew in a bunch within a few feet of the grave.

Then they waited in silence for what seemed a long time. The hooting of a distant owl was all the sound that troubled the dead stillness. Tom's reflections grew oppressive. He must force some talk. So he said in a whisper:

"Hucky, do you believe the dead people like it for us to be here?"
Huckleberry whispered:

"I wisht I knowed. It's awful solemn like, *ain't* it?"

"I bet it is."

There was a considerable pause, while the boys canvassed this
matter inwardly. Then Tom whispered:

"Say, Hucky—do you reckon Hoss Williams hears us talking?"

"O' course he does. Least his sperrit does."

Tom, after a pause:

"I wish I'd said *Mister* Williams. But I never meant any harm.
Everybody calls him Hoss."

"A body can't be too partic'lar how they talk 'bout these-yer
dead people, Tom."

This was a damper, and conversation died again. Presently Tom
seized his comrade's arm and said:

"Sh!"

"What is it, Tom?" And the two clung together with beating
hearts.

"Sh! There 'tis again! Didn't you hear it?"

"I—"

"There! Now you hear it."

"Lord, Tom they're coming! They're coming, sure. What'll we
do?"

"I dono. Think they'll see us?"

"O, Tom, they can see in the dark, same as cats. I wisht I hadn't
come."

"O, don't be afeard. *I* don't believe they'll bother us. We ain't
doing any harm. If we keep perfectly still, maybe they won't notice
us at all."

"I'll try to, Tom, but Lord I'm all of a shiver."

"Listen!"

The boys bent their heads together and scarcely breathed. A
muffled sound of voices floated up from the far end of the
graveyard.

"Look! See there!" whispered Tom. "What is it?"

"It's devil-fire. O, Tom, this is awful."

Some vague figures approached through the gloom, swinging an
old-fashioned tin lantern that freckled the ground with
innumerable little spangles of light. Presently Huckleberry
whispered with a shudder:

"It's the devils sure enough. Three of 'em! Lordy, Tom, we're
goners! Can you pray?"

"I'll try, but don't you be afeard. They ain't going to hurt us.
Now I lay me down to sleep, I—"

"Sh!"

"What is it, Huck?"

"They're *humans!* One of 'em is, anyway. One of 'em's old Muff

Potter's voice."

"No—tain't so, is it?"

"I bet I know it. Don't you stir nor budge. *He* ain't sharp enough to notice us. Drunk, same as usual, likely—blamed old rip!"

"All right, I'll keep still. Now they're stuck. Can't find it. Here they come again. Now they're hot. Cold again. Hot again. Red hot! They're p'inted right, this time. Say Huck, I know another o' them voices; it's Injun Joe."

"That's so—that murderin' half-breed! I'd druther they was devils a dern sight. What kin they be up to?"

The whispers died wholly out, now, for the three men had reached the grave and stood within a few feet of the boys' hiding-place.

"Here it is," said the third voice; and the owner of it held the lantern up and revealed the face of young Dr. Robinson.

Potter and Injun Joe were carrying a handbarrow with a rope and a couple of shovels on it. They cast down their load and began to open the grave. The doctor put the lantern at the head of the grave and came and sat down with his back against one of the elm trees. He was so close the boys could have touched him.

"Hurry, men!" he said in a low voice; "the moon might come out at any moment."

They growled a response and went on digging. For some time there was no noise but the grating sound of the spades discharging their freight of mould and gravel. It was very monotonous. Finally a spade struck upon the coffin with a dull woody accent, and within another minute or two the men had hoisted it out on the ground. They pried off the lid with their shovels, got out the body and dumped it rudely on the ground. The moon drifted from behind the clouds and exposed the pallid face. The barrow was got ready and the corpse placed on it, covered with a blanket, and bound to its place with the rope. Potter took out a large spring-knife and cut off the dangling end of the rope and then said:

"Now the cussed thing's ready, Sawbones, and you'll just out with another five, or here she stays."

"That's the talk!" said Injun Joe.

"Look here, what does this mean?" said the doctor. "You required your pay in advance, and I've paid you."

"Yes, and you done more than that," said Injun Joe, approaching the doctor, who was now standing. "Five years ago you drove me away from your father's kitchen one night, when I come to ask for something to eat, and you said I warn't there for any good; and when I swore I'd get even with you if it took a hundred years, your father had me jailed for a vagrant. Did you think I'd forget? The Injun blood ain't in me for nothing. And now I've *got* you, and you got to *settle,* you know!"

He was threatening the doctor, with his fist in his face, by this time. The doctor struck out suddenly and stretched the ruffian on the ground. Potter dropped his knife, and exclaimed:

"Here, now, don't you hit my pard!" and the next moment he had grappled with the doctor and the two were struggling with might and main, trampling the grass and tearing the ground with their heels. Injun Joe sprang to his feet, his eyes flaming with passion, snatched up Potter's knife, and went creeping, catlike and stooping, round and round about the combatants, seeking an opportunity. All at once the doctor flung himself free, seized the heavy head board of Williams' grave and felled Potter to the earth with it—and in the same instant the half-breed saw his chance and drove the knife to the hilt in the young man's breast. He reeled and fell partly upon Potter, flooding him with his blood, and in the same moment the clouds blotted out the dreadful spectacle and the two frightened boys went speeding away in the dark.

Presently, when the moon emerged again, Injun Joe was standing over the two forms, contemplating them. The doctor murmured inarticulately, gave a long gasp or two and was still. The half-breed muttered:

"*That* score is settled—damn you."

Then he robbed the body. After which he put the fatal knife in Potter's open right hand, and sat down on the dismantled coffin. Three—four—five minutes passed, and then Potter began to stir and moan. His hand closed upon the knife; he raised it, glanced at it, and let it fall, with a shudder. Then he sat up, pushing the body from him, and gazed at it, and then around him, confusedly. His eyes met Joe's.

"Lord, how is this, Joe?" he said.

"It's a dirty business," said Joe, without moving. "What did you do it for?"

"I! I never done it!"

"Look here! That kind of talk won't wash."

Potter trembled and grew white.

"I thought I'd got sober. I'd no business to drink to-night. But it's in my head yet—worse'n when we started here. I'm all in a muddle; can't recollect anything of it hardly. Tell me, Joe—*honest, now, old feller*—did I do it? Joe, I never meant to—'pon my soul and honor I never meant to, Joe. Tell me how it was Joe. O, it's awful—and him so young and promising."

"Why you two was scuffling, and he fetched you one with the head-board and you fell flat; and then up you come, all reeling and staggering, like, and snatched the knife and jammed it into him, just as he fetched you another awful clip—and here you've laid, as dead as a wedge till now."

"O, I didn't know what I was a doing. I wish I may die this minute if I did. It was all on account of the whisky; and the excitement, I reckon. I never used a weepon in my life before, Joe.

I've fought, but never with weepons. They'll all say that. Joe, don't tell! Say you won't tell, Joe—that's a good feller. I always like you Joe, and stood up for you, too. Don't you remember? You *won't* tell, *will* you Joe?'' And the poor creature dropped on his knees before the stolid murderer, and clasped his appealing hands.

"No, you've always been fair and square with me, Muff Potter, and I won't go back on you.—There, now, that's as fair as a man can say."

"O, Joe, you're an angel. I'll bless you for this the longest day I live." And Potter began to cry.

"Come, now, that's enough of that. This ain't any time for blubbering. You be off yonder way and I'll go this. Move, now, and don't leave any tracks behind you."

Potter started on a trot that quickly increased to a run. The half-breed stood looking after him. He muttered:

"If he's as much stunned with the lick and fuddled with the rum as he had the look of being, he won't think of the knife till he's gone so far he'll be afraid to come back after it to such a place by himself—chicken-heart!"

Two or three minutes later the murdered man, the blanketed corpse, the lidless coffin and the open grave were under no inspection but the moon's. The stillness was complete again, too.

CHAPTER X

The two boys flew on and on, toward the village, speechless with horror. They glanced backward over their shoulders from time to time, apprehensively, as if they feared they might be followed. Every stump that started up in their path seemed a man and an enemy, and made them catch their breath; and as they sped by some outlying cottages that lay near the village, the barking of the aroused watch-dogs seemed to give wings to their feet.

"If we can only get to the old tannery, before we break down!" whispered Tom, in short catches between breaths, "I can't stand it much longer."

Huckleberry's hard pantings were his only reply, and the boys fixed their eyes on the goal of their hopes and bent to their work to win it. They gained steadily on it, and at last, breast to breast they burst through the open door and fell grateful and exhausted in the sheltering shadows beyond. By and by their pulses slowed down, and Tom whispered:

"Huckleberry, what do you reckon 'll come of this?"

"If Dr. Robinson dies, I reckon hangin 'll come of it."

"Do you though?"

"Why I *know* it, Tom."

Tom thought a while, then he said:

"Who'll tell? We?"

"What are you talking about? S'pose something happened and
Injun Joe *didn't* hang? Why he'd kill us some time or other, just as
dead sure as we're a laying here."

"That's just what I was thinking to myself, Huck."

"If anybody tells, let Muff Potter do it, if he's fool enough. He's
generally drunk enough."

Tom said nothing—went on thinking. Presently he whispered:

"Huck, Muff Potter don't *know* it. How can he tell?"

"What's the reason he don't know it?"

"Because he'd just got that whack when Injun Joe done it. D'you
reckon he could see anything? D' you reckon he knowed anything?"

"By hokey, that's so Tom!"

"And besides, look-a-here—maybe that whack done for *him*!"

"No, 'taint likely Tom. He had liquor in him; I could see that; and
besides, he always has. Well when pap's full, you might take and
belt him over the head with a church and you couldn't phase him.
He says so, his own self. So it's the same with Muff Potter, of course.
But if a man was dead sober, I reckon maybe that whack might
fetch him; I dono."

After another reflective silence, Tom said:

"Hucky, you sure you can keep mum?"

"Tom, we *got* to keep mum. *You* know that. That Injun devil
wouldn't make any more of drownding us than a couple of cats,
if we was to squeak 'bout this and they didn't hang him. Now
look-a-here, Tom, less take and swear to one another—that's what
we got to do—swear to keep mum."

"I'm agreed. It's the best thing. Would you just hold hands and
swear that we—"

"O, no, that wouldn't do for this. That's good enough for little
rubbishy common things—specially with gals, cuz *they* go back
on you anyway, and blab if they get in a huff—but there orter be
writing 'bout a big thing like this. And blood."

Tom's whole being applauded this idea. It was deep, and dark,
and awful; the hour, the circumstances, the surroundings, were in
keeping with it. He picked up a clean pine shingle that lay in the
moonlight, took a little fragment of "red keel" out of his pocket,
got the moon on his work, and painfully scrawled these lines,
emphasizing each slow down-stroke by clamping his tongue between
his teeth, and letting up the pressure on the up-strokes:

"Huck Finn and
Tom Sawyer swears
they will keep mum
about this and they

wish they may drop
down dead in their
tracks if they ever
tell and Rot."

Huckleberry was filled with admiration of Tom's facility in writing, and the sublimity of his language. He at once took a pin from his lapel and was going to prick his flesh, but Tom said:

"Hold on! Don't do that. A pin's brass. It might have verdigrease on it."

"What's verdigrease?"

"It's p'ison. That's what it is. You just swaller some of it once—you'll see."

So Tom unwound the thread from one of his needles, and each boy pricked the ball of his thumb and squeezed out a drop of blood. In time, after many squeezes, Tom managed to sign his initials, using the ball of his little finger for a pen. Then he showed Huckleberry how to make an H and an F, and the oath was complete. They buried the shingle close to the wall, with some dismal ceremonies and incantations, and the fetters that bound their tongues were considered to be locked and the key thrown away.

A figure crept stealthily through a break in the other end of the ruined building, now, but they did not notice it.

"Tom," whispered Huckleberry, "does this keep us from *ever* telling *always?*"

"Of course it does. It don't make any difference *what* happens, we got to keep mum. We'd drop down dead—don't *you* know that?"

"Yes, I reckon that's so."

They continued to whisper for some little time. Presently a dog set up a long, lugubrious howl just outside—within ten feet of them. The boys clasped each other suddenly, in an agony of fright.

"Which of us does he mean?" gasped Huckleberry.

"I dono—peep through the crack. Quick!"

"No, *you*, Tom!"

"I can't—I can't *do* it, Huck!"

"Please, Tom. There 'tis again!"

"O, lordy, I'm thankful!" whispered Tom. "I know his voice. It's Bull Harbison."*

"O, that's good—I tell you, Tom, I was most scared to death; I'd a bet anything it was a *stray* dog."

The dog howled again. The boys' hearts sank once more.

"O, my! that ain't no Bull Harbison!" whispered Huckleberry. "*Do*, Tom!"

Tom, quaking with fear, yielded, and put his eye to the crack. His whisper was hardly audible when he said:

"O, Huck, IT'S A STRAY DOG!"

"Quick, Tom, quick! Who does he mean?"

"Huck, he must mean us both—we're right together."

"O, Tom, I reckon we're goners. I reckon there ain't no mistake

---

*If Mr. Harbison had owned a slave named Bull, Tom would have spoken of him as "Harbison's Bull," but a son or a dog of that name was "Bull Harbison."

'bout where *I'll* go to. I been so wicked."

"Dad fetch it! This comes of playing hookey and doing everything a feller's told *not* to do. I might a been good, like Sid, if I'd tried—but no, I wouldn't, of course. But if ever I get off this time, I lay I'll just *waller* in Sunday-schools!" And Tom began to snuffle a little.

"*You* bad!" and Huckleberry began to snuffle too. "Consound it, Tom Sawyer, you're just old pie, 'longside o'wshat *I* am. O, *lordy*, lordy, lordy, I wisht I only had half your chance."

Tom choked off and whispered:

"Look, Hucky, Look! He's got his *back* to us!"

Hucky looked, with joy in his heart.

"Well he has, by jingoes! Did he before?"

"Yes, he did. But I, like a fool, never thought. O, this is bully, you know. *Now* who can he mean?"

The howling stopped. Tom pricked up his ears.

"Sh! What's that?" he whispered.

"Sounds like—like hogs grunting. No—it's somebody snoring. Tom."

"That *is* it? Where 'bouts is it, Huck?"

"I bleeve it's down at 'tother end. Sounds so, anyway. Pap used to sleep there, sometimes, 'long with the hogs, but laws bless you, he just lifts things when *he* snores. Besides, I reckon he ain't ever coming back to this town any more."

The spirit of adventure rose in the boys' souls once more.

"Hucky, do you das't to go if I lead?"

"I don't like to, much. Tom, s'pose it's Injun Joe!"

Tom quailed. But presently the temptation rose up strong again and the boys agreed to try, with the understanding that they would take to their heels if the snoring stopped. So they went tip-toeing stealthily down, the one behind the other. When they had got to within five steps of the snorer, Tom stepped on a stick, and it broke with a sharp snap. The man moaned, writhed a little, and his face came into the moonlight. It was Muff Potter. The boys' hearts had stood still, and their hopes too, when the man moved, but their fears passed away now. They tip-toed out, through the broken weather-boarding, and stopped at a little distance to exchange a parting word. That long, lugubrious howl rose on the night air again! They turned and saw the strange dog standing within a few feet of where Potter was lying, and *facing* Potter, with his nose pointing heavenward.

"O, geeminy it's *him!*" exclaimed both boys, in a breath.

"Say, Tom—they say a stray dog come howling around Johnny Miller's house, 'bout midnight, as much as two weeks ago; and a whippoorwill came in and lit on the bannisters and sung, the very same evening; and there ain't anybody dead there yet."

"Well I know that. And suppose there ain't. Didn't Gracie Miller fall in the kitchen fire and burn herself terrible the very next

Saturday?"

"Yes, but she ain't *dead*. And what's more, she's getting better, too."

"All right, you wait and see. She's a goner, just as dead sure as Muff Potter's a goner. That's what the niggers say, and they know all about these kind of things, Huck."

Then they separated, cogitating. When Tom crept in at his bedroom window, the night was almost spent. He undressed with excessive caution, and fell asleep congratulating himself that nobody knew of his escapade. He was not aware that the gently-snoring Sid was awake, and had been so for an hour.

When Tom awoke, Sid was dressed and gone. There was a late look in the light, a late sense in the atmosphere. He was startled. Why had he not been called—persecuted till he was up, as usual? The thought filled him with bodings. Within five minutes he was dressed and down stairs, feeling sore and drowsy. The family were still at table, but they had finished breakfast. There was no voice of rebuke; but there were averted eyes; there was a silence and an air of solemnity that struck a chill to the culprit's heart. He sat down and tried to seem gay, but it was up-hill work; it roused no smile, no response, and he lapsed into silence and let his heart sink down to the depths.

After breakfast his aunt took him aside, and Tom almost brightened in the hope that he was going to be flogged; but it was not so. His aunt wept over him and asked him how he could go and break her old heart so; and finally told him to go on, and ruin himself and bring her grey hairs with sorrow to the grave, for it was no use for her to try any more. This was worse than a thousand whippings, and Tom's heart was sorer now than his body. He cried, he pleaded for forgiveness, promised reform over and over again and then received his dismissal, feeling that he had won but an imperfect forgiveness and established but a feeble confidence.

He left the presence too miserable to even feel revengeful toward Sid; and so the latter's prompt retreat through the back gate was unnecessary. He moped to school gloomy and sad, and took his flogging, along with Joe Harper, for playing hooky the day before, with the air of one whose heart was busy with heavier woes and wholly dead to trifles. Then he betook himself to his seat, rested his elbows on his desk and his jaws in his hands and stared at the wall with the stony stare of suffering that has reached the limit and can no further go. His elbow was pressing against some hard substance. After a long time he slowly and sadly changed his position, and took up this object with a sigh. It was in a paper. He unrolled it. A long, lingering, colossal sigh followed, and his heart broke. It was his brass andiron knob!

This final feather broke the camel's back.

· CHAPTER XI

Close upon the hour of noon the whole village was suddenly electrified with the ghastly news. No need of the as yet undreamed-of telegraph; the tale flew from man to man, from group to group, from house to house, with little less than telegraphic speed. Of course the schoolmaster gave holiday for that afternoon; the town would have thought strangely of him if he had not.

A gory knife had been found close to the murdered man, and it had been recognized by somebody as belonging to Muff Potter— so the story ran. And it was said that a belated citizen had come upon Potter washing himself in the "branch" about one or two o'clock in the morning, and that Potter had at once sneaked off— suspicious circumstances, especially the washing, which was not a habit with Potter. It was also said that the town had been ransacked for this "murderer," (the public are not slow in the matter of sifting evidence and arriving at a verdict), but that he could not be found. Horsemen had departed down all the roads in every direction, and the Sheriff "was confident" that he would be captured before night.

All the town was drifting toward the graveyard. Tom's heart-break vanished and he joined the procession, not because he would not a thousand times rather go anywhere else, but because an awful, unaccountable fascination drew him on. Arrived at the dreadful place, he wormed his small body through the crowd and saw the dismal spectacle. It seemed to him an age since he was there before. Somebody pinched his arm. He turned, and his eyes met Huckleberry's. Then both looked elsewhere at once, and wondered if anybody had noticed anything in their mutual glance. But everybody was talking, and intent upon the grisly spectacle before them.

"Poor fellow!" "Poor young fellow!" "This ought to be a lesson to grave-robbers!" "Muff Potter'll hang for this if they catch him!" This was the drift of remark; and the minister said, "It was a judgment; His hand is here."

Now Tom shivered from head to heel; for his eye fell upon the stolid face of Injun Joe. At this moment the crowd began to sway and struggle, and voices shouted, "It's him! he's coming himself!"

"Who? Who?" from twenty voices.

"Muff Potter!"

"Hallo, he's stopped!—Look out, he's turning! Don't let him get away!"

People in the branches of the trees over Tom's head, said he wasn't trying to get away—he only looked doubtful and perplexed.

"Infernal impudence!" said a bystander; "wanted to come and take a quiet look at his work, I reckon—didn't expect any company."

The crowd fell apart, now, and the Sheriff came through,

ostentatiously leading Potter by the arm. The poor fellow's face was haggard, and his eyes showed the fear that was upon him. When he stood before the murdered man, he shook as with a palsy, and he put his face in his hands and burst into tears.

"I didn't do it, friends," he sobbed; "'pon my word and honor I never done it."

"Who's accused you?" shouted a voice.

This shot seemed to carry home. Potter lifted his face and looked around him with a pathetic hopelessness in his eyes. He saw Injun Joe, and exclaimed:

"O, Injun Joe, you promised me you'd never—"

"Is that your knife?" and it was thrust before him by the Sheriff.

Potter would have fallen if they had not caught him and eased him to the ground. Then he said:

"Something told me 't if I didn't come back and get—" He shuddered; then waved his nerveless hand with a vanquished gesture and said, "Tell 'em, Joe, tell 'em—it ain't any use any more."

Then Huckleberry and Tom stood dumb and staring, and heard the stony-hearted liar reel off his serene statement, they expecting every moment that the clear sky would deliver God's lightnings upon his head, and wondering to see how long the stroke was delayed. And when he had finished and still stood alive and whole, their wavering impulse to break their oath and save the poor betrayed prisoner's life faded and vanished away, for plainly this miscreant had sold himself to Satan and it would be fatal to meddle with the property of such a power as that.

"Why didn't you leave? What did you want to come here for?" somebody said.

"I couldn't help it—I couldn't help it," Potter moaned. "I wanted to run away, but I couldn't seem to come anywhere but here." And he fell to sobbing again.

Injun Joe repeated his statement, just as calmly, a few minutes afterward on the inquest, under oath/ and the boys, seeing that the lightnings were still withheld, were confirmed in their belief that Joe had sold himself to the devil. He was now become, to them, the most balefully interesting object they had ever looked upon, and they could not take their fascinated eyes from his face.

They inwardly resolved to watch him, nights, when opportunity should offer, in the hope of getting a glimpse of his dread master.

Injun Joe helped to raise the body of the murdered man and put it in a wagon for removal; and it was whispered through the shuddering crowd that the wound bled a little! The boys thought that this happy circumstance would turn suspicion in the right direction; but they were disappointed, for more than one villager remarked:

"It was within three feet of Muff Potter when it done it."

Tom's fearful secret and gnawing conscience disturbed his sleep for as much as a week after this; and at breakfast one morning Sid said:

"Tom, you pitch around and talk in your sleep so much that you keep me awake about half the time."

Tom blanched and dropped his eyes.

"It's a bad sign," said Aunt Polly, gravely. "What you got on your mind, Tom?"

"Nothing. Nothing 't I know of." But the boy's hand shook so that he spilled his coffee.

"And you do talk such stuff," Sid said. "Last night you said 'it's blood, it's blood, that's what it is!' You said that over and over. And you said, 'Don't torment me so—I'll tell!' Tell *what*? What is it you'll tell?"

Everything was swimming before Tom. There is no telling what might have happened, now, but luckily the concern passed out of Aunt Polly's face and she came to Tom's relief without knowing it. She said:

"Sho! It's that dreadful murder. I dream about it most every night myself, Sometimes I dream it's me that done it."

Mary said she had been affected much the same way. Sid seemed satisfied. Tom got out of the presence as quick as he plausibly could, and after that he complained of toothache for a week, and tied up his jaws every night. He never knew that Sid lay nightly watching, and frequently slipped the bandage free and then leaned on his elbow listening a good while at a time, and afterward slipped the bandage back to its place again. Tom's distress of mind wore off gradually and the toothache grew irksome and was discarded. If Sid really managed to make anything out of Tom's disjointed mutterings, he kept it to himself.

It seemed to Tom that his schoolmates never would get done holding inquests on dead cats, and thus keeping his trouble present to his mind. Sid noticed that Tom never was coroner at one of these inquiries, though it had been his habit to take the lead in all new enterprises; he noticed, too, that Tom never acted as a witness,—and that was strange; and Sid did not overlook the fact that Tom even showed a marked aversion to these inquests, and always avoided them when he could. Sid marveled, but said nothing. However, even inquests went out of vogue at last, and ceased to torture Tom's conscience.

Every day or two, during this time of sorrow, Tom watched his opportunity and went to the little grated jail-window and smuggled such small comforts through to the "murderer" as he could get hold of. The jail was a trifling little brick den that stood in a marsh at the edge of the village, and no guards were afforded for it; indeed it was seldom occupied. These offerings greatly helped to ease Tom's conscience.

The villagers had a strong desire to tar-and-feather Injun Joe and ride him on a rail, for body-snatching, but so formidable was his character that nobody could be found who was willing to take the lead in the matter, so it was dropped. He had been careful to begin both of his inquest-statements with the fight, without confessing the grave-robbery that preceded it; therefore it was deemed wisest not to try the case in the courts at present.

CHAPTER XII

One of the reasons why Tom's mind had drifted away from its secret troubles was, that it had found a new and weighty matter to interest itself about. Becky Thatcher had stopped coming to school. Tom had struggled with his pride a few days, and tried to "whistle her down the wind," but failed. He began to find himself hanging around her father's house, nights, and feeling very miserable. She was ill. What if she should die! There was distraction in the thought. He no longer took an interest in war, nor even in piracy. The charm of life was gone; there was nothing but dreariness left. He put his hoop away, and his bat; there was no joy in them any more. His aunt was concerned. She began to try all manner of remedies on him. She was one of those people who are infatuated with patent medicines and all new-fangled methods of producing health or mending it. She was an inveterate experimenter in these things. When something fresh in this line came out she was in a fever, right away, to try it; not on herself, for she was never ailing, but on anybody else that came handy. She was a subscriber for all the "Health" periodicals and phreneological frauds; and the solemn ignorance they were inflated with was breath to her nostrils. All the "rot" they contained about ventilation, and how to go to bed, and how to get up, and what to eat, and what to drink, and how much exercise to take, and what frame of mind to keep one's self in, and what sort of clothing to wear, was all gospel to her, and she never observed that her health-journals of the current month customarily upset everything they had recommended the month before. She was as simple-hearted and honest as the day was long, and so she was an easy victim. She gathered together her quack periodicals and her quack medicines, and thus armed with death, went about on her pale horse, metaphorically speaking, with "hell following after." But she never suspected that she was not an angel of healing and the balm of Gilead in disguise, to the suffering neighbors.

The water treatment was new, now, and Tom's low condition was a windfall to her. She had him out at daylight every morning, stood him up in the woodshed and drowned him with a deluge of cold water; then she scrubbed him down with a towel like a file, and so brought him to; then she rolled him up in a wet sheet and

put him away under blankets till she sweated his soul clean and
"the yellow stains of it came through his pores"—as Tom said.

Yet notwithstanding all this, the boy grew more and more
melancholy and pale and dejected. She added hot baths, sitz baths,
shower baths and plunges. The boy remained as dismal as a hearse.
She began to assist the water with a slim oatmeal diet and blister
plasters. She calculated his capacity as she would a jug's, and filled
him up every day with quack cure-alls.

Tom had become indifferent to persecution by this time. This
phase filled the old lady's heart with consternation. This indifference
must be broken up at any cost. Now she heard of Pain-killer for the
first time. She ordered a lot at once. She tasted it and was filled
with gratitude. It was simply fire in a liquid form. She dropped
the water treatment and everything else, and pinned her faith to
Pain-killer. She gave Tom a tea-spoonful and watched with the
deepest anxiety for the result. Her troubles were instantly at rest,
her soul at peace again; for the "indifference" was broken up.
The boy could not have shown a wilder, heartier interest, if she had
built a fire under him.

Tom felt that it was time to wake up; this sort of life might be
romantic enough, in his blighted condition, but it was getting to
have too little sentiment and too much distracting variety about it.
So he thought over various plans for relief, and finally hit upon
that of professing to be fond of Pain-killer. He asked for it so often
that he became a nuisance, and his aunt ended by telling him to
help himself and quit bothering her. If it had been Sid, she would
have had no misgivings to alloy her delight; but since it was Tom,
she watched the bottle clandestinely. She found that the medicine
did really diminish, but it did not occur to her that the boy was
mending the health of a crack in the sitting-room floor with it.

One day Tom was in the act of dosing the crack when his aunt's
yellow cat came along, purring, eyeing the teaspoon avariciously,
and begging for a taste. Tom said.

"Don't ask for it unless you want it, Peter."

But Peter signified that he did want it.

"You better make sure."

Peter was sure.

"Now you've asked for it, and I'll give it to you, because there
ain't anything mean about *me;* but if you find you don't like it,
you musn't blame anybody but your own self."

Peter was agreeable. So Tom pried his mouth open and poured
down the Pain-killer. Peter sprang a couple of yards in the air, and
then delivered a war-whoop and set off round and round the room,
banging against furniture, upsetting flower pots and making
general havoc. Next he rose on his hind feet and pranced around,
in a frenzy of enjoyment, with his head over his shoulder and his
voice proclaiming his unappeasable happiness. Then he went tearing

around the house again spreading chaos and destruction in his path. Aunt Polly entered in time to see him throw a few double summersets, deliver a final mighty hurrah, and sail through the open window, carrying the rest of the flower-pots with him. The old lady stood petrified with astonishment, peering over her glasses; Tom lay on the floor expiring with laughter.

"Tom, what on earth ails that cat?"

"*I* don't know, aunt," gasped the boy.

"Why I never see anything like it. What *did* make him act so?"

"Deed I don't know Aunt Polly; cats always act so when they're having a good time."

"They do, do they?" There was something in the tone that made Tom apprehensive.

"Yes'm. That is, I believe they do."

"You *do*?"

"Yes'm."

The old lady was bending down, Tom watching, with interest emphasized by anxiety. Too late he divined her "drift." The handle of the tell-tale tea-spoon was visible under the bed-valance. Aunt Polly took it, held it up. Tom winced, and dropped his eyes. Aunt Polly raised him by the usual handle—his ear—and cracked his head soundly with her thimble.

"Now, sir, what did you want to treat that poor dumb beast so, for?"

"I done it out of pity for him—because he hadn't any aunt."

"Hadn't any aunt!—you numscull. What has that got to do with it?"

"Heaps. Because if he'd a had one she'd a burnt him out herself! She'd a roasted his bowels out of him 'thout any more feeling than if he was a human!"

Aunt Polly felt a sudden pang of remorse. This was putting the thing in a new light; what was cruelty to a cat *might* be cruelty to a boy, too. She began to soften; she felt sorry. Her eyes watered a little, and she put her hand on Tom's head and said gently:

"I was meaning for the best, Tom. And Tom, it *did* do you good."

Tom looked up in her face with just a preceptible twinkle peeping through his gravity:

"I know you was meaning for the best, aunty, and so was I with Peter. It done *him* good, too. I never see him get around so since—"

"O, go 'long with you, Tom, before you aggravate me again. And you try and see if you can't be a good boy, for once, and you needn't take any more medicine."

Tom reached school ahead of time. It was noticed that this strange thing had been occurring every day latterly. And now, as usual of late, he hung about the gate of the school-yard instead of playing with his comrades. He was sick, he said, and he looked it.

He tried to seem to be looking everywhere but whither he really was looking—down the road. Presently Jeff Thatcher hove in sight, and Tom's face lighted; he gazed a moment, and then turned sorrowfully away. When Jeff arrived, Tom accosted him, and "led up" warily to opportunities for remark about Becky, but the giddy lad never could see the bait. Tom watched and watched, hoping whenever a frisking frock came in sight, and hating the owner of it as soon as he saw she was not the right one. At last frocks ceased to appear, and he dropped hopelessly into the dumps; he entered the empty school house and sat down to suffer. Then one more frock passed in at the gate, and Tom's heart gave a great bound. The next instant he was out, and "going on" like an Indian; yelling, laughing, chasing boys, jumping over the fence at risk of life and limb, throwing hand-springs, standing on his head—doing all the heroic things he could conceive of, and keeping a furtive eye out, all the while, to see if Becky Thatcher was noticing. But she seemed to be unconscious of it all; she never looked. Could it be posssble that she was not aware that he was there? He carried his exploits to her immediate vicinity; came war-whooping around, snatched a boy's cap, hurled it to the roof of the school-house, broke through a group of boys, tumbling them in every direction, and fell sprawling, himself, under Becky's nose, almost upsetting her—and she turned, with her nose in the air, and he heard her say. "Mf! some people think they're mighty smart—always showing off!"

Tom's cheeks burned. He gathered himself up and sneaked off, crushed and crestfallen.

CHAPTER XIII

Tom's mind was made up now. He was gloomy and desperate. He was a forsaken, friendless boy, he said; nobody loved him; when they found out what they had driven him to, perhaps they would be sorry; he had tried to do right and get along, but they would not let him; since nothing would do them but to be rid of him, let it be so; and let them blame *him* for the consequences—why shouldn't they? What right had the friendless to complain? Yes, they had forced him to it at last; he would lead a life of crime. There was no choice.

By this time he was far down Meadow Lane, and the bell for school to "take up" tinkled faintly upon his ear. He sobbed, now, to think he should never, never hear that old familiar sound any more—it was very hard, but it was forced on him; since he was driven out into the cold world, he must submit—but he forgave them. Then the sobs came thick and fast.

Just at this point he met his soul's sworn comrade, Joe Harper—hard-eyed, and with evidently a great and dismal purpose in his heart. Plainly here were "two souls with but a single thought."

Tom, wiping his eyes with his sleeve, began to blubber out something about a resolution to escape from hard usage and lack of sympathy at home by roaming abroad into the great world never to return; and ended by hoping that Joe would not forget him.

But it transpired that this was a request which Joe had just been going to make of Tom, and had come to hunt him up for that purpose. His mother had whipped him for drinking some cream which he had never tasted and knew nothing about; it was plain that she was tired of him and wished him to go; if she felt that way, there was nothing for him to do but succumb; he hoped she would be happy, and never regret having driven her poor boy out into the unfeeling world to suffer and die.

As the two boys walked sorrowing along, they made a new compact to stand by each other and be brothers and never separate till death relieved them of their troubles. Then they began to lay their plans. Joe was for being a hermit, and living on crusts in a remote cave, and dying, some time, of cold, and want, and grief; but after listening to Tom, he conceded that there were some conspicuous advantages about a life of crime, and so he consented to be a pirate.

Three miles below St. Petersburg, at a point where the Mississippi river was a trifle over a mile wide, there was a long, narrow, wooded island, with a shallow bar at the head of it, and this offered well as a rendezvous. It was not inhabited; it lay far over toward the further shore, abreast a dense and almost wholly unpeopled forest. So Jackson's Island was chosen. Who were to be the subjects of their piracies, was a matter that did not occur to them. Then they hunted up Huckleberry Finn, and he joined them promptly, for all careers were one to him; he was indifferent. They presently separated to meet at a lonely spot on the river bank two miles above the village at the favorite hour—which was midnight. There was a small log raft there which they meant to capture. Each would bring hooks and lines, and such provision as he could steal in the most dark and mysterious way—as became outlaws. And before the afternoon was done, they had all managed to enjoy the sweet glory of spreading the fact that pretty soon the town would "hear something." All who got this vague hint were cautioned to "be mum and wait."

About midnight Tom arrived with a boiled ham and a few trifles, and stopped in a dense undergrowth on a small bluff overlooking the meeting-place. It was starlight, and very still. The mighty river lay like an ocean at rest. Tom listened a moment, but no sound disturbed the quiet. Then he gave a low, distinct whistle. It was answered from under the bluff. Tom whistled twice more; these signals were answered in the same way. Then a guarded voice said:

"Who goes there?"

"Tom Sawyer, the Black Avenger of the Spanish Main. Name your names."

"Huck Finn the Red-Handed, and Joe Harper the Terror of the Seas." Tom had furnished these titles, from his favorite literature.

"Tis well. Give the countersign."

Two hoarse whispers delivered the same awful word simultaneously to the brooding night:

"BLOOD!"

Then Tom tumbled his ham over the bluff and let himself down after it, tearing both skin and clothes to some extent in the effort. There was an easy, comfortable path along the shore under the bluff, but it lacked the advantages of difficulty and danger so valued by a pirate.

The Terror of the Seas had brought a side of bacon, and had about worn himself out with getting it there. Finn the Red-Handed had stolen a skillet and a quantity of half-cured leaf tobacco, and had also brought a few corn-cobs to make pipes with. But none of the pirates smoked or "chewed" but himself. The Black Avenger of the Spanish Main said it would never do to start without some fire. That was a wise thought; matches were hardly known there in that day. They saw a fire smouldering upon a great raft a hundred yards above, and they went stealthily thither and helped themselves to a chunk. They made an imposing adventure of it, saying "Hist!" every now and then, and suddenly halting with finger on lip; moving with hands on imaginary dagger-hilts; and giving orders in dismal whispers that if "the foe" stirred, to "let him have it to the hilt," because "dead men tell no tales." They knew well enough that the raftsmen were all down at the village laying in stores or having a spree, but still that was no excuse for their conducting this thing in an unpiratical way.

They shoved off, presently, Tom in command, Huck at the after oar and Joe at the forward. Tom stood amidships, gloomy-browed, and with folded arms, and gave his orders in a low, stern whisper:

"Luff, and bring her to the wind!"

"Aye-aye, sir!"

"Steady it is, sir!"

"Aye-aye, sir!"

"Steady, stead-y-y-y!"

"Steady it is, sir!"

"Let her go off a point!"

"Point it is, sir!"

As the boys steadily and monotonously drove the raft toward mid-stream it was no doubt understood that these orders were given only for "style," and were not intended to mean anything in particular.

"What sail's she carrying?"

"Courses, tops'ls and flying-jib, sir."

"Send the r'yals up! Lay out aloft, there, half a dozen of ye,—foretopmaststuns'l! Lively, now!"

"Aye-aye, sir!"

"Shake out that maintogalans'l! Sheets and braces! *Now,* my hearties!"

"Aye-aye, sir!"

"Hellum-a-lee—hard a port! Stand by to meet her when she comes! Port, port! *Now,* men! With a will! Stead-y-y-y!"

"Steady it is, sir!"

The raft drew beyond the middle of the river; the boys pointed her head right, and then lay on their oars. The river was not high, so there was not more than a two or three-mile current. Hardly a word was said during the next three-quarters of an hour. Now the raft was passing before the distant town. Two or three glimmering lights showed where it lay, peacefully sleeping, beyond the vague vast sweep of star-gemmed water, unconscious of the tremendous event that was happening. The Black Avenger stood still with folded arms, "looking his last" upon the scene of his former joys and his later sufferings, and wishing "she" could see him now, abroad on the wild sea, facing peril and death with dauntless heart, going to his doom with a grim smile on his lips. It was but a small strain on his imagination to remove Jackson's Island beyond eye-shot of the village, and so he "looked his last" with a broken and satisfied heart. The other pirates were looking their last, too; and they all looked so long that they came near letting the current drift them out of the range of the island. But they discovered the danger in time, and made shift to avert it. About two o'clock in the morning the raft grounded on the bar two hundred yards above the head of the island, and they waded back and forth until they had landed their freight. Part of the little raft's belongings consisted of an old sail, and this they spread over a nook in the bushes for a tent to shelter their provisions; but they themselves would sleep in the open air in good weather, as became outlaws.

They built a fire against the side of a great log twenty or thirty steps within the sombre depths of the forest, and then cooked some bacon in the frying-pan for supper, and used up half of the corn "pone" stock they had brought. It seemed glorious sport to be feasting in that wild free way in the virgin forest of an unexplored and uninhabited island, far from the haunts of men, and they said they never would return to civilization. The climbing fire lit up their faces and threw its ruddy glare upon the pillared tree trunks of their forest temple, and upon the varnished foliage and festooning vines.

When the last crisp slice of bacon was gone, and the last allowance of corn pone devoured, the boys stretched themselves out on the grass, filled with contentment. They could have found a cooler place, but they would not deny themselves such a romantic feature as the roasting camp-fire.

"*Ain't* it gay?" said Joe.

"It's *nuts!*" said Tom. "What would the boys say if they could see us?"

"Say? Well they'd just die to be here—hey Hucky!"

"I reckon so," said Huckleberry; "anyways *I*'m suited. I don't want nothing better'n this. I don't ever get enough to eat, gen'ally—and here they can't come and pick at a feller and bullyrag him so."

"It's just the life for me," said Tom. "You don't have to get up, mornings, and you don't have to go to school, and wash, and all that blame foolishness. You see a pirate don't have to do *anything,* Joe, when he's ashore, but a hermit *he* has to be praying considerable, and then he don't have any fun, anyway, all by himself that way."

"O yes, that's so," said Joe, "but I hadn't thought much about it, you know. I'd a good deal rather be a pirate, now that I've tried it."

"You see," said Tom, "people don't go much on hermits, now-a-days, like they used to in old times, but a pirate's always respected. And a hermit's got to sleep on the hardest place he can find, and put sack-cloth and ashes on his head, and stand out in the rain, and—"

"What does he put sack-cloth and ashes on his head for?" inquired Huck.

"*I* dono. But they've *got* to do it. Hermits always do. You'd have to do that if you was a hermit."

"Dern'd if I would," said Huck.

"Well what would you do?"

"I dono. But I wouldn't do that."

"Why Huck, you'd *have* to. How'd you get around it?"

"Why I just wouldn't stand it. I'd run away."

"Run away! Well you *would* be a nice old slouch of a hermit. You'd be a disgrace."

The Red-Handed made no response, being better employed. He had finished gouging out a cob, and now he fitted a weed stem to it, loaded it with tobacco, and was pressing a coal to the charge and blowing a cloud of fragrant smoke—he was in the full bloom of luxurious contentment. The other pirates envied him this majestic vice, and secretly resolved to acquire it shortly. Presently Huck said:

"What does pirates have to do?"

Tom said:

"Oh they have just a bully time—take ships, and burn them, and get the money and bury it in awful places in their island where there's ghosts and things to watch it, and kill everybody in the ships—make 'em walk a plank."

"And they carry the women to the island," said Joe; "they don't kill the women."

"No," assented Tom, "they don't kill the women—they're too noble. And the women's always beautiful, too."

"And don't they wear the bulliest clothes! Oh, no! All gold and silver and di'monds," said Joe, with enthusiasm.

"Who?" said Huck.

"Why the pirates."

Huck scanned his own clothing forlornly.

"I reckon I ain't dressed fitten for a pirate," said he, with a regretful pathos in his voice; "but I ain't got none but these."

But the other boys told him the fine clothes would come fast enough, after they should have begun their adventures. They made him understand that his poor rags would do to begin with, though it was customary for wealthy pirates to start with a proper wardrobe.

Gradually their talk died out and drowsiness began to steal upon the eyelids of the little waifs. The pipe dropped from the fingers of the Red-Handed, and he slept the sleep of the conscience-free and the weary. The Terror of the Seas and the Black Avenger of the Spanish Main had more difficulty in getting to sleep. They said their prayers inwardly, and lying down, since there was nobody there with authority to make them kneel and recite aloud; in truth they had a mind not to say them at all, but they were afraid to proceed to such lengths as that, lest they might call down a sudden and special thunderbolt from Heaven. Then at once they reached and hovered upon the imminent verge of sleep—but an intruder came, now, that would not "down." It was conscience. They began to feel a vague fear that they had been doing wrong to run away; and next they thought of the stolen meat, and then the real torture came. They tried to argue it away by reminding conscience that they had purloined sweetmeats and apples scores of times; but conscience was not to be appeased by such thin plausibilities; it seemed to them, in the end, that there was no getting around the stubborn fact that taking sweetmeats was only "hooking," while taking bacon and hams and such valuables was plain simple *stealing*—and there was a command against that in the Bible. So they inwardly resolved that so long as they remained in the business, their piracies should not again be sullied with the crime of stealing. Then conscience granted a truce, and these curiously inconsistent pirates fell peacefully to sleep.

CHAPTER XIV

When Tom awoke in the morning, he wondered where he was. He sat up and rubbed his eyes and looked around. Then he comprehended. It was the cool gray dawn, and there was a delicious sense of repose and peace in the deep pervading calm and silence of the woods. Not a leaf stirred; not a sound obtruded upon great

Nature's meditation. Beaded dew-drops stood upon the leaves and grasses. A white layer of ashes covered the fire, and a thin blue breath of smoke rose straight into the air. Joe and Huck still slept.

Now, far away in the woods a bird called; another answered; presently the hammering of a woodpecker was heard. Gradually the cool dim gray of the morning whitened, and as gradually sounds multiplied and life manifested itself. The marvel of Nature shaking off sleep and going to work unfolded itself to the musing boy. A little green worm came crawling over a dewy leaf, lifting two-thirds of his body into the air from time to time and "sniffing around," then proceeding again—for he was measuring, Tom said; and when the worm approached him, of its own accord, he sat as still as a stone, with his hopes rising and falling, by turns, as the creature still came toward him or seemed inclined to go elsewhere; and when at last it considered a painful moment with its curved body in the air and then came decisively down upon Tom's leg and began a journey over him, his whole heart was glad—for that meant that he was going to have a new suit of clothes—without the shadow of a doubt a gaudy piratical uniform. Now a procession of ants appeared, from nowhere in particular, and went about their labors; one struggled manfully by with a dead spider five times as big as itself in its arms, and lugged it straight up a tree-trunk. A brown spotted lady-bug climbed the dizzy height of a grass blade, and Tom bent down close to it and said, "Lady-bug, lady-bug, fly away home, your house is on fire, your children's alone," and she took wing and went off to see about it—which did not surprise the boy, for he knew of old that this insect was credulous about conflagrations and he had practiced upon its simplicity more than once. A tumble-bug came next, heaving sturdily at its ball, and Tom touched the creature, to see it shut its legs against its body and pretend to be dead. The birds were fairly rioting by this time. A cat-bird, the northern mocker, lit in a tree over Tom's head, and trilled out her imitations of her neighbors in a rapture of enjoyment; then a shrill jay swept down, a flash of blue flame, and stopped on a twig almost within the boy's reach, cocked his head to one side and eyed the strangers with a consuming curiosity; a gray squirrel and a big fellow of the "fox" kind came skurrying along, sitting up at intervals to inspect and chatter at the boys, for the wild things had probably never seen a human being before and scarcely knew whether to be afraid or not. All Nature was wide awake and stirring, now; long lances of sunlight pierced down through the dense foliage far and near, and a few butterflies came fluttering upon the scene.

Tom stirred up the other pirates and they all clattered away with a shout, and in a minute or two were stripped and chasing after and tumbling over each other in the shallow limpid water of the white sand-bar. They felt no longing for the little village sleeping in the distance beyond the majestic waste of water. A vagrant current or a slight rise in the river had carried off their raft, but this only gratified them, since its going was something like burning the bridge between them and civilization.

They came back to camp wonderfully refreshed, glad-hearted, and ravenous; and they soon had the camp-fire blazing up again. Huck found a spring of clear cold water close by, and the boys made cups of broad oak or hickory leaves, and felt that water, sweetened with such a wild-wood charm as that, would be a good enough substitute for coffee. While Joe was slicing bacon for breakfast, Tom and Huck asked him to hold on a minute; they stepped to a promising nook in the river bank and threw in their lines; almost immediately they had reward. Joe had not had time to get impatient before they were back again with some handsome bass, a couple of sun-perch and a small catfish—provisions enough for quite a family. They fried the fish with the bacon and were astonished; for no fish had ever seemed so delicious before. They did not know that the quicker a fresh water fish is on the fire after he is caught the better he is; and they reflected little upon what a sauce open air sleeping, open air exercise, bathing, and a large ingredient of hunger makes, too.

They lay around in the shade, after breakfast, while Huck had a smoke, and then went off through the woods on an exploring expedition. They tramped gaily along, over decaying logs, through tangled underbrush, among solemn monarchs of the forest, hung from their crowns to the ground with a drooping regalia of grape-vines. Now and then they came upon snug nooks carpeted with grass and jeweled with flowers.

They found plenty of things to be delighted with but nothing to be astonished at. They discovered that the island was about three miles long and a quarter of a mile wide, and that the shore it lay closest to was only separated from it by a narrow channel hardly two hundred yards wide. They took a swim about every hour, so it was close upon the middle of the afternoon when they got back to camp. They were too hungry to stop to fish, but they fared sumptuously upon cold ham, and then threw themselves down in the shade to talk. But the talk soon began to drag, and then died. The stillness, the solemnity that brooded in the woods, and the sense of loneliness, began to tell upon the spirits of the boys. They fell to thinking. A sort of undefined longing crept upon them. This took dim shape, presently—it was budding home-sickness. Even Finn the Red-Handed was dreaming of his door-steps and empty hogsheads. But they were all ashamed of their weakness, and none was brave enough to speak his thought.

For some time, now, the boys had been dully conscious of a peculiar sound in the distance, just as one sometimes is of the ticking of a clock which he takes no distinct note of. But now this mysterious sound became more pronounced, and forced a recognition. The boys started, glanced at each other, and then each assumed a listening attitude. There was a long silence, profound and unbroken; then a deep, sullen boom came floating down out of the distance.

"What is it!" exclaimed Joe, under his breath.

"I wonder," said Tom in a whisper.

"Tain't thunder," said Huckleberry, in an awed tone, "becuz thunder—"

"Hark!" said Tom. "Listen—don't talk."

They waited a time that seemed an age, and then the same muffled boom troubled the solemn hush.

"Let's go and see."

They sprang to their feet and hurried to the shore toward the town. They parted the bushes on the bank and peered out over the water. The little steam ferry boat was about a mile below the village, drifting with the current. Her broad deck seemed crowded with people. There were a great many skiffs rowing about or floating with the stream in the neighborhood of the ferry boat, but the boys could not determine what the men in them were doing. Presently a great jet of white smoke burst from the ferry boat's side, and as it expanded and rose in a lazy cloud, that same dull throb of sound was borne to the listeners again.

"I know now!" exclaimed Tom; "somebody's drownded!"

"That's it!" said Huck; "they done that last summer, when Bill Turner got drownded; they shoot a cannon over the water, and that makes him come up to the top. Yes, and they take loaves of bread and put quicksilver in 'em and set 'em afloat, and wherever there's anybody that's drownded, they'll float right there and stop."

"Yes, I've heard about that," said Joe. "I wonder what makes the bread do that."

"Oh, it ain't the bread, so much," said Tom; "I reckon it's mostly what they *say* over it before they start it out."

"But they don't say anything over it," said Huck. "I've seen 'em and they don't."

"Well that's funny," said Tom. "But maybe they say it to themselves. Of *course* they do. Anybody might know that."

The other boys agreed that there was reason in what Tom said, because an ignorant lump of bread, uninstructed by an incantation, could not be expected to act very intelligently when sent upon an errand of such gravity.

"By jings I wish I was over there, now," said Joe.

"I do too," said Huck. "I'd give heaps to know who it is."

The boys still listened and watched. Presently a revealing thought flashed through Tom's mind, and he exclaimed:

"Boys, I know who's drownded—it's us!"

They felt like heroes in an instant. Here was a gorgeous triumph;

they were missed; they were mourned; hearts were breaking on their account; tears were being shed; accusing memories of unkindnesses to these poor lost lads were rising up, and unavailing regrets and remorse were being indulged; and best of all, the departed were the talk of the whole town, and the envy of all the boys, as far as this dazzling notoriety was concerned. This was fine. It was worth while to be a pirate, after all.

As twilight drew on, the ferry boat went back to her accustomed business and the skiffs disappeared. The pirates returned to camp. They were jubilant with vanity over their new grandeur and the illustrious trouble they were making. They caught fish, cooked supper and ate it, and then fell to guessing at what the village was thinking and saying about them; and the pictures they drew of the public distress on their account were gratifying to look upon—from their point of view. But when the shadows of night closed them in, they gradually ceased to talk and sat gazing into the fire, with their minds evidently wandering elsewhere. The excitement was gone, now, and Tom and Joe could not keep back thoughts of certain persons at home who were not enjoying this fine frolic as much as they were. Misgivings came; they grew troubled and unhappy; a sigh or two escaped, unawares. By and by Joe timidly ventured upon a round-about "feeler" as to how the others might look upon a return to civilization—not right now, but—

Tom withered him with derision! Huck, being uncommitted, as yet, joined in with Tom, and the waverer quickly "explained," and was glad to get out of the scrape with as little taint of chicken-hearted home-sickness clinging to his garments as he could. Mutiny was effectually laid to rest for the moment.

As the night deepened, Huck began to nod, and presently to snore. Joe followed next. Tom lay upon his elbow motionless, for some time, watching the two intently. At last he got up cautiously, on his knees, and went searching among the grass and the flickering reflections flung by the camp-fire. He picked up and inspected several large semi-cylinders of the thin white bark of a sycamore, and finally chose two which seemed to suit him. Then he knelt by the fire and painfully wrote something upon each of these with his "red keel;" one he rolled up and put in his jacket pocket, and the other he put in Joe's hat and removed it to a little distance from the owner. And he also put into the hat certain school-boy treasures of almost inestimable value—among them a lump of chalk, an India rubber ball, three fish-hooks, and one of that kind of marbles known as a "sure 'nough crystal." Then he tip-toed his way cautiously among the trees till he felt that he was out of hearing, and straightway broke into a keen run in the direction of the sand-bar.

CHAPTER XV

A few minutes later Tom was in the shoal water of the bar, wading toward the Illinois shore. Before the depth reached his middle he was half way over; the current would permit no more wading, now, so he struck out confidently to swim the remaining hundred yards. He swam quartering up stream, but still was swept downward rather faster than he had expected. However, he reached the shore finally, and drifted along till he found a low place and drew himself out. He put his hand on his jacket pocket, found his piece of bark safe, and then struck through the woods, following the shore, with streaming garments. Shortly before ten o'clock he came out into an open place opposite the village, and saw the ferry boat lying in the shadow of the trees and the high bank. Everything was quiet under the blinking stars. He crept down the bank, watching with all his eyes, slipped into the water, swam three or four strokes and climbed into the skiff that did "yawl" duty at the boat's stern. He laid himself down under the thwarts and waited, panting.

Presently the cracked bell tapped and a voice gave the order to "cast off." A minute or two later the skiff's head was standing high up, against the boat's swell, and the voyage was begun. Tom felt happy in his success, for he knew it was the boat's last trip for the night. At the end of a long twelve or fifteen minutes the wheels stopped, and Tom slipped overboard and swam ashore in the dusk, landing fifty yards down stream, out of danger of possible stragglers.

He flew along unfrequented alleys, and shortly found himself at his aunt's back fence. He Climbed over, approached the "ell" and looked in at the sitting-room window, for a light was burning there. There sat Aunt Polly, Sid, Mary, and Joe Harper's mother, grouped together, talking. They were by the bed, and the bed was between them and the door. Tom went to the door and began to softly lift the latch; then he pressed gently and the door yielded a crack; he continued pushing cautiously, and quaking every time it creaked, till he judged he might squeeze through on his knees; and so he put his head through and began, warily.

"What makes the candle blow so?" said Aunt Polly. Tom hurried up. "Why that door's open, I believe. Why of course it is. No end of strange things now. Go 'long and shut it, Sid."

Tom disappeared under the bed just in time. He lay and "breathed" himself for a time, and then crept to where he could almost touch his aunt's foot.

"But as I was saying," said Aunt Polly, "he warn't *bad,* so to say—only misch*ee*vous. Only just giddy, and harum-scarum, you know. He warn't any more responsible than a colt. *He* never meant any harm, and he was the best-hearted boy that ever was"—and she began to cry.

"It was just so with my Joe—always full of his devilment, and up to every kind of mischief, but he was just as unselfish and kind as he could be—and laws bless me, to think I went and whipped him for taking that cream, never once recollecting that I throwed it out myself because it was sour, and I never to see him again in this world, never, never, never, poor abused boy!" And Mrs. Harper sobbed as if her heart would break.

"I hope Tom's better off where he is," said Sid, "but if he'd been better in some ways—"

"*Sid!*" Tom felt the glare of the old lady's eye, though he could not see it. "Not a word against my Tom, now that he's gone! God'll take care of *him*—never you trouble *your*self, sir! Oh, Mrs. Harper, I don't know how to give him up! I don't know how to give him up! He was such a comfort to me, although he tormented my old heart out of me, 'most."

"The Lord Giveth and the Lord hath taken away,—Blessed be the name of the Lord! But it's *so* hard—Oh, it's so hard! Only last Saturday my Joe busted a fire-cracker right under my nose and I knocked him sprawling. Little did I know then, how soon—O, if it was to do over again I'd hug him and bless him for it."

"Yes, yes, yes, I know just how you feel, Mrs. Harper, I know just exactly how you feel. No longer ago than yesterday noon, my Tom took and filled the cat full of Pain-killer, and I did think the cretur would tear the house down. And God forgive me, I cracked Tom's head with my thimble, poor boy, poor dead boy. But he's out of all his troubles now. And the last words I ever heard him say was to reproach—"

But this memory was too much for the old lady, and she broke entirely down. Tom was snuffling, now, himself—and more in pity of himself than anybody else. He could hear Mary crying, and putting in a kindly word for him from time to time. He began to have a nobler opinion of himself than ever before. Still he was sufficiently touched by his aunt's grief to long to rush out from under the bed and overwhelm her with joy—and the theatrical gorgeousness of the thing appealed strongly to his nature, too, but he resisted and lay still.

He went on listening, and gathered by odds and ends that it was conjectured at first that the boys had got drowned while taking a swim; then the small raft had been missed; next, certain boys said the missing lads had promised that the village should "hear something" soon; the wise-heads had "put this and that together" and decided that the lads had gone off on that raft and would turn up at the next town below, presently; but toward noon the raft had been found, lodged against the Missouri shore some five or six miles below the village,—and then hope perished; they must be drowned, else hunger would have driven them home by nightfall if not sooner. It was believed that the search for the bodies had been a fruitless effort merely because the drowning must have occurred in mid-channel, since the boys, being good swimmers, would otherwise have escaped to shore. This was Wednesday night. If the bodies continued missing until Sunday, all hope would be given over, and the funerals would be preached on that morning. Tom shuddered.

Mrs. Harper gave a sobbing good-night and turned to go. Then with a mutual impulse the two bereaved women flung themselves into each other's arms and had a good, consoling cry, and then parted. Aunt Polly was tender far beyond her wont, in her good-night to Sid and Mary. Sid snuffled a bit and Mary went off crying with all her heart.

Aunt Polly knelt down and prayed for Tom so touchingly, so appealingly, and with such measureless love in her words and her old trembling voice, that he was weltering in tears again, long before she was through.

He had to keep still long after she went to bed, for she kept making broken-hearted ejaculations from time to time, tossing unrestfully, and turning over. But at last she was still, only moaning a little in her sleep. Now the boy stole out, rose gradually by the bedside, shaded the candle-light with his hand, and stood regarding her. His heart was full of pity for her. He took out his sycamore scroll and placed it by the candle. But something occurred to him, and he lingered considering. His face lighted with a happy solution of his thought; he put the bark hastily in his pocket. Then he bent over and kissed the faded lips, and straightway made his stealthy exit, latching the door behind him.

He threaded his way back to the ferry landing, found nobody at large there, and walked boldly on board the boat, for he knew she was tenantless except that there was a watchman, who always turned in and slept like a graven image. He untied the skiff at the stern, slipped into it, and was soon rowing cautiously up stream. When he had pulled a mile above the village, he started quartering across and bent himself stoutly to his work. He hit the landing on the other side neatly, for this was a familiar bit of work to him. He was moved to capture the skiff, arguing that it might be considered a ship and therefore legitimate prey for a pirate, but he knew a thorough search would be made for it and that might end in revelations. So he stepped ashore and entered the wood.

He sat down and took a long rest, torturing himself meantime to keep awake, and then started wearily down the home-stretch. The night was far spent. It was broad daylight before he found himself fairly abreast the island bar. He rested again until the sun was well up and gilding the great river with its splendor, and then he plunged into the stream. A little later he paused, dripping, upon the threshold of the camp, and heard Joe say:

"No, Tom's true-blue, Huck, and he'll come back. He won't desert. He knows that would be a disgrace to a pirate, and Tom's too proud for that sort of thing. He's up to something or other. Now I wonder what?"

"Well, the things is ours, anyway, ain't they?"

"Pretty near, but not yet, Huck. The writing says they are if he ain't back here to breakfast."

"Which he is!" exclaimed Tom, with fine dramatic effect, stepping grandly into camp.

A sumptuous breakfast of bacon and fish was shortly provided, and as the boys set to work upon it, Tom recounted (and adorned) his adventures. They were a vain and boastful company of heroes when the tale was done. Then Tom hid himself away in a shady nook to sleep till noon, and the other pirates got ready to fish and explore.

CHAPTER XVI

After dinner all the gang turned out to hunt for turtle eggs on the bar. They went about poking sticks into the sand, and when they found a soft place they went down on their knees and dug with their hands. Sometimes they would take fifty or sixty eggs out of one hole. They were perfectly round white things a trifle smaller than an English walnut. They had a famous fried-egg feast that night, and another on Friday morning.

After breakfast they went whooping and prancing out on the bar, and chased each other round and round, shedding clothes as they went, until they were naked, and then continued the frolic far away up the shoal water of the bar, against the stiff current, which latter tripped their legs from under them from time to time and greatly increased the fun. And now and then they stooped in a group and splashed water in each other's faces with their palms, gradually approaching each other, with averted faces to avoid the strangling sprays and finally gripping and struggling till the best man ducked his neighbor, and then they all went under in a tangle of white legs and arms and came up blowing, sputtering, laughing and gasping for breath at one and the same time.

When they were well exhausted, they would run out and sprawl on the dry, hot sand, and lie there and cover themselves up with it, and by and by break for the water again and go through the original performance once more. Finally it occurred to them that their naked skin represented flesh-colored "tights" very fairly; so they drew a ring in the sand and had a circus—with three clowns in it, for none would yield this proudest post to his neighbor.

Next they got their marbles and played "knucks" and "ring-taw" and "keeps" till that amusement grew stale. Then Joe and Huck had another swim, but Tom would not venture, because

he found that in kicking off his trousers he had kicked his string
of rattlesnake rattles off his ankle, and he wondered how he had
escaped cramp so long without the protection of this mysterious
charm. He did not venture again until he had found it, and by that
time the other boys were tired and ready to rest. They gradually
wandered apart, dropped into the "dumps," and fell to gazing
longingly across the wide river to where the village lay drowsing
in the sun. Tom found himself writing "BECKY" in the sand with
his big toe; he scratched it out, and was angry with himself for his
weakness. But he wrote it again, nevertheless; he could not help
it. He erased it once more and then took himself out of temptation
by driving the other boys together and joining them.

But Joe's spirits had gone down almost beyond resurrection.
He was so homesick that he could hardly endure the misery of it.
The tears lay very near the surface. Huck was melancholy, too.
Tom was down-hearted, but tried hard not to show it. He had a
secret which he was not ready to tell, yet, but if this mutinous
depression was not broken up soon, he would have to bring it out.
He said, with a great show of cheerfulness:

"I bet there's been pirates on this island before, boys. We'll
explore it again. They've hid treasures here somewhere. How'd
you feel to light on a rotten chest full of gold and silver—hey?"

But it roused only a faint enthusiasm, which faded out, with no
reply. Tom tried one or two other seductions; but they failed, too.
It was discouraging work. Joe sat poking up the sand with a stick
and looking very gloomy. Finally he said:

"O, boys, let's give it up. I want to go home. It's so lonesome."

"Oh, no, Joe, you'll feel better by and by," said Tom. "Just think
of the fishing that's here."

"I don't care for fishing. I want to go home."

"But Joe, there ain't such another swimming place anywhere."

"Swimming'a no good. I don't seem to care for it somehow, when
there ain't anybody to say I shan't go in. I mean to go home."

"O, shucks! Baby! You want to see your mother, I reckon."

"Yes, I *do* want to see my mother—and you would too, if you
had one. I ain't any more baby than you are." And Joe snuffled a
little.

"Well, we'll let the cry-baby go home to his mother, *won't* we
Huck? Poor thing—does it want to see its mother? And so it shall.
You like it here, *don't* you Huck? We'll stay, won't we?"

Huck said "Y-e-s"—without any heart in it.

"I'll never speak to you again as long as I live," said Joe, rising.
"There now!" And he moved moodily away and began to dress
himself.

"Who cares!" said Tom. "Nobody wants you to. Go 'long home
and get laughed at. O, you're a nice pirate. Huck and me ain't
cry-babies. We'll stay, won't we Huck? Let him go if he wants to.

I reckon we can get along without him per'aps."

But Tom was uneasy, nevertheless, and was alarmed to see Joe go sullenly on with his dressing. And then it was discomforting to see Huck eyeing Joe's preparations so wistfully, and keeping up such an ominous silence. Presently, without a parting word, Joe began to wade off toward the Illinois shore. Tom's heart began to sink. He glanced at Huck. Huck could not bear the look, and dropped his eyes. Then he said:

"I want to go, too, Tom. It was getting so lonesome anyway, and now it'll be worse. Let's go too, Tom."

"I won't! You can all go, if you want to. I mean to stay."

"Tom, I better go."

"Well go 'long—who's hendering you."

Huck began to pick up his scattered clothes. He said:

"Tom, I wisht you'd come too. Now you think it over. We'll wait for you when we get to shore."

"Well you'll wait a blame long time, that's all."

Huck started sorrowfully away, and Tom stood looking after him, with a strong desire tugging at his heart to yield his pride and go along too. He hoped the boys would stop, but they still waded slowly on. It suddenly dawned on Tom that it was become very lonely and still. He made one final struggle with his pride, and then darted after his comrades, yelling:

"Wait! Wait! I want to tell you something!"

They presently stopped and turned around. When he got to where they were, he began unfolding his secret, and they listened moodily till at last they saw the "point" he was driving at, and then they set up a war-whoop of applause and said it was "splendid!" and said if he had told them at first, they wouldn't have started away. He made a plausible excuse; but his real reason had been the fear that not even the secret would keep them with him any very great length of time, and so he had meant to hold it in reserve as a last seduction.

The lads came gaily back and went at their sports again with a will, chattering all the time about Tom's stupendous plan and admiring the genius of it. After a dainty egg and fish dinner, Tom said he wanted to learn to smoke, now. Joe caught at the idea and said he would like to try, too. So Huck made pipes and filled them. These novices had never smoked anything before but cigars made of grape-vine and they "bit" the tongue and were not considered manly, anyway.

Now they stretched themselves out on their elbows and began to puff, charily, and with slender confidence. The smoke had an unpleasant taste, and they gagged a little, but Tom said:

"Why it's just as easy! If I'd a knowed *this* was all, I'd a learnt long ago."

"So would I," said Joe. "It's just nothing."

"Why many a time I've looked at people smoking, and thought well I wish I could do that; but I never thought I could," said Tom.

"That's just the way with me, hain't it Huck? You've heard me talk just that way—haven't you Huck? I'll leave it to Huck if I haven't."

"Yes—heaps of times," said Huck.

"Well I have too," said Tom; "O, hundreds of times. Once down by the slaughter-house. Don't you remember, Huck? Bob Tanner was there, and Johnny Miller, and Jeff Thatcher, when I said it. Don't you remember Huck, 'bout me saying that?"

"Yes, that's so," said Huck. "That was the day after I lost a white alley. No, 'twas the day before."

"There—I told you so," said Tom. "Huck recollects it."

"I bleeve I could smoke this pipe all day," said Joe. "*I* could smoke it all day. But I bet you Jeff Thatcher couldn't."

"Jeff Thatcher! Why he'd keel over just with two draws. Just let him try it once. *He'd* see!"

"I bet he would. And Johnny Miller—I wish I could see Johnny Miller tackle it once."

"O, dont *I*!" said Joe, "Why I bet you Johnny Miller couldn't any more do this than nothing. Just one little snifter would fetch *him*."

"'Deed it would, Joe. Say—I wish the boys could see us now."
"So do I."

"Say—boys, don't say anything about it, and some time when they're around, I'll come up to you and say 'Joe, got a pipe? I want a smoke.' And you'll say, kind of careless like, as if it warn't anything, you'll say, 'Yes, I got my *old* pipe, and another one, but my tobacker ain't very good.' And I'll say, 'Oh, that's all right, if it's *strong* enough.' And then you'll out with the pipes, and we'll light up just as ca'm, and then just see 'em look!"

"By jings that'll be gay, Tom! I wish it was *now*!"

"So do I! And when we tell 'em we learned when we was off pirating, won't they wish they'd been along?"

"O, I reckon not! I'll just *bet* they will!"

So the talk ran on. But presently it began to flag a trifle, and grow disjointed. The silences widened; the expectoration marvelously increased. Every pore inside the boys' cheeks became a spouting fountain; they could scarcely bail out the cellars under their tongues fast enough to prevent an inundation; little overflowings down their throats occurred in spite of all they could do, and sudden retchings followed every time. Both boys were looking very pale and miserable, now. Joe's pipe dropped from his nerveless fingers. Tom's followed. Both fountains were going furiously and both pumps bailing with might and main. Joe said feebly:

"I've lost my knife. I reckon I better go and find it."

Tom said, with quivering lips and halting utterance:

"I'll help you. You go over that way and I'll hunt around by the spring. No, you needn't come, Huck—we can find it."

So Huck sat down again, and waited an hour. Then he found it lonesome, and went to find his comrades. They were wide apart in the woods, both very pale, both fast asleep. But something informed him that if they had had any trouble they had got rid of it.

They were not talkative at supper that night. They had a humble look, and when Huck prepared his pipe after the meal and was going to prepare theirs, they said no, they were not feeling very well—something they ate at dinner had disagreed with them.

About midnight Joe awoke, and called the boys. There was a brooding oppressiveness in the air that seemed to bode something. The boys huddled themselves together and sought the friendly companionship of the fire, though the dull dead heat of the breathless atmosphere was stifling. They sat still, intent and waiting. The solemn hush continued. Beyond the light of the fire everything was swallowed up in the blackness of darkness. Presently there came a quivering glow that vaguely revealed the foliage for a moment and then vanished. By and by another came, a little stronger. Then another. Then a faint moan came sighing through the branches of the forest and the boys felt a fleeting breath upon their cheeks, and shuddered with the fancy that the Spirit of the Night had gone by. There was a pause. Now a wierd flash turned night into day and showed every little grass-blade, separate and distinct, that grew about their feet. And it showed three white, startled faces, too. A deep peal of thunder went rolling and tumbling down the heavens and lost itself in sullen rumblings in the distance. A sweep of chilly air passed by, rustling all the leaves and snowing the flaky ashes broadcast about the fire. Another fierce glare lit up the forest and an instant crash followed that seemed to rend the tree-tops right over the boys' heads. They clung together in terror, in the thick gloom that followed. A few big raindrops fell pattering upon the leaves.

"Quick! boys, go for the tent!" exclaimed Tom.

They sprang away, stumbling over roots and among vines in the dark, no two plunging in the same direction. A furious blast roared through the trees, making everything sing as it went. One blinding flash after another came, and peal on peal of deafening thunder. And now a drenching rain poured down and the rising hurricane drove it in sheets along the ground. The boys cried out to each other, but the roaring wind and the booming thunder-blasts drowned their voices utterly. However one by one they straggled in at last and took shelter under the tent, cold, scared, and streaming with water; but to have company in misery seemed something to be grateful for. They could not talk, the old sail flapped so furiously, even if the other noises would have allowed them. The tempest rose higher and higher, and presently the sail tore loose from its fastenings and went winging away on the blast. The boys seized each others' hands and fled, with many tumblings and bruises, to the shelter of a great oak that stood upon the river bank. Now the battle was at its highest. Under the ceaseless conflagration of lightning that flamed in the skies, everything below stood out in clean-cut and shadowless distinctness: the bending trees, the billowy river, white with foam, the driving spray of spume-flakes, the dim outlines of the high bluffs on the other side, glimpsed through the drifting cloud-rack and the slanting veil of rain. Every little while some giant tree yielded the fight and fell crashing through the younger growth; and the unflagging thunder-peals came now in ear-splitting explosive bursts, keen and sharp, and unspeakably appalling. The storm culminated in one matchless effort that seemed likely to tear the island to pieces, burn it up, drown it to the tree tops, blow it away, and deafen every creature in it, all at one and the same moment. It was a wild night for homeless young heads to be out in.

But at last the battle was done, and the forces retired with weaker and weaker threatenings and grumblings, and peace resumed her sway. The boys went back to camp, a good deal awed; but they found there was still something to be thankful for, because the great sycamore, the shelter of their beds, was a ruin, now, blasted by the lightnings, and they were not under it when the catastrophe happened.

Everything in camp was drenched, the camp-fire as well; for they were but heedless lads, like their generation, and had made no provision against rain. Here was matter for dismay, for they were soaked through and chilled. They were eloquent in their distress; but they presently discovered that the fire had eaten so far up under the great log it had been built against, (where it curved upward and separated itself from the ground,) that a hand-breadth or so of it had escaped wetting; so they patiently wrought until, with shreds and bark gathered from the undersides of sheltered logs, they coaxed the fire to burn again. Then they piled on great dead boughs till they had a roaring furnace and were glad-hearted once more. They dried their boiled ham and had a feast, and after that they sat by the fire and expanded and glorified their midnight adventure until morning, for there was not a dry spot to sleep on, anywhere around.

As the sun began to steal in upon the boys, drowsiness came over them and they went out on the sand-bar and lay down to sleep. They got scorched out by and by, and drearily set about getting breakfast. After the meal they felt rusty, and stiff-jointed, and a little homesick once more. Tom saw the signs, and fell to cheering up the pirates as well as he could. But they cared nothing for marbles, or circus, or swimming, or anything. He reminded them of the imposing secret, and raised a ray of cheer. While it lasted, he got them interested in a new device. This was to knock off being pirates, for a while, and be Indians for a change. They were attracted by this idea; so it was not long before they were stripped, and striped from head to heel with black mud, like so many zebras,— all of them chiefs, of course—and then they went tearing through the woods to attack an English settlement.

By and by they separated into three hostile tribes, and darted upon each other from ambush with dreadful war-whoops, and killed and scalped each other by thousands. It was a gory day. Consequently it was an extremely satisfactory one.

They assembled in camp toward supper time, hungry and happy; but now a difficulty arose—hostile Indians could not break the bread of hospitality together without first making peace, and this was a simple impossibility without smoking a pipe of peace. There was no other process that ever they had heard of. Two of the savages almost wished they had remained pirates. However, there was no other way; so with such show of cheerfulness as they could muster they called for the pipe and took their whiff as it passed, in due form.

And behold they were glad they had gone into savagery, for they had gained something; they found that they could now smoke a little without having to go and hunt for a lost knife; they did not get sick enough to be seriously uncomfortable. They were not likely to fool away this high promise for lack of effort. No, they practiced cautiously, after supper, with right fair success, and so they spent a jubilant evening. They were prouder and happier in their new acquirement than they would have been in the scalping and skinning of the Six Nations. We will leave them to smoke and chatter and brag, since we have no further use for them at present.

CHAPTER XVII

But there was no hilarity in the little town that same tranquil Saturday afternoon. The Harpers, and Aunt Polly's family, were being put into mourning, with great grief and many tears. An unusual quiet possessed the village, although it was ordinarily quiet enough, in all conscience. The villagers conducted their concerns with an absent air, and talked little; but they sighed often. The Saturday holiday seemed a burden to the children. They had no heart in their sports, and gradually gave them up.

In the afternoon Becky Thatcher found herself moping about the deserted school-house yard, and feeling very melancholy. But she found nothing there to comfort her. She soliloquised:

"Oh, if I only had his brass andiron-knob again! But I haven't got anything now to remember him by." And she choked back a little sob.

Presently she stopped, and said to herself:

"It was right here. O, if it was to do over again, I wouldn't say that—I wouldn't say it for the whole world. But he's gone now; I'll never never never see him any more."

This thought broke her down and she wandered away, with the tears rolling down her cheeks. Then quite a group of boys and girls,—playmates of Tom's and Joe's—came by, and stood looking over the paling fence and talking in reverent tones of how Tom did so-and-so, the last time they saw him, and how Joe said this and that small trifle (pregnant with awful prophecy, as they could easily see now!)—and each speaker pointed out the exact spot where the lost lads stood at the time, and then added something like "and I was a standing just so—just as I am now, and as if you was him— I was as close as that—and he smiled, just this way—and then something seemed to go all over me, like,—awful, you know—and I never thought what it meant, of course, but I can see now!"

Then there was a dispute about who saw the dead boys last in life, and many claimed that dismal distinction, and offered evidences, more or less tampered with by the witness; and when it was ultimately decided who *did* see the departed last, and exchanged the last words with them, the lucky parties took upon themselves a sort of sacred importance, and were gaped at and envied by all the rest. One poor chap, who had no other grandeur to offer, said with tolerably manifest pride in the remembrance:

"Well, Tom Sawyer he licked me once."

But that bid for glory was a failure. Most of the boys could say that, and so that cheapened the distinction too much. The group loitered away, still recalling memories of the lost heroes, in awed voices.

When the Sunday-school hour was finished, the next morning, the bell began to toll, instead of ringing in the usual way. It was a very still Sabbath, and the mournful sound seemed in keeping with the musing hush that lay upon nature. The villagers began to gather, loitering a moment in the vestibule to converse in whispers about the sad event. But there was no whispering in the house; only the funereal rustling of dresses as the women gathered to their seats, disturbed the silence there. None could remember when the little church had been so full before. There was finally a waiting pause, an expectant dumbness, and then Aunt Polly entered, followed by Sid and Mary, and they by the Harper family, all in deep black, and the whole congregation, the old minister as well, rose reverently and stood, until the mourners were seated in the front pew. There was another communing silence, broken at intervals by muffled sobs, and then the minister spread his hands abroad and prayed. A moving hymn was sung, and the text followed: "I am the Resurrection and the Life."

As the service proceeded, the clergyman drew such pictures of the graces, the winning ways and the rare promise of the lost lads, that every soul there, thinking he recognized these pictures, felt a pang in remembering that he had persistently blinded himself to them, always before, and had as persistently seen only faults and flaws in the poor boys. The minister related many a touching incident in the lives of the departed, too, which illustrated their sweet, generous natures, and the people could easily see, now, how noble and beautiful those episodes were, and remembered with grief that at the time they occurred they had seemed rank rascalities, well deserving of the cowhide. The congregation became more and more moved, as the pathetic tale went on, till at last the whole company broke down and joined the weeping mourners in a chorus of anguished sobs, the preacher himself giving way to his feelings, and crying in the pulpit.

There was a rustle in the gallery, which nobody noticed; a moment later the church door creaked; the minister raised his streaming eyes above his handkerchief, and stood transfixed! First one and then another pair of eyes followed the minister's, and then almost with one impulse the congregation rose and stared while the three dead boys came marching up the aisle, Tom in the lead, Joe next, and Huck, a ruin of drooping rags, sneaking sheepishly in the rear! They had been hid in the unused gallery listening to their own funeral sermon!

Aunt Polly, Mary and the Harpers threw themselves upon their restored ones, smothered them with kisses and poured out thanksgivings, while poor Huck stood abashed and uncomfortable, not knowing exactly what to do or where to hide from so many unwelcoming eyes. He wavered, and started to slink away, but Tom seized him and said:

"Aunt Polly, it ain't fair. Somebody's got to be glad to see Huck."

"And so they shall. I'm glad to see him, poor motherless thing!" And the loving attentions Aunt Polly lavished upon him were the one thing capable of making him more uncomfortable than he was before.

Suddenly the minister shouted at the top of his voice: "Praise God from whom all blessings flow—SING!—and put your hearts in it!"

And they did. Old Hundred swelled up with a triumphant burst, and while it shook the rafters Tom Sawyer the Pirate looked around upon the envying juveniles about him and confessed in his heart that this was the proudest moment of his life.

As the "sold" congregation trooped out they said they would almost be willing to be made ridiculous again to hear Old Hundred sung like that once more.

Tom got more cuffs and kisses that day—according to Aunt Polly's varying moods—than he had earned before in a year; and he hardly knew which expressed the most gratefulness to God and affection for himself.

CHAPTER XVIII

That was Tom's great secret—the scheme to return home with his brother pirates and attend their own funerals. They had paddled over to the Missouri shore on a log, at dusk on Saturday, landing five or six miles below the village; they had slept in the woods at the edge of the town till nearly daylight, and had then crept through back lanes and alleys and finished their sleep in the gallery of the church among a chaos of invalided benches.

At breakfast, Monday morning, Aunt Polly and Mary were very loving to Tom, and very attentive to his wants. There was an unusual amount of talk. In the course of it Aunt Polly said:

"Well, I don't say it wasn't a fine joke, Tom, to keep everybody suffering 'most a week so you boys had a good time, but it is a pity you could be so hard-hearted as to let *me* suffer so. If you could come over on a log to go to your funeral, you could have come over and give me a hint some way that you warn't *dead,* but only run off."

"Yes, you could have done that, Tom," said Mary; "and I believe you would if you had thought of it."

"Would you Tom?" said Aunt Polly, her face lighting wistfully.

"Say, now, would you, if you'd thought of it? "

"I—well I don't know. 'Twould a spoiled everything."

"Tom, I hoped you loved me that much," said Aunt Polly, with a grieved tone that discomforted the boy. "It would been something if you'd cared enough to *think* of it, even if you didn't *do* it."

"Now auntie, that ain't any harm," pleaded Mary; "it's only Tom's giddy way—he is always in such a rush that he never thinks of anything."

"More's the pity. Sid would have thought. And Sid would have come and *done* it, too. Tom, you'll look back, some day, when it's too late, and wish you'd cared a little more for me when it would have cost you so little."

"Now auntie, you know I do care for you," said Tom.

"I'd know it better if you acted more like it."

"I wish now I'd thought," said Tom, with a repentant tone; "but I dreamed about you, anyway. That's something, ain't it?"

"It ain't much—a cat does that much—but it's better than nothing. What did you dream?"

"Why Wednesday night I dreamt that you was sitting over there by the bed, and Sid was sitting by the wood-box, and Mary next to him."

"Well, so we did. So we always do. I'm glad your dreams could take even that much trouble about us."

"And I dreamt that Joe Harper's mother was here."

"Why, she *was* here! Did you dream any more?"

"O, lots. But it's so dim, now."

"Well, *try* to recollect—can't you?"

"Some how it seems to me that the wind—the wind blowed the—the—"

"Try harder, Tom! The wind did blow something. Come!"

Tom pressed his fingers on his forehead an anxious minute, and then said:

"I've got it now! I've got it now! It blowed the candle!"

"Mercy on us! Go on, Tom—go on!"

"And it seems to me that you said, 'Why I believe that that door—' "

"Go *on,* Tom!"

"Just let me study a moment—just a moment. Oh, yes—you said you believed the door was open."

"As I'm sitting here, I did! Didn't I, Mary! Go on!"

"And then—and then—well I won't be certain, but it seems like as if you made Sid go and—and—"

"Well? Well? What did I make him do, Tom? What did I make him do?"

"You made him—you—O, you made him shut it."

"Well for the land's sake! I never heard the beat of that in all my days! Don't tell *me* there ain't anything in dreams, any more. Sereny Harper shall know of this before I'm an hour older. I'd like to see her get around *this* with her rubbage 'bout superstition. Go on, Tom!"

"Oh, it's all getting just as bright as day, now. Next you said I warn't *bad,* only mischeevous and harum-scarum, and not any more responsible than—than—I think it was a colt, or something."

"And so it was! Well, goodness gracious! Go on, Tom!"

"And then you began to cry."

"So I did. So I did. Not the first time, neither. And then—"

"Then Mrs. Harper she began to cry, and said Joe was just the same and she wished she hadn't whipped him for taking cream when she'd thowed it out her own self—"

"Tom! The sperrit was upon you! You was a prophecying—that's what you was doing! Land alive, go on, Tom!"

"Then Sid he said—he said—"

"I don't think I said anything," said Sid.

"Yes you did, Sid," said Mary.

"Shut your heads and let Tom go on! What did he say, Tom?"

"He said—I *think* he said he hoped I was better off where I was gone to, but if I'd been better sometimes—"

"*There,* d'you hear that! It was his very words!"

"And you shut him up sharp."

"I lay I did! There must a been an angel there. There *was* an angel there, somewheres!"

"And Mrs. Harper told about Joe scaring her with a fire-cracker, and you told about Peter and the Pain-killer—"

"Just as true as I live!"

"And then there was a whole lot of talk 'bout dragging the river for us, and 'bout having the funeral Sunday, and then you and old Miss Harper hugged and cried, and she went."

"It happened just so! It happened just so, as sure as I'm a sitting in these very tracks. Tom you couldn't told it more like, if you'd a seen it! And *then* what? Go on, Tom?"

"Then I thought you prayed for me—and I could see you and hear every word you said. And you went to bed, and I was so sorry, that I took and wrote on a piece of sycamore, *'We ain't dead—we are only off being pirates,"* and put it on the table by the candle; and then you looked so good, laying there asleep, that I thought I went and leaned over and kissed you on the lips."

"Did you, Tom, *did* you! I just forgive you everything for that!" And she siezed the boy in a crushing embrace that made him feel like the guiltiest of villains.

"It was very kind, even though it was only a—dream," Sid soliloquised just audibly.

"Shut up Sid! A body does just the same in a dream as he'd do if he was awake. Here's a big Milum apple I've been saving for you Tom, if you was ever found again—now go 'long to school. I'm thankful to the good God and Father of us all I've got you back, that's long-suffering and merciful of them that believe on Him and keep His word, though goodness knows I'm unworthy of it, but if only the worthy ones got His blessings and His hand to help them over the rough places, there's few enough would smile here or ever enter into His rest when the long night comes. Go 'long Sid, Mary, Tom—take yourselves off—you've hendered me long enough."

The children left for school, and the old lady to call on Mrs. Harper and vanquish her realism with Tom's marvelous dream. Sid had better judgment than to utter the thought that was in his mind as he left the house. It was this: "Pretty thin—as long a dream as that, without any mistakes in it!"

What a hero Tom was become, now! He did not go skipping and prancing, but moved with a dignified swagger as became a pirate who felt that the public eye was on him. And indeed it was; he tried not to seem to see the looks or hear the remarks as he passed along, but they were food and drink to him. Smaller boys than himself flocked at his heels, as proud to be seen with him, and tolerated by him, as if he had been the drummer at the head of a procession or the elephant leading a menagerie into town. Boys of his own size pretended not to know he had been away at all; but they were consuming with envy, nevertheless. They would have given anything to have that swarthy sun-tanned skin of his, and his glittering notoriety; and Tom would not have parted with either for a circus.

At school the children made so much of him and of Joe, and delivered such eloquent admiration from their eyes, that the two

heroes were not long in becoming insufferably "stuck-up." They
began to tell their adventures to hungry listeners—but they only
began; it was not a thing likely to have an end, with imaginations
like theirs to furnish material. And finally, when they got out their
pipes and went serenely puffing around, the very summit of glory
was reached.

Tom decided that he could be independent of Becky Thatcher
now. Glory was sufficient. He would live for glory. Now that he was
distinguished, maybe she would be wanting to "make up." Well, let
her—she should see that he could be as indifferent as some other
people. Presently she arrived. Tom pretended not to see her. He
moved away and joined a group of boys and girls and began to talk.
Soon he observed that she was tripping gayly back and forth with
flushed face and dancing eyes, pretending to be busy chasing schoolmates, and screaming with laughter when she made a capture; but
he noticed that she always made her captures in his vicinity, and that
she seemed to cast a conscious eye in his direction at such times, too.
It gratified all the vicious vanity that was in him; and so, instead of
winning him it only "set him up" the more and made him the more
diligent to avoid betraying that he knew she was about. Presently she
gave over skylarking, and moved irresolutely about, sighing once or
twice and glancing furtively and wistfully toward Tom. Then she
observed that now Tom was talking more particularly to Amy
Lawrence than to any one else. She felt a sharp pang and grew
disturbed and uneasy at once. She tried to go away, but her feet were
treacherous, and carried her to the group instead. She said to a girl
almost at Tom's elbow—with sham vivacity:

"Why Mary Austin! you bad girl, why didn't you come to Sunday-
school?"

"I did come—didn't you see me?"

"Why no! Did you? Where did you sit?

"I was in Miss Peter's class, where I always go. I saw *you.* "

"Did you? Why it's funny I didn't see you. I wanted to tell you
about the pic-nic."

"O, that's jolly. Who's going to give it?"

"My ma's going to let me have one."

"O, goody; I hope she'll let *me* come."

"Well she will. The pic-nic's for me. She'll let anybody come that
I want, and I want you."

"That's ever so nice. When is it going to be?"

"By and by. Maybe about vacation."

"O, won't it be fun! You going to have all the girls and boys?"

"Yes, every one that's friends to me—or wants to be;" and she
glanced ever so furtively at Tom, but he talked right along to Amy
Lawrence about the terrible storm on the island, and how the
lightning tore the great sycamore tree "all to flinders" while he was
"standing within three feet of it."

"O, may I come?" said Gracie Miller.

"Yes."

"And me?" said Sally Rogers.

"Yes."

"And me, too?" said Susy Harper. "And Joe?"

"Yes."

And so on, with clapping of joyful hands till all the group had begged for invitations but Tom and Amy. Then Tom turned coolly away, still talking, and took Amy with him. Becky's lips trembled and the tears came to her eyes; she hid these signs with a forced gayety and went on chattering, but the life had gone out of the pic-nic, now, and out of everything else; she got away as soon as she could and hid herself and had what her sex calls "a good cry." Then she sat moody, with wounded pride till the bell rang. She roused up, now, with a vindictive cast in her eye, and gave her plaited tails a shake and said she know what *she'd* do.

At recess Tom continued his flirtation with Amy with jubilant self-satisfaction. And he kept drifting about to find Becky and lacerate her with the performance. At last he spied her, but there was a sudden falling of his mercury. She was sitting cosily on a little bench behind the school-house looking at a picture book with Alfred Temple—and so absorbed were they, and their heads so close together over the book that they did not seem to be conscious of anything in the world besides. Jealousy ran red hot through Tom's veins. He began to hate himself for throwing away the chance Becky had offered for a reconciliation. He called himself a fool, and all the hard names he could think of. He wanted to cry with vexation. Amy chatted happily along, as they walked, for her heart was singing, but Tom's tongue had lost its function. He did not hear what Amy was saying, and whenever she paused expectantly he could only stammer an awkward assent, which was as often misplaced as otherwise. He kept drifting to the rear of the school-house, again and again, to sear his eye-balls with the hateful spectacle there. He could not help it. And it maddened him to see, as he thought he saw, that Becky Thatcher never once suspected that he was even in the land of the living. But she did see, nevertheless; and she knew she was winning her fight, too, and was glad to see him suffer as she had suffered.

Amy's happy prattle became intolerable. Tom hinted at things he had to attend to; things that must be done; and time was fleeting. But in vain—the girl chirped on. Tom thought, "O hang her, ain't I ever going to get rid of her?" At last he *must* be attending to those things—and she said artlessly that she would be "around" when school let out. And he hastened away, hating her for it.

"Any other boy!" Tom thought, grating his teeth. "Any boy in the whole town but that Saint Louis smarty that thinks he dresses so fine and is aristocracy! O, all right, I licked you the first day you ever saw this town, mister, and I'll lick you again! You just wait till I catch you out! I'll just take and—"

And he went through the motions of thrashing an imaginary boy—
pummeling the air, and kicking and gouging. "Oh, you do, do you?
You holler 'nough, do you? Now, then, let that learn you!" And so
the imaginary flogging was finished to his satisfacton.

Tom fled home at noon. His conscience could not endure any
more of Amy's grateful happiness, and his jealousy could bear no
more of the other distress. Becky resumed her picture-inspections
with Alfred, but as the minutes dragged along and no Tom came to
suffer, her triumph began to cloud and she lost interest; gravity
and absent-mindedness followed, and then melancholy; two or
three times she pricked up her ear at a footstep, but it was a false
hope; no Tom came. At last she grew entirely miserable and wished
she hadn't carried it so far. When poor Alfred, seeing that he was
losing her, he did not know how, and kept exclaiming: "O here's a
jolly one! look at this!" she lost patience at last, and said, "Oh,
don't bother me! I don't care for them!" and burst into tears, and
got up and walked away.

Alfred dropped alongside and was going to try to comfort her,
but she said:

"Go away and leave me alone, can't you! I hate you!"

So the boy halted, wondering what he could have done—for she
had said she would look at pictures all through the nooning—and
she walked on, crying. Then Alfred went musing into the deserted
schoolhouse. He was humiliated and angry. He easily guessed his
way to the truth—the girl had simply made a convenience of him to
vent her spite upon Tom Sawyer. He was far from hating Tom the
less when this thought occurred to him. He wished there was some
way to get that boy into trouble without much risk to himself.
Tom's spelling fell under his eye. Here was his opportunity. He
gratefully opened to the lesson for the afternoon and poured ink
upon the page.

Becky, glancing in at a window behind him at the moment, saw
the act, and moved on, without discovering herself. She started
homeward, now, intending to find Tom and tell him; Tom would be
thankful and their troubles would be healed. Before she was half
way home, however, she had changed her mind. The thought of
Tom's treatment of her when she was talking about her pic-nic came
scorching back and filled her with shame. She resolved to let him get
whipped on the damaged spelling-book's account, and to hate him
forever, into the bargain.

CHAPTER XIX

Tom arrived at home in a dreary mood, and the first thing his aunt
said to him showed him that he had brought his sorrows to an
unpromising market:

"Tom, I've got a notion to skin you alive!"

"Auntie, what have I done?"

"Well, you've done enough. Here I go over to Sereny Harper, like an old softy, expecting I'm going to make her believe all that rubbage about that dream, when lo and behold you she'd found out from Joe that you was over here and heard all the talk we had that night. Tom I don't know what is to become of a boy that will act like that. It makes me feel so bad to think you could let me go to Sereny Harper and make such a fool of myself and never say a word."

This was a new aspect of the thing. His smartness of the morning had seemed to Tom a good joke before, and very ingenious. It merely looked mean and shabby now. He hung his head and could not think of anything to say for a moment. Then he said:

"Auntie, I wish I hadn't done it—but I didn't think."

"O, child, you never think. You never think of anything but your own selfishness. You could think to come all the way over here from Jackson's island in the night to laugh at our troubles, and you could think to fool me with a lie about a dream; but you couldn't ever think to pity us and save us from sorrow."

"Auntie, I know now it was mean, but I didn't mean to be mean. I didn't, honest. And besides I didn't come over here to laugh at you that night."

"What did you come for, then?"

"It was to tell you not to be uneasy about us, because we hadn't got drowned."

"Tom, Tom, I would be the thankfullest soul in this world if I could believe you ever had as good a thought as that, but you know you never did—and *I* know it, Tom."

"Indeed and 'deed I did, auntie—I wish I may never stir if I didn't."

"O, Tom, don't lie—don't do it. It only makes things a hundred times worse."

"It ain't a lie, auntie, it's the truth. I wanted to keep you from grieving—that was all that made me come."

"I'd give the whole world to believe that—it would cover up a power of sins Tom. I'd 'most be glad you'd run off and acted so bad. But it aint reasonable; because, why didn't you tell me, child?"

"Why, you see, auntie, when you got to talking about the funeral, I just got all full of the idea of our coming and hiding in the church, and I couldn't somehow bear to spoil it. So I just put the bark back in my pocket and kept mum."

"What bark?"

"The bark I had wrote on to tell you we'd gone pirating. I wish, now, you'd waked up when I kissed you—I do, honest."

The hard lines in his aunt's face relaxed and a sudden tenderness dawned in her eyes.

"*Did* you kiss me, Tom?"

"Why yes I did."

"Are you sure you did, Tom?"

"Why yes I did, auntie—certain sure."

"What did you kiss me for, Tom?"

"Because I loved you so, and you laid there moaning and I was so sorry."

The words sounded like truth. The old lady could not hide a tremor in her voice when she said:

"Kiss me again, Tom!—and be off with you to school, now, and don't bother me any more."

The moment he was gone, she ran to a closet and got out the ruin of a jacket which Tom had gone pirating in. Then she stopped with it in her hand, and said to herself:

"No, I don't dare. Poor boy, I reckon he's lied about it—but it's a blessed, blessed lie, there's such comfort come from it. I hope the Lord—I *know* the Lord will forgive him, because it was such goodheartedness in him to tell it. But I don't want to find out it's a lie. I won't look."

She put the jacket away, and stood by musing a minute. Twice she put out her hand to take the garment again, and twice she refrained. Once more she ventured, and this time she fortified herself with the thought: "It's a good lie— it's a good lie—I won't let it grieve me." So she sought the jacket pocket. A moment later she was reading Tom's piece of bark through flowing tears and saying: "I could forgive the boy, now, if he'd committed a million sins!"

CHAPTER XX

There was something about Aunt Polly's manner, when she kissed Tom, that swept away his low spirits and made him light-hearted and happy again. He started to school and had the luck of coming upon Becky Thatcher at the head of Meadow Lane. His mood always determined his manner. Without a moment's hesitation he ran to her and said:

"I acted mighty mean to-day, Becky, and I'm so sorry. I won't ever, ever do that way again, as long as ever I live—please make up, won't you?"

The girl stopped and looked him scornfully in the face:

"I'll thank you to keep yourself *to* yourself, Mr. Thomas Sawyer. I'll never speak to you again."

She tossed her head and passed on. Tom was so stunned that he had not even presence of mind enough to say "Who cares, Miss Smarty?" until the right time to say it had gone by. So he said nothing. But he was in a fine rage, nevertheless. He moped into the school-yard wishing she were a boy, and imagining how he would trounce her if she were. He presently encountered her and delivered a stinging remark as he passed. She hurled one in return, and the angry breach was complete. It seemed to Becky, in her hot resentment, that she could hardly wait for school to "take in," she was so impatient to see Tom flogged for the injured spelling-book. If she had had any lingering notion of exposing Alfred Temple, Tom's offensive fling had driven it entirely away.

Poor girl, she did not know how fast she was nearing trouble herself. The master, Mr. Dobbins, had reached middle age with an unsatisfied ambition. The darling of his desires was, to be a doctor, but poverty had decreed that he should be nothing higher than a village schoolmaster. Every day he took a mysterious book out of his desk and absorbed himself in it at times when no classes were reciting. He kept that book under lock and key. There was not an urchin in school but was perishing to have a glimpse of it, but the chance never came. Every boy and girl had a theory about the nature of that book; but no two theories were alike, and there was no way of getting at the facts in the case. Now, as Becky was passing by the desk, which stood near the door, she noticed that the key was in the lock! It was a precious moment. She glanced around; found herself alone, and the next instant she had the book in her hands. The title-page—Professor somebody's "Anatomy"—carried no information to her mind; so she began to turn the leaves. She came at once upon a handsomely engraved and colored frontispiece—a human figure, stark naked. At that moment a shadow fell on the page and Tom Sawyer stepped in at the door, and caught a glimpse of the picture. Becky snatched at the book to close it, and had the hard luck to tear the pictured page half down the middle. She thrust the volume into the desk, turned the key, and burst out crying with shame and vexation.

"Tom Sawyer, you are just as mean as you can be, to sneak up on a person and look at what they're looking at."

"How could *I* know you was looking at anything?"

"You ought to be ashamed of yourself Tom Sawyer; you know you're going to tell on me, and O, what shall I do, what shall I do! I'll be whipped, and I never was whipped in school."

Then she stamped her little foot and said:

"*Be* so mean if you want to! *I* know something that's going to happen. You just wait and you'll see! Hateful, hateful, hateful!"— and she flung out of the house with a new explosion of crying.

Tom stood still, rather flustered by this onslaught. Presently he said to himself:

"What a curious kind of a fool a girl is. Never been licked in school! Shucks. What's a licking! That's just like a girl—they're so thin-skinned and chicken hearted. Well, of course *I* ain't going to tell old Dobbins on this little fool, because there's other ways of getting even on her, that ain't so mean; but what of it? Old Dobbins will ask who it was tore his book. Nobody'll answer. Then he'll do just the way he always does—ask first one and then t'other, and when he comes to the right girl he'll know it, without any telling. Girl's faces always tell on them. They ain't got any back-bone. She'll get licked. Well, it's a kind of a tight place for Becky Thatcher, because there ain't any way out of it.'' Tom conned the thing a moment longer and then added: "All right, though; she'd like to see me in just such a fix—let her sweat it out!''

Tom joined the mob of skylarking scholars outside. In a few moments the master arrived and school "took in." Tom did not feel a strong interest in his studies. Every time he stole a glance at the girls' side of the room Becky's face troubled him. Considering all things, he did not want to pity her, and yet it was all he could do to help it. He could get up no exultation that was really worthy the name. Presently the spelling-book discovery was made, and Tom's mind was entirely full of his own matters for a while after that. Becky roused up from her lethargy of distress and showed good interest in the proceedings. She did not expect that Tom could get out of his trouble by denying that he spilt the ink on the book himself; and she was right. The denial only seemed to make the thing worse for Tom. Becky supposed she would be glad of that, and she tried to believe she was glad of it, but she found she was not certain. When the worst came to the worst, she had an impulse to get up and tell on Alfred Temple, but she made an effort and forced herself to keep still—because, said she to herself, "he'll tell about me tearing the picture sure. I wouldn't say a word, not to save his life!''

Tom took his whipping and went back to his seat not at all broken-hearted, for he thought it was possible that he had unknowingly upset the ink on the spelling-book himself, in some skylarking bout—he had denied it for form's sake and because it was custom, and had stuck to the denial from principle.

A whole hour drifted by, the master sat nodding in his throne, the air was drowsy with the hum of study. By and by, Mr. Dobbins straightened himself up, yawned, then unlocked his desk, and reached for his book, but seemed undecided whether to take it out or leave it. Most of the pupils glanced up languidly, but there were two among them that watched his movements with intent eyes. Mr. Dobbins fingered his book absently for a while, then took it out and settled himself in his chair to read! Tom shot a glance at Becky. He had seen a hunted and helpless rabbit look as she did, with a gun leveled at its head. Instantly he forgot his quarrel with her. Quick—something must be done! done in a flash, too! But the very imminence of the emergency paralyzed his invention. Good!—he had an inspiration! He would run and snatch the book, spring through the door and fly. But his resolution shook for one little instant, and the chance was lost— the master opened the volume. If Tom only had the wasted opportunity back again! Too late. There was no help for Becky

now, he said. The next moment the master faced the school.
Every eye sunk under his gaze. There was that in it which smote
even the innocent with fear. There was silence while one might
count ten, the master was gathering his wrath. Then he spoke;

"Who tore this book?"

There was not a sound. One could have heard a pin drop. The
stillness continued; the master searched face after face for signs
of guilt.

"Benjamin Rogers, did you tear this book?"

A denial. Another pause.

"Joseph Harper, did you?"

Another denial. Tom's uneasiness grew more and more
intense under the slow torture of these proceedings. The master
scanned the ranks of boys—considered a while, then turned to the
girls:

"Amy Lawrence?"

A shake of the head.

"Gracie Miller?"

The same sign.

"Susan Harper, did you do this?"

Another negative. The next girl was Becky Thatcher. Tom was
trembling from head to foot with excitement and a sense of the
hopelessness of the situation.

"Rebecca Thatcher," [Tom glanced at her face—it was white
with terror,]—"did you tear—no, look me in the face"—[her
hands rose in appeal]—"did you tear this book?"

A thought shot like lightning through Tom's brain. He sprang
to his feet and shouted—"*I* done it!"

The school stared in perplexity at this incredible folly. Tom
stood a moment, to gather his dismembered faculties; and when
he stepped forward to go to his punishment the surprise, the
gratitude, the adoration that shone upon him out of poor Becky's
eyes seemed pay enough for a hundred floggings. Inspired by the
splendor of his own act, he took without an outcry the most
merciless flaying that even Mr. Dobbins had ever administered;
and also received with indifference the added cruelty of a
command to remain two hours after school should be dismissed—
for he knew who would wait for him outside till his captivity was
done, and not count the tedious time as loss, either.

Tom went to bed that night planning vengeance against Alfred
Temple; for with shame and repentance Becky had told him all,
not forgetting her own treachery; but even the longing for
vengeance had to give way, soon, to pleasanter musings, and he
fell asleep at last, with Becky's latest words lingering dreamily
in his ear—

"Tom, how *could* you be so noble!"

CHAPTER XXI

Vacation was approaching. The schoolmaster, always severe, grew severer and more exacting than ever, for he wanted the school to make a good showing on "Examination" day. His rod and his ferule were seldom idle now—at least among the smaller pupils. Only the biggest boys, and young ladies of eighteen and twenty escaped lashing. Mr. Dobbins's lashings were very vigorous ones, too; for although he carried, under his wig, a perfectly bald and shiny head, he had only reached middle age and there was no sign of feebleness in his muscle. As the great day approached, all the tyranny that was in him came to the surface; he seemed to take a vindictive pleasure in punishing the least shortcomings. The consequence was, that the smaller boys spent their days in terror and suffering and their nights in plotting revenge. They threw away no opportunity to do the master a mischief. But he kept ahead all the time. The retribution that followed every vengeful success was so sweeping and majestic that the boys always retired from the field badly worsted. At last they conspired together and hit upon a plan that promised a dazzling victory. They swore-in the sign-painter's boy, told him the scheme, and asked his help. He had his own reasons for being delighted, for the master boarded in his father's family and had given the boy ample cause to hate him. The master's wife would go on a visit to the country in a few days, and there would be nothing to interfere with the plan; the master always prepared himself for great occasions by getting pretty well fuddled, and the sign-painter's boy said that when the dominie had reached the proper condition on Examination Evening he would "manage the thing" while he napped in his chair; then he would have him awakened at the right time and hurried away to school.

In the fullness of time the interesting occasion arrived. At eight in the evening the schoolhouse was brilliantly lighted, and adorned with wreaths and festoons of foliage and flowers. The master sat throned in his great chair upon a raised platform, with his blackboard behind him. He was looking tolerably mellow. Three rows of benches on each side and six rows in front of him were occupied by the dignitaries of the town and by the parents of the pupils. To his left, back of the rows of citizens, was a spacious temporary platform upon which were seated the scholars who were to take part in the exercises of the evening; rows of small boys, washed and dressed to an intolerable state of discomfort; rows of gawky big boys; snow-banks of girls and young ladies clad in lawn and muslin and conspiciously conscious of their bare arms, their grandmothers' ancient trinkets, their bits of pink and blue ribbon and the flowers in their hair. All the rest of the house was filled with non-participating scholars.

The exercises began. A very little boy stood up and sheepishly recited, "You'd scarce expect one of my age to speak in public on the stage, etc"—accompanying himself with the painfully exact and spasmodic gestures which a machine might have used—supposing the machine to be a trifle out of order. But he got through safely, though cruelly scared, and got a fine round of applause when he made his manufactured bow and retired.

A little shame-faced girl lisped "Mary had a little lamb, etc.," performed a compassion-inspiring curtsy, got her meed of applause, and sat down flushed and happy.

Tom Sawyer stepped forward with conceited confidence and soared into the unquenchable and indestructible "Give me liberty or give me death" speech, with fine fury and frantic gesticulation, and broke down in the middle of it. A ghastly stage-fright siezed him, his legs quaked under him and he was like to choke. True, he had the manifest sympathy of the house—but he had the house's silence, too, which was even worse than its sympathy. The master frowned, and this completed the disaster. Tom struggled a while and then retired, utterly defeated. There was a weak attempt at applause, but it died early.

"The Boy stood on the Burning Deck" followed; also "The Assyrian Came Down," and other declamatory gems. Then there were reading exercises, and a spelling fight. The meager Latin class recited with honor. The prime feature of the evening was in order, now—original "compositions" by the young ladies. Each in her turn stepped forward to the edge of the platform, cleared her throat, held up her manuscript (tied with dainty ribbon), and proceeded to read, with labored attention to "expression" and punctuation. The themes were the same that had been illuminated upon similar occasions by their mothers before them, their grandmothers, and doubtless all their ancestors in the female line clear back to the Crusades. "Friendship" was one; "Memories of Other Days;" "Religion in History;" "Dream Land;" "The Advantages of Culture;" "Forms of Political Government Compared and Contrasted;" "Melancholy;" "Filial Love;" "Heart Longings," etc., etc.

A prevalent feature in these compositions was a nursed and petted melancholy; another was a wasteful and opulent gush of "fine language;" another was a tendency to lug in by the ears particularly prized words and phrases until they were worn entirely out; and a peculiarity that conspicuously marked and marred them was the inveterate and intolerable sermon that wagged its crippled tail at the end of each and every one of them. No matter what the subject might be, a brain-racking effort was made to squirm it into some aspect or other that the moral and religious mind could contemplate with edification. The glaring insincerity of these sermons was not sufficient to compass the banishment of the fashion from the schools, and it is not sufficient to-day; it never will be sufficient while the world stands, perhaps. There is no school in all our land where the young ladies do not feel obliged to close their compositions with a sermon; and you will find that the sermon of the most frivolous and least religious girl in the school is always the longest and the most relentlessly pious. But, enough of this. Homely truth is unpalatable.

Let us return to the "Examination." The first composition that was read was one entitled "Is this, then, Life?" Perhaps the reader can endure an extract from it:

"In the common walks of life, with what delightful emotions does the youthful mind look forward to some anticipated scene of festivity! Imagination is busy sketching rose-tinted pictures of joy. In fancy, the voluptuous votary of fashion sees herself amid the festive throng, 'the observed of all observers.' Her graceful form, arrayed in snowy robes, is whirling through the mazes of the joyous dance; her eye is brightest, her step is lightest in the gay assembly.

"In such delicious fancies time quickly glides by, and the welcome hour arrives for her entrance into the elysian world, of which she has had such bright dreams. How fairy-like does every thing appear to her enchanted vision! each new scene is more charming than the last. But after a while she finds that beneath this goodly exterior, all is vanity: the flattery which once charmed her soul, now grates harshly upon her ear; the ball-room has lost its charms; and with wasted health and imbittered heart, she turns away with the conviction that earthly pleasures cannot satisfy the longings of the soul!"

And so forth and so on. There was a buzz of gratification from time to time during the reading, accompanied by whispered ejaculations of "How sweet!" "How eloquent!" "So true!" etc., and after the thing had closed with a peculiarly afflicting sermon the applause was enthusiastic.

Then arose a slim, melancholy girl, whose face had the "interesting" paleness that comes of pills and indigestion, and read a "poem." Two stanzas of it will do:

A MISSOURI MAIDEN'S FAREWELL TO ALABAMA.

ALABAMA, good-bye! I love thee well!
  But yet for awhile do I have thee now!
Sad, yes, sad thoughts of thee my heart doth swell,
  And burning recollections throng my brow!
For I have wandered through thy flowery woods;
  Have roamed and read near Tallapoosa's stream;
Have listened to Tallassee's warring floods,
  And wooed on Coosa's side Aurora's beam.

Yet shame I not to bear an o'er-full heart,
  Nor blush to turn behind my tearful eyes;
'Tis from no stranger land I now must part,
  'Tis to no strangers left I yield these sighs.
Welcome and home were mine within this State,
  Whose vales I leave—whose spires fade fast from me
And cold must be mine eyes, and heart, and tête,
  When, dear Alabama! they turn cold on thee!

There were very few there who knew what *"tête"* meant, but the poem was very satisfactory, nevertheless.

Next appeared a dark complexioned, black eyed, black haired young lady, who paused an impressive moment, assumed a tragic expression and began to read in a measured, solemn tone.

A VISION.

Dark and tempestuous was night. Around the throne on high not a single star quivered; but the deep intonations of the heavy thunder constantly vibrated upon the ear; whilst the terrific lightning revelled in angry mood through the cloudy chambers of heaven, seeming to scorn the power exerted over its terror by the illustrious Franklin! Even the boisterous winds unanimously came forth from their mystic homes, and blustered about as if to enhance by their aid the wildness of the scene.

At such a time, so dark, so dreary, for human sympathy my very spirit sighed; but instead thereof,

"My dearest friend, my counsellor, my comforter and guide—
My joy in grief, my second bliss in Joy," came to my side.

She moved like one of those bright beings pictured in the sunny walks of fancy's Eden by the romantic and young, a queen of beauty unadorned save by her own transcendent loveliness. So soft was her step, it failed to make even a sound, and but for the magical thrill imparted by her genial touch, as other unobtrusive beauties, she would have glided away unperceived—unsought. A strange sadness rested upon her features, like icy tears upon the robe of December, as she pointed to the contending elements without, and bade me contemplate the two beings presented.

This nightmare occupied some ten pages of manuscript and wound up with a sermon so destructive of all hope to non-Presbyterians that it took the first prize. This composition was considered to be the very finest effort of the evening. The mayor of the village, in delivering the prize to the author of it, made a warm speech in which he said that it was by far the most "eloquent" thing he had ever listened to, and that Daniel Webster himself might well be proud of it.

It may be remarked, in passing, that the number of

compositions in which the word "beauteous" was over-fondled, and human experience referred to as "life's page," was up to the usual average.

Now the master, mellow almost to the verge of geniality, put his chair aside, turned his back to the audience, and began to draw a map of America on the blackboard, to exercise the geography class upon. But he made a sad business of it with his unsteady hand, and a smothered titter rippled over the house. He knew what the matter was and set himself to right it. He sponged out lines and re-made them; but he only distorted them more than ever, and the tittering was more pronounced. He threw his entire attention upon his work, now, as if determined not to be put down by the mirth. He felt that all eyes were fastened upon him; he imagined he was succeeding, and yet the tittering continued; it even manifestly increased. And well it might. There was a garret above, pierced with a scuttle over his head; and down through this scuttle came a cat, suspended around the haunches by a string; she had a rag tied about her head and jaws to keep her from mewing; as she slowly descended she curved upward and clawed at the string, she swung downward and clawed at the intangible air. The tittering rose higher and higher— the cat was within six inches of the absorbed teacher's head—down, down, a little lower, and she grabbed his wig with her desperate claws, clung to it and was snatched up into the garret in an instant with her trophy still in her possession! And how the light did blaze abroad from the master's bald pate—for the sign-painter's boy had *gilded* it!

That broke up the meeting. The boys were avenged. Vacation had come.

NOTE.—The pretended "compositions" quoted in this chapter are taken without alteration from a volume entitled "Prose and Poetry, by a Western Lady"—but they are exactly and precisely after the school-girl pattern and hence are much happier than any mere imitations could be.

CHAPTER XXII

Tom joined the new order of Cadets of Temperance, being attracted by the showy character of their "regalia." He promised to abstain from smoking, chewing and profanity as long as he remained a member. Now he found out a new thing—namely, that to promise not to do a thing is the surest way in the world to make a body want to go and do that very thing. Tom soon found himself tormented with a desire to drink and swear; the desire grew to be so intense that nothing but the hope of a chance to display himself in his red sash kept him from withdrawing from the order. Fourth of July was coming; but he soon gave that up—gave it up before he had worn his shackles over forty-eight

hours—and fixed his hopes upon old Judge Frazer, justice of
the peace, who was apparently on his death-bed and would have
a big public funeral, since he was so high an official. During
three days Tom was deeply concerned about the Judge's condition
and hungry for news of it. Sometimes his hopes ran high—so high
that he would venture to get out his regalia and practice before
the looking glass. But the Judge had a most discouraging way of
fluctuating. At last he was pronounced upon the mend—and then
convalescent. Tom was disgusted; and felt a sense of injury, too.
He handed in his resignation at once—and that night the Judge
suffered a relapse and died. Tom resolved that he would never
trust a man like that again.

The funeral was a fine thing. The Cadets paraded in a style
calculated to kill the late member with envy. Tom was a free boy
again, however—there was something in that. He could drink and
swear, now—but found to his surprise that he did not want to.
The simple fact that he could, took the desire away, and the charm
of it.

Tom presently wondered to find that his coveted vacation was
beginning to hang a little heavily on his hands.

He attempted a diary—but nothing happened during three
days, and so he abandoned it.

The first of all the negro minstrel shows came to town, and
made a sensation. Tom and Joe Harper got up a band of
performers and were happy for two days.

Even the Glorious Fourth was in some sense a failure, for it
rained hard, there was no procession in consequence, and the
greatest man in the world (as Tom supposed) Mr. Benton, an
actual United States Senator, proved an overwhelming
disappointment—for he was not twenty-five feet high, nor even
anywhere in the neighborhood of it.

A circus came. The boys played circus for three days afterward
in tents made of rag carpeting—admission, three pins for boys,
two for girls—and then circusing was abandoned.

A phrenologist and a mesmerizer came—and went again and
left the village duller and drearier than ever.

There were some boys-and-girls' parties, but they were so few
and so delightful that they only made the aching voids between
ache the harder.

Becky Thatcher was gone to her Constantinople home to stay
with her parents during vacation—so there was no bright side
to life anywhere.

The dreadful secret of the murder was a chronic misery. It
was a very cancer for permanency and pain.

Then came the measles.

During two long weeks Tom lay a prisoner, dead to the
world and its happenings. He was very ill, he was interested in

nothing. When he got upon his feet at last and moved feebly down town, a melancholy change had come over everything and every creature. There had been a "revival," and everybody had "got religion," not only the adults, but even the boys and girls. Tom went about, hoping against hope for the sight of one blessed sinful face, but disappointment crossed him everywhere. He found Joe Harper studying a Testament, and turned sadly away from the depressing spectacle. He sought Ben Rogers, and found him visiting the poor with a basket of tracts. He hunted up Jim Hollis, who called his attention to the precious blessing of his late measles as a warning. Every boy he encountered added another ton to his depression; and when, in desperation, he flew for refuge at last to the bosom of Huckleberry Finn and was received with a scriptural quotation, his heart broke and he crept home and to bed realizing that he alone of all the town was lost, forever and forever.

And that night there came on a terrific storm, with driving rain, awful claps of thunder and blinding sheets of lightning. He covered his head with the bedclothes and waited in a horror of suspense for his doom; for he had not the shadow of a doubt that all this hubbub was about him. He believed he had taxed the forbearance of the powers above to the extremity of endurance and that this was the result. It might have seemed to him a waste of pomp and ammunition to kill a bug with a battery of artillery, but there seemed nothing incongruous about the getting up such an expensive thunder storm as this to knock the turf from under an insect like himself.

By and by the tempest spent itself and died without accomplishing its object. The boy's first impulse was to be grateful, and reform. His second was to wait—for there might not be any more storms.

The next day the doctors were back; Tom had relapsed. The three weeks he spent on his back this time seemed an entire age. When he got abroad at last he was hardly grateful that he had been spared, remembering how lonely was his estate, how companionless and forlorn he was. He drifted listlessly down the street and found Jim Hollis acting as judge in a juvenile court that was trying a cat for murder, in the presence of her victim, a bird. He found Joe Harper and Huck Finn up an alley eating a stolen melon. Poor lads! they—like Tom—had suffered a relapse.

CHAPTER XXIII

At last the sleepy atmosphere was stirred—and vigorously: the murder trial came on in the court. It became the absorbing topic of village talk immediately. Tom could not get away from it. Every reference to the murder sent a shudder to his heart, for his troubled conscience and fears almost persuaded him that these remarks were put forth in his hearing as "feelers;" he did not see how he could be suspected of knowing anything about the murder, but still he could not be comfortable in the midst of this gossip. It kept him in a cold shiver all the time. He took Huck to a lonely place to have a talk with him. It would be some relief to unseal his tongue for a little while; to divide his burden of distress with another sufferer. Moreover, he wanted to assure himself that Huck had remained discreet.

"Huck, have you ever told anybody about—that?"

"Bout what?"

"You know what."

"Oh—'course I haven't."

"Never a word?"

"Never a solitary word, so help me. What makes you ask?"

"Well, I was afeard."

"Why Tom Sawyer, we wouldn't be alive two days if that got found out. *You* know that."

Tom felt more comfortable. After a pause:

"Huck, they couldn't anybody get you to tell, could they?"

"Get me to tell? Why if I wanted that half-breed devil to drownd me they could get me to tell. They ain't no different way."

"Well, that's all right, then. I reckon we're safe as long as we keep mum. But let's swear again, anyway. It's more surer."

"I'm agreed."

So they swore again with dread solemnities.

"What is the talk around, Huck? I've heard a power of it."

"Talk? Well, it's just Muff Potter, Muff Potter, Muff Potter all the time. It keeps me in a sweat, constant, so's I want to hide som'ers."

"That's just the same way they go on round me. I reckon he's a goner. Don't you feel sorry for him, sometimes?"

"Most always—most always. He ain't no account; but then he hain't ever done anything to hurt anybody. Just fishes a little, to get money to get drunk on—and loafs around considerable; but lord we all do that—leastways most of us,—preachers and such like. But he's kind of good—he give me half a fish, once, when there warn't enough for two; and lots of times he's kind of stood by me when I was out of luck."

"Well, he's mended kites for me, Huck, and knitted hooks on to my line. I wish we could get him out of there."

"My! we couldn't get him out Tom. And besides, 'twouldn't do any good; they'd ketch him again."

"Yes—so they would. But I hate to hear 'em abuse him so like the dickens when he never done—that."

"I do too, Tom. Lord, I hear 'em say he's the bloodiest looking villain in this country, and they wonder he wasn't ever hung before."

"Yes, they talk like that, all the time. I've heard 'em say that if he was to get free they'd lynch him."

"And they'd do it, too."

The boys had a long talk, but it brought them little comfort. As the twilight drew on, they found themselves hanging about the neighborhood of the little isolated jail, perhaps with an undefined hope that something would happen that might clear away their difficulties. But nothing happened; there seemed to be no angels or fairies interested in this luckless captive.

The boys did as they had often done before—went to the·cell grating and gave Potter some tobacco and matches. He was on the ground floor and there were no guards.

His gratitude for their gifts had always smote their consciences before—it cut deeper than ever, this time. They felt cowardly and treacherous to the last degree when Potter said:

"You've been mighty good to me, boys—better'n anybody else in this town. And I don't forget it, I don't. Often I says to myself, says I, 'I used to mend all the boys' kites and things, and show 'em what I could, and now they've all forgot old Muff when he's in trouble; but Tom don't, and Huck don't—*they* don't forget him,' says I, 'and I don't forget them.' Well, boys, I done an awful thing—drunk and crazy at the time—that's the only way I account for it—and now I got to swing for it, and it's right. Right, and *best,* too I reckon—hope so, anyway. Well, we won't talk about that. I don't want to make *you* feel bad; you've befriended me. But what I want to say, is, don't *you* ever get drunk—then you won't ever get here. Stand a little furder west— so—that's it; it's a prime comfort to see faces that's friendly when a body's in such a muck of trouble, and there don't none come here but yourn. Good friendly faces—good friendly faces. Git up on one another's backs and let me touch 'em. That's it. Shake hands—yourn'll come through the bars, but mine's too big. Little hands, and weak—but they've helped Muff Potter a power, and they'd help him more if they could."

Tom went home miserable, and his dreams that night were full of horrors. The next day and the day after, he hung about the court room, drawn by an almost irresistible impulse to go in, but forcing himself to stay out. Huck was having the same experience. They studiously avoided each other. Each wandered away, from time to time, but the same dismal fascination always brought them back presently. Tom kept his ears open when idlers sauntered out of the court room, but invariably heard distressing news—the toils were closing more and more relentlessly around poor Potter. At the end of the second day the village talk was to the effect that Injun Joe's evidence stood firm and unshaken, and that there was not the slightest question as to what the jury's verdict would be.

Tom was out late, that night, and came to bed through the window. He was in a tremendous state of excitement. It was hours before he got to sleep. All the village flocked to the Court house the next morning, for this was to be the great day. Both sexes were about equally represented in the packed audience. After a long wait the jury filed in and took their places; shortly afterward, Potter, pale and haggard, timid and hopeless, was brought in, with chains upon him, and seated where all the curious eyes could stare at him; no less conspicuous was Injun Joe, stolid as ever. There was another pause, and then the judge arrived and the sheriff proclaimed the opening of the court. The usual whisperings among the lawyers and gathering together of papers followed. These details and accompanying delays worked up an atmosphere of preparation that was as impressive as it was fascinating.

Now a witness was called who testified that he found Muff Potter washing in the brook, at an early hour of the morning that the murder was discovered, and that he immediately sneaked away. After some further questioning, counsel for the prosecution said—

"Take the witness."

The prisoner raised his eyes for a moment, but dropped them again when his own council said—

"I have no questions to ask him."

The next witness proved the finding of the knife near the corpse. Counsel for the prosecution said:

"Take the witness."

"I have no questions to ask him," Potter's lawyer replied.

A third witness swore he had often seen the knife in Potter's possession.

"Take the witness."

Counsel for Potter declined to question him. The faces of the audience began to betray annoyance. Did this attorney mean to throw away his client's life without an effort?

Several witnesses deposed concerning Potter's guilty behavior when brought to the scene of the murder. They were allowed to leave the stand without being cross-questioned.

Every detail of the damaging circumstances that occurred in the graveyard upon that morning which all present remembered so well, was brought out by credible witnesses, but none of them were cross-examined by Potter's lawyer. The perplexity and dissatisfaction of the house expressed itself in murmurs and provoked a reproof from the bench. Counsel for the prosecution now said:

"By the oaths of citizens whose simple word is above suspicion, we have fastened this awful crime beyond all possibility of question, upon the unhappy prisoner at the bar. We rest our case here."

A groan escaped from poor Potter, and he put his face in his hands and rocked his body softly to and fro, while a painful silence reigned in the courtroom. Many men were moved, and many women's compassion testified itself in tears. Counsel for the defence rose and said:

"Your honor, in our remarks at the opening of this trial, we foreshadowed our purpose to prove that our client did this fearful deed while under the influence of a blind and irresponsible delirium produced by drink. We have changed our mind. We shall not offer that plea." [Then to the clerk]: "Call Thomas Sawyer!"

A puzzled amazement awoke in every face in the house, not even excepting Potter's. Every eye fastened itself with wondering interest upon Tom as he rose and took his place upon the stand. The boy looked wild enough, for he was badly scared. The oath was administered.

"Thomas Sawyer, where were you on the seventeenth of June, about the hour of midnight?"

Tom glanced at Injun Joe's iron face and his tongue failed him. The audience listened breathless, but the words refused to come. After a few moments, however, the boy got a little of his strength back, and managed to put enough of it into his voice to make part of the house hear:

"In the graveyard!"

"A little bit louder, please. Don't be afraid. You were—"

"In the graveyard."

A contemptuous smile flitted across Injun Joe's face.

"Were you anywhere near Horse Williams's grave?"

"Yes, sir."

"Speak up—just a trifle louder. How near were you?"

"Near as I am to you."

"Were you hidden, or not?"

"I was hid."

"Where?"

"Behind the elms that's on the edge of the grave."

Injun Joe gave a barely perceptible start.

"Any one with you?"

"Yes, sir. I went there with—"

"Wait—wait a moment. Never mind mentioning your companion's name. We will produce him at the proper time. Did you carry anything there with you."

Tom hesitated and looked confused.

"Speak out my boy—don't be diffident. The truth is always respectable. What did you take there?"

"Only a —a—dead cat."

There was a ripple of mirth, which the court checked.

"We will produce the skeleton of that cat. Now my boy, tell us everything that occurred—tell it in your own way—don't skip anything, and don't be afraid."

Tom began—hesitatingly at first, but as he warmed to his subject his words flowed more and more easily; in a little while every sound ceased but his own voice; every eye fixed itself upon him; with parted lips and bated breath the audience hung upon his words, taking no note of time, rapt in the ghastly fascinations of the tale. The strain upon pent emotion reached its climax when the boy said—

"—and as the doctor fetched the board around and Muff Potter fell, Injun Joe jumped with the knife and—"

Crash! Quick as lightning the half-breed sprang for a window, tore his way through all opposers, and was gone!

CHAPTER XXIV

Tom was a glittering hero once more—the pet of the old, the envy of the young. His name even went into immortal print, for the village paper magnified him. There were some that believed he would be President, yet, if he escaped hanging.

As usual, the fickle, unreasoning world took Muff Potter to its bosom and fondled him as lavishly as it had abused him before. But that sort of conduct is to the world's credit; therefore it is not well to find fault with it.

Tom's days were days of splendor and exultation to him, but his nights were seasons of horror. Injun Joe infested all his dreams, and always with doom in his eye. Hardly any temptation could persuade the boy to stir abroad after nightfall. Poor Huck was in the same state of wretchedness and terror, for Tom had told the whole story to the lawyer the night before the great day of the trial, and Huck was sore afraid that his share in the business might leak out, yet, notwithstanding Injun Joe's flight had saved him the suffering of testifying in court. The poor fellow had got the attorney to promise secrecy, but what of that? Since Tom's harrassed conscience had managed to drive him to the lawyer's house by night and wring a dread tale from lips that had been sealed with the dismalest and most formidable of oaths, Huck's confidence in the human race was well nigh obliterated.

Daily Muff Potter's gratitude made Tom glad he had spoken; but nightly he wished he had sealed up his tongue.

Half the time Tom was afraid Injun Joe would never be captured; the other half he was afraid he would be. He felt sure he never could draw a safe breath again until that man was dead and he had seen the corpse.

Rewards had been offered, the country had been scoured, but no

Injun Joe was found. One of those omniscient and awe-inspiring marvels, a detective, came up from St. Louis, moused around, shook his head, looked wise, and made that sort of astounding success which members of that craft usually achieve. That is to say he "found a clew." But you can't hang a "clew" for murder and so after that detective had got through and gone home, Tom felt just as insecure as he was before.

The slow days drifted on, and each left behind it a slightly lightened weight of apprehension.

CHAPTER XXV

There comes a time in every rightly constructed boy's life when he has a raging desire to go somewhere and dig for hidden treasure. This desire suddenly came upon Tom one day. He sailed out to find Joe Harper, but failed of success. Next he sought Ben Rogers; he had gone fishing. Presently he stumbled upon Huck Finn the Red-Handed. Huck would answer. Tom took him to a private place and opened the matter to him confidentially. Huck was willing. Huck was always willing to take a hand in any enterprise that offered entertainment and required no capital, for he had a troublesome superabundance of that sort of time which is *not* money. "Where'll we dig?" said Huck.

"O, most anywhere."

"Why, is it hid all around?"

"No indeed it ain't. It's hid in mighty particular places, Huck— sometimes on islands, sometimes in rotten chests under the end of a limb of an old dead tree, just where the shadow falls at midnight; but mostly under the floor in ha'nted houses."

"Who hides it?"

"Why robbers, of course—who'd you reckon? Sunday-school sup'rintendents?"

"I don't know. If 'twas mine I wouldn't hide it; I'd spend it and have a good time."

"So would I. But robbers don't do that way. They always hide it and leave it there."

"Don't they come after it any more?"

"No, they think they will, but they generally forget the marks, or else they die. Anyway it lays there a long time and gets rusty; and by and by somebody finds an old yellow paper that tells how to find the marks—a paper that's got to be ciphered over about a week because it's mostly signs and hy'roglyphics."

"Hyro-which?"

"Hy'roglyphics—pictures and things, you know, that don't seem to mean anything."

"Have you got one of them papers, Tom?"

"No."

"Well then, how you going to find the marks?"

"I don't want any marks. They always bury it under a ha'nted house or on an island, or under a dead tree that's got one limb sticking out. Well, we've tried Jackson's Island a little, and we can try it again some time; and there's the old ha'nted house up the Still-House branch, and there's lots of dead limb trees—dead loads of 'em."

"Is it under all of them?"

"How you talk! No!"

"Then how you going to know which one to go for?"

"Go for all of 'em!"

"Why Tom, it'll take all summer."

"Well, what of that? Suppose you find a brass pot with a hundred dollars in it, all rusty and gay, or a rotten chest full of di'monds. How's that?"

Huck's eyes glowed.

"That's bully. Plenty bully enough for me. Just you gimme the hundred dollars and I don't want no di'monds."

"All right. But I bet you *I* ain't going to throw off on di'monds. Some of 'em's worth twenty dollars apiece—there ain't any, hardly, but's worth six bits or a dollar."

"No! Is that so?"

"Cert'nly—anybody'll tell you so. Hain't you ever seen one, Huck?"

"Not as I remember."

"O, kings have slathers of them."

"Well, I don't know no kings, Tom."

"I reckon you don't. But if you was to go to Europe you'd see a raft of 'em hopping around."

"Do they hop?"

"Hop?—your granny! No!"

"Well what did you say they did, for?"

"Shucks, I only meant you'd *see* 'em—not hopping, of course— what do they want to hop for?—but I mean you'd just see 'em— scattered around, you know, in a kind of a general way. Like that old hump-backed Richard."

"Richard? What's his other name?"

"He didn't have any other name. Kings don't have any but a given name."

"No?"

"But they don't."

"Well, if they like it, Tom, all right; but I don't want to be a king and have only just a given name, like a nigger. But say—where you going to dig first?"

"Well, I don't know. S'pose we tackle that old dead-limb tree on the hill t'other side of Still-House branch?"

"I'm agreed."

So they got a crippled pick and a shovel, and set out on their three-mile tramp. They arrived hot and panting, and threw themselves down in the shade of a neighboring elm to rest and have a smoke.

"I like this," said Tom.

"So do I."

"Say, Huck, if we find a treasure here, what you going to do with your share?"

"Well I'll have pie and a glass of soda every day, and I'll go to every circus that comes along. I bet I'll have a gay time."

"Well ain't you going to save any of it?"

"Save it? What for?"

"Why so as to have something to live on, by and by."

"O, that ain't any use. Pap would come back to thish-yer town some day and get his claws on it if I didn't hurry up, and I tell you he'd clean it out pretty quick. What you going to do with yourn, Tom?"

"I'm going to buy a new drum, and a sure-'nough sword, and a red neck-tie and a bull pup, and get married."

"Married!"

"That's it."

"Tom, you—why you ain't in your right mind."

"Wait—you'll see."

"Well that's the foolishest thing you could do. Look at pap and my mother. Fight! Why they used to fight all the time. I remember, mighty well."

"That ain't anything. The girl I'm going to marry won't fight."

"Tom, I reckon they're all alike. They'll all comb a body. Now you better think 'bout this a while. I tell you better. What's the name of the gal?"

"It ain't a gal at all—it's a girl."

"It's all the same, I reckon; some says gal, some says girl—both's right, like enough. Anyway, what's her name, Tom?"

"I'll tell you some time—not now."

"All right—that'll do. Only if you get married I'll be more lonesomer than ever."

"No you won't. You'll come and live with me. Now stir out of this and we'll go to digging."

They worked and sweated for half an hour. No result. They toiled another half hour. Still no result. Huck said:

"Do they always bury it as deep as this?"

"Sometimes—not always. Not generally. I reckon we haven't got the right place."

So they chose a new spot and began again. The labor dragged a little, but still they made progress. They pegged away in silence for some time. Finally Huck leaned on his shovel, swabbed the beaded drops from his brow with his sleeve, and said:

"Where you going to dig next, after we get this one?"

"I reckon maybe we'll tackle the old tree that's over yonder on Cardiff Hill back of the widow's."

"I reckon that'll be a good one. But won't the widow take it away from us Tom? It's on her land."

"*She* take it away! Maybe she'd like to try it once. Whoever finds one of these hid treasures, it belongs to him. It don't make any difference whose land it's on."

That was satisfactory. The work went on. By and by Huck said:—

"Blame it, we must be in the wrong place again. What do you think?"

"It *is* mighty curious Huck. I don't understand it. Sometimes witches interfere. I reckon maybe that's what's the trouble now."

"Shucks, witches ain't got no power in the daytime."

"Well, that's so. I didn't think of that. Oh, *I* know what the matter is! What a blamed lot of fools we are! You got to find out where the shadow of the limb falls at midnight, and that's where you dig!"

"Then consound it, we've fooled away all this work for nothing. Now hang it all, we got to come back in the night. It's an awful long way. Can you get out?"

"I bet I will. We've got to do it to night, too, because if some body sees these holes they'll know in a minute what's here and they'll go for it."

"Well, I'll come around and maow to night."

"All right. Let's hide the tools in the bushes."

The boys were there that night, about the appointed time. They sat in the shadow waiting. It was a lonely place, and an hour made solemn by old traditions. Spirits whispered in the rustling leaves, ghosts lurked in the murky nooks, the deep baying of a hound floated up out of the distance, an owl answered with his sepulchral note. The boys were subdued by these solemnities, and talked little. By and by they judged that twelve had come; they marked where the shadow fell, and began to dig. Their hopes commenced to rise. Their interest grew stronger, and their industry kept pace with it. The hole deepened and still deepened, but every time their hearts jumped to hear the pick strike upon something, they only suffered a new disappointment. It was only a stone or a chunk. At last Tom said:—

"It ain't any use, Huck, we're wrong again."

"Well but we *can't* be wrong. We spotted the shadder to a dot."

"I know it, but then there's another thing."

"What's that?"

"Why we only guessed at the time. Like enough it was too late or too early."

Huck dropped his shovel.

"That's it," said he. "That's the very trouble. We got to give this one up. We can't ever tell the right time, and besides this kind of thing's too awful, here this time of night with witches and ghosts of fluttering around so. I feel as if something's behind me all the time; and I'm afeared to turn around, becuz maybe there's others in front a-waiting for a chance. I been creeping all over, ever since I got here."

"Well, I've been pretty much so, too, Huck. They most always put in a dead man when they bury a treasure under a tree, to look out for it."

"Lordy!"

"Yes, they do. I've always heard that."

"Tom I don't like to fool around much where there's dead people. A body's bound to get into trouble with 'em, sure."

"I don't like to stir 'em up, either. S'pose this one here was to stick his skull out and say something!"

"Don't, Tom! It's awful."

"Well it just is. Huck, I don't feel comfortable a bit."

"Say, Tom, let's give this place up, and try somewheres else."

"All right, I reckon we better."

"What'll it be?"

Tom considered a while; and then said—

"The ha'nted house. That's it!"

"Blame it, I don't like ha'nted houses Tom. Why they're a dern sight worse'n dead people. Dead people might talk, maybe, they they don't come sliding around in a shroud, when you ain't noticing, and peep over your shoulder all of a sudden and grit their teeth, the way a ghost does. I couldn't stand such a thing as that, Tom—nobody could."

"Yes, but Huck, ghosts don't travel around only at night. They won't hender us from digging there in the day time."

"Well that's so. But you know mighty well people don't go about that ha'nted house in the day nor the night."

"Well, that's mostly because they don't like to go where a man's been murdered, anyway—but nothing's ever been seen around that house except in the night—just some blue lights slipping by the windows—no regular ghosts."

"Well where you see one of them blue lights flickering around, Tom, you can bet there's a ghost mighty close behind it. It stands to reason. Becuz *you* know that they don't let anybody but ghosts use 'em."

"Yes, that's so. But anyway they don't come around in the daytime, so what's the use of our being afeared?"

"Well, all right. We'll tackle the ha'nted house if you say so—but I reckon it's taking chances."

They had started down the hill by this time. There in the middle of the moonlit valley below them stood the "ha'nted" house, utterly isolated, its fences gone long ago, rank weeds smothering the very doorsteps, the chimney crumbled to ruin, the window-sashes vacant, a corner of the roof caved in. The boys gazed a while, half expecting to see a blue light flit past the window; then talking in a low tone, as befitted the time and the circumstances, they struck far off to the right, to give the haunted house a wide berth, and took their way homeward through the woods that adorned the rearward side of Cardiff Hill.

CHAPTER XXVI

About noon the next day the boys arrived at the dead tree; they had come for their tools. Tom was impatient to go to the haunted house; Huck was measurably so, also—but suddenly said—

"Lookyhere, Tom, do you know what day it is?"

Tom mentally ran over the days of the week, and then quickly lifted his eyes with a startled look in them—

"My! I never once thought of it, Huck!"

"Well I didn't neither, but all at once it popped onto me that it was Friday."

"Blame it, a body can't be too careful, Huck. We might a got into an awful scrape, tackling such a thing on a Friday."

"*Might!* Better say we *would!* There's some lucky days, maybe, but Friday ain't."

"Any fool knows that. I don't reckon *you* was the first that found it out, Huck."

"Well, I never said I was, did I? And Friday ain't all, neither. I had a rotten bad dream last night—dreampt about rats."

"No! Sure sign of trouble. Did they fight?"

"No."

"Well that's good, Huck. When they don't fight it's only a sign that there's trouble around, you know. All we got to do is to look mighty sharp and keep out of it. We'll drop this thing for today, and play. Do you know Robin Hood, Huck?"

"No. Who's Robin Hood?"

"Why he was one of the greatest men that was ever in England— and the best. He was a robber."

"Cracky, I wisht I was. Who did he rob?"

"Only sheriffs and bishops and rich people and kings, and such like. But he never bothered the poor. He loved 'em. He always divided up with 'em perfectly square."

"Well, he must 'a' been a brick."

"I bet you he was, Huck. Oh, he was the noblest man that ever was. They ain't such men now, I can tell you. He could lick any man in England, with one hand tied behind him; and he could take his yew bow and plug a ten cent piece every time, a mile and a half."

"What's a *yew* bow?"

"*I* don't know. It's some kind of a bow, of course. And if he hit that dime only on the edge he would set down and cry—and curse. But we'll play Robin Hood—it's noble fun. I'll learn you."

"I'm agreed."

So they played Robin Hood all the afternoon, now and then casting a yearning eye down upon the haunted house and passing a remark about the morrow's prospect and possibilities there. As the sun began to sink into the west they took their way homeward athwart the long shadows of the trees and soon were buried from sight in the forests of Cardiff Hill.

On Saturday, shortly after noon, the boys were at the dead tree again. They had a smoke and a chat in the shade, and then dug a little in their last hole, not with great hope, but merely because Tom said there were so many cases where people had given up a treasure after getting down within six inches of it, and then somebody else had come along and turned it up with a single thrust of a shovel. The thing failed this time, however, so the boys shouldered their tools and went away feeling that they had not trifled with fortune but had fulfilled all the requirements that belong to the business of treasure-hunting.

When they reached the haunted house there was something so wierd and grisly about the dead silence that reigned there under the baking sun, and something so depressing about the loneliness and desolation of the place, that they were afraid, for a moment, to venture in. Then they crept to the door and took a trembling peep. They saw a weed-grown, floorless room, unplastered, an ancient fireplace, vacant windows, a ruinous staircase; and here, there, and everywhere, hung ragged and abandoned cobwebs. They presently entered, softly, with quickened pulses, talking in whispers, ears alert to catch the slightest sound, and muscles tense and ready for instant retreat.

In a little while familiarity modified their fears and they gave the place a critical and interested examination, rather admiring their own boldness, and wondering at it, too. Next they wanted to look up stairs. This was something like cutting off retreat, but they got to daring each other, and of course there could be but one result—they threw their tools into a corner and made the ascent. Up there were the same signs of decay. In one corner they found a closet that promised mystery, but the promise was a fraud—there was nothing in it. Their courage was up now and well in hand. They were about to go down and begin work when—

"Sh!" said Tom.

"What is it?" whispered Huck, blanching with fright.

"Sh!.....There!.....Hear it?"

"Yes!.....O, my! Let's run!"

"Keep still! Don't you budge! They're coming right toward the door."

The boys stretched themselves upon the floor with their eyes to knot holes in the planking, and lay waiting, in a misery of fear.

"They've stopped.....No—coming......Here they are. Don't

whisper another word, Huck. My goodness, I wish I was out of this!"

Two men entered. Each boy said to himself: "There's the old deaf and dumb Spaniard that's been about town once or twice lately—never saw t'other man before."

"T'other" was a ragged, unkempt creature, with nothing very pleasant in his face. The Spaniard was wrapped in a *serapè;* he had bushy white whiskers; long white hair flowed from under his sombrero, and he wore green goggles. When they came in, "T'other" was talking in a low voice; they sat down on the ground, facing the door, with their backs to the wall, and the speaker continued his remarks. His manner became less guarded and his words more distinct as he proceeded:

"No," said he, "I've thought it all over, and I don't like it. It's dangerous."

"Dangerous!" grunted the "deaf and dumb" Spaniard,—to the vast surprise of the boys. "Milksop!"

This voice made the boys gasp and quake. It was Injun Joe's! There was silence for some time. Then Joe said:

"What's any more dangerous than that job up yonder—but nothing's come of it."

"That's different. Away up the river so, and not another house about. 'Twon't ever be known that we tried, anyway, long as we didn't succeed."

"Well, what's more dangerous than coming here in the day time! —anybody would suspicion us that saw us."

"*I* know that. But there warn't any other place as handy after that fool of a job. I want to quit this shanty. I wanted to yesterday, only it warn't any use trying to stir out of here, with those infernal boys playing over there on the hill right in full view."

"Those infernal boys," quaked again under the inspiration of this remark, and thought how lucky it was that they had remembered it was Friday and concluded to wait a day. They wished in their hearts they had waited a year.

The two men got out some food and made a luncheon. After a long and thoughtful silence, Injun Joe said:

"Look here, lad—you go back up the river where you belong. Wait there till you hear from me. I'll take the chances on dropping into this town just once more, for a look. We'll do that 'dangerous' job after I've spied around a little and think things look well for it. Then for Texas! We'll leg it together!"

This was satisfactory. Both men presently fell to yawning, and Injun Joe said:

"I'm dead for sleep! It's your turn to watch."

He curled down in the weeds and soon began to snore. His comrade stirred him once or twice and he became quiet. Presently the watcher began to nod; his head drooped lower and lower, both men began to snore now.

The boys drew a long, grateful breath. Tom whispered—

"Now's our chance—come!"

Huck said:

"I can't—I'd die if they was to wake."

Tom urged—Huck held back. At last Tom rose slowly and softly, and started alone. But the first step he made wrung such a hideous creak from the crazy floor that he sank down almost dead with fright. He never made a second attempt. The boys lay there counting the dragging moments till it seemed to them that time must be done and eternity growing gray; and then they were grateful to note that at last the sun was setting.

Now one snore ceased. Injun Joe sat up, stared around—smiled grimly upon his comrade, whose head was drooping upon his knees—stirred him up with his foot and said—

"Here! *You're* a watchman, ain't you! All right, though—nothing's happened."

"My! have I been asleep?"

"Oh, partly, partly. Nearly time for us to be moving, pard. What'll we do with what little swag we've got left?"

"I don't know—leave it here as we've always done, I reckon. No use to take it away till we start south. Six hundred and fifty in silver's something to carry."

"Well—all right—it won't matter to come here once more."

"No—but I'd say come in the night as we used to do—it's better."

"Yes; but look here; it may be a good while before I get the right chance at that job; accidents might happen; 'tain't in such a very good place; we'll just regularly bury it—and bury it deep."

"Good idea," said the comrade, who walked across the room, knelt down, raised one of the rearward hearthstones and took out a bag that jingled pleasantly. He subtracted from it twenty or thirty dollars for himself and as much for Injun Joe and passed the bag to the latter, who was on his knees in the corner, now, digging with his bowie knife.

The boys forgot all their fears, all their miseries in an instant. With gloating eyes they watched every movement. Luck!—the splendor of it was beyond all imagination! Six hundred dollars was money enough to make half a dozen boys rich! Here was treasure-hunting under the happiest auspices—there would not be any bothersome uncertainty as to where to dig. They nudged each other every moment—eloquent nudges and easily understood, for they simply meant—"O, but ain't you glad *now* we're here!"

Joe's knife struck upon something.

"Hello!" said he.

"What is it?" said his comrade.

"Half-rotten plank—no it's a box, I believe. Here—bear a hand and we'll see what it's here for. Never mind, I've broke a hole.

He reached his hand in and drew it out—

"Man, it's money!"

The two men examined the handful of coins. They were gold. The boys above were as excited as themselves, and as delighted.

Joe's comrade said—

"We'll make quick work of this. There's an old rusty pick over amongst the weeds in the corner the other side of the fire-place—I saw it a minute ago."

He ran and brought the boys' pick and shovel. Injun Joe took the pick, looked it over critically, shook his head, muttered something to himself, and then began to use it. The box was soon unearthed. It was not very large; it was iron bound and had been very strong before the slow years had injured it. The men contemplated the treasure a while in blissful silence.

"Pard, there's thousands of dollars here," said Injun Joe.

"'Twas always said that Murrel's gang used around here one summer," the stranger observed.

"I know it," said Injun Joe; "and this looks like it, I should say."

"Now you won't need to do that job."

The half-breed frowned. Said he—

"You don't know me. Least you don't know all about that thing. 'Tain't robbery altogether—it's revenge!" and a wicked light flamed in his eyes. "I'll need your help in it. When it's finished—then Texas. Go home to your Nance and your kids, and stand by till you hear from me."

"Well—if you say so, what'll we do with this—bury it again?"

"Yes. [Ravishing delight overhead.] No! by the great Sachem, no! [Profound distress overhead.] I'd nearly forgot. That pick had fresh earth on it! [The boys were sick with terror in a moment.] What business has a pick and a shovel here? What business with fresh earth on them? Who brought them here—and where are they gone? Have you heard anybody?—seen anybody? What! bury it again and leave them to come and see the ground disturbed? Not exactly—not exactly. We'll take it to my den."

"Why of course! Might have thought of that before. You mean Number One?"

"No—Number Two—under the cross. The other place is bad—too common."

"All right. It's nearly dark enough to start."

Injun Joe got up and went about from window to window cautiously peeping out. Presently he said:

"Who could have brought those tools here? Do you reckon they can be up stairs?"

The boys' breath forsook them. Injun Joe put his hand on his knife, halted a moment, undecided, and then turned toward the stairway. The boys thought of the closet, but their strength was gone. The steps came creaking up the stairs—the intolerable distress of the situation woke the stricken resolution of the lads—they were about to spring for the closet, when there was a crash of rotten timbers and Injun Joe landed on the ground amid the *débris* of the ruined stairway. He gathered himself up cursing, and his comrade said:

"Now what's the use of all that? If it's anybody, and they're up there, let them *stay* there—who cares? If they want to jump down, now, and get into trouble, who objects? It will be dark in fifteen minutes—and then let them follow us if they want to. I'm willing. In my opinion, whoever hove those things in here caught a sight of us and took us for ghosts or devils or something. I'll bet they're running yet."

Joe grumbled a while; then he agreed with his friend that what daylight was left ought to be economized in getting things ready for leaving. Shortly afterward they slipped out of the house in the deepening twilight, and moved toward the river with their precious box.

Tom and Huck rose up, weak but vastly relieved, and stared after them through the chinks between the logs of the house. Follow? Not they. They were content to reach ground again without broken necks, and take the townward track over the hill. They did not talk much. They were too much absorbed in hating themselves—hating the ill luck that made them take the spade and the pick there. But for that, Injun Joe never would have suspected. He would have hidden the silver with the gold to wait there till his "revenge" was satisfied, and then he would have had the misfortune to find that money turn up missing. Bitter, bitter luck that the tools were ever brought there!

They resolved to keep a lookout for that Spaniard when he should come to town spying out for chances to do his revengeful job, and follow him to "Number Two," wherever that might be. Then a ghastly thought occurred to Tom:

"Revenge?" What if he means *us*, Huck!"

"O, don't!" said Huck, nearly fainting.

They talked it all over, and as they entered town they agreed to believe that he might possibly mean somebody else—at least that he might at least mean nobody but Tom, since only Tom had testified.

Very, very small comfort it was to Tom to be alone in danger! Company would be a palpable improvement, he thought.

CHAPTER XXVII

The adventure of the day mightily tormented Tom's dreams that night. Four times he had his hands on that rich treasure and four times it wasted to nothingness in his fingers as sleep forsook him and wakefulness brought back the hard reality of his misfortune. As he lay in the early morning recalling the incidents of his great adventure, he noticed that they seemed curiously subdued and far away—somewhat as if they had happened in another world, or in a time long gone by. Then it occurred to him that the great adventure itself must be a dream! There was one very strong argument in favor of this idea—namely, that the quantity of coin he had seen was too vast to be real. He had never seen as much as fifty dollars in one mass before, and he was like all boys of his age and station in life, in that he imagined that all references to "hundreds" and "thousands" were mere fanciful forms of speech, and that no such sums really existed in the world. He never had supposed for a moment that so large a sum as a hundred dollars was to be found in actual money in any one's possession. If his notions of hidden treasure had been analyzed, they would have been bound to consist of a handful of real dimes and a bushel of vague, splendid, graspable dollars.

But the incidents of his adventure grew sensibly sharper and clearer under the attrition of thinking them over, and so he presently found himself leaning to the impression that the thing might not have been a dream, after all. This uncertainty must be swept away. He would snatch a hurried breakfast and go and find Huck.

Huck was sitting on the gunwale of a flatboat, listlessly dangling his feet in the water and looking very melancholy. Tom concluded to let Huck lead up to the subject. If he did not do it, then the adventure would be proved to have been only a dream.

"Hello, Huck!"

"Hello, yourself."

Silence, for a minute.

"Tom, if we'd a left the blame tools at the dead tree, we'd 'a' got the money. O, ain't it awful!"

" 'Tain't a dream, then, 'tain't a dream! Somehow I most wish it was. Dog'd if I don't, Huck."

"What ain't a dream?"

"Oh, that thing yesterday. I been half thinking it was."

"Dream! If them stairs hadn't broke down you'd 'a' seen how much dream it was! I've had dreams enough all night—with that patch-eyed Spanish devil going for me all through 'em—rot him!"

"No, not rot him. *Find* him! Track the money!"

"Tom, we'll never find him. A feller don't have only once chance for such a pile—and that one's lost. I'd feel mighty shaky if I was to see him, anyway."

"Well, so'd I; but I'd like to see him, anyway—and track him out —to his Number Two."

"Number Two—yes, that's it. I been thinking 'bout that. But I can't make nothing out of it. What do you reckon it is?"

"I dono. It's too deep. Say, Huck—maybe it's the number of a house!"

"Goody! . . . . . . No, Tom, that ain't it. If it is, it ain't in this one-horse town. They ain't no numbers here."

"Well, that's so. Lemme think a minute. Here—it's the number of a room—in a tavern, you know!"

"O, that's the trick! They ain't only two taverns. We can find out quick."

"You stay here, Huck, till I come."

Tom was off at once. He did not care to have Huck's company in public places. He was gone half an hour. He found that in the best tavern, No. 2 had been occupied by a young lawyer, and was still so occupied. In the less ostentatious house No. 2 was a mystery. The tavern-keeper's young son said it was kept locked all the time, and he never saw anybody go into or come out of it except at night; he did not know any particular reason for this state of things; had had some little curiosity, but it was rather feeble; had made the most of the mystery by entertaining himself with the idea that the room was "ha'nted;" had noticed that there was a light in there the night before.

"That's what I've found out, Huck. I reckon that's the very No. 2 we're after."

"I reckon it is, Tom. Now what you going to do?"

"Lemme think."

Tom thought a long time. Then he said:

"I'll tell you. The back door of that No. 2 is the door that comes out into that little close alley between the tavern and the old rattle-trap of a brick store. Now you get hold of all the door-keys you can find, and I'll nip all of Auntie's and the first dark night we'll go there and try 'em. And mind you keep a lookout for Injun Joe, because he said he was going to drop into town and spy around once more for a chance to get his revenge. If you see him, you just follow him; and if he don't go to that No. 2, that ain't the place."

"Lordy I don't want to foller him by myself!"

"Why it'll be night, sure. He mightn't ever see you—and if he did, maybe he'd never think anything."

"Well, if it's pretty dark I reckon I'll track him. I dono—I dono. I'll try."

"You bet I'll follow him, if it's dark, Huck. Why he might 'a' found out he couldn't get his revenge, and be going right after that money."

"It's so, Tom, it's so. I'll foller him; I will, by jingoes!"

"Now you're *talking!* Don't you ever weaken, Huck, and I won't."

CHAPTER XXVIII

That night Tom and Huck were ready for their adventure. They hung around the neighborhood of the tavern until after nine, one watching the alley at a distance and the other the tavern door. Nobody entered the alley or left it; nobody resembling the Spaniard entered or left the tavern door. The night promised to be a fair one; so Tom went home with the understanding that if a considerable degree of darkness came on, Huck was to come and "maow," whereupon he would slip out and try the keys. But the night remained clear, ahd Huck closed his watch and retired to bed in an empty sugar hogshead about twelve.

Tuesday the boys had the same ill luck. Also Wednesday. But Thursday night promised better. Tom slipped out in good season with his aunt's old tin lantern, and a large towel to blindfold it with. He hid the lantern in Huck's sugar hogshead and the watch began. An hour before midnight the tavern closed up and its lights (the only ones thereabouts) were put out. No Spaniard had been seen. Nobody had entered or left the alley. Everything was auspicious. The blackness of darkness reigned, the perfect stillness was interrupted only by occasional mutterings of distant thunder.

Tom got his lantern, lit it in the hogshead, wrapped it closely in the towel, and the two adventurers crept in the gloom toward the tavern. Huck stood sentry and Tom felt his way into the alley. Then there was a season of waiting anxiety that weighed upon Huck's spirits like a mountain. He began to wish he could see a flash from the lantern—it would frighten him, but it would at least tell him that Tom was alive yet. It seemed hours since Tom had disappeared. Surely he must have fainted; maybe he was dead; maybe his heart had burst under terror and excitement. In his uneasiness Huck found himself drawing closer and closer to the alley; fearing all sorts of dreadful things, and momentarily expecting some catastrophe to happen that would take away his breath. There was not much to take away, for he seemed only able to inhale it by thimblefuls, and his heart would soon wear itself out, the way it was beating. Suddenly there was a flash of light and Tom came tearing by him:

"Run!" said he; "run, for your life!"

He needn't have repeated it; once was enough; Huck was making thirty or forty miles an hour before the repetition was uttered. The boys never stopped till they reached the shed of a deserted slaughterhouse at the lower end of the village. Just as they got within its shelter the storm burst and the rain poured down. As soon as Tom got his breath he said:

"Huck, it was awful! I tried two of the keys, just as soft as I could; but they seemed to make such a power of racket that I couldn't hardly get my breath I was so scared. They wouldn't turn in the lock, either. Well, without noticing what I was doing, I took hold of the knob, and open comes the door! It warn't locked! I hopped in, and shook off the towel, and, *great Caesar's ghost!*"

"What!—what 'd you see, Tom!"

"Huck, I most stepped onto Injun Joe's hand!"

"No!"

"Yes! He was laying there, sound asleep on the floor, with his old patch on his eye and his arms spread out."

"Lordy, what did you do? Did he wake up?"

"No, never budged. Drunk, I reckon. I just grabbed that towel and started!"

"I'd never 'a' thought of the towel, I bet!"

"Well, *I* would. My aunt would make me mighty sick if I lost it."

"Say, Tom, did you see that box?"

"Huck, I didn't wait to look around. I didn't see the box, I didn't see the cross. I didn't see anything but a bottle and a tin cup on the floor by Injun Joe; yes, and I saw two barrels and lots more bottles in the room. Don't you see, now, what's the matter with that ha'nted room?"

"How?"

"Why it's ha'nted with whisky! Maybe *all* the Temperance Taverns have got a ha'nted room, hey Huck?"

"Well I reckon maybe that's so. Who'd 'a' thought such a thing? But say, Tom, now's a mighty good time to get that box, if Injun Joe's drunk."

"It is, that! You try it!"

Huck shuddered.

"Well, no—I reckon not."

"And *I* reckon not, Huck. Only one bottle alongside of Injun Joe ain't enough. If there'd been three, he'd be drunk enough and I'd do it."

There was a long pause for reflection, and then Tom said:

"Lookyhere, Huck, less not try that thing any more till we know Injun Joe's not in there. It's too scary. Now if we watch every night, we'll be dead sure to see him go out some time or other, and then we'll snatch that box quicker'n lightning."

"Well, I'm agreed. I'll watch the whole night long, and I'll do it every night, too, if you'll do the other part of the job."

"All right, I will. All you got to do is to trot up Hooper street a block and maow—and if I'm asleep, you throw some gravel at the window and that'll fetch me."

"Agreed, and good as wheat!"

"Now Huck, the storm's over, and I'll go home. It'll begin to be daylight in a couple of hours. You go back and watch that long, will you?"

"I said I would, Tom, and I will. I'll ha'nt that tavern every night for a year! I'll sleep all day and I'll stand watch all night."

"That's all right. Now where you going to sleep?"

"In Ben Rogers's hayloft. He lets me, and so does his pap's nigger man, Uncle Jake. I tote water for Uncle Jake whenever he wants me to, and any time I ask him he gives me a little something to eat if he can spare it. That's a mighty good nigger, Tom. He likes me, becuz I don't ever act as if I was above him. Sometimes I've set right down and eat *with* him. But you needn't tell that. A body's got to do things when he's awful hungry he wouldn't want to do as a steady thing."

"Well, if I don't want you in the day time, I'll let you sleep. I won't come bothering around. Any time you see something's up, in the night, just skip right around and maow."

CHAPTER XXIX

The first thing Tom heard on Friday morning was a glad piece of news—Judge Thatcher's family had come back to town the night before. Both Injun Joe and the treasure sunk into secondary importance for a moment, and Becky took the chief place in the boy's interest. He saw her and they had an exhausting good time playing "hi-spy" and "gully-keeper" with a crowd of their schoolmates. The day was completed and crowned in a peculiarly satisfactory way: Becky teased her mother to appoint the next day for the long-promised and long-delayed picnic, and she consented. The child's delight was boundless; and Tom's not more moderate. The invitations were sent out before sunset, and straightway the young folks of the village were thrown into a fever of preparation and pleasurable anticipation. Tom's excitement enabled him to keep awake until a pretty late hour, and he had good hopes of hearing Huck's "maow," and of having his treasure to astonish Becky and the pic-nickers with, next day; but he was disappointed. No signal came that night.

Morning came, eventually, and by ten or eleven o'clock a giddy and rollicking company were gathered at Judge Thatcher's, and everything was ready for a start. It was not the custom for elderly people to mar pic-nics with their presence. The children were considered safe enough under the wings of a few young ladies of eighteen and a few young gentlemen of twenty-three or thereabouts. The old steam ferry-boat was chartered for the occasion; presently the gay throng filed up the main street laden with provision baskets. Sid was sick and had to miss the fun; Mary remained at home to entertain him. The last thing Mrs. Thatcher said to Becky, was—

"You'll not get back till late. Perhaps you'd better stay all night with some of the girls that live near the ferry landing, child."

"Then I'll stay with Susy Harper, mamma."

"Very well. And mind and behave yourself and don't be any trouble."

Presently, as they tripped along, Tom said to Becky:

"Say—I'll tell you what we'll do. 'Stead of going to Joe Harper's we'll climb right up the hill and stop at the Widow Douglas's. She'll have ice cream! She has it most every day—dead loads of it. And she'll be awful glad to have us."

"O, that will be fun!"

Then Becky reflected a moment and said:

"But what will mamma say?"

"How'll she ever know?"

The girl turned the idea over in her mind, and said reluctantly:

"I reckon it's wrong—but—"

"But shucks! Your mother won't know, and so what's the harm? All she wants is that you'll be safe; and I bet you she'd 'a' said go there if she'd 'a' thought of it. I know she would!"

The widow Douglas's splendid hospitality was a tempting bait. It and Tom's persuasions presently carried the day. So it was decided to say nothing to anybody about the night's programme. Presently it occurred to Tom that maybe Huck might come this very night and give the signal. The thought took a deal of the spirit out of his anticipations. Still he could not bear to give up the fun at Widow Douglas's. And why should he give it up, he reasoned—the signal did not come the night before, so why should it be any more likely to come to-night? The sure fun of the evening outweighed the uncertain treasure; and boy like, he determined to yield to the stronger inclination and not allow himself to think of the box of money another time that day.

Three miles below town the ferry-boat stopped at the mouth of a woody hollow and tied up. The crowd swarmed ashore and soon the forest distances and craggy heights echoed far and near with shoutings and laughter. All the different ways of getting hot and tired were gone through with, and by and by the rovers straggled back to camp fortified with responsible appetites, and then the destruction of the good things began. After the feast there was a refreshing season of rest and chat in the shade of spreading oaks. By and by somebody shouted—"Who's ready for the cave?"

Everybody was. Bundles of candles were procured, and straightway there was a general scamper up the hill. The mouth of the cave was up the hillside—an opening shaped like a letter A. It's massive oaken door stook unbarred. Within was a small chamber, chilly as an ice-house and walled by Nature with solid limestone that was dewy with a cold sweat. It was romantic and mysterious to stand here in the deep gloom and look out upon the green valley shining in the sun. But the impressiveness of the situation quickly wore off, and the romping began again. The moment a candle was lighted there was a general rush upon the owner of it; a struggle and a gallant defense followed, but the candle was soon knocked down or blown out, and then there was a glad clamor of laughter and a new chase. But all things have an end. By and by the procession went filing down the steep descent of the main avenue, the flickering rank of lights dimly revealing the lofty walls of rock almost to their point of junction sixty feet overhead. This main avenue was not more than eight or ten feet wide. Every few steps other lofty and still narrower crevices branched from it on either hand—for McDougal's cave was but a vast labyrinth of crooked isles that ran into each other and out again and led nowhere. It was said that one might wander days and nights together through its intricate tangle of rifts and chasms, and never find the end of the cave; and that he might go down, and down, and still down, into the earth, and it was just the same—labyrinth underneath labyrinth, and no end to any of them. No man "knew" the cave. That was an impossible thing. Most of the young men knew a portion of it, and it was not customary to venture much beyond this known portion. Tom Sawyer knew as much of the cave as any one.

The procession moved along the main avenue some three-quarters of a mile, and then groups and couples began to slip aside into branch avenues, fly along the dismal corridors, and take each other by surprise at points where the corridors joined again. Parties were able to elude each other for the space of half an hour without going beyond the "known" ground.

By and by, one group after another came straggling back to the mouth of the cave, panting, hilarious, smeared from head to foot with tallow drippings, daubed with clay, and entirely delighted with the success of the day. Then they were astonished to find that they had been taking no note of time and that night was about at hand. The clanging bell had been calling for half an hour. However, this sort of close to the day's adventures was romantic and therefore satisfactory. When the ferry-boat with her wild freight pushed into the stream, nobody cared sixpence for the wasted time but the captain of the craft.

Huck was already upon his watch when the ferry-boat's lights went glinting past the wharf. He heard no noise on board, for the young people were as subdued and still as people usually are who are nearly tired to death. He wondered what boat it was, and why she did not stop at the wharf—and then he dropped her out of his mind and put his attention upon his business. The night was growing cloudy and dark. Ten o'clock came, and the noise of vehicles ceased, scattered lights began to wink out, all straggling foot passengers disappeared, the village betook itself to its slumbers and left the small watcher alone with the silence and the ghosts. Eleven o'clock came, and the tavern lights were put out; darkness everywhere, now. Huck waited what seemed a weary long time, but nothing happened. His faith was weakening. Was there any use? Was there really any use? Why not give it up and turn in?

A noise fell upon his ear. He was all attention in an instant. The alley door closed softly. He sprang to the corner of the brick store. The next moment two men brushed by him, and one seemed to have something under his arm. It must be that box! So they were going to remove the treasure. Why call Tom now? It would be absurd—the men would get away with the box and never be found again. No, he would stick to their wake and follow them; he would trust to the darkness for security from discovery. So communing with himself, Huck stepped out and glided along behind the men, cat-like, with bare feet, allowing them to keep just far enough ahead not to be invisible.

They moved up the river street three blocks, then turned to the left up a cross street. They went straight ahead, then, until they came to the path that led up Cardiff Hill; this they took. They passed by the old Welchman's house, half way up the hill without hesitating, and still climbed upward. Good, thought Huck, they will bury it in the old quarry. But they never stopped at the quarry. They passed on, up the summit. They plunged into the narrow path between the tall sumach bushes, and were at once hidden in the gloom. Huck closed up and shortened his distance, now, for they would never be able to see him. He trotted along a while; then slackened his pace, fearing he was gaining too fast; moved on a piece, then stopped altogether; listened; no sound; none, save that he seemed to hear the beating of his own heart. The hooting of an owl came from over the hill—ominous sound! But no footsteps. Heavens, was everything lost! He was about to spring with winged feet, when a man cleared his throat not four feet from him! Huck's heart shot into his throat, but he swallowed it again; and then he stood there shaking as if a dozen agues had taken charge of him at once, and so weak that he thought he must surely fall to the ground. He knew where he was. He knew he was within five steps of the stile leading into Widow Douglas's grounds. Very well, he thought, let them bury it there; it won't be hard to find.

Now there was a voice—a very low voice—Injun Joe's:

"Damn her, maybe she's got company—there's lights, late as it is."

"I can't see any."

This was that stranger's voice—the stranger of the haunted house. A deadly chill went to Huck's heart—this, then, was the "revenge" job! His thought was, to fly. Then he remembered that the Widow Douglas had been kind to him more than once, and maybe these men were going to murder her. He wished he dared venture to warn her; but he knew he didn't dare—they might come and catch him. He thought all this and more in the moment that elapsed between the stranger's remark and Injun Joe's next—which was—

"Because the bush is in your way. Now—this way—now you see, don't you?"

"Yes. Well there *is* company there, I reckon. Better give it up."

"Give it up, and I just leaving this country forever! Give it up and maybe never have another chance. I tell you again, as I've told you before, I don't care for her swag—you may have it. But her husband was rough on me—many times he was rough on me—and mainly he was the justice of the peace that jugged me for a vagrant. And that ain't all. It ain't a millionth part of it! He had me *horsewhipped!*—horsewhipped in front of the jail, like a nigger!—with all the town looking on! HORSEWHIPPED!—do you understand? He took advantage of me and died. But I'll take it out of *her*."

"Oh, don't kill her! Don't do that!"

"Kill? Who said anything about killing? I would kill *him* if he was here; but not her. When you want to get revenge on a woman you don't kill her—bosh! you go for her looks. You slit her nostrils—you notch her ears like a sow!"

"By God, that's—"

"Keep your opinion to yourself! It will be safest for you. I'll tie her to the bed. If she bleeds to death, is that my fault? I'll not cry, if she does. My friend, you'll help in this thing—for *my* sake— that's why you're here—I mightn't be able alone. If you flinch, I'll kill you. Do you understand that? And if I have to kill you, I'll kill her—and then I reckon nobody'll ever know much about who done this business."

"Well, if it's got to be done, let's get at it. The quicker the better— I'm all in a shiver."

"Do it *now?* And company there? Look here—I'll get suspicious of you, first thing you know. No—we'll wait till the lights are out—there's no hurry."

Huck felt that a silence was going to ensue—a thing still more awful than any amount of murderous talk; so he held his breath and stepped gingerly back; planted his foot carefully and firmly, after balancing, one-legged, in a precarious way and almost toppling over, first on one side and then on the other. He took another step back, with the same elaboration and the same risks; then another and another, and—a twig snapped under his foot! His breath stopped and he listened. There was no sound—the stillness was perfect. His gratitude was measureless. Now he turned in his tracks, between the walls of sumach bushes—turned himself as carefully as if he were a ship—and then stepped quickly but cautiously along. When he emerged at the quarry he felt secure, and so he picked up his nimble heels and flew. Down, down he sped, till he reached the Welchman's. He banged at the door, and presently the heads of the old man and his two stalwart sons were thrust from windows.

"What's the row there? Who's banging? What do you want?"

"Let me in—quick! I'll tell everything."

"Why who are you?"

"Huckleberry Finn—quick, let me in!"

"Huckleberry Finn, indeed! It ain't a name to open many doors, I judge! But let him in, lads, and let's see what's the trouble."

"Please don't ever tell *I* told you," were Huck's words when he got in "Please don't—I'd be killed, sure—but the Widow's been good friends to me sometimes, and I want to tell—I *will* tell if you'll promise you won't ever say it was me."

"By George he *has* got something to tell, or he wouldn't act so!" exclaimed the old man; "out with it and nobody here'll ever tell, lad."

Three minutes later the old man and his sons, well armed, were up the hill, and just entering the sumach path on tip-toe, their weapons in their hands. Huck accompanied them no further. He hid behind a great bowlder and fell to listening. There was a lagging, anxious silence, and then all of a sudden there was an explosion of firearms and a cry.

Huck waited for no particulars. He sprang away and sped down the hill as fast as his legs could carry him.

CHAPTER XXX

As the earliest suspicion of dawn appeared on Sunday morning, Huck came groping up the hill and rapped gently at the old Welchman's door. The inmates were asleep but it was a sleep that was set on a hair-trigger, on account of the exciting episode of the night. A call came from a window—

"Who's there!"

Huck's scared voice answered in a low tone:

"Please let me in! It's only Huck Finn!"

"It's a name that can open this door night or day, lad!—and welcome!"

These were strange words to the vagabond boy's ears, and the pleasantest he had ever heard. He could not recollect that the closing word had ever been applied in his case before. The door was quickly unlocked, and he entered. Huck was given a seat and the old man and his brace of tall sons speedily dressed themselves.

"Now my boy I hope you're good and hungry, because breakfast will be ready as soon as the sun's up, and we'll have a piping hot one, too—make yourself easy about that! I and the boys hoped you'd turn up and stop here last night."

"I was awful scared," said Huck, "and I run. I took out when the pistols went off, and I didn't stop for three mile. I've come now becuz I wanted to know about it, you know; and I came before daylight becuz I didn't want to run acrost them devils, even if they was dead."

"Well, poor chap, you do look as if you'd had a hard night of it— but there's a bed here for you when you've had your breakfast. No, they ain't dead, lad—we are sorry enough for that. You see we knew right where to put our hands on them, by your description; so we crept along on tip-toe till we got within fifteen feet of them—dark as a cellar that sumach path was—and just then I found I was going to sneeze. It was the meanest kind of luck! I tried to keep it back, but no use—'twas bound to come, and it did come! I was in the lead with my pistol raised, and when the sneeze started those scoundrels a-rustling to get out of the path, I sung out, 'Fire, boys!' and blazed away at the place where the rustling was. So did the boys. But they were off in a jiffy, those villains, and we after them, down through the woods. I judge we never touched them. They fired a shot apiece as they started, but their bullets whizzed by and didn't do us any harm. As soon as we lost the sound of their feet we quit chasing, and went down and stirred up the constables. They got a posse together, and went off to guard the river bank, and as soon as it is light the sheriff and a gang are going to beat up the woods. My boys will be with them presently. I wish we had some sort of description of those rascals—'twould help a good deal. But you could'nt see what they were like, in the dark, lad, I suppose?"

"O, yes, I saw them down town and follered them."

"Splendid! Describe them—describe them, my boy!"

"One's the old deaf and dumb Spaniard that's ben around here once or twice, and t'other's a mean looking ragged—"

"That's enough, lad, we know the men! Happened on them in the woods back of the widow's one day, and they slunk away. Off with you, boys, and tell the sheriff—get your breakfast to-morrow morning!"

The Welchman's sons departed at once. As they were leaving the room Huck sprang up and exclaimed:

"Oh, please don't tell *any*body it was me that blowed on them! Oh, please!"

"All right if you say it, Huck, but you ought to have the credit of what you did."

"Oh, no, no! Please don't tell!"

When the young men were gone, the old Welchman said—

"They won't tell—and I won't. But why don't you want it known?"

Huck would not explain, further than to say that he already knew too much about one of those men and would not have the man know that he knew anything against him for the whole world—he would be killed for knowing it, sure.

The old man promised secrecy once more, and said:

"How did you come to follow these fellows, lad? Were they looking suspicious?"

Huck was silent while he framed a duly cautious reply. Then he said:

"Well, you see, I'm a kind of a hard lot,—least everybody says so, and I don't see nothing agin it—and sometimes I can't sleep much, on accounts of thinking about it and sort of trying to strike out a new way of doing. That was the way of it last night. I couldn't sleep, and so I come along up street 'bout midnight, a-turning it all over, and when I got to that old shackly brick store by the Temperance Tavern, I backed up agin the wall to have another think. Well, just then along comes these two chaps slipping along close by me, with something under their arm and I reckoned they'd stole it. One was a-smoking, and t'other one wanted a light; so they stopped right before me and the cigars lit up their faces and I see that the big one was the deaf and dumb Spaniard, by his white whiskers and the patch on his eye, and t'other one was a rusty, ragged looking devil."

"Could you see the rags by the light of the cigars?"

This staggered Huck for a moment. Then he said:

"Well, I don't know—but somehow it seems as if I did."

"Then they went on, and you—"

"Follered 'em—yes. That was it. I wanted to see what was up— they sneaked along so. I dogged 'em to the widder's stile, and stood in the dark and heard the ragged one beg for the widder, and the Spaniard swear he'd spile her looks just as I told you and your two—"

"What! The *deaf and dumb* man said all that!"

Huck had made another terrible mistake! He was trying his best to keep the old man from getting the faintest hint of who the Spaniard might be, and yet his tongue seemed determined to get him into trouble in spite of all he could do. He made several efforts to creep out of his scrape, but the old man's eye was upon him and he made blunder after blunder. Presently the Welchman said:

"My boy, don't be afraid of me. I wouldn't hurt a hair of your head for all the world. No—I'd protect you—I'd protect you. This Spaniard is not deaf and dumb; you've let that slip without intending it; you can't cover that up now. You know something about that Spaniard that you want to keep dark. Now trust me—tell me what it is, and trust me—I won't betray you."

Huck looked into the old man's honest eyes a moment, then bent over and whispered in his ear—

" 'Tain't a Spaniard—it's Injun Joe!"

The Welchman almost jumped out of his chair. In a moment he said:

"It's all plain enough, now. When you talked about notching ears and slitting noses I judged that that was your own embellishment, because white men don't take that sort of revenge. But an Injun! That's a different matter altogether."

During breakfast the talk went on, and in the course of it the old man said that the last thing which he and his sons had done, before going to bed, was to get a lantern and examine the stile and its vicinity for marks of blood. They found none, but captured a bulky bundle of—

"Of WHAT?"

If the words had been lightning they could not have leaped with a more stunning suddenness from Huck's blanched lips. His eyes were staring wide, now, and his breath suspended—waiting for the answer. The Welchman started—stared in return—three seconds— five seconds—ten—then replied—

"Of burglar's tools. Why what's the *matter* with you?"

Huck sank back, panting gently, but deeply, unutterably grateful. The Welchman eyed him gravely, curiously—and presently said—

"Yes, burglar's tools. That appears to relieve you a good deal. But what did give you that turn? What were *you* expecting we'd found?"

Huck was in a close place—the inquiring eye was upon him—he

would have given anything for material for a plausible answer—
nothing suggested itself—the inquiring eye was boring deeper and
deeper—a senseless reply offered—there was no time to weigh it, so
at a venture he uttered it—feebly:

"Sunday-school books, maybe."

Poor Huck was too distressed to smile, but the old man laughed
loud and joyously, shook up the details of his anatomy from head to
foot, and ended by saying that such a laugh was money in a man's
pocket, because it cut down the doctor's bills like everything. Then
he added:

"Poor old chap, you're white and jaded—you ain't well a bit—no
wonder you're a little flighty and off your balance. But you'll come
out of it. Rest and sleep will fetch you out all right, I hope."

Huck was irritated to think he had been such a goose and
betrayed such a suspicious excitement, for he had dropped the idea
that the parcel brought from the tavern was the treasure, as soon as
he had heard the talk at the widow's stile. He had only *thought* it was
not the treasure, however—he had not known that it wasn't—and so
the suggestion of a captured bundle was too much for his self-
possession. But on the whole he felt glad the little episode had
happened, for now he knew beyond all question that that bundle was
not *the* bundle, and so his mind was at rest and exceedingly
comfortable. In fact everything seemed to be drifting just in the right
direction, now; the treasure must be still in No. 2, the men would be
captured and jailed that day, and he and Tom could seize the gold
that night without any trouble or any fear of interruption.

Just as breakfast was completed there was a knock on the door.
Huck jumped for a hiding place, for he had no mind to be connected
even remotely with the late event. The Welchman admitted several
ladies and gentlemen, among them the widow Douglas, and noticed
that groups of citizens were climbing up the hill—to stare at the
stile. So the news had spread.

The Welchman had to tell the story of the night to the visitors. The
widow's gratitude for her preservation was outspoken.

"Don't say a word about it madam. There's another that you're
more beholden to than you are to me and my boys, maybe, but he
don't allow me to tell his name. We wouldn't have been there but for
him."

Of course this excited a curiosity so vast that it almost belittled the
main matter—but the Welchman allowed it to eat into the vitals of
his visitors, and through them be transmitted to the whole town, for
he refused to part with his secret. When all else had been learned,
the widow said:

"I went to sleep reading in bed and slept straight through all that
noise. Why didn't you come and wake me?"

"We judged it warn't worth while. Those fellows warn't likely to
come again—they hadn't any tools left to work with, and what was

the use of waking you up and scaring you to death? My three negro men stood guard at your house all the rest of the night. They've just come back."

More visitors came, and the story had to be told and re-told for a couple of hours more.

There was no Sabbath-school during day-school vacation, but everybody was early at church. The stirring event was well canvassed. News came that not a sign of the two villains had been yet discovered. When the sermon was finished, Judge Thatcher's wife dropped alongside of Mrs. Harper as she moved down the aisle with the crowd and said:

"Is my Becky going to sleep all day? I just expected she would be tired to death."

"Your Becky?"

"Yes," with a startled look,—"didn't she stay with you last night?"

"Why, no."

Mrs. Thatcher turned pale, and sank into a pew, just as Aunt Polly, talking briskly with a friend, passed by. Aunt Polly said:

"Good morning, Mrs. Thatcher. Good morning Mrs. Harper. I've got a boy that's turned up missing. I reckon my Tom staid at your house last night—one of you. And now he's afraid to come to church. I've got to settle with him."

Mrs. Thatcher shook her head feebly and turned paler than ever.

"He didn't stay with us," said Mrs. Harper, beginning to look uneasy. A marked anxiety came into Aunt Polly's face.

"Joe Harper, have you seen my Tom this morning?"

"No'm."

"When did you see him last?"

Joe tried to remember, but was not sure he could say. The people had stopped moving out of church. Whispers passed along, and a boding uneasiness took possession of every countenance. Children were anxiously questioned, and young teachers. They all said they had not noticed whether Tom and Becky were on board the ferry-boat on the homeward trip; it was dark; no one thought of inquiring if any one was missing. One young man finally blurted out his fear that they were still in the cave! Mrs. Thatcher swooned away. Aunt Polly fell to crying and wringing her hands.

The alarm swept from lip to lip, from group to group, from street to street, and within five minutes the bells were wildly clanging and the whole town was up! The Cardiff Hill episode sank into instant insignificance, the burglars were forgotten, horses were saddled, skiffs were manned, the ferry-boat ordered out, and before the horror was half an hour old, two hundred men were pouring down high-road and river toward the cave.

All the long afternoon the village seemed empty and dead. Many women visited Aunt Polly and Mrs. Thatcher and tried to comfort them. They cried with them, too, and that was still better than words. All the tedious night the town waited for news; but when the morning dawned at last, all the word that came was, "Send more candles—and send food." Mrs. Thatcher was almost crazed; and Aunt Polly also. Judge Thatcher sent messages of hope and encouragement from the cave, but they conveyed no real cheer.

The old Welchman came home toward daylight, spattered with candle grease, smeared with clay, and almost worn out. He found Huck still in the bed that had been provided for him, and delirious with fever. The physicians were all at the cave, so the Widow Douglas came and took charge of the patient. She said she would do her best by him, because, whether he was good, bad, or indifferent, he was the Lord's, and nothing that was the Lord's was a thing to be neglected. The Welchman said Huck had good spots in him, and the widow said—

"You can depend on it. That's the Lord's mark. He don't leave it off. He never does. Puts it somewhere on every creature that comes from his hands."

Early in the forenoon parties of jaded men began to straggle into the village, but the strongest of the citizens continued searching. All the news that could be gained was that remotenesses of the cavern were being ransacked that had never been visited before; that every corner and crevice was going to be thoroughly searched; that wherever one wandered through the maze of passages, lights were to be seen flitting hither and thither in the distance, and shoutings and pistol shots sent their hollow reverberations to the ear down the sombre aisles. In one place, far from the section usually traversed by tourists, the names "BECKY & TOM" had been found traced upon the rocky wall with candle smoke, and near at hand a grease-soiled bit of ribbon. Mrs. Thatcher recognized the ribbon and cried over it. She said it was the last relic she should ever have of her child; and that no other memorial of her could ever be so precious, because this one parted latest from the living body before the awful death came. Some said that now and then, in the cave, a far-away speck of light would glimmer, and then a glorious shout would burst forth and a score of men go trooping down the echoing aisle—and then a sickening disappointment always followed; the children were not there; it was only a searcher's light.

Three dreadful days and nights dragged their tedious hours along, and the village sank into a hopeless stupor. No one had heart for anything. The accidental discovery, just made, that the proprietor of the Temperance Tavern kept liquor on his premises, scarcely fluttered the public pulse, tremendous as the fact was. In a lucid interval, Huck feebly led up to the subject of taverns, and finally asked—dimly dreading the worst—if anything had been discovered at the Temperance Tavern since he had been ill?

"Yes," said the widow.

Huck started up in bed, wild-eyed:

"What! What was it?"

"Liquor!—and the place has been shut up. Lie down, child— what a turn you did give me!"

"Only tell me just one thing—only just one—please! Was it Tom Sawyer that found it?"

The widow burst into tears, "Hush, hush, child, hush! I've told you before, you must *not* talk. You are very, very sick!"

Then nothing but liquor had been found; there would have been a great pow-wow if it had been the gold. So the treasure was gone forever—gone forever! But what could she be crying about? Curious that she should cry.

These thoughts worked their dim way through Huck's mind, and under the weariness they gave him he fell asleep. The widow said to herself:

"There—he's asleep, poor wreck. Tom Sawyer find it! Pity but somebody could find Tom Sawyer! Ah, there ain't many left, now, that's got hope enough, or strength enough, either, to go on searching."

CHAPTER XXXI

Now to return to Tom and Becky's share in the pic-nic. They tripped along the murky aisles with the rest of the company, visiting the familiar wonders of the cave—wonders dubbed with rather over-descriptive names, such as "The Drawing-Room," "The Cathedral," "Aladdin's Palace," and so on. Presently the hide-and-seek frolicking began, and Tom and Becky engaged in it with zeal until the exertion began to grow a trifle wearisome; then they wandered down a sinuous avenue holding their candles aloft and reading the tangled web-work of names, dates, post-office addresses and mottoes with which the rocky walls had been frescoed (in candle smoke). Still drifting along and talking, they scarcely noticed that they were now in a part of the cave whose walls were not frescoed. They smoked their own names under an overhanging shelf and moved on. Presently they came to a place where a little stream of water, trickling over a ledge and carrying a limestone sediment with it, had, in the slow-dragging ages, formed a laced and ruffled Niagara in gleaming and imperishable stone. Tom squeezed his small body behind it in order to illuminate it for Becky's gratification. He found that it curtained a sort of steep natural stairway which was enclosed between narrow walls, and at once the ambition to be a discoverer seized him. Becky responded to his call, and they made a smokemark for future guidance, and started upon their quest. They wound this way and that, far down into the secret depths of the cave, made another mark, and branched off in search of novelties to tell the upper world about. In one place they found a spacious cavern, from whose ceiling depended a multitude of shining stalactites of the length and circumference of a man's leg; they walked all about it, wondering and admiring, and presently left it by one of the numerous passages that opened into it. This shortly brought them to a bewitching spring, whose basin was encrusted with a frost work of glittering crystals; it was in the midst of a cavern whose walls were supported by many fantastic pillars which had been formed by the joining of great stalactites and stalagmites together, the result of the ceaseless water-drip of centuries. Under the roof vast knots of bats had packed themselves together, thousands in a bunch; the lights disturbed the creatures and they came flocking down by hundreds, squeaking and darting furiously at the candles. Tom knew their ways and the danger of this sort of conduct. He siezed Becky's hand and hurried her into the first corridor that offered; and none too soon, for a bat struck Becky's light out with its wing while she was passing out of the cavern. The bats chased the children a good distance; but the fugitives plunged into every new passage that offered, and at last got rid of the perilous things. Tom found a subterranean lake, shortly, which stretched its dim length away until its shape was lost in the shadows. He wanted to explore its borders, but concluded that it would be best to sit down and rest a while, first. Now, for the first time, the deep stillness of the place laid a clammy hand upon the spirits of the children. Becky said—

"Why, I didn't notice, but it seems ever so long since I heard any of the others."

"Come to think, Becky, we are away down below them—and I don't know how far away north, or south, or east, or whichever it is. We couldn't hear them here."

Becky grew apprehensive.

"I wonder how long we've been down here, Tom. We better start back."

"Yes, I reckon we better. P'raps we better."

"Can you find the way, Tom? It's all a mixed-up crookedness to me."

"I reckon I could find it—but then the bats. If they put both our candles out it will be an awful fix. Let's try some other way, so as not to go through there."

"Well. But I hope we won't get lost. It would be so awful!" and the girl shuddered at the thought of the dreadful possibilities.

They started through a corridor, and traversed it in silence a long way, glancing at each new opening, to see if there was anything familiar about the look of it; but they were all strange. Every time Tom made an examination, Becky would watch his face for an encouraging sign, and he would say cheerily—

"Oh, it's all right. This ain't the one, but we'll come to it right away!"

But he felt less and less hopeful with each failure, and presently began to turn off into diverging avenues at sheer random, in desperate hope of finding the one that was wanted. He still said it was "all right," but there was such a leaden dread at his heart, that the words had lost their ring and sounded just as if he had said, "All is lost!" Becky clung to his side in an anguish of fear, and tried hard to keep back the tears, but they would come. At last she said:

"O, Tom, never mind the bats, let's go back that way! We seem to get worse and worse off all the time."

Tom stopped.

"Listen!" said he.

Profound silence; silence so deep that even their breathings were conspicuous in the hush. Tom shouted. The call went echoing down the empty aisles and died out in the distance in a faint sound that resembled a ripple of mocking laughter.

"Oh, don't do it again, Tom, it is too horrid," said Becky.

"It is horrid, but I better, Becky; they *might* hear us, you know" and he shouted again.

The "might" was even a chillier horror than the ghostly laughter, it so confessed a perishing hope. The children stood still and listened; there was no result. Tom turned upon the back track at once, and hurried his steps. It was but a little while before a certain indecision in his manner revealed another fearful fact to Becky—he could not find his way back!

"O, Tom, you didn't make any marks!"

"Becky I was such a fool! Such a fool! I never thought we might want to come back! No—I can't find the way. It's all mixed up."

"Tom, Tom, we're lost! we're lost! We never can get out of this awful place! O, why *did* we ever leave the others!"

She sank to the ground and burst into such a frenzy of crying that Tom was appalled with the idea that she might die, or lose her reason. He sat down by her and put his arms around her; she buried her face in his bosom, she clung to him, she poured out her terrors, her unavailing regrets, and the far echoes turned them all to jeering laughter. Tom begged her to pluck up hope again, and she said she could not. He fell to blaming and abusing himself for getting her into this miserable situation; this had a better effect. She said she would try to hope again, she would get up and follow wherever he might lead if only he would not talk like that any more. For he was no more to blame than she, she said.

So they moved on again—aimlessly—simply at random—all they could do was to move, keep moving. For a little while, hope made a show of reviving—not with any reason to back it, but only because it is its nature to revive when the spring has not been taken out of it by age and familiarity with failure.

By and by Tom took Becky's candle and blew it out. This economy meant so much! Words were not needed. Becky understood, and her hope died again. She knew that Tom had a whole candle and three or four pieces in his pockets—yet he must economise.

By and by, fatigue began to assert its claims; the children tried to pay no attention, for it was dreadful to think of sitting down when time was grown to be so precious; moving, in some direction, in any direction, was at least progress and might bear fruit; but to sit down was to invite death and shorten its pursuit.

At last Becky's frail limbs refused to carry her farther. She sat down. Tom rested with her, and they talked of home, and the friends there, and the comfortable beds and above all, the light! Becky cried, and Tom tried to think of some way of comforting her, but all his encouragements were grown threadbare with use, and sounded like sarcasms. Fatigue bore so heavily upon Becky that she drowsed off to sleep. Tom was grateful. He sat looking into her drawn face and saw it grow smooth and natural under the influence of pleasant dreams; and by and by a smile dawned and rested there. The peaceful face reflected somewhat of peace and healing into his own spirit, and his thoughts wandered away to by-gone times and dreamy memories. While he was deep in his musings, Becky woke up with a breezy little laugh—but it was stricken dead upon her lips, and a groan followed it.

"Oh, how *could* I sleep! I wish I never, never had waked! No! No, I don't, Tom! Don't look so! I won't say it again."

"I'm glad you've slept, Becky; you'll feel rested, now, and we'll find the way out."

"We can try, Tom; but I've seen such a beautiful country in my dream. I reckon we are going there."

"Maybe not, maybe not. Cheer up, Becky, and let's go on trying."

They rose up and wandered along, hand in hand and hopeless. They tried to estimate how long they had been in the cave, but all they knew was that it seemed days and weeks, and yet it was plain that this could not be, for their candles were not gone yet. A long time after this—they could not tell how long—Tom said they must go softly and listen for dripping water—they must find a spring. They found one presently, and Tom said it was time to rest again. Both were cruelly tired, yet Becky said she thought she could go on a little farther. She was surprised to hear Tom dissent. She could not understand it. They sat down, and Tom fastened his candle to the wall in front of them with some clay. Thought was soon busy; nothing was said for some time. Then Becky broke the silence:

"Tom, I am so hungry!"

Tom took something out of his pocket.

"Do you remember this?" said he.

Becky almost smiled.

"It's our wedding cake, Tom."

"Yes—I wish it was as big as a barrel, for it's all we've got."

"I saved it from the pic-nic for us to dream on, Tom, the way grown-up people do with wedding cake—but it'll be our—"

She dropped the sentence where it was. Tom divided the cake and Becky ate with good appetite, while Tom nibbled at his moiety. There was abundance of cold water to finish the feast with. By and by Becky suggested that they move on again. Tom was silent a moment. Then he said:

"Becky, can you bear it if I tell you something?"

Becky's face paled, but she thought she could.

"Well then, Becky, we must stay here, where there's water to drink. That little piece is our last candle!"

Becky gave loose to tears and wailings. Tom did what he could to comfort her but with little effect. At length Becky said:

"Tom!"

"Well, Becky?"

"They'll miss us and hunt for us!"

"Yes, they will! Certainly they will!"

"Maybe they're hunting for us now, Tom."

"Why I reckon maybe they are. I hope they are."

"When would they miss us, Tom?"

"When they get back to the boat, I reckon."

"Tom, it might be dark, then—would they notice we hadn't come?"

"I don't know. But anyway, your mother would miss you as soon as they got home."

A frightened look in Becky's face brought Tom to his senses and he saw that he had made a blunder. Becky was not to have gone home that night! The children became silent and thoughtful. In a moment a new burst of grief from Becky showed Tom that the thing in his mind had struck hers also—that the Sabbath morning might be half spent before Mrs. Thatcher discovered that Becky was not at Mrs. Harper's.

The children fastened their eyes upon their bit of candle and watched it melt slowly and pitilessly away; saw the half inch of wick stand alone at last; saw the feeble flame rise and fall, climb the thin column of smoke, linger at its top a moment, and then— the horror of utter darkness reigned!

How long afterward it was that Becky came to a slow consciousness that she was crying in Tom's arms, neither could tell. All that they knew was, that after what seemed a mighty stretch of time, both awoke out of a dead stupor of sleep and resumed their miseries once more. Tom said it might be Sunday, now—maybe Monday. He tried to get Becky to talk, but her sorrows were too oppressive, all her hopes were gone. Tom said that they must have been missed long ago, and no doubt the search was going on. He would shout and maybe some one would come. He tried it; but in the darkness the distant echoes sounded so hideously that he tried it no more.

The hours wasted away, and hunger came to torment the captives again. A portion of Tom's half of the cake was left; they divided and ate it. But they seemed hungrier than before. The poor morsel of food only whetted desire.

By and by Tom said:

"*Sh!* Did you hear that?"

Both held their breath and listened. There was a sound like the faintest, far-off shout. Instantly Tom answered it, and leading Becky by the hand, started groping down the corridor in its direction. Presently he listened again; again the sound was heard, and apparently a little nearer.

"It's them!" said Tom; "they're coming! Come along Becky— we're all right now!"

The joy of the prisoners was almost overwhelming. Their speed was slow, however, because pitfalls were somewhat common, and had to be guarded against. They shortly came to one and had to stop. It might be three feet deep, it might be a hundred—there was no passing it at any rate. Tom got down on his breast and reached as far down as he could. No bottom. They must stay there and wait until the searchers came. They listened; evidently the distant shoutings were growing more distant! a moment or two more and they had gone altogether. The heart-sinking misery of it! Tom whooped until he was hoarse, but it was of no use. He talked hopefully to Becky; but an age of anxious waiting passed and no sounds came again.

The children groped their way back to the spring. The weary time dragged on; they slept again, and awoke famished and woe-stricken. Tom believed it must be Tuesday by this time.

Now an idea struck him. There were some side passages near at hand. It would be better to explore some of these than bear the weight of the heavy time in idleness. He took a kite-line from his pocket, tied it to a projection, and he and Becky started, Tom in the lead, unwinding the line as he groped along. At the end of twenty steps the corridor ended in a "jumping-off place." Tom got down on his knees and felt below, and then as far around the corner as he could reach with his hands conveniently; he made an effort to stretch yet a little further to the right, and at that moment, not twenty yards away, a human hand, holding a candle, appeared from behind a rock! Tom lifted up a glorious shout, and instantly that hand was followed by the body it belonged to— Injun Joe's! Tom was paralyzed; he could not move. He was vastly gratified the next moment, to see the "Spaniard" take to his heels and get himself out of sight. Tom wondered that Joe had not recognized his voice and come over and killed him for testifying in court. But the echoes must have disguised the voice. Without doubt, that was it, he reasoned. Tom's fright weakened every muscle in his body. He said to himself that if he had strength enough to get back to the spring he would stay there, and nothing should tempt him to run the risk of meeting Injun Joe again. He was careful to keep from Becky what it was he had seen. He told her he had only shouted "for luck."

But hunger and wretchedness rise superior to fears in the long run. Another tedious wait at the spring and another long sleep brought changes. The children awoke tortured with a raging hunger. Tom believed that it must be Wednesday or Thursday or even Friday or Saturday, now, and that the search had been given over. He proposed to explore another passage. He felt willing to risk Injun Joe and all other terrors. But Becky was very weak. She had sunk into a dreary apathy and would not be roused. She said she would wait, now, where she was, and die—it would not be long. She told Tom to go with the kite-line and explore if he chose; but she implored him to come back every little while and speak to her; and she made him promise that when the awful time came, he would stay by her and hold her hand until all was over.

Tom kissed her, with a choking sensation in his throat, and made a show of being confident of finding the searchers or an escape from the cave; then he took the kite-line in his hand and went groping down one of the passages on his hands and knees, distressed with hunger and sick with bodings of coming doom.

CHAPTER XXXII

Tuesday afternoon came, and waned to the twilight. The village of St. Petersburg still mourned. The lost children had not been found. Public prayers had been offered up for them, and many and many a private prayer that had the petitioner's whole heart in it; but still no good news came from the cave. The majority of the searchers had given up the quest and gone back to their daily avocations, saying that it was plain the children could never be found. Mrs. Thatcher was very ill, and a great part of the time delirious. People said it was heartbreaking to hear her call her child, and raise her head and listen a whole minute at a time, then lay it wearily down again with a moan. Aunt Polly had drooped into a settled melancholy, and her gray hair had grown almost white. The village went to its rest on Tuesday night, sad and forlorn.

Away in the middle of the night a wild peal burst from the village bells, and in a moment the streets were swarming with frantic half-clad people, who shouted, "Turn out! turn out! they're found! they're found!" Tin pans and horns were added to the din, the population massed itself and moved toward the river, met the children coming in an open carriage drawn by shouting citizens, thronged around it, joined its homeward march, and swept magnificently up the main street roaring huzzah after huzzah!

The village was illuminated; nobody went to bed again; it was the greatest night the little town had ever seen. During the first half hour a procession of villagers filed through Judge Thatcher's house, siezed the saved ones and kissed them, squeezed Mrs. Thatcher's hand, tried to speak but couldn't—and drifted out raining tears all over the place.

Aunt Polly's happiness was complete, and Mrs. Thatcher's nearly so. It would be complete, however, as soon as the messenger dispatched with the great news to the cave should get the word to her husband. Tom lay upon a sofa with an eager auditory about him and told the history of the wonderful adventure, putting in many striking additions to adorn it withal; and closed with a description of how he left Becky and went on an exploring expedition; how he followed two avenues as far as his kite-line would reach; how he followed a third to the fullest stretch of the kite-line, and was about to turn back when he glimpsed a far-off speck that looked like daylight; dropped the line and groped toward it, pushed his head and shoulders through a small hole and saw the broad Mississippi rolling by! And if it had only happened to be night he would not have seen that speck of daylight and would not have explored that passage any more! He told how he went back for Becky and broke the good news and she told him not to fret her with such stuff, for she was tired, and knew she was going to die, and wanted to. He described how he labored with her and convinced her; and how she almost died for joy when she had groped to where she actually saw the blue speck of daylight; how he pushed his way out at the hole and then helped her out; how they sat there and cried for gladness; how some men came along in a skiff and Tom hailed them and told them their situation and their famished condition; how the men didn't believe the wild tale at first, "because," said they, "you are five miles down the river below the valley the cave is in"—then took them aboard, rowed to a house, gave them supper, made them rest till two or three hours after dark and then brought them home.

Before day-dawn, Judge Thatcher and the handful of searchers with him were tracked out, in the cave, by the twine clews they had strung behind them, and informed of the great news.

Three days and nights of toil and hunger in the cave were not to be shaken off at once, as Tom and Becky soon discovered. They were bedridden all of Wednesday and Thursday, and seemed to grow more and more tired and worn, all the time. Tom got about, a little, on Thursday, was down town Friday, and nearly as whole as ever Saturday; but Becky did not leave her room until Sunday, and then she looked as if she had passed through a wasting illness.

Tom learned of Huck's sickness and went to see him on Friday, but could not be admitted to the bedroom; neither could he on Saturday or Sunday. He was admitted daily after that, but was warned to keep still about his adventure and introduce no exciting topic. The widow Douglas staid by to see that he obeyed. At home Tom learned of the Cardiff Hill event; also that the "ragged man's" body had eventually been found in the river near the ferry landing; he had been drowned while trying to escape, perhaps.

About a fortnight after Tom's rescue from the cave, he started off to visit Huck, who had grown plenty strong enough, now, to hear exciting talk, and Tom had some that would interest him, he thought. Judge Thatcher's house was on Tom's way, and he stopped to see Becky. The Judge and some friends set Tom to talking, and some one asked him ironically if he wouldn't like to go to the cave again. Tom said he thought he wouldn't mind it. The Judge said:

"Well, there are others just like you, Tom, I've not the least doubt. But we have taken care of that. Nobody will get lost in that cave any more."

"Why?"

"Because I had its big door sheathed with boiler iron two weeks ago, and triple-locked—and I've got the keys."

Tom turned as white as a sheet.

"What's the matter, boy! Here, run, somebody! Fetch a glass of water!"

The water was brought and thrown into Tom's face.

"Ah, now you're all right. What was the matter with you, Tom?"

"Oh, Judge, Injun Joe's in the cave!"

CHAPTER XXXIII

Within a few minutes the news had spread, and a dozen skiff-loads of men were on their way to McDougal's cave, and the ferry-boat, well filled with passengers, soon followed. Tom Sawyer was in the skiff that bore Judge Thatcher.

When the cave door was unlocked, a sorrowful sight presented itself in the dim twilight of the place. Injun Joe lay stretched upon the ground, dead, with his face close to the crack of the door, as if his longing eyes had been fixed, to the latest moment, upon the light and the cheer of the free world outside. Tom was touched, for he knew by his own experience how this wretch had suffered. His pity was moved, but nevertheless he felt an abounding sense of relief and security, now, which revealed to him in a degree which he had not fully appreciated before how vast a weight of dread had been lying upon him since the day he lifted his voice against this bloody-minded outcast.

Injun Joe's bowie knife lay close by, its blade broken in two. The great foundation-beam of the door had been chipped and hacked through, with tedious labor; useless labor, too, it was, for the native rock formed a sill outside it, and upon that stubborn material the knife had wrought no effect; the only damage done was to the knife itself. But if there had been no stony obstruction there the labor would have been useless still, for if the beam had been wholly cut away Injun Joe could not have squeezed his body under the door, and he knew it. So he had only hacked that place in order to be doing something—in order to pass the weary time—in order to employ his tortured faculties. Ordinarily one could find half a dozen bits of candle stuck around in the crevices of this vestibule, left there by tourists; but there were none now. The prisoner had searched them out and eaten them. He had also contrived to catch a few bats, and these, also, he had eaten, leaving only their claws. The poor unfortunate had starved to death. In one place near at hand, a stalagmite had been slowly growing up from the ground for ages, builded by the water-drip from a stalactite overhead. The captive had broken off the stalagmite, and upon the stump had placed a stone, wherein he had scooped a shallow hollow to catch the precious drop that fell once in every three minutes with the dreary regularity of a clock-tick—a dessert spoonful once in four and twenty hours. That drop was falling when the Pyramids were new; when Troy fell; when the foundations of Rome were laid; when Christ was crucified; when the Conqueror created the British empire; when Columbus sailed; when the massacre at Lexington was "news." It is falling now; it will still be falling when all these things shall have sunk down the afternoon of history, and the twilight of tradition, and been swallowed up in the thick night of oblivion. Has everything a purpose and a mission? Did this drop fall patiently during five thousand years to be ready for this flitting human insect's need? and has it another important object to accomplish ten thousand years to come? No matter. It is many and many a year since the hapless half-breed scooped out the stone to catch the priceless drops, but to this day the tourist stares longest at that pathetic stone and that slow dropping water when he comes to see the wonders of McDougal's cave. Injun Joe's cup stands first in the list of the cavern's marvels; even "Aladdin's Palace" cannot rival it.

Injun Joe was buried near the mouth of the cave; and people flocked there in boats and wagons from the towns and from all the farms and hamlets for seven miles around; they brought their children, and all sorts of provisions, and confessed that they had had almost as satisfactory a time at the funeral as they could have had at the hanging.

This funeral stopped the further growth of one thing—the petition to the Governor for Injun Joe's pardon. The petition had been largely signed; many tearful and eloqer⁺ neetings had been held, and a committee of sappy women been appointed to go in deep mourning and wail around the governor, and implore him to be a merciful ass and trample his duty under foot. Injun Joe was believed to have killed five citizens of the village, but what of that? If he had been Satan himself there would have been plenty of weaklings ready to scribble their names to a pardon-petition, and drip a tear on it from their permanently impaired and leaky water-works.

The morning after the funeral Tom took Huck to a private place to have an important talk. Huck had learned all about Tom's adventure from the Welchman and the widow Douglas, by this time, but Tom said he reckoned there was one thing they had not told him; that thing was what he wanted to talk about now. Huck's face saddened. He said:

"I know what it is. You got into No. 2 and never found anything but whisky. Nobody told me it was you; but I just knowed it must 'a' ben you, soon as I heard 'bout that whisky business; and I knowed you hadn't got the money becuz you'd 'a' got at me some way or other and told me even if you was mum to everybody else. Tom, something's always told me we'd never get holt of that swag."

"Why Huck, *I* never told on that tavern-keeper. *You* know his tavern was all right the Saturday I went to the pic-nic. Don't you remember you was to watch there that night?"

"Oh, yes! Why it seems 'bout a year ago. It was that very night that I follered Injun Joe to the widder's."

"*You* followed him?"

"Yes—but you keep mum. I reckon Injun Joe's left friends behind him, and I don't want 'em souring on me and doing me mean tricks. If it hadn't ben for me he'd be down in Texas now, all right."

Then Huck told his entire adventure in confidence to Tom, who had only heard of the Welchmen's part of it before.

"Well," said Huck, presently, coming back to the main question, "whoever nipped the whisky in No. 2, nipped the money too, I reckon—anyways it's a goner for us, Tom."

"Huck, that money wasn't ever in No. 2!"

"What!" Huck searched his comrade's face keenly. "Tom, have you got on the track of that money again?"

"Huck, it's in the cave!"

Huck's eyes blazed.

"Say it again, Tom!"

"The money's in the cave!"

"Tom,—honest injun, now—is it fun, or earnest?"

"Earnest, Huck—just as earnest as ever I was in my life. Will you go in there with me and help get it out?"

"I bet I will! I will if it's where we can blaze our way to it and not get lost."

"Huck, we can do that without the least little bit of trouble in the world."

"Good as wheat! What makes you think the money's—"

"Huck, you just wait till we get in there. If we don't find it I'll agree to give you my drum and everything I've got in the world. I will, by jings."

"All right—it's a whiz. When do you say?"

"Right now, if you say it. Are you strong enough?"

"Is it far in the cave? I ben on my pins a little, three or four days, now, but I can't walk more'n a mile, Tom—least I don't think I could."

"It's about five mile into there the way anybody but me would go, Huck, but there's a mighty short cut that they don't anybody but me know about. Huck, I'll take you right to it in a skiff. I'll float the skiff down there, and I'll pull it back again all by myself. You needn't ever turn your hand over."

"Less start right off, Tom."

"All right. We want some bread and meat, and our pipes, and a little bag or two, and two or three kite-strings, and some of these new fangled things they call lucifer matches. I tell you many's the time I wished I had some when I was in there before."

A trifle after noon the boys borrowed a small skiff from a citizen who was absent, and got under way at once. When they were several miles below "Cave Hollow," Tom said:

"Now you see this bluff here looks all alike all the way down from the cave hollow—no houses, no wood-yards, bushes all alike. But do you see that white place up yonder where there's been a landslide? Well that's one of my marks. We'll get ashore, now."

They landed.

"Now Huck, where we're a-standing you could touch that hole I got out of with a fishing-pole. See if you can find it."

Huck searched all the place about, and found nothing. Tom proudly marched into a thick clump of sumach bushes and said—

"Here you are! Look at it, Huck; it's the snuggest hole in this country. You just keep mum about it. All along I've been wanting to be a robber, but I knew I'd got to have a thing like this, and where to run across it was the bother. We've got it now, and we'll keep it quiet, only we'll let Joe Harper and Ben Rogers in—because of course there's got to be a Gang, or else there wouldn't be any style about it. Tom Sawyer's Gang—it sounds splendid, don't it, Huck?"

"Well, it just does, Tom. And who'll we rob?"

"Oh, most anybody. Waylay people—that's mostly the way."

"And kill them?"

"No—not always. Hive them in the cave till they raise a ransom."

"What's a ransom?"

"Money. You make them raise all they can, off'n their friends;

and after you've kept them a year, if it ain't raised then you kill them. That's the general way. Only you don't kill the women. You shut up the women, but you don't kill them. They're always beautiful and rich, and awfully scared. You take their watches and things, but you always take your hat off and talk polite. They ain't anybody as polite as robbers—you'll see that in any book. Well the women get to loving you, and after they've been in the cave a week or two weeks they stop crying and after that you couldn't get them to leave. If you drove them out they'd turn right around and come back. It's so in all the books."

"Why it's real bully, Tom. I b'lieve it's better'n to be a pirate."

"Yes, it's better in some ways, because it's close to home and circuses and all that."

By this time everything was ready and the boys entered the hole, Tom in the lead. They toiled their way to the farther end of the tunnel, then made their spliced kite-strings fast and moved on. A few steps brought them to the spring and Tom felt a shudder quiver all through him. He showed Huck the fragment of candle-wick perched on a lump of clay against the wall, and described how he and Becky had watched the flame struggle and expire.

The boys began to quiet down to whispers, now, for the stillness and gloom of the place oppressed their spirits. They went on, and presently entered and followed Tom's other corridor until they reached the "jumping-off place." The candles revealed the fact that it was not really a precipice, but only a steep clay hill twenty or thirty feet high. Tom whispered—

"Now I'll show you something, Huck."

He held his candle aloft and said—

"Look as far around the corner as you can. Do you see that? There—on the big rock over yonder—done with candle smoke."

"Tom, its a *cross!*"

"*Now* where's your Number Two? '*Under the cross,*' hey? Right yonder's where I saw Injun Joe poke up his candle, Huck!"

Huck stared at the mystic sign a while, and then said with a shaky voice—

"Tom, less git out of here!"

"What! and leave the treasure?"

"Yes—leave it. Injun Joe's ghost is round about there, certain."

"No it ain't, Huck, no it ain't. It would ha'nt the place where he died—away out at the mouth of the cave—five mile from here."

"No, Tom, it wouldn't. It would hang round the money. I know the ways of ghosts, and so do you."

Tom began to fear that Huck was right. Misgivings gathered in his mind. But presently an idea occurred to him—

"Looky here, Huck, what fools we're making of ourselves! Injun Joe's ghost ain't a going to come around where there's a cross!"

The point was well taken. It had its effect.

"Tom I didn't think of that. But that's so. It's luck for us, that cross is. I reckon we'll climb down there and have a hunt for that box."

Tom went first, cutting rude steps in the clay hill as he descended. Huck followed. Four avenues opened out of the small cavern which the great rock stood in. The boys examined three of them with no result. They found a small recess in the one nearest the base of the rock, with a pallet of blankets spread down in it; also an old suspender, some bacon rhind, and the well gnawed bones of two or three fowls. But there was no money box. The lads searched and re-searched this place, but in vain. Tom said:

"He said *under* the cross. Well, this comes nearest to being under the cross. It can't be under the rock itself, because that sets solid on the ground."

They searched everywhere once more, and then sat down discouraged. Huck could suggest nothing. By and by Tom said:

"Looky here, Huck, there's foot-prints and some candle grease on the clay about one side of this rock, but not on the other sides. Now what's that for? I bet you the money *is* under the rock. I'm going to dig in the clay."

"That ain't no bad notion, Tom!" said Huck with animation.

Tom's "real Barlow" was out at once, and he had not dug four inches before he struck wood.

"Hey, Huck!—you hear that?"

Huck began to dig and scratch now. Some boards were soon uncovered and removed. They had concealed a natural chasm which led under the rock. Tom got into this and held his candle as far under the rock as he could, but said he could not see to the end of the rift. He proposed to explore. He stooped and passed under; the narrow way descended gradually. He followed its winding course, first to the right, then to the left, Huck at his heels. Tom turned a short curve, by and by, and exclaimed—

"My goodness, Huck, looky here!"

It was the treasure box, sure enough, occupying a snug little cavern, along with an empty powder keg, a couple of guns in leather cases, two or three pairs of old moccasins, a leather belt, and some other rubbish well soaked with the water-drip.

"Got it at last!" said Huck, plowing among the tarnished coins with his hand. "My, but we're rich, Tom!"

"Huck, I always reckoned we'd get it. It's just too good to believe, but we *have* got it, sure! Say—let's not fool around here. Let's snake it out. Lemme see if I can lift the box."

It weighed about fifty pounds. Tom could lift it, after an awkward fashion, but could not carry it conveniently.

"I thought so," he said; *they* carried it like it was heavy, that day at the ha'nted house. I noticed that. I reckon I was right to think of fetching the little bags along."

The money was soon in the bags and the boys took it up to the cross-rock.

"Now less fetch the guns and things," said Huck.

"No, Huck—leave them there. They're just the tricks to have when we go to robbing. We'll keep them there all the time, and we'll hold our orgies there, too. It's an awful snug place for orgies."

"What's orgies?"

"*I* dono. But robbers always have orgies, and of course we've got to have them, too. Come along, Huck, we've been in here a long time. It's getting late, I reckon. I'm hungry, too. We'll eat and smoke when we get to the skiff."

They presently emerged into the clump of sumach bushes, looked warily out, found the coast clear, and were soon lunching and smoking in the skiff. As the sun dipped toward the horizon they pushed out and got under way. Tom skimmed up the shore through the long twilight, chatting cheerily with Huck, and landed shortly after dark.

"Now Huck," said Tom, "we'll hide the money in the loft of the widow's wood-shed, and I'll come up in the morning and we'll count it and divide, and then we'll hunt up a place out in the woods for it where it will be safe. Just you lay quiet here and watch the stuff till I run and hook Benny Taylor's little wagon; I won't be gone a minute."

He disappeared, and presently returned with the wagon, put the two small sacks into it, threw some old rags on top of them, and started off, dragging his cargo behind him. When the boys reached the Welchman's house, they stopped to rest. Just as they were about to move on, the Welchman stepped out and said:

"Hallo, who's that?"

"Huck and Tom Sawyer."

"Good! Come along with me, boys, you are keeping everybody waiting. Here—hurry up, trot ahead—I'll haul the wagon for you. Why, it's not as light as it might be. Got bricks in it?—or old metal?"

"Old metal," said Tom.

"I judged so; the boys in this town will take more trouble and fool away more time, hunting up six bit's worth of old iron to sell to the foundry than they would to make twice the money at regular work. But that's human nature—hurry along, hurry along!"

The boys wanted to know what the hurry was about.

"Never mind; you'll see, when we get to the Widow Douglas's."

Huck said with some apprehension—for he was long used to being falsely accused—

"Mr. Jones, *we* haven't been doing nothing."

The Welchman laughed.

"Well, I don't know, Huck, my boy. I don't know about that.

Ain't you and the widow good friends?"

"Yes. Well, she's been good friends to me, any ways."

"All right, then. What do you want to be afraid for?"

This question was not entirely answered in Huck's slow mind before he found himself pushed, along with Tom, into Mrs. Douglas's drawing-room. Mr. Jones left the wagon near the door and followed.

The place was grandly lighted, and everybody that was of any consequence in the village was there. The Thatchers were there, the Harpers, the Rogerses, Aunt Polly, Sid, Mary, the minister, the editor, and a great many more, and all dressed in their best. The widow received the boys as heartily as any one could well receive two such looking beings. They were covered with clay and candle grease. Aunt Polly blushed crimson with humiliation, and frowned and shook her head at Tom. Nobody suffered half as much as the two boys did, however. Mr. Jones said:

"Tom wasn't at home, yet, so I gave him up; but I stumbled on him and Huck right at my door, so I just brought them along in a hurry."

"And you did just right," said the widow:—"Come with me, boys."

She took them to a bed chamber and said:

"Now wash and dress yourselves. Here are two new suits of clothes—shirts, socks, everything complete. They're Huck's—no, no thanks, Huck—Mr. Jones bought one and I the other. But they'll fit both of you. Get into them. We'll wait—come down when you are slicked up enough."

Then she left.

CHAPTER XXXIV

Huck said: "Tom, we can slope, if we can find a rope. The window ain't high from the ground."

"Shucks, what do you want to slope for?"

"Well I ain't used to that kind of a crowd. I can't stand it. I ain't going down there, Tom."

"O, bother! It ain't anything. I don't mind it a bit. I'll take care of you."

Sid appeared.

"Tom," said he, "Auntie has been waiting for you all the afternoon. Mary got your Sunday clothes ready, and everybody's been fretting about you. Say—ain't this grease and clay, on your clothes?"

"Now Mr. Siddy, you jist 'tend to your own business. What's all this blow-out about, anyway?"

"It's one of the widow's parties that she's always having. This time its for the Welchman and his sons, on account of that scrape they helped her out of the other night. And say—I can tell you something, if you want to know."

"Well, what?"

"Why old Mr. Jones is going to try to spring something on the people here to-night, but I overheard him tell auntie to-day about it, as a secret, but I reckon it's not much of a secret now. Everybody knows—the widow, too, for all she tries to let on she don't. Mr. Jones was bound Huck should be here—couldn't get along with his grand secret without Huck, you know!"

"Secret about what, Sid?"

"About Huck tracking the robbers to the widow's. I reckon Mr. Jones was going to make a grand time over his surprise, but I bet you it will drop pretty flat."

Sid chuckled in a very contented and satisfied way.

"Sid, was it you that told?"

"O, never mind who it was. Somebody told—that's enough."

"Sid, there's only one person in this town mean enough to do that, and that's you. If you had been in Huck's place you'd 'a' sneaked down the hill and never told anybody on the robbers. You can't do any but mean things, and you can't bear to see anybody praised for doing good ones. There—no thanks, as the widow says"—and Tom cuffed Sid's ears and helped him to the door with several kicks. "Now go and tell auntie if you dare—and to-morrow you'll catch it!"

Some minutes later the widow's guests were at the supper table, and a dozen children were propped up at little side tables in the same room, after the fashion of that country and that day. At the proper time Mr. Jones made his little speech, in which he thanked the widow for the honor she was doing himself and his sons, but said that there was another person whose modesty—

And so forth and so on. He sprung his secret about Huck's share in the adventure in the finest dramatic manner he was master of, but the surprise it occasioned was largely counterfeit and not as clamorous and effusive as it might have been under happier circumstances. However, the widow made a pretty fair show of astonishment, and heaped so many compliments and so much gratitude upon Huck that he almost forgot the nearly intolerable discomfort of his new clothes in the entirely intolerable discomfort of being set up as a target for everybody's gaze and everybody's laudations.

The widow said she meant to give Huck a home under her roof and have him educated; and that when she could spare the money she would start him in business in a modest way. Tom's chance was come. He said:

"Huck don't need it. Huck's rich!"

Nothing but a heavy strain upon the good manners of the company kept back the due and proper complimentary laugh at this pleasant joke. But the silence was a little awkward. Tom broke it—

"Huck's got money. Maybe you don't believe it, but he's got lots of it. Oh, you needn't smile—I reckon I can show you. You just wait a minute."

Tom ran out of doors. The company looked at each other with a perplexed interest—and inquiringly at Huck, who was tongue-tied.

"Sid, what ails Tom?" said Aunt Polly. "He—well, there ain't ever any making of that boy out. I never—"

Tom entered, struggling with the weight of his sacks, and Aunt Polly did not finish her sentence. Tom poured the mass of yellow coin upon the table and said—

"There—what did I tell you? Half of it's Huck's and half of it's mine!"

The spectacle took the general breath away. All gazed, nobody spoke for a moment. Then there was a unanimous call for an explanation. Tom said he could furnish it, and he did. The tale was long, but brim full of interest. There was scarcely an interruption from anyone to break the charm of its flow. When he had finished, Mr. Jones said—

"I thought I had fixed up a little surprise for this occasion, but it don't amount to anything now. This one makes it sing mighty small, I'm willing to allow."

The money was counted. The sum amounted to a little over twelve thousand dollars. It was more than any one present had ever seen at one time before, though several persons were there who were worth considerably more than that in property.

CHAPTER XXXV

The reader may rest satisfied that Tom's and Huck's windfall made a mighty stir in the poor little village of St. Petersburg. So vast a sum, all in actual cash, seemed next to incredible. It was talked about, gloated over, glorified, until the reason of many of the citizens tottered under the strain of the unhealthy excitement. Every "haunted" house in St. Petersburg and the neighboring villages was dissected, plank by plank, and its foundations dug up and ransacked for hidden treasure—and not by boys, but men—pretty grave, unromantic men, too, some of them. Wherever Tom and Huck appeared they were courted, admired, stared at. The boys were not able to remember that their remarks had possessed weight before; but now their sayings were treasured and repeated; everything they did seemed somehow to be regarded as remarkable; they had evidently lost the power of doing and saying commonplace things; moreover, their past history was raked up and discovered to bear marks of conspicuous

originality. The village paper published biographical sketches of
the boys.

The widow Douglas put Huck's money out at six per cent., and
Judge Thatcher did the same with Tom's at Aunt Polly's
request. Each lad had an income, now, that was simply
prodigious—a dollar for every week-day in the year and half of
the Sundays. It was just what the minister got—no, it was what
he was promised—he generally couldn't collect it. A dollar and
a quarter a week would board, lodge and school a boy in those
old simple days—and clothe him and wash him, too, for that
matter.

Judge Thatcher had conceived a great opinion of Tom. He said
that no commonplace boy would ever have got his daughter out
of the cave. When Becky told her father, in strict confidence, how
Tom had taken her whipping at school, the Judge was visibly
moved; and when she pleaded grace for the mighty lie which
Tom had told in order to shift that whipping from her shoulders
to his own, the Judge said with a fine outburst that it was a noble,
a generous, a magnanimous lie—a lie that was worthy to hold up
its head and march down through history breast to breast with
George Washington's lauded Truth about the hatchet! Becky
thought her father had never looked so tall and so superb as
when he walked the floor and stamped his foot and said that. She
went straight off and told Tom about it.

Judge Thatcher hoped to see Tom a great lawyer or a great
soldier some day. He said he meant to look to it that Tom should
be admitted to the National military academy and afterwards
trained in the best law school in the country, in order that he
might be ready for either career or both.

Huck Finn's wealth and the fact that he was now under the
widow Douglas's protection, introduced him into society—no,
dragged him into it, hurled him into it—and his sufferings were
almost more than he could bear. The widow's servants kept him
clean and neat, combed and brushed, and they bedded him
nightly in unsympathetic sheets that had not one little spot or
stain which he could press to his heart and know for a friend.
He had to eat with knife and fork; he had to use napkin, cup and
plate; he had to learn his book, he had to go to church; he had
to talk so properly that speech was become insipid in his mouth;
whithersoever he turned, the bars and shackles of civilization
shut him in and bound him hand and foot.

He bravely bore his miseries three weeks, and then one day
turned up missing. For forty-eight hours the widow hunted for
him everywhere in great distress. The public were profoundly
concerned; they searched high and low, they dragged the river
for his body. Early the third morning Tom Sawyer wisely went
poking among some old empty hogsheads down behind the

abandoned slaughter-house, and in one of them he found the refugee. Huck had slept there; he had just breakfasted upon some stolen odds and ends of food, and was lying off, now, in comfort with his pipe. He was unkempt, uncombed, and clad in the same old ruin of rags that had made him picturesque in the days when he was free and happy. Tom routed him out, told him the trouble he had been causing, and urged him to go home. Huck's face lost its tranquil content, and took a melancholy cast. He said:

"Don't talk about it, Tom. I've tried it, and it don't work; it don't work, Tom. It ain't for me; I ain't used to it. The widder's good to me, and friendly; but I can't stand them ways. She makes me git up just at the same time every morning; she makes me wash, they comb me all to thunder; she won't let me sleep in the wood-shed; I got to wear them blamed clothes that just smothers me, Tom; they don't seem to any air git through 'em, somehow; and they're so rotten nice that I can't set down, nor lay down, nor roll around anywher's; I hain't slid on a cellar-door for—well, it 'pears to be years; I got to go to church and sweat and sweat—I hate them ornery sermons! I can't ketch a fly in there, I can't chaw, I got to wear shoes all Sunday. The widder eats by a bell; she goes to bed by a bell; she gits up by a bell— everything's so awful reg'lar a body can't stand it."

"Well, everybody does that way, Huck."

"Tom, it don't make no difference. I ain't everybody, and I can't *stand* it. It's awful to be tied up so. And grub comes too easy—I don't take no interest in vittles, that way. I got to ask, to go a-fishing; I got to ask, to go in a-swimming—dern'd if I hain't got to ask to do everything. Well, I'd got to talk so nice it wasn't no comfort—I'd got to go up in the attic and rip out a while, every day, to git a taste in my mouth, or I'd a died, Tom. The widder wouldn't let me smoke; she wouldn't let me yell, she wouldn't let me gape, nor stretch, nor scratch, before folks—" [Then with a spasm of special irritation and injury],—"And dad fetch it, she prayed all the time! I never *see* such a woman! I *had* to shove, Tom—I just had to. And besides, that school's going to open, and I'd a had to go to it—well, I wouldn't stand *that,* Tom. Lookyhere, Tom, being rich ain't what it's cracked up to be. It's just worry and worry, and sweat and sweat, and a-wishing you was dead all the time. Now these clothes suits me, and this bar'l suits me, and I ain't ever going to shake 'em any more. Tom, I wouldn't ever got into all this trouble if it hadn't 'a' been for that money; now you just take my sheer of it, along with your'n, and gimme a ten-center sometimes—not many times, becuz I don't give a dern for a thing 'thout it's tollable hard to git—and you go and beg off for me with the widder."

"Oh, Huck, you know I can't do that. 'Taint fair; and besides if you'll try this thing just a while longer you'll come to like it."

"Like it! Yes—the way I'd like a hot stove if I was to set on it long enough. No, Tom, I won't be rich, and I won't live in them cussed smothery houses. I like the woods, and the river, and hogsheads, and I'll stick to 'em, too. Blame it all! just as we'd got guns, and a cave, and all just fixed to rob, here this dern foolishness has got to come up and spile it all!"

Tom saw his opportunity—

"Lookyhere, Huck, being rich ain't going to keep me back from turning robber."

"No! Oh, good-licks, are you in real dead-wood earnest, Tom?"

"Just as dead earnest as I'm a sitting here. But Huck, we can't let you into the gang if you ain't respectable, you know."

Huck's joy was quenched.

"Can't let me in, Tom? Didn't you let me go for a pirate?"

"Yes, but that's different. A robber is more high-toned than what a pirate is—as a general thing. In most countries they're awful high up in the nobility—dukes and such."

"Now Tom, hain't you always ben friendly to me? You wouldn't shet me out, would you, Tom? You wouldn't do that, now, *would* you, Tom?"

"Huck, I wouldn't want to, and I *don't* want to—but what would people say? Why they'd say, 'Mph! Tom Sawyer's Gang! pretty low characters in it!' They'd mean you, Huck. You wouldn't like that, and I wouldn't."

Huck was silent for some time, engaged in a mental struggle. Finally he said:

"Well, I'll go back to the widder for a month and tackle it and see if I can come to stand it, if you'll let me b'long to the gang, Tom."

"All right, Huck, it's a whiz! Come along, old chap, and I'll ask the widow to let up on you a little, Huck."

"Will you Tom—now will you? That's good. If she'll let up on some of the roughest things, I'll smoke private and cuss private, and crowd through or bust. When you going to start the gang and turn robbers?"

"Oh, right off. We'll get the boys together and have the initiation to-night, maybe."

"Have the which?"

"Have the initiation."

"What's that?"

"It's to swear to stand by one another, and never tell the gang's secrets, even if you're chopped all to flinders, and kill anybody and all his family that hurts one of the gang."

"That's gay—that's mighty gay, Tom, I tell you."

"Well I bet it is. And all that swearing's got to be done at midnight, in the lonesomest, awfulest place you can find—a ha'nted house is the best, but they're all ripped up now."

"Well, midnight's good, anyway, Tom."

"Yes, so it is. And you've got to swear on a coffin, and sign it with blood."

"Now that's something *like!* Why it's a million times bullier than pirating. I'll stick to the widder till I rot, Tom; and if I git to be a reg'lar ripper of a robber, and everybody talking 'bout it, I reckon she'll be proud she snaked me in out of the wet."

CONCLUSION

So endeth this chronicle. It being strictly a history of a *boy,* it must stop here; the story could not go much further without becoming the history of *a man.* When one writes a novel about grown people, he knows exactly where to stop—that is, with a marriage; but when he writes of juveniles, he must stop where he best can.

Most of the characters that perform in this book still live, and are prosperous and happy. Some day it may seem worth while to take up the story of the younger ones again and see what sort of men and women they turned out to be; therefore it will be wisest not to reveal any of that part of their lives at present.

"The Journals of Germany" appeared as an appendix to A Tramp Abroad, *published by The American Publishing Company of Hartford, Connecticut, in 1880. This short essay was received with great public enthusiasm.*

THE JOURNALS OF GERMANY

The daily journals of Hamburg, Frankfort, Baden, Munich, and Augsburg are all constructed on the same general plan. I speak of these because I am more familiar with them than with any other German papers. They contain no "editorials" whatever; no "personals,"—and this is rather a merit than a demerit, perhaps; no funny-paragraph column; no police court reports; no reports of proceedings of higher courts; no information about prize fights or other dog fights, horse races, walking matches, yachting contests, rifle matches, or other sporting matters of any sort; no reports of banquet-speeches; no department of curious odds and ends of floating fact and gossip; no "rumors" about anything or anybody; no prognostications or prophecies about anything or anybody; no lists of patents granted or sought, or any reference to such things; no abuse of public officials, big or little, or complaints against them, or praises of them; no religious columns Saturdays, no rehash of cold sermons Mondays; no "weather indications"; no "local item" unveilings of what is happening in town—nothing of a local nature, indeed, is mentioned, beyond the movements of some prince, or the proposed meeting of some deliberative body.

After so formidable a list of what one can't find in a German daily, the question may well be asked, What *can* be found in it? It is easily answered: A child's handful of telegrams, mainly about European national and international political movements; letter-correspondence about the same things; market reports. There you have it. That is what a German daily is made of. A German daily is the slowest and saddest and dreariest of the inventions of man. Our own dailies infuriate the reader, pretty often; the German daily only stupefies him. Once a week the German daily of the highest class lightens up its heavy columns,—that is, it thinks it

lightens them up,—with a profound, an abysmal, book criticism;
a criticism which carries you down, down, down into the scientific
bowels of the subject,—for the German critic is nothing if not
scientific,—and when you come up at last and scent the fresh air
and see the bonny daylight once more, you resolve without a
dissenting voice that a book criticism is a mistaken way to lighten
up a German daily. Sometimes, in place of the criticism, the first-
class daily gives you what it thinks is a gay and chipper essay,—
about ancient Grecian funeral customs, or the ancient Egyptian
method of tarring a mummy, or the reasons for believing that some
of the peoples who existed before the flood did not approve of cats.
These are not unpleasant subjects; they are not uninteresting
subjects; they are even exciting subjects,—until one of these massive
scientists gets hold of them. He soon convinces you that even these
matters can be handled in such a way as to make a person
low-spirited.

As I have said, the average German daily is made up solely of
correspondence,—a trifle of it by telegraph, the rest of it by mail.
Every paragraph has the side-head, "London," "Vienna," or some
other town, and a date. And always, before the name of the town, is
placed a letter or a sign, to indicate who the correspondent is, so that
the authorities can find him when they want to hang him. Stars,
crosses, triangles, squares, half-moons, suns,—such are some of the
signs used by correspondents.

Some of the dailies move too fast, others too slowly. For instance,
my Heidelberg daily was always twenty-four hours old when it
arrived at the hotel; but one of my Munich evening papers used to
come a full twenty-four hours before it was due.

Some of the less important dailies give one a tablespoonful of a
continued story every day; it is strung across the bottom of the page,
in the French fashion. By subscribing for the paper for five years I
judge that a man might succeed in getting pretty much all of the
story.

If you ask a citizen of Munich which is the best Munich daily
journal, he will always tell you that there is only one good Munich
daily, and that it is published in Augsburg, forty or fifty miles away.
It is like saying that the best daily paper in New York is published
out in New Jersey somewhere. Yes, the Augsburg *Allgemeine
Zeitung* is "the best Munich paper," and it is the one I had in my
mind when I was describing a "first-class German daily" above.
The entire paper, opened out, is not quite as large as a single page
of the New York *Herald.* It is printed on both sides, of course; but
in such large type that its entire contents could be put, in *Herald*
type, upon a single page of the *Herald,*—and there would still be
room enough on the page for the *Zeitung's* "supplement" and some
portion of the *Zeitung's* next day's contents.

Such is the first-class daily. The dailies actually printed in

Munich are all called second-class by the public. If you ask which is the best of these second-class papers they say there is no difference; one is as good as another. I have preserved a copy of one of them; it is called the *Munchener Tages-Anzeiger,* and bears date January 25, 1879. Comparisons are odious, but they need not be malicious; and without any malice I wish to compare this journal, published in a German city of 170,000 inhabitants, with journals of other countries. I know of no other way to enable the reader to "size" the thing.

A column of an average daily paper in America contains from 1,800 to 2,500 words; the reading matter in a single issue consists of from 25,000 to 50,000 words. The reading matter in my copy of the Munich journal consists of a total of 1,654 words,—for I counted them. That would be nearly a column of one of our dailies. A single issue of the bulkiest daily newspaper in the world—the London *Times*—often contains 100,000 words of reading matter. Considering that the *Daily Anzeiger* issues the usual twenty-six numbers per month, the reading matter in a single number of the London *Times* would keep it in "copy" two months and a half!

The *Anzeiger* is an eight-page paper; its page is one inch wider and one inch longer than a foolscap page; that is to say, the dimensions of its page are somewhere between those of a schoolboy's slate and a lady's pocket handkerchief. One-fourth of the first page is taken up with the heading of the journal; this gives it a rather top-heavy appearance; the rest of the first page is reading matter; all of the second page is reading matter; the other six pages are devoted to advertisements.

The reading matter is compressed into two hundred and five small pica lines, and is lighted up with eight pica head-lines. The bill of fare is as follows: First, under a pica head-line, to enforce attention and respect, is a four-line sermon urging mankind to remember that, although they are pilgrims here below, they are yet heirs of heaven; and that "When they depart from earth they soar to heaven." Perhaps a four-line sermon in a Saturday paper is the sufficient German equivalent of the eight or ten columns of sermons which the New Yorkers get in their Monday morning papers. The latest news (two days old) follows the four-line sermon, under the pica head-line "Telegrams,"—these are "telegraphed" with a pair of scissors out of the *Augsburger Zeitung* of the day before. These telegrams consist of fourteen and two-thirds lines from Berlin, fifteen lines from Vienna, and two and five-eighths lines from Calcutta. Thirty-three small pica lines of telegraphic news in a daily journal in a King's Capital of 170,000 inhabitants is surely not an overdose. Next we have the pica heading, "News of the Day," under which the following facts are set forth: Prince Leopold is going on a visit to Vienna, six lines; Prince Arnulph is coming back from Russia, two lines; the Landtag will meet at ten o'clock in the

morning and consider an election law, three lines and one word
over; a city government item, five and one-half lines; prices of
tickets to the proposed grand Charity Ball, twenty-three lines,—
for this one item occupies almost one-fourth of the entire first page;
there is to be a wonderful Wagner concert in Frankfurt-on-the-
Main, with an orchestra of one hundred and eight instruments,
seven and one-half lines. That concludes the first page. Eighty-five
lines, altogether, on that page, including three headlines. About
fifty of those lines, as one perceives, deal with local matters; so the
reporters are not overworked.

Exactly one-half of the second page is occupied with an opera
criticism, fifty-three lines (three of them being headlines), and
"Death Notices," ten lines.

The other half of the second page is made up of two paragraphs
under the head of "Miscellaneous News." One of these paragraphs
tells about a quarrel between the Czar of Russia and his eldest son,
twenty-one and a half lines; and the other tells about the atrocious
destruction of a peasant child by its parents, forty lines, or one-
fifth of the total of the reading matter contained in the paper.

Consider what a fifth part of the reading matter of an American
daily paper issued in a city of 170,000 inhabitants amounts to!
Think what a mass it is. Would any one suppose I could so snugly
tuck away such a mass in a chapter of this book that it would be
difficult to find it again if the reader lost his place? Surely not. I will
translate that child murder word for word, to give the reader a
realizing sense of what a fifth part of the reading matter of a Munich
daily actually is when it comes under measurement of the eye:

"From Oberkreuzberg, January 21, the *Donau Zeitung* receives
a long account of a crime, which we shorten as follows: In
Rametuach, a village near Eppenschlag, lived a young married
couple with two children, one of which, a boy aged five, was born
three years before the marriage. For this reason, and also because
a relative at Iggensbach had bequeathed M400 ($100) to the boy,
the heartless father considered him in the way; so the unnatural
parents determined to sacrifice him in the cruelest possible manner.
They proceeded to starve him slowly to death, meantime frightfully
maltreating him,—as the village people now make known, when it
is too late. The boy was shut up in a hole, and when people passed
by he cried, and implored them to give him bread. His
long-continued tortures and deprivations destroyed him at last,
on the third of January. The sudden (*sic*) death of the child created
suspicion, the more so as the body was immediately clothed and
laid upon the bier. Therefore the coroner gave notice, and an inquest
was held on the 6th. What a pitiful spectacle was disclosed then!
The body was a complete skeleton. The stomach and intestines were
utterly empty; they contained nothing whatever. The flesh on the
corpse was not as thick as the back of a knife, and incisions in it

brought not a drop of blood. There was not a piece of sound skin the size of a dollar on the whole body; wounds, scars, bruises, discolored extravasated blood, everywhere,—even on the soles of the feet there were wounds. The cruel parents asserted that the boy had been so bad that they had been obliged to use severe punishments, and that he finally fell over a bench and broke his neck. However, they were arrested two weeks after the inquest and put in the prison at Deggendorf."

Yes, they were arrested "two weeks after the inquest." What a home sound that has. That kind of police briskness rather more reminds me of my native land than German journalism does.

I think a German daily journal doesn't do any good to speak of, but at the same time it doesn't do any harm. That is a very large merit, and should not be lightly weighed nor lightly thought of.

The German humorous papers are beautifully printed upon fine paper, and the illustrations are finely drawn, finely engraved, and are not vapidly funny, but deliciously so. So, also, generally speaking, are the two or three terse sentences which accompany the pictures. I remember one of these pictures: A most dilapidated tramp is ruefully contemplating some coins which lie in his open palm. He says: "Well, begging is getting played out. Only about five marks ($1.25) for the whole day; many an official makes more!" And I call to mind a picture of a commercial traveler who is about to unroll his samples:

Merchant (pettishly).—No, don't. I don't want to buy anything!

Drummer.—If you please, I was only going to show you—

Merchant.—But I don't wish to see them!

Drummer (after a pause, pleadingly).—But do you mind letting *me* look at them! I haven't seen them for three weeks!

The Prince and the Pauper *was published in the United States in book form by James R. Osgood and Company of Boston in 1882. There is a controversy surrounding the first publication of the book. Supposedly, Twain resided in Canada for two weeks in order to get, as a Canadian citizen, copyright protection for his book. His case was thrown out of court. Mark Twain then pled for protection of copyright on the basis that* The Prince and the Pauper *was first printed in England in 1881.*

THE PRINCE AND THE PAUPER

I will set down a tale as it was told to me by one who had it of his father, which latter had it of *his* father, this last having in like manner had it of *his* father—and so on, back and still back, three hundred years and more, the fathers transmitting it to the sons and so preserving it. It may be history, it may be only a legend, a tradition. It may have happened, it may not have happened: but it *could* have happened. It may be that the wise and the learned believed it in the old days; it may be that only the unlearned and the simple loved it and credited it.

HUGH LATIMER, *Bishop of Worcester,* to LORD CROMWELL, *on the birth of the* PRINCE OF WALES *(afterward* EDWARD VI.).

FROM THE NATIONAL MANUSCRIPTS PRESERVED BY THE BRITISH GOVERNMENT.

HUGH LATIMER, *Bishop of Worcester, to* LORD CROMWELL, *on the birth of the* PRINCE OF WALES (*afterward* EDWARD VI.).

FROM THE NATIONAL MANUSCRIPTS PRESERVED BY THE BRITISH GOVERNMENT.

Ryght honorable, *Salutem in Christo Jesu,* and Syr here ys no lesse joynge and rejossynge in thes partees for the byrth of our prynce, hoom we hungurde for so longe, then ther was (I trow), *inter vicinos* att the byrth of S. I. Baptyste, as thys berer, Master Erance, can telle you. Gode gyffe us alle grace, to yelde dew thankes to our Lorde Gode, Gode of Inglonde, for verely He hathe shoyd Hym selff Gode of Inglonde, or rather an Inglyssh Gode, yf we consydyr and pondyr welle alle Hys procedynges with us from tyme to tyme. He hath overcumme alle our yllnesse with Hys excedynge goodnesse, so that we ar now moor then compellyd to serve Hym, seke Hys glory, promott Hys wurde, yf the Devylle of alle Devylles be natt in us. We have now the stooppe of vayne trustes ande the stey of vayne expectations; lett us alle pray for hys preservatione. And I for my partt wylle wyssh that hys Grace allways have, and evyn now from the begynynge, Governares, Instructores and offyceres of ryght judgmente, *ne optimum ingenium non optima educatione depravetur.*

Butt whatt a grett fowlle am I! So, whatt devotione shoyth many tymys but lytelle dyscretione! Ande thus the Gode of Inglonde be ever with you in alle your procedynges.

The 19 of October.

Youres, H. L. B. of Wurcestere, now att Hartlebury.

Yf you wolde excytt thys berere to be moore hartye ayen the abuse of ymagry or mor forwarde to promotte the veryte, ytt myght doo goode. Natt that ytt came of me, butt of your selffe, &c.

(Addressed) To the Ryght Honorable Loorde P. Sealle hys synguler gode Lorde.

CHAPTER I

THE BIRTH OF THE PRINCE AND THE PAUPER

In the ancient city of London, on a certain autumn day in the second quarter of the sixteenth century, a boy was born to a poor family of the name of Canty, who did not want him. On the same day another English child was born to a rich family of the name of Tudor, who did want him. All England wanted him too. England had so longed for him, and hoped for him, and prayed God for him, that, now that he was really come, the people went nearly mad for joy. Mere acquaintances hugged and kissed each other and cried. Everybody took a holiday, and high and low, rich and poor, feasted and danced and sang, and got very mellow; and they kept this up for days and nights together. By day, London was a sight to see, with gay banners waving from every balcony and house-top, and splendid pageants marching along. By night, it was again a sight to see, with its great bonfires at every corner, and its troops of revelers making merry around them. There was no talk in all England but of the new baby, Edward Tudor, Prince of Wales, who lay lapped in silks and satins, unconscious of all this fuss, and not knowing that great lords and ladies were tending him and watching over him—and not caring, either. But there was no talk about the other baby, Tom Canty, lapped in his poor rags, except among the family of paupers whom he had just come to trouble with his presence.

CHAPTER II

TOM'S EARLY LIFE

Let us skip a number of years.

London was fifteen hundred years old, and was a great town—for that day. It had a hundred thousand inhabitants—some think double as many. The streets were very narrow, and crooked, and dirty, especially in the part where Tom Canty lived, which was not far from London Bridge. The houses were of wood, with the second story projecting over the first, and the third sticking its elbows out beyond the second. The higher the houses grew, the broader they grew. They were skeletons of strong criss-cross beams, with solid material between, coated with plaster. The beams were painted red or blue or black, according to the owner's taste, and this gave the houses a very picturesque look. The windows were small, glazed with little diamond-shaped panes, and they opened outward, on hinges, like doors.

The house which Tom's father lived in was up a foul little pocket called Offal Court, out of Pudding Lane. It was small, decayed, and rickety, but it was packed full of wretchedly poor families. Canty's tribe occupied a room on the third floor. The mother and father had a sort of bedstead in the corner; but Tom, his grandmother, and his two sisters, Bet and Nan, were not restricted—they had all the floor to themselves, and might sleep where they chose. There were the remains of a blanket or two, and some bundles of ancient and dirty straw, but these could not rightly be called beds, for they were not organized; they were kicked into a general pile, mornings, and selections made from the mass at night, for service.

Bet and Nan were fifteen years old—twins. They were good-hearted girls, unclean, clothed in rags, and profoundly ignorant. Their mother was like them. But the father and the grandmother were a couple of fiends. They got drunk whenever they could; then they fought each other or anybody else who came in the way; they cursed and swore always, drunk or sober; John Canty was a thief, and his mother a beggar. They made beggars of the children, but failed to make thieves of them. Among, but not of, the dreadful rabble that inhabited the house, was a good old priest whom the King had turned out of house and home with a pension of a few farthings, and he used to get the children aside and teach them right ways secretly. Father Andrew also taught Tom a little Latin, and how to read and write; and would have done the same with the girls, but they were afraid of the jeers of their friends, who could not have endured such a queer accomplishment in them.

All Offal Court was just such another hive as Canty's house. Drunkenness, riot, and brawling were the order, there, every night and nearly all night long. Broken heads were as common as hunger in that place. Yet little Tom was not unhappy. He had a hard time of it, but did not know it. It was the sort of time that all the Offal Court boys had, therefore he supposed it was the correct and comfortable thing. When he came home empty handed at night, he knew his father would curse him and thrash him first, and that when he was done the awful grandmother would do it all over again and improve on it; and that away in the night his starving mother would slip to him stealthily with any miserable scrap or crust she had been able to save for him by going hungry herself, notwithstanding she was often caught in that sort of treason and soundly beaten for it by her husband.

No, Tom's life went along well enough, especially in summer. He only begged just enough to save himself, for the laws against mendicancy were stringent, and the penalties heavy; so he put in a good deal of his time listening to good Father Andrew's charming old tales and legends about giants and fairies, dwarfs and genii, and enchanted castles, and gorgeous kings and princes. His head grew to be full of these wonderful things, and many a night as he lay in the dark on his scant and offensive straw, tired, hungry, and smarting from a thrashing, he unleashed his imagination and soon forgot his aches and pains in delicious picturings to himself of the charmed life of a petted prince in a regal palace. One desire came in time to haunt him day and night: it was to see a real prince, with his own eyes. He spoke of it once to some of his Offal Court comrades; but they jeered him and scoffed him so unmercifully that he was glad to keep his dream to himself after that.

He often read the priest's old books and got him to explain and enlarge upon them. His dreamings and readings worked certain changes in him, by and by. His dream-people were so fine that he grew to lament his shabby clothing and his dirt, and to wish to be clean and better clad. He went on playing in the mud just the same, and enjoying it, too; but instead of splashing around in the Thames solely for the fun of it, he began to find an added value in it because of the washings and cleansings it afforded.

Tom could always find something going on around the Maypole in Cheapside, and at the fairs; and now and then he and the rest of London had a chance to see a military parade when some famous unfortunate was carried prisoner to the Tower, by land or boat. One summer's day he saw poor Anne Askew and three men burned at the stake in Smithfield, and heard an ex-Bishop preach a sermon to them which did not interest him. Yes, Tom's life was varied and pleasant enough, on the whole.

By and by Tom's reading and dreaming about princely life wrought such a strong effect upon him that he began to *act* the prince, unconsciously. His speech and manners became curiously ceremonious and courtly, to the vast admiration and amusement of his intimates. But Tom's influence among these young people began to grow, now, day by day; and in time he came to be looked up to, by them, with a sort of wondering awe, as a superior being. He seemed to know so much! and he could do and say such marvellous things! and withal, he was so deep and wise! Tom's remarks, and Tom's performances, were reported by the boys to their elders; and these, also, presently began to discuss Tom Canty, and to regard him as a most gifted and extraordinary creature. Full grown people brought their perplexities to Tom for solution, and were often astonished at the wit and wisdom of his decisions. In fact he was become a hero to all who knew him except his own family—these, only, saw nothing in him.

Privately, after a while, Tom organized a royal court! He was the prince; his special comrades were guards, chamberlains, equerries, lords and ladies in waiting, and the royal family. Daily the mock prince was received with elaborate ceremonials borrowed by Tom from his romantic readings; daily the great affairs of the mimic kingdom were discussed in the royal council, and daily his mimic highness issued decrees to his imaginary armies, navies, and viceroyalties.

After which, he would go forth in his rags and beg a few farthings, eat his poor crust, take his customary cuffs and abuse, and then stretch himself upon his handful of foul straw, and resume his empty grandeurs in his dreams.

And still his desire to look just once upon a real prince, in the flesh, grew upon him, day by day, and week by week, until at last it absorbed all other desires, and became the one passion of his life.

One January day, on his usual begging tour, he tramped despondently up and down the region round about Mincing Lane and Little East Cheap, hour after hour, bare-footed and cold, looking in at cook-shop windows and longing for the dreadful pork-pies and other deadly inventions displayed there—for to him these were dainties fit for the angels; that is, judging by the smell, they were—for it had never been his good luck to own and eat one. There was a cold drizzle of rain; the atmosphere was murky; it was a melancholy day. At night Tom reached home so wet and tired and hungry that it was not possible for his father and grandmother to observe his forlorn condition and not be moved—after their fashion; wherefore they gave him a brisk cuffing at once and sent him to bed. For a long time his pain and hunger, and the swearing and fighting going on in the building, kept him awake; but at last his thoughts drifted away to far, romantic lands, and he fell asleep in the company of jewelled and gilded princelings who lived in vast palaces, and had servants salaaming before them or flying to execute their orders. And then, as usual, he dreamed that *he* was a princeling himself.

All night long the glories of his royal estate shone upon him; he moved among great lords and ladies, in a blaze of light, breathing perfumes, drinking in delicious music, and answering the reverent obeisances of the glittering throng as it parted to make way for him, with here a smile, and there a nod of his princely head.

And when he awoke in the morning and looked upon the wretchedness about him, his dream had had its usual effect—it had intensified the sordidness of his surroundings a thousand fold. Then came bitterness, and heart-break, and tears.

CHAPTER III

TOM'S MEETING WITH THE PRINCE

Tom got up hungry, and sauntered hungry away, but with his thoughts busy with the shadowy splendors of his night's dreams. He wandered here and there in the city, hardly noticing where he was going, or what was happening around him. People jostled him and some gave him rough speech; but it was all lost on the musing boy. By and by he found himself at Temple Bar, the farthest from home he had ever travelled in that direction. He stopped and considered a moment, then fell into his imaginings again, and passed on outside the walls of London. The Strand had ceased to be a country-road then, and regarded itself as a street, but by a strained construction;

for, though there was a tolerably compact row of houses on one side of it, there were only some scattering great buildings on the other, these being palaces of rich nobles, with ample and beautiful grounds stretching to the river,—grounds that are now closely packed with grim acres of brick and stone.

Tom discovered Charing Village presently, and rested himself at the beautiful cross built there by a bereaved king of earlier days; then idled down a quiet, lovely road, past the great cardinal's stately palace, toward a far more mighty and majestic palace beyond,—Westminster. Tom stared in glad wonder at the vast pile of masonry, the wide-spreading wings, the frowning bastions and turrets, the huge stone gateway, with its gilded bars and its magnificent array of colossal granite lions, and the other signs and symbols of English royalty. Was the desire of his soul to be satisfied at last? Here, indeed, was a king's palace. Might he not hope to see a prince now,—a prince of flesh and blood, if Heaven were willing?

At each side of the gilded gate stood a living statue, that is to say, an erect and stately and motionless man-at-arms, clad from head to heel in shining steel armor. At a respectful distance were many country folk, and people from the city, waiting for any chance glimpse of royalty that might offer. Splendid carriages, with splendid people in them and splendid servants outside, were arriving and departing by several other noble gateways that pierced the royal enclosure.

Poor little Tom, in his rags, approached, and was moving slowly and timidly past the sentinels, with a beating heart and a rising hope, when all at once he caught sight through the golden bars of a spectacle that almost made him shout for joy. Within was a comely boy, tanned and brown with sturdy out-door sports and exercises, whose clothing was all of lovely silks and satins, shining with jewels; at his hip a little jewelled sword and dagger; dainty buskins on his feet, with red heels; and on his head a jaunty crimson cap, with drooping plumes fastened with a great sparkling gem. Several gorgeous gentlemen stood near,—his servants, without a doubt. Oh! he was a prince—a prince, a living prince, a real prince—without the shadow of a question; and the prayer of the pauper-boy's heart was answered at last.

Tom's breath came quick and short with excitement, and his eyes grew big with wonder and delight. Every thing gave way in his mind instantly to one desire: that was to get close to the prince, and have a good, devouring look at him. Before he knew what he was about, he had his face against the gate-bars. The next instant one of the soldiers snatched him rudely away, and sent him spinning among the gaping crowd of country gawks and London idlers. The soldier said,—

"Mind thy manners, thou young beggar!"

The crowd jeered and laughed; but the young prince sprang
to the gate with his face flushed, and his eyes flashing with
indignation, and cried out,—

"How dar'st thou use a poor lad like that! How dar'st thou use
the King my father's meanest subject so! Open the gates, and let
him in!"

You should have seen that fickle crowd snatch off their hats then.
You should have heard them cheer, and shout, "Long live the
Prince of Wales!"

The soldiers presented arms with their halberds, opened the
gates, and presented again as the little Prince of Poverty passed in,
in his fluttering rags, to join hands with the Prince of Limitless
Plenty.

Edward Tudor said,—

"Thou lookest tired and hungry: thou'st been treated ill. Come
with me."

Half a dozen attendants sprang forward to—I don't know what;
interfere, no doubt. But they were waved aside with a right royal
gesture, and they stopped stock still where they were, like so many
statues. Edward took Tom to a rich apartment in the palace, which
he called his cabinet. By his command a repast was brought such as
Tom had never encountered before except in books. The prince,
with princely delicacy and breeding, sent away the servants, so that
his humble guest might not be embarrassed by their critical
presence; then he sat near by, and asked questions while Tom ate.

"What is thy name, lad?"

"Tom Canty, an' it please thee, sir."

" 'Tis an odd one. Where dost live?"

"In the city, please thee, sir. Offal Court, out of Pudding Lane."

"Offal Court! Truly 'tis another odd one. Hast parents?"

"Parents have I, sir, and a grand-dam likewise that is but
indifferently precious to me, God forgive me if it be offence to say
it—also twin sisters, Nan and Bet."

"Then is thy grand-dam not over kind to thee, I take it."

"Neither to any other is she, so please your Worship. She hath a
wicked heart, and worketh evil all her days."

"Doth she mistreat thee?"

"There be times that she stayeth her hand, being asleep or
overcome with drink; but when she hath her judgment clear again,
she maketh it up to me with goodly beatings."

A fierce look came into the little prince's eyes, and he cried out,—

"What! Beatings?"

"Oh, indeed, yes, please you, sir."

"*Beatings!*—and thou so frail and little. Hark ye: before the
night come, she shall hie her to the Tower. The King my father"—

"In sooth, you forget, sir, her low degree. The Tower is for the
great alone."

"True, indeed. I had not thought of that. I will consider of her punishment. Is thy father kind to thee?"

"Not more than Gammer Canty, sir."

"Fathers be alike, mayhap. Mine hath not a doll's temper. He smiteth with a heavy hand, yet spareth me: he spareth me not always with his tongue, though, sooth to say. How doth thy mother use thee?"

"She is good, sir, and giveth me neither sorrow nor pain of any sort. And Nan and Bet are like to her in this."

"How old be these?"

"Fifteen, an' it please you, sir."

"The Lady Elizabeth, my sister, is fourteen, and the Lady Jane Grey, my cousin, is of mine own age, and comely and gracious withal; but my sister the Lady Mary, with her gloomy mien and— Look you: do thy sisters forbid their servants to smile, lest the sin destroy their souls?"

"They? Oh, dost think, sir, that *they* have servants?"

The little prince contemplated the little pauper gravely a moment, then said,—

"And prithee, why not? Who helpeth them undress at night? who attireth them when they rise?"

"None, sir. Wouldst have them take off their garment, and sleep without,—like the beasts?"

"Their garment! Have they but one?"

"Ah, good your worship, what would they do with more? Truly they have not two bodies each."

"It is a quaint and marvellous thought! Thy pardon, I had not meant to laugh. But thy good Nan and thy Bet shall have raiment and lackeys enow, and that soon, too: my cofferer shall look to it. No, thank me not; 'tis nothing. Thou speakest well; thou hast an easy grace in it. Art learned?"

"I know not if I am or not, sir. The good priest that is called Father Andrew taught me, of his kindness, from his books."

"Know'st thou the Latin?"

"But scantly, sir, I doubt."

"Learn it, lad: 'tis hard only at first. The Greek is harder; but neither these nor any tongues else, I think, are hard to the Lady Elizabeth and my cousin. Thou shouldst hear those damsels at it! But tell me of thy Offal Court. Hast thou a pleasant life there?"

"In truth, yes, so please you, sir, save when one is hungry. There be Punch-and-Judy shows, and monkeys,—oh, such antic creatures! and so bravely dressed!—and there be plays wherein they that play do shout and fight till all are slain, and 'tis so fine to see, and costeth but a farthing—albeit 'tis main hard to get the farthing, please your worship."

"Tell me more."

"We lads of Offal Court do strive against each other with the cudgel, like to the fashion of the 'prentices, sometimes."

The prince's eyes flashed. Said he,—

"Marry, that would I not mislike. Tell me more."

"We strive in races, sir, to see who of us shall be fleetest."

"That would I like also. Speak on."

"In summer, sir, we wade and swim in the canals and in the river, and each doth duck his neighbor, and spatter him with water, and dive and shout and tumble and"—

" 'Twould be worth my father's kingdom but to enjoy it once! Prithee go on."

"We dance and sing about the Maypole in Cheapside; we play in the sand, each covering his neighbor up; and times we make mud pastry—oh, the lovely mud, it hath not its like for delightfulness in all the world!—we do fairly wallow in the mud, sir, saving your worship's presence."

"Oh, prithee, say no more, 'tis glorious! If that I could but clothe me in raiment like to thine, and strip my feet, and revel in the mud once, just once, with none to rebuke me or forbid, meseemeth I could forego the crown!"

"And if that I could clothe me once, sweet sir, as thou art clad— just once"—

"Oho, wouldst like it? Then so shall it be. Doff thy rags, and don these splendors, lad! It is a brief happiness, but will be not less keen for that. We will have it while we may, and change again before any come to molest."

A few minutes later the little Prince of Wales was garlanded with Tom's fluttering odds and ends, and the little Prince of Pauperdom was tricked out in the gaudy plumage of royalty. The two went and stood side by side before a great mirror, and lo, a miracle: there did not seem to have been any change made! They stared at each other, then at the glass, then at each other again. At last the puzzled princeling said,—

"What dost thou make of this?"

"Ah, good your worship, require me not to answer. It is not meet that one of my degree should utter the thing."

"Then will *I* utter it. Thou hast the same hair, the same eyes, the same voice and manner, the same form and stature, the same face and countenance, that I bear. Fared we forth naked, there is none could say which was you, and which the Prince of Wales. And, now that I am clothed as thou wert clothed, it seemeth I should be able the more nearly to feel as thou didst when the brute soldier— Hark ye, is not this a bruise upon your hand?"

"Yes; but it is a slight thing, and your worship knoweth that the poor man-at-arms"—

"Peace! It was a shameful thing and a cruel!" cried the little prince, stamping his bare foot. "If the King—Stir not a step till I come again! It is a command!"

In a moment he had snatched up and put away an article of national importance that lay upon a table, and was out at the door and flying through the palace grounds in his bannered rags, with a hotface and glowing eyes. As soon as he reached the great gate, he seized the bars, and tried to shake them, shouting,—

"Open! Unbar the gates!"

The soldier that had maltreated Tom obeyed promptly; and as the prince burst through the portal, half-smothered with royal wrath, the soldier fetched him a sounding box on the ear that sent him whirling to the roadway, and said,—

"Take that, thou beggar's spawn, for what thou got'st me from his Highness!"

The crowd roared with laughter. The prince picked himself out of the mud, and made fiercely at the sentry, shouting,—

"I am the Prince of Wales, my person is sacred; and thou shalt hang for laying thy hand upon me!"

The soldier brought his halberd to a present-arms and said mockingly,—

"I salute your gracious Highness." Then angrily, "Be off, thou crazy rubbish!"

Here the jeering crowd closed around the poor little prince, and hustled him far down the road, hooting him, and shouting, "Way for his royal Highness! way for the Prince of Wales!"

CHAPTER IV

THE PRINCE'S TROUBLES BEGIN

After hours of persistent pursuit and persecution, the little prince was at last deserted by the rabble and left to himself. As long as he had been able to rage against the mob, and threaten it royally, and royally utter commands that were good stuff to laugh at, he was very entertaining; but when weariness finally forced him to be silent, he was no longer of use to his tormentors, and they sought amusement elsewhere. He looked about him, now, but could not recognize the locality. He was with the city of London—that was all he knew. He moved on, aimlessly, and in a little while the houses thinned, and the passers-by were infrequent. He bathed his bleeding feet in the brook which flowed then where Farringdon Street now is; rested a few moments, then passed on, and presently came upon a great space with only a few scattered houses in it, and a prodigious church. He recognized this church. Scaffoldings were about, everywhere, and swarms of workmen; for it was undergoing elaborate repairs. The prince took heart at once—he felt that his troubles were at an end, now. He said to himself, "It is the ancient Grey Friars' church, which the king my father hath taken from the monks and given for a home forever for poor and forsaken children, and new-named it Christ's Church. Right gladly will they serve the son of him who hath done so generously by them—and the more that that son is himself as poor and as forlorn as any that be sheltered here this day, or ever shall be."

He was soon in the midst of a crowd of boys who were running, jumping, playing at ball and leap-frog and otherwise disporting themselves, and right noisily, too. They were all dressed alike, and in the fashion which in that day prevailed among serving-men and 'prentices*—that is to say, each had on the crown of his head a flat black cap about the size of a saucer, which was not useful as a covering, it being of such scanty dimensions, neither was it ornamental; from beneath it the hair fell, unparted, to the middle of the forehead, and was cropped straight around; a clerical band at the neck; a blue gown that fitted closely and hung as low as the knees or lower; full sleeves, a broad red belt; bright yellow stockings, gartered above the knees; low shoes with large metal buckles. It was a sufficiently ugly costume.

The boys stopped their play and flocked about the prince, who said with native dignity—

"Good lads, say to your master that Edward Prince of Wales desireth speech with him."

A great shout went up, at this, and one rude fellow said—

"Marry, art thou his grace's messenger, beggar?"

The prince's face flushed with anger, and his ready hand flew to his hip, but there was nothing there. There was a storm of laughter, and one boy said—

"Didst mark that? He fancied he had a sword—belike he is the prince himself."

This sally brought more laughter. Poor Edward drew himself up proudly and said—

"I am the prince; and it ill beseemeth you that feed upon the king my father's bounty to use me so."

This was vastly enjoyed, as the laughter testified. The youth who had first spoken, shouted to his comrades—

"Ho, swine, slaves, pensioners of his grace's princely father, where be your manners? Down on your marrow bones, all of ye, and do reverence to his kingly port and royal rags!"

With boisterous mirth they dropped upon their knees in a body and did mock homage to their prey. The prince spurned the nearest boy with his foot, and said fiercely—

"Take thou that, till the morrow come and I build thee a gibbet!"

Ah, but this was not a joke—this was going beyond fun. The laughter ceased on the instant, and fury took its place. A dozen shouted—

"Hale him forth! To the horse-pond, to the horse-pond! Where be the dogs? Ho, there, Lion! ho, Fangs!"

Then followed such a thing as England had never seen before—

*See Note 1, at end of the volume.

the sacred person of the heir to the throne rudely buffeted by plebeian hands, and set upon and torn by dogs.

As night drew to a close that day, the prince found himself far down in the close-built portion of the city. His body was bruised, his hands were bleeding, and his rags were all besmirched with mud. He wandered on and on, and grew more and more bewildered, and so tired and faint he could hardly drag one foot after the other. He had ceased to ask questions of any one, since they brought him only insult instead of information. He kept muttering to himself, "Offal Court—that is the name; if I can but find it before my strength is wholly spent and I drop, then am I saved—for his people will take me to the palace and prove that I am none of theirs, but the true prince, and I shall have mine own again." And now and then his mind reverted to his treatment by those rude Christ's Hospital boys, and he said, "When I am king, they shall not have bread and shelter only, but also teachings out of books; for a full belly is little worth where the mind is starved, and the heart. I will keep this diligently in my remembrance, that this day's lesson be not lost upon me, and my people suffer thereby; for learning softeneth the heart and breedeth gentleness and charity."*

The lights began to twinkle, it came on to rain, the wind rose, and a raw and gusty night set in. The houseless prince, the homeless heir to the throne of England, still moved on, drifting deeper into the maze of squalid alleys where the swarming hives of poverty and misery were massed together.

Suddenly a great drunken ruffian collared him and said—

"Out to this time of night again, and hast not brought a farthing home, I warrant me! If it be so, an' I do not break all the bones in thy lean body, then am I not John Canty, but some other."

The prince twisted himself loose, unconsciously brushed his profaned shoulder, and eagerly said—

"O, art *his* father, truly? Sweet heaven grant it be so—then wilt thou fetch him away and restore me!"

"*His* father? I know not what thou mean'st; I but know I am *thy* father, as thou shalt soon have cause to"—

"O, jest not, palter not, delay not!—I am worn, I am wounded, I can bear no more. Take me to the king my father, and he will make thee rich beyond thy wildest dreams. Believe me, man, believe me!— I speak no lie, but only the truth!—put forth thy hand and save me! I am indeed the Prince of Wales!"

The man stared down, stupefied, upon the lad, then shook his head and muttered—

"Gone stark mad as any Tom o' Bedlam!"—then collared him once more, and said with a coarse laugh and an oath, "But mad or no mad, I and thy Gammer Canty will soon find where the soft places in thy bones lie, or I'm no true man!"

With this he dragged the frantic and struggling prince away, and

*See Note 2, at end of the volume.

disappeared up a front court followed by a delighted and noisy swarm of human vermin.

CHAPTER V

TOM AS A PATRICIAN

Tom Canty, left alone in the prince's cabinet, made good use of his opportunity. He turned himself this way and that before the great mirror, admiring his finery; then walked away, imitating the prince's high-bred carriage, and still observing results in the glass. Next he drew the beautiful sword, and bowed, kissing the blade, and laying it across his breast, as he had seen a noble knight do, by way of salute to the lieutenant of the Tower, five or six weeks before, when delivering the great lords of Norfolk and Surrey into his hands for captivity. Tom played with the jewelled dagger that hung upon his thigh; he examined the costly and exquisite ornaments of the room; he tried each of the sumptuous chairs, and thought how proud he would be if the Offal Court herd could only peep in and see him in his grandeur. He wondered if they would believe the marvellous tale he should tell when he got home, or if they would shake their heads, and say his overtaxed imagination had at last upset his reason.

At the end of half an hour it suddenly occurred to him that the prince was gone a long time; then right away he began to feel lonely; very soon he fell to listening and longing, and ceased to toy with the pretty things about him; he grew uneasy, then restless, then distressed. Suppose some one should come, and catch him in the prince's clothes, and the prince not there to explain. Might they not hang him at once, and inquire into his case afterward? He had heard that the great were prompt about small matters. His fears rose higher and higher; and trembling he softly opened the door to the antechamber, resolved to fly and seek the prince, and, through him, protection and release. Six gorgeous gentlemen-servants and two young pages of high degree, clothed like butterflies, sprung to their feet, and bowed low before him. He stepped quickly back, and shut the door. He said,—

"Oh, they mock at me! They will go and tell. Oh! why came I here to cast away my life?"

He walked up and down the floor, filled with nameless fears, listening, starting at every trifling sound. Presently the door swung open, and a silken page said,—

"The Lady Jane Grey."

The door closed, and a sweet young girl, richly clad, bounded towards him. But she stopped suddenly, and said in a distressed voice,—

"Oh, what aileth thee, my lord?"

Tom's breath was nearly failing him; but he made shift to stammer out,—

"Ah, be merciful, thou! In sooth I am no lord, but only poor Tom Canty of Offal Court in the city. Prithee let me see the prince, and he will of his grace restore to me my rags, and let me hence unhurt. Oh, be thou merciful, and save me!"

By this time the boy was on his knees, and supplicating with his eyes and uplifted hands as well as with his tongue. The young girl seemed horror-stricken. She cried out—

"O my lord, on thy knees?—and to *me!*"

Then she fled away in fright; and Tom, smitten with despair, sank down, murmuring—

"There is no help, there is no hope. Now will they come and take me."

Whilst he lay there benumbed with terror, dreadful tidings were speeding through the palace. The whisper, for it was whispered always, flew from menial to menial, from lord to lady, down all the long corridors, from story to story, from saloon to saloon, "The prince hath gone mad, the prince hath gone mad!" Soon every saloon, every marble hall, had its groups of glittering lords and ladies, and other groups of dazzling lesser folk, talking earnestly together in whispers, and every face had in it dismay. Presently a splendid official came marching by these groups, making solemn proclamation,—

"IN THE NAME OF THE KING.

Let none list to his false and foolish matter, upon pain of death, nor discuss the same, nor carry it abroad. In the name of the King!"

The whisperings ceased as suddenly as if the whisperers had been stricken dumb.

Soon there was a general buzz along the corridors, of "The prince! See, the prince comes!"

Poor Tom came slowly walking past the low-bowing groups, trying to bow in return, and meekly gazing upon his strange surroundings with bewildered and pathetic eyes. Great nobles walked upon each side of him, making him lean upon them, and so steady his steps. Behind him followed the court-physicians and some servants.

Presently Tom found himself in a noble apartment of the palace, and heard the door close behind him. Around him stood those who had come with him.

Before him, at a little distance, reclined a very large and very fat man, with a wide, pulpy face, and a stern expression. His large head was very gray; and his whiskers, which he wore only around his face, like a frame, were gray also. His clothing was of rich stuff but old, and slightly frayed in places. One of his swollen legs had a pillow under it, and was wrapped in bandages. There was silence now; and there was no head there but was bent in reverence, except this man's. This stern-countenanced invalid was the dread Henry VIII. He said,—and his face grew gentle as he began to speak,—

"How now, my lord Edward, my prince? Hast been minded to cozen me, the good King thy father, who loveth thee, and kindly useth thee, with a sorry jest?"

Poor Tom was listening, as well as his dazed faculties would let him, to the beginning of this speech; but when the words "me the good King" fell upon his ear, his face blanched, and he dropped as instantly upon his knees as if a shot had brought him there. Lifting up his hands, he exclaimed,—

"Thou the *King?* Then am I undone indeed!"

This speech seemed to stun the King. His eyes wandered from face to face aimlessly, then rested, bewildered, upon the boy before him. Then he said in a tone of deep disappointment,—

"Alack, I had believed the rumor disproportioned to the truth; but I fear me 'tis not so." He breathed a heavy sigh, and said in a gentle voice, "Come to thy father, child: thou art not well."

Tom was assisted to his feet, and approached the Majesty of England, humble and trembling. The King took the frightened face between his hands, and gazed earnestly and lovingly into it awhile, as if seeking some grateful sign of returning reason there, then pressed the curly head against his breast, and patted it tenderly. Presently he said,—

"Dost thou know thy father, child? Break not mine old heart; say thou know'st me. Thou *dost* know me, dost thou not?"

"Yea: thou art my dread lord the King, whom God preserve!"

"True, true—that is well—be comforted, tremble not so; there is none here who would hurt thee; there is none here but loves thee. Thou art better now; thy ill dream passeth—is't not so? And thou knowest thyself now also—is't not so? Thou wilt not miscall thyself again, as they say thou didst a little while agone?"

"I pray thee of thy grace believe me, I did but speak the truth, most dread lord; for I am the meanest among thy subjects, being a pauper born, and 'tis by a sore mischance and accident I am here, albeit I was therein nothing blameful. I am but young to die, and thou canst save me with one little word. Oh speak it, sir!"

"Die? Talk not so, sweet prince—peace, peace, to thy troubled heart—thou shalt not die!"

Tom dropped upon his knees with a glad cry,—

"God requite thy mercy, oh my King, and save thee long to bless thy land!" Then springing up, he turned a joyful face toward the two lords in waiting, and exclaimed, "Thou heard'st it! I am not to die: the King hath said it!" There was no movement, save that all bowed with grave respect; but no one spoke. He hesitated, a little confused, then turned timidly toward the King, saying, "I may go now?"

"Go? Surely, if thou desirest. But why not tarry yet a little? Whither wouldst go?"

Tom dropped his eyes, and answered humbly,—

"Peradventure I mistook; but I did think me free, and so was I moved to seek again the kennel where I was born and bred to misery, yet which harboreth my mother and my sisters, and so is home to me; whereas these pomps and splendors where unto I am not used— oh, please you, sir, to let me go!"

The King was silent and thoughtful a while, and his face betrayed a growing distress and uneasiness. Presently he said, with something of hope in his voice,—

"Perchance he is but mad upon this one strain, and hath his wits unmarred as toucheth other matter. God send it may be so! We will make trial."

Then he asked Tom a question in Latin, and Tom answered him lamely in the same tongue. The King was delighted, and showed it. The lords and doctors manifested their gratification also. The King said,—

" 'Twas not according to his schooling and ability, but sheweth that his mind is but diseased, not stricken fatally. How say you, sir?"

The physician addressed bowed low, and replied,—

"It jumpeth with mine own conviction, sir, that thou hast divined aright."

The King looked pleased with this encouragement, coming as it did from so excellent authority, and continued with good heart,—

"Now mark ye all: we will try him further."

He put a question to Tom in French. Tom stood silent a moment, embarrassed by having so many eyes centred upon him, then said diffidently,—

"I have no knowledge of this tongue, so please your majesty."

The king fell back upon his couch. The attendants flew to his assistance; but he put them aside, and said,—

"Trouble me not— it is nothing but a scurvy faintness. Raise me! there, 'tis sufficient. Come hither, child; there, rest thy poor troubled head upon thy father's heart, and be at peace. Thou'lt soon be well; 'tis but a passing fantasy. Fear thou not; thou'lt soon be well."

Then he turned toward the company: his gentle manner changed, and baleful lightnings began to play from his eyes. He said,—

"List ye all! This my son is mad; but it is not permanent. Over-study hath done this, and somewhat too much of confinement. Away with his books and teachers! see ye to it. Pleasure him with sports, beguile him in wholesome ways, so that his health come again." He raised himself higher still, and went on with energy. He raised himself higher still, and went on with energy.

"He is mad; but he is my son, and England's heir; and, mad or sane, still shall he reign! And hear ye further, and proclaim it: whoso speaketh of this his distemper worketh against the peace and order of these realms, and shall to the gallows!... Give me to drink—I burn: This sorrow sappeth my strength.... There, take away the cup.... Support me. There, that is well. Mad, is he? Were he a thousand times mad, yet is he Prince of Wales, and I the King will confirm it. This very morrow shall he be installed in his princely dignity in due and ancient form. Take instant order for it, my lord Hertford."

"The King's majesty knoweth that the Hereditary Great Marshal of England lieth attainted in the Tower. It were not meet that one attainted"—

"Peace! Insult not mine ears with his hated name. Is this man to live forever? Am I to be balked of my will? Is the prince to tarry uninstalled, because, forsooth, the realm lacketh an earl marshal free of treasonable taint to invest him with his honors? No, by the splendor of God! Warn my parliament to bring me Norfolk's doom before the sun rise again, else shall they answer for it grievously!"*

Lord Hertford said,—

"The King's will is law;" and, rising, returned to his former place.

Gradually the wrath faded out of the old King's face, and he said,—

"Kiss me, my prince. There ... what fearest thou? Am I not thy loving father?"

"Thou art good to me that am unworthy, O mighty and gracious lord: that in truth I know. But—but—it grieveth me to think of him that is to die, and"—

"Ah, 'tis like thee, 'tis like thee! I know thy heart is still the same, even though thy mind hath suffered hurt, for thou wert ever of a gentle spirit. But this duke standeth between thee and thine honors: I will have another in his stead that shall bring no taint to his great office. Comfort thee, my prince: trouble not thy poor head with this matter."

"But is it not I that speed him hence, my liege? How long might he not live, but for me?"

"Take no thought of him, my prince: he is not worthy. Kiss me once again, and go to thy trifles and amusements; for my malady distresseth me. I am aweary, and would rest. Go with thine uncle Hertford and thy people, and come again when my body is refreshed."

Tom, heavy-hearted, was conducted from the presence, for this last sentence was a death-blow to the hope he had cherished that now he would be set free. Once more he heard the buzz of low voices exclaiming, "The prince, the prince comes!"

His spirits sank lower and lower as he moved between the glittering files of bowing courtiers; for he recognized that he was indeed a captive now, and might remain forever shut up in this gilded cage, a forlorn and friendless prince, except God in his

*See Note 3, at end of the volume.

mercy take pity on him and set him free.

And, turn where he would, he seemed to see floating in the air the severed head and the remembered face of the great Duke of Norfolk, the eyes fixed on him reproachfully.

His old dreams had been so pleasant; but this reality was so dreary!

CHAPTER VI

TOM RECEIVES INSTRUCTIONS

Tom was conducted to the principal apartment of a noble suite, and made to sit down—a thing which he was loath to do, since there were elderly men and men of high degree about him. He begged them to be seated, also, but they only bowed their thanks or murmured them, and remained standing. He would have insisted, but his "uncle" the earl of Hertford whispered in his ear—

"Prithee, insist not, my lord; it is not meet that they sit in thy presence."

The lord St. John was announced, and after making obeisance to Tom, he said—

"I come upon the king's errand, concerning a matter which requireth privacy. Will it please your royal highness to dismiss all that attend you here, save my lord the earl of Hertford?"

Observing that Tom did not seem to know how to proceed, Hertford whispered him to make a sign with his hand and not trouble himself to speak unless he chose. When the waiting gentlemen had retired, lord St. John said—

"His majesty commandeth, that for due and weighty reasons of state, the prince's grace shall hide his infirmity in all ways that be within his power, till it be passed and he be as he was before. To wit, that he shall deny to none that he is the true prince, and heir to England's greatness; that he shall uphold his princely dignity, and shall receive, without word or sign of protest, that reverence and observance which unto it do appertain of right and ancient usage; that he shall cease to speak to any of that lowly birth and life his malady hath conjured out of the unwholesome imaginings of o'erwrought fancy; that he shall strive with diligence to bring unto his memory again those faces which he was wont to know—and where he faileth he shall hold his peace, neither betraying by semblance of surprise, or other sign, that he hath forgot; that upon occasions of state, whensoever any matter shall perplex him as to the thing he should do or the utterance he should make, he shall show nought of unrest to the curious that look on, but take advice in that matter of the lord Hertford, or my humble self, which are commanded of the king to be upon this service and close at call, till this commandment be dissolved. Thus saith the king's majesty, who sendeth greeting to your royal highness and prayeth that God will of His mercy quickly heal you and have you now and ever in his holy keeping."

The lord St. John made reverence and stood aside. Tom replied, resignedly—

"The king hath said it. None may palter with the king's command, or fit it to his ease, where it doth chafe, with deft evasions. The king shall be obeyed."

Lord Hertford said—

"Touching the king's majesty's ordainment concerning books and such like serious matters, it may peradventure please your highness to ease your time with lightsome entertainment, lest you go wearied to the banquet and suffer harm thereby."

Tom's face showed enquiring surprise; and a blush followed when he saw lord St. John's eyes bent sorrowfully upon him. His lordship said—

"Thy memory still wrongeth thee, and thou hast shown surprise— but suffer it not to trouble thee, for 'tis a matter that will not bide, but depart with thy mending malady. My lord of Hertford speaketh of the city's banquet which the king's majesty did promise two months flown, your highness should attend. Thou recallest it now?"

"It grieves me to confess it had indeed escaped me," said Tom, in a hesitating voice; and blushed again.

At that moment the lady Elizabeth and the lady Jane Grey were announced. The two lords exchanged significant glances, and Hertford stepped quickly toward the door. As the young girls passed him, he said in a low voice—

"I pray ye, ladies, seem not to observe his humors, nor show surprise when his memory doth lapse—it will grieve you to note how it doth stick at every trifle."

Meanwhile lord St. John was saying in Tom's ear—

"Please you sir, keep diligently in mind his majesty's desire. Remember all thou canst—*Seem* to remember all else. Let them not perceive that thou art much changed from thy wont, for thou knowest how tenderly thy old play-fellows bear thee in their hearts and how 'twould grieve them. Art willing, sir, that I remain?— and thine uncle?"

Tom signified assent with a gesture and a murmured word, for he was already learning, and in his simple heart was resolved to acquit himself as best he might, according to the king's command.

In spite of every precaution, the conversation among the young people became a little embarrassing, at times. More than once, in truth, Tom was near to breaking down and confessing himself unequal to his tremendous part; but the tact of the princess Elizabeth saved him, or a word from one or the other of the vigilant lords, thrown in apparently by chance, had the same happy effect. Once the little lady Jane turned to Tom and dismayed him with this question—

"Hast paid thy duty to the queen's majesty today, my lord?"

Tom hesitated, looked distressed, and was about to stammer out something at hazard, when lord St. John took the word and answered for him with the easy grace of a courtier accustomed to encounter delicate difficulties and to be ready for them—

"He hath indeed, madam, and she did greatly hearten him, as touching his majesty's condition; is it not so, your highness?"

Tom mumbled something that stood for assent, but felt that he was getting upon dangerous ground. Somewhat later it was mentioned that Tom was to study no more at present, whereupon her little ladyship exclaimed—

" 'Tis a pity, 'tis such a pity! Thou wert proceeding bravely. But bide thy time in patience; it will not be for long. Thou'lt yet be graced with learning like thy father, and make thy tongue master of as many languages as his, good my prince."

"My father!" cried Tom, off his guard for the moment. "I trow he cannot speak his own so that any but the swine that wallow in the styes may tell his meaning; and as for learning of any sort so-ever"—

He looked up and encountered a solemn warning in my lord St. John's eyes.

He stopped, blushed, then continued low and sadly: "Ah, my malady persecuteth me again, and my mind wandereth. I meant the king's grace no irreverence."

"We know it, sir," said the princess Elizabeth, taking her "brother's" hand between her two palms, respectfully but caressingly; "trouble not thyself as to that. The fault is none of thine, but thy distemper's."

"Thou'rt a gentle comforter, sweet lady," said Tom, gratefully, "and my heart moveth me to thank thee for't, an' I may be so bold."

Once the giddy little lady Jane fired a simple Greek phrase at Tom. The princess Elizabeth's quick eye saw by the serene blankness of the target's front that the shaft was overshot; so she tranquilly delivered a return volley of sounding Greek on Tom's behalf, and then straightway changed the talk to other matters.

Time wore on pleasantly, and likewise smoothly, on the whole. Snags and sandbars grew less and less frequent, and Tom grew more and more at his ease, seeing that all were so lovingly bent upon helping him and overlooking his mistakes. When it came out that the little ladies were to accompany him to the Lord Mayor's banquet in the evening, his heart gave a bound of relief and delight, for he felt that he should not be friendless, now, among that multitude of strangers, whereas, an hour earlier, the idea of their going with him would have been an insupportable terror to him.

Tom's guardian angels, the two lords, had had less comfort in the interview than the other parties to it. They felt much as if they were piloting a great ship through a dangerous channel; they were on the alert constantly, and found their office no child's play. Wherefore, at last, when the ladies' visit was drawing to a close and the lord Guilford Dudley was announced, they not only felt that their charge had been sufficiently taxed for the present, but also that they themselves were not in the best condition to take their ship back and make their anxious voyage all over again. So they respectfully advised Tom to excuse himself, which he was very glad to do, although a slight shade of disappointment might have been observed upon my lady Jane's face when she heard the splendid stripling denied admittance.

There was a pause, now, a sort of waiting silence which Tom could not understand. He glanced at lord Hertford, who gave him a sign— but he failed to understand that, also. The ready Elizabeth came to the rescue with her usual easy grace. She made reverence and said,—

"Have we leave of the prince's grace my brother to go?"

Tom said—

"Indeed your ladyships can have whatsoever of me they will, for the asking; yet would I rather give them any other thing that in my poor power lieth, than leave to take the light and blessing of their presence hence. Give ye good den, and God be with ye!" Then he smiled inwardly at the thought, " 'tis not for nought I have dwelt but among princes in my reading, and taught my tongue some slight trick of their broidered and gracious speech withal!"

When the illustrious maidens were gone, Tom turned wearily to his keepers and said—

"May it please your lordships to grant me leave to go into some corner and rest me!"

Lord Hertford said—

"So please your highness, it is for you to command, it is for us to obey. That thou shouldst rest, is indeed a needful thing, since thou must journey to the city presently."

He touched a bell, and a page appeared, who was ordered to desire the presence of Sir William Herbert. This gentleman came straightway, and conducted Tom to an inner apartment. Tom's first movement, there, was to reach for a cup of water; but a silk-and-velvet servitor seized it, dropped upon one knee, and offered it to him on a golden salver.

Next, the tired captive sat down and was going to take off his bushkins, timidly asking leave with his eye, but another silk-and-velvet discomforter went down upon his knees and took the office from him. He made two or three further efforts to help himself, but being promptly forestalled each time, he finally gave up, with a sigh of resignation and a murmured "Beshrew me but I marvel they do not require to breathe for me also!" Slippered, and wrapped in a sumptuous robe, he laid himself down at last to rest, but not to sleep, for his head was too full of thoughts and the room too full of people. He could not dismiss the former, so they staid;

he did not know enough to dismiss the latter, so they staid also, to his vast regret,—and theirs.

Tom's departure had left his two noble guardians alone. They mused a while, with much headshaking and walking the floor, then lord St. John said—

"Plainly, what dost thou think?"

"Plainly, then, this. The king is near his end, my nephew is mad, mad will mount the throne, and mad remain. God protect England, since she will need it!"

"Verily it promiseth so, indeed. But . . . have you no misgivings as to . . . as to" . . .

The speaker hesitated, and finally stopped. He evidently felt that he was upon delicate ground. Lord Hertford stopped before him, looked into his face with a clear, frank eye, and said—

"Speak on—there is none to hear but me. Misgivings as to what?"

"I am full loath to word the thing that is in my mind, and thou so near to him in blood, my lord. But craving pardon if I do offend, seemeth it not strange that madness could so change his port and manner!—not but that his port and speech are princely still, but that they *differ* in one unweighty trifle or another, from what his custom was aforetime. Seemeth it not strange that madness should filch from his memory his father's very lineaments; the customs and observances that are his due from such as be about him; and, leaving him his Latin, strip him of his Greek and French? My lord, be not offended, but ease my mind of its disquiet and receive my grateful thanks. It haunteth me, his saying he was not the prince, and so"—

"Peace, my lord, thou utterest treason! Hast forgot the king's command? Remember I am party to thy crime, if I but listen."

St. John paled, and hastened to say—

"I was in fault, I do confess it. Betray me not, grant me this grace out of thy courtesy, and I will neither think nor speak of this thing more. Deal not hardly with me, sir, else am I ruined."

"I am content, my lord. So thou offend not again, here or in the ears of others, it shall be as though thou hadst not spoken. But thou needst not have misgivings. He is my sister's son; are not his voice, his face, his form, familiar to me from his cradle? Madness can do all the odd conflicting things thou seest in him, and more. Dost not recall how that the old Baron Marley, being mad, forgot the favor of his own countenance that he had known for sixty years, and held it was another's; nay, even claimed he was the son of Mary Magdalene, and that his head was made of Spanish glass; and sooth to say, he suffered none to touch it, lest by mischance some heedless hand might shiver it. Give thy misgivings easement, good my lord. This is the very prince, I know him well—and soon will be thy king; it may advantage thee to bear this in mind and more dwell upon it than the other."

After some further talk, in which the lord St. John covered up his mistake as well as he could by repeated protests that his faith was thoroughly grounded, now, and could not be assailed by doubts again, the lord Hertford relieved his fellow keeper, and sat down to keep watch and ward alone. He was soon deep in meditation. And evidently the longer he thought, the more he was bothered. By and by he began to pace the floor and mutter.

"Tush, he *must* be the prince! Will any he in all the land maintain there can be two, not of one blood and birth, so marvellously twinned? And even were it so, 'twere yet a stranger miracle that chance should cast the one into the other's place. Nay, 'tis folly, folly, folly!"

Presently he said—

"Now were he impostor and called himself prince, look you *that* would be natural; that would be reasonable. But lived ever an impostor yet, who, being called prince by the king, prince by the court, prince by all, *denied* his dignity and pleaded against his exaltation? *No!* By the soul of St. Swithin, no! This is the true prince, gone mad!"

CHAPTER VII

TOM'S FIRST ROYAL DINNER

Somewhat after one in the afternoon, Tom resignedly underwent the ordeal of being dressed for dinner. He found himself as finely clothed as before, but every thing different, every thing changed, from his ruff to his stockings. He was presently conducted with much state to a spacious and ornate apartment, where a table was already set for one. Its furniture was all of massy gold, and beautifued with designs which well-nigh made it priceless, since they were the work of Benvenuto. The room was half filled with noble servitors. A chaplain said grace, and Tom was about to fall to, for hunger had long been constitutional with him, but was interrupted by my lord the Earl of Berkeley, who fastened a napkin about his neck; for the great post of Diaperers to the Princes of Wales was hereditary in this nobleman's family. Tom's cupbearer was present, and forestalled all his attempts to help himself to wine. The Taster to his highness the Prince of Wales was there also, prepared to taste any suspicious dish upon requirement, and run the risk of being poisoned.

He was only an ornamental appendage at this time, and was seldom called to exercise his function; but there had been times, not many generations past, when the office of taster had its perils, and was not a grandeur to be desired. Why they did not use a dog or a plumber seems strange; but all the ways of royalty are strange. My lord d'Arcy, First Groom of the Chamber, was there, to do goodness knows what; but there he was—let that suffice. The Lord Chief

Butler was there, and stood behind Tom's chair, overseeing the
solemnities, under command of the Lord Great Steward and the
Lord Head Cook, who stood near. Tom had three hundred and
eighty-four servants beside these; but they were not all in that room,
of course, nor the quarter of them; neither was Tom aware yet that
they existed.

All those that were present had been well drilled within the
hour to remember that the prince was temporarily out of his head,
and to be careful to show no surprise at his vagaries. These
"vagaries" were soon on exhibition before them; but they only
moved their compassion and their sorrow, not their mirth. It was a
heavy affliction to them to see the beloved prince so stricken.

Poor Tom ate with his fingers mainly; but no one smiled at it, or
even seemed to observe it. He inspected his napkin curiously, and
with deep interest, for it was of a very dainty and beautiful fabric,
then said with simplicity,—

"Prithee take it away, lest in mine unheedfulness it be soiled."

The Hereditary Diaperer took it away with reverent manner, and
without word or protest of any sort.

Tom examined the turnips and the lettuce with interest, and
asked what they were, and if they were to be eaten; for it was only
recently that men had begun to raise these things in England in
place of importing them as luxuries from Holland.* His question
was answered with grave respect, and no surprise manifested. When
he had finished his dessert, he filled his pockets with nuts; but
nobody appeared to be aware of it, or disturbed by it. But the next
moment he was himself disturbed by it, and showed discomposure;
for this was the only service he had been permitted to do with his
own hands during the meal, and he did not doubt that he had done
a most improper and unprincely thing. At that moment the muscles
of his nose began to twitch, and the end of that organ to lift and
wrinkle. This continued, and Tom began to evince a growing
distress. He looked appealingly, first at one and then another of the
lords about him, and tears came into his eyes. They sprang forward
with dismay in their faces, and begged to know his trouble. Tom
said with genuine anguish,—

"I crave your indulgence: my nose itcheth cruelly. What is the
custom and usage in this emergence? Prithee speed, for 'tis but a
little time that I can bear it."

None smiled; but all were sore perplexed, and looked one to the
other in deep tribulation for counsel. But behold, here was a dead
wall, and nothing in English history to tell how to get over it.
The Master of Ceremonies was not present: there was no one who
felt safe to venture upon this uncharted sea, or risk the attempt to
solve this solemn problem. Alas! there was no Hereditary Scratcher.
Meantime the tears had overflowed their banks, and begun to
trickle down Tom's cheeks. His twitching nose was pleading more

*See Note 4, at end of volume.

urgently than ever for relief. At last nature broke down the barriers of etiquette: Tom lifted up an inward prayer for pardon if he was doing wrong, and brought relief to the burdened hearts of his court by scratching his nose himself.

His meal being ended, a lord came and held before him a broad, shallow, golden dish with fragrant rose-water in it, to cleanse his mouth and fingers with; and my lord the Hereditary Diaperer stood a napkin for his use. Tom gazed at the dish a puzzled moment or two, then raised it to his lips, and gravely took a draught. Then he returned it to the waiting lord, and said,—

"Nay, it likes me not, my lord: it hath a pretty flavor, but it wanteth strength."

This new eccentricity of the prince's ruined mind made all the hearts about him ache; but the sad sight moved none to merriment.

Tom's next unconscious blunder was to get up and leave the table just when the chaplain had taken his stand behind his chair and with uplifted hands, and closed, uplifted eyes, was in the act of beginning the blessing. Still nobody seemed to perceive that the prince had done a thing unusual.

By his own request, our small friend was now conducted to his private cabinet, and left there alone to his own devices. Hanging upon hooks in the oaken wainscoting were the several pieces of a suit of shining steel armor, covered all over with beautiful designs exquisitely inlaid in gold. This martial panoply belonged to the true prince,—a recent present from Madam Parr the Queen. Tom put on the greaves, the gauntlets, the plumed helmet, and such other pieces as he could don without assistance, and for a while was minded to call for help and complete the matter, but bethought him of the nuts he had brought away from dinner, and the joy it would be to eat them with no crowd to eye him, and no Grand Hereditaries to pester him with undesired services; so he restored the pretty things to their several places, and soon was cracking nuts, and feeling almost naturally happy for the first time since God for his sins had made him a prince. When the nuts were all gone, he stumbled upon some inviting books in a closet, among them one about the etiquette of the English court. This was a prize. He lay down upon a sumptuous divan, and proceeded to instruct himself with honest zeal. Let us leave him there for the present.

CHAPTER VIII

THE QUESTION OF THE SEAL

About five o'clock Henry VIII. awoke out of an unrefreshing nap, and muttered to himself, "Troublous dreams, troublous dreams! Mine end is now at hand: so say these warnings, and my failing pulses do confirm it." Presently a wicked light flamed up in his eye, and he muttered, "Yet will not I die till *he* go before."

His attendants perceiving that he was awake, one of them asked his pleasure concerning the Lord Chancellor, who was waiting without.

"Admit him, admit him!" exclaimed the King eagerly.

The Lord Chancellor entered, and knelt by the King's couch, saying,—

"I have given order, and, according to the King's command, the peers of the realm, in their robes, do now stand at the bar of the House, where, having comfirmed the Duke of Norfolk's doom, they humbly wait his majesty's further pleasure in the matter."

The King's face lit up with a fierce joy. Said he,—

"Lift me up! In mine own person will I go before my Parliament, and with mine own hand will I seal the warrant that rids me of"—

His voice failed; an ashen pallor swept the flush from his cheeks; and the attendants eased him back upon his pillows, and hurriedly assisted him with restoratives. Presently he said sorrowfully,—

"Alack, how have I longed for this sweet hour! and lo, too late it cometh, and I am robbed of this so coveted chance. But speed ye, speed ye! let others do this happy office sith 'tis denied to me. I put my great seal in commission: choose thou the lords that shall compose it, and get ye to your work. Speed ye, man! Before the sun shall rise and set again, bring me his head that I may see it."

"According to the King's command, so shall it be. Will 't please your majesty to order that the Seal be now restored to me, so that I may forth upon the business?"

"The seal! Who keepeth the Seal but thou?"

"Please your majesty, you did take it from me two days since, saying it should no more do its office till your own royal hand should use it upon the Duke of Norfolk's warrant."

"Why, so in sooth I did: I do remember it. . . . What did I with it? . . . I am very feeble. . . . So oft these days doth my memory play the traitor with me. . . . 'Tis strange, strange"—

The King dropped into inarticulate mumblings, shaking his gray head weakly from time to time, and gropingly trying to recollect what he had done with the Seal. At last my lord Hertford ventured to kneel and offer information,—

"Sire, if that I may be so bold, here be several that do remember with me how that you gave the Great Seal into the hands of his highness the Prince of Wales to keep against the day that"—

"True, most true!" interrupted the King. "Fetch it! Go: time flieth!"

Lord Hertford flew to Tom, but returned to the King before very long, troubled and empty-handed. He delivered himself to this effect,—

"It grieveth me, my lord the King, to bear so heavy and unwelcome tidings; but it is the will of God that the prince's affliction abideth still, and he cannot recall to mind that he received the Seal. So came I quickly to report, thinking it were waste of precious time, and little worth withal, that any should attempt to search the long array of chambers and saloons that belong unto his royal high"—

A groan from the King interrupted my lord at this point. After a little while his majesty said, with a deep sadness in his tone,—

"Trouble him no more, poor child. The hand of God lieth heavy upon him, and my heart goeth out in loving compassion for him, and sorrow that I may not bear his burden on mine own old trouble-weighted shoulders, and so bring him peace."

He closed his eyes, fell to mumbling, and presently was silent. After a time he opened his eyes again, and gazed vacantly around until his glance rested upon the kneeling Lord Chancellor. Instantly his face flushed with wrath,—

"What, thou here yet! By the glory of God, an' thou gettest not about that traitor's business, thy mitre shall have holiday the morrow for lack of a head to grace withal!"

The trembling Chancellor answered,—

"Good your majesty, I cry you mercy! I but waited for the Seal."

"Man, hast lost thy wits? The small Seal which aforetime I was wont to take with me abroad lieth in my treasury. And, since the Great Seal hath flown away, shall not it suffice? Hast lost thy wits? Begone! And hark ye,—come no more till thou do bring his head."

The poor Chancellor was not long in removing himself from this dangerous vicinity; nor did the commission waste time in giving the royal assent to the work of the slavish Parliament, and appointing the morrow for the beheading of the premier peer of England, the luckless Duke of Norfolk.*

CHAPTER IX

THE RIVER PAGEANT

At nine in the evening the whole vast riverfront of the palace was blazing with light. The river itself, as far as the eye could reach citywards, was so thickly covered with watermen's boats and with pleasure-barges, all fringed with colored lanterns, and gently agitated by the waves, that it resembled a glowing and limitless garden of flowers stirred to soft motion by summer winds. The grand terrace of stone steps leading down to the water, spacious enough to mass the army of a German principality upon, was a picture to see, with its ranks of royal halberdiers in polished armor, and its troops of brilliantly costumed servitors flitting up and down, and to and fro, in the hurry of preparation.

Presently a command was given, and immediately all living creatures vanished from the steps. Now the air was heavy with the

*See Note 5, at end of volume.

hush of suspense and expectancy. As far as one's vision could carry, he might see the myriads of people in the boats rise up, and shade their eyes from the glare of lanterns and torches, and gaze toward the palace.

A file of forty or fifty state barges drew up to the steps. They were richly gilt, and their lofty prows and sterns were elaborately carved. Some of them were decorated with banners and streamers; some with cloth-of-gold and arras embroidered with coats-of-arms; others with silken flags that had numberless little silver bells fastened to them, which shook out tiny showers of joyous music whenever the breezes fluttered them; others of yet higher pretensions, since they belonged to nobles in the prince's immediate service, had their sides picturesquely fenced with shields gorgeously emblazoned with armorial bearings. Each state barge was towed by a tender. Besides the rowers, these tenders carried each a number of men-at-arms in glossy helmet and breastplate, and a company of musicians.

The advance-guard of the expected procession now appeared in the great gateway, a troop of halberdiers. "They were dressed in striped hose of black and tawny, velvet caps graced at the sides with silver roses, and doublets of murrey and blue cloth, embroidered on the front and back with the three feathers, the prince's blazon, woven in gold. Their halberd staves were covered with crimson velvet, fastened with gilt nails, and ornamented with gold tassels. Filing off on the right and left, they formed two long lines, extending from the gateway of the palace to the water's edge. A thick, rayed cloth or carpet was then unfolded, and laid down between them by attendants in the gold-and-crimson liveries of the prince. This done, a flourish of trumpets resounded from within. A lively prelude arose from the musicians on the water; and two ushers with white wands marched with a slow and stately pace from the portal. They were followed by an officer bearing the civic mace, after whom came another carrying the city's sword; then several sergeants of the city guard, in their full accoutrements, and with badges on their sleeves; then the garter king-at-arms, in his tabard; then several knights of the bath, each with a white lace on his sleeve; then their esquires; then the judges, in their robes of scarlet and coifs; then the lord high chancellor of England, in a robe of scarlet, open before, and purfled with minever; then a deputation of aldermen, in their scarlet cloaks; and then the heads of the different civic companies, in their robes of state. Now came twelve French gentlemen, in splendid habiliments, consisting of pourpoints of white damask barred with gold, short mantles of crimson velvet lined with violet taffeta, and carnation-colored *hauts-de-chausses,* and took their way down the steps. They were of the suite of the French ambassador, and were followed by twelve cavaliers of the suite of the Spanish ambassador, clothed in black velvet, unrelieved by any ornament. Following these came several great English nobles with their attendants."

There was a flourish of trumpets within; and the prince's uncle, the future great Duke of Somerset, emerged from the gateway, arrayed in a "doublet of black cloth-of-gold, and a cloak of crimson satin flowered with gold, and ribanded with nets of silver." He turned, doffed his plumed cap, bent his body in a low reverence, and began to step backward, bowing at each step. A prolonged trumpet-blast followed, and a proclamation, "Way for the high and mighty, the Lord Edward, Prince of Wales!" High aloft on the palace walls a long line of red tongues of flame leaped forth with a thunder-crash: the massed world on the river burst into a mighty roar of welcome; and Tom Canty, the cause and hero of it all, stepped into view, and slightly bowed his princely head.

He was "magnificently habited in a doublet of white satin, with a front-piece of purple cloth-of-tissue, powdered with diamonds, and edged with ermine. Over this he wore a mantle of white cloth-of-gold, pounced with the triple-feather crest, lined with blue satin, set with pearls and precious stones, and fastened with a clasp of brilliants. About his neck hung the order of the Garter, and several princely foreign orders;" and wherever light fell upon him jewels responded with a blinding flash. O Tom Canty, born in a hovel, bred in the gutters of London, familiar with rags and dirt and misery, what a spectacle is this!

CHAPTER X

THE PRINCE IN THE TOILS

We left John Canty dragging the rightful prince into Offal Court, with a noisy and delighted mob at his heels. There was but one person in it who offered a pleading word for the captive, and he was not heeded: he was hardly even heard, so great was the turmoil. The prince continued to struggle for freedom, and to rage against the treatment he was suffering, until John Canty lost what little patience was left in him, and raised his oaken cudgel in a sudden fury over the prince's head. The single pleader for the lad sprang to stop the man's arm, and the blow descended upon his own wrist. Canty roared out,—

"Thou'lt meddle, wilt thou? Then have thy reward."

His cudgel crashed down upon the meddler's head: there was a groan, a dim form sank to the ground among the feet of the crowd, and the next moment it lay there in the dark alone. The mob pressed on, their enjoyment nothing disturbed by this episode.

Presently the prince found himself in John Canty's abode, with the door closed against the outsiders. By the vague light of a tallow candle which was thrust into a bottle, he made out the main features of the loathsome den, and also the occupants of it. Two frowsy girls and a middle-aged woman cowered against the wall in one corner, with the aspect of animals habituated to harsh usage, and expecting and dreading it now. From another corner stole a withered hag with streaming gray hair and malignant eyes. John Canty said to this one,—

"Tarry! There's fine mummeries here. Mar them not till thou'st enjoyed them; then let thy hand be heavy as thou wilt. Stand forth, lad. Now say thy foolery again, an' thou'st not forgot it. Name thy name. Who art thou?"

The insulted blood mounted to the little prince's cheek once more, and he lifted a steady and indignant gaze to the man's face, and said,—

"'Tis but ill-breeding in such as thou to command me to speak. I tell thee now, as I told thee before, I am Edward, Prince of Wales, and none other."

The stunning surprise of this reply nailed the hag's feet to the floor where she stood, and almost took her breath. She stared at the prince in stupid amazement, which so amused her ruffianly son, that he burst into a roar of laughter. But the effect upon Tom Canty's mother and sisters was different. Their dread of bodily injury gave way at once to distress of a different sort. They ran forward with woe and dismay in their faces, exclaiming,—

"O poor Tom, poor lad!"

The mother fell on her knees before the prince, put her hands upon his shoulders, and gazed yearningly into his face through her rising tears. Then she said,—

"O my poor boy! thy foolish reading hath wrought its woful work at last, and ta'en thy wit away. Ah! why didst thou cleave to it when I so warned thee 'gainst it? Thou'st broke thy mother's heart."

The prince looked into her face, and said gently,—

"Thy son is well, and hath not lost his wits, good dame. Comfort thee: let me to the palace where he is, and straightway will the King my father restore him to thee."

"The King thy father! O my child! unsay these words that be freighted with death for thee, and ruin for all that be near to thee. Shake off this grewsome dream. Call back thy poor wandering memory. Look upon me. Am not I thy mother that bore thee, and loveth thee?"

The prince shook his head, and reluctantly said,—

"God knoweth I am loath to grieve thy heart; but truly have I never looked upon thy face before."

The woman sank back to a sitting posture on the fllor, and, covering her eyes with her hands, gave way to heart-broken sobs and wailings.

"Let the show go on!" shouted Canty. "What, Nan! what, Bet! Mannerless wenches! will ye stand in the prince's presence? Upon your knees, ye pauper scum, and do him reverence!"

He followed this with another horse-laugh. The girls began to plead timidly for their brother; and Nan said,—

"An' thou wilt but let him to bed, father, rest and sleep will heal his madness: prithee, do."

"Do, father," said Bet: "he is more worn than is his wont. To-morrow will he be himself again, and will beg with diligence, and come not empty home again."

This remark sobered the father's joviality, and brought his mind to business. He turned angrily upon the prince, and said,—

"The morrow must we pay two pennies to him that owns this hole; two pennies, mark ye,—all this money for a half-year's rent, else out of this we go. Show what thou'st gathered with thy lazy begging."

The prince said,—

"Offend me not with thy sordid matters. I tell thee again I am the King's son."

A sounding blow upon the prince's shoulder from Canty's broad palm sent him staggering into goodwife Canty's arms, who clasped him to her breast, and sheltered him from a pelting rain of cuffs and slaps by interposing her own person.

The frightened girls retreated to their corner; but the grandmother stepped eagerly forward to assist her son. The prince sprang away from Mrs. Canty, exclaiming,—

"Thou shalt not suffer for me, madam. Let these swine do their will upon me alone."

This speech infuriated the swine to such a degree that they set about their work without waste of time. Between them they belabored the boy right soundly, and then gave the girls and their mother a beating for showing sympathy for the victim.

"Now," said Canty, "to bed, all of ye. The entertainment has tired me."

The light was put out, and the family retired. As soon as the snorings of the head of the house and his mother showed that they were asleep, the young girls crept to where the prince lay, and covered him tenderly from the cold with straw and rags; and their mother crept to him also, and stroked his hair, and cried over him, whispering broken words of comfort and compassion in his ear the while. She had saved a morsel for him to eat, also; but the boy's pains had swept away all appetite,—at least for black and tasteless crusts. He was touched by her brave and costly defence of him, and by her commiseration; and he thanked her in very noble and princely words, and begged her to go to her sleep and try to forget her sorrows. And he added that the King his father would not let her loyal kindness and devotion go unrewarded. This return to his "madness" broke her heart anew, and she strained him to her breast again and again and then went back, drowned in tears, to her bed.

As she lay thinking and mourning, the suggestion began to creep into her mind that there was an undefinable something about this boy that was lacking in Tom Canty, mad or sane. She could not describe it, she could not tell just what it was, and yet her sharp mother-instinct seemed to detect it and perceive it. What if the boy were really not her son, after all? O, absurd! She almost smiled at the idea, spite of her griefs and troubles. No matter, she found that it was an idea that would not "down," but persisted in haunting her. It pursued her, it harassed her, it clung to her, and refused to be put away or ignored. At last she perceived that there was not going to be any peace for her until she should devise a test that should prove, clearly and without question, whether this lad was her son or not, and so banish these wearing and worrying doubts. Ah yes, this was plainly the right way out of the difficulty; therefore she set her wits to work at once to contrive that test. But it was an easier thing to propose than to accomplish. She turned over in her mind one promising test after another, but was obliged to relinquish them all—none of them were absolutely sure, absolutely perfect; and an imperfect one could not satisfy her. Evidently she was racking her head in vain—it seemed manifest that she must give the matter up. While this depressing thought was passing through her mind, her ear caught the regular breathing of the boy, and she knew he had fallen asleep. And while she listened, the measured breathing was broken by a soft, startled cry, such as one utters in a troubled dream. This chance occurrence furnished her instantly with a plan worth all her labored tests combined. She at once set herself feverishly, but noiselessly, to work, to relight her candle, muttering to herself, "Had I but seen him *then,* I should have known! Since that day, when he was little, that the powder burst in his face, he hath never been startled of a sudden out of his dreams or out of his thinkings, but he hath cast his hand before his eyes, even as he did that day, and not as others would do it, with the palm inward, but always with the palm turned outward—I have seen it a hundred times, and it hath never varied nor ever failed. Yes, I shall soon know, now!"

By this time she had crept to the slumbering boy's side, with the candle, shaded, in her hand. She bent heedfully and warily over him, scarcely breathing, in her suppressed excitement, and suddenly flashed the light in his face and struck the floor by his ear with her knuckles. The sleeper's eyes sprung wide open, and he cast a startled stare about him—but he made no special movement with his hands.

The poor woman was smitten almost helpless with surprise and grief; but she contrived to hide her emotions, and to soothe the boy to sleep again; then she crept apart and communed miserably with herself upon the disastrous result of her experiment. She tried to believe that her Tom's madness had banished this habitual gesture of his; but she could not do it. "No," she said, "his *hands* are not mad, they could not unlearn so old a habit in so brief a time. O, this is a heavy day for me!"

Still, hope was as stubborn, now, as doubt had been before; she could not bring herself to accept the verdict of the test; she must try the thing again—the failure must have been only an accident; so she startled the boy out of his sleep a second and a third time, at intervals—with the same result which had marked the first test—then she dragged herself to bed, and fell sorrowfully asleep, saying, "But I cannot give him up—O, no, I cannot, I cannot—he *must* be my boy!"

The poor mother's interruptions having ceased, and the prince's pains having gradually lost their power to disturb him, utter weariness at last sealed his eyes in a profound and restful sleep. Hour after hour slipped away, and still he slept like the dead. Thus four or five hours passed. Then his stupor began to lighten. Presently while half asleep and half awake, he murmured—

"Sir William!"

After a moment—

"Ho, Sir William Herbert! Hie thee hither, and list to the strangest dream that ever. . .Sir William! Dost hear? Man, I did think me changed to a pauper, and. . .Ho there! Guards! Sir William! What! is there no groom of the chamber in waiting? Alack it shall go hard with"—

"What aileth thee?" asked a whisper near him. "Who art thou calling?"

"Sir William Herbert. Who art thou?"

"I? Who should I be, but thy sister Nan? O, Tom, I had forgot! Thou'rt mad yet—poor lad thou'rt mad yet, would I had never woke to know it again! But prithee master thy tongue, lest we be all beaten till we die!"

The startled prince sprang partly up, but a sharp reminder from his stiffened bruises brought him to himself, and he sunk back among his foul straw with a moan and the ejaculation—

"Alas, it was no dream, then!"

In a moment all the heavy sorrow and misery which sleep had banished were upon him again, and he realized that he was no longer a petted prince in a palace, with the adoring eyes of a nation upon him, but a pauper, an outcast, clothed in rags, prisoner in a den fit only for beasts, and consorting with beggars and thieves.

In the midst of his grief he began to be conscious of hilarious noises and shoutings, apparently but a block or two away. The next moment there were several sharp raps at the door; John Canty ceased from snoring and said—

"Who knocketh? What wilt thou?"

A voice answered—

"Know'st thou who it was thou laid thy cudgel on?"

"No. Neither know I, nor care."

"Belike thou'lt change thy note eftsoons. An' thou would save thy neck, nothing but flight may stead thee. The man is this moment delivering up the ghost. 'Tis the priest, Father Andrew!''

"God-a-mercy!" exclaimed Canty. He roused his family, and hoarsely commanded, "Up with ye all and fly—or bide where ye are and perish!"

Scarcely five minutes later the Canty household were in the street and flying for their lives. John Canty held the prince by the wrist, and hurried him along the dark way, giving him this caution in a low voice—

"Mind thy tongue, thou mad fool, and speak not our name. I will choose me a new name, speedily, to throw the law's dogs off the scent. Mind thy tongue, I tell thee!"

He growled these words to the rest of the family—

"If it so chance that we be separated, let each make for London bridge; whoso findeth himself as far as the last linen-draper's shop on the bridge, let him tarry there till the others be come, then will we flee into Southwark together."

At this moment the party burst suddenly out of darkness into light; and not only into light, but into the midst of a multitude of singing, dancing, and shouting people, massed together on the river frontage. There was a line of bonfires stretching as far as one could see, up and down the Thames; London bridge was illuminated; Southwark bridge likewise; the entire river was aglow with the flash and sheen of colored lights; and constant explosions of fireworks filled the skies with an intricate commingling of shooting splendors and a thick rain of dazzling sparks that almost turned night into day; everywhere were crowds of revellers; all London seemed to be at large.

John Canty delivered himself of a furious curse and commanded a retreat; but it was too late. He and his tribe were swallowed up in that swarming hive of humanity, and hopelessly separated from each other in an instant. We are not considering that the prince was one of his tribe; Canty still kept his grip upon him. The prince's heart was beating high with hopes of escape, now. A burly waterman, considerably exalted with liquor, found himself rudely shoved, by Canty, in his efforts to plough through the crowd; he laid his great hand on Canty's shoulder and said—

"Nay, wither so fast, friend? Dost canker thy soul with sordid business when all that be leal men and true make holiday?"

"Mine affairs are mine own, they concern thee not," answered Canty, roughly; "take away thy hand and let me pass."

"Sith that is thy humor, thou'lt *not* pass, till thou'st drunk to the Prince of Wales, I tell thee that," said the waterman, barring the way resolutely.

"Give me the cup, then, and make speed, make speed!"

Other revellers were interested by this time. They cried out—

"The loving-cup, the loving-cup! make the sour knave drink the loving-cup, else will we feed him to the fishes."

So a huge loving-cup was brought; the waterman, grasping it by one of its handles, and with his other hand bearing up the end of an imaginary napkin, presented it in due and ancient form to Canty, who had to grasp the opposite handle with one of his hands and take off the lid with the other, according to ancient custom.* This left the prince hand-free for a second, of course. He wasted no time, but dived among the forest of legs about him and disappeared. In another moment he could not have been harder to find, under that tossing sea of life, if its billows had been the Atlantic's and he a lost sixpence.

He very soon realized this fact, and straightway busied himself about his own affairs without further thought of John Canty. He quickly realized another thing, too. To wit, that a spurious Prince of Wales was being feasted by the city in his stead. He easily concluded that the pauper lad, Tom Canty, had deliberatley taken advantage of his stupendous opportunity and become a usurper.

Therefore there was but one course to pursue—find his way to the Guildhall, make himself known, and denounce the impostor. He also made up his mind that Tom should be allowed a reasonable time for spiritual preparation, and then be hanged, drawn and quartered, according to the law and usage of the day, in cases of high treason.

CHAPTER XI

AT GUILDHALL

The royal barge, attended by its gorgeous fleet, took its stately way down the Thames through the wilderness of illuminated boats. The air was laden with music; the river banks were beruffled with joy-flames; the distant city lay in a soft luminous glow from its countless invisible bonfires; above it rose many a slender spire into the sky, incrusted with sparkling lights, wherefore in their remoteness they seemed like jeweled lances thrust aloft; as the fleet swept along, it was greeted from the banks with a continuous hoarse roar of cheers and the ceaseless flash and boom of artillery.

To Tom Canty, half buried in his silken cushions, these sounds and this spectacle were a wonder unspeakably sublime and astonishing. To his little friends at his side, the princess Elizabeth and the lady Jane Grey, they were nothing.

Arrived at the Dowgate, the fleet was towed up the limpid Walbrook (whose channel has now been for two centuries buried out of sight under acres of buildings,) to Bucklersbury, past houses and under bridges populous with merry-makers and brilliantly lighted, and at last came to a halt in a basin where now is Barge Yard, in the centre of the ancient city of London. Tom disembarked, and he and his gallant procession crossed Cheapside and made a

*See Note 6, at end of volume.

short march through the Old Jewry and Basinghall Street to the
Guildhall.

Tom and his little ladies were received with due ceremony by the
Lord Mayor and the Fathers of the City, in their gold chains and
scarlet robes of state, and conducted to a rich canopy of state at the
head of the great hall, preceded by heralds making proclamation,
and by the Mace and the City Sword. The lords and ladies who were
to attend upon Tom and his two small friends took their places
behind their chairs.

At a lower table the court grandees and other guests of noble
degree were seated, with the magnates of the city; the commoners
took places at a multitude of tables on the main floor of the hall.
From their lofty vantage-ground, the giants Gog and Magog, the
ancient guardians of the city, contemplated the spectacle below
them with eyes grown familiar to it in forgotten generations. There
was a bugle-blast and a proclamation, and a fat butler appeared in
a high perch in the leftward wall, followed by his servitors bearing
with impressive solemnity a royal Baron of Beef, smoking hot and
ready for the knife.

After grace, Tom, (being instructed) rose—and the whole house
with him—and drank from a portly golden loving-cup with the
princess Elizabeth; from her it passed to the lady Jane, and then
traversed the general assemblage. So the banquet began.

By midnight the revelry was at its height. Now came one of those
picturesque spectacles so admired in that old day. A description of it
is still extant in the quaint wording of a chronicler who witnessed it:

"Space being made, presently entered a baron and an earl
appareled after the Turkish fashion in long robes of bawdkin
powdered with gold; hats on their heads of crimson velvet, with great
rolls of gold, girded with two swords, called scimitars, hanging by
great bawdricks of gold. Next came yet another baron and another
earl, in two long gowns of yellow satin, traversed with white satin,
and in every bend of white was a bend of crimson satin, after the
fashion of Russia, with furred hats of gray on their heads; either of
them having an hatchet in their hands, and boots with *pykes*"
(points a foot long), "turned up. And after them came a knight,
then the Lord High Admiral, and with him five nobles, in doublets
of crimson velvet, voyded low on the back and before to the
cannellbone, laced on the breasts with chains of silver; and, over
that, short cloaks of crimson satin, and on their heads hats after
the dancers' fashion, with pheasants' feathers in them. These were
appareled after the fashion of Prussia. The torch-bearers, which
were about an hundred, were appareled in crimson satin and green,
like Moors, their faces black. Next came in a *mommarye.* Then the
minstrels, which were disguised, danced; and the lords and ladies
did wildly dance also, that it was a pleasure to behold."

And while Tom, in his high seat, was gazing upon this "wild" dancing, lost in admiration of the dazzling commingling of kaleidoscopic colors which the whirling turmoil of gaudy figures below him presented, the ragged but real little prince of Wales was proclaiming his rights and his wrongs, denouncing the impostor, and clamoring for admission at the gates of Guildhall! The crowd enjoyed this episode prodigiously, and pressed forward and craned their necks to see the small rioter. Presently they began to taunt him and mock at him, purposely to goad him into a higher and still more entertaining fury. Tears of mortification sprung to his eyes, but he stood his ground and defied the mob right royally. Other taunts followed, added mockings stung him, and he exclaimed,—

"I tell ye again, you pack of unmannerly curs, I am the prince of Wales! And all forlorn and friendless as I be, with none to give me word of grace or help me in my need, yet will not I be driven from my ground, but will maintain it!"

"Though thou be prince or no prince, 'tis all one, thou be'st a gallant lad, and not friendless neither! Here stand I by thy side to prove it; and mind I tell thee thou might'st have a worser friend than Miles Hendon and yet not tire thy legs with seeking. Rest thy small jaw, my child, I talk the language of these base kennel-rats like to a very native."

The speaker was a sort of Don Caesar de Bazan in dress, aspect, and bearing. He was tall, trim-built, muscular. His doublet and trunks were of rich material, but faded and threadbare, and their goldlace adornments were sadly tarnished; his ruff was rumpled and damaged; the plume in his slouched hat was broken and had a bedraggled and disreputable look; at his side he wore a long rapier in a rusty iron sheath; his swaggering carriage marked him at once as a ruffler of the camp. The speech of this fantastic figure was received with an explosion of jeers and laughter. Some cried, " 'Tis another prince in disguise!" " 'Ware thy tongue, friend, belike he is dangerous!" "Marry, he looketh it—mark his eye!" "Pluck the lad from him—to the horse-pond wi' the cub!"

Instantly a hand was laid upon the prince, under the impulse of this happy thought; as instantly the stranger's long sword was out and the meddler went to the earth under a sounding thump with the flat of it. The next moment a score of voices shouted "Kill the dog! kill him! kill him!" and the mob closed in on the warrior, who backed himself against a wall and began to lay about him with his long weapon like a madman. His victims sprawled this way and that, but the mob-tide poured over their prostrate forms and dashed itself against the champion with undiminished fury. His moments seemed numbered, his destruction certain, when suddenly a trumpet-blast sounded, a voice shouted, "Way for the king's messenger!" and a troop of horsemen came charging down upon the mob, who fled out of harm's reach as fast as their legs could carry them. The bold stranger caught up the prince in his arms, and was soon far away from danger and the multitude.

Return we within the Guildhall. Suddenly, high above the jubilant roar and thunder of the revel, broke the clear peal of a bugle-note. There was instant silence,—a deep hush; then a single voice rose—that of the messenger from the palace—and began to pipe forth a proclamation, the whole multitude standing, listening. The closing words, solemnly pronounced, were—

"The king is dead!"

The great assemblage bent their heads upon their breasts with one accord; remained so, in profound silence, a few moments; then all sunk upon their knees in a body, stretched out their hands toward Tom, and a mighty shout burst forth that seemed to shake the building—

"Long live the king!"

Poor Tom's dazed eyes wandered abroad over this stupefying spectacle, and finally rested dreamily upon the kneeling princesses beside him, a moment, then upon the earl of Hertford. A sudden purpose dawned in his face. He said, in a low tone, at lord Hertford's ear—

"Answer me truly, on thy faith and honor! Uttered I here a command, the which none but a king might hold privilege and prerogative to utter, would such commandment be obeyed, and none rise up to say me nay?"

"None, my liege, in all these realms. In thy person bides the majesty of England. Thou art the king—thy word is law."

Tom responded, in a strong, earnest voice, and with great animation—

"Then shall the king's law be law of mercy, from this day, and never more be law of blood! Up from thy knees and away! To the Tower and say the king decrees the duke of Norfolk shall not die!"*

The words were caught up and carried eagerly from lip to lip far and wide over the hall, and as Hertford hurried from the presence, another prodigious shout burst forth—

"The reign of blood is ended! Long live Edward, king of England!"

CHAPTER XII

THE PRINCE'S TROUBLES BEGIN

As soon as Miles Hendon and the little prince were clear of the mob, they struck down through back lanes and alleys toward the river. Their way was unobstructed until they approached London Bridge; then they ploughed into the multitude again, Hendon keeping a fast grip upon the prince's—no, the king's—wrist. The tremendous news was already abroad, and the boy learned it from a

*See Note 7, at end of volume.

thousand voices at once—"The king is dead!" The tidings struck a chill to the heart of the poor little waif, and sent a shudder through his frame. He realized the greatness of his loss, and was filled with a bitter grief; for the grim tyrant who had been such a terror to others had always been gentle with him. The tears sprung to his eyes and blurred all objects. For an instant he felt himself the most forlorn, outcast, and forsaken of God's creatures—then another cry shook the night with its far-reaching thunders: "Long live King Edward the Sixth!" and this made his eyes kindle, and thrilled him with pride to his fingers' ends. "Ah," he thought, "how grand and strange it seems—I AM KING!"

Our friends threaded their way slowly through the throngs upon the Bridge. This structure, which had stood for six hundred years, and had been a noisy and populous thoroughfare all that time, was a curious affair, for a closely packed rank of stores and shops, with family quarters overhead, stretched along both sides of it, from one bank of the river to the other. The Bridge was a sort of town to itself; it had its inn, its beer houses, its bakeries, its haberdasheries, its food markets, its manufacturing industries, and even its church. It looked upon the two neighbors which it linked together—London and Southwark—as being well enough, as suburbs, but not otherwise particularly important. It was a close corporation, so to speak; it was a narrow town, of a single street a fifth of a mile long, its population was but a village population, and everybody in it knew all his fellow townsmen intimately, and had known their fathers and mothers before them—and all their little family affairs into the bargain. It had its aristocracy, of course— its fine old families of butchers, and bakers, and what-not, who had occupied the same old premises for five or six hundred years, and knew the great history of the Bridge from beginning to end, and all its strange legends; and who always talked bridgy talk, and thought bridgy thoughts, and lied in a long, level, direct, substantial bridgy way. It was just the sort of population to be narrow and ignorant and self-conceited. Children were born on the Bridge, were reared there, grew to old age and finally died without ever having set a foot upon any part of the world but London Bridge alone. Such people would naturally imagine that the mighty and interminable procession which moved through its street night and day, with its confused roar of shouts and cries, its neighings and bellowings and bleatings and its muffled thunder-tramp, was the one great thing in this world, and themselves somehow the proprietors of it. And so they were in effect—at least they could exhibit it from their windows, and did—for a consideration— whenever a returning king or hero gave it a fleeting splendor, for there was no place like it for affording a long, straight, uninterrupted view of marching columns.

Men born and reared upon the Bridge found life unendurably

dull and inane, elsewhere. History tells of one of these who left the Bridge at the age of seventy-one and retired to the country. But he could only fret and toss in his bed; he could not go to sleep, the deep stillness was so painful, so awful, so oppressive. When he was worn out with it, at last, he fled back to his old home, a lean and haggard spectre, and fell peacefully to rest and pleasant dreams under the lulling music of the lashing waters and the boom and crash and thunder of London Bridge.

In the times of which we are writing, the Bridge furnished "object lessons" in English history, for its children—namely, the livid and decaying heads of renowned men impaled upon iron spikes atop of its gateways. But we digress.

Hendon's lodgings were in the little inn on the Bridge. As he neared the door with his small friend, a rough voice said—

"So, thou'rt come at last! Thou'lt not escape again, I warrant thee; and if pounding thy bones to a pudding can teach thee somewhat, thou'lt not keep us waiting another time, mayhap"—and John Canty put out his hand to seize the boy.

Miles Hendon stepped in the way, and said—

"Not too fast, friend. Thou art needlessly rough, methinks. What is the lad to thee?"

"If it be any business of thine to make and meddle in others' affairs, he is my son."

" 'Tis a lie!" cried the little king, hotly.

"Boldly said, and I believe thee, whether thy small head-piece be sound or cracked, my boy. But whether this scurvy ruffian be thy father or no, 'tis all one, he shall not have thee to beat thee and abuse, according to his threat, so thou prefer to abide with me."

"I do, I do—I know him not, I loathe him, and will die before I will go with him."

"Then 'tis settled, and there is nought more to say."

"We will see, as to that!" exclaimed John Canty, striding past Hendon to get at the boy; "by force shall he"—

"If thou do but touch him, thou animated offal, I will spit thee like a goose!" said Hendon, barring the way and laying his hand upon his sword hilt. Canty drew back. "Now mark ye," continued Hendon, "I took this lad under my protection when a mob of such as thou would have mishandled him, mayhap killed him; dost imagine I will desert him now to a worser fate?—for whether thou art his father or no,—and sooth to say, I think it is a lie—a decent swift death were better for such a lad than life in such brute hands as thine. So go thy ways, and set quick about it, for I like not much bandying of words, being not overpatient in my nature."

John Canty moved off, muttering threats and curses, and was swallowed from sight in the crowd. Hendon ascended three flights of stairs to his room, with his charge, after ordering a meal to be sent thither. It was a poor apartment, with a shabby bed and some odds and ends of old furniture in it, and was vaguely lighted by a couple of sickly candles. The little king dragged himself to the bed and lay down upon it, almost exhausted with hunger and fatigue. He had been on his feet a good part of a day and a night, for it was now two or three o'clock in the morning, and had eaten nothing meantime. He murmured drowsily—

"Prithee call me when the table is spread," and sunk into a deep sleep immediately.

A smile twinkled in Hendon's eye, and he said to himself—

"By the mass, the little beggar takes to one's quarters and usurps one's bed with as natural and easy a grace as if he owned them— with never a by-your-leave or so-please-it-you, or anything of the sort. In his diseased ravings he called himself the prince of Wales, and bravely doth he keep up the character. Poor little friendless rat, doubtless his mind has been disordered with ill usage. Well, I will be his friend; I have saved him, and it draweth me strongly to him; already I love the bold-tongued little rascal. How soldier-like he faced the smutty rabble and flung back his high defiance! And what a comely, sweet and gentle face he hath, now that sleep hath conjured away its troubles and its griefs. I will teach him, I will cure his malady; yea, I will be his elder brother, and care for him and watch over him; and whoso would shame him or do him hurt, may order his shroud, for though I be burnt for it he shall need it!"

He bent over the boy and contemplated him with kind and pitying interest, tapping the young cheek tenderly and smoothing back the tangled curls with his great brown hand. A slight shiver passed over the boy's form. Hendon muttered—

"See, now, how like a man it was to let him lie here uncovered and fill his body with deadly rheums. Now what shall I do? 'twill wake him to take him up and put him within the bed, and he sorely needeth sleep."

He looked about for extra covering, but finding none, doffed his doublet and wrapped the lad in it, saying, "I am used to nipping air and scant apparel, 'tis little I shall mind the cold"—then walked up and down the room to keep his blood in motion, soliloquizing, as before.

"His injured mind persuades him he is prince of Wales; 'twill be odd to have a prince of Wales still with us, now that he that *was* the prince is prince no more, but king,—for this poor mind is set upon the one fantasy, and will not reason out that now it should cast by the prince and call itself the king. . . . If my father liveth still, after these seven years that I have heard naught from home in my foreign dungeon, he will welcome the poor lad and give him generous shelter for my sake; so will my good elder brother, Arthur; my other brother, Hugh—but I will crack his crown, an *he* interfere, the fox-hearted, ill-conditioned animal! Yes, thither will we fare— and straightway, too."

A servant entered with a smoking meal, disposed it upon a small deal table, placed the chairs, and took his departure, leaving such cheap lodgers as these to wait upon themselves. The door slammed after him, and the noise woke the boy, who sprung to a sitting posture, and shot a glad glance about him; then a grieved look came into his face and he murmured, to himself, with a deep sigh, "Alack, it was but a dream, woe is me." Next he noticed Miles Hendon's doublet—glanced from that to Hendon, comprehended the sacrifice that had been made for him, and said, gently—

"Thou art good to me, yes, thou art very good to me. Take it and put it on—I shall not need it more."

Then he got up and walked to the washstand in the corner, and stood there, waiting. Hendon said in a cheery voice—

"We'll have a right hearty sup and bite, now, for every thing is savory and smoking hot, and that and thy nap together will make thee a little man again, never fear!"

The boy made no answer, but bent a steady look, that was filled with grave surprise, and also somewhat touched with impatience, upon the tall knight of the sword. Hendon was puzzled, and said—

"What's amiss?"

"Good sir, I would wash me."

"O, is that all! Ask no permission of Miles Hendon for aught thou cravest. Make thyself perfectly free here, and welcome, with all that are his belongings."

Still the boy stood, and moved not; more, he tapped the floor once or twice with his small impatient foot. Hendon was wholly perplexed. Said he—

"Bless us, what is it?"

"Prithee pour the water, and make not so many words!"

Hendon, suppressing a horse-laugh, and saying to himself, "By all the saints, but this is admirable!" stepped briskly forward and did the small insolent's bidding; then stood by, in a sort of stupefaction, until the command, "Come—the towel!" woke sharply up. He took up a towel, from under the boy's nose, and handed it to him, without comment. He now proceeded to comfort his own face with a wash, and while he was at it his adopted child seated himself at the table and prepared to fall to. Hendon despatched his ablutions with alacrity, then drew back the other chair and was about to place himself at table, when the boy said, indignantly—

"Forbear! Wouldst sit in the presence of the king?"

This blow staggered Hendon to his foundations. He muttered to himself, "Lo, the poor thing's madness is up with the time! it hath changed with the great change that is come to the realm, and now in fancy is he *king!* Good lack, I must humor the conceit, too—there is no other way—faith, he would order me to the Tower, else!"

And pleased with this jest, he removed the chair from the table, took his stand behind the king, and proceeded to wait upon him in the courtliest way he was capable of.

When the king ate, the rigor of his royal dignity relaxed a little, and with his growing contentment came a desire to talk. He said—

"I think thou callest thyself Miles Hendon, if I heard thee aright?"

"Yes, sire," Miles replied; then observed to himself, "If I *must* humor the poor lad's madness, I must sire him, I must majesty him, I must not go by halves, I must stick at nothing that belongeth to the part I play, else shall I play it ill and work evil to this charitable and kindly cause."

The king warmed his heart with a second glass of wine, and said— "I would know thee—tell me thy story. Thou hast a gallant way with thee, a noble—art nobly born?"

"We are of the tail of the nobility, good your majesty. My father is a baronet—one of the smaller lords, by knight service*—Sir Richard Hendon, of Hendon Hall, by Monk's Holm in Kent."

"The name has escaped my memory. Go on—tell me thy story."

"'Tis not much, your majesty, yet perchance it may beguile a short half hour for want of a better. My father, Sir Richard, is very rich, and of a most generous nature. My mother died whilst I was yet a boy. I have two brothers: Arthur, my elder, with a soul like to his father's; and Hugh, younger than I, a mean spirit, covetous, treacherous, vicious, underhanded—a reptile. Such was he from the cradle; such was he ten years past, when I last saw him—a ripe rascal at nineteen, I being twenty, then, and Arthur twenty-two. There is none other of us but the lady Edith, my cousin—she was sixteen, then—beautiful, gentle, good, the daughter of an earl, the last of her race, heiress of a great fortune and a lapsed title. My father was her guardian. I loved her and she loved me; but she was betrothed to Arthur from the cradle, and Sir Richard would not suffer the contract to be broken. Arthur loved another maid, and bade us be of good cheer and hold fast to the hope that delay and luck together would some day give success to our several causes. Hugh loved the lady Edith's fortune, though in truth he said it was herself he loved—but then 'twas his way, alway, to say one thing and mean the other. But he lost his arts upon the girl: he could deceive my father, but none else. My father loved him best of us all, and trusted and believed him; for he was the youngest child and others hated him—these qualities being in all ages sufficient to win a parent's dearest love; and he had a smooth persuasive tongue, with an admirable gift of lying—and these be qualities which do mightily assist a blind affection to cozen itself. I was wild—in troth I might go yet farther and say *very* wild, though 'twas a wildness of an innocent sort, since it hurt none but me, brought shame to none, nor loss, nor had in it any taint of crime or baseness, or what might

*He refers to the order of baronets, or baronettes,—the *barones minores,* as distinct from the parliamentary barons;—not, it need hardly be said, the baronets of later creation.

not beseem mine honorable degree.

"Yet did my brother Hugh turn these faults to good account—he seeing that our brother Arthur's health was but indifferent, and hoping the worst might work him profit were I swept out of the path—so,—but 'twere a long tale, good my liege, and little worth the telling. Briefly, then, this brother did deftly magnify my faults and make them crimes; ending his base work with finding a silken ladder in mine apartments—conveyed thither by his own means—and did convince my father by this, and suborned evidence of servants and other lying knaves, that I was minded to carry off my Edith and marry with her, in rank defiance of his will.

"Three years of banishment from home and England might make a soldier and a man of me, my father said, and teach me some degree of wisdom. I fought out my long probation in the continental wars, tasting sumptuously of hard knocks, privation and adventure; but in my last battle I was taken captive, and during the seven years that have waxed and waned since then, a foreign dungeon hath harbored me. Through wit and courage I won to the free air at last, and fled hither straight; and am but just arrived, right poor in purse and raiment, and poorer still in knowledge of what these dull seven years have wrought at Hendon Hall, its people and belongings. So please you, sir, my meagre tale is told."

"Thou hast been shamefully abused!" said the little king, with a flashing eye. "But I will right thee—by the cross will I! The king hath said it."

Then, fired by the story of Miles's wrongs, he loosed his tongue and poured the history of his own recent misfortunes into the ears of his astonished listener. When he had finished, Miles said to himself—

"Lo, what an imagination he hath! Verily this is no common mind; else, crazed or sane, it could not weave so straight and gaudy a tale as this out of the airy nothings wherewith it hath wrought this curious romaunt. Poor ruined little head, it shall not lack friend or shelter whilst I bide with the living. He shall never leave my side; he shall be my pet, my little comrade. And he shall be cured!— aye, made whole and sound—then will he make himself a name—and proud shall I be to say, 'Yes, he is mine—I took him, a homeless little ragamuffin, but I saw what was in him, and I said his name would be heard someday—behold him, observe him—was I right?' "

The king spoke—in a thoughtful, measured voice—

"Thou didst save me injury and shame, perchance my life, and so my crown. Such service demandeth rich reward. Name thy desire, and so it be within the compass of my royal power, it is thine."

This fantastic suggestion startled Hendon out of his revery. He was about to thank the king and put the matter aside with saying he had only done his duty and desired no reward, but a wiser thought came into his head, and he asked leave to be silent a few moments and consider the gracious offer—an idea which the king gravely approved, remarking that it was best to be not too hasty with a thing of such great import.

Miles reflected during some moments, then said to himself, "Yes, that is the thing to do—by any other means it were impossible to get at it—and certes, this hour's experience has taught me 'twould be most wearing and inconvenient to continue it as it is. Yes, I will propose it; 'twas a happy accident that I did not throw the chance away." Then he dropped upon one knee and said—

"My poor service went not beyond the limit of a subject's simple duty, and therefore hath no merit; but since your majesty is pleased to hold it worthy some reward, I take heart of grace to make petition to this effect. Near four hundred years ago, as your grace knoweth, there being ill blood betwixt John, King of England, and the King of France, it was decreed that two champions should fight together in the lists, and so settle the dispute by what is called the arbitrament of God. These two kings, and the Spanish king, being assembled to witness and judge the conflict, the French champion appeared; but so redoubtable was he, that our English knights refused to measure weapons with him. So the matter, which was a weighty one, was like to go against the English monarch by default. Now in the Tower lay the lord de Courcy, the mightiest arm in England, stripped of his honors and possessions, and wasting with long captivity. Appeal was made to him; he gave assent, and came forth arrayed for battle; but no sooner did the Frenchman glimpse his huge frame and hear his famous name but he fled away, and the French king's cause was lost. King John restored de Courcy's titles and possessions, and said, 'Name thy wish and thou shalt have it, though it cost me half my kingdom;' whereat de Courcy, kneeling, as I do now, made answer, 'This, then, I ask, my liege; that I and my successors may have and hold the privilege of remaining covered in the presence of the kings of England, henceforth while the throne shall last.' The boon was granted, as your majesty knoweth; and there hath been no time, these four hundred years, that that line has failed of an heir; and so, even unto this day, the head of that ancient house still weareth his hat or helm before the king's majesty, without let or hindrance, and this none other may do.* Invoking this precedent in aid of my prayer, I beseech the king to grant to me but this once grace and privilege—to my more than sufficient reward—and none other, to wit: that I and my heirs, forever, may *sit* in the presence of the majesty of England!"

"Rise, Sir Miles Hendon, Knight," said the king, gravely—giving the accolade with Hendon's sword—"rise, and seat thyself. Thy petition is granted. Whilst England remains, and the crown continues, the privilege shall not lapse."

His majesty walked apart, musing, and Hendon dropped into a chair at table, observing to himself, " 'Twas a brave thought, and

*The lords of Kingsale, descendants of de Courcy, still enjoy this curious privilege.

hath wrought me a mighty deliverance; my legs are grievously wearied. An' I had not thought of that, I must have had to stand for weeks, till my poor lad's wits are cured." After a little, he went on, "And so I become a knight of the Kingdom of Dreams and Shadows! A most odd and strange position, truly, for one so matter-of-fact as I. I will not laugh—no, God forbid, for this thing which is so substanceless to me is *real* to him. And to me, also, in one way, it is not a falsity, for it reflects with truth the sweet and generous spirit that is in him." After a pause: "Ah, what if he should call me by my fine title before folk!—there'd be a merry contrast betwixt my glory and my raiment! But no matter: let him call me what he will, so it please him; I shall be content."

CHAPTER XIII

THE DISAPPEARANCE OF THE PRINCE

A heavy drowsiness presently fell upon the two comrades. The king said—

"Remove these rags"—meaning his clothing.

Hendon disappareled the boy without dissent or remark, tucked him up in bed, then glanced about the room, saying to himself, ruefully, "He hath taken my bed again, as before—marry, what shall *I* do?" The little king observed his perplexity, and dissipated it with a word. He said, sleepily—

"Thou wilt sleep athwart the door, and guard it." In a moment more he was out of his troubles, in a deep slumber.

"Dear heart, he should have been born a king!" muttered Hendon, admiringly; "he playeth the part to a marvel."

Then he stretched himself across the door, on the floor, saying contentedly—

"I have lodged worse for seven years; 'twould be but ill gratitude to Him above to find fault with this."

He dropped asleep as the dawn appeared. Toward noon he rose, uncovered his unconscious ward—a section at a time—and took his measure with a string. The king awoke, just as he had completed his work, complained of the cold, and asked what he was doing.

" 'Tis done, now, my liege," said Hendon; "I have a bit of business outside, but will presently return; sleep thou again—thou needest it. There—let me cover thy head also—thou'lt be warm the sooner."

The king was back in dreamland before this speech was ended. Miles slipped softly out, and slipped as softly in again, in the course of thirty or forty minutes, with a complete second-hand suit of boy's clothing, of cheap material, and showing signs of wear; but tidy, and suited to the season of the year. He seated himself, and began to overhaul his purchase, mumbling to himself—

"A longer purse would have got a better sort, but when one has not the long purse one must be content with what a short one may do—

> " 'There was a woman in our town,
> In our town did dwell'—

"He stirred, methinks—I must sing in a less thunderous key; 'tis not good to mar his sleep, with this journey before him and he so wearied out, poor chap. . . . This garment—'tis well enough—a stitch here and another one there will set it aright. This other is better, albeit a stitch or two will not come amiss in it, likewise. . . . *These* be very good and sound, and will keep his small feet warm and dry—an odd new thing to him, belike, since he has doubtless been used to foot it bare, winters and summers the same. . . . Would thread were bread, seeing one getteth a year's sufficiency for a farthing, and such a brave big needle without cost, for mere love. Now shall I have the demon's own time to thread it!"

And so he had. He did as men have always done, and probably always will do, to the end of time—held the needle still, and tried to thrust the thread through the eye, which is the opposite of a woman's way. Time and time again the thread missed the mark, going sometimes on one side of the needle, sometimes on the other, sometimes doubling up against the shaft; but he was patient, having been through these experiences before, when he was soldiering. He succeeded at last, and took up the garment that had lain waiting, meantime, across his lap, and began his work.

"The inn is paid—the breakfast that is to come, included—and there is wherewithal left to buy a couple of donkeys and meet our little costs for the two or three days betwixt this and the plenty that awaits us at Hendon Hall—

> " 'She loved her hus'—

"Boby o' me! I have driven the needle under my nail! . . . It matters little—'tis not a novelty—yet 'tis not a convenience, neither. . . . We shall be merry there, little one, never doubt it! Thy troubles will vanish, there, and likewise thy sad distemper—

> " 'She loved her husband dearilee,
> But another man'—

"These be noble large stitches!"—holding the garment up and viewing it admiringly—"they have a grandeur and a majesty that do cause these small stingy ones of the tailor-man to look mighty paltry and plebeian—

> " 'She loved her husband dearilee,
> But another man he loved she,'—

"Mary, 'tis done—a goodly piece of work, too, and wrought with expedition. Now will I wake him, apparel him, pour for him, feed him, and then will we hie us to the mart by the Tabard inn in Southwark and—be pleased to rise, my liege!—he answereth not—what ho, my liege!—of a truth must I profane his sacred person with a touch, sith his slumber is deaf to speech. What!"

He threw back the covers—the boy was gone!

He stared about him in speechless astonishment for a moment; noticed for the first time that his ward's ragged raiment was also missing, then he began to rage and storm, and shout for the innkeeper.—At that moment a servant entered with the breakfast.

"Explain, thou limb of Satan, or thy time is come!" roared the man of war, and made so savage a spring toward the waiter that this latter could not find his tongue, for the instant, for fright and surprise. "Where is the boy?"

In disjointed and trembling syllables the man gave the information desired.

"You were hardly gone from the place, your worship, when a youth came running and said it was your worship's will that the boy come to you straight, at the bridge-end on the Southwark side. I brought him hither; and when he woke the lad and gave his message, the lad did grumble some little for being distrubed 'so early,' as he called it, but straightway trussed on his rags and went with the youth, only saying it had been better manners that your worship came yourself, not sent a stranger—and so"—

"And so thou'rt a fool!—a fool, and easily cozened—hang all thy breed! Yet mayhap no hurt is done. Possibly no harm is meant the boy. I will go fetch him. Make the table ready. Stay! the coverings of the bed were disposed as if one lay beneath them—happened that by accident?"

"I know not, good your worship. I saw the youth meddle with them—he that came for the boy."

"Thousand deaths! 'twas done to deceive me— 'tis plain 'twas done to gain time. Hark ye! Was that youth alone?"

"All alone, your worship."

"Art sure?"

"Sure, your worship."

"Collect thy scattered wits—bethink thee—take time, man."

After a moment's thought, the servant said—

"When he came, none came with him; but now I remember me that as the two stepped into the throng of the Bridge, a ruffian-looking man plumged out from some near place; and just as he was joining them"—

"What *then?*—out with it!" thundered the impatient Hendon, interrupting.

"Just then the crowd lapped them up and closed them in, and I saw no more, being called by my master, who was in a rage because

a joint that the scrivener had ordered was forgot, though I take all
the saints to witness that to blame *me* for that miscarriage were
like holding the unborn babe to judgment for sins com"—

"Out of my sight, idiot! Thy prating drives me mad! Hold!
whither art flying? Canst not bide still an instant? Went they toward
Southwark?"

"Even so, your worship—for, as I said before, as to that detestable
joint, the babe unborn is no whit more blameless than"—

"Art here *yet!* And prating still? Vanish, lest I throttle thee!"
The servitor vanished. Hendon followed after him, passed him,
and plunged down the stairs two steps at a stride, muttering,
" 'Tis that scurvy villain that claimed he was his son. I have lost thee,
my poor little mad master—it is a bitter thought—and I had come
to love thee so! No! by book and bell, *not* lost! Not lost, for I will
ransack the land till I find thee again. Poor child, yonder is his
breakfast—and mine, but I have no hunger now—so, let the rats
have it—speed, speed! that is the word!" As he wormed his swift
way through the noisy multitudes upon the Bridge, he several times
said to himself—clinging to the thought as if it were a particularly
pleasing one—"He grumbled, but he *went*—he went, yes, because
he thought Miles Hendon asked it, sweet lad—he would ne'er have
done it for another, I know it well!"

CHAPTER XIV

"LE ROI EST MORT—VIVE LE ROI"

Toward daylight of the same morning, Tom Canty stirred out of
a heavy sleep and opened his eyes in the dark. He lay silent a few
moments, trying to analyze his confused thoughts and impressions,
and get some sort of meaning out of them, then suddenly he burst
out in a rapturous but guarded voice—

"I see it all, I see it all! Now God be thanked, I am indeed awake
at last! Come, joy! vanish, sorrow! Ho, Nan! Bet! kick off your straw
and hie ye hither to my side, till I do pour into your unbelieving ears
the wildest madcap dream that ever the spirits of night did conjure
up to astonish the soul of man withal! . . . Ho, Nan, I say! Bet!" . . .

A dim form appeared at his side, and a voice said—

"Wilt deign to deliver thy commands!"

"Commands? . . . O, woe is me, I know thy voice! Speak, thou—
who am I?"

"Thou? In sooth, yesternight wert thou the prince of Wales, to-
day art thou my most gracious liege, Edward, King of England."

Tom buried his head among his pillows, murmuring plaintively—

"Alack, it was no dream! Go to thy rest, sweet sir—leave me to
my sorrows."

Tom slept again, and after a time he had this pleasant dream. He thought it was summer and he was playing, all alone, in the fair meadow called Goodman's Fields, when a dwarf only a foot high, with long red whiskers and a humped back appeared to him suddenly and said, "Dig, by that stump." He did so, and found twelve bright new pennies—wonderful riches! Yet this was not the best of it; for the dwarf said—

"I know thee. Thou art a good lad and deserving; thy distresses shall end, for the day of thy reward is come. Dig here every seventh day, and thou shalt find always the same treasure, twelve bright new pennies. Tell none—keep the secret."

Then the dwarf vanished, and Tom flew to Offal Court with his prize, saying to himself, "Every night will I give my father a penny; he will think I begged it, it will glad his heart, and I shall no more be beaten. One penny every week the good priest that teacheth me shall have; mother, Nan and Bet the other four. We be done with hunger and rags, now, done with fears and frets and savage usage."

In his dream he reached his sordid home all out of breath, but with eyes dancing with grateful enthusiasm; cast four of his pennies into his mother's lap and cried out—

"They are for thee!—all of them, every one!—for thee and Nan and Bet—and honestly come by, not begged nor stolen!"

The happy and astonished mother strained him to her breast and exclaimed—

"It waxeth late—may it please your majesty to rise?"

Ah, that was not the answer he was expecting. The dream had snapped asunder—he was awake.

He opened his eyes—the richly clad First Lord of the Bedchamber was kneeling by his couch. The gladness of the lying dream faded away—the poor boy recognized that he was still a captive and a king. The room was filled with courtiers clothed in purple mantles—the mourning color—and with noble servants of the monarch. Tom sat up in bed and gazed out from the heavy silken curtains upon this fine company.

The weighty business of dressing began, and one courtier after another knelt and paid his court and offered to the little King his condolences upon his heavy loss, whilst the dressing proceeded. In the beginning, a shirt was taken up by the Chief Equerry in Waiting, who passed it to the First Lord of the Buckhounds, who passed it to the Second Gentleman of the Bedchamber, who passed it to the Head Ranger of Windsor Forest, who passed it to the Third Groom of the Stole, who passed it to the Chancellor Royal of the Duchy of Lancaster, who passed it to the Master of the Wardrobe, who passed it to Norroy King-at-Arms, who passed it to the Constable of the Tower, who passed it to the Chief Steward of the Household, who passed it to the Hereditary Grand Diaperer, who passed it to the Lord High Admiral of England, who passed it to the Archbishop of

Canterbury, who passed it to the First Lord of the Bedchamber, who took what was left of it and put it on Tom. Poor little wondering chap, it reminded him of passing buckets at a fire.

Each garment in its turn had to go through this slow and solemn process; consequently Tom grew very weary of the ceremony; so weary that he felt an almost gushing gratefulness when he at last saw his long silken hose begin the journey down the line and knew that the end of the matter was drawing near. But he exulted too soon. The first Lord of the Bedchamber received the hose and was about to encase Tom's legs in them, when a sudden flush invaded his face and he hurriedly hustled the things back into the hands of the Archbishop of Canterbury with an astounded look and a whispered, "See, my lord!"—pointing to a something connected with the hose. The Archbishop paled, then flushed, and passed the hose to the Lord High Admiral, whispering, "See, my lord!" The Admiral passed ths hose to the Hereditary Grand Diaperer, and had hardly breath enough in his body to ejaculate, "See, my lord!" The hose drifted backward along the line, to the Chief Steward of the Household, the Constable of the Tower, Norroy King-at-Arms, the Master of the Wardrobe, the Chancellor Royal of the Duchy of Lancaster, the Third Groom of the Stole, the Head Ranger of Windsor Forest, the Second Gentleman of the Bedchamber, the First Lord of the Buckhounds,—accompanied always with that amazed and frightened "See! see!"—till they finally reached the hands of the Chief Equerry in Waiting, who gazed a moment, with a pallid face, upon what had caused all this dismay, then hoarsely whispered, "Body of my life, a tag gone from a truss point!—to the Tower with the Head Keeper of the King's Hose!"—after which he leaned upon the shoulder of the First Lord of the Buckhounds to regather his vanished strength whilst fresh hose, without any damaged strings to them, were brought.

But all things must have an end, and so in time Tom Canty was in a condition to get out of bed. The proper official poured water, the proper official engineered the washing, the proper official stood by with a towel, and by and by Tom got safely through the purifying stage and was ready for the services of the Hairdresser-royal. When he at length emerged from this master's hands, he was a gracious figure and as pretty as a girl, in his mantle and trunks of purple satin, and purple-plumed cap. He now moved in state toward his breakfast room, through the midst of the courtly assemblage; and as he passed, these fell back, leaving his way free, and dropped upon their knees.

After breakfast he was conducted, with regal ceremony, attended by his great officers and his guard of fifty Gentlemen Pensioners bearing gilt battle-axes, to the throne-room, where he proceeded to transact business of state. His "uncle," lord Hertford, took his stand by the throne, to assist the royal mind with wise counsel.

The body of illustrious men named by the late king as his executors, appeared, to ask Tom's approval of certain acts of theirs— rather a form, and yet not wholly a form, since there was no Protector as yet. The Archbishop of Canterbury made report of the decree of the Council of Executors concerning the obsequies of his late most illustrious majesty, and finished by reading the signatures of the Executors, to wit: the Archbishop of Canterbury; the Lord Chancellor of England; William Lord St. John; John Lord Russell; Edward Earl of Hertford; John Viscount Lisle; Cuthbert Bishop of Durham—

Tom was not listening—an earlier clause of the document was puzzling him. At this point he turned and whispered to lord Hertford—

"What day did he say the burial hath been appointed for?"

"The 16th of the coming month, my liege."

" 'Tis a strange folly. Will he keep?"

Poor chap, he was still new to the customs of royalty; he was used to seeing the forlorn dead of Offal Court hustled out of the way with a very different sort of expedition. However, the lord Hertford set his mind at rest with a word or two.

A secretary of state presented an order of the Council appointing the morrow at eleven for the reception of the foreign ambassadors, and desired the king's assent.

Tom turned an inquiring look toward Hertford, who whispered—

"Your majesty will signify consent. They come to testify their royal masters' sense of the heavy calamity which hath visited your grace and the realm of England."

Tom did as he was bidden. Another secretary began to read a preamble concerning the expenses of the late king's household, which had amounted to £28,000 during the preceding six months— a sum so vast that it made Tom Canty gasp; he gasped again when the fact appeared that £20,000 of this money was still owing and unpaid;* and once more when it appeared that the king's coffers were about empty, and his twelve hundred servants much embarrassed for lack of the wages due them. Tom spoke out, with lively apprehension.

"We be going to the dogs, 'tis plain. 'Tis meet and necessary that we take a smaller house and set the servants at large, sith they be of no value but to make delay, and trouble one with offices that harass the spirit and shame the soul, they misbecoming any but a doll, that hath nor brains nor hands to help itself withal. I remember me of a small house that standeth over against the fish-market, by Billingsgate"—

A sharp pressure upon Tom's arm stopped his foolish tongue and sent a blush to his face; but no countenance there betrayed any sign that this strange speech had been remarked or given concern.

A secretary made report that forasmuch as the late king had

* Hume.

provided in his will for conferring the ducal degree upon the earl of
Hertford and raising his brother, Sir Thomas Seymour, to the
peerage, and likewise Hertford's son to an earldom, together with
similar aggrandizements to other great servants of the crown, the
Council had resolved to hold a sitting on the 16th of February for the
delivering and confirming of these honors; and that meantime, the
late king not having granted, in writing, estates suitable to the
support of these dignities, the Council, knowing his private wishes
in that regard, had thought proper to grant to Seymour " £500
lands," and to Hertford's son "800 pound lands, and 300 pound of
the next bishop's lands which should fall vacant,"—his present
majesty being willing.*

Tom was about to blurt out something about the propriety of
paying the late King's debts first, before squandering all this money;
but a timely touch upon his arm, from the thoughtful Hertford,
saved him this indiscretion; wherefore he gave the royal assent,
without spoken comment, but with much inward discomfort. While
he sat reflecting, a moment, over the ease with which he was doing
strange and glittering miracles, a happy thought shot into his mind:
why not make his mother Duchess of Offal Court and give her an
estate? But a sorrowful thought swept it instantly away: he was only
a king in name, these grave veterans and great nobles were his
masters; to them his mother was only the creature of a diseased
mind; they would simply listen to his project with unbelieving ears,
then send for the doctor.

The dull work went tediously on. Petitions were read, and
proclamations, patents, and all manner of wordy, repetitious and
wearisome papers relating to the public business; and at last Tom
sighed pathetically and murmured to himself, "In what have I
offended, that the good God should take me away from the fields
and the free air and the sunshine, to shut me up here and make me
a king and afflict me so?" Then his poor muddled head nodded a
while, and presently dropped to his shoulder; and the business of
the empire came to a stand-still for want of that august factor, the
ratifying power. Silence ensued, around the slumbering child, and
the sages of the realm ceased from their deliberations.

During the forenoon, Tom had an enjoyable hour, by permission
of his keepers, Hertford and St. John, with the lady Elizabeth and
the little lady Jane Grey; though the spirits of the princesses were
rather subdued by the mighty stroke that had fallen upon the royal
house; and at the end of the visit his "elder sister"—afterwards the
"Bloody Mary" of history—chilled him with a solemn interview
which had but one merit in his eyes, its brevity. He had a few
moments to himself, and then a slim lad of about twelve years of
age was admitted to his presence, whose clothing, except his snowy
ruff and the laces about his wrists, was of black,—doublet, hose and
all. He bore no badge of mourning but a knot of purple ribbon on his

* Hume.

shoulder. He advanced hesitatingly, with head bowed and bare, and dropped upon one knee in front of Tom. Tom sat still and contemplated him soberly for a moment. Then he said—

"Rise, lad. Who art thou? What wouldst have?"

The boy rose, and stood at graceful ease, but with an aspect of concern in his face. He said—

"Of a surety thou must remember me, my lord. I am thy whipping-boy."

"My *whipping*-boy?"

"The same, your grace. I am Humphrey—Humphrey Marlow."

Tom perceived that here was some one whom his keepers ought to have posted him about. The situation was delicate. What should he do?—pretend that he knew this lad, and then betray by his every utterance, that he had never heard of him before? No, that would not do. An idea came to his relief: accidents like this might be likely to happen with some frequency, now that business urgencies would often call Hertford and St. John from his side, they being members of the council of executors; therefore perhaps it would be well to strike out a plan himself to meet the requirements of such emergencies. Yes, that would be a wise course—he would practise on this boy, and see what sort of success he might achieve. So he stroked his brow, perplexedly, a moment or two, and presently said—

"Now I seem to remember thee somewhat—but my wit is clogged and dim with suffering"—

"Alack, my poor master!" ejaculated the whipping-boy, with feeling; adding, to himself, "In truth 'tis as they said—his mind is gone—alas, poor soul! But misfortune catch me, how am I forgetting! they said one might not seem to observe that aught is wrong with him."

"'Tis strange how my memory doth wanton with me these days," said Tom. "But mind it not—I mend apace—a little clew doth often serve to bring me back again the things and names which had escaped me. [And not they, only, forsooth, but e'en such as I ne'er heard before—as this lad shall see.] Give thy business speech."

"'Tis matter of small weight, my liege, yet will I touch upon it an' it please your grace. Two days gone by, when your majesty faulted thrice in your Greek—in the morning lessons,—dost remember it?"

"Y-e-s—methinks I do. [It is not much of a lie—an' I had meddled with the Greek at all, I had not faulted simply thrice, but forty times.] Yes, I do recall it, now—go on."

—"The master, being wroth with what he termed such slovenly and doltish work, did promise that he would soundly whip me for it —and"—

"Whip *thee!*" said Tom, astonished out of his presence of mind. "Why should he whip *thee* for faults of mine?"

"Ah, your grace forgetteth again. He always scourgeth me, when thou dost fail in thy lessons."

"True, true—I had forgot. Thou teachest me in private—then if I fail, he argueth that thy office was lamely done, and"—

"O, my liege, what words are these? I, the humblest of thy servants, presume to teach *thee?*"

"Then where is thy blame? What riddle is this? Am I in truth gone mad, or is it thou? Explain—speak out."

"But good your majesty, there's nought that needeth simplifying. —None may visit the sacred person of the prince of Wales with blows; wherefore when he faulteth, 'tis I that take them; and meet it is and right, for that it is mine office and my livelihood."*

Tom stared at the tranquil boy, observing to himself, "Lo, it is a wonderful thing,—a most strange and curious trade; I marvel they have not hired a boy to take my combings and my dressings for me— would heaven they would!—an' they will do this thing, I will take my lashings in mine own person, giving God thanks for the change." Then he said aloud—

"And hast thou been beaten, poor friend, according to the promise?"

"No, good your majesty, my punishment was appointed for this day, and peradventure it may be annulled, as unbefitting the season of mourning that is come upon us; I know not, and so have made bold to come hither and remind your grace about your gracious promise to intercede in my behalf"—

"With the master? To save thee thy whipping?"

"Ah thou dost remember!"

"My memory mendeth, thou seest. Set thy mind at ease—thy back shall go unscathed—I will see to it."

"O, thanks, my good lord!" cried the boy, dropping upon his knee again. "Mayhap I have ventured far enow; and yet" . . .

Seeing Master Humphrey hesitate, Tom encouraged him to go on, saying he was "in the granting mood."

"Then will I speak it out, for it lieth near my heart. Sith thou art no more prince of Wales but King, thou canst order matters as thou wilt, with none to say thee nay; wherefore it is not in reason that thou wilt longer vex thyself with dreary studies, but wilt burn thy books and turn thy mind to things less irksome. Then am I ruined, and mine orphan sisters with me!"

"Ruined? Prithee how?"

"My back is my bread, O my gracious liege! if it go idle, I starve. An' thou cease from study, mine office is gone, thou'lt need no whipping-boy. Do not turn me away!"

Tom was touched with this pathetic distress. He said, with a right royal burst of generosity—

"Discomfort thyself no further, lad. Thine office shall be permanent in thee and thy line, forever." Then he struck the boy a light blow on the shoulder with the flat of his sword, exclaiming,

*See Note 8, at end of volume.

"Rise, Humphrey Marlow, Hereditary Grand Whipping-Boy to the royal house of England! Banish sorrow—I will betake me to my books again, and study so ill that they must in justice treble thy wage, so mightily shall the business of thine office be augmented."

The grateful Humphrey responded fervidly—

"Thanks, O most noble master, this princely lavishness doth far surpass my most distempered dreams of fortune. Now shall I be happy all my days, and all the house of Marlow after me."

Tom had wit enough to perceive that here was a lad who could be useful to him. He encouraged Humphrey to talk, and he was nothing loath. He was delighted to believe that he was helping in Tom's "cure"; for always, as soon as he had finished calling back to Tom's diseased mind the various particulars of his experiences and adventures in the royal school-room and elsewhere about the palace, he noticed that Tom was then able to "recall" the circumstances quite clearly. At the end of an hour Tom found himself well freighted with very valuable information concerning personages and matters pertaining to the Court; so he resolved to draw instruction from this source daily; and to this end he would give order to admit Humphrey to the royal closet whenever he might come, provided the majesty of England was not engaged with other people. Humphrey had hardly been dismissed when my lord Hertford arrived with more trouble for Tom.

He said that the lords of the Council, fearing that some overwrought report of the king's damaged health might have leaked out and got abroad, they deemed it wise and best that his majesty should begin to dine in public after a day or two—his wholesome complexion and vigorous step, assisted by a carefully guarded repose of manner and ease and grace of demeanor, would more surely quiet the general pulse—in case any evil rumors *had* gone about—than any other scheme that could be devised.

Then the earl proceeded, very delicately, to instruct Tom as to the observances proper to the stately occasion, under the rather thin disguise of "reminding" him concerning things already known to him; but to his vast gratification it turned out that Tom needed very little help in this line—he had been making use of Humphrey in that direction, for Humphrey had mentioned that within a few days he was to begin to dine in public; having gathered it from the swift-winged gossip of the Court. Tom kept these facts to himself however.

Seeing the royal memory so improved, the earl ventured to apply a few tests to it, in an apparently casual way, to find out how far its amendment had progressed. The results were happy, here and there, in spots—spots where Humphrey's tracks remained—and on the whole my lord was greatly pleased and encouraged. So encouraged was he, indeed, that he spoke up and said in a quite hopeful voice—

"Now am I persuaded that if your majesty will but tax your memory yet a little further, it will resolve the puzzle of the Great Seal

—a loss which was of moment yesterday, although of none to-day, since its term of service ended with our late lord's life. May it please your grace to make the trial?"

Tom was at sea—a Great Seal was a something which he was totally unacquainted with. After a moment's hesitation, he looked up innocently and asked—

"What was it like, my Lord?"

The earl started, almost imperceptibly, muttering to himself, "Alack, his wits are flown again!—it was ill wisdom to lead him on to strain them"—then he deftly turned the talk to other matters, with the purpose of sweeping the unlucky Seal out of Tom's thoughts —a purpose which easily succeeded.

CHAPTER XV

TOM AS KING

The next day the foreign ambassadors came, with their gorgeous trains; and Tom, throned in awful state, received them. The splendors of the scene delighted his eye and fired his imagination, at first, but the audience was long and dreary, and so were most of the addresses—wherefore, what began as a pleasure, grew into weariness and homesickness by and by. Tom said the words which Hertford put into his mouth from time to time, and tried hard to acquit himself satisfactorily, but he was too new to such things, and too ill at ease to accomplish more than a tolerable success. He looked sufficiently like a king, but he was ill able to feel like one. He was cordially glad when the ceremony was ended.

The larger part of his day was "wasted"—as he termed it, in his own mind—in labors pertaining to his royal office. Even the two hours devoted to certain princely pastimes and recreations were rather a burden to him, than otherwise, they were so fettered by restrictions and ceremonious observances. However he had a private hour with his whipping-boy which he counted clear gain, since he got both entertainment and needful information out of it.

The third day of Tom Canty's Kingship came and went much as the others had done, but there was a lifting of his cloud in one way— he felt less uncomfortable than at first; he was getting a little used to his circumstances and surroundings; his chains still galled, but not all the time; he found that the presence and homage of the great afflicted and embarrassed him less and less sharply with every hour that drifted over his head.

But for one single dread, he could have seen the fourth day approach without serious distress—the dining in public; it was to begin that day. There were greater matters in the programme—for on that day he would have to preside at a Council which would take his views and commands concerning the policy to be pursued toward various foreign nations scattered far and near over the great globe; on that day, too, Hertford would be formally chosen to the grand office of Lord Protector; other things of note were appointed for that fourth day, also, but to Tom they were all insignificant compared with the ordeal of dining all by himself with a multitude of curious eyes fastened upon him and a multitude of mouths whispering comments upon his performance,—and upon his mistakes, if he should be so unlucky as to make any.

Still, nothing could stop that fourth day, and so it came. It found poor Tom low-spirited and absent-minded, and this mood continued; he could not shake it off. The ordinary duties of the morning dragged upon his hands, and wearied him. Once more he felt the sense of captivity heavy upon him.

Late in the forenoon he was in a large audience chamber, conversing with the earl of Hertford and dully awaiting the striking of the hour appointed for a visit of ceremony from a considerable number of great officials and courtiers.

After a little while, Tom, who had wandered to a window and become interested in the life and movement of the great highway beyond the palace gates—and not idly interested, but longing with all his heart to take part in person in its stir and freedom—saw the van of a hooting and shouting mob of disorderly men, women and children of the lowest and poorest degree approaching from up the road.

"I would I knew what 'tis about!" he exclaimed, with all a boy's curiosity in such happenings.

"Thou art the king!" solemnly responded the earl, with a reverence. "Have I your grace's leave to act?"

"O blithely, yes! O gladly, yes!" exclaimed Tom, excitedly, adding to himself with a lively sense of satisfaction, "In truth, being a king is not all dreariness—it hath its compensations and conveniences."

The earl called a page, and sent him to the captain of the guard with the order—

"Let the mob be halted, and inquiry made concerning the occasion of its movement. By the king's command!"

A few seconds later a long rank of the royal guards, cased in flashing steel, filed out at the gates and formed across the highway in front of the multitude. A messenger returned, to report that the crowd was following a man, a woman, and a young girl to execution for crimes committed against the peace and dignity of the realm.

Death—and a violent death—for these poor unfortunates! The thought wrung Tom's heartstrings. The spirit of compassion took control of him, to the exclusion of all other considerations; he never thought of the offended laws, or of the grief or loss which these three criminals had inflicted upon their victims, he could think of nothing but the scaffold and the grisly fate hanging over the heads of the condemned. His concern made him even forget, for the moment, that he was but the false shadow of a king, not the substance; and before he knew it he had blurted out the command—

"Bring them here!"

Then he blushed scarlet, and a sort of apology sprung to his lips; but observing that his order had wrought no sort of surprise in the earl or the waiting page, he suppressed the words he was about to utter. The page, in the most matter-of-course way, made a profound obeisance and retired backward out of the room to deliver the command. Tom experienced a glow of pride and a renewed sense of the compensating advantages of the kingly office. He said to himself, "Truly it is like what I used to feel when I read the old priest's tales, and did imagine mine own self a prince, giving law and command to all, saying, 'Do this, do that,' whilst none durst offer let or hindrance to my will."

Now the doors swung open; one high-sounding title after another was announced, the personages owning them followed, and the place was quickly half filled with noble folk and finery. But Tom was hardly conscious of the presence of these people, so wrought up was he and so intensely absorbed in that other and more interesting matter. He seated himself, absently, in his chair of state, and turned his eyes upon the door with manifestations of impatient expectancy; seeing which, the company forbore to trouble him, and fell to chatting a mixture of public business and court gossip one with another.

In a little while the measured tread of military men was heard approaching, and the culprits entered the presence in charge of an under-sheriff and escorted by a detail of the king's guard. The civil officer knelt before Tom, then stood aside; the three doomed persons knelt, also, and remained so; the guard took position behind Tom's chair. Tom scanned the prisoners curiously. Something about the dress or appearance of the man had stirred a vague memory in him. "Methinks I have seen this man ere now . . . but the when or the where fail me"—such was Tom's thought. Just then the man glanced quickly up, and quickly dropped his face again, not being able to endure the awful port of sovereignty; but the one full glimpse of the face, which Tom got, was sufficient. He said to himself: "Now is the matter clear; this is the stranger that plucked Giles Witt out of the Thames, and saved his life, that windy, bitter first day of the New Year—a brave, good deed—pity he hath been doing baser ones and got himself in this sad case . . . . I have not forgot the day, neither the hour; by reason that an hour after, upon the stroke of eleven, I did get a hiding by the hand of Gammer Canty which was of so goodly and admired severity that all that went before or followed after it were but fondlings and caresses by comparison."

Tom now ordered that the woman and the girl be removed from the presence for a little time; then addressed himself to the under-sheriff, saying—

"Good sir, what is this man's offence?"

The officer knelt, and answered—

"So please your majesty, he hath taken the life of a subject by poison."

Tom's compassion for the prisoner, and admiration of him as the daring rescuer of a drowning boy, experienced a most damaging shock.

"The thing was proven upon him?" he asked.

"Most clearly, sire."

Tom sighed, and said—

"Take him away—he hath earned his death. 'Tis a pity, for he was a brave heart—na—na, I mean he hath the *look* of it!"

The prisoner clasped his hands together with sudden energy, and wrung them despairingly, at the same time appealing imploringly to the "King" in broken and terrified phrases—

"O my lord the king, an' thou canst pity the lost, have pity upon me! I am innocent—neither hath that wherewith I am charged been more than but lamely proved—yet I speak not of that; the judgment is gone forth against me and may not suffer alteration; yet in mine extremity I beg a boon, for my doom is more than I can bear. A grace, a grace, my lord the king! in thy royal compassion grant my prayer—give commandment that I be hanged!"

Tom was amazed. This was not the outcome he had looked for.

"Odds my life, a strange *boon!* Was it not the fate intended thee?"

"O good my liege, not so! It is ordered that I be *boiled alive!*"

The hideous surprise of these words almost made Tom spring from his chair. As soon as he could recover his wits he cried out—

"Have thy wish, poor soul! an' thou had poisoned a hundred men thou shouldst not suffer so miserable a death."

The prisoner bowed his face to the ground and burst into passionate expressions of gratitude—ending with—

"If ever thou shouldst know misfortune—which God forbid!—may thy goodness to me this day be remembered and requited!"

Tom turned to the earl of Hertford, and said—

"My lord, is it believable that there was warrant for this man's ferocious doom?"

"It is the law, your grace—for poisoners. In Germany coiners be boiled to death in *oil*—not cast in of a sudden, but by a rope let down into the oil by degrees, and slowly; first the feet, then the legs, then"—

"O prithee no more, my lord, I cannot bear it!" cried Tom, covering his eyes with his hands to shut out the picture. "I beseech your good lordship that order be taken to change this law—O, let no more poor creatures be visited with its tortures."

The earl's face showed profound gratification, for he was a man of merciful and generous impulses—a thing not very common with his class in that fierce age. He said—

"These your grace's noble words have sealed its doom. History will remember it to the honor of your royal house."

The under-sheriff was about to remove his prisoner; Tom gave him a sign to wait; then he said—

"Good sir, I would look into this matter further. The man has said his deed was but lamely proved. Tell me what thou knowest."

"If the king's grace please, it did appear upon the trial, that this man entered into a house in the hamlet of Islington where one lay sick—three witnesses say it was at ten of the clock in the morning and two say it was some minutes later—the sick man being alone at the time, and sleeping—and presently the man came forth again, and went his way. The sick man died within the hour, being torn with spasms and retchings."

"Did any see the poison given? Was poison found?"

"Marry, no, my liege."

"Then how doth one know there was poison given at all?"

"Please your majesty, the doctors testified that none die with such symptoms but by poison."

Weighty evidence, this—in that simple age. Tom recognized its formidable nature, and said—

"The doctor knoweth his trade—belike they were right. The matter hath an ill look for this poor man."

"Yet was not this all, your majesty; there is more and worse. Many testified that a witch, since gone from the village, none know whither, did foretell, and speak it privately in their ears, that the sick man *would die by poison*—and more, that a stranger would give it—a stranger with brown hair and clothed in a worn and common garb; and surely this prisoner doth answer woundily to the bill. Please your majesty to give the circumstance that solemn weight which is its due, seeing it was *foretold.*"

This was an argument of tremendous force, in that superstitious day. Tom felt that the thing was settled; if evidence was worth anything, this poor fellow's guilt was proved. Still he offered the prisoner a chance, saying—

"If thou canst say aught in thy behalf, speak."

"Nought that will avail, my king. I am innocent, yet cannot I make it appear. I have no friends, else might I show that I was not in Islington that day; so also might I show that at that hour they name I was above a league away, seeing I was at Wapping Old Stairs; yea more, my King, for I could show, that whilst they say I was *taking* life, I was *saving* it. A drowning boy"—

"Peace! Sheriff, name the day the deed was done!"

"At ten in the morning, or some minutes later, the first day of the new year, most illustrous"—

"Let the prisoner go free—it is the king's will!"

Another blush followed this unregal outburst, and he covered his indecorum as well as he could by adding—

"It enrageth me that a man should be hanged upon such idle, hare-brained evidence!"

A low buzz of admiration swept through the assemblage. It was not admiration of the decree that had been delivered by Tom, for the propriety or expediency of pardoning a convicted poisoner was a thing which few there would have felt justified in either admitting or admiring—no, the admiration was for the intelligence and spirit which Tom had displayed. Some of the low-voiced remarks were to this effect—

"This is no mad king—he hath his wits sound."

"How sanely he put his questions—how like his former natural self was this abrupt, imperious disposal of the matter!"

"God be thanked his infirmity is spent! This is no weakling, but a king. He hath borne himself like to his own father."

The air being filled with applause, Tom's ear necessarily caught a little of it. The effect which this had upon him was to put him greatly at his ease, and also to charge his system with very gratifying sensations.

However, his juvenile curiosity soon rose superior to these pleasant thoughts and feelings; he was eager to know what sort of deadly mischief the woman and the little girl could have been about; so, by his command the two terrified and sobbing creatures were brought before him.

"What is it that these have done?" he inquired of the sheriff.

"Please your majesty, a black crime is charged upon them, and clearly proven: wherefore the judges have decreed, according to the law, that they be hanged. They sold themselves to the devil—such is their crime."

Tom shuddered. He had been taught to abhor people who did this wicked thing. Still, he was not going to deny himself the pleasure of feeding his curiosity, for all that; so he asked—

"Where was this done?—and when?"

"On a midnight, in December—in a ruined church, your majesty."

Tom shuddered again.

"Who was there present?"

"Only these two, your grace—and *that other.* "

"Have these confessed?"

"Nay, not so, sire—they do deny it."

"Then prithee, how was it known?"

"Certain witnesses did see them wending thither, good your majesty; this bred the suspicion, and dire effects have since confirmed and justified it. In particular, it is in evidence that through the wicked power so obtained, they did invoke and bring about a storm that wasted all the region round about. Above forty witnesses have proved the storm; and sooth one might have had a thousand, for all had reason to remember it, sith all had suffered by it."

"Certes this is a serious matter." Tom turned this dark piece of scoundrelism over in his mind a while, then asked—

"Suffered the woman, also, by the storm?"

Several old heads among the assemblage nodded their recognition of the wisdom of this question. The sheriff, however, saw nothing consequential in the inquiry; he answered, with simple directness—

"Indeed, did she, your majesty, and most righteously, as all aver. Her habitation was swept away, and herself and child left shelterless."

"Methinks the power to do herself so ill a turn was dearly bought. She had been cheated, had she paid for a farthing for it; that she paid her soul, and her child's, argueth that she is mad; if she is mad she knoweth not what she doth, therefore sinneth not."

The elderly heads nodded recognition of Tom's wisdom once more, and one individual murmured, "An' the king be mad himself, according to report, then is it a madness of a sort that would improve the sanity of some I wot of, if by the gentle providence of God they could but catch it."

"What age hath the child?" asked Tom.

"Nine years, please your majesty."

"By the law of England may a child enter into covenant and sell itself, my lord?" asked Tom, turning to a learned judge.

"The law doth not permit a child to make or meddle in any weighty matter, good my liege, holding that its callow wit unfitteth it to cope with the riper wit and evil schemings of them that are its elders. The *devil* may buy a child, if he so choose, and the child agree thereto, but not an Englishman—in this latter case the contract would be null and void."

"It seemeth a rude unchristian thing, and ill contrived, that English law denieth privileges to Englishmen, to waste them on the devil!" cried Tom, with honest heat.

This novel view of the matter excited many smiles, and was stored away in many heads to be repeated about the court as evidence of Tom's originality as well as progress toward mental health.

The elder culprit had ceased from sobbing, and was hanging upon Tom's words with an excited interest and a growing hope. Tom noticed this, and it strongly inclined his sympathies toward her in her perilous and unfriended situation. Presently he asked—

"How wrought they, to bring the storm?"

"*By pulling off their stockings, sire.*"

This astonished Tom, and also fired his curiosity to fever heat. He said, eagerly—

"It is wonderful! Hath it always this dread effect?"

"Always, my liege—at least if the woman desire it, and utter the needful words, either in her mind or with her tongue."

Tom turned to the woman, and said with impetuous zeal—

"Exert thy power—I would see a storm!"

There was a sudden paling of cheeks in the superstitious assemblage, and a general, though unexpressed, desire to get out of the place—all of which was lost upon Tom, who was dead to everything but the proposed cataclysm. Seeing a puzzled and astonished look in the woman's face, he added, excitedly—

"Never fear—thou shalt be blameless. More—thou shalt go free— none shall touch thee. Exert thy power."

"O, my lord the king, I have it not—I have been falsely accused."

"Thy fears stay thee. Be of good heart, thou shalt suffer no harm. Make a storm—it mattereth not how small a one—I require nought great or harmful, but indeed prefer the opposite—do this and thy life is spared—thou shalt go out free, with thy child, bearing the king's pardon, and safe from hurt or malice from any in the realm."

The woman prostrated herself, and protested, with tears, that she had no power to do the miracle, else she would gladly win her child's life, alone, and be content to lose her own, if by obedience to the king's command so precious a grace might be acquired.

Tom urged—the woman still adhered to her declarations. Finally he said—

"I think the woman hath said true. An' *my* mother were in her place and gifted with the devil's functions, she had not stayed a moment to call her storms and lay the whole land in ruins, if the saving of my forfeit life were the price she got! It is argument that other mothers are made in like mould. Thou art free, good wife— thou and thy child—for I do think thee innocent. *Now* thou'st nought to fear, being pardoned—pull off thy stockings!—an' thou canst make me a storm, thou shalt be rich!"

The redeemed creature was loud in her gratitude, and proceeded to obey, whilst Tom looked on with eager expectancy, a little marred by apprehension; the courtiers at the same time manifesting decided discomfort and uneasiness. The woman stripped her own feet and her little girl's also, and plainly did her best to reward the king's generosity with an earthquake, but it was all a failure and a disappointment. Tom sighed, and said—

"There, good soul, trouble thyself no further, thy power is departed out of there. Go thy way in peace; and if it return to thee at any time, forget me not, but fetch me a storm."*

* See Notes to Chapter 15 at the end of the volume.

CHAPTER XVI

THE STATE DINNER

The dinner hour drew near—yet strangely enough, the thought brought but slight discomfort to Tom, and hardly any terror. The morning's experiences had wonderfully built up his confidence; the poor little ash-cat was already more wonted to his strange garret, after four days' habit, than a mature person could have become in a full month. A child's facility in accommodating itself to circumstances was never more strikingly illustrated.

Let us privileged ones hurry to the great banqueting room and have a glance at matters there whilst Tom is being made ready for the imposing occasion. It is a spacious apartment, with gilded pillars and pilasters, and pictured walls and ceilings. At the door stand tall guards, as rigid as statues, dressed in rich and picturesque costumes, and bearing halberds. In a high gallery which runs all around the place is a band of musicians and a packed company of citizens of both sexes, in brilliant attire. In the centre of the room, upon a raised platform, is Tom's table. Now let the ancient chronicler speak:

"A gentleman enters the room bearing a rod, and along with him another bearing a table-cloth, which, after they have both kneeled three times with the utmost veneration, he spreads upon the table, and after kneeling again they both retire; then come two others, one with the rod again, the other with a salt-cellar, a plate, and bread; when they have kneeled as the others had done, and placed what was brought upon the table, they too retire with the same ceremonies performed by the first; at last come two nobles, richly clothed, one bearing a tasting-knife, who, after prostrating themselves in the most graceful manner, approach and rub the table with bread and salt, with as much awe as if the king had been present."*

So end the solemn preliminaries. Now, far down the echoing corridors we hear the bugle-blast, and the indistinct cry, "Place for the king! way for the king's most excellent majesty!" These sounds are momently repeated—they grow nearer and nearer—and presently, almost in our faces, the martial note peals and the cry rings out, "Way for the king!" At this instant the shining pageant appears, and files in at the door, with a measured march. Let the chronicler speak again:

"First come Gentlemen, Barons, Earls, Knights of the Garter, all richly dressed and bareheaded; next comes the Chancellor, between two, one of which carries the royal sceptre, the other the Sword of State in a red scabbard, studded with golden fleurs-de-lis, the point upwards; next comes the King himself—whom, upon his appearing, twelve trumpets and many drums salute with a great burst of welcome, whilst all in the galleries rise in their places, crying "God

*Leigh Hunt's "The Town," p. 408, quotation from an early tourist.

save the King!" After him come nobles attached to his person, and on his right and left march his guard of honor, his fifty Gentlemen Pensioners, with gilt battle-axes."

This was all fine and pleasant. Tom's pulse beat high and a glad light was in his eye. He bore himself right gracefully, and all the more so because he was not thinking of how he was doing it, his mind being charmed and occupied with the blithe sights and sounds about him—and besides, nobody can be very ungraceful in nicely-fitting beautiful clothes after he has grown a little used to them—especially if he is for the moment unconscious of them. Tom remembered his instructions, and acknowledged his greeting with a slight inclination of his plumed head, and a courteous "I thank ye, my good people."

He seated himself at table, without removing his cap; and did it without the least embarrassment; for to eat with one's cap on was the one solitary royal custom upon which the kings and the Cantys met upon common ground, neither party having any advantage over the other in the matter of old familiarity with it. The pageant broke up and grouped itself picturesquely, and remained bareheaded.

Now, to the sound of gay music, the Yeomen of the Guard entered, —"the tallest and mightiest men in England, they being selected in this regard"—but we will let the chronicler tell about it:

"The Yeomen of the Guard entered, bareheaded, clothed in scarlet, with golden roses upon their backs; and these went and came, bringing in each turn a course of dishes, served in plate. These dishes were received by a gentleman in the same order they were brought, and placed upon the table, while the taster gave to each guard a mouthful to eat of the particular dish he had brought, for fear of any poison."

Tom made a good dinner, notwithstanding he was conscious that hundreds of eyes followed each morsel to his mouth and watched him eat it with an interest which could not have been more intense if it had been a deadly explosive and was expected to blow him up and scatter him all over the place. He was careful not to hurry, and equally careful not to do any thing whatever for himself, but wait till the proper official knelt down and did it for him. He got through without a mistake—flawless and precious triumph.

When the meal was over at last and he marched away in the midst of his bright pageant, with the happy noises in his ears of blaring bugles, rolling drums and thundering acclamations, he felt that if he had seen the worst of dining in public, it was an ordeal which he would be glad to endure several times a day if by that means he could but buy himself free from some of the more formidable requirements of his royal office.

CHAPTER XVII

FOO-FOO THE FIRST

Miles Hendon hurried along toward the Southwark end of the bridge, keeping a sharp lookout for the persons he sought, and hoping and expecting to overtake them presently. He was disappointed in this, however. By asking questions, he was enabled to track them part of the way through Southwark; then all traces ceased, and he was perplexed as to how to proceed. Still, he continued his efforts as best he could during the rest of the day. Nightfall found him leg-weary, half famished, and his desire as far from accomplishment as ever; so he supped at the Tabard inn and went to bed, resolved to make an early start in the morning, and give the town an exhaustive search. As he lay thinking and planning, he presently began to reason thus: The boy would escape from the ruffian, his reputed father, if possible; would he go back to London and seek his former haunts? no, he would not do that, he would avoid recapture. What, then, would he do? Never having had a friend in the world, or a protector, until he met Miles Hendon, he would naturally try to find that friend again, provided the effort did not require him to go toward London and danger. He would strike for Hendon Hall, that is what he would do, for he knew Hendon was homeward bound and there he might expect to find him. Yes, the case was plain to Hendon—he must lose no more time in Southwark, but move at once through Kent, toward Monk's Holm, searching the wood and inquiring as he went. Let us return to the vanished little king, now.

The ruffian whom the waiter at the inn on the bridge saw "about to join" the youth and the king, did not exactly join them, but fell in close behind them and followed their steps. He said nothing. His left arm was in a sling, and he wore a large green patch over his left eye; he limped slightly, and used an oaken staff as a support. The youth led the king a crooked course through Southwark, and by and by struck into the high road beyond. The king was irritated, now, and said he would stop here—it was Hendon's place to come to him, not his to go to Hendon. He would not endure such insolence; he would stop where he was. The youth said—

"Thou'lt tarry here, and thy friend lying wounded in the wood yonder? So be it, then."

The king's manner changed at once. He cried out—

"Wounded? And who hath dared to do it? But that is apart; lead on, lead on! Faster, sirrah! art shod with lead? Wounded, is he? Now though the doer of it be a duke's son, he shall rue it!"

It was some distance to the wood, but the space was speedily traversed. The youth looked about him, discovered a bough sticking in the ground, with a small bit of rag tied to it, then led the way into the forest, watching for similar boughs and finding them at intervals: they were evidently guides to the point he was aiming at. By and by an open place was reached, where were the charred remains of a farm-house, and near them a barn which was falling to ruin and decay. There was no sign of life anywhere, and utter silence prevailed. The youth entered the barn, the king following eagerly upon his heels. No one there! The king shot a surprised and suspicious glance at the youth, and asked—

"Where is he?"

A mocking laugh was his answer. The king was in a rage in a moment; he seized a billet of wood and was in the act of charging upon the youth when another mocking laugh fell upon his ear. It was from the lame ruffian, who had been following at a distance. The king turned and said angrily—

"Who art thou? What is thy business here?"

"Leave thy foolery," said the man, "and quiet thyself. My disguise is none so good that thou canst pretend thou knowest not thy father through it."

"Thou art not my father. I knew thee not. I am the king. If thou hast hid my servant, find him for me, or thou shalt sup sorrow for what thou hast done."

John Canty replied, in a stern and measured voice—

"It is plain thou art mad, and I am loth to punish thee; but if thou provoke me, I must. Thy prating doth no harm here, where there are no ears that need to mind thy follies, yet is it well to practice thy tongue to wary speech, that it may do no hurt when our quarters change. I have done a murder, and may not tarry at home—neither shalt thou, seeing I need thy service. My name is changed, for wise reasons; it is Hobbs—John Hobbs; thine is Jack—charge thy memory accordingly. Now, then, speak. Where is thy mother? where are thy sisters? They came not to the place appointed—knowest thou whither they went?"

The king answered, sullenly—

"Trouble me not with these riddles. My mother is dead; my sisters are in the palace."

The youth near by burst into a derisive laugh, and the king would have assaulted him, but Canty—or Hobbs, as he now called himself —prevented him, and said—

"Peace, Hugo, vex him not; his mind is astray, and thy ways fret him. Sit thee down, Jack, and quiet thyself; thou shalt have a morsel to eat, anon."

Hobbs and Hugo fell to talking together, in low voices, and the king removed himself as far as he could from their disagreeable company. He withdrew into the twilight of the farther end of the barn, where he found the earthen floor bedded a foot deep with straw. He lay down here, drew straw over himself in lieu of blankets, and was soon absorbed in thinking. He had many griefs, but the minor ones were swept almost into forgetfulness by the supreme one, the loss of his father. To the rest of the world the name of Henry VIII. brought a shiver, and suggested an ogre whose nostrils breathed destruction and whose hand dealt scourgings and death; but to this boy the name brought only sensations of pleasure, the figure it invoked wore a countenance that was all gentleness and affection. He called to mind a long succession of loving passages between his father and himself, and dwelt fondly upon them, his unstinted tears attesting how deep and real was the grief that possessed his heart. As the afternoon wasted away, the lad, wearied with his troubles, sunk gradually into a tranquil and healing slumber.

After a considerable time—he could not tell how long—his senses struggled to a half-consciousness, and as he lay with closed eyes vaguely wondering where he was and what had been happening, he noted a murmurous sound, the sullen beating of rain upon the roof. A snug sense of comfort stole over him, which was rudely broken, the next moment, by a chorus of piping cackles and coarse laughter. It startled him disagreeably, and he unmuffled his head to see whence this interruption proceeded. A grim and unsightly picture met his eye. A bright fire was burning in the middle of the floor, at the other end of the barn; and around it, and lit weirdly up by the red glare, lolled and sprawled the motliest company of tattered gutterscum and ruffians, of both sexes, he had ever read or dreamed of. There were huge, stalwart men, brown with exposure, long-haired, and clothed in fantastic rags; there were middle-sized youths, of truculent countenance, and similarly clad; there were blind mendicants, with patched or bandaged eyes; crippled ones, with wooden legs and crutches; there was a villain-looking peddler with his pack; a knife-grinder, a tinker, and a barber-surgeon, with the implements of their trades; some of the females were hardly-grown girls, some were at prime, some were old and wrinkled hags, and all were loud, brazen, foul-mouthed; and all soiled and slatternly; there were three sore-faced babies; there were a couple of starveling curs, with strings about their necks, whose office was to lead the blind.

The night was come, the gang had just finished feasting, an orgy was beginning, the can of liquor was passing from mouth to mouth. A general cry broke forth—

"A song! a song from the Bat and Dick Dot-and-go-One!"

One of the blind men got up, and made ready by casting aside the patches that sheltered his excellent eyes, and the pathetic placard which recited the cause of his calamity. Dot-and-go-One disencumbered himself of his timber leg and took his place, upon sound and healthy limbs, beside his fellow-rascal; then they roared out a rollicking ditty, and were re-enforced by the whole crew, at the end of each stanza, in a rousing chorus. By the time the last stanza was reached, the half-drunken enthusiasm had risen to such a pitch, that everybody joined in and sang it clear through from the beginning, producing a volume of villainous sound that made the rafters quake. These were the inspiring words:

> "Bien Darkmans then, Bouse Mort and Ken,
>   The bien Coves bings awast,
>   On Chates to trine by Rome Coves dine
>   For his long lib at last.
>   Bing'd out bien Morts and toure, and toure,
>   Bing out of the Rome vile bine,
>   And toure the Cove that cloy'd your duds,
>   Upon the Chates to trine."*

Conversation followed; not in the thieves' dialect of the song, for that was only used in talk when unfriendly ears might be listening. In the course of it it appeared that "John Hobbs" was not altogether a new recruit, but had trained in the gang at some former time. His later history was called for, and when he said he had "accidentally" killed a man, considerable satisfaction was expressed; when he added that the man was a priest, he was roundly applauded, and had to take a drink with everybody. Old acquaintances welcomed him joyously, and new ones were proud to shake him by the hand. He was asked why he had "tarried away so many months." He answered—

"London is better than the country, and safer these late years, the laws be so bitter and so diligently enforced. An' I had not had that accident, I had staid there. I had resolved to stay, and never more venture country-wards—but the accident has ended that."

He inquired how many persons the gang numbered now. The "Ruffler," or chief, answered—

"Five and twenty sturdy budges, bulks, files, clapperdogeons and maunders, counting the dells and doxies and other morts.† Most are here, the rest are wandering eastward, along the winter lay. We follow at dawn."

"I do not see the Wen among the honest folk about me. Where may he be?"

"Poor lad, his diet is brimstone, now, and over hot for a delicate taste. He was killed in a brawl, somewhere about midsummer."

"I sorrow to hear that; the Wen was a capable man, and brave."

"That was he, truly. Black Bess, his dell, is of us yet, but absent on the eastward tramp; a fine lass, of nice ways and orderly conduct, none ever seeing her drunk above four days in the seven."

"She was ever strict—I remember it well—a goodly wench and worthy all commendation. Her mother was more free and less particular; a troublesome and ugly tempered beldame, but furnished with a wit above the common."

*From "The English Rogue;" London, 1665.

†Canting terms for various kinds of thieves, beggars and vagabonds, and their female companions.

"We lost her through it. Her gift of palmistry and other sorts of fortune-telling begot for her at last a witch's name and fame. The law roasted her to death at a slow fire. It did touch me to a sort of tenderness to see the gallant way she met her lot—cursing and reviling all the crowd that gaped and gazed around her, whilst the flames licked upward toward her face and catched her thin locks and crackled about her old gray head—cursing them, said I?—cursing them! why an' thou shouldst live a thousand years thou'dst never hear so masterful a cursing. Alack, her art died with her. There be base and weakling imitations left, but no true blasphemy."

The Ruffler sighed; the listeners sighed in sympathy; a general depression fell upon the company for a moment, for even hardened outcasts like these are not wholly dead to sentiment, but are able to feel a fleeting sense of loss and affliction at wide intervals and under peculiarly favoring circumstances—as in cases like to this, for instance, when genius and culture depart and leave no heir. However, a deep drink all round soon restored the spirits of the mourners.

"Have any others of our friends fared hardly?" asked Hobbs.

"Some—yes. Particularly new comers—such as small husbandmen turned shiftless and hungry upon the world because their farms were taken from them to be changed to sheep ranges. They begged, and were whipped at the cart's tail, naked from the girdle up, till the blood ran; then set in the stocks to be pelted; they begged again, were whipped again, and deprived of an ear; they begged a third time—poor devils, what else could they do?—and were branded on the cheek with a red hot iron, then sold for slaves; they ran away, were hunted down, and hanged. 'Tis a brief tale, and quickly told. Others of us have fared less hardly. Stand forth, Yokel, Burns, and Hodge—show your adornments!"

These stood up and stripped away some of their rags, exposing their backs, criss-crossed with ropy old welts left by the lash; one turned up his hair and showed the place where a left ear had once been; another showed a brand upon his shoulder—the letter V— and a mutilated ear; the third said:

"I am Yokel, once a farmer and prosperous, with loving wife and kids—now am I somewhat different in estate and calling; and the wife and kids are gone; mayhap they are in heaven, maybe in—in the other place—but the kindly God be thanked, they bide no more in *England!* My good old blameless mother strove to earn bread by nursing the sick; one of these died, the doctors knew not how, so my mother was burnt for a witch, whilst my babes looked on and wailed. English law!—up, all, with your cups!—now altogether and with a cheer!—drink to the merciful English law that delivered *her* from the English hell! Thank you, mates, one and all. I begged, from house to house—I and the wife—bearing with us the hungry kids— but it was crime to be hungry in England—so they stripped us and lashed us through three towns!—for its lash drank deep of my

Mary's blood and its blessed deliverance came quick. She lies there, in the potter's field, safe from all harms. And the kids—well, whilst the law lashed me from town to town, they starved. Drink lads—only a drop—a drop to the poor kids, that never did any creature harm. I begged again—begged for a crust, and got the stocks and lost an ear—see, here bides the stump; I begged again, and here is the stump of the other to keep me minded of it. And still I begged again, and was sold for a slave—here on my cheek under this stain, if I washed it off, ye might see the red S the branding-iron left there! A Slave! Do ye understand that word! An English Slave!—that is he that stands before ye. I have run from my master, and when I am found—the heavy curse of heaven fall on the law of the land that hath commanded it!—I shall hang!"*

A ringing voice came through the murky air—

"Thou shalt *not!*—and this day the end of that law is come!"

All turned, and saw the fantastic figure of the little king approaching hurriedly; as it emerged into the light and was clearly revealed, a general explosion of inquiries broke out:

"Who is it? *What* is it? Who art thou, manikin?"

The boy stood confused in the midst of all those surprised and questioning eyes, and answered with princely dignity—

"I am Edward, king of England."

A wild burst of laughter followed, partly of derision and partly of delight in the excellence of the joke. The king was stung. He said sharply—

"Ye mannerless vagrants, is this your recognition of the royal boon I have promised?"

He said more, with angry voice and excited gesture, but it was lost in a whirlwind of laughter and mocking exclamations. "John Hobbs" made several attempts to make himself heard above the din, and at last succeeded—saying—

"Mates, he is my son, a dreamer, a fool, and stark mad—mind him not—he thinketh he *is* the king."

"I *am* the king," said Edward, turning toward him, "as thou shalt know to thy cost, in good time. Thou hast confessed a murder—thou shalt swing for it."

"*Thou'lt* betray me!—*thou?* An' I get my hand upon thee"—

"Tut-tut!" said the burly Ruffler, interposing in time to save the king, and emphasizing this service by knocking Hobbs down with his fist, "hast respect for neither Kings *nor* Rufflers? An' thou insult my presence so again, I'll hang thee up myself." Then he said to his majesty, "Thou must make no threats against thy mates, lad; and thou must guard thy tongue from saying evil of them elsewhere. *Be* king, if it please thy mad humor, but be not harmful in it. Sink the title thou hast uttered,—'tis treason; we be bad men, in some few trifling ways, but none among us is so base as to be traitor to his king; we be loving and loyal hearts, in that regard. Note if I speak

* See Note 10, at end of volume.

truth. Now—all together: 'Long live Edward, king of England!' "

"LONG LIVE EDWARD, KING OF ENGLAND!"

The response came with such a thundergust from the motley crew that the crazy building vibrated to the sound. The little king's face lighted with pleasure for an instant, and he slightly inclined his head and said with grave simplicity—

"I thank you, my good people."

This unexpected result threw the company into convulsions of merriment. When something like quiet was presently come again, the Ruffler said, firmly, but with an accent of good nature—

"Drop it, boy, 'tis not wise, nor well. Humor thy fancy, if thou must, but choose some other title."

A tinker shrieked out a suggestion—

"Foo-foo the First, King of the Mooncalves!"

The title "took," at once, every throat responded, and a roaring shout went up, of—

"Long live Foo-foo the First, King of the Mooncalves!" followed by hootings, cat-calls, and peals of laughter.

"Hale him forth, and crown him!"

"Robe him!"

"Sceptre him!"

"Throne him!"

These and twenty other cries broke out at once; and almost before the poor little victim could draw a breath he was crowned with a tin basin, robed in a tattered blanket, throned upon a barrel, and sceptred with the tinker's soldering-iron. Then all flung themselves upon their knees about him and sent up a chorus of ironical wailings, and mocking supplications, whilst they swabbed their eyes with their soiled and ragged sleeves and aprons—

"Be gracious to us, O, sweet king!"

"Trample not upon thy beseeching worms, O noble majesty!"

"Pity thy slaves, and comfort them with a royal kick!"

"Cheer us and warm us with they gracious rays, O flaming sun of sovereignty!"

"Sanctify the ground with the touch of thy foot, that we may eat the dirt and be ennobled!"

"Deign to spit upon us, O sire, that our children's children may tell of thy princely condescension, and be proud and happy forever!"

But the humorous tinker made the "hit" of the evening and carried off the honors. Kneeling, he pretended to kiss the king's foot, and was indignantly spurned; whereupon he went about begging for a rag to paste over the place upon his face which had been touched by the foot, saying it must be preserved from contact with the vulgar air, and that he should make his fortune by going on the highway and exposing it to view at the rate of a hundred shillings a sight. He made himself so killingly funny that he was the envy and admiration of the whole mangy rabble.

Tears of shame and indignation stood in the little monarch's
eyes; and the thought in his heart was, "Had I offered them a deep
wrong they could not be more cruel—yet have I proffered nought but
to do them a kindness—and it is thus they use me for it!"

CHAPTER XVIII

THE PRINCE WITH THE TRAMPS

The troop of vagabonds turned out at early dawn, and set forward
on their march. There was a lowering sky overhead, sloppy ground
under foot, and a winter chill in the air. All gayety was gone from
the company; some were sullen and silent, some were irritable and
petulant, none were gentle-humored, all were thirsty.

The Ruffler put "Jack" in Hugo's charge, with some brief
instructions, and commanded John Canty to keep away from him
and let him alone; he also warned Hugo not to be too rough with
the lad.

After a while the weather grew milder, and the clouds lifted
somewhat. The troop ceased to shiver, and their spirits began to
improve. They grew more and more cheerful, and finally began to
chaff each other and insult passengers along the highway. This
showed that they were awaking to an appreciation of life and its
joys once more. The dread in which their sort was held was apparent
in the fact that everybody gave them the road, and took their ribald
insolences meekly, without venturing to talk back. They snatched
linen from the hedges, occasionally, in full view of the owners, who
made no protest, but only seemed grateful that they did not take the
hedges, too.

By and by they invaded a small farm house and made themselves
at home while the trembling farmer and his people swept the larder
clean to furnish a breakfast for them. They chucked the housewife
and her daughters under the chin whilst receiving the food from
their hands, and made coarse jests about them, accompanied with
insulting epithets and bursts of horse-laughter. They threw bones
and vegetables at the farmer and his sons, kept them dodging all
the time, and applauded uproariously when a good hit was made.
They ended by buttering the head of one of the daughters who
resented some of their familiarities. When they took their leave
they threatened to come back and burn the house over the heads of
the family if any report of their doings got to the ears of the
authorities.

About noon, after a long and weary tramp, the gang came to a
halt behind a hedge on the outskirts of a considerable village. An
hour was allowed for rest, then the crew scattered themselves
abroad to enter the village at different points to ply their various
trades.—"Jack" was sent with Hugo. They wandered hither and

thither for some time, Hugo watching for opportunities to do a
stroke of business but finding none—so he finally said—

"I see nought to steal; it is a paltry place. Wherefore we will beg."

"*We*, forsooth! Follow thy trade—it befits thee. But *I* will not
beg."

"Thou'lt not beg!" exclaimed Hugo, eying the king with surprise.
"Prithee, since when hast thou reformed?"

"What dost thou mean?"

"Mean? Hast thou not begged the streets of London all thy life?"

"I? Thou idiot!"

"Spare thy compliments—thy stock will last the longer. Thy
father says thou hast begged all thy days. Mayhap he lied.
Peradventure you will even make so bold as to *say* he lied," scoffed
Hugo.

"Him *you* call my father? Yes, he lied."

"Come, play not thy merry game of madman so far, mate; use it
for thy amusement, not thy hurt. An' I tell him this, he will scorch
thee finely for it."

"Save thyself the trouble. I will tell him."

"I like thy spirit, I do in truth; but I do not admire thy judgment.
Bone-rackings and bastings be plenty enow in this life, without
going out of one's way to invite them. But a truce to these matters;
I believe your father. I doubt not he can lie; I doubt not he *doth*
lie, upon occasion, for the best of us do that; but there is no occasion
here. A wise man does not waste so good a commodity as lying for
nought. But come; sith it is thy humor to give over begging,
wherewithal shall we busy ourselves? With robbing kitchens?"

The king said, impatiently—

"Have done with this folly—you weary me!"

Hugo replied, with temper—

"Now harkee, mate; you will not beg, you will not rob; so be it.
But I will tell you what you *will* do. You will play decoy whilst *I* beg.
Refuse, an' you think you may venture!"

The king was about to reply contemptuously, when Hugo said,
interrupting—

"Peace! Here comes one with a kindly face. Now will I fall down
in a fit. When the stranger runs to me, set you up a wail, and fall
upon your knees, seeming to weep; then cry out as if all the devils
of misery were in your belly, and say, 'O, sir, it is my poor afflicted
brother, and we be friendless; o' God's name cast through your
merciful eyes one pitiful look upon a sick, forsaken and most
miserable wretch; bestow one little penny out of thy riches upon
one smitten of God and ready to perish!'—and mind you, keep you
on wailing, and abate not till we bilk him of his penny, else shall
you rue it."

Then immediately Hugo began to moan, and groan, and roll his
eyes, and reel and totter about; and when the stranger was close at

hand, down he sprawled before him, with a shriek, and began to writhe and wallow in the dirt, in seeming agony.

"O dear, O dear!" cried the benevolent stranger. "O poor soul, poor soul, how he doth suffer! There—let me help thee up."

"O, noble sir, forbear, and God love you for a princely gentleman—but it giveth me cruel pain to touch me when I am taken so. My brother there will tell your worship how I am racked with anguish when these fits be upon me. A penny, dear sir, a penny, to buy a little food; then leave me to my sorrows."

"A penny! thou shalt have three, thou hapless creature"—and he fumbled in his pocket with nervous haste and got them out. "There, poor lad, take them, and most welcome. Now come hither, my boy, and help me carry thy stricken brother to yon house, where"—

"I am not his brother," said the king, interrupting.

"What! not his brother?"

"O hear him!" groaned Hugo, then privately ground his teeth. "He denies his own brother—and he with one foot in the grave!"

"Boy, thou art indeed hard of heart, if this is thy brother. For shame!—and he scarce able to move hand or foot. If he is not thy brother, who is he, then?"

"A beggar and a thief! He has got your money and has picked your pocket likewise. An' thou wouldst do a healing miracle, lay thy staff over his shoulders and trust Providence for the rest."

But Hugo did not tarry for the miracle. In a moment he was up and off like the wind, the gentleman following after and raising the hue and cry lustily as he went. The king, breathing deep gratitude to Heaven for his own release, fled in the opposite direction and did not slacken his pace until he was out of harm's reach. He took the first road that offered, and soon put the village behind him. He hurried along, as briskly as he could, during several hours, keeping a nervous watch over his shoulder for pursuit; but his fears left him at last, and a grateful sense of security took their place. He recognized, now, that he was hungry; and also very tired. So he halted at a farm house; but when he was about to speak, he was cut short and driven rudely away. His clothes were against him. He wandered on, wounded and indignant, and was resolved to put himself in the way of light treatment no more. But hunger is pride's master; so as the evening drew near, he made an attempt at another farm house; but here he fared worse than before; for he was called hard names and was promised arrest as a vagrant except he moved on promptly.

The night came on, chilly and overcast; and still the footsore monarch labored slowly on. He was obliged to keep moving, for every time he sat down to rest he was soon penetrated to the bone with the cold. All his sensations and experiences, as he moved through the solemn gloom and the empty vastness of the night, were new and strange to him. At intervals he heard voices approach, pass by, and fade into silence; and as he saw nothing more of the bodies they belonged to than a sort of formless drifting blur, there was something spectral and uncanny about it all that made him shudder. Occasionally he caught the twinkle of a light—always far away, apparently—almost in another world; if he heard the tinkle of a sheep's bell, it was vague, distant, indistinct; the muffled lowing of the herds floated to him on the night wind in vanishing cadences, a mournful sound; now and then came the complaining howl of a dog over viewless expanses of field and forest; all sounds were remote; they made the little king feel that all life and activity were far removed from him, and that he stood solitary, companionless, in the centre of a measureless solitude.

He stumbled along, through the grewsome fascinations of this new experience, startled occasionally by the soft rustling of the dry leaves overhead, so like human whispers they seemed to sound; and by and by he came suddenly upon the freckled light of a tin lantern near at hand. He stepped back into the shadows and waited. The lantern stood by the open door of a barn. The king waited some time—there was no sound, and nobody stirring. He got so cold, standing still, and the hospitable barn looked so enticing, that at last he resolved to risk everything and enter. He started swiftly and stealthily, and just as he was crossing the threshold he heard voices behind him. He darted behind a cask, within the barn, and stooped down. Two farm laborers came in, bringing the lantern with them, and fell to work, talking meanwhile. Whilst they moved about with the light, the king made good use of his eyes and took the bearings of what seemed to be a good sized stall at the further end of the place, purposing to grope his way to it when he should be left to himself. He also noted the position of a pile of horse blankets, midway of the route, with the intent to levy upon them for the service of the crown of England for one night.

By and by the men finished and went away, fastening the door behind them and taking the lantern with them. The shivering king made for the blankets, with as good speed as the darkness would allow; gathered them up and then groped his way safely to the stall. Of two of the blankets he made a bed, then covered himself with the remaining two. He was a glad monarch, now, though the blankets were old and thin, and not quite warm enough; and besides gave out a pungent horsy odor that was almost suffocatingly powerful.

Although the king was hungry and chilly, he was also so tired and so drowsy that these latter influences soon began to get the advantage of the former, and he presently dozed off into a state of semi-consciousness. Then, just as he was on the point of losing himself wholly, he distinctly felt something touch him! He was broad awake in a moment, and gasping for breath. The cold horror of that mysterious touch in the dark almost made his heart stand still. He lay motionless, and listened, scarcely breathing. But nothing stirred, and there was no sound. He continued to listen, and wait, during what seemed a long time, but still nothing stirred, and there was no sound. So he began to drop into a drowse once more, at last; and all at once he felt that mysterious touch again! It was a grisly thing, this light touch from this noiseless and invisible presence; it made the boy sick with ghostly fears. What should he do? That was the question; but he did not know how to answer it. Should he leave these reasonably comfortable quarters and fly from this inscrutable horror? But fly whither? He could not get out of the barn; and the idea of scurrying blindly hither and thither in the dark, within the captivity of the four walls, with this phantom gliding after him, and visiting him with that soft hideous touch upon cheek or shoulder at every turn, was intolerable. But to stay where he was, and endure this living death all night?—was that better? No. What, then, was there left to do? Ah, there was but one course; he knew it well—he must put out his hand and find that thing!

It was easy to think this; but it was hard to brace himself up to try it. Three times he stretched his hand a little way out into the dark, gingerly; and snatched it suddenly back, with a gasp—not because it had encountered any thing, but because he had felt so sure it was just *going* to. But the fourth time, he groped a little further, and his hand lightly swept against something soft and warm. This petrified him, nearly, with fright—his mind was in such a state that he could imagine the thing to be nothing else than a corpse, newly dead and still warm. He thought he would rather die than touch it again. But he thought this false thought because he did not know the immortal strength of human curiosity. In no long time his hand was tremblingly groping again—against his judgment, and without his consent—but groping persistently on, just the same. It encountered a bunch of long hair; he shuddered, but followed up the hair and found what seemed to be a warm rope; followed up the rope and found an innocent calf!—for the rope was not a rope at all, but the calf's tail.

The king was cordially ashamed of himself for having gotten all that fright and misery out of so paltry a matter as a slumbering calf; but he need not have felt so about it, for it was not the calf that frightened him but a dreadful non-existent something which the calf stood for; and any other boy, in those old superstitious times, would have acted and suffered just as he had done.

The king was not only delighted to find that the creature was only a calf, but delighted to have the calf's company; for he had been feeling so lonesome and friendless that the company and comradeship of even this humble animal was welcome. And he had been so buffeted, so rudely entreated by his own kind, that it was a real comfort to him to feel that he was at last in the society of a fellow creature that had at least a soft heart and a gentle spirit, whatever loftier attributes might be lacking. So he resolved to waive rank and make friends with the calf.

While stroking its sleek warm back—for it lay near him and within easy reach—it occurred to him that this calf might be utilized in more ways than one. Whereupon he re-arranged his bed, spreading it down close to the calf; then he cuddled himself up to the calf's back, drew the covers up over himself and his friend, and in a minute or two was as warm and comfortable as he had ever been in the downy couches of the regal palace of Westminster.

Pleasant thoughts came, at once; life took on a cheerfuller seeming. He was free of the bonds of servitude and crime, free of the companionship of base and brutal outlaws; he was warm, he was sheltered; in a word, he was happy. The night wind was rising; it swept by in fitful gusts that made the old barn quake and rattle, then its forces died down at intervals, and went moaning and wailing around corners and projections—but it was all music to the king, now that he was snug and comfortable: let it blow and rage, let it batter and bang, let it moan and wail, he minded it not, he only enjoyed it. He merely snuggled the closer to his friend, in a luxury of warm contentment, and drifted blissfully out of consciousness into a deep and dreamless sleep that was full of serenity and peace. The distant dogs howled, the melancholy kine complained, and the winds went on raging, whilst furious sheets of rain drove along the roof; but the majesty of England slept on, undisturbed, and the calf did the same, it being a simple creature and not easily troubled by storms or embarrassed by sleeping with a king.

CHAPTER XIX

THE PRINCE WITH THE PEASANTS

When the king awoke in the early morning, he found that a wet but thoughtful rat had crept into the place during the night and made a cosey bed for itself in his bosom. Being disturbed, now, it scampered away. The boy smiled, and said, "Poor fool, why so fearful? I am as forlorn as thou. 'Twould be a shame in me to hurt the helpless, who am myself so helpless. Moreover, I owe you thanks for a good omen; for when a king has fallen so low that the very rats do make a bed of him, it surely meaneth that his fortunes be upon the turn, since it is plain he can no lower go."

He got up and stepped out of the stall, and just then he heard the sound of children's voices. The barn door opened and a couple of little girls came in. As soon as they saw him their talking and laughing ceased, and they stopped and stood still, gazing at him with strong curiosity; they presently began to whisper together, then they approached nearer, and stopped again to gaze and whisper. By and

by they gathered courage and began to discuss him aloud. One
said—

"He hath a comely face."

The other added—

"And pretty hair."

"But is ill clothed enow."

"And how starved he looketh."

They came still nearer, sidling shyly around and about him,
examining him minutely from all points, as if he were some strange
new kind of animal; but warily and watchfully, the while, as if they
half feared he might be a sort of animal that would bite, upon
occasion. Finally they halted before him, holding each other's
hands, for protection, and took a good satisfying stare with their
innocent eyes; then one of them plucked up all her courage and
inquired with honest directness—

"Who art thou, boy?"

"I am the king," was the grave answer.

The children gave a little start, and their eyes spread themselves
wide open and remained so during a speechless half minute. Then
curiosity broke the silence—

"The *king?* What king?"

"The king of England."

The children looked at each other—then at him—then at each
other again—wonderingly, perplexedly—then one said—

"Didst hear him, Margery?—he saith he is the king. Can that be
true?"

"How can it be else but true, Prissy? Would he say a lie? For look
you, Prissy, an' it were not true, it *would* be a lie. It surely would be.
Now think on't. For all things that be not true, be lies—thou canst
make nought else out of it."

It was a good tight argument, without a leak in it anywhere; and
it left Prissy's half-doubts not a leg to stand on. She considered a
moment, then put the king upon his honor with the simple remark—

"If thou art truly the king, then I believe thee."

"I am truly the king."

This settled the matter. His majesty's royalty was accepted
without further question or discussion, and the two little girls began
at once to inquire into how he came to be where he was, and how he
came to be so unroyally clad, and whither he was bound, and all
about his affairs. It was a mighty relief to him to pour out his
troubles where they would not be scoffed at or doubted; so he told
his tale with feeling, forgetting even his hunger for the time; and it
was received with the deepest and tenderest sympathy by the gentle
little maids. But when he got down to his latest experiences and
they learned how long he had been without food, they cut him short
and hurried him away to the farm-house to find a breakfast for him.

The king was cheerful and happy, now, and said to himself,

"When I am come to mine own again, I will always honor little children, remembering how that these trusted me and believed in me in my time of trouble; whilst they that were older, and thought themselves wiser, mocked at me and held me for a liar."

The children's mother received the king kindly, and was full of pity; for his forlorn condition and apparently crazed intellect touched her womanly heart. She was a widow, and rather poor; consequently she had seen trouble enough to enable her to feel for the unfortunate. She imagined that the demented boy had wandered away from his friends or keepers; so she tried to find out whence he had come, in order that she might take measures to return him; but all her references to neighboring towns and villages, and all her inquiries in the same line, went for nothing—the boy's face, and his answers, too, showed that the things she was talking of were not familiar to him. He spoke earnestly and simply about court matters; and broke down, more than once, when speaking of the late king "his father;" but whenever the conversation changed to baser topics, he lost interest and became silent.

The woman was mightily puzzled; but she did not give up. As she proceeded with her cooking, she set herself to contriving devices to surprise the boy into betraying his real secret. She talked about cattle—he showed no concern; then about sheep—the same result— so her guess that he had been a shepherd boy was an error; she talked about mills; and about weavers, tinkers, smiths, trades and tradesmen of all sorts; and about Bedlam, and jails, and charitable retreats; but no matter, she was baffled at all points. Not altogether, either; for she argued that she had narrowed the thing down to domestic service. Yes, she was sure she was on the right track, now— he must have been a house servant. So she led up to that. But the result was discouraging. The subject of sweeping appeared to weary him; fire-building failed to stir him; scrubbing and scouring awoke no enthusiasm. Then the goodwife touched, with a perishing hope, and rather as a matter of form, upon the subject of cooking. To her surprise, and her vast delight, the king's face lighted at once! Ah, she had hunted him down at last, she thought; and she was right proud too, of the devious shrewdness and tact which had accomplished it.

Her tired tongue got a chance to rest, now; for the king's, inspired by gnawing hunger and the fragrant smells that came from the sputtering pots and pans, turned itself loose and delivered itself up to such an eloquent dissertation upon certain toothsome dishes, that within three minutes the woman said to herself, "Of a truth I was right—he hath holpen in a kitchen!" Then he broadened his bill of fare, and discussed it with such appreciation and animation, that the goodwife said to herself, "Good lack! how can he know so many dishes, and so fine ones withal? For these belong only upon the tables of the rich and great. Ah, now I see! ragged outcast as he is, he must have served in the palace before his reason went astray; yes, he must have helped in the very kitchen of the king himself! I will test him."

Full of eagerness to prove her sagacity, she told the king to mind the cooking a moment—hinting that he might manufacture and add a dish or two, if he chose—then she went out of the room and gave her children a sign to follow after. The king muttered—

"Another English king had a commission like to this, in a bygone time—it is nothing against my dignity to undertake an office which the great Alfred stooped to assume. But I will try to better serve my trust than he; for he let the cakes burn."

The intent was good, but the performance was not answerable to it; for this king, like the other one, soon fell into deep thinkings concerning his vast affairs, and the same calamity resulted—the cookery got burned. The woman returned in time to save the breakfast from entire destruction; and she promptly brought the king out of his dreams with a brisk and cordial tongue-lashing. Then, seeing how troubled he was, over his violated trust, she softened at once and was all goodness and gentleness toward him.

The boy made a hearty and satisfying meal, and was greatly refreshed and gladdened by it. It was a meal which was distinguished by this curious feature, that rank was waived on both sides; yet neither recipient of the favor was aware that it had been extended. The goodwife had intended to feed this young tramp with broken victuals in a corner, like any other tramp, or like a dog; but she was so remorseful for the scolding she had given him, that she did what she could to atone for it by allowing him to sit at the family table and eat with his betters, on ostensible terms of equality with them; and the king, on his side, was so remorseful for having broken his trust, after the family had been so kind to him, that he forced himself to atone for it by humbling himself to the family level, instead of requiring the woman and her children to stand and wait upon him while he occupied their table in the solitary state due his birth and dignity. It does us all good to unbend sometimes. This good woman was made happy all the day long by the applauses she got out of herself for her magnanimous condescension to a tramp; and the king was just as self-complacent over his gracious humility toward a humble peasant woman.

When breakfast was over, the housewife told the king to wash up the dishes. This command was a staggerer, for a moment, and the king came near rebelling: but then he said to himself, "Alfred the Great watched the cakes; doubtless he would have washed the dishes, too—therefore will I essay it."

He made a sufficiently poor job of it; and to his surprise, too, for the cleaning of wooden spoons and trenchers had seemed an easy thing to do. It was a tedious and troublesome piece of work, but he finished it at last. He was becoming impatient to get away on his journey now; however, he was not to lose this thrifty dame's society so easily. She furnished him some little odds and ends of employment, which he got through with after a fair fashion and with some credit. Then she set him and the little girls to paring some winter apples; but he was so awkward at this service, that she retired him from it and gave him a butcher knife to grind. Afterward she kept him carding wool until he began to think he had laid the good King Alfred about far enough in the shade for the present, in the matter of showy menial heroisms that would read picturesquely in story-books and histories, and so he was half minded to resign. And when, just after the noonday dinner, the goodwife gave him a basket of kittens to drown, he did resign. At least he was just going to resign—for he felt that he must draw the line somewhere, and it seemed to him that to draw it at kitten-drowning was about the right thing—when there was an interruption. The interruption was John Canty—with a peddler's pack on his back—and Hugo!

The King discovered these rascals approaching the front gate before they had had a chance to see him; so he said nothing about drawing the line, but took up his basket of kittens and stepped quietly out the back way, without a word. He left the creatures in an outhouse, and hurried on, into a narrow lane at the rear.

CHAPTER XX

THE PRINCE AND THE HERMIT

The high hedge hid him from the house, now; and so, under the impulse of a deadly fright, he let out all his forces and sped toward a wood in the distance. He never looked back until he had almost gained the shelter of the forest; then he turned and descried two figures in the distance. That was sufficient; he did not wait to scan them critically, but hurried on, and never abated his pace till he was far within the twilight depths of the wood. Then he stopped; being persuaded that he was now tolerably safe. He listened intently, but the stillness was profound and solemn—awful, even, and depressing to the spirits. At wide intervals his straining ear did detect sounds, but they were so remote, and hollow, and mysterious, that they seemed not to be real sounds, but only the moaning and complaining ghosts of departed ones. So the sounds were yet more dreary than the silence which they interrupted.

It was his purpose, in the beginning, to stay where he was, the rest of the day; but a chill soon invaded his perspiring body, and he was at last obliged to resume movement in order to get warm. He struck straight through the forest, hoping to pierce to a road presently, but he was disappointed in this. He travelled on and on; but the farther he went, the denser the wood became, apparently. The gloom began to thicken, by and by, and the king realized that the night was coming on. It made him shudder to think of spending it in such an uncanny place; so he tried to hurry faster, but he only made the less speed, for he could not now see well enough to choose his steps judiciously; consequently he kept tripping over roots and tangling himself in vines and briers.

And how glad he was when at last he caught the glimmer of a light! He approached it warily, stopping often to look about him and listen. It came from an unglazed window-opening in a little hut. He heard a voice, now, and felt a disposition to run and hide; but he changed his mind at once, for this voice was praying, evidently. He glided to the one window of the hut, raised himself on tiptoe, and stole a glance within. The room was small; its floor was the natural earth, beaten hard by use; in a corner was a bed of rushes and a ragged blanket or two; near it was a pail, a cup, a basin, and two or three pots and pans; there was a short bench and a three-legged stool; on the hearth the remains of a fagot fire were smouldering; before a shrine, which was lighted by a single candle, knelt an aged man, and on an old wooden box at his side, lay an open book and a human skull. The man was of large, bony frame; his hair and whiskers were very long and snowy white; he was clothed in a robe of sheepskins which reached from his neck to his heels.

"A holy hermit!" said the king to himself; "now am I indeed fortunate."

The hermit rose from his knees; the king knocked. A deep voice responded—

"Enter!—but leave sin behind, for the ground whereon thou shalt stand is holy!"

The king entered, and paused. The hermit turned a pair of gleaming, unrestful eyes upon him, and said—

"Who art thou?"

"I am the king," came the answer, with placid simplicity.

"Welcome, king!" cried the hermit, with enthusiasm. Then, bustling about with feverish activity, and constantly saying "Welcome, welcome," he arranged his bench, seated the king on it, by the hearth, threw some fagots on the fire, and finally fell to pacing the floor, with a nervous stride.

"Welcome! Many have sought sanctuary here, but they were not worthy, and were turned away. But a king who casts his crown away, and despises the vain splendors of his office, and clothes his body in rags, to devote his life to holiness and the mortification of the flesh— he is worthy, he is welcome!—here shall he abide all his days till death come." The king hastened to interrupt and explain, but the hermit paid no attention to him—did not even hear him, apparently, but went right on with his talk, with a raised voice and a growing energy. "And thou shalt be at peace here. None shall find out thy refuge to disquiet thee with supplications to return to that empty and foolish life which God hath moved thee to abandon. Thou shalt pray, here; thou shalt study the Book; thou shalt meditate upon the follies and delusions of this world, and upon the sublimities of the world to come; thou shalt feed upon crusts and herbs, and scourge thy body with whips, daily, to the purifying of thy soul. Thou shalt wear a hair shirt next thy skin; thou shalt drink water, only; and thou shalt be at peace; yes, wholly at peace; for whoso comes to seek thee shall go his way again, baffled; he shall not find thee, he shall not molest thee."

The old man, still pacing back and forth, ceased to speak aloud, and began to mutter. The king seized this opportunity to state his case; and he did it with an eloquence inspired by uneasiness and apprehension. But the hermit went on muttering, and gave no heed. And still muttering, he approached the king and said, impressively—

" 'Sh! I will tell you a secret!" He bent down to impart it, but checked himself, and assumed a listening attitude. After a moment or two he went on tiptoe to the window-opening, put his head out and peered around in the gloaming, then came tip-toeing back again, put his face close down to the king's, and whispered—

"I am an archangel!"

The king started violently, and said to himself, "Would God I were with the outlaws again; for lo, now am I the prisoner of a madman!" His apprehensions were heightened, and they showed plainly in his face. In a low, excited voice, the hermit continued—

"I see you feel my atmosphere! There's awe in your face! None may be in this atmosphere and not be thus affected; for it is the very atmosphere of heaven. I go thither and return, in the twinkling of an eye. I was made an archangel on this very spot, it is five years ago, by angels sent from heaven to confer that awful dignity. Their presence filled this place with an intolerable brightness. And they knelt to me, king! yes, they knelt to me! for I was greater than they. I have walked in the courts of heaven, and held speech with the patriarch. Touch my hand—be not afraid—touch it. There—now thou has touched a hand which has been clasped by Abraham and Isaac and Jacob! For I have walked in the golden courts, I have seen the Deity face to face!" He paused, to give this speech effect; then his face suddenly changed, and he started to his feet again, saying, with angry energy, "Yes, I am an archangel; *a mere archangel!*— I that might have been pope! It is verily true. I was told it from heaven in a dream, twenty years ago; ah, yes I was to be pope!—and I *should* have been pope, for Heaven had said it—but the king dissolved my religious house, and I, poor obscure unfriended monk, was cast homeless upon the world, robbed of my mighty destiny!" Here he began to mumble again, and beat his forehead in futile rage, with his fist; now and then articulating a venomous curse, and now and then a pathetic "Wherefore I am nought but an archangel— I that should have been pope!"

So he went on, for an hour, whilst the poor little king sat and suffered. Then all at once the old man's frenzy departed, and he became all gentleness. His voice softened, he came down out of his clouds, and fell to prattling along so simply and so humanely, that he soon won the king's heart completely. The old devotee moved the boy nearer to the fire and made him comfortable; doctored his small bruises and abrasions with a deft and tender hand; and then set about preparing and cooking a supper—chatting pleasantly all the time, and occasionally stroking the lad's cheek or patting his head, in such a gently caressing way that in a little while all the fear and repulsion inspired by the archangel were changed to reverence and affection for the man.

This happy state of things continued while the two ate the supper; then, after a prayer before the shrine, the hermit put the boy to bed, in a small adjoining room, tucking him in as snugly and lovingly as a mother might; and so, with a parting caress, left him and sat down by the fire, and began to poke the brands about in an absent and aimless way. Presently he paused; then tapped his forehead several times with his fingers, as if trying to recall some thought which had escaped from his mind. Apparently he was unsuccessful. Now he started quickly up, and entered his guest's room, and said—

"Thou art king?"

"Yes," was the response, drowsily uttered.

"What king?"

"Of England."

"Of England! Then Henry is gone!"

"Alack, it is so. I am his son."

A black frown settled down upon the hermit's face, and he clenched his bony hands with a vindictive energy. He stood a few moments, breathing fast and swallowing repeatedly, then said in a husky voice—

"Dost know it was he that turned us out into the world houseless and homeless?"

There was no response. The old man bent down and scanned the boy's reposeful face and listened to his placid breathing. "He sleeps—sleeps soundly;" and the frown vanished away and gave place to an expression of evil satisfaction. A smile flitted across the dreaming boy's features. The hermit muttered, "So—his heart is happy;" and he turned away. He went stealthily about the place, seeking here and there for something; now and then halting to listen, now and then jerking his head around and casting a quick glance toward the bed; and always muttering, always mumbling to himself. At last he found what he seemed to want—a rusty old butcher knife and a whetstone. Then he crept to his place by the fire, sat himself down, and began to whet the knife softly on the stone, still muttering, mumbling, ejaculating. The winds sighed around the lonely place, the mysterious voices of the night floated by out of the distances. The shining eyes of venturesome mice and rats peered out at the old man from cracks and coverts, but he went on with his work, rapt absorbed, and noted none of these things.

At long intervals he drew his thumb along the edge of his knife, and nodded his head with satisfaction. "It grows sharper," he said; "yes, it grows sharper."

He took no note of the flight of time, but worked tranquilly on, entertaining himself with his thoughts, which broke out occasionally in articulate speech:

"His father wrought us evil, he destroyed us—and is gone down into the eternal fires! Yes, down into the eternal fires! He escaped us—but it was God's will, yes it was God's will, we must not repine. But he hath not escaped the fires! no, he hath not escaped the fires, the consuming, unpitying, remoreseless fires—and *they* are everlasting!"

And so he wrought; and still wrought; mumbling—chuckling a low rasping chuckle, at times—and at times breaking again into words:

"It was his father that did it all. I am but an archangel—but for him, I should be pope!"

The king stirred. The hermit sprang noiselessly to the bedside, and went down upon his knees, bending over the prostrate form with his knife uplifted. The boy stirred again; his eyes came open for an instant, but there was no speculation in them, they saw nothing; the next moment his tranquil breathing showed that his sleep was sound once more.

The hermit watched and listened, for a time, keeping his position and scarcely breathing; then he slowly lowered his arm, and presently crept away, saying,—

"It is long past midnight—it is not best that he should cry out, lest by accident some one be passing."

He glided about his hovel, gathering a rag here, a thong there, and another one yonder; then he returned, and by careful and gentle handling, he managed to tie the king's ankles together without waking him. Next he essayed to tie the wrists; he made several attempts to cross them, but the boy always drew one hand or the other away, just as the cord was ready to be applied; but at last, when the archangel was almost ready to despair, the boy crossed his hands himself, and the next moment they were bound. Now a bandage was passed under the sleeper's chin and brought up over his head and tied fast—and so softly, so gradually, and so deftly were the knots drawn together and compacted, that the boy slept peacefully through it all without stirring.

CHAPTER XXI

HENDON TO THE RESCUE

The old man glided away, stooping, stealthily, cat-like, and
brought the low bench. He seated himself upon it, half his body in
the dim and flickering light, and the other half in shadow; and so,
with his craving eyes bent upon the slumbering boy, he kept his
patient vigil there, heedless of the drift of time, and softly whetted
his knife, and mumbled and chuckled; and in aspect and attitude
he resembled nothing so much as a grizzly, monstrous spider,
gloating over some hapless insect that lay bound and helpless in
his web.

After a long while, the old man, who was still gazing,—yet not
seeing, his mind having settled into a dreamy abstraction,—
observed on a sudden, that the boy's eyes were open—wide open
and staring!—staring up in frozen horror at the knife. The smile
of a gratified devil crept over the old man's face, and he said,
without changing his attitude or occupation—

"Son of Henry the Eighth, hast thou prayed?"

The boy struggled helplessly in his bonds; and at the same time
forced a smothered sound through his closed jaws, which the
hermit chose to interpret as an affirmative answer to his question.

"Then pray again. Pray the prayer for the dying!"

A shudder shook the boy's frame, and his face blenched. Then
he struggled again to free himself—turning and twisting himself
this way and that; tugging frantically, fiercely, desperately—but
uselessly—to burst his fetters: and all the while the old ogre smiled
down upon him, and nodded his head, and placidly whetted his
knife; mumbling, from time to time. "The moments are precious,
they are few and precious—pray the prayer for the dying!"

The boy uttered a despairing groan, and ceased from his
struggles, panting. The tears came, then, and trickled, one after the
other, down his face; but this piteous sight wrought no softening
effect upon the savage old man.

The dawn was coming, now; the hermit observed it, and spoke
up sharply, with a touch of nervous apprehension in his voice:

"I may not indulge this ecstasy longer! The night is already gone.
It seems but a moment—only a moment; would it had endured a
year! Seed of the Church's spoiler, close thy perishing eyes, an' thou
fearest to look upon"...

The rest was lost in inarticulate mutterings. The old man sunk
upon his knees, his knife in his hand, and bent himself over the
moaning boy—

Hark! There was a sound of voices near the cabin—the knife
dropped from the hermit's hand; he cast a sheepskin over the boy
and started up, trembling. The sounds increased, and presently the

voices became rough and angry; then came blows, and cries for help; then a clatter of swift footsteps, retreating. Immediately came a succession of thundering knocks upon the cabin door, followed by—

"Hullo-o-o! Open! And despatch, in the name of all the devils!"

O, this was the blessedest sound that had ever made music in the king's ears; for it was Miles Hendon's voice!

The hermit, grinding his teeth in impotent rage, moved swiftly out of the bedchamber, closing the door behind him; and straightway the king heard a talk, to this effect, proceeding from the "chapel:"

"Homage and greeting, reverend sir! Where is the boy—*my* boy?"

"What boy, friend?"

"What boy! Lie me no lies, sir priest, play me no deceptions!—I am not in the humor for it. Near to this place I caught the scoundrels who I judged did steal him from me, and I made them confess; they said he was at large again, and they had tracked him to your door. They showed me his very footprints. Now palter no more; for look you, holy sir, an' thou produce him not— Where is the boy?"

"O, good sir, peradventure you mean the ragged regal vagrant that tarried here the night. If such as you take interest in such as he, know, then, that I have sent him of an errand. He will be back anon."

"How soon? How soon? Come, waste not the time—cannot I overtake him? How soon will he be back?"

"Thou needst not stir; he will return quickly."

"So be it then. I will try to wait. But stop!—*you* sent him of an errand?—you! Verily, this is a lie—he would not go. He would pull thy old beard, an' thou didst offer him such an insolence. Thou hast lied, friend; thou hast surely lied! He would not go for thee nor for any man."

"For any *man*—no; haply not. But I am not a man."

"*What!* Now o' God's name what art thou, then?"

"It is a secret—mark thou reveal it not. I am an archangel!"

There was a tremendous ejaculation from Miles Hendon—not altogether unprofane—followed by—

"This doth well and truly account for his complaisance! Right well I knew he would budge nor hand nor foot in the menial service of any mortal; but lord, even a king must obey when an archangel gives the word o' command! Let me—'sh! What noise was that?"

All this while the king had been yonder, alternately quaking with terror and trembling with hope; and all the while, too, he had thrown all the strength he could into his anguished moanings, constantly expecting them to reach Hendon's ear, but always realizing, with bitterness, that they failed, or at least made no impression. So this last remark of his servant came as comes a reviving breath from fresh fields to the dying; and he exerted himself once more, and with all his energy, just as the hermit was saying—

"Noise? I heard only the wind."

"Mayhap it was. Yes, doubtless that was it. I have been hearing it faintly all the—there it is again! It is not the wind! What an odd sound! Come, we will hunt it out!"

Now the king's joy was nearly insupportable. His tired lungs did their utmost—and hopefully, too—but the sealed jaws and the muffling sheepskin sadly crippled the effort. Then the poor fellow's heart sank, to hear the hermit say—

"Ah, it came from without—I think from the copse yonder. Come, I will lead the way."

The king heard the two pass out, talking; heard their footsteps die quickly away—then he was alone with a boding, brooding, awful silence.

It seemed an age till he heard the steps and voices approaching again—and this time he heard an added sound—the trampling of hoofs, apparently. Then he heard Hendon say—

"I will not wait longer. I *cannot* wait longer. He has lost his way in this thick wood. Which direction took he? Quick—point it out to me."

"He—but wait; I will go with thee."

"Good—good! Why, truly thou art better than thy looks. Marry I do think there's not another archangel with so right a heart as thine. Wilt ride? Wilt take the wee donkey that's for my boy, or wilt thou fork thy holy legs over this ill-conditioned slave of a mule that I have provided for myself?—and had been cheated in, too, had he cost but the indifferent sum of a month's usury on a brass farthing let to a tinker out of work."

"No—ride thy mule, and lead thine ass; I am surer on mine own feet, and will walk."

"Then prithee mind the little beast for me while I take my life in my hands and make what success I may toward mounting the big one."

Then followed a confusion of kicks, cuffs, tramplings and plungings, accompanied by a thunderous intermingling of volleyed curses, and finally a bitter apostrophe to the mule, which must have broken its spirit, for hostilities seemed to cease from that moment.

With unutterable misery the fettered little king heard the voices and footsteps fade away and die out. All hope forsook him, now, for the moment, and a dull despair settled down upon his heart. "My only friend is deceived and got rid of," he said; "the hermit will return and"—He finished with a gasp; and at once fell to struggling so frantically with his bonds again, that he shook off the smothering sheepskin.

And now he heard the door open! The sound chilled him to the marrow—already he seemed to feel the knife at his throat. Horror made him close his eyes; horror made him open them again—and before him stood John Canty and Hugo!

He would have said "Thank God!" if his jaws had been free.

A moment or two later his limbs were at liberty, and his captors each gripping him by an arm, were hurrying him with all speed through the forest.

CHAPTER XXII

A VICTIM OF TREACHERY

Once more "King Foo-Foo the First" was roving with the tramps and outlaws, a butt for their coarse jests and dull-witted railleries, and sometimes the victim of small spitefulnesses at the hands of Canty and Hugo when the Ruffler's back was turned. None but Canty and Hugo really disliked him. Some of the others liked him, and all admired his pluck and spirit. During two or three days, Hugo, in whose ward and charge the king was, did what he covertly could to make the boy uncomfortable; and at night, during the customary orgies, he amused the company by putting small indignities upon him—always as if by accident. Twice he stepped upon the king's toes—accidentally—and the king, as became his royalty, was contemptuously unconscious of it and indifferent to it; but the third time Hugo entertained himself in that way, the king felled him to the ground with a cudgel, to the prodigious delight of the tribe. Hugo, consumed with anger and shame, sprang up, seized a cudgel, and came at his small adversary in a fury. Instantly a ring was formed around the gladiators, and the betting and cheering began. But poor Hugo stood no chance whatsoever. His frantic and lubberly 'prentice-work found but a poor market for itself when pitted against an arm which had been trained by the first masters of Europe in single-stick, quarter-staff, and every art and trick of swordsmanship. The little king stood, alert but at graceful ease, and caught and turned aside the thick rain of blows with a facility and precision which set the motley on-lookers wild with admiration; and every now and then, when his practised eye detected an opening, and a lightning-swift rap upon Hugo's head followed as a result, the storm of cheers and laughter that swept the place was something wonderful to hear. At the end of fifteen minutes, Hugo, all battered, bruised, and the target for a pitiless bombardment of ridicule, slunk from the field; and the unscathed hero of the fight was seized and borne aloft upon the shoulders of the joyous rabble to the place of honor beside the Ruffler, where with vast ceremony he was crowned King of the Game-Cocks; his meaner title being at the same time solemnly cancelled and annulled, and a decree of banishment from the gang pronounced against any who should henceforth utter it.

All attempts to make the king serviceable to the troop had failed. He had stubbornly refused to act; moreover he was always trying to escape. He had been thrust into an unwatched kitchen, the first day of his return; he not only came forth empty handed, but tried to rouse the housemates. He was sent out with a tinker to help him at his work; he would not work; moreover he threatened the tinker with his own soldering-iron; and finally both Hugo and the tinker found their hands full with the mere matter of keeping him from getting away. He delivered the thunders of his royalty upon the heads of all who hampered his liberties or tried to force him to service. He was sent out, in Hugo's charge, in company with a slatternly woman and a diseased baby, to beg; but the result was not encouraging—he declined to plead for the mendicants, or be a party to their cause in any way.

Thus several days went by; and the miseries of this tramping life, and the weariness and sordidness and meanness and vulgarity of it, became gradually and steadily so intolerable to the captive that he began at last to feel that his release from the hermit's knife must prove only a temporary respite from death, at best.

But at night, in his dreams, these things were forgotten, and he was on his throne, and master again. This, of course, intensified the sufferings of the awakening—so the mortifications of each succeeding morning of the few that passed between his return to bondage and the combat with Hugo, grew bitterer and bitterer, and harder and harder to bear.

The morning after that combat, Hugo got up with a heart filled with vengeful purposes against the king. He had two plans, in particular. One was to inflict upon the lad what would be, to his proud spirit and "imagined" royalty, a peculiar humiliation; and if he failed to accomplish this, his other plan was to put a crime of some kind upon the king and then betray him into the implacable clutches of the law.

In pursuance of the first plan, he proposed to put a "clime" upon the king's leg; rightly judging that that would mortify him to the last and perfect degree; and as soon as the clime should operate, he meant to get Canty's help, and *force* the king to expose his leg in the highway and beg for alms. "Clime" was the cant term for a sore, artificially created. To make a clime, the operator made a paste or poultice of unslaked lime, soap, and the rust of old iron, and spread it upon a piece of leather, which was then bound tightly upon the leg. This would presently fret off the skin, and make the flesh raw and angry-looking; blood was then rubbed upon the limb, which, being fully dried, took on a dark and repulsive color. Then a bandage of soiled rags was put on in a cleverly careless way which would allow the hideous ulcer to be seen and move the compassion of the passer-by.*

Hugo got the help of the tinker whom the king had cowed with the soldering-iron; they took the boy out on a tinkering tramp, and as soon as they were out of sight of the camp they threw him down and the tinker held him while Hugo bound the poultice tight and fast upon his leg.

The king raged and stormed, and promised to hang the two the moment the sceptre was in his hand again; but they kept a firm grip upon him and enjoyed his impotent struggling and jeered at his threats. This continued until the poultice began to bite; and in no long time its work would have been perfected, if there had been no interruption. But there was; for about this time the "slave" who had made the speech denouncing England's laws, appeared on the scene and put an end to the enterprise, and stripped off the poultice and bandage.

The King wanted to borrow his deliverer's cudgel and warm the jackets of the two rascals on the spot; but the man said no, it would bring trouble—leave the matter till night; the whole tribe being together, then, the outside world would not venture to interfere or interrupt. He marched the party back to camp and reported the affair to the Ruffler, who listened, pondered, and then decided that the king should not be again detailed to beg, since it was plain he was worthy of something higher and better— wherefore, on the spot he promoted him from the mendicant rank and appointed him to steal!

Hugo was overjoyed. He had already tried to make the king steal, and failed; but there would be no more trouble of that sort, now, for of course the king would not dream of defying a distinct command delivered directly from headquarters. So he planned a raid for that very afternoon, purposing to get the king in the law's grip in the course of it; and to do it, too, with such ingenious strategy, that it should seem to be accidental and unintentional; for the King of the Game-Cocks was popular, now, and the gang might not deal over-gently with an unpopular member who played so serious a treachery upon him as the delivering him over to the common enemy, the law.

Very well. All in good time Hugo strolled off to a neighboring village with his prey; and the two drifted slowly up and down one street after another, the one watching sharply for a sure chance to achieve his evil purpose, and the other watching as sharply for a chance to dart away and get free of his infamous captivity forever.

Both threw away some tolerably fair-looking opportunities; for both, in their secret hearts, were resolved to make absolutely sure work this time, and neither meant to allow his fevered desires to seduce him into any venture that had much uncertainty about it.

Hugo's chance came first. For at last a woman approached who

*From "The English Rogue;" London, 1665.

carried a fat package of some sort in a basket. Hugo's eyes sparkled with sinful pleasure as he said to himself, "Breath o' my life, an' I can but put *that* upon him, 'tis good-den and God keep thee, King of the Game-Cocks!" He waited and watched—outwardly patient, but inwardly consuming with excitement—till the woman had passed by, and the time was ripe; then said, in a low voice—"Tarry here till I come again," and darted stealthily after the prey.

The king's heart was filled with joy—he could make his escape, now, if Hugo's quest only carried him far enough away.

But he was to have no such luck. Hugo crept behind the woman, snatched the package, and came running back, wrapping it in an old piece of blanket which he carried on his arm. The hue and cry was raised in a moment, by the woman, who knew her loss by the lightening of her burden, although she had not seen the pilfering done. Hugo thrust the bundle into the king's hands without halting, saying,—

"Now speed ye after me with the rest, and cry 'Stop thief!' but mind ye lead them astray!"

The next moment Hugo turned a corner and darted down a crooked alley,—and in another moment or two he lounged into view again, looking innocent and indifferent, and took up a position behind a post to watch results.

The insulted king threw the bundle on the ground; and the blanket fell away from it just as the woman arrived, with an augmenting crowd at her heels; she seized the king's wrist with one hand, snatched up her bundle with the other, and began to pour out a tirade of abuse upon the boy while he struggled, without success, to free himself from her grip.

Hugo had seen enough—his enemy was captured and the law would get him, now—so he slipped away, jubilant and chuckling, and wended campwards, framing a judicious version of the matter to give to the Ruffler's crew as he strode along.

The king continued to struggle in the woman's grasp, and now and then cried out, in vexation—

"Unhand me, thou foolish creature; it was not I that bereaved thee of thy paltry goods."

The crowd closed around, threatening the king and calling him names; a brawny blacksmith in leather apron, and sleeves rolled to his elbows, made a reach for him, saying he would trounce him well, for a lesson; but just then a long sword flashed in the air and fell with convincing force upon the man's arm, flat-side down, the fantastic owner of it remarking pleasantly at the same time—

"Marry, good souls, let us proceed gently, not with ill blood and uncharitable words. This is matter for the law's consideration, not private and unofficial handling. Loose thy hold from the boy, good-wife."

The blacksmith averaged the stalwart soldier with a glance, then went muttering away, rubbing his arm; the woman released the boy's wrist reluctantly; the crowd eyed the stranger unlovingly, but prudently closed their mouths. The king sprang to his deliverer's side, with flushed cheeks and sparkling eyes, exclaiming—

"Thou has lagged sorely, but thou comest in good season, now'. Sir Miles; carve me this rabble to rags!"

CHAPTER XXIII

THE PRINCE A PRISONER

Hendon forced back a smile, and bent down and whispered in the king's ear—

"Softly, softly, my prince, wag thy tongue warily—nay, suffer it not to wag at all. Trust in me—all shall go well in the end." Then he added, to himself: "*Sir* Miles! Bless me, I had totally forgot I was a knight! Lord how marvellous a thing it is, the grip his memory doth take upon his quaint and crazy fancies! . . . An empty and foolish title is mine, and yet it is something to have deserved it, for I think it is more honor to be held worthy to be a spectre-knight in his Kingdom of Dreams and Shadows, than to be held base enough to be an earl in some of the *real* kingdoms of this world."

The crowd fell apart to admit a constable, who approached and was about to lay his hand upon the king's shoulder, when Hendon said—

"Gently, good friend, withhold your hand—he shall go peaceably; I am responsible for that. Lead on, we will follow."

The officer led, with the woman and her bundle; Miles and the king followed after, with the crowd at their heels. The King was inclined to rebel; but Hendon said to him in a low voice—

"Reflect, sire—your laws are the wholesome breath of your own royalty; shall their source resist them, yet require the branches to respect them? Apparently one of these laws has been broken; when the king is on his throne again, can it ever grieve him to remember that when he was seemingly a private person he loyally sunk the king in the citizen and submitted to its authority?"

"Thou art right; say no more; thou shalt see that whatsoever the king of England requires a subject to suffer under the law, he will himself suffer while he holdeth the station of a subject."

When the woman was called upon to testify before the justice of the peace, she swore that the small prisoner at the bar was the person who had committed the theft; there was none able to show the contrary, so the king stood convicted. The bundle was now unrolled, and when the contents proved to be a plump little dressed pig, the judge looked troubled, whilst Hendon turned pale, and his body was thrilled with an electric shiver of dismay; but the king remained unmoved, protected by his ignorance. The judge

meditated, during an ominous pause, then turned to the woman,
with the question—

"What dost thou hold this property to be worth?"

The woman courtesied and replied—

"Three shillings and eightpence, your worship—I could not abate
a penny and set forth the value honestly."

The justice glanced around uncomfortably upon the crowd, then
nodded to the constable and said—

"Clear the court and close the doors."

It was done. None remained but the two officials, the accused,
the accuser, and Miles Hendon. This latter was rigid and colorless,
and on his forehead big drops of cold sweat gathered, broke and
blended together, and trickled down his face. The judge turned to
the woman again, and said, in a compassionate voice—

" 'Tis a poor ignorant lad, and mayhaps was driven hard by
hunger, for these be grievous times for the unfortunate; mark you,
he hath not an evil face—but when hunger driveth— Good woman!
dost know that when one steals a thing above the value of thirteen
pence ha'penny the law saith he shall *hang* for it?"

The little king started, wide-eyed with consternation, but
controlled himself and held his peace; but not so the woman. She
sprang to her feet, shaking with fright, and cried out—

"O, good lack, what have I done! God-a-mercy, I would not
hang the poor thing for the whole world! Ah, save me from this,
your worship—what shall I do, what *can* I do?"

The justice maintained his judicial composure, and simply said—

"Doubtless it is allowable to revise the value, since it is not yet
writ upon the record."

"Then in God's name call the pig eightpence, and heaven bless
the day that freed my conscience of this awesome thing!"

Miles Hendon forgot all decorum in his delight; and surprised
the king and wounded his dignity, by throwing his arms around
him and hugging him. The woman made her grateful adieux and
started away with her pig; and when the constable opened the door
for her, he followed her out into the narrow hall. The justice
proceeded to write in his record book. Hendon, always alert,
thought he would like to know why the officer followed the woman
out; so he slipped softly into the dusky hall and listened. He heard
a conversation to this effect—

"It is a fat pig, and promises good eating; I will buy it of thee;
here is the eightpence."

"Eightpence, indeed! Thou'lt do no such thing. It cost me three
shillings and eightpence, good honest coin of the last reign, that old
Harry that's just dead ne'er touched nor tampered with. A fig for
thy eightpence!"

"Stands the wind in that quarter? Thou wast under oath, and so
swore falsely when thou saidst the value was but eightpence. Come

straightway back with me before his worship, and answer for the crime!—and then the lad will hang."

"There, there, dear heart, say no more, I am content. Give me the eightpence, and hold thy peace about the matter."

The woman went off crying; Hendon slipped back into the court room, and the constable presently followed, after hiding his prize in some convenient place. The justice wrote a while longer, then read the king a wise and kindly lecture, and sentenced him to a short imprisonment in the common jail, to be followed by a public flogging. The astounded king opened his mouth and was probably going to order the good judge to be beheaded on the spot; but he caught a warning sign from Hendon, and succeeded in closing his mouth again before he lost any thing out of it. Hendon took him by the hand, now made reverence to the justice, and the two departed in the wake of the constable toward the jail. The moment the street was reached, the inflamed monarch halted, snatched away his hand, and exclaimed—

"Idiot, dost imagine I will enter a common jail *alive?*"

Hendon bent down and said, somewhat sharply—

"*Will* you trust in me? Peace! and forbear to worsen our chances with dangerous speech. What God wills, will happen; thou canst not hurry it, thou canst not alter it; therefore wait, and be patient—'twill be time enow to rail or rejoice when what is to happen has happened."*

CHAPTER XXIV

THE ESCAPE

The short winter day was nearly ended. The streets were deserted, save for a few random stragglers, and these hurried straight along, with the intent look of people who were only anxious to accomplish their errands as quickly as possible and then snugly house themselves from the rising wind and the gathering twilight. They looked neither to the right nor to the left; they paid no attention to our party, they did not even seem to see them. Edward the Sixth wondered if the spectacle of a king on his way to jail had ever encountered such marvellous indifference before. By and by the constable arrived at a deserted market-square and proceeded to cross it. When he had reached the middle of it, Hendon laid his hand upon his arm, and said in a low voice—

"Bide a moment, good sir, there is none in hearing, and I would say a word to thee."

"My duty forbids it, sir; prithee hinder me not, the night comes on."

"Stay, nevertheless, for the matter concerns thee nearly. Turn thy back a moment and seem not to see; *let this poor lad escape.*"

*Notes to Chapter 23, at end of volume.

"This to me, sir! I arrest thee in"—

"Nay, be not too hasty. See thou be careful and commit no foolish error"—then he shut his voice down to a whisper, and said in the man's ear—"the pig thou hast purchased for eightpence may cost thee thy neck, man!"

The poor constable, taken by surprise, was speechless, at first, then found his tongue and fell to blustering and threatening; but Hendon was tranquil, and waited with patience till his breath was spent; then said—

"I have a liking to thee, friend, and would not willingly see thee come to harm. Observe, I heard it all—every word. I will prove it to thee." Then he repeated the conversation which the officer and the woman had had together in the hall, word for word, and ended with—

"There—have I set it forth correctly? Should not I be able to set it forth correctly before the judge, if occasion required?"

The man was dumb with fear and distress, for a moment; then he rallied and said with forced lightness—

" 'Tis making a mighty matter indeed, out of a jest; I but plagued the woman for mine amusement."

"Kept you the woman's pig for amusement?"

The man answered sharply—

"Nought else, good sir—I tell thee 'twas but a jest."

"I do begin to believe thee," said Hendon, with a perplexing mixture of mockery and half-conviction in his tone; "but tarry thou here a moment whilst I run and ask his worship—for nathless, he being a man experienced in law, in jests, in"—

He was moving away, still talking; the constable hesitated, fidgeted, spat out an oath or two, then cried out—

"Hold, hold, good sir—prithee wait a little—the judge! why man, he hath no more sympathy with a jest than hath a dead corpse!— come, and we will speak further. Ods body! I seem to be in evil case—and all for an innocent and thoughtless pleasantry. I am a man of family; and my wife and little ones— List to reason, good your worship; what wouldst thou of me?"

"Only that thou be blind and dumb and paralytic whilst one may count a hundred thousand—counting slowly," said Hendon, with the expression of a man who asks but a reasonable favor, and that a very little one.

"It is my destruction!" said the constable despairingly. "Ah, be reasonable, good sir; only look at this matter, on all its sides, and see how mere a jest it is—how manifestly and how plainly it is so. And even if one granted it were not a jest, it is a fault so small that e'en the grimmest penalty it could call forth would be but a rebuke and warning from the judge's lips."

Hendon replied with a solemnity which chilled the air about him—

"This jest of thine hath a name, in law,—wot you what it is?"

"I knew it not! Peradventure I have been unwise. I never dreamed it had a name—ah, sweet heaven, I thought it was original."

"Yes, it hath a name. In the law this crime is called *Non compos mentis lex talionis sic transit gloria Mundi.*"

"Ah, my God!"

"And the penalty is death!"

"God be merciful to me, a sinner!"

"By advantage taken of one in fault, in dire peril, and at thy mercy, thou hast seized goods worth above thirteen pence ha'penny, paying but a trifle for the same; and this, in the eye of the law, is constructive barratry, misprision of treason, malfeasance in office, *ad hominem expurgatis in statu quo*—and the penalty is death by the halter, without ransom, commutation, or benefit of clergy."

"Bear me up, bear me up, sweet sir, my legs do fail me! Be thou merciful—spare me this doom, and I will turn my back and see nought that shall happen."

"Good! now thou'rt wise and reasonable. And thou'll restore the pig?"

"I will, I will indeed—nor ever touch another, though heaven send it and an archangel fetch it. Go—I am blind for thy sake—I see nothing. I will say thou didst break in and wrest the prisoner from my hands by force. It is but a crazy, ancient door—I will batter it down myself betwixt midnight and the morning."

"Do it, good soul, no harm will come of it; the judge hath a loving charity for this poor lad, and will shed no tears and break no jailer's bones for his escape."

CHAPTER XXV

HENDON HALL

As soon as Hendon and the king were out of sight of the constable, his majesty was instructed to hurry to a certain place outside the town, and wait there, whilst Hendon should go to the inn and settle his account. Half an hour later the two friends were blithely jobbing eastward on Hendon's sorry steeds. The king was warm and comfortable, now, for he had cast his rags and clothed himself in the second-hand suit which Hendon had bought on London Bridge.

Hendon wished to guard against over-fatiguing the boy; he judged that hard journeys, irregular meals, and illiberal measures of sleep would be bad for his crazed mind; whilst rest, regularity, and moderate exercise would be pretty sure to hasten its cure; he longed to see the stricken intellect made well again and its diseased visions driven out of the tormented little head; therefore he resolved to move by easy stages toward the home whence he had so long been banished, instead of obeying the impulse of his impatience and hurrying along night and day.

When he and the king had journeyed about ten miles, they reached a considerable village, and halted there for the night, at a good inn. The former relations were resumed; Hendon stood behind the king's chair, while he dined, and waited upon him; undressed him when he was ready for bed; then took the floor for his own quarters, and slept athwart the door, rolled up in a blanket.

The next day, and the next day after, they jogged lazily along talking over the adventures they had met since their separation, and mightily enjoying each other's narratives. Hendon detailed all his wide wanderings in search of the king, and described how the archangel had led him a fool's journey all over the forest, and taken him back to the hut, finally, when he found he could not get rid of him. Then—he said—the old man went into the bedchamber and came staggering back looking broken-hearted, and saying he had expected to find that the boy had returned and lain down in there to rest, but it was not so. Hendon had waited at the hut all day; hope of the king's return died out, then, and he departed upon the quest again.

"And old Sanctum Sanctorum *was* truly sorry your highness came not back," said Hendon; "I saw it in his face."

"Marry I will never doubt *that!*" said the king—and then told his own story; after which, Hendon was sorry he had not destroyed the archangel.

During the last day of the trip, Hendon's spirits were soaring. His tongue ran constantly. He talked about his old father, and his brother Arthur, and told of many things which illustrated their high and generous characters; he went into loving frenzies over his Edith, and was so gladhearted that he was even able to say some gentle and brotherly things about Hugh. He dwelt a deal on the coming meeting at Hendon Hall; what a surprise it would be to everybody, and what an outburst of thanksgiving and delight there would be.

It was a fair region, dotted with cottages and orchards, and the road led through broad pasture lands whose receding expanses, marked with gentle elevations and depressions, suggested the swelling and subsiding undulations of the sea. In the afternoon the returning prodigal made constant deflections from his course to see if by ascending some hillock he might not pierce the distance and catch a glimpse of his home. At last he was successful, and cried out excitedly—

"There is the village, my prince, and there is the Hall close by! You may see the towers from here; and that wood there—that is my father's park. Ah, *now* thou'lt know what state and grandeur be! A

house with seventy rooms—think of that!and seven and twenty
servants! A brave lodging for such as we, is it not so? Come, let us
speed—my impatience will not brook further delay."

All possible hurry was made; still, it was after three o'clock before
the village was reached. The travellers scampered through it,
Hendon's tongue going all the time. "Here is the church—covered
with the same ivy—none gone, none added." "Yonder is the inn, the
old Red Lion,—and yonder is the marketplace." "Here is the
Maypole, and here the pump—nothing is altered; nothing but the
people at any rate; ten years make a change in people; some of these
I seem to know, but none know me." So his chat ran on. The end of
the village was soon reached; then the travelers struck into a
crooked, narrow road, walled in with tall hedges, and hurried briskly
along it for a half mile, then passed into a vast flower garden
through an imposing gateway whose huge stone pillars bore
sculptured armorial devices. A noble mansion was before them.

"Welcome to Hendon Hall, my king!" exclaimed Miles. "Ah, 'tis
a great day! My father and my brother, and the lady Edith will be
so mad with joy that they will have eyes and tongue for none but me
in the first transports of the meeting, and so thou'lt seem but coldly
welcomed—but mind it not; 'twill soon seem otherwise; for when I
say thou art my ward, and tell them how costly is my love for thee,
thou'lt see them take thee to their breasts for Miles Hendon's sake,
and make their house and hearts thy home forever after!"

The next moment Hendon sprang to the ground before the great
door, helped the king down, then took him by the hand and rushed
within. A few steps brought him to a spacious apartment; he
entered, seated the king with more hurry than ceremony, then ran
toward a young man who sat at a writing-table in front of a generous
fire of logs.

"Embrace me, Hugh," he cried, "and say thou'rt glad I am come
again! and call our father, for home is not home till I shall touch his
hand, and see his face, and hear his voice once more!"

But Hugh only drew back, after betraying a momentary surprise,
and bent a grave stare upon the intruder—a stare which indicated
somewhat of offended dignity, at first, then changed, in response to
some inward thought or purpose, to an expression of marvelling
curiosity, mixed with a real or assumed compassion. Presently he
said, in a mild voice—

"Thy wits seem touched, poor stranger; doubtless thou hast
suffered privations and rude buffetings at the world's hands; thy
looks and dress betoken it. Whom dost thou take me to be?"

"Take thee? Prithee for whom else than whom thou art? I take
thee to be Hugh Hendon," said Miles, sharply.

The other continued, in the same soft tone—

"And whom dost thou imagine thyself to be?"

"Imagination hath nought to do with it! Dost thou pretend thou knowest me not for thy brother Miles Hendon?"

An expression of pleased surprise flitted across Hugh's face, and he exclaimed—

"What! thou art not jesting? can the dead come to life? God be praised if it be so! Our poor lost boy restored to our arms after all these cruel years! Ah, it seems too good to be true, it *is* too good to be true—I charge thee, have pity, do not trifle with me! Quick—come to the light—let me scan thee well!"

He seized Miles by the arm, dragged him to the window, and began to devour him from head to foot with his eyes, turning him this way and that, and stepping briskly around him and about him to prove him from all points of view; whilst the returned prodigal, all aglow with gladness, smiled, laughed, and kept nodding his head and saying—

"Go on, brother, go on, and fear not; thou'lt find nor limb nor feature that cannot bide the test. Scour and scan me to thy content, my dear old Hugh—I am indeed thy old Miles, thy same old Miles, thy lost brother, is't not so? Ah, 'tis a great day—I *said* 'twas a great day! Give me thy hand, give me thy cheek—lord, I am like to die of very joy!"

He was about to throw himself upon his brother; but Hugh put up his hand in dissent, then dropped his chin mournfully upon his breast, saying with emotion—

"Ah, God of his mercy give me strength to bear this grievous disappointment!"

Miles, amazed, could not speak, for a moment; then he found his tongue, and cried out—

"*What* disappointment? Am I not thy brother?"

Hugh shook his head sadly, and said—

"I pray heaven it may prove so, and that other eyes may find the resemblances that are hid from mine. Alack, I fear me the letter spoke but too truly."

"What letter?"

"One that came from over sea, some six or seven years ago. It said my brother died in battle."

"It was a lie! Call thy father—he will know me."

"One may not call the dead."

"Dead?" Miles's voice was subdued, and his lips trembled. "My father dead!—O, this is heavy news. Half my new joy is withered now. Prithee let me see my brother Arthur—he will know me; he will know me and console me."

"He, also, is dead."

"God be merciful to me, a stricken man! Gone,—both gone—the worthy taken and the worthless spared, in me! Ah! I crave your mercy!—do not say the lady Edith"—

"Is dead? No, she lives."

"Then, God be praised, my joy is whole again! Speed thee,

brother—let her come to me! An' *she* say I am not myself,—but she
will not; no, no, *she* will know me, I were a fool to doubt it. Bring
her—bring the old servants; they, too, will know me."

"All are gone but five—Peter, Halsey, David, Bernard and
Margaret."

So saying, Hugh left the room. Miles stood musing, a while, then
began to walk the floor, muttering—

"The five arch villains have survived the two-and-twenty leal and
honest—'tis an odd thing."

He continued walking back and forth, muttering to himself; he
had forgotten the king entirely. By and by his majesty said gravely,
and with a touch of genuine compassion, though the words
themselves were capable of being interpreted ironically—

"Mind not thy mischance, good man; there be others in the world
whose identity is denied, and whose claims are derided. Thou
hast company."

"Ah, my king," cried Hendon, coloring slightly, "do not thou
condemn me—wait, and thou shalt see. I am no impostor—she will
say it; you shall hear it from the sweetest lips in England. I an
impostor? Why I know this old hall, these pictures of my ancestors,
and all these things that are about us, as a child knoweth its own
nursery. Here was I born and bred, my lord; I speak the truth; I
would not deceive thee; and should none else believe, I pray thee do
not *thou* doubt me—I could not bear it."

"I do not doubt thee," said the king, with a childlike simplicity
and faith.

"I thank thee out of my heart!" exclaimed Hendon, with a
fervency which showed that he was touched. The king added, with
the same gentle simplicity—

"Dost thou doubt *me?*"

A guilty confusion seized upon Hendon, and he was grateful that
the door opened to admit Hugh, at that moment, and saved him the
necessity of replying.

A beautiful lady, richly clothed, followed Hugh, and after her
came several liveried servants. The lady walked slowly, with her head
bowed and her eyes fixed upon the floor. The face was unspeakably
sad. Miles Hendon sprang forward, crying out—

"O, my Edith, my darling"—

But Hugh waved him back, gravely, and said to the lady—

"Look upon him. Do you know him?"

At the sound of Miles's voice the woman had started, slightly, and
her cheeks had flushed; she was trembling, now. She stood still,
during an impressive pause of several moments; then slowly lifted up
her head and looked into Hendon's eyes with a stony and frightened
gaze; the blood sank out of her face, drop by drop, till nothing
remained but the gray pallor of death; then she said, in a voice as
dead as the face, "I know him not!" and turned, with a moan and a

stifled sob, and tottered out of the room.

Miles Hendon sank into a chair and covered his face with his hands. After a pause, his brother said to the servants—

"You have observed him. Do you know him?"

They shook their heads; then the master said—

"The servants know you not, sir. I fear there is some mistake. You have seen that my wife knew you not."

"Thy *wife!*" In an instant Hugh was pinned to the wall, with an iron grip about his throat. "O, thou fox-hearted slave, I see it all! Thou'st writ the lying letter thyself, and my stolen bride and goods are its fruit. There—now get thee gone, lest I shame mine honorable soldiership with the slaying of so pitiful a manikin!"

Hugh, red-faced, and almost suffocated, reeled to the nearest chair, and commanded the servants to seize and bind the murderous stranger. They hesitated, and one of them said—

"He is armed, Sir Hugh, and we are weaponless."

"Armed? What of it, and ye so many? Upon him, I say!"

But Miles warned them to be careful what they did, and added—

"Ye know me of old—I have not changed; come on, an' it like you."

This reminder did not hearten the servants much; they still held back.

"Then go, ye paltry cowards, and arm yourselves and guard the doors, whilst I send one to fetch the watch;" said Hugh. He turned, at the threshold, and said to Miles, "You'll find it to your advantage to offend not with useless endeavors at escape."

"Escape? Spare thyself discomfort, an' that is all that troubles thee. For Miles Hendon is master of Hendon Hall and all its belongings. He will remain—doubt it not."

CHAPTER XXVI

DISOWNED

The king sat musing a few moments, then looked up and said—

" 'Tis strange—most strange. I cannot account for it."

"No, it is not strange, my liege. I know him, and this conduct is but natural. He was a rascal from his birth."

"O, I spake not of *him,* Sir Miles."

"Not of him? Then of what? What is it that is strange?"

"That the king is not missed."

"How? Which? I doubt I do not understand."

"Indeed! Doth it not strike you as being passing strange that the land is not filled with couriers and proclamations describing my person and making search for me? Is it no matter for commotion and distress that the head of the State is gone?—that I am vanished away and lost?"

"Most true, my king, I had forgot." Then Hendon sighed, and muttered to himself, "Poor ruined mind—still busy with its pathetic dream."

"But I have a plan that shall right us both. I will write a paper, in three tongues—Latin, Greek and English—and thou shalt haste away with it to London in the morning. Give it to none but my uncle, the lord Hertford; when he shall see it, he will know and say I wrote it. Then he will send for me."

"Might it not be best, my prince, that we wait, here, until I prove myself and make my rights secure to my domains? I should be so much the better able then to"—

The king interrupted him imperiously—

"Peace! What are thy paltry domains, thy trivial interests, contrasted with matters which concern the weal of a nation and the integrity of a throne!" Then he added, in a gentle voice, as if he were sorry for his severity, "Obey and have no fear; I will right thee, I will make thee whole—yes, more than whole. I shall remember, and requite."

So saying, he took the pen, and set himself to work. Hendon contemplated him lovingly, a while, then said to himself—

"An' it were dark, I should think it *was* a king that spoke; there's no denying it, when the humor's upon him he doth thunder and lighten like your true king—now where got he that trick? See him scribble and scratch away contentedly at his meaningless pot-hooks, fancying them to be Latin and Greek—and except my wit shall serve me with a lucky device for diverting him from his purpose, I shall be forced to pretend to post away to-morrow on this wild errand he hath invented for me."

The next moment Sir Miles's thoughts had gone back to the recent episode. So absorbed was he in his musings, that when the king presently handed him the paper which he had been writing, he received it and pocketed it without being conscious of the act. "How marvellous strange she acted," he muttered. "I think she knew me—and I think she did *not* know me. These opinions do conflict, I perceive it plainly; I cannot reconcile them, neither can I, by argument, dismiss either of the two, or even persuade one to outweigh the other. The matter standeth simply thus: she *must* have known my face, my figure, my voice, for how could it be otherwise? yet she *said* she knew me not, and that is proof perfect, for she cannot lie. But stop—I think I begin to see. Peradventure he hath influenced her—commanded her—compelled her, to lie. That is the solution! The riddle is unriddled. She seemed dead with fear—yes, she was under his compulsion. I will seek her; I will find her; now that he is away, she will speak her true mind. She will remember the old times when we were little playfellows together, and this will soften her heart, and she will no more betray me, but will confess me. There is no treacherous blood in her—no, she was always honest and true. She has loved me in those old days—this is my security; for whom one has loved, one cannot betray."

He stepped eagerly toward the door; at that moment it opened, and the lady Edith entered. She was very pale, but she walked with a firm step, and her carriage was full of grace and gentle dignity. Her face was as sad as before.

Miles sprang forward, with a happy confidence, to meet her, but she checked him with a hardly perceptible gesture, and he stopped where he was. She seated herself, and asked him to do likewise. Thus simply did she take the sense of old-comradeship out of him, and transform him into a stranger and a guest. The surprise of it, the bewildering unexpectedness of it, made him begin to question, for a moment, if he *was* the person he was pretending to be, after all. The lady Edith said—

"Sir, I have come to warn you. The mad cannot be persuaded out of their delusions, perchance; but doubtless they may be persuaded to avoid perils. I think this dream of yours hath the seeming of honest truth to you, and therefore is not criminal—but do not tarry here with it; for here it is dangerous." She looked steadily into Miles's face, a moment, then added, impressively, "It is the more dangerous for that you *are* much like what our lost lad must have grown to be, if he had lived."

"Heavens, madame, but I *am* he!"

"I truly think you think it, sir. I question not your honesty in that—I but warn you, that is all. My husband is master in this region; his power hath hardly any limit; the people prosper or starve, as he wills. If you resembled not the man whom you profess to be, my husband might bid you pleasure yourself with your dream in peace; but trust me, I know him well, I know what he will do; he will say to all, that you are but a mad impostor, and straightway all will echo him." She bent upon Miles that same steady look once more, and added: "If you *were* Miles Hendon, and he knew it and all the region knew it—consider what I am saying, weigh it well—you would stand in the same peril, your punishment would be no less sure; he would deny you and denounce you, and none would be bold enough to give you countenance."

"Most truly I believe it," said Miles, bitterly.

"The power that can command one life-long friend to betray and disown another, and be obeyed, may well look to be obeyed in quarters where bread and life are on the stake and no cobweb ties of loyalty and honor are concerned."

A faint tinge appeared for a moment in the lady's cheek, and she dropped her eyes to the floor; but her voice betrayed no emotion when she proceeded—

"I have warned you, I must still warn you, to go hence. This man will destroy you, else. He is a tyrant who knows no pity. I, who am

his fettered slave, know this. Poor Miles, and Arthur, and my dear
guardian, Sir Richard, are free of him, and at rest—better that
you were with them than that you bide here in the clutches of this
miscreant. Your pretensions are a menace to his title and
possessions; you have assaulted him in his own house—you are
ruined if you stay. Go—do not hesitate. If you lack money, take this
purse, I beg of you, and bribe the servants to let you pass. O be
warned, poor soul, and escape while you may."

Miles declined the purse with a gesture, and rose up and stood
before her.

"Grant me one thing," he said. "Let your eyes rest upon mine, so
that I may see if they be steady. There—now answer me. Am I
Miles Hendon?"

"No. I know you not."

"Swear it!"

The answer was low, but distinct—

"I swear."

"O, this passes belief!"

"Fly! Why will you waste the precious time? Fly and save
yourself."

At that moment the officers burst into the room and a violent
struggle began; but Hendon was soon overpowered and dragged
away. The king was taken, also, and both were bound, and led to
prison.

CHAPTER XXVII

IN PRISON

The cells were all crowded; so the two friends were chained in
a large room where persons charged with trifling offenses were
commonly kept. They had company, for there were some twenty
manacled or fettered prisoners here, of both sexes and of varying
ages,—an obscene and noisy gang. The king chafed bitterly over the
stupendous indignity thus put upon his royalty, but Hendon was
moody and taciturn. He was pretty thoroughly bewildered. He had
come home, a jubilant prodigal, expecting to find everybody wild
with joy over his return; and instead had got the cold shoulder and
a jail. The promise and the fulfilment differed so widely, that the
effect was stunning; he could not decide whether it was most tragic
or most grotesque. He felt much as a man might who had danced
blithely out to enjoy a rainbow, and got struck by lightning.

But gradually his confused and tormenting thoughts settled down
into some sort of order, and then his mind centred itself upon
Edith. He turned her conduct over, and examined it in all lights,
but he could not make any thing satisfactory out of it. Did she know
him?—or didn't she know him? It was a perplexing puzzle, and

occupied him a long time: but he ended, finally, with the conviction that she did know him, and had repudiated him for interested reasons. He wanted to load her name with curses now; but this name had so long been sacred to him that he found he could not bring his tongue to profane it.

Wrapped in prison blankets of a soiled and tattered condition, Hendon and the king passed a troubled night. For a bribe the jailer had furnished liquor to some of the prisoners; singing of ribald songs, fighting, shouting, and carousing, was the natural consequence. At last, a while after midnight, a man attacked a woman and nearly killed her by beating her over the head with his manacles before the jailer could come to the rescue. The jailer restored peace by giving the man a sound clubbing about the head and shoulders—then the carousing ceased; and after that, all had an opportunity to sleep who did not mind the annoyance of the moanings and groanings of the two wounded people.

During the ensuing week, the days and nights were of a monotonous sameness, as to events; men whose faces Hendon remembered more or less distinctly, came, by day, to gaze at the "impostor" and repudiate and insult him; and by night the carousing and brawling went on, with symmetrical regularity. However, there was a change of incident at last. The jailer brought in an old man, and said to him—

"The villain is in this room—cast thy old eyes about and see if thou canst say which is he."

Hendon glanced up, and experienced a pleasant sensation for the first time since he had been in the jail. He said to himself, "This is Blake Andrews, a servant all his life in my father's family— a good honest soul, with a right heart in his breast. That is, formerly. But none are true, now; all are liars. This man will know me—and will deny me, too, like the rest."

The old man gazed around the room, glanced at each face in turn, and finally said—

"I see none here but paltry knaves, scum o' the streets. Which is he?"

The jailer laughed.

"Here," he said; "scan this big animal, and grant me an opinion."

The old man approached, and looked Hendon over, long and earnestly, then shook his head and said—

"Marry, *this* is no Hendon—nor ever was!"

"Right! Thy old eyes are sound yet. An' I were Sir Hugh, I would take the shabby carle and"—

The jailer finished by lifting himself a-tip-toe with an imaginary halter, at the same time making a gurgling noise in his throat suggestive of suffocation. The old man said, vindictively—

"Let him bless God an' he fare no worse. An' *I* had the handling o' the villain, he should roast, or I am no true man!"

The jailer laughed a pleasant hyena laugh, and said—

"Give him a piece of thy mind, old man—they all do it. Thou'lt find it good diversion."

Then he sauntered toward his ante-room and disappeared. The old man dropped upon his knees and whispered—

"God be thanked, thou'rt come again, my master! I believed thou wert dead these seven years, and lo, here thou art alive! I knew thee the moment I saw thee; and main hard work it was to keep a stony countenance and seem to see none here but tuppeny knaves and rubbish o' the streets. I am old and poor, Sir Miles; but say the word and I will go forth and proclaim the truth though I be strangled for it."

"No," said Hendon, "thou shalt not. It would ruin thee, and yet help but little in my cause. But I thank thee; for thou hast given me back somewhat of my lost faith in my kind."

The old servant became very valuable to Hendon and the king; for he dropped in several times a day to "abuse" the former, and always smuggled in a few delicacies to help out the prison bill of fare; he also furnished the current news. Hendon reserved the dainties for the king; without them his majesty might not have survived, for he was not able to eat the coarse and wretched food provided by the jailer. Andrews was obliged to confine himself to brief visits, in order to avoid suspicion; but he managed to impart a fair degree of information each time—information delivered in a low voice, for Hendon's benefit, and interlarded with insulting epithets delivered in a louder voice, for the benefit of other hearers.

So, little by little, the story of the family came out. Arthur had been dead six years. This loss, with the absence of news from Hendon, impaired the father's health; he believed he was going to die, and he wished to see Hugh and Edith settled in life before he passed away; but Edith begged hard for delay, hoping for Miles's return; then the letter came which brought the news of Miles's death; the shock prostrated Sir Richard; he believed his end was very near, and he and Hugh insisted upon the marriage; Edith begged for and obtained a month's respite; then another, and finally a third; the marriage then took place, by the death-bed of Sir Richard. It had not proved a happy one. It was whispered about the country that shortly after the nuptials the bride found among her husband's papers several rough and incomplete drafts of the fatal letter, and had accused him of precipitating the marriage— and Sir Richard's death, too—by a wicked forgery. Tales of cruelty to the lady Edith and the servants were to be heard on all hands; and since the father's death Sir Hugh had thrown off all soft disguises and become a pitiless master toward all who in any way depended upon him and his domains for bread.

There was a bit of Andrews's gossip which the king listened to with a lively interest—

"There is rumor that the king is mad. But in charity forbear to say *I* mentioned it, for 'tis death to speak of it, they say."

His majesty glared at the old man and said—

"The king is *not* mad, good man—and thou'lt find it to thy advantage to busy thyself with matters that nearer concern thee than this seditious prattle."

"What doth the lad mean?" said Andrews, surprised at this brisk assault from such an unexpected quarter. Hendon gave him a sign, and he did not pursue his question, but went on with his budget—

"The late king is to be buried at Windsor in a day or two—the 16th of the month,—and the new king will be crowned at Westminster the 20th."

"Methinks they must needs find him first," muttered his majesty; then added, confidently, "but they will look to that—and so also shall I."

"In the name of"—

But the old man got no further—a warning sign from Hendon checked his remark. He resumed the thread of his gossip—

"Sir Hugh goeth to the coronation—and with grand hopes. He confidently looketh to come back a peer, for he is high in favor with the Lord Protector."

"What Lord Protector?" asked his majesty.

"His grace the Duke of Somerset."

"What Duke of Somerset?"

"Marry, there is but one—Seymour, Earl of Hertford."

The king asked, sharply—

"Since when is *he* a duke, and Lord Protector?"

"Since the last day of January."

"And prithee who made him so?"

"Himself and the great Council—with help of the king."

His majesty started violently. "The *king!*" he cried. "*What* king, good sir?"

"What king, indeed! (God-a-mercy, what aileth the boy?) Sith we have but one, 'tis not difficult to answer—his most sacred majesty King Edward the Sixth—whom God preserve! Yea, and a dear and gracious little urchin is he, too; and whether he be mad or no—and they say he mendeth daily—his praises are on all men's lips; and all bless him, likewise, and offer prayers that he may be spared to reign long in England; for he began humanely, with saving the old duke of Norfolk's life, and now is he bent on destroying the cruelest of the laws that harry and oppress the people."

This news struck his majesty dumb with amazement, and plunged him into so deep and dismal a revery that he heard no more of the old man's gossip. He wondered if the "little urchin" was the beggar-boy whom he left dressed in his own garments in the palace. It did not seem possible that this could be, for surely his manners

and speech would betray him if he pretended to be the prince of
Wales—then he would be driven out, and search made for the true
prince. Could it be that the Court had set up some sprig of the
nobility in his place? No, for his uncle would not allow that—he
was all-powerful and could and would crush such a movement, of
course. The boy's musings profited him nothing; the more he tried
to unriddle the mystery the more perplexed he became, the more his
head ached, and the worse he slept. His impatience to get to London
grew hourly, and his captivity became almost unendurable.

Hendon's arts all failed with the king—he could not be comforted,
but a couple of women who were chained near him, succeeded
better. Under their gentle ministrations he found peace and learned
a degree of patience. He was very grateful, and came to love them
dearly and to delight in the sweet and soothing influence of their
presence. He asked them why they were in prison, and when they
said they were Baptists, he smiled, and inquired—

"Is that a crime to be shut up for, in a prison? Now I grieve, for
I shall lose ye—they will not keep ye long for such a little thing."

They did not answer; and something in their faces made him
uneasy. He said, eagerly—

"You do not speak—be good to me, and tell me—there will be no
other punishment? Prithee tell me there is no fear of that."

They tried to change the topic, but his fears were aroused, and
he pursued it—

"Will they scourge thee? No, no, they would not be so cruel!
Say they would not. Come, they *will* not, will they?"

The women betrayed confusion and distress, but there was no
avoiding an answer, so one of them said, in a voice choked with
emotion—

"O, thou'lt break our hearts, thou gentle spirit! God will help
us to bear our"—

"It is a confession!" the king broke in. "Then they *will* scourge
thee, the stonyhearted wretches! But O, thou must not weep, I
cannot bear it. Keep up thy courage—I shall come to my own in time
to save thee from this bitter thing, and I will do it!"

When the king awoke in the morning, the women were gone.

"They are saved!" he said, joyfully; then added, despondently,
"but woe is me!—for they were my comforters."

Each of them had left a shred of ribbon pinned to his clothing,
in token of remembrance. He said he would keep these things
always; and that soon he would seek out these dear good friends of
his and take them under his protection.

Just then the jailer came in with some subordinates and
commanded that the prisoners be conducted to the jail-yard. The
king was overjoyed—it would be a blessed thing to see the blue sky
and breathe the fresh air once more. He fretted and chafed at the
slowness of the officers, but his turn came at last and he was

released from his staple and ordered to follow the other prisoners, with Hendon.

The court or quadrangle, was stone-paved, and open to the sky. The prisoners entered it through a massive archway of masonry, and were placed in file, standing, with their backs against the wall. A rope was stretched in front of them, and they were also guarded by their officers. It was a chill and lowering morning, and a light snow which had fallen during the night whitened the great empty space and added to the general dismalness of its aspect. Now and then a wintry wind shivered through the place and sent the snow eddying hither and thither.

In the centre of the court stood two women, chained to posts. A glance showed the king that these were his good friends. He shuddered, and said to himself, "Alack, they are not gone free, as I had thought. To think that such as these should know the lash!— in England! Ay there's the shame of it—not in Heathenesse, but Christian England! They will be scourged; and I, whom they have comforted and kindly entreated, must look on and see the great wrong done; it is strange, so strange! that I, the very source of power in this broad realm, am helpless to protect them. But let these miscreants look well to themselves, for there is a day coming when I will require of them a heavy reckoning for this work. For every blow they strike now, they shall feel a hundred, then."

A great gate swung open and a crowd of citizens poured in. They flocked around the two women, and hid them from the king's view. A clergyman entered and passed through the crowd, and he also was hidden. The king now heard talking, back and forth, as if questions were being asked and answered, but he could not make out what was said. Next there was a deal of bustle and preparation, and much passing and repassing of officials through that part of the crowd that stood on the further side of the women; and whilst this proceeded a deep hush gradually fell upon the people.

Now, by command, the masses parted and fell aside, and the king saw a spectacle that froze the marrow in his bones. Fagots had been piled about the two women, and a kneeling man was lighting them!

The women bowed their heads, and covered their faces with their hands; the yellow flames began to climb upward among the snapping and crackling fagots, and wreaths of blue smoke to stream away on the wind; the clergyman lifted his hands and began a prayer—just then two young girls came flying through the great gate, uttering piercing screams, and threw themselves upon the women at the stake. Instantly they were torn away by the officers, and one of them was kept in a tight grip, but the other broke loose, saying she would die with her mother; and before she could be stopped she had flung her arms about her mother's neck again. She was torn away once more, and with her gown on fire. Two or three men held her, and the burning portion of her gown was snatched off and thrown flaming aside, she struggling all the while to free herself, and saying she would be alone in the world, now, and begging to be allowed to die with her mother. Both the girls screamed continually, and fought for freedom; but suddenly this tumult was drowned under a volley of heart-piercing shrieks of mortal agony,—the king glanced from the frantic girls to the stake, then turned away and leaned his ashen face against the wall, and looked no more. He said, "That which I have seen, in that one little moment, will never go out from my memory, but will abide there; and I shall see it all the days, and dream of it all the nights, till I die. Would God I had been blind!"

Hendon was watching the king. He said to himself, with satisfaction, "His disorder mendeth; he hath changed, and groweth gentler. If he had followed his wont, he would have stormed at these varlets, and said he was king, and commanded that the women be turned loose unscathed. Soon his delusion will pass away and be forgotten, and his poor mind will be whole again. God speed the day!"

That same day several prisoners were brought in to remain over night, who were being conveyed, under guard, to various places in the kingdom, to undergo punishment for crimes committed. The king conversed with these,—he had made it a point, from the beginning, to instruct himself for the kingly office by questioning prisoners whenever the opportunity offered—and the tale of their woes wrung his heart. One of them was a poor half-witted woman who had stolen a yard or two of cloth from a weaver—she was to be hanged for it. Another was a man who had been accused of stealing a horse; he said the proof had failed, and he had imagined that he was safe from the halter; but no—he was hardly free before he was arraigned for killing a deer in the king's park; this was proved against him, and now he was on his way to the gallows. There was a tradesman's apprentice whose case particularly distressed the king; this youth said he found a hawk, one evening, that had escaped from its owner, and he took it home with him, imagining himself entitled to it; but the court convicted him of stealing it, and sentenced him to death.

The king was furious over these inhumanities, and wanted Hendon to break jail and fly with him to Westminster, so that he could mount his throne and hold out his sceptre in mercy over these unfortunate people and save their lives. "Poor child," sighed Hendon, "these woful tales have brought his malady upon him again—alack, but for his evil hap, he would have been well in a little time."

Among these prisoners was an old lawyer—a man with a strong face and a dauntless mien. Three years past, he had written a pamphlet against the Lord Chancellor, accusing him of injustice, and had been punished for it by the loss of his ears in the pillory, and degradation from the bar, and in addition had been fined £3000 and sentenced to imprisonment for life. Lately he had repeated his offence; and in consequence was now under sentence to lose *what remained of his ears*, pay a fine of £5000, be branded on both cheeks, and remain in prison for life.

"These be honorable scars," he said, and turned back his gray hair and showed the mutilated stubs of what had once been his ears.

The king's eye burned with passion. He said—

"None believe in me—neither wilt thou. But no matter—within the compass of a month thou shalt be free; and more, the laws that have dishonored thee, and shamed the English name, shall be swept from the statute books. The world is made wrong, kings should go to school to their own laws, at times, and so learn mercy."*

CHAPTER XXVIII

THE SACRIFICE

Meantime Miles was growing sufficiently tired of confinement and inaction. But now his trial came on, to his great gratification, and he thought he could welcome any sentence provided a further imprisonment should not be a part of it. But he was mistaken about that. He was in a fine fury when he found himself described as a "sturdy vagabond" and sentenced to sit two hours in the pillory for bearing that character and for assaulting the master of Hendon Hall. His pretensions as to brothership with his prosecutor, and rightful heirship to the Hendon honors and estates, were left contemptuously unnoticed, as being not even worth examination.

He raged and threatened, on his way to punishment, but it did no good; he was snatched roughly along, by the officers, and got an occasional cuff, besides, for his unreverent conduct.

The king could not pierce through the rabble that swarmed behind; so he was obliged to follow in the rear, remote from his good friend and servant. The king had been nearly condemned to the stocks, himself, for being in such bad company, but had been let off with a lecture and a warning, in consideration of his youth. When the crowd at last had left, he flitted feverishly from point to point around the outer rim, hunting a place to get through; and at last, after a deal of difficulty and delay, succeeded. There sat his poor henchman in the degrading stocks, the sport and butt of a dirty mob—he, the body servant of the king of England! Edward had heard the sentence pronounced, but he had not realized the half that it meant. His anger began to rise as the sense of this new indignity which had been put upon him sank home; it jumped to summer heat, the next moment, when he saw an egg sail through the air and crush itself against Hendon's cheek, and heard the crowd roar its

*See Notes to Chapter 27, at end of volume.

enjoyment of the episode. He sprang across the open circle and confronted the officer in charge, crying—

"For shame! This is my servant—set him free! I am the—"

"O, peace!" exclaimed Hendon, in a panic, "thou'lt destroy thyself. Mind him not, officer, he is mad."

"Give thyself no trouble as to the matter of minding him, good man, I have small mind to mind him; but as to teaching him somewhat, to that I am well inclined." He turned to a subordinate and said, "Give the little fool a taste or two of the lash, to mend his manners."

"Half a dozen will better serve his turn," suggested Sir Hugh, who had ridden up, a moment before, to take a passing glance at the proceedings.

The king was seized. He did not even struggle, so paralyzed was he with the mere thought of the monstrous outrage that was proposed to be inflicted upon his sacred person. History was already defiled with the record of the scourging of an English king with whips—it was an intolerable reflection that he must furnish a duplicate of that shameful page. He was in the toils, there was no help for him: he must either take his punishment or beg for its remission. Hard conditions; he would take the stripes—a king might do that, but a king could not beg.

But meantime, Miles Hendon was resolving the difficulty. "Let the child go," said he; "ye heartless dogs, do ye not see how young and frail he is? Let him go—I will take his lashes."

"Marry, a good thought,—and thanks for it," said Sir Hugh, his face lighting with a sardonic satisfaction. "Let the little beggar go, and give this fellow a dozen in his place—an honest dozen, well laid on." The king was in the act of entering a fierce protest, but Sir Hugh silenced him with the potent remark, "Yes, speak up, do, and free thy mind—only, mark ye, that for each word you utter he shall get six strokes the more."

Hendon was removed from the stocks, and his back laid bare; and whilst the lash was applied the poor little king turned away his face and allowed unroyal tears to channel his cheeks unchecked. "Ah, brave good heart," he said to himself, "this loyal deed shall never perish out of my memory. I will not forget it—and neither shall *they!*" he added, with passion. Whilst he mused, his appreciation of Hendon's magnanimous conduct grew to greater and still greater dimensions in his mind, and so also did his gratefulness for it. Presently he said to himself, "Who saves his prince from wounds and possible death—and this he did for me—performs high service; but it is little—it is nothing!—O, less than nothing!—when 'tis weighed against the act of him who saves his prince from SHAME!"

Hendon made no outcry, under the scourge, but bore the heavy blows with soldierly fortitude. This, together with his redeeming the boy by taking his stripes for him, compelled the respect of even that forlorn and degraded mob that was gathered there; and its gibes and hootings died away, and no sound remained but the sound of the falling blows. The stillness that pervaded the place, when Hendon found himself once more in the stocks, was in strong contrast with the insulting clamor which had prevailed there so little a while before. The king came softly to Hendon's side, and whispered in his ear—

"Kings cannot ennoble thee, thou good, great soul, for One who is higher than kings hath done that for thee; but a king can confirm thy nobility to men." He picked up the scourge from the ground, touched Hendon's bleeding shoulders lightly with it, and whispered, "Edward of England dubs thee earl!"

Hendon was touched. The water welled to his eyes, yet at the same time the grisly humor of the situation and circumstances so undermined his gravity that it was all he could do to keep some sign of his inward mirth from showing outside. To be suddenly hoisted, naked and gory, from the common stocks to the Alpine altitude and splendor of an Earldom, seemed to him the last possibility in the line of the grotesque. He said to himself, "Now am I finely tinselled, indeed! The spectre-knight of the Kingdom of Dreams and Shadows is become a spectre-earl!—a dizzy flight for a callow wing! An' this go on, I shall presently be hung like a very may-pole with fantastic gauds and make-believe honors. But I shall value them, all valueless as they are, for the love that doth bestow them. Better these poor mock dignities of mine, that come unasked, from a clean hand and a right spirit, than real ones bought by servility from grudging and interested power."

The dreaded Sir Hugh wheeled his horse about, and as he spurred away, the living wall divided silently to let him pass, and as silently closed together again. And so remained; nobody went so far as to venture a remark in favor of the prisoner, or in compliment to him; but no matter, the absence of abuse was a sufficient homage in itself. A late comer who was not posted as to the present circumstances, and who delivered a sneer at the "impostor" and was in the act of following it with a dead cat, was promptly knocked down and kicked out, without any words, and then the deep quiet resumed sway once more.

CHAPTER XXIX

TO LONDON

When Hendon's term of service in the stocks was finished, he was released and ordered to quit the region and come back no more. His sword was restored to him, and also his mule and his donkey. He mounted and rode off, followed by the king, the crowd opening with quiet respectfulness to let them pass, and then dispersing when they were gone.

Hendon was soon absorbed in thought. There were questions of high import to be answered. What should he do? Whither should he go? Powerful help must be found, somewhere, or he must relinquish his inheritance and remain under the imputation of being an impostor besides. Where could he hope to find this powerful help? Where, indeed! It was a knotty question. By and by a thought occurred to him which pointed to a possibility—the slenderest of slender possibilities, certainly, but still worth considering, for lack of any other that promised any thing at all. He remembered what old Andrews had said about the young king's goodness and his generous championship of the wronged and unfortunate. Why not go and try to get speech of him and beg for justice? Ah, yes, but could so fantastic a pauper get admission to the august presence of a monarch? Never mind—let that matter take care of itself; it was a bridge that would not need to be crossed till he should come to it. He was an old campaigner, and used to inventing shifts and expedients; no doubt he would be able to find a way. Yes, he would strike for the capital. Maybe his father's old friend Sir Humphrey Marlow would help him—"good old Sir Humphrey, Head Lieutenant of the late king's kitchen, or stables, or something"—Miles could not remember just what or which. Now that he had something to turn his energies to, a distinctly defined object to accomplish, the fog of humiliation and depression which had settled down upon his spirits lifted and blew away, and he raised his head and looked about him. He was surprised to see how far he had come; the village was away behind him. The king was jogging along in his wake, with his head bowed; for he, too, was deep in plans and thinkings. A sorrowful misgiving clouded Hendon's new-born cheerfulness: would the boy be willing to go again to a city where, during all his brief life, he had never known any thing but ill usage and pinching want? But the question must be asked; it could not be avoided; so Hendon reined up, and called out—

"I had forgotten to inquire whither we are bound. Thy commands, my liege?"

"To London!"

Hendon moved on again, mightily contented with the answer—but astounded at it, too.

The whole journey was made without an adventure of importance. But it ended with one. About ten o'clock on the night of the 19th of February, they stepped upon London Bridge, in the midst of a writhing, struggling jam of howling and hurrahing people, whose beer-jolly faces stood out strongly in the glare from manifold torches—and at that instant the decaying head of some former duke or other grandee tumbled down between them, striking Hendon on the elbow and then bounding off among the hurrying confusion of feet. So evanescent and unstable are men's works, in this world!—

the late good king is but three weeks dead and three days in his grave, and already the adornments which he took such pains to select from prominent people for his noble bridge are falling. A citizen stumbled over that head, and drove his own head into the back of somebody in front of him, who turned and knocked down the person that came handy, and was promptly laid out himself by that person's friend. It was the right ripe time for a free fight, for the festivities of the morrow—Coronation Day—were already beginning; everybody was full of strong drink and patriotism; within five minutes the free fight was occupying a good deal of ground; within ten or twelve it covered an acre or so, and was become a riot. By this time Hendon and the king were hopelessly separated from each other and lost in the rush and turmoil of the roaring masses of humanity. And so we leave them.

CHAPTER XXX

TOM'S PROGRESS

Whilst the true King wandered about the land poorly clad, poorly fed, cuffed and derided by tramps one while, herding with thieves and murderers in a jail another, and called idiot and impostor by all impartially, the mock King Tom Canty enjoyed a quite different experience.

When we saw him last, royalty was just beginning to have a bright side for him. This bright side went on brightening more and more every day: in a very little while it was become almost all sunshine and delightfulness. He lost his fears; his misgivings faded out and died; his embarrassments departed, and gave place to an easy and confident bearing. He worked the whipping-boy mine to ever-increasing profit.

He ordered my Lady Elizabeth and my Lady Jane Grey into his presence when he wanted to play or talk, and dismissed them when he was done with them, with the air of one familiarly accustomed to such performances. It no longer confused him to have these lofty personages kiss his hand at parting.

He came to enjoy being conducted to bed in state at night, and dressed with intricate and solemn ceremony in the morning. It came to be a proud pleasure to march to dinner attended by a glittering procession of officers of state and gentlemen-at-arms; insomuch, indeed, that he doubled his guard of gentlemen-at-arms, and made them a hundred. He liked to hear the bugles sounding down the long corridors, and the distant voices responding, "Way for the King!"

He even learned to enjoy sitting in throned state in council, and seeming to be something more than the Lord Protector's mouth-piece. He liked to receive great ambassadors and their gorgeous trains, and listen to the affectionate messages they brought from illustrious monarchs who called him "brother." O happy Tom Canty, late of Offal Court!

He enjoyed his splendid clothes, and ordered more: he found his four hundred servants too few for his proper grandeur, and trebled them. The adulation of salaaming courtiers came to be sweet music to his ears. He remained kind and gentle, and a sturdy and determined champion of all that were oppressed, and he made tireless war upon unjust laws: yet upon occasion, being offended, he could turn upon an earl, or even a duke, and give him a look that would make him tremble. Once, when his royal "sister," the grimly, holy Lady Mary, set herself to reason with him against the wisdom of his course in pardoning so many people who would otherwise be jailed, or hanged, or burned, and reminded him that their august late father's prisons had sometimes contained as high as sixty thousand convicts at one time, and that during his admirable reign he had delivered seventy-two thousand thieves and robbers over to death by the executioner,* the boy was filled with generous indignation, and commanded her to go to her closet, and beseech God to take away the stone that was in her breast, and give her a human heart.

Did Tom Canty never feel troubled about the poor little rightful prince who had treated him so kindly, and flown out with such hot zeal to avenge him upon the insolent sentinel at the palace-gate? Yes; his first royal days and nights were pretty well sprinkled with painful thoughts about the lost prince, and with sincere longings for his return, and happy restoration to his native rights and splendors. But as time wore on, and the prince did not come, Tom's mind became more and more occupied with his new and enchanting experiences, and by little and little the vanished monarch faded almost out of his thoughts; and finally, when he did intrude upon them at intervals, he was become an unwelcome spectre, for he made Tom feel guilty and ashamed.

Tom's poor mother and sisters travelled the same road out of his mind. At first he pined for them, sorrowed for them, longed to see them, but later, the thought of their coming some day in their rags and dirt, and betraying him with their kisses, and pulling him down from his lofty place, and dragging him back to penury and degradation and the slums, made him shudder. At last they ceased to trouble his thoughts almost wholly. And he was content, even glad; for, whenever their mournful and accusing faces did rise before him now, they made him feel more despicable than the worms that crawl.

At midnight of the 19th of February, Tom Canty was sinking to sleep in his rich bed in the palace, guarded by his loyal vassals, and surrounded by the pomps of royalty, a happy boy; for to-morrow was the day appointed for his solemn crowning as King of England. At that same hour, Edward, the true king, hungry and thirsty, soiled

*Hume's England.

and draggled, worn with travel, and clothed in rags and shreds,—
his share of the results of the riot,—was wedged in among a crowd
of people who were watching with deep interest certain hurrying
gangs of workmen who streamed in and out of Westminster Abbey,
busy as ants: they were making the last preparation for the royal
coronation.

CHAPTER XXXI

THE RECOGNITION PROCESSION

When Tom Canty awoke the next morning, the air was heavy with
a thunderous murmur: all the distances were charged with it. It was
music to him; for it meant that the English world was out in its
strength to give loyal welcome to the great day.

Presently Tom found himself once more the chief figure in a
wonderful floating pageant on the Thames; for by ancient custom
the "recognition procession" through London must start from the
Tower, and he was bound thither.

When he arrived there, the sides of the venerable fortress seemed
suddenly rent in a thousand places, and from every rent leaped a
red tongue of flame and a white gush of smoke; a deafening
explosion followed, which drowned the shoutings of the multitude,
and made the ground tremble; the flame-jets, the smoke, and the
explosions, were repeated over and over again with marvellous
celerity, so that in a few moments the old Tower disappeared in the
vast fog of its own smoke, all but the very top of the tall pile called
the White Tower: this, with its banners, stood out above the dense
bank of vapor as a mountain-peak projects above a cloud-rack.
as a mountain-peak projects above a cloud-rack.

Tom Canty, splendidly arrayed, mounted a prancing war-steed,
whose rich trappings almost reached to the ground; his "uncle,"
the Lord Protector Somerset, similarly mounted, took place in his
rear; the King's Guard formed in single ranks on either side, clad
in burnished armor; after the protector followed a seemingly
interminable procession of resplendent nobles attended by their
vassals; after these came the lord mayor and the aldermanic body,
in crimson velvet robes, and with their gold chains across their
breasts; and after these the officers and members of all the guilds
of London, in rich raiment, and bearing the showy banners of the
several corporations. Also in the procession, as a special guard of
honor through the city, was the Ancient and Honorable Artillery
Company,—an organization already three hundred years old at that
time, and the only military body in England possessing the privilege
(which it still possesses in our day) of holding itself independent
of the commands of Parliament. It was a brilliant spectacle, and was
hailed with acclamations all along the line, as it took its stately way

through the packed multitudes of citizens. The chronicler says, "The King, as he entered the city, was received by the people with prayers, welcomings, cries, and tender words, and all signs which argue an earnest love of subjects toward their sovereign; and the King, by holding up his glad countenance to such as stood afar off, and most tender language to those that stood nigh his Grace, showed himself no less thankful to receive the people's good will than they to offer it. To all that wished him well, he gave thanks. To such as bade 'God save his Grace,' he said in return, 'God save you all!' and added that 'he thanked them with all his heart.' Wonderfully transported were the people with the loving answers and gestures of their King."

In Fenchurch Street a "fair child, in costly apparel," stood on a stage to welcome his Majesty to the city. The last verse of his greeting was in these words:

"Welcome, O King! as much as hearts can think;
  Welcome again, as much as tongue can tell,—
Welcome to joyous tongues, and hearts that will not shrink:
  God thee preserve, we pray, and wish thee ever well."

The people burst forth in a glad shout, repeating with one voice what the child had said. Tom Canty gazed abroad over the surging sea of eager faces, and his heart swelled with exultation; and he felt that the one thing worth living for in this world was to be a king, and a nation's idol. Presently he caught sight, at a distance, of a couple of his ragged Offal Court comrades,—one of them the lord high admiral in his late mimic court, the other the first lord of the bedchamber in the same pretentious fiction; and his pride swelled higher than ever. Oh, if they could only recognize him now! What unspeakable glory it would be, if they could recognize him, and realize that the derided mock king of the slums and back alleys was become a real king, with illustrious dukes and princes for his humble menials, and the English world at his feet! But he had to deny himself, and choke down his desire, for such a recognition might cost more than it would come to: so he turned away his head, and left the two soiled lads to go on with their shoutings and glad adulations, unsuspicious of whom it was they were lavishing them upon.

Every now and then rose the cry, "A largess! a largess!" and Tom responded by scattering a handful of bright new coins abroad for the multitude to scramble for.

The chronicler says, "At the upper end of Gracechurch Street, before the sign of the Eagle, the city had erected a gorgeous arch, beneath which was a stage, which stretched from one side of the street to the other. This was a historical pageant, representing the King's immediate progenitors. There sat Elizabeth of York in the

midst of an immense white rose, whose petals formed elaborate
furbelows around her; by her side was Henry VII., issuing out of a
vast red rose, disposed in the same manner: the hands of the royal
pair were locked together, and the wedding-ring ostentatiously
displayed. From the red and white roses proceeded a stem, which
reached up to a second stage, occupied by Henry VIII., issuing from
a red-and-white rose, with the effigy of the new king's mother, Jane
Seymour, represented by his side. One branch sprang from this pair,
which mounted to a third stage, where sat the effigy of Edward VI.
himself, enthroned in royal majesty; and the whole pageant was
framed with wreaths of roses, red and white.''

This quaint and gaudy spectacle so wrought upon the rejoicing
people, that their acclamations utterly smothered the small voice
of the child whose business it was to explain the thing in eulogistic
rhymes. But Tom Canty was not sorry; for this loyal uproar was
sweeter music to him than any poetry, no matter what its quality
might be. Whithersoever Tom turned his happy young face, the
people recognized the exactness of his effigy's likeness to himself,
the flesh and blood counterpart; and new whirlwinds of applause
burst forth.

The great pageant moved on, and still on, under one triumphal
arch after another, and past a bewildering succession of spectacular
and symbolical tableaux, each of which typified and exalted some
virtue, or talent, or merit, of the little king's. ''Throughout the whole
of Cheapside, from every penthouse and window, hung banners
and streamers; and the richest carpets, stuffs, and cloth-of-gold
tapestried the streets,—specimens of the great wealth of the stores
within; and the splendor of this thoroughfare was equalled in the
other streets, and in some even surpassed.''

''And all these wonders and these marvels are to welcome
me—me!'' murmured Tom Canty.

The mock king's cheeks were flushed with excitement, his eyes
were flashing, his senses swam in a delirium of pleasure. At this
point, just as he was raising his hand to fling another rich largess,
he caught sight of a pale, astounded face which was strained forward
out of the second rank of the crowd, its intense eyes riveted upon
him. A sickening consternation struck through him; he recognized
his mother! and up flew his hand, palm outward, before his eyes,—
that old involuntary gesture, born of a forgotten episode, and
perpetuated by habit. In an instant more she had torn her way out
of the press, and past the guards, and was at his side. She embraced
his leg, she covered it with kisses, she cried, ''O my child, my
darling!'' lifting toward him a face that was transfigured with joy
and love. The same instant an officer of the King's Guard snatched
her away with a curse, and sent her reeling back whence she came
with a vigorous impulse from his strong arm. The words ''I do not
know you, woman!'' were falling from Tom Canty's lips when this

piteous thing occurred; but it smote him to the heart to see her treated so; and as she turned for a last glimpse of him, whilst the crowd was swallowing her from his sight, she seemed so wounded, so broken-hearted, that a shame fell upon him which consumed his pride to ashes and withered his stolen royalty. His grandeurs were striken valueless: they seemed to fall away from him like rotten rags.

The procession moved on, and still on, through ever augmenting splendors and ever augmenting tempests of welcome; but to Tom Canty they were as if they had not been. He neither saw nor heard. Royalty had lost its grace and sweetness; its pomps were become a reproach. Remorse was eating his heart out. He said, "Would God I were free of my captivity!"

He had unconsciously dropped back into the phraseology of the first days of his compulsory greatness.

The shining pageant still went winding like a radiant and interminable serpent down the crooked lanes of the quaint old city, and through the huzzaing hosts; but still the King rode with bowed head and vacant eyes, seeing only his mother's face and that wounded look in it.

"Largess, largess!" The cry fell upon an unheeding ear.

"Long live Edward of England!" It seemed as if the earth shook with the explosion; but there was no response from the King. He heard it only as one hears the thunder of the surf when it is blown to the ear out of a great distance, for it was smothered under another sound which was still nearer, in his own breast, in his accusing conscience,—a voice which kept repeating those shameful words, "I do not know you, woman!"

The words smote upon the King's soul as the strokes of a funeral bell smite upon the soul of a surviving friend when they remind him of secret treacheries suffered at his hands by him that is gone.

New glories were unfolded at every turning; new wonders, new marvels, sprung into view; the pent clamors of waiting batteries were released; new raptures poured from the throats of the waiting multitudes: but the King gave no sign, and the accusing voice that went moaning through his comfortless breast was all the sound he heard.

By and by the gladness in the faces of the populace changed a little, and became touched with a something like solicitude or anxiety: an abatement in the volume of applause was observable too. The lord protector was quick to notice these things: he was as quick to detect the cause. He spurred to the King's side, bent low in his saddle, uncovered, and said,—

"My liege, it is an ill time for dreaming. The people observe thy downcast head, thy clouded mien, and they take it for an omen. Be advised: unveil the sun of royalty, and let it shine upon these boding vapors, and disperse them. Lift up they face, and smile upon the people."

So saying, the duke scattered a handful of coins to right and left, then retired to his place. The mock king did mechanically as he had been bidden. His smile had no heart in it, but few eyes were near enough or sharp enough to detect that. The noddings of his plumed head as he saluted his subjects were full of grace and graciousness; the largess which he delivered from his hand was royally liberal: so the people's anxiety vanished, and the acclamations burst forth again in as mighty a volume as before.

Still once more, a little before the progress was ended, the duke was obliged to ride forward, and make remonstrance. He whispered,—

"O dread sovereign! shake off these fatal humors: the eyes of the world are upon thee." Then he added with sharp annoyance, "Perdition catch that crazy pauper! 'twas she that hath disturbed your Highness."

The gorgeous figure turned a lustreless eye upon the duke, and said in a dead voice,—

"She was my mother!"

"My God!" groaned the protector as he reined his horse backward to his post, "the omen was pregnant with prophecy. He is gone mad again!"

CHAPTER XXXII

CORONATION DAY

Let us go backward a few hours, and place ourselves in Westminster Abbey, at four o'clock in the morning of this memorable Coronation Day. We are not without company; for although it is still night, we find the torch-lighted galleries already filling up with people who are well content to sit still and wait seven or eight hours till the time shall come for them to see what they may not hope to see twice in their lives—the coronation of a king. Yes, London and Westminster have been astir ever since the warning guns boomed at three o'clock, and already crowds of untitled rich folk who have bought the privilege of trying to find sitting-room in the galleries are flocking in at the entrances reserved for their sort.

The hours drag along, tediously enough. All stir has ceased for some time, for every gallery has long ago been packed. We may sit, now, and look and think at our leisure. We have glimpses, here and there and yonder, through the dim cathedral twilight, of portions of many galleries and balconies, wedged full with people, the other portions of these galleries and balconies being cut off from sight by intervening pillars and architectural projections. We have in view the whole of the great north transept—empty, and waiting for England's privileged ones. We see also the ample area or platform, carpeted with rich stuffs, whereon the throne stands. The throne occupies the centre of the platform, and is raised above it upon an elevation of four steps. Within the seat of the throne is enclosed a rough flat rock—the stone of Scone—which many generations of Scottish kings sat on to be crowned, and so it in time became holy enough to answer a like purpose for English monarchs. Both the throne and its footstool are covered with cloth of gold.

Stillness reigns, the torches blink dully, the time drags heavily. But at last the lagging daylight asserts itself, the torches are extinguished, and a mellow radiance suffuses the great spaces. All features of the noble building are distinct, now, but soft and dreamy, for the sun is lightly veiled with clouds.

At seven o'clock the first break in the drowsy monotony occurs; for on the stroke of this hour the first peeress enters the transept, clothed like Solomon for splendor, and is conducted to her appointed place by an official clad in satins and velvets, whilst a duplicate of him gathers up the lady's long train, follows after, and, when the lady is seated, arranges the train across her lap for her. He then places her footstool according to her desire, after which he puts her coronet where it will be convenient to her hand when the time for the simultaneous coronetting of the nobles shall arrive.

By this time the peeresses are flowing in in a glittering stream, and satin-clad officials are flitting and glinting everywhere, seating them and making them comfortable. The scene is animated enough, now. There is stir and life, and shifting color everywhere. After a time, quiet reigns again; for the peeresses are all come, and are all in their places—a solid acre, or such a matter, of human flowers, resplendent in variegated colors, and frosted like a Milky Way with diamonds. There are all ages, here: brown, wrinkled, whitehaired dowagers who are able to go back, and still back, down the stream of time, and recall the crowning of Richard III. and the troublous days of that old forgotten age; and there are handsome middle-aged dames; and lovely and gracious young matrons; and gentle and beautiful young girls, with beaming eyes and fresh complexions, who may possibly put on their jewelled coronets awkwardly when the great time comes; for the matter will be new to them, and their excitement will be a sore hindrance. Still this may not happen, for the hair of all these ladies has been arranged with a special view to the swift and successful lodging of the crown in its place when the signal comes.

We have seen that this massed array of peeresses is sown thick with diamonds, and we also see that it is a marvellous spectacle—but now we are about to be astonished in earnest. About nine, the clouds suddenly break away and a shaft of sunshine cleaves the mellow atmosphere, and drifts slowly along the ranks of ladies; and every rank it touches flames into a dazzling splendor of many-colored fires, and we tingle to our finger-tips with the electric thrill that is shot through us by the surprise and the beauty of the spectacle! Presently a special envoy from some distant corner of the Orient, marching with the general body of foreign ambassadors, crosses this bar of sunshine, and we catch our breath, the glory that streams and flashes and palpitates about him is so overpowering; for he is crusted from head to heels with gems, and his slightest movement showers a dancing radiance all around him.

Let us change the tense for convenience. The time drifted along,— one hour—two hours—two hours and a half; then the deep booming of artillery told that the king and his grand procession had arrived at last; so the waiting multitude rejoiced. All knew that a further delay must follow, for the king must be prepared and robed for the solemn ceremony; but this delay would be pleasantly occupied by the assembling of the peers of the realm in their stately robes. These were conducted ceremoniously to their seats, and their coronets placed conveniently at hand; and meanwhile the multitude in the galleries were alive with interest, for most of them were beholding for the first time, dukes, earls and barons, whose names had been historical for five hundred years. When all were finally seated, the spectacle from the galleries and all coigns of vantage was complete; a gorgeous one to look upon and to remember.

Now the robed and mitred great heads of the church, and their attendants, filed in upon the platform, and took their appointed places; these were followed by the Lord Protector and other great officials, and these again by a steel-clad detachment of the Guard.

There was a waiting pause; then, at a signal, a triumphant peal of music burst forth, and Tom Canty, clothed in a long robe of cloth of gold, appeared at a door, and stepped upon the platform. The entire multitude rose, and the ceremony of the Recognition ensued.

Then a noble anthem swept the Abbey with its rich waves of sound; and thus heralded and welcomed, Tom Canty was conducted to the throne. The ancient ceremonies went on, with impressive solemnity, whilst the audience gazed; and as they drew nearer and nearer to completion, Tom Canty grew pale, and still paler, and a deep and steadily deepening woe and despondency settled down upon his spirits and upon his remorseful heart.

At last the final act was at hand. The Archbishop of Canterbury lifted up the crown of England from its cushion and held it out over the trembling mock-king's head. In the same instant a rainbow-radiance flashed along the spacious transept; for with one impulse every individual in the great concourse of nobles lifted a coronet and poised it over his or her head,—and paused in that attitude.

A deep hush pervaded the Abbey. At this impressive moment, a startling apparition intruded upon the scene—an apparition observed by none in the absorbed multitude, until it suddenly appeared, moving up the great central aisle. It was a boy,

bare-headed, ill shod, and clothed in coarse plebeian garments
that were falling to rags. He raised his hand with a solemnity which
ill comported with his soiled and sorry aspect, and delivered this
note of warning—

"I forbid you to set the crown of England upon that forfeited
head. *I* am the king!"

In an instant several indignant hands were laid upon the boy; but
in the same instant Tom Canty, in his regal vestments, made a
swift step forward and cried out in a ringing voice—

"Loose him and forbear! He *is* the king!"

A sort of panic of astonishment swept the assemblage, and they
partly rose in their places and started in a bewildered way at one
another and at the chief figures in this scene, like persons who
wondered whether they were awake and in their senses, or asleep
and dreaming. The Lord Protector was as amazed as the rest, but
quickly recovered himself and exclaimed in a voice of authority—

"Mind not his Majesty, his malady is upon him again—seize the
vagabond!"

He would have been obeyed, but the mock-king stamped his foot
and cried out—

"On your peril! Touch him not, he is the king!"

The hands were withheld; a paralysis fell upon the house; no one
moved, no one spoke; indeed no one knew how to act or what to say,
in so strange and surprising an emergency. While all minds were
struggling to right themselves, the boy still moved steadily forward,
with high port and confident mien; he had never halted from the
beginning; and while the tangled minds still floundered helplessly,
he stepped upon the platform, and the mock-king ran with a glad
face to meet him; and fell on his knees before him and said—

"O, my lord the king, let poor Tom Canty be first to swear fealty
to thee, and say 'Put on thy crown and enter into thine own
again!' "

The Lord Protector's eye fell sternly upon the new-comer's face;
but straightway the sternness vanished away, and gave place to an
expression of wondering surprise. This thing happened also to the
other great officers. They glanced at each other, and retreated a
step by a common and unconscious impulse. The thought in each
mind was the same: "What a strange resemblance!"

The Lord Protector reflected a moment or two, in perplexity, then
he said, with grave respectfulness—

"By your favor, sir, I desire to ask certain questions which'"—

"I will answer them, my lord."

The duke asked him many questions about the court, the late
king, the prince, the princesses,—the boy answered them correctly
and without hesitating. He described the rooms of state in the
palace, the late king's apartments, and those of the Prince of Wales.

It was strange; it was wonderful; yes, it was unaccountable—so all said that heard it. The tide was beginning to turn, and Tom Canty's hopes to run high, when the Lord Protector shook his head and said—

"It is true it is most wonderful—but it is no more than our lord the king likewise can do." This remark, and this reference to himself as still the king, saddened Tom Canty, and he felt his hopes crumbling from under him. "These are not *proofs,*" added the Protector.

The tide was turning very fast, now, very fast indeed—but in the wrong direction; it was leaving poor Tom Canty stranded on the throne, and sweeping the other out to sea. The Lord Protector communed with himself—shook his head—the thought forced itself upon him, "It is perilous to the State and to us all, to entertain so fateful a riddle as this; it could divide the nation and undermine the throne." He turned and said—

"Sir Thomas, arrest this—no, hold!" His face lighted, and he confronted the ragged candidate with this question—

"Where lieth the Great Seal? Answer me this truly, and the riddle is unriddled; for only he that was Prince of Wales *can* so answer! On so trivial a thing hang a throne and a dynasty!"

It was a lucky thought, a happy thought. That it was so considered by the great officials was manifested by the silent applause that shot from eye to eye around their circle in the form of bright approving glances. Yes, none but the true prince could dissolve the stubborn mystery of the vanished Great Seal—this forlorn little impostor had been taught his lesson well, but here his teachings must fail, for his teacher himself could not answer *that* question—ah, very good, very good indeed; now we shall be rid of this troublesome and perilous business in short order! And so they nodded invisibly and smiled inwardly with satisfaction, and looked to see this foolish lad stricken with a palsy of guilty confusion. How surprised they were, then, to see nothing of the sort happen—how they marvelled to hear him answer up promptly, in a confident and untroubled voice, and say—

"There is nought in this riddle that is difficult." Then, without so much as a by-your-leave to anybody, he turned and gave this command, with the easy manner of one accustomed to doing such things: "My lord St. John, go you to my private cabinet in the palace—for none knoweth the place better than you—and, close down the door that opens from the ante-chamber, you shall find in the wall a brazen nail-head; press upon it and a little jewel-closet will fly open which not even you do know of—no, nor any soul else, in all the world but me and the trusty artisan that did contrive it for me. The first thing that falleth under your eye will be the Great Seal—fetch it hither."

All the company wondered at this speech, and wondered still more to see the little mendicant pick out this peer without hesitancy or apparent fear of mistake, and call him by name with such a placidly convincing air of having known him all his life. The peer was almost surprised into obeying. He even made a movement as if to go, but quickly recovered his tranquil attitude and confessed his blunder with a blush. Tom Canty turned upon him and said, sharply—

"Why dost thou hesitate? Hast not heard the king's command? Go!"

The lord St. John made a deep obeisance—and it was observed that it was a significantly cautious and non-committal one, it not being delivered at either of the kings, but at the neutral ground about half way between the two—and took his leave.

Now began a movement of the gorgeous particles of that official group which was slow, scarcely perceptible, and yet steady and persistent—a movement such as is observed in a kaleidoscope that is turned slowly, whereby the components of one splendid cluster fall away and join themselves to another—a movement which little by little, in the present case, dissolved the glittering crowd that stood about Tom Canty and clustered it together again in the neighborhood of the new-comer. Tom Canty stood almost alone. Now ensued a brief season of deep suspense and waiting—during which even the few faint-hearts still remaining near Tom Canty gradually scraped together courage enough to glide, one by one, over to the majority. So at last Tom Canty, in his royal robes and jewels, stood wholly alone and isolated from the world, a conspicuous figure, occupying an eloquent vacancy.

Now the lord St. John was seen returning. As he advanced up the mid-aisle the interest was so intense that the low murmur of conversation in the great assemblage died out and was succeeded by a profound hush, a breathless stillness, through which his footfalls pulsed with a dull and distant sound. Every eye was fastened upon him as he moved along. He reached the platform, paused a moment, then moved toward Tom Canty with a deep obeisance, and said—

"Sire, the Seal is not there!"

A mob does not melt away from the presence of a plague-patient with more haste than the band of pallid and terrified courtiers melted away from the presence of the shabby little claimant of the Crown. In a moment he stood all alone, without friend or supporter, a target upon which was concentrated a bitter fire of scornful and angry looks. The Lord Protector called out fiercely—

"Cast the beggar into the street, and scourge him through the town—the paltry knave is worth no more consideration!"

Officers of the guard sprang forward to obey, but Tom Canty waved them off and said—

"Back! Whoso touches him perils his life!"

The Lord Protector was perplexed, in the last degree. He said to the lord St. John—

"Searched you well?—but it boots not to ask that. It doth seem passing strange. Little things, trifles, slip out of one's ken, and one does not think it matter for surprise; but how a so bulky thing as the Seal of England can vanish away and no man be able to get track of it again—a massy golden disk"—

Tom Canty, with beaming eyes, sprang forward and shouted—

"Hold, that is enough! Was it round?—and thick? and had it letters and devices graved upon it?—Yes? O, *now* I know what this Great Seal is that there's been such worry and bother about! An' ye had described it to me, ye could have had it three weeks ago. Right well I know where it lies; but it was not I that put it there—first."

"Who, then, my liege?" asked the Lord Protector.

"He that stands there—the rightful king of England. And he shall tell you himself where it lies—then you will believe he knew it of his own knowledge. Bethink thee, my king—spur thy memory—it was the last, the very *last* thing thou didst that day before thou didst rush forth from the palace, clothed in my rags, to punish the soldier that insulted me."

A silence ensued, undisturbed by a movement or a whisper, and all eyes were fixed upon the new-comer, who stood, with bent head and corrugated brow, groping in his memory among a thronging multitude of valueless recollections for one single little elusive fact, which, found, would seat him upon a throne—unfound, would leave him as he was, for good and all—a pauper and an outcast. Moment after moment passed—still the boy struggled silently on, and gave no sign. But at last he heaved a sigh, shook his head slowly, and said, with a trembling lip and in a despondent voice—

"I call the scene back—all of it—but the Seal hath no place in it." He paused, then looked up, and said with gentle dignity, "My lords and gentlemen, if ye will rob your rightful sovereign of his own for lack of this evidence which he is not able to furnish, I may not stay ye, being powerless. But"—

"O, folly, O, madness, my king!" cried Tom Canty, in a panic, "wait!—think! Do not give up!—the cause is not lost! Nor *shall* be, neither! List to what I say—follow every word—I am going to bring that morning back again, every hap just as it happened. We talked—I told you of my sisters, Nan and Bet—ah, yes, you remember that; and about mine old grandam—and the rough games of the lads of Offal Court—yes, you remember these things also; very well, follow me still, you shall recall every thing. You gave me food and drink, and did with princely courtesy send away the servants, so that my low breeding might not shame me before them—ah, yes, this also you remember."

As Tom checked off his details, and the other boy nodded his head in recognition of them, the great audience and the officials stared in puzzled wonderment; the tale sounded like true history, yet how could this impossible conjunction between a prince and a beggar boy have come about? Never was a company of people so perplexed, so interested, and so stupefied, before.

"For a jest, my prince, we did exchange garments. Then we stood before a mirror; and so alike were we that both said it seemed as if there had been no change made—yes, you remember that. Then you noticed that the soldier had hurt my hand—look! here it is, I cannot yet even write with it, the fingers are so stiff. At this your Highness sprang up, vowing vengeance upon that soldier, and ran toward the door—you passed a table—that thing you call the Seal lay on that table—you snatched it up and looked eagerly about, as if for a place to hide it—your eye caught sight of"—

"There, 'tis sufficient!—and the dear God be thanked!" exclaimed the ragged claimant, in a mighty excitement. "Go, my good St. John,—in an arm-piece of the Milanese armor that hangs on the wall, thou'lt find the Seal!"

"Right, my king! right!" cried Tom Canty; "*now* the sceptre of England is thine own; and it was better for him that would dispute it that he had been born dumb! Go, my lord St. John, give thy feet wings!"

The whole assemblage was on its feet, now, and well nigh out of its mind with uneasiness, apprehension, and consuming excitement. On the floor and on the platform a deafening buzz of frantic conversation burst forth, and for some time nobody knew any thing or heard any thing or was interested in any thing but what his neighbor was shouting into his ear, or he was shouting into his neighbor's ear. Time—nobody knew how much of it— swept by unheeded and unnoted.—At last a sudden hush fell upon the house, and in the same moment St. John appeared upon the platform and held the Great Seal aloft in his hand. Then such a shout went up!

"Long live the true King!"

For five minutes the air quaked with shouts and the crash of musical instruments, and was white with a storm of waving handkerchiefs; and through it all a ragged lad, the most conspicuous figure in England, stood, flushed and happy and proud, in the centre of the spacious platform, with the great vassals of the kingdom kneeling around him.

Then all rose, and Tom Canty cried out—

"Now, O, my king, take these regal garments back, and give poor Tom, thy servant, his shreds and remnants again."

The Lord Protector spoke up—

"Let the small varlet be stripped and flung into the Tower."

But the new king, the true king, said—

"I will not have it so. But for him I had not got my crown again—none shall lay a hand upon him to harm him. And as for thee, my good uncle, my Lord Protector, this conduct of thine is not grateful toward this poor lad, for I hear he hath made thee a duke"—the Protector blushed—"yet he was not a king; wherefore, what is thy fine title worth, now? To-morrow you shall sue to me, *through him,* for its confirmation, else no duke, but a simple earl, shalt thou remain."

Under this rebuke, his grace the duke of Somerset retired a little from the front for the moment. The king turned to Tom, and said, kindly—

"My poor boy, how was it that you could remember where I hid the Seal when I could not remember it myself?"

"Ah, my king, that was easy, since I used it divers days."

"Used it,—yet could not explain where it was?"

"I did not know it was *that* they wanted. They did not describe it, your majesty."

"Then how used you it?"

The red blood began to steal up into Tom's cheeks, and he dropped his eyes and was silent.

"Speak up, good lad, and fear nothing," said the king. "How used you the Great Seal of England?"

Tom stammered a moment, in a pathetic confusion, then got it out—

"To crack nuts with!"

Poor child, the avalanche of laughter that greeted this, nearly swept him off his feet. But if a doubt remained in any mind that Tom Canty was not the king of England and familiar with the august appurtenances of royalty, this reply disposed of it utterly.

Meantime the sumptuous robe of state had been removed from Tom's shoulders to the king's, whose rags were effectually hidden from sight under it. Then the coronation ceremonies were resumed; the true king was anointed and the crown set upon his head, whilst cannon thundered the news to the city, and all London seemed to rock with applause.

CHAPTER XXXIII

EDWARD AS KING

Miles Hendon was picturesque enough before he got into the riot on London Bridge—he was more so when he got out of it. He had but little money when he got in, none at all when he got out. The pickpockets had stripped him of his last farthing.

But no matter, so he found his boy. Being a soldier, he did not go at his task in a random way, but set to work, first of all, to arrange his campaign.

What would the boy naturally do? Where would he naturally go? Well—argued Miles—he would naturally go to his former haunts, for that is the instinct of unsound minds, when homeless and forsaken, as well as of sound ones. Whereabouts were his former haunts? His rags, taken together with the low villain who seemed to know him and who even claimed to be his father, indicated that his home was in one or another of the poorest and meanest districts of London. Would the search for him be difficult, or long? No, it was likely to be easy and brief. He would not hunt for the boy, he would hunt for a crowd; in the centre of a big crowd or a little one, sooner or later, he should find his poor little friend, sure; and the mangy mob would be entertaining itself with pestering and aggravating the boy, who would be proclaiming himself king, as usual. Then Miles Hendon would cripple some of those people, and carry off his little ward, and comfort and cheer him with loving words, and the two would never be separated any more.

So Miles started on his quest. Hour after hour he tramped through back alleys and squalid streets, seeking groups and crowds, and finding no end of them, but never any sign of the boy. This greatly surprised him, but did not discourage him. To his notion, there was nothing the matter with his plan of campaign; the only miscalculation about it was that the campaign was becoming a lengthy one, whereas he had expected it to be short.

When daylight arrived, at last, he had made many a mile, and canvassed many a crowd, but the only result was that he was tolerably tired, rather hungry, and very sleepy. He wanted some breakfast, but there was no way to get it. To beg for it did not occur to him; as to pawning his sword, he would as soon have thought of parting with his honor; he could spare some of his clothes—yes, but one could as easily find a customer for a disease as for such clothes.

At noon he was still tramping—among the rabble which followed after the royal procession, now; for he argued that this regal display would attract his little lunatic powerfully. He followed the pageant through all its devious windings about London, and all the way to Westminster and the Abbey. He drifted here and there amongst the multitudes that were massed in the vicinity for a weary long time, baffled and perplexed, and finally wandered off, thinking, and trying to contrive some way to better his plan of campaign. By and by, when he came to himself out of his musings, he discovered that the town was far behind him and that the day was growing old. He was near the river, and in the country; it was a region of fine rural seats—not the sort of district to welcome clothes like his.

It was not at all cold; so he stretched himself on the ground in the lee of a hedge to rest and think. Drowsiness presently began to settle upon his senses; the faint and far-off boom of cannon was wafted to his ear, and he said to himself "The new king is crowned," and straightway fell asleep. He had not slept or rested, before, for more than thirty hours. He did not wake again until near the middle of the next morning.

He got up, lame, stiff, and half famished, washed himself in the river, stayed his stomach with a pint or two of water, and trudged off toward Westminster grumbling at himself for having wasted so much time. Hunger helped him to a new plan, now; he would try to get speech with old Sir Humphrey Marlow and borrow a few marks, and—but that was enough of a plan for the present; it would be time enough to enlarge it when this first stage should be accomplished.

Toward eleven o'clock he approached the palace; and although a host of showy people were about him, moving in the same direction, he was not inconspicuous—his costume took care of that. He watched these people's faces narrowly, hoping to find a charitable one whose possessor might be willing to carry his name to the old lieutenant—as to trying to get into the palace himself, that was simply out of the question.

Presently our whipping-boy passed him, then wheeled about and scanned his figure well, saying to himself, "An' that is not the very vagabond his majesty is in such a worry about, then am I an ass—though belike I was that before. He answereth that description to a rag—that God should make two such, would be to cheapen miracles, by wasteful repetition. I would I could contrive an excuse to speak with him."

Miles Hendon saved him the trouble; for he turned about, then, as a man generally will when somebody mesmerizes him by gazing hard at him from behind; and observing a strong interest in the boy's eyes, he stepped toward him and said—

"You have just come out from the palace; do you belong there?"

"Yes, your worship."

"Know you Sir Humphrey Marlow?"

The boy started, and said to himself, "Lord! mine old departed father!" Then he answered, aloud, "Right well, your worship."

"Good—is he within?"

"Yes," said the boy; and added, to himself, "within his grave."

"Might I crave your favor to carry my name to him, and say I beg to say a word in his ear?"

"I will despatch the business right willingly, fair sir."

"Then say Miles Hendon, son of Sir Richard, is here without—I shall be greatly bounden to you, my good lad."

The boy looked disappointed—"the king did not name him so," he said to himself—"but it mattereth not, this is his twin brother, and can give his majesty news of 'tother Sir-Odds-and-Ends, I warrant." So he said to Miles, "Step in there a moment, good sir, and wait till I bring you word."

Hendon retired to the place indicated—it was a recess sunk in the palace wall, with a stone bench in it—a shelter for sentinels in bad weather. He had hardly seated himself when some halberdiers, in charge of an officer, passed by. The officer saw him, halted his men, and commanded Hendon to come forth. He obeyed, and was promptly arrested as a suspicious character prowling within the precincts of the palace. Things began to look ugly. Poor Miles was going to explain, but the officer roughly silenced him, and ordered his men to disarm him and search him.

"God of his mercy grant that they find somewhat," said poor Miles; "I have searched enow, and failed, yet is my need greater than theirs."

Nothing was found but a document. The officer tore it open, and Hendon smiled when he recognized the "pot-hooks" made by his lost little friend that black day at Hendon Hall. The officer's face grew dark as he read the English paragraph, and Miles blenched to the opposite color as he listened.

"Another new claimant of the crown!" cried the officer. "Verily they breed like rabbits, to-day. Seize the rascal, men, and see ye keep him fast whilst I convey this precious paper within and send it to the king."

He hurried away, leaving the prisoner in the grip of the halberdiers.

"Now is my evil luck ended at last," muttered Hendon, "for I shall dangle at a rope's end for a certainty, by reason of that bit of writing. And what will become of my poor lad!—ah, only the good God knoweth."

By and by he saw the officer coming again, in a great hurry; so he plucked his courage together, purposing to meet his trouble as became a man. The officer ordered the men to loose the prisoner and return his sword to him; then bowed respectfully, and said—

"Please you sir, to follow me."

Hendon followed, saying to himself, "An' I were not travelling to death and judgment, and so must needs economize in sin, I would throttle this knave for his mock courtesy."

The two traversed a populous court, and arrived at the grand entrance of the palace, where the officer, with another bow, delivered Hendon into the hands of a gorgeous official, who received him with profound respect and led him forward through a great hall, lined on both sides with rows of splendid flunkies (who made reverential obeisance as the two passed along, but fell into death-throes of silent laughter at our stately scare-crow the moment his back was turned), and up a broad staircase, among flocks of fine folk, and finally conducted him into a vast room, clove a passage for him through the assembled nobility of England, then made a bow, reminded him to take his hat off, and left him standing in the middle of the room, a mark for all eyes, for plenty of indignant frowns, and for a sufficiency of amused and derisive smiles.

Miles Hendon was entirely bewildered. There sat the young king, under a canopy of state, five steps away, with his head bent down

and aside, speaking with a sort of human bird of paradise—a duke,
maybe; Hendon observed to himself that it was hard enough to be
sentenced to death in the full vigor of life, without having this
peculiarly public humiliation added. He wished the king would
hurry about it—some of the gaudy people near by were becoming
pretty offensive. At this moment the king raised his head slightly
and Hendon caught a good view of his face. The sight nearly took
his breath away!—He stood gazing at the fair young face like one
transfixed; then presently ejaculated—

"Lo, the lord of the Kingdom of Dreams and Shadows on his
throne!"

He muttered some broken sentences, still gazing and marvelling;
then turned his eyes around and about, scanning the gorgeous
throng and the splendid saloon, murmuring "But these are *real*—
verily these are *real*—surely it is not a dream."

He stared at the king again—and thought, "*Is* it a dream?...or
is he the veritable sovereign of England, and not the friendless poor
Tom o' Bedlam I took him for—who shall solve me this riddle?"

A sudden idea flashed in his eye, and he strode to the wall,
gathered up a chair, brought it back, planted it on the floor, and
sat down in it!

A buzz of indignation broke out, a rough hand was laid upon
him, and a voice exclaimed,—

"Up, thou mannerless clown!—wouldst sit in the presence of
the king?"

The disturbance attracted his majesty's attention, who stretched
forth his hand and cried out—

"Touch him not, it is his right!"

The throng fell back, stupefied. The king went on—

"Learn ye all, ladies, lords and gentlemen, that this is my trusty
and well-beloved servant, Miles Hendon, who interposed his good
sword and saved his prince from bodily harm and possible death—
and for this he is a knight, by the king's voice. Also learn, that for
a higher service, in that he saved his sovereigh stripes and shame,
taking these upon himself, he is a peer of England, Earl of Kent,
and shall have gold and lands meet for the dignity. More—the
privilege which he hath just exercised is his by royal grant; for we
have ordained that the chiefs of his line shall have and hold the
right to sit in thé presence of the majesty of England henceforth,
age after age, so long as the crown shall endure. Molest him not."

Two persons, who, through delay, had only arrived from the
country during this morning, and had now been in this room only
five minutes, stood listening to these words and looking at the king,
then at the scare-crow, then at the king again, in a sort of torpid
bewilderment. These were Sir Hugh and the Lady Edith. But the
new Earl did not see them. He was still staring at the monarch, in a
dazed way, and muttering—

"O, body o' me! *This* my pauper! This my lunatic! This is he whom *I* would show what grandeur was, in my house of seventy rooms and seven and twenty servants! This is he who had never known aught but rags for raiment, kicks for comfort, and offal for diet! This is he whom *I* adopted and would make respectable! Would God I had a bag to hide my head in!"

Then his manners suddenly came back to him, and he dropped upon his knees, with his hands between the king's, and swore allegiance and did homage for his lands and titles. Then he rose and stood respectfully aside, a mark still for all eyes—and much envy, too.

Now the king discovered Sir Hugh, and spoke out, with wrathful voice and kindling eye—

"Strip this robber of his false show and stolen estates, and put him under lock and key till I have need of him."

The late Sir Hugh was led away.

There was a stir at the other end of the room, now; the assemblage fell apart, and Tom Canty, quaintly but richly clothed, marched down, between these living walls, preceded by an usher. He knelt before the king, who said—

"I have learned the story of these past few weeks, and am well pleased with thee. Thou hast governed the realm with right royal gentleness and mercy. Thou hast found thy mother and thy sisters again? Good; they shall be cared for—and thy father shall hang, if thou desire it and the law consent. Know, all ye that hear my voice, that from this day, they that abide in the shelter of Christ's Hospital and share the king's bounty, shall have their minds and hearts fed, as well as their baser parts; and this boy shall dwell there, and hold the chief place in its honorable body of governors, during life. And for that he hath been a king, it is meet that other than common observance shall be his due; wherefore, note this his dress of state, for by it he shall be known, and none shall copy it; and wheresoever he shall come, it shall remind the people that he hath been royal, in his time, and none shall deny him his due of reverence or fail to give him salutation. He hath the throne's protection, he hath the crown's support, he shall be known and called by the honorable title of the King's Ward."

The proud and happy Tom Canty rose and kissed the king's hand, and was conducted from the presence. He did not waste any time, but flew to his mother, to tell her and Nan and Bet all about it and get them to help him enjoy the great news.*

*See Notes to Chapter 33 at end of the volume.

CONCLUSION

JUSTICE AND RETRIBUTION

When the mysteries were all cleared up, it came out, by confession of Hugh Hendon, that his wife had repudiated Miles by his command, that day at Hendon Hall—a command assisted and supported by the perfectly trustworthy promise that if she did not deny that he was Miles Hendon, and stand firmly to it, he would have her life; whereupon she said take it, she did not value it—and she would not repudiate Miles; then the husband said he would spare her life but have Miles assassinated! This was a different matter; so she gave her word and kept it.

Hugh was not prosecuted for his threats or for stealing his brother's estates and title, because the wife and brother would not testify against him—and the former would not have been allowed to do it, even if she had wanted to. Hugh deserted his wife and went over to the continent, where he presently died; and by and by the earl of Kent married his relict. There were grand times and rejoicings at Hendon village when the couple paid their first visit to the Hall.

Tom Canty's father was never heard of again.

The king sought out the farmer who had been branded and sold as a slave, and reclaimed him from his evil life with the Ruffler's gang, and put him in the way of a comfortable livelihood.

He also took that old lawyer out of prison and remitted his fine. He provided good homes for the daughters of the two Baptist women whom he saw burned at the stake, and roundly punished the official who laid the undeserved stripes upon Miles Hendon's back.

He saved from the gallows the boy who had captured the stray falcon, and also the woman who had stolen a remnant of cloth from a weaver; but he was too late to save the man who had been convicted of killing a deer in the royal forest.

He showed favor to the justice who had pitied him when he was supposed to have stolen a pig, and he had the gratification of seeing him grow in the public esteem and become a great and honored man.

As long as the king lived he was fond of telling the story of his adventures, all through, from the hour that the sentinel cuffed him away from the palace gate till the final midnight when he deftly mixed himself into a gang of hurrying workmen and so slipped into the Abbey and climbed up and hid himself in the Confessor's tomb, and then slept so long, next day, that he came within one of missing the Coronation altogether. He said that the frequent rehearsing of the precious lesson kept him strong in his purpose to make its teachings yield benefits to his people; and so, whilst his life was spared he should continue to tell the story, and thus keep its sorrowful spectacles fresh in his memory and the springs of pity replenished in his heart.

Miles Hendon and Tom Canty were favorites of the king, all through his brief reign, and his sincere mourners when he died. The good earl of Kent had too much good sense to abuse his peculiar privilege but he exercised it twice after the instance we have seen of it before he was called from the world; once at the accession of Queen Mary, and once at the accession of Queen Elizabeth. A descendant of his exercised it at the accession of James I. Before this one's son chose to use the privilege, near a quarter of a century had elapsed, and the "privilege of the Kents" had faded out of most people's memories; so, when the Kent of that day appeared before Charles I. and his court and sat down in the sovereign's presence to assert and perpetuate the right of his house, there was a fine stir, indeed! But the matter was soon explained and the right confirmed. The last earl of the line fell in the wars of the Commonwealth fighting for the king, and the odd privilege ended with him.

Tom Canty lived to be a very old man, a handsome, white-haired old fellow, of grave and benignant aspect. As long as he lasted he was honored; and he was also reverenced, for his striking and peculiar costume kept the people reminded that "in his time he had been royal;" so, wherever he appeared the crowd fell apart, making way for him, and whispering, one to another, "Doff thy had, it is the King's Ward!"—and so they saluted, and got his kindly smile in return—and they valued it, too, for his was an honorable history.

Yes, King Edward VI. lived only a few years, poor boy, but he lived them worthily. More than once, when some great dignitary, some gilded vassal of the crown, made argument against his leniency, and urged that some law which he was bent upon amending was gentle enough for its purpose, and wrought no suffering or oppression which any one need mightily mind, the young king turned the mournful eloquence of his great compassionate eyes upon him and answered—

"What dost *thou* know of suffering and oppression? I and my people know, but not thou."

The reign of Edward VI. was a singularly merciful one for those harsh times. Now that we are taking leave of him let us try to keep this in our minds, to his credit.

NOTES

NOTE 1.—Page 605.

Christ's Hospital Costume.

It is most reasonable to regard the dress as copied from the costume of the citizens of London of that period, when long blue coats were the common habit of apprentices and serving-men, and yellow stockings were generally worn; the coat fits closely to the body, but has loose sleeves, and beneath is worn a sleeveless yellow under-coat; around the waist is a red leathern girdle; a clerical band around the neck, and a small flat black cap, about the size of a saucer, completes the costume.—*Timbs' "Curiosities of London."*

NOTE 2.—Page 606.

It appears that Christ's Hospital was not originally founded as a *school;* its object was to rescue children from the streets, to shelter, feed, clothe them, etc.—*Timbs' "Curiosities of London."*

NOTE 3.—Page 611.

The Duke of Norfolk's Condemnation Commanded.

The King was now approaching fast towards his end; and fearing lest Norfolk should escape him, he sent a message to the Commons, by which he desired them to hasten the bill, on pretence that Norfolk enjoyed the dignity of earl marshal, and it was necessary to appoint another, who might officiate at the ensuing ceremony of installing his son Prince of Wales.—*Hume,* vol. iii. p. 307.

NOTE 4.—Page 618

It was not till the end of this reign [Henry VIII] that any salads, carrots, turnips, or other edible roots were produced in England. The little of these vegetables that was used, was formerly imported from Holland and Flanders. Queen Catherine, when she wanted a salad, was obliged to despatch a messenger thither on purpose.—*Hume's History of England,* vol. iii. p. 314.

NOTE 5.—Page 621.

Attainder of Norfolk.

The house of peers, without examining the prisoner, without trial or evidence, passed a bill of attainder against him and sent it down to the commons.... The obsequious commons obeyed his [the King's] directions; and the King, having affixed the royal assent to the bill by commissioners, issued orders for the execution of Norfolk on the morning of the twenty-ninth of January, [the next day.]—*Hume's England,* vol. iii. p. 306.

NOTE 6.—Page 629.

The Loving-Cup.

The loving-cup, and the peculiar ceremonies observed in drinking from it, are older than English history. It is thought that both are Danish importations. As far back as knowledge goes, the loving-cup has always been drunk at English banquets. Tradition explains the ceremonies in this way: in the rude ancient times it was deemed a wise precaution to have both hands of both drinkers employed, lest while the pledger pledged his love and fidelity to the pledgee the pledgee take that opportunity to slip a dirk into him!

NOTE 7.—Page 632.

The Duke of Norfolk's Narrow Escape.

Had Henry VIII survived a few hours longer, his order for the duke's execution would have been carried into effect. "But news being carried to the Tower that the King himself had expired that night, the lieutenant deferred obeying the warrant; and it was not thought advisable by the Council to begin a new reign by the death of the greatest nobleman in the Kingdom, who had been condemned by a sentence so unjust and tyrannical."—*Hume's England,* vol. iii. p. 307.

NOTE 8.—Page 649.

The Whipping-Boy

James I and Charles II had whipping-boys when they were little fellows, to take their punishment for them when they fell short in their lessons; so I have ventured to furnish my small prince with one, for my own purposes.

NOTES TO CHAPTER XV.—Page 658.

Character of Hertford.

The young king discovered an extreme attachment to his uncle, who was, in the main, a man of moderation and probity.—*Hume's England,* vol. iii. p. 324.

But if he [the Protector] gave offence by assuming too much state, he deserves great praise on account of the laws passed this session, by which the rigor of former statutes was much mitigated, and some security given to the freedom of the constitution. All laws were repealed which extended the crime of treason beyond the statute of the twenty-fifth of Edward III; all laws enacted during the late reign extending the crime of felony; all the former laws against Lollardy or heresy, together with the statute of the Six Articles. None were to be accused for words, but within a month after they were spoken. By these repeals several of the most rigorous laws that ever had passed in England were annulled; and some dawn, both of civil and religious liberty, began to appear to the people. A repeal also passed of that law, the destruction of all laws, by which the king's proclamation was made of equal force with a statute.—*Ibid.,* vol. iii. p. 339.

Boiling to Death.

In the reign of Henry VIII, poisoners were, by act of parliament, condemned to be *boiled to death.* This act was repealed in the following reign.

In Germany, even in the 17th century, this horrible punishment was inflicted on coiners and counterfeiters. Taylor, the Water Poet, describes an execution he witnessed in Hamburg, in 1616. The judgment pronounced against a coiner of false money was that he should "be *boiled to death in oil:* not thrown into the vessel at once, but with a pulley or rope to be hanged under the armpits, and then let down into the oil *by degrees;* first the feet, and next the legs, and so to boil his flesh from his bones alive."—*Dr. J. Hammond Trumbull's "Blue Laws, True and False,"* p. 13.

The Famous Stocking Case.

A woman and her daughter, *nine years old,* were hanged in Huntingdon for selling their souls to the devil, and raising a storm by pulling off their stockings!—*Ibid.,* p. 20.

NOTE 10.—Page 666.

Enslaving.

So young a king, and so ignorant a peasant were likely to make mistakes—and this is an instance in point. This peasant was suffering from this law *by anticipation;* the king was venting his indignation against a law which was not yet in existence: for this hideous statute was to have birth in this little king's own reign. However, we know, from the humanity of his character, that it could never have been suggested by him.

NOTES TO CHAPTER XXIII.—Page 691.

Death for Trifling Larcenies.

When Connecticut and New Haven were framing their first codes, larceny above the value of twelve pence was a capital crime in England—as it had been since the time of Henry I.—*Dr. J. Hammond Trumbull's "Blue Laws, True and False,"* p. 17.

The curious old book called "The English Rogue" makes the limit thirteen pence ha'penny; death being the portion of any who steal a thing "above the value of thirteen pence ha'penny."

NOTES TO CHAPTER XXVII.—Page 708.

From many descriptions of larceny, the law expressly took away the benefit of clergy; to steal a horse, or a *hawk,* or woolen cloth from the weaver, was a hanging matter. So it was, to kill a deer from the king's forest, or to export sheep from the Kingdom.—*Dr. J. Hammond Trumbull's "Blue Laws, True and False,"* p. 13.

William Prynne, a learned barrister, was sentenced—[long after Edward the Sixth's time]—to lose both his ears in the pillory; to degradation from the bar; a fine of £3,000, and imprisonment for life. Three years afterwards, he gave new offence to Laud, by publishing a pamphlet against the hierarchy. He was again prosecuted, and was sentenced to lose *what remained of his ears;* to pay a fine of £5,000; to be *branded on both cheeks* with the letters S. L. (for Seditious Libeller,) and to remain in prison for life. The severity of this sentence was equalled by the savage rigor of its execution.— *Ibid.,* p. 12.

NOTES TO CHAPTER XXXII.—Page 731.

Christ's Hospital, or Blue Coat School, "the Noblest Institution in the World."

The ground on which the Priory of the Grey Friars stood was conferred by Henry the Eighth on the Corporation of London, [who caused the institution there of a home for poor boys and girls.] Subsequently, Edward the Sixth caused the old priory to be properly repaired, and founded within it that noble establishment called the Blue Coat School, or Christ's Hospital, for the *education* and maintenance of orphans and the children of indigent persons. . . . . Edward would not let him [Bishop Ridley] depart till the letter was written, [to the Lord Mayor,] and then charged him to deliver it himself, and signify his special request and commandment that no time might be lost in proposing what was convenient, and apprising him of the proceedings. The work was zealously undertaken, Ridley himself engaging in it; and the result was, the founding of Christ's Hospital for the Education of Poor Children. [The king endowed several other charities at the same time.] "Lord God," said he, "I yield thee most hearty thanks that thou hast given me life thus long, to finish this work to the glory of thy name!" That innocent and most exemplary life was drawing rapidly to its close, and in a few days he rendered up his spirit to his Creator, praying God to defend the realm from Papistry.—*J. Heneage Jesse's "London, its Celebrated Characters and Places."*

In the Great Hall hangs a large picture of King Edward VI seated on his throne, in a scarlet and ermined robe, holding the sceptre in his left hand, and presenting with the other the Charter to the kneeling Lord Mayor. By his side stands the Chancellor, holding the seals, and next to him are other officers of state. Bishop Ridley kneels before him with uplifted hands, as if supplicating a blessing on the event; whilst the Aldermen, etc., with the Lord Mayor, kneel on both sides, occupying the middle ground of the picture; and lastly, in front, are a double row of boys on one side, and girls on the other, from the master and matron down to the boy and girl who have stepped forward from their respective rows, and kneel with raised hands before the king.—*Timbs' "Curiosities of London,"* p. 98.

Christ's Hospital, by ancient custom, possesses the privilege of addressing the Sovereign on the occasion of his or her coming into the City to partake of the hospitality of the Corporation of London. —*Ibid.*

The Dining-Hall, with its lobby and organ-gallery, occupies the entire story, which is 187 feet long, 51 feet wide, and 47 feet high; it is lit by nine large windows, filled with stained glass on the south side; and is, next to Westminster Hall, the noblest room in the metropolis. Here the boys, now about 800 in number, dine; and here are held the "Suppings in Public," to which visitors are admitted by tickets, issued by the Treasurer and by the Governors of Christ's Hospital. The tables are laid with cheese in wooden bowls; beer in wooden piggins, poured from leathern jacks; and bread brought in large baskets. The official company enter; the Lord Mayor, or President, takes his seat in a state chair, made of oak from St. Catherine's Church by the Tower; a hymn is sung, accompanied by the organ; a "Grecian," or head boy, reads the prayers from the pulpit, silence being enforced by three drops of a wooden hammer. After prayer the supper commences, and the visitors walk between the tables. At its close, the "tradeboys" take up the baskets, bowls, jacks, piggins, and candlesticks, and pass in procession, the bowing to the Governors being curiously formal. This spectacle was witnessed by Queen Victoria and Prince Albert in 1845.

Among the more eminent Blue Coat boys are Joshua Barnes, editor of Anacreon and Euripides; Jeremiah Markland, the eminent critic, particularly in Greek literature; Camden, the antiquary; Bishop Stillingfleet; Samuel Richardson, the novelist; Thomas Mitchell, the translator of Aristophanes; Thomas Barnes, many years editor of the London *Times;* Coleridge, Charles Lamb, and Leigh Hunt.

No boy is admitted before he is seven years old, or after he is nine; and no boy can remain in the school after he is fifteen, King's boys and "Grecians" alone excepted. There are about 500 Governors, at the head of whom are the Sovereign and the Prince of Wales. The qualification for a Governor is payment of £500.— *Ibid.*

GENERAL NOTE

ONE *hears much about the "hideous Blue-Laws of Connecticut," and is accustomed to shudder piously when they are mentioned. There are people in America—and even in England!—who imagine that they were a very monument of malignity, pitilessness, and inhumanity; whereas, in reality they were about the first* SWEEPING DEPARTURE FROM JUDICIAL ATROCITY *which the "civilized" world had seen. This humane and kindly Blue-Law code, of two hundred and forty years ago, stands all by itself, with ages of bloody law on the further side of it, and a century and three-quarters of bloody English law on* THIS *side of it.*

There has never been a time—under the Blue-Laws or any other— when above FOURTEEN *crimes were punishable by death in Connecticut. But in England, within the memory of men who are still hale in body and mind,* TWO HUNDRED AND TWENTY-THREE *crimes were punishable by death!* * *These facts are worth knowing—and worth thinking about, too.*

*See Dr. J. Hammond Trumbull's "Blue Laws, True and False," p. 11.

ON THE DECAY OF THE
ART OF LYING

"On the Decay of the Art of Lying" appeared first in *the book* The Stolen White Elephant, Etc., *published in 1882 by James R. Osgood and Company, Boston.*

ON THE DECAY OF THE ART OF LYING

ESSAY, FOR DISCUSSION, READ AT A MEETING OF THE HISTORICAL AND ANTIQUARIAN CLUB OF HARTFORD, AND OFFERED FOR THE THIRTY-DOLLAR PRIZE. NOW FIRST PUBLISHED.*

Observe, I do not mean to suggest that the *custom* of lying has suffered any decay or interruption—no, for the Lie, as a Virtue, a Principle, is eternal; the Lie, as a recreation, a solace, a refuge in time of need, the fourth Grace, the tenth Muse, man's best and surest friend, is immortal, and cannot perish from the earth while this Club remains. My complaint simply concerns the decay of the *art* of lying. No high-minded man, no man of right feeling, can contemplate the lumbering and slovenly lying of the present day without grieving to see a noble art so prostituted. In this veteran presence I naturally enter upon this theme with diffidence; it is like an old maid trying to teach nursery matters to the mothers in Israel. It would not become me to criticise you, gentlemen, who are nearly all my elders—and my superiors, in this thing—and so, if I should here and there *seem* to do it, I trust it will in most cases be more in a spirit of admiration than of fault-finding; indeed if this finest of the fine arts had everywhere received the attention, encouragement, and conscientious practice and development which this Club has devoted to it, I should not need to utter this lament, or shed a single tear. I do not say this to flatter: I say it in a spirit of just and appreciative recognition. [It had been my intention, at this point, to mention names and give illustrative specimens, but indications observable about me admonished me to beware of particulars and confine myself to generalities.]

No fact is more firmly established than that lying is a necessity of our circumstances—the deduction that it is then a Virtue goes

*Did not take the prize.

without saying. No virtue can reach its highest usefulness without careful and diligent cultivation—therefore, it goes without saying, that this one ought to be taught in the public schools—at the fireside—even in the newspapers. What chance has the ignorant, uncultivated liar against the educated expert? What chance have I against Mr. Per—against a lawyer? *Judicious* lying is what the world needs. I sometimes think it were even better and safer not to lie at all than to lie injudiciously. An awkward, unscientific lie is often as ineffectual as the truth.

Now let us see what the philosophers say. Note that venerable proverb: Children and fools *always* speak the truth. The deduction is plain—adults and wise persons *never* speak it. Parkman, the historian, says, "The principle of truth may itself be carried into an absurdity." In another place in the same chapter he says, "The saying is old that truth should not be spoken at all times; and those whom a sick conscience worries into habitual violation of the maxim are imbeciles and nuisances." It is strong language, but true. None of us could *live* with an habitual truth-teller; but thank goodness none of us has to. An habitual truth-teller is simply an impossible creature; he does not exist; he never has existed. Of course there are people who *think* they never lie, but it is not so—and this ignorance is one of the very things that shame our so-called civilization. Everybody lies—every day; every hour; awake; asleep; in his dreams; in his joy; in his mourning; if he keeps his tongue still, his hands, his feet, his eyes, his attitude, will convey deception—and purposely. Even in sermons—but that is a platitude.

In a far country where I once lived the ladies used to go around paying calls, under the humane and kindly pretence of wanting to see each other; and when they returned home, they would cry out with a glad voice, saying, "We made sixteen calls and found fourteen of them out"—not meaning that they found out anything against the fourteen—no, that was only a colloquial phrase to signify that they were not at home—and their manner of saying it expressed their lively satisfaction in that fact. Now their pretence of wanting to see the fourteen—and the other two whom they had been less lucky with—was that commonest and mildest form of lying which is sufficiently described as a deflection from the truth. Is it justifiable? Most certainly. It is beautiful, it is noble; for its object is, *not* to reap profit, but to convey a pleasure to the sixteen. The iron-souled truth-monger would plainly manifest, or even utter the fact that he didn't want to see those people—and he would be an ass, and inflict a totally unnecessary pain. And next, those ladies in that far country—but never mind, they had a thousand pleasant ways of lying, that grew out of gentle impulses, and were a credit to their intelligence and an honor to their hearts. Let the particulars go.

The men in that far country were liars, every one. Their mere

howdy-do was a lie, because *they* didn't care how you did, except
they were undertakers. To the ordinary inquirer you lied in return;
for you made no conscientious diagnosis of your case, but answered
at random, and usually missed it considerably. You lied to the
undertaker, and said your health was failing—a wholly
commendable lie, since it cost you nothing and pleased the other
man. If a stranger called and interrupted you, you said with your
hearty tongue, "I'm glad to see you," and said with your heartier
soul, "I wish you were with the cannibals and it was dinner-time."
When he went, you said regretfully, *"Must* you go?" and followed it
with a "Call again;" but you did no harm, for you did not deceive
anybody nor inflict any hurt, whereas the truth would have made
you both unhappy.

I think that all this courteous lying is a sweet and loving art, and
should be cultivated. The highest perfection of politeness is only a
beautiful edifice, built, from the base to the dome, of graceful and
gilded forms of charitable and unselfish lying.

What I bemoan is the growing prevalence of the brutal truth.
Let us do what we can to eradicate it. An injurious truth has no merit
over an injurious lie. Neither should ever be uttered. The man who
speaks an injurious truth lest his soul be not saved if he do
otherwise, should reflect that that sort of a soul is not strictly worth
saving. The man who tells a lie to help a poor devil out of trouble, is
one of whom the angels doubtless say, "Lo, here is an heroic soul
who casts his own welfare into jeopardy to succor his neighbor's;
let us exalt this magnanimous liar."

An injurious lie is an uncommendable thing; and so, also, and in
the same degree, is an injurious truth—a fact which is recognized
by the law of libel.

Among other common lies, we have the *silent* lie—the deception
which one conveys by simply keeping still and concealing the truth.
Many obstinate truth-mongers indulge in this dissipation,
imagining that if they *speak* no lie, they lie not at all. In that far
country where I once lived, there was a lovely spirit, a lady whose
impulses were always high and pure, and whose character answered
to them. One day I was there at dinner, and remarked, in a general
way, that we are all liars. She was amazed, and said, "Not *all?*"
It was before "Pinafore's" time, so I did not make the response
which would naturally follow in our day, but frankly said, "Yes,
all—we are all liars; there are no exceptions." She looked almost
offended, and said, "Why, do you include *me?*" "Certainly," I said.
"I think you even rank as an expert." She said, " 'Sh—'sh! the
children!" So the subject was changed in deference to the children's
presence, and we went on talking about other things. But as soon
as the young people were out of the way, the lady came warmly
back to the matter and said, "I have made it the rule of my life to
never tell a lie; and I have never departed from it in a single

instance." I said, "I don't mean the least harm or disrespect, but really you have been lying like smoke ever since I've been sitting here. It has caused me a good deal of pain, because I am not used to it." She required of me an instance—just a single instance. So I said—

"Well, here is the unfilled duplicate of the blank which the Oakland hospital people sent to you by the hand of the sick-nurse when she came here to nurse your little nephew through his dangerous illness. This blank asks all manner of questions as to the conduct of that sick-nurse: 'Did she ever sleep on her watch? Did she ever forget to give the medicine?' and so forth and so on. You are warned to be very careful and explicit in your answers, for the welfare of the service requires that the nurses be promptly fined or otherwise punished for derelictions. You told me you were perfectly delighted with that nurse—that she had a thousand perfections and only one fault: you found you never could depend on her wrapping Johnny up half sufficiently while he waited in a chilly chair for her to rearrange the warm bed. You filled up the duplicate of this paper, and sent it back to the hospital by the hand of the nurse. How did you answer this question—'Was the nurse at any time guilty of a negligence which was likely to result in the patient's taking cold?' Come—everything is decided by a bet here in California: ten dollars to ten cents you lied when you answered that question." She said, "I didn't; *I left it blank!*" "Just so—you have told a *silent* lie; you have left it to be inferred that you had no fault to find in that matter." She said, "Oh, was that a lie? And how *could* I mention her one single fault, and she so good?—it would have been cruel." I said, "One ought always to lie, when one can do good by it; your impulse was right, but your judgment was crude; this comes of unintelligent practice. Now observe the result of this inexpert deflection of yours. You know Mr. Jones's Willie is lying very low with scarlet-fever; well, your recommendation was so enthusiastic that that girl is there nursing him, and the worn-out family have all been trustingly sound asleep for the last fourteen hours, leaving their darling with full confidence in those fatal hands, because you, like young George Washington, have a reputa— However, if you are not going to have anything to do, I will come around to-morrow and we'll attend the funeral together, for, of course, you'll naturally feel a peculiar interest in Willie's case—as personal a one, in fact, as the undertaker."

But that was all lost. Before I was half-way through she was in a carriage and making thirty miles an hour toward the Jones mansion to save what was left of Willie and tell all she knew about the deadly nurse. All of which was unnecessary, as Willie wasn't sick; I had been lying myself. But that same day, all the same, she sent a line to the hospital which filled up the neglected blank, and stated the *facts,* too, in the squarest possible manner.

Now, you see, this lady's fault was *not* in lying, but only in lying injudiciously. She should have told the truth, *there,* and made it up to the nurse with a fraudulent compliment further along in the paper. She could have said, "In one respect this sick-nurse is perfection—when she is on watch, she never snores." Almost any little pleasant lie would have taken the sting out of that troublesome but necessary expression of the truth.

Lying is universal—we *all* do it; we all *must* do it. Therefore, the wise thing is for us diligently to train ourselves to lie thoughtfully, judiciously; to lie with a good object, and not an evil one; to lie for others' advantage, and not our own; to lie healingly, charitably, humanely, not cruelly, hurtfully, maliciously; to lie gracefully and graciously, not awkwardly and clumsily; to lie firmly, frankly, squarely, with head erect, not haltingly, tortuously, with pusillanimous mien, as being ashamed of our high calling. Then shall we be rid of the rank and pestilent truth that is rotting the land; then shall we be great and good and beautiful, and worthy dwellers in a world where even benign Nature habitually lies, except when she promises execrable weather. Then— But I am but a new and feeble student in this gracious art; I cannot instruct *this* Club.

Joking aside, I think there is much need of wise examination into what sorts of lies are best and wholesomest to be indulged, seeing we *must* all lie and *do* all lie, and what sorts it may be best to avoid—and this is a thing which I feel I can confidently put into the hands of this experienced Club—a ripe body, who may be termed, in this regard, and without undue flattery, Old Masters.

The Adventures of Huckleberry Finn *never appeared in its entirety prior to publication. This was unusual in the days of serialized novels. Parts of it did appear in the* Chicago Times, *January 1885, and in* Century Magazine, *February 1885. Released in 1885, it was the first book issued by Mark Twain's publishing company, C.L. Webster, New York.*

THE ADVENTURES OF HUCKLEBERRY FINN

EXPLANATORY.

In this book a number of dialects are used, to wit: the Missouri negro dialect; the extremest form of the backwoods South-Western dialect; the ordinary "Pike-County" dialect; and four modified varieties of this last. The shadings have not been done in a haphazard fashion, or by guess-work; but pains-takingly, and with the trustworthy guidance and support of personal familiarity with these several forms of speech.

I make this explanation for the reason that without it many readers would suppose that all these characters were trying to talk alike and not succeeding.

THE AUTHOR.

CHAPTER I

You don't know about me, without you have read a book by the name of "The Adventures of Tom Sawyer," but that ain't no matter. That book was made by Mr. Mark Twain, and he told the truth, mainly. There was things which he stretched, but mainly he told the truth. That is nothing. I never seen anybody but lied, one time or another, without it was Aunt Polly, or the widow, or maybe Mary. Aunt Polly—Tom's Aunt Polly, she is—and Mary, and the Widow Douglas, is all told about in that book—which is mostly a true book; with some stretchers, as I said before.

Now the way that the book winds up, is this: Tom and me found the money that the robbers hid in the cave, and it made us rich. We got six thousand dollars apiece—all gold. It was an awful sight of money when it was piled up. Well, Judge Thatcher, he took it and put it out at interest, and it fetched us a dollar a day apiece, all the year round—more than a body could tell what to do with. The Widow Douglas, she took me for her son, and allowed she would sivilize me; but it was rough living in the house all the time, considering how dismal regular and decent the widow was in all her ways; and so when I couldn't stand it no longer, I lit out. I got into my old rags, and my sugar-hogshead again, and was free and satisfied. But Tom Sawyer, he hunted me up and said he was going to start a band of robbers, and I might join if I would go back to the widow and be respectable. So I went back.

The widow she cried over me, and called me a poor lost lamb, and she called me a lot of other names, too, but she never meant no harm by it. She put me in them new clothes again, and I couldn't do nothing but sweat and sweat, and feel all cramped up. Well, then, the old thing commenced again. The widow rung a bell for supper, and you had to come to time. When you got to the table you couldn't go right to eating, but you had to wait for the widow to tuck down her head and grumble a little over the victuals, though there warn't really anything the matter with them. That is, nothing only everything was cooked by itself. In a barrel of odds and ends it is different; things get mixed up, and the juice kind of swaps around, and the things go better.

After supper she got out her book and learned me about Moses and the Bulrushers; and I was in a sweat to find out all about him; but by-and-by she let it out that Moses had been dead a considerable long time; so then I didn't care no more about him; ᵇ⁻⁻⁻⁻ I don't take no stock in dead people.

ᵇⁱoon I wanted to smoke, and asked the widow to let me. ᵇⁱouldn't. She said it was a mean practice and wasn't clean, ᵇt try to not do it any more. That is just the way with some ᵇʸey get down on a thing when they don't know nothing ᵇʳe she was a bothering about Moses, which was no kin to her, and no use to anybody, being gone, you see, yet finding a power of fault with me for doing a thing that had some good in it. And she took snuff too; of course that was all right, because she done it herself.

Her sister, Miss Watson, a tolerable slim old maid, with goggles on, had just come to live with her, and took a set at me now, with a spelling-book. She worked me middling hard for about an hour, and then the widow made her ease up. I couldn't stood it much longer. Then for an hour it was deadly dull, and I was fidgety. Miss Watson would say, "Dont put your feet up there, Huckleberry;" and "dont scrunch up like that, Huckleberry—set up straight;" and pretty soon she would say, "Don't gap and stretch like that, Huckleberry—why don't you try to behave?" Then she told me all about the bad place, and I said I wished I was there. She got mad, then, but I didn't mean no harm. All I wanted was to go somewheres; all I wanted was a change, I warn't particular. She said it was wicked to say what I said; said she wouldn't say it for the whole world; *she* was going to live so as to go to the good place. Well, I couldn't see no advantage in going where she was going, so I made up my mind I wouldn't try for it. But I never said so, because it would only make trouble, and wouldn't do no good.

Now she had got a start, and she went on and told me all about the good place. She said all a body would have to do there was to go around all day long with a harp and sing, forever and ever. So I didn't think much of it. But I never said so. I asked her if she reckoned Tom Sawyer would go there, and, she said, not by a considerable sight. I was glad about that, because I wanted him and me to be together.

Miss Watson she kept pecking at me, and it got tiresome and lonesome. By-and-by they fetched the niggers in and had prayers, and then everybody was off to bed. I went up to my room with a piece of candle and put it on the table. Then I set down in a chair by the window and tried to think of something cheerful, but it warn't no use. I felt so lonesome I most wished I was dead. The stars was shining and the leaves rustled in the woods ever so mournful; and I heard an owl, away off, who-whooing about somebody that was dead, and a whippowill and a dog crying about somebody that was going to die; and the wind was trying to whisper something to me and I couldn't make out what it was, and so it made the cold shivers run over me. Then away out in the woods I heard that kind of a sound that a ghost makes when it wants to tell about something that's on its mind and can't make itself understood, and so can't rest easy in its grave and has to go about that way every night grieving. I got so down-hearted and scared, I did wish I had some company. Pretty soon a spider went crawling up my shoulder, and I flipped it off and it lit in the candle; and before I could budge it was all shriveled up. I didn't need anybody to tell me that that was an awful bad sign and would fetch me some bad luck, so I was scared and most shook the clothes off of me. I got up and turned around in my tracks three times and crossed my breast every time; and then I tied up a little lock of my hair with a thread to keep witches away. But I hadn't no confidence. You do that when you've lost a horse-shoe that you've found, instead of nailing it up over the door, but I hadn't ever heard anybody say it was any way to keep off bad luck when you'd killed a spider.

I set down again, a shaking all over, and got out my pipe for a smoke; for the house was all as still as death, now, and so the widow wouldn't know. Well, after a long time I heard the clock away off in the town go boom—boom—boom—twelve licks—and all still again—stiller than ever. Pretty soon I heard a twig snap, down in the dark amongst the trees—something was a stirring. I set still and listened. Directly I could just barely hear a *"me-yow! me-yow!"* down there. That was good! Says I, *"me-yow! me-yow!"* as soft as I could, and then I put out the light and scrambled out of the window onto the shed. Then I slipped down to the ground and crawled in amongst the trees, and sure enough there was Tom Sawyer waiting for me.

CHAPTER II

We went tip-toeing along a path amongst the trees back towards the end of the widow's garden, stooping down so as the branches wouldn't scrape our heads. When we was passing by the kitchen I fell over a root and made a noise. We scrouched down and laid still. Miss Watson's big nigger, named Jim, was setting in the kitchen door; we could see him pretty clear, because there was a light behind him. He got up and stretched his neck out about a minute, listening. Then he says,

"Who dah?"

He listened some more; then he come tip-toeing down and stood right between us; we could a touched him, nearly. Well, likely it was minutes and minutes that there warn't a sound, and we all there so close together. There was a place on my ankle that got to itching; but I dasn't scratch it; and then my ear begun to itch; and next my back, right between my shoulders. Seemed like I'd die if I couldn't scratch. Well, I've noticed that thing plenty of times since. If you are with the quality, or at a funeral, or trying to go to sleep when you ain't sleepy—if you are anywheres where it won't do for you to scratch, why you will itch all over in upwards of a thousand places. Pretty soon Jim says:

"Say—who is you? Whar is you? Dog my cats ef I didn' hear sumf'n. Well, I knows what I's gwyne to do. I's gwyne to set down here and listen tell I hears it agin."

So he set down on the ground betwixt me and Tom. He leaned

his back up against a tree, and stretched his legs out till one of them most touched one of mine. My nose begun to itch. It itched till the tears come into my eyes. But I dasn't scratch. Then it begun to itch on the inside. Next I got to itching underneath. I didn't know how I was going to set still. This miserableness went on as much as six or seven minutes; but it seemed a sight longer than that. I was itching in eleven different places now. I reckoned I couldn't stand it more'n a minute longer, but I set my teeth hard and got ready to try. Just then Jim begun to breathe heavy; next he begun to snore—and then I was pretty soon comfortable again.

Tom he made a sign to me—kind of a little noise with his mouth—and we went creeping away on our hands and knees. When we was ten foot off, Tom whispered to me and wanted to tie Jim to the tree for fun; but I said no; he might wake and make a disturbance, and then they'd find out I warn't in. Then Tom said he hadn't got candles enough, and he would slip in the kitchen and get some more. I didn't want him to try. I said Jim might wake up and come. But Tom wanted to resk it; so we slid in there and got three candles, and Tom laid five cents on the table for pay. Then we got out, and I was in a sweat to get away; but nothing would do Tom but he must crawl to where Jim was, on his hands and knees, and play something on him. I waited, and it seemed a good while, everything was so still and lonesome.

As soon as Tom was back, we cut along the path, around the garden fence, and by-and-by fetched up on the steep top of the hill the other side of the house. Tom said he slipped Jim's hat off of his head and hung it on a limb right over him, and Jim stirred a little, but he didn't wake. Afterwards Jim said the witches bewitched him and put him in a trance, and rode him all over the State, and then set him under the trees again and hung his hat on a limb to show who done it. And next time Jim told it he said they rode him down to New Orleans; and after that, every time he told it he spread it more and more, till by-and-by he said they rode him all over the world, and tired him most to death, and his back was all over saddle-boils. Jim was monstrous proud about it, and he got so he wouldn't hardly notice the other niggers. Niggers would come miles to hear Jim tell about it, and he was more looked up to than any nigger in that country. Strange niggers would stand with their mouths open and look him all over, same as if he was a wonder. Niggers is always talking about witches in the dark by the kitchen fire; but whenever one was talking and letting on to know all about such things, Jim would happen in and say, "Hm! What you know 'bout witches?" and that nigger was corked up and had to take a back seat. Jim always kept that five-center piece around his neck with a string and said it was a charm the devil give to him with his own hands and told him he could cure anybody with it and fetch witches whenever he wanted to, just by saying something to it; but

he never told what it was he said to it. Niggers would come from all
around there and give Jim anything they had, just for a sight of that
five-center piece; but they wouldn't touch it, because the devil had
had his hands on it. Jim was most ruined, for a servant, because he
got so stuck up on account of having seen the devil and been rode
by witches.

Well, when Tom and me got to the edge of the hill-top, we looked
away down into the village and could see three or four lights
twinkling, where there was sick folks, may be; and the stars over
us was sparkling ever so fine; and down by the village was the river,
a whole mile broad, and awful still and grand. We went down the
hill and found Jo Harper, and Ben Rogers, and two or three more
of the boys, hid in the old tanyard. So we unhitched a skiff and
pulled down the river two mile and a half, to the big scar on the
hillside, and went ashore.

We went to a clump of bushes, and Tom made everybody swear
to keep the secret, and then showed them a hole in the hill, right in
the thickest part of the bushes. Then we lit the candles and crawled
in on our hands and knees. We went about two hundred yards, and
then the cave opened up. Tom poked about amongst the passages
and pretty soon ducked under a wall where you wouldn't a noticed
that there was a hole. We went along a narrow place and got into
a kind of room, all damp and sweaty and cold, and there we stopped.
Tom says:

"Now we'll start this band of robbers and call it Tom Sawyer's
Gang. Everybody that wants to join has got to take an oath, and
write his name in blood."

Everybody was willing. So Tom got out a sheet of paper that he
had wrote the oath on, and read it. It swore every boy to stick to the
band, and never tell any of the secrets; and if anybody done
anything to any boy in the band, whichever boy was ordered to kill
that person and his family must do it, and he mustn't eat and he
mustn't sleep till he had killed them and hacked a cross in their
breasts, which was the sign of the band. And nobody that didn't
belong to the band could use that mark, and if he did he must be
sued; and if he done it again he must be killed. And if anybody that
belonged to the band told the secrets, he must have his throat
cut, and then have his carcass burnt up and the ashes scattered all
around, and his name blotted off of the list with blood and never
mentioned again by the gang, but have a curse put on it and be
forgot, forever.

Everybody said it was a real beautiful oath, and asked Tom if he
got it out of his own head. He said, some of it, but the rest was out
of pirate books, and robber books, and every gang that was
high-toned had it.

Some thought it would be good to kill the *families* of boys that told
the secrets. Tom said it was a good idea, so he took a pencil and

wrote it in. Then Ben Rogers says:

"Here's Huck Finn, he hain't got no family—what you going to do 'bout him?"

"Well, hain't he got a father?" says Tom Sawyer.

"Yes, he's got a father, but you can't never find him, these days. He used to lay drunk with the hogs in the tanyard, but he hain't been seen in these parts for a year or more."

They talked it over, and they was going to rule me out, because they said every boy must have a family or somebody to kill, or else it wouldn't be fair and square for the others. Well, nobody could think of anything to do—everybody was stumped, and set still. I was most ready to cry; but all at once I thought of a way, and so I offered them Miss Watson—they could kill her. Everybody said:

"Oh, she'll do, she'll do. That's all right. Huck can come in."

Then they all stuck a pin in their fingers to get blood to sign with, and I made my mark on the paper.

"Now," says Ben Rogers, "what's the line of business of this Gang?"

"Nothing only robbery and murder," Tom said.

"But who are we going to rob? houses—or cattle—or——"

"Stuff! stealing cattle and such things ain't robbery, it's burglary," says Tom Sawyer. "We ain't burglars. That ain't no sort of style. We are highwaymen. We stop stages and carriages on the road, with masks on, and kill the people and take their watches and money."

"Must we always kill the people?"

"Oh, certainly. It's best. Some authorities think different, but mostly it's considered best to kill them. Except some that you bring to the cave here and keep them till they're ransomed."

"Ransomed? What's that?"

"I don't know. But that's what they do. I've seen it in books; and so of course that's what we've got to do."

"But how can we do it if we don't know what it is?"

"Why blame it all, we've *got* to do it. Don't I tell you it's in the books? Do you want to go to doing different from what's in the books, and get things all muddled up?"

"Oh, that's all very fine to *say,* Tom Sawyer, but how in the nation are these fellows going to be ransomed if we don't know how to do it to them? that's the thing *I* want to get at. Now what do you *reckon* it is?"

"Well I don't know. But per'aps if we keep them till they're ransomed, it means that we keep them till they're dead."

"Now, that's something *like.* That'll answer. Why couldn't you said that before? We'll keep them till they're ransomed to death— and a bothersome lot they'll be, too, eating up everything and always trying to get loose."

"How you talk, Ben Rogers. How can they get loose when there's a guard over them, ready to shoot them down if they move a peg?"

"A guard. Well, that *is* good. So somebody's got to set up all night and never get any sleep, just so as to watch them. I think that's foolishness. Why can't a body take a club and ransom them as soon as they get here?"

"Because it ain't in the books so—that's why. Now Ben Rogers, do you want to do things regular, or don't you?—that's the idea. Don't you reckon that the people that made the books knows what's the correct thing to do? Do you reckon *you* can learn 'em anything? Not by a good deal. No, sir, we'll just go on and ransom them in the regular way."

"All right. I don't mind; but I say it's a fool way, anyhow. Say— do we kill the women, too?"

"Well, Ben Rogers, if I was as ignorant as you I wouldn't let on. Kill the women? No—nobody ever saw anything in the books like that. You fetch them to the cave, and you're always as polite as pie to them; and by-and-by they fall in love with you and never want to go home any more."

"Well, if that's the way, I'm agreed, but I don't take no stock in it. Mighty soon we'll have the cave so cluttered up with women, and fellows waiting to be ransomed, that there won't be no place for the robbers. But go ahead, I ain't got nothing to say."

Little Tommy Barnes was asleep, now, and when they waked him up he was scared, and cried, and said he wanted to go home to his ma, and didn't want to be a robber any more.

So they all made fun of him, and called him cry-baby, and that made him mad, and he said he would go straight and tell all the secrets. But Tom give him five cents to keep quiet, and said we would all go home and meet next week and rob somebody and kill some people.

Ben Rogers said he couldn't get out much, only Sundays, and so he wanted to begin next Sunday; but all the boys said it would be wicked to do it on Sunday, and that settled the thing. They agreed to get together and fix a day as soon as they could, and then we elected Tom Sawyer first captain and Jo Harper second captain of the Gang, and so started home.

I clumb up the shed and crept into my window just before day was breaking. My new clothes was all greased up and clayey, and I was dog-tired.

CHAPTER III

Well, I got a good going-over in the morning, from old Miss Watson, on account of my clothes; but the widow she didn't scold, but only cleaned off the grease and clay and looked so sorry that I thought I would behave a while if I could. Then Miss Watson she took me in the closet and prayed, but nothing come of it. She told me to pray every day, and whatever I asked for I would get it. But it warn't so. I tried it. Once I got a fish-line, but no hooks. It warn't any good to me without hooks. I tried for the hooks three or four times, but somehow I couldn't make it work. By-and-by, one day, I asked Miss Watson to try for me, but she said I was a fool. She never told me why, and I couldn't make it out no way.

I set down, one time, back in the woods, and had a long think about it. I says to myself, if a body can get anything they pray for, why don't Deacon Winn get back the money he lost on pork? Why can't the widow get back her silver snuff-box that was stole? Why can't Miss Watson fat up? No, says I to myself, there ain't nothing in it. I went and told the widow about it, and she said the thing a body could get by praying for it was "spiritual gifts." This was too many for me, but she told me what she meant—I must help other people, and do everything I could for other people, and look out for them all the time, and never think about myself. This was including Miss Watson, as I took it. I went out in the woods and turned it over in my mind a long time, but I couldn't see no advantage about it—except for the other people—so at last I reckoned I wouldn't worry about it any more, but just let it go. Sometimes the widow would take me one side and talk about Providence in a way to make a body's mouth water; but maybe next day Miss Watson would take hold and knock it all down again. I judged I could see that there was two Providences, and a poor chap would stand considerable show with the widow's Providence, but if Miss Watson's got him there warn't no help for him any more. I thought it all out, and reckoned I would belong to the widow's, if he wanted me, though I couldn't make out how he was agoing to be any better off then that what he was before, seeing I was so ignorant and so kind of low-down and ornery.

Pap he hadn't been seen for more than a year, and that was comfortable for me; I didn't want to see him no more. He used to always whale me when he was sober and could get his hands on me; though I used to take to the woods most of the time when he was around. Well, about this time he was found in the river drowned, about twelve mile above town, so people said. They judged it was him, anyway; said this drowned man was just his size, and was ragged, and had uncommon long hair—which was all like pap—but they couldn't make nothing out of the face, because it had been in the water so long it warn't much like a face at all. They said he was floating on his back in the water. They took him and buried him on the bank. But I warn't comfortable long, because I happened to think of something. I knowed mighty well that a drownded man don't float on his back, but on his face. So I knowed, then, that this warn't pap, but a woman dressed up in a man's clothes. So I was uncomfortable again. I judged the old man would turn up again by-and-by, though I wished he wouldn't.

We played robber now and then about a month, and then I
resigned. All the boys did. We hadn't robbed nobody, we hadn't
killed any people, but only just pretended. We used to hop out of
the woods and go charging down on hog-drovers and women in
carts taking garden stuff to market, but we never hived any of them.
Tom Sawyer called the hogs "ingots," and he called the turnips and
stuff "julery" and we would go to the cave and pow-wow over what
we had done and how many people we had killed and marked. But
I couldn't see no profit in it. One time Tom sent a boy to run about
town with a blazing stick, which he called a slogan (which was the
sign for the Gang to get together), and then he said he had got
secret news by his spies that next day a whole parcel of Spanish
merchants and rich A-rabs was going to camp in Cave Hollow with
two hundred elephants, and six hundred camels, and over a
thousand "sumter" mules, all loaded down with di'monds, and they
didn't have only a guard of four hundred soldiers, and so we would
lay in ambuscade, as he called it, and kill the lot and scoop the
things. He said we must slick up our swords and guns, and get ready.
He never could go after even a turnip-cart but he must have the
swords and guns all scoured up for it; though they was only lath
and broom-sticks, and you might scour at them till you rotted
and then they warn't worth a mouthful of ashes more than what
they was before. I didn't believe we could lick such a crowd of
Spaniards and A-rabs, but I wanted to see the camels and elephants,
so I was on hand next day, Saturday, in the ambuscade; and when
we got the word, we rushed out of the woods and down the hill.
But there warn't no Spaniards and A-rabs, and there warn't no
camels nor no elephants. It warn't anything but a Sunday-school
picnic, and only a primer-class at that. We busted it up, and chased
the children up the hollow; but we never got anything but some
doughnuts and jam, though Ben Rogers got a rag doll, and Jo
Harper got a hymn-book and a tract; and then the teacher charged
in and made us drop everything and cut. I didn't see no di'monds,
and I told Tom Sawyer so. He said there was loads of them there,
anyway; and he said there was A-rabs there, too, and elephants
and things. I said, why couldn't we see them, then? He said if I
warn't so ignorant, but had read a book called "Don Quixote,"
I would know without asking. He said it was all done by
enchantment. He said there was hundreds of soldiers there, and
elephants and treasure, and so on, but we had enemies which he
called magicians, and they had turned the whole thing into an
infant Sunday school, just out of spite. I said, all right, then the
thing for us to do was to go for the magicians. Tom Sawyer said
I was a numskull.

"Why," says he, "a magician could call up a lot of genies, and
they would hash you up like nothing before you could say Jack
Robinson. They are as tall as a tree and as big around as a church."

"Well," I says, "s'pose we got some genies to help *us*—can't we lick the other crowd then?"

"How you going to get them?"

"I don't know. How do *they* get them?"

"Why they rub an old tin lamp or an iron ring, and then the genies come tearing in, with the thunder and lightning a-ripping around and the smoke a-rolling, and everything they're told to do they up and do it. They don't think nothing of pulling a shot tower up by the roots, and belting a Sunday-school superintendent over the head with it—or any other man."

"Who makes them tear around so?"

"Why, whoever rubs the lamp or the ring. They belong to whoever rubs the lamp or the ring, and they've got to do whatever he says. If he tells them to build a palace forty miles long, out of di'monds, and fill it full of chewing gum, or whatever you want, and fetch an emperor's daughter from China for you to marry, they've got to do it—and they've got to do it before sun-up next morning, too. And more—they've got to waltz that palace around over the country wherever you want it, you understand."

"Well," says I, "I think they are a pack of flatheads for not keeping the palace themselves 'stead of fooling them away like that. And what's more—if I was one of them I would see a man in Jericho before I would drop my business and come to him for the rubbing of an old tin lamp."

"How you talk, Huck Finn. Why, you'd *have* to come when he rubbed it, whether you wanted to or not."

"What, and I as high as a tree and as big as a church? All right, then; I *would* come; but I lay I'd make that man climb the highest tree there was in the country."

"Shucks, it ain't no use to talk to you, Huck Finn. You don't seem to know anything, somehow—perfect sap-head."

I thought all this over for two or three days, and then I reckoned I would see if there was anything in it. I got an old tin lamp and an iron ring and went out in the woods and rubbed and rubbed till I sweat like an Injun, calculating to build a palace and sell it; but it warn't no use, none of the genies come. So then I judged that all that stuff was only just one of Tom Sawyer's lies. I reckoned he believed in the A-rabs and the elephants, but as for me I think different. It had all the marks of a Sunday school.

CHAPTER IV

Well, three or four months run along, and it was well into the winter, now. I had been to school most all the time, and could spell, and read, and write just a little, and could say the multiplication table up to six times seven is thirty-five, and I don't reckon I could ever get any further than that if I was to live forever. I don't take no stock in mathematics, anyway.

At first I hated the school, but by-and-by I got so I could stand it. Whenever I got uncommon tired I played hookey, and the hiding I got next day done me good and cheered me up. So the longer I went to school the easier it got to be. I was getting sort of used to the widow's ways, too, and they warn't so raspy on me. Living in a house, and sleeping in a bed, pulled on me pretty tight, mostly, but before the cold weather I used to slide out and sleep in the woods, sometimes, and so that was a rest to me. I liked the old ways best, but I was getting so I liked the new ones, too, a little bit. The widow said I was coming along slow but sure, and doing very satisfactory. She said she warn't ashamed of me.

One morning I happened to turn over the salt-cellar at breakfast. I reached for some of it as quick as I could, to throw over my left shoulder and keep off the bad luck, but Miss Watson was in ahead of me, and crossed me off. She says, "Take your hands away, Huckleberry—what a mess you are always making." The widow put in a good word for me, but that warn't going to keep off the bad luck, I knowed that well enough. I started out, after breakfast, feeling worried and shaky, and wondering where it was going to fall on me, and what it was going to be. There is ways to keep off some kinds of bad luck, but this wasn't one of them kind; so I never tried to do anything, but just poked along low-spirited and on the watch-out.

I went down the front garden and clumb over the stile, where you go through the high board fence. There was an inch of new snow on the ground, and I seen somebody's tracks. They had come up from the quarry and stood around the stile a while, and then went on around the garden fence. It was funny they hadn't come in, after standing around so. I couldn't make it out. It was very curious, somehow. I was going to follow around, but I stooped down to look at the tracks first. I didn't notice anything at first, but next I did. There was a cross in the left boot-heel made with big nails, to keep off the devil.

I was up in a second and shinning down the hill. I looked over my shoulder every now and then, but I didn't see nobody. I was at Judge Thatcher's as quick as I could get there. He said:

"Why, my boy, you are all out of breath. Did you come for your interest?"

"No sir," I says; "is there some for me?"

"Oh, yes, a half-yearly is in, last night. Over a hundred and fifty dollars. Quite a fortune for you. You better let me invest it along with your six thousand, because if you take it you'll spend it."

"No sir," I says, "I don't want to spend it. I don't want it at all— nor the six thousand, nuther. I want you to take it; I want to give it to you—the six thousand and all."

He looked surprised. He couldn't seem to make it out. He says:

"Why, what can you mean, my boy?"

I says, "Don't you ask me no questions about it, please. You'll take it—won't you?"

He says:

"Well I'm puzzled. Is something the matter?"

"Please take it," says I, "and don't ask me nothing—then I won't have to tell no lies."

He studied a while, and then he says:

"Oho-o. I think I see. You want to *sell* all your property to me—not give it. That's the correct idea."

Then he wrote something on a paper and read it over, and says:

"There—you see it says 'for a consideration.' That means I have bought it of you and paid you for it. Here's a dollar for you. Now, you sign it."

So I signed it, and left.

Miss Watson's nigger, Jim, had a hair-ball as big as your fist, which had been took out of the fourth stomach of an ox, and he used to do magic with it. He said there was a spirit inside of it, and it knowed everything. So I went to him that night and told him pap was here again, for I found his tracks in the snow. What I wanted to know, was, what he was going to do, and was he going to stay? Jim got out his hair-ball, and said something over it, and then he held it up and dropped it on the floor. It fell pretty solid, and only rolled about an inch. Jim tried it again, and then another time, and it acted just the same. Jim got down on his knees and put his ear against it and listened. But it warn't no use; he said it wouldn't talk. He said sometimes it wouldn't talk without money. I told him I had an old slick counterfeit quarter that warn't no good because the brass showed through the silver a little, and it wouldn't pass nohow, even if the brass didn't show, because it was so slick it felt greasy, and so that would tell on it every time. (I reckoned I wouldn't say nothing about the dollar I got from the judge.) I said it was pretty bad money, but maybe the hair-ball would take it, because maybe it wouldn't know the difference. Jim smelt it, and bit it, and rubbed it, and said he would manage so the hair-ball would think it was good. He said he would split open a raw Irish potato and stick the quarter in between and keep it there all night, and next morning you couldn't see no brass, and it wouldn't feel greasy no more, and so anybody in town would take it in a minute, let alone a hair-ball. Well, I knowed a potato would do that, before, but I had forgot it.

Jim put the quarter under the hair-ball and got down and listened again. This time he said the hair-ball was all right. He said it would tell my whole fortune if I wanted it to. I says, go on. So the hair-ball talked to Jim, and Jim told it to me. He says:

"Yo' ole father doan' know, yit, what he's a-gwyne to do.

Sometimes he spec he'll go 'way, en den agin he spec he'll stay. De bes' way is to res' easy en let de ole man take his own way. Dey's two angels hoverin' roun' 'bout him. One uv 'em is white en shiny, en 'tother one is black. De white one gits him to go right, a little while, den de black one sail in en bust it all up. A body can't tell, yit, which one gwyne to fetch him at de las'. But you is all right. You gwyne to have considable trouble in yo' life, en considable joy. Sometimes you gwyne to git hurt, en sometimes you gwyne to git sick; but every time you's gwyne to git well agin. Dey's two gals flyin' 'bout you in yo' life. One uv 'em's light en 'tother one is dark. One is rich en 'tother is po'. You's gwyne to marry de po' one fust en de rich one by-en-by. You wants to keep 'way fum de water as much as you kin, en don't run no resk, 'kase it's down in de bills dat you's gwyne to git hung."

When I lit my candle and went up to my room that night, there set pap, his own self!

CHAPTER V

I had shut the door to. Then I turned around, and there he was. I used to be scared of him all the time, he tanned me so much. I reckoned I was scared now, too; but in a minute I see I was mistaken. That is, after the first jolt, as you may say, when my breath sort of hitched—he being so unexpected; but right away after, I see I warn't scared of him worth bothering about.

He was most fifty, and he looked it. His hair was long and tangled and greasy, and hung down, and you could see his eyes shining through like he was behind vines. It was all black, no gray; so was his long, mixed-up whiskers. There warn't no color in his face, where his face showed; it was white; not like another man's white, but a white to make a body sick, a white to make a body's flesh crawl— a tree-toad white, a fish-belly white. As for his clothes—just rags, that was all. He had one ankle resting on 'tother knee; the boot on that foot was busted, and two of his toes stuck through, and he worked them now and then. His hat was laying on the floor; an old black slouch with the top caved in, like a lid.

I stood a-looking at him; he set there a-looking at me, with his chair tilted back a little. I set the candle down. I noticed the window was up; so he had clumb in by the shed. He kept a-looking me all over. By-and-by he says:

"Starchy clothes—very. You think you're a good deal of a big-bug, *don't* you?"

"Maybe I am, maybe I ain't," I says.

"Don't you give me none o' your lip," says he. "You've put on considerable many frills since I been away. I'll take you down a peg before I get done with you. You're educated, too, they say; can read and write. You think you're better'n your father, now, don't you, because he can't? *I*'ll take it out of you. Who told you you might meddle with such hifalut'n foolishness, hey?—who told you you could?"

"The widow. She told me."

"The widow, hey?—and who told the widow she could put in her shovel about a thing that ain't none of her business?"

"Nobody never told her."

"Well, I'll learn her how to meddle. And looky here—you drop that school, you hear? I'll learn people to bring up a boy to put on airs over his own father and let on to be better'n what *he* is. You lemme catch you fooling around that school again, you hear? Your mother couldn't read, and she couldn't write, nuther, before she died. None of the family couldn't, before *they* died. *I* can't; and here you're a-swelling yourself up like this. I ain't the man to stand it—you hear? Say—lemme hear you read."

I took up a book and begun something about General Washington and the wars. When I'd read about a half a minute, he fetched the book a whack with his hand and knocked it across the house. He says:

"It's so. You can do it. I had my doubts when you told me. Now looky here; you stop that putting on frills. I won't have it. I'll lay for you, my smarty; and if I catch you about that school I'll tan you good. First you know you'll get religion, too. I never see such a son."

He took up a little blue and yaller picture of some cows and a boy, and says:

"What's this?"

"It's something they give me for learning my lessons good."

He tore it up, and says—

"I'll give you something better—I'll give you a cowhide."

He set there a-mumbling and a-growling a minute, and then he says—

"*Ain't* you a sweet-scented dandy, though? A bed; and bedclothes; and a look'n-glass; and a piece of carpet on the floor— and your own father got to sleep with the hogs in the tanyard. I never see such a son. I bet I'll take some o' these frills out o' you before I'm done with you. Why there ain't no end to your airs— they say you're rich. Hey?—how's that?"

"They lie—that's how."

"Looky here—mind how you talk to me; I'm a-standing about all I can stand, now—so don't gimme no sass. I've been in town two days, and I hain't heard nothing but about you being' rich. I heard about it away down the river, too. That's why I come. You git me that money to-morrow—I want it."

"I hain't got no money."

"It's a lie. Judge Thatcher's got it. You git it. I want it."

"I hain't got no money, I tell you. You ask Judge Thatcher; he'll tell you the same."

"All right. I'll ask him; and I'll make him pungle, too, or I'll
know the reason why. Say—how much you got in your pocket? I
want it."

"I hain't got only a dollar, and I want that to—"

"It don't make no difference what you want it for—you just
shell it out."

He took it and bit it to see if it was good, and then he said he
was going down town to get some whisky; said he hadn't had a drink
all day. When he had got out on the shed, he put his head in again,
and cussed me for putting on frills and trying to be better than him;
and when I reckoned he was gone, he come back and put his head
in again, and told me to mind about that school, because he was
going to lay for me and lick me if I didn't drop that.

Next day he was drunk, and he went to Judge Thatcher's and
bullyragged him and tried to make him give up the money, but he
couldn't, and then he swore he'd make the law force him.

The judge and the widow went to law to get the court to take me
away from him and let one of them be my guardian; but it was a
new judge that had just come, and he didn't know the old man;
so he said courts mustn't interfere and separate families if they
could help it; said he'd druther not take a child away from its father.
So Judge Thatcher and the widow had to quit on the business.

That pleased the old man till he couldn't rest. He said he'd
cowhide me till I was black and blue if I didn't raise some money
for him. I borrowed three dollars from Judge Thatcher, and pap
took it and got drunk and went a-blowing around and cussing and
whooping and carrying on; and he kept it up all over town, with a
tin pan, till most midnight; then they jailed him, and next day they
had him before court, and jailed him again for a week. But he said
he was satisfied; said he was boss of his son, and he'd make it warm
for *him*.

When he got out the new judge said he was agoing to make a man
of him. So he took him to his own house, and dressed him up clean
and nice, and had him to breakfast and dinner and supper with the
family, and was just old pie to him, so to speak. And after supper
he talked to him about temperance and such things till the old man
cried, and said he'd been a fool, and fooled away his life; but now
he was agoing to turn over a new leaf and be a man nobody
wouldn't be ashamed of, and he hoped the judge would help him
and not look down on him. The judge said he could hug him for
them words; so *he* cried, and his wife she cried again; pap said he'd
been a man that had always been misunderstood before, and the
judge said he believed it. The old man said that what a man wanted
that was down, was sympathy; and the judge said it was so; so they
cried again. And when it was bedtime, the old man rose up and held
out his hand, and says:

"Look at it gentlemen, and ladies all; take ahold of it; shake it. There's a hand that was the hand of a hog; but it ain't so no more; it's the hand of a man that's started in on a new life, and 'll die before he'll go back. You mark them words—don't forget I said them. It's a clean hand now; shake it—don't be afeard."

So they shook it, one after the other, all around, and cried. The judge's wife she kissed it. Then the old man he signed a pledge— made his mark. The judge said it was the holiest time on record, or something like that. Then they tucked the old man into a beautiful room, which was the spare room, and in the night sometime he got powerful thirsty and clumb out onto the porch-roof and slid down a stanchion and traded his new coat for a jug of forty-rod, and clumb back again and had a good old time; and towards daylight he crawled out again, drunk as a fiddler, and rolled off the porch and broke his left arm in two places and was most froze to death when somebody found him after sun-up. And when they come to look at that spare room, they had to take soundings before they could navigate it.

The judge he felt kind of sore. He said he reckoned a body could reform the ole man with a shot-gun, maybe, but he didn't know no other way.

CHAPTER VI

Well, pretty soon the old man was up and around again, and then he went for Judge Thatcher in the courts to make him give up that money, and he went for me, too, for not stopping school. He catched me a couple of times and thrashed me, but I went to school just the same, and dodged him or out-run him most of the time. I didn't want to go to school much, before, but I reckoned I'd go now to spite pap. That law trial was a slow business; appeared like they warn't ever going to get started on it; so every now and then I'd borrow two or three dollars off of the judge for him, to keep from getting a cowhiding. Every time he got money he got drunk; and every time he got drunk he raised Cain around town; and every time he raised Cain he got jailed. He was just suited—this kind of thing was right in his line.

He got to hanging around the widow's too much, and so she told him at last, that if he didn't quit using around there she would make trouble for him. Well, *wasn't* he mad? He said he would show who was Huck Finn's boss. So he watched out for me one day in the spring, and catched me, and took me up the river about three mile, in a skiff, and crossed over to the Illinois shore where it was woody and there warn't no houses but an old log hut in a place where the timber was so thick you couldn't find it if you didn't know where it was.

He kept me with him all the time, and I never got a chance to run off. We lived in that old cabin, and he always locked the door and put the key under his head, nights. He had a gun which he had stole, I reckon, and we fished and hunted, and that was what we lived on. Every little while he locked me in and went down to the store, three miles, to the ferry, and traded fish and game for whisky and fetched it home and got drunk and had a good time, and licked me. The widow she found out where I was, by-and-by, and she sent a man over to try to get hold of me, but pap drove him off with the gun, and it warn't long after that till I was used to being where I was, and liked it, all but the cowhide part.

It was kind of lazy and jolly, laying off comfortable all day, smoking and fishing, and no books nor study. Two months or more run along, and my clothes got to be all rags and dirt, and I didn't see how I'd ever got to like it so well at the widow's, where you had to wash, and eat on a plate, and comb up, and go to bed and get up regular, and be forever bothering over a book and have old Miss Watson pecking at you all the time. I didn't want to go back no more. I had stopped cussing, because the widow didn't like it; but now I took to it again because pap hadn't no objections. It was pretty good times up in the woods there, take it all around.

But by-and-by pap got too handy with his hick'ry, and I couldn't stand it. I was all over welts. He got to going away so much, too, and locking me in. Once he locked me in and was gone three days. It was dreadful lonesome. I judged he had got drowned and I wasn't ever going to get out any more. I was scared. I made up my mind I would fix up some way to leave there. I had tried to get out of that cabin many a time, but I couldn't find no way. There warn't a window to it big enough for a dog to get through. I couldn't get up the chimbly, it was too narrow. The door was thick solid oak slabs. Pap was pretty careful not to leave a knife or anything in the cabin when he was away; I reckon I had hunted the place over as much as a hundred times; well, I was 'most all the time at it, because it was about the only way to put in the time. But this time I found something at last; I found an old rusty wood-saw without any handle; it was laid in between a rafter and the clapboards of the roof. I greased it up and went to work. There was an old horse-blanket nailed against the logs at the far end of the cabin behind the table, to keep the wind from blowing through the chinks and putting the candle out. I got under the table and raised the blanket and went to work to saw a section of the big bottom log out, big enough to let me through. Well, it was a good long job, but I was getting towards the end of it when I heard pap's gun in the woods. I got rid of the signs of my work, and dropped the blanket and hid my saw, and pretty soon pap come in.

Pap warn't in a good humor—so he was his natural self. He said he was down to town, and everything was going wrong. His lawyer said he reckoned he would win his lawsuit and get the money, if they ever got started on the trial; but then there was ways to put it off a long time, and Judge Thatcher knowed how to do it. And he said people allowed there'd be another trial to get me away from him and give me to the widow for my guardian, and they guessed it would win, this time. This shook me up considerable, because I didn't want to go back to the widow's any more and be so cramped up and sivilized, as they called it. Then the old man got to cussing, and cussed everything and everybody he could think of, and then cussed them all over again to make sure he hadn't skipped any, and after that he polished off with a kind of a general cuss all round, including a considerable parcel of people which he didn't know the names of, and so called them what's-his-name, when he got to them, and went right along with his cussing.

He said he would like to see the widow get me. He said he would watch out, and if they tried to come any such game on him he knowed of a place six or seven mile off, to stow me in, where they might hunt till they dropped and they couldn't find me. That made me pretty uneasy again, but only for a minute; I reckoned I wouldn't stay on hand till he got that chance.

The old man made me go to the skiff and fetch the things he had got. There was a fifty-pound sack of corn meal, and a side of bacon, ammunition, and a four-gallon jug of whisky, and an old book and two newspapers for wadding, besides some tow. I toted up a load, and went back and set down on the bow of the skiff to rest. I thought it all over, and I reckoned I would walk off with the gun and some lines, and take to the woods when I run away. I guessed I wouldn't stay in one place, but just tramp right across the country, mostly night times, and hunt and fish to keep alive, and so get so far away that the old man nor the widow couldn't ever find me any more. I judged I would saw out and leave that night if pap got drunk enough, and I reckoned he would. I got so full of it I didn't notice how long I was staying, till the old man hollered and asked me whether I was asleep or drownded.

I got the things all up to the cabin, and then it was about dark. While I was cooking supper the old man took a swig or two and got sort of warmed up, and went to ripping again. He had been drunk over in town, and laid in the gutter all night, and he was a sight to look at. A body would a thought he was Adam, he was just all mud. Whenever his liquor begun to work, he most always went for the govment. This time he says:

"Call this a govment! why, just look at it and see what it's like. Here's the law a-standing ready to take a man's son away from him—a man's own son, which he has had all the trouble and all the anxiety and all the expense of raising. Yes, just as that man has got that son raised at last, and ready to go to work and begin to do suthin' for *him* and give him a rest, the law up and goes for him. And they call *that* govment! That ain't all, nuther. The law backs

that old Judge Thatcher up and helps him to keep me out o' my
property. Here's what the law does. The law takes a man worth six
thousand dollars and upards, and jams him into an old trap of a
cabin like this, and lets him go round in clothes that ain't fitten
for a hog. They call that govment! A man can't get his rights in a
govment like this. Sometimes I've a mighty notion to just leave the
country for good and all. Yes, and I *told* 'em so; I told old
Thatcher so to his face. Lots of 'em heard me, and can tell what I
said. Says I, for two cents I'd leave the blamed country and never
come anear it agin. Them's the very words. I says, look at my hat—if
you call it a hat—but the lid raises up and the rest of it goes down
till it's below my chin, and then it ain't rightly a hat at all, but more
like my head was shoved up through a jint o' stove-pipe. Look at it,
says I—such a hat for me to wear—one of the wealthiest men in
this town, if I could git my rights.

"Oh, yes, this is a wonderful govment, wonderful. Why, looky
here. There was a free nigger there, from Ohio; a mulatter, most as
white as a white man. He had the whitest shirt on you ever see, too,
and the shiniest hat; and there ain't a man in that town that's got
as fine clothes as what he had; and he had a gold watch and chain,
and a silver-headed cane—the awfulest old gray-headed nabob in
the State. And what do you think? they said he was a p'fessor in a
college, and could talk all kinds of languages, and knowed
everything. And that ain't the wust. They said he could *vote,* when
he was at home. Well, that let me out. Thinks I, what is the country
a-coming to? It was 'lection day, and I was just about to go and vote,
myself, if I warn't too drunk to get there; but when they told me
there was a State in this country where they'd let that nigger vote,
I drawed out. I says I'll never vote agin. Them's the very words I
said; they all heard me; and the country may rot for all me—
I'll never vote agin as long as I live. And to see the cool way of that
nigger—why, he wouldn't a give me the road if I hadn't shoved him
out o' the way. I says to the people, why ain't this nigger put up at
auction and sold?—that's what I want to know. And what do you
reckon they said? Why, they said he couldn't be sold till he'd been
in the State six months, and he hadn't been there that long yet.
There, now—that's a specimen. They call that a govment that can't
sell a free nigger till he's been in the State six months. Here's a
govment that calls itself a govment, and lets on to be a govment,
and thinks it is a govment, and yet's got to set stock-still for six
whole months before it can take ahold of a prowling, thieving,
infernal, white-shirted free nigger, and——"

Pap was 'agoing on so, he never noticed where his old limber legs
was taking him to, so he went head over heels over the tub of salt
pork, and barked both shins, and the rest of his speech was all the
hottest kind of language—mostly hove at the nigger and the
govment, though he give the tub some, too, all along, here and

there. He hopped around the cabin considerable, first on one leg and then on the other, holding first one shin and then the other one, and at last he let out with his left foot all of a sudden and fetched the tub a rattling kick. But it warn't good judgment, because that was the boot that had a couple of his toes leaking out of the front end of it; so now he raised a howl that fairly made a body's hair raise, and down he went in the dirt, and rolled there, and held his toes; and the cussing he done then laid over anything he had ever done previous. He said so his own self, afterwards. He had heard old Sowberry Hagan in his best days, and he said it laid over him, too; but I reckon that was sort of piling it on, maybe.

After supper pap took the jug, and said he had enough whisky there for two drunks and one delirium tremens. That was always his word. I judged he would be blind drunk in about an hour, and then I would steal the key, or saw myself out, one or 'tother. He drank, and drank, and tumbled down on his blankets, by-and-by; but luck didn't run my way. He didn't go sound asleep, but was uneasy. He groaned, and moaned, and thrashed around this way and that, for a long time. At last I got so sleepy I couldn't keep my eyes open, all I could do, and so before I knowed what I was about I was sound asleep, and the candle burning.

I don't know how long I was asleep, but all of a sudden there was an awful scream and I was up. There was pap, looking wild and skipping around every which way and yelling about snakes. He said they was crawling up his legs; and then he would give a jump and scream, and say one had bit him on the cheek—but I couldn't see no snakes. He started and run round and round the cabin, hollering "take him off! take him off! he's biting me on the neck!" I never see a man look so wild in the eyes. Pretty soon he was all fagged out, and fell down panting; then he rolled over and over, wonderful fast, kicking things every which way, and striking and grabbing at the air with his hands, and screaming, and saying there was devils ahold of him. He wore out, by-and-by, and laid still a while, moaning. Then he laid stiller, and didn't make a sound. I could hear the owls and the wolves, away off in the woods, and it seemed terrible still. He was laying over by the corner. By-and-by he raised up, part way, and listened, with his head to one side. He says very low:

"Tramp—tramp—tramp; that's the dead; tramp—tramp— tramp; they're coming after me; but I won't go— Oh, they're here! don't touch me—don't! hands off—they're cold; let go— Oh, let a poor devil alone!"

Then he went down on all fours and crawled off begging them to let him alone, and he rolled himself up in his blanket and wallowed in under the old pine table, still a-begging; and then he went to crying. I could hear him through the blanket.

By-and-by he rolled out and jumped up on his feet looking wild, and he see me and went for me. He chased me round and round the place, with a clasp-knife, calling me the Angel of Death and saying he would kill me and then I couldn't come for him no more. I begged, and told him I was only Huck, but he laughed *such* a screechy laugh, and roared and cussed, and kept on chasing me up. Once when I turned short and dodged under his arm he made a grab and got me by the jacket between my shoulders, and I thought I was gone; but I slid out of the jacket quick as lightning, and saved myself. Pretty soon he was all tired out, and dropped down with his back against the door, and said he would rest a minute and then kill me. He put his knife under him, and said he would sleep and get strong, and then he would see who was who.

So he dozed off, pretty soon. By-and-by I got the old split-bottom chair and clumb up, as easy as I could, not to make any noise, and got down the gun. I slipped the ramrod down it to make sure it was loaded, and then I laid it across the turnip barrel, pointing towards pap, and set down behind it to wait for him to stir. And how slow and still the time did drag along.

CHAPTER VII

"Git up! what you 'bout!"

I opened my eyes and looked around, trying to make out where I was. It was after sun-up, and I had been sound asleep. Pap was standing over me, looking sour—and sick, too. He says—

"What you doin' with this gun?"

I judged he didn't know nothing about what he had been doing, so I says:

"Somebody tried to get in, so I was laying for him."

"Why didn't you roust me out?"

"Well I tried to, but I couldn't; I couldn't budge you."

"Well, all right. Don't stand there palavering all day, but out with you and see if there's a fish on the lines for breakfast. I'll be along in a minute."

He unlocked the door and I cleared out, up the river bank. I noticed some pieces of limbs and such things floating down, and a sprinkling of bark; so I knowed the river had begun to rise. I reckoned I would have great times, now, if I was over at the town. The June rise used to be always luck for me; because as soon as that rise begins, here comes cord-wood floating down, and pieces of log rafts—sometimes a dozen logs together; so all you have to do is to catch them and sell them to the wood yards and the sawmill.

I went along up the bank with one eye out for pap and 'tother one out for what the rise might fetch along. Well, all at once, here comes a canoe; just a beauty, too, about thirteen or fourteen foot long, riding high like a duck. I shot head first off of the bank, like

a frog, clothes and all on, and struck out for the canoe. I just
expected there'd be somebody laying down in it, because people
often done that to fool folks, and when a chap had pulled a skiff
out most to it they'd raise up and laugh at him. But it warn't so
this time. It was a drift-canoe, sure enough, and I clumb in and
paddled her ashore. Thinks I, the old man will be glad when he
sees this—she's worth ten dollars. But when I got to shore pap
wasn't in sight yet, and as I was running her into a little creek like
a gully, all hung over with vines and willows, I struck another idea;
I judged I'd hide her good, and then, stead of taking to the woods
when I run off, I'd go down the river about fifty mile and camp in
one place for good, and not have such a rough time tramping on
foot.

It was pretty close to the shanty, and I thought I heard the old
man coming, all the time; but I got her hid; and then I out and
looked around a bunch of willows, and there was the old man down
the path apiece just drawing a bead on a bird with his gun. So he
hadn't seen anything.

When he got along, I was hard at it taking up a "trot" line. He
abused me a little for being so slow, but I told him I fell in the river
and that was what made me so long. I knowed he would see I was
wet, and then he would be asking questions. We got five cat-fish
off of the lines and went home.

While we laid off, after breakfast, to sleep up, both of us being
about wore out, I got to thinking that if I could fix up some way to
keep pap and the widow from trying to follow me, if would be a
certainer thing than trusting to luck to get far enough off before
they missed me; you see, all kinds of things might happen. Well, I
didn't see no way for a while, but by-and-by pap raised up a minute,
to drink another barrel of water, and he says:

"Another time a man comes a-prowling round here, you roust
me out, you hear? That man warn't here for no good. I'd a shot him.
Next time, you roust me out, you hear?"

Then he dropped down and went to sleep again—but what he
had been saying give me the very idea I wanted. I says to myself,
I can fix it now so nobody won't think of following me.

About twelve o'clock we turned out and went along up the bank.
The river was coming up pretty fast, and lots of drift-wood going
by on the rise. By-and-by, along comes part of a log raft—nine logs
fast together. We went out with the skiff and towed it ashore. Then
we had dinner. Anybody but pap would a waited and seen the day
through, so as to catch more stuff; but that warn't pap's style. Nine
logs was enough for one time; he must shove right over to town and
sell. So he locked me in and took the skiff and started off towing the
raft about half-past three. I judged he wouldn't come back that
night. I waited till I reckoned he had got a good start, then I out
with my saw and went to work on that log again. Before he was

'tother side of the river I was out of the hole; him and his raft was just a speck on the water away off yonder.

I took the sack of corn meal and took it to where the canoe was hid, and shoved the vines and branches apart and put it in; then I done the same with the side of bacon; then the whisky jug; I took all the coffee and sugar there was, and all the ammunition; I took the wadding; I took the bucket and gourd, I took a dipper and a tin cup, and my old saw and two blankets, and the skillet and the coffee-pot. I took fish-lines and matches and other things— everything that was worth a cent. I cleaned out the place. I wanted an axe, but there wasn't any, only the one out at the wood pile, and I knowed why I was going to leave that. I fetched out the gun, and now I was done.

I had wore the ground a good deal, crawling out of the hole and dragging out so many things. So I fixed that as good as I could from the outside by scattering dust on the place, which covered up the smoothness and the sawdust. Then I fixed the piece of log back into its place, and put two rocks under it and one against it to hold it there,—for it was bent up at that place, and didn't quite touch ground. If you stood four or five foot away and didn't know it was sawed, you wouldn't ever notice it; and besides, this was the back of the cabin and it warn't likely anybody would go fooling around there.

It was all grass clear to the canoe; so I hadn't left a track. I followed around to see. I stood on the bank and looked out over the river. All safe. So I took the gun and went up a piece into the woods and was hunting around for some birds, when I see a wild pig; hogs soon went wild in them bottoms after they had got away from the prairie farms. I shot this fellow and took him into camp.

I took the axe and smashed in the door—I beat it and hacked it considerable, a-doing it. I fetched the pig in and took him back nearly to the table and hacked into his throat with the ax, and laid him down on the ground to bleed—I say ground, because it *was* ground—hard packed, and no boards. Well, next I took an old sack and put a lot of big rocks in it,—all I could drag—and I started it from the pig and dragged it to the door and through the woods down to the river and dumped it in, and down it sunk, out of sight. You could easy see that something had been dragged over the ground. I did wish Tom Sawyer was there, I knowed he would take an interest in this kind of business, and throw in the fancy touches. Nobody could spread himself like Tom Sawyer in such a thing as that.

Well, last I pulled out some of my hair, and bloodied the ax good, and stuck it on the back side, and slung the ax in the corner. Then I took up the pig and held him to my breast with my jacket (so he couldn't drip) till I got a good piece below the house and then dumped him into the river. Now I thought of something else. So I went and got the bag of meal and my old saw out of the canoe and fetched them to the house. I took the bag to where it used to stand, and ripped a hole in the bottom of it with the saw, for there warn't no knives and forks on the place—pap done everything with his clasp-knife, about the cooking. Then I carried the sack about a hundred yards across the grass and through the willows east of the house, to a shallow lake that was five mile wide and full of rushes—and ducks too, you might say, in the season. There was a slough or a creek leading out of it on the other side, that went miles away, I don't know where, but it didn't go to the river. The meal sifted out and made a little track all the way to the lake. I dropped pap's whetstone there too, so as to look like it had been done by accident. Then I tied up the rip in the meal sack with a string, so it wouldn't leak no more, and took it and my saw to the canoe again.

It was about dark, now; so I dropped the canoe down the river under some willows that hung over the bank, and waited for the moon to rise. I made fast to a willow; then I took a bite to eat, and by-and-by laid down in the canoe to smoke a pipe and lay out a plan. I says to myself, they'll follow the track of that sackful of rocks to the shore and then drag the river for me. And they'll follow that meal track to the lake and go browsing down the creek that leads out of it to find the robbers that killed me and took the things. They won't ever hunt the river for anything but my dead carcass. They'll soon get tired of that, and won't bother no more about me. All right; I can stop anywhere I want to. Jackson's Island is good enough for me; I know that island pretty well, and nobody ever comes there. And then I can paddle over to town, nights, and slink around and pick up things I want. Jackson's Island's the place.

I was pretty tired, and the first thing I knowed, I was asleep. When I woke up I didn't know where I was, for a minute. I set up and looked around, a little scared. Then I remembered. The river looked miles and miles across. The moon was so bright I could a counted the drift logs that went a slipping along, black and still, hundred of yards out from shore. Everything was dead quiet, and it looked late, and *smelt* late. You know what I mean—I don't know the words to put it in.

I took a good gap and a stretch, and was just going to unhitch and start, when I heard a sound away over the water. I listened. Pretty soon I made it out. It was that dull kind of a regular sound that comes from oars working in rowlocks when it's a still night. I peeped out through the willow branches, and there it was—a skiff, away across the water. I couldn't tell how many was in it. It kept a-coming, and when it was abreast of me I see there warn't but one man in it. Thinks I, maybe it's pap, though I warn't expecting him. He dropped below me, with the current, and by-and-by he come a-swinging up shore in the easy water, and he went by so close I could a reached out the gun and touched him. Well, it *was* pap, sure enough—and sober, too, by the way he laid to his oars.

I didn't lose no time. The next minute I was a-spinning down stream soft but quick in the shade of the bank. I made two mile and a half, and then struck out a quarter of a mile or more towards the middle of the river, because pretty soon I would be passing the ferry landing and people might see me and hail me. I got out amongst the drift-wood and then laid down in the bottom of the canoe and let her float. I laid there and had a good rest and a smoke out of my pipe, looking away into the sky, not a cloud in it. The sky looks ever so deep when you lay down on your back in the moonshine; I never knowed it before. And how far a body can hear on the water such nights! I heard people talking at the ferry landing. I heard what they said, too, every word of it. One man said it was getting towards the long days and the short nights, now. 'Tother one said *this* warn't one of the short ones, he reckoned— and then they laughed, and he said it over again and they laughed again; then they waked up another fellow and told him, and laughed, but he didn't laugh; he ripped out something brisk and said let him alone. The first fellow said he 'lowed to tell it to his old woman—she would think it was pretty good; but he said that warn't nothing to some things he had said in his time. I heard one man say it was nearly three o'clock, and he hoped daylight wouldn't wait more than about a week longer. After that, the talk got further and further away, and I couldn't make out the words any more, but I could hear the mumble; and now and then a laugh, too, but it seemed a long ways off.

I was away below the ferry now. I rose up and there was Jackson's Island, about two mile and a half down stream, heavy-timbered and standing up out of the middle of the river, big and dark and solid, like a steamboat without any lights. There warn't any signs of the bar at the head—it was all under water, now.

It didn't take me long to get there. I shot past the head at a ripping rate, the current was so swift, and then I got into the dead water and landed on the side towards the Illinois shore. I run the canoe into a deep dent in the bank that I knowed about; I had to part the willow branches to get in; and when I made fast nobody could a seen the canoe from the outside.

I went up and set down on a log at the head of the island and looked out on the big river and the black driftwood, and away over to the town, three mile away, where there was three or four lights twinkling. A monstrous big lumber raft was about a mile up stream, coming along down, with a lantern in the middle of it. I watched it come creeping down, and when it was most abreast of where I stood I heard a man say, "Stern oars, there! heave her head to stabboard!" I heard that just as plain as if the man was by my side.

There was a little gray in the sky, now; so I stepped into the woods and laid down for a nap before breakfast.

CHAPTER VIII

The sun was up so high when I waked, that I judged it was after eight o'clock. I laid there in the grass and the cool shade, thinking about things and feeling rested and ruther comfortable and satisfied. I could see the sun out at one or two holes, but mostly it was big trees all about, and gloomy in there amongst them. There was freckled places on the ground where the light sifted down through the leaves, and the freckled places swapped about a little, showing there was a little breeze up there. A couple of squirrels set on a limb and jabbered at me very friendly.

I was powerful lazy and comfortable—didn't want to get up and cook breakfast. Well, I was dozing off again, when I thinks I hears a deep sound of "boom!" away up the river. I rouses up and rests on my elbow and listens; pretty soon I hears it again. I hopped up and went and looked out at a hole in the leaves, and I see a bunch of smoke laying on the water a long ways up—about abreast the ferry. And there was the ferry-boat full of people, floating along down. I knowed what was the matter, now. "Boom!" I see the white smoke squirt out of the ferry-boat's side. You see, they was firing cannon over the water, trying to make my carcass come to the top.

I was pretty hungry, but it warn't going to do for me to start a fire, because they might see the smoke. So I set there and watched the cannon-smoke and listened to the boom. The river was a mile wide, there, and it always looks pretty on a summer morning—so I was having a good enough time seeing them hunt for my remainders, if I only had a bite to eat. Well, then I happened to think how they always put quicksilver in loaves of bread and float them off because they always go right to the drownded carcass and stop there. So says I, I'll keep a lookout, and if any of them's floating around after me, I'll give them a show. I changed to the Illinois edge of the island to see what luck I could have, and I warn't disappointed. A big double loaf come along, and I most got it, with a long stick, but my foot slipped and she floated out further. Of course I was where the current set in the closest to the shore—I knowed enough for that. But by-and-by along comes another one, and this time I won. I took out the plug and shook out the little dab of quicksilver, and set my teeth in. It was "baker's bread"— what the quality eat—none of your low-down corn-pone.

I got a good place amongst the leaves, and set there on a log, munching the bread and watching the ferry-boat, and very well satisfied. And then something struck me. I says, now I reckon the widow or the parson or somebody prayed that this bread would find me, and here it has gone and done it. So there ain't no doubt but there is something in that thing. That is, there's something in it when a body like the widow or the parson prays, but it don't work for me, and I reckon it don't work for only just the right kind.

I lit a pipe and had a good long smoke and went on watching. The ferry-boat was floating with the current, and I allowed I'd have a chance to see who was aboard when she come along, because she would come in close, where the bread did. When she'd got pretty well along down towards me, I put out my pipe and went to where I fished out the bread, and laid down behind a log on the bank in a little open place. Where the log forked I could peep through.

By-and-by she come along, and she drifted in so close that they could a run out a plank and walked ashore. Most everybody was on the boat. Pap, and Judge Thatcher, and Bessie Thatcher, and Jo Jo Harper, and Tom Sawyer, and his old Aunt Polly, and Sid and Mary, and plenty more. Everybody was talking about the murder, but the captain broke in and says:

"Look sharp, now; the current sets in the closest here, and maybe he's washed ashore and got tangled amongst the brush at the water's edge. I hope so, anyway."

I didn't hope so. They all crowded up and leaned over the rails, nearly in my face, and kept still, watching with all their might. I could see them first-rate, but they couldn't see me. Then the captain sung out:

"Stand away!" and the cannon let off such a blast right before me that it made me deef with the noise and pretty near blind with the smoke, and I judged I was gone. If they'd a had some bullets in, I reckon they'd a got the corpse they was after. Well, I see I warn't hurt, thanks to goodness. The boat floated on and went out of sight around the shoulder of the island. I could hear the booming, now and then, further and further off, and by-and-by after an hour, I didn't hear it no more. The island was three mile long. I judged they had got to the foot, and was giving it up. But they didn't yet a while. They turned around the foot of the island and started up the channel on the Missouri side, under steam, and booming once in a while as they went. I crossed over to that side and watched them. When they got abreast the head of the island they quit shooting and dropped over to the Missouri shore and went home to the town.

I knowed I was all right now. Nobody else would come a-hunting after me. I got my traps out of the canoe and made me a nice camp in the thick woods. I made a kind of a tent out of my blankets to put my things under so the rain couldn't get at them. I catched a cat-fish and haggled him open with my saw, and towards sundown I started my camp fire and had supper. Then I set out a line to catch some fish for breakfast.

When it was dark I set by my camp fire smoking, and feeling pretty satisfied; but by-and-by it got sort of lonesome, and so I went and set on the bank and listened to the currents washing along, and counted the stars and drift-logs and rafts that come down, and then went to bed; there ain't no better way to put in time when you are lonesome; you can't stay so, you soon get over it.

And so for three days and nights. No difference—just the same thing. But the next day I went exploring around down through the island. I was boss of it; it all belonged to me, so to say, and I wanted to know all about it; but mainly I wanted to put in the time. I found plenty strawberries, ripe and prime; and green summer-grapes, and green razberries; and the green blackberries was just beginning to show. They would all come handy by-and-by, I judged.

Well, I went fooling along in the deep woods till I judged I warn't far from the foot of the island. I had my gun along, but I hadn't shot nothing; it was for protection; thought I would kill some game nigh home. About this time I mighty near stepped on a good sized snake, and it went sliding off through the grass and flowers, and I after it, trying to get a shot at it. I clipped along, and all of a sudden I bounded right on to the ashes of a camp fire that was still smoking.

My heart jumped up amongst my lungs. I never waited for to look further, but uncocked my gun and went sneaking back on my tip-toes as fast as ever I could. Every now and then I stopped a second, amongst the thick leaves, and listened; but my breath come so hard I couldn't hear nothing else. I slunk along another piece further, then listened again; and so on, and so on; if I see a stump, I took it for a man; if I trod on a stick and broke it, it made me feel like a person had cut one of my breaths in two and I only got half, and the short half, too.

When I got to camp I warn't feeling very brash, there warn't much sand in my craw; but I says, this ain't no time to be fooling around. So I got all my traps into my canoe again so as to have them out of sight, and I put out the fire and scattered the ashes around to look like an old last year's camp, and then clumb a tree.

I reckon I was up in the tree two hours; but I didn't see nothing, I didn't hear nothing—I only *thought* I heard and seen as much as a thousand things. Well, I couldn't stay up there forever; so at last I got down, but I kept in the thick woods and on the lookout all the time. All I could get to eat was berries and what was left over from breakfast.

By the time it was night I was pretty hungry. So when it was good and dark, I slid out from shore before moonrise and paddled over to the Illinois bank—about a quarter of a mile. I went out in the woods and cooked a supper, and I had about made up my mind I would stay there all night, when I hear a *plunkety-plunk, plunkety-plunk,* and says to myself, horses coming; and next I hear people's voices. I got everything into the canoe as quick as I could, and then went creeping through the woods to see what I could find out. I hadn't got far when I hear a man say:

"We better camp here, if we can find a good place; the horses is about beat out. Let's look around."

I didn't wait, but shoved out and paddled away easy. I tied up in the old place, and reckoned I would sleep in the canoe.

I didn't sleep much. I couldn't, somehow, for thinking. And every time I waked up I thought somebody had me by the neck. So the sleep didn't do me no good. By-and-by I says to myself, I can't live this way; I'm agoing to find out who it is that's here on the island with me; I'll find it out or bust. Well, I felt better, right off.

So I took my paddle and slid out from shore just a step or two, and then let the canoe drop along down amongst the shadows. The moon was shining, and outside of the shadows it made it most as light as day. I poked along well onto an hour, everything still as rocks and sound asleep. Well by this time I was most down to the foot of the island. A little ripply, cool breeze begun to blow, and that was as good as saying the night was about done. I give her a turn with the paddle and brung her nose to shore; then I got my gun and slipped out and into the edge of the woods. I set down there on a log and looked out through the leaves. I see the moon go off watch and the darkness begin to blanket the river. But in a little while I see a pale streak over the tree-tops, and knowed the day was coming. So I took my gun and slipped off towards where I had run across that camp fire, stopping every minute or two to listen. But I hadn't no luck, somehow; I couldn't seem to find the place. But by-and-by, sure enough, I catched a glimpse of fire, away through the trees. I went for it, cautious and slow. By-and-by I was close enough to have a look, and there laid a man on the ground. It most give me the fan-tods. He had a blanket around his head, and his head was nearly in the fire. I set there behind a clump of bushes, in about six foot of him, and kept my eyes on him steady. It was getting gray daylight, now. Pretty soon he gapped, and stretched himself, and hove off the blanket, and it was Miss Watson's Jim! I bet I was glad to see him. I says:

"Hello, Jim!" and skipped out.

He bounced up and stared at me wild. Then he drops down on his knees, and puts his hands together and says:

"Doan' hurt me—don't! I hain't ever done no harm to a ghos'. I awluz liked dead people, en done all I could for 'em. You go en git in de river agin, whah you b'longs, en doan' do nuffin to Ole Jim, 'at 'uz awluz yo' fren'."

Well, I warn't long making him understand I warn't dead. I was ever so glad to see Jim. I warn't lonesome, now. I told him I warn't afraid of *him* telling the people where I was. I talked along, but he only set there and looked at me; never said nothing. Then I says:

"It's good daylight. Le's get breakfast. Make up your camp fire good."

"What's de use er makin' up de camp fire to cook strawbries en sich truck? But you got a gun, hain't you? Den we kin git sumfn better den strawbries."

"Strawberries and such truck," I says. "Is that what you live on?"

"I couldn't git nuffn else," he says.

"Why, how long you been on the island, Jim?"

"I come heah de night arter you's killed."

"What, all that time?"

"Yes-indeedy."

"And ain't you had nothing but that kind of rubbage to eat?"

"No, sah—nuffn else."

"Well, you must be most starved, ain't you?"

"I reck'n I could eat a hoss. I think I could. How long you ben on de islan'?"

"Since the night I got killed."

"No! W'y, what has you lived on? But you got a gun. Oh, yes, you got a gun. Dat's good. Now you kill sumfn en I'll make up de fire."

So we went over to where the canoe was, and while he built a fire in a grassy open place amongst the trees, I fetched meal and bacon and coffee, and coffee-pot and frying-pan, and sugar and tin cups, and the nigger was set back considerable, because he reckoned it was all done with witchcraft. I catched a good big cat-fish, too, and Jim cleaned him with his knife, and fried him.

When breakfast was ready, we lolled on the grass and eat it smoking hot. Jim laid it in with all his might, for he was most about starved. Then when we had got pretty well stuffed, we laid off and lazied.

By-and-by Jim says:

"But looky here, Huck, who wuz it dat 'uz killed in dat shanty, ef it warn't you?"

Then I told him the whole thing, and he said it was smart. He said Tom Sawyer couldn't get up no better plan than what I had. Then I says:

"How do you come to be here, Jim, and how'd you get here?"

He looked pretty uneasy, and didn't say nothing for a minute. Then he says:

"Maybe I better not tell."

"Why, Jim?"

"Well, dey's reasons. But you wouldn' tell on me ef I 'uz to tell you, would you, Huck?"

"Blamed if I would, Jim."

"Well, I b'lieve you, Huck. I—I *run off.*"

"Jim!"

"But mind, you said you wouldn't tell—you know you said you wouldn't tell, Huck."

"Well, I did. I said I wouldn't, and I'll stick to it. Honest *injun* I will. People would call me a low down Ablitionist and despise me for keeping mum—but that don't make no difference. I ain't agoing to tell, and I ain't agoing back there anyways. So now, le's know all about it."

"Well, you see, it 'uz dis way. Ole Missus—dat's Miss Watson—

she pecks on me all de time, en treats me pooty rough, but she awluz said she wouldn' sell me down to Orleans. But I noticed dey wuz a nigger trader roun' de place considable, lately, en I begin to git oneasy. Well, one night I creeps to de do', pooty late, en de do' warn't quite shet, en I hear ole missus tell de widder she gwyne to sell me down to Orelans, but she didn' want to, but she could git eight hund'd dollars for me, en it 'uz sich a big stack o' money she couldn' resis'. De widder she try to git her to say she wouldn't do it, but I never waited to hear de res'. I lit out mighty quick, I tell you.

"I tuck out en shin down de hill en 'spec to steal a skift 'long de sho' som'ers 'bove de town, but dey wuz people a-stirrin' yit, so I hid in de ole tumble-down cooper shop on de bank to wait for everybody to go 'way. Well, I wuz dah all night. Dey wuz somebody roun' all de time. 'Long 'bout six in de mawnin', skifts begin to go by, en 'bout eight er nine every skift dat went 'long wuz talkin' 'bout how yo' pap come over to de town en say you's killed. Dese las' skifts wuz full o' ladies en genlmen agoin' over for to see de place. Sometimes dey'd pull up at de sho' en take a res' b'fo' dey started acrost, so by de talk I got to know all 'bout de killin'. I 'uz powerful sorry you's killed, Huck, but I ain't no mo', now.

"I laid dah under de shavins all day. I' uz hungry, but I warn't afeared; bekase I knowed ole missus en de widder wuz goin' to start to de camp-meetn' right arter breakfas' en be gone all day, en dey knows I goes off wid de cattle 'bout daylight, so dey wouldn' 'spec to see me roun' de place, en so dey wouldn' miss me tell arter dark in de evenin'. De yuther servants wouldn' miss me, kase dey'd shin out en take holiday, soon as de ole folks 'uz out'n de way.

"Well, when it come dark I tuck out up de river road, en went 'bout two mile er more to whah dey warn't no houses. I'd made up my mine 'bout what I's agwyne to do. You see ef I kep' on tryin' to git away afoot, de dogs 'ud track me; ef I stole a skift to cross over, dey'd miss dat skift, you see, en dey'd know 'bout whah I'd lan' on de yuther side en whah to pick up my track. So I says, a raff if what I's arter; it doan' *make* no track.

"I see a light a-comin' roun' de p'int, bymeby, so I wade' in en shove' a log ahead of' me, en swum more'n half-way acrost de river, en got in 'mongst de drift-wood, en kep' my head down low, en kinder swum agin de current tell de raff come along. Den I swum to de stern uv it, en tuck aholt. It clouded up en 'uz pooty dark for a little while. So I clumb up en laid down on de planks. De men 'uz all 'way yonder in de middle, whah de lantern wuz. De river wuz arisin' en dey wuz a good current; so I reck'n'd 'at by fo' in de mawnin' I'd be twenty-five mile down de river, en den I'd slip in, jis' b'fo' daylight, en swim asho' en take to de woods on de Illinoi side.

"But I didn' have no luck. When we 'uz mos' down to de head er de islan', a man begin to come aft wid de lantern. I see it warn't

no use fer to wait, so I slid overboard, en struck out fer de islan'. Well,
I had a notion I could lan' mos' anywhers, but I couldn't—bank
too bluff. I 'uz mos' to de foot er de islan' b'fo' I foun' a good place.
I went into de woods en judged I wouldn' fool wid raffs no mo',
long as dey move de lantern roun' so. I had my pipe en a plug er dog-
leg, en some matches in my cap, en dey warn't wet, so I 'uz all right."

"And so you ain't had no meat nor bread to eat all this time?
Why didn't you get mud-turkles?"

"How you gwyne to git'm? You can't slip up on um en grab um;
it in de night? en I warn't gwyne to show mysef on de bank in de
daytime."

"Well, that's so. You've had to keep in the woods all the time, of
course. Did you hear 'em shooting the cannon?"

"Oh, yes. I knowed dey was arter you. I see um go by heah;
watched um thoo de bushes."

Some young birds come along, flying a yard or two at a time and
lighting. Jim said it was a sign it was going to rain. He said it was a
sign when young chickens flew that way, and so he reckoned it was
the same way when young birds done it. I was going to catch some
of them, but Jim wouldn't let me. He said it was death. He said his
father laid mighty sick once, and some of them catched a bird, and
his old granny said his father would die, and he did.

And Jim said you musn't count the things you are going to cook
for dinner, because that would bring bad luck. The same if you
shook the table-cloth after sundown. And he said if a man owned
a bee-hive, and that man died, the bees must be told about it
before sun-up next morning, or else the bees would all weaken down
and quit work and die. Jim said bees wouldn't sting idiots; but I
didn't believe that, because I had tried them lots of times myself,
and they wouldn't sting me.

I had heard about some of these things before, but not all of them.
Jim knowed all kinds of signs. He said he knowed most everything.
I said it looked to me like all the signs was about bad luck, and so
I asked him if there warn't any good-luck signs. He says:

"Mighty few—an' *dey* ain' no use to a body. What you want to
know when good luck's a-comin' for? want to keep it off?" And
he said: "Ef you's got hairy arms en a hairy breas', it's a sign dat
you's agwyne to be rich. Well, dey's some use in a sign like dat,
'kase it's so fur ahead. You see, maybe you's got to be po' a long time
fust, en so you might git discourage' en kill yo'sef 'f you did n' know
by de sign dat you gwyne to be rich bymeby."

"Have you got hairy arms and a hairy breast, Jim?"

"What's de use to ax dat question? don' you see I has?"

"Well, are you rich?"

"No, but I ben rich wunst, and gwyne to be rich agin. Wunst I
had foteen dollars, but I tuck to specalat'n', en got busted out."

"What did you speculate in, Jim?"

"Well, fust I tackled stock."

"What kind of stock?"

"Why, live stock. Cattle, you know. I put ten dollars in a cow. But I ain' gwyne to resk no mo' money in stock. De cow up 'n' died on my han's."

"So you lost the ten dollars."

"No, I didn' lose it all. I on'y los' 'bout nine of it. I sole de hide en taller for a dollar en ten cents."

"You had five dollars and ten cents left. Did you speculate any more?"

"Yes. You know dat one-laigged nigger dat b'longs to old Misto Bradish? well, he sot up a bank, en say anybody dat put in a dollar would git fo' dollars mo' at de en' er de year. Well, all de niggers went in, but dey didn' have much. I wuz de on'y one dat had much. So I stuck out for mo' dan fo' dollars, en I said 'f I didn' git it I'd start a bank mysef. Well o' course dat nigger want' to keep me out er de business, bekase he say dey warn't business 'nough for two banks, so he say I could put in my five dollars en he pay me thirty-five at de en' er de year.

"So I done it. Den I reck'n'd I'd inves' de thirty-five dollars right off en keep things a-movin'. Dey wuz a nigger name' Bob, dat had ketched a wood-flat, en his marster didn' know it; en I bought it off'n him en told him to take de thirty-five dollars when de en' er de year come; but somebody stole de wood-flat dat night, en nex' day de one-laigged nigger say de bank's busted. So dey didn' none uv us git no money."

"What did you do with the ten cents, Jim?"

"Well, I 'uz gwyne to spen' it, but I had a dream, en de dream tole me to give it to a nigger name' Balum—Balum's Ass dey call him for short, he's one er dem chuckle-heads, you know. But he's lucky, dey say, en I see I warn't lucky. De dream say let Balum inves' de ten cents en he'd make a raise for me. Well, Balum he tuck de money, en when he wuz in church he hear de preacher say dat whoever give to de po' len' to de Lord, en boun' to git his money back a hund'd times. So Balum he tuck en give de ten cents to de po,' en laid low to see what wuz gwyne to come of it."

"Well, what did come of it, Jim?"

"Nuffn' never come of it. I couldn' manage to k'leck dat money no way; en Balum he couldn'. I ain' gwyne to len' no mo' money 'dout I see de security. Boun' to git yo' money back a hund'd times, de preacher says! Ef I could git de ten *cents* back, I'd call it squah, en be glad er de chanst."

"Well, it's all right, anyway, Jim, long as you're going to be rich again some time or other."

"Yes—en I's rich now, come to look at it. I owns mysef, en I's wuth eight hund'd dollars. I wisht I had de money, I wouldn' want no mo'."

CHAPTER IX

I wanted to go and look at a place right about the middle of the island, that I'd found when I was exploring; so we started, and soon got to it, because the island was only three miles long and a quarter of a mile wide.

This place was a tolerable long steep hill or ridge, about forty foot high. We had a rough time getting to the top, the sides was so steep and the bushes so thick. We tramped and clumb around all over it, and by-and-by found a good big cavern in the rock, most up to the top on the side towards Illinois. The cavern was as big as two or three rooms bunched together, and Jim could stand up straight in it. It was cool in there. Jim was for putting our traps in there, right away, but I said we didn't want to be climbing up and down there all the time.

Jim said if we had the canoe hid in a good place, and had all the traps in the cavern, we could rush there if anybody was to come to the island, and they would never find us without dogs. And besides, he said them little birds had said it was going to rain, and did I want the things to get wet?

So we went back and got the canoe and paddled up abreast the cavern, and lugged all the traps up there. Then we hunted up a place close by to hide the canoe in, amongst the thick willows. We took some fish off of the lines and set them again, and begun to get ready for dinner.

The door of the cavern was big enough to roll a hogshead in, and on one side of the door the floor stuck out a little bit and was flat and a good place to build a fire on. So we built it there and cooked dinner.

We spread the blankets inside for a carpet, and eat our dinner in there. We put all the other things handy at the back of the cavern. Pretty soon it darkened up and begun to thunder and lighten; so the birds was right about it. Directly it begun to rain, and it rained like all fury, too, and I never see the wind blow so. It was one of these regular summer storms. It would get so dark that it looked all blue-black outside, and lovely; and the rain would thrash along by so thick that the trees off a little ways looked dim and spider-webby; and here would come a blast of wind that would bend the trees down and turn up the pale underside of the leaves; and then a perfect ripper of a gust would follow along and set the branches to tossing their arms as if they was just wild; and next, when it was just about the bluest and blackest—*fst!* it was as bright as glory and you'd have a little glimpse of tree-tops a-plunging about, away off yonder in the storm, hundreds of yards further than you could see before; dark as sin again in a second, and now you'd hear the thunder let go with an

awful crash and then go rumbling, grumbling, tumbling down the
sky towards the under side of the world, like rolling empty barrels
down stairs, where it's long stairs and they bounce a good deal, you
know.

"Jim, this is nice," I says. "I wouldn't want to be nowhere else but
here. Pass me along another hunk of fish and some hot corn-bread."

"Well, you wouldn't a ben here, 'f it hadn't a ben for Jim. You'd
a ben down dah in de woods widout any dinner, en gittn' mos'
drownded, too, dat you would, honey. Chickens knows when its
gwyne to rain, en so do de birds, chile."

The river went on raising and raising for ten or twelve days, till at
last it was over the banks. The water was three or four foot deep on
the island in the low places and on the Illinois bottom. On that side
it was a good many miles wide; but on the Missouri side it was the
same old distance across—a half a mile—because the Missouri shore
was just a wall of high bluffs.

Daytimes we paddled all over the island in the canoe. It was
mighty cool and shady in the deep woods even if the sun was blazing
outside. We went winding in and out amongst the trees; and
sometimes the vines hung so thick we had to back away and go some
other way. Well, on every old broken-down tree, you could see
rabbits, and snakes, and such things; and when the island had been
overflowed a day or two, they got so tame, on account of being
hungry, that you could paddle right up and put your hand on them if
you wanted to; but not the snakes and turtles—they would slide off
in the water. The ridge our cavern was in, was full of them. We could
a had pets enough if we'd wanted them.

One night we catched a little section of a lumber raft—nice pine
planks. It was twelve foot wide and fifteen or sixteen foot long, and
the top stood above water six or seven inches, a solid level floor. We
could see saw-logs go by in the daylight, sometimes, but we let them
go; we didn't show ourselves in daylight.

Another night, when we was up at the head of the island, just
before daylight, here comes a frame house down, on the west side.
She was a two-story, and tilted over, considerable. We paddled out
and got aboard—clumb in at an up-stairs window. But it was too
dark to see yet, so we made the canoe fast and set in her to wait for
daylight.

The light begun to come before we got to the foot of the island.
Then we looked in at the window. We could make out a bed, and a
table, and two old chairs, and lots of things around about on the
floor; and there was clothes hanging against the wall. There was
something laying on the floor in the far corner that looked like a
man. So Jim says:

"Hello, you!"

But it didn't budge. So I hollered again, and then Jim says:

"De man ain't asleep—he's dead. You hold still—I'll go en see."

He went and bent down and looked, and says:

"It's a dead man. Yes, indeedy; naked, too. He's ben shot in de back. I reck'n he's ben dead two er three days. Come in, Huck, but doan' look at his face—it's too gashly."

I didn't look at him at all. Jim throwed some old rags over him, but he needn't done it; I didn't want to see him. There was heaps of old greasy cards scattered around over the floor, and old whisky bottles, and a couple of masks made out of black cloth; and all over the walls was the ignorantest kind of words and pictures, made with charcoal. There was two old dirty calico dresses, and a sun-bonnet, and some women's under-clothes, hanging against the wall, and some men's clothing, too. We put the lot into the canoe; it might come good. There was a boy's old speckled straw hat on the floor; I took that too. And there was a bottle that had had milk in it; and it had a rag stopper for a baby to suck. We would a took the bottle, but it was broke. There was a seedy old chest, and an old hair trunk with the hinges broke. They stood open, but there warn't nothing left in them that was any account. They stood open, but there warn't nothing left in them that was any account. The way things was scattered about, we reckoned the people left in a hurry and warn't fixed so as to carry off most of their stuff.

We got an old tin lantern, and a butcher knife without any handle, and a bran-new Barlow knife worth two bits in any store, and a lot of tallow candles, and a tin candlestick, and a gourd, and a tin cup, and a ratty old bed-quilt off the bed, and a reticule with needles and pins and beeswax and buttons and thread and all such truck in it, and a hatchet and some nails, and a fish-line as thick as my little finger, with some monstrous hooks on it, and a roll of buckskin, and a leather dog-collar, and a horse-shoe, and some vials of medicine that didn't have no label on them; and just as we was leaving I found a tolerable good curry-comb, and Jim he found a ratty old fiddle-bow, and a wooden leg. The straps was broke off of it, but barring that, it was a good enough leg, though it was too long for me and not long enough for Jim, and we couldn't find the other one, though we hunted all around.

And so, take it all around, we made a good haul. When we was ready to shove off, we was a quarter of a mile below the island, and it was pretty broad day; so I made Jim lay down in the canoe and cover up with the quilt, because if he set up, people could tell he was a nigger a good ways off. I paddled over to the Illinois shore, and drifted down most a half a mile doing it. I crept up the dead water under the bank and hadn't no accidents and didn't see nobody. We got home all safe.

CHAPTER X

After breakfast I wanted to talk about the dead man and guess out how he come to be killed, but Jim didn't want to. He said it would fetch bad luck; and besides, he said, he might come and ha'nt us; he said a man that warn't buried was more likely to go a-ha'nting around than one that was planted and comfortable. That sounded pretty reasonable, so I didn't say no more; but I couldn't keep from studying over it and wishing I knowed who shot the man, and what they done it for.

We rummaged the clothes we'd got, and found eight dollars in silver sewed up in the lining of an old blanket overcoat. Jim said he reckoned the people in that house stole the coat, because if they'd a knowed the money was there they wouldn't a left it. I said I reckoned they killed him, too; but Jim didn't want to talk about that. I says:

"Now you think it's bad luck; but what did you say when I fetched in the snake-skin that I found on the top of the ridge day before yesterday? You said it was the worst bad luck in the world to touch a snake-skin with my hands. Well, here's your bad luck! We've raked in all this truck and eight dollars besides. I wish we could have some bad luck like this every day, Jim."

"Never you mind, honey, never you mind. Don't you git too peart. It's a-comin'. Mind I tell you, it's a-comin'."

It did come, too. It was a Tuesday that we had that talk. Well, after dinner Friday, we was laying around in the grass at the upper end of the ridge, and got out of tobacco. I went to the cavern to get some, and found a rattlesnake in there. I killed him, and curled him up on the foot of Jim's blanket, ever so natural, thinking there'd be some fun when Jim found him there. Well, by night I forgot all about the snake, and when Jim flung himself down on the blanket while I struck a light, the snake's mate was there, and bit him.

He jumped up yelling, and the first thing the light showed was the varmit curled up and ready for another spring. I laid him out in a second with a stick, and Jim grabbed pap's whisky jug and begun to pour it down.

He was barefooted, and the snake bit him right on the heel. That all comes of my being such a fool as to not remember that wherever you leave a dead snake its mate always comes there and curls around it. Jim told me to chop off the snake's head and throw it away, and then skin the body and roast a piece of it. I done it, and he eat it and said it would help cure him. He made me take off the rattles and tie them around his wrist, too. He said that that would help. Then I slid out quiet and throwed the snakes clear away amongst the bushes; for I warn't going to let Jim find out it was all my fault, not if I could help it.

Jim sucked and sucked at the jug, and now and then he got out of his head and pitched around and yelled; but every time he come to

to himself he went to sucking at the jug again. His foot swelled up
pretty big, and so did his leg; but by-and-by the drunk begun to
come, and so I judged he was all right; but I'd druther been bit with
a snake than pap's whisky.

Jim was laid up for four days and nights. Then the swelling was all
gone and he was around again. I made up my mind I wouldn't ever
take aholt of a snake-skin again with my hands, now that I see what
had come of it. Jim said he reckoned I would believe him next time.
And he said that handling a snake-skin was such awful bad luck
that maybe we hadn't got to the end of it yet. He said he druther see
the new moon over his left shoulder as much as a thousand times
than take up a snake-skin in his hand. Well, I was getting to feel that
way myself, though I've always reckoned that looking at the new
moon over your left shoulder is one of the carelessest and foolishest
things a body can do. Old Hank Bunker done it once, and bragged
about it; and in less than two years he got drunk and fell off of the
shot tower and spread himself out so that he was just a kind of a
layer, as you may say; and they slid him edgeways between two barn
doors for a coffin, and buried him so, so they say, but I didn't see it.
Pap told me. But anyway, it all come of looking at the moon that
way, like a fool.

Well, the days went along, and the river went down between its
banks again; and about the first thing we done was to bait one of the
big hooks with a skinned rabbit and set it and catch a cat-fish that
was as big as a man, being six foot two inches long, and weighed over
two hundred pounds. We couldn't handle him, of course; he would a
flung us into Illinois. We just set there and watched him rip and tear
around till he drownded. We found a brass button in his stomach,
and a round ball, and lots of rubbage. We split the ball open with the
hatchet, and there was a spool in it. Jim said he'd had it there a long
time, to coat it over so and make a ball of it. It was as big a fish as
was ever catched in the Mississippi, I reckon. Jim said he hadn't ever
seen a bigger one. He would a been worth a good deal over at the
village. They peddle out such a fish as that by the pound in the
market house there; everybody buys some of him; his meat's as white
as snow and makes a good fry.

Next morning I said it was getting slow and dull, and I wanted to
get a stirring up, some way. I said I reckoned I would slip over the
river and find out what was going on. Jim liked that notion; but he
said I must go in the dark and look sharp. Then he studied it over
and said, couldn't I put on some of them old things and dress up
like a girl? That was a good notion, too. So we shortened up one
of the calico gowns and I turned up my trowser-legs to my knees and
got into it. Jim hitched it behind with the hooks, and it was a fair fit.
I put on the sun-bonnet and tied it under my chin, and then for a
body to look in and see my face was like looking down a joint of
stove-pipe. Jim said nobody would know me, even in the daytime,

hardly. I practiced around all day to get the hang of the things, and by-and-by I could do pretty well in them, only Jim said I didn't walk like a girl; and he said I must quit pulling up my gown to get at my britches pocket. I took notice, and done better.

I started up the Illinois shore in the canoe just after dark.

I started across to the town from a little below the ferry landing, and the drift of the current fetched me in at the bottom of the town. I tied up and started along the bank. There was a light burning in a little shanty that hadn't been lived in for a long time, and I wondered who had took up quarters there. I slipped up and peeped in at the window. There was a woman about forty year old in there, knitting by a candle that was on a pine table. I didn't know her face; she was a stranger, for you couldn't start a face in that town that I didn't know. Now this was lucky, because I was weakening; I was getting afraid I had come; people might know my voice and find me out. But if this woman had been in such a little town two days she could tell me all I wanted to know; so I knocked at the door, and made up my mind I wouldn't forget I was a girl.

CHAPTER XI

"Come in," says the woman, and I did. She says:

"Take a cheer."

I done it. She looked me all over with her little shiny eyes, and says:

"What might your name be?"

"Sarah Williams."

"Where 'bouts do you live? In this neighborhood?"

"No'm. In Hookerville, seven miles below. I've walked all the way and I'm all tired out."

"Hungry, too, I reckon. I'll find you something."

"No'm, I ain't hungry. I was so hungry I had to stop two mile below here at a farm; so I ain't hungry no more. It's what makes me so late. My mother's down sick, and out of money and everything, and I come to tell my uncle Abner Moore. He lives at the upper end of the town, she says. I hain't ever been here before. Do you know him?"

"No; but I don't know everybody yet. I haven't lived here quite two weeks. It's a considerable ways to the upper end of the town. You better stay here all night. Take off your bonnet."

"No," I says, "I'll rest a while, I reckon, and go on. I ain't afeared of the dark."

She said she wouldn't let me go by myself, but her husband would be in by-and-by, maybe in a hour and a half, and she'd send him along with me. Then she got to talking about her husband, and about her relations up the river, and her relations down the river, and about how much better off they used to was, and how they didn't know but they'd made a mistake coming to our town, instead of letting well alone—and so on and so on, till I was afeard *I* had made a mistake coming to her to find out what was going on in the town; but by-and-by she dropped onto pap and the murder, and then I was pretty willing to let her clatter right along. She told about me and Tom Sawyer finding the six thousand dollars (only she got it ten) and all about pap and what a hard lot he was, and what a hard lot I was, and at last she got down to where I was murdered. I says:

"Who done it? We've heard considerable about these goings on, down in Hookerville, but we don't know who 'twas that killed Huck Finn."

"Well, I reckon there's a right smart chance of people *here* that'd like to know who killed him. Some thinks old Finn done it himself."

"No—is that so?"

"Most everybody thought it at first. He'll never know how nigh he come to getting lynched. But before night they changed around and judged it was done by a runaway nigger named Jim."

"Why *he*—"

I stopped. I reckoned I better keep still. She run on, and never noticed I had put in at all.

"The nigger run off the very night Huck Finn was killed. So there's a reward out for him—three hundred dollars. And there's a reward out for old Finn too—two hundred dollars. You see, he come to town the morning after the murder, and told about it, and was out with 'em on the ferry-boat hunt, and right away after he up and left. Before night they wanted to lynch him, but he was gone, you see. Well, next day they found out the nigger was gone; they found out he hadn't ben seen sence ten o'clock the night the murder was done. So then they put it on him, you see, and while they was full of it, next day back comes old Finn and went boo-hooing to Judge Thatcher to get money to hunt for the nigger all over Illinois with. The judge give him some, and that evening he got drunk and was around till after midnight with a couple of mighty hard looking strangers, and then went off with them. Well, he hain't come back sence, and they ain't looking for him back till this thing blows over a little, for people thinks now that he killed his boy and fixed things so folks would think robbers done it, and then he'd get Huck's money without having to bother a long time with a lawsuit. People do say he warn't any too good to do it. Oh, he's sly, I reckon. If he don't come back for a year, he'll be all right. You can't prove anything on him, you know; everything will be quieted down then, and he'll walk into Huck's money as easy as nothing."

"Yes, I reckon so, 'm. I don't see nothing in the way of it. Has everybody quit thinking the nigger done it?"

"Oh, no, not everybody. A good many thinks he done it. But they'll get the nigger pretty soon, now, and maybe they can scare it out of him."

"Why, are they after him yet?"

"Well, you're innocent, ain't you! Does three hundred dollars lay round every day for people to pick up? Some folks thinks the nigger ain't far from here. I'm one of them—but I hain't talked it around. A few days ago I was talking with an old couple that lives next door in the log shanty, and they happened to say hardly anybody ever goes to that island over yonder that they call Jackson's Island. Don't anybody live there? says I. No, nobody, says they. I didn't say any more, but I done some thinking. I was pretty near certain I'd seen smoke over there, about the head of the island, a day or two before that, so I says to myself, like as not that nigger's hiding over there; anyway, says I, it's worth the trouble to give the place a hunt. I hain't seen any smoke sence, so I reckon maybe he's gone, if it was him; but husband's going over to see—him and another man. He was gone up the river; but he got back to-day and I told him as soon as he got here two hours ago."

I had got so uneasy I couldn't set still. I had to do something with my hands; so I took up a needle off of the table and went to threading it. My hands shook, and I was making a bad job of it. When the woman stopped talking, I looked up, and she was looking at me pretty curious, and smiling a little. I put down the needle and thread and let on to be interested—and I was, too—and says:

"Three hundred dollars is a power of money. I wish my mother could get it. Is your husband going over there to-night?"

"Oh, yes. He went up town with the man I was telling you of, to get a boat and see if they could borrow another gun. They'll go over after midnight."

"Couldn't they see better if they was to wait till daytime?"

"Yes. And couldn't the nigger see better, too? After midnight he'll likely be asleep, and they can slip around through the woods and hunt up his camp fire all the better for the dark, if he's got one."

"I didn't think of that."

The woman kept looking at me pretty curious, and I didn't feel a bit comfortable. Pretty soon she says:

"What did you say your name was, honey?"

"M—Mary Williams."

Somehow it didn't seem to me that I said it was Mary before, so I didn't look up; seemed to me I said it was Sarah; so I felt sort of cornered, and was afeared maybe I was looking it, too. I wished the woman would say something more; the longer she set still, the uneasier I was. But now she says:

"Honey, I thought you said it was Sarah when you first come in?"

"Oh, yes'm, I did. Sarah Mary Williams. Sarah's my first name. Some calls me Sarah, some calls me Mary."

"Oh, that's the way of it?"

"Yes'm."

I was feeling better, then, but I wished I was out of there, anyway.

I couldn't look up yet.

Well, the woman fell to talking about how hard times was, and how poor they had to live, and how the rats was as free as if they owned the place, and so forth, and so on, and then I got easy again. She was right about the rats. You'd see one stick his nose out of a hole in the corner every little while. She said she had to have things handy to throw at them when she was alone, or they wouldn't give her no peace. She showed me a bar of lead, twisted up into a knot, and said she was a good shot with it generly, but she'd wrenched her arm a day or two ago, and didn't know whether she could throw true, now. But she watched for a chance, and directly she banged away at a rat, but she missed him wide, and said "Ouch!" it hurt her arm so. Then she told me to try for the next one. I wanted to be getting away before the old man got back, but of course I didn't let on. I got the thing, and the first rat that showed his nose I let drive, and if he'd a stayed where he was he'd a been a tolerable sick rat. She said that that was first-rate, and she reckoned I would hive the next one. She went and got the lump of lead and fetched it back and brought along a hank of yarn, which she wanted me to help her with. I held up my two hands and she put the hank over them and went on talking about her and her husband's matters. But she broke off to say:

"Keep your eye on the rats. You better have the lead in your lap, handy."

So she dropped the lump into my lap, just at that moment, and I clapped my legs together on it and she went on talking. But only about a minute. Then she took off the hank and looked me straight in the face, but very pleasant, and says:

"Come, now—what's your real name?"

"Wh-what, mum?"

"What's your real name? Is it Bill, or Tom, or Bob?—or what is it?"

I reckon I shook like a leaf, and I didn't know hardly what to do. But I says:

"Please to don't poke fun at a poor girl like me, mum. If I'm in the way, here, I'll—"

"No, you won't. Set down and stay where you are. I ain't going to hurt you, and I ain't going to tell on you, nuther. You just tell me your secret, and trust me. I'll keep it; and what's more, I'll help you. So'll my old man, if you want him to. You see, you're a runaway 'prentice—that's all. It ain't anything. There ain't any harm in it. You've been treated bad, and you made up your mind to cut. Bless you, child, I wouldn't tell on you. Tell me all about it, now—that's a good boy."

So I said it wouldn't be no use to try to play it any longer, and I would just make a clean breast and tell her everything, but she mustn't go back on her promise. Then I told her my father and mother was dead, and the law had bound me out to a mean old farmer in the country thirty mile back from the river, and he treated me so bad I couldn't stand it no longer; he went away to be gone a couple of days, and so I took my chance and stole some of his daughter's old clothes, and cleared out, and I had been three nights coming the thirty miles; I traveled nights, and hid day-times and slept, and the bag of bread and meat I carried from home lasted me all the way and I had a plenty. I said I believed my uncle Abner Moore would take care of me, and so that was why I struck out for this town of Goshen."

"Goshen, child? This ain't Goshen. This is St. Petersburg. Goshen's ten mile further up the river. Who told you this was Goshen?"

"Why, a man I met at day-break this morning, just as I was going to turn into the woods for my regular sleep. He told me when the roads forked I must take the right hand, and five mile would fetch me to Goshen."

"He was drunk I reckon. He told you just exactly wrong."

"Well, he did act like he was drunk, but it ain't no matter now. I got to be moving along. I'll fetch Goshen before day-light."

"Hold on a minute. I'll put you up a snack to eat. You might want it."

So she put me up a snack, and says:

"Say—when a cow's laying down, which end of her gets up first? Answer up prompt, now—don't stop to study over it. Which end gets up first?"

"The hind end, mum."

"Well, then, a horse?"

"The for'rard end, mum."

"Which side of a tree does the most moss grow on?"

"North side."

"If fifteen cows is browsing on a hillside, how many of them eats with their heads pointed the same direction?"

"The whole fifteen, mum."

"Well, I reckon you *have* lived in the country. I thought maybe you was trying to hocus me again. What's your real name, now?"

"George Peters, mum."

"Well, try to remember it, George. Don't forget and tell me it's Elexander before you go, and then get out by saying it's George-Elexander when I catch you. And don't go about women in that old calico. You do a girl tolerable poor, but you might fool men, maybe. Bless you, child, when you set out to thread a needle, don't hold the thread still and fetch the needle up to it; hold the needle still and poke the thread at it—that's the way a woman most always does; but a man always does 'tother way. And when you throw at a rat or anything, hitch yourself up a tip-toe, and fetch your hand up over your head as awkard as you can, and miss your rat about six or

seven foot. Throw stiff-armed from the shoulder, like there was a
pivot there for it to turn on—like a girl; not from the wrist and
elbow, with your arm out to one side, like a boy. And mind you,
when a girl tries to catch anything in her lap, she throws her knees
apart; she don't clap them together, the way you did when you
catched you catched the lump of lead. Why, I spotted you for a boy
when you was threading the needle; and I contrived the other things
just to make certain. Now trot along to your uncle, Sarah Mary
Williams George Elexander Peters, and if you get into trouble you
send word to Mrs. Judith Loftus, which is me, and I'll do what I can
to get you out of it. Keep the river road, all the way, and next time
you tramp, take shoes and socks with you. The river road's a rocky
one, and your feet 'll be in a condition when you get to Goshen, I
reckon."

I went up the bank about fifty yards, and then I doubled on my
tracks and slipped back to where my canoe was, a good piece below
the house. I jumped in and was off in a hurry. I went up stream far
enough to make the head of the island, and then started across.
I took off the sun-bonnet, for I didn't want no blinders on, then.
When I was about the middle, I hear the clock begin to strike; so
I stops and listens; the sound come faint over the water, but clear—
eleven. When I struck the head of the island I never waited to blow,
though I was most winded, but I shoved right into the timber where
my old camp used to be, and started a good fire there on a high-and-
dry spot.

Then I jumped in the canoe and dug out for our place a mile and a
half below, as hard as I could go. I landed, and slopped through the
timber and up the ridge and into the cavern. There Jim laid, sound
asleep on the ground. I roused him out and says:

"Git up and hump yourself, Jim! There ain't a minute to lose.
They're after us!"

Jim never asked no questions, he never said a word; but the way he
worked for the next half an hour showed about how he was scared.
By that time everything we had in the world was on our raft and she
was ready to be shoved out from the willow cove where she was hid.
We put out the camp fire at the cavern the first thing, and didn't
show a candle outside after that.

I took the canoe out from shore a little piece and took a look, but
if there was a boat around I couldn't see it, for stars and shadows
ain't good to see by. Then we got out the raft and slipped along down
in the shade, past the foot of the island dead still, never saying a
word.

CHAPTER XII

It must a been close onto one o'clock when we got below the
island at last, and the raft did seem to go mighty slow. If a boat

was to come along, we was going to take to the canoe and break for the Illinois shore; and it was well a boat didn't come, for we hadn't ever thought to put the gun into the canoe, or a fishing-line or anything to eat. We was in ruther too much of a sweat to think of so many things. It warn't good judgment to put *everything* on the raft.

If the men went to the island, I just expect they found the camp fire I built, and watched it all night for Jim to come. Anyways, they stayed away from us, and if my building the fire never fooled them it warn't no fault of mine. I played it as low-down on them as I could.

When the first streak of day begun to show, we tied up to a tow-head in a big bend on the Illinois side, and hacked off cottonwood branches with the hatchet and covered up the raft with them so she looked like there had been a cave-in in the bank there. A tow-head is a sand-bar that has cotton-woods on it as thick as harrow-teeth.

We had mountains on the Missouri shore and heavy timber on the Illinois side, and the channel was down the Missouri shore at that place, so we warn't afraid of anybody running across us. We laid there all day and watched the rafts and steamboats spin down the Missouri shore, and up-bound steamboats fight the big river in the middle. I told Jim all about the time I had jabbering with that woman; and Jim said she was a smart one, and if she was to start after us herself *she* wouldn't set down and watch a camp fire—no, sir, she'd fetch a dog. Well, then, I said, why couldn't she tell her husband to fetch a dog? Jim said he bet she did think of it by the time the men was ready to start, and he believed they must a gone up town to get a dog and so they lost all that time, or else we wouldn't be here on a tow-head sixteen or seventeen mile below the village—no, indeedy, we would be in that same old town again. So I said I didn't care what was the reason they didn't get us, as long as they didn't.

When it was beginning to come on dark, we poked our heads out of the cottonwood thicket and looked up, and down, and across; nothing in sight; so Jim took up some of the top planks of the raft and built a snug wigwam to get under in blazing weather and rainy, and to keep the things dry. Jim made a floor for the wigwam, and raised it a foot or more above the level of the raft, so now the blankets and all the traps was out of the reach of steamboat waves. Right in the middle of the wigwam we made a layer of dirt about five or six inches deep with a frame around it for to hold it to its place; this was to build a fire on in sloppy weather or chilly; the wigwam would keep it from being seen. We made an extra steering oar, too, because one of the others might get broke, on a snag or something. We fixed up a short forked stick to hang the old lantern on; because we must always light the lantern whenever we see a steamboat coming down stream, to keep from getting run over; but we wouldn't have to light it for upstream boats unless we see

we was in what they call a "crossing;" for the river was pretty high
yet, very low banks being still a little under water; so up-bound
boats didn't always run the channel, but hunted easy water.

This second night we run between seven and eight hours, with a
current that was making over four mile an hour. We catched fish,
and talked, and we took a swim now and then to keep off sleepiness.
It was kind of solemn, drifting down the big still river, laying on our
backs looking up at the stars, and we didn't ever feel like talking
loud, and it warn't often that we laughed, only a little kind of low
chuckle. We had mighty good weather, as a general thing, and
nothing ever happened to us at all, that night, nor the next, nor the
next.

Every night we passed towns, some of them away up on black
hillsides, nothing but just a shiny bed of lights, not a house could
you see. The fifth night we passed St. Louis, and it was like the
whole world lit up. In St. Petersburg they used to say there was
twenty or thirty thousand people in St. Louis, but I never believed
it till I see that wonderful spread of lights at two o'clock that still
night. There warn't a sound there; everybody was asleep.

Every night, now, I used to slip ashore, towards ten o'clock, at
some little village, and buy ten or fifteen cents' worth of meal or
bacon or other stuff to eat; and sometimes I lifted a chicken that
warn't roosting comfortable, and took him along. Pap always said,
take a chicken when you get a chance, because if you don't want
him yourself you can easy find somebody that does, and a good deed
ain't ever forgot. I never see pap when he didn't want the chicken
himself, but that is what he used to say, anyway.

Mornings, before daylight, I slipped into corn fields and borrowed
a watermelon, or a mush-melon, or a punkin, or some new corn, or
things of that kind. Pap always said it warn't no harm to borrow
things, if you was meaning to pay them back, sometime; but the
widow said it warn't anything but a soft name for stealing, and no
decent body would do it. Jim said he reckoned the widow was partly
right and pap was partly right; so the best way would be for us to
pick out two or three things from the list and say we wouldn't borrow
them anymore—then he reckoned it wouldn't be no harm to borrow
the others. So we talked it over all one night, drifting along down the
river, trying to make up our minds whether to drop the watermelons,
or the cantelopes, or the mushmelons, or what. But towards daylight
we got it all settled satisfactory, and concluded to drop crabapples
and p'simmons. We warn't feeling just right, before that, but it was
all comfortable now. I was glad the way it come out, too, because
crabapples ain't ever good, and the p'simmons wouldn't be ripe for
two or three months yet.

We shot a water-fowl, now and then, that got up too early in the
morning or didn't go to bed early enough in the evening. Take it
all around, we lived pretty high.

The fifth night below St. Louis we had a big storm after midnight, with a power of thunder and lightning, and the rain poured down in a solid sheet. We stayed in the wigwam and let the raft take care of itself. When the lightning glared out we could see a big straight river ahead, and high rocky bluffs on both sides. By-and-by says I, "Hel-*lo,* Jim, looky yonder!" It was a steamboat that had killed herself on a rock. We was drifting straight down for her. The lightning showed her very distinct. She was leaning over, with part of her upper deck above water, and you could see every little chimbly-guy clean and clear, and a chair by the big bell, with an old slouch hat hanging on the back of it when the flashes come.

Well, it being away in the night, and stormy, and all so mysterious-like, I felt just the way any other boy would a felt when I see that wreck laying there so mournful and lonesome in the middle of the river. I wanted to get aboard of her and slink around a little, and see what there was there. So I says:

"Le's land on her, Jim."

But Jim was dead against it, at first. He says:

"I doan' want to go fool'n 'long er no wrack. We's doin' blame' well, en we better let blame' well alone, as de good book says. Like as not dey's a watchman on dat wrack.'

"Watchman your grandmother," I says; "there ain't nothing to watch but the texas and the pilot-house; and do you reckon anybody's going to resk his life for a texas and a pilot-house such a night as this, when it's likely to break up and wash off down the river any minute?" Jim couldn't say nothing to that, so he didn't try. "And besides," I says, "we might borrow something worth having, out of the captain's stateroom. Seegars, *I* bet you—and cost five cents apiece, solid cash. Steamboat captains is always rich, and get sixty dollars a month, and *they* don't care a cent what a thing costs, you know, long as they want it. Stick a candle in your pocket; I can't rest, Jim, till we give her a rummaging. Do you reckon Tom Sawyer would ever go by this thing? Not for pie, he wouldn't. He'd call it an adventure—that's what he'd call it; and he'd land on that wreck if it was his last act. And wouldn't he throw style into it?—wouldn't he spread himself, nor nothing? Why, you'd think it was Christopher C'lumbus discovering Kingdom-Come. I wish Tom Sawyer *was* here."

Jim he grumbled a little, but give in. He said we mustn't talk any more than we could help, and then talk mighty low. The lightning showed us the wreck again, just in time, and we fetched the starboard derrick, and made fast there.

The deck was high out, here. We went sneaking down the slope of it to labboard, in the dark, towards the texas, feeling our way slow with our feet, and spreading our hands out to fend off the guys, for it was so dark we couldn't see no sign of them. Pretty soon we struck the forward end of the skylight, and clumb onto it; and the next step fetched us in front of the captain's door, which was open, and by Jimminy, away down through the texas-hall we see a light! and all in the same second we seem to hear low voices in yonder!

Jim whispered and said he was feeling powerful sick, and told me to come along. I says, all right; and was going to start for the raft; but just then I heard a voice wail out and say:

"Oh, please don't, boys; I swear I won't ever tell!"

Another voice said, pretty loud:

"It's a lie, Jim Turner. You've acted this way before. You always want more'n your share of the truck, and you've always got it, too, because you've swore 't if you didn't you'd tell. But this time you've said it jest one time too many. You're the meanest, treacherousest hound in this country."

By this time Jim was gone for the raft. I was just a-biling with curiosity; and I says to myself, Tom Sawyer wouldn't back out now, and so I won't either; I'm agoing to see what's going on here. So I dropped on my hands and knees, in the little passage, and crept aft in the dark, till there warn't but about one stateroom betwixt me and the cross-hall of the texas. Then, in there I see a man stretched on the floor and tied hand and foot, and two men standing over him, and one of them had a dim lantern in his hand, and the other one had a pistol. This one kept pointing the pistol at the man's head on the floor and saying—

"I'd *like* to! And I orter, too, a mean skunk!"

The man on the floor would shrivel up, and say: "Oh, please don't, Bill—I hain't ever goin' to tell."

And every time he said that, the man with the lantern would laugh, and say:

" 'Deed you *ain't!* You never said no truer thing 'n that, you bet you." And once he said: "Hear him beg! and yit if we hadn't got the best of him and tied him, he'd a killed us both. And what *for?* Jist for noth'n. Jist because we stood on our *rights*—that's what for. But I lay you ain't agoin' to threaten nobody any more, Jim Turner. Put *up* that pistol, Bill."

Bill says:

"I don't want to, Jake Packard. I'm for killin' him—and didn't he kill old Hatfield jist the same way—and don't he deserve it?"

"But I don't *want* him killed, and I've got my reasons for it."

"Bless yo' heart for them words, Jake Packard! I'll never forgit you, long's I live!" says the man on the floor, sort of blubbering.

Packard didn't take no notice of that, but hung up his lantern on a nail, and started towards where I was, there in the dark, and motioned Bill to come. I crawfished as fast as I could, about two yards, but the boat slanted so that I couldn't make very good time; so to keep from getting run over and catched I crawled into a stateroom on the upper side. The man came a-pawing along in the dark, and when Packard got to my stateroom, he says:

"Here—come in here."

And in he come, and Bill after him. But before they got in, I was up in the upper berth, cornered, and sorry I come. Then they stood there, with their hands on the ledge of the berth, and talked. I couldn't see them, but I could tell where they was, by the whisky they'd been having. I was glad I didn't drink whisky; but it wouldn't made much difference, anyway, because most of the time they couldn't a treed me because I didn't breathe. I was too scared. And besides, a body *couldn't* breathe, and hear such talk. They talked low and earnest. Bill wanted to kill Turner. He says:

"He's said he'll tell, and he will. If we was to give both our shares to him *now*, it wouldn't make no difference after the row, and the way we've served him. Shore's you're born, he'll turn State's evidence; now you hear *me*. I'm for putting him out of his troubles."

"So'm I," says Packard, very quiet.

"Blame it, I'd sorter begun to think you wasn't. Well, then, that's all right. Les' go and do it."

"Hold on a minute; I hain't had my say yit. You listen to me. Shooting's good, but there's quieter ways if the thing's *got* to be done. But what *I* say, is this; it ain't good sense to go court'n around after a halter, if you can git at what you're up to in some way that's jist as good and at the same time don't bring you into no resks. Ain't that so?"

"You bet it is. But how you goin' to manage it this time?"

"Well, my idea is this: we'll rustle around and gether up whatever pickins we've overlooked in the staterooms, and shove for shore and hide the truck. Then we'll wait. Now I say it ain't agoin' to be more'n two hours befo' this wrack breaks up and washes off down the river. See? He'll be drownded, and won't have nobody to blame for it but his own self. I reckon that's a considerble sight better'n killin' of him. I'm unfavorable to killin' a man as long as you can git around it; it ain't good sense, it ain't good morals. Ain't I right?"

"Yes—I reck'n you are. But s'pose she *don't* break up and wash off?"

"Well, we can wait the two hours, anyway, and see, can't we?"

"All right, then; come along."

So they started, and I lit out, all in a cold sweat, and scrambled forward. It was dark as pitch there; but I said in a kind of a coarse whisper, "Jim!" and he answered up, right at my elbow, with a sort of a moan, and I says:

"Quick, Jim, it ain't no time for fooling around and moaning; there's a gang of murderers in yonder, and if we don't hunt up their boat and set her drifting down the river so these fellows can't get away from the wreck, there's one of 'em going to be in a bad fix. But if we find their boat we can put *all* of 'em in a bad fix—for the Sheriff'll get 'em. Quick—hurry! I'll hunt the labboard side, you hunt the stabboard. You start at the raft, and—"

"Oh, my lordy, lordy! *Raf'*? Dey ain' no raf' no mo', she done broke loose en gone!—'en here we is!"

CHAPTER XIII

Well, I catched my breath and most fainted. Shut up on a wreck with such a gang as that! But it warn't no time to be sentimentering. We'd *got* to find that boat, now—had to have it for ourselves. So we went a-quaking and shaking down the stabboard side, and slow work it was, too—seemed a week before we got to the stern. No sign of a boat. Jim said he didn't believe he could go any further—so scared he hadn't hardly any strength left, he said. But I said come on, if we get left on this wreck, we are in a fix, sure. So on we prowled, again. We struck for the stern of the texas, and found it, and then scrabbled along forwards on the skylight, hanging on from shutter to shutter, for the edge of the skylight was in the water. When we got pretty close to the cross-hall door, there was the skiff, sure enough! I could just barely see her. I felt ever so thankful. In another second I would a been aboard of her; but just then the door opened. One of the men stuck his head out, only about a couple of foot from me, and I thought I was gone; but he jerked it in again, and says:

"Heave that blame lantern out o' sight, Bill!"

He flung a bag of something into the boat, and then got in himself, and set down. It was Packard. Then Bill *he* come out and got in. Packard says, in a low voice:

"All ready—shove off!"

I couldn't hardly hang onto the shutters, I was so weak. But Bill says:

"Hold on—'d you go through him?"

"No. Didn't you?"

"No. So he's got his share o' the cash, yet."

"Well, then, come along—no use to take truck and leave money."

"Say—won't he suspicion what we're up to?"

"Maybe he won't. But we got to have it anyway. Come along."

So they got out and went in.

The door slammed to, because it was on the careened side; and in a half second I was in the boat, and Jim come a tumbling after me. I out with my knife and cut the rope, and away we went!

We didn't touch an oar, and we didn't speak nor whisper, nor hardly even breathe. We went gliding swift along, dead silent, past the tip of the paddlebox, and past the stern; then in a second or two more we was a hundred yards below the wreck, and the darkness soaked her up, every last sign of her, and we was safe, and knowed it.

When we was three or four hundred yards down stream, we see

the lantern show like a little spark at the texas door, for a second,
and we knowed by that that the rascals had missed their boat, and
was beginning to understand that they was in just as much trouble,
now, as Jim Turner was.

Then Jim manned the oars, and we took out after our raft. Now
was the first time that I begun to worry about the men—I reckon
I hadn't had time to before. I begun to think how dreadful it was,
even for murderers, to be in such a fix. I says to myself, there ain't
no telling but I might come to be a murderer myself, yet, and then
how would *I* like it? So says I to Jim:

"The first light we see, we'll land a hundred yards below it or
above it, in a place where it's a good hiding-place for you and the
skiff, and then I'll go and fix up some kind of a yarn, and get
somebody to go for that gang and get them out of their scrape, so
they can be hung when their time comes."

But that idea was a failure; for pretty soon it begun to storm
again, and this time worse than ever. The rain poured down, and
never a light showed; everybody in bed, I reckon. We boomed along
down the river, watching for lights and watching for our raft. After
a long time the rain let up, but the clouds staid, and the lightning
kept whimpering, and by-and-by a flash showed us a black thing
ahead, floating, and we made for it.

It was the raft, and mighty glad was we to get aboard of it again.
We seen a light, now, away down to the right, on shore. So I said
I would go for it. The skiff was half full of plunder which that gang
had stole, there on the wreck. We hustled it onto the raft in a pile,
and I told Jim to float along down, and show a light when he judged
he had gone about two mile, and keep it burning till I come; then I
manned my oars and shoved for the light. As I got down towards
it, three or four more showed—up on a hillside. It was a village. I
closed in above the shore-light, and laid on my oars and floated.
As I went by, I see it was a lantern hanging on the jackstaff of a
double-hull ferry-boat. I skimmed around for the watchman,
a-wondering whereabouts he slept; and by-and-by I found him
roosting on the bitts, forward, with his head down between his
knees. I give his shoulder two or three little shoves, and begun to cry.

He stirred up, in a kind of a startlish way; but when he see it was
only me, he took a good gap and stretch, and then he says:

"Hello, what's up? Don't cry, bub. What's the trouble?"

I says:

"Pap, and mam, and sis, and—"

Then I broke down. He says:

"Oh, dang it, now, *don't* take on so, we all has to have our
troubles and this'n 'll come out all right. What's the matter with
'em?"

"They're—they're—are you the watchman of the boat?"

"Yes," he says, kind of pretty-well-satisfied like. "I'm the captain and the owner, and the mate, and the pilot, and watchman, and head deck-hand; and sometimes I'm the freight and passengers. I ain't as rich as old Jim Hornback, and I can't be so blame' generous and good to Tom, Dick and Harry as what he is, and slam around money the way he does; but I've told him a many a time 't I wouldn't trade places with him; for, says I, a sailor's life's the life for me, and I'm derned if *I'd* live two mile out o' town, where there ain't nothing ever goin' on, not for all his spondulicks and as much more on top of it. Says I—"

I broke in and says:

"They're in an awful peck of trouble, and——"

"*Who* is?"

"Why, pap, and mam, and sis, and Miss Hooker; and if you'd take your ferry-boat and go up there——"

"Up where? Where are they?"

"On the wreck."

"What wreck?"

"Why, there ain't but one."

"What, you don't mean the *Walter Scott?*"

"Yes."

"Good land! what are they doin' *there,* for gracious sakes?"

"Well, they didn't go there a-purpose."

"I bet they didn't! Why, great goodness, there ain't no chance for 'em if they don't git off mighty quick! Why, how in the nation did they ever git into such a scrape?"

"Easy enough. Miss Hooker was a-visiting, up there to the town——"

"Yes, Booth's Landing—go on."

"She was a-visiting, there at Booth's Landing, and just in the edge of the evening she started over with her nigger woman in the horse-ferry, to stay all night at her friend's house, Miss What-you-may-call-her, I disremember her name, and they lost their steering-oar, and swung around and went a-floating down, stern-first, about two mile, and saddle-baggsed on the wreck, and the ferry man and the nigger woman and the horses was all lost, but Miss Hooker she made a grab and got aboard the wreck. Well, about an hour after dark, we come along down in our trading-scow, and it was so dark we didn't notice the wreck till we was right on it; and so *we* saddle-baggsed; but all of us was saved but Bill Whipple—and oh, he *was* the best cretur!—I most wish't it had been me, I do."

"My George! It's the beatenest thing I ever struck. And *then* what did you all do."

"Well, we hollered and took on, but it's so wide there, we couldn't make nobody hear. So pap said somebody got to get ashore and get help somehow. I was the only one that could swim, so I made a dash for it, and Miss Hooker she said if I didn't strike help sooner, come here and hunt up her uncle, and he'd fix the thing. I made the land

about a mile below, and been fooling along ever since, trying to get
people to do something, but they said, 'What, in such a night and
such a current? there ain't no sense in it; go for the steam-ferry.'
Now if you'll go, and——"

"By Jackson, I'd *like* to, and blame it I don't know but I will;
but who is the dingnation's agoin' to *pay* for it? Do you reckon your
pap——"

"Why *that's* all right. Miss Hooker she told me, *particular,*
that her uncle Hornback——"

"Great guns! is *he* her uncle? Looky here, you break for that
light over yonder-way, and turn out west when you git there, and
about a quarter of a mile out you'll come to the tavern; tell 'em to
dart you out to Jim Hornback's and he'll foot the bill. And don't
you fool around any, because he'll want to know the news. Tell him
I'll have his niece all safe before he can get to town. Hump yourself,
now; I'm agoing up around the corner here, to roust out my
engineer."

I struck for the light, but as soon as he turned the corner I went
back and got into my skiff and bailed her out and then pulled up
shore in the easy water about six hundred yards, and tucked myself
in among some woodboats; for I couldn't rest easy till I could see the
ferry-boat start. But take it all around, I was feeling ruther
comfortable on accounts of taking all this trouble for that gang,
for not many would a done it. I wished the widow knowed about
it. I judged she would be proud of me for helping these rapscallions,
because rapscallions and dead beats is the kind the widow and
good people takes the most interest in.

Well, before long, here comes the wreck, dim and dusky, sliding
along down! A kind of cold shiver went through me, and then I
struck out for her. She was very deep, and I see in a minute there
warn't much chance for anybody being alive in her. I pulled all
around her and hollered a little, but there wasn't any answer; all
dead still. I felt a little bit heavy-hearted about the gang, but not
much, for I reckoned if they could stand it, I could.

Then here comes the ferry-boat; so I shoved for the middle of the
river on a long down-stream slant; and when I judged I was out of
eye-reach, I laid on my oars, and looked back and see her go and
smell around the wreck for Miss Hooker's remainders, because the
captain would know her uncle Hornback would want them; and
then pretty soon the ferry-boat give it up and went for shore, and I
laid into my work and went a-booming down the river.

It did seem a powerful long time before Jim's light showed up;
and when it did show, it looked like it was a thousand mile off. By
the time I got there the sky was beginning to get a little gray in the
east; so we struck for an island, and hid the raft, and sunk the skiff,
and turned in and slept like dead people.

CHAPTER XIV

By-and-by, when we got up, we turned over the truck the gang had stole off of the wreck, and found boots, and blankets, and clothes, and all sorts of other things, and a lot of books, and a spyglass, and three boxes of seegars. We hadn't ever been this rich before, in neither of our lives. The seegars was prime. We laid off all the afternoon in the woods talking, and me reading the books, and having a general good time. I told Jim all about what happened inside the wreck, and at the ferry-boat; and I said these kinds of things was adventures; but he said he didn't want no more adventures. He said that when I went in the texas and he crawled back to get on the raft and found her gone, he nearly died; because he judged it was all up with *him,* anyway it could be fixed; for if he didn't get saved he would get drownded; and if he did get saved, whoever saved him would send him back home so as to get the reward, and then Miss Watson would sell him South, sure. Well, he was right; he was most always right; he had an uncommon level head, for a nigger.

I read considerable to Jim about kings, and dukes, and earls, and such, and how gaudy they dressed, and how much style they put on, and called each other your majesty, and your grace, and your lordship, and so on, 'stead of mister; and Jim's eyes bugged out, and he was interested. He says:

"I didn' know dey was so many un um. I hain't hearn 'bout none un um, skasely, but ole King Sollermun, onless you counts dem kings dat's in a pack er k'yards. How much do a king git?"

"Get?" I says; "why, they get a thousand dollars a month if they want it; they can have just as much as they want; everything belongs to them."

"*Ain'* dat gay? En what dey got to do, Huck?"

"*They* don't do nothing! Why how you talk. They just set around."

"No—is dat so?"

"Of course it is. They just set around. Except maybe when there's a war; then they go to the war. But other times they just lazy around; or go hawking—just hawking and sp— Sh!—d'you hear a noise?"

We skipped out and looked; but it warn't nothing but the flutter of a steamboat's wheel, away down coming around the point; so we come back.

"Yes," says I, "and other times, when things is dull, they fuss with the parlyment; and if everybody don't go just so he v their heads off. But mostly they hang round the harem."

"Roun' de which?"

"Harem."

"What's de harem?"

"The place where he keep his wives. Don't you know a

harem? Solomon had one; he had about a million wives."

"Why, yes, dat's so; I—I'd done forgot it. A harem's a bo'd'n-house, I reck'n. Mos' likely dey has rackety times in de nussery. En I reck'n de wives quarrels considable; en dat 'crease de racket. Yit dey say Sollermun de wises' man dat ever live'. I doan' take no stock in dat. Bekase why: would a wise man want to live in de mids' er sich a blimblammin' all de time? No—'deed he wouldn't. A wise man 'ud take en buil' a biler-factry; en den he could shet *down* de biler-factry when he want to res'."

"Well, but he *was* the wisest man, anyway; because the widow she told me so, her own self."

"I doan k'yer what de widder say, he *warn't* no wise man, nuther. He had some er de dad-fetchedes' ways I ever see. Does you know 'bout dat chile dat he 'uz gwyne to chop in two?"

"Yes, the widow told me all about it."

"*Well*, den! Warn' dat de beatenes' notion in de worl'? You jes' take en look at it a minute. Dah's de stump, dah—dat's one er de women; heah's you—dat's de yuther one; I's Sollermun; en dish-yer dollar bill's de chile. Bofe un you claims it. What does I do? Does I shin aroun' mongs' de neighbors en fine out which un you de bill *do* b'long to, en han' it over to de right one, all safe en soun', de way dat anybody dat had any gumption would? No—I take en whack de bill in *two,* en give half un it to you, en de yuther half to de yuther woman. Dat's de way Sollermun was gwyne to do wid de chile. Now I want to ast you: what's de use er dat half a bill?—can't buy noth'n wid it. En what use is a half a chile? I would'n give a dern for a million un um."

"But hang it, Jim, you've clean missed the point—blame it, you've missed it a thousand mile."

"Who? Me? Go 'long. Doan' talk to *me* 'bout yo' pints. I reck'n I knows sense when I sees it; en dey ain' no sense in sich doin's as dat. De 'spute warn't 'bout a half a chile, de 'spute was 'bout a whole chile; en de man dat think he kin settle a 'spute 'bout a whole chile wid a half a chile, doan' know enough to come in out'n de rain. Doan' talk to me 'bout Sollermun, Huck, I knows him by de back."

"But I tell you you don't get the point."

"Blame de pint! I reck'n I knows what I knows. En mine you, de *real* pint is down furder—it's down deeper. It lays in de way Sollermun was raised. You take a man dat's got on'y one er two chillen; is dat man gwyne to be waseful o' chillen? No, he ain't; he can't 'ford it. *He* know how to value 'em. But you take a man dat's got 'bout five million chillen runnin' roun' de house, en it's diffunt. *He* as soon chop a chile in two as a cat. Dey's plenty mo'. A chile er two, mo' er less, warn't no consekens to Sollermun, dad fetch him!"

I never see such a nigger. If he got a notion in his head once, there 't no getting it out again. He was the most down on Solomon of any nigger I ever see. So I went to talking about other kings, and let Solomon slide. I told about Louis Sixteenth that got his head cut off in France long time age; and about his little boy the dolphin, that would a been a king, but they took and shut him up in jail, and some say he died there.

"Po' little chap."

"But some says he got out and got away, and come to America."

"Dat's good! But he'll be pooty lonesome—dey ain' no kings here, is dey, Huck?"

"No."

"Den he cain't git no situation. What he gwyne to do?"

"Well, I don't know. Some of them gets on the police, and some of them learns people how to talk French."

"Why, Huck, doan' de French people talk de same way we does?"

"*No,* Jim; you couldn't understand a word they said—not a single word."

"Well, now, I be ding-busted! How do dat come?"

"*I* don't know; but it's so. I got some of their jabber out of a book. Spose a man was to come to you and say *Polly-voo-franzy*—what would you think?"

"I wouldn' think nuff'n; I'd take en bust him over de head. Dat is, if he warn't white. I wouldn't 'low no nigger to call me dat."

"Shucks, it ain't calling you anything. It's only saying do you know how to talk French."

"Well, den, why couldn't he *say* it?"

"Why, he *is* a-saying it. That's a Frenchman's *way* of saying it."

"Well, it's a blame' ridicklous way, en I doan' want to hear no mo' 'bout it. Dey ain' no sense in it."

"Looky here, Jim; does a cat talk like we do?"

"No, a cat don't."

"Well, does a cow?"

"No, a cow don't, nuther."

"Does a cat talk like a cow, or a cow talk like a cat?"

"No, dey don't."

"It's natural and right for 'em to talk different from each other, ain't it?"

"Course."

"And ain't it natural and right for a cat and a cow to talk different from *us?*"

"Why, mos' sholy it is."

"Well, then, why ain't it natural and right for a *Frenchman* to talk different from us? You answer me that."

"Is a cat a man, Huck?"

"No."

"Well, den, dey ain't no sense in a cat talkin' like a man. Is a cow a man?—er is a cow a cat?"

"No, she ain't either of them."

"Well, den, she ain' got no business to talk like either one er the yuther of 'em. Is a Frenchman a man?"

"Yes."

"Well, den! Dad blame it, why doan' he *talk* like a man? You answer me *dat!"*

I see it warn't no use wasting words—you can't learn a nigger to argue. So I quit.

CHAPTER XV

We judged that three nights more would fetch us to Cairo, at the bottom of Illinois, where the Ohio River comes in, and that was what we was after. We would sell the raft and get on a steamboat and go way up the Ohio amongst the free States, and then be out of trouble.

Well, the second night a fog begun to come on, and we made for a tow-head to tie to, for it wouldn't do to try to run in fog; but when I paddled ahead in the canoe, with the line, to make fast, there warn't anything but little saplings to tie to. I passed the line around one of them right on the edge of the cut bank, but there was a stiff current, and the raft come booming down so lively she tore it out by the roots and away she went. I see the fog closing down, and it made me so sick and scared I couldn't budge for most a half a minute it seemed to me—and then there warn't no raft in sight; you couldn't see twenty yards. I jumped into the canoe and run back to the stern and grabbed the paddle and set her back a stroke. But she didn't come. I was in such a hurry I hadn't untied her. I got up and tried to untie her, but I was so excited my hands shook so I couldn't hardly do anything with them.

As soon as I got started I took out after the raft, hot and heavy, right down the tow-head. That was all right as far as it went, but the tow-head warn't sixty yards long, and the minute I flew by the foot of it I shot out into the solid white fog, and hadn't no more idea which way I was going than a dead man.

Thinks I, it won't do to paddle; first I know I'll run into the bank or a tow-head or something; I got to set still and float, and yet it's mighty fidgety business to have to hold your hands still at such a time. I whooped and listened. Away down there, somewheres, I hears a small whoop, and up comes my spirits. I went tearing after it, listening sharp to hear it again. The next time it come, I see I warn't heading for it but heading away to the right of it. And the next time, I was heading away to the left of it—and not gaining on it much, either, for I was flying around, this way and that and 'tother, but it was going straight ahead all the time.

I did wish the fool would think to beat a tin pan, and beat it all the time, but he never did, and it was the still places between the whoops that was making the trouble for me. Well, I fought along, and directly I hears the whoop *behind* me. I was tangled good, now. That was somebody else's whoop, or else I was turned around.

I throwed the paddle down. I heard the whoop again; it was behind me yet, but in a different place; it kept coming, and kept changing its place, and I kept answering, till by-and-by it was in front of me again and I knowed the current had swung the canoe's head down stream and I was all right, if that was Jim and not some other raftsman hollering. I couldn't tell nothing about voices in a fog; for nothing don't look natural nor sound natural in a fog.

The whooping went on, and in about a minute I come a booming down on a cut bank with smoky ghosts of big trees on it, and the current throwed me off to the left and shot by, amongst a lot of snags that fairly roared, the current was tearing by them so swift.

In another second or two it was solid white and still again. I set perfectly still, then, listening to my heart thump, and I reckon I didn't draw a breath while it thumped a hundred.

I just give up, then. I knowed what the matter was. That cut bank was an island, and Jim had gone down 'tother side of it. It warn't no tow-head, that you could float by in ten minutes. It had the big timber of a regular island; it might be five or six mile long and more than a half a mile wide.

I kept quiet, with my ears cocked, about fifteen minutes, I reckon. I was floating along, of course, four or five mile an hour; but you don't ever think of that. No, you *feel* like you are laying dead still on the water; and if a little glimpse of a snag slips by, you don't think to yourself how fast *you're* going, but you catch your breath and think, my! how that snag's tearing along. If you think it ain't dismal and lonesome out in a fog that way, by yourself, in the night, you try it once—you'll see.

Next, for about a half an hour, I whoops now and then; at last I hears the answer a long ways off, and tries to follow it, but I couldn't do it, and directly I judged I'd got into a nest of tow-heads, for I had little dim glimpses of them on both sides of me, sometimes just a narrow channel between; and some that I couldn't see, I knowed was there, because I'd hear the wash of the current against the old dead brush and trash that hung over the banks. Well, I warn't long losing the whoops, down amongst the tow-heads; and I only tried to chase them a little while, anyway, because it was worse than chasing a Jack-o-lantern. You never knowed a sound dodge around so, and swap places so quick and so much.

I had to claw away from the bank pretty lively, four or five times, to keep from knocking the islands out of the river; and so I judged the raft must be butting into the bank every now and then, or else it would get further ahead and clear out of hearing—it was floating a little faster than what I was.

Well, I seemed to be in the open river again, by-and-by, but I couldn't hear no sign of a whoop nowheres. I reckoned Jim had fetched up on a snag, maybe, and it was all up with him. I was good and tired, so I laid down in the canoe and said I wouldn't bother no more. I didn't want to go to sleep, of course; but I was so sleepy I couldn't help it; so I thought I would take just one little cat-nap.

But I reckon it was more than a cat-nap, for when I waked up the stars was shining bright, the fog was all gone, and I was spinning down a big bend stern first. First I didn't know where I was; I thought I was dreaming; and when things begun to come back to me, they seemed to come up dim out of last week.

It was a monstrous big river here, with the tallest and the thickest kind of timber on both banks; just a solid wall, as well as I could see, by the stars. I looked away down stream, and seen a black speck on the water. I took out after it; but when I got to it it warn't nothing but a couple of saw-logs made fast together. Then I see another speck, and chased that; then another, and this time I was right. It was the raft.

When I got to it Jim was setting there with his head down between his knees, asleep, with his right arm hanging over the steering oar. The other oar was smashed off, and the raft was littered up with leaves and branches and dirt. So she'd had a rough time.

I made fast and laid down under Jim's nose on the raft, and begun to gap, and stretch my fists out against Jim, and says:

"Hello, Jim, have I been asleep? Why didn't you stir me up?"

"Goodness gracious, is dat you, Huck? En you ain' dead—you ain' drownded—you's back agin? It's too good for true, honey, it's too good for true. Lemme look at you, chile, lemme feel o' you. No, you ain' dead! you's back agin,' live en soun', jis de same old Huck—de same ole Huck, thanks to goodness!"

"What's the matter with you, Jim? You been a drinking?"

"Drinkin'? Has I ben a drinkin'? Has I had a chance to be a drinkin'?"

"Well, then, what makes you talk so wild?"

"How does I talk wild?"

"*How?* why, hain't you been talking about my coming back, and all that stuff, as if I'd been gone away?"

"Huck—Huck Finn, you look me in de eye; look me in de eye. *Hain't* you ben gone away?"

"Gone away? Why, what in the nation do you mean? *I* hain't been gone anywheres. Where would I go to?"

"Well, looky here, boss, dey's sumf'n wrong, dey is. Is I *me,* or who *is* I? Is I heah, or whah *is* I? Now dat's what I wants to know?"

"Well, I think you're here, plain enough, but I think you're a tangle-headed old fool, Jim."

"I is, is I? Well you answer me dis. Didn't you tote out de line in de canoe, fer to make fas' to de tow-head?"

"No, I didn't. What tow-head? I hain't seen no tow-head."

"You hain't seen no tow-head? Looky here—didn't de line pull

loose en de raf' go a hummin' down de river, en leave you en de
canoe behine in de fog?"

"What fog?"

"Why *de* fog. De fog dat's ben aroun' all night. En didn't you
whoop, en didn't I whoop, tell we got mix' up in de islands en one un
us got los' en 'tother one was jis' as good as los', 'kase he didn'
know whah he wuz? En didn't I bust up agin a lot er dem islands
en have a turrible time en mos' git drownded? Now ain' dat so,
boss—ain't it so? You answer me dat."

"Well, this is too many for me, Jim. I hain't seen no fog, nor no
islands, nor no troubles, nor nothing. I been setting here talking
with you all night till you went to sleep about ten minutes ago, and
I reckon I done the same. You couldn't a got drunk in that time,
so of course you've been dreaming."

"Dad fetch it, how is I gwyne to dream all dat in ten minutes?"

"Well, hang it all, you did dream it, because there didn't any
of it happen."

"But Huck, it's all jis' as plain to me as——"

"It don't make no difference how plain it is, there ain't nothing
in it. I know, because I've been here all the time."

Jim didn't say nothing for about five minutes, but set there
studying over it. Then he says:

"Well, den, I reck'n I did dream it, Huck; but dog my cats ef
it ain't de powerfullest dream I ever see. En I hain't ever had no
dream b'fo' dat's tired me like dis one."

"Oh, well, that's all right, because a dream does tire a body like
everything, sometimes. But this one was a staving dream—tell me
all about it, Jim."

So Jim went to work and told me the whole thing right through,
just as it happened, only he painted it up considerable. Then he said
he must start in and " 'terpret" it, because it was sent for a warning.
He said the first tow-head stood for a man that would try to do
us some good, but the current was another man that would get us
away from him. The whoops was warnings that would come to us
every now and then, and if we didn't try hard to make out to
understand them they'd just take us into bad luck, 'stead of keeping
us out of it. The lot of tow-heads was troubles we was going to get
into with quarrelsome people and all kinds of mean folks, but if
we minded our business and didn't talk back and aggravate them,
we would pull through and get out of the fog and into the big clear
river, which was the free States, and wouldn't have no more trouble.

It had clouded up pretty dark just after I got onto the raft, but it
was clearing up again, now.

"Oh, well, that's all interpreted well enough, as far as it goes,
Jim," I says; "but what does *these* things stand for?"

It was the leaves and rubbish on the raft, and the smashed oar.
You could see them first rate, now.

Jim looked at the trash, and then looked at me, and back at the trash again. He had got the dream fixed so strong in his head that he couldn't seem to shake it loose and get the facts back into its place again, right away. But when he did get the thing straightened around, he looked at me steady, without ever smiling, and says:

"What do dey stan' for? I's gwyne to tell you. When I got all wore out wid work, en wid de callin' for you, en went to sleep, my heart wuz mos' broke bekase you wuz los', en I didn' k'yer no mo' what become er me en de raf'. En when I wake up en fine you back agin', all safe en soun', de tears come en I could a got down on my knees en kiss' yo' foot I's so thankful. En all you wuz thinkin 'bout wuz how you could make a fool uv old Jim wid a lie. Dat truck dah is *trash*; en trash is what people is dat puts dirt on de head er dey fren's en makes 'em ashamed."

Then he got up slow, and walked to the wigwam, and went in there, without saying anything but that. But that was enough. It made me feel so mean I could almost kissed *his* foot to get him to take it back.

It was fifteen minutes before I could work myself up to go and humble myself to a nigger—but I done it, and I warn't ever sorry for it afterwards, neither. I didn't do him no more mean tricks, and I wouldn't done that one if I'd a knowed it would make him feel that way.

CHAPTER XVI

We slept most all day, and started out at night, a little ways behind a monstrous long raft that was as long going by as a procession. She had four long sweeps at each end, so we judged she carried as many as thirty men, likely. She had five big wig-wams aboard, wide apart, and an open camp fire in the middle, and a tall flag-pole at each end. There was a power of style about her. It *amounted* to something being a raftsman on such a craft as that.

We went drifting down into a big bend, and the night clouded up and got hot. The river was very wide, and was walled with solid timber on both sides; you couldn't see a break in it hardly ever, or a light. We talked about Cairo, and wondered whether we would know it when we got to it. I said likely we wouldn't, because I had heard say there warn't but about a dozen houses there, and if they didn't happen to have them lit up, how was we going to know we was passing a town? Jim said if the two big rivers joined together there, that would show. But I said maybe we might think we was passing the foot of an island and coming into the same old river again. That disturbed Jim—and me too. So the question was, what to do? I said, paddle ashore the first time a light showed, and tell them pap was behind, coming along with a trading-scow, and was a green hand at the business, and wanted to know how far it was to

Cairo. Jim thought it was a good idea, so we took a smoke on it and waited.

There warn't nothing to do, now, but to look out sharp for the town, and not pass it without seeing it. He said he'd be mighty sure to see it, because he'd be a free man the minute he seen it, but if he missed it he'd be in the slave country again and no more show for freedom. Every little while he jumps up and says:

"Dah she is!"

But it warn't. It was Jack-o-lanterns, or lightning-bugs; so he set down again, and went to watching, same as before. Jim said it made him all over trembly and feverish to be so close to freedom. Well, I can tell you it made me all over trembly and feverish, too, to hear him, because I begun to get it through my head that he *was* most free—and who was to blame for it? Why, *me.* I couldn't get that out of my conscience, no how nor no way. It got to troubling me so I couldn't rest; I couldn't stay still in one place. It hadn't ever come home to me before, what this thing was that I was doing. But now it did; and it staid with me, and scorched me more and more. I tried to make out to myself that *I* warn't to blame, because *I* didn't run Jim off from his rightful owner; but it warn't no use, conscience up and says, every time, "But you knowed he was running for his freedom, and you could a paddled ashore and told somebody." That was so—I couldn't get around that, noway. That was where it pinched. Conscience says to me, "What had poor Miss Watson done to you, that you could see her nigger go off right under your eyes and never say one single word? What did that poor old woman do to you, that you could treat her so mean? Why, she tried to learn you your book, she tried to learn you your manners, she tried to be good to you every way she knowed how. *That's* what she done."

I got to feeling so mean and so miserable I most wished I was dead. I fidgeted up and down the raft, abusing myself to myself, and Jim was fidgeting up and down past me. We neither of us could keep still. Every time he danced around and says, "Dah's Cairo!" it went through me like a shot, and I thought if it *was* Cairo I reckoned I would die of miserableness.

Jim talked out loud all the time while I was talking to myself. He was saying how the first thing he would do when he got to a free State he would go to saving up money and never spend a single cent, and when he got enough he would buy his wife, which was owned on a farm close to where Miss Watson lived; and then they would both work to buy the two children, and if their master wouldn't sell them, they'd get an Ab'litionist to go and steal them.

It most froze me to hear such talk. He wouldn't ever dared to talk such talk in his life before. Just see what a difference it made in him the minute he judged he was about free. It was according to the old saying, "give a nigger an inch and he'll take an ell." Thinks I, this is what comes of my not thinking. Here was this nigger which I had as good as helped to run away, coming right out flat-footed and saying he would steal his children—children that belonged to a man I didn't even know; a man that hadn't ever done me no harm.

I was sorry to hear Jim say that, it was such a lowering of him. My conscience got to stirring me up hotter than ever, until at last I says to it. "Let up on me—it ain't too late, yet—I'll paddle ashore at the first light, and tell." I felt easy, and happy, and light as a feather, right off. All my troubles was gone. I went to looking out sharp for a light, and sort of singing to myself. By-and-by one showed. Jim sings out:

"We's safe, Huck, we's safe! Jump up and crack yo' heels, dat's de good ole Cairo at las', I jis knows it!"

I says:

"I'll take the canoe and go see, Jim. It mightn't be, you know."

He jumped and got the canoe ready, and put his old coat in the bottom for me to set on, and give me the paddle; and as I shoved off, he says:

"Pooty soon I'll be a-shout'n for joy, en I'll say, it's all on accounts o' Huck; I's a free man, en I couldn't ever ben free ef it hadn' ben for Huck; Huck done it. Jim won't ever forgit you, Huck; you's de bes' fren' Jim's ever had; en you's de *only* fren' ole Jim's got now."

I was paddling off, all in a sweat to tell on him; but when he says this, it seemed to kind of take the tuck all out of me. I went along slow then, and I warn't right down certain whether I was glad I started or whether I warn't. When I was fifty yards off, Jim says:

"Dah you goes, de ole true Huck; de on'y white genlman dat ever kep' his promise to ole Jim."

Well, I just felt sick. But I says, I *got* to do it—I can't get *out* of it. Right then, along comes a skiff with two men in it, with guns, and they stopped and I stopped. One of them says:

"What's that, yonder?"

"A piece of a raft," I says.

"Do you belong on it?"

"Yes, sir."

"Any men on it?"

"Only one, sir."

"Well, there's five niggers run off to-night, up yonder above the head of the bend. Is your man white or black?"

I didn't answer up prompt. I tried to, but the words wouldn't come. I tried, for a second or two, to brace up and out with it, but I warn't man enough—hadn't the spunk of a rabbit. I see I was weakening; so I just give up trying, and up and says—

"He's white."

"I reckon we'll go and see for ourselves."

"I wish you would," says I, "because it's pap that's there, and maybe you'd help me tow the raft ashore where the light is. He's sick—and so is mam and Mary Ann."

"Oh, the devil! we're in a hurry, boy. But I s'pose we've got to. Come—buckle to you paddle, and let's get along."

I buckled to my paddle and they laid to their oars. When we had made a stroke or two, I says:

"Pap'll be mighty much obleeged to you, I can tell you. Everybody goes away when I want them to help me tow the raft ashore, and I can't do it by myself."

"Well, that's infernal mean. Odd, too. Say, boy, what's the matter with your father?"

"It's the—a—the—well, it ain't anything, much."

They stopped pulling. It warn't but a mighty little ways to the raft now. One says:

"Boy, that's a lie. What *is* the matter with your pap? Answer up square now, and it'll be the better for you."

"I will, sir, I will, honest—but don't leave us, please. It's the—the—gentlemen, if you'll only pull ahead, and let me heave you the head-line, you won't have to come a-near the raft—please do."

"Set her back, John, set her back!" says one. They backed water. "Keep away, boy—keep to looard. Confound it, I just expect the wind has blowed it to us. Your pap's got the small-pox, and you know it precious well. Why didn't you come out and say so? Do you want to spread it all over?"

"Well," says I, a-blubbering, "I've told everybody before, and then they just went away and left us."

"Poor devil, there's something in that. We are right down sorry for you, but we—well, hang it, we don't want the small-pox, you see. Look here, I'll tell you what to do. Don't you try to land by yourself, or you'll smash everything to pieces. You float along down about twenty miles and you'll come to a town on the left-hand side of the river. It will be long after sun-up, then, and when you ask for help, you tell them your folks are all down with chills and fever. Don't be a fool again, and let people guess what is the matter. Now we're trying to do you a kindness; so you just put twenty miles between us, that's a good boy. It wouldn't do any good to land yonder where the light is—it's only a wood-yard. Say—I reckon your father's poor, and I'm bound to say he's in pretty hard luck. Here—I'll put a twenty dollar gold piece on this board, and you get it when it floats by. I feel mighty mean to leave you, but my kingdom! it won't do to fool with small-pox, don't you see?"

"Hold on, Parker," says the other man, "here's a twenty to put on the board for me. Good-bye, boy, you do as Mr. Parker told you, and you'll be all right."

"That's so, my boy—good-bye, good-bye. If you see any runaway niggers, you get help and nab them, and you can make some money by it."

"Good-bye, sir," says I, "I won't let no runaway niggers get by me if I can help it."

They went off, and I got aboard the raft, feeling bad and low, because I knowed very well I had done wrong, and I see it warn't no use for me to try to learn to do right; a body that don't get *started* right when he's little, ain't got no show—when the pinch comes there ain't nothing to back him up and keep him to his work, and so he gets beat. Then I thought a minute, and says to myself, hold on,— s'pose you'd a done right and give Jim up; would you felt better than what you do now? No, says I, I'd feel bad—I'd feel just the same way I do now. Well, then, says I, what's the use you learning to do right, when it's troublesome to do right and ain't no trouble to do wrong, and the wages is just the same? I was stuck. I couldn't answer that. So I reckoned I wouldn't bother no more about it, but after this always do whichever come handiest at the time.

I went into the wigwam; Jim warn't there. I looked all around; he warn't anywhere. I says:

"Jim!"

"Here I is, Huck. Is dey out o' sight yit? Don't talk loud."

He was in the river, under the stern oar, with just his nose out. I told him they was out of sight, so he come aboard. He says:

"I was a-listenin' to all de talk, en I slips into de river en was gwyne to shove for sho' if dey come aboard. Den I was gwyne to swim to de raf' agin when dey was gone. But lawsy, how you did fool 'em, Huck! Dat *wuz* de smartes' dodge! I tell you, chile, I 'speck it save' ole Jim—ole Jim ain't gwyne to forgit you for dat, honey."

Then we talked about the money. It was a pretty good raise, twenty dollars apiece. Jim said we could take deck passage on a steamboat now, and the money would last us as far as we wanted to go in the free States. He said twenty mile more warn't far for the raft to go, but he wished we was already there.

Towards daybreak we tied up, and Jim was mighty particular about hiding the raft good. Then he worked all day fixing things in bundles, and getting all ready to quit rafting.

That night about ten we hove in sight of the lights of a town away down in a left-hand bend.

I went off in the canoe, to ask about it. Pretty soon I found a man out in the river with a skiff, setting a trot-line. I ranged up and says:

"Mister, is that town Cairo?"

"Cairo? no. You must be a blame' fool."

"What town is it, mister?"

"If you want to know, go and find out. If you stay here botherin' around me for about a half a minute longer, you'll get something you won't want."

I paddled to the raft. Jim was awful disappointed, but I said never mind, Cairo would be the next place, I reckoned.

We passed another town before daylight, and I was going out
again; but it was high ground, so I didn't go. No high ground about
Cairo, Jim said. I had forgot it. We laid up for the day, on a
tow-head tolerable close to the left-hand bank. I begun to
suspicion something. So did Jim. I says:

"Maybe we went by Cairo in the fog that night."

He says:

"Doan' less' talk about it, Huck. Po' niggers can't have no luck.
I awluz 'spected dat rattle-snake skin warn't done wid it's work."

"I wish I'd never seen that snake-skin, Jim—I do wish I'd never
laid eyes on it."

"It ain't yo' fault, Huck; you didn' know. Don't you blame
yo'self 'bout it."

When it was daylight, here was the clear Ohio water in shore, sure
enough, and outside was the old regular Muddy! So it was all up
with Cairo.

We talked it all over. It wouldn't do to take to the shore; we
couldn't take the raft up the stream, of course. There warn't no way
but to wait for dark, and start back in the canoe and take the
chances. So we slept all day amongst the cotton-wood thicket, so
as to be fresh for the work, and when we went back to the raft
about dark the canoe was gone!

We didn't say a word for a good while. There warn't anything to
say. We both knowed well enough it was some more work of the
rattle-snake skin; so what was the use to talk about it? It would only
look like we was finding fault, and that would be bound to fetch
more bad luck—and keep on fetching it, too, till we knowed enough
to keep still.

By-and-by we talked about what we better do, and found there
warn't no way but just to go along down with the raft till we got a
chance to buy a canoe to go back in. We warn't going to borrow
it when there warn't anybody around, the way pap would do, for that
might set people after us.

So we shoved out, after dark, on the raft.

Anybody that don't believe yet, that it's foolishness to handle a
snake-skin, after all that snake-skin done for us, will believe it now,
if they read on and see what more it done for us.

The place to buy canoes is off of rafts laying up at shore. But we
didn't see no rafts laying up; so we went along during three hours
and more. Well, the night got gray, and ruther thick, which is the
next meanest thing to fog. You can't tell the shape of the river, and
you can't see no distance. It got to be very late and still, and then
along comes a steamboat up the river. We lit the lantern, and
judged she would see it. Up-stream boats didn't generly come close
to us; they go out and follow the bars and hunt for easy water under
the reefs; but nights like this they bull right up the channel against
the whole river.

We could hear her pounding along, but we didn't see her good till she was close. She aimed right for us. Often they do that and try to see how close they can come without touching; sometimes the wheel bites off a sweep, and then the pilot sticks his head out and laughs, and thinks he's mighty smart. Well, here she comes, and we said she was going to try to shave us; but she didn't seem to be sheering off a bit. She was a big one, and she was coming in a hurry, too, looking like a black cloud with rows of glow-worms around it; but all of a sudden she bulged out, big and scary, with a long row of wide-open furnace doors shining like red-hot teeth, and her monstrous bows and guards hanging right over us. There was a yell at us, and a jingling of bells to stop the engines, a pow-wow of cussing, and whistling of steam—and as Jim went overboard on one side and I on the other, she come smashing straight through the raft.

I dived—and I aimed to find the bottom, too, for a thirty-foot wheel had got to go over me, and I wanted it to have plenty of room. I could always stay under water a minute; this time I reckon I staid under water a minute and a half. Then I bounced for the top in a hurry, for I was nearly busting. I popped out to my arm-pits and blowed the water out of my nose, and puffed a bit. Of course there was a booming current; and of course that boat started her engines again ten seconds after she stopped them, for they never cared much for raftsmen; so now whe was churning along up the river, out of sight in the thick weather, though I could hear her.

I sung out for Jim about a dozen times, but I didn't get any answer; so I grabbed a plank that touched me while I was "treadin water," and struck out for shore, shoving it ahead of me. But I made out to see that the drift of the current was towards the left-hand shore, which meant that I was in a crossing; so I changed off and went that way.

It was one of these long, slanting, two-mile crossings; so I was a good long time in getting over. I made a safe landing, and clum up the bank. I couldn't see but a little ways, but I went poking along over rough ground for a quarter of a mile or more, and then I run across a big old-fashioned double log house before I noticed it. I was going to rush by and get away, but a lot of dogs jumped out and went to howling and barking at me, and I knowed better than to move another peg.

CHAPTER XVII

In about half a minute somebody spoke out of a window, without putting his head out, and says:

"Be done, boys! Who's there?"

I says:

"It's me."

"Who's me?"

"George Jackson, sir."

"What do you want?"

"I don't want nothing, sir. I only want to go along by, but the dogs won't let me."

"What are you prowling around here this time of night, for—hey?"

"I warn't prowling around, sir; I fell overboard off of the steamboat."

"Oh, you did, did you? Strike a light there, somebody. What did you say your name was?"

"George Jackson, sir. I'm only a boy."

"Look here; if you're telling the truth, you needn't be afraid—nobody'll hurt you. But don't try to budge; stand right where you are. Rouse out Bob and Tom, some of you, and fetch the guns. George Jackson, is there anybody with you?"

"No, sir, nobody."

I heard the people stirring around in the house, now, and see a light. The man sung out:

"Snatch that light away, Betsy, you old fool—ain't you got any sense? Put it on the floor behind the front door. Bob, if you and Tom are ready, take your places."

"All ready."

"Now, George Jackson, do you know the Shepherdsons?"

"No, sir—I never heard of them."

"Well, that may be so, and it mayn't. Now, all ready. Step forward, George Jackson. And mind, don't you hurry—come mighty slow. If there's anybody with you, let him keep back—if the shows himself he'll be shot. Come along, now. Come slow; push the door open, yourself—just enough to squeeze in, d' you hear?"

I didn't hurry, I couldn't if I'd a wanted to. I took one slow step at a time, and there warn't a sound, only I thought I could hear my heart. The dogs were as still as the humans, but they followed a little behind me. When I got to the three log door-steps, I heard them unlocking and unbarring and unbolting. I put my hand on the door and pushed it a little and a little more, till somebody said, "There, that's enough—put your head in." I done it, but I judged they would take it off.

The candle was on the floor, and there they all was, looking at me, and me at them, for about a quarter of a minute. Three big men with guns pointed at me, which made me wince, I tell you; the oldest, gray and about sixty, the other two thirty or more—all of them fine and handsome—and the sweetest old gray-headed lady, and back of her two young women which I couldn't see right well. The old gentleman says:

"There—I reckon it's all right. Come in."

As soon as I was in, the old gentleman he locked the door and barred it and bolted it, and told the young men to come in with their guns, and they all went in a big parlor that had a new rag carpet on the floor, and got together in a corner that was out of range of the front windows—there warn't none on the side. They held the candle, and took a good look at me, and all said, "Why *he* ain't a Shepherdson—no, there ain't any Shepherdson about him." Then the old man said he hoped I wouldn't mind being searched for arms, because he didn't mean no harm by it—it was only to make sure. So he didn't pry into my pockets, but only felt outside with his hands, and said it was all right. He told me to make myself easy and at home, and tell all about myself; but the old lady says:

"Why bless you, Saul, the poor thing's as wet as he can be; and don't you reckon it may be he's hungry?"

"True for you, Rachel—I forgot."

So the old lady says:

"Betsy" (this was a nigger woman), "you fly around and get him something to eat, as quick as you can, poor thing; and one of you girls go and wake up Buck and tell him— Oh, here he is himself. Buck, take this little stranger and get the wet clothes off from him and dress him up in some of yours that's dry."

Buck looked about as old as me—thirteen or fourteen or along there, though he was a little bigger than me. He hadn't on anything but a shirt, and he was very frowsy-headed. He come in gaping and digging one fist into his eyes, and he was dragging a gun along with the other one. He says:

"Ain't they no Shepherdsons around?"

They said, no, 'twas a false alarm.

"Well," he says, "if they'd a ben some, I reckon I'd a got one."

They all laughed, and Bob says:

"Why, Buck, they might have scalped us all, you've been so slow in coming."

"Well, nobody come after me, and it ain't right. I'm always kep' down; I don't get no show."

"Never mind, Buck, my boy," says the old man, "you'll have show enough, all in good time, don't you fret about that. Go 'long with you now, and do as your mother told you."

When we got up stairs to his room, he got me a coarse shirt and a round-about and pants of his, and I put them on. While I was at it he asked me what my name was, but before I could tell him, he started to telling me about a blue jay and a young rabbit he had catched in the woods day before yesterday, and he asked me where Moses was when the candle went out. I said I didn't know; I hadn't heard about it before, no way.

"Well, guess," he says.

"How'm I going to guess," says I, "when I never heard tell about it before?"

"But you can guess, can't you? It's just as easy."

"*Which* candle?" I says.

"Why, any candle," he says.

"I don't know where he was," says I; "where was he?"

"Why he was in the *dark!* That's where he was!"

"Well, if you knowed where he was, what did you ask me for?"

"Why, blame it, it's a riddle, don't you see? Say, how long are you going to stay here? You got to stay always. We can just have booming times—they don't have no school now. Do you own a dog? I've got a dog—and he'll go in the river and bring out chips that you throw in. Do you like to comb up, Sundays, and all that kind of foolishness? You bet I don't, but ma she makes me. Confound these ole britches, I reckon I'd better put 'em on, but I'd ruther not, it's so warm. Are you all ready? All right—come along, old hoss."

Cold corn-pone, cold corn-beef, butter and butter-milk—that is what they had for me down there, and there ain't nothing better that ever I've come across yet. Buck and his ma and all of them smoked cob pipes, except the nigger woman, which was gone, and the two young women. They all smoked and talked, and I eat and talked. The young women had quilts around them, and their hair down their backs. They all asked me questions, and I told them how pap and me and all the family was living on a little farm down at the bottom of Arkansaw, and my sister Mary Ann run off and got married and never was heard of no more, and Bill went to hunt them and he warn't heard of no more, and Tom and Mort died, and then there warn't nobody but just me and pap left, and he was just trimmed down to nothing, on account of his troubles; so when he died I took what there was left, because the farm didn't belong to us, and started up the river, deck passage, and fell overboard; and that was how I come to be here. So they said I could have a home there as long as I wanted it. Then it was most daylight, and everybody went to bed, and I went to bed with Buck, and when I waked up in the morning, drat it all, I had forgot what my name was. So I laid there about an hour trying to think, and when Buck waked up, I says:

"Can you spell, Buck?"

"Yes," he says.

"I bet you can't spell my name," says I.

"I bet you what you dare I can," says he.

"All right," says I, "go ahead."

"G-o-r-g-e J-a-x-o-n—there now," he says.

"Well," says I, "you done it, but I didn't think you could. It ain't no slouch of a name to spell—right off without studying."

I set it down, private, because somebody might want *me* to spell it, next, and so I wanted to be handy with it and rattle it off like I was used to it.

It was a mighty nice family, and a mighty nice house, too. I hadn't seen no house out in the country before that was so nice and had so much style. It didn't have an iron latch on the front door, nor a

wooden one with a buckskin string, but a brass knob to turn, the
same as houses in a town. There warn't no bed in the parlor, not a
sign of a bed; but heaps of parlors in towns has beds in them. There
was a big fireplace that was bricked on the bottom, and the bricks
was kept clean and red by pouring water on them and scrubbing
them with another brick; sometimes they washed them over with red
water-paint that they call Spanish-brown, same as they do in town.
They had big brass dog-irons that could hold up a saw-log. There
was a clock on the middle of the mantel-piece, with a picture of a
town painted on the bottom half of the glass front, and a round place
in the middle of it for the sun, and you could see the pendulum swing
behind it. It was beautiful to hear that clock tick; and sometimes
when one of these peddlers had been along and scoured her up and
got her in good shape, she would start in and strike a hundred and
fifty before she got tuckered out. They wouldn't took any money
for her.

Well, there was a big outlandish parrot on each side of the clock,
made out of something like chalk, and painted up gaudy. By one of
the parrots was a cat made of crockery, and a crockery dog by the
other; and when you pressed down on them they squeaked, but
didn't open their mouths nor look different nor interested. They
squeaked through underneath. There was a couple of big wild-
turkey-wing fans spread out behind those things. On a table in the
middle of the room was a kind of a lovely crockery basket that had
apples and oranges and peaches and grapes piled up in it which was
much redder and yellower and prettier than real ones is, but they
warn't real because you could see where pieces had got chipped off
and showed the white chalk or whatever it was, underneath.

This table had a cover made out of beautiful oil-cloth, with a red
and blue spread-eagle painted on it, and a painted border all
around. It come all the way from Philadelphia, they said. There was
some books too, piled up perfectly exact, on each corner of the table.
One was a big family Bible, full of pictures. One was "Pilgrim's
Progress," about a man that left his family it didn't say why. I read
considerable in it now and then. The statements was interesting, but
tough. Another was "Friendship's Offering," full of beautiful stuff
and poetry; but I didn't read the poetry. Another was Henry Clay's
Speeches, and another was Dr. Gunn's Family Medicine, which told
you all about what to do if a body was sick or dead. There was a
Hymn Book, and a lot of other books. And there was nice split-
bottom chairs, and perfectly sound, too—not bagged down in the
middle and busted, like an old basket.

They had pictures hung on the walls—mainly Washingtons and
Lafayettes, and battles, and Highland Marys, and one called
"Signing the Declaration." There was some that they called
crayons, which one of the daughters which was dead made her own
self when she was only fifteen years old. They was different from

any pictures I ever see before; blacker, mostly, than is common.
One was a woman in a slim black dress, belted small under the
arm-pits, with bulges like a cabbage in the middle of the sleeves,
and a large black scoop-shovel bonnet with a black veil, and white
slim ankles crossed about with black tape, and very wee black
slippers, like a chisel, and she was leaning pensive on a tombstone
on her right elbow, under a weeping willow, and her other hand
hanging down her side holding a white handkerchief and a reticule,
and underneath the picture it said "Shall I Never See Thee More
Alas." Another one was a young lady with her hair all combed up
straight to the top of her head, and knotted there in front of a comb
like a chair-back, and she was crying into a handerchief and had a
dead bird laying on its back in her other hand with its heels up,
and underneath the picture it said "I Shall Never Hear Thy Sweet
Chirrup More Alas." There was one where a young lady was at a
window looking up at the moon, and tears running down her cheeks;
and she had an open letter in one hand with black sealing-wax
showing on one edge of it, and she was mashing a locket with a
chain to it against her mouth, and underneath the picture it said
"And Art Thou Gone Yes Thou Art Gone Alas." These was all
nice pictures, I reckon, but I didn't somehow seem to take to them,
because if ever I was down a little, they always give me the fan-tods.
Everybody was sorry she died, because she had laid out a lot more of
these pictures to do, and a body could see by what she had done
what they had lost. But I reckoned, that with her disposition, she
was having a better time in the graveyard. She was at work on what
they said was her greatest picture when she took sick, and every day
and every night it was her prayer to be allowed to live till she got it
done, but she never got the chance. It was a picture of a young
woman in a long white gown, standing on the rail of a bridge all
ready to jump off, with her hair all down her back, and looking up
to the moon, with the tears running down her face, and she had
two arms folded across her breast, and two arms stretched out in
front, and two more reaching up towards the moon—and the idea
was, to see which pair would look best and then scratch out all the
other arms; but, as I was saying, she died before she got her mind
made up, and now they kept this picture over the head of the bed in
her room, and every time her birthday come they hung flowers on
it. Other times it was hid with a little curtain. The young woman in
the picture had a kind of a nice sweet face, but there was so many
arms it made her look too spidery, seemed to me.

This young girl kept a scrap-book when she was alive, and used
to paste obituaries and accidents and cases of patient suffering in
it out of the *Presbyterian Observer,* and write poetry. This is what
she wrote about a boy by the name of Stephen Dowling Bots that
fell down a well and was drownded:

820

ODE TO STEPHEN DOWLING BOTS, DEC'D.

And did young Stephen sicken,
    And did young Stephen die?
And did the sad hearts thicken,
    And did the mourners cry?

No; such was not the fate of
    Young Stephen Dowling Bots;
Though sad hearts round him thickened,
    'Twas not from sickness' shots.

No whooping-cough did rack his frame,
    Nor measles drear, with spots;
Not these impaired the sacred name
    Of Stephen Dowling Bots.

Despised love struck not with woe
    That head of curly knots,
Nor stomach troubles laid him low.
    Young Stephen Dowling Bots.

O no. Then list with tearful eye,
    Whilst I his fate do tell.
His soul did from this cold world fly,
    By falling down a well.

They got him out and emptied him;
    Alas it was too late;
His spirit was gone for to sport aloft
    In the realms of the good and great.

If Emmeline Grangerford could make poetry like that before she was fourteen, there ain't no telling what she could a done by-and-by. Buck said she could rattle off poetry like nothing. She didn't ever have to stop to think. He said she would slap down a line, and if she couldn't find anything to rhyme with it she would just scratch it out and slap down another one, and go ahead. She warn't particular, she could write about anything you choose to give her to write about, just so it was sadful. Every time a man died, or a woman died, or a child died, she would be on hand with her "tribute" before he was cold. She called them tributes. The neighbors said it was the doctor first, then Emmeline, then the undertaker—the undertaker never got in ahead of Emmeline but once, and then she hung fire on a rhyme for the dead person's name, which was Whistler. She warn't ever the same, after that; she never complained, but she kind of pined away and did not live long. Poor thing, many's the time I made myself go up to the little room that used to be hers and get out her poor old scrap-book and read in it when her pictures had been aggravating me and I had soured on her a little. I liked all that family, dead ones and all, and warn't going to let anything come between us. Poor Emmeline made poetry about all the dead people when she was alive, and it didn't seem right that there warn't nobody to make some about her, now she was gone; so I tried to sweat out a verse or two myself, but I couldn't seem to make it go, somehow. They kept Emmeline's room trim and nice and all the things fixed in it just the way she liked to have them when she was alive, and nobody ever slept there. The old lady took care of the room herself, though there was plenty of niggers, and she sewed there a good deal and read her Bible there, mostly.

Well, as I was saying about the parlor, there was beautiful curtains on the windows; white, with pictures painted on them, of castles with vines all down the walls, and cattle coming down to drink. There was a little old piano, too, that had tin pans in it, I reckon, and nothing was ever so lovely as to hear the young ladies sing, "The Last Link is Broken" and play "The Battle of Prague" on it. The walls of all the rooms was plastered, and most had carpets on 'he floors, and the whole house was whitewashed on the outside.

It was a double house, and the big open place betwixt them was roofed and floored; and sometimes the table was set there in the middle of the day, and it was a cool, comfortable place. Nothing couldn't be better. And warn't the cooking good, and just bushels of it too!

CHAPTER XVIII

Col. Grangerford was a gentleman, you see. He was a gentleman all over; and so was his family. He was well born, as the saying is, and that's worth as much in a man as it is in a horse, so the Widow Douglass said, and nobody ever denied that she was of the first aristocracy in our town; and pap he always said it, too, though he warn't no more quality than a mud-cat, himself. Col. Grangerford was very tall and very slim, and had a darkish-paly complexion, not a sign of red in it anywheres; he was cleanshaved every morning, all over his thin face, and he had the thinnest kind of lips, and the thinnest kind of nostrils, and a high nose, and heavy eyebrows, and the blackest kind of eyes, sunk so deep back that they seemed like they was looking out of caverns at you, as you may say. His forehead was high, and his hair was black and straight, and hung to his shoulders. His hands was long and thin, and every day of his life he put on a clean shirt and a full suit from head to foot made out of linen so white it hurt your eyes to look at it; and on Sundays he wore a blue tail-coat with brass buttons on it. He carried a mahogany cane with a silver head to it. There warn't no frivolishness about him, not a bit, and he warn't ever loud. He was as kind as he could be—you could feel that, you know, and so you had confidence.

Sometimes he smiled, and it was good to see; but when he straightened himself up like a liberty-pole, and the lightning begun to flicker out from under his eyebrows you wanted to climb a tree first, and find out what the matter was afterwards. He didn't ever have to tell anybody to mind their manners—everybody was always good mannered where he was. Everybody loved to have him around, too; he was sunshine most always—I mean he made it seem like good weather. When he turned into a cloud-bank it was awful dark for a half a minute and that was enough; there wouldn't nothing go wrong again for a week.

When him and the old lady come down in the morning, all the family got up out of their chairs and give them good-day, and didn't set down again till they had set down. Then Tom and Bob went to the sideboard where the decanters was, and mixed a glass of bitters and handed it to him, and he held it in his hand and waited till Tom's and Bob's was mixed, and then they bowed and said "Our duty to you, sir, and madam;" and *they* bowed the least bit in the world and said thank you, and so they drank, all three, and Bob and Tom poured a spoonful of water on the sugar and the mite of whisky or apple brandy in the bottom of their tumblers, and give it to me and Buck, and we drank to the old people too.

Bob was the oldest, and Tom next. Tall, beautiful men with very broad shoulders and brown faces, and long black hair and black eyes. They dressed in white linen from head to foot, like the old gentleman, and wore broad Panama hats.

Then there was Miss Charlotte, she was twenty-five, and tall and proud and grand, but as good as she could be, when she warn't stirred up; but when she was, she had a look that would make you wilt in your tracks, like her father. She was beautiful.

So was her sister, Miss Sophia, but it was a different kind. She was gentle and sweet, like a dove, and she was only twenty.

Each person had their own nigger to wait on them—Buck, too. My nigger had a monstrous easy time, because I warn't used to having anybody do anything for me, but Buck's was on the jump most of the time.

This was all there was of the family, now; but there used to be more—three sons; they got killed; and Emmeline that died.

The old gentleman owned a lot of farms, and over a hundred niggers. Sometimes a stack of people would come there, horseback, from ten or fifteen mile around, and stay five or six days, and have such junketings round about and on the river, and dances and picnics in the woods, day-times, and balls at the house, nights. These people was mostly kin-folks of the family. The men brought their guns with them. It was a handsome lot of quality, I tell you.

There was another clan of aristocracy around there—five or six families—mostly of the name of Shepherdson. They was as high-toned, and well born, and rich and grand, as the tribe of

Grangerfords. The Shepherdsons and the Grangerfords used the same steamboat landing, which was about two mile above our house; so sometimes when I went up there with a lot of our folks I used to see a lot of the Shepherdsons there, on their fine horses.

One day Buck and me was away out in the woods, hunting, and heard a horse coming. We was crossing the road. Buck says:

"Quick! Jump for the woods!"

We done it, and then peeped down the woods through the leaves. Pretty soon a splendid young man come galloping down the road, setting his horse easy and looking like a soldier. He had his gun across his pommel. I had seen him before. It was young Harney Shepherdson. I heard Buck's gun go off at my ear, and Harney's hat tumbled off from his head. He grabbed his gun and rode straight to the place where we was hid. But we didn't wait. We started through the woods on a run. The woods warn't thick, so I looked over my shoulder, to dodge the bullet, and twice I seen Harney cover Buck with his gun; and then he rode away the way he come— to get his hat, I reckon, but I couldn't see. We never stopped running till we got home. The old gentleman's eyes blazed a minute—'twas pleasure, mainly, I judged—then his face sort of smoothed down, and he says, kind of gentle:

"I don't like that shooting from behind a bush. Why didn't you step into the road, my boy?"

"The Shepherdsons don't, father. They always take advantage."

Miss Charlotte she held her head up like a queen while Buck was telling his tale, and her nostrils spread and her eyes snapped. The two young men looked dark, but never said nothing. Miss Sophia she turned pale, but the color come back when she found the man warn't hurt.

Soon as I could get Buck down by the corn-cribs under the trees by ourselves, I says:

"Did you want to kill him, Buck?"

"Well, I bet I did."

"What did he do to you?"

"Him? He never done nothing to me."

"Well, then, what did you want to kill him for?"

"Why nothing—only it's on account of the feud."

"What's a feud?"

"Why, where was you raised? Don't you know what a feud is?"

"Never heard of it before—tell me about it."

"Well," says Buck, "a feud is this way. A man has a quarrel with another man, and kills him; then that other man's brother kills *him*; then the other brothers, on both sides, goes for one another; then the *cousins* chip in—and by-and-by everybody's killed off, and there ain't no more feud. But it's kind of slow, and takes a long time."

"Has this one been going on long, Buck?"

"Well I should *reckon!* it started thirty year ago, or som'ers along there. There was trouble 'bout something and then a lawsuit to settle it; and the suit went agin one of the men, and so he up and shot the man that won the suit—which he would naturally do, of course. Anybody would."

"What was the trouble about, Buck?—land?"

"I reckon maybe—I don't know."

"Well, who done the shooting?—was it a Grangerford or a Shepherdson?"

"Laws, how do *I* know? it was so long ago."

"Don't anybody know?"

"Oh, yes, pa knows, I reckon, and some of the other old folks; but they don't know, now, what the row was about in the first place."

"Has there been many killed, Buck?"

"Yes—right smart chance of funerals. But they don't always kill. Pa's got a few buck-shot in him; but he don't mind it 'cuz he don't weigh much anyway. Bob's been carved up some with a bowie, and Tom's been hurt once or twice."

"Has anybody been killed this year, Buck?"

"Yes, we got one and they got one. 'Bout three months ago, my cousin Bud, fourteen year old, was riding through the woods, on t'other side of the river, and didn't have no weapon with him, which was blame' foolishness, and in a lonesome place he hears a horse a-coming behind him, and sees old Baldy Shepherdson a-linkin' after him with his gun in his hand and his white hair a-flying in the wind; and 'stead of jumping off and taking to the brush, Bud 'lowed he could outrun him; so they had it, nip and tuck, for five mile or more, the old man a-gaining all the time; so at last Bud seen it warn't any use, so he stopped and faced around so as to have the bullet holes in front, you know, and the old man he rode up and shot him down. But he didn't git much chance to enjoy his luck, for inside of a week our folks laid *him* out."

"I reckon that old man was a coward, Buck."

"I reckon he *warn't* a coward. Not by a blame' sight. There ain't a coward amongst them Shepherdsons—not a one. And there ain't no cowards amongst the Grangerfords, either. Why, that old man kep' up his end in a fight one day, for a half an hour, against three Grangerfords, and come out winner. They was all a-horseback; he lit off of his horse and got behind a little wood-pile, and kep' his horse before him to stop the bullets; but the Grangerfords staid on their horses and capered around the old man, and peppered away at him, and he peppered away at them. Him and his horse both went home pretty leaky and crippled, but the Grangerfords had to be *fetched* home—and one of 'em was dead, and another died the next day. No, sir, if a body's out hunting for cowards, he don't want to fool away any time amongst them Shepherdsons, becuz they don't breed any of that *kind.*"

Next Sunday we all went to church, about three mile, everybody
a-horseback. The men took their guns along, so did Buck, and kept
them between their knees or stood them handy against the wall.
The Shepherdsons done the same. It was pretty ornery preaching—
all about brotherly love, and such-like tiresomeness; but everybody
said it was a good sermon, and they all talked it over going home,
and had such a powerful lot to say about faith, and good works
and free grace, and preforeordestination, and I don't know what all,
that it did seem to me to be one of the roughest Sundays I had run
across yet.

About an hour after dinner everybody was dozing around, some
in their chairs and some in their rooms, and it got to be pretty dull.
Buck and a dog was stretched out on the grass in the sun, sound
asleep. I went up to our room, and judged I would take a nap myself.
I found that sweet Miss Sophia standing in her door, which was
next to ours, and she took me in her room and shut the door very
soft, and asked me if I liked her, and I said I did; and she asked me
if I would do something for her and not tell anybody, and I said I
would. Then she said she'd forgot her Testament, and left it in the
seat at church, between two other books and would I slip out quiet
and go there and fetch it to her, and not say nothing to nobody.
I said I would. So I slid out and slipped off up the road, and there
warn't anybody at the church, except maybe a hog or two, for there
warn't any lock on the door, and hogs likes a puncheon floor in
summer-time because it's cool. If you notice, most folks don't go to
church only when they've got to; but a hog is different.

Says I to myself something's up—it ain't natural for a girl to be
in such a sweat about a Testament; so I give it a shake, and out
drops a little piece of paper with *"Half-past two"* wrote on it with
a pencil. I ransacked it, but couldn't find anything else. I couldn't
make anything out of that, so I put the paper in the book again, and
when I got home and up stairs, there was Miss Sophia in her door
waiting for me. She pulled me in and shut the door; then she looked
in the Testament till she found the paper, and as soon as she read
it she looked glad; and before a body could think, she grabbed me
and give me a squeeze, and said I was the best boy in the world, and
not to tell anybody. She was mighty red in the face, for a minute, and
her eyes lighted up and it made her powerful pretty. I was a good
deal astonished, but when I got my breath I asked her what the
paper was about, and she asked me if I had read it, and I said no,
and she asked me if I could read writing, and I told her "no, only
coarse-hand," and then she said the paper warn't anything but a
book-mark to keep her place, and I might go and play now.

I went off down to the river, studying over this thing, and pretty
soon I notice that my nigger was following along behind. When we
was out of sight of the house, he looked back and around a second,
and then comes a-running and says:

"Mars Jawge, if you'll come down into de swamp, I'll show you a whole stack o' water-moccasins."

Thinks I, that's mighty curious; he said that yesterday. He oughter know a body don't love water-moccasins enough to go around hunting for them. What is he up to anyway? So I says—

"All right, trot ahead."

I followed a half a mile, then he struck out over the swamp and waded ankle deep as much as another half mile. We come to a little flat piece of land which was dry and very thick with trees and bushes and vines, and he says—

"You shove right in dah, jist a few steps, Mars Jawge, dah's whah dey is. I's seed 'm befo', I don't k'yer to see 'em no mo'."

Then he slopped right along and went away, and pretty soon the trees hid him. I poked into the place a-ways, and come to a little open patch as big as a bedroom, all hung around with vines, and found a man laying there asleep—and by jings it was my old Jim!

I waked him up, and I reckoned it was going to be a grand surprise to him to see me again, but it warn't. He nearly cried, he was so glad, but he warn't surprised. Said he swum along behind me, that night, and heard me yell every time, but dasn't answer, because he didn't want nobody to pick *him* up, and take him into slavery again. Says he—

"I got hurt a little, en couldn't swim fas', so I wuz a considable ways behine you, towards de las'; when you landed I reck'ned I could ketch up wid you on de lan' 'dout havin' to shout at you, but when I see dat house I begin to go slow. I 'uz off too fur to hear what dey say to you—I wuz 'fraid o' de dogs—but when it 'uz all quiet agin, I knowed you's in de house, so I struck out for de woods to wait for day. Early in de mawnin' some er de niggers come along, gwyne to de fields, en dey tuck me en showed me dis place, whah de dogs can't track me on accounts o' de water, en dey brings me truck to eat every night, en tells me how you's a gitt'n along."

"Why didn't you tell my Jack to fetch me here sooner, Jim?"

"Well, 'twarn't no use to 'sturb you, Huck, tell we could do sumfn—but we's all right, now. I ben a-buyin' pots en pans en vittles, as I got a chanst, en a patchin' up de raf', nights, when——"

"*What* raft, Jim?"

"Our ole raf'."

"You mean to say our old raft warn't smashed all to flinders?"

"No, she warn't. She was tore up a good deal—one en' of her was—but dey warn't no great harm done, on'y our traps was mos' all los'. Ef we hadn' dive' so deep en swum so fur under water, en de night hadn' ben so dark, en we warn't so sk'yerd, en ben sich punkin-heads, as de sayin' is, we'd a seed de raf'. But it's jis' as well we didn't, 'kase now she's all fixed up agin mos' as good as new, en we's got a new lot o' stuff, too, in de place o' what 'uz los'."

"Why, how did you get hold of the raft again, Jim—did you catch her?"

"How I gwyne to ketch her, en I out in de woods? No, some er de niggers foun' her ketched on a snag, along heah in de ben', en dey hid her in a crick, 'mongst de willows, en dey wuz so much jawin' 'bout which un 'um she b'long to de mos', dat I come to heah 'bout it pooty soon, so I ups en settles de trouble by tellin' 'um she don't b'long to none uv um, but to you en me; en I ast'm if dey gwyne to grab a young white genlman's propaty, en git a hid'n for it? Den I gin 'm ten cents apiece, en dey 'uz mighty well satisfied, en wisht some mo' raf's 'ud come along en make 'm rich agin. Dey's mighty good to me, dese niggers is, en whatever I wants 'm to do fur me, I doan' have to ast 'm twice, honey. Dat Jack's a good nigger, en pooty smart."

"Yes, he is. He ain't ever told me you was here; told me to come, and he'd show me a lot of water-moccasins. If anything happens, *he* ain't mixed up in it. He can say he never seen us together, and it'll be the truth."

I don't want to talk much about the next day. I reckon I'll cut it pretty short. I waked up about dawn, and was agoing to turn over and go to sleep again, when I noticed how still it was—didn't seem to be anybody stirring. That warn't usual. Next I notice that Buck was up and gone. Well, I gets up, a-wondering, and goes down stairs—nobody around; everything as still as a mouse. Just the same outside; thinks I, what does it mean? Down by the wood-pile I comes across my Jack, and says:

"What's it all about?"

Says he:

"Don't you know, Mars Jawge?"

"No," says I, "I don't."

"Well, den, Miss Sophia's run off! 'deed she has. She run off in de night, sometime—nobody don't know jis' when—run off to git married to dat young Harney Shepherdson, you know—leastways, so dey 'spec. De fambly foun' it out, 'bout half an hour ago—maybe a little mo'—en I *tell* you dey warn't no time los'. Sich another hurryin' up guns en hosses *you* never see! De women folks has gone for to stir up de relations, en ole Mars Saul en de boys tuck dey guns en rode up de river road for to try to ketch dat young man en kill him 'fo' he kin git acrost de river wid Miss Sophia. I reck'n dey's gwyne to be mighty rough times."

"Buck went off 'thout waking me up."

"Well I reck'n he *did!* Dey warn't gwyne to mix you up in it. Mars Buck he loaded up his gun en 'lowed he's gwyne to fetch home a Shepherdson or bust. Well, dey'll be plenty un 'm dah, I reck'n, en you bet you he'll fetch one if he gits a chanst."

I took up the river road as hard as I could put. By-and-by I begin to hear guns a good ways off. When I come in sight of the log store and the wood-pile where the steamboats lands, I worked along under the trees and brush till I got to a good place, and then I clumb up into the forks of a cotton-wood that was out of reach, and watched. There was a wood-rank four foot high, a little ways in front of the tree, and first I was going to hide behind that; but maybe it was luckier I didn't.

There was four or five men cavorting around on their horses in the open place before the log store, cussing and yelling, and trying to get at a couple of young chaps that was behind the wood-rank alongside of the steamboat landing—but they couldn't come it. Every time one of them showed himself on the river side of the wood-pile he got shot at. The two boys was squatting back to back behind the pile, so they could watch both ways.

By-and-by the men stopped cavorting around and yelling. They started riding towards the store; then up gets one of the boys, draws a steady bead over the wood-rank, and drops one of them out of his saddle. All the men jumped off of their horses and grabbed the hurt one and started to carry him to the store; and that minute the two boys started on the run. They got half-way to the tree I was in before the men noticed. Then the men see them, and jumped on their horses and took out after them. They gained on the boys, but it didn't do no good, the boys had too good a start; they got to the wood-pile that was in front of my tree, and slipped in behind it, and so they had the bulge on the men again. One of the boys was Buck, and the other was a slim young chap about nineteen years old.

The men ripped around awhile, and then rode away. As soon as they was out of sight, I sung out to Buck and told him. He didn't know what to make of my voice coming out of the tree, at first. He was awful surprised. He told me to watch out sharp and let him know when the men come in sight again; said they was up to some devilment or other—wouldn't be gone long. I wished I was out of that tree, but I dasn't come down. Buck begun to cry and rip, and 'lowed that him and his cousin Joe (that was the other young chap) would make up for this day, yet. He said his father and his two brothers was killed, and two or three of the enemy. Said the Shepherdsons laid for them, in ambush. Buck said his father and brothers ought to waited for their relations—the Shepherdsons was too strong for them. I asked him what was become of young Harney and Miss Sophia. He said they'd got across the river and was safe. I was glad of that; but the way Buck did take on because he didn't manage to kill Harney that day he shot at him—I hain't ever heard anything like it.

All of a sudden, bang! bang! bang! goes three or four guns—the men had slipped around through the woods and come in from behind without their horses! The boys jumped for the river—both of them hurt—and as they swum down the current the men run along the bank shooting at them and singing out, "Kill them, kill them!" It made me so sick I most fell out of the tree. I ain't agoing to tell

all that happened—it would make me sick again if I was to do that.
I wished I hadn't ever come ashore that night, to see such things.
I ain't ever going to get shut of them—lots of times I dream about
them.

I staid in the tree till it begun to get dark, afraid to come down.
Sometimes I heard guns away off in the woods; and twice I seen
little gangs of men gallop past the log store with guns; so I reckoned
the trouble was still agoing on. I was mighty down-hearted; so I
made up my mind I wouldn't ever go anear that house again,
because I reckoned I was to blame, somehow. I judged that that
piece of paper meant that Miss Sophia was to meet Harney
somewheres at half-past two and run off; and I judged I ought to
told her father about the paper and the curious way she acted, and
then maybe he would a locked her up and this awful mess wouldn't
ever happened.

When I got down out of the tree, I crept along down the river
bank a piece, and found the two bodies laying in the edge of the
water, and tugged at them till I got them ashore; then I covered
up their faces, and got away as quick as I could. I cried a little when
I was covering up Buck's face, for he was mighty good to me.

It was just dark, now. I never went near the house, but struck
through the woods and made for the swamp. Jim warn't on his
island, so I tramped off in a hurry for the crick, and crowded
through the willows, red-hot to jump aboard and get out of that
awful country—the raft was gone! My souls, but I was scared! I
couldn't get my breath for most a minute. Then I raised a yell. A
voice not twenty-five foot from me, says—

"Good lan'! is dat you, honey? Doan' make no noise."

It was Jim's voice—nothing ever sounded so good before. I run
along the bank a piece and got aboard, and Jim he grabbed me and
hugged me, he was so glad to see me. He says—

"Laws bless you, chile, I 'uz right down sho' you's dead agin.
Jack's been heah, he say he reck'n you's ben shot, kase you didn'
come home no mo'; so I's jes' dis minute a startin' de raf' down
towards de mouf er de crick, so's to be all ready for to shove out en
leave soon as Jack comes agin en tells me for certain you *is* dead.
Lawsy, I's mighty glad to git you back agin, honey."

I says—

"All right—that's mighty good; they won't find me, and they'll
think I've been killed, and floated down the river—there's
something up there that'll help them to think so—so don't you lose
no time, Jim, but just shove off for the big water as fast as ever you
can."

I never felt easy till the raft was two mile below there and out
in the middle of the Mississippi. Then we hung up our signal
lantern, and judged that we was free and safe once more. I hadn't
had a bite to eat since yesterday; so Jim he got out some

corn-dodgers and buttermilk, and pork and cabbage, and greens—
there ain't nothing in the world so good, when it's cooked right—
and whilst I eat my supper we talked, and had a good time. I was
powerful glad to get away from the feuds, and so was Jim to get
away from the swamp. We said there warn't no home like a raft,
after all. Other places do seem so cramped up and smothery, but a
raft don't. You feel mighty free and easy and comfortable on a raft.

CHAPTER XIX

Two or three days and nights went by; I reckon I might say they
swum by, they slid along so quiet and smooth and lovely. Here is
the way we put in the time. It was a monstrous big river down
there—sometimes a mile and a half wide; we run nights, and laid
up and hid day-times; soon as night was most gone, we stopped
navigating and tied up—nearly always in the dead water under a
tow-head; and then cut young cottonwoods and willows and hid the
raft with them. Then we set out the lines. Next we slid into the river
and had a swim, so as to freshen up and cool off; then we set down
on the sandy bottom where the water was about knee deep, and
watched the daylight come. Not a sound, anywheres—perfectly
still—just like the whole world was asleep, only sometimes the
bull frogs a-cluttering, maybe. The first thing to see, looking away
over the water, was a kind of dull line—that was the woods on
t'other side—you couldn't make nothing else out; then a pale place
in the sky; then more paleness, spreading around; then the river
softened up, away off, and warn't black any more, but gray; you
could see little dark spots drifting along, ever so far away—trading
scows, and such things; and long black streaks—rafts; sometimes
you could hear a sweep screaking; or jumbled up voices, it was so
still, and sounds come so far; and by-and-by you could see a streak
on the water which you know by the look of the streak that there's
a snag there in a swift current which breaks on it and makes that
streak look that way; and you see the mist curl up off of the water,
and the east reddens up, and the river, and you make out a log
cabin in the edge of the woods, away on the bank on t'other side of
the river, being a wood-yard, likely, and piled by them cheats so you
can throw a dog through it anywheres; then the nice breeze springs
up and comes fanning you from over there, so cool and fresh, and
sweet to smell, on account of the woods and the flowers; but
sometimes not that way, because they've left dead fish laying
around, gars, and such, and they do get pretty rank; and next
you've got the full day, and everything smiling in the sun, and the
song-birds just going it!

A little smoke couldn't be noticed, now, so we would take some
fish off of the lines, and cook up a hot breakfast. And afterwards
we would watch the lonesomeness of the river, and kind of lazy

along, and by-and-by lazy off to sleep. Wake up, by-and-by, and
look to see what done it, and maybe see a steamboat, coughing along
up stream, so far off towards the other side you couldn't tell nothing
about her only whether she was stern-wheel or side-wheel,
then for about an hour there wouldn't be nothing to hear nor
nothing to see—just solid lonesomeness. Next you'd see a raft sliding
by, away off yonder, and maybe a galoot on it chopping, because
they're most always doing it on a raft; you'd see the ax flash, ane
come down—you don't hear nothing; you see that ax go up again,
and by the time it's above the man's head, then you hear the
k'chunk!—it had took all that time to come over the water. So we
would put in the day, lazying around, listening to the stillness.
Once there was a thick fog, and the rafts and things that went by
was beating tin pans so the steamboats wouldn't run over them.
A scow or a raft went by so close we could hear them talking and
cussing and laughing—heard them plain; but we couldn't see no
sign of them; it made you feel crawly, it was like spirits carrying on
that way in the air. Jim said he believed it was spirits; but I says:

   "No, spirits wouldn't say, 'dern the dern fog.' "

   Soon as it was night, out we shoved; when we got her out to about
the middle, we let her alone, and let her float wherever the current
wanted her to; then we lit the pipes, and dangled our legs in the
water and talked about all kinds of things—we was always naked,
day and night, whenever the mosquitoes would let us—the new
clothes Buck's folks made for me was too good to be comfortable,
and besides I didn't go much on clothes, nohow.

   Sometimes we'd have that whole river all to ourselves for the
longest time. Yonder was the banks and the islands, across the
water; and maybe a spark—which was a candle in a cabin window—
and sometimes on the water you could see a spark or two—on a raft
or a scow, you know; and maybe you could hear a fiddle or a song
coming over from one of them crafts. It's lovely to live on a raft.
We had the sky, up there, all speckled with stars, and we used to lay
on our backs and look up at them, and discuss about whether they
was made, or only just happened—Jim he allowed they was made,
but I allowed they happened; I judged it would have took too long
to *make* so many. Jim said the moon could a *laid* them; well, that
looked kind of reasonable, so I didn't say nothing against it,
because I've seen a frog lay most as many, so of course it could
be done. We used to watch the stars that fell, too, and see them
streak down. Jim allowed they'd got spoiled and was hove out of the
nest.

   Once or twice of a night we would see a steamboat slipping along
in the dark, and now and then she would belch a whole world of
sparks up out of her chimbleys, and they would rain down in the
river and look awful pretty; then she would turn a corner and her
lights would wink out and her pow-wow shut off and leave the

river still again; and by-and-by her waves would get to us, a long time after she was gone, and joggle the raft a bit, and after that you wouldn't hear nothing for you couldn't tell how long, except maybe frogs or something.

After midnight the people on shore went to bed, and then for two or three hours the shores was black—no more sparks in the cabin windows. These sparks was our clock—the first one that showed again meant morning was coming, so we hunted a place to hide and tie up, right away.

One morning about day-break, I found a canoe and crossed over a chute to the main shore—it was only two hundred yards—and paddled about a mile up a crick amongst the cypress woods, to see if I couldn't get some berries. Just as I was passing a place where a kind of a cow-path crossed the crick, here comes a couple of men tearing up the path as tight as they could foot it. I thought I was a goner, for whenever anybody was after anybody I judged it was *me*—or maybe Jim. I was about to dig out from there in a hurry, but they was pretty close to me then, and sung out and begged me to save their lives—said they hadn't been doing nothing, and was being chased for it—said there was men and dogs a-coming. They wanted to jump right in, but I says—

"Don't you do it. I don't hear the dogs and horses yet; you've got time to crowd through the brush and get up the crick a little ways; then you take to the water and wade down to me and get in—that'll throw the dogs off the scent."

They done it, and soon as they was aboard I lit out for our tow-head, and in about five or ten minutes we heard the dogs and the men away off, shouting. We heard them come along towards the crick, but couldn't see them; they seemed to stop and fool around a while; then, as we got further and further away all the time, we couldn't hardly hear them at all; by the time we had left a mile of woods behind us and struck the river, everything was quiet, and we paddled over to the tow-head and hid in the cotton-woods and was safe.

One of these fellows was about seventy, or upwards, and had a bald head and very gray whiskers. He had an old battered-up slouch hat on, and a greasy blue woolen shirt, and ragged old blue jeans britches stuffed into his boot tops, and home-knit galluses—no, he only had one. He had an old long-tailed blue jeans coat with slick brass buttons, flung over his arm, and both of them had big fat ratty-looking carpet-bags.

The other fellow was about thirty and dressed about as ornery. After breakfast we all laid off and talked, and the first thing that come out was that these chaps didn't know one another.

"What got you into trouble?" says the baldhead to t'other chap.

"Well, I'd been selling an article to take the tartar off the teeth—and it does take it off, too, and generly the enamel along with it—

but I staid about one night longer than I ought to, and was just in the act of sliding out when I ran across you on the trail this side of town, and you told me they were coming, and begged me to help you to get off. So I told you I was expecting trouble myself and would scatter out *with* you. That's the whole yarn—what's yourn?"

"Well, I'd ben a-runnin' a little temperance revival thar, 'bout a week, and was the pet of the women-folks, big and little, for I was makin' it mighty warm for the rummies, I *tell* you, and takin' as much as five or six dollars a night—ten cents a head, children and niggers free—and business a growin' all the time; when somehow or another a little report got around, last night, that I had a way of puttin' in my time with a private jug, on the sly. A nigger rousted me out this mornin', and told me the people was getherin' on the quiet, with their dogs and horses, and they'd be along pretty soon and give me 'bout half an hour's start, and then run me down, if they could; and if they got me they'd tar and feather me and ride me on a rail, sure. I didn't wait for no breakfast—I warn't hungry."

"Old man," says the young one, "I reckon we might double-team it together; what do you think?"

"I ain't undisposed. What's your line—mainly?"

"Jour printer, by trade; do a little in patent medicines; theatre-actor—tragedy, you know; take a turn at mesmerism and phrenology when there's a chance; teach singing-geography school for a change; sling a lecture, sometimes—oh, I do lots of things— most anything that comes handy, so it ain't work. What's your lay?"

"I've done considerble in the doctoring way in my time. Layin' on o' hands is my best holt—for cancer, and paralysis, and sich things; and I k'n tell a fortune pretty good, when I've got somebody along to find out the facts for me. Preachin's my line, too; and workin' camp-meetin's; and missionaryin' around."

Nobody never said anything for a while; then the young man hove a sigh and says—

"Alas!"

"What're you alassin' about?" says the baldhead.

"To think I should have lived to be leading such a life, and be degraded down into such company." And he begun to wipe the corner of his eye with a rag.

"Dern your skin, ain't the company good enough for you?" says the baldhead, pretty pert and uppish.

"Yes, it *is* good enough for me; it's as good as I deserve; for who fetched me so low, when I was so high? *I* did myself. I don't blame *you,* gentlemen—far from it; I don't blame anybody. I deserve it all. Let the cold world do its worst; one thing I know—there's a grave somewhere for me. The world may go on just as its always done, and take everything from me—loved ones, property, everything—but it can't take that. Some day I'll lie down in it and forget it all, and my poor broken heart will be at rest." He went on a-wiping.

"Drot your pore broken heart," says the baldhead; "what are you heaving your pore broken heart at *us* f'r? *We* hain't done nothing."

"No, I know you haven't. I ain't blaming you, gentlemen. I brought myself down—yes, I did it myself. It's right I should suffer—perfectly right—I don't make any moan."

"Brought you down from whar? Whar was you brought down from?"

"Ah, you would not believe me; the world never believes—let it pass—'tis no matter. The secret of my birth——"

"The secret of your birth? Do you mean to say——"

"Gentlemen," says the young man, very solemn, "I will reveal it to you, for I feel I may have confidence in you. By rights I am a duke!"

Jim's eyes bugged out when he heard that; and I reckon mine did, too. Then the baldhead says: "No! you can't mean it?"

"Yes. My great-grandfather, eldest son of the Duke of Bridgewater, fled to this country about the end of the last century, to breathe the pure air of freedom; married here, and died, leaving a son, his own father dying about the same time. The second son of the late duke seized the title and estates—the infant real duke was ignored. I am the lineal descendant of that infant—I am the rightful Duke of Bridgewater; and here am I, forlorn, torn from my high estate, hunted of men, despised by the cold world, ragged, worn, heart-broken, and degraded to the companionship of felons on a raft!"

Jim pitied him ever so much, and so did I. We tried to comfort him, but he said it warn't much use, he couldn't be much comforted; said if we was a mind to acknowledge him, that would do him more good than most anything else; so we said we would, if he would tell us how. He said we ought to bow, when we spoke to him, and say "Your Grace," or "My Lord," or "Your Lordship"— and he wouldn't mind it if we called him plain "Bridgewater," which he said was a title, anyway, and not a name; and one of us ought to wait on him at dinner, and do any little thing for him he wanted done.

Well, that was all easy, so we done it. All through dinner Jim stood around and waited on him, and says, "Will yo' Grace have some o' dis, or some o' dat?" and so on, and a body could see it was mighty pleasing to him.

But the old man got pretty silent, by-and-by—didn't have much to say and didn't look pretty comfortable over all that petting that was going on around that duke. He seemed to have something on his mind. So, along in the afternoon, he says:

"Looky here, Bilgewater," he says, "I'm nation sorry for you, but you ain't the only person that's had troubles like that."

"No?"

"No, you ain't. You ain't the only person that's ben snaked down wrongfully out'n a high place."

"Alas!"

"No, you ain't the only person that's had a secret of his birth." And by jings, *he* begins to cry.

"Hold! What do you mean?"

"Bilgewater, kin I trust you?" says the old man, still sort of sobbing.

"To the bitter death!" He took the old man by the hand and squeezed it, and says, "The secret of your being: speak!"

"Bilgewater, I am the late Dauphin!"

You bet you Jim and me stared, this time. Then the duke says: "You are what?"

"Yes, my friend, it is too true—your eyes is lookin' at this very moment on the pore disappeared Dauphin, Looy the Seventeen, son of Looy the Sixteen and Marry Antonette."

"You! At your age! No! You mean you're the late Charlemagne; you must be six or seven hundred years old, at the very least."

"Trouble has done it, Bilgewater, trouble has done it; trouble has brung these gray hairs and this premature balditude. Yes, gentlemen, you see before you, in blue jeans and misery, the wanderin', exiled, trampled-on and sufferin' rightful King of France."

Well, he cried and took on so, that me and Jim didn't know hardly what to do, we was so sorry—and so glad and proud we'd got him with us, too. So we set in, like we done before with the duke, and tried to comfort *him.* But he said it warn't no use, nothing but to be dead and done with it all could do him any good; though he said it often made him feel easier and better for a while if people treated him according to his rights, and got down on one knee to speak to him, and always called him "Your Majesty," and waited on him first at meals, and didn't set down in his presence till he asked them. So Jim and me set to majestying him, and doing this and that and t'other for him, and standing up till he told us we might set down. This done him heaps of good, and so he got cheerful and comfortable. But the duke kind of soured on him, and didn't look a bit satisfied with the way things was going; still, the king acted real friendly towards him, and said the duke's great-grandfather and all the other Dukes of Bilgewater was a good deal thought of by *his* father and was allowed to come to the palace considerable; but the duke staid huffy a good while, till by-and-by the king says:

"Like as not we got to be together a blamed long time, on this h-yer raft, Bilgewater, and so what's the use o' your bein' sour? It'll only make things oncomfortable. It ain't my fault I warn't born a duke, it ain't your fault you warn't born a king—so what's the use to worry? Make the best o' things the way you find 'em, says I—that's my motto. This ain't no bad thing that we've struck here—plenty grub and an easy life—come, give us your hand, Duke, and less all be friends."

The duke done it, and Jim and me was pretty glad to see it. It took away all the uncomfortableness, and we felt mighty good over it, because it would a been a miserable business to have any unfriendliness on the raft; for what you want, above all things, on a raft, is for everybody to be satisfied, and feel right and kind towards the others.

It didn't take me long to make up my mind that these liars warn't no kings nor dukes, at all, but just low-down humbugs and frauds. But I never said nothing, never let on; kept it to myself; it's the best way; then you don't have no quarrels, and don't get into no trouble. If they wanted us to call them kings and dukes, I hadn't no objections, 'long as it would keep peace in the family; and it warn't no use to tell Jim, so I didn't tell him. If I never learnt nothing else out of pap, I learnt that the best way to get along with his kind of people is to let them have their own way.

CHAPTER XX

They asked us considerable many questions; wanted to know what we covered up the raft that way for, and laid by in the day-time instead of running—was Jim a runaway nigger? Says I—

"Goodness sakes, would a runaway nigger run *south?*"

No, they allowed he wouldn't. I had to account for things some way, so I says:

"My folks was living in Pike County, in Missouri, where I was born, and they all died off but me and pa and my brother Ike. Pa, he 'lowed he'd break up and go down and live with Uncle Ben, who's got a little one-horse place on the river, forty-four mile below Orleans. Pa was pretty poor, and had some debts; so when he'd squared up there warn't nothing left but sixteen dollars and our nigger, Jim. That warn't enough to take us fourteen hundred mile, deck passage nor no other way. Well, when the river rose, pa had a streak of luck one day; he ketched this piece of a raft; so we reckoned we'd go down to Orleans on it. Pa's luck didn't hold out; a steamboat run over the forrard corner of the raft, one night, and we all went overboard and dove under the wheel; Jim and me come up, all right, but pa was drunk, and Ike was only four years old, so they never come up no more. Well, for the next day or two we had considerable trouble, because people was always coming out in skiffs and trying to take Jim away from me, saying they believed he was a runaway nigger. We don't run day-times no more, now; nights they don't bother us."

The duke says—

"Leave me alone to cipher out a way so we can run in the day-time if we want to. I'll think the thing over—I'll invent a plan that'll fix it. We'll let it alone for to-day, because of course we don't want to go by that town yonder in daylight—it mightn't be healthy."

Towards night it begun to darken up and look like rain; the heat lightning was squirting around, low down in the sky, and the leaves was beginning to shiver—it was going to be pretty ugly, it was easy to see that. So the duke and the king went to overhauling our wigwam, to see what the beds was like. My bed was a straw tick—better than Jim's, which was a corn-shuck tick; there's always cobs around about in a shuck tick, and they poke into you and hurt; and when you roll over, the dry shucks sound like you was rolling over in a pile of dead leaves; it makes such a rustling that you wake up. Well, the duke allowed he would take my bed; but the king allowed he wouldn't. He says—

"I should a reckoned the difference in rank would a sejested to you that a corn-shuck bed warn't just fitten for me to sleep on. Your Grace'll take the shuck bed yourself."

Jim and me was in a sweat again, for a minute, being afraid there was going to be some more trouble amongst them; so we was pretty glad when the duke says—

" 'Tis my fate to be always ground into the mire under the iron heel of oppression. Misfortune has broken my once haughty spirit; I yield, I submit; 'tis my fate. I am alone in the world—let me suffer; I can bear it."

We got away as soon as it was good and dark. The king told us to stand well out towards the middle of the river, and not show a light till we got a long ways below the town. We come in sight of the little bunch of lights by-and-by—that was the town, you know—and slid by, about a half a mile out, all right. When we was three-quarters of a mile below, we hoisted up our signal lantern; and about ten o'clock it come on to rain and blow and thunder and lighten like everything; so the king told us to both stay on watch till the weather got better; then him and the duke crawled into the wigwam and turned in for the night. It was my watch below, till twelve, but I wouldn't a turned in, anyway, if I'd had a bed; because a body don't see such a storm as that every day in the week, not by a long sight. My souls, how the wind did scream along! And every second or two there'd come a glare that lit up the white-caps for a half a mile around, and you'd see the islands looking dusty through the rain, and the trees thrashing around in the wind; then comes a *h-wack!*—bum! bum! bumble-umble-um-bum-bum-bum-bum—and the thunder would go rumbling and grumbling away, and quit—and then *rip* comes another flash and another sockdolager. The waves most washed me off the raft, sometimes, but I hadn't any clothes on, and didn't mind. We didn't have no trouble about snags; the lightning was glaring and flittering around so constant that we could see them plenty soon enough to throw her head this way or that and miss them.

I had the middle watch, you know, but I was pretty sleepy by that time, so Jim he said he would stand the first half of it for me; he was always mighty good, that way, Jim was. I crawled into the wigwam, but the king and the duke had their legs sprawled around so there warn't no show for me; so I laid outside—I didn't mind the rain, because it was warm, and the waves warn't running so high, now. About two they come up again, though, and Jim was going to call me, but he changed his mind because he reckoned they warn't high enough yet to do any harm; but he was mistaken about that, for pretty soon all of a sudden along comes a regular ripper, and washed me overboard. It most killed Jim a-laughing. He was the easiest nigger to laugh that ever was, anyway.

I took the watch, and Jim he laid down and snored away; and by-and-by the storm let up for good and all; and the first cabin-light that showed, I rousted him out and we slid the raft into hiding-quarters for the day.

The king got out an old ratty deck of cards, after breakfast, and him and the duke played seven-up a while, five cents a game. Then they got tired of it, and allowed they would "lay out a campaign," as they called it. The duke went down into his carpet-bag and fetched up a lot of little printed bills, and read them out loud. One bill said "The celebrated Dr. Armand de Montalban of Paris," would "lecture on the Science of Phrenology" at such and such a place, on the blank day of blank, at ten cents admission, and "furnish charts of character at twenty-five cents apiece." The duke said that was *him*. In another bill he was the "world renowned Shaksperean tragedian, Garrick the Younger, of Drury Lane, London." In other bills he had a lot of other names and done other wonderful things, like finding water and gold with a "divining rod," "dissipating witch-spells," and so on. By-and-by he says—

"But the histrionic muse is the darling. Have you ever trod the boards, Royalty?"

"No," says the king.

"You shall, then, before you're three days older, Fallen Grandeur," says the duke. "The first good town we come to, we'll hire a hall and do the sword-fight in Richard III. and the balcony scene in Romeo and Juliet. How does that strike you?"

"I'm in, up to the hub, for anything that will pay, Bilgewater, but you see I don't know nothing about play-actn', and hain't ever seen much of it. I was too small when pap used to have 'em at the palace. Do you reckon you can learn me?"

"Easy!"

"All right. I'm jist a-freezn' for something fresh, anyway. Less commence, right away."

So the duke he told him all about who Romeo was, and who Juliet was, and said he was used to being Romeo, so the king could be Juliet.

"But if Juliet's such a young gal, Duke, my peeled head and my white whiskers is goin' to look oncommon odd on her, maybe."

"No, don't you worry—these country jakes won't ever think of that. Besides, you know, you'll be in costume, and that makes all the difference in the world; Juliet's in a balcony, enjoying the moonlight before she goes to bed, and she's got on her night-gown and her ruffled night-cap. Here are the costumes for the parts."

He got out two or three curtain-calico suits, which he said was meedyevil armor for Richard III. and t'other chap, and a long white cotton night-shirt and a ruffled night-cap to match. The king was satisfied; so the duke got out his book and read the parts over in the most splendid spread-eagle way, prancing around and acting at the same time, to show how it had got to be done; then he give the book to the king and told him to get his part by heart.

There was a little one-horse town about three mile down the bend, and after dinner the duke said he had ciphered out his idea about how to run in daylight without it being dangersome for Jim; so he allowed he would go down to the town and fix that thing. The king allowed he would go too, and see if he couldn't strike something. We was out of coffee, so Jim said I better go along with them in the canoe and get some.

When we got there, there warn't nobody stirring; streets empty, and perfectly dead and still, like Sunday. We found a sick nigger sunning himself in a back yard, and he said everybody that warn't too young or too sick or too old, was gone to camp-meeting, about two mile back in the woods. The king got the directions, and allowed he'd go and work that camp-meeting for all it was worth, and I might go, too.

The duke said what he was after was a printing office. We found it; a little bit of a concern, up over a carpenter shop—carpenters and printers all gone to the meeting, and no doors locked. It was a dirty, littered-up place, and had ink marks, and handbills with pictures of horses and runaway niggers on them, all over the walls. The duke shed his coat and said he was all right, now. So me and the king lit out for the camp-meeting.

We got there in about a half an hour, fairly dripping, for it was a most awful hot day. There was as much as a thousand people there, from twenty mile around. The woods was full of teams and wagons, hitched everywheres, feeding out of the wagon troughs and stomping to keep off the flies. There was sheds made of poles and roofed over with branches, where they had lemonade and gingerbread to sell, and piles of watermelons and green corn and such-like truck.

The preaching was going on under the same kinds of sheds, only they was bigger and held crowds of people. The benches was made out of outside slabs of logs, with holes bored in the round side to drive sticks into for legs. They didn't have no backs. The preachers had high platforms to stand on, at one end of the sheds. The women had on sun-bonnets; and some had linsey-woolsey frocks, some gingham ones, and a few of the young ones had on calico. Some of the young men was barefooted, and some of the children didn't have on any clothes but just a tow-linen shirt. Some of the old women was knitting, and some of the young folks was courting on the sly.

The first shed we come to, the preacher was lining out a hymn. He lined out two lines, everybody sung it, and it was kind of grand to hear it, there was so many of them and they done it in such a rousing way; then he lined out two more for them to sing—and so on. The people woke up more and more, and sung louder and louder; and towards the end, some begun to groan, and some begun to shout. Then the preacher begun to preach; and begun in earnest, too; and went weaving first to one side of the platform and then the other, and then a leaning down over the front of it, with his arms and his body going all the time, and shouting his words out with all his might; and every now and then he would hold up his Bible and spread it open, and kind of pass it around this way and that, shouting, "It's the brazen serpent in the wilderness! Look upon it and live!" And people would shout out, "Glory!—A-a-men!" And so he went on, and the people groaning and crying and saying amen:

"Oh, come to the mourners' bench! come, black with sin! (amen!) come, sick and sore! (amen!) come, lame and halt, and blind! (amen!) come, pore and needy, sunk in shame! (a-a-men!) come all that's worn, and soiled, and suffering!—come with a broken spirit! come with a contrite heart! come in your rags and sin and dirt! the waters that cleanse is free, the door of heaven stands open—oh, enter in and be at rest!" (a-a-men! glory, glory hallelujah!)

And so on. You couldn't make out what the preacher said, any more, on account of the shouting and crying. Folks got up, everywheres in the crowd, and worked their way, just by main strength, to the mourners' bench, with the tears running down their faces; and when all the mourners had got up there to the front benches in a crowd, they sung, and shouted, and flung themselves down on the straw, just crazy and wild.

Well, the first I knowed, the king got agoing; and you could hear him over everybody; and next he went a-charging up on to the platform and the preacher he begged him to speak to the people, and he done it. He told them he was a pirate—been a pirate for thirty years, out in the Indian Ocean, and his crew was thinned out considerable, last spring, in a fight, and he was home now, to take out some fresh men, and thanks to goodness he'd been robbed last night, and put ashore off of a steamboat without a cent, and he was glad of it, it was the blessedest thing that ever happened to him, because he was a changed man now, and happy for the first time in his life; and poor as he was, he was going to start right off and work his way back to the Indian Ocean and put in the rest of his life trying to turn the pirates into the true path; for he could do it better than anybody else, being acquainted with all the pirate crews in that ocean; and though it would take him a long time to get there, without money, he would get there anyway, and every time he convinced a pirate he would say to him, "Don't you thank me, don't you give me no credit, it all belongs to them dear people in Pokeville camp-meeting, natural brothers and benefactors of the race—and that dear preacher there, the truest friend a pirate ever had!"

And then he busted into tears, and so did everybody. Then somebody sings out, "Take up a collection for him, take up a collection!" Well, a half a dozen made a jump to do it, but somebody sings out, "Let *him* pass the hat around!" Then everybody said it, the preacher too.

So the king went all through the crowd with his hat, swabbing his eyes, and blessing the people and praising them and thanking them for being so good to the poor pirates away off there; and every little while the prettiest kind of girls with the tears running down their cheeks, would up and ask him would he let them kiss him, for to remember him by; and he always done it; and some of them he hugged and kissed as many as five or six times—and he was invited to stay a week; and everybody wanted him to live in their houses, and said they'd think it was an honor; but he said as this was the last day of the camp-meeting he couldn't do no good, and besides he was in a sweat to get to the Indian Ocean right off and go to work on the pirates.

When we got back to the raft and he come to count up, he found he had collected eighty-seven dollars and seventy-five cents. And then he had fetched away a three-gallon jug of whisky, too, that he found under a wagon when we was starting home through the woods. The king said, take it all around, it laid over any day he'd ever put in in the missionarying line. He said it warn't no use talking, heathens don't amount to shucks, alongside of pirates, to work a camp-meeting with.

The duke was thinking *he'd* been doing pretty well, till the king come to show up, but after that he didn't think so so much. He had set up and printed off two little jobs for farmers, in that printing office—horse bills—and took the money, four dollars. And he had got in ten dollars worth of advertisements for the paper, which he said he would put in for four dollars if they would pay in advance—so they done it. The price of the paper was two dollars a year, but he took in three subscriptions for half a dollar apiece on condition of them paying him in advance; they were going to pay in cord-wood and onions, as usual, but he said he had just bought the concern and knocked down the price as low as he could afford it, and was going to run it for cash. He set up a little piece of poetry, which he made, himself, out of his own head—three verses—kind of sweet and saddish—the name of it was, "Yes, crush, cold world, this breaking heart"—and he left that all set up and ready to print in the paper and didn't charge nothing for it. Well, he took in nine dollars and a half, and said he'd done a pretty square day's work for it.

Then he showed us another little job he'd printed and hadn't charged for, because it was for us. It had a picture of a runaway nigger, with a bundle on a stick, over his shoulder, and "$200 reward" under it. The reading was all about Jim, and just described him to a dot. It said he run away from St. Jacques' plantation, forty mile below New Orleans, last winter, and likely went north, and whoever would catch him and send him back, he could have the reward and expenses.

"Now," says the duke, "after to-night we can run in the daytime if we want to. Whenever we see anybody coming, we can tie Jim hand and foot with a rope, and lay him in the wigwam and show this handbill and say we captured him up the river, and were too poor to travel on a steamboat, so we got this little raft on credit from our friends and are going down to get the reward. Handcuffs and chains would look still better on Jim, but it wouldn't go well with the story of us being so poor. Too much like jewelry. Ropes are the correct thing—we must preserve the unities, as we say on the boards."

We all said the duke was pretty smart, and there couldn't be no trouble about running daytimes. We judged we could make miles enough that night to get out of the reach of the pow-wow we reckoned the duke's work in the printing office was going to make in that little town—then we could boom right along, if we wanted to.

We laid low and kept still, and never shoved out till nearly ten o'clock; then we slid by, pretty wide away from the town, and didn't hoist our lantern till we was clear out of sight of it.

When Jim called me to take the watch at four in the morning, he says—

"Huck, does you rek'n we gwyne to run acrost any mo' kings on dis trip?"

"No," I says, "I reckon not."

"Well," says he, "dat's all right, den. I doan' mine one er two kings, but dat's enough. Dis one's powerful drunk, en de duke ain' much better."

I found Jim had been trying to get him to talk French, so he could hear what it was like; but he said he had been in this country so long, and had so much trouble, he'd forgot it.

CHAPTER XXI

It was after sun-up, now, but we went right on, and didn't tie up. The king and the duke turned out, by-and-by, looking pretty rusty; but after they'd jumped overboard and took a swim, it chippered them up a good deal. After breakfast the king he took a seat on a corner of the raft, and pulled off his boots and rolled up his britches, and let his legs dangle in the water, so as to be comfortable, and lit his pipe, and went to getting his Romeo and Juliet by heart. When he had got it pretty good, him and the duke begun to practice it together. The duke had to learn him over and over again, how to say every speech; and he made him sigh, and put his hand on his heart, and after while he said he done it pretty well; "only," he says, "you mustn't bellow out *Romeo!* that way, like a bull—you must say it soft, and sick, and languishy, so—R-o-o-meo! that is the idea; for Juliet's a dear sweet mere child of a girl, you know, and she don't bray like a jackass."

Well, next they got a couple of long swords that the duke made out of oak laths, and begun to practice the sword-fight—the duke called himself Richard III.; and the way they laid on, and pranced around the raft was grand to see. But by-and-by the king tripped and fell overboard, and after that they took a rest, and had a talk about all kinds of adventures they'd had in other times along the river.

After dinner, the duke says:

"Well, Capet, we'll want to make this a first-class show, you know, so I guess we'll add a little more to it. We want a little something to answer encores with, anyway."

"What's onkores, Bilgewater?"

The duke told him, and then says:

"I'll answer by doing the Highland fling or the sailor's hornpipe; and you—well, let me see—oh, I've got it—you can do Hamlet's soliloquy."

"Hamlet's which?"

"Hamlet's soliloquy, you know; the most celebrated thing in Shakespeare. Ah, it's sublime, sublime! Always fetches the house. I haven't got it in the book—I've only got one volume—but I reckon I can piece it out from memory. I'll just walk up and down a minute, and see if I can call it back from recollection's vaults."

So he went to marching up and down, thinking, and frowning horrible every now and then; then he would hoist up his eyebrows; next he would squeeze his hand on his forehead and stagger back and kind of moan; next he would sigh, and next he'd let on to drop a tear. It was beautiful to see him. By-and-by he got it. He told us to give attention. Then he strikes a most noble attitude, with one leg shoved forwards, and his arms stretched away up, and his head

tilted back, looking up at the sky; and then he begins to rip and
rave and grit his teeth; and after that, all through his speech he
howled, and spread around, and swelled up his chest, and just
knocked the spots out of any acting ever *I* see before. This is the
speech—I learned it, easy enough, while he was learning it to the
king:

> To be, or not to be; that is the bare bodkin
> That makes calamity of so long life;
> For who would fardels bear, till Birnam Wood do come to Dunsinane,
> But that the fear of something after death
> Murders the innocent sleep,
> Great nature's second course,
> And makes us rather sling the arrows of outrageous fortune
> Than fly to others that we know not of.
> There's the respect must give us pause:
> Wake Duncan with thy knocking! I would thou couldst:
> For who would bear the whips and scorns of time,
> The oppressor's wrong, the proud man's contumely,
> The law's delay, and the quietus which his pangs might take,
> In the dead waste and middle of the night, when churchyards yawn
> In customary suits of solemn black,
> But that the undiscovered country from whose bourne no
>   traveler returns,
> Breathes forth contagion on the world,
> And thus the native hue of resolution, like the poor cat i' the adage,
> Is sicklied o'er with care,
> And all the clouds that lowered o'er our housetops,
> With this regard their currents turn awry,
> And lose the name of action.
> 'Tis a consummation devoutly to be wished. But soft you, the
>   fair Ophelia;
> Ope not they ponderous and marble jaws,
> But get thee to a nunnery—go!

Well, the old man he liked that speech, and he mighty soon got it
so he could do it first rate. It seemed like he was just born for it; and
when he had his hand in and was excited, it was perfectly lovely the
way he would rip and tear and rair up behind when he was getting
it off.

The first chance we got, the duke he had some show bills printed;
and after that, for two or three days, as we floated along, the raft
was a most uncommon lively place, for there warn't nothing but
sword-fighting and rehearsing—as the duke called it—going on all
the time. One morning, when we was pretty well down the State of
Arkansaw, we come in sight of a little one-horse town in a big bend;
so we tied up about three-quarters of a mile above it, in the mouth
of a crick which was shut in like a tunnel by the cypress trees, and
all of us but Jim took the canoe and went down there to see if there
was any chance in that place for our show.

We struck it mighty lucky; there was going to be a circus there
that afternoon, and the country people was already beginning to
come in, in all kinds of old shackly wagons, and on horses. The
circus would leave before night, so our show would have a pretty
good chance. The duke he hired the court house, and we went
around and stuck up our bills. They read like this:

Shaksperean Revival! ! !
Wonderful Attraction!
For One Night Only!
The world renowned tragedians,
David Garrick the younger, of Drury Lane Theatre, London,
and
Edmund Kean the elder, of the Royal Haymarket Theatre, White-
chapel, Pudding Lane, Piccadilly, London, and the
Royal Continental Theatres, in their sublime
Shaksperean Spectacle entitled
The Balcony Scene
in
Romeo and Juliet! ! !

Romeo . . . . Mr. Garrick
Juliet . . . . Mr. Kean

Assisted by the whole strength of the company!
New costumes, new scenery, new appointments!
Also:
The thrilling, masterly, and blood-curdling
Broad-sword conflict
In Richard III. ! ! !

Richard III . . . . Mr. Garrick.
Richmond . . . . Mr. Kean.

also:
(by special request,)
Hamlet's Immortal Soliloquy! !
By the Illustrious Kean!
Done by him 300 consecutive nights in Paris!
For One Night Only,
On account of imperative European engagements!
Admission 25 cents; children and servants, 10 cents.

Then we went loafing around the town. The stores and houses
was most all old shackly dried-up frame concerns that hadn't ever
been painted; they was set up three or four foot above ground on
stilts, so as to be out of reach of the water when the river was
overflowed. The houses had little gardens around them, but they
didn't seem to raise hardly anything in them but jimpson weeds,
and sunflowers, and ash-piles, and old curled-up boots and shoes,
and pieces of bottles, and rags, and played-out tin-ware. The fences
was made of different kinds of boards, nailed on at different times;
and they leaned every which-way, and had gates that didn't generly

have but one hinge—a leather one. Some of the fences had been whitewashed, some time or another, but the duke said it was in Clumbus's time, like enough. There was generly hogs in the garden, and people driving them out.

All the stores was along one street. They had white-domestic awnings in front, and the country people hitched their horses to the awning-posts. There was empty dry-goods boxes under the awnings, and loafers roosting on them all day long, whittling them with their Barlow knives; and chawing tobacco, and gaping and yawning and stretching—a mighty ornery lot. They generly had on yellow straw hats most as wide as an umbrella, but didn't wear no coats nor waistcoats; they called one another Bill, and Buck, and Hank, and Joe, and Andy, and talked lazy and drawly, and used considerable many cuss-words. There was as many as one loafer leaning up against every awning-post, and he most always had his hands in his britches pockets, except when he fetched them out to lend a chaw of tobacco or scratch. What a body was hearing amongst them, all the time was—

"Gimme a chaw 'v tobacker, Hank."

"Cain't—I hain't got but one chaw left. Ask Bill."

Maybe Bill he gives him a chaw; maybe he lies and says he ain't got none. Some of them kinds of loafers never has a cent in the world, nor a chaw of tobacco of their own. They get all their chawing by borrowing—they say to a fellow, "I wisht you'd len' me a chaw, Jack, I just this minute give Ben Thompson the last chaw I had"—which is a lie, pretty much every time; it don't fool nobody but a stranger; but Jack ain't no stranger, so he says—

"*You* give him a chaw, did you? so did your sister's cat's grandmother. You pay me back the chaws you've awready borry'd off'n me, Lafe Buckner, then I'll loan you one or two ton of it, and won't charge you no back intrust, nuther."

"Well, I *did* pay you back some of it wunst."

"Yes, you did—'bout six chaws. You borry'd store tobacker and paid back nigger-head."

Store tobacco is flat black plug, but these fellows mostly chaws the natural leaf twisted. When they borrow a chaw, they don't generly cut it off with a knife, but they set the plug in between their teeth, and gnaw with their teeth and tug at the plug with their hands till they get it in two—then sometimes the one that owns the tobacco looks mournful at it when it's handed back, and says, sarcastic—

"Here, gimme the *chaw*, and you take the *plug*."

All the streets and lanes was just mud, they warn't nothing else *but* mud—mud as black as tar, and nigh about a foot deep in some places; and two or three inches deep in *all* the places. The hogs loafed and grunted around, everywheres. You'd see a muddy sow and a litter of pigs come lazying along the street and whollop

herself right down in the way, where folks had to walk around her,
and she'd stretch out, and shut her eyes and wave her ears, whilst
the pigs was milking her, and look as happy as if she was on salary.
And pretty soon you'd hear a loafer sing out, "Hi! *so* boy! sick him,
Tige!" and away the sow would go, squealing most horrible, with a
dog or two swinging to each ear, and three or four dozen more
a-coming; and then you would see all the loafers get up and watch
the thing out of sight, and laugh at the fun and look grateful for
the noise. Then they'd settle back again till there was a dog-fight.
There couldn't anything wake them up all over, and make them
happy all over, like a dog-fight—unless it might be putting
turpentine on a stray dog and setting fire to him, or tying a tin pan
to his tail and see him run himself to death.

On the river front some of the houses was sticking out over the
bank, and they was bowed and bent, and about ready to tumble in.
The people had moved out of them. The bank was caved away
under one corner of some others, and that corner was hanging over.
People lived in them yet, but it was dangersome, because sometimes
a strip of land as wide as a house caves in at a time. Sometimes a
belt of land a quarter of a mile deep will start in and cave along
and cave along till it all caves into the river one summer. Such a
town as that has to be always moving back, and back, and back,
because the river's always gnawing at it.

The nearer it got to noon that day, the thicker and thicker was
the wagons and horses in the streets, and more coming all the time.
Families fetched their dinners with them, from the country, and eat
them in the wagons. There was considerable whiskey drinking
going on, and I seen three fights. By-and-by somebody sings out—

"Here comes old Boggs!—in from the country for his little old
monthly drunk—here he comes, boys!"

All the loafers looked glad—I reckoned they was used to having
fun out of Boggs. One of them says—

"Wonder who he's a gwyne to chaw up this time. If he'd a
chawed up all the men he's ben a gwyne to chaw up in the last
twenty year, he'd have considerble ruputation, now."

Another one says, "I wisht old Boggs'd threaten me, 'cuz then
I'd know I warn't gwyne to die for a thousan' year."

Boggs comes a-tearing along on his horse, whooping and yelling
like an Injun, and singing out—

"Cler the track, thar. I'm on the waw-path, and the price uv
coffins is a gwyne to raise."

He was drunk, and weaving about in his saddle; he was over fifty
year old, and had a very red face. Everybody yelled at him, and
laughed at him, and sassed him, and he sassed back, and said he'd
attend to them and lay them out in their regular turns, but he
couldn't wait now, because he'd come to town to kill old Colonel
Sherburn, and his motto was, "meat first, and spoon vittles to top

off on."

He sees me, and rode up and says—

"Whar'd you come f'm, boy? You prepared to die?"

Then he rode on. I was scared; but a man says—

"He don't mean nothing; he's always a carryin' on like that, when he's drunk. He's the best-naturedest old fool in Arkansaw—never hurt nobody, drunk nor sober."

Boggs rode up before the biggest store in town and bent his head down so he could see under the curtain of the awning, and yells—

"Come out here, Sherburn! Come out and meet the man you've swindled. You're the houn' I'm after, and I'm a gwyne to have you, too!"

And so he went on, calling Sherburn everything he could lay his tongue to, and the whole street packed with people listening and laughing and going on. By-and-by a proud-looking man about fifty-five—and he was a heap the best dressed man in that town, too—steps out of the store, and the crowd drops back on each side to let him come. He says to Boggs, mighty ca'm and slow—he says:

"I'm tired of this; but I'll endure it till one o'clock. Till one o'clock, mind—no longer. If you open you mouth against me only once, after that time, you can't travel so far but I will find you."

Then he turns and goes in. The crowd looked mighty sober; nobody stirred, and there warn't no more laughing. Boggs rode off blackguarding Sherburn as loud as he could yell, all down the street; and pretty soon back he comes and stops before the store, still keeping it up. Some men crowded around him and tried to get him to shut up, but he wouldn't; they told him it would be one o'clock in about fifteen minutes, and so he *must* go home—he must go right away. But it didn't do no good. He cussed away, with all his might, and throwed his hat down in the mud and rode over it, and pretty soon away he went a-raging down the street again, with his gray hair a-flying. Everybody that could get a chance at him tried their best to coax him off of his horse so they could lock him up and get him sober; but it warn't no use—up the street he would tear again, and give Sherburn another cussing. By-and-by somebody says—

"Go for his daughter!—quick, go for his daughter; sometimes he'll listen to her. If anybody can persuade him, she can."

So somebody started on a run. I walked down street a ways, and stopped. In above five or ten minutes, here comes Boggs again—but not on his horse. He was a-reeling across the street towards me, bareheaded, with a friend on both sides of him aholt of his arms and hurrying him along. He was quiet, and looked uneasy; and he warn't hanging back any, but was doing some of the hurrying himself. Somebody sings out—

"Boggs!"

I looked over there to see who said it, and it was that Colonel

Sherburn. He was standing perfectly still, in the street, and had a pistol raised in his right hand—not aiming it, but holding it out with the barrel tilted up towards the sky, The same second I see a young girl coming on the run, and two men with her. Boggs and the men turned round to see who called him, and when they see the pistol the men jumped to one side, and the pistol barrel come down slow and steady to a level—both barrels cocked. Boggs throws up both of his hands, and says, "O Lord, don't shoot!" Bang! goes the first shot, and he staggers back clawing at the air—bang! goes the second one, and he tumbles backwards onto the ground, heavy and solid, with his arms spread out. That young girl screamed out, and comes rushing, and down she throws herself on her father, crying, and saying, "Oh, he's killed him, he's killed him!" The crowd closed up around them, and shouldered and jammed one another, with their necks stretched, trying to see, and people on the inside trying to shove them back, and shouting, "Back, back! give him air, give him air!"

Colonel Sherburn he tossed his pistol onto the ground, and turned around on his heels and walked off.

They took Boggs to a little drug store, the crowd pressing around, just the same, and the whole town following, and I rushed and got a good place at the window, where I was close to him and could see in. They laid him on the floor, and put one large Bible under his head, and opened another one and spread it on his breast—but they tore open his shirt first, and I seen where one of the bullets went in. He made about a dozen long gasps, his breast lifting the Bible up when he drawed in his breath, and letting it down again when he breathed it out—and after that he laid still; he was dead. Then they pulled his daughter away from him, screaming and crying, and took her off. She was about sixteen, and very sweet and gentle-looking, but awful pale and scared.

Well, pretty soon the whole town was there, squirming and scrouging and pushing and shoving to get at the window and have a look, but people that had the places wouldn't give them up, and folks behind them was saying all the time, "Say, now, you've looked enough, you fellows; 'taint right and 'taint fair, for you to stay thar all the time, and never give nobody a chance; other folks has their rights as well as you."

There was considerable jawing back, so I slid out, thinking maybe there was going to be trouble. The streets was full, and everybody was excited. Everybody that seen the shooting was telling how it happened, and there was a big crowd packed around each one of these fellows, stretching their necks and listening. One long lanky man, with long hair and a big white fur stove-pipe hat on the back of his head, and a crooked-handled cane, marked out the places on the ground where Boggs stood, and where Sherburn stood, and the people following him around from one place to t'other and watching everything he done, and bobbing their heads to show they understood, and stooping a little and resting their hands on their thighs to watch him mark the places on the ground with his cane; and then he stood up straight and stiff where Sherburn had stood, frowning and having his hat-brim down over his eyes, and sung out, "Boggs!" and then fetched his cane down slow to a level, and says "Bang!" staggered backwards, says "Bang!" again, and fell down flat on his back. The people that had seen the thing said he done it perfect; said it was just exactly the way it all happened. Then as much as a dozen people got out their bottles and treated him.

Well, by-and-by somebody said Sherburn ought to be lynched. In about a minute everybody was saying it; so away they went, mad and yelling, and snatching down every clothes-line they come to, to do the hanging with.

CHAPTER XXII

They swarmed up the street towards Sherburn's house, a-whooping and yelling and raging like Injuns, and everything had to clear the way or get run over and tromped to mush, and it was awful to see. Children was heeling it ahead of the mob, screaming and trying to get out of the way; and every window along the road was full of women's heads, and there was nigger boys in every tree, and bucks and wenches looking over every fence; and as soon as the mob would get nearly to them they would break and skaddle back out of reach. Lots of the women and girls was crying and taking on, scared most to death.

They swarmed up in front of Sherburn's palings as thick as they could jam together, and you couldn't hear yourself think for the noise. It was a little twenty-foot yard. Some sung out "Tear down the fence! tear down the fence!" Then there was a racket of rippings and tearing and smashing, and down she goes, and the front wall of the crowd begins to roll in like a wave.

Just then Sherburn steps out on to the roof of his little front porch, with a double-barrel gun in his hand, and takes his stand, perfectly ca'm and deliberage, not saying a word. The racket stoppped, and the wave sucked back.

Sherburn never said a word—just stood there, looking down. The stillness was awful creepy and uncomfortable. Sherburn run his eye slow along the crowd; and wherever it struck, the people tried a little to outgaze him, but they couldn't; they dropped their eyes and looked sneaky. Then pretty soon Sherburn sort of laughed; not the pleasant kind, but the kind that makes you feel like when you are eating bread that's got sand in it.

Then he says, slow and scornful:

"The idea of *you* lynching anybody! It's amusing. The idea of you thinking you had pluck enough to lynch a *man!* Because you're

brave enough to tar and feather poor friendless cast-out women
that come along here, did that make you think you had grit
enough to lay your hands on a *man?* Why, a *man's* safe in the
hands of ten thousand of your kind—as long as it's day-time and
you're not behind him.

"Do I know you? I know you clear through. I was born and
raised in the South, and I've lived in the North; so I know the
average all around. The average man's a coward. In the North he
lets anybody walk over him that wants to, and goes home and prays
for a humble spirit to bear it. In the South one man, all by himself,
has stopped a stage full of men, in the day-time, and robbed the
lot. Your newspapers call you a brave people so much that you
think you *are* braver than any other people—whereas you're just *as*
brave, and no braver. Why don't your juries hang murderers?
Because they're afraid the man's friends will shoot them in the
back, in the dark—and it's just what they *would* do.

"So they always acquit; and then a *man* goes in the night, with a
hundred masked cowards at his back, and lynches the rascal. Your
mistake is, that you didn't bring a man with you; that's one
mistake, and the other is that you didn't come in the dark, and
fetch your masks. You brought *part* of a man—Buck Harkness,
there—and if you hadn't had him to start you, you'd a taken it out
in blowing.

"You didn't want to come. The average man don't like trouble
and danger. *You* don't like trouble and danger. But if only *half* a
man—like Buck Harkness, there—shouts 'Lynch him, lynch him!'
you're afraid to back down—afraid you'll be found out to be what
you are—*cowards*—and so you raise a yell, and hang yourselves
onto that half-a-man's coat tail, and come raging up here, swearing
what big things you're going to do. The pitifulest thing out is a
mob; that's what an army is—a mob; they don't fight with courage
that's born in them, but with courage that's borrowed from their
mass, and from their officers. But a mob without any *man* at the
head of it, is *beneath* pitifulness. Now the thing for *you* to do, is to
droop your tails and go home and crawl in a hole. If any real
lynching's going to be done, it will be done in the dark, Southern
fashion; and when they come they'll bring their masks, and fetch a
man along. Now *leave*—and take your half-a-man with you"—
tossing his gun up across his left arm and cocking it, when he says
this.

The crowd washed back sudden, and then broke all apart and
went tearing off every which way, and Buck Harkness he heeled it
after them, looking tolerable cheap. I could a staid, if I'd a wanted
to, but I didn't want to.

I went to the circus, and loafed around the back side till the
watchman went by, and then dived in under the tent. I had my
twenty-dollar gold piece and some other money, but I reckoned I

better save it, because there ain't no telling how soon you are going
to need it, away from home and amongst strangers, that way. You
can't be too careful. I ain't opposed to spending money on circuses,
when there ain't no other way, but there ain't no use in *wasting* it
on them.

It was a real bully circus. It was the splendidest sight that ever
was, when they all come riding in, two and two, a gentleman and
lady, side by side, the men just in their drawers and under-shirts,
and no shoes nor stirrups, and resting their hands on their thighs,
easy and comfortable—there must a' been twenty of them—and
every lady with a lovely complexion, and perfectly beautiful, and
looking just like a gang of real sure-enough queens, and dressed in
clothes that cost millions of dollars, and just littered with
diamonds. It was a powerful fine sight; I never see anything so
lovely. And then one by one they got up and stood, and went
a-weaving around the ring so gentle and wavy and graceful, the
men looking ever so tall and airy and straight, with their heads
bobbing and skimming along, away up there under the tent-roof,
and every lady's rose-leafy dress flapping soft and silky around her
hips, and she looking like the most loveliest parasol.

And then faster and faster they went, all of them dancing, first
one foot stuck out in the air and then the other, the horses leaning
more and more, and the ring-master going round and round the
centre-pole, cracking his whip and shouting "hi!—hi!" and the
clown cracking jokes behind him; and by-and-by all hands dropped
the reins, and every lady put her knuckles on her hips and every
gentleman folded his arms, and then how the horses did lean over
and hump themselves! And so, one after the other they all skipped
off into the ring and made the sweetest bow I ever see, and then
scampered out, and everybody clapped their hands and went just
about wild.

Well, all through the circus they done the most astonishing
things; and all the time that clown carried on so it most killed the
people. The ring-master couldn't ever say a word to him but he was
back at him quick as a wink with the funniest thing a body ever
said; and how he ever *could* think of so many of them, and so
sudden and so pat, was what I couldn't noway understand. Why, I
couldn't a thought of them in a year. And by-and-by a drunk man
tried to get into the ring—said he wanted to ride; said he could ride
as well as anybody that ever was. They argued and tried to keep
him out, but he wouldn't listen, and the whole show come to a
standstill. Then the people begun to holler at him and make fun of
him, and that made him mad, and he begun to rip and tear; so
that stirred up the poeple, and a lot of men begun to pile down off
of the benches and swarm towards the ring, saying, "Knock him
down! throw him out!" and one or two women begun to scream. So,
then, the ring-master he made a little speech, and said he hoped

there wouldn't be no disturbance, and if the man would promise he wouldn't make no more trouble, he would let him ride, if he thought he could stay on the horse. So everybody laughed and said all right, and the man got on. The minute he was on, the horse begun to rip and tear and jump and cavort around, with two circus men hanging onto his bridle trying to hold him, and the drunk man hanging onto his neck, and his heels flying in the air every jump, and the whole crowd of people standing up shouting and laughing till the tears rolled down. And at last, sure enough, all the circus men could do, the horse broke loose, and away he went like the very nation, round and round the ring, with that sot laying down on him and hanging to his neck, with first one leg hanging most to the ground on the side, and then t'other one on t'other side, and the people just crazy. It warn't funny to me, though; I was all of a tremble to see his danger. But pretty soon he struggled up astraddle and grabbed the bridle, a-reeling this way and that; and the next minute he sprung up and dropped the bridle and stood! and the horse agoing like a house afire too. He just stood there, a-sailing around as easy and comfortable as if he warn't ever drunk in his life—and then he begun to pull off his clothes and sling them. He shed them so thick they kind of clogged up the air, and altogether he shed seventeen suits. And then, there he was, slim and handsome, and dressed the gaudiest and prettiest you ever saw, and he lit into that horse with his whip and made him fairly hum—and finally skipped off, and made his bow and danced off to the dressing-room, and everybody just a-howling with pleasure and astonishment.

Then the ring-master he see how he had been fooled, and he *was* the sickest ring-master you ever see, I reckon. Why, it was one of his own men! He had got up that joke all out of his own head, and never let on to nobody. Well, I felt sheepish enough, to be took in so, but I wouldn't a been in that ring-master's place, not for a thousand dollars. I don't know; there may be bullier circuses than what that one was, but I never struck them yet. Anyways it was plenty good enough for *me;* and wherever I run across it, it can have all of my custom, every time.

Well, that night we had *our* show; but there warn't only about twelve people there; just enough to pay expenses. And they laughed all the time, and that made the duke mad; and everybody left, anyway, before the show was over, but one boy which was asleep. So the duke said these Arkansaw lunkheads couldn't come up to Shakspeare; what they wanted was low comedy—and may be something ruther worse than low comedy, he reckoned. He said he could size their style. So next morning he got some big sheets of wrapping-paper and some black paint, and drawed off some handbills and stuck them up all over the village. The bills said:

AT THE COURT HOUSE!

FOR 3 NIGHTS ONLY!

The World-Renowned Tragedians

DAVID GARRICK THE YOUNGER!

AND

EDMUND KEAN THE ELDER!

Of the London and Continental
Theatres,
In their Thrilling Tragedy of
THE KING'S CAMELOPARD

OR

THE ROYAL NONESUCH!!!

Admission 50 cents.

Then at the bottom was the biggest line of all—which said:

LADIES AND CHILDREN NOT ADMITTED.

"There," says he, "if that line don't fetch them, I don't know
Arkansaw!"

CHAPTER XXIII

Well, all day him and the king was hard at it, rigging up a stage,
and a curtain, and a row of candles for footlights; and that night
the house was jam full of men in no time. When the place couldn't
hold no more, the duke he quit tending door and went around the
back way and come onto the stage and stood up before the curtain,
and made a little speech, and praised up this tragedy, and said it
was the most thrillingest one that ever was; and so he went on
a-bragging about the tragedy and about Edmund Kean the Elder,
which was to play the main principal part in it; and at last when
he'd got everybody's expectations up high enough, he rolled up the
curtain, and the next minute the king come a-prancing out on all
fours, naked; and he was painted all over, ring-streaked-and-
striped, all sorts of colors, as splendid as a rainbow. And—but
never mind the rest of his outfit, it was just wild, but it was awful
funny. The people most killed themselves laughing; and when the
king got done capering, and capered off behind the scenes, they
roared and clapped and stormed and haw-hawed till he come back
and done it over again; and after that, they made him do it another
time. Well, it would a made a cow laugh to see the shines that old
idiot cut.

Then the duke he lets the curtain down, and bows to the people,
and says the great tragedy will be performed only two nights more,
on accounts of pressing London engagements, where the seats is all
sold aready for it in Drury Lane; and then he makes them another
bow, and says if he has succeeded in pleasing and instructing them,
he will be deeply obleeged if they will mention it to their friends

and get them to come and see it.

Twenty people sings out:

"What, is it over? Is that *All?*"

The duke says yes. Then there was a fine time. Everybody sings out "sold," and rose up mad, and was agoing for that stage and them tragedians. But a big fine-looking man jumps up on a bench, and shouts:

"Hold on! Just a word, gentlemen." They stopped to listen. "We are sold—mighty badly sold. But we don't want to be the laughing-stock of this whole town, I reckon, and never hear the last of this thing as long as we live. *No.* What we want, is to get out of here quiet, and talk this show up, and sell the *rest* of the town. Then we'll all be in the same boat. Ain't that sensible?" ("You bet it is!—the jedge is right!" everybody sings out.) "All right, then—not a word about any sell. Go along home, and advise everybody to come and see the tragedy."

Next day you couldn't hear nothing around that town but how splendid that show was. House was jammed again, that night, and we sold this crowd the same way. When me and king and the duke got home to the raft, we all had a super; and by-and-by, about midnight, they made Jim and me back her out and float her down the middle of the river and fetch her in and hide her about two miles below town.

The third night the house was crammed again—and they warn't new-comers, this time, but people that was at the show the other two nights. I stood by the duke at the door, and I see that every man that went in had his pockets bulging, or something muffled up under his coat—and I see it warn't no perfumery neither, not by a long sight. I smelt sickly eggs by the barrel, and rotten cabbages, and such things; and if I know the signs of a dead cat being around, and I bet I do, there was sixty-four of them went in. I shoved in there for a minute, but it was too various for me, I couldn't stand it. Well, when the place couldn't hold no more people, the duke he give a fellow a quarter and told him to tend door for him a minute, and then he started around for the stage door, I after him; but the minute we turned the corner and was in the dark, he says:

"Walk fast, now, till you get away from the houses, and then shin for the raft like the dickens was after you!"

I done it, and he done the same. We struck the raft at the same time, and less than two seconds we was gliding down steam, all dark and still, and edging towards the middle of the river, nobody saying a word. I reckoned the poor king was in for a gaudy time of it with the audience; but nothing of the sort; pretty soon he crawls out from under the wigwam, and says:

"Well, how'd the old thing pan out this time, Duke?"

He hadn't been up town at all.

We never showed a light till we was about ten mile below that village. Then we lit up and had a supper and the king and the duke fairly laughed their bones loose over the way they'd served them people. The duke says:

"Greenhorns, flatheads! *I* knew the first house would keep mum and let the rest of the town get roped in; and I knew they'd lay for us the third night, and consider it was *their* turn now. Well, it *is* their turn, and I'd give something to know how much they'd take for it. I *would* just like to know how they're putting in their opportunity. They can turn it into a picnic, if they want to—they brought plenty provisions."

Them rapscallions took in four hundred and sixty-five dollars in that three nights. I never see money hauled in by the wagon-load like that, before.

By-and-by, when they was asleep and snoring, Jim says:

"Don't it 'sprise you, de way dem kings carries on, Huck?"

"No," I says, "it don't."

"Why don't it, Huck?"

"Well, it don't, because it's in the breed. I reckon they're all alike."

"But, Huck, dese kings o' ourn is regular rapscallions; dat's jist what dey is; dey's regular rapscallions."

"Well, that's what I'm a-saying; all kings is mostly rapscallions, as fur as I can make out."

"Is dat so?"

"You read about them once—you'll see. Look at Henry the Eight; this'n 's a Sunday-School Superintendent to *him*. And look at Charles Second, and Louis Fourteen, and Louis Fifteen, and James Second, and Edward Second, and Richard Third, and forty more; besides all them Saxon heptarchies that used to rip around so in old times and raise Cain. My, you ought to seen old Henry the Eight when he was in bloom. He *was* a blossom. He used to marry a new wife every day, and chop off her head next morning. And he would do it just as indifferent as if he was ordering up eggs. 'Fetch up Nell Gwynn," he says. They fetch her up. Next morning, 'Chop off her head!' And they chop it off. 'Fetch up Jane Shore,' he says; and up she comes. Next morning 'Chop off her head'—and they chop it off. 'Ring up Fair Rosamun.' Fair Rosamun answers the bell. Next morning, 'Chop off her head.' And he made every one of them tell him a tale every night; and he put them all in a book, and called it Domesday Book—which was a good name and stated the case. You don't know kings, Jim, but I know them; and this old rip of ourn is one of the cleanest I've struck in history. Well, Henry he takes a notion he wants to get up some trouble with this country. How does he go at it—give notice?—give the country a show? No. All of a sudden he heaves all the tea in Boston Harbor overboard, and whacks out a declaration of independence, and dares them to come on. That was *his* style—he never give anybody a chance. He had suspicions of his father, the Duke of Wellington. Well, what did he do?—ask him to show up? No—drownded him in a butt of mamsey, like a cat. Spose people left money laying around where he was—what did he do? He collared it. Spose he contracted to do a thing; and you paid him, and didn't set down there and see that he done it—what did he do? He always done the other thing. Spose he opened his mouth—what then? If he didn't shut it up powerful quick, he'd lose a lie, every time. That's the kind of a bug Henry was; and if we'd a had him along 'stead of our kings, he'd a fooled that town a heap worse than ourn done. I don't say that ourn is lambs, because they ain't, when you come right down to the cold facts; but they ain't nothing to *that* old ram, anyway. All I say is, kings is kings, and you got to make allowances. Take them all around, they're a mighty ornery lot. It's the way they're raised."

"But dis one do *smell* so like de nation, Huck."

"Well, they all do, Jim. *We* can't help the way a king smells; history don't tell no way."

"Now de duke, he's a tolerable likely man, in some ways."

"Yes, a duke's different. But not very different. This one's a middling hard lot, for a duke, When he's drunk, there ain't no near-sighted man could tell him from a king."

"Well, anyways, I doan' hanker for no mo' un um, Huck. Dese is all I kin stan'."

"It's the way I feel, too, Jim. But we've got them on our hands, and we got to remember what they are, and make allowances. Sometimes I wish we could hear of a country that's out of kings."

What was the use to tell Jim these warn't real kings and dukes? It wouldn't a done no good; and besides, it was just as I said; you couldn't tell them from the real kind.

I went to sleep, and Jim didn't call me when it was my turn. He often done that. When I waked up, just at day-break, he was setting there with his head down betwixt his knees, moaning and mourning to himself. I didn't take notice, nor let on. I knowed what it was about. He was thinking about his wife and his children, away up yonder, and he was low and homesick; because he hadn't ever been away from home before in his life; and I do believe he cared just as much for his people as white folks does for their'n. It don't seem natural, but I reckon it's so. He was often moaning and mourning that way, nights, when he judged I was asleep, and saying, "Po' little 'Lizabeth! po' little Johnny! its mighty hard; I spec' I ain't ever gwyne to see you no mo', no mo'!" He was a mighty good nigger, Jim was.

But this time I somehow got to talking to him about his wife and young ones; and by-and-by he says:

"What makes me feel so bad dis time, 'uz bekase I hear sumpn over yonder on de bank like a whack, er a slam, while ago, en it

mine me er de time I treat my little 'Lizabeth so ornery. She warn't
on'y 'bout fo' year ole, en she tuck de sk'yarlet-fever, en had a
powful rough spell; but she got well, en one day she was a-stannin'
around', en I says to her, I says:

"Shet de do'.'

"She never done it; jis' stood dah, kiner smilin' up at me. It
make me mad; en I says agin, mighty loud, I says:

" 'Doan' you hear me?—shet de do'!'

"She jis' stood de same way, kiner smilin' up. I was a-bilin'!
I says:

" 'I lay I *make* you mine!'

"En wid dat I fetch' her a slap side de head dat sont her
a-sprawlin'. Den I went into de yuther room, en 'uz gone 'bout ten
minutes; en when I come back, dah was dat do' a-stanning' open
yit, en dat chile stannin' mos' right in it, a-lookin' down and
mournin', en de tears runnin' down. My, but I *wuz* mad, I was
agwyne for de chile, but jis' den—it was a do' dat open innerds—
jis' den, 'long come de wind en slam it to, behine de chile,
ker-*blam!*—en my lan', de chile never move'! My breff mos' hop
outer me; en I feel so—so—I don't know *how* I feel. I crope out, all
a-tremblin', en crope aroun' en open de do' easy en slow, en poke
my head in behind de chile, sof' en still, en all uv a sudden, I says
pow! just' as loud as I could yell. *She never budge!* Oh, Huck, I
bust out a-cryin' en grab her up in my arms, en say, 'Oh, de po'
little thing! de Lord God Amighty fogive po' ole Jim, kaze he never
gwyne to fogive hisself as long's he live!' Oh, she was plumb deef en
dumb, Huck, plumb deef en dumb—en I'd been a-treat'n her so!"

CHAPTER XXIV

Next day, towards night, we laid up under a little willow tow-
head out in the middle, where there was a village on each side of
the river, and the duke and the king begun to lay out a plan for
working them towns. Jim he spoke to the duke, and said he hoped
it wouldn't take but a few hours, because it got mighty heavy and
tiresome to him when he had to lay all day in the wigwam tied with
the rope. You see, when we left him all alone we had to tie him,
because if anybody happened on him all by himself and not tied, it
wouldn't look much like he was a runaway nigger, you know. So the
duke said it *was* kind of hard to have to lay roped all day, and he'd
cipher out some way to get around it.

He was uncommon bright, the duke was, and he soon struck it.
He dressed Jim up in King Lear's outfit—it was a long curtain-
calico gown, and a white horse-hair wig and whiskers; and then he
took his theatre-paint and painted Jim's face and hands and ears
and neck all over a dead dull solid blue, like a man that's been
drownded nine days. Blamed if he warn't the horriblest looking

outrage I ever see. Then the duke took and wrote out a sign on a shingle so—

Sick Arab—but harmless when not out of his head.

And he nailed that shingle to a lath, and stood the lath up four or five foot in front of the wigwam. Jim was satisfied. He said it was a sight better than laying tied a couple of years every day and trembling all over every time there was a sound. The duke told him to make himself free and easy, and if anybody ever come meddling around, he must hop out of the wigwam, and carry on a little, and fetch a howl or two like a wild beast, and he reckoned they would light out and leave him alone. Which was sound enough judgment; but you take the average man, and he wouldn't wait for him to howl. Why, he didn't only look like he was dead, he looked considerable more than that.

These rapscallions wanted to try the Nonesuch again, because there was so much money in it, but they judged it wouldn't be safe, because maybe the news might a worked along down by this time. They couldn't hit no project that suited, exactly; so at last the duke said he reckoned he'd lay off and work his brains an hour or two and see if he couldn't put up something on the Arkansaw village; and the king he allowed he would drop over to t'other village, without any plan, but just trust in Providence to lead him the profitable way—meaning the devil, I reckon. We had all bought store clothes where we stopped last; and now the king put his'n on, and he did look real swell and starchy. I never knowed how clothes could change a body before. Why, before, he looked like the orneriest old rip that ever was; but now, when he'd take off his new white beaver and make a bow and do a smile, he looked that grand and good and pious that you'd say he had walked right out of the ark, and maybe was old Leviticus himself. Jim cleaned up the canoe, and I got my paddle ready. There was a big steamboat laying at the shore away up under the point, about three mile above town—been there a couple of hours, taking on freight. Says the king:

"Seein' how I'm dressed, I reckon maybe I better arrive down from St. Louis or Cincinnati, or some other big place. Go for the steamboat, Huckleberry; we'll come down to the village on her."

I didn't have to be ordered twice, to go and take a steamboat ride. I fetched the shore a half a mile above the village, and then went scooting along the bluff bank in the easy water. Pretty soon we come to a nice innocent-looking young country jake setting on a log swabbing the sweat off of his face, for it was powerful warm weather; and he had a couple of big carpet-bags by him.

"Run her nose in shore," says the king. I done it. "Wher' you bound for, young man?"

"For the steamboat; going to Orleans."

"Git aboard," says the king. "Hold on a minute, my servant 'll

he'p you with them bags. Jump out and he'p the gentleman,
Adolphus"—meaning me, I see.

I done so, and then we all three started on again. The young
chap was mighty thankful; said it was tough work toting his
baggage such weather. He asked the king where he was going, and
the king told him he'd come down the river and landed at the other
village this morning, and now he was going up a few mile to see an
old friend on a farm up there. The young fellow says:

"When I first see you, I says to myself, 'It's Mr. Wilks, sure, and
he come mighty near getting here in time.' But then I says again,
'No, I reckon it ain't him, or else he wouldn't be paddling up the
river.' You *ain't* him, are you?"

"No, my name's Blodgett—Elexander Blodgett—*Reverend*
Elexander Blodgett, I spose I must say, as I'm one o' the Lord's
poor servants. But still I'm jist as able to be sorry for Mr. Wilks for
not arriving in time, all the same, if he's missed anything by it—
which I hope he hasn't."

"Well, he don't miss any property by it, because he'll get that all
right; but he's missed seeing his brother Peter die—which he
mayn't mind, nobody can tell as to that—but his brother would a
give anything in this world to see *him* before he died; never talked
about nothing else all these three weeks; hadn't seen him since they
was boys together—and hadn't ever seen his brother William at all
—that's the deef and dumb one—William ain't more than thirty or
thirty-five. Peter and George was the only ones that come out here;
George was the married brother; him and his wife both died last
year. Harvey and William's the only ones that's left now; and, as I
was saying, they haven't got here in time."

"Did anybody send 'em word?"

"Oh, yes; a month or two ago, when Peter was first took; because
Peter said then that he sorter felt like he warn't going to get well
this time. You see, he was pretty old, and George's g'yirls was too
young to be much company for him, except Mary Jane the red-
headed one; and so he was kinder lonesome after George and his
wife died, and didn't seem to care much to live. He most
desperately wanted to see Harvey—and William too, for that matter
—because he was one of them kind that can't bear to make a will.
He left a letter behind for Harvey, and said he'd told in it where
his money was hid, and how he wanted the rest of the property
divided up so George's g'yirls would be all right—for George didn't
leave nothing. And that letter was all they could get him to put a
pen to."

"Why do you reckon Harvey don't come? Wher' does he live?"

"Oh, he lives in England—Sheffield—preaches there—hasn't
ever been in this country. He hasn't had any too much time—and
beside he mightn't a got the letter at all, you know."

"Too bad, too bad he couldn't a lived to see his brothers, poor soul. You going to Orleans, you say?"

"Yes, but that ain't only a part of it. I'm going in a ship, next Wednesday, for Ryo Janeero, where my uncle lives."

"It's a pretty long journey. But it'll be lovely; I wisht I was agoing. Is Mary Jane the oldest? How old is the others?"

"Mary Jane's nineteen, Susan's fifteen, and Joanna's about fourteen—that's the one that gives herself to good works and has a hare-lip."

"Poor things! to be left alone in the cold world so."

"Well, they could be worse off. Old Peter had friends, and they ain't going to let them come to no harm. There's Hobson, the Babtis' preacher; and Deacon Lot Hovey, and Ben Rucker, and Abner Shackleford, and Levi Bell, the lawyer; and Dr. Robinson, and their wives, and the widow Bartley, and—well, there's a lot of them; but these are the ones that Peter was thickest with, and used to write about sometimes, when he wrote home; so Harvey'll know where to look for friends when he get's here."

Well, the old man he went on asking questions till he just fairly emptied that young fellow. Blamed if he didn't inquire about everybody and everything in that blessed town, and all about all the Wilkses; and about Peter's business—which was a tanner; and about George's—which was a carpenter; and about Harvey's—which was a dissentering minister; and so on, and so on. Then he says:

"What did you want to walk all the way up to the steamboat for?"

"Because she's a big Orleans boat, and I was afeard she mightn't stop there. When they're deep they won't stop for a hail. A Cincinnati boat will, but this is a St. Louis one."

"Was Peter Wilks well off?"

"Oh, yes, pretty well off. He had houses and land, and it's reckoned he left three or four thousand in cash hid up som'ers."

"When did you say he died?"

"I didn't say, but it was last night."

"Funeral to-morrow, likely?"

"Yes, 'bout the middle of the day."

"Well, it's all terrible sad; but we've all got to go, one time or another. So what we want to do is to be prepared; then we're all right."

"Yes, sir, it's the best way. Ma used to always say that."

When we struck the boat, she was about done loading, and pretty soon she got off. The king never said nothing about going aboard, so I lost my ride, after all. When the boat was gone, the king made me paddle up another mile to a lonesome place, and then he got ashore, and says:

"Now hustle back, right off, and fetch the duke up here, and the new carpet-bags. And if he's gone over to t'other side, go over there and git him. And tell him to git himself up regardless. Shove along, now."

I see what *he* was up to; but I never said nothing, of course. When I got back with the duke, we hid the canoe and then they set down on a log, and the king told him everything, just like the young fellow had said it—every last word of it. And all the time he was a doing it, he tried to talk like an Englishman; and he done it pretty well too, for a slouch. I can't imitate him, and so I ain't agoing to try to; but he really done it pretty good. Then he says:

"How are you on the deef and dumb, Bilgewater?"

The duke said, leave him alone for that; said he had played a deef and dumb person on the histrionic boards. So then they waited for a steamboat.

About the middle of the afternoon a couple of little boats come along, but they didn't come from high enough up the river; but at last there was a big one, and they hailed her. She sent out her yawl, and we went aboard, and she was from Cincinnati; and when they found we only wanted to go four or five mile, they was booming mad, and give us a cussing, and said they wouldn't land us. But the king was ca'm. He says:

"If gentlemen kin afford to pay a dollar a mile apiece, to be took on and put off in a yawl, a steamboat kin afford to carry 'em, can't it?"

So they softened down and said it was all right; and when we got to the village, they yawled us ashore. About two dozen men flocked down, when they see the yawl a coming; and when the king says—

"Kin any of you gentlemen tell me wher' Mr. Peter Wilks lives?" they give a glance at one another, and nodded their heads, as much as to say, "What d' I tell you?" Then one of them says, kind of soft and gentle:

"I'm sorry, sir, but the best we can do is to tell you where he *did* live yesterday evening."

Sudden as winking, the ornery old cretur went all to smash, and fell up against the man, and put his chin on his shoulder, and cried down his back, and says:

"Alas, alas, our poor brother—gone, and we never got to see him; oh, it's too, *too* hard!"

Then he turns around, blubbering, and makes a lot of idiotic signs to the duke on his hands, and blamed if *he* didn't drop a carpet-bag and bust out a-crying. If they warn't the beatenest lot, them two frauds, that ever I struck.

Well, the men gethered around, and sympathized with them, and said all sorts of kind things to them, and carried their carpet-bags up the hill for them, and let them lean on them and cry, and told the king all about his brother's last moments and the king he told it all over again on his hands to the duke, and both of them took on about that dead tanner like they'd lost the twelve disciples. Well, if ever I struck anything like it, I'm a nigger. It was enough to make a body ashamed of the human race.

CHAPTER XXV

The news was all over town in two minutes, and you could see the people tearing down on the run, from every which way, some of them putting on their coats as they come. Pretty soon we was in the middle of a crowd, and the noise of the tramping was like a soldier-march. The windows and door-yards was full; and every minute somebody would say, over a fence:

"Is it *them?*"

And somebody trotting along with the gang would answer back and say,

"You bet it is."

When we got to the house, the street in front of it was packed, and the three girls was standing in the door. Mary Jane *was* red-headed, but that don't make no difference, she was most awful beautiful, and her face and her eyes was all lit up like glory, she was so glad her uncles was come. The king he spread his arms, and Mary Jane she jumped for them, and the hare-lip jumped for the duke, and there they *had* it! Everybody most, leastways women, cried for joy to see them meet again at last and have such good times.

Then the king he hunched the duke, private—I see him do it—and then he looked around and see the coffin, over in the corner on two chairs; so then, him and the duke, with a hand across each other's shoulder, and t'other hand to their eyes, walked slow and solemn over there, everybody dropping back to give them room, and all the talk and noise stopping, people saying "Sh!" and all the men taking their hats off and drooping their heads, so you could a heard a pin fall. And when they got there, they bent over and looked in the coffin, and took one sight, and then they bust out a crying so you could a heard them to Orleans, most; and then they put their arms around each other's necks, and hung their chins over each other's shoulders; and then for three minutes, or maybe four, I never see two men leak the way they done. And mind you, everybody was doing the same; and the place was that damp I never see anything like it. Then one of them got on one side of the coffin, and t'other on t'other side, and they kneeled down and rested their foreheads on the coffin, and let on to pray all to theirselves. Well, when it come to that, it worked the crowd like you never see any-thing like it, and so everybody broke down and went to sobbing right out loud—the poor girls, too; and every woman, nearly, went up to the girls, without saying a word, and kissed them, solemn, on the forehead, and then put their hand on their head, and looked up towards the sky, with the tears running down, and then busted out and went off sobbing and swabbing, and give the next woman a show. I never see anything so disgusting.

Well, by-and-by the king he gets up and comes forward a little, and works himself up and slobbers out a speech, all full of tears and flapdoodle about its being a sore trial for him and his poor brother to lose the diseased, and to miss seeing diseased alive, after the long journey of four thousand mile, but its a trial that's sweetened and sanctified to us by this dear sympathy and these holy tears, and so he thanks them out of his heart and out of his brother's heart, because out of their mouths they can't, words being too weak and cold, and all that kind of rot and slush, till it was just sickening; and then he blubbers out a pious goody-goody Amen, and turns himself loose and goes to crying fit to bust.

And the minute the words was out of his mouth somebody over in the crowd struck up the doxolojer, and everybody joined in with all their might, and it just warmed you up and made you feel as good as church letting out. Music *is* a good thing; and after all that soul-butter and hogwash, I never see it freshen up things so, and sound so honest and bully.

Then the king begins to work his jaw again, and says how him and his nieces would be glad if a few of the main principal friends of the family would take supper here with them this evening, and help set up with the ashes of the diseased; and says if his poor brother laying yonder could speak, he knows who he would name, for they was names that was very dear to him and mentioned often in his letters; so he will name the same, to-wit, as follows, vizz:— Rev. Mr. Hobson, and Deacon Lot Hovey, and Mr. Ben Rucker, and Abner Shackleford, and Levi Bell, and Dr. Robinson, and their wives, and the widow Bartley.

Rev. Hobson and Dr. Robinson was down to the end of the town, a-hunting together; that is, I mean the doctor was shipping a sick man to t'other world, and the preacher was pinting him right. Lawyer Bell was away up to Louisville on some business. But the rest was on hand, and so they all come and shook hands with the king and thanked him and talked to him; and then they shook hands with the duke, and didn't say nothing but just kept a-smiling and bobbing their heads like a passel of sapheads whilst he made all sorts of signs with his hands and said "Goo-goo—goo-goo-goo," all the time, like a baby that can't talk.

So the king he blatted along, and managed to inquire about pretty much everybody and dog in town, by his name, and mentioned all sorts of little things that happened one time or another in the town, or to George's family, or to Peter; and he always let on that Peter wrote him the things, but that was a lie, he got every blessed one of them out of that young flathead that we canoed up to the steamboat.

Then Mary Jane she fetched the letter her father left behind, and the king he read it out loud and cried over it. It give the dwelling-house and three thousand dollars, gold, to the girls; and it give the tanyard (which was doing a good business), along with some other houses and land (worth about seven thousand), and three thousand dollars in gold to Harvey and William, and told where the six thousand cash was hid, down cellar. So these two frauds said they'd go and fetch it up, and have everything square and above-board; and told me to come with a candle. We shut the cellar door behind us, and when they found the bag they spilt it out on the floor, and it was a lovely sight, all them yaller-boys. My, the way the king's eyes did shine! He slaps the duke on the shoulder, and says:

"Oh, *this* ain't bully, nor noth'n! Oh, no, I reckon not! Why, Biljy, it beats the Nonesuch, *don't* it!"

The duke allowed it did. They pawed the yaller-boys, and sifted them through their fingers and let them jingle down on the floor; and the king says:

"It ain't no use talkin'; being' brothers to a rich dead man, and representatives of furrin heirs that's got left, is the line for you and me, Bilge. Thish-yer comes of trust'n to Providence. It's the best way, in the long run. I've tried 'em all, and ther' ain't no better way."

Most everybody would a been satisfied with the pile, and took it on trust; but no, they must count it. So they counts it, and it comes out four hundred and fifteen dollars short. Says the king:

"Dern him, I wonder what he done with that four hundred and fifteen dollars?"

They worried over that a while, and ransacked all around for it. Then the duke says:

"Well, he was a pretty sick man, and likely he made a mistake— I reckon that's the way of it. The best way's to let it go, and keep still about it. We can spare it."

"Oh, shucks, yes, we can *spare* it. I don't k'yer noth'n 'bout that —it's the *count* I'm thinkin' about. We want to be awful square and open and above-board, here, you know. We want to lug this h-yer money up stairs and count it before everybody—then ther' ain't noth'n suspicious. But when the dead man says ther's six thous'n dollars, you know, we don't want to—"

"Hold on," says the duke. "Less make up the deffisit"—and he begun to haul out yaller-boys out of his pocket.

"It's a most amaz'n' good idea, duke—you *have* got a rattlin' clever head on you," says the king. "Blest if the old Nonesuch ain't a heppin' us out agin"—and *he* begun to haul out yaller-jackets and stack them up.

It most busted them, but they made up the six thousand clean and clear.

"Say," says the duke, "I got another idea. Le's go up stairs and count this money, and then take and *give it to the girls.*"

"Good land, duke, lemme hug you! It's the most dazzling idea 'at ever a man struck. You have cert'nly got the most astonishin' head I ever see. Oh, this is the boss dodge, ther' ain't no mistake 'bout it. Let 'em fetch along their suspicions now, if they want to—this'll lay 'em out."

When we got up stairs, everybody gethered around the table, and the king he counted it and stacked it up, three hundred dollars in a pile—twenty elegant little piles. Everybody looked hungry at it, and licked their chops. Then they raked it into the bag again, and I see the king begin to swell himself up for another speech. He says:

"Friends all, my poor brother that lays yonder, has done generous by them that's left behind in the vale of sorrers. He has done generous by these-yer poor little lambs that he loved and sheltered, and that's left fatherless and motherless. Yes, and we that knowed him, knows that he would a done *more* generous by 'em if he hadn't ben afeard o' woundin' his dear William and me. Now, *wouldn't* he? Ther' ain't no question 'bout it, in *my* mind. Well, then—what kind o' brothers would it be, that'd stand in his way at sech a time? And what kind o' uncles would it be that'd rob—yes, *rob*—sech poor sweet lambs as these 'at he loved so, at sech a time? If I know William—and I *think* I do—he—well, I'll jest ask him." He turns around and begins to make a lot of signs to the duke with his hands; and the duke he looks at him stupid and leather-headed a while, then all of a sudden he seems to catch his meaning, and jumps for the king, goo-gooing with all his might for joy, and hugs him about fifteen times before he lets up. Then the king says, "I knowed it; I reckon *that* 'll convince anybody the way *he* feels about it. Here, Mary Jane, Susan, Joanner, take the money—take it *all*. It's the gift of him that lays yonder, cold but joyful."

Mary Jane she went for him, Susan and the hare-lip went for the duke, and then such another hugging and kissing I never see yet. And everybody crowded up with the tears in their eyes, and most shook the hands off of them frauds, saying all the time:

"You *dear* good souls?—how *lovely!*—how *could* you!"

Well, then, pretty soon all hands got to talking about the diseased again, and how good he was, and what a loss he was, and all that; and before long a big iron-jawed man worked himself in there from outside, and stood a listening and looking, and not saying anything; and nobody saying anything to him either, because the king was talking and they was all busy listening. The king was saying—in the middle of something he'd started in on—

"—they bein' partickler friends o' the diseased. That's why they're invited here this evenin'; but to-morrow we want *all* to come—everybody; for he respected everybody, he liked everybody, and so it's fitten that his funeral orgiess h'd be public."

And so he went a-mooning on and on, liking to hear himself talk, and every little while he fetched in his funeral orgies again, till the duke he couldn't stand it no more; so he writes on a little scrap of paper, *"obsequies,* you old fool," and folds it up and goes to goo-gooing and reaching it over people's heads to him. The king he reads it, and puts it in his pocket, and says:

"Poor William, afflicted as he is, his *heart's* aluz right. Asks me to invite everybody to come to the funeral—wants me to make 'em all welcome. But he needn't a worried—it was jest what I was at."

Then he weaves along again, perfectly ca'm, and goes to dropping in his funeral orgies again every now and then, just like he done before. And when he done it the third time, he says:

"I say orgies, not because it's the common term, because it ain't —obsequies bein' the common term—but because orgies is the right term. Obsequies ain't used in England no more, now—it's gone out. We say orgies now, in England. Orgies is better, because it means the thing you're after, more exact. It's a word that's made up out'n the Greek *orgo,* outside, open, abroad; and the Hebrew *jeesum,* to plant, cover up; hence in*ter.* So, you see, funeral orgies is an open er public funeral."

He was the *worst* I ever struck. Well, the iron-jawed man he laughed right in his face. Everybody was shocked. Everybody says, "Why *doctor!*" and Abner Shackleford says:

"Why, Robinson, hain't you heard the news? This is Harvey Wilks."

The king he smiled eager, and shoved out his flapper, and says: *"Is* it my poor brother's dear good friend and physician? I—"

"Keep your hands off of me!" says the doctor. *"You* talk like an Englishman—*don't* you? It's the worse imitation I ever heard. *You* Peter Wilks's brother. You're a fraud, that's what you are!"

Well, how they all took on! They crowded around the doctor, and tried to quiet him down, and tried to explain to him, and tell him how Harvey'd showed in forty ways that he *was* Harvey, and knowed everybody by name, and the names of the very dogs, and begged and *begged* him not to hurt Harvey's feelings and the poor girls' feelings, and all that; but it warn't no use, he stormed right along, and said any man that pretended to be an Englishman and couldn't imitate the lingo no better than what he did, was a fraud and a liar. The poor girls was hanging to the king and crying; and all of a sudden the doctor ups and turns on *them.* He says:

"I was your father's friend, and I'm your friend; and I warn you *as* a friend, and an honest one, that wants to protect you and keep you out of harm and trouble, to turn your backs on that scoundrel, and have nothing to do with him, the ignorant tramp, with his idiotic Greek and Hebrew as he calls it. He is the thinnest kind of an impostor—has come here with a lot of empty names and facts which he has picked up somewheres, and you take them for *proofs,* and are helped to fool yourselves by these foolish friends here, who ought to know better. Mary Jane Wilks, you know me for your

friend, and for your unselfish friend, too. Now listen to me; turn
this pitiful rascal out—I *beg* you to do it. Will you?''

Mary Jane straightened herself up, and my, but she was
handsome! She says:

"*Here* is my answer." She hove up the bag of money and put it
in the king's hands, and says, "Take this six thousand dollars, and
invest for me and my sisters any way you want to, and don't give us
no receipt for it."

Then she put her arm around the king on one side, and Susan
and the hare-lip done the same on the other. Everybody clapped
their hands and stomped on the floor like a perfect storm, whilst the
king held up his head and smiled proud. The doctor says:

"All right, I wash *my* hands of the matter. But I warn you all
that a time's coming when you're going to feel sick whenever you
think of this day"—and away he went.

"All right, doctor," says the king, kinder mocking him, "we'll
try and get 'em to send for you"—which made them all laugh, and
they said it was a prime good hit.

CHAPTER XXVI

Well when they was all gone, the king he asks Mary Jane how
they was off for spare rooms, and she said she had one spare room,
which would do for Uncle William, and she'd give her own room to
Uncle Harvey, which was a little bigger, and she would turn into the
room with her sisters and sleep on a cot; and up garret was a little
cubby, with a pallet in it. The king said the cubby would do for his
valley—meaning me.

So Mary Jane took us up, and she showed them their rooms,
which was plain but nice. She said she'd have her frocks and a lot
of other traps took out of her room if they was in Uncle Harvey's
way, but he said they warn't. The frocks was hung along the wall,
and before them was a curtain made out of calico that hung down
to the floor. There was an old hair trunk in one corner, and a guitar
box in another, and all sorts of little knickknacks and jimcracks
around, like girls brisken up a room with. The king said it was all
the more homely and more pleasanter for these fixings, and so don't
disturb them. The duke's room was pretty small, but plenty good
enough, and so was my cubby.

That night they had a big supper, and all them men and women
was there, and I stood behind the king and the duke's chairs and
waited on them, and the niggers waited on the rest. Mary Jane
she set at the head of the table, with Susan along side of her, and
said how bad the biscuits was, and how mean the preserves was,
and how ornery and tough the fried chickens was—and all that
kind of rot, the way women always do for to force out compliments;
and the people all knowed everything was tip-top, and said so—said

"How *do* you get biscuits to brown so nice?" and "Where, for the land's sake *did* you get these amaz'n pickles?" and all that kind of humbug talky-talk, just the way people always does at a supper, you know.

And when it was all done, me and the hare-lip had supper in the kitchen off of the leavings, whilst the others was helping the niggers clean up the things. The hare-lip she got to pumping me about England, and blest if I didn't think the ice was getting mighty thin, sometimes. She says:

"Did you ever see the king?"

"Who? William Fourth? Well, I bet I have—he goes to our church." I knowed he was dead years ago, but I never let on. So when I says he goes to our church, she says:

"What—regular?"

"Yes—regular. His pew's right over opposite ourn—on 'tother side the pulpit."

"I thought he lived in London?"

"Well, he does. Where *would* he live?"

"But I thought *you* lived in Sheffield?"

I see I was up a stump. I had to let on to get choked with a chicken bone, so as to get time to think how to get down again. Then I says:

"I mean he goes to our church regular when he's in Sheffield. That's only in the summer-time, when he comes there to take the sea baths."

"Why, how you talk—Sheffield ain't on the sea."

"Well, who said it was?"

"Why, you did."

"I *didn't,* nuther."

"You did!"

"I didn't."

"You did."

"I never said nothing of the kind."

"Well, what *did* you say, then?"

"Said he come to take the sea *baths*—that's what I said."

"Well, then! how's he going to take the sea baths if it ain't on the sea?"

"Looky here," I says; "did you ever see any Congress water?"

"Yes."

"Well, did you have to go to Congress to get it?"

"Why, no."

"Well, neither does William Fourth have to go to the sea to get a sea bath."

"How does he get it, then?"

"Gets it the way people down here gets Congress-water—in barrels. There in the palace at Sheffield they've got furnaces, and he wants his water hot. They can't bile that amount of water away off there at the sea. They haven't got no conveniences for it."

"Oh, I see, now. You might a said that in the first place and saved time."

When she said that, I see I was out of the woods again, and so I was comfortable and glad. Next, she says:

"Do you go to church, too?"

"Yes—regular."

"Where do you set?"

"Why, in our pew."

"*Whose* pew?"

"Why, *ourn*—your Uncle Harvey's."

"His'n? What does *he* want with a pew?"

"Wants it to set in. What did you *reckon* he wanted with it?"

"Why, I thought he'd be in the pulpit."

Rot him, I forgot he was a preacher. I see I was up a stump again, so I played another chicken bone and got another think. Then I says:

"Blame it, do you suppose there ain't but one preacher to a church?"

"Why, what do they want with more?"

"What!—to preach before a king? I never see such a girl as you. They don't have no less than seventeen."

"Seventeen! My land! Why, I wouldn't set out such a string as that, not if I *never* got to glory. It must take 'em a week."

"Shucks, they don't *all* of 'em preach the same day—only *one* of 'em."

"Well, then, what does the rest of 'em do?"

"Oh, nothing much. Loll around, pass the plate—and one thing or another. But mainly they don't do nothing."

"Well, then, what are they *for*?"

"Why, they're for *style*. Don't you know nothing?"

"Well, I don't *want* to know no such foolishness as that. How is servants treated in England? Do they treat 'em better 'n we treat our niggers?"

"*No!* A servant ain't nobody there. They treat them worse than dogs."

"Don't they give 'em holidays, the way we do, Christmas and New Year's week, and Fourth of July?"

"Oh, just listen! A body could tell *you* hain't ever been to England, by that. Why, Hare-l—why, Joanna, they never see a holiday from year's end to year's end; never got to the circus, nor theatre, nor nigger shows, nor nowheres."

"Nor church?"

"Nor church."

"But *you* always went to church."

Well, I was gone up again. I forgot I was the old man's servant. But next minute I whirled in on a kind of an explanation how a valley was different from a common servant, and *had* to go to church whether he wanted to or not, and set with the family, on account of it's being the law. But I didn't do it pretty good, and when I got done I see she warn't satisfied. She says:

"Honest injun, now, hain't you been telling me a lot of lies?"

"Honest injun," says I.

"None of it at all?"

"None of it at all. Not a lie in it," says I.

"Lay your hand on this book and say it."

I see it warn't nothing but a dictionary, so I laid my hand on it and said it. So then she looked a little better satisfied, and says:

"Well, then, I'll believe some of it; but I hope to gracious if I'll believe the rest."

"What is it you won't believe, Joe?" says Mary Jane, stepping in with Susan behind her. "It ain't right nor kind for you to talk so to him, and him a stranger and so far from his people. How would you like to be treated so?"

"That's always your way, Maim—always sailing in to help somebody before they're hurt. I hain't done nothing to him. He's told some stretchers, I reckon; and I said I wouldn't swallow it all; and that's every bit and grain I *did* say. I reckon he can stand a little thing like that, can't he?"

"I don't care whether 'twas little or whether 'twas big, he's here in our house and a stranger, and it wasn't good of you to say it. If you was in his place, it would make you feel ashamed; and so you oughtn't to say a thing to another person that will make *them* feel ashamed."

"Why, Maim, he said——"

"It don't make no difference what he *said*—that ain't the thing. The thing is for you to treat him *kind,* and not be saying things to make him remember he ain't in his own country and amongst his own folks."

I says to myself, *this* is a girl that I'm letting that old reptle rob her of her money!

Then Susan *she* waltzed in; and if you'll believe me, she did give Hare-lip hark from the tomb!

Says I to myself, And this is *another* one that I'm letting him rob her of her money!

Then Mary Jane she took another inning, and went in sweet and lovely again—which was her way—but when she got done there warn't hardly anything left o' poor Hare-lip. So she hollered.

"All right, then," says the other girls, "you just ask his pardon."

She done it, too. And she done it beautiful. She done it so beautiful it was good to hear; and I wished I could tell her a thousand lies, so she could do it again.

I says to myself, this is *another* one that I'm letting him rob her of her money. And when she got through, they all jest laid theirselves out to make me feel at home and know I was amongst friends. I felt so ornery and low down and mean, that I says to myself, My mind's made up; I'll hive that money for them or bust.

So then I lit out—for bed, I said, meaning some time or another. When I got by myself, I went to thinking the thing over. I says to myself, shall I go to that doctor, private, and blow on these frauds? No—that won't do. He might tell who told him; then the king and the duke would make it warm for me. Shall I go, private, and tell Mary Jane? No—I dasn't do it. Her face would give them a hint, sure; they've got the money, and they'd slide right out and get away with it. If she was to fetch in help, I'd get mixed up in the business, before it was done with, I judge. No, there ain't no good way but one. I got to steal that money, somehow; and I got to steal it some way that they won't suspicion that I done it. They've got a good thing, here; and they ain't agoing to leave till they've played this family and this town for all they're worth, so I'll find a chance time enough. I'll steal it, and hide it; and by-and-by, when I'm away down the river, I'll write a letter and tell Mary Jane where it's hid. But I better hive it to-night, if I can, because the doctor maybe hasn't let up as much as he lets on he has; he might scare them out of here, yet.

So, thinks I, I'll go and search them rooms. Up stairs the hall was dark, but I found the duke's room, and started to paw around it with my hands; but I recollected it wouldn't be much like the king to let anybody else take care of that money but his own self; so then I went to his room and begun to paw around there. But I see I couldn't do nothing without a candle, and I dasn't light one, of course. So I judged I'd got to do the other thing—lay for them, and eavesdrop. About that time, I hears their footsteps coming, and was going to skip under the bed; I reached for it, but it wasn't where I thought it would be; but I touched the curtain that hid Mary Jane's frocks, so I jumped in behind that and snuggled in amongst the gowns, and stood there perfectly still.

They come in and shut the door; and the first thing the duke done was to get down and look under the bed. Then I was glad I hadn't found the bed when I wanted it. And yet, you know, it's kind of natural to hide under the bed when you are up to anything private. They sets down, then, and the king says:

"Well, what is it? and cut it middlin' short, because it's better for us to be down there a whoopin'-up the mournin', than up here givin' em a chance to talk us over."

"Well, this is it, Capet. I ain't easy; I ain't comfortable. That doctor lays on my mind. I wanted to know your plans. I've got a notion, and I think it's a sound one."

"What is it, duke?"

"That we better glide out of this, before three in the morning, and clip it down the river with what we've got. Specially, seeing we got it so easy—*given* back to us, flung at our heads, as you may say, when of course we allowed to have to steal it back. I'm for knocking off and lighting out."

That made me feel pretty bad. About an hour or two ago, it would a been a little different, but now it made me feel bad and disappointed. The king rips out and says:

"What! And not sell out the rest o' the property? March off like a passel o' fools and leave eight or nine thous'n dollars' worth o' property layin' around jest sufferin' to be scooped in?—and all good salable stuff, too."

The duke he grumbled; said the bag of gold was enough, and he didn't want to go no deeper—didn't want to rob a lot of orphans of *everything* they had.

"Why, how you talk!" says the king. "We shan't rob 'em of nothing at all but jest this money. The people that *buys* the property is the suff'rers; because as soon's it's found out 'at we didn't own it—which won't be long after we've slid—the sale won't be valid, and it'll all go back to the estate. These-yer orphans'll git their house back agin, and that's enough for *them;* they're young and spry, and k'n easy earn a livin'. *They* ain't agoing to suffer. Why, jest think—there's thous'n's and thous'n's that ain't nigh so well off. Bless you, *they* ain't got noth'n to complain of."

Well, the king he talked him blind; so at last he give in, and said all right, but said he believed it was blame foolishness to stay, and that doctor hanging over them. But the king says:

"Cuss the doctor! What do we k'yer for *him?* Hain't we got all the fools in town on our side? and ain't that a big enough majority in any town?"

So they got ready to go down stairs again. The duke says:

"I don't think we put that money in a good place."

That cheered me up. I'd begun to think I warn't going to get a hint of no kind to help me. The king says:

"Why?"

"Because Mary Jane'll be in mourning from this out; and first you know the nigger that does up the rooms will get an order to box these duds up and put 'em away; and do you reckon a nigger can run across money and not borrow some of it?"

"Your head's level, agin, duke," says the king; and he come a fumbling under the curtain two or three foot from where I was. I stuck tight to the wall, and kept mighty still, though quivery; and I wondered what them fellows would say to me if they catched me; and I tried to think what I'd better do if they did catch me. But the king he got the bag before I could think more than about a half a thought, and he never suspicioned I was around. They took and shoved the bag through a rip in the straw tick that was under the feather bed, and crammed it in a foot or two amongst the straw and said it was all right, now, because a nigger only makes up the feather bed, and don't turn over the straw tick only about twice a year, and so it warn't in no danger of getting stole, now.

But I knowed better. I had it out of there before they was half-way down stairs. I groped along up to my cubby, and hid it there till I could get a chance to do better. I judged I better hide it outside of the house somewheres, because if they missed it they would give the house a good ransacking. I knowed that very well. Then I turned in, with my clothes all on; but I couldn't a gone to sleep, if I'd a wanted to, I was in such a sweat to get through with the business. By-and-by I heard the king and the duke come up; so I rolled off of my pallet and laid with my chin at the top of my ladder and waited to see if anything was going to happen. But nothing did.

So I held on till all the late sounds had quit and the early ones hadn't begun, yet; and then I slipped down the ladder.

CHAPTER XXVII

I crept to their doors and listened; they was snoring, so I tip-toed along, and got down stairs all right. There warn't a sound anywheres. I peeped through a crack of the dining-room door, and see the men that was watching the corpse all sound asleep on their chairs. The door was open into the parlor, where the corpse was laying, and there was a candle in both rooms. I passed along, and the parlor door was open; but I see there warn't nobody in there but the remainders of Peter; so I shoved on by; but the front door was locked, and the key wasn't there. Just then I heard somebody coming down the stairs, back behind me. I run in the parlor, and took a swift look around, and the only place I see to hide the bag was in the coffin. The lid was shoved along about a foot, showing the dead man's face down in there, with a wet cloth over it, and his shroud on. I tucked the money-bag in under the lid, just down beyond where his hands was crossed, which made me creep, they was so cold, and then I run back across the room and in behind the door.

The person coming was Mary Jane. She went to the coffin, very soft, and kneeled down and looked in; then she put up her handkerchief and I see she begun to cry, though I couldn't hear her, and her back was to me. I slid out, and as I passed the dining-room I thought I'd make sure them watchers hadn't seen me; so I looked through the crack and everything was all right. They hadn't stirred.

I slipped up to bed, feeling ruther blue, on accounts of the thing playing out that way after I had took so much trouble and run so much resk about it. Says I, if it could stay where it is, all right; because when we get down the river a hundred mile or two, I could write back to Mary Jane, and she could dig him up again and get it; but that ain't the thing that's going to happen; the thing that's going to happen is, the money'll be found when they come to screw on the lid. Then the king'll get it again, and it'll be a long day before he gives anybody another chance to smouch it from him. Of course I *wanted* to slide down and get it out of there, but I dasn't try it. Every minute it was getting earlier, now, and pretty soon some of them watchers would begin to stir, and I might get catched— catched with six thousand dollars in my hands that nobody hadn't hired me to take care of. I don't wish to be mixed up in no such business as that, I says to myself.

When I got down stairs in the morning, the parlor was shut up, and the watchers was gone. There warn't nobody around but the family and the widow Bartley and our tribe. I watched their faces to see if anything had been happening, but I couldn't tell. Towards the middle of the day the undertaker come, with his man, and they set the coffin in the middle of the room on a couple of chairs, and then set all our chairs in rows, and borrowed more from the neighbors till the hall and the parlor and the dining-room was full. I see the coffin lid was the way it was before, but I dasn't go to look in under it, with folks around.

Then the people begun to flock in, and the beats and the girls took seats in the front row at the head of the coffin, and for a half an hour the people filed around slow, in single rank, and looked down at the dead man's face a minute, and some dropped in a tear, and it was all very still and solemn, only the girls and the beats holding handkerchiefs to their eyes and keeping their heads bent, and sobbing a little. There warn't no other sound but the scraping of the feet on the floor, and blowing noses—because people always blows them more at a funeral than they do at other places except church.

When the place was packed full, the undertaker he slid around in his black gloves with his softy soothering ways, putting on the last touches, and getting people and things all shipshape and comfortable, and making no more sound than a cat. He never spoke; he moved people around, he squeezed in late ones, he opened up passage-ways, and done it all with nods, and signs with his hands. Then he took his place over against the wall. He was the softest, glidingest, stealthiest man I ever see; and there warn't no more smile to him than there is to a ham.

They had borrowed a melodeum—a sick one; and when everything was ready, a young woman set down and worked it, and it was pretty skreeky and colicky, and everybody joined in and sung, and Peter was the only one that had a good thing, according to my notion. Then the Reverend Hobson opened up, slow and solemn, and begun to talk; and straight off the most outrageous row busted out in the cellar a body ever heard; it was only one dog, but he made a most powerful racket, and he kept it up, right along; the parson he had to stand there, over the coffin, and wait—you couldn't hear yourself think. It was right down awkward, and nobody didn't seem to know what to do. But pretty soon they see that long-legged undertaker make a sign to the preacher as much as to say, "Don't you worry—just depend on me." Then he stooped down and begun to glide along the wall, just his shoulders showing over the people's heads. So he glided along, and the pow-wow and racket getting more and more outrageous all the time; and at last, when he had gone around two sides of the room, he disappears down cellar. Then, in about two seconds we heard a whack, and the dog he finished up with a most amazing howl or two, and then everything was dead still, and the parson begun his solemn talk where he left off. In a minute or two here comes this undertaker's back and shoulders gliding along the wall again; and so he glided, and glided, around three sides of the room, and then rose up, and shaded his mouth with his hands, and stretched his neck out towards the preacher, over the people's heads, and says, in a kind of a coarse whisper, *"He had a rat!"* Then he drooped down and glided along the wall again to his place. You could see it was a great satisfaction to the people, because naturally they wanted to know. A little thing like that don't cost nothing, and it's just the little things that makes a man to be looked up to and liked. There warn't no more popular man in town than what that undertaker was.

Well, the funeral sermon was very good, but pison long and tiresome; and then the king he shoved in and got off some of his usual rubbage, and at last the job was through, and the undertaker begun to sneak up on the coffin with his screw-driver. I was in a sweat then, and watched him pretty keen. But he never meddled at all; just slid the lid along, as soft as mush, and screwed it down tight and fast. So there I was! I didn't know whether the money was in there, or not. So, says I, spose somebody has hogged that bag on the sly?—now how do *I* know whether to write to Mary Jane or not? 'Spose she dug him up and didn't find nothing—what would she think of me? Blame it, I says, I might get hunted up and jailed; I'd better lay low and keep dark, and not write at all; the thing's awful mixed, now; trying to better it, I've worsened it a hundred times, and I wish to goodness I'd just let it alone, dad fetch the whole business!

They buried him, and we come back home, and I went to watching faces again—I couldn't help it, and I couldn't rest easy. But nothing come of it; the faces didn't tell me nothing.

The king he visited around, in the evening, and sweetened every body up, and made himself ever so friendly; and he give out the idea that his congregation over in England would be in a sweat about him, so he must hurry and settle up the estate right away, and leave for home. He was very sorry he was so pushed, and so was everybody; they wished he could stay longer, but they said they could see it couldn't be done. And he said of course him and

William would take the girls home with them; and that pleased everybody too, because then the girls would be well fixed, and amongst their own relations; and it pleased the girls, too—tickled them so they clean forgot they ever had a trouble in the world; and told him to sell out as quick as he wanted to, they would be ready. Them poor things was that glad and happy it made my heart ache to see them getting fooled and lied to so, but I didn't see no safe way for me to chip in and change the general tune.

Well, blamed if the king didn't bill the house and the niggers and all the property for auction straight off—sale two days after the funeral; but anybody could buy private beforehand if they wanted to.

So the next day after the funeral, along about noontime, the girls' joy got the first jolt; a couple of nigger traders come along, and the king sold them the niggers reasonable, for three-day drafts as they called it, and away they went, the two sons up the river to Memphis, and their mother down the river to Orleans. I thought them poor girls and them niggers would break their hearts for grief; they cried around each other, and took on so it most made me down sick to see it. The girls said they hadn't ever dreamed of seeing the family separated or sold away from the town. I can't ever get it out of my memory, the sight of them poor miserable girls and niggers hanging around each other's necks and crying; and I reckon I couldn't a stood it all but would a had to bust out and tell on our gang if I hadn't knowed the sale warn't no account and the niggers would be back home in a week or two.

The thing made a big stir in the town, too, and a good many come out flat-footed and said it was scandalous to separate the mother and the children that way. It injured the frauds some; but the old fool he bulled right along, spite of all the duke could say or do, and I tell you the duke was powerful uneasy.

Next day was auction day. About broad-day in the morning, the king and the duke come up in the garret and woke me up, and I see by their look that there was trouble. The king says:

"Was you in my room night before last?"

"No, your majesty"—which was the way I always called him when nobody but our gang warn't around.

"Was you in there yisterday er last night?"

"No, your majesty."

"Honor bright, now—no lies."

"Honor bright, your majesty, I'm telling you the truth. I hain't been anear your room since Miss Mary Jane took you and the duke and showed it to you."

The duke says:

"Have you seen anybody else go in there?"

"No, your grace, not as I remember, I believe."

"Stop and think."

I studied a while, and see my chance, then I says:

"Well, I see the niggers go in there several times."

Both of them give a little jump; and looked like they hadn't ever expected it, and then like they *had.* Then the duke says:

"What, *all* of them?"

"No—leastways not all at once. That is, I don't think I ever see them all come *out* at once but just one time."

"Hello—when was that?"

"It was the day we had the funeral. In the morning. It warn't early, because I overslept. I was just starting down the ladder, and I see them."

"Well, go on, *go* on—what did they do? How'd they act?"

"They didn't do nothing. And they didn't act anyway, much, as fur as I see. They tip-toed away; so I seen, easy enough, that they'd shoved in there to do up your majesty's room, or something, sposing you was up; and found you *warn't* up, and so they was hoping to slide out of the way of trouble without waking you up, if they hadn't already waked you up."

"Great guns, *this* is a go!" says the king; and both of them looked pretty sick, and tolerable silly. They stood there a thinking and scratching their heads, a minute, and then the duke he bust into a kind of a little raspy chuckle, and says:

"It does beat all, how neat the niggers played their hand. They let on to be *sorry* they was going out of this region! and I believed they *was* sorry. And so did you, and so did everybody. Don't ever tell *me* any more that a nigger ain't got any histrionic talent. Why, the way they played that thing, it would fool *anybody.* In my opinion there's a fortune in 'em. If I had capital and a theatre, I wouldn't want a better lay out than that—and here we've gone and sold 'em for a song. Yes, and ain't privileged to sing the song, yet. Say, where *is* that song?—that draft."

"In the bank for to be collected. Where *would* it be?"

"Well, *that's* all right then, thank goodness."

Says I, kind of timid-like:

"Is something gone wrong?"

The king whirls on me and rips out:

"None o' your business! You keep your head shet, and mind y'r own affairs—if you got any. Long as you're in this town, don't you forget *that,* you hear?" Then he says to the duke, "We got to jest swaller it, and say noth'n: mum's the word for *us.*"

As they was starting down the ladder, the duke he chuckles again, and says:

"Quick sales *and* small profits! It's a good business—yes."

The king snarls around on him and says,

"I was trying to do for the best, in sellin' 'm out so quick. If the profits has turned out to be none, lackin' considable, and none to carry, is it my fault any more'n it's yourn?"

"Well, *they'd* be in this house yet, and we *wouldn't* if I could a got my advice listened to."

The king sassed back, as much as was safe for him, and then swapped around and lit into *me* again. He give me down the banks for not coming and *telling* him I see the niggers come out of his room acting that way—said any fool would a *knowed* something was up. And then waltzed in and cussed *himself* a while; and said it all come of him not laying late and taking his natural rest that morning, and he'd be blamed if he'd ever do it again. So they went off a jawing; and I felt dreadful glad I'd worked it all off onto the niggers and yet hadn't done the niggers no harm by it.

CHAPTER XXVIII

By-and-by it was getting-up time; so I come down the ladder and started for down stairs, but as I come to the girls' room, the door was open, and I see Mary Jane setting by her old hair trunk, which was open and she'd been packing things in it—getting ready to go to England. But she had stopped now, with a folded gown in her lap, and had her face in her hands, crying. I felt awful bad to see it; of course anybody would. I went in there, and says:

"Miss Mary Jane, you can't abear to see people in trouble, and *I* can't—most always. Tell me about it."

So she done it. And it was the niggers—I just expected it. She said the beautiful trip to England was most about spoiled for her; she didn't know *how* she was ever going to be happy there, knowing the mother and the children warn't ever going to see each other no more—and then busted out bitterer than ever, and flung up her hands, and says:

"Oh, dear, dear, to think they ain't *ever* going to see each other any more!"

"But they *will*—and inside of two weeks—and I *know* it!" says I.

Laws it was out before I could think!—and before I could budge, she throws her arms around my neck, and told me to say it *again,* say it *again,* say it *again!*

I see I had spoke too sudden, and said too much, and was in a close place. I asked her to let me think a minute; and she set there, very impatient and excited, and handsome, but looking kind of happy and eased-up, like a person that's had a tooth pulled out. So I went to studying it out. I says to myself, I reckon a body that ups and tells the truth when he is in a tight place, is taking considerable many resks, though I ain't had no experience, and can't say for certain; but it looks so to me, anyway; and yet here's a case where I'm blest if it don't look to me like the truth is better, and actuly *safer,* than a lie. I must lay it by in my mind, and think it over some time or other, it's so kind of strange and unregular. I never see nothing like it. Well, I says to myself at last, I'm agoing to chance it;

I'll up and tell the truth this time, though it does seem most like setting down on a kag of powder and touching it off just to see where you'll go to. Then I says:

"Miss Mary Jane, is there any place out of town a little ways, where you could go and stay three or four days?"

"Yes—Mr. Lothrop's. Why?"

"Never mind why, yet. If I'll tell you how I know the niggers will see each other again—inside of two weeks—here in this house—and *prove* how I know it—will you go to Mr. Lothrop's and stay four days?"

"Four days!" she says; "I'll stay a year!"

"All right," I says, "I don't want nothing more out of *you* than just your word—I druther have it than another man's kiss-the-Bible." She smiled, and reddened up very sweet, and I says, "If you don't mind it, I'll shut the door—and bolt it."

Then I come back and set down again, and says:

"Don't you holler. Just set still, and take it like a man. I got to tell the truth, and you want to brace up, Miss Mary, because it's a bad kind, and going to be hard to take, but there ain't no help for it. These uncles of yourn ain't no uncles at all—they're a couples of frauds—regular dead-beats. There, now we're over the worst of it—you can stand the rest middling easy."

It jolted her up like everything, of course; but I was over the shoal water now, so I went right along, her eyes a blazing higher and higher all the time, and told her every blame thing, from where we first struck that young fool going up to the steamboat, clear through to where she flung herself onto the king's breast at the front door and he kissed her sixteen or seventeen times—and then up she jumps, with her face afire like sunset, and says:

"The brute! Come—don't waste a minute—not a *second*—we'll have them tarred and feathered, and flung in the river!"

Says I:

"Cert'nly. But do you mean, *before* you go to Mr. Lothrop's, or——"

"Oh," she says, "what am I *thinking* about!" she says, and set right down again. "Don't mind what I said—please don't—you *won't* now, *will* you?" Laying her silky hand on mine in that kind of a way that I said I would die first. "I never thought. I was so stirred up," she says; "now go on, and I won't do so any more. You tell me what to do, and whatever you say, I'll do it."

"Well," I says, "it's a rough gang, them two frauds, and I'm fixed so I got to travel with them a while longer, whether I want to or not—I druther not tell you why—and if you was to blow on them this town would get me out of their claws, and *I'd* be all right, but there'd be another person that you don't know about who'd be in big trouble. Well, we got to save *him,* hain't we? Of course. Well, then, we won't blow on them."

Saying them words put a good idea in my head. I see how maybe I could get me and Jim rid of the frauds; get them jailed here, and then leave. But I didn't want to run the raft in day-time, without anybody aboard to answer questions but me; so I didn't want the plan to begin working till pretty late to-night. I says:

"Miss Mary Jane, I'll tell you what we'll do—and you won't have to stay at Mr. Lothrop's so long, nuther. How fur is it?"

"A little short of four miles—right out in the country, back here."

"Well, that'll answer. Now you go along out there, and lay low till nine or half-past, to-night, and then get them to fetch you home again—tell them you've thought of something. If you get here before eleven, put a candle in this window, and if I don't turn up, wait *till* eleven, and *then* if I don't turn up it means I'm gone, and out of the way, and safe. Then you come out and spread the news around, and get these beats jailed."

"Good," she says, "I'll do it."

"And if it just happens so that I don't get away, but get took up along with them, you must up and say I told you the whole thing beforehand, and you must stand by me all you can."

"Stand by you, indeed I will. They sha'n't touch a hair of your head!" she says, and I see her nostrils spread and her eyes snap when she said it, too.

"If I get away, I sha'n't be here," I says, "to prove these rapscallions ain't your uncles, and I couldn't do it if I *was* here. I could swear they was beats and bummers, that's all; though that's worth something. Well, there's others can do that better than what I can—and they're people that ain't going to be doubted as quick as I'd be. I'll tell you how to find them. Gimme a pencil and a piece of paper. There—'*Royal Nonesuch, Bricksville.*' Put it away, and don't lose it. When the court wants to find out something about these two, let them send up to Bricksville and say they've got the men that played the Royal Nonesuch, and ask for some witnesses—why, you'll have that entire town down here before you can hardly wink, Miss Mary. And they'll come a-biling, too."

I judged we had got everything fixed about right now. So I says:

"Just let the auction go right along, and don't worry. Nobody don't have to pay for the things they buy till a whole day after the auction, on accounts of the short notice, and they ain't going out of this till they get that money—and the way we've fixed it the sale ain't going to count, and they ain't going to *get* no money. It's just like the way it was with the niggers—it warn't no sale, and the niggers will be back before long. Why, they can't collect the money for the *niggers*, yet—they're in the worst kind of a fix, Miss Mary."

"Well," she says, "I'll run down to breakfast now, and then I'll start straight for Mr. Lothrop's."

" 'Deed, *that* ain't the ticket, Miss Mary Jane," I says, "by no manner of means; go *before* breakfast."

"Why?"

"What did you reckon I wanted you to go at all for, Miss Mary?"

"Well, I never thought—and come to think, I don't know. What was it?"

"Why, it's because you ain't one of these leather-face people. I don't want no better book that what your face is. A body can set down and read it off like coarse print. Do you reckon you can go and face your uncles, when they come to kiss you good-morning, and never——"

"There, there, don't! Yes, I'll go before breakfast—I'll be glad to. And leave my sisters with them?"

"Yes—never mind about them. They've got to stand it yet a while. They might suspicion something if all of you was to go. I don't want you to see them, nor your sisters, nor nobody in this town—if a neighbor was to ask how is your uncles this morning, your face would tell something. No, you go right along, Miss Mary Jane, and I'll fix it with all of them. I'll tell Miss Susan to give your love to your uncles and say you've went away for a few hours for to get a little rest and change, or to see a friend, and you'll be back to-night or early in the morning."

"Gone to see a friend is all right, but I won't have my love given to them."

"Well, then, it sha'n't be." It was well enough to tell her so—no harm in it. It was only a little thing to do, and no trouble; and it's the little things that smoothes people's roads the most, down here below; it would make Mary Jane comfortable, and it wouldn't cost nothing. Then I says: "There's one more thing—that bag of money."

"Well, they've got that; and it makes me feel pretty silly to think how they got it."

"No, you're out, there. They hain't got it."

"Why, who's got it?"

"I wish I knowed, but I don't. I had it, because I stole it from them: and I stole it to give to you; and I know where I hid it, but I'm afraid it ain't there no more. I'm awful sorry, Miss Mary Jane, I'm just as sorry as I can be; but I done the best I could; I did, honest. I come nigh getting caught, and I had to shove it into the first place I come to, and run—and it warn't a good place."

"Oh, stop blaming yourself—it's too bad to do it, and I won't allow it—you couldn't help it; it wasn't your fault. Where did you hide it?"

I didn't want to set her to thinking about her troubles again; and I couldn't seem to get my mouth to tell her what would make her see that corpse laying in the coffin with that bag of money on his stomach. So for a minute I didn't say nothing—then I says:

"I'd ruther not *tell* you where I put it, Miss Mary Jane, if you don't mind letting me off; but I'll write it for you on a piece of paper, and you can read it along the road to Mr. Lothrop's, if you want to. Do you reckon that'll do?"

"Oh, yes."

So I wrote: "I put it in the coffin. It was in there when you was crying there, away in the night. I was behind the door, and I was mighty sorry for you, Miss Mary Jane."

It made my eyes water a little, to remember her crying there all by herself in the night, and them devils laying there right under her own roof, shaming her and robbing her; and when I folded it up and give it to her, I see the water come into her eyes, too; and she shook me by the hand, hard, and says:

"*Good*-bye—I'm going to do everything just as you've told me; and if I don't ever see you again, I sha'n't ever forget you, and I'll think of you a many and a many a time, and I'll *pray* for you, too!" —and she was gone.

Pray for me! I reckoned if she knowed me she'd take a job that was more nearer her size. But I bet she done it, just the same—she was just that kind. She had the grit to pray for Judus if she took the notion—there warn't no backdown to her, I judge. You may say what you want to, but in my opinion she had more sand in her than any girl I ever see; in my opinion she was just full of sand. It sounds like flattery, but it ain't no flattery. And when it comes to beauty—and goodness too—she lays over them all. I hain't ever seen her since that time that I see her go out of that door; no, I hain't ever seen her since, but I reckon I've thought of her a many and a many a million times, and of her saying she would pray for me; and if ever I'd a thought it would do any good for me to pray for *her,* blamed if I wouldn't a done it or bust.

Well, Mary Jane she lit out the back way, I reckon; because nobody see her go. When I struck Susan and the hare-lip, I says:

"What's the name of them people over on t'other side of the river that you all goes to see sometimes?"

They says:

"There's several; but it's the Proctors, mainly."

"That's the name," I says; "I most forgot it. Well, Miss Mary Jane she told me to tell you she's gone over there in a dreadful hurry—one of them's sick."

"Which one?"

"I don't know; leastways I kinder forget; but I think it's——"

"Sakes alive, I hope it ain't *Hanner?*"

"I'm sorry to say it," I says, "but Hanner's the very one."

"My goodness—and she so well only last week! Is she took bad?"

"It ain't no name for it. They set up with her all night, Miss Mary Jane said, and they don't think she'll last many hours."

"Only think of that, now! What's the matter with her!"

I couldn't think of anything reasonable, right off that way, so I says:

"Mumps."

"Mumps your granny! They don't set up with people that's got the mumps."

HANNER WITH THE MUMPS.

"They don't, don't they? You better bet they do with *these* mumps. These mumps is different. It's a new kind, Miss Mary Jane said."

"How's it a new kind?"

"Because it's mixed up with other things."

"What other things?"

"Well, measles, and whooping-cough, and erysiplas, and consumption, and yaller jandees, and brain fever, and I don't know what all."

"My land! And they call it the *mumps?*"

"That's what Miss Mary Jane said."

"Well, what in the nation do they call it the *mumps* for?"

"Why, because it *is* the mumps. That's what it starts with."

"Well, ther' ain't no sense in it. A body might stump his toe, and take pison, and fall down the well, and break his neck, and bust his brains out, and somebody come along and ask what killed him, and some numskull up and say, 'Why he stumped his *toe*.' Would ther' be any sense in that? *No*. And thar' ain't no sense in *this*, nuther. Is it ketching?"

"Is it *ketching*? Why, how you talk. Is a *harrow* catching?—in the dark? If you don't hitch onto one tooth, you're bound to on another, ain't you? And you can't get away with that tooth without fetching the whole harrow along, can you? Well, these kind of mumps is a kind of a harrow, as you may say— and it ain't no slouch of a harrow, nuther, you come to get it hitched on good."

"Well, it's awful, *I* think," says the hare-lip. "I'll go to Uncle Harvey and——"

"Oh, yes," I says, "I *would*. Of *course* I would. I wouldn't lose no time."

"Well, why wouldn't you?"

"Just look at it a minute, and maybe you can see. Hain't your uncles obleeged to get along home to England as fast as they can? And do you reckon they'd be mean enough to go off and leave you to go all that journey by yourselves? *You* know they'll wait for you. So fur, so good. Your uncle Harvey's a preacher, ain't he? Very well, then; is a *preacher* going to deceive a steamboat clerk? Is he going to deceive a *ship clerk?*—so as to get them to let Miss Mary Jane go aboard? Now *you* know he ain't. What *will* he do, then? Why, he'll say, 'It's a great pity, but my church matters has got to get along the best way they can; for my niece has been exposed to the dreadful pluribus-unum mumps, and so it's my bounden duty to set down here and wait the three months it takes to show on her if she's got it.' But never mind, if you think it's best to tell your uncle Harvey——"

"Shucks, and stay fooling around here when we could all be having good times in England whilst we was waiting to find out whether Mary Jane's got it or not? Why, you talk like a muggins."

"Well, anyway, maybe you better tell some of the neighbors."

"Listen at that, now. You do beat all, for natural stupidness. Can't you *see* that they'd go and tell? Ther' ain't no way but just to not tell anybody at *all*."

"Well, maybe you're right—yes, I judge you *are* right."

"But I reckon we ought to tell Uncle Harvey she's gone out a while, anyway, so he won't be uneasy about her?"

"Yes, Miss Mary Jane she wanted you to do that. She says, 'Tell them to give Uncle Harvey and William my love and a kiss, and say I've run over the river to see Mr.—Mr.—what *is* the name of that rich family your uncle Peter used to think so much of?—I mean the one that——"

"Why, you must mean the Apthorps, ain't it?"

"Of course; bother them kind of names, a body can't ever seem to remember them, half the time, somehow. Yes, she said, say she has run over for to ask the Apthorps to be sure and come to the auction and buy this house, because she allowed her uncle Peter would ruther they had it than anybody else; and she's going to stick to them till they say they'll come, and then, if she ain't too tired, she's coming home; and if she is, she'll be home in the morning anyway. She said, don't say nothing about the Proctors, but only about the Apthorps—which'll be perfectly true, because she *is* going there to speak about their buying the house; I know it, because she told me so, herself."

"All right," they said, and cleared out to lay for their uncles, and give them the love and the kisses, and tell them the message.

Everything was all right now. The girls wouldn't say nothing because they wanted to go to England; and the king and the duke would ruther Mary Jane was off working for the auction than around in reach of Doctor Robinson. I felt very good; I judged I had done it pretty neat—I reckoned Tom Sawyer couldn't a done it no neater himself. Of course, he would a throwed more style into it, but I can't do that very handy, not being brung up to it.

Well, they held the auction in the public square, along towards the end of the afternoon, and it strung along, and strung along, and the old man he was on hand and looking his level pisonest, up there longside of the auctioneer, and chipping in a little Scripture, now and then, or a little goody-goody saying, of some kind, and the duke he was around goo-gooing for sympathy all he knowed how, and just spreading himself generly.

But by-and-by the thing dragged through, and everything was sold. Everything but a little old trifling lot in the graveyard. So they'd got to work *that* off—I never see such a girafft as the king was for wanting to swallow *everything*. Well, whilst they was at it, a steamboat landed, and in about two minutes up comes a crowd a whooping and yelling and laughing and carrying on, and singing out:

"*Here's* your opposition line! here's your two sets o' heirs to old Peter Wilks—and you pays your money and you takes your choice!"

CHAPTER XXIX

They was fetching a very nice looking old gentleman along, and a nice looking younger one, with his right arm in a sling. And my souls, how the people yelled, and laughed, and kept it up. But I didn't see no joke about it, and I judged it would strain the duke and the king some to see any. I reckoned they'd turn pale. But no, nary a pale did *they* turn. The duke he never let on he suspicioned what was up, but just went a goo-gooing around, happy and satisfied, like a jug that's googling out buttermilk; and as for the king, he just gazed and gazed down sorrowful on them newcomers like it give him the stomach-ache in his very heart to think there could be such frauds and rascals in the world. Oh, he done it admirable. Lots of the principal people gethered around the king, to let him see they was on his side. That old gentleman that had just come looked all puzzled to death. Pretty soon he begun to speak, and I see, straight off, he pronounced *like* an Englishman, not the king's way, though the king's *was* pretty good, for an imitation. I can't give the old gent's words, nor I can't imitate him; but he turned around to the crowd, and says, about like this:

"This is a surprise to me which I wasn't looking for; and I'll acknowledge, candid and frank, I ain't very well fixed to meet it and answer it; for my brother and me has had misfortunes, he's broke his arm, and our baggage got put off at a town above here, last night in the night by a mistake. I am Peter Wilks's brother Harvey, and this is his brother William, which can't hear nor speak —and can't even make signs to amount to much; now 't he's only got one hand to work them with. We are who we say we are; and in a day or two, when I get the baggage, I can prove it. But, up till then, I won't say nothing more, but go to the hotel and wait."

So him and the new dummy started off; and the king he laughs, and blethers out:

"Broke his arm—*very* likely *ain't* it?—and very convenient, too, for a fraud that's got to make signs, and hain't learnt how. Lost their baggage! That's *mighty* good!—and mighty ingenious—under the *circumstances!*"

So he laughed again; and so did everybody else, except three or four, or maybe half a dozen. One of these was that doctor; another one was a sharp looking gentleman, with a carpet-bag of the old-fashioned kind made out of carpet-stuff, that had just come off of the steamboat and was talking to him in a low voice, and glancing towards the king now and then and nodding their heads—it was Levi Bell, the lawyer that was gone up to Louisville; and another one was a big rough husky that come along and listened to all the old gentleman said, and was listening to the king now. And when the king got done, this husky up and says:

"Say, looky here; if you are Harvey Wilks, when'd you come to this town?"

"The day before the funeral, friend," said the king.

"But what time o' day?"

"In the evenin'—'bout an hour er two before sundown."

"*How'd* you come?"

"I come down on the *Susan Powell,* from Cincinnati."

"Well, then, how'd you come to be up at the Pint in the *mornin'* —in a canoe?"

"I warn't up at the Pint in the mornin'."

"It's a lie."

Several of them jumped for him and begged him not to talk that way to an old man and a preacher.

"Preacher be hanged, he's a fraud and a liar. He was up at the Pint that mornin'. I live up there, don't I? Well, I was up there, and he was up there. I *see* him there. He come in a canoe, along with Tim Collins and a boy."

The doctor he up and says:

"Would you know the boy again if you was to see him, Hines?"

"I reckon I would, but I don't know. Why, yonder he is, now. I know him perfectly easy."

It was me he pointed at. The doctor says:

"Neighbors, I don't know whether the new couple is frauds or not; but if *these* two ain't frauds, I am an idiot, that's all. I think it's our duty to see that they don't get away from here till we've looked into this thing. Come along, Hines; come along, the rest of you. We'll take these fellows to the tavern and affront them with t'other couple, and I reckon we'll find out *something* before we get through."

It was nuts for the crowd, though maybe not for the king's friends; so we all started. It was about sundown. The doctor he led me along by the hand, and was plenty kind enough, but he never let *go* my hand.

We all got in a big room in the hotel, and lit up some candles, and fetched in the new couple. First, the doctor says:

"I don't wish to be too hard on these two men, but *I* think they're frauds, and they may have complices that we don't know nothing about. If they have, won't the complices get away with that bag of gold Peter Wilks left? It ain't unlikely. If these men ain't frauds, they won't object to sending for that money and letting us keep it till they prove they're all right—ain't that so?"

Everybody agreed to that. So I judged they had our gang in a pretty tight place, right at the outstart. But the king he only looked sorrowful, and says:

"Gentlemen, I wish the money was there, for I ain't got no disposition to throw anything in the way of a fair, open, out-and-out investigation o' this misable business; but alas, the money ain't there; you k'n send and see, if you want to."

"Where is it, then?"

"Well, when my niece give it to me to keep for her, I took and hid it inside o' the straw tick o' my bed, not wishin' to bank it for the next few days we'd be here, and considerin' the bed a safe place, we not bein' used to niggers, and suppos'n' 'em honest, like servants in England. The niggers stole it the very next mornin' after I had went down stairs; and when I sold 'em, I hadn't missed the money yit, so they got clean away with it. My servant here k'n tell you 'bout it gentlemen."

The doctor and several said "Shucks!" and I see nobody didn't altogether believe him. One man asked me if I see the niggers steal it. I said no, but I see them sneaking out of the room and hustling away, and I never thought nothing, only I reckoned they was afraid they had waked up my master and was trying to get away before he made trouble with them. That was all they asked me. Then the doctor whirls on me and says:

"Are *you* English too?"

I says yes; and him and some others laughed, and said, "Stuff!"

Well, then they sailed in on the general investigation, and there we had it, up and down, hour in, hour out, and nobody said a word about supper, nor ever seemed to think about it—and so they kept it up, and kept it up; and it *was* the worst mixed-up thing you ever see. They made the king tell his yarn, and they made the old gentleman tell his'n; and anybody but a lot of prejudiced chuckleheads would a *seen* that the old gentleman was spinning truth and t'other one lies. And by-and-by they had me up to tell what I knowed. The king he give me a left handed look out of the corner of his eye, and so I knowed enough to talk on the right side. I begun to tell about Sheffield, and how we lived there, and all about the English Wilkses, and so on; but I didn't get pretty fur till the doctor begun to laugh; and Levi Bell, the lawyer, says:

"Set down, my boy, I wouldn't strain myself, if I was you. I reckon you ain't used to lying, it don't seem to come handy; what you want is practice. You do it pretty awkward."

I didn't care nothing for the compliment, but I was glad to be let off, anyway.

The doctor he started to say something, and turns and says:

"If you'd been in town at first, Levi Bell—"

The king broke in and reached out his hand, and says:

"Why, is this my poor dead brother's old friend that he's wrote so often about?"

The lawyer and him shook hands, and the lawyer smiled and looked pleased, and they talked right along a while, and then got to one side and talked low; and at last the lawyer speaks up and says:

"That'll fix it. I'll take the order and send it, along with your brother's, and then they'll know it's all right."

So they got some paper and a pen, and the king he set down and twisted his head to one side, and chawed his tongue, and scrawled off something; and then they give the pen to the duke—and then for the first time, the duke looked sick. But he took the pen and wrote. So then the lawyer turns to the new old gentleman and says:

"You and your brother please write a line or two and sign your names."

The old gentleman wrote, but nobody couldn't read it. The lawyer looked powerful astonished, and says:

"Well, it beats *me*"—and snaked a lot of old letters out of his pocket, and examined them, and then examined the old man's writing, and then *them* again; and then says: "These old letters is from Harvey Wilks; and here's *these* two's handwritings, and anybody can see *they* didn't write them" (the king and the duke looked sold and foolish, I tell you, to see how the lawyer had took them in), "and here's *this* old gentleman's handwriting, and anybody can tell, easy enough, *he* didn't write them—fact is, the scratches he makes ain't properly *writing*, at all. Now here's some letters from—"

The new old gentleman says—

"If you please, let me explain. Nobody can read my hand but my brother there—so he copies for me. It's *his* hand you've got there, not mine."

"*Well!*" says the lawyer, "this *is* a state of things. I've got some of Williams's letters too; so if you'll get him to write a line or so we can com—"

"He *can't* write with his left hand," says the old gentleman. "If he could use his right hand, you would see that he wrote his own letters and mine too. Look at both, please—they're by the same hand."

The lawyer done it, and says:

"I believe it's so—and if it ain't so, there's a heap stronger resemblance than I'd noticed before, anyway. Well, well, well! I thought we was right on the track of a slution, but it's gone to grass, partly. But anyway, *one* thing is proved—*these* two ain't either of 'em Wilkses"—and he wagged his head towards the king and the duke.

Well, what do you think?—that muleheaded old fool wouldn't give in *then!* Indeed he wouldn't. Said it warn't no fair test. Said his brother William was the cussedest joker in the world, and hadn't *tried* to write—*he* see William was going to play one of his jokes the minute he put the pen to paper. And so he warmed up and went warbling and warbling right along, till he was actuly beginning to believe what he was saying, *himself*—but pretty soon the new old gentleman broke in, and says:

"I've thought of something. Is there anybody here that helped to lay out my br—helped to lay out the late Peter Wilks for burying?"

"Yes," says somebody, "me and Ab Turner done it. We're both here."

Then the old man turns towards the king, and says:

"Perhaps this gentleman can tell me what was tatooed on his breast?"

Blamed if the king didn't have to brace up mighty quick, or he'd a squshed down like a bluff bank that the river has cut under, it took him so sudden—and mind you, it was a thing that was calculated to make most *anybody* sqush to get fetched such a solid one as that without any notice—because how was *he* going to know what was tatooed on the man? He whitened a little; he couldn't help it; and it was mighty still in there, and everybody bending a little forwards and gazing at him. Says I to myself, *Now* he'll throw up the sponge—there ain't no more use. Well, did he? A body can't hardly believe it, but he didn't. I reckon he thought he'd keep the thing up till he tired them people out, so they'd thin out, and him and the duke could break loose and get away. Anyway, he set there, and pretty soon he begun to smile, and says:

"Mf! It's a *very* tough question, *ain't* it! *Yes,* sir, I k'n tell you what's tatooed on his breast. It's jest a small, thin, blue arrow— that's what it is; and if you don't look clost, you can't see it. *Now* what do you say—hey?"

Well, *I* never see anything like that old blister for clean out-and-out cheek.

The new old gentleman turns brisk towards Ab Turner and his pard, and his eye lights up like he judged he'd got the king *this* time, and says:

"There—you've heard what he said! Was there any such mark on Peter Wilks's breast?"

Both of them spoke up and says:

"We didn't see no such mark."

"Good!" says the old gentleman. "Now, what you *did* see on his breast was a small dim P, and a B (which is an initial he dropped when he was young), and a W, with dashes between them, so: P-B-W"—and he marked them that way on a piece of paper. "Come—ain't that what you saw?"

Both of them spoke up again, and says:

"No, we *didn't.* We never seen any marks at all."

Well, everybody *was* in a state of mind, now; and they sings out:

"The whole *bilin'* of 'm's frauds! Le's duck 'em! le's drown 'em! le's ride 'em on a rail!" and everybody was whooping at once, and there was a rattling pow-wow. But the lawyer he jumps on the table and yells, and says:

"Gentlemen—*gentlemen!* Hear me just a word—just a *single* word—if you PLEASE! There's one way yet—let's go and dig up the corpse and look."

That took them.

"Horray!" they all shouted, and was starting right off; but the lawyer and the doctor sung out:

"Hold on, hold on! Collar all these four men and the boy, and fetch *them* along, too!"

"We'll do it!" they all shouted: "and if we don't find them marks we'll lynch the whole gang!"

I *was* scared, now, I tell you. But there warn't no getting away, you know. They gripped us all, and marched us right along, straight for the graveyard, which was a mile and a half down the river, and the whole town at our heels, for we made noise enough, and it was only nine in the evening.

As we went by our house I wished I hadn't sent Mary Jane out of town; because now if I could tip her the wink, she'd light out and save me, and blow on our dead-beats.

Well, we swarmed along down the river road, just carrying on like wild-cats; and to make it more scary, the sky was darking up, and the lightning beginning to wink and flitter, and the wind to shiver amongst the leaves. This was the most awful trouble and most dangersome I ever was in; and I was kinder stunned; everything was going so different from what I had allowed for; stead of being fixed so I could take my own time, if I wanted to, and see all the fun, and have Mary Jane at my back to save me and set me free when the close-fit come, here was nothing in the world betwixt me and sudden death but just them tatoo-marks. If they didn't find them—

I couldn't bear to think about it; and yet, somehow, I couldn't think about nothing else. It got darker and darker, and it was a beautiful time to give the crowd a slip; but that big husky had me by the wrist—Hines—and a body might as well try to give Goliar the slip. He dragged me right along, he was so excited; and I had to run to keep up.

When they got there they swarmed into the graveyard and washed over it like an overflow. And when they got to the grave, they found they had about a hundred times as many shovels as they wanted, but nobody hadn't thought to fetch a lantern. But they sailed into digging, anyway, by the flicker of the lightning, and sent a man to the nearest house a half a mile off, to borrow one.

So they dug and dug, like everything; and it got awful dark, and the rain started, and the wind swished and swushed along, and the lightning come brisker and brisker, and the thunder boomed; but them people never took no notice of it, they was so full of this business; and one minute you could see everything and every face in that big crowd, and the shovelfuls of dirt sailing up out of the grave, and the next second the dark wiped it all out, and you couldn't see nothing at all.

At last they got out the coffin, and begun to unscrew the lid, and then such another crowding, and shouldering, and shoving as there was, to scrouge in and get a sight, you never see; and in the dark, that way, it was awful. Hines he hurt my wrist dreadful, pulling and tugging so, and I reckon he clean forgot I was in the world, he was so excited and panting.

All of a sudden the lightning let go a perfect sluice of white glare, and somebody sings out:

"By the living jingo, here's the bag of gold on his breast!"

Hines lets out a whoop, like everybody else, and dropped my wrist and give a big surge to bust his way in and get a look, and the way I lit out and shinned for the road in the dark, there ain't nobody can tell.

I had the road all to myself, and I fairly flew—leastways I had it all to myself except the solid dark, and the now-and-then glares, and the buzzing of the rain, and the thrashing of the wind, and the splitting of the thunder; and sure as you are born I did clip it along!

When I struck the town, I see there warn't nobody out in the storm, so I never hunted for no back streets, but humped it straight through the main one; and when I begun to get towards our house I aimed my eye and set it. No light there; the house all dark—which made me feel sorry and disappointed, I didn't know why. But at last, just as I was sailing by, *flash* comes the light in Mary Jane's window! and my heart swelled up sudden, like to bust; and the same second the house and all was behind me in the dark, and wasn't ever going to be before me no more in this world. She *was* the best girl I ever see, and had the most sand.

The minute I was far enough above the town to see I could make the towhead, I begun to look sharp for a boat to borrow; and the first time the lightning showed me one that wasn't chained, I snatched it and shoved. It was a canoe, and warn't fastened with nothing but a rope. The towhead was a rattling big distance off, away out there in the middle of the river, but I didn't lose no time; and when I struck the raft at last, I was so fagged I would a just laid down to blow and gasp if I could afforded it. But I didn't. As I sprung aboard I sung out:

"Out with you Jim, and set her loose! Glory be to goodness, we're shut of them!"

Jim lit out, and was a coming for me with both arms spread, he was so full of joy; but when I glimpsed him in the lightning, my heart shot up in my mouth, and I went overboard backwards; for I forgot he was old King Lear and a drownded A-rab all in one, and it most scared the livers and lights out of me. But Jim fished me out, and was going to hug me and bless me, and so on, he was so glad I was back and we was shut of the king and the duke, but I says:

"Not now—have it for breakfast, have it for breakfast! Cut loose and let her slide!"

So, in two seconds, away we went, a sliding down the river, and it *did* seem so good to be free again and all by ourselves on the big river and nobody to bother us. I had to skip around a bit, and jump up and crack my heels a few times, I couldn't help it; but about the third crack, I noticed a sound that I knowed mighty well—and held my breath and listened and waited—and sure enough, when the next flash busted out over the water, here they come!—and just a laying to their oars and making their skiff hum! It was the king and the duke.

So I wilted right down onto the planks, then, and give up; and it was all I could do to keep from crying.

CHAPTER XXX

When they got aboard, the king went for me, and shook me by
the collar, and says:

"Tryin' to give us the slip, was ye, you pup! Tired of our
company—hey?"

I says:

"No, your majesty, we warn't—*please* don't, your majesty!"

"Quick, then, and tell us what *was* your idea, or I'll shake the
insides out o' you!"

"Honest, I'll tell you everything, just as it happened, your
majesty. The man that had aholt of me was very good to me, and
kept saying he had a boy about as big as me that died last year,
and he was sorry to see a boy in such a dangerous fix; and when
they was all took by surprise by finding the gold, and made a rush
for the coffin, he lets go of me and whispers, 'Heel it, now, or they'll
hang ye, sure!' and I lit out. It didn't seem no good for *me* to stay
—*I* couldn't do nothing, and I didn't want to be hung if I could get
away. So I never stopped running till I found the canoe; and when I
got here I told Jim to hurry, or they'd catch me and hang me yet,
and said I was afeard you and the duke wasn't alive, now, and I was
awful sorry, and so was Jim, and was awful glad when we see you
coming, you may ask Jim if I didn't."

Jim said it was so; and the king told him to shut up, and said,
"Oh, yes, it's *mighty* likely!" and shook me up again, and said he
reckoned he'd drownd me. But the duke says:

"Leggo the boy, you old idiot! Would *you* a done any different?
Did you inquire around for *him,* when you got loose? I don't
remember it."

So the king let go of me, and begun to cuss that town and
everybody in it. But the duke says:

"You better a blame sight give *yourself* a good cussing, for you're
the one that's entitled to it most. You hain't done a thing, from the
start, that had any sense in it, except coming out so cool and
cheeky with that imaginary blue-arrow mark. That *was* bright—it
was right down bully; and it was the thing that saved us. For if it
hadn't been for that, they'd a jailed us till them Englishmen's
baggage come—and then—the penitentiary, you bet! But that trick
took 'em to the graveyard, and the gold done us a still bigger
kindness; for if the excited fools hadn't let go all holts and made
that rush to get a look, we'd a slept in our cravats to-night—cravats
warranted to *wear,* too—longer than we'd need 'em."

They was still a minute—thinking—then the king says, kind of
absent-minded like:

"Mf! And we reckoned the *niggers* stole it!"

That made me squirm!

"Yes," says the duke, kinder slow, and deliberate, and sarcastic,

"*We* did."

After about a half a minute, the king drawls out:

"Leastways—*I* did."

The duke says, pretty brisk:

"On the contrary—*I* did."

The king kind of ruffles up, and says:

"Looky here, Bilgewater, what'r you referrin' to?"

The duke says, pretty brish:

"When it comes to that, maybe you'll let me ask, what was *you* referring to?"

"Shucks!" says the king, very sarcastic; "but *I* don't know—maybe you was asleep, and didn't know what you was about."

The duke bristles right up, now, and says:

"Oh, let *up* on this cussed nonsense—do you take me for a blame' fool? Don't you reckon *I* know who hid that money in that coffin?"

"*Yes,* sir! I know you *do* know—because you done it yourself!"

"It's a lie!"—and the duke went for him. The king sings out:

"Take y'r hands off!—leggo my throat!—I take it all back!"

The duke says:

"Well, you just own up, first, that you *did* hide that money there, intending to give me the slip one of these days, and come back and dig it up, and have it all to yourself."

"Wait jest a minute, duke—answer me this one question, honest and fair; if you didn't put the money there, say it, and I'll b'lieve you, and take back everything I said."

"You old scoundrel, I didn't, and you know I didn't. There, now!"

"Well, then, I b'lieve you. But answer me only jest this one more—now *don't* git mad; didn't you have it in your *mind* to hook the money and hide it?"

The duke never said nothing for a little bit; then he says:

"Well—I don't care if I *did,* I didn't *do* it, anyway. But you not only had it in mind to do it, but you *done* it."

"I wisht I may never die if I done it, duke, and that's honest. I won't say I warn't *goin'* to do it, because I *was;* but you—I mean somebody—got in ahead o' me."

"It's a lie! You done it, and you got to *say* you done it, or—"

The king begun to gurgle, and then he gasps out:

" 'Nough!—*I own up!*"

I was very glad to hear him say that, it made me feel much more easier than what I was feeling before. So the duke took his hands off, and says:

"If you ever deny it again, I'll drown you. It's *well* for you to set there and blubber like a baby—it's fitten for you, after the way you've acted. I never see such an old ostrich for wanting to gobble everything—and I a trusting you all the time, like you was my own

father. You ought to been ashamed of yourself to stand by and hear
it saddled onto a lot of poor niggers and you never say a word for
'em. It makes me feel ridiculous to think I was soft enough to
believe that rubbage. Cuss you, I can see, now, why you was so
anxious to make up the deffesit—you wanted to get what money
I'd got out of the Nonesuch and one thing or another, and scoop
it *all!*"

The king says, timid, and still a snuffling:

"Why, duke, it was you that said make up the deffersit, it
warn't me."

"Dry up! I don't want to hear no more *out* of you!" says the
duke. "And *now* you see what you *got* by it. They've got all their
own money back, and all of *ourn* but a shekel or two, *besides*.
G'long to bed—and don't you deffersit *me* no more deffersits, long
's *you* live!"

So the king sneaked into the wigwam, and took to his bottle for
comfort; and before long the duke tackled *his* bottle; and so in
about a half an hour they was as thick as thieves again, and the
tighter they got, the lovinger they got; and went off a snoring in
each other's arms. They both got powerful mellow, but I noticed the
king didn't get mellow enough to forget to remember to not deny
about hiding the money-bag again. That made me feel easy and
satisfied. Of course when they got to snoring, we had a long gabble,
and I told Jim everything.

CHAPTER XXXI

We dasn't stop again at any town, for days and days; kept right
along down the river. We was down south in the warm weather,
now, and a mighty long ways from home. We begun to come to
trees with Spanish moss on them, hanging down from the limbs like
long gray beards. It was the first I ever see it growing, and it made
the woods look solemn and dismal. So now the frauds reckoned
they was out of danger, and they begun to work the villages again.

First they done a lecture on temperance; but they didn't make
enough for them both to get drunk on. Then in another village they
started a dancing school; but they didn't know no more how to
dance than a kangaroo does; so the first prance they made, the
general public jumped in and pranced them out of town. Another
time they tried to go at yellocution; but they didn't yellocute long
till the audience got up and give them a solid good cussing and
made them skip out. They tackled missionarying, and
mesmerizering, and doctoring, and telling fortunes, and a little of
everything; but they couldn't seem to have no luck. So at last they
got just about dead broke, and laid around the raft, as she floated
along, thinking, and thinking, and never saying nothing, by the half
a day at a time, and dreadful blue and desperate.

And at last they took a change, and begun to lay their heads together in the wigwam and talk low and confidential two or three hours at a time. Jim and me got uneasy. We didn't like the look of it. We judged they was studying up some kind of worse deviltry than ever. We turned it over and over, and at last we made up our minds they was going to break into somebody's house or store, or was going into the counterfeit-money business, or something. So then we was pretty scared, and made up an agreement that we wouldn't have nothing in the world to do with such actions, and if we ever got the least show we would give them the cold shake, and clear out and leave them behind. Well, early one morning we hid the raft in a good safe place about two mile below a little bit of a shabby village, named Pikesville, and the king he went ashore, and told us all to stay hid whilst he went up to town and smelt around to see if anybody had got any wind of the Royal Nonesuch there yet. ("House to rob, you *mean*," says I to myself, "and when you get through robbing it you'll come back here and wonder what's become of me and Jim and the raft—and you'll have to take it out in wondering.") And he said if he warn't back by midday, the duke and me would know it was all right, and we was to come along.

So we staid where we was. The duke he fretted and sweated around, and was in a mighty sour way. He scolded us for everything, and we couldn't seem to do nothing right; he found fault with every little thing. Something was a-brewing, sure. I was good and glad when midday come and no king; we could have a change, anyway—and maybe a chance for *the* change, on top of it. So me and the duke went up to the village, and hunted around there for the king, and by-and-by we found him in the back room of a little low doggery, very tight, and a lot of loafers bullyragging him for sport, and he a cussing and threatening with all his might, and so tight he couldn't walk, and couldn't do nothing to them. The duke he begun to abuse him for an old fool, and the king begun to sass back; and the minute they was fairly at it, I lit out, and shook the reefs out of my hind legs, and spun down the river road like a deer—for I see our chance; and I made up my mind that it would be a long day before they ever see me and Jim again. I got down there all out of breath but loaded up with joy, and sung out—

"Set her loose, Jim, we're all right, now!"

But there warn't no answer, and nobody come out of the wigwam. Jim was gone! I set up a shout—and then another—and then another one; and run this way and that in the woods, whooping and screeching; but it warn't no use—old Jim was gone. Then I set down and cried; I couldn't help it. But I couldn't set still long. Pretty soon I went out on the road, trying to think what I better do, and I run across a boy walking, and asked him if he'd seen a strange nigger, dressed so and so, and he says:

"Yes."

"Whereabouts?" says I.

"Down to Silas Phelps's place, two mile below here. He's a runaway nigger, and they've got him. Was you looking for him?"

"You bet I ain't! I run across him in the woods about an hour or two ago, and he said if I hollered he'd cut my livers out—and told me to lay down and stay where I was; and I done it. Been there ever since; afeard to come out."

"Well," he says, "you needn't be afeard no more, becuz they've got him. He run off f'm down South, som'ers."

"It's a good job they got him."

"Well, I *reckon!* There's two hundred dollars reward on him. It's like picking up money out'n the road."

"Yes, it is—and *I* could a had it if I'd been big enough; I see him *first.* Who nailed him?"

"It was an old fellow—a stranger—and he sold out his chance in him for forty dollars becuz he's got to go up the river and can't wait. Think o' that, now! You bet *I'd* wait, if it was seven year."

"That's me, every time," says I. "But maybe his chance ain't worth no more than that, if he'll sell it so cheap. Maybe there's something ain't straight about it."

"But it *is,* though—straight as a string. I see the handbill myself. It tells all about him, to a dot—paints him like a picture, and tells the plantation he's frum, below Newr*leans.* No-sirree-*bob,* they ain't no trouble 'bout *that* speculation, you bet you. Say, gimme a chaw tobacker, won't ye?"

I didn't have none, so he left. I went to the raft, and set down in the wigwam to thing. But I couldn't come to nothing. I thought till I wore my head sore, but I couldn't see no way out of the trouble. After all this long journey, and after all we'd done for them scoundrels, here was it all come to nothing, everything all busted up and ruined, because they could have the heart to serve Jim such a trick as that, and make him a slave again all his life, and amongst strangers, too, for forty dirty dollars.

Once I said to myself it would be a thousand times better for Jim to be a slave at home where his family was, as long as he'd *got* to be a slave, and so I'd better write a letter to Tom Sawyer and tell him to tell Miss Watson where he was. But I soon give up that notion, for tow things: she'd be made and disgusted at his rascality and ungratefulness for leaving her, and so she'd sell him straight down the river again; and if she didn't, everybody naturally despises an ungrateful nigger, and they'd make Jim feel it all the time, and so he'd feel ornery and disgraced. And then think of *me!* It would get all around, the Huck Finn helped a nigger to get his freedom; and if I was to ever see anybody from that town again, I'd be ready to get down and lick his boots for shame. That's just the way: a person does a low-down thing, and then he don't want to take no consequences of it. Thinks as long as he can hide it, ain't no disgrace. That was my fix exactly. The more I studied about this, the more my conscience went to grinding me, and the more wicked and low-down and ornery I got to feeling. And at last, when it hit me all of a sudden that here was the plain hand of Providence slapping me in the face and letting me know my wickedness was being watched all the time from up there in heaven, whilst I was stealing a poor old woman's nigger that hadn't ever done me no harm, and now was showing me there's One that's always on the lookout, and ain't agoing to allow no such miserable doings to go only just so fur and no further, I most dropped in my tracks I was so scared. Well, I tried the best I could to kinder soften it up somehow for myself, by saying I was brung up wicked, and so I warn't so much to blame; but something inside of me kept saying, "There was the Sunday school, you could a gone to it; and if you'd a done it they'd a learnt you, there, that people that acts as I'd been acting about that nigger goes to everlasting fire."

It made me shiver. And I about made up my mind to pray; and see if I couldn't try to quit being the kind of a boy I was, and be better. So I kneeled down. But the words wouldn't come. Why wouldn't they? It warn't no use to try and hide it from Him. Nor from *me*, neither. I knowed very well why they wouldn't come. It was because my heart warn't right; it was because I warn't square; it was because I was playing double. I was letting *on* to give up sin, but away inside of me I was holding on to the biggest one of all. I was trying to make my mouth *say* I would do the right thing and the clean thing, and go and write to that nigger's owner and tell where he was; but deep down in me I knowed it was a lie—and He knowed it. You can't pray a lie—I found that out.

So I was full of trouble, full as I could be; and didn't know what to do. At last I had an idea; and I says, I'll go and write the letter—and *then* see if I can pray. Why, it was astonishing, the way I felt as light as a feather, right straight off, and my troubles all gone. So I got a piece of paper and a pencil, all glad and excited, and set down and wrote:

> Miss Watson your runaway nigger Jim is down here two mile below Pikesville and Mr. Phelps has got him and he will give him up for the reward if you send. HUCK FINN.

I felt good and all washed clean of sin for the first time I had ever felt so in my life, and I knowed I could pray now. But I didn't do it straight off, but laid the paper down and set there thinking— thinking how good it was all this happened so, and how near I come to being lost and going to hell. And went on thinking. And got to thinking over our trip down the river; and I see Jim before me, all the time, in the day, and in the nighttime, sometimes moonlight, sometimes storms, and we a floating along, talking, and singing, and laughing. But somehow I couldn't seem to strike no places to harden me against him, but only the other kind. I'd see him standing my watch on top of his'n, stead of calling me, so I could go on sleeping; and see him how glad he was when I come back out of the fog; and when I come to him again in the swamp, up there where the feud was; and such-like times; and would always call me honey, and pet me, and do everything he could think of for me, and how good he always was; and at last I struck the time I saved him by telling the men we had small-pox aboard, and he was so grateful, and said I was the best friend old Jim ever had in the world, and the *only* one he's got now; and then I happened to look around, and see that paper.

It was a close place. I took it up, and held it in my hand. I was a trembling, because I'd got to decide, forever, betwixt two things, and I knowed it. I studied a minute, sort of holding my breath, and then says to myself:

"All right, then, I'll *go* to hell"—and tore it up.

It was awful thoughts, and awful words, but they was said. And I let them stay said; and never thought no more about reforming. I shoved the whole thing out of my head; and said I would take up wickedness again, which was in my line, being brung up to it, and the other warn't. And for a starter, I would go to work and steal Jim out of slavery again; and if I could think up anything worse, I would do that, too; because as long as I was in, and in for good, I might as well go the whole hog.

Then I set to thinking over how to get at it, and turned over considerable many ways in my mind; and at last fixed up a plan that suited me. So then I took the bearings of a woody island that was down the river a piece, and as soon as it was fairly dark I crept out with my raft and went for it, and hid it there, and then turned in. I slept the night through, and got up before it was light, and had my breakfast, and put on my store clothes, and tied up some others and one thing or another in a bundle, and took the canoe and cleared for shore. I landed below where I judged was Phelps's place, and hid my bundle in the woods, and then filled up the canoe with water, and loaded rocks into her and sunk her where I could find her again when I wanted her, about a quarter of a mile below a little steam sawmill that was on the bank.

Then I struck up the road, and when I passed the mill I see a sign on it, "Phelps's Sawmill," and when I come to the farm-houses, two or three hundred yards further along, I kept my eyes peeled, but didn't see nobody around, though it was good daylight, now. But I didn't mind, because I didn't want to see nobody just yet—I only wanted to get the lay of the land. According to my plan, I was going to turn up there from the village, not from below. So I just took a look, and shoved along, straight for town. Well, the very first man I see, when I got there, was the duke. He was sticking up a bill for the Royal Nonesuch—three-night performance—like that other time. *They* had the cheek, them frauds! I was right on him, before I could shirk. He looked astonished, and says:

"Hel-*lo!* Where'd *you* come from?" Then he says, kind of glad and eager, "Where's the raft?—got her in a good place?"

I says:

"Why, that's just what I was agoing to ask your grace."

Then he didn't look so joyful—and says:

"What was your idea for asking *me?*" he says.

"Well," I says, "when I see the king in that doggery yesterday, I says to myself, we can't get him home for hours, till he's soberer; so I went a loafing around town to put in the time, and wait. A man up and offered me ten cents to help him pull a skiff over the river and back to fetch a sheep, and so I went along; but when we was dragging him to the boat, and the man left me aholt of the rope and went behind him to shove him along, he was too strong for me, and jerked loose and run, and we after him. We didn't have no dog, and so we had to chase him all over the country till we tired him out. We never got him till dark, then we fetched him over, and I started down for the raft. When I got there and see it was gone, I says to myself, 'they've got into trouble and had to leave; and they've took my nigger, which is the only nigger I've got in the world, and now I'm in a strange country, and ain't got no property no more, nor nothing, and no way to make my living;' so I set down and cried. I slept in the woods all night. But what *did* become of the raft then?—and Jim, poor Jim!"

"Blamed if *I* know—that is, what's become of the raft. That old fool had made a trade and got forty dollars, and when we found him in the doggery the loafers had matched half dollars with him and got every cent but what he'd spent for whisky; and when I got him home late last night and found the raft gone, we said, 'That little rascal has stole our raft and shook us, and run off down the river.' "

"I wouldn't shake my *nigger,* would I?—the only nigger I had in the world, and the only property."

"We never thought of that. Fact is, I reckon we'd come to consider him our nigger; yes, we did consider him so—goodness knows we had trouble enough for him. So when we see the raft was gone, and we flat broke, there warn't anything for it but to try the Royal Nonesuch another shake. And I've pegged along ever since, dry as a powderhorn. Where's that ten cents? Give it here."

I had considerable money, so I give him ten cents, but begged him to spend it for something to eat, and give me some, because it was all the money I had, and I hadn't had nothing to eat since yesterday. He never said nothing. The next minute he whirls on me and says:

"Do you reckon that nigger would blow on us? We'd skin him if he done that!"

"How can he blow? Hain't he run off?"

"No! That old fool sold him, and never divided with me, and the money's gone."

"*Sold* him?" I says, and begun to cry; "why, he was *my* nigger, and that was my money. Where is he?—I want my nigger."

"Well, you can't *get* your nigger, that's all—so dry up your blubbering. Looky here—do you think *you'd* venture to blow on us? Blamed if I think I'd trust you. Why, if you *was* to blow on us—"

He stopped, but I never see the duke look so ugly out of his eyes before. I went on a-whimpering, and says:

"I don't want to blow on nobody; and I ain't got no time to blow, nohow. I got to turn out and find my nigger."

He looked kinder bothered, and stood there with his bills fluttering on his arm, thinking, and wrinkling up his forehead. At last he says:

"I'll tell you something. We got to be here three days. If you'll promise you won't blow, and won't let the nigger blow, I'll tell you where to find him."

So I promised, and he says:

"A farmer by the name of Silas Ph—" and then he stopped. You see he started to tell me the truth; but when he stopped, that way, and begun to study and think again, I reckoned he was changing his mind. And so he was. He wouldn't trust me; he wanted to make sure of having me out of the way the whole three days. So pretty soon he says: "The man that bought him is named Abram Foster— Abram G. Foster—and he lives forty mile back here in the country, on the road to Lafayette."

"All right," I says, "I can walk it in three days. And I'll start this very afternoon."

"No you won't, you'll start *now;* and don't you lose any time about it, neither, nor do any gabbling by the way. Just keep a tight tongue in your head and move right along, and then you won't get into trouble with *us,* d'ye hear?"

That was the order I wanted, and that was the one I played for. I wanted to be left free to work my plans.

"So clear out," he says; "and you can tell Mr. Foster whatever you want to. Maybe you can get him to believe that Jim *is* your nigger—some idiots don't require documents—leastways I've heard there's such down South here. And when you tell him the handbill and the reward's bogus, maybe he'll believe you when you explain to him what the idea was for getting 'em out. Go 'long, now, and tell him anything you want to; but mind you don't work your jaw any *between* here and there."

So I left, and struck for the back country. I didn't look around, but I kinder felt like he was watching me. But I knowed I could tire him out at that. I want straight out in the country as much as a mile, before I stopped; then I doubled back through the woods towards Phelps's. I reckoned I better start in on my plan straight off, without

fooling around, because I wanted to stop Jim's mouth till these
fellows could get away. I didn't want no trouble with their kind. I'd
seen all I wanted to of them, and wanted to get entirely shut
of them.

CHAPTER XXXII

When I got there it was all still and Sunday-like, and hot and
sunshiny—the hands was gone to the fields; and there was them
kind of faint dronings of bugs and flies in the air that makes it seem
so lonesome and like everybody's dead and gone; and if a breeze
fans along and quivers the leaves, it makes you feel mournful,
because you feel like it's spirits whispering—spirits that's been
dead ever so many years—and you always think they're talking
about *you*. As a general thing it makes a body wish *he* was dead, too,
and done with it all.

Phelps's was one of these little one-horse cotton plantations;
and they all look alike. A rail fence round a two-acre yard; a stile,
made out of logs sawed off and up-ended, in steps, like barrels of
a different length, to climb over the fence with, and for the women
to stand on when they are going to jump onto a horse; some sickly
grass-patches in the big yard, but mostly it was bare and smooth,
like an old hat with the nap rubbed off; big double log house for the
white folks—hewed logs, with the chinks stopped up with mud or
mortar, and these mud-stripes been whitewashed some time or
another; round-log kitchen, with a big broad, open but roofed
passage joining it to the house; log smoke-house back of the kitchen;
three little log nigger-cabins in a row t'other side the smokehouse;
one little hut all by itself away down against the back fence, and
some out-buildings down a piece the other side; ash-hopper, and big
kettle to bile soap in, by the little hut; bench by the kitchen door,
with bucket of water and a gourd; hound asleep there, in the sun;
more hounds asleep, round about; about three shade-trees away
off in a corner; some currant bushes and gooseberry bushes in one
place by the fence; outside of the fence a garden and a water-melon
patch; then the cotton fields begins; and after the fields, the woods.

I went around and clumb over the back stile by the ash-hopper,
and started for the kitchen. When I got a little ways, I heard the dim
hum of a spinning-wheel wailing along up and sinking along down
again; and then I knowed for certain I wished I was dead—for that
is the lonesomest sound in the whole world.

I went right along, not fixing up any particular plan, but just
trusting to Providence to put the right words in my mouth when the
time come; for I'd noticed that Providence always did put the right
words in my mouth, if I left it alone.

When I got half-way, first one hound and then another got up and
went for me, and of course I stopped and faced them, and kept

still. And such another pow-wow as they made! In a quarter of a minute I was a kind of a hub of a wheel, as you may say—spokes made out of dogs—circle of fifteen of them packed together around me, with their necks and noses stretched up towards me, a barking and howling; and more a coming; you could see them sailing over fences and around corners from everywheres.

A nigger woman come tearing out of the kitchen with a rolling-pin in her hand, singing out, "Begone! *you* Tige! you Spot! begone, sah!" and she fetched first one and then another of them a clip and sent him howling, and then the rest followed; and the next second, half of them come back, wagging their tails around me and making friends with me. There ain't no harm in a hound, nohow.

And behind the woman comes a little nigger girl and two little nigger boys, without anything on but tow-linen shirts, and they hung onto their mother's gown, and peeped out from behind her at me, bashful, the way they always do. And here comes the white woman running from the house, about forty-five or fifty year old, bareheaded, and her spinning-stick in her hand; and behind her comes her little white children, acting the same way the little niggers was doing. She was smiling all over so she could hardly stand—and says:

"It's *you,* at last!—*ain't* it?"

I out with a "Yes'm," before I thought.

She grabbed me and hugged me tight; and then gripped me by both hands and shook and shook; and the tears come in her eyes, and run down over; and she couldn't seem to hug and shake enough, and kept saying, "You don't look as much like your mother as I reckoned you would, but law sakes, I don't care for that, I'm *so* glad to see you! Dear, dear, it does seem like I could eat you up! Children, it's your cousin Tom!—tell him howdy."

But they ducked their heads, and put their fingers in their mouths, and hid behind her. So she run on:

"Lize, hurry up and get him a hot breakfast, right away—or did you get your breakfast on the boat?"

I said I had got it on the boat. So then she started for the house, leading me by the hand, and the children tagging after. When we got there, she set me down in a split-bottomed chair, and set herself down on a little low stool in front of me, holding both of my hands, and says:

"Now I can have a *good* look at you; and laws-a-me, I've been hungry for it a many and a many a time, all these long years, and it's come at last! We been expecting you a couple of days and more. What's kep' you?—boat get aground?"

"Yes'm—she——"

"Don't say yes'm—say Aunt Sally. Where'd she get aground?"

I didn't rightly know what to say, because I didn't know whether the boat would be coming up the river or down. But I go

a good deal on instinct; and my instinct said she would be coming
up—from down towards Orleans. That did'nt help me much,
though; for I didn't know the names of bars down that way. I see
I'd got to invent a bar, or forget the name of the one we got aground
on—or— Now I struck an idea, and fetched it out:

"It warn't the grounding—that didn't keep us back but a little.
We blowed out a cylinder-head."

"Good gracious! anybody hurt?"

"No'm. Killed a nigger."

"Well, it's lucky; because sometimes people do get hurt. Two
years ago last Christmas, your uncle Silas was coming up from
Newrleans on the old *Lally Rook,* and she blowed out a cylinder-
head and crippled a man. And I think he died afterwards. He was
a Babtist. Your uncle Silas knowed a family in Baton Rouge that
knowed his people very well. Yes, I remember, now he *did* die.
Mortification set in, and they had to amputate him. But it didn't
save him. Yes, it was mortification—that was it. He turned blue all
over, and died in the hope of a glorious resurrection. They say he
was a sight to look at. Your uncle's been up to the town every day to
fetch you. And he's gone again, not more'n an hour ago; he'll be
back any minute, now. You must a met him on the road, didn't
you?—oldish man, with a—"

"No, I didn't see nobody, Aunt Sally. The boat landed just at
daylight, and I left my baggage on the wharf-boat and went looking
around the town and out a piece in the country, to put in the time
and not get here too soon; and so I come down the back way."

"Who'd you give the baggage to?"

"Nobody."

"Why, child, it'll be stole!"

"Not where *I* hid it I reckon it won't," I says.

"How'd you get your breakfast so early on the boat?"

It was kinder thin ice, but I says:

"The captain see me standing around, and told me I better have
something to eat before I went ashore; so he took me in the texas
to the officers' lunch, and give me all I wanted."

I was getting so uneasy I couldn't listen good. I had my mind on
the children all the time; I wanted to get them out to one side, and
pump them a little, and find out who I was. But I couldn't get no
show, Mrs. Phelps kept it up and run on so. Pretty soon she made
the cold chills streak all down my back, because she says:

"But here we're a running on this way, and you hain't told me a
word about Sis, nor any of them. Now I'll rest my works a little, and
you start up yourn; just tell me *everything*—tell me all about 'm
all—every one of 'm; and how they are, and what they're doing,
and what they told you to tell me; and every last thing you can
think of."

Well, I see I was up a stump—and up it good. Providence had

stood by me this far, all right, but I was hard and tight aground,
now. I see it warn't a bit of use to try to go ahead—I'd *got* to throw
up my hand. So I says to myself, here's another place where I got to
resk the truth. I opened my mouth to begin; but she grabbed me and
hustled me in behind the bed, and says:

"Here he comes! stick your head down lower—there, that'll do;
you can't be seen, now. Don't you let on you're here. I'll play a joke
on him. Children, don't you say a word."

I see I was in a fix, now. But it warn't no use to worry; there warn't
nothing to do but just hold still, and try and be ready to stand from
under when the lightning struck.

I had just one little glimpse of the old gentleman when he come in,
then the bed hid him. Mrs. Phelps she jumps for him and says:

"Has he come?"

"No," says her husband.

"Good-*ness* gracious!" she says, "what in the world *can* have
become of him?"

"I can't imagine," says the old gentleman; "and I must say, it
makes me dreadful uneasy."

"Uneasy!" she says, "I'm ready to go distracted! He *must* a come;
and you've missed him along the road. I *know* it's so—something
tells me so."

"Why Sally, I *couldn't* miss him along the road—*you* know that."

"But oh, dear, dear, what *will* Sis say! He must a come! You
must a missed him. He——"

"Oh, don't distress me any more'n I'm already distressed. I don't
know what in the world to make of it. I'm at my wit's end, and I
don't mind acknowledging 't I'm right down scared. But there's
no hope that he's come; for he *couldn't* come and me miss him.
Sally, it's terrible—just terrible—something's happened to the
boat, sure!"

"Why, Silas! Look yonder!—up the road!—ain't that somebody
coming?"

He sprung to the window at the head of the bed, and that give
Mrs. Phelps the chance she wanted. She stooped down quick, at the
foot of the bed, and give me a pull, and out I come; and when he
turned back from the window, there she stood, a-beaming and
a-smiling like a house afire, and I standing pretty meek and sweaty
alongside. The old gentleman stared, and says:

"Why, who's that?"

"Who do you reckon 't is?"

"I haint no idea. Who *is* it?"

"It's *Tom Sawyer!*"

By jings, I most slumped through the floor. But there warn't no
time to swap knives; the old man grabbed me by the hand and
shook, and kept on shaking; and all the time, how the woman did
dance around and laugh and cry; and then how they both did fire off

questions about Sid, and Mary, and the rest of the tribe.

But if they was joyful, it warn't nothing to what I was; for it was like being born again, I was so glad to find out who I was. Well, they froze to me for two hours; and at last when my chin was so tired it couldn't hardly go, any more, I had told them more about my family—I mean the Sawyer family—than ever happened to any six Sawyer families. And I explained all about how we blowed out a cylinder-head at the mouth of White River and it took us three days to fix it. Which was all right, and worked first rate; because *they* didn't know but what it would take three days to fix it. If I'd a called it a bolt-head it would a done just as well.

Now I was feeling pretty comfortable all down one side, and pretty uncomfortable all up the other. Being Tom Sawyer was easy and comfortable; and it stayed easy and comfortable till by-and-by I hear a steamboat coughing along down the river—then I says to myself, spose Tom Sawyer come down on that boat?—and spose he steps in here, any minute, and sings out my name before I can throw him a wink to keep quiet? Well, I couldn't *have* it that way—it wouldn't do at all. I must go up the road and waylay him. So I told the folks I reckoned I would go up to the town and fetch down my baggage. The old gentleman was for going along with me, but I said no, I could drive the horse myself, and I druther he wouldn't take no trouble about me.

CHAPTER XXXIII

So I started for town, in the wagon, and when I was half-way I see a wagon coming, and sure enough it was Tom Sawyer, and I stopped and waited till he come along. I says "Hold on!" and it stopped alongside, and his mouth opened up like a trunk, and staid so; and he swallowed two or three times like a person that's got a dry throat, and then says:

"I hain't ever done you no harm. You know that. So then, what you want to come back and ha'nt *me* for?"

I says:

"I hain't come back—I hain't been *gone.*"

When he heard my voice, it righted him up some, but he warn't quite satisfied yet. He says:

"Don't you play nothing on me, because I wouldn't on you. Honest injun, now, you ain't a ghost?"

"Honest injun, I ain't," I says.

"Well—I—I—well, that ought to settle it, of course; but I can't somehow seem to understand it, no way. Looky here, warn't you ever murdered *at all?*"

"No. I warn't ever murdered at all—I played it on them. You come in here and feel of me if you don't believe me."

So he done it; and it satisfied him; and he was that glad to see me again, he didn't know what to do. And he wanted to know all about it right off; because it was a grand adventure, and mysterious, and so it hit him where he lived. But I said, leave it alone till by-and-by; and told his driver to wait, and we drove off a little piece, and I told him the kind of a fix I was in, and what did he reckon we better do? He said, let him alone a minute, and don't disturb him. So he thought and thought, and pretty soon he says:

"It's all right, I've got it. Take my trunk in your wagon, and let on it's your'n; and you turn back and fool along slow, so as to get to the house about the time you ought to; and I'll go towards town a piece, and take a fresh start, and get there a quarter or a half an hour after you; and you needn't let on to know me, at first."

I says:

"All right; but wait a minute. There's one more thing—a thing that *nobody* don't know but me. And that is, there's a nigger here that I'm a trying to steal out of slavery—and his name is *Jim*—old Miss Watson's Jim."

He says:

"What! Why Jim is——"

He stopped and went to studying. I says:

"*I* know what you'll say. You'll say it's dirty low-down business; but what if it is?—*I*'m low down; and I'm agoing to steal him, and I want you to keep mum and not let on. Will you?"

His eye lit up, and he says:

"I'll *help* you steal him!"

Well, I let go all holts then, like I was shot. It was the most astonishing speech I ever heard—and I'm bound to say Tom Sawyer fell, considerable, in my estimation. Only I couldn't believe it. Tom Sawyer a *nigger stealer!*

"Oh, shucks," I says, "you're joking."

"I ain't joking, either."

"Well, then," I says, "joking or no joking, if you hear anything said about a runaway nigger, don't forget to remember that *you* don't know nothing about him, and *I* don't know nothing about him."

Then we took the trunk and put it in my wagon, and he drove off his way, and I drove mine. But of course I forgot all about driving slow, on accounts of being glad and full of thinking; so I got home a heap too quick for that length of a trip. The old gentleman was at the door, and he says:

"Why, this is wonderful. Who ever would a thought it was in that mare to do it. I wish we'd a timed her. And she hain't sweated a hair—not a hair. It's wonderful. Why, I wouldn't take a hundred dollars for that horse now; I wouldn't honest; and yet I'd a sold her for fifteen before, and thought 'twas all she was worth."

That's all he said. He was the innocentest, best old soul I ever see. But it warn't surprising; because he warn't only just a farmer, he was a preacher, too, and had a little one-horse log church down back of the plantation, which he built it himself at his own expense, for a church and school-house, and never charged nothing for his preaching, and it was worth it, too. There was plenty other farmer-preachers like that, and done the same way, down South.

In about half an hour Tom's wagon drove up to the front stile, and Aunt Sally she see it through the window because it was only about fifty yards, and says:

"Why, there's somebody come! I wonder who 'tis? Why, I do believe it's a stranger. Jimmy" (that's one of the children), "run and tell Lize to put on another plate for dinner."

Everybody made a rush for the front door, because, of course, a stranger don't come *every* year, and so he lays over the yaller fever, for interest, when he does come. Tom was over the stile and starting for the house; the wagon was spinning up the road for the village, and we was all bunched in the front door. Tom had his store clothes on, and an audience—and that was always nuts for Tom Sawyer. In them circumstances it warn't no trouble to him to throw in an amount of style that was suitable. He warn't a boy to meeky along up that yard like a sheep; no, he come ca'm and important, like the ram. When he got afront of us, he lifts his hat ever so gracious and dainty, like it was the lid of a box that had butterflies asleep in it and he didn't want to disturb them, and says:

"Mr. Archibald Nichols, I presume?"

"No, my boy," says the old gentleman, "I'm sorry to say 't your driver has deceived you; Nichols's place is down a matter of three mile more. Come in, come in."

Tom he took a look back over his shoulder, and says, "Too late— he's out of sight."

"Yes, he's gone, my son, and you must come in and eat your dinner with us; and then we'll hitch up and take you down to Nichols's."

"Oh, I *can't* make you so much trouble; I couldn't think of it. I'll walk—I don't mind the distance."

"But we won't *let* you walk—it wouldn't be Southern hospitality to do it. Come right in."

"Oh, *do*," says Aunt Sally; "it ain't a bit of trouble to us, not a bit in the world. You *must* stay. It's a long, dusty three mile, and we *can't* let you walk. And besides, I've already told 'em to put on another plate, when I see you coming; so you mustn't disappoint us. Come right in, and make yourself at home."

So Tom he thanked them very hearty and handsome, and let himself be persuaded, and come in; and when he was in, he said he was a stranger from Hicksville, Ohio, and his name was William Thompson—and he made another bow.

Well, he run on, and on, and on, making up stuff about Hicksville and everybody in it he could invent, and I getting a little nervous,

and wondering how this was going to help me out of my scrape;
and at last, still talking along, he reached over and kissed Aunt
Sally right on the mouth, and then settled back again in his chair,
comfortable, and was going on talking; but she jumped up and
wiped it off with the back of her hand, and says:

"You owdacious puppy!"

He looked kind of hurt, and says:

"I'm surprised at you, m'am."

"You're s'rp— Why, what do you reckon *I* am? I've a good notion
to take and—say, what do you mean by kissing me?"

He looked kind of humble, and says:

"I didn't mean nothing, m'am. I didn't mean no harm. I—I—
thought you'd like it."

"Why, you born fool!" She took up the spining-stick, and it
looked like it was all she could do to keep from giving him a crack
with it. "What made you think I'd like it?"

"Well, I don't know. Only, they—they—told me you would."

"*They* told you I would. Whoever told you's *another* lunatic. I
never heard the beat of it. Who's *they?*"

"Why—everybody. They all said so, m'am."

It was all she could do to hold in; and her eyes snapped, and her
fingers worked like she wanted to scratch him; and she says:

"Who's 'everybody?' Out with their names—or ther'll be an idiot
short."

He got up and looked distressed, and fumbled his hat, and says:

"I'm sorry, and I warn't expecting it. They told me to. They all
told me to. They all said kiss her; and said she'll like it. They all
said it—every one of them. But I'm sorry, m'am, and I won't do it
no more—I won't, honest."

"You won't, won't you? Well, I sh'd *reckon* you won't!"

"No'm, I'm honest about it; I won't ever do it again. Till you ask
me."

"Till I *ask* you! Well, I never see the beat of it in my born days!
I lay you'll be the Methusalem-numskull of creation before ever *I*
ask you—or the likes of you."

"Well," he says, "it does surprise me so. I can't make it out,
somehow. They said you would, and I thought you would. But—"
He stopped and looked around slow, like he wished he could run
across a friendly eye, somewhere's; and fetched up on the old
gentleman's, and says, "Didn't *you* think she'd like me to kiss her,
sir?"

"Why, no, I—I—well, no, I b'lieve I didn't."

Then he looks on around, the same way, to me—and says:

"Tom, didn't *you* think Aunt Sally'd open out her arms and say,
'Sid Sawyer——' "

"My land!" she says, breaking in and jumping for him, "you
impudent young rascal, to fool a body so—" and was going to hug

him, but he fended her off, and says:

"No, not till you've asked me, first."

So she didn't lose no time, but asked him; and hugged him and kissed him, over and over again, and then turned him over to the old man, and he took what was left. And after they got a little quiet again, she says:

"Why, dear me, I never see such a surprise. We warn't looking for *you*, at all, but only Tom. Sis never wrote to me about anybody coming but him."

"It's because it warn't *intended* for any of us to come but Tom," he says; "but I begged and begged, and at the last minute she let me come, too; so, coming down the river, me and Tom thought it would be a first-rate surprise for him to come here to the house first, and for me to by-and-by tag along and drop in and let on to be a stranger. But it was a mistake, Aunt Sally. This ain't no healthy place for a stranger to come."

"No—not impudent whelps, Sid. You ought to had your jaws boxed; I hain't been so put out since I don't know when. But I don't care, I don't mind the terms—I'd be willing to stand a thousand such jokes to have you here. Well, to think of that performance! I don't deny it, I was most putrified with astonishment when you give me that smack."

We had dinner out in that broad open passage betwixt the house and the kitchen; and there was things enough on that table for seven families—and all hot, too; none of your flabby tough meat that's laid in a cupboard in a damp cellar all night and tastes like a hunk of old cold cannibal in the morning. Uncle Silas he asked a pretty long blessing over it, but it was worth it; and it didn't cool it a bit, neither, the way I've seen them kind of interruptions do, lots of times.

There was a considerable good deal of talk, all the afternoon, and me and Tom was on the lookout all the time, but it warn't no use, they didn't happen to say nothing about my runaway nigger, and we was afraid to try to work up to it. But at supper, at night, one of the little boys says:

"Pa, mayn't Tom and Sid and me go to the show?"

"No," says the old man, "I reckon there ain't going to be any; and you couldn't go if there was; because the runaway nigger told Burton and me all about that scandalous show, and Burton said he would tell the people; so I reckon they've drove the owdacious loafers out of town before this time."

So there it was!—but *I* couldn't help it. Tom and me was to sleep in the same room and bed; so, being tired, we bid good-night and went up to bed, right after supper, and clumb out of the window and down the lightning-rod, and shoved for the town; for I didn't believe anybody was going to give the king and the duke a hint, and so, if I didn't hurry up and give them one they'd get into trouble sure.

On the road Tom he told me all about how it was reckoned I was murdered, and how pap disappeared, pretty soon, and didn't come back no more, and what a stir there was when Jim run away; and I told Tom all about our Royal Nonesuch rapscallions, and as much of the raft-voyage as I had time to; and as we struck into the town and up through the middle of it—it was as much as half after eight, then—here comes a raging rush of people, with torches, and an awful whooping and yelling, and banging tin pans and blowing horns; and we jumped to one side to let them go by; and as they went by, I see they had the king and the duke astraddle of a rail— that is, I knowed it *was* the king and the duke, though they was all over tar and feathers, and didn't look like nothing in the world that was human—just looked like a couple of monstrous big soldier-plumes. Well, it made me sick to see it; and I was sorry for them poor pitiful rascals, it seemed like I couldn't ever feel any hardness against them any more in the world. It was a dreadful thing to see. Human beings *can* be awful cruel to one another.

We see we was too late—couldn't do no good. We asked some stragglers about it, and they said everybody went to the show looking very innocent; and laid low and kept dark till the poor old king was in the middle of his cavortings on the stage; then somebody give a signal, and the house rose up and went for them.

So we poked along back home, and I warn't feeling so brash as I was before, but kind of ornery, and humble, and to blame, somehow—though *I* hadn't done nothing. But that's always the way; it don't make no difference whether you do right or wrong, a person's conscience ain't got no sense, and just goes for him *anyway*. If I had a yaller dog that didn't know no more than a person's conscience does, I would pison him. It takes up more room than all the rest of a person's insides, and yet ain't no good, nohow. Tom Sawyer he says the same.

CHAPTER XXXIV

We stopped talking, and got to thinking.

By-and-by Tom says:

"Looky here, Huck, what fools we are, to not think of it before! I bet I know where Jim is."

"No! Where?"

"In that hut down by the ash-hopper. Why, looky here. When we was at dinner, didn't you see a nigger man go in there with some vittles?"

"Yes."

"What did you think the vittles was for?"

"For a dog."

"So'd I. Well, it wasn't for a dog."

"Why?"

"Because part of it was watermelon."

"So it was—I noticed it. Well, it does beat all, that I never thought about a dog not eating watermelon. It shows how a body can see and don't see at the same time."

"Well, the nigger unlocked the padlock when he went in, and he locked it again when he come out. He fetched uncle a key, about the time we got up from table—same key, I bet. Watermelon shows man, lock shows prisoner; and it ain't likely there's two prisoners on such a little plantation, and where the people's all so kind and good. Jim's the prisoner. All right—I'm glad we found it out detective fashion; I wouldn't give shucks for any other way. Now you work your mind and study out a plan to steal Jim, and I will study out one, too; and we'll take the one we like the best."

What a head for just a boy to have! If I had Tom Sawyer's head, I wouldn't trade it off to be a duke, nor mate of a steamboat, nor clown in a circus, nor nothing I can think of. I went to thinking out a plan, but only just to be doing something; I knowed very well where the right plan was going to come from. Pretty soon, Tom says:

"Ready?"

"Yes," I says.

"All right—bring it out."

"My plan is this," I says. "We can easy find out if it's Jim in there. Then get up my canoe to-morrow night, and fetch my raft over from the island. Then the first dark night that comes, steal the key out of the old man's britches, after he goes to bed, and shove off down the river on the raft, with Jim, hiding daytimes and running nights, the way me and Jim used to do before. Wouldn't that plan work?"

"*Work?* Why cert'nly, it would work, like rats a fighting. But it's too blame' simple; there ain't nothing *to* it. What's the good of a plan that ain't no more trouble than that? It's as mild as goose-milk. Why, Huck, it wouldn't make no more talk than breaking into a soap factory."

I never said nothing, because I warn't expecting nothing different; but I knowed mighty well that whenever he got *his* plan ready it wouldn't have none of them objections to it.

And it didn't. He told me what it was, and I see in a minute it was worth fifteen of mine, for style, and would make Jim just as free a man as mine would, and maybe get us all killed besides. So I was satisfied, and said we would waltz in on it. I needn't tell what it was, here, because I knowed it wouldn't stay the way it was. I knowed he would be changing it around, every which way, as we went along, and heaving in new bullinesses wherever he got a chance. And that is what he done.

Well, one thing was dead sure; and that was, that Tom Sawyer was in earnest and was actuly going to help steal that nigger out of slavery. That was the thing that was too many for me. Here was a boy that was respectable, and well brung up; and had a character to lose; and folks at home that had characters; and he was bright and not leather-headed; and knowing and not ignorant; and not mean, but kind; and yet here he was, without any more pride, or rightness, or feeling, than to stoop to this business, and make himself a shame, and his family a shame, before everybody. I *couldn't* understand it, no way at all. It was outrageous, and I knowed I ought to just up and tell him so; and so be his true friend, and let him quit the thing right where he was, and save himself. And I *did* start to tell him; but he shut me up, and says:

"Don't you reckon I know what I'm about? Don't I generly know what I'm about?"

"Yes."

"Didn't I *say* I was going to help steal the nigger?"

"Yes."

"*Well* then."

That's all he said, and that's all I said. It warn't no use to say any more; because when he said he'd do a thing, he always done it. But *I* couldn't make out how he was willing to go into this thing; so I just let it go, and never bothered no more about it. If he was bound to have it so, *I* couldn't help it.

When we got home, the house was all dark and still; so we went on down to the hut by the ash-hopper, for to examine it. We went through the yard, so as to see what the hounds would do. They knowed us, and didn't make no more noise than country dogs is always doing when anything comes by in the night. When we got to the cabin, we took a look at the front and the two sides; and on the side I warn't acquainted with—which was the north side—we found a square window-hole, up tolerable high, with just one stout board nailed across it. I says:

"Here's the ticket. This hole's big enough for Jim to get through, if we wrench off the board."

Tom says:

"It's as simple as tit-tat-toe, three-in-a-row, and as easy as playing hooky. I should *hope* we can find a way that's a little more complicated than *that,* Huck Finn."

"Well then," I says, "how'll it do to saw him out, the way I done before I was murdered, that time?"

"That's more *like,*" he says. "It's real mysterious, and troublesome, and good," he says; "but I bet we can find a way that's twice as long. There ain't no hurry; le's keep on looking around."

Betwixt the hut and the fence, on the back side, was a lean-to, that joined the hut at the eaves, and was made out of plank. It was as long as the hut, but narrow—only about six foot wide. The door to it was at the south end, and was padlocked. Tom he went to the soap kettle, and searched around and fetched back the iron thing they lift the lid with; so he took it and prized out one of the staples. The chain fell down, and we opened the door and went in, and shut it, and struck a match, and see the shed was only built against the cabin and hadn't no connection with it; and there warn't no floor to the shed, nor nothing in it but some old rusty played-out hoes, and spades, and picks, and a crippled plow. The match went out, and so did we, and shoved in the staple again, and the door was locked as good as ever. Tom was joyful. He says:

"Now we're all right. We'll *dig* him out. It'll take about a week!"

Then we started for the house, and I went in the back door—you only have to pull a buckskin latch-string, they don't fasten the doors—but that warn't romantical enough for Tom Sawyer: no way would do him but he must climb up the lightning-rod. But after he got up half-way about three times, and missed fire and fell every time, and the last time most busted his brains out, he thought he'd got to give it up; but after he was rested, he allowed he would give her one more turn for luck, and this time he made the trip.

In the morning we was up at break of day, and down to the nigger cabins to pet the dogs and make friends with the nigger that fed Jim—if it *was* Jim that was being fed. The niggers was just getting through breakfast and starting for the fields; and Jim's nigger was piling up a tin pan with bread and meat and things; and whilst the others was leaving, the key come from the house.

This nigger had a good-natured, chuckle-headed face, and his wool was all tied up in little bunches with thread. That was to keep witches off. He said the witches was pestering him awful, these nights, and making him see all kinds of strange things, and hear all kinds of strange words and noises, and he didn't believe he was ever witched so long, before, in his life. He got so worked up, and got to running on so about his troubles, he forgot all about what he'd been agoing to do. So Tom says:

"What's the vittles for? Going to feed the dogs?"

The nigger kind of smiled around gradually over his face, like when you heave a brickbat in a mud puddle, and he says:

"Yes, Mars Sid, a dog. Cur'us dog, too. Does you want to go en look at 'im?"

"Yes."

I hunched Tom, and whispers:

"You going, right here in the day-break? *That* warn't the plan."

"No, it warn't—but it's the plan *now*."

So, drat him, we went along, but I didn't like it much. When we got in, we couldn't hardly see anything, it was so dark; but Jim was there, sure enough, and could see us; and he sings out:

"Why, *Huck!* En good *lan'!* ain' dat Misto Tom?"

I just knowed how it would be; I just expected it. *I* didn't know nothing to do; and if I had, I couldn't a done it; because that nigger busted in and says:

"Why, de gracious sakes! do he know you genlmen?"

We could see pretty well, now. Tom he looked at the nigger, steady and kind of wondering, and says:

"Does *who* know us?"

"Why, dish-yer runaway nigger."

"I don't reckon he does; but what put that into your head?"

"What *put* it dar? Didn' he jis' dis minute sing out like he knowed you?"

Tom says, in a puzzled-up kind of way:

"Well, that's mighty curious. *Who* sung out? *When* did he sing out? *What* did he sing out?" And turns to me, perfectly c'am, and says, "Did *you* hear anybody sing out?"

Of course there warn't nothing to be said but the one thing; so I says:

"No; *I* ain't heard nobody say nothing."

Then he turns to Jim, and looks him over like he never see him before; and says:

"Did you sing out?"

"No, sah," says Jim; "*I* hain't said nothing, sah."

"Not a word?"

"No, sah, I hain't said a word."

"Did you ever see us before?"

"No, sah; not as *I* knows on."

So Tom turns to the nigger, which was looking wild and distressed, and says, kind of severe:

"What do you reckon's the matter with you, anyway? What made you think somebody sung out?"

"Oh, it's de dad-blame' witches, sah, en I wisht I was dead, I do. Dey's awluz at it, sah, en dey do mos' kill me, dey sk'yers me so. Please to don't tell nobody 'bout it sah, er ole Mars Silas he'll scole me; 'kase he say dey *ain't* no witches. I jis' wish to goodness he was heah now—*den* what would he say! I jis' bet he couldn' fine no way to git aroun' it *dis* time. But it's awluz jis' so; people dat's *sot,* stays sot; dey won't look into nothn' en fine it out f'r deyselves, en when *you* fine it out en tell um 'bout it, dey doan' b'lieve you."

Tom give him a dime, and said we wouldn't tell nobody; and told him to buy some more thread to tie up his wool with; and then looks at Jim, and says:

"I wonder if Uncle Silas is going to hang this nigger. If I was to catch a nigger that was ungrateful enough to run away, *I* wouldn't give him up, I'd hang him." And whilst the nigger stepped to the door to look at the dime and bite it to see if it was good, he whispers to Jim, and says:

"Don't ever let on to know us. And if you hear any digging going on nights, it's us: we're going to set you free."

Jim only had time to grab us by the hand and squeeze it, then the nigger come back, and we said we'd come again some time if the nigger wanted us to; and he said he would, more particular if it was

dark, because the witches went for him mostly in the dark, and it
was good to have folks around then.

CHAPTER XXXV

It would be most an hour, yet, till breakfast, so we left, and struck
down into the woods; because Tom said we got to have *some* light
to see how to dig by, and a lantern makes too much, and might get
us into trouble; what we must have was a lot of them rotten chunks
that's called fox-fire and just makes a soft kind of a glow when you
lay them in a dark place. We fetched an armful and hid it in the
weeds, and set down to rest, and Tom says, kind of dissatisfied:

"Blame it, this whole thing is just as easy and awkard as it can be.
And so it makes it so rotten difficult to get up a difficult plan. There
ain't no watchman to be drugged—now there *ought* to be a
watchman. There ain't even a dog to give a sleeping-mixture to.
And there's Jim chained by one leg, with a ten-foot chain, to the
leg of his bed: why, all you got to do is to lift up the bedstead and
slip off the chain. And Uncle Silas he trusts everybody; sends the
key to the punkin-headed nigger, and don't send nobody to watch
the nigger. Jim could a got out of that window hole before this, only
there wouldn't be no use trying to travel with a ten-foot chain on his
leg. Why, drat it, Huck, it's the stupidest arrangement I ever see.
You got to invent *all* the difficulties. Well, we can't help it, we got
to do the best we can with the materials we've got. Anyhow, there's
one thing—there's more honor in getting him out through a lot of
difficulties and dangers, where there warn't one of them furnished
to you by the people who it was their duty to furnish them, and you
had to contrive them all out of your own head. Now look at just
that one thing of the lantern. When you come down to the cold
facts, we simply got to *let on* that a lantern's resky. Why, we could
work with a torchlight procession if we wanted to, *I* believe. Now,
whilst I think of it, we got to hunt up something to make a saw out
of, the first chance we get."

"What do we want of a saw?"

"What do we *want* of it? Hain't we got to saw the leg of Jim's
bed off, so as to get the chain loose?"

"Why, you just said a body could lift up the bedstead and slip
the chain off."

"Well, if that ain't just like you, Huck Finn. You *can* get up the
infant-schooliest ways of going at a thing. Why, hain't you ever read
any books at all?—Baron Trenck, nor Casanova, nor Benvenuto
Chelleeny, nor Henri IV., nor none of them heroes? Whoever heard
of getting a prisoner loose in such an old-maidy was as that? No;
the way all the best authorities does, is to saw the bed-leg in two,
and leave it just so, and swallow the sawdust, so it can't be found,
and put some dirt and grease around the sawed place so the very

keenest seneskal can't see no sign of it's being sawed, and thinks the bed-leg is perfectly sound. Then, the night you're ready, fetch the leg a kick, down she goes; slip off your chain, and there you are. Nothing to do but hitch your rope-ladder to the battlements, shin down it, break your leg in the moat—because a rope-ladder is nineteen foot too short, you know—and there's your horses and your trusty vassles, and they scoop you up and fling you across a saddle and away you go, to your native Langudoc, or Navarre, or wherever it is. It's gaudy, Huck. I wish there was a moat to this cabin. If we get time, the night of the escape, we'll dig one."

I says:

"What do we want of a moat, when we're going to snake him out from under the cabin?"

But he never heard me. He had forgot me and everything else. He had his chin in his hand, thinking. Pretty soon, he sighs, and shakes his head; then sighs again, and says:

"No, it wouldn't do—there ain't necessity enough for it."

"For what?" I says.

"Why, to saw Jim's leg off," he says.

"Good land!" I says, "why, there ain't *no* necessity for it. And what would you want to saw his leg off for, anyway?"

"Well, some of the best authorities has done it. They couldn't get the chain off, so they just cut their hand off, and shoved. And a leg would be better still. But we got to let that go. There ain't necessity enough in this case; and besides, Jim's a nigger and wouldn't understand the reasons for it, and how it's the custom in Europe; so we'll let it go. But there's one thing—he can have a rope-ladder; we can tear up our sheets and make him a rope-ladder easy enough. And we can send it to him in a pie; it's mostly done that way. And I've et worse pies."

"Why, Tom Sawyer, how you talk," I says; "Jim ain't got no use for a rope ladder."

"He *has* got use for it. How *you* talk, you better say; you don't know nothing about it. He's *got* to have a rope ladder; they all do."

"What in the nation can he *do* with it?"

"*Do* with it? He can hide it in his bed, can't he? That's what they all do; and *he's* got to, too. Huck, you don't ever seem to want to do anything that's regular; you want to be starting something fresh all the time. Spose he *don't* do nothing with it? ain't it there in his bed, for a clew, after he's gone? and don't you reckon they'll want clews? Of course they will. And you wouldn't leave them any? That would be a *pretty* howdy-do, *wouldn't* it! I never heard of such a thing."

"Well," I says, "if it's in the regulations, and he's got to have it, all right, let him have it; because I don't wish to go back on no regulations; but there's one thing, Tom Sawyer—if we go to tearing up our sheets to make Jim a rope-ladder, we're going to get into trouble with Aunt Sally, just as sure as you're born. Now, the way I look at it, a hickry-bark ladder don't cost nothing, and don't waste nothing, and is just as good to load up a pie with, and hide in a straw tick, as any rag ladder you can start; and as for Jim, he ain't had no experience, and so *he* don't care what kind of a——"

"Oh, shucks, Huck Finn, if I was as ignorant as you, I'd keep still—that's what *I'd* do. Who ever heard of a state prisoner escaping by a hickry-bark ladder? Why, it's perfectly ridiculous."

"Well, all right, Tom, fix it your own way; but if you'll take my advice, you'll let me borrow a sheet off of the clothes-line."

He said that would do. And that give him another idea, and he says:

"Borrow a shirt, too."

"What do we want of a shirt, Tom?"

"Want it for Jim to keep a journal on."

"Journal your granny—*Jim* can't write."

"Spose he *can't* write—he can make marks on the shirt, can't he, if we make him a pen out of an old pewter spoon or a piece of an old iron barrel-hoop?"

"Why, Tom, we can pull a feather out of a goose and make him a better one; and quicker, too."

"*Prisoners* don't have geese running around the donjon-keep to pull pens out of, you muggins. They *always* make their pens out of the hardest, toughest, troublesomest piece of old brass candlestick or something like that they can get their hands on; and it takes them weeks and weeks, and months and months to file it out, too, because they've got to do it by rubbing it on the wall. *They* wouldn't use a goose-quill if they had it. It ain't regular."

"Well, then, what'll we make him the ink out of?"

"Many makes it out of iron-rust and tears; but that's the common sort and women; the best authorities uses their own blood. Jim can do that; and when he wants to send any little common ordinary mysterious message to let the world know where he's captivated, he can write it on the bottom of a tin plate with a fork and throw it out of the window. The Iron Mask always done that, and it's a blame' good way, too."

"Jim ain't got no tin plates. They feed him in a pan."

"That ain't anything; we can get him some."

"Can't nobody *read* his plates."

"That ain't got nothing to *do* with it, Huck Finn. All *he's* got to do is to write on the plate and throw it out. You don't *have* to be able to read it. Why, half the time you can't read anything a prisoner writes on a tin plate, or anywhere else."

"Well, then, what's the sense in wasting the plates?"

"But it's *somebody's* plates, ain't it?"

"Well, spos'n it is? What does the *prisoner* care whose——"

"Why, blame it all, it ain't the *prisoner's* plates."

He broke off there, because we heard the breakfast-horn blowing.

So we cleared out for the house.

Along during that morning I borrowed a sheet and a white shirt off of the clothes-line; and I found an old sack and put them in it, and we went down and got the fox-fire, and put that in too. I called it borrowing, because that was what pap always called it; but Tom said it warn't borrowing, it was stealing. He said we was representing prisoners; and prisoners don't care how they get a thing so they get it, and nobody don't blame them for it, either. It ain't no crime in a prisoner to steal the thing he needs to get away with, Tom said; it's his right; and so, as long as we was representing a prisoner, we had a perfect right to steal anything on this place we had the least use for, to get ourselves out of prison with. He said if we warn't prisoners it would be a very different thing, and nobody but a mean ornery person would steal when he warn't a prisoner. So we allowed we would steal everything there was that come handy. And yet he made a mighty fuss, one day, after that, when I stole a watermelon out of the nigger patch and eat it; and he made me go and give the niggers a dime, without telling them what it was for. Tom said that what he meant was, we could steal anything we *needed*. Well, I says, I needed the watermelon. But he said I didn't need it to get out of prison with, there's where the difference was. He said if I'd a wanted it to hide a knife in, and smuggle it to Jim to kill the seneskal with, it would a been all right. So I let it go at that, though I couldn't see no advantage in my representing a prisoner, if I got to set down and chaw over a lot of gold-leaf distinctions like that, every time I see a chance to hog a watermelon.

Well, as I was saying, we waited that morning till everybody was settled down to business, and nobody in sight around the yard; then Tom he carried the sack into the lean-to whilst I stood off a piece to keep watch. By-and-by he come out, and we went and set down on the wood-pile, to talk. He says:

"Everything's all right, now, except tools: and that's easy fixed."

"Tools?" I says.

"Yes."

"Tools for what?"

"Why, to dig with. We ain't agoing to *gnaw* him out, are we?"

"Ain't them old crippled picks and things in there good enough to dig a nigger out with?" I says.

He turns on me looking pitying enough to make a body cry, and says:

"Huck Finn, did you *ever* hear of a prisoner having picks and shovels, and all the modern conveniences in his wardrobe to dig himself out with? Now I want to ask you—if you got any reasonableness in you at all—what kind of a show would *that* give him to be a hero? Why, they might as well lend him the key, and done with it. Picks and shovels—why they wouldn't furnish 'em to a king."

"Well, then," I says, "if we don't want the picks and shovels, what do we want?"

"A couple of case-knives."

"To dig the foundations out from under that cabin with?"

"Yes."

"Confound it, it's foolish, Tom."

"It don't make no difference how foolish it is, it's the *right* way— and it's the regular way. And there ain't no *other* way, that ever *I* heard of, and I've read all the books that gives any information about these things. They always dig out with a case-knife—and not through dirt, mind you; generly it's through solid rock. And it takes them weeks and weeks and weeks, and for ever and ever. Why, look at one of them prisoners in the bottom dungeon of the Castle Deef, in the harbor of Marseilles, that dug himself out that way; how long was *he* at it, you reckon?"

"I don't know."

"Well, guess."

"I don't know. A month and a half?"

"Thirty-seven year—and he come out in China. *That's* the kind. I wish the bottom of *this* fortress was solid rock."

"Jim don't know nobody in China."

"What's *that* got to do with it? Neither did that other fellow. But you're always a-wandering off on a side issue. Why can't you stick to the main point?"

"All right—*I* don't care where he comes out, so he *comes* out; and Jim don't, either, I reckon. But there's one thing, anyway—Jim's too old to be dug out with a case-knife. He won't last."

"Yes he will *last,* too. You don't reckon it's going to take thirty-seven years to dig out through a *dirt* foundation, do you?"

"How long will it take, Tom?"

"Well, we can't resk being as long as we ought to, because it mayn't take very long for Uncle Silas to hear from down there by New Orleans. He'll hear Jim ain't from there. Then his next move will be to advertise Jim, or something like that. So we can't resk being as long digging him out as we ought to. By rights I reckon we ought to be a couple of years; but we can't. Things being so uncertain, what I recommend is this: that we really dig right in, as quick as we can; and after that, we can *let on,* to ourselves, that we was at it thirty-seven years. Then we can snatch him out and rush him away the first time there's an alarm. Yes, I reckon that'll be the best way."

"Now, there's *sense* in that," I says. "Letting on don't cost nothing; letting on ain't no trouble; and if it's any object, I don't mind letting on we was at it a hundred and fifty year. It wouldn't strain me none, after I got my hand in. So I'll mosey along now, and smouch a couple of case-knives."

"Smouch three," he says; "we want one to make a saw out of."

"Tom, if it ain't unregular and irreligious to sejest it," I says, "there's an old rusty saw-blade around yonder sticking under the weatherboarding behind the smoke-house."

He looked kind of weary and discouraged-like, and says:

"It ain't no use to try to learn you nothing, Huck. Run along and smouch the knives—three of them." So I done it.

CHAPTER XXXVI

As soon as we reckoned everybody was asleep, that night, we went down the lightning-rod, and shut ourselves up in the lean-to, and got out our pile of fox-fire, and went to work. We cleared everything out of the way, about four or five foot along the middle of the bottom log. Tom said he was right behind Jim's bed now, and we'd dig in right under it, and when we got through there couldn't nobody in the cabin ever know there was any hole there, because Jim's counterpin hung down most to the ground, and you'd have to raise it up and look under to see the hole. So we dug and dug, with the case-knives, till most midnight; and then we was dog-tired, and our hands was blistered, and yet you couldn't see we'd done anything, hardly. At last I says:

"This ain't no thirty-seven year job, this is a thirty-eight year job, Tom Sawyer."

He never said nothing. But he sighed, and pretty soon he stopped digging, and then for a good little while I knowed he was thinking. Then he says:

"It ain't no use, Huck, it ain't agoing to work. If we was prisoners it would, because then we'd have as many years as we wanted, and no hurry; and we wouldn't get but a few minutes to dig, every day, while they was changing watches, and so our hands wouldn't get blistered, and we could keep it up right along, year in and year out, and do it right, and the way it ought to be done. But *we* can't fool along, we got to rush; we ain't got no time to spare. If we was to put in another night this way, we'd have to knock off for a week to let our hands get well—couldn't touch a case-knife with them sooner."

"Well, then, what we going to do, Tom?"

"I'll tell you. It ain't right, and it ain't moral, and I wouldn't like it to get out—but there ain't only just the one way; we got to dig him out with the picks, and *let on* it's case-knives."

"Now you're *talking!"* I says; "your head gets leveler and leveler all the time, Tom Sawyer," I says. "Picks is the thing, moral or no moral; and as for me, I don't care shucks for the morality of it, nohow. When I start in to steal a nigger, or a watermelon, or a Sunday-school book, I ain't no ways particular how it's done so it's done. What I want is my nigger; or what I want is my

watermelon; or what I want is my Sunday-school book; and if a
pick's the handiest thing, that's the thing I'm agoing to dig that
nigger or that watermelon or that Sunday-school book out with;
and I don't give a dead rat what the authorities thinks about it
nuther."

"Well," he says, "there's excuse for picks and letting-on in a
case like this; if it warn't so, I wouldn't approve of it, nor I wouldn't
stand by and see the rules broke—because right is right, and wrong
is wrong, and a body ain't got no business doing wrong when he
ain't ignorant and knows better. It might answer for *you* to dig
Jim out with a pick, *without* any letting-on, because you don't know
no better; but it wouldn't for me, because I do know better. Gimme
a case-knife."

He had his own by him, but I handed him mine. He flung it
down, and says:

"Gimme a *case-knife.*"

I didn't know just what to do—but then I thought. I scratched
around amongst the old tools, and got a pick-ax and give it to him,
and he took it and went to work, and never said a word.

He was always just that particular. Full of principle.

So then I got a shovel, and then we picked and shoveled, turn
about, and made the fur fly. We stuck to it about a half an hour,
which was as long as we could stand up; but we had a good deal
of a hole to show for it. When I got up stairs, I looked out at the
window and see Tom doing his level best with the lightning-rod,
but he couldn't come it, his hands was so sore. At last he says:

"It ain't no use, it can't be done. What you reckon I better do?
Can't you think up no way?"

"Yes," I says, "but I reckon it ain't regular. Come up the stairs,
and let on it's a lightning-rod."

So he done it.

Next day Tom stole a pewter spoon and a brass candlestick in
the house, for to make some pens for Jim out of, and six tallow
candles; and I hung around the nigger cabins, and laid for a chance,
and stole three tin plates. Tom said it wasn't enough; but I said
nobody wouldn't ever see the plates that Jim throwed out, because
they'd fall in the dog-fennel and jimpson weeds under the
window-hole—then we could tote them back and he could use them
over again. So Tom was satisfied. Then he says:

"Now, the thing to study out is, how to get the things to Jim."

"Take them in through the hole," I says, "when we get it done."

He only just looked scornful, and said something about nobody
ever heard of such an idiotic idea, and then he went to studying.
By-and-by he said he had ciphered out two or three ways, but there
warn't no need to decide on any of them yet. Said we'd got to post
Jim first.

That night we went down the lightning-rod a little after ten, and

took one of the candles along, and listened under the window-hole, and heard Jim snoring; so we pitched it in, and it didn't wake him. Then we whirled in with the pick and shovel, and in about two hours and a half the job was done. We crept in under Jim's bed and into the cabin, and pawed around and found the candle and lit it, and stood over Jim a while, and found him looking hearty and healthy, and then we woke him up gentle and gradual. He was so glad to see us he most cried; and called us honey, and all the pet names he could think of; and was for having us hunt up a cold chisel to cut the chain off of his leg with, right away, and clearing out without losing any time. But Tom he showed him how unregular it would be, and set down and told him all about our plans, and how we could alter them in a minute any time there was an alarm; and not to be the least afraid, because we would see he got away, *sure.*
So Jim he said it was all right, and we set there and talked over old times a while, and then Tom asked a lot of questions, and when Jim told him Uncle Silas come in every day or two to pray with him, and Aunt Sally come in to see if he was comfortable and had plenty to eat, and both of them was kind as they could be, Tom says:

"*Now* I know how to fix it. We'll send you some things by them."

I said, "Don't do nothing of the kind; it's one of the most jackass ideas I ever struck;" but he never paid no attention to me; went right on. It was his way when he'd got his plans set.

So he told Jim how we'd have to smuggle in the rope-ladder pie, and the other large things, by Nat, the nigger that fed him, and he must be on the lookout, and not be surprised, and not let Nat see him open them; and we would put small things in uncle's coat pockets and he must steal them out; and we would tie things to aunt's apron strings or put them in her apron pocket, if we got a chance; and told him what they would be and what they was for. And told him how to keep a journal on the shirt with his blood, and all that. He told him everything. Jim he couldn't see no sense in the most of it, but he allowed we was white folks and knowed better than him; so he was satisfied, and said he would do it all just as Tom said.

Jim had plenty corn-cob pipes and tobacco; so we had a right down good sociable time; then we crawled out through the hole, and so home to bed, with hands that looked like they'd been chawed. Tom was in high spirits. He said it was the best fun he ever had in his life, and the most intellectural; and said if he only could see his way to it we would keep it up all the rest of our lives and leave Jim to our children to get out; for he believed Jim would come to like it better and better the more he got used to it. He said that in that way it could be strung out to as much as eighty year, and would be the best time on record. And he said it would make us all celebrated that had a hand in it.

In the morning we went out to the wood-pile and chopped up the

brass candlestick into handy sizes, and Tom put them and the
pewter spoon in his pocket. Then we went to the nigger cabins,
and while I got Nat's notice off, Tom shoved a piece of candlestick
into the middle of a corn-pone that was in Jim's pan, and we went
along with Nat to see how it would work, and it just worked noble;
when Jim bit into it it most mashed all his teeth out; and there
warn't ever anything could a worked better. Tom said so himself.
Jim he never let on but what it was only just a piece of rock or
something like that that's always getting into bread, you know;
but after that he never bit into nothing but what he jabbed his fork
into it three or four places, first.

And whilst we was a standing there in the dimmish light, here
comes a couple of the hounds bulging in, from under Jim's bed;
and they kept on piling in till there was eleven of them, and there
warn't hardly room in there to get your breath. By jings, we forgot
to fasten that lean-to door. The nigger Nat he only just hollered
"witches!" once, and keeled over onto the floor amongst the dogs,
and begun to groan like he was dying. Tom jerked the door open
and flung out a slab of Jim's meat, and the dogs went for it, and in
two seconds he was out himself and back again and shut the door,
and I knowed he'd fixed the other door too. Then he went to work
on the nigger, coaxing him and petting him, and asking him if he'd
been imagining he saw something again. He raised up, and blinked
his eyes around, and says:

"Mars Sid, you'll say I's a fool, but if I didn't b'lieve I see most
a million dogs, er devils, er some'n, I wisht I may die right heah in
dese tracks. I did, mos' sholy. Mars Sid, I *felt* um—I *felt* um, sah;
dey was all over me. Dad fetch it, I jus' wisht I could git my han's
on one er dem witches jis' wunst —on'y jis' wunst—it's all *I*'d ast.
But mos'ly I wisht dey'd lemme 'lone, I does."

Tom says:

"Well, I tell you what *I* think. What makes them come here
just at this runaway nigger's breakfast-time? It's because they're
hungry; that's the reason. You make them a witch pie; that's the
thing for *you* to do."

"But my lan', Mars Sid, how's *I* gwyne to make 'm a witch pie?
I doan' know how to make it. I hain't ever hearn er sich a thing
b'fo.' "

"Well, then, I'll have to make it myself."

"Will you do it, honey?—will you? I'll wusshup de groun' und'
yo' foot, I will!"

"All right, I'll do it, seeing it's you, and you've been good to us
and showed us the runaway nigger. But you got to be mighty
careful. When we come around, you turn your back; and then
whatever we've put in the pan, don't you let on you see it at all. And
don't you look, when Jim unloads the pan—something might
happen, I don't know what. And above all, don't you *handle* the

witch-things."

"*Hannel* 'm Mars Sid? What *is* you a talkin' 'bout? I wouldn' lay de weight er my finger on um, not f'r ten hund'd thous'n' billion dollars, I wouldn't."

CHAPTER XXXVII

That was all fixed. So then we went away and went to the rubbage-pile in the back yard where they keep the old boots, and rags, and pieces of bottles, and wore-out tin things, and all such truck, and scratched around and found an old tin washpan and stopped up the holes as well as we could, to bake the pie in, and took it down cellar and stole it full of flour, and started for breakfast and found a couple of shingle-nails that Tom said would be handy for a prisoner to scrabble his name and sorrows on the dungeon walls with, and dropped one of them in Aunt Sally's apron pocket which was hanging on a chair, and t'other we stuck in the band of Uncle Silas's hat, which was on the bureau, because we heard the children say their pa and ma was going to the runaway nigger's house this morning, and then went to breakfast, and Tom dropped the pewter spoon in Uncle Silas's coat pocket, and Aunt Sally wasn't come yet, so we had to wait a little while.

And when she come she was hot, and red, and cross, and couldn't hardly wait for the blessing; and then she went to sluicing out coffee with one hand and cracking the handiest child's head with her thimble with the other, and says:

"I've hunted high, and I've hunted low, and it does beat all, what *has* become of your other shirt."

My heart fell down amongst my lungs and livers and things, and a hard piece of corn-crust started down my throat after it and got met on the road with a cough and was shot across the table and took one of the children in the eye and curled him up like a fishing-worm, and let a cry out of him the size of a war-whoop, and Tom he turned kinder blue around the gills, and it all amounted to a considerable state of things for about a quarter of a minute or as much as that, and I would a sold out for half price if there was a bidder. But after that we was all right again—it was the sudden surprise of it that knocked us so kind of cold. Uncle Silas he says:

"It's most uncommon curious, I can't understand it. I know perfectly well I took it *off,* because——"

"Because you hain't got but one *on.* Just *listen* at the man! *I* know you took it off, and know it by a better way than your wool-gathering memory, too, because it was on the clo'es-line yesterday—I see it there myself. But it's gone—that's the long and the short of it, and you'll just have to change to a red flann'l one till I can get time to make a new one. And it'll be the third I've made in two years; it just keeps a body on the jump to keep you in shirts;

and whatever you do manage to *do* with 'm all, is more'n *I* can make out. A body'd think you *would* learn to take some sort of care of 'em, at your time of life."

"I know it, Sally, and I do try all I can. But it oughtn't to be altogether my fault, because you know I don't see them nor have nothing to do with them except when they're on me; and I don't believe I've ever lost one of them *off* of me."

"Well, it ain't *your* fault if you haven't, Silas—you'd a done it if you could, I reckon. And the shirt ain't all that's gone, nuther. Ther's a spoon gone; and *that* ain't all. There was ten, and now ther's only nine. The calf got the shirt I reckon, but the calf never took the spoon, *that's* certain."

"Why, what else is gone, Sally?"

"Ther's six *candles* gone—that's what. The rats could a got the candles, and I reckon they did; I wonder they don't walk off with the whole place, the way you're always going to stop their holes and don't do it; and if they warn't fools they'd sleep in your hair, Silas—*you'd* never find it out; but you can't lay the *spoon* on the rats, and that I *know*."

"Well, Sally, I'm in fault, and I acknowledge it; I've been remiss; but I won't let to-morrow go by without stopping up them holes."

"Oh, I wouldn't hurry, next year'll do. Matilda Angelina Araminta *Phelps!*"

Whack comes the thimble, and the child snatches her claws out of the sugar-bowl without fooling around any. Just then, the nigger woman steps onto the passage, and says:

"Missus, dey's a sheet gone."

"A *sheet* gone! Well, for the land's sake!"

"I'll stop up them holes *to-day*," says Uncle Silas, looking sorrowful.

"Oh, *do* shet up!—spose the rats took the *sheet? Where's* it gone, Lize?"

"Clah to goodness I hain't no notion, Miss Sally. She wuz on de clo's-line yistiddy, but she done gone; she ain' dah no mo,' now."

"I reckon the world *is* coming to an end. I *never* see the beat of it, in all my born days. A shirt, and a sheet, and a spoon, and six can——"

"Missus," comes a young yaller wench, "dey's a brass cannelstick miss'n."

"Cler out from here, you hussy, er I'll take a skillet to ye!"

Well, she was just a biling. I begun to lay for a chance; I reckoned I would sneak out and go for the woods till the weather moderated. She kept a raging right along, running her insurrection all by herself, and everybody else mighty meek and quiet; and at last Uncle Silas, looking kind of foolish, fishes up that spoon out of his pocket. She stopped, with her mouth open and her hands up; and as for me, I wished I was in Jerusalem or somewheres. But not long; because she says:

"It's *just* as I expected. So you had it in your pocket all the time; and like as not you've got the other things there, too. How'd it get there?"

"I reely don't know, Sally," he says, kind of apologizing, "or you know I would tell. I was a-studying over my text in Acts Seventeen, before breakfast, and I reckon I put it in there, not noticing, meaning to put my Testament in, and it must be so, because my Testament ain't in, but I'll go and see, and if the Testament is where I had it, I'll know I didn't put it in, and that will show that I laid the Testament down and took up the spoon, and——"

"Oh, for the land's sake! Give a body a rest! Go 'long now, the whole kit and biling of ye; and don't come nigh me again till I've got back my peace of mind."

I'd a heard her, if she'd a said it to herself, let alone speaking it out; and I'd a got up and obeyed her, if I'd a been dead. As we was passing through the setting-room, the old man he took up his hat, and the shingle-nail fell out on the floor, and he just merely picked it up and laid it on the mantel-shelf, and never said nothing, and went out. Tom see him do it, and remembered about the spoon, and says:

"Well, it ain't no use to send things by *him* no more, he ain't reliable." Then he says: "But he done us a good turn with the spoon anyway, without knowing it, and so we'll go and do him one without *him* knowing it—stop up his rat-holes."

There was a noble good lot of them, down cellar, and it took us a whole hour, but we done the job tight and good, and ship-shape. Then we heard steps on the stairs, and blowed out our light, and hid; and here comes the old man, with a candle in one hand and a bundle of stuff in t'other, looking as absent-minded as year before last. He went a mooning around, first to one rat-hole and then another, till he'd been to them all. Then he stood about five minutes, picking tallow-drip off of his candle and thinking. Then he turns off slow and dreamy towards the stairs, saying:

"Well, for the life of me I can't remember when I done it. I could show her now that I warn't to blame on account of the rats. But never mind—let it go. I reckon it wouldn't do no good."

And so he went on a mumbling up stairs, and then we left. He was a mighty nice old man. And always is.

Tom was a good deal bothered about what to do for a spoon, but he said we'd got to have it; so he took a think. When he had ciphered it out, he told me how we was to do; then we went and waited around the spoon-basket till we see Aunt Sally coming, and then Tom went to counting the spoons and laying them out to one side, and I slid one of them up my sleeve, and Tom says:

"Why, Aunt Sally, there ain't but nine spoons, *yet.*"

She says:

"Go 'long to your play, and don't bother me. I know better, I counted 'm myself."

"Well, I've counted them twice, Aunty, and *I* can't make but nine."

She looked out of all patience, but of course she come to count—anybody would.

"I declare to gracious ther' *ain't* but nine!" she says. "Why, what in the world—plague *take* the things, I'll count 'm again."

So I slipped back the one I had, and when she got done counting, she says:

"Hang the troublesome rubbage, there's *ten,* now!" and she looked huffy and bothered both. But Tom says:

"Why, Aunty, *I* don't think there's ten."

"You numskull, didn't you see me *count* 'm?"

"I know, but——"

"Well, I'll count 'm *again.*"

So I smouched one, and they come out nine same as the other time. Well, she *was* in a tearing way—just a trembling all over, she was so mad. But she counted and counted, till she got that addled she'd start to count-in the *basket* for a spoon, sometimes; and so, three times they come out right, and three times they come out wrong. Then she grabbed up the basket and slammed it across the house and knocked the cat galley-west; and she said cle'r out and let her have some peace, and if we come bothering around her again betwixt that and dinner, she'd skin us. So we had the odd spoon; and dropped it in her apron pocket whilst she was a giving us our sailing-orders, and Jim got it all right, along with her shingle-nail, before noon. We was very well satisfied with this business, and Tom allowed it was worth twice the trouble it took, because he said *now* she couldn't ever count them spoons twice alike again to save her life; and wouldn't believe she'd counted them right, if she *did;* and said that after she'd about counted her head off, for the next three days, he judged she'd give it up and offer to kill anybody that wanted her to ever count them any more.

So we put the sheet back on the line, that night, and stole one out of her closet; and kept on putting it back and stealing it again, for a couple of days, till she didn't know how many sheets she had, any more, and said she didn't *care,* and warn't agoing to bullyrag the rest of her soul out about it, and wouldn't count them again not to save her life, she druther die first.

So we was all right now, as to the shirt and the sheet and the spoon and the candles, by the help of the calf and the rats and the mixed-up counting; and as to the candlestick, it warn't no consequence, it would blow over by-and-by.

But that pie was a job; we had no end of trouble with that pie. We fixed it up away down in the woods, and cooked it there; and we got it done at last, and very satisfactory, too; but not all in one day; and we had to use up three wash-pans full of flour, before we got through, and we got burnt pretty much all over, in places, and eyes put out with the smoke, because, you see, we didn't want nothing but a crust, and we couldn't prop it up right, and she would always cave in. But of course we thought of the right way at last; which was to cook the ladder, too, in the pie. So then we laid in with Jim, the second night, and tore up the sheet all in little strings, and twisted them together, and long before daylight we had a lovely rope, that you could a hung a person with. We let on it took nine months to make it.

And in the forenoon we took it down to the woods, but it wouldn't go in the pie. Being made of a whole sheet, that way, there was rope enough for forty pies, if we'd a wanted them, and plenty left over for soup, or sausage, or anything you choose. We could a had a whole dinner.

But we didn't need it. All we needed was just enough for the pie, and so we throwed the rest away. We didn't cook none of the pies in the washpan, afraid the solder would melt; but Uncle Silas he had a noble brass warming-pan which he thought considerable of, because it belonged to one of his ancestors with a long wooden handle that come over from England with William the Conqueror in the *Mayflower* or one of them early ships and was hid away up garret with a lot of other old pots and things that was valuable, not on account of being any account because they warn't, but on account of them being relicts, you know, and we snaked her out, private, and took her down there, but she failed on the first pies, because we didn't know how, but she come up smiling on the last one. We took and lined her with dough, and set her in the coals, and loaded her up with rag-rope, and put on a dough roof, and shut down the lid, and put hot embers on top, and stood off five foot, with the long handle, cool and comfortable, and in fifteen minutes she turned out a pie that was a satisfaction to look at. But the person that et it would want to fetch a couple of kags of toothpicks along, for if that rope-ladder wouldn't cramp him down to business, I don't know nothing what I'm talking about, and lay him in enough stomach-ache to last him till next time, too.

Nat didn't look, when we put the witch-pie in Jim's pan; and we put the three tin plates in the bottom of the pan under the vittles; and so Jim got everything all right, and as soon as he was by himself he busted into the pie and hid the rope-ladder inside of his straw tick, and scratched some marks on a tin plate and throwed it out of the window-hole.

CHAPTER XXXVIII

Making them pens was a distressid-tough job, and so was the saw; and Jim allowed the inscription was going to be the toughest of all. That's the one which the prisoner has to scrabble on the wall. But we had to have it; Tom said we'd *got* to; there warn't no case of a state prisoner not scrabbling his inscription to leave behind, and his coat of arms.

"Look at Lady Jane Grey," he says; "look at Gilford Dudley; look at old Northumberland! Why, Huck, spose it *is* considerble trouble?—what you going to do?—how you going to get around it? Jim's *got* to do his inscription and coat of arms. They all do."

Jim says:

"Why, Mars Tom, I hain't got no coat o' arms; I hain't got nuffn but dish-yer old shirt, en you knows I got to keep de journal on dat."

"Oh, you don't understand, Jim; a coat of arms is very different."

"Well," I says, "Jim's right, anyway, when he says he hain't got no coat of arms, because he hain't."

"I reckon *I* knowed that," Tom says, "but you bet he'll have one before he goes out of this—because he's going out *right,* and there ain't going to be no flaws in his record."

So whilst me and Jim filed away at the pens on a brickbat apiece, Jim a making his'n out of the brass and I making mine out of the spoon, Tom set to work to think out the coat of arms. By-and-by he said he'd struck so many good ones he didn't hardly know which to take, but there was one which he reckoned he'd decide on. He says:

"On the scutcheon we'll have a bend *or* in the dexter base, a saltire *murrey* in the fess, with a dog, couchant, for common charge, and under his foot a chain enbattled, for slavery, with a chevron *vert* in a chief engrailed, and three invected lines on a field *azure,* with the nombril points rampant on a dancette indented; crest, a runaway nigger, *sable,* with his bundle over his shoulder on a bar sinister: and a couple of gules for supporters, which is you and me; motto, *Maggiore fretta, minore atto.* Got it out of a book—means, the more haste, the less speed."

"Geewhillikins," I says, "but what does the rest of it mean?"

"We ain't got no time to bother over that," he says, "we got to dig in like all git-out."

"Well, anyway," I says, "what's *some* of it? What's a fess?"

"A fess—a fess is—*you* don't need to know what a fess is. I'll show him how to make it when he gets to it."

"Shucks, Tom," I says, "I think you might tell a person. What's a bar sinister?"

"Oh, *I* don't know. But he's got to have it. All the nobility does."

That was just his way. If it didn't suit him to explain a thing to you, he wouldn't do it. You might pump at him a week, it wouldn't make no difference.

He'd got all that coat of arms business fixed, so now he started in to finish up the rest of that part of the work, which was to plan out a mournful inscription—said Jim got to have one, like they all done. He made up a lot, and wrote them out on a paper, and read them off, so:

1. *Here a captive heart busted.*
2. *Here a poor prisoner, forsook by the world and friends, fretted out his sorrowful life.*
3. *Here a lonely heart broke, and a worn spirit went to its rest, after thirty-seven years of solitary captivity.*
4. *Here, homeless and friendless, after thirty-seven years of bitter captivity, perished a noble stranger, natural son of Louis XIV.*

Tom's voice trembled, whilst he was reading them, and he most broke down. When he got done, he couldn't no way make up his mind which one for Jim to scrabble onto the wall, they was all so good; but at last he allowed he would let him scrabble them all on. Jim said it would take him a year to scrabble such a lot of truck onto the logs with a nail, and he didn't know how to make letters, besides; but Tom said he would block them out for him, and then he wouldn't have nothing to do but just follow the lines. Then pretty soon he says:

"Come to think, the logs ain't agoing to do; they don't have log walls in a dungeon: we got to dig the inscriptions into a rock. We'll fetch a rock."

Jim said the rock was worse than the logs; he said it would take him such a pison long time to dig them into a rock, he wouldn't ever get out. But Tom said he would let me help him do it. Then he took a look to see how me and Jim was getting along with the pens. It was most pesky tedious hard work and slow, and didn't give my hands no show to get well of the sores, and we didn't seem to make no headway, hardly. So Tom says:

"I know how to fix it. We got to have a rock for the coat of arms and mournful inscriptions, and we can kill two birds with that same rock. There's a gaudy big grindstone down at the mill, and we'll smouch it, and carve the things on it, and file out the pens and the saw on it, too."

It warn't no slouch of an idea; and it warn't no slouch of a grindstone nuther; but we allowed we'd tackle it. It warn't quite midnight, yet, so we cleared out for the mill, leaving Jim at work. We smouched the grindstone, and set out to roll her home, but it was a most nation tough job. Sometimes, do what we could, we couldn't keep her from falling over, and she come mighty near mashing us, every time. Tom said she was going to get one of us, sure, before we got through. We got her half way; and then we was plumb played out, and most drownded with sweat. We see it

warn't no use, we got to go and fetch Jim. So he raised up his bed
and slid the chain off of the bed-leg, and wrapt it round his neck,
and we crawled out through our hole and down there, and Jim and
me laid into that grindstone and walked her along like nothing;
and Tom superintended. He could out-superintend any boy I ever
see. He knowed how to do everything.

Our hole was pretty big, but it warn't big enough to get the
grindstone through; but Jim he took the pick and soon made it big
enough. Then Tom marked out them things on it with the nail,
and set Jim to work on them, with the nail for a chisel and an iron
bolt from the rubbage in the lean-to for a hammer, and told him to
work till the rest of his candle quit on him, and then he could go to
bed, and hide the grindstone under his straw tick and sleep on
it. Then we helped him fix his chain back on the bed-leg, and was
ready for bed ourselves. But Tom thought of something, and says:

"You got any spiders in here, Jim?"

"No, sah, thanks to goodness I hain't, Mars Tom."

"All right, we'll get you some."

"But bless you, honey, I doan' *want* none. I's afeard un um. I
jis' 's soon have rattlesnakes aroun'."

Tom thought a minute or two, and says:

"It's a good idea. And I reckon it's been done. It *must* a been
done; it stands to reason. Yes, it's a prime good idea. Where could
you keep it?"

"Keep what, Mars Tom?"

"Why, a rattlesnake."

"De goodness gracious alive, Mars Tom! Why, if dey was a
rattlesnake to come in heah, I'd take en bust right out thoo dat
log wall, I would, wid my head."

"Why, Jim, you woulnd't be afraid of it, after a little. You could
tame it."

"*Tame* it!"

"Yes—easy enough. Every animal is grateful for kindness and
petting, and they wouldn't *think* of hurting a person that pets them.
Any book will tell you that. You try—that's all I ask; just try for two
or three days. Why, you can get him so, in a little while, that he'll
love you; and sleep with you; and won't stay away from you a
minute; and will let you wrap him round your neck and put his head
in your mouth."

"*Please,* Mars Tom—*doan'* talk so! I can't *stan'* it! He'd *let*
me shove his head in my mouf—fer a favor, hain't it? I lay he'd wait
a pow'ful long time 'fo' I *ast* him. En mo' en dat, I doan *want* him
to sleep wid me."

"Jim, don't act so foolish. A prisoner's *got* to have some kind of
a dumb pet, and if a rattlesnake hain't ever been tried, why, there's
more glory to be gained in your being the first to ever try it than
any other way you could ever think of to save your life."

"Why, Mars Tom, I doan' *want* no sich glory. Snake take 'n bite Jim's chin off, den *whah* is de glory? No, sah, I doan' want no sich doin's."

"Blame it, can't you *try?* I only *want* you to try—you needn't keep it up if it don't work."

"But de trouble all *done,* ef de snake bite me while I's a tryin' him. Mars Tom, I's willin' to tackle mos' anything 'at ain't onreasonable, but ef you en Huck fetches a rattlesnake in heah for me to tame, I's gwyne to *leave,* dat's *shore.*"

"Well, then, let it go, let it go, if you're so bullheaded about it. We can get you some garter-snakes and you can tie some buttons on their tails, and let on they're rattlesnakes, and I reckon that'll have to do."

"I k'n stan' *dem,* Mars Tom, but blame' 'f I couldn' get along widout um, I tell you dat. I never knowed b'fo', 't was so much bother and trouble to be a prisoner."

"Well, it *always* is, when it's done right. You got any rats around here?"

"No, sah, I hain't seed none."

"Well, we'll get you some rats."

"Why, Mars Tom, I doan' *want* no rats. Dey's de dad-blamedest creturs to sturb a body, en rustle roun' over 'im, en bite his feet, when he's tryin' to sleep, I ever see. No, sah, gimme g'yarter-snakes, 'f I's got to have 'm, but doan' gimme no rats, I ain' got no use f'r um, skasely."

"But Jim, you *got* to have 'em—they all do. So don't make no more fuss about it. Prisoners ain't ever without rats. There ain't no instance of it. And they train them, and pet them, and learn them tricks, and they get to be as sociable as flies. But you got to play music to them. You got anything to play music on?"

"I ain' got nuffn but a coase comb en a piece o' paper, en a juice-harp; but I reck'n dey wouldn' take no stock in a juice-harp."

"Yes they would. *They* don't care what kind of music 'tis. A jews-harp's plenty good enough for a rat. All animals likes music—in a prison they dote on it. Specially, painful music; and you can't get no other kind out of a jews-harp. It always interest them; they come out to see what's the matter with you. Yes, you're all right; you're fixed very well. You want to set on your bed, nights, before you go to sleep, and early in the mornings, and play your jews-harp; play The Last Link is Broken—that's the thing that'll scoop a rat, quicker'n anything else: and when you've played about two minutes, you'll see all the rats, and the snakes, and spiders, and things begin to feel worried about you, and come. And they'll just fairly swarm over you, and have a noble good time."

"Yes, *dey* will, I reck'n, Mars Tom, but what kine er time is *Jim* havin'? Blest if I kin see de pint. But I'll do it ef I got to. I reck'n I better keep de animals satisfied, en not have no trouble in de house."

Tom waited to think over, and see if there wasn't nothing else; and pretty soon he says:

"Oh—there's one thing I forgot. Could you raise a flower here, do you reckon?"

"I doan' know but maybe I could, Mars Tom; but it's tolable dark in heah, en I ain' got no use f'r no flower, nohow, en she'd be a pow'ful sight o' trouble."

"Well, you try it, anyway. Some other prisoners has done it."

"One er dem big cat-tail-lookin' mullen-stalks would grow in heah, Mars Tom, I reck'n, but she wouldn' be wuth half de trouble she'd coss."

"Don't you believe it. We'll fetch you a little one, and you plant it in the corner, over there, and raise it. And don't call it mullen. call it Pitchiola—that's its right name, when it's in a prison. And you want to water it with your tears."

"Why, I got plenty spring water, Mars Tom."

"You don't *want* spring water; you want to water it with your tears. It's the way they always do."

"Why, Mars Tom, I lay I kin raise one er dem mullen-stalks twyste wid spring water whiles another man's a *start'n* one wid tears."

"That ain't the idea. You *got* to do it with tears."

"She'll die on my han's, Mars Tom, she sholy will; kase I doan' skasely ever cry."

So Tom was stumped. But he studied it over, and then said Jim would have to worry along the best he could with an onion. He promised he would go to the nigger cabins and drop one, private, in Jim's coffee-pot, in the morning. Jim said he would "jis' 's soon have tobacker in his coffee;" and found so much fault with it, and with the work and bother of raising the mullen, and jews-harping the rats, and petting and flattering up the snakes and spiders and things, on top of all the other work he had to do on pens, and inscriptions, and journals, and things, which made it more trouble and worry and responsibility to be a prisoner than anything he ever undertook, that Tom most lost all patience with him; and said he was just loadened down with more gaudier chances than a prisoner ever had in the world to make a name for himself, and yet he didn't know enough to appreciate them, and they was just about wasted on him. So Jim he was sorry, and said he wouldn't behave so no more, and then me and Tom shoved for bed.

CHAPTER XXXIX

In the morning we went up to the village and bought a wire rat trap and fetched it down, and unstopped the best rat hole, and in about an hour we had fifteen of the bulliest kind of ones; and then we took it and put it in a safe place under Aunt Sally's bed. But while we was gone for spiders, little Thomas Franklin Benjamin Jefferson Elexander Phelps found it there, and opened the door of it to see if the rats would come out, and they did; and Aunt Sally she come in, and when we got back she was a standing on top of the bed raising Cain, and the rats was doing what they could to keep off the dull times for her. So she took and dusted us both with the hickry, and we was as much as two hours catching another fifteen or sixteen, drat that meddlesome cub, and they warn't the likeliest, nuther, because the first haul was the pick of the flock. I never see a likelier lot of rats than what that first haul was.

We got a splendid stock of sorted spiders, and bugs, and frogs, and caterpillars, and one thing or another; and we like-to got a hornet's nest, but we didn't. The family was at home. We didn't give it right up, but staid with them as long as we could; because we allowed we'd tired them out or they'd got to tire us out, and they done it. Then we got allycumpain and rubbed on the places, and was pretty near all right again, but couldn't set down convenient. And so we went for the snakes, and grabbed a couple of dozen garters and house-snakes, and put them in a bag, and put it in our room, and by that time it was supper time, and a rattling good honest day's work; and hungry?—oh, no, I reckon not! And there warn't a blessed snake up there, when we went back—we didn't half tie the sack, and they worked out, somehow, and left. But it didn't matter much, because they was still on the premises somewheres. So we judged we could get some of them again. No, there warn't no real scarcity of snakes about the house for a considerble spell. You'd see them dripping from the rafters and places, every now and then; and they generly landed in your plate, or down the back of your neck, and most of the time where you didn't want them. Well, they was handsome, and striped, and there warn't no harm in a million of them; but that never made no difference to Aunt Sally, she despised snakes, be the breed what they might, and she couldn't stand them no way you could fix it; and every time one of them flopped down on her, it didn't make no difference what she was doing, she would just lay that work down and light out. I never see such a woman. And you could hear her whoop to Jericho. You couldn't get her to take aholt of one of them with the tongs. And if she turned over and found one in bed, she would scramble out and lift a howl that you would think the house was afire. She disturbed the old man so, that he said he could most wish there hadn't ever been no snakes created. Why, after every last snake had been gone clear out of the house for

as much as a week, Aunt Sally warn't over it yet; she warn't near
over it; when she was setting thinking about something, you could
touch her on the back of her neck with a feather and she would jump
right out of her stockings. It was very curious. But Tom said all
women was just so. He said they was made that way; for some reason
or other.

We got a licking every time one of our snakes come in her way;
and she allowed these lickings warn't nothing to what she would do
if we ever loaded up the place again with them. I didn't mind the
lickings, because they didn't amount to nothing; but I minded the
trouble we had, to lay in another lot. But we got them laid in, and all
the other things; and you never see a cabin as blithesome as Jim's
was when they'd all swarm out for music and go for him. Jim didn't
like the spiders, and the spiders didn't like Jim; and so they'd lay
for him and make it mighty warm for him. And he said that between
the rats, and the snakes, and the grindstone, there warn't no room
in bed for him, skasely; and when there was, a body couldn't sleep,
it was so lively, and it was always lively, he said, because *they* never
all slept at one time, but took turn about, so when the snakes was
asleep the rats was on deck, and when the rats turned in the snakes
come on watch, so he always had one gang under him, in his way,
and t'other gang having a circus over him, and if he got up to hunt
a new place, the spiders would take a chance at him as he crossed
over. He said if he ever got out, this time, he wouldn't ever be a
prisoner again, not for a salary.

Well, by the end of three weeks, everything was in pretty good
shape. the shirt was sent in early, in a pie, and every time a rat bit
Jim he would get up and write a little in his journal whilst the ink
was fresh; the pens was made, the inscriptions and so on was all
carved on the grindstone; the bed-leg was sawed in two, and we had
et up the sawdust, and it give us a most amazing stomach-ache.
We reckoned we was all going to die, but didn't. It was the most
undigestible sawdust I ever see; and Tom said the same. But as I
was saying, we'd got all the work done, now, at last; and we was
all pretty much fagged out, too, but mainly Jim. The old man had
wrote a couple of times to the plantation below Orleans to come and
get their runaway nigger, but hadn't got no answer, because there
warn't no such plantation; so he allowed he would advertise Jim in
the St. Louis and New Orleans papers; and when he mentioned the
St. Louis ones, it give me the cold shivers, and I see we hadn't no
time to lose. So Tom said, now for the nonnamous letters.

"What's them?" I says.

"Warnings to the people that something is up. Sometimes it's
done one way, sometimes another. But there's always somebody
spying around, that gives notice to the governor of the castle. When
Louis XVI. was going to light out of the Tooleries, a servant girl done
it. It's a very good way, and so is the nonnamous letters. We'll use

them both. And it's usual for the prisoner's mother to change clothes with him, and she stays in, and he slides out in her clothes. We'll do that too."

"But looky here, Tom, what do we want to *warn* anybody for, that something's up? Let them find it out for themselves—it's their lookout."

"Yes, I know; but you can't depend on them. It's the way they've acted from the very start—left us to do *everything*. They're so confiding and mullet-headed they don't take notice of nothing at all. So if we don't *give* them notice, there won't be nobody nor nothing to interfere with us, and so after all our hard work and trouble this escape 'll go off perfectly flat: won't amount to nothing—won't be nothing *to* it."

"Well, as for me, Tom, that's the way I'd like."

"Shucks," he says, and looked disgusted. So I says:

"But I ain't going to make no complaint. Anyway that suits me. What you going to do about the servant-girl?"

"You'll be her. You slide in, in the middle of the night, and hook that yaller girl's frock."

"Why, Tom, that'll make trouble next morning; because of course she prob'bly hain't got any but that one."

"I know; but you don't want it but fifteen minutes, to carry the nonnamous letter and shove it under the front door."

"All right, then, I'll do it; but I could carry it just as handy in my own togs."

"You wouldn't look like a servant-girl *then*, would you?"

"No, but there won't be nobody to see what I look like, *anyway*."

"That ain't got nothing to do with it. The thing for us to do, is just to do our *duty*, and not worry about whether anybody *sees* us do it or not. Hain't you got no principle at all?"

"All right, I ain't saying nothing; I'm the servant-girl. Who's Jim's mother?"

"I'm his mother. I'll hook a gown from Aunt Sally."

"Well, then, you'll have to stay in the cabin when me and Jim leaves."

"Not much. I'll stuff Jim's clothes full of straw and lay it on his bed to represent his mother in disguise, and Jim 'll take the nigger woman's gown off of me and wear it, and we'll all evade together. When a prisoner of style escapes, it's called an evasion. It's always called so when a king escapes, f'rinstance. And the same with a king's son; it don't make no difference whether he's a natural one or an unnatural one."

So Tom he wrote the nonnamous letter, and I smouched the yaller wench's frock, that night, and put it on, and shoved it under the front door, the way Tom told me to. It said:

Beware. Trouble is brewing. Keep a sharp lookout.   UNKNOWN FRIEND.

Next night we stuck a picture which Tom drawed in blood, of a skull and crossbones, on the front door; and next night another one of a coffin, on the back door. I never see a family in such a sweat. They couldn't been worse scared if the place had a been full of ghosts laying for them behind everything and under the beds and shivering through the air. If a door banged, Aunt Sally she jumped, and said "ouch!" if anything fell, she jumped and said "ouch!" if you happened to touch her, when she warn't noticing, she done the same; she couldn't face noway and be satisfied, because she allowed there was something behind her every time—so she was always a whirling around, sudden, and saying "ouch," and before she'd get two-thirds around, she'd whirl back again, and say it again; and she was afraid to go to bed, but she dasn't set up. So the thing was working very well, Tom said; he said he never see a thing work more satisfactory. He said it showed it was done right.

So he said, now for the grand bulge! So the very next morning at the streak of dawn we got another letter ready, and was wondering what we better do with it, because we heard them say at supper they was going to have a nigger on watch at both doors all night. Tom he went down the lightning-rod to spy around; and the nigger at the back door was asleep, and he stuck it in the back of his neck and come back. This letter said:

Don't betray me, I wish to be your friend. There is a desprate gang of cutthroats from over in the Ingean Territory going to steal your runaway nigger to-night, and they have been trying to scare you so as you will stay in the house and not bother them. I am one of the gang, but have got relliggion and wish to quit it and lead a honest life again, and will betray the helish design. They will sneak down from northards, along the fence at midnight exact, with a false key, and go in the nigger's cabin to get him. I am to be off a piece and blow a tin horn if I see any danger; but stead of that, I will ba like a sheep soon as they get in and not blow at all, then whilst they are getting his chains loose, you slip there and lock them in, and can kill them at your leasure. Don't do anything but just the way I am telling you, if you do they will suspicion something and raise whoopjamboreehoo. I do not wish any reward but to know I have done the right thing.

UNKNOWN FRIEND.

CHAPTER XL

We was feeling pretty good, after breakfast, and took my canoe and went over the river a fishing, with a lunch, and had a good time, and took a look at the raft and found her all right, and got home late to supper, and found them in such a sweat and worry they didn't know which end they was standing on, and made us go right off to bed the minute we was done supper, and wouldn't tell us what the trouble was, and never let on a word about the new letter, but didn't need to, because we knowed as much about it as anybody did, and as soon as we was half up stairs and her back was turned, we slid for the cellar cubboard and loaded up a good lunch and took it up to our room and went to bed, and got up about half-past eleven, and Tom put on Aunt Sally's dress that he stole and was going to start with the lunch, but says:

"Where's the butter?"

"I laid out a hunk of it," I says, "on a piece of a corn-pone."

"Well, you *left* it laid out, then—it ain't here."

"We can get along without it," I says.

"We can get along *with* it, too," he says; "just you slide down cellar and fetch it. And then mosey right down the lightning-rod and come along. I'll go and stuff the straw into Jim's clothes to represent his mother in disguise, and be ready to *ba* like a sheep and shove soon as you get there."

So out he went, and down cellar went I. The hunk of butter, big as a person's fist, was where I had left it, so I took up the slab of corn-pone with it on, and blowed out my light, and started up stairs, very stealthy, and got up to the main floor all right, but here comes Aunt Sally with a candle, and I clapped the truck in my hat, and clapped my hat on my head, and the next second she see me; and she says:

"You been down cellar?"

"Yes'm."

"What you been doing down there?"

"Noth'n."

"*Noth'n!*"

"No'm."

"Well, then, what possessed you to go down there, this time of night?"

"I don't know'm."

"You don't *know*? Don't answer me that way, Tom, I want to know what you been *doing* down there?"

"I hain't been doing a single thing, Aunt Sally, I hope to gracious if I have."

I reckoned she'd let me go, now, and as a generl thing she would; but I spose there was so many strange things going on she was just in a sweat about every little thing that warn't yard-stick straight; so she says, very decided:

"You just march into that setting-room and stay there till I come. You been up to something you no business to, and I lay I'll find out what it is before *I'm* done with you."

So she went away as I opened the door and walked into the setting-room. My, but there was a crowd there! Fifteen farmers, and every one of them had a gun. I was most powerful sick, and slunk to a chair and set down. They was setting around, some of them talking a little, in a low voice, and all of them fidgety and uneasy, but trying to look like they warn't; but I knowed they was, because they was always taking off their hats, and putting them on, and scratching their heads, and changing their seats, and fumbling with their buttons. I warn't easy myself, but I didn't take my hat off, all the same.

I did wish Aunt Sally would come, and get done with me, and lick me, if she wanted to, and let me get away and tell Tom how we'd overdone this thing, and what a thundering hornet's nest we'd got ourselves into, so we could stop fooling around, straight off, and clear out with Jim before these rips got out of patience and come for us.

At last she come, and begun to ask me questions, but I *couldn't* answer them straight, I didn't know which end of me was up; because these men was in such a fidget now, that some was wanting to start right *now* and lay for them desperadoes, and saying it warn't but a few minutes to midnight; and others was trying to get them to hold on and wait for the sheep-signal; and here was aunty pegging away at the questions, and me a shaking all over and ready to sink down in my tracks I was that scared; and the place getting hotter and hotter, and the butter beginning to melt and run down my neck and behind my ears: and pretty soon, when one of them says, "*I'm* for going and getting in the cabin *first,* and right *now,* and catching them when they come," I most dropped; and a streak of butter come a trickling down my forehead, and Aunt Sally she see it, and turns white as a sheet, and says:

"For the land's sake what *is* the matter with the child!—he's got the brain fever as shore as you're born, and they're oozing out!"

And everybody runs to see, and she snatches off my hat, and out comes the bread, and what was left of the butter, and she grabbed me, and hugged me, and says:

"Oh, what a turn you did give me! and how glad and grateful I am it ain't no worse; for luck's against us, and it never rains but it pours, and when I see that truck I thought we'd lost you, for I knowed by the color and all, it was just like your brains would be if— Dear, dear, whyd'nt you *tell* me that was what you'd been down there for, *I* wouldn't a cared. Now cler out to bed, and don't lemme see no more of you till morning!"

I was up stairs in a second, and down the lightning-rod in another one, and shinning through the dark for the lean-to. I couldn't hardly get my words out, I was so anxious; but I told Tom as quick as I could, we must jump for it, now, and not a minute to lose—the house full of men, yonder, with guns!

His eyes just blazed; and he says:

"No!—is that so? *Ain't* it bully! Why, Huck, if it was to do over again, I bet I could fetch two hundred! If we could put it off till—"

"Hurry! *hurry!*" I says. "Where's Jim?"

"Right at your elbow; if you reach out your arm you can touch him. He's dressed and everything's ready. Now we'll slide out and give the sheep-signal."

But then we heard the tramp of men, coming to the door, and heard them begin to fumble with the padlock; and heard a man say:

"I *told* you we'd be too soon; they haven't come—the door is locked. Here I'll lock some of you into the cabin and you lay for 'em in the dark and kill 'em when they come; and the rest scatter around a piece, and listen if you can hear 'em coming."

So in they come, but couldn't see us in the dark, and most trod on us whilst we was hustling to get under the bed. But we got under all right, and out through the hole, swift but soft—Jim first, me next, and Tom last, which was according to Tom's orders. Now we was in the lean-to, and heard trampings close by outside. So we crept to the door, and Tom stopped us there and put his eye to the crack, but couldn't make out nothing, it was so dark; and whispered and said he would listen for the steps to get further, and when he nudged us Jim must glide out first, and him last. So he set his ear to the crack and listened, and listened, and listened, and the steps a scraping around, out there, all the time; and at last he nudged us, and we slid out, and stooped down, not breathing, and not making the least noise, and slipped stealthy towards the fence, in Injun file, and got to it, all right, and me and Jim over it; but Tom's britches catched fast on a splinter on the top rail, and then he hear the steps coming, so he had to pull loose, which snapped the splinter and made a noise; and as he dropped in our tracks and started, somebody sings out:

"Who's that? Answer, or I'll shoot!"

But we didn't answer; we just unfurled our heels and shoved. Then there was a rush, and a *bang, bang, bang!* and the bullets fairly whizzed around us! We heard them sing out:

"Here they are! They've broke for the river! after 'em, boys! And turn loose the dogs!"

So here they come, full tilt. We could hear them, because they wore boots, and yelled, but we didn't wear no boots, and didn't yell. We was in the path to the mill; and when they got pretty close onto us, we dodged into the bush and let them go by, and then dropped in behind them. They'd had all the dogs shut up, so they wouldn't scare off the robbers; but by this time somebody had let them loose, and here they come, making pow-wow enough for a million; but they was our dogs; so we stopped in our tracks till they catched up; and when they see it warn't nobody but us, and no excitement to offer them, they only just said howdy, and tore right ahead towards the shouting and clattering; and then we up steam again and whizzed along after them till we was nearly to the mill, and then struck up through the bush to where my canoe was tied, and hopped in and pulled for dear life towards the middle of the river, but didn't make no more noise than we was obleeged to. Then we struck out, easy and comfortable, for the island where my raft was; and we could hear them yelling and barking at each other all up

and down the bank, till we was so far away the sounds got dim and
died out. And when we stepped onto the raft, I says:

"*Now,* old Jim, you're a free man *again,* and I bet you won't ever
be a slave no more."

"En a mighty good job it wuz, too, Huck. It 'uz planned
beautiful, en it 'uz *done* beautiful; en dey ain't *nobody* kin git up a
plan dat's mo' mixed-up en splendid den what dat one wuz."

We was all as glad as we could be, but Tom was the gladdest of
all, because he had a bullet in the calf of his leg.

When me and Jim heard that, we didn't feel so brash as what we
did before. It was hurting him considerble, and bleeding; so we
laid him in the wigwam and tore up one of the duke's shirts for to
bandage him, but he says:

"Gimme the rags, I can do it myself. Don't stop, now; don't fool
around here, and the evasion booming along so handsome; man
the sweeps, and set her loose! Boys, we done it elegant!—'deed we
did. I wish *we'd* a had the handling of Louis XVI., there wouldn't
a been no 'Son of Saint Louis, ascend to heaven!' wrote down in
his biography: no, sir, we'd a whooped him over the *border*—that's
what we'd a done with *him*—and done it just as slick as nothing at
all, too. Man the sweeps—man the sweeps!"

But me and Jim was consulting—and thinking. And after we'd
thought a minute, I says:

"Say it, Jim."

So he says:

"Well, den, dis is de way it look to me, Huck. Ef it wuz *him* dat
'uz bein' sot free, en one er de boys wuz to git shot, would he say,
'Go on en save me, nemmine 'bout a doctor f'r to save dis one? Is
dat like Mars Tom Sawyer? Would he say dat? You *bet* he
wouldn't! *Well,* den, is *Jim* gwyne to say it? No, sah—I doan'
budge a step out'n dis place, 'dout a *doctor;* not it it's forty year!"

I knowed he was white inside, and I reckoned he'd say what he
did say—so it was all right, now, and I told Tom I was agoing for a
doctor. He raised considerble row about it, but me and Jim stuck
to it and wouldn't budge; so he was for crawling out and setting the
raft loose himself; but we wouldn't let him. Then he give us a piece
of his mind—but it didn't do no good.

So when he see me getting the canoe ready, he says:

"Well, then, if you're bound to go, I'll tell you the way to do,
when you get to the village. Shut the door, and blindfold the doctor
tight and fast, and make him swear to be silent as the grave, and
put a purse full of gold in his hand, and then take and lead him all
around the back alleys and everywheres, in the dark, and then
fetch him here in the canoe, in a roundabout way amongst the
islands and search him and take his chalk away from him, and
don't give it back to him till you get him back to the village, or else
he will chalk this raft so he can find it again. It's the way they all do."

So I said I would, and left, and Jim was to hide in the woods when he see the doctor coming, till he was gone again.

CHAPTER XLI

The doctor was an old man; a very nice, kind-looking old man, when I got him up. I told him me and my brother was over on Spanish Island hunting, yesterday afternoon, and camped on a piece of a raft we found, and about midnight he must a kicked his gun in his dreams, for it went off and shot him in the leg, and we wanted him to go over there and fix it and not say nothing about it, nor let anybody know, because we wanted to come home this evening, and surprise the folks.

"Who is your folks?" he says.

"The Phelpses, down yonder."

"Oh," he says. And after a minute, he says: "How'd you say he got shot?"

"He had a dream," I says, "and it shot him."

"Singular dream," he says.

So he lit up his lantern, and got his saddle-bags, and we started. But when he see the canoe, he didn't like the look of her—said she was big enough for one, but didn't look pretty safe for two. I says:

"Oh, you needn't be afeard, sir, she carried the three of us, easy enough."

"What three?"

"Why, me and Sid, and—and—and *the guns;* that's what I mean."

"Oh," he says.

But he put his foot on the gunnel, and rocked her; and shook his head, and said he reckoned he'd look around for a bigger one. But they was all locked and chained; so he took my canoe, and said for me to wait till he come back, or I could hunt around further, or maybe I better go down home and get them ready for the surprise, if I wanted to. But I said I didn't; so I told him just how to find the raft, and then he started.

I struck an idea, pretty soon. I says to myself, spos'n he can't fix that leg just in three shakes of a sheep's tail, as the saying is? spos'n it takes him three or four days? What are we going to do?— lay around there till he lets the cat out of the bag? No, sir, I know what *I'll* do. I'll wait, and when he comes back, if he says he's got to go any more, I'll get down there, too, if I swim; and we'll take and tie him, and keep him, and shove out down the river; and when Tom's done with him, we'll give him what it's worth, or all we got, and then let him get shore.

So then I crept into a lumber pile to get some sleep; and next time I waked up the sun was away up over my head! I shot out and went for the doctor's house, but they told me he'd gone away in the night, some time or other, and warn't back yet. Well, thinks I, that looks powerful bad for Tom, and I'll dig out for the island, right off. So away I shoved, and turned the corner, and nearly rammed my head into Uncle Silas's stomach! He says:

"Why, *Tom!* Where you been, all this time, you rascal?"

"*I* hain't been nowheres," I says, "only just hunting for the runaway nigger—me and Sid."

"Why, where ever did you go?" he says. "Your aunt's been mighty uneasy."

"She needn't," I says, "because we was all right. We followed the men and the dogs, but they out-run us, and we lost them; but we thought we heard them on the water, so we got a canoe and took out after them, and crossed over but couldn't find nothing of them; so we cruised along up-shore till we got kind of tired and beat out; and tied up the canoe and went to sleep, and never waked up till about an hour ago, then we paddled over here to hear the news, and Sid's at the post-office to see what he can hear, and I'm a branching out to get something to eat for us, and then we're going home."

So then we went to the post-office to get "Sid"; but just as I suspicioned, he warn't there; so the old man he got a letter out of the office, and we waited a while longer but Sid didn't come; so the old man said come along, let Sid foot it home, or canoe-it, when he got done fooling around—but we would ride. I couldn't get him to let me stay and wait for Sid; and he said there warn't no use in it, and I must come along, and let Aunt Sally see we was all right.

When we got home, Aunt Sally was that glad to see me she laughed and cried both, and hugged me, and give me one of them lickings of hern that don't amount to shucks, and said she'd serve Sid the same when he come.

And the place was plumb full of farmers and farmers' wives, to dinner; and such another clack a body never heard. Old Mrs. Hotchkiss was the worst; her tongue was agoing all the time. She says:

"Well, Sister Phelps, I've ransacked that-air cabin over an' I b'lieve the nigger was crazy. I says so to Sister Damrell—didn't I, Sister Damrell?—s'I, he's crazy, s'I—them's the very words I said. You all hearn me: He's crazy, s'I; everything shows it, s'I. Look at that-air grindstone, s'I; want to tell *me* 't any cretur 'tis in his right mind's agoin' to scrabble all them crazy things onto a grindstone, s'I? Here sich 'n' sich a person busted his heart; 'n' here so 'n' so pegged along for thirty-seven year, 'n' all that—natcherl son o' Louis somebody, 'n' sich everlast'n rubbage. He's plumb crazy, s'I; it's what I says in the fust place, it's what I says in the middle, 'n' it's what I says last 'n' all the time—the nigger's crazy—crazy's

Nebokoodneezer, s'I."

"An' look at that-air ladder made out'n rags, Sister Hotchkiss," says old Mrs. Damrell, "what in the name o' goodness *could* he every want of—"

"The very words I was a-sayin' no longer ago th'n this minute to Sister Utterback, 'n' she'll tell you so herself. Sh-she, look at that-air rag ladder, sh-she; 'n' s'I, yes, *look* at it, s'I. Sh-she, Sister Hotchkiss, sh-she—"

"But how in the nation'd they ever *git* that grindstone *in* there, *any*-way? 'n' who dug that-air *hole*? 'n' who—"

"My very *words*, Brer Penrod! I was a-sayin'—pass that-air sasser o' m'lasses, won't ye?—I was a-sayin' to Sister Dunlap, jist this minute, how *did* they git that grindstone in there, s'I. Without *help*, mind you—'thout *help*! *Thar's* wher' 'tis. Don't tell *me*, s'I; there *wuz* help, s'I; 'n' ther' wuz a *plenty* help, too, s'I; ther's ben a *dozen* a-helpin' that nigger, 'n' I lay I'd skin every last nigger on this place, but *I'd* find out who done it, s'I; 'n' moreover, s'I—"

"A *dozen* says you!—*forty* couldn't a done everything that's been done. Look at them case-knife saws and things, how tedious they've been made; look at that bed-leg sawed off with 'm, a week's work for six men; look at that nigger made out'n straw on the bed; and look at——"

"You may *well* say it, Brer Hightower! It's jist as I was a-sayin' to Brer Phelps, his own self. S'e, what do *you* think of it, Sister Hotchkiss, s'e? think o' what, Brer Phelps, s'I? think o' that bed-leg sawed off that a way, s'e? *think* of it, s'I? I lay it never sawed *itself* off, s'I—somebody *sawed* it, s'I; that's my opinion, take it or leave it, it mayn't be no 'count, s'I, but sich as 't is, it's my opinion, s'I, 'n' if anybody k'n start a better one, s'I, let him *do* it, s'I, that's all. I says to Sister Dunlap, s'I——"

"Why, dog my cats, they must a ben a house-full o' niggers in there every night for four weeks, to a done all that work, Sister Phelps. Look at that shirt—every last inch of it kivered over with secret African writ'n done with blood! Must a ben a raft uv 'm at it right along, all the time, amost. Why, I'd give two dollars to have it read to me; 'n' as for the niggers that wrote it, I 'low I'd take 'n' lash 'm t'll——"

"People to *help* him, Brother Marples! Well, I reckon you'd *think* so, if you'd a been in this house for a while back. Why, they've stole everything they could lay their hands on—and we a watching, all the time, mind you. They stole that shirt right off o' the line! and as for that sheet they made the rag ladder out of ther' ain't no telling how many times they *didn't* steal that; and flour, and candles, and candlesticks, and spoons, and the old warming-pan, and most a thousand things that I disremember, now, and my new calico dress; and me, and Silas, and my Sid and Tom on the constant watch day *and* night, as I was a telling you,

and not a one of us could catch hide nor hair, nor sight nor sound
of them; and here at the last minute, lo and behold you, they slides
right in under our noses, and fools us, and not only fools *us* but the
Injun Territory robbers too, and actuly gets *away* with that nigger,
safe and sound, and that with sixteen men and twenty-two dogs
right on their very heels at that very time! I tell you, it just bangs
anything i ever *heard* of. Why, *sperits* couldn't a done better, and
been no smarter. And I reckon they must a *been* sperits—because,
you know our dogs, and ther' ain't no better; well, them dogs never
even got on the *track* of 'm, once! You explain *that* to me, if you
can!—*any* of you!"

   "Well, it does beat——"
   "Laws alive, I never——"
   "So help me, I wouldn't a be——"
   "*House*-thieves as well as——"
   "Goodnessgracioussakes, I'd a ben afeard to *live* in sich a——"
   " 'Fraid to *live!*—why, I was that scared I das'nt hardly go to
bed, or get up, or lay down, or *set* down, Sister Ridgeway. Why,
they'd steal the very—why, goodness sakes, you can guess what
kind of a fluster *I* was in by the time midnight come, last night. I
hope to gracious if I warn't afraid they'd steal some o' the family!
I was just to that pass, I didn't have no reasoning faculties no
more. It looks foolish enough, *now,* in the day-time; but I says to
myself, there's my two poor boys asleep, 'way up stairs in that
lonesome room, and I declare to goodness I was that uneasy 't I
crep' up there and locked 'em in! I *did*. And anybody would.
Because, you know, when you get scared, that way, and it keeps
running on, and getting worse and worse, all the time, and your
wits gets to addling, and you get to doing all sorts o' wild things,
and by-and-by you think to yourself, spos'n *I* was a boy, and was
away up there, and the door ain't locked, and you——" She
stopped, looking kind of wondering, and then she turned her head
around slow, and when her eye lit on me—I got up and took a
walk.

   Says I to myself, I can explain better how we come to not be in
that room this morning, if I go out to one side and study over it a
little. So I done it. But I dasn't go fur, or she'd a sent for me. And
when it was late in the day, the people all went, and then I come in
and told her the noise and shooting waked up me and "Sid," and
the door was locked, and we wanted to see the fun, so we went
down the lightning-rod, and both of us got hurt a little, and we
didn't never want to try *that* no more. And then I went on and told
her all what I told Uncle Silas before; and then she said she'd
forgive us, and maybe it was all right enough anyway, and about
what a body might expect of boys, for all boys was a pretty harum-
scarum lot, as fur as she could see; and so, as long as no harm
hadn't come of it, she judged she better put in her time being

grateful we was alive and well and she had us still, stead of fretting over what was past and done. So then she kissed me, and patted me on the head, and dropped into a kind of a brown study; and pretty soon jumps up, and says:

"Why, lawsamercy, it's most night, and Sid not come yet! What *has* become of that boy?"

I see my chance; so I skips up and says:

"I'll run right up to town and get him," I says.

"No you won't," she says. "You'll stay right wher' you are; *one's* enough to be lost at a time. If he ain't here to supper, your uncle'll go."

Well, he warn't there to supper; so right after supper uncle went.

He come back about ten, a little bit uneasy; hadn't run across Tom's track. Aunt Sally was a good *deal* uneasy; but Uncle Silas he said there warn't no occasion to be—boys will be boys, he said, and you'll see this one turn up in the morning, all sound and right. So she had to be satisfied. But she said she'd set up for him a while, anyway, and keep a light burning, so he could see it.

And then when I went up to bed she come up with me and fetched her candle, and tucked me in, and mothered me so good I felt mean, and like I couldn't look her in the face; and she set down on the bed and talked with me a long time, and said what a splendid boy Sid was, and didn't seem to want to ever stop talking about him; and kept asking me every now and then, if I reckoned he could a got lost, or hurt, or maybe drownded, and might be laying at this minute, somewheres, suffering or dead, and she not by him to help him, and so the tears would drip down, silent, and I would tell her that Sid was all right, and would be home in the morning, sure; and she would squeeze my hand, or maybe kiss me, and tell me to say it again, and keep on saying it, because it done her good, and she was in so much trouble. And when she was going away, she looked down in my eyes, so steady and gentle, and says:

"The door ain't going to be locked, Tom; and there's the window and the rod; but you'll be good, *won't* you? And you won't go? For *my* sake."

Laws knows I *wanted* to go, bad enough, to see about Tom, and was all intending to go; but after that, I wouldn't a went, not for kingdoms.

But she was on my mind, and Tom was on my mind; so I slept very restless. And twice I went down the rod, away in the night, and slipped around front, and see her setting there by her candle in the window with her eyes towards the road and the tears in them; and I wished I could do something for her, but I couldn't, only to swear that I wouldn't never do nothing to grieve her any more. And the third time, I waked up at dawn, and slid down, and she was there yet, and her candle was most out, and her old gray head was resting on her hand, and she was asleep.

CHAPTER XLII

The old man was up town again, before breakfast, but couldn't get no track of Tom; and both of them set at the table, thinking, and not saying nothing, and looking mournful, and their coffee getting cold, and not eating anything. And by-and-by the old man says:

"Did I give you the letter?"

"What letter?"

"The one I got yesterday out of the post-office."

"No, you didn't give me no letter."

"Well, I must a forgot it."

So he rummaged his pockets, and then went off somewheres where he had laid it down, and fetched it, and give it to her. She says:

"Why, it's from St. Petersburg—it's from Sis."

I allowed another walk would do me good; but I couldn't stir. But before she could break it open, she dropped it and run—for she see something. And so did I. It was Tom Sawyer on a mattress; and that old doctor; and Jim, in *her* calico dress, with his hands tied behind him; and a lot of people. I hid the letter behind the first thing that come handy, and rushed. She flung herself at Tom, crying, and says:

"Oh, he's dead, he's dead, I know he's dead!"

And Tom he turned his head a little, and muttered something or other, which showed he warn't in his right mind; then she flung up her hands, and says:

"He's alive, thank God! And that's enough!" and she snatched a kiss of him, and flew for the house to get the bed ready, and scattering orders right and left at the niggers and everybody else, as fast as her tongue could go, every jump of the way.

I followed the men to see what they was going to do with Jim; and the old doctor and Uncle Silas followed after Tom into the house. The men was very huffy, and some of them wanted to hang Jim, for an example to all the other niggers around there, so they wouldn't be trying to run away, like Jim done, and making such a raft of trouble, and keeping a whole family scared most to death for days and nights. But the others said, don't do it, it wouldn't answer at all, he ain't our nigger, and his owner would turn up and make us pay for him, sure. So that cooled them down a little, because the people that's always the most anxious for to hang a nigger that hain't done just right, is always the very ones that ain't the most anxious to pay for him when they've got their satisfaction out of him.

They cussed Jim considerble, though, and give him a cuff or two, side the head, once in a while, but Jim never said nothing, and he never let on to know me, and they took him to the same cabin, and put his own clothes on him, and chained him again, and not to no bed-leg, this time, but to a big staple drove into the bottom log, and chained his hands, too, and both legs, and said he warn't to have nothing but bread and water to eat, after this, till his owner come or he was sold at auction, because he didn't come in a certain length of time, and filled up our hole, and said a couple of farmers with guns must stand watch around about the cabin every night, and a bull-dog tied to the door in the day-time; and about this time they was through with the job and was tapering off with a kind of generl good-bye cussing, and then the old doctor comes and takes a look, and says:

"Don't be no rougher on him than you're obleeged to, because he ain't a bad nigger. When I got to where I found the boy, I see I couldn't cut the bullet out without some help, and he warn't in no condition for me to leave, to go and get help; and he got a little worse and a little worse, and after a long time he went out of his head, and wouldn't let me come anigh him, any more, and said if I chalked his raft he'd kill me, and no end of wild foolishness like that, and I see I couldn't do anything at all with him; so I says, I got to have *help,* somehow; and the minute I says it, out crawls this nigger from somewhere, and says he'll help, and he done it, too, and done it very well. Of course I judged he must be a runaway nigger, and there I *was!* and there I had to stick, right straight along all the rest of the day, and all night. It was a fix, I tell you! I had a couple of patients with the chills, and of course I'd of liked to run up to town and see them, but I dasn't, because the nigger might get away, and then I'd be to blame; and yet never a skiff come close enough for me to hail. So there I had to stick, plumb till daylight this morning; and I never see a nigger that was a better nuss or faithfuller, and yet he was resking his freedom to do it, and was all tired out, too, and I see plain enough he'd been worked main hard, lately. I liked the nigger for that; I tell you, gentlemen, a nigger like that is worth a thousand dollars—and kind treatment, too. I had everything I needed, and the boy was doing as well there as he would a done at home—better, maybe, because it was so quiet; but there I *was,* with both of 'm on my hands; and there I had to stick, till about dawn this morning; then some men in a skiff come by, and as good luck would have it, the nigger was setting by the pallet with his head propped on his knees, sound asleep; so I motioned them in, quiet, and they slipped up on him and grabbed him and tied him before he knowed what he was about, and we never had no trouble. And the boy being in a kind of a flighty sleep, too, we muffled the oars and hitched the raft on, and towed her over very nice and quiet, and the nigger never made the least row nor said a word, from the start. He ain't no bad nigger, gentlemen; that's what I think about him."

Somebody says:

"Well, it sounds very good, doctor, I'm obleeged to say."

Then the others softened up a little, too, and I was mighty thankful to that old doctor for doing Jim that good turn; and I was glad it was according to my judgment of him, too; because I thought he had a good heart in him and was a good man, the first time I see him. Then they all agreed that Jim had acted very well, and was deserving to have some notice took of it, and reward. So every one of them promised, right out and hearty, that they wouldn't cuss him no more.

Then they come out and locked him up. I hoped they was going to say he could have one or two of the chains took off, because they was rotten heavy, or could have meat and greens with his bread and water, but they didn't think of it, and I reckoned it warn't best for me to mix in, but I judged I'd get the doctor's yarn to Aunt Sally, somehow or other, as soon as I'd got through the breakers that was laying just ahead of me. Explanations, I mean, of how I forgot to mention about Sid being shot, when I was telling how him and me put in that dratted night paddling around hunting the runaway nigger.

But I had plenty time. Aunt Sally she stuck to the sick-room all day and all night; and every time I see Uncle Silas mooning around, I dodged him.

Next morning I heard Tom was a good deal better, and they said Aunt Sally was gone to get a nap. So I slips to the sick-room, and if I found him awake I reckoned we could put up a yarn for the family that would wash. But he was sleeping, and sleeping very peaceful, too; and pale, not fire-faced the way he was when he come. So I set down and laid for him to wake. In about a half an hour, Aunt Sally comes gliding in, and there I was, up a stump again! She motioned me to be still, and set down by me, and begun to whisper, and said we could all be joyful now, because all the symptoms was first rate, and he'd been sleeping like that for ever so long, and looking better and peacefuller all the time, and ten to one he'd wake up in his right mind.

So we set there watching, and by-and-by he stirs a bit, and opened his eyes very natural, and takes a look, and says:

"Hello, why I'm at *home!* How's that? Where's the raft?"

"It's all right," I says.

"And *Jim?*"

"The same," I says, but couldn't say it pretty brash. But he never noticed, but says:

"Good! Splendid! *Now* we're all right and safe! Did you tell Aunty?"

I was going to say yes; but she chipped in and says:

"About what, Sid?"

"Why, about the way the whole thing was done."

"What whole thing?"

"Why, *the* whole thing. There ain't but one; how we set the runaway nigger free—me and Tom."

"Good land! Set the run— What *is* the child talking about! Dear, dear, out of his head again!"

"*No,* I ain't out of my HEAD; I know all what I'm talking about. We *did* set him free—me and Tom. We laid out to do it, and we *done* it. And we done it elegant, too." He'd got a start, and she never checked him up, just set and stared and stared, and let him clip along, and I see it warn't no use for *me* to put in. "Why, Aunty, it cost us a power of work—weeks of it—hours and hours, every night, whilst you was all asleep. And we had to steal candles, and the sheet, and the shirt, and your dress, and spoons, and tin plates, and case-knives, and the warming-pan, and the grindstone, and flour, and just no end of things, and you can't think what work it was to make the saws, and pens, and inscriptions, and one thing or another, and you can't think *half* the fun it was. And we had to make up the pictures of coffins and things, and nonnamous letters from the robbers, and get up and down the lighting-rod, and dig the hole into the cabin, and make the rope-ladder and send it in cooked up in a pie, and send in spoons and things to work with, in your apron pocket"——

"Mercy sakes!"

——"and load up the cabin with rats and snakes and so on, for company for Jim; and then you kept Tom here so long with the butter in his hat that you come near spiling the whole business, because the men come before we was out of the cabin, and we had to rush, and they heard us and let drive at us, and I got my share, and we dodged out of the path and let them go by, and when the dogs come they warn't interested in us, but went for the most noise, and we got our canoe, and made for the raft, and was all safe, and Jim was a free man, and we done it all by ourselves, and *wasn't* it bully, Aunty!"

"Well, I never heard the likes of it in all my born days! So it was *you,* you little rapscallions, that's been making all this trouble, and turned everybody's wits clean inside out and scared us all most to death. I've as good a notion as ever I had in my life, to take it out o' you this very minute. To think, here I've been, night after night, a—*you* just get well once, you young scamp, and I lay I'll tan the Old Harry out o' both o' ye!"

But Tom, he *was* so proud and joyful, he just *couldn't* hold in, and his tongue just *went* it—she a-chipping in, and spitting fire all along, and both of them going it at once, like a cat-convention; and she says:

"*Well,* you get all the enjoyment you can out of it *now,* for mind I tell you if I catch you meddling with him again——"

"Meddling with *who?*" Tom says, dropping his smile and looking surprised.

"With *who?* Why, the runaway nigger, of course. Who'd you reckon?"

Tom looks at me very grave, and says:

"Tom, didn't you just tell me he was all right? Hasn't he got away?"

"*Him?*" says Aunt Sally; "the runaway nigger? 'Deed he hasn't. They've got him back, safe and sound, and he's in that cabin again, on bread and water, and loaded down with chains, till he's claimed or sold!"

Tom rose square up in bed, with his eye hot, and his nostrils opening and shutting like gills, and sings out to me:

"They hain't no *right* to shut him up! *Shove!*—and don't you lose a minute. Turn him loose! he ain't no slave; he's as free as any cretur that walks this earth!"

"What *does* the child mean?"

"I mean every word I *say,* Aunt Sally, and if somebody don't go, *I'*ll go. I've knowed him all his life, and so has Tom, there. Old Miss Watson died two months ago, and she was ashamed she ever was going to sell him down the river, and *said* so; and she let him free in her will."

"Then what on earth did *you* want to set him free for, seeing he was already free?"

"Well, that *is* a question, I must say; and *just* like women! Why, I wanted the *adventure* of it; and I'd a waded neck-deep in blood to—goodness alive, AUNT POLLY!"

If she warn't standing right there, just inside the door, looking as sweet and contented as an angel half-full of pie, I wish I may never!

Aunt Sally jumped for her, and most hugged the head off of her, and cried over her, and I found a good enough place for me under the bed, for it was getting pretty sultry for *us,* seemed to me. And I peeped out, and in a little while Tom's Aunt Polly shook herself loose and stood there looking across at Tom over her spectacles—kind of grinding him into the earth, you know. And then she says:

"Yes, you *better* turn y'r head away—I would if I was you, Tom."

"Oh, deary me!" says Aunt Sally; "*is* he changed so? Why, that ain't *Tom* it's Sid; Tom's—Tom's—why, where is Tom? He was here a minute ago."

"You mean where's Huck *Finn*—that's what you mean! I reckon I hain't raised such a scamp as my Tom all these years, not to know him when I *see* him. That *would* be a pretty howdy-do. Come out from under that bed, Huck Finn."

So I done it. But not feeling brash.

Aunt Sally she was one of the mixed-upest looking persons I ever see; except one, and that was Uncle Silas, when he come in, and they told it all to him. It kind of made him drunk, as you may say, and he didn't know nothing at all the rest of the day, and preached a prayer-meeting sermon that night that give him a rattling reputation, because the oldest man in the world couldn't a understood it. So Tom's Aunt Polly, she told all about who I was, and what; and I had to up and tell how I was in such a tight place that when Mrs. Phelps took me for Tom Sawyer—she chipped in and says, "Oh, go on and call me Aunt Sally, I'm used to it, now, and 'taint no need to change"—that when Aunt Sally took me for Tom Sawyer, I had to stand it—there warn't no other way, and I knowed he wouldn't mind, because it would be nuts for him, being a mystery, and he'd make an adventure out of it and be perfectly satisfied. And so it turned out, and he let on to be Sid, and made things as soft as he could for me.

And his Aunt Polly she said Tom was right about old Miss Watson setting Jim free in her will; and so, sure enough, Tom Sawyer had gone and took all that trouble and bother to set a free nigger free! and I couldn't ever understand, before, until that minute and that talk, how he *could* help a body set a nigger free, with his bringing-up.

Well, Aunt Polly she said that when Aunt Sally wrote to her that Tom and *Sid* had come, all right and safe, she says to herself:

"Look at that, now! I might have expected it, letting him go off that way without anybody to watch him. So now I got to go and trapse all the way down the river, eleven hundred mile, and find out what that creetur's up to, *this* time; as long as I couldn't seem to get any answer out of you about it."

"Why, I never heard nothing from you," says Aunt Sally.

"Well, I wonder! Why, I wrote to you twice, to ask you what you could mean by Sid being here."

"Well, I never got 'em, Sis."

Aunt Polly, she turns around slow and severe, and says:

"You, Tom!"

"Well—*what?*" he says, kind of pettish.

"Don't you what *me,* you impudent thing—hand out them letters."

"What letters?"

"*Them* letters. I be bound, if I have to take aholt of you I'll——"

"They're in the trunk. There, now. And they're just the same as they was when I got them out of the office. I hain't looked into them, I hain't touched them. But I knowed they'd make trouble, and I thought if you warn't in no hurry, I'd——"

"Well, you *do* need skinning, there ain't no mistake about it. And I wrote another one to tell you I was coming; and I spose he——"

"No, it come yesterday; I hain't read it yet, but *it's* all right, I've got that one."

I wanted to offer to bet two dollars she hadn't, but I reckoned maybe it was just as safe to not to. So I never said nothing.

CHAPTER THE LAST

The first time I catched Tom, private, I asked him what was his
idea, time of the evasion?—what it was he'd planned to do if the
evasion worked all right and he managed to set a nigger free that
was already free before? And he said, what he had planned in his
head, from the start, if we got Jim out all safe, was for us to run
him down the river, on the raft, and have adventures plumb to the
mouth of the river, and then tell him about his being free, and take
him back up home on a steamboat, in style, and pay him for his
lost time, and write word ahead and get out all the niggers around,
and have them waltz him into town with a torchlight procession
and a brass band, and then he would be a hero, and so would we.
But I reckened it was about as well the way it was.

We had Jim out of the chains in no time, and when Aunt Polly
and Uncle Silas and Aunt Sally found out how good he helped the
doctor nurse Tom, they made a heap of fuss over him, and fixed
him up prime, and give him all he wanted to eat, and a good time,
and nothing to do. And we had him up to the sick-room; and had a
high talk; and Tom give Jim forty dollars for being prisoner for us
so patient, and doing it up so good, and Jim was pleased most to
death, and busted out, and says:

"*Dah*, now, Huck, what I tell you?—what I tell you up dah on
Jackson islan'? I *tole* you I got a hairy breas', en what's de sign un
it; en I *tole* you I ben rich wunst, en gwineter to be rich *again;*
en it's come true; en heah she *is! Dah,* now! doan' talk to *me*—
signs is *signs,* mine I tell you; en I knowed jis' 's well 'at I 'uz
gwineter be rich agin as I's a stannin' heah dis minute!"

And then Tom he talked along, and talked along, and says, le's
all three slide out of here, one of these nights, and get an outfit, an
go for howling adventures amongst the Injuns, over in the
Territory, for a couple of weeks or two; and I says, all right, that
suits me, but I aint got no money for to buy the outfit, and I reckon
I couldn't get none from home, because it's likely pap's been back
before now, and got it all away from Judge Thatcher and drunk
it up.

"No he hain't," Tom says; "it's all there, yet—six th
dollars and more; and your pap hain't ever been back
Hadn't when I come away, anyhow."

Jim says, kind of solemn:

"He ain't a comin' back no mo', Huck."

I says:

"Why, Jim?"

"Nemmine why, Huck—but he ain't comin'

But I kept at him; so at last he says:

"Doan' you 'member de house dat was f
dey wuz a man in dah, kivered up, en I w

and didn' let you come in? Well, den, you k'n git yo' money when you wants it: kase dat wuz him."

Tom's most well, now, and got his bullet around his neck on a watch-guard for a watch, and is always seeing what time it is, and so there ain't nothing more to write about, and I am rotten glad of it, because if I'd a knowed what a trouble it was to make a book I wouldn't a tackled it and aint't agoing to no more. But I reckon I got to light out for the Territory ahead of the rest, because Aunt Sally she's going to adopt me and sivilize me and I can't stand it. I been there before.

THE END. YOURS TRULY, HUCK FINN

A CONNECTICUT YANKEE
IN KING ARTHUR'S COURT

A Connecticut Yankee in King Arthur's Court *was first published in 1889 by C.L. Webster, New York. In spite of the author's direct control over the production of the book, the Preface, written for the first edition, did not appear in print until Harper and Brothers published the Author's National Edition nearly twenty years later — long after C.L. Webster went bankrupt.*

A CONNECTICUT YANKEE IN KING ARTHUR'S COURT

PREFACE

The ungentle laws and customs touched upon in this tale are historical, and the episodes which are used to illustrate them are also historical. It is not pretended that these laws and customs existed in England in the sixth century; no, it is only pretended that inasmuch as they existed in the English and other civilizations of far later times, it is safe to consider that it is no libel upon the sixth century to suppose them to have been in practice in that day also. One is quite justified in inferring that whatever one of these laws or customs was lacking in that remote time, its place was competently filled by a worse one.

The question as to whether there is such a thing as divine right of kings is not settled in this book. It was found too difficult. That the executive head of a nation should be a person of lofty character and extraordinary ability, was manifest and indisputable; that none but the Deity could select that head unerringly, was also manifest and indisputable; that the Deity ought to make that selection, then, was likewise manifest and indisputable; consequently, that He does make it, as claimed, was an unavoidable deduction. I mean, until the author of this book encountered the Pompadour, and Lady Castlemaine and some other executive heads of that kind; these were found so difficult to work into the scheme, that it was judged better to take the other tack in this book, (which must be issued this fall,) and then go into training and settle the question in another book. It is of course a thing which ought to be settled, and I am not going to have anything particular to do next winter anyway.

MARK TWAIN.

A WORD OF EXPLANATION

It was in Warwick Castle that I came across the curious stranger whom I am going to talk about. He attracted me by three things: his candid simplicity, his marvelous familiarity with ancient armor, and the restfulness of his company—for he did all the talking. We fell together, as modest people will, in the tail of the herd that was being shown through, and he at once began to say things which interested me. As he talked along, softly, pleasantly, flowingly, he seemed to drift away imperceptibly out of this world and time, and into some remote era and old forgotten country; and so he gradually wove such a spell about me that I seemed to move among the spectres and shadows and dust and mold of a gray antiquity, holding speech with a relic of it! Exactly as I would speak of my nearest personal friends or enemies, or my most familiar neighbors, he spoke of Sir Bedivere, Sir Bors de Ganis, Sir Launcelot of the Lake, Sir Galahad, and all the other great names of the Table Round—and how old, old, unspeakably old and faded and dry and musty and ancient he came to look as he went on! Presently he turned to me and said, just as one might speak of the weather, or any other common matter—

"You know about transmigration of souls; do you know about transposition of epochs—and bodies?"

I said I had not heard of it. He was so little interested—just as when people speak of the weather—that he did not notice whether I made him any answer or not. There was half a moment of silence, immediately interrupted by the droning voice of the salaried cicerone:

"Ancient hauberk, date of the sixth century, time of King Arthur and the Round Table; said to have belonged to the knight Sir Sagramor le Desirous; observe the round hole through the chain-mail in the left breast; can't be accounted for; supposed to have been done with a bullet since invention of firearms—perhaps maliciously by Cromwell's soldiers."

My acquaintance smiled—not a modern smile, but one that must have gone out of general use many, many centuries ago—and muttered apparently to himself:

"Wit ye well, *I saw it done*." Then, after a pause, added: "I did it myself."

By the time I had recovered from the electric surprise of this remark, he was gone.

All that evening I sat by my fire at the Warwick Arms, steeped in a dream of the olden time, while the rain beat upon the windows, and the wind roared about the eaves and corners. From time to time I dipped into old Sir Thomas Malory's enchanting book, and fed at its rich feast of prodigies and adventures, breathed in the fragrance of its obsolete names, and dreamed again. Midnight being come at length, I read another tale, for a night-cap—this which here follows, to wit:

HOW SIR LAUNCELOT SLEW TWO GIANTS, AND MADE A CASTLE FREE

Anon withal came there upon him two great giants, well armed, all save the heads, with two horrible clubs in their hands. Sir Launcelot put his shield afore him, and put the stroke away of the one giant, and with his sword he clave his head asunder. When his fellow saw that, he ran away as he were wood,* for fear of the horrible strokes, and Sir Launcelot after him with all his might, and smote him on the shoulder, and clave him to the middle. Then Sir Launcelot went into the hall, and there came afore him three score ladies and damsels, and all kneeled unto him, and thanked God and him of their deliverance. For, sir, said they, the most part of us have been here this seven year their prisoners, and we have worked all manner of silk works for our meat, and we are all great gentlewomen born, and blessed be the time, knight, that ever thou wert born; for thou hast done the most worship that ever did knight in the world, that will we bear record, and we all pray you to tell us your name, that we may tell our friends who delivered us out of prison. Fair damsels, he said, my name is Sir Launcelot du Lake. And so he departed from them and betaught them unto God. And then he mounted upon his horse, and rode into many strange and wild countries, and through many waters and valleys, and evil was he lodged. And at the last by fortune him happened against a night to come to a fair courtilage, and therein he found an old gentlewoman that lodged him with a good-will, and there he had good cheer for him and his horse. And when time was, his host brought him into a fair garret over the gate to his bed. There Sir Launcelot unarmed him, and set his harness by him, and went to bed, and anon he fell on sleep. So, soon after there came one on horseback, and knocked at the gate in great haste. And when Sir Launcelot heard this he rose up, and looked out at the window, and saw by the moonlight three knights come riding after that one man, and all three lashed on him at once with swords, and that one knight turned on them knightly again and defended him. Truly, said Sir Launcelot, yonder one knight shall I help, for it were shame for me to see three knights on one, and if he be slain I am partner of his death. And therewith he took his harness and went out at a window by a sheet down to the four knights, and then Sir Launcelot said on high, Turn you knights unto me, and leave your fighting with that knight. And then they all three left Sir Kay, and turned unto Sir Launcelot, and there began great battle, for they alight all three, and strake many strokes at Sir Launcelot, and assailed him on every side. Then Sir Kay dressed him for to have holpen Sir Launcelot. Nay, sir, said he, I will none of your help, therefore as ye will have my help let me alone with them. Sir Kay for the pleasure of the knight suffered him for to do his will, and so stood aside. And then anon within six strokes Sir Launcelot had stricken them to the earth.

And then they all three cried, Sir knight, we yield us unto you as man of might matchless. As to that, said Sir Launcelot, I will not take your yielding unto me, but so that ye yield you unto Sir Kay the seneschal, on that covenant I will save your lives and else not. Fair knight, said they, that

*Demented.

were we loath to do; for as for Sir Kay we chased him hither, and had overcome him had ye not been; therefore, to yield us unto him it were no reason. Well, as to that, said Sir Launcelot, advise you will, for ye may choose whether ye will die or live, for an ye be yielden, it shall be unto Sir Kay. Fair knight, then they said, in saving our lives we will do as thou commandest us. Then shall ye, said Sir Launcelot, on Whitsunday next coming go unto the court of King Arthur, and there shall ye yield you unto Queen Guenever, and put you all three in her grace and mercy, and say that Sir Kay sent you thither to be her prisoners. On the morn Sir Launcelot arose early, and left Sir Kay sleeping: and Sir Launcelot took Sir Kay's armor and his shield and armed him, and so he went to the stable and took his horse, and took his leave of his host, and so he departed. Then soon after arose Sir Kay and missed Sir Launcelot: and then he espied that he had his armor and his horse. Now by my faith I know well that he will grieve some of the court of King Arthur: for on him knights will be bold, and deem that it is I, and that will beguile them; and because of his armor and shield I am sure I shall ride in peace. And then soon after departed Sir Kay, and thanked his host.

As I laid the book down there was a knock at the door, and my stranger came in. I gave him a pipe and a chair, and made him welcome. I also comforted him with a hot Scotch whiskey; gave him another one; then still another—hoping always for his story. After a fourth persuader, he drifted into it himself, in a quite simple and natural way:

THE STRANGER'S HISTORY

I am an American. I was born and reared in Hartford, in the State of Connecticut—anyway, just over the river, in the country. So I am a Yankee of the Yankees—and practical; yes, and nearly barren of sentiment, I suppose—or poetry, in other words. My father was a blacksmith, my uncle was a horse doctor, and I was both, along at first. Then I went over to the great arms factory and learned my real trade; learned all there was to it; learned to make everything: guns, revolvers, cannon, boilers, engines, all sorts of labor-saving machinery. Why, I could make anything a body wanted—anything in the world, it didn't make any difference what; and if there wasn't any quick new-fangled way to make a thing, I could invent one— and do it as easy as rolling off a log. I became head superintendent; had a couple of thousand men under me.

Well, a man like that is a man that is full of fight—that goes without saying. With a couple of thousand rough men under one, one has plenty of that sort of amusement. I had, anyway. At last I met my match, and I got my dose. It was during a misunderstanding conducted with crowbars with a fellow we used to call Hercules. He laid me out with a crusher alongside the head that made everything crack, and seemed to spring every joint in my skull and made it overlap its neighbor. Then the world went out in darkness, and I didn't feel anything more, and didn't know anything at all—at least for a while.

When I came to again, I was sitting under an oak tree, on the grass, with a whole beautiful and broad country landscape all to myself—nearly. Not entirely; for there was a fellow on a horse, looking down at me—a fellow fresh out of a picture-book. He was in oldtime iron armor from head to heel, with a helmet on his head the shape of a nail-keg with slits in it; and he had a shield, and a sword, and a prodigious spear; and his horse had armor on, too, and a steel horn projecting from his forehead, and gorgeous red and green silk trappings that hung down all around him like a bed-quilt, nearly to the ground.

"Fair sir, will ye just?" said this fellow.

"Will I which?"

"Will ye try a passage of arms for land or lady or for—"

"What are you giving me?" I said. "Get along back to your circus, or I'll report you."

Now what does this man do but fall back a couple of hundred yards and then come rushing at me as hard as he could tear, with his nail-keg bent down nearly to his horse's neck and his long spear pointed straight ahead. I saw he meant business, so I was up the tree when he arrived.

He allowed that I was his property, the captive of his spear. There was argument on his side—and the bulk of the advantage—so I judged it best to humor him. We fixed up an agreement whereby I was to go with him and he was not to hurt me. I came down, and we started away, I walking by the side of his horse. We marched comfortably along, through glades and over brooks which I could not remember to have seen before—which puzzled me and made me wonder—and yet we did not come to any circus or sign of a circus. So I gave up the idea of a circus, and concluded he was from an asylum. But we never came to an asylum—so I was up a stump, as you may say. I asked him how far we were from Hartford. He said he had never heard of the place; which I took to be a lie, but allowed it to go at that. At the end of an hour we saw a far-away town sleeping in a valley by a winding river; and beyond it on a hill, a vast gray fortress, with towers and turrets, the first I had ever seen out of a picture.

"Bridgeport?" said I, pointing.

"Camelot," said he.

My stranger had been showing signs of sleepiness. He caught himself nodding, now, and smiled one of those pathetic, obsolete smiles of his, and said:

"I find I can't go on; but come with me, I've got it all written out, and you can read it if you like."

In his chamber, he said: "First, I kept a journal; then by-and-by, after years, I took the journal and turned it into a book. How long ago that was!"

"Begin here—I've already told you what goes before." He was steeped in drowsiness by this time. As I went out at his door I heard him murmur sleepily: "Give you good den, fair sir."

I sat down by my fire and examined my treasure. The first part of it—the great bulk of it—was parchment, and yellow with age. I scanned a leaf particularly and saw that it was a palimpsest. Under the old dim writing of the Yankee historian appeared traces of a penmanship which was older and dimmer still—Latin words and sentences: fragments from old monkish legends, evidently. I turned to the place indicated by my stranger and began to read—as follows:

THE TALE OF THE LOST LAND

CHAPTER I

CAMELOT

"Camelot—Camelot," said I to myself. "I don't seem to remember hearing of it before. Name of the asylum, likely."

It was a soft, reposeful summer landscape, as lovely as a dream, and as lonesome as Sunday. The air was full of the smell of flowers, and the buzzing of insects, and the twittering of birds, and there were no people, no wagons, there was no stir of life, nothing going on. The road was mainly a winding path with hoof-prints in it, and now and then a faint trace of wheels on either side in the grass—wheels that apparently had a tire as broad as one's hand.

Presently a fair slip of a girl, about ten years old, with a cataract of golden hair streaming down over her shoulders, came along. Around her head she wore a hoop of flame-red poppies. It was as sweet an outfit as ever I saw, what there was of it. She walked indolently along, with a mind at rest, its peace reflected in her innocent face. The circus man paid no attention to her; didn't even seem to see her. And she—she was no more startled at his fantastic make-up than if she was used to his like every day of her life. She was going by as indifferently as she might have gone by a couple of cows; but when she happened to notice me, *then* there was a change! Up went her hands, and she was turned to stone; her mouth dropped open, her eyes stared wide and timorously, she was the picture of astonished curiosity touched with fear. And there she stood gazing, in a sort of stupefied fascination, till we turned a corner of the wood and were lost to her view. That she should be startled at me instead of at the other man, was too many for me; I couldn't make head or tail of it. And that she should seem to consider me a spectacle, and totally overlook her own merits in that respect, was another puzzling thing, and a display of magnanimity, too, that was surprising in one so young. There was food for thought here. I moved along as one in a dream.

As we approached the town, signs of life began to appear. At intervals we passed a wretched cabin, with a thatched roof, and about it small fields and garden patches in an indifferent state of cultivation. There were people, too; brawny men, with long, coarse, uncombed hair that hung down over their faces and made them look like animals. They and the women, as a rule, wore a coarse tow-linen robe that came well below the knee, and a rude sort of sandals, and many wore an iron collar. The small boys and girls were always naked; but nobody seemed to know it. All of these people stared at me, talked about me, ran into the huts and fetched out their families to gape at me; but nobody ever noticed that other fellow, except to make him humble salutation and get no response for their pains.

In the town were some substantial windowless houses of stone scattered among a wilderness of thatched cabins; the streets were mere crooked alleys, and unpaved; troops of dogs and nude children played in the sun and made life and noise; hogs roamed and rooted contentedly about, and one of them lay in a reeking wallow in the middle of the main thoroughfare and suckled her family. Presently there was a distant blare of military music; it came nearer, still nearer, and soon a noble cavalcade wound into view, glorious with plumed helmets and flashing mail and flaunting banners and rich doublets and horse-cloths and gilded spear heads; and through the muck and swine, and naked brats, and joyous dogs, and shabby huts it took its gallant way, and in its wake we followed. Followed through one winding alley and then another,—and climbing, always climbing—till at last we gained the breezy height where the huge castle stood. There was an exchange of bugle blasts; then a parley from the walls, where men-at-arms, in hauberk and morion marched back and forth with halberd at shoulder under flapping banners with the rude figure of a dragon displayed upon them; and then the great gates were flung open, the drawbridge was lowered, and the head of the cavalcade swept forward under the frowning arches; and we, following, soon found ourselves in a great paved court, with towers and turrets stretching up into the blue air on all the four sides; and all about us the dismount was going on, and much greeting and ceremony, and running to and fro, and a gay display of moving and intermingling colors, and an altogether pleasant stir and noise and confusion.

CHAPTER II

KING ARTHUR'S COURT

The moment I got a chance I slipped aside privately and touched an ancient common looking man on the shoulder and said, in an insinuating, confidential way—

"Friend, do me a kindness. Do you belong to the asylum, or are you just here on a visit or something like that?"

He looked me over stupidly, and said—

"Marry, fair sir, me seemeth—"

"That will do," I said; "I reckon you are a patient."

I moved away, cogitating, and at the same time keeping an eye out for any chance passenger in his right mind that might come along and give me some light. I judged I had found one, presently; so I drew him aside and said in his ear—

"If I could see the head keeper a minute—only just a minute—"

"Prithee do not let me."

"Let you *what?*"

"*Hinder* me, then, if the word please thee better." Then he went on to say he was an under-cook and could not stop to gossip, though he would like it another time; for it would comfort his very liver to know where I got my clothes. As he started away he pointed and said yonder was one who was idle enough for my purpose, and was seeking me besides, no doubt. This was an airy slim boy in shrimp-colored tights that made him look like a forked carrot; the rest of his gear was blue silk and dainty laces and ruffles; and he had long yellow curls, and wore a plumed pink satin cap tilted complacently over his ear. By his look, he was good-natured; by his gait, he was satisfied with himself. He was pretty enough to frame. He arrived, looked me over with a smiling and impudent curiosity; said he had come for me, and informed me that he was a page.

"Go 'long," I said; "you ain't more than a paragraph."

It was pretty severe, but I was nettled. However, it never phazed him; he didn't appear to know he was hurt. He began to talk and laugh, in happy, thoughtless, boyish fashion, as we walked along, and made himself old friends with me at once; asked me all sorts of questions about myself and about my clothes, but never waited for an answer—always chattered straight ahead, as if he didn't know he had asked a question and wasn't expecting any reply, until at last he happened to mention that he was born in the beginning of the year 513.

It made the cold chills creep over me! I stopped, and said, a little faintly:

"Maybe I didn't hear you just right. Say it again—and say it slow. What year was it?"

"513."

"513! You don't look it! Come, my boy, I am a stranger and friendless; be honest and honorable with me. Are you in your right mind?"

He said he was.

"Are these other people in their right minds?"

He said they were.

"And this isn't an asylum? I mean, it isn't a place where they cure crazy people?"

He said it wasn't.

"Well, then," I said, "either I am a lunatic, or something just as awful has happened. Now tell me, honest and true, where am I?"

"IN KING ARTHUR'S COURT."

I waited a minute, to let that idea shudder its way home, and then said:

"And according to your notions, what year is it now?"

"528—nineteenth of June."

I felt a mournful sinking at the heart, and muttered: "I shall never see my friends again—never, never again. They will not be born for more than thirteen hundred years yet."

I seemed to believe the boy, I didn't know why. *Something* in me seemed to believe him—my consciousness, as you may say; but my reason didn't. My reason straightway began to clamor; that was natural. I didn't know how to go about satisfying it, because I knew that the testimony of men wouldn't serve—my reason would say they were lunatics, and throw out their evidence. But all of a sudden I stumbled on the very thing, just by luck. I knew that the only total eclipse of the sun in the first half of the sixth century occurred on the 21st of June, A.D. 528, O.S., and began at 3 minutes after 12 noon. I also knew that no total eclipse of the sun was due in what to *me* was the present year—*i. e.,* 1879. So, if I could keep my anxiety and curiosity from eating the heart out of me for forty-eight hours, I should then find out for certain whether this boy was telling me the truth or not.

Wherefore, being a practical Connecticut man, I now shoved this whole problem clear out of my mind till its appointed day and hour should come, in order that I might turn all my attention to the circumstances of the present moment, and be alert and ready to make the most out of them that could be made. One thing at a time, is my motto—and just play that thing for all it is worth, even if it's only two pair and a jack. I made up my mind to two things; if it was still the nineteenth century and I was among lunatics and couldn't get away, I would presently boss that asylum or know the reason why; and if on the other hand it was really the sixth century, all right, I didn't want any softer thing: I would boss the whole country inside of three months; for I judged I would have the start of the best-educated man in the kingdom by a matter of thirteen hundred years and upwards. I'm not a man to waste time after my mind's made up and there's work on hand; so I said to the page—

"Now, Clarence, my boy—if that might happen to be your name—I'll get you to post me up a little if you don't mind. What is the name of that apparition that brought me here?"

"My master and thine? That is the good knight and great lord Sir Kay the Seneschal, foster brother to our liege the king."

"Very good; go on, tell me everything."

He made a long story of it; but the part that had immediate interest for me was this. He said I was Sir Kay's prisoner, and that in the due course of custom I would be flung into a dungeon and left there on scant commons until my friends ransomed me—unless I chanced to rot, first. I saw that the last chance had the best show, but I didn't waste any bother about that; time was too precious. The page said, further, that dinner was about ended in the great hall by this time, and that as soon as the sociability and the heavy drinking should begin, Sir Kay would have me in and exhibit me before King Arthur and his illustrious knights seated at the Table Round, and would brag about his exploit in capturing me, and would probably exaggerate the facts a little, but it wouldn't be good form for me to correct him, and not over safe, either; and when I was done being exhibited, then ho for the dungeon; but he, Clarence, would find a way to come and see me every now and then, and cheer me up, and help me get word to my friends.

Get word to my friends! I thanked him; I couldn't do less; and about this time a lackey came to say I was wanted; so Clarence led me in and took me off to one side and sat down by me.

Well, it was a curious kind of spectacle, and interesting. It was an immense place, and rather naked—yes, and full of loud contrasts. It was very, very lofty; so lofty that the banners descending from the arched beams and girders away up there floated in a sort of twilight; there was a stone-railed gallery at each end, high up, with musicians in the one, and women, clothed in stunning colors, in the other. The floor was of big stone flags laid in black and white squares, rather battered by age and use, and needing repair. As to ornament, there wasn't any, strictly speaking; though on the walls hung some huge tapestries which were probably taxed as works of art; battle-pieces, they were, with horses shaped like those which children cut out of paper or create in gingerbread; with men on them in scale armor whose scales are represented by round holes—so that the man's coat looks as if it had been done with a biscuit-punch. There was a fireplace big enough to camp in; and its projecting sides and hood, of carved and pillared stone-work, had the look of a cathedral door. Along the walls stood men-at-arms, in breastplate and morion, with halberds for their only weapon—rigid as statues; and that is what they looked like.

In the middle of this groined and vaulted public square was an oaken table which they called the Table Round. It was as large as a circus ring; and around it sat a great company of men dressed in such various and splendid colors that it hurt one's eyes to look at them. They wore their plumed hats, right along, except that whenever one addressed himself directly to the king, he lifted his hat a trifle just as he was beginning his remark.

Mainly they were drinking—from entire ox horns; but a few were still munching bread or gnawing beef bones. There was about an average of two dogs to one man; and these sat in expectant attitudes till a spent bone was flung to them, and then they went for it by brigades and divisions, with a rush, and there ensued a fight which filled the prospect with a tumultuous chaos of plunging heads and bodies and flashing tails, and the storm of howlings and barkings deafened all speech for the time; but that was no matter, for the dog-fight was always a bigger interest anyway; the men rose, sometimes, to observe it the better and bet on it, and the ladies and the musicians stretched themselves out over their balusters with the same object; and all broke into delighted ejaculations from time to time. In the end, the winning dog stretched himself out comfortably with his bone between his paws, and proceeded to growl over it, and gnaw it, and grease the floor with it, just as fifty others were already doing; and the rest of the court resumed their previous industries and entertainments.

As a rule the speech and behavior of these people were gracious and courtly; and I noticed that they were good and serious listeners when anybody was telling anything—I mean in a dog-fightless interval. And plainly, too, they were a childlike and innocent lot; telling lies of the stateliest pattern with a most gentle and winning naivety, and ready and willing to listen to anybody else's lie, and believe it, too. It was hard to associate them with anything cruel or dreadful; and yet they dealt in tales of blood and suffering with a guileless relish that made me almost forget to shudder.

I was not the only prisoner present. There were twenty or more. Poor devils, many of them were maimed, hacked, carved, in a frightful way: and their hair, their faces, their clothing, were caked with black and stiffened drenchings of blood. They were suffering sharp physical pain, of course; and weariness, and hunger and thirst, no doubt; and at least none had given them the comfort of a wash, or even the poor charity of a lotion for their wounds; yet you never heard them utter a moan or a groan, or saw them show any sign of restlessness, or any disposition to complain. The thought was forced upon me: "The rascals—*they* have served other people so in their day; it being their own turn, now, they were not expecting any better treatment than this; so their philosophical bearing is not an outcome of mental training, intellectual fortitude, reasoning; it is mere animal training; they are white Indians."

CHAPTER III

KNIGHTS OF THE TABLE ROUND

Mainly the Round Table talk was monologues—narrative accounts of the adventures in which these prisoners were captured and their friends and backers killed and stripped of their steeds and armor. As a general thing—as far as I could make out—these murderous adventures were not forays undertaken to avenge injuries, nor to settle old disputes or sudden fallings out; no, as a rule they were simply duels between strangers—duels between people who had never even been introduced to each other, and between whom existed no cause of offence whatever. Many a time I had seen a couple of boys, strangers, meet by chance, and say simultaneously, "I can lick you," and go at it on the spot; but I had always imagined until now that that sort of thing belonged to children only, and was a sign and mark of childhood; but here were these big boobies sticking to it and taking pride in it clear up into full age and beyond. Yet there was something very engaging about these great simple-hearted creatures, something attractive and lovable. There did not seem to be brains enough in the entire nursery, so to speak, to bait a fish-hook with; but you didn't seem to mind that, after a little, because you soon saw that brains were not needed in a society like that, and, indeed would have marred it, hindered it, spoiled its symmetry—perhaps rendered its existence impossible.

There was a fine manliness observable in almost every face; and in some a certain loftiness and sweetness that rebuked your belittling criticisms and stilled them. A most noble benignity and purity reposed in the countenance of him they called Sir Galahad, and likewise in the king's also; and there was majesty and greatness in the giant frame and high bearing of Sir Launcelot of the Lake.

There was presently an incident which centred the general interest upon this Sir Launcelot. At a sign from a sort of master of ceremonies, six or eight of the prisoners rose and came forward in a body and knelt on the floor and lifted up their hands toward the ladies' gallery and begged the grace of a word with the queen. The most conspicuously situated lady in that massed flower-bed of feminine show and finery inclined her head by way of assent, and then the spokesman of the prisoners delivered himself and his fellows into her hands for free pardon, ransom, captivity or death, as she in her good pleasure might elect; and this, as he said, he was doing by command of Sir Kay the Seneschal, whose prisoners they were, he having vanquished them by his single might and prowess in sturdy conflict in the field.

Surprise and astonishment flashed from face to face all over the house; the queen's gratified smile faded out at the name of Sir Kay, and she looked disappointed; and the page whispered in my ear with an accent and manner expressive of extravagant derision—

"Sir *Kay,* forsooth! Oh, call me pet names, dearest, call me a marine! In twice a thousand years shall the unholy invention of man labor at odds to beget the fellow to this majestic lie!"

Every eye was fastened with severe inquiry upon Sir Kay. But he was equal to the occasion. He got up and played his hand like a major—and took every trick. He said he would state the case, exactly according to the facts; he would tell the simple straight-forward tale, without comment of his own; "and then," said he, "if ye find glory and honor due, ye will give it unto him who is the mightiest man of his hands that ever bare shield or strake with sword in the ranks of Christian battle—even him that sitteth there!" and he pointed to Sir Launcelot. Ah, he fetched them; it was a rattling good stroke. Then he went on and told how Sir Launcelot, seeking adventures, some brief time gone by, killed seven giants at one sweep of his sword, and set a hundred and forty-two captive maidens free; and then went further, still seeking adventures, and found him (Sir Kay) fighting a desperate fight against nine foreign knights, and straightway took the battle solely into his own hands, and conquered the nine; and that night Sir Launcelot rose quietly, and dressed him in Sir Kay's armor and took Sir Kay's horse and gat him away into distant lands, and vanquished sixteen knights in one pitched battle and thirty-four in another; and all these and the former nine he made to swear that about Whitsuntide they would ride to Arthur's court and yield them to Queen Guenever's hands as captives of Sir Kay the Seneschal, spoil of his knightly prowess; and now here were these half-dozen, and the rest would be along as long as they might be healed of their desperate wounds.

Well, it was touching to see the queen blush and smile, and look embarrassed and happy, and fling furtive glances at Sir Launcelot that would have got him shot in Arkansas, to a dead certainty.

Everybody praised the valor and magnanimity of Sir Launcelot; and as for me, I was perfectly amazed, that one man, all by himself, should have been able to beat down and capture such battalions of practised fighters. I said as much to Clarence; but this mocking featherhead only said—

"An Sir Kay had had time to get another skin of sour wine into him, ye had seen the accompt doubled."

I looked at the boy in sorrow; and as I looked I saw the cloud of a deep despondency settle upon his countenance. I followed the direction of his eye, and saw that a very old and white-bearded man, clothed in a flowing black gown, had risen and was standing at the table upon unsteady legs, and feebly swaying his ancient head and surveying the company with his watery and wandering eye. The same suffering look that was in the page's face was observable in all the faces around—the look of dumb creatures who know that they must endure and make no moan.

"Marry, we shall have it again," sighed the boy; "that same old weary tale that he hath told a thousand times in the same words, and that he *will* tell till he dieth, every time he hath gotten his barrel full and feeleth his exaggeration-mill a-working. Would God I had died or I saw this day!"

"Who is it?"

"Merlin, the mighty liar and magician, perdition singe him for the weariness he worketh with his one tale! But that men fear him for that he hath the storms and the lightnings and all the devils that be in hell at his beck and call, they would have dug his entrails out these many years ago to get at that tale and squelch it. He telleth it always in the third person, making believe he is too modest to glorify himself—maledictions light upon him, misfortune be his dole! Good friend, prithee call me for evensong."

The boy nestled himself upon my shoulder and pretended to go to sleep. The old man began his tale; and presently the lad was asleep in reality; so also were the dogs, and the court, the lackeys, and the files of men-at-arms. The droning voice droned on; a soft snoring arose on all sides and supported it like a deep and subdued accompaniment of wind instruments. Some heads were bowed upon folded arms, some lay back with open mouths that issued unconscious music; the flies buzzed and bit, unmolested, the rats swarmed softly out from a hundred holes, and pattered about, and made themselves at home everywhere; and one of them sat up like a squirrel on the king's head and held a bit of cheese in its hands and nibbled it, and dribbled the crumbs in the king's face with naive and impudent irreverence. It was a tranquil scene, and restful to the weary eye and the jaded spirit.

This was the old man's tale. He said:

"Right so the king and Merlin departed, and went until an hermit that was a good man and a great leech. So the hermit searched all his wounds and gave him good salves; so the king was there three days, and then were his wounds well amended that he might ride and go, and so departed. And as they rode, Arthur said, I have no sword. No force,* said Merlin, hereby is a sword that shall be yours and I may. So they rode till they came to a lake, the which was a fair water and broad, and in the midst of the lake Arthur was ware of an arm clothed in white samite, that held a fair sword in that hand. Lo, said Merlin, yonder is that sword that I spake of. With that they saw a damsel going upon the lake. What damsel is that? said Arthur. That is the Lady of the lake, said Merlin; and within that lake is a rock, and therein is as fair a place as any on earth, and richly beseen, and this damsel will come to you anon, and then speak ye fair to her that she will give you that sword. Anon withal came the damsel unto Arthur and saluted him, and he her again. Damsel, said Arthur, what sword is that, that yonder the arm holdeth above the water? I would it were mine, for I have no sword. Sir Arthur King, said the damsel, that sword is mine, and if ye will give me a gift when I ask it you, ye shall have it. By my faith, said Arthur, I will give you what gift ye will ask. Well, said the damsel, go ye into yonder barge and row yourself to the sword, and take it and the scabbard with you, and I will ask my gift when I see my time. So Sir Arthur and Merlin alight, and tied

*No matter.

their horses to two trees, and so they went into the ship, and when
they came to the sword that the hand held, Sir Arthur took it up by
the handles, and took it with him. And the arm and the hand went
under the water; and so they came unto the land and rode forth.
And then Sir Arthur saw a rich pavilion. What signifieth yonder
pavilion? It is the knight's pavilion, said Merlin, that ye fought
with last, Sir Pellinore, but he is out, he is not there; he hath ado
with a knight of yours, that hight Egglame, and they have fought
and he hath chased him even to Carlion, and we shall meet with
him anon in the highway. That is well said, said Arthur, now have
I a sword, now will I wage battle with him, and be avenged on him.
Sir, ye shall not so, said Merlin, for the knight is weary of fighting
and chasing, so that ye shall have no worship to have ado with him;
also, he will not lightly be matched of one knight living; and
therefore it is my counsel, let him pass, for he shall do you good
service in short time, and his sons, after his days. Also ye shall see
that day in short space ye shall be right glad to give him your sister
to wed. When I see him, I will do as ye advise me, said Arthur.
Then Sir Arthur looked on the sword, and liked it passing well.
Whether liketh you better, said Merlin, the sword or the scabbard?
Me liketh better the sword, said Arthur. Ye are more unwise, said
Merlin, for the scabbard is worth ten of the sword, for while ye
have the scabbard upon you ye shall never lose no blood, be ye
never so sore wounded; therefore, keep well the scabbard always
with you. So they rode unto Carlion, and by the way they met with
Sir Pellinore; but Merlin had done such a craft that Pellinore saw
not Arthur, and he passed by without any words. I marvel, said
Arthur, that the knight would not speak. Sir, said Merlin, he saw
you not; for and he had seen you ye had not lightly departed. So
they came unto Carlion, whereof his knights were passing glad.
And when they heard of his adventures they marvelled that he
would jeopard his person so alone. But all men of worship said it
was merry to be under such a chieftain that would put his person in
adventure as other poor knights did."

CHAPTER IV

SIR DINADAN THE HUMORIST

It seemed to me that this quaint lie was most simply and
beautifully told; but then I had heard it only once, and that makes
a difference; it was pleasant to the others when it was fresh, no
doubt.

Sir Dinadan the Humorist was the first to awake, and he soon
roused the rest with a practical joke of a sufficiently poor quality.
He tied some metal mugs to a dog's tail and turned him loose, and

he tore around and around the place in a frenzy of fright, with all
the other dogs bellowing after him and battering and crashing
against everything that came in their way and making altogether a
chaos of confusion and a most deafening din and turmoil; at which
every man and woman of the multitude laughed till the tears
flowed, and some fell out of their chairs and wallowed on the floor
in ecstasy. It was just like so many children. Sir Dinadan was so
proud of his exploit that he could not keep from telling over and
over again, to weariness, how the immortal idea happened to occur
to him; and as is the way with humorists of his breed, he was still
laughing at it after everybody else had got through. He was so set
up that he concluded to make a speech—of course a humorous
speech. I think I never heard so many old played-out jokes strung
together in my life. He was worse than the minstrels, worse than
the clown in the circus. It seemed peculiarly sad to sit here, thirteen
hundred years before I was born and listen again to poor, flat,
worm-eaten jokes that had given me the dry gripes when I was a
boy thirteen hundred years afterwards. It about convinced me that
there isn't any such thing as a new joke possible. Everybody
laughed at these antiquities—but then they always do; I had
noticed that, centuries later. However, of course the scoffer didn't
laugh—I mean the boy. No, he scoffed; there wasn't anything he
wouldn't scoff at. He said the most of Sir Dinadan's jokes were
rotten and the rest were petrified. I said "petrified" was good; as I
believed, myself, that the only right way to classify the majestic
ages of some of those jokes was by geologic periods. But that neat
idea hit the boy in a blank place, for geology hadn't been invented
yet. However, I made a note of the remark, and calculated to
educate the commonwealth up to it if I pulled through. It is no use
to throw a good thing away merely because the market isn't ripe
yet.

Now Sir Kay arose and began to fire up on his history-mill with
me for fuel. It was time for me to feel serious, and I did. Sir Kay
told how he had encountered me in a far land of barbarians, who
all wore the same ridiculous garb that I did—a garb that was a
work of enchantment, and intended to make the wearer secure
from hurt by human hands. However, he had nullified the force of
the enchantment by prayer, and had killed my thirteen knights in
a three-hours' battle, and taken me prisoner, sparing my life in
order that so strange a curiosity as I was might be exhibited to the
wonder and admiration of the king and the court. He spoke of me
all the time, in the blandest way, as "this prodigious giant," and
"this horrible sky-towering monster," and "this tusked and taloned
man-devouring ogre;" and everybody took in all this bosh in the
naivest way, and never smiled or seemed to notice that there was
any discrepancy between these watered statistics and me. He said
that in trying to escape from him I sprang into the top of a tree two

hundred cubits high at a single bound, but he dislodged me with a stone the size of a cow, which "all-to brast" the most of my bones, and then swore me to appear at Arthur's court for sentence. He ended by condemning me to die at noon on the 21st; and was so little concerned about it that he stopped to yawn before he named the date.

I was in a dismal state by this time; indeed, I was hardly enough in my right mind to keep the run of a dispute that sprung up as to how I had better be killed, the possibility of the killing being doubted by some, because of the enchantment in my clothes. And yet it was nothing but an ordinary suit of fifteen-dollar slop-shops. Still, I was sane enough to notice this detail, to wit: many of the terms used in the most matter-of-fact way by this great assemblage of the first ladies and gentlemen in the land would have made a Comanche blush. Indelicacy is too mild a term to convey the idea. However, I had read "Tom Jones," and "Roderick Random," and other books of that kind, and knew that the highest and first ladies and gentlemen in England had remained little or no cleaner in their talk, and in the morals and conduct which such talk implies, clear up to a hundred years ago; in fact clear into our own nineteenth century—in which century, broadly speaking, the earliest samples of the real lady and real gentleman discoverable in English history—or in European history, for that matter—may be said to have made their appearance. Suppose the mouths of his characters, had allowed the characters to speak for themselves? We should have had talk from Rachel and Ivanhoe and the soft lady Rowena which would embarrass a tramp in our day. However, to the unconsciously indelicate all things are delicate. King Arthur's people were not aware that they were indecent, and I had presence of mind enough not to mention it.

They were so troubled about my enchanted clothes that they were mightily relieved, at last, when old Merlin swept the difficulty away for them with a common-sense hint. He asked them why they were so dull—why didn't it occur to them to strip me. In half a minute I was as naked as a pair of tongs! And dear, dear, to think of it: I was the only embarrassed person there. Everybody discussed me; and did it as unconcernedly as if I had been a cabbage. Queen Guenever was as naively interested as the rest, and said she had never seen anybody with legs just like mine before. It was the only compliment I got—if it was a compliment.

Finally, I was carried off in one direction, and my perilous clothes in another. I was shoved into a dark and narrow cell in a dungeon, with some scant remnants for dinner, some mouldy straw for a bed, and no end of rats for company.

CHAPTER V

AN INSPIRATION

I was so tired that even my fears were not able to keep me awake long.

When I next came to myself, I seemed to have been asleep a very long time. My first thought was, "Well, what an astonishing dream I've had! I reckon I've waked only just in time to keep from being hanged or drowned or burned, or something. . . . I'll nap again till the whistle blows, and then I'll go down to the arms factory and have it out with Hercules."

But just then I heard the harsh music of rusty chains and bolts, a light flashed in my eyes, and that butterfly, Clarence, stood before me! I gasped with surprise; my breath almost got away from me.

"What!" I said, "you here yet? Go along with the rest of the dream! scatter!"

But he only laughed, in his light-hearted way, and fell to making fun of my sorry plight.

"All right," I said resignedly, "let the dream go on; I'm in no hurry."

"Prithee what dream?"

"What dream? Why, the dream that I am in Arthur's court—a person who never existed; and that I am talking to you, who are nothing but a work of the imagination."

"Oh, la, indeed! and is it a dream that you're to be burned to-morrow? Ho-ho—answer me that!"

The shock that went through me was distressing. I now began to reason that my situation was in the last degree serious, dream or no dream; for I knew by past experience of the life-like intensity of dreams, that to be burned to death, even in a dream, would be very far from being a jest, and was a thing to be avoided, by any means, fair or foul, that I could contrive. So I said beseechingly:

"Ah, Clarence, good boy, only friend I've got,—for you *are* my friend, aren't you?—don't fail me; help me to devise some way of escaping from this place!"

"Now do but hear thyself! Escape? Why, man, the corridors are in guard and keep of men-at-arms."

"No doubt, no doubt. But how many, Clarence? Not many, I hope?"

"Full a score. One may not hope to escape." After a pause—hesitatingly: "and there be other reasons—and weightier."

"Other ones? What are they?"

"Well, they say—oh, but I daren't, indeed I daren't!"

"Why, poor lad, what is the matter? Why do you blench? Why do you tremble so?"

"Oh, in sooth, there is need! I do want to tell you, but—"

"Come, come, be brave, be a man—speak out, there's a good lad!"

He hesitated, pulled one way by desire, the other way by fear; then he stole to the door and peeped out, listening; and finally crept close to me and put his mouth to my ear and told me his fearful news in a whisper, and with all the cowering apprehension of one who was venturing upon awful ground and speaking of things whose very mention might be freighted with death.

"Merlin, in his malice, has woven a spell about this dungeon, and there bides not the man in these kingdoms that would be desperate enough to essay to cross its lines with you! Now God pity me, I have told it! Ah, be kind to me, be merciful to a poor boy who means thee well; for an thou betray me I am lost!"

I laughed the only really refreshing laugh I had had for some time; and shouted—

"Merlin has wrought a spell! *Merlin,* forsooth! That cheap old humbug, that maundering old ass? Bosh, pure bosh, the silliest bosh in the world! Why, it does seem to me that of all the childish, idiotic, chuckle-headed, chicken-livered superstitions that ev— oh, damn Merlin!"

But Clarence had slumped to his knees before I had half finished, and he was like to go out of his mind with fright.

"Oh, beware! These are awful words! Any moment these walls may crumble upon us if you say such things. Oh call them back before it is too late!"

Now this strange exhibition gave me a good idea and set me to thinking. If everybody about here was so honestly and sincerely afraid of Merlin's pretended magic as Clarence was, certainly a superior man like me ought to be shrewd enough to contrive some way to take advantage of such a state of things. I went on thinking, and worked out a plan. Then I said:

"Get up. Pull yourself together; look me in the eye. Do you know why I laughed?"

"No—but for our blessed Lady's sake, do it no more."

"Well, I'll tell you why I laughed. Because I'm a magician myself."

"Thou!" The boy recoiled a step, and caught his breath, for the thing hit him rather sudden; but the aspect which he took on was very, very respectful, I took quick note of that; it indicated that a humbug didn't need to have a reputation in this asylum; people stood ready to take him at his word, without that. I resumed:

"I've known Merlin seven hundred years, and he—"

"Seven hun—"

"Don't interrupt me. He has died and come alive again thirteen times, and travelled under a new name every time: Smith, Jones, Robinson, Jackson, Peters, Haskins, Merlin—a new alias every time

he turns up. I knew him in Egypt three hundred years ago; I knew
him in India five hundred years ago—he is always blethering
around in my way, everywhere I go; he makes me tired. He don't
amount to shucks, as a magician; knows some of the old common
tricks, but has never got beyond the rudiments, and never will. He
is well enough for the provinces—one-night stands and that sort of
thing, you know—but dear me, *he* oughtn't to set up for an
expert—anyway not where there's a real artist. Now look here,
Clarence, I am going to stand your friend, right along, and in
return you must be mine. I want you to do me a favor. I want you
to get word to the king that I am a magician myself—and the
Supreme Grand High-yu-Muck-amuck and head of the tribe, at
that; and I want him to be made to understand that I am just
quietly arranging a little calamity here that will make the fur fly in
these realms if Sir Kay's project is carried out and any harm comes
to me. Will you get that to the king for me?"

The poor boy was in such a state that he could hardly answer
me. It was pitiful to see a creature so terrified, so unnerved, so
demoralized. But he promised everything; and on my side he made
me promise over and over again that I would remain his friend,
and never turn against him or cast any enchantments upon him.
Then he worked his way out, staying himself with his hand along
the wall, like a sick person.

Presently this thought occurred to me: how heedless I have been!
When the boy gets calm, he will wonder why a great magician like
me should have begged a boy like him to help me get out of this
place; he will put this and that together, and will see that I am a
humbug.

I worried over that heedless blunder for an hour, and called
myself a great many hard names, meantime. But finally it occurred
to me all of a sudden that these animals didn't reason; that *they*
never put this and that together; that all their talk showed that
they didn't know a discrepancy when they saw it. I was at
rest, then.

But as soon as one is at rest, in this world, off he goes on
something else to worry about. It occurred to me that I had made
another blunder: I had sent the boy off to alarm his betters with a
threat—I intending to invent a calamity at my leisure; now the
people who are the readiest and eagerest and willingest to swallow
miracles are the very ones who are hungriest to see you perform
them; suppose I should be called on for a sample? Suppose I
should be asked to name my calamity? Yes, I had made a blunder;
I ought to have invented my calamity first. "What shall I do? what
can I say, to gain a little time?" I was in trouble again; in the
deepest kind of trouble: . . . "There's a footstep!—they're coming.
If I had only just a moment to think. . . . Hoof, I've got it. I'm
all right."

You see, it was the eclipse. It came into my mind, in the nick of time, how Columbus, or Cortez, or one of those people, played an eclipse as a saving trump once, on some savages, and I saw my chance. I could play it myself, now; and it wouldn't be any plagiarism, either, because I should get it in nearly a thousand years ahead of those parties.

Clarence came in, subdued, distressed, and said:

"I hasted the message to our liege the king, and straightway he had me to his presence. He was frighted even to the marrow, and was minded to give order for your instant enlargement, and that you be clothed in fine raiment and lodged as befitted one so great; but then came Merlin and spoiled all; for he persuaded the king that you are mad, and know not whereof you speak; and said your threat is but foolishness and idle vaporing. They disputed long, but in the end, Merlin, scoffing, said, 'Wherefore hath he not *named* his brave calamity? Verily it is because he cannot.' This thrust did in a most sudden sort close the king's mouth, and he could offer naught to turn the argument; and so, reluctant, and full loth to do you the discourtesy, he yet prayeth you to consider his perplexed case, as noting how the matter stands, and name the calamity—if so be you have determined the nature of it and the time of its coming. Oh, prithee delay not; to delay at such a time were to double and treble the perils that already compass thee about. Oh, be thou wise—name the calamity!"

I allowed silence to accumulate while I got my impressiveness together, and then said:

"How long have I been shut up in this hole?"

"Ye were shut up when yesterday was well spent. It is 9 of the morning now."

"No! Then I have slept well, sure enough. Nine in the morning now! And yet it is the very complexion of midnight, to a shade. This is the 20th, then?"

"The 20th—yes."

"And I am to be burned alive to-morrow." The boy shuddered.

"At high noon."

"Now then, I will tell you what to say." I paused, and stood over that cowering lad a whole minute in awful silence; then, in a voice deep, measured, charged with doom, I began, and rose by dramatically graded stages to my colossal climax, which I delivered in as sublime and noble a way as ever I did such a thing in my life: "Go back and tell the king that at that hour I will smother the whole world in the dead blackness of midnight; I will blot out the sun, and he shall never shine again; the fruits of the earth shall rot for lack of light and warmth, and the peoples of the earth shall famish and die, to the last man!"

I had to carry the boy out myself, he sunk into such a collapse. I handed him over to the soldiers, and went back.

CHAPTER VI

THE ECLIPSE

In the stillness and the darkness, realization soon began to supplement knowledge. The mere knowledge of a fact is pale; but when you come to *realize* your fact, it takes on color. It is all the difference between hearing of a man being stabbed to the heart, and seeing it done. In the stillness and the darkness, the knowledge that I was in deadly danger took to itself deeper and deeper meaning all the time; a something which was realization crept inch by inch through my veins and turned me cold.

But it is a blessed provision of nature that at times like these, as soon as a man's mercury has got down to a certain point there comes a revulsion, and he rallies. Hope springs up, and cheerfulness along with it, and then he is in good shape to do something for himself, if anything can be done. When my rally came, it came with a bound. I said to myself that my eclipse would be sure to save me, and make me the greatest man in the kingdom besides; and straightway my mercury went up to the top of the tube, and my solicitudes all vanished. I was as happy a man as there was in the world. I was even impatient for to-morrow to come, I so wanted to gather-in that great triumph and be the centre of all the nation's wonder and reverence. Besides, in a business way it would be the making of me; I knew that.

Meantime there was one thing which had got pushed into the background of my mind. That was the half-conviction that when the nature of my proposed calamity should be reported to those superstitious people, it would have such an effect that they would want to compromise. So, by-and-by when I heard footsteps coming, that thought was recalled to me, and I said to myself, "As sure as anything, it's the compromise. Well, if it is good, all right, I will accept; but if it isn't, I mean to stand my ground and play my hand for all it is worth."

"The stake is ready. Come!"

The stake! The strength went out of me, and I almost fell down. It is hard to get one's breath at such a time, such lumps come into one's throat and such gaspings; but as soon as I could speak, I said:

"But this is a mistake—the execution is to-morrow."

"Order changed; been set forward a day. Haste thee!"

I was lost. There was no help for me. I was dazed, stupefied; I had no command over myself; I only wandered purposelessly about like one out of his mind; so the soldiers took hold of me, and pulled me along with them, out of the cell and along the maze of underground corridors, and finally into the fierce glare of daylight and the upper world. As we stepped into the vast enclosed court of the castle I got a shock; for the first thing I saw was the stake, standing in the centre, and near it the piled fagots and a monk. On all four sides of the court the seated multitudes rose rank above rank, forming sloping terraces that were rich with color. The king and the queen sat in their thrones, the most conspicuous figures there, of course.

To note all this, occupied but a second. The next second Clarence had slipped from some place of concealment and was pouring news into my ear, his eyes beaming with triumph and gladness. He said:

" 'Tis through *me* the change was wrought! And main hard have I worked to do it, too. But when I revealed to them the calamity in store, and saw how mighty was the terror it did engender, then saw I also that this was the time to strike! Wherefore I diligently pretended, unto this and that and the other one, that your power against the sun could not reach its full until the morrow; and so if any would save the sun and the world, you must be slain to-day, whilst your enchantments are but in the weaving and lack potency. Odsbodikins, it was but a dull lie, a most indifferent invention, but you should have seen them seize it and swallow it, in the frenzy of their fright, as it were salvation sent from heaven; and all the while was I laughing in my sleeve the one moment, to see them so cheaply deceived, and glorifying God the next, that He was content to let the meanest of His creatures be His instrument to the saving of thy life. Ah, how happy has the matter sped! You will not need to do the sun a *real* hurt—ah, forget not that, on your soul forget it not! Only make a little darkness—only the littlest little darkness, mind, and cease with that. It will be sufficient. They will see that I spoke falsely,—being ignorant, as they will fancy—and with the falling of the first shadow of that darkness you shall see them go mad with fear; and they will set you free and make you great! Go to thy triumph, now! But remember—ah, good friend, I implore thee remember my supplication, and do the blessed sun no hurt. For *my* sake, thy true friend."

I choked out some words through my grief and misery; as much as to say I would spare the sun; for which the lad's eyes paid me back with such deep and loving gratitude that I had not the heart to tell him his good-hearted foolishness had ruined me and sent me to my death.

As the soldiers assisted me across the court the stillness was so profound that if I had been blindfold I should have supposed I was in a solitude instead of walled in by four thousand people. There was not a movement perceptible in those masses of humanity; they were as rigid as stone images, and as pale; and dread sat upon every countenance. This hush continued while I was being chained to the stake; it still continued while the fagots were carefully and tediously piled about my ankles, my knees, my thighs, my body. Then there was a pause, and a deeper hush, if possible, and a man knelt down at my feet with a glazing torch; the multitude strained forward, gazing, and parting slightly from their seats without knowing it; the monk raised his hands above my head, and his eyes toward the blue sky, and began some words in Latin; in this attitude he droned on and on, a little while, and then stopped. I waited two or three moments; then looked up; he was standing there petrified. With a common impulse the multitude rose slowly up and stared into the sky. I followed their eyes; as sure as guns, there was my eclipse beginning! The life went boiling through my veins; I was a new man! The rim of black spread slowly into the sun's disk, my heart beat higher and higher, and still the assemblage and the priest stared into the sky, motionless. I knew that this gaze would be turned upon me, next. When it was, I was ready. I was in one of the most grand attitudes I ever struck, with my arm stretched up pointing to the sun. It was a noble effect. You could *see* the shudder sweep the mass like a wave. Two shouts rang out, one close upon the heels of the other:

"Apply the torch!"

"I forbid it!"

The one was from Merlin, the other from the king. Merlin started from his place—to apply the torch himself, I judged. I said:

"Stay where you are. If any man moves—even the king—before I give him leave, I will blast him with thunder, I will consume him with lightnings!"

The multitude sank meekly into their seats, and I was just expecting they would. Merlin hesitated a moment or two, and I was on pins and needles during that little while. Then he sat down, and I took a good breath; for I knew I was master of the situation now. The king said:

"Be merciful, fair sir, and essay no further in this perilous matter, lest disaster follow. It was reported to us that your powers could not attain unto their full strength until the morrow; but—"

"Your Majesty thinks the report may have been a lie? It *was* a lie."

That made an immense effect; up went appealing hands everywhere, and the king was assailed with a storm of supplications that I might be bought off at any price, and the calamity stayed. The king was eager to comply. He said:

"Name any terms, reverend sir, even to the halving of my kingdom; but banish this calamity, spare the sun!"

My fortune was made. I would have taken him up in a minute, but *I* couldn't stop an eclipse; the thing was out of the question. So I asked time to consider. The king said—

"How long—ah, how long, good sir? Be merciful; look, it groweth darker, moment by moment. Prithee how long?"

"Not long. Half an hour—maybe an hour."

There were a thousand pathetic protests, but I couldn't shorten up any, for I couldn't remember how long a total eclipse lasts. I was in a puzzled condition, anyway, and wanted to think. Something was wrong about that eclipse, and the fact was very unsettling. If this wasn't the one I was after, how was I to tell whether this was the sixth century, or nothing but a dream? Dear me, if I could only prove it was the latter! Here was a glad new hope. If the boy was right about the date, and this was surely the 20th, it *wasn't* the sixth century. I reached for the monk's sleeve, in considerable excitement, and asked him what day of the month it was.

Hang him, he said it was the *twenty-first!* It made me turn cold to hear him. I begged him not to make any mistake about it; but he was sure; he knew it was the 21st. So, that feather-headed boy had botched things again! The time of the day was right for the eclipse; I had seen that for myself, in the beginning, by the dial that was near by. Yes, I *was* in King Arthur's court, and I might as well make the most out of it I could.

The darkness was steadily growing, the people becoming more and more distressed. I now said:

"I have reflected, Sir King. For a lesson, I will let this darkness proceed, and spread night in the world; but whether I blot out the sun for good, or restore it, shall rest with you. These are the terms, to wit: You shall remain king over all your dominions, and receive all the glories and honors that belong to the kingship; but you shall appoint me your perpetual minister and executive, and give me for my services one per cent. of such actual increase of revenue over and above its present amount as I may succeed in creating for the state. If I can't live on that, I sha'n't ask anybody to give me a lift. Is it satisfactory?"

There was a prodigious roar of applause, and out of the midst of it the king's voice rose, saying:

"Away with his bonds, and set him free! and do him homage, high and low, rich and poor, for he is become the king's right hand, is clothed with power and authority, and his seat is upon the highest step of the throne! Now sweep away his creeping night, and bring the light and cheer again, that all the world may bless thee."

But I said:

"That a common man should be shamed before the world, is nothing; but it were dishonor to the *king* if any that saw his minister naked should not also see him delivered from his shame. If I might ask that my clothes be brought again—"

"They are not meet," the king broke in. "Fetch raiment of another sort; clothe him like a prince!"

My idea worked. I wanted to keep things as they were till the eclipse was total, otherwise they would be trying again to get me to dismiss the darkness, and of course I couldn't do it. Sending for the clothes gained some delay, but not enough. So I had to make another excuse. I said it would be but natural if the king should change his mind and repent to some extent of what he had done under excitement; therefore I would let the darkness grow a while, and if at the end of a reasonable time the king had kept his mind the same, the darkness should be dismissed. Neither the king nor anybody else was satisfied with that arrangement, but I had to stick to my point.

It grew darker and darker and blacker and blacker, while I struggled with those awkward sixth-century clothes. It got to be pitch dark, at last, and the multitude groaned with horror to feel the cold uncanny night breezes fan through the place and see the stars come out and twinkle in the sky. At last the eclipse was total, and I was very glad of it, but everybody else was in misery; which was quite natural. I said:

"The king, by his silence, still stands to the terms." Then I lifted up my hands—stood just so a moment—then I said, with the most awful solemnity: "Let the enchantment dissolve and pass harmless away!"

There was no response, for a moment, in that deep darkness and that graveyard hush. But when the silver rim of the sun pushed itself out, a moment or two later, the assemblage broke loose with a vast shout and came pouring down like a deluge to smother me with blessings and gratitude; and Clarence was not the last of the wash, be sure.

CHAPTER VII

MERLIN'S TOWER

Inasmuch as I was now the second personage in the Kingdom, as far as political power and authority were concerned, much was made of me. My raiment was of silks and velvets and cloth of gold, and by consequence was very showy, also uncomfortable. But habit would soon reconcile me to my clothes; I was aware of that. I was given the choicest suite of apartments in the castle, after the king's. They were aglow with loud-colored silken hangings, but the stone floors had nothing but rushes on them for a carpet, and they misfit rushes at that, being not all of one breed. As for conveniences properly speaking, there weren't any. I mean *little* conveniences; it is the little conveniences that make the real comfort of life. The big oaken chairs, graced with rude carvings, were well enough, but that was the stopping-place. There was no soap, no matches, no looking-glass—except a metal one, about as powerful as a pail of water. And not a chromo. I had been used to chromos for years, and I saw now that without my suspecting it a passion for art had got worked into the fabric of my being, and was become a part of me. It made me homesick to look around over this proud and gaudy but heartless barrenness and remember that in our house in East Hartford, all unpretending as it was, you couldn't go into a room but you would find an insurance-chromo, or at least a three-color God-Bless-Our-Home over the door; and in the parlor we had nine. But here, even in my grand room of state, there wasn't anything in the nature of a picture except a thing the size of a bed-quilt, which was either woven or knitted, (it had darned places in it,) and nothing in it was the right color or the right shape; and as for proportions, even Raphael himself couldn't have botched them more formidably, after all his practice on those nightmares they call his "celebrated Hampton court cartoons." Raphael was a bird. We had several of his chromos; one was his "Miraculous Draught of Fishes," where he puts in a miracle of his own—puts three men into a canoe which wouldn't have held a dog without upsetting. I always admired to study R.'s art, it was so fresh and unconventional.

There wasn't even a bell or a speaking-tube in the castle. I had a great many servants, and those that were on duty lolled in the anteroom; and when I wanted one of them I had to go and call for him. There was no gas, there were no candles; a bronze dish half full of boarding-house butter with a blazing rag floating in it was the thing that produced what was regarded as light. A lot of these hung along the walls and modified the dark, just toned it down enough to make it dismal. If you went out at night, your servants carried torches. There were no books, pens, paper, or ink, and no glass in the openings they believed to be windows. It is a little thing—glass is—until it is absent, then it becomes a big thing. But perhaps the worst of all was, that there wasn't any sugar, coffee, tea or tobacco. I saw that I was just another Robinson Crusoe cast away on an uninhabited island, with no society but some more or less tame animals, and if I wanted to make life bearable I must do as he did—invent, contrive, create, reorganize things; set brain and hand to work, and keep them busy. Well, that was in my line.

One thing troubled me along at first—the immense interest which people took in me. Apparently the whole nation wanted a look at me. It soon transpired that the eclipse had scared the British world almost to death: that while it lasted the whole country, from one end to the other, was in a pitiable state of panic, and the churches, hermitages, and monkeries overflowed with praying and weeping poor creatures who thought the end of the world was come. Then had followed the news that the producer of this awful event was a stranger, a mighty magician at Arthur's court; that he could have blown out the sun like a candle, and was just going to do it when his mercy was purchased, and he then dissolved his enchantments, and was now recognized and honored as the man who had by his unaided might saved the globe from destruction and its peoples from extinction. Now if you consider that everybody believed that, and not only believed it but never even dreamed of doubting it, you will easily understand that there was not a person in all Britain that would not have walked fifty miles to get a sight of me. Of course I was all the talk—all other subjects were dropped; even the king became suddenly a person of minor interest and notoriety. Within twenty-four hours the delegations began to arrive, and from that time onward for a fortnight they kept coming. The village was crowded, and all the countryside. I had to go out a dozen times a day and show myself to these reverent and awe-stricken multitudes. It came to be a great burden, as to time and trouble, but of course it was at the same time compensatingly agreeable to be so celebrated and such a centre of homage. It turned Brer Merlin green with envy and spite, which was a great satisfaction to me. But there was one thing I couldn't understand; nobody had asked for an autograph. I spoke to Clarence about it. By George, I had to explain to him what it was. Then he said nobody in the country could read or write but a few dozen priests. Land! think of that.

There was another thing that troubled me a little. Those multitudes presently began to agitate for another miracle. That was natural. To be able to carry back to their far homes the boast that they had seen the man who could command the sun, riding in the heavens, and be obeyed, would make them great in the eyes of their neighbors, and envied by them all; but to be able to also say they had seen him work a miracle themselves—why, people would come a distance to see *them*. The pressure got to be pretty strong. There was going to be an eclipse of the moon, and I knew the date and hour, but it was too far away. Two years. I would have given a good deal for license to hurry it up and use it now when there was a big market for it. It seemed a great pity to have it wasted, so, and come lagging along at a time when a body wouldn't have any use for it as like as not. If it had been booked for only a month away, I could have sold it short; but as matters stood, I couldn't seem to cipher out any way to make it do me any good, so I gave up trying. Next, Clarence found that old Merlin was making himself busy on the sly among those people. He was spreading a report that I was a humbug, and that the reason I didn't accommodate the people with a miracle was because I couldn't. I saw that I must do something. I presently thought out a plan.

By my authority as executive I threw Merlin into prison—the same cell I had occupied myself. Then I gave public notice by herald trumpet that I should be busy with affairs of state for a fortnight, but about the end of that time I would take a moment's leisure and blow up Merlin's stone tower by fires from heaven; in the meantime, whoso listened to evil reports about me, let him beware. Furthermore, I would perform but this one miracle at this time, and no more; if it failed to satisfy and any murmured, I would turn the murmurers into horses, and make them useful. Quiet ensued.

I took Clarence into my confidence, to a certain degree, and we went to work privately. I told him that this was a sort of miracle that required a trifle of preparation, and that it would be sudden death to ever talk about these preparations to anybody. That made his mouth safe enough. Clandestinely we made a few bushels of first-rate blasting-powder, and I superintended my armorers while they constructed a lightning-rod and some wires. This old stone tower was very massive—and rather ruinous, too, for it was Roman, and four hundred years old. Yes, and handsome, after a rude fashion, and clothed with ivy from base to summit, as with a shirt of scale mail. It stood on a lonely eminence, in good view from the castle, and about half a mile away.

Working by night, we stowed the powder in the tower—dug stones out, on the inside, and buried the powder in the walls themselves, which were fifteen feet thick at the base. We put in a peck at a time, in a dozen places. We could have blown up the Tower of London with these charges. When the thirteenth night was come we put up our lightning-rod, bedded it in one of the batches of powder, and ran wires from it to the other batches. Everybody had shunned that locality from the day of my proclamation, but on the morning of the fourteenth I thought best to warn the people, through the heralds, to keep clear away—a quarter of a mile away. Then added, by command, that at some time during the twenty-four hours I would consummate the miracle, but would first give a brief notice; by flags on the castle towers, if in the daytime, by torch-baskets in the same places if at night.

Thunder-showers had been tolerably frequent of late, and I was not much afraid of a failure; still, I shouldn't have cared for a delay of a day or two; I should have explained that I was busy with affairs of state, yet, and the people must wait.

Of course we had a blazing sunny day—almost the first one without a cloud for three weeks; things always happen so. I kept secluded, and watched the weather. Clarence dropped in from time to time and said the public excitement was growing and growing all the time, and the whole country filling up with human masses as far as one could see from the battlements. At last the wind sprang up and a cloud appeared—in the right quarter, too, and just at nightfall. For a little while I watched that distant cloud spread and blacken, then I judged it was time for me to appear. I ordered the torch-baskets to be lit, and Merlin liberated and sent to me. A quarter of an hour later I ascended the parapet and there found the king and the court assembled and gazing off in the darkness toward Merlin's Tower. Already the darkness was so heavy that one could not see far; these people, and the old turrets, being partly in deep shadow and partly in the red glow from the great torch-baskets overhead, made a good deal of a picture.

Merlin arrived in a gloomy mood. I said:

"You wanted to burn me alive when I had not done you any harm, and latterly you have been trying to injure my professional reputation. Therefore I am going to call down fire and blow up your tower, but it is only fair to give you a chance; now if you think you can break my enchantments and ward off the fires, step to the bat, it's your innings."

"I can, fair sir, and I will. Doubt it not."

He drew an imaginary circle on the stones of the roof, and burnt a pinch of powder in it which sent up a small cloud of aromatic smoke, whereat everybody fell back, and began to cross themselves and get uncomfortable. Then he began to mutter and make passes in the air with his hands. He worked himself up slowly and gradually into a sort of frenzy, and got to thrashing around with his arms like the sails of a windmill. By this time the storm had about reached us; the gusts of wind were flaring the torches and making the shadows swash about, the first heavy drops of rain were falling, the world abroad was black as pitch, the lightning began to wink fitfully. Of course my rod would be loading itself now. In fact, things were imminent. So I said:

"You have had time enough. I have given you every advantage, and not interfered. It is plain your magic is weak. It is only fair that I begin now."

I made about three passes in the air, and then there was an awful crash and that old tower leaped into the sky in chunks, along with a vast volcanic fountain of fire that turned night to noonday, and showed a thousand acres of human beings grovelling on the ground in a general collapse of consternation. Well, it rained mortar and masonry the rest of the week. This was the report; but probably the facts would have modified it.

It was an effective miracle. The great bothersome temporary population vanished. There were a good many thousand tracks in the mud the next morning, but they were all outward bound. If I had advertised another miracle I couldn't have raised an audience with a sheriff.

Merlin's stock was flat. The king wanted to stop his wages; he even wanted to banish him, but I interfered. I said he would be useful to work the weather, and attend to small matters like that, and I would give him a lift now and then when his poor little parlor-magic soured on him. There wasn't a rag of his tower left, but I had the government rebuild it for him, and advised him to take boarders; but he was too high-toned for that. And as for being grateful, he never even said thank-you. He was a rather hard lot, take him how you might; but then you couldn't fairly expect a man to be sweet that had been set back so.

CHAPTER VIII

THE BOSS

To be vested with enormous authority is a fine thing; but to have the on-looking world consent to it is a finer. The tower episode solidified my power, and made it impregnable. If any were perchance disposed to be jealous and critical before that, they experienced a change of heart, now. There was not any one in the kingdom who would have considered it good judgment to meddle with my matters.

I was fast getting adjusted to my situation and circumstances. For a time, I used to wake up, mornings, and smile at my "dream," and listen for the Colt's factory whistle; but that sort of thing played itself out, gradually, and at last I was fully able to realize that I was actually living in the sixth century, and in Arthur's court, not a lunatic asylum. After that, I was just as much at home in that century as I could have been in any other; and as for preference, I wouldn't have traded it for the twentieth. Look at the opportunities here for a man of knowledge, brains, pluck and enterprise to sail in and grow up with the country. The grandest field that ever was; and all my own; not a competitor; not a man who wasn't a baby to me in acquirements and capacities; whereas, what would I amount to in the twentieth century? I should be foreman of a factory, that is about all; and could drag a seine down-street any day and catch a hundred better men than myself.

What a jump I had made! I couldn't keep from thinking about it, and contemplating it, just as one does who has struck oil. There was nothing back of me that could approach it, unless it might be Joseph's case; and Joseph's only approached it, it didn't equal it, quite. For it stands to reason that as Joseph's splendid financial ingenuities advantaged nobody but the king, the general public must have regarded him with a good deal of disfavor, whereas I had done my entire public a kindness in sparing the sun, and was popular by reason of it.

I was no shadow of a king; I was the substance; the king himself was the shadow. My power was colossal; and it was not a mere name, as such things have generally been, it was the genuine article. I stood here, at the very spring and source of the second great period of the world's history; and could see the trickling stream of that history gather, and deepen and broaden, and roll its mighty tides down the far centuries; and I could note the upspringing of adventurers like myself in the shelter of its long array of thrones: De Montforts, Gavestons, Mortimers, Villierses; the war-making, campaign-directing wantons of France, and

Charles the Second's sceptre-wielding drabs; but nowhere in the procession was my full-sized fellow visible. I was a Unique; and glad to know that that fact could not be dislodged or challenged for thirteen centuries and a half, for sure.

Yes, in power I was equal to the king. At the same time there was another power that was a trifle stronger than both of us put together. That was the Church. I do not wish to disguise that fact. I couldn't, if I wanted to. But never mind about that, now; it will show up, in its proper place, later on. It didn't cause me any trouble in the beginning—at least any of consequence.

Well, it was a curious country, and full of interest. And the people! They were the quaintest and simplest and trustingest race; why, they were nothing but rabbits. It was pitiful for a person born in a wholesome free atmosphere to listen to their humble and hearty outpourings of loyalty toward their king and Church and nobility; as if they had any more occasion to love and honor king and Church and noble than a slave has to love and honor the lash, or a dog has to love and honor the stranger that kicks him! Why, dear me, *any* kind of royalty, howsoever modified, *any* kind of aristocracy, howsoever pruned, is rightly an insult; but if you are born and brought up under that sort of arrangment you probably never find it out for yourself, and don't believe it when somebody else tells you. It is enough to make a body ashamed of his race to think of the sort of froth that has always occupied its thrones without shadow of right or reason, and the seventh-rate people that have always figured as its aristocracies—a company of monarchs and nobles who, as a rule, would have achieved only poverty and obscurity if left, like their betters, to their own exertions.

The most of King Arthur's British nation were slaves, pure and simple, and bore that name, and wore the iron collar on their necks; and the rest were slaves in fact, but without the name; they imagined themselves men and freemen, and called themselves so. The truth was, the nation as a body was in the world for one object, and one only: to grovel before king and Church and noble; to slave for them, sweat blood for them, starve that they might be fed, work that they might play, drink misery to the dregs that they might be happy, go naked that they might wear silks and jewels, pay taxes that they might be spared from paying them, be familiar all their lives with the degrading language and postures of adulation that they might walk in pride and think themselves the gods of this world. And for all this, the thanks they got were cuffs and contempt; and so poor-spirited were they that they took even this sort of attention as an honor.

Inherited ideas are a curious thing, and interesting to observe and examine. I had mine, the king and his people had theirs. In both cases they flowed in ruts worn deep by time and habit, and the man who should have proposed to divert them by reason and argument would have had a long contract on his hands. For instance, those people had inherited the idea that all men without title and a long pedigree, whether they had great natural gifts and acquirements or hadn't, were creatures of no more consideration than so many animals, bugs, insects; whereas I had inherited the idea that human daws who can consent to masquerade in the peacock-shams of inherited dignities and unearned titles, are of no good but to be laughed at. The way I was looked upon was odd, but it was natural. You know how the keeper and the public regard the elephant in the menagerie: well, that is the idea. They are full of admiration of his vast bulk and his prodigious strength; they speak with pride of the fact that he can do a hundred marvels which are far and away beyond their own powers; and they speak with the same pride of the fact that in his wrath he is able to drive a thousand men before him. But does that make him one of *them?* No; the raggedest tramp in the pit would smile at the idea. He couldn't comprehend it; couldn't take it in; couldn't in any remote way conceive of it. Well, to the king, the nobles, and all the nation, down to the very slaves and tramps, I was just that kind of an elephant, and nothing more. I was admired, also feared; but it was as an animal is admired and feared. The animal is not reverenced, neither was I; I was not even respected. I had no pedigree, no inherited title; so in the king's and nobles' eyes I was mere dirt; the people regarded me with wonder and awe, but there was no reverence mixed with it; through the fore of inherited ideas they were not able to conceive of anything being entitled to that except pedigree and lordship. There you see the hand of that awful power, the Roman Catholic Church. In two or three little centuries it had converted a nation of men to a nation of worms. Before the day of the Church's supremacy in the world, men were men, and held their heads up, and had a man's pride and spirit and independence; and what of greatness and position a person got, he got mainly by achievement, not by birth. But then the Church came to the front, with an axe to grind; and she was wise, subtle, and knew more than one way to skin a cat—or a nation; she invented "divine right of kings," and propped it all around, brick by brick, with the Beatitudes—wrenching them from their good purpose to make them fortify an evil one; she preached (to the commoner,) humility, obedience to superiors, the beauty of self-sacrifice; she preached (to the commoner,) meekness under insult; preached (still to the commoner, always to the commoner,) patience, meanness of spirit, non-resistance under oppression; and she introduced heritable ranks and aristocracies, and taught all the Christian populations of the earth to bow down to them and worship them. Even down to my birth-century that poison was still in the blood of Christendom, and the best of English commoners was still content to see his inferiors impudently continuing to hold a number of positions, such as lordships and the throne, to which the grotesque laws of his country did not allow him to aspire; in fact he was not merely contented with this strange condition of things, he was even able to persuade himself that he was proud of it. It seems to show that there isn't anything you can't stand, if you are only born and bred to it. Of course that taint, that reverence for rank and title, had been in our American blood, too—I know that; but when I left America it had disappeared—at least to all intents and purposes. The remnant of it was restricted to the dudes and dudesses. When a disease has worked its way down to that level, it may fairly be said to be out of the system.

But to return to my anomalous position in King Arthur's kingdom. Here I was, a giant among pigmies, a man among children, a master intelligence among intellectual moles: by all rational measurement the one and only actually great man in that whole British world; and yet there and then, just as in the remote England of my birth-time, the sheep-witted earl who could claim long descent from a king's leman, acquired at second-hand from the slums of London, was a better man than I was. Such a personage was fawned upon in Arthur's realm and reverently looked up to by everybody, even though his dispositions were as mean as his intelligence, and his morals as base as his lineage. There were times when *he* could sit down in the king's presence, but I couldn't. I could have got a title easily enough, and that would have raised me a large step in everybody's eyes; even in the king's, the giver of it. But I didn't ask for it; and I declined it when it was offered. I couldn't have enjoyed such a thing with my notions; and it wouldn't have been fair, anyway, because as far back as I could go, our tribe had always been short of the bar sinister. I couldn't have felt really and satisfactorily fine and proud and set-up over any title except one that should come from the nation itself, the only legitimate source; and such an one I hoped to win; and in the course of years of honest and honorable endeavor, I did win it and did wear it with a high and clean pride. This title fell casually from the lips of a blacksmith, one day, in a village, was caught up as a happy thought and tossed from mouth to mouth with a laugh and an affirmative vote; in ten days it had swept the kingdom, and was become as familiar as the king's name. I was never known by any other designation afterwards, whether in the nation's talk or in grave debate upon matters of state at the council-board of the sovereign. This title, translated into modern speech, would be THE BOSS. Elected by the nation. That suited me. And it was a pretty high title. There were very few THE'S, and I was one of them. If you spoke of the duke, or the earl, or the bishop, how could anybody tell which one you meant? But if you spoke of The King or The Queen or The Boss, it was different.

Well, I liked the king, and *as* king I respected him—respected the office; at least respected it as much as I was capable of respecting any unearned supremacy; but as *men* I looked down upon him and his nobles—privately. And he and they liked me, and respected my office; but as an animal, without birth or sham title, they looked down upon me—and were not particularly private about it, either. I didn't charge for my opinion about them, and they didn't charge for their opinion about me: the account was square, the books balanced, everybody was satisfied.

CHAPTER IX

THE TOURNAMENT

They were always having grand tournaments there at Camelot; and very stirring and picturesque and ridiculous human bull-fights they were, too, but just a little wearisome to the practical mind. However, I was generally on hand—for two reasons: a man must not hold himself aloof from the things which his friends and his community have at heart if he would be liked—especially as a statesman; and both as businessman and statesman I wanted to study the tournament and see if I couldn't invent an improvement on it. That reminds me to remark, in passing, that the very first official thing I did, in my administration—and it was on the very first day of it, too—was to start a patent office, for I knew that a country without a patent office and good patent laws was just a crab, and couldn't travel any way but sideways or backwards.

Things ran along, a tournament nearly every week; and now and then the boys used to want me to take a hand—I mean Sir Launcelot and the rest—but I said I would by-and-by; no hurry yet, and too much government machinery to oil up and set to rights and start a-going.

We had one tournament which was continued from day to day during more than a week, and as many as five hundred knights took part in it, from first to last. They were weeks gathering. They came on horseback from everywhere; from the very ends of the country, and even from beyond the sea; and many brought ladies and all brought squires, and troops of servants. It was a most gaudy and gorgeous crowd, as to costumery, and very characteristic of the country and the time, in the way of high animal spirits, innocent indecencies of language, and happy-hearted indifference to morals. It was fight or look on, all day and every day; and sing, gamble, dance, carouse half the night every night. They had a most noble good time. You never saw such people. Those banks of beautiful ladies, shining in their barbaric splendors, would see a knight sprawl from his horse in the lists with a lance-shaft the thickness of your ankle clean through him and the blood spouting, and instead of fainting they would clap their hands and crowd each other for a better view; only sometimes one would dive into her handkerchief, and look ostentatiously broken-hearted, and then you could lay two to one that there was a scandal there somewhere and she was afraid the public hadn't found it out.

The noise at night would have been annoying to me ordinarily, but I didn't mind it in the present circumstances, because it kept me from hearing the quacks detaching legs and arms from the day's cripples. They ruined an uncommon good old cross-cut saw for me, and broke the saw-buck, too, but I let it pass. And as for my axe— well, I made up my mind that the next time I lent an axe to a surgeon I would pick my century.

I not only watched this tournament from day to day, but detailed an intelligent priest from my Department of Public Morals and Agriculture, and ordered him to report it; for it was my purpose by-and-by, when I should have gotten the people along far enough, to start a newspaper. The first thing you want in a new country, is a patent office; then work up your school system; and after that, out with your paper. A newspaper has its faults, and plenty of them, but no matter, it's hark from the tomb for a dead nation, and don't you forget it. You can't resurrect a dead nation without it; there isn't any way. So I wanted to sample things, and be finding out what sort of reporter-material I might be able to rake together out of the sixth century when I should come to need it.

Well, the priest did very well, considering. He got in all the details, and that is a good thing in a local item: you see he had kept books for the undertaker-department of his church when he was younger, and there, you know. the money's in the details; the more details, the more swag: bearers, mutes, candles, prayers,— everything counts; and if the bereaved don't buy prayers enough you mark up your candles with a forked pencil, and your bill shows up all right. And he had a good knack at getting in the complimentary thing here and there about a knight that was likely to advertise—no, I mean a knight that had influence; and he also had a neat gift of exaggeration, for in his time he had kept door for a pious hermit who lived in a sty and worked miracles.

Of course his novice's report lacked whoop and crash and lurid description, and therefore wanted the true ring; but its antique wording was quaint and sweet and simple, and full of the fragrances and flavors of the time, and these little merits made up in a measure for its more important lacks. Here is an extract from it:

Then Sir Brian de les Isles and Grummore Grummorsum, knights of the castle, encountered with Sir Aglovale and Sir Tor, and Sir Tor smote down Sir Grummore Grummorsum to the earth. Then came in Sir Carados of the dolorous tower, and Sir Turquine, knights of the castle, and there encountered with them Sir Percivale de Galis and Sir Lamorak de Galis, that were two brethren, and then encountered Sir Percivale with Sir Carados, and either brake their spears unto their hands, and then Sir

Turquine with Sir Lamorak, and either of them smote down other, horse and all, to the earth, and either parties rescued other and horsed them again. And Sir Arnold, and Sir Gauter, knights of the castle, encountered with Sir Brandiles and Sir Kay, and these four knights encountered mightily, and brake their spears to their hands. Then came Sir Pertolope from the castle, and there encountered with him Sir Lionel, and there Sir Pertolope the green knight smote down Sir Lionel, brother to Sir Launcelot. All this was marked by noble heralds, who bare him best, and their names. Then Sir Bleobaris brake his spear upon Sir Gareth, but of that stroke Sir Bleobaris fell to the earth. When Sir Galihodin saw that, he bad Sir Gareth keep him, and Sir Gareth smote him to the earth. Then Sir Galihud gat a spear to avenge his brother, and in the same wise Sir Gareth served him, and Sir Dinadan and his brother La Cote Male Taile, and Sir Sagramore le Desirous, and Sir Dodinas le Savage; all these he bare down with one spear. When King Agwisance of Ireland saw Sir Gareth fare so he marvelled what he might be, that one time seemed green, and another time, at his again coming, he seemed blue. And thus at every course that he rode to and fro he changed his color, so that there might neither king nor knight have ready cognizance of him. Then Sir Agwisance the King of Ireland encountered with Sir Gareth, and there Sir Gareth smote him from his horse, saddle and all. And then came King Carados of Scotland, and Sir Gareth smote him down horse and man. And in the same wise he served King Uriens of the land of Gore. And then there came in Sir Bagdemagus, and Sir Gareth smote him down horse and man to the earth. And Bagdemagus's son Meliganus brake a spear upon Sir Gareth mightily and knightly. And then Sir Galahault the noble prince cried on high, Knight with the many colors, well hast thou justed; now make thee ready that I may just with thee. Sir Gareth heard him, and he gat a great spear, and so they encountered together, and there the prince brake his spear; but Sir Gareth smote him upon the left side of the helm, that he reeled here and there, and he had fallen down had not his men recovered him. Truly said King Arthur, that knight with the many colors is a good knight. Wherefore the king called unto him Sir Launcelot, and prayed him to encounter with that knight. Sir, said Launcelot, I may as well find in my heart for to forbear him at this time, for he hath had travail enough this day, and when a good knight doth so well upon some day, it is no good knight's part to let him of his worship. and, namely, when he seeth a knight hath done so great labour: for peradventure, said Sir Launcelot, his quarrel is here this day, and peradventure he is best beloved with this lady of all that be here, for I see well he paineth himself and enforceth him to do great deeds, and therefore, said Sir Launcelot, as for me, this day he shall have the honour: though it lay in my power to put him from it, I would not.

There was an unpleasant little episode that day, which for reasons of state I struck out of my priest's report. You will have noticed that Garry was doing some great fighting in the engagement. When I say Garry I mean Sir Gareth. Garry was my private pet name for him; it suggests that I had a deep affection for him, and that was the case. But is was a private pet name only, and never spoken aloud to any one, much less to him; being a noble, he would not have endured a familiarity like that from me. Well, to proceed: I sat in the private box set apart for me as the king's minister. While Sir Dinadan was waiting for his turn to enter the lists, he came in there and sat down and began to talk; for he was always making up to me, because I was a stranger and he liked to have a fresh market for his jokes, the most of them having reached that stage of wear where the teller has to do the laughing himself while the other person looks sick. I had always responded to his efforts as well as I could, and felt a very deep and real kindness for him, too, for the reason that if by malice of fate he knew the one particular anecdote which I had heard oftenest and had most hated and most loathed all my life, he had at least spared it me. It was one which I had heard attributed to every humorous person who had ever stood on American soil, from Columbus down to Artemus Ward. It was about a humorous lecturer who flooded an ignorant audience with the killingest jokes for an hour and never got a laugh; and then when he was leaving, some gray simpletons wrung him gratefully by the hand and said it had been the funniest thing they had ever heard, and "it was all they could do to keep from laughin' right out in meetin'." That anecdote never saw the day that it was worth the telling; and yet I had sat under the telling of it hundreds and thousands and millions and billions of times, and cried and cursed all the way through. Then who can hope to know what my feelings were, to hear this armor-plated ass start in on it again, in the murky twilight of tradition, before the dawn of history, while even Lactantius might be referred to as "the late Lactantius," and the Crusades wouldn't be born for five hundred years yet? Just as he finished, the call-boy came; so, haw-hawing like a demon, he went rattling and clanking out like a crate of loose castings, and I knew nothing more. It was some minutes before I came to, and then I opened my eyes just in time to see Sir Gareth fetch him an awful welt, and I unconsciously out with the prayer, "I hope to gracious he's killed!" But by ill-luck, before I had got half through with the words, Sir Gareth crashed into Sir Sagramor le Desirous and sent him thundering over his horse's crupper, and Sir Sagramor caught my remark and thought I meant it for *him*.

Well, whenever one of those people got a thing into his head, there was no getting it out again. I knew that, so I saved my breath, and offered no explanations. As soon as Sir Sagramor got well, he notified me that there was a little account to settle between us, and he named a day three or four years in the future; place of settlement, the lists where the offence had been given. I said I would be ready when he got back. You see, he was going for the Holy Grail. The boys all took a flier at the Holy Grail now and then. It was a several years' cruise. They always put in the long absence snooping around, in the most conscientious way, though none of them had any idea where the Holy Grail really was, and I don't think any of them actually expected to find it, or would have known what to do with

it if he *had* run across it. You see, it was just the Northwest Passage
of that day, as you may say; that was all. Every year expeditions
went out holy grailing, and next year relief expeditions went out to
hunt for *them*. There was worlds of reputation in it, but no money.
Why, they actually wanted *me* to put in! Well, I should smile.

CHAPTER X

BEGINNINGS OF CIVILIZATION

The Round Table soon heard of the challenge, and of course it
was a good deal discussed, for such things interested the boys. The
king thought I ought now to set forth in quest of adventures, so that
I might gain renown and be the more worthy to meet Sir Sagramor
when the several years should have rolled away. I excused myself
for the present; I said it would take me three or four years yet to get
things well fixed up and going smoothly; then I should be ready;
all the chances were that at the end of that time Sir Sagramor would
still be out grailing, so no valuable time would be lost by the
postponement; I should then have been in office six or seven years,
and I believed my system and machinery would be so well developed
that I could take a holiday without its working any harm.

I was pretty well satisfied with what I had already accomplished.
In various quiet nooks and corners I had the beginnings of all sorts
of industries under way—nuclei of future vast factories, the iron and
steel missionaries of my future civilization. In these were gathered
together the brightest young minds I could find, and I kept agents
out raking the country for more, all the time. I was training a crowd
of ignorant folk into experts—experts in every sort of handiwork
and scientific calling. These nurseries of mine went smoothly and
privately along undisturbed in their obscure country retreats, for
nobody was allowed to come into their precincts without a special
permit—for I was afraid of the Church.

I had started a teacher-factory and a lot of Sunday-schools the
first thing; as a result, I now had an admirable system of graded
schools in full blast in those places, and also a complete variety of
Protestant congregations all in a prosperous and growing condition.
Everybody could be any kind of a Christian he wanted to; there
was perfect freedom in that matter. But I confined public religious
teaching to the churches and the Sunday-schools, permitting
nothing of it in my other educational buildings. I could have given
my own sect the preference and made everybody a Presbyterian
without any trouble, but that would have been to affront a law of
human nature: spiritual wants and instincts are as various in the
human family as are physical appetites, complexions, and features,
and a man is only at his best, morally, when he is equipped with the

religious garment whose color and shape and size most nicely accommodate themselves to the spiritual complexion, angularities, and stature of the individual who wears it; and besides I was afraid of a united Church; it makes a mighty power, the mightiest conceivable, and then when it by-and-by gets into selfish hands, as it is always bound to do, it means death to human liberty, and paralysis to human thought.

All mines were royal property, and there were a good many of them. They had formerly been worked as savages always work mines—holes grubbed in the earth and the mineral brought up in sacks of hide by hand, at the rate of a ton a day; but I had begun to put the mining on a scientific basis as early as I could.

Yes, I had made pretty handsome progress when Sir Sagramor's challenge struck me.

Four years rolled by—and then! Well, you would never imagine it in the world. Unlimited power *is* the ideal thing when it is in safe hands. The despotism of heaven is the one absolutely perfect government. An earthly despotism would be the absolutely perfect earthly government, if the conditions were the same, namely, the despot the perfectest individual of the human race, and his lease of life perpetual. But as a perishable perfect man must die, and leave his despotism in the hands of an imperfect successor, an earthly despotism is not merely a bad form of government, it is the worst form that is possible.

My works showed what a despot could do with the resources of a kingdom at his command. Unsuspected by this dark land, I had the civilization of the nineteenth century booming under its very nose! It was fenced away from the public view, but there it was, a gigantic and unassailable fact—and to be heard from, yet, if I lived and had luck. There it was, as sure a fact, and as substantial a fact as any serene volcano, standing innocent with its smokeless summit in the blue sky and giving no sign of the rising hell in its bowels. My schools and churches were children four years before; they were grown-up, now; my shops of that day were vast factories, now; where I had a dozen trained men then, I had a thousand, now; where I had one brilliant expert then, I had fifty now. I stood with my hand on the cock, so to speak, ready to turn it on and flood the midnight world with light at any moment. But I was not going to do the thing in that sudden way. It was not my policy. The people could not have stood it; and moreover I should have had the Established Roman Catholic Church on my back in a minute.

No, I had been going cautiously all the while. I had had confidential agents trickling through the country some time, whose office was to undermine knighthood by imperceptible degrees, and to gnaw a little at this and that and the other superstition, and so prepare the way gradually for a better order of things. I was turning on my light one-candle-power at a time, and meant to continue to do so.

I had scattered some branch schools secretly about the kingdom, and they were doing very well. I meant to work this racket more and more, as time wore on, if nothing occurred to frighten me. One of my deepest secrets was my West Point—my military academy. I kept that most jealously out of sight; and I did the same with my naval academy which I had established at a remote seaport. Both were prospering to my satisfaction.

Clarence was twenty-two now, and was my head executive, my right hand. He was a darling; he was equal to anything; there wasn't anything he couldn't turn his hand to. Of late I had been training him for journalism, for the time seemed about right for a start in the newspaper line; nothing big, but just a small weekly for experimental circulation in my civilization-nurseries. He took to it like a duck; there was an editor concealed in him, sure. Already he had doubled himself in one way; he talked sixth century and wrote nineteenth. His journalistic style was climbing, steadily; it was already up to the back settlement Alabama mark, and couldn't be told from the editorial output of that region either by matter or flavor.

We had another large departure on hand, too. This was a telegraph and a telephone; our first venture in this line. These wires were for private service only, as yet, and must be kept private until a riper day should come. We had a gang of men on the road, working mainly by night. They were stringing ground wires; we were afraid to put up poles, for they would attract too much inquiry. Ground wires were good enough, in both instances, for my wires were protected by an insulation of my own invention which was perfect. My men had orders to strike across country, avoiding roads, and establishing connection with any considerable towns whose lights betrayed their presence, and leaving experts in charge. Nobody could tell you how to find any place in the kingdom, for nobody ever went intentionally to any place, but only struck it by accident in his wanderings, and then generally left it without thinking to inquire what its name was. At one time and another we had sent out topographical expeditions to survey and map the kingdom, but the priests had always interfered and raised trouble. So we had given the thing up, for the present; it would be poor wisdom to antagonize the Church.

As for the general condition of the country, it was as it had been when I arrived in it, to all intents and purposes. I had made changes, but they were necessarily slight, and they were not noticeable. Thus far, I had not even meddled with taxation, outside of the taxes which provided the royal revenues. I had systematized those, and put the service on an effective and righteous basis. As a result, these revenues were already quadrupled, and yet the burden was so much more equably distributed than before, that all the kingdom felt a sense of relief, and the praises of my administration were hearty and general.

Personally, I struck an interruption, now, but I did not mind it, it could not have happened at a better time. Earlier it could have annoyed me, but now everything was in good hands and swimming right along. The king had reminded me several times, of late, that the postponement I had asked for, four years before, had about run out, now. It was a hint that I ought to be starting out to seek adventures and get up a reputation of a size to make me worthy of the honor of breaking a lance with Sir Sagramor, who was still out grailing, but was being hunted for by various relief expeditions, and might be found any year, now. So you see I was expecting this interruption; it did not take me by surprise.

CHAPTER XI

THE YANKEE IN SEARCH OF ADVENTURES

There never was such a country for wandering liars; and they were of both sexes. Hardly a month went by without one of these tramps arriving; and generally loaded with a tale about some princess or other wanting help to get her out of some far-away castle where she was held in captivity by a lawless scoundrel, usually a giant. Now you would think that the first thing the king would do after listening to such a novelette from an entire stranger, would be to ask for credentials—yes, and a pointer or two as to locality of castle, best route to it, and so on. But nobody ever thought of so simple and common-sense a thing as that. No, everybody swallowed these people's lies whole, and never asked a question of any sort or about anything. Well, one day when I was not around, one of these people came along—it was a she one, this time—and told a tale of the usual pattern. Her mistress was a captive in a vast and gloomy castle, along with forty-four other young and beautiful girls, pretty much all of them princesses; they had been languishing in that cruel captivity for twenty-six years; the masters of the castle were three stupendous brothers, each with four arms and one eye—the eye in the centre of the forehead, and as big as a fruit. Sort of fruit not mentioned; their usual slovenliness in statistics.

Would you believe it? The king and the whole Round Table were in raptures over this preposterous opportunity for adventure. Every knight of the Table jumped for the chance, and begged for it; but to their vexation and chagrin the king conferred it upon me, who had not asked for it at all.

By an effort, I contained my joy when Clarence brought me the news. But he—he could not contain his. His mouth gushed delight and gratitude in a steady discharge—delight in my good fortune, gratitude to the king for this splendid mark of his favor for me. He could keep neither his legs nor his body still, but pirouetted about the place in an airy ecstasy of happiness.

On my side, I could have cursed the kindness that conferred upon me this benefaction, but I kept my vexation under the surface for policy's sake, and did what I could to let on to be glad. Indeed, I *said* I was glad. And in a way it was true; I was as glad as a person is when he is scalped.

Well, one must make the best of things, and not waste time with useless fretting, but get down to business and see what can be done. In all lies there is wheat among the chaff; I must get at the wheat in this case: so I sent for the girl and she came. She was a comely enough creature, and soft and modest, but if signs went for anything, she didn't know as much as a lady's watch. I said—

"My dear, have you been questioned as to particulars?"

She said she hadn't.

"Well, I didn't expect you had, but I thought I would ask to make sure; it's the way I've been raised. Now you mustn't take it unkindly if I remind you that as we don't know you, we must go a little slow. You may be all right, of course, and we'll hope that you are; but to take it for granted isn't business. *You* understand that. I'm obliged to ask you a few questions; just answer up fair and square, and don't be afraid. Where do you live, when you are at home?"

"In the land of Moder, fair sir."

"Land of Moder. I don't remember hearing of it before. Parents living?"

"As to that, I know not if they be yet on live, sith it is many years that I have lain shut up in the castle."

"Your name, please?"

"I hight the Demoiselle Alisande la Carteloise, an it please you."

"Do you know anybody here who can identify you?"

"That were not likely, fair lord, I being come hither now for the first time."

"Have you brought any letters—any documents—any proofs that you are trustworthy and truthful?"

"Of a surety, no; and wherefore should I? Have I not a tongue, and cannot I say all that myself?"

"But *your* saying it, you know, and somebody else's saying it, is different."

"Different? How might that be? I fear me I do not understand."

"Don't *understand?* Land of—why, you see—you see—why, great Scott, can't you understand a little thing like that? Can't you understand the difference between your—*why* do you look so innocent and idiotic!"

"I? In truth I know not, but an it were the will of God."

"Yes, yes, I reckon that's about the size of it. Don't mind my seeming excited; I'm not. Let us change the subject. Now as to this castle, with forty-five princesses in it, and three ogres at the head of it, tell me—where is this harem?"

"Harem?"

"The *castle,* you understand; where is the castle?"

"Oh, as to that, it is great, and strong, and well beseen, and lieth in a far country. Yes, it is many leagues."

"How many?"

"Ah, fair sir, it were woundily hard to tell, they are so many, and do so lap the one upon the other, and being made all in the same image and tincted with the same color, one may not know the one league from its fellow, nor how to count them except they be taken apart, and ye wit well it were God's work to do that, being not within man's capacity; for ye will note—"

"Hold on, hold on, never mind about the distance; *whereabouts* does the castle lie? What's the direction from here?"

"Ah, please you sir, it hath no direction from here; by reason that the road lieth not straight, but turneth evermore; wherefore the direction of its place abideth not, but is sometime under the one sky and anon under another, whereso if ye be minded that it is in the east, and wend thitherward, ye shall observe that the way of the road doth yet again turn upon itself by the space of half a circle, and this marvel happing again and yet again and still again, it will grieve you that you had thought by vanities of the mind to thwart and bring to naught the will of Him that giveth not a castle a direction from a place except it pleaseth Him, and if it please Him not, will the rather that even all castles and all directions thereunto vanish out of the earth, leaving the places wherein they tarried desolate and vacant, so warning His creatures that where He will He will, and where He will not He—"

"Oh, that's all right, that's all right, give us a rest; never mind about the direction, *hang* the direction—I beg pardon, I beg a thousand pardons, I am not well to-day; pay no attention when I soliloquize, it is an old habit, an old, bad habit, and hard to get rid of when one's digestion is all disordered with eating food that was raised forever and ever before he was born; good land! a man can't keep his functions regular on spring chickens thirteen hundred years old. But come—never mind about that; let's—have you got such a thing as a map of that region about you? Now a good map—"

"Is it peradventure that manner of thing which of late the unbelievers have brought from over the great seas, which, being boiled in oil, and an onion and salt added thereto, doth—"

"What, a map? What are you talking about? Don't you know what a map is? There, there, never mind, don't explain, I hate explanations; they fog a thing up so that you can't tell anything about it. Run along, dear; good-day; show her the way, Clarence."

Oh, well, it was reasonably plain, now, why these donkeys didn't prospect these liars for details. It may be that this girl had a fact in her somewhere, but I don't believe you could have sluiced it out with a hydraulic; nor got it with the earlier forms of blasting, even; it was a case for dynamite. Why, she was a perfect ass; and yet the king and his knights had listened to her as if she had been a leaf out of the gospel. It kind of sizes up the whole party. And think of the simple ways of this court: this wandering wench hadn't any more trouble to get access to the king in his palace than she would have had to get into the poor-house in my day and country. In fact he was glad to see her, glad to hear her tale; with that adventure of hers to offer, she was as welcome as a corpse is to a coroner.

Just as I was ending-up these reflections, Clarence came back. I remarked upon the barren result of my efforts with the girl; hadn't got hold of a single point that could help me to find the castle. The youth looked a little surprised, or puzzled, or something, and intimated that he had been wondering to himself what I had wanted to ask the girl all those questions for.

"Why, great guns," I said, "don't I want to find the castle? And how else would I go about it?"

"La, sweet your worship, one may lightly answer that, I ween. She will go with thee. They always do. She will ride with thee."

"Ride with me? Nonsense!"

"But of a truth she will. She will ride with thee. Thou shalt see."

"What? She browse around the hills and scour the woods with me—alone—and I as good as engaged to be married? Why, it's scandalous. Think how it would look."

My, the dear face that rose before me! The boy was eager to know all about this tender matter. I swore him to secrecy and then whispered her name—"Puss Flanagan." He looked disappointed, and said he didn't remember the countess. How natural it was for the little courtier to give her a rank. He asked me where she lived.

"In East Har—" I came to myself and stopped, a little confused; then I said, "Never mind, now; I'll tell you sometime."

And might he see her? Would I let him see her some day?

It was but a little thing to promise—thirteen hundred years or so—and he so eager, so I said Yes. But I sighed; I couldn't help it. And yet there was no sense in sighing, for she wasn't born yet. But that is the way we are made: we don't reason, where we feel; we just feel.

My expedition was all the talk that day and that night, and the boys were very good to me, and made much of me, and seemed to have forgotten their vexation and disappointment, and come to be as anxious for me to hive those ogres and set those ripe old virgins loose as if it were themselves that had the contract. Well, they *were* good children—but just children, that is all. And they gave me no end of points about how to scout for giants, and how to scoop them in; and they told me all sorts of charms against enchantments, and gave me salves and other rubbish to put on my wounds. But it never occurred to one of them to reflect that if I was such a wonderful necromancer as I was pretending to be, I ought not to need salves or instructions, or charms against enchantments, and least of all, arms

and armor, on a foray of any kind—even against fire-spouting
dragons, and devils hot from perdition, let alone such poor
adversaries as these I was after, these commonplace ogres of the
back settlements.

I was to have an early breakfast, and start at dawn, for that was
the usual way; but I had the demon's own time with my armor, and
this delayed me a little. It is troublesome to get into, and there is so
much detail. First you wrap a layer or two of blanket around your
body, for a sort of cushion and to keep off the cold iron; then you put
on your sleeves and shirt of chain-mail—these are made of small
steel links woven together, and they form a fabric so flexible that if
you toss your shirt onto the floor, it slumps into a pile like a peck of
wet fish-net; it is very heavy and is nearly the uncomfortablest
material in the world for a night-shirt, yet plenty used it for that—
tax collectors, and reformers, and one-horse kings with a defective
title, and those sorts of people; then you put on your shoes—flat-
boats roofed over with interleaving bands of steel—and screw your
clumsy spurs into the heels. Next you buckle your greaves on your
legs, and your cuisses on your thighs; then come your backplate and
your breastplate, and you begin to feel crowded; then you hitch onto
the breastplate the half-petticoat of broad overlapping bands of steel
which hangs down in front but is scolloped out behind so you can sit
down, and isn't any real improvement on an inverted coal scuttle,
either for looks or for wear, or to wipe your hands on; next you belt
on your sword; then you put your stove-pipe joints onto your arms,
your iron gauntlets onto your hands, your iron rat-trap onto your
head, with a rag of steel web hitched onto it to hang over the back of
your neck—and there you are, snug as a candle in a candle-mould.
This is no time to dance. Well, a man that is packed away like that,
is a nut that isn't worth the cracking, there is so little of the meat,
when you get down to it, by comparison with the shell.

The boys helped me, or I never could have got in. Just as we
finished, Sir Bedivere happened in, and I saw that as like as not I
hadn't chosen the most convenient outfit for a long trip. How stately
he looked; and tall and broad and grand. He had on his head a
conical steel casque that only came down to his ears, and for visor
had only a narrow steel bar that extended down to his upper lip and
protected his nose; and all the rest of him, from neck to heel, was
flexible chain-mail, trousers and all. But pretty much all of him was
hidden under his outside garment, which of course was of chain-
mail, as I said, and hung straight from his shoulders to his ankles;
and from his middle to the bottom, both before and behind, was
divided, so that he could ride and let the skirts hang down on each
side. He was going grailing, and it was just the outfit for it, too. I
would have given a good deal for that ulster, but it was too late now
to be fooling around. The sun was just up, the king and the court
were all on hand to see me off and wish me luck; so it wouldn't be

etiquette for me to tarry. You don't get on your horse yourself; no,
if you tried it you would get disappointed. They carry you out, just
as they carry a sun-struck man to the drug store, and put you on,
and help get you to rights, and fix your feet in the stirrups; and all
the while you do feel so strange and stuffy and like somebody else—
like somebody that has been married on a sudden, or struck by
lightning, or something like that, and hasn't quite fetched around,
yet, and is sort of numb, and can't just get his bearings. Then they
stood up the mast they called a spear, in its socket by my left foot,
and I gripped it with my hand; lastly they hung my shield around my
neck, and I was all complete and ready to up anchor and get to sea.
Everybody was as good to me as they could be, and a maid of honor
gave me the stirrup-cup her own self. There was nothing more to
do, now, but for that damsel to get up behind me on a pillion, which
she did, and put an arm or so around me to hold on.

And so we started; and everybody gave us a goodbye and waved
their handkerchiefs or helmets. And everybody we met, going down
the hill and through the village was respectful to us, except some
shabby little boys on the outskirts. They said—

"Oh, what a guy!" And hove clods at us.

In my experience boys are the same in all ages. They don't respect
anything, they don't care for anything or anybody. They say "Go up,
baldhead" to the prophet going his unoffending way in the gray of
antiquity; they sass me in the holy gloom of the Middle Ages; and I
had seen them act the same way in Buchanan's administration; I
remember, because I was there and helped. The prophet had his
bears and settled with his boys; and I wanted to get down and settle
with mine, but it wouldn't answer, because I couldn't have got up
again. I hate a country without a derrick.

CHAPTER XII

SLOW TORTURE

Straight off, we were in the country. It was most lovely and
pleasant in those sylvan solitudes in the early cool morning in the
first freshness of autumn. From hill-tops we saw fair green valleys
lying spread out below, with streams winding through them, and
island-groves of trees here and there, and huge lonely oaks scattered
about and casting black blots of shade; and beyond the valleys we
saw the ranges of hills, blue with haze, stretching away in billowy
perspective to the horizon, with at wide intervals a dim fleck of white
or gray on a wave-summit, which we knew was a castle. We crossed
broad natural lawns sparkling with dew, and we moved like spirits,
the cushioned turf giving out no sound of foot-fall; we dreamed
along through glades in a mist of green light that got its tint from the

sun-drenched roof of leaves over-head, and by our feet the clearest and coldest of runlets went frisking and gossiping over its reefs and making a sort of whispering music comfortable to hear; and at times we left the world behind and entered into the solemn great deeps and rich gloom of the forest, where furtive wild things whisked and scurried by and were gone before you could even get your eye on the place where the noise was; and where only the earliest birds were turning out and getting to business with a song here and a quarrel yonder and a mysterious far-off hammering and drumming for worms on a tree-trunk away somewhere in the impenetrable remotenesses of the woods. And by-and-by out we would swing again into the glare.

About the third or fourth or fifth time that we swung out into the glare—it was along there somewhere, a couple of hours or so after sun-up—it wasn't as pleasant as it had been. It was beginning to get hot. This was quite noticeable. We had a very long pull, after that, without any shade. Now it is curious how progressively little frets grow and multiply after they once get a start. Things which I didn't mind at all, at first, I began to mind now—and more and more, too, all the time. The first ten or fifteen times I wanted my handkerchief I didn't seem to care; I got along, and said never mind, it isn't any matter, and dropped it out of my mind. But now it was different; I wanted it all the time; it was nag, nag, nag, right along, and no rest; I couldn't get it out of my mind; and so at last I lost my temper and said hang a man that would make a suit of armor without any pockets in it. You see I had my handkerchief in my helmet; and some other things; but it was that kind of a helmet that you can't take off by yourself. That hadn't occurred to me when I put it there; and in fact I didn't know it. I supposed it would be particularly convenient there. And so now, the thought of its being there, so handy and close by, and yet not get-at-able, made it all the worse and the harder to bear. Yes, the thing that you can't get is the thing that you want, mainly; every one has noticed that. Well, it took my mind off from everything else; took it clear off, and centred it in my helmet; and mile after mile, there it stayed, imagining the handkerchief, picturing the handkerchief; and it was bitter and aggravating to have the salt sweat keep trickling down into my eyes, and I couldn't get at it. It seems like a little thing, on paper, but it was not a little thing at all; it was the most real kind of misery. I would not say it if it was not so. I made up my mind that I would carry along a reticule next time, let it look how it might, and people say what they would. Of course these irons dudes of the Round Table would think it was scandalous, and maybe raise Sheol about it, but as for me, give me comfort first, and style afterwards. So we jogged along, and now and then we struck a stretch of dust, and it would tumble up in clouds and get into my nose and make me sneeze and cry; and of course I said things I oughtn't to have said,

I don't deny that. I am not better than others. We couldn't seem to meet anybody in this lonesome Britain, not even an ogre; and in the mood I was in then, it was well for the ogre; that is, an ogre with a handkerchief. Most knights would have thought of nothing but getting his armor; but so I got his bandanna, he could keep his hardware, for all me.

Meantime it was getting hotter and hotter in there. You see, the sun was beating down and warming up the iron more and more all the time. Well, when you are hot, that way, every little thing irritates you. When I trotted, I rattled like a crate of dishes, and that annoyed me; and moreover I couldn't seem to stand that shield slatting and banging, now about my breast, now around my back; and if I dropped into a walk my joints creaked and screeched in that wearisome way that a wheelbarrow does, and as we didn't create any breeze at that gait, I was like to get fried in that stove; and besides, the quieter you went the heavier the iron settled down on you and the more and more tons you seemed to weigh every minute. And you had to be always changing hands, and passing your spear over to the other foot, it got so irksome for one hand to hold it long at a time.

Well, you know, when you perspire that way, in rivers, there comes a time when you—when you—well, when you itch. You are inside, your hands are outside; so there you are; nothing but iron between. It is not a light thing, let it sound as it may. First it is one place; then another; then some more; and it goes on spreading and spreading, and at last the territory is all occupied, and nobody can imagine what you feel like, nor how unpleasant it is. And when it had got to the worst, and it seemed to me that I could not stand anything more, a fly got in through the bars and settled on my nose, and the bars were stuck and wouldn't work, and I couldn't get the visor up; and I could only shake my head, which was baking hot by this time, and the fly—well, you know how a fly acts when he has got a certainty—he only minded the shaking enough to change from nose to lip, and lip to ear, and buzz and buzz all around in there, and keep on lighting and biting, in a way that a person already so distressed as I was, simply could not stand. So I gave in, and got Alisande to unship the helmet and relieve me of it. Then she emptied the conveniences out of it and fetched it full of water, and I drank and then stood up and she poured the rest down inside the armor. One cannot think how refreshing it was. She continued to fetch and pour until I was well soaked and thoroughly comfortable.

It was good to have a rest—and peace. But nothing is quite perfect in this life, at any time. I had made a pipe a while back, and also some pretty fair tobacco; not the real thing, but what some of the Indians use: the inside bark of the willow, dried. These comforts had been in the helmet, and now I had them again, but no matches.

Gradually, as the time wore along, one annoying fact was borne in upon my understanding—that we were weather-bound. An armed novice cannot mount his horse without help and plenty of it. Sandy was not enough; not enough for me, anyway. We had to wait until somebody should come along. Waiting, in silence, would have been agreeable enough, for I was full of matter for reflection, and wanted to give it a chance to work. I wanted to try and think out how it was that rational or even half-rational men could ever have learned to wear armor, considering its inconveniences; and how they had managed to keep up such a fashion for generations when it was plain that what I had suffered to-day they had had to suffer all the days of their lives. I wanted to think that out; and moreover I wanted to think out some way to reform this evil and persuade the people to let the foolish fashion die out; but thinking was out of the question in the circumstances. You couldn't think, where Sandy was. She was a quite biddable creature and good-hearted, but she had a flow of talk that was as steady as a mill, and made your head sore like the drays and wagons in a city. If she had had a cork she would have been a comfort. But you can't cork that kind; they would die. Her clack was going all day, and you would think something would surely happen to her works, by-and-by; but no, they never got out of order; and she never had to slack up for words. She could grind, and pump, and churn and buzz by the week, and never stop to oil up or blow out. And yet the result was just nothing but wind. She never had any ideas, any more than a fog has. She was a perfect blatherskite; I mean for jaw, jaw, jaw, talk, talk, talk, jabber, jabber, jabber; but just as good as she could be. I hadn't minded her mill that morning, on account of having that hornet's nest of other troubles; but more than once in the afternoon I had to say—

"Take a rest, child; the way you are using up all the domestic air, the kingdom will have to go to importing it by to-morrow, and it's a low enough treasury without that."

CHAPTER XIII

FREEMEN!

Yes, it is strange how little a while at a time a person can be contented. Only a little while back, when I was riding and suffering, what a heaven this peace, this rest, this sweet serenity in this secluded shady nook by this purling stream would have seemed, where I could keep perfectly comfortable all the time by pouring a dipper of water into my armor now and then; yet already I was getting dissatisfied; partly because I could not light my pipe—for although I had long ago started a match factory, I had forgotten to bring matches with me—and partly because we had nothing to eat.

Here was another illustration of the childlike improvidence of this age and people. A man in armor always trusted to chance for his food on a journey, and would have been scandalized at the idea of hanging a basket of sandwiches on his spear. There was probably not a knight of all the Round Table combination who would not rather have died than been caught carrying such a thing as that on his flagstaff. And yet there could not be anything more sensible. It had been my intention to smuggle a couple of sandwiches into my helmet, but I was interrupted in the act, and had to make an excuse and lay them aside, and a dog got them.

Night approached, and with it a storm. The darkness came on fast. We must camp, of course. I found a good shelter for the demoiselle under a rock, and went off and found another for myself. But I was obliged to remain in my armor, because I could not get it off by myself and yet could not allow Alisande to help, because it would have seemed so like undressing before folk. It would not have amounted to that in reality, because I had clothes on underneath; but the prejudices of one's breeding are not gotten rid of just at a jump, and I knew that when it came to stripping off that bob-tailed iron petticoat I should be embarrassed.

With the storm came a change of weather; and the stronger the wind blew, and the wilder the rain lashed around, the colder and colder it got. Pretty soon, various kinds of bugs and ants and worms and things began to flock in out of the wet and crawl down inside my armor to get warm; and while some of them behaved well enough, and smuggled up amongst my clothes and got quiet, the majority were of a restless, uncomfortable sort, and never stayed still, but went on prowling and hunting for they did not know what; especially the ants, which went tickling along in wearisome procession from one end of me to the other by the hour, and are a kind of creatures which I never wish to sleep with again. It would be my advice to persons situated in this way, to not roll or thrash around, because this excites the interest of all the different sorts of animals and makes every last one of them want to turn out and see what is going on, and this makes things worse than they were before, and of course makes you objurgate harder, too, if you can. Still, if one did not roll and thrash around he would die; so perhaps it is as well to do one way as the other, there is no real choice. Even after I was frozen solid I could still distinguish that tickling, just as a corpse does when he is taking electric treatment. I said I would never wear armor after this trip.

All those trying hours whilst I was frozen and yet was in a living fire, as you may say, on account of that swarm of crawlers, that same unaswerable question kept circling and circling through my tired head: How do people stand this miserable armor? How have they managed to stand it all these generations? How can they sleep at night for dreading the tortures of next day?

When the morning came at last, I was in a bad enough plight:
seedy, drowsy, fagged, from want of sleep; weary from thrashing
around, famished from long fasting; pining for a bath, and to get
rid of the animals; and crippled with rheumatism. And how had it
fared with the nobly born, the titled aristocrat, the Demoiselle
Alisande la Carteloise? Why, she was as fresh as a squirrel; she had
slept like the dead; and as for a bath, probably neither she nor any
other noble in the land had ever had one, and so she was not missing
it. Measured by modern standards, they were merely modified
savages, those people. This noble lady showed no impatience to get
to breakfast—and that smacks of the savage, too. On their journeys
those Britons were used to long fasts, and knew how to bear them;
and also how to freight up against probable fasts before starting,
after the style of the Indian and the anaconda. As like as not, Sandy
was loaded for a three-day stretch.

We were off before sunrise, Sandy riding and I limping along
behind. In half an hour we came upon a group of ragged poor
creatures who had assembled to mend the thing which was regarded
as a road. They were as humble as animals to me; and when I
proposed to breakfast with them, they were so flattered, so
overwhelmed by this extraordinary condescension of mine that at
first they were not able to believe that I was in earnest. My lady put
up her scornful lip and withdrew to one side; she said in their
hearing that she would as soon think of eating with the other cattle
—a remark which embarrassed these poor devils merely because
it referred to them, and not because it insulted or offended them,
for it didn't. And yet they were not slaves, not chattels. By a
sarcasm of law and phrase they were freemen. Seven-tenths of the
free population of the country were of just their class and degree:
small "independent" farmers, artisans, etc.; which is to say, they
were the nation, the actual Nation; they were about all of it that was
useful, or worth saving, or really respectworthy; and to subtract
them would have been to subtract the Nation and leave behind some
dregs, some refuse, in the shape of a king, nobility and gentry, idle,
unproductive, acquainted mainly with the arts of wasting and
destroying, and of no sort of use or value in any rationally
constructed world. And yet, by ingenious contrivance, this gilded
minority, instead of being in the tail of the procession where it
belonged, was marching head up and banners flying, at the other
end of it; had elected itself to be the Nation, and these innumerable
clams had permitted it so long that they had come at last to accept
it as a truth; and not only that, but to believe it right and as it should
be. The priests had told their fathers and themselves that this
ironical state of things was ordained of God; and so, not reflecting
upon how unlike God it would be to amuse himself with sarcasms,
and especially such poor transparent ones as this, they had dropped
the matter there and become respectfully quiet.

The talk of these meek people had a strange enough sound in a formerly American ear. They were freemen, but they could not leave the estates of their lord or their bishop without his permission; they could not prepare their own bread, but must have their corn ground and their bread baked at his mill and his bakery, and pay roundly for the same; they could not sell a piece of their own property without paying him a handsome percentage of the proceeds, nor buy a piece of somebody else's without remembering him in cash for the privilege; they had to harvest his grain for him gratis, and be ready to come at a moment's notice, leaving their own crop to destruction by the threatened storm; they had to let him plant fruit trees in their fields, and then keep their indignation to themselves when his heedless fruit gatherers trampled the grain around the trees; they had to smother their anger when his hunting parties galloped through their fields laying waste the result of their patient toil; they were not allowed to keep doves themselves, and when the swarms from my lord's dovecote settled on their crops they must not lose their temper and kill a bird, for awful would the penalty be; when the harvest was at last gathered, then came the procession of robbers to levy their blackmail upon it: first the Church carted off its fat tenth, then the king's commissioner took his twentieth, then my lord's people made a mighty inroad upon the remainder; after which, the skinned freeman had liberty to bestow the remnant in his barn, in case it was worth the trouble; there were taxes, and taxes, and taxes, and more taxes, and taxes again, and yet other taxes—upon this free and independent pauper, but none upon his lord the baron or the bishop, none upon the wasteful nobility or the all-devouring Church; if the baron would sleep unvexed, the freeman must sit up all night after his day's work and whip the ponds to keep the frogs quiet; if the freeman's daughter— but no, that last infamy of monarchical government is unprintable; and finally, if the freeman, grown desperate with his tortures, found his life unendurable under such conditions, and sacrificed it and fled to death for mercy and refuge, the gentle Church condemned him to eternal fire, the gentle law buried him at midnight at the cross-roads with a stake through his back, and his master the baron or the bishop confiscated all his property and turned his widow and his orphans out of doors.

And here were these freemen assembled in the early morning to work on their lord the bishop's road three days each—gratis; every head of a family, and every son of a family, three days each, gratis, and a day or so added for their servants. Why, it was like reading about France and the French, before the ever-memorable and blessed Revolution, which swept a thousand years of such villany away in one swift tidal-wave of blood—one: a settlement of that hoary debt in the proportion of half a drop of blood for each hogshead of it that had been pressed by slow tortures out of that

people in the weary stretch of ten centuries of wrong and shame
and misery the like of which was not to be mated but in hell. There
were two "Reigns of Terror," if we would but remember it and
consider it; the one wrought murder in hot passion, the other in
heartless cold blood; the one lasted mere months, the other had
lasted a thousand years; the one inflicted death upon ten thousand
persons, the other upon a hundred millions; but our shudders are
all for the "horrors" of the minor Terror, the momentary Terror,
so to speak; whereas, what is the horror of swift death by the axe,
compared with life-long death from hunger, cold, insult, cruelty
and heart-break? What is swift death by lightning compared with
death by slow fire at the stake? A city cemetery could contain the
coffins filled by that brief Terror which we have all been so diligently
taught to shiver at and mourn over; but all France could hardly
contain the coffins filled by that older and real Terror—that
unspeakably bitter and awful Terror which none of us has been
taught to see in its vastness or pity as it deserves.

These poor ostensible freemen who were sharing their breakfast
and their talk with me, were as full of humble reverence for their
king and Church and nobility as their worst enemy could desire.
There was something pitifully ludicrous about it. I asked them if
they supposed a nation of people ever existed, who, with a free vote
in every man's hand, would elect that a single family and its
descendants should reign over it forever, whether gifted or boobies,
to the exclusion of all other families—including the voter's; and
would also elect that a certain hundred families should be raised
to dizzy summits of rank, and clothed-on with offensive
transmissible glories and privileges to the exclusion of the rest of the
nations's families—*including his own.*

They all looked unhit, and said they didn't know; that they had
never thought about it before, and it hadn't ever occurred to them
that a nation could be so situated that every man *could* have a say
in the government. I said I had seen one—and that it would last
until it had an Established Church. Again they were all unhit—at
first. But presently one man looked up and asked me to state that
proposition again; and state it slowly, so it could soak into his
understanding. I did it; and after a little he had the idea, and he
brought his fist down and said *he* didn't believe a nation where every
man had a vote would voluntarily get down in the mud and dirt in
any such way; and that to steal from a nation its will and preference
must be a crime and the first of all crimes.

I said to myself:

"This one's a man. If I were backed by enough of his sort, I would
make a strike for the welfare of this country, and try to prove myself
its loyalest citizen by making a wholesome change in its system of
government."

You see my kind of loyalty was loyalty to one's country, not to its
institutions or its office-holders. The country is the real thing, the

substantial thing, the eternal thing; it is the thing to watch over, and care for, and be loyal to; institutions are extraneous, they are its mere clothing, and clothing can wear out, become ragged, cease to be comfortable, cease to protect the body from winter, disease, and death. To be loyal to rags, to shout for rags, to worship rags, to die for rags—that is a loyalty of unreason, it is pure animal; it belongs to monarchy, was invented by monarchy; let monarchy keep it. I was from Connecticut, whose Constitution declares "that all political power is inherent in the people, and all free governments are founded on their authority and instituted for their benefit; and that they have *at all times* an undeniable and indefeasible right to *alter their form of government* in such a manner as they may think expedient."

Under that gospel, the citizen who thinks he sees that the commonwealth's political clothes are worn out, and yet holds his peace and does not agitate for a new suit, is disloyal; he is a traitor. That he may be the only one who thinks he sees this decay, does not excuse him; it is his duty to agitate anyway, and it is the duty of the others to vote him down if they do not see the matter as he does.

And now here I was, in a country where a right to say how the country should be governed was restricted to six persons in each thousand of its population. For the nine hundred and ninety-four to express dissatisfaction with the regnant system and propose to change it, would have made the whole six shudder as one man, it would have been so disloyal, so dishonorable, such putrid black treason. So to speak, I was become a stockholder in a corporation where nine hundred and ninety-four of the members furnished all the money and did all the work, and the other six elected themselves a permanent board of direction and took all the dividends. It seemed to me that what the nine hundred and ninety-four dupes needed was a new deal. The thing that would have best suited the circus side of my nature would have been to resign the Boss-ship and get up an insurrection and turn it into a revolution; but I knew that the Jack Cade or the Wat Tyler who tried such a thing without first educating his materials up to revolution-grade is almost absolutely certain to get left. I had never been accustomed to getting left, even if I do say it myself. Wherefore, the "deal" which had been for some time working into shape in my mind was of a quite different pattern from the Cade-Tyler sort.

So I did not talk blood and insurrection to that man there who sat munching black bread with that abused and mistaught herd of human sheep, but took him aside and talked matter of another sort to him. After I had finished, I got him to lend me a little ink from his veins; and with this and a sliver I wrote on a piece of bark—

Put him in the Man-Factory—

and gave it to him, and said—

"Take it to the palace at Camelot and give it into the hands of

Amyas le Poulet, whom I call Clarence, and he will understand."

"He is a priest, then," said the man, and some of the enthusiasm went out of his face.

"How—a priest? Didn't I tell you that no chattel of the Church, no bond-slave of pope or bishop can enter my Man-Factory? Didn't I tell you that *you* couldn't enter unless your religion, whatever it might be, was your own free property?"

"Marry, it is so, and for that I was glad; wherefore it liked me not, and bred in me a cold doubt, to hear of this priest being there."

"But he isn't a priest, I tell you."

The man looked far from satisfied. He said:

"He is not a priest, and yet can read?"

"He is not a priest and yet can read—yes, and write, too, for that matter. I taught him myself." The man's face cleared. "And it is the first thing that you yourself will be taught in that Factory—"

"I? I would give blood out of my heart to know that art. Why, I will be your slave, your—"

"No you won't, you won't be anybody's slave. Take your family and go along. Your lord the bishop will confiscate your small property, but no matter, Clarence will fix you all right."

CHAPTER XIV

"DEFEND THEE, LORD!"

I paid three pennies for my breakfast, and a most extravagant price it was, too, seeing that one could have breakfasted a dozen persons for that money; but I was feeling good by this time, and I had always been a kind of spendthrift anyway; and then these people had wanted to give me the food for nothing, scant as their provision was, and so it was a grateful pleasure to emphasize my appreciation and sincere thankfulness with a good big financial lift where the money would do so much more good than it would in my helmet, where, these pennies being made of iron and not stinted in weight, my half-dollar's worth was a good deal of a burden to me. I spent money rather too freely in those days, it is true; but one reason for it was that I hadn't got the proportions of things entirely adjusted, even yet, after so long a sojourn in Britain— hadn't got along to where I was able to absolutely realize that a penny in Arthur's land and a couple of dollars in Connecticut were about one and the same thing: just twins, as you may say, in purchasing power. If my start from Camelot could have been delayed a very few days I could have paid these people in beautiful new coins from our own mint, and that would have pleased me; and them, too, not less. I had adopted the American values exclusively. In a week or two now, cents, nickels, dimes, quarters and half-dollars, and also a trifle of gold, would be trickling in thin but steady streams all through the commercial veins of the kingdom, and I looked to see this new blood freshen up its life.

The farmers were bound to throw in something, to sort of offset my liberality, whether I would or no; so I let them give me a flint and steel; and as soon as they had comfortably bestowed Sandy and me on our horse, I lit my pipe. When the first blast of smoke shot out through the bars of my helmet, all those people broke for the woods, and Sandy went over backwards and struck the ground with a dull thud. They thought I was one of those fire-belching dragons they had heard so much about from knights and other professional liars. I had infinite trouble to persuade those people to venture back within explaining distance. Then I told them that this was only a bit of enchantment which would work harm to none but my enemies. And I promised, with my hand on my heart, that if all who felt no enmity toward me would come forward and pass before me they should see that only those who remained behind would be struck dead. The procession moved with a good deal of promptness. There were no casualties to report, for nobody had curiosity enough to remain behind to see what would happen.

I lost some time, now, for these big children, their fears gone, became so ravished with wonder over my awe-compelling fireworks that I had to stay there and smoke a couple of pipes out before they would let me go. Still the delay was not wholly unproductive, for it took all that time to get Sandy thoroughly wonted to the new thing, she being so close to it, you know. It plugged up her conversation-mill, too, for a considerable while, and that was a gain. But above all other benefits accruing, I had learned something. I was ready for any giant or any ogre that might come along, now.

We tarried with a holy hermit, that night, and my opportunity came about the middle of the next afternoon. We were crossing a vast meadow by way of short-cut, and I was musing absently, hearing nothing, seeing nothing, when Sandy suddenly interrupted a remark which she had begun that morning, with the cry—

"Defend thee, lord!—peril of life is toward!"

And she slipped down from the horse and ran a little way and stood. I looked up and saw, far off in the shade of a tree, half a dozen armed knights and their squires; and straightway there was bustle among them and tightening of saddle-girths for the mount. My pipe was ready and would have been lit, if I had not been lost in thinking about how to banish oppression from this land and restore to all its people their stolen rights and manhood without disobliging anybody. I lit up at once, and by the time I had got a good head of reserved steam on, here they came. All together, too; none of those chivalrous magnanimities which one reads so much about—one courtly rascal at a time, and the rest standing by to see fair play. No, they came in a body, they came with a whirr and a rush, they came like a volley from a battery; came with heads low down, plumes streaming out behind, lances advanced at a level. It was a handsome sight, a beautiful sight—for a man up a tree. I laid my lance in rest and waited, with my heart beating, till the iron wave was just ready to break over me, then spouted a column of white smoke through the bars of my helmet. You should have seen the wave go to pieces and scatter! This was a finer sight than the other one.

But these people stopped, two or three hundred yards away, and this troubled me. My satisfaction collapsed, and fear came; I judged I was a lost man. But Sandy was radiant; and was going to be eloquent, but I stopped her, and told her my magic had miscarried, somehow or other, and she must mount, with all despatch, and we must ride for life. No, she wouldn't. She said that my enchantment had disabled those knights; they were not riding on, because they couldn't; wait, they would drop out of their saddles presently, and we would get their horses and harness. I could not deceive such trusting simplicity, so I said it was a mistake; that when my fireworks killed at all, they killed instantly; no, the men would not die, there was something wrong about my apparatus, I couldn't tell what; but we must hurry and get away, for those people would attack us again, in a minute. Sandy laughed and said—

"Lack-a-day, sir, they be not of that breed! Sir Launcelot will give battle to dragons, and will abide by them, and will assail them again, and yet again, and still again, until he do conquer and destroy them; and so likewise will Sir Pellinore and Sir Aglovale and Sir Carados, and mayhap others, but there be none else that will venture it, let the idle say what the idle will. And, la, as to yonder base rufflers, think ye they have not their fill, but yet desire more?"

"Well, then, what are they waiting, for? Why don't they leave? Nobody's hindering. Good land, I'm willing to let by-gones be by-gones, I'm sure."

"Leave, is it? Oh, give thyself easement as to that. They dream not of it, no, not they. They wait to yield them."

"Come—really, is that 'sooth'—as you people say? If they want to, why don't they?"

"It would like them much; but an ye wot how dragons are esteemed, ye would not hold them blamable. They fear to come."

"Well, then, suppose I go to them instead, and—"

"Ah, wit ye well they would not abide your coming. I will go."

And she did. She was a handy person to have along on a raid. I would have considered this a doubtful errand, myself. I presently saw the knights riding away, and Sandy coming back. That was a relief. I judged she had somehow failed to get the first innings—I mean in the conversation; otherwise the interview wouldn't have been so short. But it turned out that she had managed the business well; in fact admirably. She said that when she told those people

I was The Boss, it hit them where they lived; "smote them sore with fear and dread" was her word; and then they were ready to put up with anything she might require. So she swore them to appear at Arthur's court within two days and yield them, with horse and harness, and be my knights henceforth, and subject to my command. How much better she managed that thing than I should have done it myself! She was a daisy.

CHAPTER XV

SANDY'S TALE

"And so I'm proprietor of some knights," said I, as we rode off. "Who would ever have supposed that I should live to list up assets of that sort. I shan't know what to do with them; unless I raffle them off. How many of them are there, Sandy?"

"Seven, please you, sir, and their squires."

"It is a good haul. Who are they? Where do they hang out?"

"Where do they hang out?"

"Yes, where do they live?"

"Ah, I understood thee not. That will I tell eftsoons." Then she said musingly, and softly, turning the words daintily over her tongue: "Hang they out —hang they out—where hang—where do they hang out; eh, right so; where do they hang out. Of a truth the phrase hath a fair and winsome grace, and is prettily worded withal. I will repeat it anon and anon in mine idlesse, whereby I may peradventure learn it. Where do they hang out. Even so! already it falleth trippingly from my tongue, and forasmuch as—"

"Don't forget the cow-boys, Sandy."

"Cow-boys?"

"Yes; the knights, you know: You were going to tell me about them. A while back, you remember. Figuratively speaking, game's called."

"Game—"

"Yes, yes, yes! Go to the bat. I mean, get to work on your statistics, and don't burn so much kindling getting your fire started. Tell me about the knights."

"I will well, and lightly will begin. So they two departed and rode into a great forest. And—"

"Great Scott!"

You see, I recognized my mistake at once. I had set her works a-going; it was my own fault; she would be thirty days getting down to those facts. And she generally began without a preface and finished without a result. If you interrupted her she would either go right along without noticing, or answer with a couple of words, and go back and say the sentence over again. So, interruptions only did harm; and yet I had to interrupt, and interrupt pretty frequently, too, in order to save my life; a person would die if he let her monotony drip on him right along all day.

"Great Scott!" I said in my distress. She went right back and began over again:

"So they two departed and rode into a great forest. And—"

"*Which* two?"

"Sir Gawaine and Sir Uwaine. And so they came to an abbey of monks, and there were well lodged. So on the morn they heard their masses in the abbey, and so they rode forth till they came to a great forest; then was Sir Gawaine ware in a valley by a turret, of twelve fair damsels, and two knights armed on great horses, and the damsels went to and fro by a tree. And then was Sir Gawaine ware how there hung a white shield on that tree, and ever as the damsels came by it they spit upon it, and some threw mire upon the shield—"

"Now, if I hadn't seen the like myself in this country, Sandy, I wouldn't believe it. But I've seen it, and I can just see those creatures now, parading before that shield and acting like that. The women here do certainly act like all possessed. Yes, and I mean your best, too, society's very choicest brands. The humblest hello-girl along ten thousand miles of wire could teach gentleness, patience, modesty, manners, to the highest duchess in Arthur's land."

"Hello-girl?"

"Yes, but don't you ask me to explain; it's a new kind of girl; they don't have them here; one often speaks sharply to them when they are not the least in fault, and he can't get over feeling sorry for it and ashamed of himself in thirteen hundred years, it's such shabby mean conduct and so unprovoked; the fact is, no gentlemen ever does it—though I—well, I myself, if I've got to confess—"

"Peradventure she—"

"Never mind her; never mind her; I tell you I couldn't ever explain her so you would understand."

"Even so be it, sith ye are so minded. Then Sir Gawaine and Sir Uwaine went and saluted them, and asked them why they did that despite to the shield. Sirs, said the damsels, we shall tell you. There is a knight in this country that owneth this white shield, and he is a passing good man of his hands, but he hateth all ladies and gentlewomen, and therefore we do all this despite to the shield. I will say you, said Sir Gawaine, it beseemeth evil a good knight to despise all ladies and gentlewomen, and peradventure though he hate you he hath some cause, and peradventure he loveth in some other places ladies and gentlewomen, and to be loved again, and he such a man of prowess as ye speak of—"

"Man of prowess—yes, that is the man to please them, Sandy. Man of brains—that is a thing they never think of. Tom Sayers—John Heenan—John L. Sullivan—pity but you could be here. You would have your legs under the Round Table and a 'Sir' in front of your names within the twenty-four hours; and you could bring about a new distribution of the married princesses and duchesses of the Court in another twenty-four. The fact is, it is just a sort of polished-up court of Comanches, and there isn't a squaw in it who doesn't stand ready at the dropping of a hat to desert to the buck with the biggest string of scalps at his belt."

"—and he be such a man of prowess as ye speak of, said Sir Gawaine. Now what is his name? Sir, said they, his name is Marhaus the king's son of Ireland."

"Son of the king of Ireland, you mean; the other form doesn't mean anything. And look out and hold on tight now, we must jump this gully. . . . There, we are all right now. This horse belongs in the circus; he is born before his time."

"I know him well, said Sir Uwaine, he is a passing good knight as any is on live."

"*On live.* If you've got a fault in the world, Sandy, it is that you are a shade too archaic. But it isn't any matter."

"—for I saw him once proved at a justs where many knights were gathered, and that time there might no man withstand him. Ah, said Sir Gawaine, damsels, methinketh ye are to blame, for it is to suppose he that hung that shield there will not be long therefrom, and then may those knights match him on horseback, and that is more your worship than thus; for I will abide no longer to see a knight's shield dishonored. And therewith Sir Uwaine and Sir Gawaine departed a little from them, and then were they ware where Sir Marhaus came riding on a great horse straight toward them. And when the twelve damsels saw Sir Marhaus they fled into the turret as they were wild, so that some of them fell by the way. Then the one of the knights of the tower dressed his shield, and said on high, Sir Marhaus defend thee. And so they ran together that the knight brake his spear on Marhaus, and Sir Marhaus smote him so hard that he brake his neck and the horse's back—"

"Well, that is just the trouble about this state of things, it ruins so many horses."

"That saw the other knight of the turret, and dressed him toward Marhaus, and they went so eagerly together, that the knight of the turret was soon smitten down, horse and man, stark dead—"

"*Another* horse gone; I tell you it is a custom that ought to be broken up. I don't see how people with any feeling can applaud and support it."

* * * * * *

"So these two knights came together with great random—"

I saw that I had been asleep and missed a chapter, but I didn't say anything. I judged that the Irish knight was in trouble with the visitors by this time, and this turned out to be the case.

"—that Sir Uwaine smote Sir Marhaus that his spear brast in pieces on the shield, and Sir Marhaus smote him so sore that horse and man he bare to the earth, and hurt Sir Uwaine on the left side—"

"The truth is, Alisande, these archaics are a little *too* simple; the vocabulary is too limited, and so, by consequence, descriptions suffer in the matter of variety; they run too much to level Saharas of fact, and not enough to picturesque detail; this throws about them a certain air of the monotonous; in fact the fights are all alike; a couple of people come together with great random—random is a good word, and so is exegesis, for that matter, and so is holocaust, and defalcation, and usufruct and a hundred others, but land! a body ought to discriminate—they come together with great random, and a spear is brast, and one party break his shield and the other one goes down, horse and man, over his horse-tail and brake his neck, and then the next candidate comes randoming in, and brast *his* spear, and the other man brast his shield, and down *he* goes, horse and man, over his horse-tail, and brake *his* neck, and then there's another elected, and another and another and still another, till the material is all used up; and when you come to figure up results, you can't tell one fight from another, nor who whipped; and as a *picture*, of living, raging, roaring battle, sho! why, it's pale and noiseless—just ghosts scuffling in a fog. Dear me, what would this barren vocabulary get out of the mightiest spectacle?—the burning of Rome in Nero's time, for instance? Why, it would merely say, 'Town burned down; no insurance; boy brast a window, fireman brake his neck!' Why, *that* ain't a picture!"

It was a good deal of a lecture, I thought, but it didn't disturb Sandy, didn't turn a feather; her steam soared steadily up again, the minute I took off the lid:

"Then Sir Marhaus turned his horse and rode toward Gawaine with his spear. And when Sir Gawaine saw that, he dressed his shield, and they aventred their spears, and they came together with all the might of their horses, that either knight smote other so hard in the midst of their shields, but Sir Gawaine's spear brake—"

"I knew it would."

—"but Sir Marhaus's spear held; and therewith Sir Gawaine and his horse rushed down to the earth—"

"Just so—and brake his back."

—"and lightly Sir Gawaine rose upon his feet and pulled out his sword, and dressed him toward Sir Marhaus on foot, and therewith either came unto other eagerly, and smote together with their swords, that their shields flew in cantels, and they bruised their helms and their hauberks, and wounded either other. But Sir Gawaine, fro it passed nine of the clock, waxed by the space of three hours ever stronger and stronger, and thrice his might was increased. All this espied Sir Marhaus, and had great wonder how his might increased, and so they wounded other passing sore; and then when it was come noon—"

The pelting sing-song of it carried me forward to scenes and sounds of my boyhood days:

"N-e-e-ew Haven! ten minutes for refreshments—knductr 'll strike the gong-bell two minutes before train leaves—passengers for the Shore-line please take seats in the rear k'yar, this k'yar don't go no furder—*ahh*-pls, *aw*-rnjz, b'*nan*ners, *s-a-n-d*'ches. p——*op*-corn!"

——"and waxed past noon and drew toward evensong. Sir Gawaine's strength feebled and waxed passing faint, that unnethes he might dure any longer, and Sir Marhaus was then bigger and bigger—"

"Which strained his armor, of course; and yet little would one of these people mind a small thing like that."

—"and so, Sir Knight, said Sir Marhaus, I have well felt that ye are a passing good knight, and a marvellous man of might as ever I felt any, while it lasteth, and our quarrels are not great, and therefore it were a pity to do you hurt, for I feel you are passing feeble. Ah, said Sir Gawaine, gentle knight, ye say the word that I should say. And therewith they took off their helms and either kissed other, and there they swore together either to love other as brethren—"

But I lost the thread there, and dozed off to slumber, thinking about what a pity it was that men with such superb strength— strength enabling them to stand up cased in cruelly burdensome iron and drenched with perspiration, and hack and batter and bang each other for six hours on a stretch—should not have been born at a time when they could put it to some useful purpose. Take a jackass, for instance: a jackass has that kind of strength, and puts it to a useful purpose, and is valuable to this world because he *is* a jackass; but a nobleman is not valuable because he is a jackass. It is a mixture that is always ineffectual, and should never have been attempted in the first place. And yet, once you start a mistake, the trouble is done and you never know what is going to come of it.

When I came to myself again and began to listen, I perceived that I had lost another chapter, and that Alisande had wandered a long way off with her people.

"And so they rode and came into a deep valley full of stones, and thereby they saw a fair stream of water; above thereby was the head of the stream, a fair fountain, and three damsels sitting thereby. In this country, said Sir Marhaus, came never knight since it was christened, but he found strange adventures—"

"This is not good form, Alisande. Sir Marhaus the king's son of Ireland talks like all the rest; you ought to give him a brogue, or at least a characteristic expletive; by this means one would recognize him as soon as he spoke, without his ever being named. It is a common literary device with the great authors. You should make

him say, 'In this country, be jabers, came never knight since it was
christened, but he found strange adventures, be jabers.' You see
how much better that sounds."

—"came never knight but he found strange adventures, be jabers.
Of a truth it doth indeed, fair lord, albeit 'tis passing hard to say,
though peradventure that will not tarry but better speed with usage.
And then they rode to the damsels, and either saluted other, and the
eldest had a garland of gold about her head, and she was
threescore winter of age or more—"

"The *damsel* was?"

"Even so, dear lord—and her hair was white under the garland—"

"Celluloid teeth, nine dollars a set, as like as not—the loose-fit
kind, that go up and down like a portcullis when you eat, and fall
out when you laugh."

"The second damsel was of thirty winter of age, with a circlet of
gold about her head. The third damsel was but fifteen year of age—"

Billows of thought came rolling over my soul, and the voice faded
out of my hearing!

Fifteen! Break—my heart! oh, my lost darling! Just her age who
was so gentle, and lovely, and all the world to me, and whom I shall
never see again! How the thought of her carries me back over wide
seas of memory to a vague dim time, a happy time, so many, many
centuries hence, when I used to wake in the soft summer mornings,
out of sweet dreams of her, and say "Hello, Central!" just to hear
her dear voice come melting back to me with a "Hello, Hank!"
that was music of the spheres to my enchanted ear. She got three
dollars a week, but she was worth it.

I could not follow Alisande's further explanation of who our
captured knights were, now—I mean in case she should ever get to
explaining who they were. My interest was gone, my thoughts were
far away, and sad. By fitful glimpses of the drifting tale, caught
here and there and now and then, I merely noted in a vague way that
each of these three knights took one of these three damsels up
behind him on his horse, and one rode north, another east, the other
south, to seek adventures, and meet again and lie, after year and
day. Year and day—and without baggage. It was of a piece with the
general simplicity of the country.

The sun was now setting. It was about three in the afternoon when
Alisande had begun to tell me who the cowboys were; so she had
made pretty good progress with it—for her. She would arrive some
time or other, no doubt, but she was not a person who could be
hurried.

We were approaching a castle which stood on high ground; a
huge, strong, venerable structure, whose gray towers and
battlements were charmingly draped with ivy, and whose whole
majestic mass was drenched with splendors flung from the sinking

sun. It was the largest castle we had seen, and so I thought it might
be the one we were after, but Sandy said no. She did not know who
owned it; she said she had passed it without calling, when she went
down to Camelot.

CHAPTER XVI

MORGAN LE FAY

If knights errant were to be believed, not all castles were desirable
places to seek hospitality in. As a matter of fact, knights errant were
not persons to be believed—that is, measured by modern standards
of veracity; yet, measured by the standards of their own time, and
scaled accordingly, you got the truth. It was very simple: you
discounted a statement ninety-seven per cent.; the rest was fact.
Now after making this allowance, the truth remained that if I could
find out something about a castle before ringing the door-bell—I
mean hailing the warders—it was the sensible thing to do. So I was
pleased when I saw in the distance a horseman making the bottom
turn of the road that wound down from this castle.

As we approached each other, I saw that he wore a plumed
helmet, and seemed to be otherwise clothed in steel, but bore a
curious addition also—a stiff square garment like a herald's
tabard. However, I had to smile at my own forgetfulness when I
got nearer and read this sign on his tabard:

"Persimmons's Soap—All the Prime-Donne Use It."

That was a little idea of my own, and had several wholesome
purposes in view toward the civilizing and uplifting of this nation.
In the first place, it was a furtive, underhand blow at this nonsense
of knight errantry, though nobody suspected that but me. I had
started a number of these people out—the bravest knights I could
get—each sandwiched between bulletin-boards bearing one device
or another, and I judged that by-and-by when they got to be
numerous enough they would begin to look ridiculous; and then,
even the steel-clad ass that *hadn't* any board would himself begin
to look ridiculous because he was out of the fashion.

Secondly, these missionaries would gradually, and without
creating suspicion or exciting alarm, introduce a rudimentary
cleanliness among the nobility, and from them it would work down
to the people, if the priests could be kept quiet. This would
undermine the Church. I mean would be a step toward that. Next,
education—next, freedom—and then she would begin to crumble.
It being my conviction that any Established Church is an established

crime, and established slave-pen, I had no scruples, but was willing to assail it in any way or with any weapon that promised to hurt it. Why, in my own former day—in remote centuries not yet stirring in the womb of time—there were old Englishmen who imagined that they had been born in a free country: a "free" country with the Corporation Act and the Test still in force in it—timbers propped against men's liberties and dishonored consciences to shore up an Established Anachronism with.

My missionaries were taught to spell out the gilt signs on their tabards—the showy gilding was a neat idea, I could have got the king to wear a bulletin-board for the sake of that barbaric splendor—they were to spell out these signs and then explain to the lords and ladies what soap was; and if the lords and ladies were afraid of it, get them to try it on a dog. The missionary's next move was to get the family together and try it on himself; he was to stop at no experiment, however desperate, that could convince the nobility that soap was harmless; if any final doubt remained, he must catch a hermit—the woods were full of them; saints they called themselves, and saints they were believed to be. They were unspeakably holy, and worked miracles, and everybody stood in awe of them. If a hermit could survive a wash, and that failed to convince a duke, give him up, let him alone.

Whenever my missionaries overcame a knight errant on the road they washed him, and when he got well they swore him to go and get a bulletin-board and disseminate soap and civilization the rest of his days. As a consequence the workers in the field were increasing by degrees, and the reform was steadily spreading. My soap factory felt the strain early. At first I had only two hands; but before I had left home I was already employing fifteen, and running night and day; and the atmospheric result was getting so pronounced that the king went sort of fainting and gasping around and said he did not believe he could stand it much longer, and Sir Launcelot got so that he did hardly anything but walk up and down the roof and swear, although I told him it was worse up there than anywhere else, but he said he wanted plenty of air; and he was always complaining that a palace was no place for a soap factory, anyway, and said if a man was to start one in his house he would be damned if he wouldn't strangle him. There were ladies present, too, but much these people ever cared for that; they would swear before children, if the wind was their way when the factory was going.

This missionary knight's name was La Cote Male Taile, and he said that this castle was the abode of Morgan le Fay, sister of King Arthur, and wife of King Uriens, monarch of a realm about as big as the District of Columbia—you could stand in the middle of it and throw bricks into the next kingdom. "Kings" and "Kingdoms" were as thick in Britain as they had been in little Palestine in

Joshua's time, when people had to sleep with their knees pulled up because they couldn't stretch out without a passport.

La Cote was much depressed, for he had scored here the worst failure of his campaign. He had not worked off a cake; yet he had tried all the tricks of the trade, even to the washing of a hermit; but the hermit died. This was indeed a bad failure, for this animal would now be dubbed a martyr, and would take his place among the saints of the Roman calendar. Thus made he his moan, this poor Sir La Cote Male Taile, and sorrowed passing sore. And so my heart bled for him, and I was moved to comfort and stay him. Wherefore I said—

"Forbear to grieve, fair knight, for this is not a defeat. We have brains, you and I; and for such as have brains there are no defeats, but only victories. Observe how we will turn this seeming disaster into an advertisement; an advertisement for our soap; and the biggest one, to draw, that was ever thought of; an advertisement that will transform that Mount Washington defeat into a Matterhorn victory. We will put on your bulletin-board, *'Patronized by the Elect.'* How does that strike you?"

"Verily, it is wonderly bethought!"

"Well, a body is bound to admit that for just a modest little one-line ad, it's a corker."

So the poor colporteur's griefs vanished away. He was a brave fellow, and had done mighty feats of arms in his time. His chief celebrity rested upon the events of an excursion like this one of mine, which he had once made with a damsel named Maledisant, who was as handy with her tongue as was Sandy, though in a different way, for her tongue churned forth only railings and insult, whereas Sandy's music was of a kindlier sort. I knew his story well, and so I knew how to interpret the compassion that was in his face when he bade me farewell. He supposed I was having a bitter hard time of it.

Sandy and I discussed his story, as we rode along, and she said that La Cote's bad luck had begun with the very beginning of that trip; for the king's fool had overthrown him on the first day, and in such cases it was customary for the girl to desert to the conqueror, but Maledisant didn't do it; and also persisted afterward in sticking to him, after all his defeats. But, said I, suppose the victor should decline to accept his spoil? She said that that wouldn't answer—he must. He couldn't decline; it wouldn't be regular. I made a note of that. If Sandy's music got to be too burdensome, some time, I would let a knight defeat me, on the chance that she would desert to him.

In due time we were challenged by the warders, from the castle walls, and after a parley admitted. I have nothing pleasant to tell about that visit. But it was not a disappointment, for I knew Mrs. le Fay by reputation, and was not expecting anything pleasant. She was held in awe by the whole realm, for she had made everybody believe she was a great sorceress. All her ways were wicked, all her

instincts devilish. She was loaded to the eye-lids with cold malice,
All her history was black with crime; and among her crimes murder
was common. I was most curious to see her; as curious as I could
have been to see Satan. To my surprise she was beautiful; black
thoughts had failed to make her expression repulsive, age had
failed to wrinkle her satin skin or mar its bloomy freshness. She
could have passed for old Urien's grand-daughter, she could have
been mistaken for sister to her own son.

As soon as we were fairly within the castle gates we were ordered
into her presence. King Uriens was there, a kind-faced old man with
a subdued look; and also the son, Sir Uwaine le Blanchemains, in
whom I was of course interested on account of the tradition that he
had once done battle with thirty knights, and also on account of
his trip with Sir Gawaine and Sir Marhaus, which Sandy had
been aging me with. But Morgan was the main attraction, the
conspicuous personality here; she was head chief of this household,
that was plain. She caused us to be seated, and then she began
with all manner of pretty graces and graciousnesses, to ask me
questions. Dear me, it was like a bird or a flute, or something,
talking. I felt persuaded that this woman must have been
misrepresented, lied about. She trilled along, and trilled along, and
presently a handsome young page, clothed like the rainbow, and
as easy and undulatory of movement as a wave, came with something
on a golden salver, and kneeling to present it to her, overdid his
graces and lost his balance, and so fell lightly against her knee.
She slipped a dirk into him in as matter-of-course a way as another
person would have harpooned a rat!

Poor child, he slumped to the floor, twisted his silken limbs in
one great straining contortion of pain, and was dead. Out of the old
king was wrung an involuntary "O-h!" of compassion. The look he
got, made him cut it suddenly short and not put any more hyphens
in it. Sir Uwaine, at a sign from his mother, went to the ante-room
and called some servants, and meanwhile madame went rippling
sweetly along with her talk.

I saw that she was a good housekeeper, for while she talked she
kept a corner of her eye on the servants to see that they made no
balks in handling the body and getting it out; when they came with
fresh clean towels, she sent back for the other kind; and when they
had finished wiping the floor and were going, she indicated a
crimson fleck the size of a tear which their duller eyes had
overlooked. It was plain to me that La Cote Male Taile had failed
to see the mistress of the house. Often, how louder and clearer than
any tongue, does dumb circumstantial evidence speak.

Morgan le Fay rippled along as musically as ever. Marvellous
woman. And what a glance she had: when it fell in reproof upon
those servants, they shrunk and quailed as timid people do when
the lightning flashes out of a cloud. I could have got the habit

myself. It was the same with that poor old Brer Uriens; he was always on the ragged edge of apprehension; she could not even turn toward him but he winced.

In the midst of the talk I let drop a complimentary word about King Arthur, forgetting for the moment how this woman hated her brother. That one little compliment was enough. She clouded up like a storm; she called for her guards, and said—

"Hale me these varlets to the dungeons."

That struck cold on my ears, for her dungeons had a reputation. Nothing occurred to me to say—or do. But not so with Sandy. As the guard laid a hand upon me, she piped up with the tranquilest confidence, and said—

"God's wownds, dost thou covet destruction, thou maniac? It is The Boss!"

Now what a happy idea that was!—and so simple; yet it would never have occurred to me. I was born modest; not all over, but in spots; and this was one of the spots.

The effect upon madame was electrical. It cleared her countenance and brought back her smiles and all her persuasive graces and blandishments; but nevertheless she was not able to entirely cover up with them the fact that she was in a ghastly fright. She said:

"La, but do list to thine handmaid! as if one gifted with powers like to mine might say the thing which I have said unto one who has vanquished Merlin, and not be jesting. By mine enchantments I foresaw your coming, and by them I knew you when you entered here. I did but play this little jest with hope to surprise you into some display of your art, as not doubting you would blast the guards with occult fires, consuming them to ashes on the spot, a marvel much beyond mine own ability, yet one which I have long been childishly curious to see."

The guards were less curious, and got out as soon as they got permission.

CHAPTER XVII

A ROYAL BANQUET

Madame seeing me pacific and unresentful, no doubt judged that I was deceived by her excuse; for her fright dissolved away, and she was soon so importunate to have me give an exhibition and kill somebody, that the thing grew to be embarrassing. However, to my relief she was presently interrupted by the call to prayers. I will say this much for the nobility: that, tyrannical, murderous, rapacious and morally rotten as they were, they were deeply and enthusiastically religious. Nothing could divert them from the

regular and faithful performance of the pieties enjoined by the
Church. More than once I had seen a noble who had gotten his
enemy at a disadvantage, stop to pray before cutting his throat;
more than once I had seen a noble, after ambushing and
despatching his enemy, retire to the nearest wayside shrine and
humbly give thanks, without ever waiting to rob the body. There
was to be nothing finer or sweeter in the life of even Benvenuto
Cellini, that rough-hewn saint, ten centuries later. All of the nobles
of Britain, with their families, attended divine service morning and
night daily, in their private chapels, and even the worst of them had
family worship five or six times a day besides. The credit of this
belonged entirely to the Church. Although I was no friend to that
Catholic Church, I was obliged to admit this. And often, in spite of
me, I found myself saying. "What would this country be without
the Church?"

After prayers we had dinner in a great banqueting hall which was
lighted by hundreds of grease-jets, and everything was as fine and
lavish and rudely splendid as might become the royal degree of the
hosts. At the head of the hall, on a dais, was the table of the king,
queen, and their son, Prince Uwaine. Stretching down the hall from
this, was the general table, on the floor. At this, above the salt, sat
the visiting nobles and the grown members of their families, of both
sexes,—the resident Court, in effect—sixty-one persons; below the
salt sat minor officers of the household, with their principal
subordinates: altogether a hundred and eighteen persons sitting,
and about as many liveried servants standing behind their chairs, or
serving in one capacity or another. It was a very fine show. In a
gallery a band with cymbals, horns, harps and other horrors, opened
the proceedings with what seemed to be the crude first-draft or
original agony of the wail known to later centuries as "In the Sweet
Bye and Bye." It was new, and ought to have been rehearsed a little
more. For some reason or other the queen had the composer hanged,
after dinner.

After this music, the priest who stood behind the royal table said a
noble long grace in ostensible Latin. Then the battalion of waiters
broke away from their posts, and darted, rushed, flew, fetched and
carried, and the mighty feeding began; no words anywhere, but
absorbing attention to business. The rows of chops opened and shut
in vast unison, and the sound of it was like to the muffled burr of
subterranean machinery.

The havoc continued an hour and a half, and unimaginable was
the destruction of substantials. Of the chief feature of the feast—the
huge wild boar that lay stretched out so portly and imposing at the
start—nothing was left but the semblance of a hoop-skirt; and he
was but the type and symbol of what had happened to all the
other dishes.

With the pastries and so-on, the heavy drinking began—and the talk. Gallon after gallon of wine and mead disappeared, and everybody got comfortable, then happy, then sparklingly joyous—both sexes,—and by-and-by pretty noisy. Men told anecdotes that were terrific to hear, but nobody blushed; and when the nub was sprung, the assemblage let go with a horse-laugh that shook the fortress. Ladies answered back with historiettes that would almost have made Queen Margaret of Navarre or even the great Elizabeth of England hide behind a handkerchief, but nobody hid here, but only laughed—howled, you may say. In pretty much all of these dreadful stories, ecclesiastics were the hardy heroes, but that didn't worry the chaplain any, he had his laugh with the rest; more than that, upon invitation he roared out a song which was of as daring a sort as any that was sung that night.

By midnight everybody was fagged out, and sore with laughing; and as a rule, drunk: some weepingly, some affectionately, some hilariously, some quarrelsomely, some dead and under the table. Of the ladies, the worst spectacle was a lovely young duchess, whose wedding-eve this was; and indeed she was a spectacle, sure enough. Just as she was she could have sat in advance for the portrait of the young daughter of the Regent d'Orleans, at the famous dinner whence she was carried, foul-mouthed, intoxicated and helpless, to her bed, in the lost and lamented days of the Ancient Regime.

Suddenly, even while the priest was lifting his hands, and all conscious heads were bowed in reverent expectation of the coming blessing, there appeared under the arch of the far-off door at the bottom of the hall, an old and bent and white-haired lady, leaning upon a crutch-stick; and she lifted the stick and pointed it toward the queen and cried out—

"The wrath and curse of God fall upon you, woman without pity, who have slain mine innocent grandchild and made desolate this old heart that had nor chick nor friend nor stay nor comfort in all this world but him!"

Everybody crossed himself in a grisly fright, for a curse was an awful thing to those people; but the queen rose up majestic, with the death-light in her eye, and flung back this ruthless command:

"Lay hands on her! To the stake with her!"

The guards left their posts to obey. It was a shame; it was a cruel thing to see. What could be done? Sandy gave me a look; I knew she had another inspiration. I said—

"Do what you choose."

She was up and facing toward the queen in a moment. She indicated me, and said:

"Madame, *he* saith this may not be. Recall the commandment, or he will dissolve the castle and it shall vanish away like the instable fabric of a dream!"

Confound it, what a crazy contract to pledge a person to! What if the queen—

But my consternation subsided there, and my panic passed off; for the queen, all in a collapse, made no show of resistance but gave a countermanding sign and sunk into her seat. When she reached it she was sober. So were many of the others. The assemblage rose, whiffed ceremony to the winds, and rushed for the door like a mob; overturning chairs, smashing crockery, tugging, struggling, shouldering, crowding—anything to get out before I should change my mind and puff the castle into the measureless dim vacancies of space. Well, well, well, they *were* a superstitious lot. It is all a body can do to conceive of it.

The poor queen was so scared and humbled that she was even afraid to hang the composer without first consulting me. I was very sorry for her—indeed any one would have been, for she was really suffering; so I was willing to do anything that was reasonable, and had no desire to carry things to wanton extremities. I therefore considered the matter thoughtfully, and ended by having the musicians ordered into our presence to play that Sweet Bye and Bye again, which they did. Then I saw that she was right, and gave her permission to hang the whole band. This little relaxation of sternness had a good effect upon the queen. A statesman gains little by the arbitrary exercise of iron-clad authority upon all occasions that offer, for this wounds the just pride of his subordinates, and thus tends to undermine his strength. A little concession, now and then, where it can do no harm, is the wiser policy.

Now that the queen was at ease in her mind once more, and measurably happy, her wine naturally began to assert itself again, and it got a little the start of her. I mean it set her music going—her silver bell of a tongue. Dear me, she was a master talker. It would not become me to suggest that it was pretty late and that I was a tired man and very sleepy. I wished I had gone off to bed when I had the chance. Now I must stick it out; there was no other way. So she tinkled along and along, in the otherwise profound and ghostly hush of the sleeping castle, until by-and-by there came, as if from deep down under us, a faraway sound, as of a muffled shriek—with an expression of agony about it that made my flesh crawl. The queen stopped, and her eyes lighted with pleasure; she tilted her graceful head as a bird does when it listens. The sound bored its way up through the stillness again.

"What is it?" I said.

"It is a truly a stubborn soul, and endureth long. It is many hours now."

"Endureth what?"

"The rack. Come—ye shall see a blithe sight. An he yield not his secret now, ye shall see him torn asunder."

What a silky smooth hellion she was; and so composed and serene, when the cords all down my legs were hurting in sympathy with that man's pain. Conducted by mailed guards bearing flaring torches, we tramped along echoing corridors, and down stone stairways dank and dripping, and smelling of mould and ages of imprisoned night—a chill, uncanny journey and a long one, and not made the shorter or the cheerier by the sorceress's talk, which was about this sufferer and his crime. He had been accused by an anonymous informer, of having killed a stag in the royal preserves. I said—

"Anonymous testimony isn't just the right thing, your Highness. It were fairer to confront the accused with the accuser."

"I had not thought of that, it being but of small consequence. But an I would, I could not, for that the accuser came masked by night, and told the forester, and straightway got him hence again, and so the forester knoweth him not."

"Then is this Unknown the only person who saw the stag killed?"

"Marry, *no* man *saw* the killing, but this Unknown saw this hardy wretch near to the spot where the stag lay, and came with right loyal zeal and betrayed him to the forester."

"So the Unknown was near the dead stag, too? Isn't it just possible that he did the killing himself? His loyal zeal—in a mask— looks just a shade suspicious. But what is your Highness's idea for racking the prisoner? Where is the profit?"

"He will not confess, else; and then were his soul lost. For his crime his life is forfeited by the law—and of a surety will I see that he payeth it!—but it were peril to my own soul to let him die unconfessed and unabsolved. Nay, I were a fool to fling me into hell for *his* accommodation."

"But, your Highness, suppose he has nothing to confess?"

"As to that, we shall see, anon. An I rack him to death and he confess not, it will peradventure show that he had indeed naught to confess—ye will grant that that is sooth? Then shall I not be damned for an unconfessed man that had naught to confess—wherefore, I shall be safe."

It was the stubborn unreasoning of the time. It was useless to argue with her. Arguments have no chance against petrified training; they wear it as little as the waves wear a cliff. And her training was everybody's. The brightest intellect in the land would not have been able to see that her position was defective.

As we entered the rack-cell I caught a picture that will not go from me; I wish it would. A native young giant of thirty or thereabouts, lay stretched upon the frame on his back, with his wrists and ankles tied to ropes which led over windlasses at either end. There was no color in him; his features were contorted and set, and sweat-drops stood upon his forehead. A priest bent over him on each side; the executioner stood by; guards were on duty; smoking torches stood in sockets along the walls; in a corner crouched a poor young creature, her face drawn with anguish, a half-wild and hunted look in her eyes, and in her lap lay a little child asleep. Just as we stepped across the threshold the executioner gave his machine a slight turn, which wrung a cry from both the prisoner and the woman; but I shouted and the executioner released the strain without waiting to see who spoke. I could not let this horror go on; it would have killed me to see it. I asked the queen to let me clear the place and speak to the prisoner privately; and when she was going to object I spoke in a low voice and said I did not want to make a scene before her servants, but I must have my way; for I was King Arthur's representative, and was speaking in his name. She saw she had to yield. I asked her to indorse me to these people, and then leave me. It was not pleasant for her, but she took the pill; and even went further than I was meaning to require. I only wanted the backing of her own authority; but she said—

"Ye will do in all things as this lord shall command. It is The Boss."

It was certainly a good word to conjure with: you could see it by the squirming of these rats. The queen's guards fell into line, and she and they marched away, with their torch-bearers, and woke the echoes of the cavernous tunnels with the measured beat of their retreating foot-falls. I had the prisoner taken from the rack and placed upon his bed, and medicaments applied to his hurts, and wine given him to drink. The woman crept near and looked on, eagerly, lovingly, but timorously,—like one who fears a repulse; indeed, she tried furtively to touch the man's forehead, and jumped back, the picture of fright, when I turned unconsciously toward her. It was pitiful to see.

"Lord," I said, "stroke him, lass, if you want to. Do anything you're a mind to; don't mind me."

Why, her eyes were as grateful as an animal's, when you do it a kindness that it understands. The baby was out of her way and she had her cheek against the man's in a minute, and her hands fondling his hair, and her happy tears running down. The man revived, and caressed his wife with his eyes, which was all he could do. I judged I might clear the den, now, and I did; cleared it of all but the family and myself. Then I said—

"Now my friend, tell me your side of this matter; I know the other side."

The man moved his head in sign of refusal. But the woman looked pleased—as it seemed to me—pleased with my suggestion. I went on:

"You know of me?"

"Yes. All do, in Arthur's realms."

"If my reputation has come to you right and straight, you should not be afraid to speak."

The woman broke in, eagerly:

"Ah, fair my lord, do thou persuade him! Thou canst an thou

wilt. Ah, he suffereth so; and it is for me—for *me!* And how can I bear it? I would I might see him die—a sweet, swift death; oh, my Hugo, I cannot bear this one!"

And she fell to sobbing and grovelling about my feet, and still imploring. Imploring what? The man's death? I could not quite get the bearings of the thing. But Hugo interrupted her and said—

"Peace! Ye wit not what ye ask. Shall I starve whom I love, to win a gentle death? I wend thou knewest me better."

"Well," I said, "I can't quite make this out. It is a puzzle. Now—"

"Ah, dear my lord, an ye will but persuade him! Consider how these his tortures wound me! Oh, and he will not speak!—whereas, the healing, the solace that lie in a blessed swift death—"

"What *are* you maundering about? He's going out from here a free man and whole—he's not going to die."

The man's white face lit up, and the woman flung herself at me in a most surprising explosion of joy, and cried out—

"He is saved!—for it is the king's word by the mouth of the king's servant—Arthur, the king whose word is gold!"

"Well, then you do believe I can be trusted, after all. Why didn't you before?"

"Who doubted? Not I, indeed; and not she."

"Well, why wouldn't you tell me your story, then?"

"Ye had made no promise; else had it been otherwise."

"I see, I see. . . . And yet I believe I don't quite see, after all. You stood the torture and refused to confess; which shows plain enough to even the dullest understanding that you had nothing to confess—"

"*I,* my lord? How so? It was I that killed the deer!"

"You *did?* Oh, dear, this is the most mixed-up business that ever—"

"Dear lord, I begged him on my knees to confess, but—"

"You *did!* It gets thicker and thicker. What did you want him to do that for?"

"Sith it would bring him a quick death and save him all this cruel pain."

"Well—yes, there is reason in that. But *he* didn't want the quick death."

"He? Why, of surety he *did.*"

"Well, then, why in the world *didn't* he confess?"

"Ah, sweet sir, and leave my wife and chick without bread and shelter?"

"Oh, heart of gold, now I see it! The bitter law takes the convicted man's estate and beggars his widow and his orphans. They could torture you to death, but without conviction or confession they could not rob your wife and baby. You stood by them like a man; and *you*—true wife and true woman that you are—you would have brought him release from torture at cost to yourself of slow starvation and death—well, it humbles a body to think what your sex can do when it comes to self-sacrifice. I'll book you both for my colony; you'll like it there; it's a Factory where I'm going to turn groping and grubbing automata into *men*."

CHAPTER XVIII

IN THE QUEEN'S DUNGEONS

Well, I arranged all that; and I had the man sent to his home. I had a great desire to rack the executioner; not because he was a good, pains-taking and pain-giving official,—for surely it was not to his discredit that he performed his functions well—but to pay him back for wantonly cuffing and otherwise distressing that young woman. The priests told me about this, and were generously hot to have him punished. Something of this disagreeable sort was turning up every now and then. I mean, episodes that showed that not all priests were frauds and self-seekers, but that many, even the great majority, of these that were down on the ground among the common people, were sincere and right-hearted, and devoted to the alleviation of human troubles and sufferings. Well, it was a thing which could not be helped, so I seldom fretted about it, and never many minutes at a time; it has never been my way to bother much about things which you can't cure. But I did not like it, for it was just the sort of thing to keep people reconciled to an Established Church. We *must* have a religion—it goes without saying—but my idea is, to have it cut up into forty free sects, so that they will police each other, as had been the case in the United States in my time. Concentration of power in a political machine is bad; and an Established Church is only a political machine; it was invented for that; it is nursed, cradled, preserved for that; it is an enemy to human liberty, and does no good which it could not better do in a split-up and scattered condition. That wasn't law; it wasn't gospel: it was only an opinion—my opinion, and I was only a man, one man: so it wasn't worth any more than the pope's—or any less, for that matter.

Well, I couldn't rack the executioner, neither would I overlook the just complaint of the priests. The man must be punished somehow or other, so I degraded him from his office and made him leader of the band—the new one that was to be started. He begged hard, and said he couldn't play—a plausible excuse, but too thin; there wasn't a musician in the country that could.

The queen was a good deal outraged, next morning, when she found she was going to have neither Hugo's life nor his property. But I told her she must bear this cross; that while by law and custom she certainly was entitled to both the man's life and his property, there were extenuating circumstances, and so in Arthur the king's name I had pardoned him. The deer was ravaging the man's fields, and he had killed it in sudden passion, and not for gain; and he had carried it into the royal forest in the hope that that might make detection of the misdoer impossible. Confound her, I couldn't make her see that sudden passion is an extenuating circumstance in the killing of venison—or of a person—so I gave it up and let her sulk it out. I *did* think I was going to make her see it by remarking that her own sudden passion in the case of the page modified that crime.

"Crime!" she exclaimed. "How thou talkest! Crime, forsooth! Man, I am going to *pay* for him!"

Oh, it was no use to waste sense on her. Training—training is everything; training is all there is *to* a person. We speak of nature; it is folly; there is no such thing as nature; what we call by that misleading name is merely heredity and training. We have no thoughts of our own, no opinions of our own; they are transmitted to us, trained into us. All that is original in us, and therefore fairly creditable or discreditable to us, can be covered up and hidden by the point of a cambric needle, all the rest being atoms contributed by, and inherited from, a procession of ancestors that stretches back a billion years to the Adam-clam or grasshopper or monkey from whom our race has been so tediously and ostentatiously and unprofitably developed. And as for me, all that I think about in this plodding sad pilgrimage, this pathetic drift between the eternities, is to look out and humbly live a pure and high and blameless life, and save that one microscopic atom in me that is truly *me:* the rest may land in Sheol and welcome for all I care.

No, confound her, her intellect was good, she had brains enough, but her training made her an ass—that is, from a many-centuries-later point of view. To kill the page was no crime—it was her right; and upon her right she stood, serenely and unconscious of offence. She was a result of generations of training in the unexamined and unassailed belief that the law which permitted her to kill a subject when she chose was a perfectly right and righteous one.

Well, we must give even Satan his due. She deserved a compliment for one thing; and I tried to pay it, but the words stuck in my throat. She had a right to kill the boy, but she was in no wise obliged to pay for him. That was law for some other people, but not for her. She knew quite well that she was doing a large and generous thing to pay for that lad, and that I ought in common fairness to come out with something handsome about it, but I couldn't—my mouth refused. I couldn't help seeing, in my fancy, that poor old grandma with the broken heart, and that fair young creature lying butchered, his little silken pomps and vanities laced with his golden blood. How could she *pay* for him! *Whom* could she pay? And so, well knowing that this woman, trained as she had been, deserved praise, even

adulation, I was yet not able to utter it, trained as *I* had been. The
best I could do was to fish up a compliment from outside, so to
speak—and the pity of it was, that it was true:

"Madame, your people will adore you for this."

Quite true, but I meant to hang her for it some day, if I lived.
Some of those laws were too bad, altogether too bad. A master
might kill his slave for nothing: for mere spite, malice, or to pass the
time—just as we have seen that the crowned head could do it with
his slave, that is to say, anybody. A gentleman could kill a free
commoner, and pay for him—cash or garden-truck. A noble could
kill a noble without expense, as far as the law was concerned, but
reprisals in kind were to be expected. *Any*body could kill *some*body,
except the commoner and the slave; these had no privileges. If they
killed, it was murder, and the law wouldn't stand murder. It made
short work of the experimenter—and of his family too, if he
murdered somebody who belonged up among the ornamental ranks.
If a commoner gave a noble even so much as a Damiens-scratch
which didn't kill or even hurt, he got Damiens's dose for it just the
same; they pulled him to rags and tatters with horses, and all the
world came to see the show, and crack jokes, and have a good time;
and some of the performances of the best people present were as
tough, and as properly unprintable, as any that have been printed by
the pleasant Casanova in his chapter about the dismemberment of
Louis X V.'s poor awkward enemy.

I had had enough of this grisly place by this time, and wanted to
leave, but I couldn't, because I had something on my mind that
my conscience kept prodding me about, and wouldn't let me forget.
If I had the remaking of man, he wouldn't have any conscience. It
is one of the most disagreeable things connected with a person;
and although it certainly does a great deal of good, it cannot be
said to pay, in the long run; it would be much better to have less
good and more comfort. Still, this is only my opinion, and I am only
one man; others, with less experience, may think differently. They
have a right to their view. I only stand to this: I have noticed my
conscience for many years, and I know it is more trouble and bother
to me than anything else I started with. I suppose that in the
beginning I prized it, because we prize anything that is ours; and
yet how foolish it was to think so. If we look at it in another way,
we see how absurd it is: if I had an anvil in me would I prize
it? Of course not. And yet when you come to think, there is no real
difference between a conscience and an anvil—I mean for comfort.
I have noticed it a thousand times. And you could dissolve an anvil
with acids, when you couldn't stand it any longer; but there isn't
any way that you can work off a conscience—at least so it will stay
worked off; not that I know of, anyway.

There was something I wanted to do before leaving, but it was a
disagreeable matter, and I hated to go at it. Well, it bothered me all

the morning. I could have mentioned it to the old king, but what would be the use?—he was but an extinct volcano; he had been active in his time, but his fire was out, this good while, he was only a stately ash-pile, now; gentle enough, and kindly enough for my purpose, without doubt, but not usable. He was nothing, this so-called king: the queen was the only power there. And she was a Vesuvius. As a favor, she might consent to warm a flock of sparrows for you, but then she might take that very opportunity to turn herself loose and bury a city. However, I reflected that as often as any other way, when you are expecting the worst, you get something that is not so bad, after all.

So I braced up and placed my matter before her royal Highness. I said I had been having a general jail-delivery at Camelot and among neighboring castles, and with her permission I would like to examine her collection, her bric-a-brac—that is to say, her prisoners. She resisted; but I was expecting that. But she finally consented. I was expecting that, too, but not so soon. That about ended my discomfort. She called her guards and torches, and we went down into the dungeons. These were down under the castle's foundations, and mainly were small cells hollowed out of the living rock. Some of these cells had no light at all. In one of them was a woman, in foul rags, who sat on the ground, and would not answer a question, or speak a word, but only looked up at us once or twice, through a cobweb of tangled hair, as if to see what casual thing it might be that was disturbing with sound and light the meaningless dull dream that was become her life; after that, she sat bowed, with her dirt-caked fingers idly interlocked in her lap, and gave no further sign. This poor rack of bones was a woman of middle age, apparently; but only apparently; she had been there nine years, and was eighteen when she entered. She was a commoner, and had been sent here on her bridal night by Sir Breuse Sance Pité, a neighboring lord whose vassal her father was, and to which said lord she had refused what has since been called *le droit du seigneur;* and moreover, had opposed violence to violence and spilt half a gill of his almost sacred blood. The young husband had interfered at that point, believing the bride's life in danger, and had flung the noble out into the midst of the humble and trembling wedding guests, in the parlor, and left him there astonished at this strange treatment, and implacably embittered against both bride and groom. The said lord being cramped for dungeon-room had asked the queen to accommodate his two criminals, and here in her bastile they had been ever since; hither indeed, they had come before their crime was an hour old, and had never seen each other since. Here they were, kernelled like toads in the same rock; they had passed nine pitch dark years within fifty feet of each other, yet neither knew whether the other was alive or not. All the first years, their only question had been—asked with beseechings and tears that might have moved

stones, in time, perhaps, but hearts are not stones: "Is he alive?"
"Is she alive?" But they had never got an answer; and at last that
question was not asked any more—or any other.

I wanted to see the man, after hearing all this. He was thirty-four
years old, and looked sixty. He sat upon a squared block of stone,
with his head bent down, his forearms resting on his knees, his long
hair hanging like a fringe before his face, and he was muttering to
himself. He raised his chin and looked us slowly over, in a listless
dull way, blinking with the distress of the torchlight, then dropped
his head and fell to muttering again and took no further notice of us.
There were some pathetically suggestive dumb witnesses present.
On his wrists and ankles were cicatrices, old smooth scars, and
fastened to the stone on which he sat was a chain with manacles and
fetters attached; but this apparatus lay idle on the ground, and was
thick with rust. Chains cease to be needed after the spirit has gone
out of a prisoner.

I could not rouse the man; so I said we would take him to her,
and see—to the bride who was the fairest thing in the earth to him,
once—roses, pearls and dew made flesh, for him; a wonder-work,
the master-work of nature: with eyes like no other eyes, and voice
like no other voice, and a freshness, and lithe young grace, and
beauty, that belonged properly to the creatures of dreams—as he
thought—and to no other. The sight of her would set his stagnant
blood leaping; the sight of her—

But it was a disappointment. They sat together on the ground
and looked dimly wondering into each other's faces a while, with
a sort of weak animal curiosity; then forgot each other's presence,
and dropped their eyes, and you saw that they were away again and
wandering in some far land of dreams and shadows that we know
nothing about.

I had them taken out and sent to their friends. The queen did not
like it much. Not that she felt any personal interest in the matter,
but she thought it disrespectful to Sir Breuse Sance Pité. However, I
assured her that if he found he couldn't stand it I would fix him so
that he could.

I set forty-seven prisoners loose out of those awful rat-holes, and
left only one in captivity. He was a lord, and had killed another lord,
a sort of kinsman of the queen. That other lord had ambushed him
to assassinate him, but this fellow had got the best of him and cut
his throat. However, it was not for that that I left him jailed, but for
maliciously destroying the only public well in one of his wretched
villages. The queen was bound to hang him for killing her kinsman,
but I would not allow it: it was no crime to kill an assassin. But I
said I was willing to let her hang him for destroying the well; so she
concluded to put up with that, as it was better than nothing.

Dear me, for what trifling offences the most of those forty-seven
men and women were shut up there! Indeed, some were there for no

distinct offence at all, but only to gratify somebody's spite; and not always the queen's by any means, but a friend's. The newest prisoner's crime was a mere remark which he had made. He said he believed that men were about all alike, and one man as good as another, barring clothes. He said he believed that if you were to strip the nation naked and send a stranger through the crowd, he couldn't tell the king from a quack doctor, nor a duke from a hotel clerk. Apparently here was a man whose brains had not been reduced to an ineffectual mush by idiotic training. I set him loose and sent him to the Factory.

Some of the cells carved in the living rock were just behind the face of the precipice, and in each of these an arrow-slit had been pierced outward to the daylight, and so the captive had a thin ray from the blessed sun for his comfort. The case of one of these poor fellows was particularly hard. From his dusky swallow's hole high up in that vast wall of native rock he could peer out through the arrow-slit and see his own home off yonder in the valley; and for twenty-two years he had watched it, with heart-ache and longing, through that crack. He could see the lights shine there at night, and in the daytime he could see figures go in and come out—his wife and children, some of them, no doubt, though he could not make out, at that distance. In the course of years he noted festivities there, and tried to rejoice, and wondered if they were weddings or what they might be. And he noted funerals; and they wrung his heart. He could make out the coffin, but he could not determine its size, and so could not tell whether it was wife or child. He could see the procession form, with priests and mourners, and move solemnly away, bearing the secret with them. He had left behind him five children and a wife; and in nineteen years he had seen five funerals issue, and none of them humble enough in pomp to denote a servant. So he had lost five of his treasures; there must still be one remaining—one now infinitely, unspeakably precious,—but *which* one? wife, or child? That was the question that tortured him, by night and by day, asleep and awake. Well, to have an interest, of some sort, and half a ray of light, when you are in a dungeon, is a great support to the body and preserver of the intellect. This man was in pretty good condition yet. By the time he had finished telling me his distressful tale, I was in the same state of mind that you would have been in yourself, if you have got average human curiosity: that is to say, I was as burning up as he was to find out which member of the family it was that was left. So I took him over home myself; and an amazing kind of a surprise party it was, too—typhoons and cyclones of frantic joy, and whole Niagaras of happy tears; and by George we found the aforetime young matron graying toward the imminent verge of her half century, and the babies all men and women, and some of them married and experimenting familywise themselves—for not a soul of the tribe was dead! Conceive of the ingenious devilishness of that queen: she had a special hatred for this prisoner, and she had *invented* all those funerals herself, to scorch his heart with; and the sublimest stroke of genius of the whole thing was leaving the family-invoice a funeral *short,* so as to let him wear his poor old soul out guessing.

But for me, he never would have got out. Morgan le Fay hated him with her whole heart, and she never would have softened toward him. And yet his crime was committed more in thoughtlessness than deliberate depravity. He had said she had red hair. Well, she had; but that was no way to speak of it. When red-headed people are above a certain social grade their hair is auburn.

Consider it: among these forty-seven captives there were five whose names, offences, and dates of incarceration were no longer known! One woman and four men—all bent, and wrinkled, and mind-extinguished patriarchs. They themselves had long ago forgotten these details; at any rate they had mere vague theories about them, nothing definite and nothing that they repeated twice in the same way. The succession of priests whose office it had been to pray daily with the captives and remind them that God had put them there, for some wise purpose or other, and teach them that patience, humbleness, and submission to oppression was what He loved to see in parties of a subordinate rank, had traditions about these poor old human ruins, but nothing more. These traditions went but little way, for they concerned the length of the incarceration only, and not the names of the offences. And even by the help of tradition the only thing that could be proven was that none of the five had seen daylight for thirty-five years: how much longer this privation had lasted was not guessable. The king and the queen knew nothing about these poor creatures, except that they were heirlooms, assets inherited, along with the throne, from the former firm. Nothing of their history had been transmitted with their persons, and so the inheriting owners had considered them of no value, and had felt no interest in them. I said to the queen—

"Then why in the world didn't you set them free?"

The question was a puzzler. She didn't know *why* she hadn't; the thing had never come up in her mind. So here she was, forecasting the veritable history of future prisoners of the Castle d'If, without knowing it. It seemed plain to me now, that with her training, those inherited prisoners were merely property—nothing more, nothing less. Well, when we inherit property, it does not occur to us to throw it away, even when we do not value it.

When I brought my procession of human bats up into the open world and the glare of the afternoon sun—previously blind-folding them, in charity for eyes so long untortured by light—they were a spectacle to look at. Skeletons, scarecrows, goblins, pathetic frights, every one: legitimatest possible children of Monarchy by the Grace of God and the Established Church. I muttered absently—

"I *wish* I could photograph them!"

You have seen that kind of people who will never let on that they don't know the meaning of a new big word. The more ignorant they are, the more pitifully certain they are to pretend you haven't shot over their heads. The queen was just one of that sort, and was always making the stupidest blunders by reason of it. She hesitated a moment; then her face brightened up with sudden comprehension, and she said she would do it for me.

I thought to myself: She? why what can she know about photography? But it was a poor time to be thinking. When I looked around, she was moving on the procession with an axe!

Well, she certainly was a curious one, was Morgan le Fay. I have seen a good many kinds of women in my time, but she laid over them all, for variety. And how sharply characteristic of her this episode was. She had no more idea than a horse, of how to photograph a procession; but being in doubt, it was just like her to try to do it with an axe.

CHAPTER XIX

KNIGHT ERRANTRY AS A TRADE

Sandy and I were on the road again, next morning, bright and early. It was *so* good to open up one's lungs and take in whole luscious barrels-full of the blessed God's untainted, dew-freshened, woodland-scented air once more, after suffocating body and mind for two days and nights in the moral and physical stenches of that intolerable old buzzard-roost! I mean, for me: of course the place was all right and agreeable enough for Sandy, for she had been used to high life all her days.

Poor girl, her jaws had had a wearisome rest, now for a while, and I was expecting to get the consequences. I was right; but she had stood by me most helpfully in the castle, and had mightily supported and reinforced me with gigantic foolishnesses which were worth more for the occasion than wisdoms double their size; so I thought she had earned a right to work her mill for a while, if she wanted to, and I felt not a pang when she started it up:

"Now turn we unto Sir Marhaus that rode with the damsel of thirty winter of age southward—"

"Are you going to see if you can work up another half-stretch on the trail of the cowboys, Sandy?"

"Even so, fair my lord."

"Go ahead, then. I won't interrupt this time, if I can help it. Begin over again; start fair, and shake out all your reefs, and I will load my pipe and give good attention."

"Now turn we unto Sir Marhaus that rode with the damsel of

thirty winter of age southward. And so they came into a deep forest,
and by fortune they were nighted, and rode along in a deep way,
and at the last they came into a courtelage where abode the duke of
South Marches, and there they asked harbour. And on the morn the
duke sent unto Sir Marhaus, and bad him make him ready. And so
Sir Marhaus arose and armed him, and there was a mass sung
afore him, and he brake his fast, and so mounted on horseback
in the court of the castle, there they should do the battle. So there
was the duke already on horseback, clean armed, and his six
sons by him, and every each had a spear in his hand, and so they
encountered, whereas the duke and his two sons brake their spears
upon him, but Sir Marhaus held up his spear and touched none of
them. Then came the four sons by couples, and two of them brake
their spears, and so did the other two. And all this while Sir
Marhaus touched them not. Then Sir Marhaus ran to the duke, and
smote him with his spear that horse and man fell to the earth. And
so he served his sons. And then Sir Marhaus alight down, and bad
the duke yield him or else he would slay him. And then some of his
sons recovered, and would have set upon Sir Marhaus. Then Sir
Marhaus said to the duke, Cease thy sons, or else I will do the
uttermost to you all. When the duke saw he might not escape the
death, he cried to his sons, and charged them to yield them to Sir
Marhaus. And they kneeled all down and put the pommels of their
swords to the knight, and so he received them. And then they holp
up their father, and so by their common assent promised unto Sir
Marhaus never to be foes unto King Arthur, and thereupon at
Whitsuntide after, to come he and his sons, and put them in the
king's grace.*

"Even so standeth the history, fair Sir Boss. Now ye shall wit that
that very duke and his six sons are they whom but few days past
you also did overcome and send to Arthur's court!"

"Why, Sandy, you can't mean it!"

"An I speak not sooth, let it be the worse for me."

"Well, well, well,—now who would ever have thought it? One
whole duke and six dukelets; why, Sandy, it was an elegant haul.
Knight-errantry is a most chuckle-headed trade, and it is tedious
hard work, too, but I begin to see that there *is* money in it, after all,
if you have luck. Not that I would ever engage in it as a business;
for I wouldn't. No sound and legitimate business can be established
on a basis of speculation. A successful whirl in the knight-errantry
line—now what is it when you blow away the nonsense and come
down to the cold facts? It's just a corner in pork, that's all and
you can't make anything else out of it. You're rich—yes,—suddenly
rich—for about a day, maybe a week: then somebody corners the
market on *you*, and down goes your bucket-shop; ain't that so,
Sandy?"

*The story is borrowed, language and all, from the *Morte d'Arthur.*—M.T.

"Whethersoever it be that my mind miscarrieth, bewraying simple language in such sort that the words do seem to come endlong and overthwart—"

"There's no use in beating about the bush and trying to get around it that way, Sandy, it's *so*, just as I say, I *know* it's so. And, moreover, when you come right down to the bed-rock, knight-errantry is *worse* than pork; for whatever happens, the pork's left, and so somebody's benefited, anyway; but when the market breaks, in a knight-errantry whirl, and every knight in the pool passes in his checks, what have you got for assets? Just a rubbish-pile of battered corpses and a barrel or two of busted hardware. Can you call *those* assets? Give me pork, every time. Am I right?"

"Ah, peradventure my head being distraught by the manifold matters whereunto the confusions of these but late adventured haps and fortunings whereby not I alone nor you alone, but every each of us, meseemeth—"

"No, it's not your head, Sandy. Your head's all right, as far as it goes, but you don't know business; that's where the trouble is. It unfits you to argue about business, and you're wrong to be always trying. However, that aside, it was a good haul, anyway, and will breed a handsome crop of reputation in Arthur's court. And speaking of the cowboys, what a curious country this is for women and men that never get old. Now there's Morgan le Fay, as fresh and young as a Vassar pullet, to all appearances, and here is this old duke of the South Marches still slashing away with sword and lance at his time of life, after raising such a family as he has raised. As I understand it, Sir Gawaine killed seven of his sons, and still he had six left for Sir Marhaus and me to take into camp. And then there was that damsel of sixty winter of age still excursioning around in her frosty bloom— How old are you, Sandy?"

It was the first time I ever struck a still place in her. The mill had shut down for repairs, or something.

CHAPTER XX

THE OGRE'S CASTLE

Between six and nine we made ten miles, which was plenty for a horse carrying triple—man, woman, and armor; then we stopped for a long nooning, under some trees by a limpid brook.

Right so came by-and-by a knight riding; and as he drew near he made dolorous moan, and by the words of it I perceived that he was cursing and swearing; yet nevertheless was I glad of his coming, for that I saw he bore a bulletin-board whereon in letters all of shining gold was writ—

"USE PETERSON'S PROPHYLACTIC TOOTH-BRUSH
—ALL THE GO."

I was glad of his coming, for even by this token I knew him for knight of mine. It was Sir Madok de la Montaine, a burly great fellow whose chief distinction was that he had come within an ace of sending Sir Launcelot down over his horse-tail once. He was never long in a stranger's presence without finding some pretext or other to let out that great fact. But there was another fact of nearly the same size, which he never pushed upon anybody unasked, and yet never withheld when asked: that was, that the reason he didn't quite succeed was, that he was interrupted and sent down over horse-tail himself. This innocent vast lubber did not see any particular difference between the two facts. I liked him, for he was earnest in his work, and very valuable. And he was so fine to look at, with his broad mailed shoulders, and the grand leonine set of his plumed head, and his big shield with its quaint device of a gauntleted hand clutching a prophylactic tooth-brush, with motto: *"Try Noyoudont."* This was a tooth-wash that I was introducing.

He was aweary, he said, and indeed he looked it; but he would not alight. He said he was after the stove-polish man; and with this he broke out cursing and swearing anew. The bulletin-boarder referred to was Sir Ossaise of Surluse, a brave knight, and of considerable celebrity on account of his having tried conclusions in a tournament, once, with no less a Mogul than Sir Gaheris himself—although not successfully. He was of a light and laughing disposition, and to him nothing in this world was serious. It was for this reason that I had chosen him to work up a stove-polish sentiment. There were no stoves yet, and so there could be nothing serious about stove-polish. All that the agent needed to do was to deftly and by degrees prepare the public for the great change, and have them established in predilections toward neatness against the time when the stove should appear upon the stage.

Sir Madok was very bitter, and brake out anew with cursings. He said he had cursed his soul to rage; and yet he would not get down from his horse, neither would he take any rest, or listen to any comfort, until he should have found Sir Ossaise and settled this account. It appeared, by what I could piece together of the unprofane fragments of his statement, that he had chanced upon Sir Ossaise at dawn of the morning, and been told that if he would make a short cut across the fields and swamps and broken hills and glades, he could head off a company of travellers who would be rare customers for prophylactics and tooth-wash. With characteristic zeal Sir Madok had plunged away at once upon this quest, and after three hours of awful crosslot riding had overhauled his game. And behold, it was the five patriarchs that had been released from the dungeons the evening before! Poor old creatures, it was all of twenty years since any one of them had known what it was to be equipped with any remaining snag or remnant of a tooth.

"Blank-blank-blank him," said Sir Madok, "an I do not stove-polish him an I may find him, leave it to me; for never no knight that hight Ossaise or aught else may do me this disservice and bide on live, an I may find him, the which I have thereunto sworn a great oath this day."

And with these words, and others, he lightly took his spear and gat him thence. In the middle of the afternoon we came upon one of those very patriarchs ourselves, in the edge of a poor village. He was basking in the love of relatives and friends whom he had not seen for fifty years; and about him and caressing him were also descendants of his own body whom he had never seen at all till now; but to him these were all strangers, his memory was gone, his mind was stagnant. It seemed incredible that a man could outlast half a century shut up in a dark hole like a rat, but here were his old wife and some old comrades to testify to it. They could remember him as he was in the freshness and strength of his young manhood, when he kissed his child and delivered it to its mother's hands and went away into that long oblivion. The people at the castle could not tell within half a generation the length of time the man had been shut up there for his unrecorded and forgotten offence; but this old wife knew; and so did her old child, who stood there among her married sons and daughters trying to realize a father who had been to her a name, a thought, a formless image, a tradition, all her life, and now was suddenly concreted into actual flesh and blood and set before her face.

It was a curious situation; yet it is not on that account that I have made room for it here, but on account of a thing which seemed to me still more curious. To wit, that this dreadful matter brought from these drown-trodden people no outburst of rage against these oppressors. They had been heritors and subjects of cruelty and outrage so long that nothing could have startled them but a kindness. Yes, here was a curious revelation indeed, of the depth to which people had been sunk in slavery. Their entire being was reduced to a monotonous dead level of patience, resignation, dumb uncomplaining acceptance of whatever might befall them in this life. Their very imagination was dead. When you can say that of a man, he has struck bottom, I reckon; there is no lower deep for him.

I rather wished I had gone some other road. This was not the sort of experience for a statesman to encounter who was planning out a peaceful revolution in his mind. For it could not help bringing up the un-get-aroundable fact that, all gentle cant and philosophizing to the contrary notwithstanding, no people in the world ever did achieve their freedom by goody-goody talk and moral suasion: it being immutable law that all revolutions that will succeed, must *begin* in blood, whatever may answer afterward. If history teaches anything, it teaches that. What this folk needed, then, was a Reign of Terror and a guillotine, and I was the wrong man for them.

Two days later, toward noon, Sandy began to show signs of excitement and feverish expectancy. She said we were approaching the ogre's castle. I was surprised into an uncomfortable shock. The object of our quest had gradually dropped out of my mind; this sudden resurrection of it made it seem quite a real and startling thing, for a moment, and roused up in me a smart interest. Sandy's excitement increased every moment; and so did mine, for that sort of thing is catching. My heart got to thumping. You can't reason with your heart; it has its own laws, and thumps about things which the intellect scorns. Presently, when Sandy slid from the horse, motioned me to stop, and went creeping stealthily, with her head bent nearly to her knees, toward a row of bushes that bordered a declivity, the thumpings grew stronger and quicker. And they kept it up while she was gaining her ambush and getting her glimpse over the declivity; and also while I was creeping to her side on my knees. Her eyes were burning, now, as she pointed with her finger, and said in a panting whisper—

"The castle! The castle! Lo, where it looms!"

What a welcome disappointment I experienced! I said—

"Castle? It is nothing but a pig-sty; a pig-sty with a wattled fence around it."

She looked surprised and distressed. The animation faded out of her face; and during many moments she was lost in thought and silent. Then—

"It was not enchanted aforetime," she said in a musing fashion, as if to herself. "And how strange is this marvel, and how awful— that to the one perception it is enchanted and dight in a base and shameful aspect; yet to the perception of the other it is not enchanted, hath suffered no change, but stands firm and stately still, girt with its moat and waving its banners in the blue air from its towers. And God shield us, how it pricks the heart to see again these captives, and the sorrow deepened in their sweet faces! We have tarried along, and are to blame."

I saw my cue. The castle was enchanted to *me*, not to her. It would be wasted time to try to argue her out of her delusion, it couldn't be done; I must just humor it. So I said—

"This is a common case—the enchanting of a thing to one eye and leaving it in its proper form to another. You have heard of it before, Sandy, though you haven't happened to experience it. But no harm is done. In fact it is lucky the way it is. If these ladies were hogs to everybody and to themselves, it would be necessary to break the enchantment, and that might be impossible if one failed to find out the particular process of the enchantment. And hazardous, too; for in attempting a disenchantment without the true key, you are liable to err, and turn your hogs into dogs, and the dogs into cats, the cats into rats, and so on, and end by reducing your materials to nothing, finally, or to an odorless gas which you can't follow—which of course amounts to the same thing. But here, by good-luck, no one's eyes but mine are under the enchantment, and so it is of no consequence to dissolve it. These ladies remain ladies to you, and to themselves, and to everybody else; and at the same time they will suffer in no way from my delusion, for when I know that an ostensible hog is a lady, that is enough for me, I know how to treat her."

"Thanks, oh sweet my lord, thou talkest like an angel. And I know that thou wilt deliver them, for that thou art minded to great deeds and art as strong a knight of your hands and as brave to will and to do, as any that is on life."

"I will not leave a princess in the sty, Sandy. Are those three yonder that to my disordered eyes are starveling swine-herds—"

"The ogres? Are *they* changed also? It is most wonderful. Now am I fearful; for how canst thou strike with sure aim when five of their nine cubits of stature are to thee invisible? Ah, go warily, fair sir; this is a mightier emprise than I wend."

"You be easy, Sandy. All I need to know is, how *much* of an ogre is invisible; then I know how to locate his vitals. Don't you be afraid, I will make short work of these bunco-steerers. Stay where you are."

I left Sandy kneeling there, corpse-faced but plucky and hopeful, and rode down to the pig-sty, and struck up a trade with the swine-herds. I won their gratitude by buying out all the hogs at the lump sum of sixteen pennies, which was rather above latest quotations. I was just in time; for the Church, the lord of the manor, and the rest of the tax gatherers would have been along next day and swept off pretty much all the stock, leaving the swine-herds very short of hogs and Sandy out of princesses. But now the tax people could be paid in cash, and there would be a stake left besides. One of the men had ten children; and he said that last year when a priest came and of his ten pigs took the fattest one for tithes, the wife burst out upon him, and offered him a child and said—

"Thou beast without bowels of mercy, why leave me my child, yet rob me of the wherewithal to feed it?"

How curious. The same thing had happened in the Wales of my day, under this same old Established Church, which was supposed by many to have changed its nature when it changed its disguise.

I sent the three men away, and then opened the sty gate and beckoned Sandy to come—which she did; and not leisurely, but with the rush of a prairie-fire. And when I saw her fling herself upon those hogs, with tears of joy running down her cheeks, and strain them to her heart, and kiss them, and caress them, and call them reverently by grand princely names, I was ashamed of her, ashamed of the human race.

We had to drive those hogs home—ten miles; and no ladies were ever more fickle-minded or contrary. They would stay in no road,

no path; they broke out through the brush on all sides, and flowed
away in all directions, over rocks, and hills, and the roughest places
they could find. And they must not be struck, or roughly accosted;
Sandy could not bear to see them treated in ways unbecoming their
rank. The troublesomest old sow of the lot had to be called my
Lady, and your Highness, like the rest. It is annoying and difficult
to scour around after hogs, in armor. There was one small countess,
with an iron ring in her snout and hardly any hair on her back, that
was the devil for perversity. She gave me a race of an hour, over all
sorts of country, and then we were right where we had started
from, having made not a rod of real progress. I seized her at last by
the tail, and brought her along, squealing. When I overtook Sandy,
she was horrified, and said it was in the last degree indelicate to drag
a countess by her train.

We got the hogs home just at dark—most of them. The princess
Nerovens de Morganore was missing, and two of her ladies in
waiting: namely, Miss Angela Bohun, and the Demoiselle Elaine
Courtemains, the former of these two being a young black sow with a
white star in her forehead, and the latter a brown one with thin legs
and a slight limp in the forward shank on the starboard side—a
couple of the tryingest blisters to drive, that I ever saw. Also among
the missing were several mere baronesses—and I wanted them to
stay missing; but no, all that sausage-meat had to be found; so
servants were sent out with torches to scour the woods and hills to
that end.

Of course the whole drove was housed in the house, and great
guns!—well, I never saw anything like it. Nor ever heard anything
like it. And never smelt anything like it. It was like an insurrection
in a gasometer.

CHAPTER XXI

THE PILGRIMS

When I did get to bed at last I was unspeakably tired; the
stretching out, and the relaxing of the long-tense muscles, how
luxurious, how delicious! but that was as far as I could get—sleep
was out of the question, for the present. The ripping and tearing and
squealing of the nobility up and down the halls and corridors was
pandemonium come again, and kept me broad awake. Being awake,
my thoughts were busy of course; and mainly they busied
themselves with Sandy's curious delusion. Here she was, as sane a
person as the kingdom could produce; and yet, from my point of
view she was acting like a crazy woman. My land, the power of
training! of influence! of education! It can bring a body up to believe
anything. I had to put myself in Sandy's place to realize that she was
not a lunatic. Yes, and put her in mine, to demonstrate how easy it

is to seem a lunatic to a person who has not been taught as you have been taught. If I had told Sandy I had seen a wagon, uninfluenced by enchantment, spin along fifty miles an hour; had seen a man, unequipped with magic powers, get into a basket and soar out of sight among the clouds; and had listened, without any necromancer's help, to the conversation of a person who was several hundred miles away, Sandy would not merely have supposed me to be crazy, she would have thought she knew it. Everybody around her believed in enchantments; nobody had any doubts; to doubt that a castle could be turned into a sty, and its occupants into hogs, would have been the same as my doubting, among Connecticut people, the actuality of the telephone and its wonders,—and in both cases would be absolute proof of a diseased mind, an unsettled reason. Yes, Sandy was sane; that must be admitted. If I also would be sane—to Sandy—I must keep my superstitions about unenchanted and unmiraculous locomotives, balloons and telephones, to myself. Also, I believed that the world was not flat, and hadn't pillars under it to support it, nor a canopy over it to turn off a universe of water that occupied all space above: but as I was the only person in the kingdom afflicted with such impious and criminal opinions, I recognized that it would be good wisdom to keep quiet about this matter, too, if I did not wish to be suddenly shunned and forsaken by everybody as a madman.

The next morning Sandy assembled the swine in the dining-room and gave them their breakfast, waiting upon them personally and manifesting in every way the deep reverence which the natives of her island, ancient and modern, have always felt for rank, let its outward casket and the mental and moral contents be what they may. I could have eaten with the hogs if I had had birth approaching my lofty official rank; but I hadn't, and so accepted the unavoidable slight and made no complaint. Sandy and I had our breakfast at the second table. The family were not at home. I said:

"How many are in the family, Sandy, and where do they keep themselves?"

"Family?"

"Yes."

"Which family, good my lord?"

"Why, this family; your own family."

"Sooth to say, I understand you not. I have no family."

"No family? Why, Sandy, isn't this your home?"

"Now how indeed might that be? I have no home."

"Well, then, whose house is this?"

"Ah, wit you well I would tell you an I knew myself."

"Well, then, whose house is this?"

"Ah, wit you well I would tell you an I knew myself."

"Come—you don't even know these people? Then who invited us here?"

"None invited us. We but came; that is all."

"Why, woman, this is a most extraordinary performance. The effrontery of it is beyond admiration. We blandly march into a man's house, and cram it full of the only really valuable nobility the sun has yet discovered in the earth, and then it turns out that we don't even know the man's name. How did you ever venture to take this extravagant liberty? I supposed, of course, it was your home. What will the man say?"

"What will he say? Forsooth what can he say but give thanks?"

"Thanks for what?"

Her face was filled with a puzzled surprise:

"Verily, thou troublest mine understanding with strange words. Do ye dream that one of his estate is like to have the honor twice in his life to entertain company such as we have brought to grace his house withal?"

"Well, no—when you come to that. No, it's an even bet that this is the first time he has had a treat like this."

"Then let him be thankful, and manifest the same by grateful speech and due humility; he were a dog, else, and the heir and ancestor of dogs."

To my mind, the situation was uncomfortable. It might become more so. It might be a good idea to muster the hogs and move on. So I said:

"The day is wasting, Sandy. It is time to get the nobility together and be moving."

"Wherefore, fair sir and Boss?"

"We want to take them to their home, don't we?"

"La, but list to him! They be of all the regions of the earth! Each must hie to her own home; wend you we might do all these journeys in one so brief life as He hath appointed that created life, and thereto death likewise with help of Adam, who by sin done through persuasion of his helpmeet, she being wrought upon and bewrayed by the beguilements of the great enemy of man, that serpent hight Satan, aforetime consecrated and set apart unto that evil work by overmastering spite and envy begotten in his heart through fell ambitions that did blight and mildew a nature erst so white and pure whenso it hove with the shining multidudes its brethren-born in glade and shade of that fair heaven wherein all such as native be to that rich estate and—"

"Great Scott!"

"My lord?"

"Well, you know we haven't got time for this sort of thing. Don't you see, we could distribute these people around the earth in less time than it is going to take you to explain that we can't. We mustn't talk now, we must act. You want to be careful; you mustn't let your mill get the start of you that way, at a time like this. To business, now—and sharp's the word. Who is to take the aristocracy home?"

"Even their friends. These will come for them from the far parts of the earth."

This was lightning from a clear sky, for unexpectedness; and the relief of it was like pardon to a prisoner. She would remain to deliver the goods, of course.

"Well, then, Sandy, as our enterprise is handsomely and successfully ended, I will go home and report; and if ever another one—"

"I also am ready; I will go with thee."

This was recalling the pardon.

"How? You will go with me? Why should you?"

"Will I be traitor to my knight, dost think? That were dishonor. I may not part from thee until in knightly encounter in the field some overmatching champion shall fairly win and fairly wear me. I were to blame an I thought that that might ever hap."

"Elected for the long term," I sighed to myself. "I may as well make the best of it." So then I spoke up and said:

"All right; let us make a start."

While she was gone to cry her farewells over the pork, I gave that whole peerage away to the servants. And I asked them to take a duster and dust around a little where the nobilities had mainly lodged and promenaded, but they considered that that would be hardly worth while, and would moreover be a rather grave departure from custom, and therefore likely to make talk. A departure from custom—that settled it; it was a nation capable of committing any crime but that. The servants said they would follow the fashion, a fashion grown sacred through immemorial observance: they would scatter fresh rushes in all the rooms and halls, and then the evidence of the aristocratic visitation would be no longer visible. It was a kind of satire on Nature; it deposited the history of the family in a stratified record; and the antiquary could dig through it and tell by the remains of each period what changes of diet the family had introduced successively for a hundred years.

The first thing we struck that day was a procession of pilgrims. It was not going our way, but we joined it nevertheless; for it was hourly being borne in upon me, now, that if I would govern this country wisely, I must be posted in the details of its life, and not at second hand but by personal observation and scrutiny.

This company of pilgrims resembled Chaucer's in this: that it had in it a sample of about all the upper occupations and professions the country could show, and a corresponding variety of costume. There were young men and old men, young women and old women, lively folk and grave folk. They rode upon mules and horses, and there was not a side-saddle in the party; for this specialty was to remain unknown in England for nine hundred years yet.

It was a pleasant, friendly, sociable herd; pious, happy, merry, and full of unconscious coarsenesses and innocent indecencies.

What they regarded as the merry tale went the continual round and caused no more embarrassment than it would have caused in the best English society twelve centuries later. Practical jokes worthy of the English wits of the first quarter of the far-off nineteenth century were sprung here and there and yonder along the line, and compelled the delightedest applause; and sometimes when a bright remark was made at one end of the procession and started on its travels toward the other, you could note its progress all the way by the sparkling spray of laughter it threw off from its bows as it plowed along; and also by the blushes of the mules in its wake.

Sandy knew the goal and purpose of this pilgrimage and she posted me. She said:

"They journey to the Valley of Holiness, for to be blessed of the godly hermits and drink of the miraculous waters and be cleansed from sin."

"Where is this watering place?"

"It lieth a two day journey hence, by the borders of the land that hight the Cuckoo Kingdom."

"Tell me about it. Is it a celebrated place?"

"Oh, of a truth, yes. There be none more so. Of old time there lived there an abbot and his monks. Belike were none in the world more holy than these; for they gave themselves to study of pious books, and spoke not the one to the other, or indeed to any, and ate decayed herbs and naught thereto, and slept hard, and prayed much, and washed never; also they wore the same garment until it fell from their bodies through age and decay. Right so came they to be known of all the world by reason of these holy austerities, and visited by rich and poor, and reverenced."

"Proceed."

"But always there was lack of water there. Whereas, upon a time, the holy abbot prayed, and for answer a great stream of clear water burst forth by miracle in a desert place. Now were the fickle monks tempted of the Fiend, and they wrought with their abbot unceasingly by beggings and beseechings that he would construct a bath; and when he was become aweary and might not resist more, he said have ye your will, then, and granted that they asked. Now mark thou what 'tis to forsake the ways of purity the which He loveth, and wanton with such as be worldly and an offence. These monks did enter into the bath and come thence washed as white as snow; and lo, in that moment His sign appeared, in miraculous rebuke! for His insulted waters ceased to flow, and utterly vanished away."

"They fared mildly, Sandy, considering how that kind of crime is regarded in this country."

"Belike; but it was their first sin; and they had been of perfect life for long, and differing in naught from the angels. Prayers, tears, torturings of the flesh, all was vain to beguile that water to flow again. Even processions; even burnt-offerings; even votive candles to the Virgin, did fail every each of them; and all in the land did marvel."

"How odd to find that even this industry has its financial panics, and at times sees its assignats and greenbacks languish to zero, and everything come to a standstill. Go on, Sandy."

"And so upon a time, after year and day, the good abbot made humble surrender and destroyed the bath. And behold, His anger was in that moment appeased, and the waters gushed richly forth again, and even unto this day they have not ceased to flow in that generous measure."

"Then I take it nobody has washed since."

"He that would essay it could have his halter free; yea, and swiftly would he need it, too."

"The community has prospered since?"

"Even from that very day. The fame of the miracle went abroad into all lands. From every land came monks to join; they came even as the fishes come, in shoals; and the monastery added building to building, and yet others to these, and so spread wide its arms and took them in. And nuns came, also; and more again, and yet more; and built over against the monastery on the yon side of the vale, and added building to building, until mighty was that nunnery. And these were friendly unto those, and they joined their loving labors together, and together they built a fair great foundling asylum midway of the valley between."

"You spoke of some hermits, Sandy."

"These have gathered there from the ends of the earth. A hermit thriveth best where there be multitudes of pilgrims. Ye shall not find no hermit of no sort wanting. If any shall mention a hermit of a kind he thinketh new and not to be found but in some far strange land, let him but scratch among the holes and caves and swamps that line that Valley of Holiness, and whatsoever be his breed, it skills not, he shall find a sample of it there."

I closed up alongside of a burly fellow with a fat good-humored face, purposing to make myself agreeable and pick up some further crumbs of fact; but I had hardly more than scraped acquaintance with him when he began eagerly and awkwardly to lead up, in the immemorial way, to that same old anecdote—the one Sir Dinadan told me, what time I got into trouble with Sir Sagramor and was challenged of him on account of it. I excused myself and dropped to the rear of the procession, sad at heart, willing to go hence from this troubled life, this vale of tears, this brief day of broken rest, of cloud and storm, of weary struggle and monotonous defeat; and yet shrinking from the change, as remembering how long eternity is, and how many have wended thither who know that anecdote.

Early in the afternoon we overtook another procession of pilgrims; but in this one was no merriment, no jokes, no laughter, no playful ways, nor any happy giddiness, whether of youth or age. Yet both were here, both age and youth; gray old men and women, strong men and women of middle age, young husbands, young wives, little boys and girls, and three babies at the breast. Even the children were smileless; there was not a face among all these half a hundred people but was cast down, and bore that set expression of hopelessness which is bred of long and hard trials and old acquaintance with despair. They were slaves. Chains led from their fettered feet and their manacled hands to a sole-leather belt about their waists; and all except the children were also linked together in a file, six feet apart, by a single chain which led from collar to collar all down the line. They were on foot, and had tramped three hundred miles in eighteen days, upon the cheapest odds and ends of food, and stingy rations of that. They had slept in these chains every night, bundled together like swine. They had upon their bodies some poor rags, but they could not be said to be clothed. Their irons had chafed the skin from their ankles and made sores which were ulcerated and wormy. Their naked feet were torn, and none walked without a limp. Originally there had been a hundred of these unfortunates, but about half had been sold on the trip. The trader in charge of them rode a horse and carried a whip with a short handle and a long heavy lash divided into several knotted tails at the end. With this whip he cut the shoulders of any that tottered from weariness and pain, and straitened them up. He did not speak; the whip conveyed his desire without that. None of these poor creatures looked up as we rode along by; they showed no consciousness of our presence. And they made no sound but one; that was the dull and awful clank of their chains from end to end of the long file, as forty-three burdened feet rose and fell in unison. The file moved in a cloud of its own making.

All these faces were gray with a coating of dust. One has seen the like of this coating upon furniture in unoccupied houses, and has written his idle thought in it with his finger. I was reminded of this when I noticed the faces of some of those women, young mothers carrying babes that were near to death and freedom, how a something in their hearts was written in the dust upon their faces, plain to see, and lord how plain to read! for it was the track of tears. One of these young mothers was but a girl, and it hurt me to the heart to read that writing, and reflect that it was come up out of the breast of such a child, a breast that ought not to know trouble yet, but only the gladness of the morning of life; and no doubt—

She reeled just then, giddy with fatigue, and down came the lash and flicked a flake of skin from her naked shoulder. It stung me as if I had been hit instead. The master halted the file and jumped from his horse. He stormed and swore at this girl, and said she had made annoyance enough with her laziness, and as this was the last chance he should have, he would settle the account now. She dropped on her knees and put up her hands and began to beg and cry and implore, in a passion of terror, but the master gave no attention. He snatched the child from her, and then made the men-slaves who were chained before and behind her throw her on the ground and hold her there and expose her body; and then he laid on with the lash like a madman till her back was flayed, she strieking and struggling the while, piteously. One of the men who was holding her turned away his face, and for this humanity he was reviled and flogged.

All our pilgrims looked on and commented—on the expert way in which the whip was handled. They were too much hardened by lifelong every-day familiarity with slavery to notice that there was anything else in the exhibition that invited comment. This was what slavery could do, in the way of ossifying what one may call the superior lobe of human feeling; for these pilgrims were kind-hearted people, and they would not have allowed that man to treat a horse like that.

I wanted to stop the whole thing and set the slave free, but that would not do. I must not interfere too much and get myself a name for riding over the country's laws and the citizen's rights roughshod. If I lived and prospered I would be the death of slavery, that I was resolved upon; but I would try to fix it so that when I became its executioner it should be by command of the nation.

Just here was the wayside shop of a smith; and now arrived a landed proprietor who had bought this girl a few miles back, deliverable here where her irons could be taken off. They were removed; then there was a squabble between the gentleman and the dealer as to which should pay the blacksmith. The moment the girl was delivered from her irons, she flung herself, all tears and frantic sobbings, into the arms of the slave who had turned away his face when she was whipped. He strained her to his breast, and smothered her face and the child's with kisses, and washed them with the rain of his tears. I suspected. I inquired. Yes, I was right: it was husband and wife. They had to be torn apart by force; the girl had to be dragged away, and she struggled and fought and shrieked like one gone mad till a turn of the road hid her from sight; and even after that, we could still make out the fading plaint of those receding shrieks. And the husband and father, with his wife and child gone, never to be seen by him again in life?—well, the look of him one might not bear at all, and so I turned away; but I knew I should never get his picture out of my mind again, and there it is to this day, to wring my heartstrings whenever I think about it.

We put up at the inn in a village just at nightfall, and when I rose next morning and looked abroad, I was ware where a knight came riding in the golden glory of the new day, and recognized him for knight of mine—Sir Ozana le Cure Hardy. He was in the gentlemen's furnishing line, and his missionarying specialty was plug hats. He was clothed all in steel, in the beautifulest armor of the time—up to where his helmet ought to have been; but he hadn't any helmet, he wore a shiny stove-pipe hat, and was as ridiculous a spectacle as one might want to see. It was another of my surreptitious schemes for extinguishing knighthood by making it grotesque and absurd. Sir Ozana's saddle was hung about with hat-boxes, and every time he overcame a wandering knight he swore him into my service and fitted him with a plug and made him wear it. I dressed and ran down to welcome Sir Ozana and get his news.

"How is trade?" I asked.

"Ye will note that I have but these four left; yet were they sixteen whenas I got me from Camelot."

"Why, you have certainly done nobly, Sir Ozana. Where have you been foraging of late?"

"I am but now come from the Valley of Holiness, please you sir."

"I am pointed for that place myself. Is there anything stirring in the monkery, more than common?"

"By the mass ye may not question it! . . . Give him good feed, boy, and stint it not, an thou valuest thy crown; so get ye lightly to the stable and do even as I bid......Sir, it is parlous news I bring, and—be these pilgrims? Then ye may not do better, good folk, than gather and hear the tale I have to tell, sith it concerneth you, forasmuch as ye go to find that ye will not find, and seek that ye will seek in vain, my life being hostage for my word, and my word and message being these, namely: That a hap has happened whereof the like has not been seen no more but once this two hundred years, which was the first and last time that that said misfortune strake the holy valley in that form by commandment of the Most High whereto by reasons just and causes thereunto contributing, wherein the matter—"

"The miraculous fount hath ceased to flow!" This shout burst from twenty pilgrim mouths at once.

"Ye say well, good people. I was verging to it, even when ye spake."

"Has somebody been washing again?"

"Nay, it is suspected, but none believe it. It is thought to be some other sin, but none wit what."

"How are they feeling about the calamity?"

"None may describe it in words. The fount is these nine days dry. The prayers that did begin then, and the lamentations in sackcloth and ashes, and the holy processions, none of these have ceased nor night nor day; and so the monks and the huns and the foundlings be all exhausted, and do hang up prayers writ upon parchment, sith that no strength is left in man to lift up voice. And at last they sent for thee, Sir Boss, to try magic and enchantment; and if you could not come, then was the messenger to fetch Merlin, and he is there these three days now, and saith he will fetch that water though he burst the globe and wreck its kingdoms to accomplish it; and right bravely doth he work his magic and call upon his hellions to hie

them hither and help, but not a whiff of moisture hath he started
yet, even so much as might qualify as mist upon a copper mirror
an ye count not the barrel of sweat he sweateth betwixt sun and sun
over the dire labors of his task; and if ye—"

Breakfast was ready. As soon as it was over I showed to Sir Ozana
these words which I had written on the inside of his hat: "*Chemical
Department, Laboratory extension, Section G. Pxxp. Send two of
first size, two of No. 3, and six of No. 4, together with the proper
complementary details—and two of my trained assistants.*" And
I said:

"Now get you to Camelot as fast as you can fly, brave knight, and
show the writing to Clarence, and tell him to have these required
matters in the Valley of Holiness with all possible despatch."

"I will well, Sir Boss," and he was off.

CHAPTER XXII

THE HOLY FOUNTAIN

The pilgrims were human beings. Otherwise they would have
acted differently. They had come a long and difficult journey, and
now when the journey was nearly finished, and they learned that the
main thing they had come for had ceased to exist, they didn't do as
horses or cats or angle-worms would probably have done—turn
back and get at something profitable—no, anxious as they had
before been to see the miraculous fountain, they were as much as
forty times as anxious now to see the place where it had used to be.
There is no accounting for human beings.

We made good time; and a couple of hours before sunset we stood
upon the high confines of the Valley of Holiness, and our eyes swept
it from end to end and noted its features. That is, its large features.
These were the three masses of buildings. They were distant and
isolated temporalities shrunken to toy constructions in the lonely
waste of what seemed a desert—and was. Such a scene is always
mournful, it is so impressively still, and looks so steeped in death.
But there was a sound here which interrupted the stillness only to
add to its mournfulness; this was the faint far sound of tolling bells
which floated fitfully to us on the passing breeze, and so faintly,
so softly, that we hardly knew whether we heard it with our ears or
with our spirits.

We reached the monastery before dark, and there the males were
given lodging, but the women were sent over to the nunnery. The
bells were close at hand, now, and their solemn booming smote upon
the ear like a message of doom. A superstitious despair possessed
the heart of every monk and published itself in his ghastly face.
Everywhere, these black-robed, soft-sandled, tallow-visaged spectres

appeared, flitted about and disappeared, noiseless as the creatures of a troubled dream, and as uncanny.

The old abbot's joy to see me was pathetic. Even to tears; but he did the shedding himself. He said:

"Delay not, son, but get to thy saving work. An we bring not the water back again, and soon, we are ruined, and the good work of two hundred years must end. And see thou do it with enchantments that be holy, for the Church will not endure that work in her cause be done by devil's magic."

"When I work, Father, be sure there will be no devil's work connected with it. I shall use no arts that come of the devil, and no elements not created by the hand of God. But is Merlin working strictly on pious lines?"

"Ah, he said he would, my son, he said he would, and took oath to make his promise good."

"Well, in that case, let him proceed."

"But surely you will not sit idle by, but help?"

"It will not answer to mix methods, Father; neither would it be professional courtesy. Two of a trade must not underbid each other. We might as well cut rates and be done with it; it would arrive at that in the end. Merlin has the contract; no other magician can touch it till he throws it up."

"But I will take it from him; it is a terrible emergency and the act is thereby justified. And if it were not so, who will give law to the Church? The Church giveth law to all; and what she wills to do, that she may do, hurt whom it may. I will take it from him; you shall begin upon the moment."

"It may not be, Father. No doubt, as you say, where power is supreme, one can do as one likes and suffer no injury; but we poor magicians are not so situated. Merlin is a very good magician in a small way, and has quite a neat provincial reputation. He is struggling along, doing the best he can, and it would not be etiquette for me to take his job until he himself abandons it."

The abbot's face lighted.

"Ah, that is simple. There are ways to persuade him to abandon it."

"No-no, Father, it skills not, as these people say. If he were persuaded against his will, he would load that well with a malicious enchantment which would balk me until I found out its secret. It might take a month. I could set up a little enchantment of mine which I call the telephone, and he could not find out its secret in a hundred years. Yes, you perceive, he might block me for a month. Would you like to risk a month in a dry time like this?"

"A month! The mere thought of it maketh me to shudder. Have it thy way, my son. But my heart is heavy with this disappointment. Leave me, and let me wear my spirit with weariness and waiting, even as I have done these ten long days, counterfeiting thus the thing that is called rest, the prone body making outward sign of repose where inwardly is none."

Of course it would have been best, all round, for Merlin to waive etiquette and quit and call it half a day, since he would never be able to start that water, for he was a true magician of the time: which is to say, the big miracles, the ones that gave him his reputation, always had the luck to be performed when nobody but Merlin was present; he couldn't start this well with all this crowd around to see; a crowd was as bad for a magician's miracle in that day as it was for a spiritualist's miracle in mine: there was sure to be some skeptic on hand to turn up the gas at the crucial moment and spoil everything. But I did not want Merlin to retire from the job until I was ready to take hold of it effectively myself; and I could not do that until I got my things from Camelot, and that would take two or three days.

My presence gave the monks hope, and cheered them up a good deal; insomuch that they ate a square meal that night for the first time in ten days. As soon as their stomachs had been properly reinforced with food, their spirits began to rise fast; when the mead began to go round they rose faster. By the time everybody was half-seas over, the holy community was in good shape to make a night of it; so we stayed by the board and put it through on that line. Matters got to be very jolly. Good old questionable stories were told that made the tears run down and cavernous mouths stand wide and the round bellies shake with laughter; and questionable songs were bellowed out in a mighty chorus that drowned the boom of the tolling bells.

At last I ventured a story myself; and vast was the success of it. Not right off, of course, for the native of those islands does not as a rule dissolve upon the early applications of a humorous thing; but the fifth time I told it, they began to crack, in places; the eighth time I told it, they began to crumble; at the twelfth repetition they fell apart in chunks; and at the fifteenth they disintegrated, and I got a broom and swept them up. This language is figurative. Those islanders—well, they are slow pay, at first, in the matter of return for your investment of effort, but in the end they make the pay of all other nations poor and small by contrast.

I was at the well next day betimes. Merlin was there, enchanting away like a beaver, but not raising the moisture. He was not in a pleasant humor; and every time I hinted that perhaps this contract was a shade too hefty for a novice he unlimbered his tongue and cursed like a bishop—French bishop of the Regency days, I mean.

Matters were about as I expected to find them. The "fountain" was an ordinary well, it had been dug in the ordinary way, and stoned up in the ordinary way. There was no miracle about it. Even the lie that had created its reputation was not miraculous; I could have told it myself, with one hand tied behind me. The well was in a dark chamber which stood in the centre of a cut-stone chapel, whose walls were hung with pious pictures of a workmanship that would have made a chromo feel good; pictures historically commemorative of curative miracles which had been achieved by the waters when nobody was looking. That is, nobody but angels: they are always on deck when there is a miracle to the fore—so as to get put in the picture, perhaps. Angels are as fond of that as a fire-company; look at the old masters.

The well-chamber was dimly lighted by lamps; the water was drawn with a windlass and chain, by monks, and poured into troughs which delivered it into stone reservoirs outside, in the chapel—when there was water to draw, I mean—and none but monks could enter the well-chamber. I entered it, for I had temporary authority to do so, by courtesy of my professional brother and subordinate. But he hadn't entered it himself. He did everything by incantations; he never worked his intellect. If he had stepped in there and used his eyes, instead of his disordered mind, he could have cured the well by natural means, and then turned it into a miracle in the customary way; but no, he was an old numskull, a magician who believed in his own magic; and no magician can thrive who is handicapped with a superstition like that.

I had an idea that the well had sprung a leak; that some of the wall stones near the bottom had fallen and exposed fissures that allowed the water to escape. I measured the chain—98 feet. Then I called in a couple of monks, locked the door, took a candle, and made them lower me in the bucket. When the chain was all paid out, the candle confirmed my suspicion; a considerable section of the wall was gone, exposing a good big fissure.

I almost regretted that my theory about the well's trouble was correct, because I had another one that had a showy point or two about it for a miracle. I remembered that in America, many centuries later, when an oil well ceased to flow, they used to blast it out with a dynamite torpedo. If I should find this well dry, and no explanation of it, I could astonish these people most nobly by having a person of no especial value drop a dynamite bomb into it. It was my idea to appoint Merlin. However, it was plain that there was no occasion for the bomb. One cannot have everything the way he would like it. A man has no business to be depressed by a disappointment, anyway; he ought to make up his mind to get even. That is what I did. I said to myself, I am in no hurry, I can wait; that bomb will come good, yet. And it did, too.

When I was above ground again, I turned out the monks, and let down a fish-line: the well was a hundred and fifty feet deep, and there was forty-one feet of water in it! I called in a monk and asked:

"How deep is the well?"

"That, sir, I wit not, having never been told."

"How does the water usually stand in it?"

"Near the top, these two centuries, as the testimony goeth, brought down to us through our predecessors."

It was true—as to recent times at least—for there was witness to it, and better witness than a monk: only about twenty or thirty feet of chain showed wear and use, the rest of it was unworn and rusty. What had happened when the well gave out that other time? Without doubt some practical person had come along and mended the leak, and then had come up and told the abbot he had discovered by divination that if the sinful bath were destroyed the well would flow again. The leak had befallen again, now, and these children would have prayed, and processioned, and tolled their bells for heavenly succor till they all dried up and blew away, and no innocent of them all would ever have thought to drop a fish-line into the well or go down in it and find out what was really the matter. Old habit of mind is one of the toughest things to get away from in the world. It transmits itself like physical form and feature; and for a man, in those days, to have had an idea that his ancestors hadn't had, would have brought him under suspicion of being illegitimate. I said to the monk:

"It is a difficult miracle to restore water in a dry well, but we will try, if my brother Merlin fails. Brother Merlin is a very passable artist, but only in the parlor-magic line, and he may not succeed; in fact is not likely to succeed. But that should be nothing to his discredit; the man that can do *this* kind of miracle knows enough to keep hotel."

"Hotel? I mind not to have heard—"

"Of hotel? It's what you call hostel. The man that can do this miracle can keep hostel. I can do this miracle; I shall do this miracle; yet I do not try to conceal from you that it is a miracle to tax the occult powers to the last strain."

"None knoweth that truth better than the brotherhood, indeed; for it is of record that aforetime it was parlous difficult and took a year. Natheless, God send you good success, and to that end will we pray."

As a matter of business it was a good idea to get the notion around that the thing was difficult. Many a small thing has been made large by the right kind of advertising. That monk was filled up with the difficulty of this enterprise; he would fill up the others. In two days the solicitude would be booming.

On my way home at noon, I met Sandy. She had been sampling the hermits. I said:

"I would like to do that, myself. This is Wednesday. Is there a matinée?"

"A which, please you sir?"

"Matinée. Do they keep open afternoons?"

"Who?"

"The hermits, of course."

"Keep open?"

"Yes, keep open. Isn't that plain enough? Do they knock off at noon?"

"Knock off?"

"Knock off?—yes, knock off. What is the matter with knock off? I never saw such a dunderhead; can't you understand anything at all? In plain terms, do they shut up shop, draw the game, bank the fires—"

"Shut up shop, draw—"

"There, never mind, let it go; you make me tired. You can't seem to understand the simplest thing."

"I would I might please thee, sir, and it is to me dole and sorrow that I fail, albeit sith I am but a simple damsel and taught of none, being from the cradle unbaptized in those deep waters of learning that do anoint with a sovereignty him that partaketh of that most noble sacrament, investing him with reverend state to the mental eye of the humble mortal who, by bar and lack of that great consecration seeth in his own unlearned estate but a symbol of that other sort of lack and loss which men do publish to the pitying eye with sackcloth trappings whereon the ashes of grief do lie bepowdered and bestrewn, and so, when such shall in the darkness of his mind encounter these golden phrases of high mystery, these shut-up-shops, and draw-the-game, and bank-the-fires, it is but by the grace of God that he burst not for envy of the mind that can beget, and tongue that can deliver so great and mellow-sounding miracles of speech, and if there do ensue confusion in that humbler mind, and failure to divine the meanings of these wonders, then if so be this miscomprehension is not vain but sooth and true, wit ye well it is the very substance of worshipful dear homage and may not lightly be misprized, nor had been, an ye had noted this complexion of my mood and mind and understood that that I would I could not, and that I could not I might not, nor yet nor might *nor* could, nor might-not nor could-not, might be by advantage turned to the desired *would*, and so I pray you mercy of my fault, and that ye will of your kindness and your charity forgive it, good my master and most dear lord."

I couldn't make it all out—that is, the details—but I got the general idea; and enough of it, too, to be ashamed. It was not fair to spring those nineteenth century technicalities upon the untutored infant of the sixth and then rail at her because she couldn't get their drift; and when she was making the honest best drive at it she could, too, and no fault of hers that she couldn't fetch the home-plate; and I apologized. Then we meandered pleasantly away toward the hermit-holes in sociable converse together, and better friends than ever.

I was gradually coming to have a mysterious and shuddery reverence for this girl; for now-a-days whenever she pulled out from

the station and got her train fairly started on one of those horizonless
transcontinental sentences of hers, it was borne in upon me that
I was standing in the awful presence of the Mother of the German
Language. I was so impressed with this, that sometimes when she
began to empty one of these sentences on me I unconsciously took
the very attitude of reverence, and stood uncovered; and if words
had been water, I had been drowned, sure. She had exactly the
German way: whatever was in her mind to be delivered, whether a
mere remark, or a sermon, or a cyclopedia, or the history of a war,
she would get it into a single sentence or die. Whenever the literary
German dives into a sentence, that is the last you are going to see of
him till he emerges on the other side of his Atlantic with his verb
in his mouth.

We drifted from hermit to hermit all the afternoon. It was a most
strange menagerie. The chief emulation among them seemed to be,
to see which could manage to be the uncleanest and most prosperous
with vermin. Their manner and attitudes were the last expression
of complacent self-righteousness. It was one anchorite's pride to
lie naked in the mud and let the insects bite him and blister him
unmolested; it was another's to lean against a rock, all day long,
conspicuous to the admiration of the throng of pilgrims, and pray;
it was another's to go naked, and crawl around on all fours; it was
another's to drag about with him, year in and year out, eighty
pounds of iron; it was another's to never lie down when he slept, but
to stand among the thorn-bushes and snore when there were
pilgrims around to look; a woman, who had the white hair of age,
and no other apparel, was black from crown to heel with forty-seven
years of holy abstinence from water. Groups of gazing pilgrims stood
around all and every of these strange objects, lost in reverent wonder,
and envious of the fleckless sanctity which these pious austerities
had won for them from an exacting heaven.

By-and-by we went to see one of the supremely great ones. He was
a mighty celebrity; his fame had penetrated all Christendom; the
noble and the renowned journeyed from the remotest lands on the
globe to pay him reverence. His stand was in the centre of the widest
part of the valley; and it took all that space to hold his crowds.

His stand was a pillar sixty feet high, with a broad platform on the
top of it. He was now doing what he had been doing every day for
twenty years up there—bowing his body ceaselessly and rapidly
almost to his feet. It was his way of praying. I timed him with a
stop-watch, and he made 1244 revolutions in 24 minutes and 46
seconds. It seemed a pity to have all this power going to waste. It
was one of the most useful motions in mechanics, the
pedal-movement; so I made a note in my memorandum-book,
purposing some day to apply a system of elastic cords to him and run
a sewing-machine with it. I afterwards carried out that scheme,
and got five years' good service out of him; in which time he turned

out upwards of eighteen thousand first-rate tow-linen shirts, which was ten a day. I worked him Sundays and all; he was going, Sundays, the same as weekdays, and it was no use to waste the power. These shirts cost me nothing but just the mere trifle for the materials—I furnished those myself, it would not have been right to make him do that—and they sold like smoke to pilgrims at a dollar and a half apiece, which was the price of fifty cows or a blooded race-horse in Arthurdom. They were regarded as a perfect protection against sin, and advertised as such by my knights everywhere, with the paint-pot and stencil-plate; insomuch that there was not a cliff or a bowlder or a dead-wall in England but you could read on it at a mile distance:

"Buy the only genuine St. Stylite; patronized by the Nobility. Patent applied for."

There was more money in the business than one knew what to do with. As it extended, I brought out a line of goods suitable for kings, and a nobby thing for duchesses and that sort, with ruffles down the fore-hatch and the running-gear clewed up with a feather-stitch to leeward and then hauled aft with a back-stay and triced up with a half-turn in the standing rigging forward of the weather-gaskets. Yes, it was a daisy.

But about that time I noticed that the motive power had taken to standing on one leg, and I found that there was something the matter with the other one; so I stocked the business and unloaded, taking Sir Bors de Ganis into camp financially along with certain of his friends: for the works stopped within a year, and the good saint got him to his rest. But he had earned it. I can say that for him.

When I saw him that first time—however, his personal condition will not quite bear description here. You can read it in the Lives of the Saints.*

CHAPTER XXIII

RESTORATION OF THE FOUNTAIN

Saturday noon I went to the well and looked on a while. Merlin was still burning smoke-powders, and pawing the air, and muttering gibberish as hard as ever, but looking pretty down-hearted, for of course he had not started even a perspiration in that well yet. Finally I said:

"How does the thing promise by this time, partner?"

"Behold, I am even now busied with trial of the powerfulest enchantment known to the princes of the occult arts in the lands

*All the details concerning the hermits, in this chapter, are from Lecky—but greatly modified. This book not being a history but only a tale, the majority of the historian's frank details were too strong for reproduction in it.—EDITOR.

of the East; an it fail me, naught can avail. Peace, until I finish."

He raised a smoke this time that darkened all the region, and must have made matters uncomfortable for the hermits, for the wind was their way, and it rolled down over their dens in a dense and billowy fog. He poured out volumes of speech to match, and contorted his body and sawed the air with his hands in a most extraordinary way. At the end of twenty minutes he dropped down panting, and about exhausted. Now arrived the abbot and several hundred monks and nuns, and behind them a multitude of pilgrims and a couple of acres of foundlings, all drawn by the prodigious smoke, and all in a grand state of excitement. The abbot inquired anxiously for results. Merlin said:

"If any labor of mortal might break the spell that binds these waters, this which I have but just essayed had done it. It has failed; whereby I do now know that that which I had feared is a truth established: the sign of this failure is, that the most potent spirit known to the magicians of the East, and whose name none may utter and live, has laid his spell upon this well. The mortal does not breathe, nor ever will, who can penetrate the secret of that spell, and without that secret none can break it. The water will flow no more forever, good Father. I have done what man could. Suffer me to go."

Of course this threw the abbot into a good deal of a consternation. He turned to me with the signs of it in his face, and said:

"Ye have heard from him. Is it true?"

"Part of it is."

"Not all, then, not all! What part is true?"

"That that spirit with the Russian name has put his spell upon the well."

"God's wownds, then are we ruined!"

"Possibly."

"But not certainly? Ye mean, not certainly?"

"That is it."

"Wherefore, ye also mean that when he saith none can break the spell—"

"Yes, when he says that, he says what isn't necessarily true. There are conditions under which an effort to break it may have some chance—that is, some small, some trifling chance—of success."

"The conditions—"

"Oh, they are nothing difficult. Only these: I want the well and the surroundings for the space of half a mile, entirely to myself from sunset to-day until I remove the ban—and nobody allowed to cross the ground but by my authority."

"Are these all?"

"Yes."

"And you have no fear to try?"

"Oh, none. One may fail, of course; and one may also succeed.

One can try, and I am ready to chance it. I have my conditions?"

"These and all others ye may name. I will issue commandment to that effect."

"Wait," said Merlin, with an evil smile. "Ye wit that he that would break this spell must know that spirit's name?"

"Yes, I know his name."

"And wit you also that to know it skills not of itself, but he must likewise pronounce it? Ha-ha! Knew ye that?"

"Yes, I knew that, too."

"You had that knowledge! Art a fool? Are ye minded to utter that name and die?"

"Utter it? Why certainly. I would utter it if it was Welsh."

"Ye are even a dead man, then; and I go to tell Arthur."

"That's all right. Take your gripsack and get along. The thing for *you* to do is to go home and work the weather, John W. Merlin."

It was a home shot, and it made him wince; for he was the worst weather-failure in the kingdom. Whenever he ordered up the danger-signals along the coast there was a week's dead calm, sure, and every time he prophesied fair weather it rained brick-bats. But I kept him in the weather bureau right along, to undermine his reputation. However, that shot raised his bile, and instead of starting home to report my death, he said he would remain and enjoy it.

My two experts arrived in the evening, and pretty well fagged, for they had travelled double tides. They had pack-mules along, and and had brought everything I needed—tools, pump, lead-pipe, Greek-fire, sheaves of big rockets, roman-candles, colored-fire sprays, electric apparatus, and a lot of sundries—everything necessary for the stateliest kind of a miracle. They got their supper and a nap, and about midnight we sallied out through a solitude so wholly vacant and complete that it quite overpassed the required conditions. We took possession of the well and its surroundings. My boys were experts in all sorts of things, from the stoning up of a well to the constructing of a mathematical instrument. An hour before sunrise we had that leak mended in ship-shape fashion, and the water began to rise. Then we stowed our fireworks in the chapel, locked up the place, and went home to bed.

Before the noon mass was over, we were at the well again; for there was a deal to do, yet, and I was determined to spring the miracle before midnight, for business reasons: for whereas a miracle worked for the Church on a week-day is worth a good deal, it is worth six times as much if you get it in on a Sunday. In nine hours the water had risen to its customary level; that is to say, it was within twenty-three feet of the top. We put in a little iron pump, one of the first turned out by my works near the capital; we bored into a stone reservoir which stood against the outer wall of the well-chamber and inserted a section of lead pipe that was long enough to reach to the door of the chapel and project beyond the threshold, where the gushing water would be visible to the two hundred and fifty acres of people I was intending should be present on the flat plain in front of this little holy hillock at the proper time.

We knocked the head out of an empty hogshead and hoisted this hogshead to the flat roof of the chapel, where we clamped it down fast, poured in gunpowder till it lay loosely an inch deep on the bottom, then we stood up rockets in the hogshead as thick as they could loosely stand, all the different breeds of rockets there are; and they made a portly and imposing sheaf, I can tell you. We grounded the wire of a pocket electrical battery in that powder, we placed a whole magazine of Greek-fire on each corner of the roof—blue on one corner, green on another, red on another, and purple on the last—and grounded a wire in each.

About two hundred yards off, in the flat, we built a pen of scantlings, about four feet high, and laid planks on it, and so made a platform. We covered it with swell tapestries borrowed for the occasion, and topped it off with the abbot's own throne. When you are going to do a miracle for an ignorant race, you want to get in every detail that will count; you want to make all the properties impressive to the public eye; you want to make matters comfortable for your head guest; then you can turn yourself loose and play your effects for all they are worth. I know the value of these things, for I know human nature. You can't throw too much style into a miracle. It costs trouble, and work, and sometimes money; but it pays in the end. Well, we brought the wires to the ground at the chapel, and brought them under the ground to the platform, and hid the batteries there. We put a rope fence a hundred feet square around the platform to keep off the common multitude, and that finished the work. My idea was, doors open at 10.30, performance to begin at 11.25 sharp. I wished I could charge admission, but of course that wouldn't answer. I instructed my boys to be in the chapel as early as 10, before anybody was around, and be ready to man the pumps at the proper time, and make the fur fly. Then we went home to supper.

The news of the disaster to the well had travelled far, by this time; and now for two or three days a steady avalanche of people had been pouring into the valley. The lower end of the valley was become one huge camp; we should have a good house, no question about that. Criers went the rounds early in the evening and announced the coming attempt, which put every pulse up to fever-heat. They gave notice that the abbot and his official suite would move in state and occupy the platform at 10.30, up to which time all the region which was under my ban must be clear; the bells would then cease from tolling, and this sign should be permission to the multitudes to close in and take their places.

I was at the platform and all ready to do the honors when the abbot's solemn procession hove in sight—which it did not do till it was nearly to the rope fence, because it was a starless black night

and no torches permitted. With it came Merlin, and took a front
seat on the platform; he was as good as his word, for once. One could
not see the multitudes banked together beyond the ban, but they
were there, just the same. The moment the bells stopped, those
banked masses broke and poured over the line like a vast black
wave, and for as much as a half-hour it continued to flow, and then
it solidified itself, and you could have walked upon a pavement of
human heads to—well, miles.

We had a solemn stage-wait, now, for about twenty minutes—a
thing I had counted on for effect; it is always good to let your
audience have a chance to work up its expectancy. At length, out of
the silence a noble Latin chant—men's voices—broke and swelled
up and rolled away into the night, a majestic tide of melody. I had
put that up, too, and it was one of the best effects I ever invented.
When it was finished I stood up on the platform and extended my
hands abroad, for two minutes, with my face uplifted—that always
produces a dead hush—and then slowly pronounced this ghastly
word with a kind of awfulness which caused hundreds to tremble,
and many women to faint:

"Constantinopolitanischerdudelsackspfeifenmachersgesellschafft!"

Just as I was moaning out the closing hunks of that word, I
touched off one of my electric connections, and all that murky world
of people stood revealed in a hideous blue glare! It was immense—
that effect! Lots of people shrieked, women curled up and quit in
every direction, foundlings collapsed by platoons. The abbot and the
monks crossed themselves nimbly and their lips fluttered with
agitated prayers. Merlin held his grip, but he was astonished clear
down to his corns; he had never seen anything to begin with that,
before. Now was the time to pile in the effects. I lifted my hands and
groaned out this word—as it were in agony—

"Nihilistendynamittheaterkaestchenssprengungsattentaets-
versuchungen!"

—and turned on the red fire! You should have heard that Atlantic
of people moan and howl when that crimson hell joined the blue!
After sixty seconds I shouted—

"Transvaaltruppentropentransporttrampelthier-
treibertrauungsthraenentragoedie!"

—and lit up the green fire! After waiting only forty seconds, this time, I spread my arms abroad and thundered out the devastating syllables of this word of words—

"Mekkamuselmannenmassenmen-chenmoerdermohrenmuttermarmormo-numentenmacher!"

—and whirled on the purple glare! There they were, all going at once, red, blue, green, purple!—four furious volcanoes pouring vast clouds of radiant smoke aloft, and spreading a blinding rainbowed noonday to the furthest confines of that valley. In the distance one could see that fellow on the pillar standing rigid against the background of sky, his seesaw stopped for the first time in twenty years. I knew the boys were at the pump, now, and ready. So I said to the abbot:

"The time is come, Father. I am about to pronounce the dread name and command the spell to dissolve. You want to brace up, and take hold of something." Then I shouted to the people: "Behold, in another minute the spell will be broken, or no mortal can break it. If it break, all will know it, for you will see the sacred water gush from the chapel door!"

I stood a few moments, to let the hearers have a chance to spread my announcement to those who couldn't hear, and so convey it to the furthest ranks, then I made a grand exhibition of extra posturing and gesturing, and shouted:

"Lo, I command the fell spirit that possesses the holy fountain to now disgorge into the skies all the infernal fires that still remain in him, and straightway dissolve his spell and flee hence to the pit, there to lie bound a thousand years. By his own dread name I command it—BGWJJILLIGKKK!"

Then I touched off the hogshead of rockets, and a vast fountain of dazzling lances of fire vomited itself toward the zenith with a hissing rush, and burst in mid-sky into a storm of flashing jewels! One mighty groan of terror started up from the massed people— then suddenly broke into a wild hosannah of joy—for there, fair and plain in the uncanny glare, they saw the freed water leaping forth! The old abbot could not speak a word, for tears and the chokings in his throat; without utterance of any sort, he folded me in his arms and mashed me. It was more eloquent than speech. And harder to get over, too, in a country where there were really no doctors that were worth a damaged nickel.

You should have seen those acres of people throw themselves down in that water and kiss it; kiss it, and pet it, and fondle it, and talk to it as if it were alive, and welcome it back with the dear names they gave their darlings, just as if it had been a friend who was long gone away and lost, and was come home again. Yes, it was pretty to see, and made me think more of them than I had done before.

I sent Merlin home on a shutter. He had caved in and gone down like a landslide when I pronounced that fearful name, and had never come to since. He never had heard that name before,—neither had I—but to him it was the right one; any jumble would have been the right one. He admitted, afterward, that that spirit's own mother could not have pronounced that name better than I did. He never could understand how I survived it, and I didn't tell him. It is only young magicians that give away a secret like that. Merlin spent three months working enchantments to try to find out the deep trick of how to pronounce that name and outlive it. But he didn't arrive.

When I started to the chapel, the populace uncovered and fell back reverently to make a wide way for me, as if I had been some kind of a superior being—and I was. I was aware of that. I took along a night-shift of monks, and taught them the mystery of the pump, and set them to work, for it was plain that a good part of the people out there were going to sit up with the water all night, consequently it was but right that they should have all they wanted of it. To those monks that pump was a good deal of a miracle itself, and they were full of wonder over it; and of admiration, too, of the exceeding effectiveness of its performance.

It was a great night, an immense night. There was reputation in it. I could hardly get to sleep for glorying over it.

CHAPTER XXIV

A RIVAL MAGICIAN

My influence in the Valley of Holiness was something prodigious now. It seemed worth while to try to turn it to some valuable account. The thought came to me the next morning, and was suggested by my seeing one of my knights who was in the soap line come riding in. According to history, the monks of this place two centuries before, had been worldly minded enough to want to wash. It might be that there was a leaven of this unrighteousness still remaining. So I sounded a Brother:

"Wouldn't you like a bath?"

He shuddered at the thought—the thought of the peril of it to the well—but he said with feeling—

"One needs not to ask that of a poor body who has not known that blessed refreshment sith that he was a boy. Would God I might wash me! but it may not be, fair sir, tempt me not; it is forbidden."

And then he sighed in such a sorrowful way that I was resolved he should have at least one layer of his real estate removed, if it sized up my whole influence and bankrupted the pile. So I went to the abbot and asked for a permit for this Brother. He blenched at the idea—I don't mean that you could see him blench, for of course you couldn't see it without you scraped him, and I didn't care enough about it to scrape him, but I knew the blench was there, just the same, and within a book-cover's thickness of the surface, too—blenched, and trembled. He said:

"Ah, son, ask aught else thou wilt, and it is thine, and freely granted out of a grateful heart—but this, oh, this! Would you drive away the blessed water again?"

"No, Father, I will not drive it away. I have mysterious knowledge which teaches me that there was an error that other time when it was thought the institution of the bath banished the fountain." A large interest began to show up in the old man's face. "My knowledge informs me that the bath was innocent of that misfortune, which was caused by quite another sort of sin."

"These are brave words—but—but right welcome, if they be true."

"They are true, indeed. Let me build the bath again, Father. Let me build it again, and the fountain shall flow forever."

"You promise this?—you promise it? Say the word—say you promise it!"

"I do promise it."

"Then will I have the first bath myself! Go—get ye to your work. Tarry not, tarry not, but go."

I and my boys were at work, straight off. The ruins of the old bath were there yet, in the basement of the monastery, not a stone missing. They had been left just so, all these lifetimes, and avoided with a pious fear, as things accursed. In two days we had it all done and the water in—a spacious pool of clear pure water that a body could swim in. It was running water, too. It came in, and went out, through the ancient pipes. The old abbot kept his word, and was the first to try it. He went down black and shaky, leaving the whole black community above troubled and worried and full of bodings; but he came back white and joyful, and the game was made! another triumph scored.

It was a good campaign that we made in that Valley of Holiness, and I was very well-satisfied, and ready to move on, now, but I struck a disappointment. I caught a heavy cold, and it started up an old lurking rheumatism of mine. Of course the rheumatism hunted up my weakest place and located itself there. This was the place where the abbot put his arms about me and mashed me, what time he was moved to testify his gratitude to me with an embrace.

When at last I got out, I was a shadow. But everybody was full of attentions and kindnesses, and these brought cheer back into my life, and were the right medicine to help a convalescent swiftly up toward health and strength again; so I gained fast.

Sandy was worn out with nursing, so I made up my mind to turn

out and go a cruise alone, leaving her at the nunnery to rest up.
My idea was to disguise myself as a freeman of peasant degree and
wander through the country a week or two on foot. This would give
me a chance to eat and lodge with the lowliest and poorest class of
free citizens on equal terms. There was no other way to inform
myself perfectly of their every-day life and the operation of the laws
upon it. If I went among them as a gentleman, there would be
restraints and conventionalities which would shut me out from their
private joys and troubles, and I should get no further than the
outside shell.

One morning I was out on a long walk to get up muscle for my
trip, and had climbed the ridge which bordered the northern
extremity of the valley, when I came upon an artificial opening in
the face of a low precipice, and recognized it by its location as a
hermitage which had often been pointed out to me from a distance
as the den of a hermit of high renown for dirt and austerity. I knew
he had lately been offered a situation in the Great Sahara, where
lions and sandflies made the hermit-life peculiarly attractive and
difficult, and had gone to Africa to take possession, so I thought I
would look in and see how the atmosphere of this den agreed with
its reputation.

My surprise was great: the place was newly swept and scoured.
Then there was another surprise. Back in the gloom of the cavern
I heard the clink of a little bell, and then this exclamation:

"Hello, Central! Is this you, Camelot?—Behold thou mayst glad
thy heart an thou hast faith to believe the wonderful when that it
cometh in unexpected guise and maketh itself manifest in
impossible places—here standeth in the flesh his mightiness The
Boss, and with thine own ears shall ye hear him speak!"

Now what a radical reversal of things this was; what a jumbling
together of extravagant incongruities; what a fantastic conjunction
of opposites and irreconcilables—the home of the bogus miracle
become the home of a real one, the den of a mediæval hermit turned
into a telephone office!

The telephone clerk stepped in the light, and I recognized one of
my young fellows. I said:

"How long has this office been established here, Ulfius?"

"But since midnight, fair Sir Boss, an it please you. We saw many
lights in the valley, and so judged it well to make a station, for that
where so many lights be needs must they indicate a town of
goodly size."

"Quite right. It isn't a town in the customary sense, but it's a good
stand, anyway. Do you know where you are?"

"Of that I have had no time to make inquiry; for whenas my
comradeship moved hence upon their labors, leaving me in charge,
I got me to needed rest, purposing to inquire when I waked, and
report the place's name to Camelot for record."

"Well, this is the Valley of Holiness."

It didn't take; I mean, he didn't start at the name, as I had supposed he would. He merely said—

"I will so report it."

"Why, the surrounding regions are filled with the noise of late wonders that have happened here! You didn't hear of them?"

"Ah, ye will remember we move by night, and avoid speech with all. We learn naught but that we get by the telephone from Camelot."

"Why *they* know all about this thing. Haven't they told you anything about the great miracle of the restoration of a holy fountain?"

"Oh, *that?* Indeed yes. But the name of *this* valley doth woundily differ from the name of *that* one; indeed to differ wider were not pos—"

"What was that name, then?"

"The Valley of Hellishness."

"*That* explains it. Confound a telephone, anyway. It is the very demon for conveying similarities of sound that are miracles of divergence from similarity of sense. But no matter, you know the name of the place now. Call up Camelot."

He did it, and had Clarence sent for. It was good to hear my boy's voice again. It was like being home. After some affectionate interchanges, and some account of my late illness, I said:

"What is new?"

"The king and queen and many of the court do start even in this hour, to go to your Valley to pay pious homage to the waters ye have restored, and cleanse themselves of sin, and see the place where the infernal spirit spouted true hell-flames to the clouds—an ye listen sharply ye may hear me wink and hear me likewise smile a smile, sith 'twas I that made selection of those flames from out our stock and sent them by your order."

"Does the king know the way to this place?"

"The king?—no, nor to any other in his realms, mayhap; but the lads that holp you with your miracle will be his guide and lead the way, and appoint the places for rests at noons and sleeps at night."

"This will bring them here—when?"

"Mid-afternoon, or later, the third day."

"Anything else in the way of news?"

"The king hath begun the raising of the standing army ye suggested to him; one regiment is complete and officered."

"The mischief! I wanted a main hand in that, myself. There is only one body of men in the kingdom that are fitted to officer a regular army."

"Yes—and ye will marvel to know there's not so much as one West Pointer in that regiment."

"What are you talking about? Are you in earnest?"

"It is truly as I have said."

"Why, this makes me uneasy. Who were chosen, and what was the method? Competitive examination?"

"Indeed I know naught of the method. I but know this—these officers be all of noble family, and are born—what is it you call it?—chuckleheads."

"There's something wrong, Clarence."

"Comfort yourself, then; for two candidates for a lieutenancy do travel hence with the king—young nobles both—and if you but wait where you are you will hear them questioned."

"That is news to the purpose. I will get one West Pointer in, anyway. Mount a man and send him to that school with a message; let him kill horses, if necessary, but he must be there before sunset to-night and say—"

"There is no need. I have laid a ground wire to the school. Prithee let me connect you with it."

It sounded good! In this atmosphere of telephones and lightning communication with distant regions, I was breathing the breath of life again after long suffocation. I realized, then, what a creepy, dull, inanimate horror this land had been to me all these years, and how I had been in such a stifled condition of mind as to have grown used to it almost beyond the power to notice it.

I gave my order to the superintendent of the Academy personally. I also asked him to bring me some paper and a fountain pen and a box or so of safety matches. I was getting tired of doing without these conveniences. I could have them, now, so I wasn't going to wear armor any more at present, and therefore could get at my pockets.

When I got back to the monastery, I found a thing of interest going on. The abbot and his monks were assembled in the great hall, observing with childish wonder and faith the performances of a new magician, a fresh arrival. His dress was the extreme of the fantastic; as showy and foolish as the sort of thing an Indian medicine-man wears. He was mowing, and mumbling, and gesticulating, and drawing mystical figures in the air and on the floor,—the regular thing, you know. He was a celebrity from Asia—so he said, and that was enough. That sort of evidence was as good as gold, and passed current everywhere.

How easy and cheap it was to be a great magician on this fellow's terms. His specialty was to tell you what any individual on the face of the globe was doing at the moment; and what he had done at any time in the past, and what he would do at any time in the future. He asked if any would like to know what the Emperor of the East was doing now? The sparkling eyes and the delighted rubbing of hands made eloquent answer—this reverend crowd *would* like to know what that monarch was at, just at this moment. The fraud went through some more mummery, and then made grave announcement:

"The high and mighty Emperor of the East doth at this moment put money in the palm of a holy begging friar—one, two, three pieces, and they be all of silver."

A buzz of admiring exclamations broke out, all around:

"It is marvellous!" "Wonderful!" "What study, what labor, to have acquired a so amazing power as this!"

Would they like to know what the Supreme Lord of Inde was doing? Yes. He told them what the Supreme Lord of Inde was doing. Then he told them what the Sultan of Egypt was at; also what the King of the Remote Seas was about. And so on and so on; and with each new marvel the astonishment at his accuracy rose higher and higher. They thought he must surely strike an uncertain place sometime; but no, he never had to hesitate, he always knew, and always with unerring precision. I saw that if this thing went on I should lose my supremacy, this fellow would capture my following, I should be left out in the cold. I must put a cog in his wheel, and do it right away, too. I said:

"If I might ask, I should very greatly like to know what a certain person is doing."

"Speak, and freely. I will tell you."

"It will be difficult—perhaps impossible."

"My art knoweth not that word. The more difficult it is, the more certainly will I reveal it to you."

You see, I was working up the interest. It was getting pretty high, too; you could see that by the craning necks all around, and the half-suspended breathing. So now I climaxed it:

"If you make no mistake—if you tell me truly what I want to know—I will give you two hundred silver pennies."

"The fortune is mine! I will tell you what you would know."

"Then tell me what I am doing with my right hand."

"Ah-h!" There was a general gasp of surprise. It had not occurred to anybody in the crowd—that simple trick of inquiring about somebody who wasn't ten thousand miles away. The magician was hit hard; it was an emergency that had never happened in his experience before, and it corked him; he didn't know how to meet it. He looked stunned, confused; he couldn't say a word. "Come," I said, "what are you waiting for? Is it possible you can answer up, right off, and tell what anybody on the other side of the earth is doing, and yet can't tell what a person is doing who isn't three yards from you? Persons behind me know what I am doing with my right hand—they will indorse you if you tell correctly." He was still dumb. "Very well, I'll tell you why you don't speak up and tell; it is because you don't know. *You* a magician! Good friends, this tramp is a mere fraud and liar."

This distressed the monks and terrified them. They were not used to hearing these awful beings called names, and they did not know what might be the consequence. There was a dead silence, now;

superstitious bodings were in every mind. The magician began to pull his wits together, and when he presently smiled an easy, nonchalant smile, it spread a mighty relief around; for it indicated that his mood was not destructive. He said:

"It hath stuck me speechless, the frivolity of this person's speech. Let all know, if perchance there be any who know it not, that enchanters of my degree deign not to concern themselves with doings of any but Kings, Princes, Emperors, them that be born in the purple and them only. Had ye asked me what Arthur the great king is doing, it were another matter, and I had told ye; but the doings of a subject interest me not."

"Oh, I misunderstood you. I thought you said 'anybody,' and so I supposed 'anybody' included—well, anybody; that is, everybody."

"It doth—anybody that is of lofty birth; and the better if he be royal."

"That, it meseemeth, might well be," said the abbot, who saw his opportunity to smooth things and avert disaster, "for it were not likely that so wonderful a gift as this would be conferred for the revelation of the concerns of lesser beings than such as be born near to the summits of greatness. Our Arthur the king—"

"Would you know of him?" broke in the enchanter.

"Most gladly, yea, and gratefully."

Everybody was full of awe and interest again, right away, the incorrigible idiots. They watched the incantations absorbingly, and looked at me with a "There, now, what can you say to that?" air, when the announcement came:

"The king is weary with the chase, and lieth in his palace these two hours sleeping a dreamless sleep."

"God's benison upon him!" said the abbot, and crossed himself; "may that sleep be to the refreshment of his body and his soul."

"And so it might be, if he were sleeping," I said, "but the king is not sleeping, the king rides."

Here was trouble again—a conflict of authority. Nobody knew which of us to believe. I still had some reputation left. The magician's scorn was stirred, and he said:

"Lo, I have seen many wonderful soothsayers and prophets and magicians in my life-days, but none before that could sit idle and see to the heart of things with never an incantation to help."

"You have lived in the woods, and lost much by it. I use incantations myself, as this good brotherhood are aware—but only on occasions of moment."

When it comes to sarcasaming, I reckon I know how to keep my end up. That jab made this fellow squirm. The abbot inquired after the queen and the court, and got this information:

"They be all on sleep, being overcome by fatigue, like as to the king."

I said:

"That is merely another lie. Half of them are about their amusements, the queen and the other half are not sleeping, they ride. Now perhaps you can spread yourself a little, and tell us where the king and queen and all that are this moment riding with them are going?"

"They sleep now, as I said; but on the morrow they will ride, for they journey toward the sea."

"And where will they be the day after to-morrow at vespers?"

"Far to the north of Camelot, and half their journey will be done."

"That is another lie, by the space of a hundred and fifty miles. Their journey will not be merely half done, it will be all done, and they will be *here*, in this valley."

That was a noble shot! It set the abbot and the monks in a whirl of excitement, and it rocked the enchanter to his base. I followed the thing right up:

"If the king does not arrive, I will have myself ridden on a rail; if he does I will ride you on a rail instead."

Next day I went up to the telephone office and found that the king had passed through two towns that were on the line. I spotted his progress on the succeeding day in the same way. I kept these matters to myself. The third day's reports showed that it he kept up his gait he would arrive by four in the afternoon. There was still no sign anywhere of interest in his coming; there seemed to be no preparations making to receive him in state; a strange thing, truly. Only one thing could explain this: that other magician had been cutting under me, sure. This was true. I asked a friend of mine, a monk, about it, and he said, yes, the magician had tried some further enchantments and found out that the court had concluded to make no journey at all, but stay at home. Think of that! Observe how much a reputation was worth in such a country. These people had seen me do the very showiest bit of magic in history, and the only one within their memory that had a positive value, and yet here they were, ready to take up with an adventurer who could offer no evidence of his powers but his mere unproven word.

However, it was not good politics to let the king come without any fuss and feathers at all, so I went down and drummed up a procession of pilgrims and smoked out a batch of hermits and started them out at two o'clock to meet him. And that was the sort of state he arrived in. The abbot was helpless with rage and humiliation when I brought him out on a balcony and showed him the head of the state marching in and never a monk on hand to offer him welcome, and no stir of life or clang of joy-bell to glad his spirit. He took one look and then flew to rouse out his forces. The next minute the bells were dinning furiously, and the various buildings were vomiting monks and nuns, who went swarming in a rush toward the coming procession; and with them went that magician— and he was on a rail, too, by the abbot's order; and his reputation was in the mud, and mine was in the sky again. Yes, a man can keep his trade-mark current in such a country, but he can't sit around and do it, he has got to be on deck and attending to business, right along.

CHAPTER XXV

A COMPETITIVE EXAMINATION

When the king travelled for change of air, or made a progress, or visited a distant noble whom he wished to bankrupt with the cost of his keep, part of the administration moved with him. It was a fashion of the time. The Commission charged with the examination of candidates for posts in the army came with the king to the Valley, whereas they could have transacted their business just as well at home. And although this expedition was strictly a holiday excursion for the king, he kept some of his business functions going, just the same. He touched for the evil, as usual; he held court in the gate at sunrise and tried cases, for he was himself Chief Justice of the King's Bench.

He shone very well in this latter office. He was a wise and humane judge, and he clearly did his honest best and fairest,—according to his lights. That is a large reservation. His lights—I mean his rearing—often colored his decisions. Whenever there was a dispute between a noble or gentleman and a person of lower degree, the king's leanings and sympathies were for the former class always, whether he suspected it or not. It was impossible that this should be otherwise. The blunting effects of slavery upon the slaveholder's moral perceptions are known and conceded, the world over; and a privileged class, an aristocracy, is but a band of slaveholders under another name. This has a harsh sound, and yet should not be offensive to any—even to the noble himself—unless the fact itself be an offence: for the statement simply formulates a fact. The repulsive feature of slavery is the *thing*, not its name. One needs but to hear an aristocrat speak of the classes that are below him to recognize—and in but indifferently modified measure—the very air and tone of the actual slaveholder; and behind these are the slaveholder's spirit, the slaveholder's blunted feeling. They are the result of the same cause in both cases: the possessor's old and inbred custom of regarding himself as a superior being. The king's judgments wrought frequent injustices, but it was merely the fault of his training, his natural and unalterable sympathies. He was as unfitted for a judgeship as would be the average mother for the position of milk-distributor to starving children in famine-time; her own children would fare a shade better than the rest.

One very curious case came before the king. A young girl, an orphan, who had a considerable estate, married a fine young fellow who had nothing. The girl's property was within a seignory held by the Church. The bishop of the diocese, an arrogant scion of the great nobility, claimed the girl's estate on the ground that she had married privately, and thus had cheated the Church out of one of its rights as lord of the seignory—the one heretofore referred to as *le droit du seigneur*. The penalty of refusal or avoidance was confiscation. The girl's defence was, that the lordship of the seignory was vested in the bishop, and the particular right here involved was not transferable, but must be exercised by the lord himself or stand vacated; and that an older law, of the Church itself, strictly barred the bishop from exercising it. It was a very odd case, indeed.

It reminded me of something I had read in my youth about the ingenious way in which the aldermen of London raised the money that built the Mansion House. A person who had not taken the Sacrament according to the Anglican rite, could not stand as a candidate for sheriff of London. Thus Dissenters were ineligible; they could not run if asked, they could not serve if elected. The aldermen, who without any question were Yankees in disguise, hit upon this neat device: they passed a by-law imposing a fine of £400 upon any one who should refuse to be a candidate for sheriff, and a fine of £600 upon any person who, after being elected sheriff, refused to serve. Then they went to work and elected a lot of Dissenters, one after another, and kept it up until they had collected £15,000 in fines; and there stands the stately Mansion House to this day, to keep the blushing citizen in mind of a long past and lamented day when a band of Yankees slipped into London and played games of the sort that has given their race a unique and shady reputation among all truly good and holy peoples that be in the earth.

The girl's case seemed strong to me; the bishop's case was just as strong. I did not see how the king was going to get out of this hole. But he got out. I append his decision:

"Truly I find small difficulty here, the matter being even a child's affair for simpleness. An the young bride had conveyed notice, as in duty bound, to her feudal lord and proper master and protector the bishop, she had suffered no loss, for the said bishop could have got a dispensation making him, for temporary conveniency, eligible to the exercise of his said right, and thus would she have kept all she had. Whereas, failing in her first duty, she hath by that failure failed in all; for whoso, clinging to a rope, severeth it above his hands, must fall; it being no defence to claim that the rest of the rope is sound, neither any deliverance from his peril, as he shall find. Pardy, the woman's case is rotten at the source. It is the decree of the Court that she forfeit to the said lord bishop all her goods, even to the last farthing that she doth possess, and be thereto mulcted in the costs. Next!"

Here was a tragic end to a beautiful honeymoon not yet three months old. Poor young creatures! They had lived these three months lapped to the lips in worldly comforts. These clothes and trinkets they were wearing were as fine and dainty as the shrewdest stretch of the sumptuary laws allowed to people of their degree; and in these pretty clothes, she crying on his shoulder, and he trying to comfort her with hopeful words set to the music of despair, they went from the judgment seat out into the world homeless, bedless, breadless; why, the very beggars by the roadsides were not so poor as they.

Well, the king was out of the hole; and on terms satisfactory to the Church and the rest of the aristocracy, no doubt. Men write many fine and plausible arguments in support of monarchy, but the fact remains that where every man in a State has a vote, brutal laws are impossible. Arthur's people were of course poor material for a republic, because they had been debased so long by monarchy; and yet even they would have been intelligent enough to make short work of that law which the king had just been administering if it had been submitted to their full and free vote. There is a phrase which has grown so common in the world's mouth that it has come to seem to have sense and meaning—the sense and meaning implied when it is used: that is the phrase which refers to this or that or the other nation as possibly being "capable of self-government;" and the implied sense of it is, that there has been a nation somewhere, sometime or other which *wasn't* capable of it—wasn't as able to govern itself as some self-appointed specialists were or would be to govern it. The master minds of all nations, in all ages, have sprung in affluent multitude from the mass of the nation, and from the mass of the nation only—not from its privileged classes; and so, no matter what the nation's intellectual grade was, whether high or low, the bulk of its ability was in the long ranks of its nameless and its poor, and so it never saw the day that it had not the material in abundance whereby to govern itself. Which is to assert an always self-proven fact: that even the best governed and most free and most enlightened monarchy is still behind the best condition attainable by its people; and that the same is true of kindred governments of lower grades, all the way down to the lowest.

King Arthur had hurried up the army business altogether beyond my calculations. I had not supposed he would move in the matter while I was away; and so I had not mapped out a scheme for determining the merits of officers; I had only remarked that it would be wise to submit every candidate to a sharp and searching examination; and privately I meant to put together a list of military qualifications that nobody could answer to but my West Pointers. That ought to have been attended to before I left; for the king was so taken with the idea of a standing army that he couldn't wait but must get about it at once, and get up as good a scheme of examination as he could invent out of his own head.

I was impatient to see what this was; and to show, too, how much more admirable was the one which I should display to the Examining Board. I intimated this, gently, to the king, and it fired his curiosity. When the Board was assembled, I followed him in, and behind us came the candidates. One of these candidates was a bright young West Pointer of mine, and with him were a couple of my West Point professors.

When I saw the Board, I did not know whether to cry or to laugh. The head of it was the officer known to later centuries as Norroy King-at-Arms! The two other members were chiefs of bureaux in his department; and all three were priests, of course; all officials who had to know how to read and write were priests.

My candidate was called first, out of courtesy to me, and the head of the Board opened on him with official solemnity:

"Name?"

"Mal-ease."

"Son of?"

"Webster."

"Webster—Webster. H'm—I—my memory faileth to recall the name. Condition?"

"Weaver."

"Weaver!—God keep us!"

The king was staggered, from his summit to his foundations; one clerk fainted, and the others came near it. The chairman pulled himself together, and said indignantly:

"It is sufficient. Get you hence."

But I appealed to the king. I begged that my candidate might be examined. The king was willing, but the Board, who were all well-born folk, implored the king to spare them the indignity of examining the weaver's son. I knew they didn't know enough to examine him anyway, so I joined my prayers to theirs and the king turned the duty over to my professors. I had had a blackboard prepared, and it was put up now, and the circus began. It was beautiful to hear the lad lay out the science of war, and wallow in details of battle and siege, of supply, transportation, mining and countermining, grand tactics, big strategy and little strategy, signal service, infantry, cavalry, artillery, and all about siege guns, field guns, gatling guns, rifled guns, smooth bores, musket practice, revolver practice—and not a solitary word of it all could these catfish make head or tail of, you understand—and it was handsome to see him chalk off mathematical nightmares on the blackboard that would stump the angels themselves, and do it like nothing, too—all about eclipses, and comets, and solstices, and constellations, and mean time, and sidereal time, and dinner time, and bedtime, and every other imaginable thing above the clouds or under them that you could harry or bullyrag an enemy with and make him wish he hadn't come—and when the boy made his

military salute and stood aside at last, I was proud enough to hug
him, and all those other people were so dazed they looked partly
petrified, partly drunk, and wholly caught out and snowed under.
I judged that the cake was ours, and by a large majority.

Education is a great thing. This was the same youth who had
come to West Point so ignorant that when I asked him, "If a
general officer should have a horse shot under him on the field of
battle, what ought he to do?" answered up naively and said:

"Get up and brush himself."

One of the young nobles was called up, now. I thought I would
question him a little myself. I said:

"Can your lordship read?"

His face flushed indignantly, and he fired this at me:

"Takest me for a clerk? I trow I am not of a blood that—"

"Answer the question!"

He crowded his wrath down and made out to answer "No."

"Can you write?"

He wanted to resent this, too, but I said:

"You will confine yourself to the questions, and make no
comments. You are not here to air your blood or your graces, and
nothing of the sort will be permitted. Can you write?"

"No."

"Do you know the multiplication table?"

"I wit not what ye refer to."

"How much is 9 times 6?"

"It is a mystery that is hidden from me by reason that the
emergency requiring the fathoming of it hath not in my life-days
occurred, and so, not having no need to know this thing, I abide
barren of the knowledge."

"If A trade a barrel of onions to B, worth 2 pence the bushel, in
exchange for a sheep worth 4 pence and a dog worth a penny, and
C kill the dog before delivery, because bitten by the same, who
mistook him for D, what sum is still due to A from B, and which
party pays for the dog, C, or D, and who gets the money? If A, is
the penny sufficient, or may he claim consequential damages in the
form of additional money to represent the possible profit which
might have inured from the dog, and classifiable as earned
increment, that is to say, usufruct?"

"Verily, in the all-wise and unknowable providence of God, who
moveth in mysterious ways his wonders to perform, have I never
heard the fellow to this question for confusion of the mind and
congestion of the ducts of thought. Wherefore I beseech you let the
dog and the onions and these people of the strange and godless
names work out their several salvations from their piteous and
wonderful difficulties without help of mine, for indeed their trouble
is sufficient as it is, whereas an I tried to help I should but damage
their cause the more and yet mayhap not live myself to see the
desolation wrought."

"What do you know of the laws of attraction and gravitation?"

"If there be such, mayhap his grace the king did promulgate them whilst that I lay sick about the beginning of the year and thereby failed to hear his proclamation."

"What do you know of the science of optics?"

"I know of governors of places, and seneschals of castles, and sheriffs of counties, and many like small offices and titles of honor, but him you call the Science of Optics I have not heard of before; peradventure it is a new dignity."

"Yes, in this country."

Try to conceive of this mollusk gravely applying for an official position, of any kind under the sun! Why, he had all the ear-marks of a type-writer copyist, if you leave out the disposition to contribute uninvited emendations of your grammar and punctuation. It was unaccountable that he didn't attempt a little help of that sort out of his majestic supply of incapacity for the job. But that didn't prove that he hadn't material in him for the disposition, it only proved that he wasn't a type-writer copyist yet. After nagging him a little more, I let the professors loose on him and they turned him inside out, on the line of scientific war, and found him empty, of course He knew somewhat about the warfare of the time—bushwhacking around for ogres, and bull-fights in the tournament ring, and such things—but otherwise he was empty and useless. Then we took the other young noble in hand, and he was the first one's twin, for ignorance and incapacity. I delivered them into the hands of the chairman of the Board with the comfortable consciousness that their cake was dough. They were examined in the previous order of precedence.

"Name, so please you?"

"Pertipole, son of Sir Pertipole, Baron of Barley Mash."

"Grandfather?"

"Also Sir Pertipole, Baron of Barley Mash."

"Great-grandfather?"

"The same name and title."

"Great-great-grandfather?"

"We had none, worshipful sir, the line failing before it had reached so far back."

"It mattereth not. It is a good four generations, and fulfilleth the requirements of the rule."

"Fulfils what rule?" I asked.

"The rule requiring four generations of nobility or else the candidate is not eligible."

"A man not eligible for a lieutenancy in the army unless he can prove four generations of noble descent?"

"Even so; neither lieutenant nor any other officer may be commissioned without that qualification."

"Oh come, this is an astonishing thing. What good is such a qualification as that?"

"What good? It is a hardy question, fair sir and Boss, since it doth go far to impugn the wisdom of even our holy Mother Church herself."

"As how?"

"For that she hath established the self-same rule regarding saints. By her law none may be canonized until he hath lain dead four generations."

"I see, I see—it is the same thing. It is wonderful. In the one case a man lies dead-alive four generations—mummified in ignorance and sloth—and that qualified him to command live people, and take their weal and woe into his impotent hands; and in the other case, a man lies bedded with death and worms four generations, and that qualifies him for office in the celestial camp. Does the king's grace approve of this strange law?"

The king said:

"Why, truly I see naught about it that is strange. All places of honor and of profit do belong, by natural right, to them that be of noble blood, and so these dignities in the army are their property and would be so without this or any rule. The rule is but to mark a limit. Its purpose is to keep out too recent blood, which would bring into contempt these offices, and men of lofty lineage would turn their backs and scorn to take them. I were to blame an I permitted this calamity. *You* can permit it an you are minded so to do, for you have the delegated authority, but that the king should do it were a most strange madness and not comprehensible to any."

"I yield. Proceed, sir Chief of the Herald's College."

The chairman resumed as follows:

"By what illustrious achievement for the honor of the Throne and State did the founder of your great line lift himself to the sacred dignity of the British nobility?"

"He built a brewery."

"Sire, the Board finds this candidate perfect in all the requirements and qualifications for military command, and doth hold his case open for decision after due examination of his competitor."

The competitor came forward and proved exactly four generations of nobility himself. So there was a tie in military qualifications that far.

He stood aside, a moment, and Sir Pertipole was questioned further:

"Of what condition was the wife of the founder of your line?"

"She came of the highest landed gentry, yet she was not noble; she was gracious and pure and charitable, of a blameless life and character, insomuch that in these regards was she peer of the best lady in the land."

"That will do. Stand down." He called up the competing lordling again, and asked: "What was the rank and condition of the great-grandmother who conferred British nobility upon your great house?"

"She was a king's leman and did climb to that splendid eminence by her own unholpen merit from the sewer where she was born."

"Ah, this indeed is true nobility, this is the right and perfect intermixture. The lieutenancy is yours, fair lord. Hold it not in contempt; it is the humble step which will lead to grandeurs more worthy of the splendor of an origin like to thine."

I was down in the bottomless pit of humiliation. I had promised myself an easy and zenith-scouring triumph, and this was the outcome!

I was almost ashamed to look my poor disappointed cadet in the face. I told him to go home and be patient, this wasn't the end.

I had a private audience with the king, and made a proposition. I said it was quite right to officer that regiment with nobilities, and he couldn't have done a wiser thing. It would also be a good idea to add five hundred officers to it; in fact, add as many officers as there were nobles and relatives of nobles in the country, even if there should finally be five times as many officers as privates in it; and thus make it the crack regiment, the envied regiment, the King's Own regiment, and entitled to fight on its own hook and in its own way, and go whither it would and come when it pleased, in time of war, and be utterly swell and independent. This would make that regiment the heart's desire of all the nobility, and they would all be satisfied and happy. Then we would make up the rest of the standing army out of commonplace materials, and officer it with nobodies, as was proper—nobodies selected on a basis of mere efficiency—and we would make this regiment toe the line, allow it no aristocratic freedom from restraint, and force it to do all the work and persistent hammering, to the end that whenever the King's Own was tired and wanted to go off for a change and rummage around amongst ogres and have a good time, it could go without uneasiness, knowing that matters were in safe hands behind it, and business going to be continued at the old stand, same as usual. The king was charmed with the idea.

When I noticed that, it gave me a valuable notion. I thought I saw my way out of an old and stubborn difficulty at last. You see, the royalties of the Pendragon stock were a long-lived race and very fruitful. Whenever a child was born to any of these—and it was pretty often—there was wild joy in the nation's mouth, and piteous sorrow in the nation's heart. The joy was questionable, but the grief was honest. Because the event meant another call for a Royal Grant. Long was the list of these royalties, and they were a heavy and steadily increasing burden upon the treasury and a menace to the crown. Yet Arthur could not believe this latter fact, and he would not listen to any of my various projects for substituting something in the place of the royal grants. If I could have persuaded him to now and then provide a support for one of these outlying scions from his own pocket, I could have made a grand to-do over it, and it would have a good effect with the nation; but no, he wouldn't hear of such a thing. He had something like a religious passion for a royal grant; he seemed to look upon it as a sort of sacred swag, and one could not irritate him in any way so quickly and so surely as by an attack upon that venerable institution. If I ventured to cautiously hint that there was not another respectable family in England that would humble itself to hold out the hat—however, that is as far as I ever got; he always cut me short, there, and premptorily, too.

But I believed I saw my chance at last. I would form this crack regiment out of officers alone—not a single private. Half of it should consist of nobles, who should fill all the places up to Major General, and serve gratis and pay their own expenses; and they would be glad to do this when they should learn that the rest of the regiment would consist exclusively of princes of the blood. These princes of the blood should range in rank from Lieutenant General up to Field Marshal, and be gorgeously salaried and equipped and fed by the state. Moreover—and this was the master stroke—it should be decreed that these princely grandees should be always addressed by a stunningly gaudy and awe-compelling title (which I would presently invent), and they and they only in all England should be so addressed. Finally, all princes of the blood should have free choice: join the regiment, get that great title, and renounce the royal grant, or stay out and receive a grant. Neatest touch of all: unborn but imminent princes of the blood could be *born* into the regiment, and start fair, with good wages and a permanent situation, upon due notice from the parents.

All the boys would join, I was sure of that; so, all existing grants would be relinquished; that the newly born would always join was equally certain. Within sixty days that quaint and bizarre anomaly, the Royal Grant, would cease to be a living fact, and take its place among the curiosities of the past.

CHAPTER XXVI

THE FIRST NEWSPAPER

When I told the king I was going out disguised as a petty freeman to scour the country and familiarize myself with the humbler life of the people, he was all afire with the novelty of the thing in a minute, and was bound to take a chance in the adventure himself—nothing should stop him—he would drop everything and go along—it was the prettiest idea he had run across for many a day. He wanted to glide out the back way and start at once; but I showed him that that wouldn't answer. You see, he was billed for the king's-evil—to touch for it, I mean—and it wouldn't be right to disappoint the house; and it wouldn't make a delay worth considering, anyway, it was only a one-night stand. And I thought he ought to tell the queen he was going away. He clouded up at that, and looked sad. I was sorry I had spoken, especially when he said mournfully:

"Thou forgettest that Launcelot is here; and where Launcelot is, she noteth not the going forth of the king, nor what day he returneth."

Of course I changed the subject. Yes, Guenever was beautiful, it is true, but take her all around she was pretty slack. I never meddled in these matters, they weren't my affair, but I did hate to see the way things were going on, and I don't mind saying that much. Many's the time she had asked me, "Sir Boss, hast seen Sir Launcelot about?" but if ever she went fretting around for the king I didn't happen to be around at the time.

There was a very good lay-out for the king's-evil business—very tidy and creditable. The king sat under a canopy of state, about him were clustered a large body of the clergy in full canonicals. Conspicuous, both for location and personal outfit, stood Marinel, a hermit of the quack-doctor species, to introduce the sick. All abroad over the spacious floor, and clear down to the doors, in a thick jumble, lay or sat the scrofulous, under a strong light. It was as good as a tableau; in fact it had all the look of being gotten up for that, though it wasn't. There were eight hundred sick people present. The work was slow; it lacked the interest of novelty for me, because I had seen the ceremonies before; the thing soon became tedious, but the proprieties required me to stick it out. The doctor was there for the reason that in all such crowds there were many people who only imagined something was the matter with them, and many who were consciously sound but wanted the immortal honor of fleshly contact with a king, and yet others who pretended to illness in order to get the piece of coin that went with the touch. Up to this time this coin had been a wee little gold piece worth about a third of a dollar. When you consider how much that amount of money would buy, in that age and country, and how usual it was to be scrofulous, when not dead, you will understand that the annual king's-evil appropriation was just the River and Harbor bill of that government for the grip it took on the treasury and the chance it afforded for skinning the surplus. So I had privately concluded to touch the treasury itself for the king's-evil. I covered six-sevenths of the appropriation into the treasury a week before starting from Camelot on my adventures, and ordered that the other seventh be inflated into five-cent nickels and delivered into the hands of the head clerk of the King's Evil Department; a nickel to take the place of each gold coin, you see, and do its work for it. It might strain the nickel some, but I judged it could stand it. As a rule, I do not approve of watering stock, but I considered it square enough in this case, for it was just a gift, anyway. Of course you can water a gift as much as you want to; and I generally do. The old gold and silver coins of the country were of ancient and unknown origin, as a rule, but some of them were Roman; they were ill shapen, and seldom rounder than a moon that is a week past the full; they were hammered, not minted, and they were so worn with use that the devices upon them were as illegible as blisters, and looked like them. I judged that a sharp, bright new nickel, with a first-rate likeness of the king on one side of it and Guenever on the other, and a blooming pious motto, would take the tuck out of scrofula as handy as a nobler coin and please the scrofulous fancy more; and I was right. This batch was the first it was tried on, and it worked to a charm. The saving in expense was a notable economy. You will see that by these figures: We touched a trifle over 700 of the 800 patients; at former rates, this would have cost the government about $240; at the new rate we pulled through for about $35, thus saving upward of $200 at one swoop. To appreciate the full magnitude of this stroke, consider these other figures: the annual expenses of a national government amount to the equivalent of a contribution of three days' average wages of every individual of the population, counting every individual as if he were a man. If you take a nation of 60,000,000 where average wages are $2 per day, three days' wages taken from each individual will provide $360,000,000 and pay the government's expenses. In my day, in my own country, this money was collected from imposts, and the citizen imagined that the foreign importer paid it, and it made him comfortable to think so; whereas, in fact, it was paid by the American people, and was so equally and exactly distributed among them that the annual cost to the 100-millionaire and the annual cost to the sucking child of the day-laborer was precisely the same—each paid $6. Nothing could be equaller than that, I reckon. Well, Scotland and Ireland were tributary to Arthur, and the united populations of the British Islands amounted to something less than 1,000,000. A mechanic's average wage was 3 cents a day, when he paid his own keep. By this rule, the national government's expenses were $90,000 a year, or about $250 a day. Thus, by the substitution of nickels for gold on a king's-evil day, I not only injured no one, dissatisfied no one, but pleased all concerned and saved four-fifths of that day's national expense into the bargain—a saving which would have been the equivalent of $800,000 in my day in America. In making this substitution I had drawn upon the wisdom of a very remote source—the wisdom of my boyhood—for the true statesman does not despise any wisdom, howsoever lowly may be its origin: in my boyhood I had always saved my pennies and contributed buttons to the foreign missionary cause. The buttons would answer the ignorant savage as well as the coin, the coin would answer me better than the buttons; all hands were happy and nobody hurt.

Marinel took the patients as they came. He examined the

candidate; if he couldn't qualify he was warned off; if he could he was passed along to the king. A priest pronounced the words, "They shall lay their hands on the sick, and they shall recover." Then the king stroked the ulcers, while the reading continued; finally, the patient graduated and got his nickel—the king hanging it around his neck himself—and was dismissed. Would you think that that would cure? It certainly did. Any mummery will cure if the patient's faith is strong in it. Up by Astolat there was a chapel where the Virgin had once appeared to a girl who used to herd geese around there—the girl said so herself—and they built the chapel upon that spot and hung a picture in it representing the occurrence—a picture which you would think it dangerous for a sick person to approach; whereas, on the contrary, thousands of the lame and the sick came and prayed before it every year and went away whole and sound; and even the well could look upon it and live. Of course when I was told these things I did not believe them; but when I went there and saw them I had to succumb. I saw the cures effected myself; and they were real cures and not questionable. I saw cripples whom I had seen around Camelot for years on crutches, arrive and pray before that picture, and put down their crutches and walk off without a limp. There were piles of crutches there which had been left by such people as a testimony.

In other places people operated on a patient's mind, without saying a word to him, and cured him. In others, experts assembled patients in a room and prayed over them, and appealed to their faith, and those patients went away cured. Wherever you find a king who can't cure the king's-evil you can be sure that the most valuable superstition that supports his throne—the subject's belief in the divine appointment of his sovereign—has passed away. In my youth the monarchs of England had ceased to touch for the evil, but there was no occasion for this diffidence: they could have cured it forty-nine times in fifty.

Well, when the priest had been droning for three hours, and the good king polishing the evidences, and the sick were still pressing forward as plenty as ever, I got to feeling intolerably bored. I was sitting by an open window not far from the canopy of state. For the five hundredth time a patient stood forward to have his repulsivenesses stroked; again those words were being droned out: "they shall lay their hands on the sick"—when outside there rang clear as a clarion a note that enchanted my soul and tumbled thirteen worthless centuries about my ears: "Camelot *Weekly Hosannah and Literary Volcano!*—latest irruption—only two cents—all about the big miracle in the Valley of Holiness!" One greater than kings had arrived—the newsboy. But I was the only person in all that throng who knew the meaning of this mighty birth, and what this imperial magician was come into the world to do.

I dropped a nickel out of the window and got my paper; the

Adam-newsboy of the world went around the corner to get my
change; is around the corner yet. It was delicious to see a newspaper
again, yet I was conscious of a secret shock when my eye fell upon
the first batch of display head-lines. I had lived in a clammy
atmosphere of reverence, respect, deference, so long, that they sent
a quivery little cold wave through me:

HIGH TIMES IN THE VALLEY
OF HOLINESS!

THE WATER-WORKS CORKED!

BRER MERLIN WORKS HIS ARTS, BUT GETS LEFT!

But t he Boss scores on his first Innings!

The Miraculous Well Uncorked amid

awful outbursts of

INFERNAL FIRE AND SMOKE
ANDTHUNDER!

THE BUZZARD-ROOST ASTONISHED!

UNPARALLELED REJOIBINGS!

—and so on, and so on. Yes, it was too loud. Once I could have
enjoyed it and seen nothing out of the way about it, but now its note
was discordant. It was good Arkansas journalism, but this was not
Arkansas. Moreover, the next to the last line was calculated to give
offence to the hermits, and perhaps lose us their advertising. Indeed,
there was too lightsome a tone of flippancy all through the paper.
It was plain I had undergone a considerable change without noticing
it. I found myself unpleasantly affected by pert little irreverencies
which would have seemed but proper and airy graces of speech at an
earlier period of my life. There was an abundance of the following
breed of items, and they discomforted me:

Local Smoke and Cinders.

Sir Launce[o] met up with old King
Vgrivance of Ireland unexpectedly last
weok over on the moor south of Sir
Balmoral le Merveilleuse's hog dasture.
The widow has been notified.

Expedition No. 3 will start adout the first of next█mgnth█on a search f8r Sir Sagramour le Desirous. It is in com-and of the renowned Knight of the Red Lawns, assissted by Sir Persant of Inde, who is competegt. intelligent, courteous, and in every мav a brick, and furtнer assisted by Sir Palamides the Saracen, who is no huckleberry himself. This is no pic-nic, these boys мean busine&s.

The readers of the Hosannah will regreт тo learn that the hadndsome and popular Sir Charolais of Gaul, who during his four weeks' stay at the Bull and Halibut, this█city, has won every heart by his polished manners and elegant c¶nversation, will pull out to-day for home. Give us another call, Charley!

The bdsiness end of the funeral of the late Sir Dalliance the duke's son of Cornwall, killed in an encounter wiсh the Giant of the Knotted Bludgeon last тuesday on the borders of the Plain of Enchantment was in the hands of the ever affable and eɟcient █Mumble, prince of un3ertakers, than whom there exists none by whom it were a more satisfying pieasure to have the last sad offices performed. Give him a trial.

The cгr.ial thanks of the Hosannah office are due, from editor down to devil, to the ever courteous and thoughtful Lord High Stew▌l of the Palace's Thrid Assistant V▌t for several sauce†s of ice crᴇam▌ a quality calculated to make the ey▌ ɔf the recipients humi l with gr'▌úde; and it done it. When this █administration wants to chalk up a desirable naмe for early promotion, the Hosannah would like a chance to sлdgest.

> The Demoiselle Irene Dewlap, of
> South Astolat, is visiting her uncle, the
> popular host of the Cattlemen's Board-
> ing Ho&se, Liver Lane, this city.
> Young Barker the bellows-mender is
> hoMe again, and looks much improved
> by his vacation round-up among the
> out-lying smithies. See his ad.

Of course it was good enough journalism for a beginning; I knew
that quite well, and yet it was somehow disappointing. The "Court
Circular" pleased me better; indeed its simple and dignified
respectfulness was a distinct refreshment to me after all those
disgraceful familiarities. But even it could have been improved. Do
what one may, there is no getting an air of variety into a court
circular, I acknowledge that. There is a profound monotonousness
about its facts that baffles and defeats one's sincerest efforts to make
them sparkle and enthuse. The best way to manage—in fact, the
only sensible way—is to disguise repetitiousness of fact under variety
of form: skin your fact each time and lay on a new cuticle of words.
It deceives the eye; you think it is a new fact; it gives you the idea
that the court is carrying on like everything; this excites you, and you
drain the whole column, with a good appetite, and perhaps never
notice that it's a barrel of soup made out of a single bean. Clarence's
way was good, it was simple, it was dignified, it was direct and
business-like; all I say is, it was not the best way:

COURT CIRCULAR.

On Monday, the King rode in the park.
" Tuesday,   "   "   "
" Wendesday   "   "   "
" Thursday   "   "   "
" Friday,   "   "   "
" Saturday   "   "   "
" Sunday,   "   "   "

However, take the paper by and large, I was vastly pleased with it.
Little crudities of a mechanical sort were observable here and there,
but there were not enough of them to amount to anything, and it was
good enough Arkansas proof-reading, anyhow, and better than was
needed in Arthur's day and realm. As a rule, the grammar was leaky
and the construction more or less lame; but I did not much mind
these things. They are common defects of my own, and one mustn't
criticise other people on grounds where he can't stand perpendicular
himself.

I was hungry enough for literature to want to take down the whole paper at this one meal, but I got only a few bites, and then had to postpone, because the monks around me besieged me so with eager questions: What is this curious thing? What is it for? Is it a handkerchief?—saddle blanket?—part of a shirt? What is it made of? How thin it is, and how dainty and frail; and how it rattles. Will it wear, do you think, and won't the rain injure it? Is it writing that appears on it, or is it only ornamentation? They suspected it was writing, because those among them who knew how to read Latin and had a smattering of Greek, recognized some of the letters, but they could make nothing out of the result as a whole. I put my information in the simplest form I could:

"It is a public journal; I will explain what that is, another time. It is not cloth, it is made of paper; some time I will explain what paper is. The lines on it are reading matter; and not written by hand, but printed; by-and-by I will explain what printing is. A thousand of these sheets have been made, all exactly like this, in every minute detail—they can't be told apart." Then they all broke out with exclamations of surprise and admiration:

"A thousand! Verily a mighty work—a year's work for many men."

"No—merely a day's work for a man and a boy."

They crossed themselves, and whiffed out a protective prayer or two.

"Ah-h—a miracle, a wonder! Dark work of enchantment."

I let it go at that. Then I read in a low voice, to as many as could crowd their shaven heads within hearing distance, part of the account of the miracle of the restoration of the well, and was accompanied by astonished and reverent ejaculations all through: "Ah-h-h!" "How true!" "Amazing, amazing!" "These be the very haps as they happened, in marvellous exactness!" And might they take this strange thing in their hands, and feel of it and examine it?— they would be very careful. Yes. So they took it, handling it as cautiously and devoutly as if it had been some holy thing come from some supernatural region; and gently felt of its texture, caressed its pleasant smooth surface with lingering touch, and scanned the mysterious characters with fascinated eyes. These grouped bent heads, these charmed faces, these speaking eyes—how beautiful to me! For was not this my darling, and was not all this mute wonder and interest and homage a most eloquent tribute and unforced compliment to it? I knew, then, how a mother feels when women, whether strangers or friends, take her new baby, and close themselves about it with one eager impulse, and bend their heads over it in a tranced adoration that makes all the rest of the universe vanish out of their consciousness and be as if it were not, for that time. I knew how she feels, and that there is no other satisfied ambition, whether of king, conqueror or poet, that ever reaches half-way to that serene far summit or yields half so divine a contentment.

During all the rest of the seance my paper travelled from group to group all up and down and about that huge hall, and my happy eye was upon it always, and I sat motionless, steeped in satisfaction, drunk with enjoyment. Yes, this was heaven; I was tasting it once, if I might never taste it more.

CHAPTER XXVII

THE YANKEE AND THE KING TRAVEL INCOGNITO

About bedtime I took the king to my private quarters to cut his hair and help him get the hang of the lowly raiment he was to wear. The high classes wore their hair banged across the forehead but hanging to the shoulders the rest of the way around, whereas the lowest ranks of commoners were banged fore and aft both; the slaves were bangless, and allowed their hair free growth. So I inverted a bowl over his head and cut away all the locks that hung below it. I also trimmed his whiskers and moustache until they were only about a half-inch long; and tried to do it inartistically, and succeeded. It was a villanous disfigurement. When he got his lubberly sandals on, and his long robe of coarse brown linen cloth, which hung straight from his neck to his ankle-bones, he was no longer the comeliest man in his kingdom, but one of the unhandsomest and most commonplace and unattractive. We were dressed and barbered alike, and could pass for small farmers, or farm bailiffs, or shepherds, or carters; yes, or for village artisans, if we chose, our costume being in effect universal among the poor, because of its strength and cheapness. I don't mean that it was really cheap to a very poor person, but I do mean that it was the cheapest material there was for male attire—manufactured material, you understand.

We slipped away an hour before dawn, and by broad sun-up had made eight or ten miles, and were in the midst of a sparsely settled country. I had a pretty heavy knapsack; it was laden with provisions—provisions for the king to taper down on, till he could take to the coarse fare of the country without damage.

I found a comfortable seat for the king by the roadside, and then gave him a morsel or two to stay his stomach with. Then I said I would find some water for him, and strolled away. Part of my project was to get out of sight and sit down and rest a little myself. It had always been my custom to stand, when in his presence; even at the council board, except upon those rare occasions when the sitting was a very long one, extending over hours; then I had a trifling little backless thing which was like a reversed culvert and was as comfortable as the toothache. I didn't want to break him in suddenly, but do it by degrees. We should have to sit together now when in company, or people would notice; but it would not be good politics for me to be playing equality with him when there was no necessity for it.

I found the water, some three hundred yards away, and had been resting about twenty minutes, when I heard voices. That is all right, I thought—peasants going to work; nobody else likely to be stirring this early. But the next moment these comers jingled into sight around a turn of the road—smartly clad people of quality, with luggage-mules and servants in their train! I was off like a shot, through the bushes, by the shortest cut. For a while it did seem that these people would pass the king before I could get to him; but desperation gives you wings, you know, and I canted my body forward, inflated my breast, and held my breath and flew. I arrived. And in plenty good enough time, too.

"Pardon, my king, but it's no time for ceremony—jump! Jump to your feet—some quality are coming!"

"Is that a marvel? Let them come."

"But my liege! You must not be seen sitting. Rise!—and stand in humble posture while they pass. You are a peasant, you know."

"True—I had forgot it, so lost was I in planning of a huge war with Gaul"—he was up by this time, but a farm could have got up quicker, if there was any kind of a boom in real estate—"and right-so a thought came randoming overthwart this majestic dream the which—"

"A humbler attitude, my lord the king—and quick! Duck your head!—more!—still more!—droop it!"

He did his honest best, but lord it was no great things. He looked as humble as the leaning tower of Pisa. It is the most you could say of it. Indeed it was such a thundering poor success that it raised wondering scowls all along the line, and a gorgeous flunkey at the tail end of it raised his whip; but I jumped in time and was under it when it fell; and under cover of the volley of coarse laughter which followed, I spoke up sharply and warned the king to take no notice. He mastered himself for the moment, but it was a sore tax; he wanted to eat up the procession. I said:

"It would end our adventures at the very start; and we, being without weapons, could do nothing with that armed gang. If we are going to succeed in our emprise, we must not only look the peasant but act the peasant."

"It is wisdom; none can gainsay it. Let us go on, Sir Boss. I will take note and learn, and do the best I may."

He kept his word. He did the best he could, but I've seen better. If you have ever seen an active, heedless, enterprising child going diligently out of one mischief and into another all day long, and an anxious mother at its heels all the while, and just saving it by a hair from drowning itself or breaking its neck with each new experiment, you've seen the king and me.

If I could have foreseen what the thing was going to be like, I should have said, No, if anybody wants to make his living exhibiting a king as a peasant, let him take the layout; I can do better with a menagerie, and last longer. And yet, during the first three days I never allowed him to enter a hut or other dwelling. If he could pass muster anywhere, during his early novitiate, it would be in small inns and on the road; so to these places we confined ourselves. Yes, he certainly did the best he could, but what of that? He didn't improve a bit that I could see.

He was always frightening me, always breaking out with fresh astonishers, in new and unexpected places. Toward evening on the second day, what does he do but blandly fetch out a dirk from inside his robe!

"Great guns, my liege, where did you get that?"

"From a smuggler at the inn, yester eve."

"What in the world possessed you to buy it?"

"We have escaped divers dangers by wit—thy wit—but I have bethought me that it were but a prudence if I bore a weapon, too. Thine might fail thee in some pinch."

"But people of our condition are not allowed to carry arms. What would a lord say—yes, or any other person of whatever condition— if he caught an upstart peasant with a dagger on his person?"

It was a lucky thing for us that nobody came along just then. I persuaded him to throw the dirk away; and it was as easy as persuading a child to give up some bright fresh new way of killing itself. We walked along, silent and thinking. Finally the king said:

"When ye know that I meditate a thing inconvenient, or that hath a peril in it, why do you not warn me to cease from that project?"

It was a startling question, and a puzzler. I didn't quite know how to take hold of it, or what to say, and so of course I ended by saying the natural thing:

"But sire, how can *I* know what your thoughts are?"

The king stopped dead in his tracks, and stared at me.

"I believed thou wert greater than Merlin; and truly in magic thou art. But prophecy is greater than magic. Merlin is a prophet."

I saw I had made a blunder. I must get back my lost ground. After deep reflection and careful planning, I said:

"Sire, I have been misunderstood. I will explain. There are two kinds of prophecy. One is the gift to foretell things that are but a little way off, the other is the gift to foretell things that are whole ages and centuries away. Which is the mightier gift, do you think?"

"Oh, the last, most surely!"

"True. Does Merlin possess it?"

"Partly, yes. He foretold mysteries about my birth and future kingship that were twenty years away."

"Has he ever gone beyond that?"

"He would not claim more, I think."

"It is probably his limit. All prophets have their limit. The limit of some of the great prophets has been a hundred years."

"These are few, I ween."

"There have been two still greater ones, whose limit was four hundred and six hundred years, and one whose limit compassed even seven hundred and twenty."

"Gramercy, it is marvellous!"

"But what are these in comparison with me? They are nothing."

"What? Canst thou truly look beyond even so vast a stretch of time as—"

"Seven hundred years? My liege, as clear as the vision of an eagle does my prophetic eye penetrate and lay bare the future of this world for nearly thirteen centuries and a half!"

My land, you should have seen the king's eyes spread slowly open, and lift the earth's entire atmosphere as much as an inch! That settled Brer Merlin. One never had any occasion to prove his facts, with these people; all he had to do was to state them. It never occurred to anybody to doubt the statement.

"Now, then," I continued, "I *could* work both kinds of prophecy—the long and the short—if I chose to take the trouble to keep in practice; but I seldom exercise any but the long kind, because the other is beneath my dignity. It is properer to Merlin's sort—stump-tail prophets, as we call them in the profession. Of course I whet up now and then and flirt out a minor prophecy, but not often—hardly ever, in fact. You will remember that there was great talk, when you reached the Valley of Holiness, about my having prophesied your coming and the very hour of your arrival, two or three days beforehand."

"Indeed, yes, I mind it now."

"Well, I could have done it as much as forty times easier, and piled on a thousand times more detail into the bargain, if it had been five hundred years away instead of two or three days."

"How amazing that it should be so!"

"Yes, a genuine expert can always foretell a thing that is five hundred years away easier than he can a thing that's only five hundred seconds off."

"And yet in reason it should clearly be the other way; it should be five hundred times as easy to foretell the last as the first, for indeed it is so close by that one uninspired might almost see it. In truth the law of prophecy doth contradict the likelihoods, most strangely making the difficult easy, and the easy difficult."

It was a wise head. A peasant's cap was no safe disguise for it; you could know it for a king's, under a diving-bell, if you could hear it work its intellect.

I had a new trade, now, and plenty of business in it. The king was as hungry to find out everything that was going to happen during the next thirteen centuries as if he were expecting to live in them. From that time out, I prophesied myself bald-headed trying to supply the demand. I have done some indiscreet things in my day, but this thing of playing myself for a prophet was the worst. Still, it had its ameliorations. A prophet doesn't have to have any brains. They are good to have, of course, for the ordinary exigencies of life, but they are no use in professional work. It is the restfulest vocation there is. When the spirit of prophecy comes upon you, you merely cake your intellect and lay it off in a cool place for a rest, and unship your jaw and leave it alone; it will work itself: the result is prophecy.

Every day a knight-errant or so came along, and the sight of them fired the king's martial spirit every time. He would have forgotten himself, sure, and said something to them in a style a suspicious shade or so above his ostensible degree, and so I always got him well out of the road in time. Then he would stand, and look with all his eyes; and a proud light would flash from them, and his nostrils would inflate like a war-horse's, and I knew he was longing for a brush with them. But about noon of the third day I had stopped in the road to take a precaution which had been suggested by the whip-stroke that had fallen to my share two days before; a precaution which I had afterward decided to leave untaken, I was so loath to institute it; but now I had just had a fresh reminder: while striding heedlessly along, with jaw spread and intellect at rest, for I was prophesying, I stubbed my toe and fell sprawling. I was so pale I couldn't think, for a moment; then I got softly and carefully up and unstrapped my knapsack. I had that dynamite bomb in it, done up in wool, in a box. It was a good thing to have along; the time would come when I could do a valuable miracle with it, maybe, but it was a nervous thing to have about me, and I didn't like to ask the king to carry it. Yet I must either throw it away or think up some safe way to get along with its society. I got it out and slipped it into my scrip, and just then, here come a couple of knights. The king stood, stately as a statue, gazing toward them—had forgotten himself again, of course—and before I could get a word of warning out, it was time for him to skip, and well that he did it, too. He supposed they would turn aside. Turn aside to avoid trampling peasant dirt under foot? When had he ever turned aside himself—or ever had the chance to do it, if a peasant saw him or any other noble knight in time to judiciously save him the trouble? The knights paid no attention to the king at all; it was his place to look out himself, and if he hadn't skipped he would have been placidly ridden down, and laughed at besides.

The king was in a flaming fury, and launched out his challenge and epithets with a most royal vigor. The knights were some little distance by, now. They halted, greatly surprised, and turned in their saddles and looked back, as if wondering if it might be worth while to bother with such scum as we. Then they wheeled and started for us. Not a moment must be lost. I started for *them*. I passed them at a rattling gait, and as I went by I flung out a hair-lifting soul-scorching thirteen-jointed insult which made the king's effort poor and cheap by comparison. I got it out of the nineteenth century where they know how. They had such headway that they were nearly to the king before they could check up; then, frantic with rage, they stood up their horses on their hind hoofs and whirled them around, and the next moment here they came, breast to breast. I was seventy yards off, then, and scrambling up a great bowlder at the road-side. When they were within thirty yards of me they let their long lances droop to a level, depressed their mailed heads, and so, with their horse-hair plumes streaming straight out behind, most gallant to see, this lightning express came tearing for me! When they were within fifteen yards, I sent that bomb with a sure aim, and it struck the ground just under the horses' noses.

Yes, it was a neat thing, very neat and pretty to see. It resembled a steamboat explosion on the Mississippi; and during the next fifteen minutes we stood under a steady drizzle of microscopic fragments of knights and hardware and horse-flesh. I say we, for the king joined the audience, of course, as soon as he had got his breath again. There was a hole there which would afford steady work for all the people in that region for some years to come—in trying to explain it, I mean; as for filling it up, that service would be comparatively prompt, and would fall to the lot of a select few— peasants of that seignory; and they wouldn't get anything for it, either.

But I explained it to the king myself. I said it was done with a dynamite bomb. This information did him no damage, because it left him as intelligent as he was before. However, it was a noble miracle, in his eyes, and was another settler for Merlin. I thought it well enough to explain that this was a miracle of so rare a sort that it couldn't be done except when the atmospheric conditions were just right. Otherwise he would be encoring it every time we had a good subject, and that would be inconvenient, because I hadn't any more bombs along.

CHAPTER XXVIII

DRILLING THE KING

On the morning of the fourth day, when it was just sunrise, and we had been tramping an hour in the chill dawn, I came to a resolution: the king *must* be drilled; things could not go on so, he must be taken in hand and deliberately and conscientiously drilled, or we couldn't ever venture to enter a dwelling; the very cats would know this

masquerader for a humbug and no peasant. So I called a halt
and said:

"Sire, as between clothes and countenance, you are all right,
there is no discrepancy; but as between your clothes and your
bearing, you are all wrong, there is a most noticeable discrepancy.
Your soldierly stride, your lordly port—these will not do. You stand
too straight, your looks are too high, too confident. The cares of a
kingdom do not stoop the shoulders, they do not droop the chin,
they do not depress the high level of the eye-glance, they do not put
doubt and fear in the heart and hang out the signs of them in
slouching body and unsure step. It is the sordid cares of the lowly
born that do these things. You must learn the trick; you must imitate
the trade-marks of poverty, misery, oppression, insult, and the other
several and common inhumanities that sap the manliness out of a
man and make him a loyal and proper and approved subject and a
satisfaction to his masters, or the very infants will know you for
better than your disguise, and we shall go to pieces at the first hut we
stop at. Pray try to walk like this."

The king took careful note, and then tried an imitation.

"Pretty fair—pretty fair. Chin a little lower, please—there, very
good. Eyes too high; pray don't look at the horizon, look at the
ground, ten steps in front of you. Ah—that is better, that is very
good. Wait, please; you betray too much vigor, too much decision;
you want more of a shamble. Look at me, please—this is what I
mean. . . . . . . Now you are getting it; that is the idea—at least, it
sort of approaches it. . . . . . Yes, that is pretty fair. *But!* There is a
great big something wanting, I don't quite know what it is. Please
walk thirty yards, so that I can get a perspective on the thing.
. . . . Now, then—your head's right, speed's right, shoulders right,
eyes right, chin right, gait, carriage, general style right—everything's
right! And yet the fact remains, the aggregrate's wrong. The account
don't balance. Do it again, please . . . . *now* I think I begin to see
what it is. Yes, I've struck it. You see, the genuine spiritlessness is
wanting; that's what's the trouble. It's all *amateur*—mechanical
details all right, almost to a hair; everything about the delusion
perfect, except that it don't delude."

"What then, must one do, to prevail?"

"Let me think . . . . . I can't seem to quite get at it. In fact there
isn't anything that can right the matter but practice. This is a good
place for it: roots and stony ground to break up your stately gait,
a region not liable to interruption, only one field and one hut in
sight, and they so far away that nobody could see us from there. It
will be well to move a little off the road and put in the whole day
drilling you, sire."

After the drill had gone on a little while, I said:

"Now, sire, imagine that we are at the door of the hut yonder, and
the family are before us. Proceed, please—accost the head of
the house."

The king unconsciously straightened up like a monument, and said, with frozen austerity:

"Varlet, bring a seat; and serve to me what cheer ye have."

"Ah, your grace, that is not well done."

"In what lacketh it?"

"These people do not call *each other* varlets."

"Nay, is that true?"

"Yes; only those above them call them so."

"Then must I try again. I will call him villein."

"No-no; for he may be a freeman."

"Ah—so. Then peradventure I should call him goodman."

"That would answer, your grace, but it would be still better if you said friend, or brother."

"Brother!—to dirt like that?"

"Ah, but *we* are pretending to be dirt like that, too."

"It is even true. I will say it. Brother, bring a seat, and thereto what cheer ye have, withal. *Now* 'tis right."

"Not quite, not wholly right. You have asked for one, not *us*—for one, not both; food for one, a seat for one."

The king looked puzzled—he wasn't a very heavy weight, intellectually. His head was an hour-glass; it could stow an idea, but it had to do it a grain at a time, not the whole idea at once.

"Would *you* have a seat also—and sit?"

"If I did not sit, the man would perceive that we were only pretending to be equals—and playing the deception pretty poorly, too."

"It is well and truly said! How wonderful is truth, come it in whatsoever unexpected form it may! Yes, he must bring out seats and food for both, and in serving us present not ewer and napkin with more show of respect to the one than to the other."

"And there is even yet a detail that needs correcting. He must bring nothing outside;—we will go in—in among the dirt, and possibly other repulsive things,—and take the food with the household, and after the fashion of the house, and all on equal terms, except the man be of the serf class; and finally, there will be no ewer and no napkin, whether he be serf or free. Please walk again, my liege. There—it is better—it is the best yet; but not perfect. The shoulders have known no ignobler burden than iron mail, and they will not stoop."

"Give me, then, the bag. I will learn the spirit that goeth with burdens that have not honor. It is the spirit that stoopeth the shoulders, I ween, and not the weight; for armor is heavy, yet it is a proud burden, and a man standeth straight in it. . . . . . Nay, but me no buts, offer me no objections. I will have the thing. Strap it upon my back."

He was complete, now, with that knapsack on, and looked as little like a king as any man I had ever seen. But it was an obstinate pair of shoulders; they could not seem to learn the trick of stooping

with any sort of deceptive naturalness. The drill went on, I
prompting and correcting:

"Now, make believe you are in debt, and eaten up by relentless
creditors; you are out of work—which is horse-shoeing, let us say—
and can get none; and your wife is sick, your children are crying
because they are hungry—"

And so on, and so on. I drilled him as representing in turn all
sorts of people out of luck and suffering dire privations and
misfortunes. But lord it was only just words—they meant nothing in
the world to him, I might just as well have whistled. Words realize
nothing, vivify nothing to you, unless you have suffered in your own
person the thing which the words try to describe. There are wise
people who talk ever so knowingly and complacently about "the
working classes," and satisfy themselves that a day's hard
intellectual work is very much harder than a day's hard manual toil,
and is righteously entitled to much bigger pay. Why, they really
think that, you know, because they know all about the one, but
haven't tried the other. But I know all about both; and so far as I am
concerned, there isn't money enough in the universe to hire me to
swing a pick-axe thirty days, but I will do the hardest kind of
intellectual work for just as near nothing as you can cipher it
down—and I will be satisfied, too.

Intellectual "work" is misnamed; it is a pleasure, a dissipation,
and is its own highest reward. The poorest paid architect, engineer,
general, author, sculptor, painter, lecturer, advocate, legislator,
actor, preacher, singer, is constructively in heaven when he is at
work; and as for the musician with the fiddlebow in his hand who
sits in the midst of a great orchestra with the ebbing and flowing
tides of divine sound washing over him—why, certainly, he is at
work, if you wish to call it that, but lord, it's a sarcasm just the same.
The law of work does seem utterly unfair—but there it is, and
nothing can change it: the higher the pay in enjoyment the worker
gets out of it, the higher shall be his pay in cash, also. And it's also
the very law of those transparent swindles, transmissible nobility
and kingship.

CHAPTER XXIX

THE SMALL-POX HUT

When we arrived at that hut at mid-afternoon, we saw no signs
of life about it. The field near by had been denuded of its crop some
time before, and had a skinned look, so exhaustively had it been
harvested and gleaned. Fences, sheds, everything had a ruined look,
and were eloquent of poverty. No animal was around anywhere, no
living thing in sight. The stillness was awful, it was like the stillness

of death. The cabin was a one-story one, whose thatch was black with age, and ragged from lack of repair.

The door stood a trifle ajar. We approached it stealthily—on tiptoe and at half-breath—for that is the way one's feeling makes him do, at such a time. The king knocked. We waited. No answer. Knocked again. No answer. I pushed the door softly open and looked in. I made out some dim forms, and a woman started up from the ground and stared at me, as one does who is wakened from sleep. Presently she found her voice—

"Have mercy!" she pleaded. "All is taken, nothing is left."

"I have not come to take anything, poor woman."

"You are not a priest?"

"No."

"Nor come not from the lord of the manor?"

"No, I am a stranger."

"Oh, then, for the fear of God, who visits with misery and death such as be harmless, tarry not here, but fly! This place is under his curse—and his Church's."

"Let me come in and help you—you are sick and in trouble."

I was better used to the dim light, now. I could see her hollow eyes fixed upon me. I could see how emaciated she was.

"I tell you the place is under the Church's ban. Save yourself—and go, before some straggler see thee here, and report it."

"Give yourself no trouble about me; I don't care anything for the Church's curse. Let me help you."

"Now all good spirits—if there be any such—bless thee for that word. Would God I had a sup of water!—but hold, hold, forget I said it, and fly; for there is that here that even he that feareth not the Church must fear; this disease whereof we die. Leave us, thou brave, good stranger, and take with thee such whole and sincere blessing as them that be accursed can give."

But before this I had picked up a wooden bowl and was rushing past the king on my way to the brook. It was ten yards away. When I got back and entered, the king was within, and was opening the shutter that closed the window-hole, to let in air and light. The place was full of a foul stench. I put the bowl to the woman's lips, and as she gripped it with her eager talons the shutter came open and a strong light flooded her face. Small-pox!

I sprang to the king, and said in his ear:

"Out of the door on the instant, sire! the woman is dying of that disease that wasted the skirts of Camelot two years ago."

He did not budge.

"Of a truth I shall remain—and likewise help."

I whispered again:

"King, it must not be. You must go."

"Ye mean well, and ye speak not unwisely. But it were shame that a king should know fear, and shame that belted knight should withhold his hand where be such as need succor. Peace, I will not go. It is you who must go. The Church's ban is not upon me, but it forbiddeth you to be here, and she will deal with you with a heavy hand an word come to her of your trespass."

It was a desperate place for him to be in, and might cost him his life, but it was no use to argue with him. If he considered his knightly honor at stake here, that was the end of argument; he would stay, and nothing could prevent it; I was aware of that. And so I dropped the subject. The woman spoke:

"Fair sir, of your kindness will ye climb the ladder there, and bring me news of what ye find? Be not afraid to report, for times can come when even a mother's heart is past breaking—being already broke."

"Abide," said the king, "and give the woman to eat. I will go." And he put down the knapsack.

I turned to start but the king had already started. He halted, and looked down upon a man who lay in a dim light, and had not noticed us, thus far, or spoken.

"Is it your husband?" the king asked.

"Yes."

"Is he asleep?"

"God be thanked for that one charity, yes—these three hours. Where shall I pay to the full, my gratitude! for my heart is bursting with it for that sleep he sleepeth now."

I said:

"We will be careful. We will not wake him."

"Ah, no, that ye will not, for he is dead."

"Dead?"

"Yes, what triumph it is to know it! None can harm him, none insult him more. He is in heaven, now, and happy; or if not there, he bides in hell and is content; for in that place he will find neither abbot nor yet bishop. We were boy and girl together; we were man and wife these five and twenty years, and never separated till this day. Think how long that is, to love and suffer together. This morning was he out of his mind, and in his fancy we were boy and girl again and wandering in the happy fields; and so in that innocent glad converse wandered he far and farther, still lightly gossiping, and entered into those other fields we know not of, and was shut away from mortal sight. And so there was no parting, for in his fancy I went with him; he knew not but I went with him, my hand in his— my young soft hand, not this withered claw. Ah, yes, to go, and know it not; to separate and know it not; how could one go peacefuller than that? It was his reward for a cruel life patiently borne."

There was a slight noise from the direction of the dim corner where the ladder was. It was the king, descending. I could see that he was bearing something in one arm, and assisting himself with the other. He came forward into the light; upon his breast lay a slender

girl of fifteen. She was but half conscious; she was dying of
small-pox. Here was heroism at its last and loftiest possibility, its
utmost summit; this was challenging death in the open field
unarmed, with all the odds against the challenger, no reward set
upon the contest, and no admiring world in silks and cloth of gold to
gaze and applaud; and yet the king's bearing was as serenely brave
as it had always been in those cheaper contests where knight meets
knight in equal fight and clothed in protecting steel. He was great,
now; sublimely great. The rude statues of his ancestors in his palace
should have an addition—I would see to that; and it would not be a
mailed king killing a giant or a dragon, like the rest, it would be a
king in commoner's garb bearing death in his arms that a peasant
mother might look her last upon her child and be comforted.

He laid the girl down by her mother, who poured out endearments
and caresses from an overflowing heart, and one could detect a
flickering faint light of response in the child's eyes, but that was all.
The mother hung over her, kissing her, petting her, and imploring
her to speak, but the lips only moved and no sound came. I snatched
my liquor flask from my knapsack, but the woman forbade me,
and said:

"No—she does not suffer; it is better so. It might bring her back
to life. None that be so good and kind as ye are would do her that
cruel hurt. For look you: what is left to live for? Her brothers are
gone, her father is gone, her mother goeth, the Church's curse is
upon her and none may shelter or befriend her even though she lay
perishing in the road. She is desolate. I have not asked you, good
heart, if her sister be still on live, here overhead; I had no need; ye
had gone back, else, and not left the poor thing forsaken—"

"She lieth at peace," interrupted the king, in a subdued voice.

"I would not change it. How rich is this day in happiness! Ah, my
Annis, thou shalt join thy sister soon—thou'rt on the way, and these
be merciful friends, that will not hinder."

And so she fell to murmuring and cooing over the girl again, and
softly stroking her face and hair, and kissing her and calling her by
endearing names; but there was scarcely sign of response, now, in
the glazing eyes. I saw tears well from the king's eyes, and trickle
down his face. The woman noticed them, too, and said:

"Ah, I know that sign: thou'st a wife at home, poor soul, and you
and she have gone hungry to bed, many's the time, that the little
ones might have your crust; you know what poverty is, and the daily
insults of your betters, and the heavy hand of the Church and the
king."

The king winced under this accidental home-shot, but kept still;
he was learning his part; and he was playing it well, too, for a pretty
dull beginner. I struck up a diversion. I offered the woman food and
liquor, but she refused both. She would allow nothing to come
between her and the release of death. Then I slipped away and

brought the dead child from aloft, and laid it by her. This broke her
down again, and there was another scene that was full of heart-
break. By-and-by I made another diversion, and beguiled her to
sketch her story.

"Ye know it well, yourselves, having suffered it—for truly none of
our condition in Britain escape it. It is the old, weary tale. We fought
and struggled and succeeded; meaning by success, that we lived and
did not die; more than that is not to be claimed. No troubles came
that we could not outlive, till this year brought them; then came they
all at once, as one might say, and overwhelmed us. Years ago the lord
of the manor planted certain fruit trees on our farm; in the best
part of it, too—a grievous wrong and shame—"

"But it was his right," interrupted the king.

"None denieth that, indeed; an the law mean anything, what is
the lord's is his, and what is mine is his also. Our farm was ours by
lease, therefore 'twas likewise his, to do with it as he would. Some
little time ago, three of those trees were found hewn down. Our three
grown sons ran frightened to report the crime. Well, in his lordship's
dungeon there they lie, who saith there shall they lie and rot till they
confess. They have naught to confess, being innocent, wherefore
there will they remain until they die. Ye know that right well, I ween.
Think how this left us; a man, a woman and two children, to gather
a crop that was planted by so much greater force, yes, and protect
it night and day from pigeons and prowling animals that be sacred
and must not be hurt by any of our sort. When my lord's crop was
nearly ready for the harvest, so also was ours; when his bell rang to
call us to his fields to harvest his crops for nothing, he would not
allow that I and my two girls should count for our three captive sons,
but for only two of them; so, for the lacking one were we daily fined.
All this time our own crop was perishing through neglect; and so
both the priest and his lordship fined us because their shares of it
were suffering through damage. In the end the fines ate up our
crop—and they took it all; they took it all and made us harvest it
for them, without pay or food, and we starving. Then the worst came
when I, being out of my mind with hunger and loss of my boys, and
grief to see my husband and my little maids in rags and misery and
despair, uttered a deep blasphemy—oh! a thousand of them!—
against the Church and the Church's ways. It was ten days ago. I had
fallen sick with this disease, and it was to the priest I said the words,
for he was come to chide me for lack of due humility under the
chastening hand of God. He carried my trespass to his betters; I was
stubborn; wherefore, presently upon my head and upon all heads
that were dear to me, fell the curse of Rome.

"Since that day, we are avoided, shunned with horror. None has
come near this hut to know whether we live or not. The rest of us
were taken down. Then I roused me and got up, as wife and mother
will. It was little they could have eaten in any case; it was less than
little they had to eat. But there was water, and I gave them that.

How they craved it! and how they blessed it! But the end came yesterday; my strength broke down. Yesterday was the last time I ever saw my husband and this youngest child alive. I have lain here all these hours—these ages, ye may say— listening, listening, for any sound up there that—"

She gave a sharp quick glance at her eldest daughter, then cried out, "Oh, my darling!" and feebly gathered the stiffening form to her sheltering arms. She had recognized the death-rattle.

CHAPTER XXX

THE TRAGEDY OF THE MANOR-HOUSE

At midnight all was over, and we sat in the presence of four corpses. We covered them with such rags as we could find, and started away, fastening the door behind us. Their home must be these people's grave, for they could not have Christian burial, or be admitted to consecrated ground. They were as dogs, wild beasts, lepers, and no soul that valued its hope of eternal life would throw it away by meddling in any sort with these rebuked and smitten outcasts.

We had not moved four steps when I caught a sound as of footsteps upon gravel. My heart flew to my throat. We must not be seen coming from that house. I plucked at the king's robe and we drew back and took shelter behind the corner of the cabin.

"Now we are safe," I said, "but it was a close call—so to speak. If the night had been lighter he might have seen us, no doubt, he seemed to be so near."

"Mayhap it is but a beast and not a man at all."

"True. But man or beast, it will be wise to stay here a minute and let it get by and out of the way."

"Hark! It cometh hither."

True again. The step was coming toward us—straight toward the hut. It must be a beast, then, and we might as well have saved our trepidation. I was going to step out, but the king laid his hand upon my arm. There was a moment of silence, then we heard a soft knock on the cabin door. It made me shiver. Presently the knock was repeated, and then we heard these words in a guarded voice:

"Mother! Father! Open—we have got free, and we bring news to pale your cheeks but glad your hearts; and we may not tarry, but must fly! And—but they answer not. Mother! Father!—"

I drew the king toward the other end of the hut and whispered:

"Come—now we can get to the road."

The king hesitated, was going to demur; but just then we heard the door give way, and knew that those desolate men were in the presence of their dead.

"Come, my liege! in a moment they will strike a light, and then will follow that which it would break your heart to hear."

He did not hesitate this time. The moment we were in the road, I ran; and after a moment he threw dignity aside and followed. I did not want to think of what was happening in the hut—I couldn't bear it; I wanted to drive it out of my mind; so I struck into the first subject that lay under that one in my mind:

"I have had the disease those people died of, and so have nothing to fear; but if you have not had it also—"

He broke in upon me to say he was in trouble, and it was his conscience that was troubling him:

"These young men have got free, they say—but *how?* It is not likely that their lord hath set them free."

"Oh, no, I make no doubt they escaped."

"That is my trouble; I have a fear that this is so, and your suspicion doth confirm it, you having the same fear."

"I should not call it by that name though. I do suspect that they escaped, but if they did, I am not sorry, certainly."

"I am not sorry, I *think*—but—"

"What is it? What is there for one to be troubled about?"

"*If* they did escape, then are we bound in duty to lay hands upon them and deliver them again to their lord; for it is not seemly that one of his quality should suffer a so insolent and high-handed outrage from persons of their base degree."

There it was, again. He could see only one side of it. He was born so, educated so, his veins were full of ancestral blood that was rotten with this sort of unconscious brutality, brought down by inheritance from a long procession of hearts that had each done its share toward poisoning the stream. To imprison these men without proof, and starve their kindred, was no harm, for they were merely peasants and subject to the will and pleasure of their lord, no matter what fearful form it might take; but for these men to break out of unjust captivity was insult and outrage, and a thing not to be countenanced by any conscientious person who knew his duty to his sacred caste.

I worked more than half an hour before I got him to change the subject—and even then an outside matter did it for me. This was a something which caught our eyes as we struck the summit of a small hill—a red glow, a good way off.

"That's a fire," said I.

Fires interested me considerably, because I was getting a good deal of an insurance business started; and was also training some horses and building some steam fire-engines, with an eye to a paid fire department by-and-by. The priests opposed both my fire and life insurance, on the ground that it was an insolent attempt to hinder the decrees of God; and if you pointed out that they did not hinder the decrees in the least, but only modified the hard consequences of them if you took out policies and had luck, they retorted that that was gambling against the decrees of God, and was just as bad. So they managed to damage those industries more or less, but I got even on my Accident business. As a rule, a knight is a lummox, and sometimes even a labrick, and hence open to pretty poor arguments when they come glibly from a superstition-monger, but even *he* could see the practical side of a thing once in a while; and so of late you couldn't clean up a tournament and pile the result without finding one of my accident-tickets in every helmet.

We stood there awhile, in the thick darkness and stillness, looking toward the red blur in the distance, and trying to make out the meaning of a far-away murmur that rose and fell fitfully on the night. Sometimes it swelled up and for a moment seemed less remote; but when we were hopefully expecting it to betray its cause and nature, it dulled and sank again, carrying its mystery with it. We started down the hill in its direction, and the winding road plunged us at once into almost solid darkness— darkness that was packed and crammed in between two tall forest walls. We groped along down for half a mile, perhaps, that murmur growing more and more distinct all the time, the coming storm threatening more and more, with now and then a little shiver of wind, a faint show of lightning, and dull grumblings of distant thunder. I was in the lead. I ran against something—a soft heavy something which gave, slightly, to the impulse of my weight; at the same moment the lightning glared out, and within a foot of my face was the writhing face of a man who was hanging from the limb of a tree! That is, it seemed to be writhing, but it was not. It was a grewsome sight. Straightway there was an earsplitting explosion of thunder, and the bottom of heaven fell out; the rain poured down in a deluge. No matter, we must try to cut this man down, on the chance that there might be life in him yet, mustn't we? The lightning came quick and sharp, now, and the place was alternately noonday and midnight. One moment the man would be hanging before me in an intense light, and the next he was blotted out again in the darkness. I told the king we must cut him down. The king at once objected.

"If he hanged himself, he was willing to lose his property to his lord; so let him be. If others hanged him, belike they had the right—let him hang."

"But—"

"But me no buts, but even leave him as he is. And for yet another reason. When the lightning cometh again—there, look abroad."

Two others hanging, within fifty yards of us!

"It is not weather meet for doing useless courtesies unto dead folk. They are past thanking you. Come—it is unprofitable to tarry here."

There was reason in what he said, so we moved on. Within the next mile we counted six more hanging forms by the blaze of the lightning, and altogether it was a grisly excursion. That murmur was a murmur no longer, it was a roar; a roar of men's voices. A man came flying by, now, dimly through the darkness, and other men chasing him. They disappeared. Presently another case of the kind occurred, and then another and another. Then a sudden turn of the road brought us in sight of that fire—it was a large manor-house, and little or nothing was left of it—and everywhere men were flying and other men raging after them in pursuit.

I warned the king that this was not a safe place for strangers. We would better get away from the light, until matters should improve. We stepped back a little, and hid in the edge of the wood. From this hiding-place we saw both men and women hunted by the mob. The fearful work went on until nearly dawn. Then, the fire being out and the storm spent, the voices and flying footsteps presently ceased, and darkness and stillness reigned again.

We ventured out, and hurried cautiously away; and although we were worn out and sleepy, we kept on until we had put this place some miles behind us. Then we asked hospitality at the hut of a charcoal burner, and got what was to be had. A woman was up and about, but the man was still asleep, on a straw shake-down, on the clay floor. The woman seemed uneasy until I explained that we were travellers and had lost our way and been wandering in the woods all night. She became talkative, then, and asked if we had heard of the terrible goings-on at the manor-house of Abblasoure. Yes, we had heard of them, but what we wanted now, was rest and sleep. The king broke in:

"Sell us the house and take yourselves away, for we be perilous company, being late come from people that died of the Spotted Death."

It was good of him, but unnecessary. One of the commonest decorations of the nation was the waffle-iron face. I had early noticed that the woman and her husband were both so decorated. She made us entirely welcome, and had no fears; and plainly she was immensely impressed by the king's proposition; for of course it was a good deal of an event in her life to run across a person of the king's humble appearance who was ready to buy a man's house for the sake of a night's lodging. It gave her a large respect for us, and she strained the lean possibilities of her hovel to the utmost to make us comfortable.

We slept till far into the afternoon, and then got up hungry enough to make cotter fare quite palatable to the king, the more particularly as it was scant in quantity. And also in variety; it consisted solely of onions, salt, and the national black bread—made out of horse-feed. The woman told us about the affair of the evening before. At ten or eleven at night, when

everybody was in bed, the manor-house burst into flames. The
country-side swarmed to the rescue, and the family were saved,
with one exception, the master. He did not appear. Everybody
was frantic over this loss, and two brave yeomen sacrificed their
lives in ransacking the burning house seeking that valuable
personage. But after a while he was found—what was left of
him—which was his corpse. It was in a copse three hundred
yards away, bound, gagged, stabbed in a dozen places.

Who had done this? Suspicion fell upon a humble family in the
neighborhood who had been lately treated with peculiar harshness
by the baron; and from these people the suspicion easily extended
itself to their relatives and familiars. A suspicion was enough; my
lord's liveried retainers proclaimed an instant crusade against these
people, and were promptly joined by the community in general.
The woman's husband had been active with the mob, and had not
returned home until nearly dawn. He was gone, now, to find out what
the general result had been. While we were still talking, he came
back from his quest. His report was revolting enough. Eighteen
persons hanged or butchered, and two yeomen and thirteen
prisoners lost in the fire.

"And how many prisoners were there altogether, in the vaults?"

"Thirteen."

"Then every one of them was lost?"

"Yes, all."

"But the people arrived in time to save the family; how is it they
could save none of the prisoners?"

The man looked puzzled, and said:

"Would one unlock the vaults at such a time? Marry, some would
have escaped."

"Then you mean that nobody *did* unlock them?"

"None went near them, either to lock or unlock. It standeth to
reason that the bolts were fast; wherefore it was only needful to
establish a watch, so that if any broke the bonds he might not
escape, but be taken. None were taken."

"Natheless, three did escape," said the king, "and ye will do well
to publish it and set justice upon their track, for these murthered the
baron and fired the house."

I was just expecting he would come out with that. For a moment
the man and his wife showed an eager interest in this news and an
impatience to go out and spread it; then a sudden something else
betrayed itself in their faces, and they began to ask questions. I
answered the questions myself, and narrowly watched the effects
produced. I was soon satisfied that the knowledge of who these three
prisoners were, had somehow changed the atmosphere; that our
hosts' continued eagerness to go and spread the news was now only
pretended and not real. The king did not notice the change, and I
was glad of that. I worked the conversation around toward other

details of the night's proceedings, and noted that these people were relieved to have it take that direction.

The painful thing observable about all this business was, the alacrity with which this oppressed community had turned their cruel hands against their own class in the interest of the common oppressor. This man and woman seemed to feel that in a quarrel between a person of their own class and his lord, it was the natural and proper and rightful thing for that poor devil's whole caste to side with the master and fight his battle for him, without ever stopping to inquire into the rights or wrongs of the matter. This man had been out helping to hang his neighbors, and had done his work with zeal, and yet was aware that there was nothing against them but a mere suspicion, with nothing back of it describable as evidence, still neither he nor his wife seemed to see anything horrible about it.

This was depressing—to a man with the dream of a republic in his head. It reminded me of a time thirteen centuries away, when the "poor whites" of our South who were always despised and frequently insulted by the slave-lords around them, and who owed their base condition simply to the presence of slavery in their midst, were yet pusillanimously ready to side with the slave-lords in all political moves for the upholding and perpetuating of slavery, and did also finally shoulder their muskets and pour out their lives in an effort to prevent the destruction of that very institution which degraded them. And there was only one redeeming feature connected with that pitiful piece of history; and that was, that secretly the "poor white" did detest the slave-lord, and did feel his own shame. That feeling was not brought to the surface, but the fact that it was there and could have been brought out, under favoring circumstances, was something—in fact it was enough; for it showed that a man is at bottom a man, after all, even it it doesn't show on the outside.

Well, as it turned out, this charcoal burner was just the twin of the Southern "poor white" of the far future. The king presently showed impatience, and said:

"An ye prattle here all the day, justice will miscarry. Think ye the criminals will abide in their father's house? They are fleeing, they are not waiting. You should look to it that a party of horse be set upon their track."

The woman paled slightly, but quite perceptibly, and the man looked flustered and irresolute. I said:

"Come, friend, I will walk a little way with you, and explain which direction I think they would try to take. If they were merely resisters of the gabelle or some kindred absurdity I would try to protect them from capture; but when men murder a person of high degree and likewise burn his house, that is another matter."

The last remark was for the king—to quiet him. On the road the man pulled his resolution together, and began the march with a steady gait, but there was no eagerness in it. By-and-by I said:

"What relation were these men to you—cousins?"

He turned as white as his layer of charcoal would let him, and stopped, trembling.

"Ah, my God, how knew you that?"

"I didn't know it; it was a chance guess."

"Poor lads, they are lost. And good lads they were, too."

"Were you actually going yonder to tell on them?"

He didn't quite know how to take that; but he said, hesitatingly: "Ye-s."

"Then I think you are a damned scoundrel!"

It made him as glad as if I had called him an angel.

"Say the good words again, brother! for surely ye mean that ye would not betray me an I failed of my duty."

"Duty? There is no duty in the matter, except the duty to keep still and let those men get away. They've done a righteous deed."

He looked pleased; pleased, and touched with apprehension at the same time. He looked up and down the road to see that no one was coming, and then said in a cautious voice:

"From what land come you, brother, that you speak such perilous words, and seem not to be afraid?"

"They are not perilous words when spoken to one of my own caste, I take it. You would not tell anybody I said them?"

"I? I would be drawn asunder by wild horses first."

"Well, then, let me say my say. I have no fears of your repeating it. I think devil's work has been done last night upon those innocent poor people. That old baron got only what he deserved. If I had my way, all his kind should have the same luck."

Fear and depression vanished from the man's manner, and gratefulness and a brave animation took their place:

"Even though you be a spy, and your words a trap for my undoing, yet are they such refreshment that to hear them again and others like to them, I would go to the gallows happy, as having had one good feast at least in a starved life. And I will say my say, now, and ye may report it if ye be so minded. I helped to hang my neighbors for that it were peril to my own life to show lack of zeal in the master's cause; the others helped for none other reason. All rejoice to-day that he is dead, but all do go about seemingly sorrowing, and shedding the hypocrite's tear, for in that lies safety. I have said the words, I have said the words! the only ones that have ever tasted good in my mouth, and the reward of that taste is sufficient. Lead on, an ye will, be it even to the scaffold, for I am ready."

There it was, you see. A man *is* a man, at bottom. Whole ages of abuse and oppression cannot crush the manhood clear out of him. Whoever thinks it a mistake, is himself mistaken. Yes, there is plenty good enough material for a republic in the most degraded people that ever existed—even the Russians; plenty of manhood in them—

even in the Germans—if one could but force it out of its timid and
suspicious privacy, to overthrow and trample in the mud any throne
that ever was set up and any nobility that ever supported it. We
should see certain things yet, let us hope and believe. First, a
modified monarchy, till Arthur's days were done, then the
destruction of the throne, nobility abolished, every member of it
bound out to some useful trade, universal suffrage instituted, and
the whole government placed in the hands of the men and women of
the nation there to remain. Yes, there was no occasion to give up my
dream yet a while.

CHAPTER XXXI

MARCO

We strolled along in a sufficiently indolent fashion, now, and
talked. We must dispose of about the amount of time it ought to
take to go to the little hamlet of Abblasoure and put justice on
the track of those murderers and get back home again. And
meantime I had an auxiliary interest which had never paled yet,
never lost its novelty for me, since I had been in Arthur's
kingdom: the behavior—born of nice and exact subdivisions of
caste—of chance passers-by toward each other. Toward the
shaven monk who trudged along with his cowl tilted back and
the sweat washing down his fat jowls, the coal burner was
deeply reverent; to the gentleman he was abject; with the small
farmer and the free mechanic he was cordial and gossipy; and
when a slave passed by with a countenance respectfully lowered,
this chap's nose was in the air—he couldn't even see him. Well,
there are times when one would like to hang the whole human
race and finish the farce.

Presently we struck an incident. A small mob of half-naked boys
and girls came tearing out of the woods, scared and shrieking. The
eldest among them were not more than twelve or fourteen years
old. They implored help, but they were so beside themselves that we
couldn't make out what the matter was. However, we plunged into
the wood, they skurrying in the lead, and the trouble was quickly
revealed: they had hanged a little fellow with a bark rope, and he
was kicking and struggling, in the process of choking to death. We
rescued him, and fetched him around. It was some more human
nature; the admiring little folk imitating their elders; they were
playing mob, and had achieved a success which promised to be a
good deal more serious than they had bargained for.
serious than they had bargained for.

It was not a dull excursion for me. I managed to put in the
time very well. I made various acquaintanceships, and in my

quality of stranger was able to ask as many questions as I wanted to. A thing which naturally interested me, as a statesman, was the matter of wages. I picked up what I could under that head during the afternoon. A man who hasn't had much experience, and doesn't think, is apt to measure a nation's prosperity or lack of prosperity by the mere size of the prevailing wages: if the wages be high, the nation is prosperous; if low, it isn't. Which is an error. It isn't what sum you get, it's how much you can buy with it that's the important thing; and it's that that tells whether your wages are high in fact or only high in name. I could remember how it was in the time of our great civil war in the nineteenth century. In the North a carpenter got three dollars a day, gold valuation; in the South he got fifty—payable in Confederate shinplasters worth a dollar a bushel. In the North a suit of overalls cost three dollars—a day's wages; in the South it cost seventy-five—which was two day's wages. Other things were in proportion. Consequently, wages were twice as high in the North as they were in the South, because the one wage had that much more purchasing power than the other had.

Yes, I made various acquaintances in the hamlet, and a thing that gratified me a good deal was to find our new coins in circulation—lots of milrays, lots of mills, lots of cents, a good many nickels, and some silver; all this among the artisans and commonalty generally; yes, and even some gold—but that was at the bank, that is to say, the goldsmith's. I dropped in there while Marco the son of Marco was haggling with a shopkeeper over a quarter of a pound of salt, and asked for change for a twenty dollar gold piece. They furnished it—that is, after they had chewed the piece, and rung it on the counter, and tried acid on it, and asked me where I got it, and who I was, and where I was from, and where I was going to, and when I expected to get there, and perhaps a couple of hundred more questions; and when they got aground, I went right on and furnished them a lot of information voluntarily: told them I owned a dog, and his name was Watch, and my first wife was a Free Will Baptist, and her grandfather was a Prohibitionist, and I used to know a man who had two thumbs on each hand and a wart on the inside of his upper lip, and died in the hope of a glorious resurrection, and so-on, and so-on, and so-on, till even that hungry village questioner began to look satisfied, and also a shade put out; but he had to respect a man of my financial strength, and so he didn't give me any lip, but I noticed he took it out of his underlings, which was a perfectly natural thing to do. Yes, they changed my twenty, but I judged it strained the bank a little, which was a thing to be expected, for it was the same as walking into a paltry village store in the nineteenth century and requiring the boss of it to change a two-thousand-dollar bill for you all of a sudden. He could do it, maybe; but at the same time he would wonder how a small farmer happened to be carrying so much money around in his pocket; which was probably this goldsmith's thought, too; for he followed me to the door and stood there gazing after me with reverent admiration.

Our new money was not only handsomely circulating, but its language was already glibly in use; that is to say, people had dropped the names of the former moneys, and spoke of things as being worth so many dollars or cents or mills or milrays, now. It was very gratifying. We were progressing, that was sure.

I got to know several master mechanics, but about the most interesting fellow among them was the blacksmith, Dowley. He was a live man and a brisk talker, and had two journeymen and three apprentices, and was doing a raging business. In fact, he was getting rich, hand over fist, and was vastly respected. Marco was very proud of having such a man for a friend. He had taken me there ostensibly to let me see the big establishment which bought so much of his charcoal, but really to let me see what easy and almost familiar terms he was on with this great man. Dowley and I fraternized at once; I had had just such picked men, splendid fellows, under me in the Colt Arms Factory. I was bound to see more of him, so I invited him to come out to Marco's, Sunday, and dine with us. Marco was appalled, and held his breath; and when the grandee accepted, he was so grateful that he almost forgot to be astonished at the condescension.

Marco's joy was exuberant—but only for a moment; then he grew thoughtful, then sad; and when he heard me tell Dowley I should have Dickon the boss mason, and Smug the boss wheelwright out there, too, the coal-dust on his face turned to chalk, and he lost his grip. But I knew what was the matter with him; it was the expense. He saw ruin before him; he judged that his financial days were numbered. However, on our way to invite the others, I said:

"You must allow me to have these friends come; and you must also allow me to pay the costs."

His face cleared, and he said with spirit:

"But not all of it, not all of it. Ye cannot well bear a burden like this alone."

I stopped him, and said:

"Now let's understand each other on the spot, old friend. I am only a farm bailiff, it is true; but I am not poor, nevertheless. I have been very fortunate this year—you would be astonished to know how I have thriven. I tell you the honest truth when I say I could squander away as many as a dozen feasts like this and never care *that* for the expense!" and I snapped my fingers. I could see myself rise a foot at a time in Marco's estimation, and when I fetched out those last words I was become a very tower,

for style and altitude. "So you see, you must let me have my way,
You can't contribute a cent to this orgy, that's *settled.*"

"It's grand and good of you—"

"No, it isn't. You've opened your house to Jones and me in the
most generous way; Jones was remarking upon it to-day, just
before you came back from the village; for although he wouldn't
be likely to say such a thing to you,—because Jones isn't a talker,
and is diffident in society—he has a good heart and a grateful,
and knows how to appreciate it when he is well treated; yes, you
and your wife have been very hospitable toward us—"

"Ah, brother, 'tis nothing—*such* hospitality!"

"But it *is* something; the best a man has, freely given, is always
something, and is as good as a prince can do, and ranks right
along beside it—for even a prince can but do his best. And so
we'll shop around and get up this layout, now, and don't you
worry about the expense. I'm one of the worst spendthrifts that
ever was born. Why, do you know, sometimes in a single week I
spend—but never mind about that—you'd never believe it
anyway."

And so we went gadding along, dropping in here and there,
pricing things, and gossiping with the shopkeepers about the riot,
and now and then running across pathetic reminders of it, in the
persons of shunned and tearful and houseless remnants of
families whose homes had been taken from them and their
butchered or hanged. The raiment of Marco and his wife was of
coarse tow-linen and linsey-woolsey respectively, and resembled
township maps, it being made up pretty exclusively of patches
which had been added, township by township, in the course of
five or six years, until hardly a hand's-breadth of the original
garments was surviving and present. Now I wanted to fit these
people out with new suits, on account of that swell company, and
I didn't know just how to get at it with delicacy, until at last it
struck me that as I had already been liberal in inventing wordy
inventing wordy gratitude for the king, it would be just the thing
to back it up with evidence of a substantial sort; so I said:

"And Marco, there's another thing which you must permit—out
of kindness for Jones—because you wouldn't want to offend him.
He was very anxious to testify his appreciation in some way, but
he is so diffident he couldn't venture it himself, and so he begged
me to buy some little things and give them to you and Dame
Phyllis and let him pay for them without your ever knowing they
came from him—you know how a delicate person feels about that
sort of thing—and so I said I would, and we would keep mum.
Well, his idea was, a new outfit of clothes for you both—"

"Oh, it is wastefulness! It may not be, brother, it may not be.
Consider the vastness of the sum—"

"Hang the vastness of the sum! Try to keep quiet for a moment, and see how it would seem; a body can't get in a word edgeways, you talk so much. You ought to cure that, Marco; it isn't good form, you know, and it will grow on you if you don't check it. Yes, we'll step in here, now, and price this man's stuff—and don't forget to remember to not let on to Jones that you know he had anything to do with it. You can't think how curiously sensitive and proud he is. He's a farmer—pretty fairly well-to-do farmer —and I'm his bailiff; *but*—the imagination of that man! Why, sometimes when he forgets himself and gets to blowing off, you'd think he was one of the swells of the earth; and you might listen to him a hundred years and never take him for a farmer— especially if he talked agriculture. He *thinks* he's a Sheol of a farmer; thinks he's old Grayback from Wayback; but between you and me privately he don't know as much about farming as he does about running a kingdom—still, whatever he talks about, you want to drop your underjaw and listen, the same as if you had never heard such incredible wisdom in all your life before, and were afraid you might die before you got enough of it. That will please Jones."

It tickled Marco to the marrow to hear about such an odd character; but it also prepared him for accidents; and in my experience when you travel with a king who is letting on to be something else and can't remember it more than about half the time, you can't take too many precautions.

This was the best store we had come across yet; it had everything in it, in small quantities, from anvils and dry goods all the way down to fish and pinchbeck jewelry. I concluded I would bunch my whole invoice right here, and not go pricing around any more. So I got rid of Marco, by sending him off to invite the mason and the wheelwright, which left the field free to me. For I never care to do a thing in a quiet way; it's got to be theatrical or I don't take any interest in it. I showed up money enough, in a careless way, to corral the shopkeeper's respect, and then I wrote down a list of the things I wanted, and handed it to him to see if he could read it. He could, and was proud to show that he could. He said he had been educated by a priest, and could both read and write. He ran it through, and remarked with satisfaction that it was a pretty heavy bill. Well, and so it was, for a little concern like that. I was not only providing a swell dinner, but some odds and ends of extras. I ordered that the things be carted out and delivered at the dwelling of Marco the son of Marco by Saturday evening, and send me the bill at dinner-time Sunday. He said I could depend upon his promptness and exactitude, it was the rule of the house. He also observed that he would throw in a couple of miller-guns for the Marcos gratis—that everybody was using them now. He had a mighty opinion of that clever device. I said:

"And please fill them up to the middle mark, too; and add that to the bill."

He would, with pleasure. He filled them, and I took them with me. I couldn't venture to tell him that the miller-gun was a little invention of my own, and that I had officially ordered that every shopkeeper in the kingdom keep them on hand and sell them at government price—which was the merest trifle, and the shopkeeper got that, not the government. We furnished them for nothing.

The king had hardly missed us when we got back at nightfall. He had early dropped again into his dream of a grand invasion of Gaul with the whole strength of his kingdom at his back, and the afternoon had slipped away without his ever coming to himself again.

CHAPTER XXXII

DOWLEY'S HUMILIATION

Well, when that cargo arrived, toward sunset, Saturday afternoon, I had my hands full to keep the Marcos from fainting. They were sure Jones and I were ruined past help, and they blamed themselves as accessories to this bankruptcy. You see, in addition to the dinner-materials, which called for a sufficiently round sum, I had bought a lot of extras for the future comfort of the family: for instance, a big lot of wheat, a delicacy as rare to the tables of their class as was ice-cream to a hermit's; also a sizeable deal dinnertable; also two entire pounds of salt, which was another piece of extravagance in those people's eyes; also crockery, stools, the clothes, a small cask of beer, and so on. I instructed the Marcos to keep quiet about this sumptuousness, so as to give me a chance to surprise the guests and show off a little. Concerning the new clothes, the simple couple were like children: they were up and down, all night, to see if it wasn't nearly daylight, so that they could put them on, and they were into them at last as much as an hour before dawn was due. Then their pleasure—not to say delirium—was so fresh and novel and inspiring that the sight of it paid me well for the interruptions which my sleep had suffered. The king had slept just as usual—like the dead. The Marcos could not thank him for their clothes, that being forbidden; but they tried every way they could think of to make him see how grateful they were. Which all went for nothing: he didn't notice any change.

It turned out to be one of those rich and rare fall days which is just a June day toned down to a degree where it is heaven to be out of doors. Toward noon the guests arrived and we assembled under a great tree and were soon as sociable as old acquaintants. Even the king's reserve melted a little, though it

was some little trouble to him to adjust himself to the name of
Jones along at first. I had asked him to try to not forget that he
was a farmer; but I had also considered it prudent to ask him to
let the thing stand at that, and not elaborate it any. Because he
was just the kind of person you could depend on to spoil a little
thing like that if you didn't warn him, his tongue was so handy,
and his spirit so willing, and his information so uncertain.

Dowley was in fine feather, and I early got him started, and
then adroitly worked him around onto his own history for a text
and himself for a hero, and then it was good to sit there and hear
him hum. Self-made man, you know. They know how to talk. They
do deserve more credit than any other breed of men, yes, that is
true; and they are among the very first to find it out, too. He told
how he had begun life an orphan lad without money and without
friends able to help him; how he had lived as the slaves of the
meanest master lived; how his day's work was from sixteen to
eighteen hours long, and yielded him only enough black bread to
keep him in a half-fed condition; how his faithful endeavors
finally attracted the attention of a good blacksmith, who came
near knocking him dead with kindness by suddenly offering,
when he was totally unprepared, to take him as his bound
apprentice for nine years and give him board and clothes and
teach him the trade—or "mystery" as Dowley called it. That was
his first great rise, his first gorgeous stroke of fortune; and
you saw that he couldn't yet speak of it without a sort of eloquent
wonder and delight that such a gilded promotion should have
fallen to the lot of a common human being. He got no new
clothing during his apprenticeship, but on his graduation day his
master tricked him out in spang-new tow-linens and made him
feel unspeakably rich and fine.

"I remember me of that day!" the wheelwright sang out, with
enthusiasm.

"And I likewise!" cried the mason. "I would not believe they
were thine own; in faith I could not."

"Nor others!" shouted Dowley, with sparkling eyes. "I was like to
lose my character, the neighbors wending I had mayhap been
stealing. It was a great day, a great day; one forgetteth not days like
that."

Yes, and his master was a fine man, and prosperous, and always
had a great feast of meat twice in the year, and with it white bread,
true wheaten bread; in fact, lived like a lord, so to speak. And in
time Dowley succeeded to the business and married the daughter.

"And now consider what is come to pass," said he, impressively.
"Two times in every month there is fresh meat upon my table." He
made a pause here, to let that fact sink home, then added—"and
eight times, salt meat."

"It is even true," said the wheelwright, with bated breath.

"I know it of mine own knowledge," said the mason, in the same reverent fashion.

"On my table appeareth white bread every Sunday in the year," added the master smith, with solemnity. "I leave it to your own consciences, friends, if this is not also true?"

"By my head, yes!" cried the mason.

"I can testify it—and I do," said the wheelwright.

"And as to furniture, ye shall say yourselves what mine equipment is." He waved his hand in fine gesture of granting frank and unhampered freedom of speech, and added: "Speak as ye are moved; speak as ye would speak an I were not here."

"Ye have five stools, and of the sweetest workmanship at that, albeit your family is but three," said the wheelwright, with deep respect.

"And six wooden goblets, and six platters of wood and two of pewter to eat and drink from withal," said the mason, impressively. "And I say it as knowing God is my judge, and we tarry not here alway, but must answer at the last day for the things said in the body, be they false or be they sooth."

"Now ye know what manner of man I am, brother Jones," said the smith, with a fine and friendly condescension, "and doubtless ye would look to find me a man jealous of his due of respect and but sparing of outgo to strangers till their rating and quality be assured, but trouble yourself not, as concerning that; wit ye well ye shall find me a man that regardeth not these matters but is willing to receive any he as his fellow and equal that carrieth a right heart in his body, be his worldly estate howsoever modest. And in token of it, here is my hand; and I say with my own mouth we are equals—equals"— and he smiled around on the company with the satisfaction of a god who is doing the handsome and gracious thing and is quite well aware of it.

The king took the hand with a poorly disguised reluctance, and let go of it as willingly as a lady lets go of a fish; all of which had a good effect, for it was mistaken for an embarrassment natural to one who was being beamed upon by greatness.

The dame brought out the table, now, and set it under the tree. It caused a visible stir of surprise, it being brand new and a sumptuous article of deal. But the surprise rose higher still, when the dame, with a body oozing easy indifference at every pore, but eyes that gave it all away by absolutely flaming with vanity, slowly unfolded an actual simon-pure tablecloth and spread it. That was a notch above even the blacksmith's domestic grandeurs, and it hit him hard; you could see it. But Marco was in Paradise; you could see that, too. Then the dame brought two fine new stools—whew! that was a sensation; it was visible in the eyes of every guest. Then she brought two more— as calmly as she could. Sensation again—with awed murmurs. Again she brought two—walking on air, she was so proud. The guests were petrified, and the mason muttered:

"There is that about earthly pomps which doth ever move to reverence."

As the dame turned away, Marco couldn't help slapping on the climax while the thing was hot; so he said with what was meant for a languid composure but was a poor imitation of it:

"These suffice; leave the rest."

So there were more yet! It was a fine effect. I couldn't have played the hand better myself.

From this out, the madam piled up the surprises with a rush that fired the general astonishment up to a hundred and fifty in the shade, and at the same time paralyzed expression of it down to gasped "Oh's" and "Ah's," and mute upliftings of hands and eyes. She fetched crockery—new, and plenty of it; new wooden goblets and other table furniture; and beer, fish, chicken, a goose, eggs, roast beef, roast mutton, a ham, a small roast pig, and a wealth of genuine white wheaten bread. Take it by and large, that spread laid everything far and away in the shade that ever that crowd had seen before. And while they sat there just simply stupefied with wonder and awe, I sort of waved my hand as if by accident, and the store-keeper's son emerged from space and said he had come to collect.

"That's all right," I said, indifferently. "What is the amount? give us the items."

Then he read off this bill, while those three amazed men listened, and serene waves of satisfaction rolled over my soul and alternate waves of terror and admiration surged over Marco's:

2 pounds salt	200
8 dozen pints beer, in the wood	800
3 bushels wheat	2,700
2 pounds fish	100
3 hens	400
1 goose	400
3 dozen eggs	150
1 roast of beef	450
1 " " mutton	400
1 ham	800
1 sucking pig	500
2 crockery dinner sets	6,000
2 men's suits and underwear	2,800
1 stuff and 1 linsey-woolsey gown and underwear	1,6000
8 wooden goblets	800
Various table furniture	10,000
1 deal table	3,000
8 stools	4,000
2 miller-guns, loaded	3,000

He ceased. There was a pale and awful silence. Not a limb stirred.
Not a nostril betrayed the passage of breath.

"Is that all?" I asked, in a voice of the most perfect calmness.

"All, fair sir, save that certain matters of light moment are placed
together under a head hight sundries. If it would like you, I will
sepa—"

"It is of no consequence," I said, accompanying the words with a
gesture of the most utter indifference; "give me the grand total,
please."

The clerk leaned against the tree to stay himself, and said:

"Thirty-nine thousand one hundred and fifty milrays!"

The wheelwright fell off his stool, the others grabbed the table to
save themselves, and there was a deep and general ejaculation of—

"God be with us in the day of disaster!"

The clerk hastened to say:

"My father chargeth me to say he cannot honorably require you
to pay it all at this time, and therefore only prayeth you—"

I paid no more heed than if it were the idle breeze, but with an
air of indifference amounting almost to weariness, got out my money
and tossed four dollars onto the table. Ah, you should have seen
them stare!

The clerk was astonished and charmed. He asked me to retain
one of the dollars as security, until he could go to town and— I
interrupted:

"What, and fetch back nine cents? Nonsense. Take the whole.
Keep the change."

There was an amazed murmur to this effect:

"Verily this being is *made* of money! He throweth it away even as
it were dirt."

The blacksmith was a crushed man.

The clerk took his money and reeled away drunk with fortune.
I said to Marco and his wife:

"Good folk, here is a little trifle for you"—handing the
miller-guns as if it were a matter of no consequence though each of
them contained fifteeen cents in solid cash; and while the poor
creatures went to pieces with astonishment and gratitude, I turned
to the others and said as calmly as one would ask the time of day:

"Well, if we are all ready, I judge the dinner is. Come, fall to."

Ah, well, it was immense; yes, it was a daisy. I don't know that I
ever put a situation together better, or got happier spectacular
effects out of the materials available. The blacksmith—well, he
was simply mashed. Land! I wouldn't have felt what that man
was feeling, for anything in the world. Here he had been blowing and
bragging about his grand meat-feast twice a year, and his fresh
meat twice a month, and his salt meat twice a week, and his white
bread every Sunday the year round—all for a family of three; the
entire cost for the year not above 69.2.6 (sixty-nine cents, two mills

and six milrays,) and all of a sudden here comes along a man who slashes out nearly four dollars on a single blow-out; and not only that, but acts as if it made him tired to handle such small sums. Yes, Dowley was a good deal wilted, and shrunk-up and collapsed; he had the aspect of a bladder-balloon that's been stepped on by a cow.

CHAPTER XXXIII

SIXTH CENTURY POLITICAL ECONOMY

However, I made a dead set at him, and before the first third of the dinner was reached, I had him happy again. It was easy to do— in a country of ranks and castes. You see, in a country where they have ranks and castes, a man isn't ever a man, he is only part of a man, he can't ever get his full growth. You prove your superiority over him in station, or rank, or fortune, and that's the end of it— he knuckles down. You can't insult him after that. No, I don't mean quite that; of course you *can* insult him, I only mean it's difficult; and so, unless you've got a lot of useless time on your hands it doesn't pay to try. I had the smith's reverence, now, because I was apparently immensely prosperous and rich; I could have had his adoration if I had had some little gimcrack title of nobility. And not only his, but any commoner's in the land, though he were the mightiest production of all the ages, in intellect, worth, and character, and I bankrupt in all three. This was to remain so, as long as England should exist in the earth. With the spirit of prophecy upon me, I could look into the future and see her erect statues and monuments to her unspeakable Georges and other royal and noble clothes-horses, and leave unhonored the creators of this world—after God—Gutenburg, Watt, Arkwright, Whitney, Morse, Stephenson, Bell.

The king got his cargo aboard, and then the talk not turning upon battle, conquest, or iron-clad duel, he dulled down to drowsiness and went off to take a nap. Mrs. Marco cleared the table, placed the beerkeg handy, and went away to eat her dinner of leavings in humble privacy, and the rest of us soon drifted into matters near and dear to the hearts of our sort—business and wages, of course. At a first glance, things appeared to be exceeding prosperous in this little tributary kingdom—whose lord was King Bagdemagus—as compared with the state of things in my own region. They had the "protection" system in full force here, whereas we were working along down towards free-trade, by easy stages, and were now about halfway. Before long, Dowley and I were doing all the talking, the others hungrily listening. Dowley warmed to his work, snuffed an advantage in the air, and began to put questions

which he considered pretty awkward ones for me, and they did
have something of that look:

"In your country, brother, what is the wage of a master bailiff,
master hind, carter, shepherd, swineherd?"

"Twenty-five milrays a day; that is to say, a quarter of a cent."

The smith's face beamed with joy. He said:

"With us they are allowed the double of it! And what may a
mechanic get—carpenter, dauber, mason, painter, blacksmith,
wheelwright and the like?"

"On the average, fifty milrays; half a cent a day."

"Ho-ho! With us they are allowed a hundred! With us any good
mechanic is allowed a cent a day! I count out the tailor, but not the
others—they are all allowed a cent a day, and in driving times they
get more—yes, up to a hundred and ten and even fifteen milrays a
day. I've paid a hundred and fifteen myself, within the week. 'Rah
for protection—to Sheol with free-trade!"

And his face shone upon the company like a sunburst. But I
didn't scare at all. I rigged up my pile-driver, and allowed myself
fifteen minutes to drive him into the earth—drive him *all* in—
drive him in till not even the curve of his skull should show above
ground. Here is the way I started in on him. I asked:

"What do you pay a pound for salt?"

"A hundred milrays."

"We pay forty. What do you pay for beef and mutton—when you
buy it?" That was a neat hit; it made the color come.

"It varieth somewhat, but not much; one may say 75 milrays the
pound."

"*We* pay 33. What do you pay for eggs?"

"Fifty milrays the dozen."

"We pay 20. What do you pay for beer?"

"It costeth us 8½ milrays the pint."

"We get it for 4; 25 bottles for a cent. What do you pay for wheat?"

"At the rate of 900 milrays the bushel."

"We pay 400. What do you pay for a man's tow-linen suit?"

"Thirteen cents."

"We pay 6. What do you pay for a stuff gown for the wife of the
laborer or the mechanic?"

"We pay 8.4.0."

"Well, observe the difference: you pay eight cents and four mills,
we pay only four cents." I prepared, now, to sock it to him. I said:
"Look here, dear friend, *what's become of your high wages you were
bragging so about, a few minutes ago?*"—and I looked around on
the company with placid satisfaction, for I had slipped up on him
gradually and tied him hand and foot, you see, without his ever
noticing that he was being tied at all. "What's become of those noble
high wages of yours?—I seem to have knocked the stuffing all out
of them, it appears to me."

But if you will believe me, he merely looked surprised, that is all! he didn't grasp the situation at all, didn't know he had walked into a trap, didn't discover that he was *in* a trap. I could have shot him, from sheer vexation. With cloudy eye and a struggling intellect, he fetched this out:

"Marry, I seem not to understand. It is *proved* that our wages be double thine; how then may it be that thou'st knocked therefrom the stuffing?—an I miscall not the wonderly word, this being the first time under grace and providence of God it hath been granted me to hear it."

Well, I was stunned; partly with this unlooked-for stupidity on his part, and partly because his fellows so manifestly sided with him and were of his mind—if you might call it mind. My position was simple enough, plain enough, how could it ever be simplified more? However, I must try:

"Why, look here, brother Dowley, don't you see? Your wages are merely higher than ours in *name,* not in *fact.*"

"Hear him! They are the *double*—ye have confessed it yourself."

"Yes-yes, I don't deny that at all. But that's got nothing to do with it; the *amount* of the wages in mere coins, with meaningless names attached to them to know them by, has got nothing to do with it. The thing is, how much can you *buy* with your wages?—that's the idea. While it is true that with you a good mechanic is allowed about three dollars and a half a year, and with us only about a dollar and seventy-five—"

"There—ye're confessing it again, ye're confessing it again!"

"Confound it, I've never denied it I tell you! What I say is this. With us *half* a dollar buys more than a *dollar* buys with you—and *therefore* it stands to reason and the commonest kind of common-sense, that our wages are *higher* than yours."

He looked dazed, and said, despairingly:

"Verily, I cannot make it out. Ye've just *said* ours are the higher, and with the same breath ye take it back."

"Oh, great Scott, isn't it possible to get such a simple thing through your head? Now look here—let me illustrate. We pay four cents for a woman's stuff gown, you pay 8.4.0, which is four mills more than *double.* What do you allow a laboring woman who works on a farm?"

"Two mills a day."

"Very good; we allow but half as much; we pay her only a tenth of a cent a day; and—"

"Again ye're conf—"

"Wait! Now, you see, the thing is very simple; this time you'll understand it. For instance, it takes your woman 42 days to earn her gown, at 2 mills a day—7 weeks' work; but ours earns hers in forty days —two days *short* of 7 weeks. Your woman has a gown, and her whole seven weeks' wages are gone; ours has a gown, and two days' wages left, to buy something else with. There—*now* you understand it!"

He looked—well, he merely looked dubious, it's the most I can say; so did the others. I waited—to let the thing work. Dowley spoke at last—and betrayed the fact that he actually hadn't gotten away from his rooted and grounded superstitions yet. He said, with a trifle of hesitancy:

"But—but—ye cannot fail to grant that two mills a day is better than one."

Shucks! Well, of course I hated to give it up. So I chanced another flyer:

"Let us suppose a case. Suppose one of your journeymen goes out and buys the following articles:

"1 pound of salt;
1 dozen eggs;
1 dozen pints of beer;
1 bushel of wheat;
1 tow-linen suit;
5 pounds of beef;
5 pounds of mutton.

"The lot will cost him 32 cents. It takes him 32 working days to earn the money—5 weeks and 2 days. Let him come to us and work 32 days at *half* the wages; he can buy all those things for a shade under 14½ cents; they will cost him a shade under 29 days' work, and he will have about half a week's wages over. Carry it through the year; he would save nearly a week's wages every two months, *your* man nothing; thus saving five or six weeks' wages in a year, *Now* I reckon you understand that 'high wages' and 'low wages' are phrases that don't mean anything in the world until you find out which of them will *buy* the most!"

It was a crusher.

But alas, it didn't crush. No, I had to give it up. What those people valued was *high wages;* it didn't seem to be a matter of any consequence to them whether the high wages would buy anything or not. They stood for "protection," and swore by it, which was reasonable enough, because interested parties had gulled them into the notion that it was protection which had created their high wages. I proved to them that in a quarter of a century their wages had advanced but 30 per cent., while the cost of living had gone up 100; and that with us, in a shorter time, wages had advanced 40 per cent. while the cost of living had gone steadily down. But it didn't do any good. Nothing could unseat their strange beliefs.

Well, I was smarting under a sense of defeat. Undeserved defeat, but what of that? That didn't soften the smart any. And to think of the circumstances! the first statesman of the age, the capablest man, the best-informed man in the entire world, the loftiest uncrowned head that had moved through the clouds of any political firmament for centuries, sitting here apparently defeated in argument by an ignorant country blacksmith! And I could see that those others were sorry for me!—which made me blush till I could smell my whiskers scorching. Put yourself in my place; feel as mean as I did, as ashamed as I felt—wouldn't *you* have struck below the belt to get even? Yes, you would; it is simply human nature. Well, that is what I did. I am not trying to justify it; I'm only saying that I was mad, and *anybody* would have done it.

Well, when I make up my mind to hit a man, I don't plan out a love-tap; no, that isn't my way; as long as I'm going to hit him at all, I'm going to hit him a lifter. And I don't jump at him all of a sudden, and risk making a blundering half-way business of it; no, I get away off yonder to one side, and work up on him gradually, so that he never suspects that I'm going to hit him at all; and by-and-by, all in a flash, he's flat of his back, and he can't tell for the life of him how it all happened. That is the way I went for brother Dowley. I started to talking lazy and comfortable, as if I was just talking to pass the time; and the oldest man in the world couldn't have taken the bearings of my starting place and guessed where I was going to fetch up:

"Boys, there's a good many curious things about law, and custom, and usage, and all that sort of thing, when you come to look at it; yes, and about the drift and progress of human opinion and movement, too. There are written laws—they perish; but there are also unwritten laws—*they* are eternal. Take the unwritten law of wages: it says they've got to advance, little by little, straight through the centuries. And notice how it works. We know what wages are now, here and there and yonder; we strike an average, and say that's the wages of to-day. We know what the wages were a hundred years ago, and what they were two hundred years ago; that's as far back as we can get, but it suffices to give us the law of progress, the measure and rate of the periodical augmentation; and so, without a document to help us, we can come pretty close to determining what the wages were three and four and five hundred years ago. Good, so far. Do we stop there? No. We stop looking backward; we face around and apply the law to the future. My friends, I can tell you what people's wages are going to be at any date in the future you want to know, for hundreds and hundreds of years."

"What, goodman, what!"

"Yes. In seven hundred years wages will have risen to six times what they are now, here in your region, and farm hands will be allowed 3 cents a day, and mechanics 6."

"I would I might die now and live then!" interrupted Smug the wheelwright, with a fine avaricious glow in his eye.

"And that isn't all; they'll get their board besides—such as it is: it won't bloat them. Two hundred and fifty years later—pay attention, now—a mechanic's wages will be—mind you, this is law, not guesswork; a mechanic's wages will then be *twenty* cents a day!"

There was a general gasp of awed astonishment. Dickon the mason murmured, with raised eyes and hands:

"More than three weeks' pay for one day's work!"

"Riches!—of a truth, yes, riches!" muttered Marco, his breath coming quick and short, with excitement.

"Wages will keep on rising, little by little, little by little, as steadily as a tree grows, and at the end of three hundred and forty years more there'll be at least *one* country where the mechanic's average wage will be *two hundred* cents a day!"

It knocked them absolutely dumb! Not a man of them could get his breath for upwards of two minutes. Then the coal burner said prayerfully:

"Might I but live to see it!"

"It is the income of an earl!" said Smug.

"An earl, say ye?" said Dowley; "ye could say more than that and speak no lie; there's no earl in the realm of Bagdemagus that hath an income like to that. Income of an earl—mf! it's the income of an angel!"

"Now then, that is what is going to happen as regards wages. In that remote day, that man will earn with *one* week's work, that bill of goods which it takes you upwards of *fifty* weeks to earn now. Some other pretty surprising things are going to happen, too. Brother Dowley, who is it that determines, every spring, what the particular wage of each kind of mechanic, laborer, and servant shall be for that year?"

"Sometimes the courts, sometimes the town council; but most of all, the magistrate. Ye may say, in general terms, it is the magistrate that fixes the wages."

"Doesn't ask any of those poor devils to *help* him fix their wages for them, does he?"

"Hm! That *were* an idea! The master that's to pay him the money is the one that's rightly concerned in that matter, ye will notice."

"Yes—but I thought the other man might have some little trifle at stake in it, too; and even his wife and children, poor creatures. The masters are these: nobles, rich men, the prosperous generally. These few, who do no work, determine what pay the vast hive shall have who *do* work. You see? They're a 'combine'—a trade union, to coin a new phrase—who band themselves together to force their lowly brother to take what they choose to give. Thirteen hundred years hence—so says the unwritten law—the 'combine' will be the other way, and then how these fine people's posterity will fume and fret and grit their teeth over the insolent tyranny of trade unions! Yes indeed! the magistrate will tranquilly arrange the wages from now clear away down into the nineteenth century; and then all of a sudden the wage-earner will consider that a couple of thousand

years or so is enough of this one-sided sort of thing; and he will
rise up and take a hand in fixing his wages himself. Ah, he will have
a long and bitter account of wrong and humiliation to settle."

"Do ye believe—"

"That he actually will help to fix his own wages? Yes, indeed.
And he will be strong and able, then."

"Brave times, brave times, of a truth!" sneered the prosperous
smith.

"Oh,—and there's another detail. In that day, a master may hire
a man for only just one day, or one week, or one month at a time, if
he wants to."

"What?"

"It's true. Morever, a magistrate won't be able to force a man to
work for a master a whole year on a stretch whether the man wants
to or not."

"Will there be *no* law or sense in that day?"

"Both of them, Dowley. In that day a man will be his own
property, not the property of magistrate and master. And he can
leave town whenever he wants to, if the wages don't suit him!—and
they can't put him in the pillory for it."

"Perdition catch such an age!" shouted Dowley, in strong
indignation. "An age of dogs, an age barren of reverence for
superiors and respect for authority! The pillory—"

"Oh, wait, brother; say no good word for that institution. *I* think
the pillory ought to be abolished."

"A most strange idea. Why?"

"Well, I'll tell you why. Is a man ever put in the pillory for a
capital crime?"

"No."

"Is it right to condemn a man to a slight punishment for a small
offence and then kill him?"

There was no answer. I had scored my first point! For the first
time, the smith wasn't up and ready. The company noticed it. Good
effect.

"You don't answer, brother. You were about to glorify the pillory
a while ago, and shed some pity on a future age that isn't going to
use it. *I* think the pillory ought to be abolished. What usually
happens when a poor fellow is put in the pillory for some little
offence that didn't amount to anything in the world? The mob try
to have some fun with him, don't they?"

"Yes."

"They begin by clodding him; and they laugh themselves to pieces
to see him try to dodge one clod and get hit with another?"

"Yes."

"Then they throw dead cats at him, don't they?"

"Yes."

"Well, then, suppose he has a few personal enemies in that mob—and here and there a man or a woman with a secret grudge against him—and suppose especially that he is unpopular in the community, for his pride, or his prosperity, or one thing or another—stones and bricks take the place of clods and cats presently, don't they?"

"There is no doubt of it."

"As a rule he is crippled for life, isn't he?—jaws broken, teeth smashed out?—or legs mutilated, gangrened, presently cut off?—or an eye knocked out, maybe both eyes?"

"It is true, God knoweth it."

"And if he is unpopular he can depend on *dying*, right there in the stocks, can't he?"

"He surely can! One may not deny it."

"I take it none of *you* are unpopular—by reason of pride or insolence, or conspicuous prosperity, or any of those things that excite envy and malice among the base scum of a village? *You* wouldn't think it much of a risk to take a chance in the stocks?"

Dowley winced, visibly. I judged he was hit. But he didn't betray it by any spoken word. As for the others, they spoke out plainly, and with strong feeling. They said they had seen enough of the stocks to know what a man's chance in them was, and they would never consent to enter them if they could compromise on a quick death by hanging.

"Well, to change the subject—for I think I've established my point that the stocks ought to be abolished. I think some of our laws are pretty unfair. For instance, if I do a thing which ought to deliver me to the stocks, and you know I did it and yet keep still and don't report me, *you* will get the stocks if anybody informs on you."

"Ah, but that would serve you but right," said Dowley, "for you *must* inform. So saith the law."

The others coincided.

"Well, all right, let it go, since you vote me down. But there's one thing which certainly isn't fair. The magistrate fixes a mechanic's wage at 1 cent a day, for instance. The law says that if any master shall venture even under utmost press of business, to pay anything *over* that cent a day, even for a single day, he shall be both fined and pilloried for it; and whoever knows he did it and doesn't inform, they also shall be fined and pilloried. Now it seems to me unfair, Dowley, and a deadly peril to all of us, that because you thoughtlessly confessed, a while ago, that within a week you have paid a cent and fifteen mil—"

Oh, I tell *you* it was a smasher! You ought to have seen them go to pieces, the whole gang. I had just slipped up on poor smiling and complacent Dowley so nice and easy and softly, that he never

suspected anything was going to happen till the blow came
crashing down and knocked him all to rags.

A fine effect. In fact as fine as any I ever produced, with so little
time to work it up in.

But I saw in a moment that I had overdone the thing a little. I
was expecting to scare them, but I wasn't expecting to scare them
to death. They were mighty near it, though. You see they had been
a whole lifetime learning to appreciate the pillory; and to have
that thing staring them in the face, and every one of them distinctly
at the mercy of me, a stranger, if I chose to go and report—well,
it was awful, and they couldn't seem to recover from the shock,
they couldn't seem to pull themselves together. Pale, shaky, dumb,
pitiful? Why, they weren't any better than so many dead men. It
was very uncomfortable. Of course I thought they would appeal to
me to keep mum, and then we would shake hands, and take a
drink all round, and laugh it off, and there an end. But no; you
see I was an unknown person, among a cruelly oppressed and
suspicious people, a people always accustomed to having advantage
taken of their helplessness, and never expecting just or kind
treatment from any but their own families and very closest
intimates. Appeal to *me* to be gentle, to be fair, to be generous? Of
course they wanted to, but they couldn't dare.

CHAPTER XXXIV

THE YANKEE AND THE KING SOLD AS SLAVES

Well, what had I better do? Nothing in a hurry, sure. I must get
up a diversion; anything to employ me while I could think, and
while these poor fellows could have a chance to come to life again.
There sat Marco, petrified in the act of trying to get the hang of his
miller-gun—turned to stone, just in the attitude he was in when my
pile-driver fell, the toy still gripped in his unconscious fingers. So
I took it from him and proposed to explain its mystery. Mystery! a
simple little thing like that; and yet it was mysterious enough, for
that race and that age.

I never saw such an awkward people, with machinery; you see,
they were totally unused to it. The miller-gun was a little
double-barrelled tube of toughened glass, with a neat little trick of
a spring to it, which upon pressure would let a shot excape. But the
shot wouldn't hurt anybody, it would only drop into your hand.In
the gun were two sizes—wee mustard-seed shot, and another sort
that were several times larger. They were money. The mustard-seed

shot represented milrays, the larger ones mills. So the gun was a purse; and very handy, too; you could pay out money in the dark with it, with accuracy; and you could carry it in your mouth; or in your vest pocket, if you had one. I made them of several sizes—one size so large that it would carry the equivalent of a dollar. Using shot for money was a good thing for the government; the metal cost nothing, and the money couldn't be counterfeited, for I was the only person in the kingdom who knew how to manage a shot tower. "Paying the shot" soon came to be a common phrase. Yes, and I knew it would still be passing men's lips, away down in the nineteenth century, yet none would suspect how and when it originated.

The king joined us, about this time, mightily refreshed by his nap, and feeling good. Anything could make me nervous now, I was so uneasy—for our lives were in danger; and so it worried me to detect a complacent something in the king's eye which seemed to indicate that he had been loading himself up for a performance of some kind or other; confound it, why must he go and choose such a time as this?

I was right. He began, straight off, in the most innocently artful, and transparent, and lubberly way, to lead up to the subject of agriculture. The cold sweat broke out all over me. I wanted to whisper in his ear, "Man, we are in awful danger! every moment is worth a principality till we get back these men's confidence; *don't* waste any of this golden time." But of course I couldn't do it. Whisper to him? It would look as if we were conspiring. So I had to sit there and look calm and pleasant while the king stood over that dynamite mine and mooned along about his damned onions and things. At first the tumult of my own thoughts, summoned by the danger-signal and swarming to the rescue from every quarter of my skull, kept up such a hurrah and confusion and fifing and drumming that I couldn't take in a word; but presently when my mob of gathering plans began to crystallize and fall into position and form line of battle, a sort of order and quiet ensued and I caught the boom of the king's batteries, as if out of remote distance:

"—were not the best way, methinks, albeit it is not to be denied that authorities differ as concerning this point, some contending that the onion is but an unwholesome berry when stricken early from the tree—"

The audience showed signs of life, and sought each other's eyes in a surprised and troubled way.

"—whileas others do yet maintain, with much show of reason, that this is not of necessity the case, instancing that plums and other like cereals do be always dug in the unripe state—"

The audience exhibited distinct distress; yes, and also fear.

"—yet are they clearly wholesome, the more especially when one doth assuage the asperities of their nature by admixture of the tranquillizing juice of the wayward cabbage—"

The wild light of terror began to glow in these men's eyes, and one of them muttered, "These be errors, every one—God hath surely smitten the mind of this farmer." I was in miserable apprehension; I sat upon thorns.

"—and further instancing the known truth that in the case of animals, the young, which may be called the green fruit of the creature, is the better, all confessing that when a goat is ripe, his fur doth heat and sore engame his flesh, the which defect, taken in connection with his several rancid habits, and fulsome appetites, and godless attitudes of mind, and bilious quality of morals—"

They rose and went for him! With a fierce shout, "The one would betray us, the other is mad! Kill them! Kill them!" they flung themselves upon us. What joy flamed up in the king's eye! He might be lame in agriculture, but this kind of thing was just in his line. He had been fasting long, he was hungry for a fight. He hit the blacksmith a crack under the jaw that lifted him clear off his feet and stretched him flat of his back. "St. George for Britain!" and he downed the wheelwright. The mason was big, but I laid him out like nothing. The three gathered themselves up and came again; went down again; came again; and kept on repeating this, with native British pluck, until they were battered to jelly, reeling with exhaustion, and so blind that they couldn't tell us from each other; and yet they kept right on, hammering away with what might was left in them. Hammering each other—for we stepped aside and looked on while they rolled, and struggled, and gouged, and pounded, and bit, with the strict and wordless attention to business of so many bulldogs. We looked on without apprehension, for they were fast getting past ability to go for help against us, and the arena was far enough from the public road to be safe from intrusion.

Well, while they were gradually playing out, it suddenly occurred to me to wonder what had become of Marco. I looked around; he was nowhere to be seen. Oh, but this was ominous! I pulled the king's sleeve, and we glided away and rushed for the hut. No Marco there, no Phyllis there! They had gone to the road for help, sure. I told the king to give his heels wings, and I would explain later. We made good time across the open ground, and as we darted into the shelter of the wood I glanced back and saw a mob of excited peasants swarm into view, with Marco and his wife at their head. They were making a world of noise, but that couldn't hurt anybody; the wood was dense, and as soon as we were well into its depths we would take to a tree and let them whistle. Ah, but then came another sound—dogs! Yes, that was quite another matter. It magnified our contract—we must find running water.

We tore along at a good gait, and soon left the sounds far behind and modified to a murmur. We struck a stream and darted into it. We waded swiftly down it, in the dim forest light, for as much as three hundred yards, and then came across an oak with a great bough sticking out over the water. We climbed up on this bough, and began to work our way along it to the body of the tree; now we began to hear those sounds more plainly; so the mob had struck our trail. For a while the sounds approached pretty fast. And then for another while they didn't. No doubt the dogs had found the place where we had entered the stream, and were now waltzing up and down the shores trying to pick up the trail again.

When we were snugly lodged in the tree and curtained with foliage, the king was satisfied, but I was doubtful. I believed we could crawl along a branch and get into the next tree, and I judged it worth while to try. We tried it, and made a success of it, though the king slipped, at the junction, and came near failing to connect. We got comfortable lodgement and satisfactory concealment among the foliage, and then we had nothing to do but listen to the hunt.

Presently we heard it coming—and coming on the jump, too; yes, and down both sides of the stream. Louder—louder—next minute it swelled swiftly up into a roar of shoutings, barkings, tramplings, and swept by like a cyclone.

"I was afraid that the overhanging branch would suggest something to them," said I, "but I don't mind the disappointment. Come, my liege, it were well that we make good use of our time. We've flanked them. Dark is coming on, presently. If we can cross the stream and get a good start, and borrow a couple of horses from somebody's pasture to use for a few hours, we shall be safe enough."

We started down, and got nearly to the lowest limb, when we seemed to hear the hunt returning. We stopped to listen.

"Yes," said I, "they're baffled, they've given it up, they're on their way home. We will climb back to our roost again, and let them go by."

So we climbed back. The king listened a moment and said:

"They still search—I wit the sign. We did best to abide."

He was right. He knew more about hunting than I did. The noise approached steadily, but not with a rush. The king said:

"They reason that we were advantaged by no parlous start of them, and being on foot are as yet no mighty way from where we took the water."

"Yes, sire, that is about it, I am afraid, though I was hoping better things."

The noise drew nearer and nearer, and soon the van was drifting under us, on both sides of the water. A voice called a halt from the other bank, and said:

"An they were so minded, they could get to yon tree by this branch that overhangs, and yet not touch ground. Ye will do well to send a man up it."

"Marry, that will we do!"

I was obliged to admire my cuteness in foreseeing this very thing and swapping trees to beat it. But don't you know, there are some things that can beat smartness and foresight? Awkwardness and stupidity can. The best swordsman in the world doesn't need to fear the second best swordsman in the world; no, the person for him to be afraid of is some ignorant antagonist who has never had a sword in his hand before; he doesn't do the thing he ought to do, and so the expert isn't prepared for him; he does the thing he ought not to do: and often it catches the expert out and ends him on the spot. Well, how could I, with all my gifts, make any valuable preparation against a near-sighted, cross-eyed, pudding-headed clown who would aim himself at the wrong tree and hit the right one? And that is what he did. He went for the wrong tree, which was of course the right one by mistake, and up he started.

Matters were serious, now. We remained still, and awaited developments. The peasant toiled his difficult way up. The king raised himself up and stood; he made a leg ready, and when the comer's head arrived in reach of it there was a dull thud, and down went the man floundering to the ground. There was a wild outbreak of anger, below, and the mob swarmed in from all around, and there we were treed, and prisoners. Another man started up; the bridging bough was detected, and a volunteer started up the tree that furnished the bridge. The king ordered me to play Horatius and keep the bridge. For a while the enemy came thick and fast; but no matter, the head man of each procession always got a buffet that dislodged him as soon as he came in reach. The king's spirits rose, his joy was limitless. He said that if nothing occurred to mar the prospect we should have a beautiful night, for on this line of tactics we could hold the tree against the whole country-side.

However, the mob soon came to that conclusion themselves; wherefore they called off the assault and began to debate other plans. They had no weapons, but there were plenty of stones, and stones might answer. We had no objections. A stone might possibly penetrate to us once in a while, but it wasn't very likely; we were well protected by boughs and foliage, and were not visible from any good aiming-point. If they would but waste half an hour in stone-throwing, the dark would come to our help. We were feeling very well satisfied. We could smile; almost laugh.

But we didn't; which was just as well, for we should have been interrupted. Before the stones had been raging through the leaves and bouncing from the boughs fifteen minutes, we began to notice a smell. A couple of sniffs of it was enough of an explanation: it was smoke! Our game was up at last. We recognized that. When smoke invites you, you have to come. They raised their pile of dry brush and damp weeds higher and higher, and when they saw the thick cloud begin to roll up and smother the tree, they broke out in a storm of joy-clamors. I got enough breath to say:

"Proceed, my liege; after you is manners."

The king gasped:

"Follow me down, and then back thyself against one side of the trunk, and leave me the other. Then will we fight. Let each pile his dead according to his own fashion and taste."

Then he descended barking and coughing, and I followed. I struck the ground an instant after him; we sprang to our appointed places, and began to give and take with all our might. The pow-wow and racket were prodigious; it was a tempest of riot and confusion and thick-falling blows. Suddenly some horsemen tore into the midst of the crowd, and a voice shouted:

"Hold—or ye are dead men!"

How good it sounded! The owner of the voice bore all the marks of a gentleman: picturesque and costly raiment, the aspect of command, a hard countenance, with complexion and features marred by dissipation. The mob fell humbly back, like so many spaniels. The gentleman inspected us critically, then said sharply to the peasants:

"What are ye doing to these people?"

"They be madmen, worshipful sir, that have come wandering we know not whence, and—"

"Ye know not whence? Do ye pretend ye know them not?"

"Most honored sir, we speak but the truth. They are strangers and unknown to any in this region; and they be the most violent and bloodthirsty madmen that ever—"

"Peace! Ye know not what ye say. They are not mad. Who are ye? And whence are ye? Explain."

"We are but peaceful strangers, sir," I said, "and travelling upon our own concerns. We are from a far country, and unacquainted here. We have purposed no harm; and yet but for your brave interference and protection these people would have killed us. As you have divined, sir, we are not mad; neither are we violent or bloodthirsty."

The gentleman turned to his retinue and said calmly:

"Lash me these animals to their kennels!"

The mob vanished in an instant; and after them plunged the horsemen, laying about them with their whips and pitilessly riding down such as were witless enough to keep the road instead of taking to the bush. The shrieks and supplications presently died away in the distance, and soon the horsemen began to straggle back. Meantime the gentleman had been questioning us more closely,

but had dug no particulars out of us. We were lavish of recognition
of the service he was doing us, but we revealed nothing more than
that we were friendless strangers from a far country. When the
escort were all returned, the gentleman said to one of his servants:

"Bring the led-horses and mount these people."

"Yes, my lord."

We were placed toward the rear, among the servants. We travelled
pretty fast, and finally drew rein some time after dark at a road-side
inn some ten or twelve miles from the scene of our troubles. My lord
went immediately to his room, after ordering his supper, and we
saw no more of him. At dawn in the morning we breakfasted and
made ready to start.

My lord's chief attendant sauntered forward at that moment with
indolent grace, and said:

"Ye have said ye should continue upon this road, which is our
direction likewise; wherefore my lord, the earl Grip, hath given
commandment that ye retain the horses and ride, and that certain of
us ride with ye a twenty mile to a fair town that hight Cambenet,
whenso ye shall be out of peril."

We could do nothing less than express our thanks and accept the
offer. We jogged along, six in the party, at a moderate and
comfortable gait, and in conversation learned that my lord Grip
was a very great personage in his own region, which lay a day's
journey beyond Cambenet. We loitered to such a degree that it was
near the middle of the forenoon when we entered the market square
of the town. We dismounted and left our thanks once more for my
lord, and then approached a crowd assembled in the centre of the
square, to see what might be the object of interest. It was the
remnant of that old peregrinating band of slaves! So they had been
dragging their chains about, all this weary time. That poor husband
was gone, and also many others; and some few purchases had been
added to the gang. The king was not interested, and wanted to move
along, but I was absorbed, and full of pity. I could not take my eyes
away from these worn and wasted wrecks of humanity. There they
sat, grouped upon the ground, silent, uncomplaining, with bowed
heads, a pathetic sight. And by hideous contrast, a redundant orator
was making a speech to another gathering not thirty steps away, in
fulsome laudation of "our glorious British liberties!"

I was boiling. I had forgotten I was a plebeian, I was remembering
I was a man. Cost what it might, I would mount that rostrum and—

Click! the king and I were handcuffed together! Our companions,
those servants, had done it; my lord Grip stood looking on. The king
burst out in a fury, and said:

"What meaneth this ill-mannered jest?"

My lord merely said to his head miscreant, coolly:

"Put up the slaves and sell them!"

Slaves! The word had a new sound—and how unspeakably awful!

The king lifted his manacles and brought them down with a deadly force; but my lord was out of the way when they arrived. A dozen of the rascal's servants sprang forward, and in a moment we were helpless, with our hands bound behind us. We so loudly and so earnestly proclaimed ourselves freemen, that we got the interested attention of that liberty-mounting orator and his patriotic crowd, and they gathered about us and assumed a very determined attitude. The orator said:

"If indeed ye are freemen, ye have nought to fear—the God-given liberties of Britain are about ye for your shield and shelter! (Applause.) Ye shall soon see. Bring forth your proofs."

"What proofs?"

"Proof that ye are freemen."

Ah—I remembered! I came to myself; I said nothing. But the king stormed out:

"Thou'rt insane, man. It were better, and more in reason, that this thief and scoundrel here prove that we are *not* freemen."

You see, he knew his own laws just as other people so often know the laws: by words, not by effects. They take a *meaning*, and get to be very vivid, when you come to apply them to yourself.

All hands shook their heads and looked disappointed; some turned away, no longer interested. The orator said—and this time in the tones of business, not of sentiment:

"An ye do not know your country's laws, it were time ye learned them. Ye are strangers to us; ye will not deny that. Ye may be freemen, we do not deny that; but also ye may be slaves. The law is clear: it doth not require the claimant to prove ye are slaves, it requireth you to prove ye are *not*."

I said:

"Dear sir, give us only time to send to Astolat; or give us only time to send to the Valley of Holiness—"

"Peace, good man, these are extraordinary requests, and you may not hope to have them granted. It would cost much time, and would unwarrantably inconvenience your master—"

"*Master*, idiot!" stormed the king. "I have no master, I myself am the m—"

"Silence, for God's sake!"

I got the words out in time to stop the king. We were in trouble enough already; it could not help us any to give these people the notion that we were lunatics.

There is no use in stringing out the details. The earl put us up and sold us at auction. This same infernal law had existed in our own South in my own time, more than thirteen hundred years later, and under it hundreds of freemen who could not prove that they were freemen had been sold into life-long slavery without the circumstance making any particular impression upon me; but the minute law and the auction block came into my personal experience, a thing which had been merely improper before became suddenly hellish. Well, that's the way we are made.

Yes, we were sold at auction, like swine. In a big town and an active market we should have brought a good price; but this place was utterly stagnant and so we sold at a figure which makes me ashamed, every time I think of it. The King of England brought seven dollars, and his prime minister nine; whereas the king was easily worth twelve dollars and I as easily worth fifteen. But that is the way things always go; if you force a sale on a dull market, I don't care what the property is, you are going to make a poor business of it, and you can make up your mind to it. If the earl had had wit enough to—

However, there is no occasion for my working my sympathies up on his account. Let him go, for the present: I took his number, so to speak.

The slave dealer bought us both, and hitched us onto that long chain of his, and we constituted the rear of his procession. We took up our line of march and passed out of Cambenet at noon; and it seemed to me unaccountably strange and odd that the King of England and his chief minister, marching manacled and fettered and yoked, in a slave convoy, could move by all manner of idle men and women, and under windows where sat the sweet and the lovely, and yet never attract a curious eye, never provoke a single remark. Dear, dear, it only shows that there is nothing diviner about a king than there is about a tramp, after all. He is just a cheap and hollow artificiality when you don't know he is a king. But reveal his quality, and dear me it takes your very breath away to look at him. I reckon we are all fools. Born so, no doubt.

CHAPTER XXXV

A PITIFUL INCIDENT

It's a world of surprises. The king brooded; this was natural. What would he brood about, should you say? Why, about the prodigious nature of his fall, of course—from the loftiest place in the world to the lowest; from the most illustrious station in the world to the obscurest; from the grandest vocation among men to the basest. No, I take my oath that the thing that gravelled him most, to start with, was not this, but the price he had fetched! He couldn't seem to get over that seven dollars. Well, it stunned me so, when I first found it out, that I couldn't believe it; it didn't seem natural. But as soon as my mental sight cleared and I got a right focus on it, I saw I was mistaken: it *was* natural. For this reason: a king is a mere artificiality, and so a king's feelings, like the impulses of an automatic doll, are mere artificialities; but as a man, he is a reality, and his feelings, as a man, are real, not phantoms. It shames the average man to be valued below his own estimate of his worth; and the king certainly wasn't anything more than an average man, if he was up that high.

Confound him, he wearied me with arguments to show that in anything like a fair market he would have fetched twenty-five dollars, sure—a thing which was plainly nonsense, and full of the baldest conceit; I wasn't worth it myself. But it was tender ground for me to argue on. In fact I had to simply shirk argument and do the diplomatic instead. I had to throw conscience aside, and brazenly concede that he ought to have brought twenty-five dollars; whereas I was quite well aware that in all the ages, the world had never seen a king that was worth half the money, and during the next thirteen centuries wouldn't see one that was worth the fourth of it. Yes, he tired me. If he began to talk about the crops; or about the recent weather; or about the condition of politics, or about dogs, or cats, or morals, or theology—no matter what—I sighed, for I knew what was coming: he was going to get out of it a palliation of that tiresome seven-dollar sale. Wherever we halted, where there was a crowd, he would give me a look which said, plainly: "if that thing could be tried over again, now, with this kind of folk, you would see a different result." Well, when he was first sold, it secretly tickled me to see him go for seven dollars; but before he was done with his sweating and worrying I wished he had fetched a hundred. The thing never got a chance to die, for every day, at one place or another, possible purchasers looked us over, and as often as any other way, their comment on the king was something like this:

"Here's a two-dollar-and-a-half chump with a thirty-dollar style. Pity but style was marketable."

At last this sort of remark produced an evil result. Our owner was a practical person and he perceived that this defect must be mended if he hoped to find a purchaser for the king. So he went to work to take the style out of his sacred majesty. I could have given the man some valuable advice, but I didn't; you mustn't volunteer advice to a slave-driver unless you want to damage the cause you are arguing for. I had found it a sufficiently difficult job to reduce the king's style to a peasant's style, even when he was a willing and anxious pupil; now then, to undertake to reduce the king's style to a slave's style—and by force—go to! it was a stately contract. Never mind the details—it will save me trouble to let you imagine them. I will only remark that at the end of a week there was plenty of evidence that lash and club and fist had done their work well; the king's body was a sight to see—and to weep over; but his spirit?—why, it wasn't even phased. Even that dull clod of a slave-driver was able to see that there can be such a thing as a slave who will remain a man till he dies; whose bones you can break, but whose manhood you can't. This man found that from his first effort down to his latest, he couldn't ever come within reach of the king but the king was ready to plunge for him, and did it. So he gave up, at last, and left the king in possession of his style unimpaired. The fact is, the king was a good deal more than a king, he was a man; and when a man is a man, you can't knock it out of him.

We had a rough time for a month, tramping to and fro in the earth, and suffering. And what Englishman was the most interested in the slavery question by that time? His grace the king! Yes; from being the most indifferent, he was become the most interested. He was become the bitterest hater of the institution I had ever heard talk. And so I ventured to ask once more a question which I had asked years before and had gotten such a sharp answer that I had not thought it prudent to meddle in the matter further. Would he abolish slavery?

His answer was as sharp as before, but it was music this time; I shouldn't ever wish to hear pleasanter, though the profanity was not good, being awkwardly put together, and with the crash-word almost in the middle instead of at the end, where of course it ought to have been.

I was ready and willing to get free, now; I hadn't wanted to get free any sooner. No, I cannot quite say that. I had wanted to, but I had not been willing to take desperate chances, and had always dissuaded the king from them. But now—ah, it was a new atmosphere! Liberty would be worth any cost that might be put upon it now. I set about a plan, and was straightway charmed with it. It would require time, yes, and patience, too, a great deal of both. One could invent quicker ways, and fully as sure ones; but none that would be as picturesque as this; none that could be made so dramatic. And so I was not going to give this one up. It might delay us months, but no matter, I would carry it out or break something.

Now and then we had an adventure. One night we were overtaken by a snow-storm while still a mile from the village we were making for. Almost instantly we were shut up as in a fog, the driving snow was so thick. You couldn't see a thing, and we were soon lost. The slave-driver lashed us desperately, for he saw ruin before him, but his lashings only made matters worse, for they drove us further from the road and from likelihood of succor. So we had to stop, at last, and slump down in the snow where we were. The storm continued until toward midnight, then ceased. By this time two of our feebler men and three of our women were dead, and others past moving and threatened with death. Our master was nearly beside himself. He stirred up the living, and made us stand, jump, slap ourselves, to restore our circulation, and he helped as well as he could with his whip.

Now came a diversion. We heard shrieks and yells, and soon a woman came running, and crying; and seeing our group, she flung herself into our midst and begged for protection. A mob of people

came tearing after her, some with torches, and they said she was a
witch who had caused several cows to die by a strange disease, and
practised her arts by help of a devil in the form of a black cat. This
poor woman had been stoned until she hardly looked human, she
was so battered and bloody. The mob wanted to burn her.

Well, now, what do you suppose our master did? When we closed
around this poor creature to shelter her, he saw his chance. He said,
burn her here, or they shouldn't have her at all. Imagine that! They
were willing. They fastened her to a post; they brought wood and
piled it about her; they applied the torch while she shrieked and
pleaded and strained her two young daughters to her breast; and our
brute, with a heart solely for business, lashed us into position about
the stake and warmed us into life and commercial value by the same
fire which took away the innocent life of that poor harmless mother.
That was the sort of master we had. I took *his* number. That
snow-storm cost him nine of his flock; and he was more brutal to us
than ever, after that, for many days together, he was so enraged
over his loss.

We had adventures, all along. One day we ran into a procession.
And such a procession! All the riffraff of the kingdom seemed to be
comprehended in it; and all drunk at that. In the van was a cart
with a coffin in it, and on the coffin sat a comely young girl of about
eighteen suckling a baby, which she squeezed to her breast in a
passion of love every little while, and every little while wiped from its
face the tears which her eyes rained down upon it; and always the
foolish little thing smiled up at her, happy and content, kneading
her breast with its dimpled fat hand, which she patted and fondled
right over her breaking heart.

Men and women, boys and girls, trotted along beside or after
the cart, hooting, shouting profane and ribald remarks, singing
snatches of foul song, skipping, dancing—a very holiday of hellions,
a sickening sight. We had struck a suburb of London, outside the
walls, and this was a sample of one sort of London society. Our
master secured a good place for us near the gallows. A priest was in
attendance, and he helped the girl climb up, and said comforting
words to her, and made the under-sheriff provide a stool for her.
Then he stood there by her on the gallows, and for a moment looked
down upon the mass of upturned faces at his feet, then out over the
solid pavement of heads that stretched away on every side occupying
the vacancies far and near, and then began to tell the story of the
case. And there was pity in his voice—how seldom a sound that
was in that ignorant and savage land! I remember every detail of
what he said, except the words he said it in; and so I change it into
my own words:

"Law is intended to mete out justice. Sometimes it fails. This
cannot be helped. We can only grieve, and be resigned, and pray for
the soul of him who falls unfairly by the arm of the law, and that his

fellows may be few. A law sends this poor young thing to death—and it is right. But another law had placed her where she must commit her crime or starve, with her child—and before God that law is responsible for both her crime and her ignominious death!

"A little while ago this young thing, this child of eighteen years, was as happy a wife and mother as any in England; and her lips were blithe with song, which is the native speech of glad and innocent hearts. Her young husband was as happy as she; for he was doing his whole duty, he worked early and late at his handicraft, his bread was honest bread well and fairly earned, he was prospering, he was furnishing shelter and sustenance to his family, he was adding his mite to the wealth of the nation. By consent of a treacherous law, instant destruction fell upon this holy home and swept it away! That young husband was waylaid and impressed, and sent to sea. The wife knew nothing of it. She sought him everywhere, she moved the hardest hearts with the supplications of her tears, the broken eloquence of her despair. Weeks dragged by, she watching, waiting, hoping, her mind going slowly to wreck under the burden of her misery. Little by little all her small possessions went for food. When she could no longer pay her rent, they turned her out of doors. She begged, while she had strength; when she was starving, at last, and her milk failing, she stole a piece of linen cloth of the value of a fourth part of a cent, thinking to sell it and save her child. But she was seen by the owner of the cloth. She was put in jail and brought to trial. The man testified to the facts. A plea was made for her, and her sorrowful story was told in her behalf. She spoke, too, by permission, and said she did steal the cloth, but that her mind was so disordered of late, by trouble, that when she was overborne with hunger all acts, criminal or other, swam meaningless through her and she knew nothing rightly, except that she was *so* hungry! For a moment all were touched, and there was disposition to deal mercifully with her, seeing that she was so young and friendless, and her case so piteous, and the law that robbed her of her support to blame as being the first and only cause of her transgression; but the prosecuting officer replied that whereas these things were all true, and most pitiful as well, still there was much small theft in these days, and mistimed mercy here would be a danger to property—Oh, my God, is there no property in ruined homes, and orphaned babes, and broken hearts that British law holds precious!—and so he must require sentence.

"When the judge put on his black cap, the owner of the stolen linen rose trembling up, his lip quivering, his face as gray as ashes; and when the awful words came, he cried out. 'Oh, poor child, poor child, I did not know it was death!' and fell as a tree falls. When they lifted him up his reason was gone; before the sun was set, he had taken his own life. A kindly man; a man whose heart was right, at bottom; add his murder to this that is to be now done here;

and charge them both where they belong—to the rulers and the bitter laws of Britain. The time is come, my child; let me pray over thee—not *for* thee, dear abused poor heart and innocent, but for them that be guilty of thy ruin and death, who need it more."

After his prayer they put the noose around the young girl's neck, and they had great trouble to adjust the knot under her ear, because she was devouring the baby all the time, wildly kissing it, and snatching it to her face and her breast, and drenching it with tears, and half moaning half shrieking all the while, and the baby crowing, and laughing, and kicking its feet with delight over what it took for romp and play. Even the hangman couldn't stand it, but turned away. When all was ready the priest gently pulled and tugged and forced the child out of the mother's arms, and stepped quickly out of her reach; but she clasped her hands, and made a wild spring toward him, with a shriek; but the rope—and the under-sheriff—held her short. Then she went on her knees and stretched out her hands and cried:

"One more kiss—Oh, my God, one more, one more,—it is the dying that begs it!"

She got it; she almost smothered the little thing. And when they got it away again, she cried out:

"Oh, my child, my darling, it will die! It has no home, it has no father, no friend, no mother—"

"It has them all!" said that good priest. "All these will I be to it till I die."

You should have seen her face then! Gratitude? Lord, what do you want with words to express that? Words are only painted fire; a look is the fire itself. She gave that look, and carried it away to the treasury of heaven, where all things that are divine belong.

CHAPTER XXXVI

AN ENCOUNTER IN THE DARK

London—to a slave—was a sufficiently interesting place. It was merely a great big village; and mainly mud and thatch. The streets were muddy, crooked, unpaved. The populace was an ever flocking and drifting swarm of rags, and splendors, of nodding plumes and shining armor. The king had a palace there; he saw the outside of it. It made him sigh; yes, and swear a little, in a poor juvenile sixth century way. We saw knights and grandees whom we knew, but they didn't know us in our rags and dirt and raw welts and bruises, and wouldn't have recognized us if we had hailed them, nor stopped to answer, either, it being unlawful to speak with slaves on a chain. Sandy passed within ten yards of me on a mule—hunting for me, I imagined. But the thing which clean broke my heart was something which happened in front of our old barrack in a square, while we were enduring the spectacle of a man being boiled to death in oil for counterfeiting pennies. It was the sight of a newsboy—and I couldn't get at him! Still, I had one comfort; here was proof that Clarence was still alive and banging away. I meant to be with him before long; the thought was full of cheer.

I had one little glimpse of another thing, one day, which gave me a great uplift. It was a wire stretching from housetop to housetop. Telegraph or telephone, sure. I did very much wish I had a little piece of it. It was just what I needed, in order to carry out my project of escape. My idea was, to get loose some night, along with the king, then gag and bind our master, change clothes with him, batter him into the aspect of a stranger, hitch him to the slave-chain, assume possession of the property, march to Camelot, and—

But you get my idea; you see what a stunning dramatic surprise I would wind up with at the palace. It was all feasible, if I could only get hold of a slender piece of iron which I could shape into a lock-pick. I could then undo the lumbering padlocks with which our chains were fastened, whenever I might choose. But I never had any luck; no such thing ever happened to fall in my way. However, my chance came at last. A gentleman who had come twice before to dicker for me, without result, or indeed any approach to a result, came again. I was far from expecting ever to belong to him, for the price asked for me from the time I was first enslaved was exorbitant, and always provoked either anger or derision, yet my master stuck stubbornly to it—twenty-two dollars. He wouldn't bate a cent. The king was greatly admired, because of his grand physique, but his kingly style was against him, and he wasn't salable; nobody wanted that kind of a slave. I considered myself safe from parting from him because of my extravagant price. No, I was not expecting to ever belong to this gentleman whom I have spoken of, but he had something which I expected would belong to me eventually, if he would but visit us often enough. It was a steel thing with a long pin to it, with which his long cloth outside garment was fastened together in front. There were three of them. He had disappointed me twice, because he did not come quite close enough to me to make my project entirely safe; but this time I succeeded; I captured the lower clasp of the three, and when he missed it he thought he had lost it on the way.

I had a chance to be glad about a minute, then straightway a chance to be sad again. For when the purchase was about to fail, as usual, the master suddenly spoke up and said what would be worded thus—in modern English:

"I'll tell you what I'll do. I'm tired supporting these two for no good. Give me twenty-two dollars for this one, and I'll throw the other one in."

The king couldn't get his breath, he was in such a fury. He began to choke and gag, and meantime the master and the gentleman moved away, discussing.

"An ye will keep the offer open—"

" 'Tis open till the morrow at this hour."

"Then will I answer you at that time," said the gentleman, and disappeared, the master following him.

I had a time of it to cool the king down, but I managed it. I whispered in his ear, to this effect:

"Your grace *will* go for nothing, but after another fashion. And so shall I. To-night we shall both be free."

"Ah! How is that?"

"With this thing which I have stolen, I will unlock these locks and cast off these chains to-night. When he comes about nine thirty to inspect us for the night, we will seize him, gag him, batter him, and early in the morning we will march out of this town, proprietors of this caravan of slaves."

That was as far as I went, but the king was charmed and satisfied. That evening we waited patiently for our fellow-slaves to get to sleep and signify it by the usual sign, for you must not take many chances on those poor fellows if you can avoid it. It is best to keep your own secrets. No doubt they fidgeted only about as usual, but it didn't seem so to me. It seemed to me that they were going to be forever getting down to their regular snoring. As the time dragged on I got nervously afraid we shouldn't have enough of it left for our needs; so I made several premature attempts, and merely delayed things by it; for I couldn't seem to touch a padlock, there in the dark, without starting a rattle out of it which interrupted somebody's sleep and made him turn over and wake some more of the gang.

But finally I did get my last iron off, and was a free man once more. I took a good breath of relief, and reached for the king's irons. Too late! in comes the master, with a light in one hand and his heavy walking-staff in the other. I snuggled close among the wallow of snorers, to conceal as nearly as possible that I was naked of irons; and I kept a sharp lookout and prepared to spring for my man the moment he should bend over me.

But he didn't approach. He stopped, gazed absently toward our dusky mass a minute, evidently thinking about something else; then set down his light, moved musingly toward the door, and before a body could imagine what he was going to do, he was out of the door and had closed it behind him.

"Quick!" said the king. "Fetch him back!"

Of course it was the thing to do, and I was up and out in a moment. But dear me, there were no lamps in those days, and it was a dark night. But I glimpsed a dim figure a few steps away. I darted for it, threw myself upon it, and then there was a state of things and lively! We fought and scuffled and struggled, and drew a crowd in no time. They took an immense interest in the fight and encouraged us all they could, and in fact couldn't have been pleasanter or more cordial if it had been their own fight. Then a tremendous row broke out behind us, and as much as half of our audience left us, with a rush, to invest some sympathy in that. Lanterns began to swing in all directions; it was the watch, gathering from far and near. Presently a halberd fell across my back, as a reminder, and I knew what it meant. I was in custody. So was my adversary. We were marched off toward prison, one on each side of the watchman. Here was disaster, here was a fine scheme gone to sudden destruction! I tried to imagine what would happen when the master should discover that it was I who had been fighting him; and what would happen if they jailed us together in the general apartment for brawlers and petty law-breakers, as was the custom; and what might—

Just then my antagonist turned his face around in my direction, the freckled light from the watchman's tin lantern fell on it, and by George he was the wrong man!

CHAPTER XXXVII

AN AWFUL PREDICAMENT

Sleep? It was impossible. It would naturally have been impossible in that noisome cavern of a jail, with its mangy crowd of drunken, quarrelsome and song-singing rapscallions. But the thing that made sleep all the more a thing not to be dreamed of, was my racking impatience to get out of this place and find out the whole size of what might have happened yonder in the slave-quarters in consequence of that intolerable miscarriage of mine.

It was a long night, but the morning got around at last. I made a full and frank explanation to the court. I said I was a slave, the property of the great Earl Grip, who had arrived just after dark at the Tabard inn in the village on the other side of the water, and had stopped there over night, by compulsion, he being taken deadly sick with a strange and sudden disorder. I had been ordered to cross to the city in all haste and bring the best physician; I was doing my best; naturally I was running with all my might; the night was dark, I ran against this common person here, who seized me by the throat and began to pummel me, although I told him my errand, and implored him, for the sake of the great earl my master's mortal peril—

The common person interrupted and said it was a lie; and was going to explain how I rushed upon him and attacked him without a a word—

"Silence, sirrah!" from the court. "Take him hence and give him a few stripes whereby to teach him how to treat the servant of a nobleman after a different fashion another time. Go!"

Then the court begged my pardon, and hoped I would not fail to tell his lordship it was in no wise the court's fault that this high-handed thing had happened. I said I would make it all right, and so took my leave. Took it just in time, too; he was starting to ask me why I didn't fetch out these facts the moment I was arrested. I said I would if I had thought of it—which was true—but that I was so battered by that man that all my wit was knocked out of me—and so forth and so on, and got myself away, still mumbling.

I didn't wait for breakfast. No grass grew under my feet. I was soon at the slave quarters. Empty—everybody gone! That is, everybody except one body—the slave-master's. It lay there all battered to pulp; and all about were the evidences of a terrific fight. There was a rude board coffin on a cart at the door, and workmen, assisted by the police, were thinning a road through the gaping crowd in order that they might bring it in.

I picked out a man humble enough in life to condescend to talk with one so shabby as I, and got his account of the matter.

"There were sixteen slaves here. They rose against their master in the night, and thou seest how it ended."

"Yes. How did it begin?"

"There was no witness but the slaves. They said the slave that was most valuable got free of his bonds and escaped in some strange way—by magic arts 'twas thought, by reason that he had no key, and the locks were neither broke nor in any wise injured. When the master discovered his loss, he was mad with despair, and threw himself upon his people with his heavy stick, who resisted and brake his back and in other and divers ways did give him hurts that brought him swiftly to his end."

"This is dreadful. It will go hard with the slaves, no doubt, upon the trial."

"Marry, the trial is over."

"Over!"

"Would they be a week, think you—and the matter so simple? They were not the half of a quarter of an hour at it."

"Why, I don't see how they could determine which were the guilty ones in so short a time."

"*Which* ones? Indeed they considered not particulars like to that. They condemned them in a body. Wit ye not the law?—which men say the Romans left behind them here when they went—that if one slave killeth his master all the slaves of that man must die for it."

"True. I had forgotten. And when will these die?"

"Belike within a four and twenty hours; albeit some say they will wait a pair of days more, if peradventure they may find the missing one meantime."

The missing one! It made me feel uncomfortable.

"Is it likely they will find him?"

"Before the day is spent—yes. They seek him everywhere. They stand at the gates of the town, with certain of the slaves who will discover him to them if he cometh, and none can pass out but he will be first examined."

"Might one see the place where the rest are confined?"

"The outside of it—yes. The inside of it—but ye will not want to see that."

I took the address of that prison, for future reference, and then sauntered off. At the first second-hand clothing shop I came to, up a back street, I got a rough rig suitable for a common seaman who might be going on a cold voyage, and bound up my face with a liberal bandage, saying I had a toothache. This concealed my worst bruises. It was a transformation. I no longer resembled my former self. Then I struck out for that wire, found it and followed it to its den. It was a little room over a butcher's shop—which meant that business wasn't very brisk in the telegraphic line. The young chap in charge was drowsing at his table. I locked the door and put the vast key in my bosom. This alarmed the young fellow, and he was going to make a noise; but I said:

"Save your wind; if you open your mouth you are dead, sure. Tackle your instrument. Lively, now! Call Camelot."

"This doth amaze me! How should such as you know aught of such matters as—"

"Call Camelot! I am a desperate man. Call Camelot, or get away from the instrument and I will do it myself."

"What—you?"

"Yes—certainly. Stop gabbling. Call the palace." He made the call.

"Now then, call Clarence."

"Clarence *who?*"

"Never mind Clarence who. Say you want Clarence; you'll get an answer."

He did so. We waited five nerve-straining minutes—ten minutes—how long it did seem!—and then came a click that was as familiar to me as a human voice; for Clarence had been my own pupil.

"Now, my lad, vacate! They would have known *my* touch, maybe, and so your call was surest; but I'm all right, now."

He vacated the place and cocked his ear to listen—but it didn't win. I used a cipher. I didn't waste any time in sociabilities with Clarence, but squared away for business, straight-off—thus:

"The king is here and in danger. We were captured and brought here as slaves. We should not be able to prove our identity—and the fact is, I am not in a position to try. Send a telegram for the palace here which will carry conviction with it."

His answer came straight back:

"They don't know anything about the telegraph; they haven't had any experience yet, the line to London is so new. Better not venture that. They might hang you. Think up something else."

Might hang us! Little he knew how closely he was crowding the facts. I couldn't think up anything for the moment. Then an idea struck me, and I started it along:

"Send five hundred picked knights with Launcelot in the lead; and send them on the jump. Let them enter by the southwest gate, and look out for the man with a white cloth around his right arm."

The answer was prompt:

"They shall start in half an hour."

"All right, Clarence; now tell this lad here that I'm a friend of yours and a dead-head; and that he must be discreet and say nothing about this visit of mine."

The instrument began to talk to the youth and I hurried away. I fell to ciphering. In half an hour it would be nine o'clock. Knights and horses in heavy armor couldn't travel very fast. These would make the best time they could, and now that the ground was in good condition, and no snow or mud, they would probably make a seven-mile gait; they would have to change horses a couple of times; they would arrive about six, or a little after; it would still be plenty light enough; they would see the white cloth which I should tie around my right arm, and I would take command. We would surround that prison and have the king out in no time. It would be showy and picturesque enough, all things considered, though I would have preferred noonday, on account of the more theatrical aspect the thing would have.

Now then, in order to increase the strings to my bow, I thought I would look up some of those people whom I had formerly recognized, and make myself known. That would help us out of our scrape, without the knights. But I must proceed cautiously, for it was a risky business. I must get into sumptuous raiment, and it wouldn't do to run and jump into it. No, I must work up to it by degrees, buying suit after suit of clothes, in shops wide apart, and getting a little finer article with each change, until I should finally reach silk and velvet, and be ready for my project. So I started.

But the scheme fell through like scat! The first corner I turned, I came plump upon one of our slaves, snooping around with a watchman. I coughed, at the moment, and he gave me a sudden look that bit right into my marrow. I judge he thought he had heard that cough before. I turned immediately into a shop and worked along down the counter, pricing things and watching out of the corner of my eye. Those people had stopped, and were talking together and looking in at the door. I made up my mind to get out the back way, if there was a back way, and I asked the shopwoman if I could step out there and look for the escaped slave, who was believed to be in hiding back there somewhere, and said I was an officer in disguise, and my pard was yonder at the door with one of the murderers in charge, and would she be good enough to step there and tell him he needn't wait, but had better go at once to the further end of the back alley and be ready to head him off when I rousted him out.

She was blazing with eagerness to see one of those already celebrated murderers, and she started on the errand at once. I slipped out the back way, locked the door behind me, put the key in my pocket and started off, chuckling to myself and comfortable.

Well, I had gone and spoiled it again, made another mistake. A double one, in fact. There were plenty of ways to get rid of that officer by some simple and plausible device, but no, I must pick out a picturesque one; it is the crying defect of my character. And then, I had ordered my procedure upon what the officer, being human, would *naturally* do; whereas when you are least expecting it, a man will now and then go and do the very thing which it's *not* natural for him to do. The natural thing for the officer to do, in this case, was to follow straight on my heels; he would find a stout oaken door, securely locked, between him and me; before he could break it down, I should be far away and engaged in slipping into a succession of baffling disguises which would soon get me into a sort of raiment which was a surer protection from meddling law-dogs in Britain than any amount of mere innocence and purity of character. But instead of doing the natural thing, the officer took me at my word, and followed my instructions. And so, as I came trotting out of that cul de sac, full of satisfaction with my own cleverness, he turned the corner and I walked right into his handcuffs. If I had known it was a cul de sac—however, there isn't any excusing a blunder like that, let it go. Charge it up to profit and loss.

Of course I was indignant, and swore I had just come ashore from a long voyage, and all that sort of thing—just to see, you know, if it woud deceive that slave. But it didn't. He knew me. Then I reproached him for betraying me. He was more surprised than hurt. He stretched his eyes wide, and said:

"What, wouldst have me let thee, of all men, escape and not hang with us, when thou'rt the very *cause* of our hanging? Go to!"

"Go to" was their way of saying "I should smile!" or "I like that!" Queer talkers, those people.

Well, there was a sort of bastard justice in his view of the case, and so I dropped the matter. When you can't cure a disaster by argument, what is the use to argue? It isn't my way. So I only said:

"You're not going to be hanged. None of us are."

Both men laughed, and the slave said:

"Ye have not ranked as a fool—before. You might better keep your reputation, seeing the strain would not be for long."

"It will stand it, I reckon. Before to-morrow we shall be out of prison, and free to go where we will, besides."

The witty officer lifted at his left ear with his thumb, made a rasping noise in his throat, and said:

"Out of prison—yes—ye say true. And free likewise to go where ye will, so ye wander not out of his grace the Devil's sultry realm."

I kept my temper, and said, indifferently:

"Now I suppose you really think we are going to hang within a day or two."

"I thought it not many minutes ago, for so the thing was decided and proclaimed."

"Ah, then you've changed your mind, is that it?"

"Even that. I only *thought*, then; I *know*, now."

I felt sarcastical, so I said:

"Oh, sapient servant of the law, condescend to tell us, then, what you *know*.

"That ye will all be hanged *to-day*, at mid-afternoon! Oho! that shot hit home! Lean upon me."

The fact is I did need to lean upon somebody. My knights couldn't arrive in time. They would be as much as three hours too late. Nothing in the world could save the King of England; nor me, which was more important. More important, not merely to me, but to the nation—the only nation on earth standing ready to blossom into civilization. I was sick. I said no more, there wasn't anything to say. I knew what the man meant; that if the missing slave was found, the postponement would be revoked, the execution take place to-day. Well, the missing slave was found.

CHAPTER XXXVIII

SIR LAUNCELOT AND KNIGHTS TO THE RESCUE

Nearing four in the afternoon. The scene was just outside the walls of London. A cool, comfortable, superb day, with a brilliant sun; the kind of day to make one want to live, not die. The multitude was prodigious and far reaching; and yet we fifteen poor devils hadn't a friend in it. There was something painful in that thought, look at it how you might. There we sat, on our tall scaffold, the butt of the hate and mockery of all those enemies. We were being made a holiday spectacle. They had built a sort of grand stand for the nobility and gentry, and these were there in full force, with their ladies. We recognized a good many of them.

The crowd got a brief and unexpected dash of diversion out of the king. The moment we were freed of our bonds he sprang up, in his fantastic rags, with face bruised out of all recognition, and proclaimed himself Arthur, King of Britain, and denounced the awful penalties of treason upon every soul there present if hair of his sacred head were touched. It startled and surprised him to hear them break into a vast roar of laughter. It wounded his dignity, and he locked himself up in silence, then, although the crowd begged him to go on, and tried to provoke him to it by cat-calls, jeers, and shouts of "Let him speak! The king! The king! his humble subjects hunger and thirst for words of wisdom out of the mouth of their master his Serene and Sacred Raggedness!"

But it went for nothing. He put on all his majesty and sat under this rain of contempt and insult unmoved. He certainly was great in his way. Absently, I had taken off my white bandage and wound it about my right arm. When the crowd noticed this, they began upon me. They said:

"Doubtless this sailor-man is his minister—observe his costly badge of office!"

I let them go on until they got tired, and then I said:

"Yes, I am his minister, The Boss; and to-morrow you will hear that from Camelot which—"

I got no further. They drowned me out with joyous derision. But presently there was silence; for the sheriffs of London, in their official robes, with their subordinates, began to make a stir which indicated that business was about to begin. In the hush which followed, our crime was recited, the death warrant read, then everybody uncovered while a priest uttered a prayer.

Then a slave was blindfolded, the hangman unslung his rope. There lay the smooth road below us, we upon one side of it, the banked multitude walling its other side—a good clear road, and kept free by the police—how good it would be to see my five hundred horsemen come tearing down it! But, no, it was out of the possibilities. I followed its receding thread out into the distance—not a horseman on it, or sign of one.

There was a jerk, and the slave hung dangling; dangling and hideously squirming, for his limbs were not tied.

A second rope was unslung, in a moment another slave was dangling.

In a minute a third slave was struggling in the air. It was dreadful. I turned away my head a moment, and when I turned back I missed the king! They were blindfolding him! I was paralyzed; I couldn't move, I was choking, my tongue was petrified. They finished blindfolding him, they led him under the rope. I couldn't shake off that clinging impotence. But when I saw them put the noose around his neck, then everything let go in me and I made a spring to the rescue—and as I made it I shot one more glance abroad—by George, here they came, a-tilting!—five hundred mailed and belted knights on bicycles!

The grandest sight that ever was seen. Lord, how the plumes streamed, how the sun flamed and flashed from the endless procession of webby wheels!

I waved my right arm as Launcelot swept in—he recognized my rag—I tore away noose and bandage, and shouted:

"On your knees, every rascal of you, and salute the king! Who fails shall sup in hell to-night!"

I always use that high style when I'm climaxing an effect. Well, it was noble to see Launcelot and the boys swarm up onto that scaffold and heave sheriffs and such overboard. And it was fine to see that astonished multitude go down on their knees and beg their lives of the king they had just been deriding and insulting. And as he stood apart, there, receiving this homage in his rags, I thought to myself, well really there *is* something peculiarly grand about the gait and bearing of a king, after all.

I was immensely satisfied. Take the whole situation all around, it was one of the gaudiest effects I ever instigated.

And presently up comes Clarence, his own self! and winks, and says, very modernly:

"Good deal of a surprise, wasn't it? I knew you'd like it. I've had the boys practising, this long time, privately; and just hungry for a chance to show off."

CHAPTER XXXIX

THE YANKEE'S FIGHT WITH THE KNIGHTS

Home again, at Camelot. A morning or two later I found the paper, damp from the press, by my plate at the breakfast table. I turned to the advertising columns, knowing I should find something of personal interest to me there. It was this:

DE PAR LE ROI.

ᴋnow that the great lord and illustrious kni8ht, ꜱIR SAGRAMOR LE DESIᴙOUS naving condescended to meet the Kinᴦ's Minister, Hank Morgan, the which is surnamed The Boss, for satisfgction of offence anciently given, these wilL engage in the lists by Camelot about tne fourth hour of tne mornmg on tne sixteenth day of this next succeeding month. The battle wiil be à l'cutrance, sith the said offence was of a deadly sort, admitting of no comPosition.

DE PAR ᴌE ᴙOᴌ

Clarence's editorial reference to this affair was to this effect:

thdrew.
woJk maintained
there since, soon
listic have with
oked interest
upon the ea
ve been m d
oy the ar s,
ent out ch y by
rterian B 1, and
some y g men
of our unde the
i guidance of tha
or aid in a known
ie great enterprise
ot ...aking pure ;
esen1
'uovement had its
origin in preven-
has ever been a
sions in our
on of Wis-
other one
ospel,
by-
e
Tne
he same
co represent
ized thirty of
needs and hear-
vhich, years ago !
'resgn was osgan-
ng, the missions,
so that both had
'o withdraw' and
much to their
grief,

It will be observed, by a gl7nce at our advertising columns, that the community is to be favore l with a treat of unusual interest in the tournament line. The names of the artists are warrant of good enterTainment. The box-office will be open at noon of the 13th; admission 3 cents, reserved seats 5 ; proceeds to go to the hospital fund The royal pair and all the Court will be present. With these exceptions, and the press and the clergy, tne free list is strictly sus¶ended. Parties are hereby warned against buying tickets of speculators; they will not be good at the door. Everybody knows and likes The Boss, everybody knows and likes Sir Sag.; come, let us give tne lads a good send-off. ReMember, tne proceeds go to a great and free charity, and one whose broad begevolence stretches out its helping hand, warm with the blood of a loving heart, to all that suffer, regardless of race, creed, condition or color—the only charity yet established in the earth which has no politico-religious stopcock on its compassion, but says Here flows the stream, let *all* come and drink! Jurn out, all hands! fetch along your doughnuts and your gum-drops and have a good time. Pie for sale on the grounds, and rocks to crack it with; also ciRcus-lemonade—three drops of lime juice to a barrel of water.

N. B. *This is the first tournament under the new law, whidh allows each combatant to use any weapon he may prefer.* You want to make a note of that.

our disappointn.
dromptly and –
two of their felo
erlain, and ot
ers have already
spoken, yo '
furnised fc
their use, n
make and
the kind
letters
of introd
duction whi
they are unif.
ing friends to us
ried, and leave the
thot kind words and
which you, m, joy.
hind ; and it is a
home matter of b
it is our durp
direct them to
now under the
g fields as are
Tnese young mer
are warm-hearted
aztrl, regions bei
not to " build .
ond,', and the
der instructi
ons of our
another man
founhati's on.,
ociety, which
They go un
say tqat " inr
ionaries to mon
say sending mi

Up to the day set, there was no talk in all Britain of anything but this combat. All other topics sank into insignificance and passed out of men's thoughts and interest. It was not because a tournament was a great matter; it was not because Sir Sagramor had found the Holy Grail, for he had not, but had failed; it was not because the second (official) personage in the kingdom was one of the duellists; no, all these features were commonplace. Yet there was abundant reason for the extraordinary interest which this coming fight was creating. It was born of the fact that all the nation knew that was not to be a duel between mere men, so to speak, but a duel between two mighty magicians; a duel not of muscle but of mind, not of human skill but of superhuman art and craft; a final struggle for supremacy between the two master enchanters of the age. It was realized that the most prodigious achievements of the most renowned knights could not be worthy of comparison with a spectacle like this; they could be but child's play, contrasted with this mysterious and awful battle of the gods. Yes, all the world knew it was going to be in reality a duel between Merlin and me, a measuring of his magic powers against mine. It was known that Merlin had been busy whole days and nights together, imbuing Sir Sagramor's arms and armor with supernal powers of offence and defence, and that he had procured for him from the spirits of the air a fleecy veil which would render the wearer invisible to his antagonist while still visible to other men. Against Sir Sagramor, so weaponed and protected, a thousand knights could accomplish nothing; against him no known enchantments could prevail. These facts were sure; regarding them there was no doubt, no reason for doubt. There was but one question: might there be still other enchantments, *unknown* to Merlin, which could render Sir Sagramor's veil transparent to me, and make his enchanted mail vulnerable to my weapons? This was the one thing to be decided in the lists. Until then the world must remain in suspense.

So the world thought there was a vast matter at stake here, and the world was right, but it was not the one they had in their minds. No, a far vaster one was upon the cast of this die: *the life of knight-errantry.* I was a champion, it was true, but not the champion of the frivolous black arts, I was the champion of hard unsentimental common-sense and reason. I was entering the lists to either destroy knight-errantry or be its victim.

Vast as the show-grounds were, there were no vacant spaces in them outside of the lists, at ten o'clock on the morning of the 16th. The mammoth grand-stand was clothed in flags, streamers, and rich tapestries, and packed with several acres of small-fry tributary kings, their suites, and the British aristocracy; with our own royal gang in the chief place, and each and every individual a flashing prism of gaudy silks and velvets—well, I never saw anything to begin with it but a fight between an Upper Mississippi sunset and the aurora borealis. The huge camp of beflagged and gay-colored tents at one end of the lists, with a stiff-standing sentinel at every door and a shining shield hanging by him for challenge, was another fine sight. You see, every knight was there who had any ambition or any caste feeling; for my feeling toward their order was not much of a secret, and so here was their chance. If I won my fight with Sir Sagramor, others would have the right to call me out as long as I might be willing to respond.

Down at our end there were but two tents; one for me, and

another for my servants. At the appointed hour the king made a sign, and the heralds, in their tabards, appeared and made proclamation, naming the combatants and stating the cause of quarrel. There was a pause, then a ringing bugle-blast, which was the signal for us to come forth. All the multitude caught their breath, and an eager curiosity flashed into every face.

Out from his tent rode great Sir Sagramor, an imposing tower of iron, stately and rigid, his huge spear standing upright in its socket and grasped in his strong hand, his grand horse's face and breast cased in steel, his body clothed in rich trappings that almost dragged the ground—oh, a most noble picture. A great shout went up, of welcome and admiration.

And then out I came. But I didn't get any shout. There was a wondering and eloquent silence, for a moment, then a great wave of laughter began to sweep along that human sea, but a warning bugle-blast cut its career short. I was in the simplest and comfortablest of gymnast costumes—flesh-colored tights from neck to heel, with blue silk puffings about my loins, and bareheaded. My horse was not above medium size, but he was alert, slender-limbed, muscled with watch-springs, and just a greyhound to go. He was a beauty, glossy as silk, and naked as he was when he was born, except for bridle and ranger-saddle.

The iron tower and the gorgeous bed-quilt came cumbrously but gracefully pirouetting down the lists, and we tripped lightly up to meet them. We halted; the tower saluted, I responded; then we wheeled and rode side by side to the grand-stand and faced our king and queen, to whom we made obeisance. The queen exclaimed:

"Alack, Sir Boss, wilt fight naked, and without lance or sword or—"

But the king checked her and made her understand, with a polite phrase or two, that this was none of her business. The bugles rang again; and we separated and rode to the ends of the lists, and took position. Now old Merlin stepped into view and cast a dainty web of gossamer threads over Sir Sagramor which turned him into Hamlet's ghost; the king made a sign, the bugles blew, Sir Sagramor laid his great lance in rest, and the next moment here he came thundering down the course with his veil flying out behind, and I went whistling through the air like an arrow to meet him—cocking my ear, the while, as if noting the invisible knight's position and progress by hearing, not sight. A chorus of encouraging shouts burst out for him, and one brave voice flung out a heartening word for me—said:

"Go it, slim Jim!"

It was an even bet that Clarence had procured that favor for me—and furnished the language, too. When that formidable lance-point was within a yard and a half of my breast I twitched my horse aside without an effort and the big knight swept by, scoring a blank. I got plenty of applause that time. We turned, braced up, and down we came again. Another blank for the knight, a roar of applause for me. This same thing was repeated once more; and it fetched such a whirlwind of applause that Sir Sagramor lost his temper, and at once changed his tactics and set himself the task of chasing me down. Why, he hadn't any show in the world at that; it was a game of tag, with all the advantage on my side; I whirled out of his path with ease whenever I chose, and once I slapped him on the back as I went to the rear. Finally I took the chase into my own hands; and after that, turn, or twist, or do what he would, he was never able to get behind me again; he found himself always in front, at the end of his manoeuvre. So he gave up that business and retired to his end of the lists. His temper was clear gone, now, and he forgot himself and flung an insult at me which disposed of mine. I slipped my lasso from the horn of my saddle, and grasped the coil in my right hand. This time you should have seen him come!—it was a business trip, sure; by his gait there was blood in his eye. I was sitting my horse at ease, and swinging the great loop of my lasso in wide circles about my head; the moment he was under way, I started for him; when the space between us had narrowed to forty feet, I sent the snaky spirals of the rope a-cleaving through the air, then darted aside and faced about and brought my trained animal to a halt with all his feet braced under him for a surge. The next moment the rope sprang taut and yanked Sir Sagramor out of the saddle! Great Scott, but there was a sensation!

Unquestionably the popular thing in this world is novelty. These people had never seen anything of that cowboy business before, and it carried them clear off their feet with delight. From all around and everywhere, the shout went up—

"Encore! encore!"

I wondered where they got the word, but there was no time to cipher on philological matters, because the whole knight-errantry hive was just humming, now, and my prospect for trade couldn't have been better. The moment my lasso was released and Sir Sagramor had been assisted to his tent, I hauled in the slack, took my station and began to swing my loop around my head again. I was sure to have use for it as soon as they could elect a successor for Sir Sagramor, and that couldn't take long where there were so many hungry candidates. Indeed, they elected one straight off—Sir Hervis de Revel.

Bzz! Here he came, like a house afire; I dodged; he passed like a flash, with my horse-hair coils settling around his neck; a second or so later, *fst!* his saddle was empty.

I got another encore; and another, and another, and still another. When I had snaked five men out, things began to look serious to the iron-clads, and they stopped and consulted together. As a result, they decided that it was time to waive etiquette and send their greatest and best against me. To the astonishment of that little world, I lassoed Sir Lamorak de Galis, and after him Sir Galahad. So you see there was simply nothing to be done, now, but play their right bower—bring out the superbest of the superb, the mightiest of the mighty, the great Sir Launcelot himself!

A proud moment for me? I should think so. Yonder was Arthur, King of Britain; yonder was Guenever; yes, and whole tribes of little provincial kings and kinglets; and in the tented camp yonder, renowned knights from many lands; and likewise the selectest body known to chivalry, the Knights of the Table Round, the most illustrious in Christendom; and biggest fact of all, the very sun of their shining system was yonder couching his lance, the focal point of forty thousand adoring eyes; and all by myself, here was I laying for him. Across my mind flitted the dear image of a certain hello-girl of West Hartford, and I wished she could see me now. In that moment, down came the Invincible, with the rush of a whirlwind— the courtly world rose to its feet and bent forward—the fateful coils went circling through the air, and before you could wink I was towing Sir Launcelot across the field on his back, and kissing my hand to the storm of waving kerchiefs and the thundercrash of applause that greeted me!

Said I to myself, as I coiled my lariat and hung it on my saddle-horn, and sat there drunk with glory, "The victory is perfect—no other will venture against me—knight-errantry is dead." Now imagine my astonishment—and everybody else's too—to hear the peculiar bugle-call which announces that another competitor is about to enter the lists! There was a mystery here; I couldn't account for this thing. Next, I noticed Merlin gliding away from me; and then I noticed that my lasso was gone! The old sleight-of-hand expert had stolen it, sure, and slipped it under his robe.

The bugle blew again. I looked, and down came Sagramor riding again, with his dust brushed off and his veil nicely re-arranged. I trotted up to meet him, and pretended to find him by the sound of his horse's hoofs. He said:

"Thou'rt quick of ear, but it will not save thee from this!" and he touched the hilt of his great sword. "An ye are not able to see it, because of the influence of the veil, know that it is no cumbrous lance, but a sword—and I ween ye will not be able to avoid it."

His visor was up; there was death in his smile. I should never be able to dodge his sword, that was plain. Somebody was going to die, this time. If he got the drop on me, I could name the corpse. We rode forward together, and saluted the royalties. This time the king was disturbed. He said:

"Where is thy strange weapon?"

"It is stolen, sire."

"Hast another at hand?"

"No, sire, I brought only the one."

Then Merlin mixed in:

"He brought but the one because there was but the one to bring. There exists none other but that one. It belongeth to the king of the Demons of the Sea. This man is a pretender, and ignorant; else he had known that that weapon can be used in but eight bouts only, and then it vanisheth away to its home under the sea."

"Then is he weaponless," said the king. "Sir Sagramor, ye will grant him leave to borrow."

"And I will lend!" said Sir Launcelot, limping up. "He is as brave a knight of his hands as any that be on live, and he shall have mine."

He put his hand on his sword to draw it, but Sir Sagramor said:

"Stay, it may not be. He shall fight with his own weapons; it was his privilege to choose them and bring them. If he has erred, on his head be it."

"Knight!" said the king. "Thou'rt overwrought with passion; it disorders thy mind. Wouldst kill a naked man?"

"An he do it, he shall answer it to me," said Sir Launcelot.

"I will answer it to any he that desireth!" retorted Sir Sagramor hotly.

Merlin broke in, rubbing his hands and smiling his lowdownest smile of malicious gratification:

"'Tis well said, right well said! And 'tis enough of parleying, let my lord the king deliver the battle signal."

The king had to yield. The bugle made proclamation, and we turned apart and rode to our stations. There we stood, a hundred yards apart, facing each other, rigid and motionless, like horsed statues. And so we remained, in a soundless hush, as much as a full minute, everybody gazing, nobody stirring. It seemed as if the king could not take heart to give the signal. But at last he lifted his hand, the clear note of the bugle followed, Sir Sagramor's long blade described a flashing curve in the air, and it was superb to see him come. I sat still. On he came. I did not move. People got so excited that they shouted to me:

"Fly, fly! Save thyself! This is murther!"

I never budged so much as an inch, till that thundering apparition had got within fifteen paces of me; then I snatched a dragoon revolver out of my holster, there was a flash and a roar, and the revolver was back in the holster before anybody could tell what had happened.

Here was a riderless horse plunging by, and yonder lay Sir Sagramor, stone dead.

The people that ran to him were stricken dumb to find that the life was actually gone out of the man and no reason for it visible, no hurt upon his body, nothing like a wound. There was a hole through the breast of his chain-mail, but they attached no importance to a little thing like that; and as a bullet-wound there produces but little blood, none came in sight because of the clothing and swaddlings under the armor. The body was dragged over to let the king and the swells look down upon it. They were stupefied with astonishment, naturally. I was requested to come and explain the miracle. But I remained in my tracks, like a statue, and said:

"If it is a command, I will come, but my lord the king knows that I am where the laws of combat require me to remain while any desire to come against me."

I waited. Nobody challenged. Then I said:

"If there are any who doubt that this field is well and fairly won, I do not wait for them to challenge me, I challenge them."

"It is a gallant offer," said the king, "and well beseems you. Whom will you name, first?"

"I name none, I challenge all! Here I stand, and dare the chivalry of England to come against me—not by individuals, but in mass!"

"What!" shouted a score of knights.

"You have heard the challenge. Take it, or I proclaim you recreant knights and vanquished, every one!'

It was a "bluff" you know. At such a time it is sound judgment to put on a bold face and play your hand for a hundred times what it is worth; forty-nine times out of fifty nobody dares to "call," and you rake in the chips. But just this once—well, things looked squally! In just no time, five hundred knights were scrambling into their saddles, and before you could wink a widely scattering drove were under way and clattering down upon me. I snatched both revolvers from the holsters and began to measure distances and calculate chances.

Bang! One saddle empty. Bang! another one. Bang—bang! and I bagged two. Well it was nip and tuck with us, and I knew it. If I spent the eleventh shot without convincing these people, the twelfth man would kill me, sure. And so I never did feel so happy as I did when my ninth downed its man and I detected the wavering in the crowd which is premonitory of panic. An instant lost now, could knock out my last chance. But I didn't lose it. I raised both revolvers and pointed them—the halted host stood their ground just about one good square moment, then broke and fled.

The day was mine. Knight-errantry was a doomed institution. The march of civilization was begun. How did I feel? Ah you never could imagine it.

And Brer Merlin? His stock was flat again. Somehow, every time the magic of fol-de-rol tried conclusions with the magic of science, the magic of fol-de-rol got left.

CHAPTER XL

THREE YEARS LATER

When I broke the back of knight-errantry that time, I no longer felt obliged to work in secret. So, the very next day I exposed my hidden schools, my mines, and my vast system of clandestine factories and work-shops to an astonished world. That is to say, I exposed the nineteenth century to the inspection of the sixth.

Well it is always a good plan to follow up an advantage promptly. The knights were temporarily down, but if I would keep them so I must just simply paralyze them—nothing short of that would answer. You see, I was "bluffing" that last time, in the field; it would be natural for them to work around to that conclusion, if I gave them a chance. So I must not give them time: and I didn't.

I renewed my challenge, engraved it on brass, posted it up where any priest could read it to them, and also kept it standing, in the advertising columns of the paper.

I not only renewed it, but added to its proportions. I said, name the day, and I would take fifty assistants and stand up *against the masses chivalry of the whole earth and destroy it.*

I was not bluffing this time. I meant what I said; I could do what I promised. There wasn't any way to misunderstand the language of that challenge. Even the dullest of the chivalry perceived that this was a plain case of "put up, or shut up." They were wise and did the latter. In all the next three years they gave me no trouble worth mentioning.

Consider the three years sped. Now look around on England. A happy and prosperous country, and strangely altered. Schools everywhere, and several colleges; a number of pretty good newspapers. Even authorship was taking a start; Sir Dinadan the Humorist was first in the field, with a volume of gray-headed jokes which I had been familiar with during thirteen centuries. If he had left out that old rancid one about the lecturer I wouldn't have said anything; but I couldn't stand that one. I suppressed the book and hanged the author.

Slavery was dead and gone; all men were equal before the law; taxation had been equalized. The telegraph, the telephone, the phonograph, the typewriter, the sewing-machine, and all the thousand willing and handy servants of steam and electricity were working their way into favor. We had a steamboat or two on the Thames, we had steam war-ships, and the beginnings of a steam commercial marine; I was getting ready to send out an expedition to discover America.

We were building several lines of railway, and our line from Camelot to London was already finished and in operation. I was shrewd enough to make all offices connected with the passenger service places of high and distinguished honor. My idea was to attract the chivalry and nobility, and make them useful and keep them out of mischief. The plan worked very well, the competition for the places was hot. The conductor of the 4.33 express was a duke, there wasn't a passenger conductor on the line below the degree of earl. They were good men, every one, but they had two defects which I couldn't cure, and so had to wink at: they wouldn't lay aside their armor, and they would "knock down" fares—I mean rob the company.

There was hardly a knight in all the land who wasn't in some useful employment. They were going from end to end of the country in all manner of useful missionary capacities; their penchant for wandering, and their experience in it, made them altogether the most effective spreaders of civilization we had. They went clothed in steel and equipped with sword and lance and battle-axe, and if they couldn't persuade a person to try a sewing-machine on the instalment plan, or a melodeon, or a barbed-wire fence, or a prohibition journal, or any of the other thousand and one things they canvassed for, they removed him and passed on.

I was very happy. Things were working steadily towards a secretly longed-for point. You see, I had two schemes in my head which were the vastest of all my projects. The one was, to overthrow the Catholic Church and set up the Protestant faith on its ruins—not as an Established Church, but a-go-as-you-please one; and the other project was, to get a decree issued by-and-by, commanding that upon Arthur's death unlimited suffrage should be introduced, and given to men and women alike—at any rate to all men, wise or unwise, and to all mothers who at middle age should be found to know nearly as much as their sons at twenty-one. Arthur was good for thirty years yet, he being about my own age—that is to say, forty—and I believed that in that time I could easily have the active part of the population of that day ready and eager for an event which should be the first of its kind in the history of the world—a rounded and complete governmental revolution without bloodshed. The result to be a republic. Well, I may as well confess, though I do feel ashamed when I think of it: I was beginning to have a base hankering to be its first president myself. Yes, there was more or less human nature in me; I found that out.

Clarence was with me as concerned the revolution, but in a modified way. His idea was a republic, without privileged orders but with a hereditary royal family at the head of it instead of an elective chief magistrate. He believed that no nation that had ever known the joy of worshipping a royal family could ever be robbed of it and not fade away and die of melancholy. I urged that kings were dangerous. He said, then have cats. He was sure that a royal family of cats would answer every purpose. They would be as useful as any other royal family, they would know as much, they would have the same virtues and the same treacheries, the same disposition to get up shindies with other royal cats, they would be laughably vain and absurd and never know it, they would be wholly inexpensive; finally, they would have as sound a divine right as any other royal house, and "Tom VII., or Tom XI., or Tom XIV. by the grace of God King," would sound as well as it would when applied to the ordinary royal tomcat with tights on. "And as a rule," said he, in his neat modern English, "the character of these cats would be considerably above the character of the average king, and this would be an immense moral advantage to the nation, for the reason that a nation always models its morals after its monarch's. The worship of royalty being founded in unreason, these graceful and harmless cats would easily become as sacred as any other royalties, and indeed more so, because it would presently be noticed that they hanged nobody, beheaded nobody, imprisoned nobody, inflicted no cruelties or injustices of any sort, and so must be worthy of a deeper love and reverence than the customary human king, and would certainly get it. The eyes of the whole harried world would soon be fixed upon this humane and gentle system, and royal butchers would presently begin to disappear; their subjects would fill the vacancies with catlings from our own royal house; we should become a factory; we should supply the thrones of the world; within forty years all Europe would be governed by cats, and we should furnish the cats. The reign of universal peace would begin then, to end no more forever......*Me-e-e-yow-ow-ow-ow—fzt!—wow!*"

Hang him, I supposed he was in earnest, and was beginning to be persuaded by him, until he exploded that cat-howl and startled me almost out of my clothes. But he never could be in earnest. He didn't know what it was. He had pictured a distinct and perfectly rational and feasible improvement upon constitutional monarchy, but he was too feather-headed to know it, or care anything about it, either. I was going to give him a scolding, but Sandy came flying in at that moment, wild with terror, and so choked with sobs that for a minute she could not get her voice. I ran and took her in my arms, and lavished caresses upon her and said, beseechingly:

"Speak, darling, speak! What is it?"

Her head fell limp upon my bosom, and she gasped, almost inaudibly:

"HELLO, CENTRAL!"

"Quick!" I shouted to Clarence; "telephone the king's homeopath to come!"

In two minutes I was kneeling by the child's crib, and Sandy was dispatching servants here, there and everywhere, all over the palace. I took in the situation almost at a glance—membraneous croup! I bent down and whispered:

"Wake up, sweetheart! Hello-Central!"

She opened her soft eyes languidly, and made out to say—

"Papa."

That was a comfort. She was far from dead, yet. I sent for
preparations of sulphur, I rousted out the croup-kettle myself;
for I don't sit down and wait for doctors when Sandy or the child
is sick. I knew how to nurse both of them, and had had experience.
This little chap had lived in my arms a good part of its small life,
and often I could soothe away its troubles and get it to laugh through
the tear-dews on its eye-lashes when even its mother couldn't.

Sir Launcelot, in his richest armor, came striding along the great
hall, now, on his way to the stock-board; he was president of the
stock-board, and occupied the Siege Perilous, which he had bought
of Sir Galahad; for the stock-board consisted of the Knights of the
Round Table, and they used the Round Table for business purposes,
now. Seats at it were worth—well, you would never believe the figure,
so it is no use to state it. Sir Launcelot was a bear, and he had put
up a corner in one of the new lines, and was just getting ready to
squeeze the shorts to-day; but what of that? He was the same old
Launcelot, and when he glanced in as he was passing the door and
found out that his pet was sick, that was enough for him; bulls and
bears might fight it out their own way for all him, he would come
right in here and stand by little Hello-Central for all he was worth.
And that was what he did. He shied his helmet into the corner, and
in half a minute he had a new wick in the alcohol lamp and was
firing up on the croup-kettle. By this time Sandy had built a blanket
canopy over the crib, and everything was ready.

Sir Launcelot got up steam, he and I loaded up the kettle with
unslaked lime and carbolic acid, with a touch of lactic acid added
thereto, then filled the thing up with water and inserted the
steam-spout under the canopy. Everything was ship-shape, now, and
we sat down on either side of the crib to stand our watch. Sandy was
so grateful and so comforted that she charged a couple of church-
wardens with willow-bark and sumach-tobacco for us, and told us
to smoke as much as we pleased, it couldn't get under the canopy,
and she was used to smoke, being the first lady in the land who had
ever seen a cloud blown. Well, there couldn't be a more contented
or comfortable sight than Sir Launcelot in his noble armor sitting
in gracious serenity at the end of a yard of snowy church-warden.
He was a beautiful man, a lovely man, and was just intended to
make a wife and children happy. But of course, Guenever—however,
it's no use to cry over what's done and can't be helped.

Well, he stood watch-and-watch with me, right straight through,
for three days and nights, till the child was out of danger; then he
took her up in his great arms and kissed her, with his plumes falling
about her golden head, then laid her softly in Sandy's lap again
and took his stately way down the vast hall, between the ranks of
admiring men-at-arms and menials, and so disappeared. And no
instinct warned me that I should never look upon him again in this

world! Lord, what a world of heart-break it is.

The doctors said we must take the child away, if we would coax her back to health and strength again. And she must have sea-air. So we took a man-of-war, and a suite of two hundred and sixty persons, and went cruising about, and after a fortnight of this we stepped ashore on the French coast, and the doctors thought it would be a good idea to make something of a stay there. The little king of that region offered us his hospitalities, and we were glad to accept. If he had had as many conveniences as he lacked, we should have been plenty comfortable enough; even as it was, we made out very well, in his queer old castle, by the help of comforts and luxuries from the ship.

At the end of a month I sent the vessel home for fresh supplies, and for news. We expected her back in three or four days. She would bring me, along with other news, the result of a certain experiment which I had been starting. It was a project of mine to replace the tournament with something which might furnish an escape for the extra steam of the chivalry, keep those bucks entertained and out of mischief, and at the same time preserve the best thing in them, which was their hardy spirit of emulation. I had had a choice band of them in private training for some time, and the date was now arriving for their first public effort.

This experiment was base-ball. In order to give the thing vogue from the start, and place it out of the reach of criticism, I chose my nines by rank, not capacity. There wasn't a knight in either team who wasn't a sceptred sovereign. As for material of this sort, there was a glut of it, always, around Arthur. You couldn't throw a brick in any direction and not cripple a king. Of course I couldn't get these people to leave off their armor; they wouldn't do that when they bathed. They consented to differentiate the armor so that a body could tell one team from the other, but that was the most they would do. So, one of the teams wore chain-mail ulsters, and the other wore plate-armor made of my new Bessemer steel. Their practice in the field was the most fantastic thing I ever saw. Being ball-proof, they never skipped out of the way, but stood still and took the result; when a Bessemer was at the bat and a ball hit him, it would bound a hundred and fifty yards, sometimes. And when a man was running, and threw himself on his stomach to slide to his base, it was like an iron-clad coming into port. At first I appointed men of no rank to act as umpires, but I had to discontinue that. These people were no easier to please than other nines. The umpire's first decision was usually his last; they broke him in two with a bat, and his friends toted him home on a shutter. When it was noticed that no umpire ever survived a game, umpiring got to be unpopular. So I was obliged to appoint somebody whose rank and lofty position under the government would protect him.

Here are the names of the nines:

BESSEMERS	ULSTERS
KING ARTHUR.	EMPEROR LUCIUS.
KING LOT OF LOTHIAN.	KING LOGRIS
KING OF NORTHGALIS.	KING MARHALT OF IRELAND.
KING MARSIL.	KING MORGANORE.
KING OF LITTLE BRITAIN.	KING MARK OF CORNWALL.
KING LABOR.	KING NENTRES OF GARLOT.
KING PELLAM OF LISTENGESE.	KING MELIODAS OF LIONES.
KING BAGDEMAGUS.	KING OF THE LAKE.
KING TOLLEME LA FEINTES.	THE SOWDAN OF SYRIA.

Umpire—CLARENCE

The first public game would certainly draw fifty thousand people; and for solid fun would be worth going around the world to see. Everything would be favorable; it was balmy and beautiful spring weather, now, and Nature was all tailored out in her new clothes.

CHAPTER XLI

THE INTERDICT

However, my attention was suddenly snatched from such matters; our child began to lose ground again, and we had to go to sitting up with her, her case became so serious. We couldn't bear to allow anybody to help, in this service, so we two stood watch-and-watch, day in and day out. Ah, Sandy, what a right heart she had, how simple, and genuine, and good she was! She was a flawless wife and mother; and yet I had married her for no other particular reason, except that by the customs of chivalry she was my property until some knight should win her from me in the field. She had hunted Britain over for me; had found me at the hanging-bout outside of London, and had straightway resumed her old place at my side in the placidest way and as of right. I was a New Englander, and in my opinion this sort of partnership would compromise her, sooner or later. She couldn't see how, but I cut argument short and we had a wedding.

Now I didn't know I was drawing a prize, yet that was what I did draw. Within the twelvemonth I became her worshipper; and ours was the dearest and perfectest comradeship that ever was. People talk about beautiful friendships between two persons of the same sex. What is the best of that sort, as compared with the friendship of man and wife, where the best impulses and highest ideals of both are the same? There is no place for comparison between the two friendships; the one is earthly, the other divine.

In my dreams, along at first, I still wandered thirteen centuries away, and my unsatisfied spirit went calling and harking all up and

down the unreplying vacancies of a vanished world. Many a time
Sandy heard that imploring cry come from my lips in my sleep.
With a grand magnanimity she saddled that cry of mine upon our
child, conceiving it to be the name of some lost darling of mine. It
touched me to tears, and it also nearly knocked me off my feet, too,
when she smiled up in my face for an earned reward, and played her
quaint and pretty surprise upon me:

"The name of one who was dear to thee is here preserved, here
made holy, and the music of it will abide alway in our ears. Now
thou'lt kiss me, as knowing the name I have given the child."

But I didn't know it, all the same. I hadn't an idea in the world,
but it would have been cruel to confess it and spoil her pretty game;
so I never let on, but said:

"Yes, I know, sweetheart—how dear and good it is of you, too!
But I want to hear these lips of yours, which are also mine, utter it
first—then its music will be perfect."

Pleased to the marrow, she murmured—

"HELLO-CENTRAL!"

I didn't laugh—I am always thankful for that—but the strain
ruptured every cartilage in me, and for weeks afterward I could hear
my bones clack when I walked. She never found out her mistake.
The first time she heard that form of salute used at the telephone
she was surprised, and not pleased; but I told her I had given order
for it: that henceforth and forever the telephone must always be
invoked with that reverent formality, in perpetual honor and
remembrance of my lost friend and her small namesake. This was
not true. But it answered.

Well, during two weeks and a half we watched by the crib, and in
our deep solicitude we were unconscious of any world outside of that
sick-room. Then our reward came: the centre of the universe turned
the corner and began to mend. Grateful? It isn't the term. There
isn't any term for it. You know that, yourself, if you've ever watched
your child through the Valley of the Shadow and seen it come back
to life and sweep night out of the earth with one all-illuminating
smile that you could cover with your hand.

Why, we were back in this world in one instant! Then we looked
the same startled thought into each other's eyes at the same
moment: more than two weeks gone, and that ship not back yet!

In another minute I appeared in the presence of my train. They
had been steeped in troubled bodings all this time—their faces
showed it. I called an escort and we galloped five miles to a hill-top
overlooking the sea. Where was my great commerce that so lately
had made these glistening expanses populous and beautiful with
its white-winged flocks? Vanished, every one! Not a sail, from verge
to verge, not a smoke-bank—just a dead and empty solitude, in
place of all that brisk and breezy life.

I went swiftly back, saying not a word to anybody. I told Sandy this ghastly news. We could imagine no explanation that would begin to explain. Had there been an invasion? an earthquake? a pestilence? Had the nation been swept out of existence? But guessing was profitless. I must go—at once. I borrowed the king's navy—a "ship" no bigger than a steam launch—and was soon ready.

The parting—ah, yes, that was hard. As I was devouring the child with last kisses, it brisked up and jabbered out its vocabulary!—the first time in more than two weeks, and it made fools of us for joy. The darling mispronunciations of childhood!—dear me, there's no music that can touch it; and how one grieves when it wastes away and dissolves into correctness, knowing it will never visit his bereaved ear again. Well, how good it was to be able to carry that gracious memory away with me!

I approached England the next morning, with the wide highway of salt water all to myself. There were ships in the harbor, at Dover, but they were naked as to sails, and there was no sign of life about them. It was Sunday; yet at Canterbury the streets were empty; strangest of all, there was not even a priest in sight, and no stroke of a bell fell upon my ear. The mournfulness of death was everywhere. I couldn't understand it. At last, in the further edge of that town I saw a small funeral procession—just a family and a few friends following a coffin—no priest; a funeral without bell, book or candle; there was a church there, close at hand, but they passed it by, weeping, and did not enter it; I glanced up at the belfry, and there hung the bell, shrouded in black, and its tongue tied back. Now I knew! Now I understood the stupendous calamity that had overtaken England. Invasion? Invasion is a triviality to it. It was the INTERDICT!

I asked no questions. I didn't need to ask any. The Church had struck; the thing for me to do was to get into a disguise, and go warily. One of my servants gave me a suit of his clothes, and when we were safe beyond the town I put them on, and from that time I travelled alone; I could not risk the embarrassment of company.

A miserable journey. A desolate silence everywhere. Even in London itself. Traffic had ceased; men did not talk or laugh, or go in groups, or even in couples; they moved aimlessly about, each man by himself, with his head down, and woe and terror at his heart. The Tower showed recent war-scars. Verily, much had been happening.

Of course I meant to take the train for Camelot. Train! Why, the station was as vacant as a cavern. I moved on. The journey to Camelot was a repetition of what I had already seen. The Monday and the Tuesday differed in no way from the Sunday. I arrived, far in the night. From being the best electric-lighted town in the kingdom and the most like a recumbent sun of anything you ever saw, it was become simply a blot—a blot upon darkness—that is to say, it was darker and solider than the rest of the darkness, and so you could see it a little better; it made me feel as if maybe it was symbolical—a sort of sign that the Church was going to *keep* the upper hand, now, and snuff out all my beautiful civilization just like that. I found no life stirring in the sombre streets. I groped my way with a heavy heart. The vast castle loomed black upon the hill-top, not a spark visible about it. The drawbridge was down, the great gate stood wide, I entered without challenge, my own heels making the only sound I heard—and it was sepulchral enough, in those huge vacant courts.

CHAPTER XLII

WAR!

I found Clarence, alone in his quarters, drowned in melancholy; and in place of the electric light, he had reinstituted the ancient rag-lamp, and sat there in a grisly twilight with all curtains drawn tight. He sprang up and rushed for me eagerly, saying:

"Oh, it's worth a billion milrays to look upon a live person again!"

He knew me as easily as if I hadn't been disguised at all. Which frightened me; one may easily believe that.

"Quick, now, tell me the meaning of this fearful disaster," I said. "How did it come about?"

"Well, if there hadn't been any Queen Guenever, it wouldn't have come so early; but it would have come, anyway. It would have come on your own account, by-and-by; by luck, it happened to come on the queen's."

"*And* Sir Launcelot's?"

"Just so."

"Give me the details."

"I reckon you will grant that during some years there has been only one pair of eyes in these kingdoms that has not been looking steadily askance at the queen and Sir Launcelot—"

"Yes, King Arthur's."

"—and only one heart that was without suspicion—"

"Yes—the king's; a heart that isn't capable of thinking evil of a friend."

"Well, the king might have gone on, still happy and unsuspecting, to the end of his days, but for one of your modern improvements—the stock-board. When you left, three miles of the London, Canterbury and Dover were ready for the rails, and also ready and ripe for manipulation in the stock-market. It was wild-cat, and everybody knew it. The stock was for sale at a give-away. What does Sir Launcelot do, but—"

"Yes, I know; he quietly picked up nearly all of it, for a song; then he bought about twice as much more, deliverable upon call;

and he was about to call when I left.''

"Very well, he did call. The boys couldn't deliver. Oh, he had them—and he just settled his grip and squeezed them. They were laughing in their sleeves over their smartness in selling stock to him at 15 and 16 and along there, that wasn't worth 10. Well, when they had laughed long enough on that side of their mouths, they rested-up that side by shifting the laugh to the other side. That was when they compromised with the Invincible at 283!"

"Good land!"

"He skinned them alive, and they deserved it—anyway, the whole kingdom rejoiced. Well, among the flayed were Sir Agravaine and Sir Mordred, nephews to the king. End of the first act. Act second, scene first, an apartment in Carlisle castle, where the court had gone for a few day's hunting. Persons present, the whole tribe of the king's nephews. Mordred and Agravaine propose to call the guileless Arthur's attention to Guenever and Sir Launcelot. Sir Gawaine, Sir Gareth, and Sir Gaheris will have nothing to do with it. A dispute ensues, with loud talk; in the midst of it, enter the king. Mordred and Agravaine spring their devastating tale upon him. *Tableau.* A trap is laid for Launcelot, by the king's command, and Sir Launcelot walks into it. He made it sufficiently uncomfortable for the ambushed witnesses—to-wit, Mordred, Agravaine, and twelve knights of lesser rank, for he killed every one them but Mordred; but of course that couldn't straighten matters between Launcelot and the king, and didn't."

"Oh, dear, only one thing could result—I see that. War, and the knights of the realm divided into a king's party and a Sir Launcelot's party."

"Yes—that was the way of it. The king sent the queen to the stake, proposing to purify her with fire. Launcelot and his knights rescued her, and in doing it slew certain good old friends of yours and mine—in fact, some of the best we ever had; to-wit, Sir Belias le Orgulous, Sir Segwarides, Sir Griflet le Fils de Dieu, Sir Brandiles, Sir Aglovale—"

"Oh, you tear out my heartstrings."

"—wait, I'm not done yet—Sir Tor, Sir Gauter, Sir Gillimer—"

"The very best man in my subordinate nine. What a handy right-fielder he was!"

"—Sir Reynold's three brothers, Sir Damus, Sir Priamus, Sir Kay the Stranger—"

"My peerless short-stop! I've seen him catch a daisy-cutter in his teeth. Come, I can't stand this!"

"—Sir Driant, Sir Lambegus, Sir Herminde, Sir Pertilope, Sir Perimones, and—whom do you think?"

"Rush! Go on."

"Sir Gaheris, and Sir Gareth—both!"

"Oh, incredible! Their love for Launcelot was indestructible."

"Well, it was an accident. They were simply on-lookers; they were unarmed, and were merely there to witness the queen's punishment. Sir Launcelot smote down whoever came in the way of his blind fury, and he killed these without noticing who they were. Here is an instantaneous photograph one of our boys got of the battle; it's for sale on every news stand. There—the figures nearest the queen are Sir Launcelot with his sword up, and Sir Gareth gasping his latest breath. You can catch the agony in the queen's face through the curling smoke. It's a rattling battle-picture."

"Indeed it is. We must take good care of it; its historical value is incalculable. Go on."

"Well, the rest of the tale is just war, pure and simple. Launcelot retreated to his town and castle of Joyous Gard, and gathered there a great following of knights. The king, with a great host, went there, and there was desperate fighting during several days, and as a result, all the plain around was paved with corpses and cast iron. Then the Church patched up a peace between Arthur and Launcelot and the queen and everybody—everybody but Sir Gawaine. He was bitter about the slaying of his brothers, Gareth and Gaheris, and would not be appeased. He notified Launcelot to get him thence, and make swift preparation, and look to be soon attacked. So Launcelot sailed to his Duchy of Guienne, with his following, and Gawaine soon followed, with an army, and he beguiled Arthur to go with him. Arthur left the kingdom in Sir Mordred's hands until you should return—"

"Ah—a king's customary wisdom!"

"Yes. Sir Mordred set himself at once to work to make his kingship permanent. He was going to marry Guenever, as a first move; but she fled and shut herself up in the Tower of London. Mordred attacked; the Bishop of Canterbury dropped down on him with the Interdict. The king returned; Mordred fought him at Dover, at Canterbury, and again at Barham Down. Then there was talk of peace and a composition. Terms, Mordred to have Cornwall and Kent during Arthur's life, and the whole kingdom afterward."

"Well, upon my word! My dream of a republic to *be* a dream, and so remain."

"Yes. The two armies lay near Salisbury. Gawaine—Gawaine's head is at Dover Castle, he fell in the fight there—Gawaine appeared to Arthur in a dream, at least his ghost did, and warned him to refrain from conflict for a month, let the delay cost what it might. But battle was precipitated by an accident. Arthur had given order that if a sword was raised during the consultation over the proposed treaty with Mordred, sound the trumpet and fall on! for he had no confidence in Mordred. Mordred had given a similar order to *his* people. Well, by-and-by an adder bit a knight's heel; the knight forgot all about the order, and made a slash at the adder with his sword. Inside of half a minute those two prodigious hosts came

together with a crash! They butchered away all day. Then the king—
however, we have started something fresh since you left—our
paper has."

"No? What is that?"

"War correspondence!"

"Why, that's good."

"Yes, the paper was booming right along, for the Interdict made
no impression, got no grip, while the war lasted. I had war
correspondents with both armies. I will finish that battle by reading
you what one of the boys says:

Then the king looked about him, and then was he ware of all his host and
of all his good knights were left no more on live but two knights, that was
Sir Lucan de Butlere, and his brother Sir Bedivere; and they were full sore
wounded. Jesu mercy, said the king, where are all my noble knights
becomen? Alas that ever I should see this doleful day. For now, said Arthur,
I am come to mine end. But would to God that I wist where were that traitor
Sir Mordred, that hath caused all this mischief. Then was King Arthur ware
where Sir Mordred leaned upon his sword among a great heap of dead men.
Now give me my spear, said Arthur unto Sir Lucan, for yonder I have espied
the traitor that all this woe hath wrought. Sir, let him be, said Sir Lucan, for
he is unhappy; and if ye pass this unhappy day, ye shall be right well
revenged upon him. Good lord, remember ye of your night's dream, and
what the spirit of Sir Gawaine told you this night, yet God of his great
goodness hath preserved you hitherto. Therefore, for God's sake, my lord,
leave off by this. For blessed be God ye have won the field: for here we be
three on live, and with Sir Mordred is none on live. And if ye leave off now,
this wicked day of destiny is past. Tide me death, betide me life, saith the
king, now I see him yonder alone, he shall never escape mine hands, for at
a better avail shall I never have him. God speed you well, said Sir Bedivere.
Then the king gat his spear in both his hands, and ran toward Sir Mordred,
crying, Traitor, now is thy death day come. And when Sir Mordred heard
Sir Arthur, he ran until him with his sword drawn in his hand. And then
King Arthur smote Sir Mordred under the shield, with a foin of his spear
throughout the body more than a fathom. And when Sir Mordred felt that
he had his death's wound, he thrust himself, with the might that he had, up
to the but of King Arthur's spear. And right so he smote his father Arthur
with his sword holden in both his hands, on the side of the head, that the
sword pierced the helmet and the brain-pan, and therewithal Sir Mordred
fell stark dead to the earth. And the noble Arthur fell in a swoon to the
earth, and there he swooned oft-times.

"That is a good piece of war correspondence, Clarence; you are
a first-rate newspaper man. Well—is the king all right? Did he get
well?"

"Poor soul, no. He is dead."

I was utterly stunned; it had not seemed to me that any wound
could be mortal to him.

"And the queen, Clarence?"

"She is a nun, in Almesbury."

"What changes! and in such a short while. It is inconceivable. What next, I wonder?"

"I can tell you what next."

"Well?"

"Stake our lives and stand by them!"

"What do you mean by that?"

"The Church is master, now. The Interdict included you with Mordred; it is not to be removed while you remain alive. The clans are gathering. The Church has gathered all the knights that are left alive, and as soon as you are discovered we shall have business on our hands."

"Stuff! With our deadly scientific war-material; with our hosts of trained—"

"Save your breath—we haven't sixty faithful left!"

"What are you saying? Our schools, our colleges, our vast workshops, our—"

"When those knights come, those establishments will empty themselves and go over to the enemy. Did you think you had educated the superstition out of those people?"

"I certainly did think it."

"Well, then, you may unthink it. They stood every strain easily—until the Interdict. Since then, they merely put on a bold outside—at heart they are quaking. Make up your mind to it—when the armies come, the mask will fall."

"It's hard news. We are lost. They will turn our own science against us."

"No they won't."

"Why?"

"Because I and a handful of the faithful have blocked that game. I'll tell you what I've done, and what moved me to it. Smart as you are, the Church was smarter. It was the Church that sent you cruising—through her servants the doctors."

"Clarence!"

"It is the truth. I know it. Every officer of your ship was the Church's picked servant, and so was every man of the crew."

"Oh, come!"

"It is just as I tell you. I did not find out these things at once, but I found them out finally. Did you send me verbal information, by the commander of the ship, to the effect that upon his return to you, with supplies, you were going to leave Cadiz—"

"Cadiz! I haven't been at Cadiz at all!"

"—going to leave Cadiz and cruise in distant seas indefinitely, for the health of your family? Did you send me that word?"

"Of course not. I would have written, wouldn't I?"

"Naturally. I was troubled and suspicious. When the commander sailed again I managed to ship a spy with him. I have never heard of vessel or spy since. I gave myself two weeks to hear from you in. Then

I resolved to send a ship to Cadiz. There was a reason why I didn't."

"What was that?"

"Our navy had suddenly and mysteriously disappeared! Also as suddenly and as mysteriously, the railway and telegraph and telephone service ceased, the men all deserted, poles were cut down, the Church laid a ban upon the electric light! I had to be up and doing—and straight off. Your life was safe—nobody in these kingdoms but Merlin would venture to touch such a magician as you without ten thousand men at his back—I had nothing to think of but how to put preparations in the best trim against your coming. I felt safe myself—nobody would be anxious to touch a pet of yours. So this is what I did. From our various works I selected all the men—boys I mean—whose faithfulness under whatsoever pressure I could swear to, and I called them together secretly and gave them their instructions. There are fifty-two of them; none younger than fourteen, and none above seventeen years old."

"Why did you select boys?"

"Because all the others were born in an atmosphere of superstition and reared in it. It is in their blood and bones. We imagined we had educated it out of them; they thought so, too; the Interdict woke them up like a thunderclap! It revealed them to themselves, and it revealed them to me, too. With boys it was different. Such as have been under our training from seven to ten years have had no acquaintance with the Church's terrors, and it was among these that I found my fifty-two. As a next move, I paid a private visit to that old cave of Merlin's—not the small one—the big one—"

"Yes, the one where we secretly established our first great electric plant when I was projecting a miracle."

"Just so. And as that miracle hadn't become necessary then, I thought it might be a good idea to utilize the plant now. I've provisioned the cave for a siege—"

"A good idea, a first-rate idea."

"I think so. I placed four of my boys there as a guard—inside, and out of sight. Nobody was to be hurt—while outside; but any attempt to enter—well, we said just let anybody try it! Then I went out into the hills and uncovered and cut the secret wires which connected your bedroom with the wires that go to the dynamite deposits under all our vast factories, mills, workshops, magazines, etc., and about midnight I and my boys turned out and connected that wire with the cave, and nobody but you and I suspects where the other end of it goes to. We laid it under ground, of course, and it was all finished in a couple of hours or so. We sha'n't have to leave our fortress, now, when we want to blow up our civilization."

"It was the right move—and the natural one; a military necessity, in the changed condition ot things. Well, what changes *have* come! We expected to be besieged in the palace some time or other, but—

however, go on."

"Next, we built a wire fence."

"Wire fence?"

"Yes. You dropped the hint of it yourself, two or three years ago."

"Oh, I remember—the time the Church tried her strength against us the first time, and presently thought it wise to wait for a hopefuler season. Well, how have you arranged the fence?"

"I start twelve immensely strong wires—naked, not insulated— from a big dynamo in the cave—dynamo with no brushes except a positive and a negative one—"

"Yes, that's right."

"The wires go out from the cave and fence in a circle of level ground a hundred yards in diameter; they make twelve independent fences, ten feet apart—that is to say, twelve circles within circles— and their ends come into the cave again."

"Right; go on."

"The fences are fastened to heavy oaken posts only three feet apart, and these posts are sunk five feet in the ground."

"That is good and strong."

"Yes. The wires have no ground-connection outside of the cave. They go out from the positive brush of the dynamo; there is a ground-connection through the negative brush; the other ends of the wire return to the cave, and each is grounded independently."

"No-no, that won't do!"

"Why?"

"It's too expensive—uses up force for nothing. You don't want any ground-connection except the one through the negative brush. The other end of every wire must be brought back into the cave and fastened independently, and *without* any ground-connection. Now, then, observe the economy of it. A cavalry charge hurls itself against the fence; you are using no power, you are spending no money, for there is only one ground-connection till those horses come against the wire; the moment they touch it they form a connection with the negative brush *through the ground,* and drop dead. Don't you see?—you are using no energy until it is needed; your lightning is there, and ready, like a load in a gun; but it isn't costing you a cent till you touch it off. Oh, yes, the single ground-connection—"

"Of course! I don't know how I overlooked that. It's not only cheaper, but it's more effectual than the other way, for if wires break or get tangled, no harm is done."

"No, especially if we have a tell-tale in the cave and disconnect the broken wire. Well, go on. The gatlings?"

"Yes—that's arranged. In the centre of the inner circle, on a spacious platform six feet high, I've grouped a battery of thirteen gatling guns, and provided plenty of ammunition."

"That's it. They command every approach, and when the Church's knights arrive, there's going to be music. The brow of the precipice over the cave—"

"I've got a wire fence there, and a gatling. They won't drop any rocks down on us."

"Well, and the glass-cylinder dynamite torpedoes?"

"That's attended to. It's the prettiest garden that was ever planted. It's a belt forty feet wide, and goes around the other fence— distance between it and the fence one hundred yards—kind of neutral ground, that space is. There isn't a single square yard of that whole belt but is equipped with a torpedo. We laid them on the surface of the ground, and sprinkled a layer of sand over them. It's an innocent looking garden, but you let a man start in to hoe it once, and you'll see."

"You tested the torpedoes?"

"Well, I was going to, but—"

"But what? Why, it's an immense oversight not to apply a—"

"Test? Yes, I know; but they're all right; I laid a few in the public road beyond our lines and they've been tested."

"Oh, that alters the case. Who did it?"

"A Church committee."

"How kind!"

"Yes. They came to command us to make submission. You see they didn't really come to test the torpedoes; that was merely an incident."

"Did the committee make a report?"

"Yes, they made one. You could have heard it a mile."

"Unanimous?"

"That was the nature of it. After that I put up some signs, for the protection of future committees, and we have had no intruders since."

"Clarence, you've done a world of work, and done it perfectly."

"We had plenty of time for it; there wasn't any occasion for hurry."

We sat silent awhile, thinking. Then my mind was made up, and I said:

"Yes, everything is ready; everything is ship-shape, no detail is wanting. I know what to do, now."

"So do I: sit down and wait."

"No, *sir!* rise up and *strike!*"

"Do you mean it?"

"Yes, indeed! The *de*fensive isn't in my line, and the *of*fensive is. That is, when I hold a fair hand—two-thirds as good a hand as the enemy. Oh, yes, we'll rise up and strike; that's our game."

"A hundred to one, you are right. When does the performance begin?"

"*Now!* We'll proclaim the Republic."

"Well, that *will* precipitate things, sure enough!"

"It will make them buzz, *I* tell you! England will be a hornet's nest before noon to-morrow, if the Church's hand hasn't lost its cunning—and we know it hasn't. Now you write and I'll dictate—thus:

"PROCLAMATION

"BE IT KNOWN UNTO ALL. Whereas the king having died and left no heir, it becomes my duty to continue the executive authority vested in me, until a government shall have been created and set in motion. The monarchy has lapsed, it no longer exists. By consequence, all political power has reverted to its original source, the people of the nation. With the monarchy, its several adjuncts died also; wherefore there is no longer a nobility, no longer a privileged class, no longer an Established Church: all men are become exactly equal, they are upon one common level, and religion is free. *A Republic is hereby proclaimed,* as being the natural estate of a nation when other authority has ceased. It is the duty of the British people to meet together immediately, and by their votes elect representatives and deliver into their hands the government."

I signed it "The Boss," and dated it from Merlin's Cave. Clarence said:

"Why, that tells where we are, and invites them to call right away."

"That is the idea. We *strike*—by the Proclamation—then it's their innings. Now have the thing set up and printed and posted, right off; that is, give the order; then, if you've got a couple of bicycles handy at the foot of the hill, ho for Merlin's Cave!"

"I shall be ready in ten minutes. What a cyclone there is going to be to-morrow when this piece of paper gets to work! . . . . . It's a pleasant old palace, this is; I wonder if we shall ever again—but never mind about that."

CHAPTER XLIII

THE BATTLE OF THE SAND-BELT

In Merlin's Cave—Clarence and I and fifty-two fresh, bright, well-educated, clean-minded young British boys. At dawn I sent an order to the factories and to all our great works to stop operations and remove all life to a safe distance, as everything was going to be blown up by secret mines, *"and no telling at what moment— therefore, vacate at once."* These people knew me, and had confidence in my word. They would clear out without waiting to part their hair, and I could take my own time about dating the explosion. You couldn't hire one of them to go back during the century, if the explosion was still impending.

We has a week of waiting. It was not dull for me, because I was

writing all the time. During the first three days, I finished turning
my old diary into this narrative form; it only required a chapter or so
to bring it down to date. The rest of the week I took up in writing
letters to my wife. It was always my habit to write to Sandy every day,
whenever we were separate, and now I kept up the habit for the love
of it, and of her, though I couldn't do anything with the letters, of
course, after I had written them. But it put in the time, you see, and
was almost like talking; it was almost as if I was saying, "Sandy, if
you and Hello-Central were here in the cave, instead of only your
photographs, what good times we could have!" And then, you know,
I could imagine the baby goo-gooing something out in reply, with its
fists in its mouth and itself stretched across its mother's lap on its
back, and she a-laughing and admiring and worshipping, and now
and then tickling under the baby's chin to set it cackling, and then
maybe throwing in a word of answer to me herself—and so on and
so on—well, don't you know, I could sit there in the cave with my
pen, and keep it up, that way, by the hour with them. Why, it was
almost like having us all together again.

I had spies out, every night, of course, to get news. Every report
made things look more and more impressive. The hosts were
gathering, gathering; down all the roads and paths of England the
knights were riding, and priests rode with them, to hearten these
original Crusaders, this being the Church's war. All the nobilities,
big and little, were on their way, and all the gentry. This was all as
was expected. We should thin out this sort of folk to such a degree
that the people would have nothing to do but just step to the front
with their republic and—

Ah, what a donkey I was! Toward the end of the week I began to
get this large and disenchanting fact through my head: that the mass
of the nation had swung their caps and shouted for the republic for
about one day, and there an end! The Church, the nobles, and the
gentry then turned one grand, all-disapproving frown upon them
and shrivelled them into sheep! From that moment the sheep had
begun to gather to the fold—that is to say, the camps—and offer
their valueless lives and their valuable wool to the "righteous cause."
Why, even the very men who had lately been slaves were in the
"righteous cause," and glorifying it, praying for it, sentimentally
slabbering over it, just like all the other commoners. Imagine such
human muck as this; conceive of this folly!

Yes, it was now "Death to the Republic!" everywhere—not a
dissenting voice. All England was marching against us! Truly this
was more than I had bargained for.

I watched my fifty-two boys narrowly; watched their faces, their
walk, their unconscious attitudes: for all these are a language—
a language given us purposely that it may betray us in times of
emergency, when we have secrets which we want to keep. I knew that
that thought would keep saying itself over and over again in their

minds and hearts, *All England is marching against us!* and ever
more strenuously imploring attention with each repetition, ever
more sharply realizing itself to their imaginations, until even in their
sleep they would find no rest from it, but hear the vague and flitting
creatures of their dreams say, *All England—*ALL ENGLAND!—*is
marching against you!* I knew all this would happen; I knew that
ultimately the pressure would become so great that it would compel
utterance; therefore, I must be ready with an answer at that time—
an answer well chosen and tranquillizing.

I was right. The time came. They *had* to speak. Poor lads, it was
pitiful to see, they were so pale, so worn, so troubled. At first their
spokesman could hardly find voice or words; but he presently got
both. This is what he said—and he put it in the neat modern English
taught him in my schools:

"We have tried to forget what we are—English boys! We have
tried to put reason before sentiment, duty before love; our minds
approve, but our hearts reproach us. While apparently it was only
the nobility, only the gentry, only the twenty-five or thirty thousand
knights left alive out of the late wars, we were of one mind, and
undisturbed by any troubling doubt; each and every one of these
fifty-two lads who stand here before you, said, 'They have chosen—
it is their affair.' But think!—the matter is altered—*all England is
marching against us!* Oh, sir, consider!—reflect!—these people are
our people, they are bone of our bone, flesh of our flesh, we love
them—do not ask us to destroy our nation!"

Well, it shows the value of looking ahead, and being ready for a
thing when it happens. If I hadn't foreseen this thing and been fixed,
that boy would have had me!—I couldn't have said a word. But I
was fixed. I said:

"My boys, your hearts are in the right place, you have thought
the worthy thought, you have done the worthy thing. You are English
boys, you will remain English boys, and you will keep that name
unsmirched. Give yourselves no further concern, let your minds be
at peace. Consider this: while all England *is* marching against us,
who is in the van? Who, by the commonest rules of war, will march
in the front? Answer me."

"The mounted host of mailed knights."

"True. They are 30,000 strong. Acres deep, they will march. Now,
observe: none but *they* will ever strike the sand-belt. Then there will
be an episode! Immediately after, the civilian multitude in the rear
will retire, to meet business engagements elsewhere. None but nobles
and gentry are knights, and *none but these* will remain to dance to
our music after that episode. It is absolutely true that we shall have
to fight nobody but these thirty thousand knights. Now speak, and
it shall be as you decide. Shall we avoid the battle, retire from the
field?"

"NO!!!"

The shout was unanimous and hearty.

"Are you—are you—well, afraid of these thirty thousand knights?"

That joke brought out a good laugh, the boys' troubles vanished away, and they went gaily to their posts. Ah, they were a darling fifty-two! As pretty as girls, too.

I was ready for the enemy, now. Let the approaching big day come along—it would find us on deck.

The big day arrived on time. At dawn the sentry on watch in the corral came into the cave and reported a moving black mass under the horizon, and a faint sound which he thought to be military music. Breakfast was just ready; we sat down and ate it.

This over, I made the boys a little speech, and then sent out a detail to man the battery, with Clarence in command of it.

The sun rose presently and sent its unobstructed splendors over the land, and we saw a prodigious host moving slowly toward us, with the steady drift and aligned front of a wave of the sea. Nearer and nearer it came, and more and more sublimely imposing became its aspect; yes, all England was there, apparently. Soon we could see the innumerable banners fluttering, and then the sun struck the sea of armor and set it all aflash. Yes, it was a fine sight; I hadn't ever seen anything to beat it.

At last we could make out details. All the front ranks, no telling how many acres deep, were horsemen—plumed knights in armor. Suddenly we heard the blare of trumpets; the slow walk burst into a gallop, and then—well, it was wonderful to see! Down swept that vast horses-shoe wave—it approached the sand-belt—my breath stood still; nearer, nearer—the strip of green turf beyond the yellow belt grew narrow—narrower still—became a mere ribbon in front of the horses—then disappeared under their hoofs. Great Scott! Why, the whole front of that host shot into the sky with a thunder-crash, and became a whirling tempest of rags and fragments; and along the ground lay a thick wall of smoke that hid what was left of the multitude from our sight.

Time for the second step in the plan of campaign! I touched a button, and shook the bones of England loose from her spine!

In that explosion all our noble civilization-factories went up in the air and disappeared from the earth. It was a pity, but it was necessary. We could not afford to let the enemy turn our own weapons against us.

Now ensued one of the dullest quarter-hours I had ever endured. We waited in a silent solitude enclosed by our circles of wire, and by a circle of heavy smoke outside of these. We couldn't see over the wall of smoke, and we couldn't see through it. But at last it began to to shred away lazily, and by the end of another quarter-hour the land was clear and our curiosity was enabled to satisfy itself. No living creature was in sight! We now perceived that additions had been

made to our defences. The dynamite had dug a ditch more than a
hundred feet wide, all around us, and cast up an embankment some
twenty-five feet high on both borders of it. As to destruction of life,
it was amazing. Moreover, it was beyond estimate. Of course we
could not *count* the dead, because they did not exist as individuals,
but merely as homogeneous protoplasm, with alloys or iron and
buttons.

No life was in sight, but necessarily there must have been some
wounded in the rear ranks, who were carried off the field under
cover of the wall of smoke; there would be sickness among the
others—there always is after an episode like that. But there would be
no reinforcements; this was the last stand of the chivalry of England;
it was all that was left of the order, after the recent annihilating
wars. So I felt quite safe in believing that the utmost force that could
for the future be brought against us would be but small; that is, of
knights. I therefore issued a congratulatory proclamation to my
army in these words:

SOLDIERS, CHAMPIONS OF HUMAN LIBERTY AND EQUALITY: Your General
congratulates you! In the pride of his strength and the vanity of his renown,
an arrogant enemy came against you. You were ready. The conflict was
brief; on your side, glorious. This mighty victory having been achieved
utterly without loss, stands without example in history. So long as the
planets shall continue to move in their orbits, the BATTLE OF THE SAND-
BELT will not perish out of the memories of men.   THE BOSS.

I read it well, and the applause I got was very gratifying to me. I
then wound up with these remarks:

"The war with the English nation, as a nation, is at an end. The
nation has retired from the field and the war. Before it can be
persuaded to return, war will have ceased. This campaign is the only
one that is going to be fought. It will be brief—the briefest in history.
Also the most destructive to life, considered from the standpoint of
proportion of casualties to numbers engaged. We are done with the
nation; henceforth we deal only with the knights. English knights
can be killed, but they cannot be conquered. We know what is before
us. While one of these men remains alive, our task is not finished,
the war is not ended. We will kill them all." [Loud and long
continued applause.]

I picketed the great embankments thrown up around our lines by
the dynamite explosion—merely a lookout of a couple of boys to
announce the enemy when he should appear again.

Next, I sent an engineer and forty men to a point just beyond our
lines on the south, to turn a mountain brook that was there, and
bring it within our lines and under our command, arranging it in
such a way that I could make instant use of it in an emergency. The
forty men were divided into two shifts of twenty each, and were to

relieve each other every two hours. In ten hours the work was accomplished.

It was nightfall, now, and I withdrew my pickets. The one who had had the northern outlook reported a camp in sight, but visible with the glass only. He also reported that a few knights had been feeling their way toward us, and had driven some cattle across our lines, but that the knights themselves had not come very near. That was what I had been expecting. They were feeling us, you see; they wanted to know if we were going to play that red terror on them again. They would grow bolder in the night, perhaps. I believed I knew what project they would attempt, because it was plainly the thing I would attempt myself if I were in their places and as ignorant as they were. I mentioned it to Clarence.

"I think you are right." said he; "it is the obvious thing for them to try."

"Well, then," I said, "if they do it they are doomed."

"Certainly."

"They won't have the slightest show in the world."

"Of course they won't."

"It's dreadful, Clarence. It seems an awful pity."

The thing disturbed me so, that I couldn't get any peace of mind for thinking of it and worrying over it. So, at last, to quiet my conscience, I framed this message to the knights:

TO THE HONORABLE THE COMMANDER OF THE INSURGENT CHIVALRY OF ENGLAND: You fight in vain. We know your strength—if one may call it by that name. We know that at the utmost you cannot bring against us above five and twenty thousand knights. Therefore, you have no chance—none whatever. Reflect: we are well equipped, well fortified, we number 54. Fifty-four what? Men? No, *minds*—the capablest in the world: a force against which mere animal might may no more hope to prevail than may the idle waves of the sea hope to prevail against the granite barriers of England. Be advised. We offer you your lives; for the sake of your families, do not reject the gift. We offer you this chance, and it is the last: throw down your arms; surrender unconditionally to the Republic, and all will be forgiven.

                            (Signed).   THE BOSS.

I read it to Clarence, and said I proposed to send it by a flag of truce. He laughed the sarcastic laugh he was born with, and said:

"Somehow it seems impossible for you to ever fully realize what these nobilities are. Now let us save a little time and trouble. Consider me the commander of the knights yonder. Now then, you are the flag of truce; approach and deliver me your message, and I will give you your answer."

I humored the idea. I came forward under an imaginary guard of the enemy's soldiers, produced my paper, and read it through. For answer, Clarence struck the paper out of my hand, pursed up a scornful lip and said with lofty disdain—

"Dismember me this animal, and return him in a basket to the base-born knave who sent him; other answer have I none!"

How empty is theory in presence of fact! And this was just fact, and nothing else. It was the thing that would have happened, there was no getting around that. I tore up the paper and granted my mistimed sentimentalities a permanent rest.

Then, to business. I tested the electric signals from the gatling platform to the cave, and made sure that they were all right; I tested and retested those which commanded the fences—these were signals whereby I could break and renew the electric current in each fence independently of the others, at will. I placed the brook-connection under the guard and authority of three of my best boys, who would alternate in two-hour watches all night and promptly obey my signal, if I should have occasion to give it—three revolver-shots in quick succession. Sentry-duty was discarded for the night, and the corral left empty of life; I ordered that quiet be maintained in the cave, and the electric lights turned down to a glimmer.

As soon as it was good and dark, I shut off the current from all of the fences, and then groped my way out to the embankment bordering our side of the great dynamite ditch. I crept to the top of it and lay there on the slant of the muck to watch. But it was too dark to see anything. As for sounds, there were none. The stillness was death-like. True, there were the usual night-sounds of the country— the whir of night-birds, the buzzing of insects, the barking of distant dogs, the mellow lowing of far-off kine—but these didn't seem to break the stillness, they only intensified it, and added a grewsome melancholy to it into the bargain.

I presently gave up looking, the night shut down so black, but I kept my ears strained to catch the least suspicious sound, for I judged I had only to wait and I shouldn't be disappointed. However, I had to wait a long time. At last I caught what you may call indistinct glimpses of sound—dulled metallic sound. I pricked up my ears, then, and held my breath, for this was the sort of thing I had been waiting for. This sound thickened, and approached—from toward the north. Presently I heard it at my own level—the ridge-top of the opposite embankment, a hundred feet or more away. Then I seemed to see a row of black dots appear along that ridge—human heads? I couldn't tell; it mightn't by anything at all; you can't depend on your eyes when your imagination is out of focus. However, the question was soon settled. I heard that metallic noise descending into the great ditch. It augmented fast, it spread all along, and it unmistakably furnished me this fact: an armed host was taking up its quarters in the ditch. Yes, these people were arranging a little surprise for us. We could expect entertainment about dawn, possibly earlier.

I groped my way back to the corral, now; I had seen enough. I went to the platform and signalled to turn the current onto the two inner fences. Then I went into the cave, and found everything satisfactory there—nobody awake but the working-watch. I woke Clarence and told him the great ditch was filling up with men, and that I believed all the knights were coming for us in a body. It was my notion that as soon as dawn approached we could expect the ditch's ambuscaded thousands to swarm up over the embankment and make an assault, and be followed immediately by the rest of their army.

Clarence said:

"They will be wanting to send a scout or two in the dark to make preliminary observations. Why not take the lightning off the outer fences, and give them a chance?"

"I've already done it, Clarence. Did you ever know me to be inhospitable?"

"No, you are a good heart. I want to go and—"

"Be a reception committee? I will go, too."

We crossed the corral and lay down together between the two inside fences. Even the dim light of the cave had disordered our eyesight somewhat, but the focus straightway began to regulate itself and soon it was adjusted for present circumstances. We had had to feel our way before, but we could make out to see the fence posts now. We started a whispered conversation, but suddenly Clarence broke off and said:

"What is that?"

"What is what?"

"That thing yonder?"

"What thing—where?"

"There beyond you a little piece—a dark something—a dull shape of some kind—against the second fence."

I gazed and he gazed. I said:

"Could it be a man, Clarence?"

"No, I think not. If you notice, it looks a lit—why, it *is* a man!—leaning on the fence."

"I certainly believe it is; let us go and see."

We crept along on our hands and knees until we were pretty close, and then looked up. Yes, it was a man—a dim great figure in armor, standing erect, with both hands on the upper wire—and of course there was a smell of burning flesh. Poor fellow, dead as a door-nail, and never knew what hurt him. He stood there like a statue—no motion about him, except that his plumes swished about a little in the night wind. We rose up and looked in through the bars of his visor, but couldn't make out whether we knew him or not—features too dim and shadowed.

We heard muffled sounds approaching, and we sank down to the ground where we were. We made out another knight vaguely; he was coming very stealthily, and feeling his way. He was near enough, now, for us to see him put out a hand, find an upper wire, then bend and step under it and over the lower one. Now he arrived at the first knight—and started slightly when he discovered him. He stood a moment—no doubt wondering why the other one didn't move on; then he said, in a low voice, "Why dreamest thou here, good Sir Mar—" then he laid his hand on the corpse's shoulder—and just uttered a little soft moan and sunk down dead. Killed by a dead man, you see—killed by a dead friend, in fact. There was something awful about it.

These early birds came scattering along after each other, about one every five minutes in our vicinity, during half an hour. They brought no armor of offence but their swords; as a rule they carried the sword ready in the hand, and put it forward and found the wires with it. We would now and then see a blue spark when the knight that caused it was so far away as to be invisible to us; but we knew what had happened, all the same; poor fellow, he had touched a charged wire with his sword and been elected. We had brief intervals of grim stillness, interrupted with piteous regularity by the clash made by the falling of an iron-clad; and this sort of thing was going on, right along, and was very creepy, there in the dark and lonesomeness.

We concluded to make a tour between the inner fences. We elected to walk upright, for convenience sake; we argued that if discerned, we should be taken for friends rather than enemies, and in any case we should be out of reach of swords, and these gentry did not seem to have any spears along. Well, it was a curious trip. Everywhere dead men were lying outside the second fence—not plainly visible, but still visible; and we counted fifteen of those pathetic statues—dead knights standing with their hands on the upper wire.

One thing seemed to be sufficiently demonstrated: our current was so tremendous that it killed before the victim could cry out. Pretty soon we detected a muffled and heavy sound, and next moment we guessed what it was. It was a surprise in force coming! I whispered Clarence to go and wake the army, and notify it to wait in silence in the cave for further orders. He was soon back, and we stood by the inner fence and watched the silent lightning do its awful work upon that swarming host. One could make out but little of detail; but he could note that a black mass was piling itself up beyond the second fence. That swelling bulk was dead men! Our camp was enclosed with a solid wall of the dead—a bulwark, a breastwork, of corpses, you may say. One terrible thing about this thing was the absence of human voices; there were no cheers, no war cries: being intent upon a surprise, these men moved as noiselessly as they could; and always when the front rank was near enough to their goal to make it proper for them to begin to get a shout ready, of course they struck the fatal line and went down without testifying.

I sent a current through the third fence, now; and almost immediately through the fourth and fifth, so quickly were the gaps filled up. I believed the time was come, now, for my climax; I believed that that whole army was in our trap. Anyway, it was high time to find out. So I touched a button and set fifty electric suns aflame on the top of our precipice.

Land, what a sight! We were enclosed in three walls of dead men! All the other fences were pretty nearly filled with the living, who were stealthily working their way forward through the wires. The sudden glare paralyzed this host, petrified them, you may say, with astonishment; there was just one instant for me to utilize their immobility in, and I didn't lose the chance. You see, in another instant they would have recovered their faculties, then they'd have burst into a cheer and made a rush, and my wires would have gone down before it; but that lost instant lost them their opportunity forever; while even that slight fragment of time was still unspent, I shot the current through all the fences and struck the whole host dead in their tracks! *There* was a groan you could *hear!* It voiced the death-pang of eleven thousand men. It swelled out on the night with awful pathos.

A glance showed that the rest of the enemy—perhaps ten thousand strong—were between us and the encircling ditch, and pressing forward to the assault. Consequently we had them *all!* and had them past help. Time for the last act of the tragedy. I fired the three appointed revolver shots—which meant:

"Turn on the water!"

There was a sudden rush and roar, and in a minute the mountain brook was raging through the big ditch and creating a river a hundred feet wide and twenty-five deep.

"Stand to your guns, men! Open fire!"

The thirteen gatlings began to vomit death into the fated ten thousand. They halted, they stood their ground a moment against that withering deluge of fire, then they broke, faced about and swept toward the ditch like chaff before a gale. A full fourth part of their force never reached the top of the lofty embankment; the three-fourths reached it and plunged over—to death by drowning.

Within ten short minutes after we had opened fire, armed resistance was totally annihilated, the campaign was ended, we fifty-four were masters of England! Twenty-five thousand men lay dead around us.

But how treacherous is fortune! In a little while—say an hour—happened a thing, by my own fault, which—but I have no heart to write that. Let the record end here.

CHAPTER XLIV

A POSTSCRIPT BY CLARENCE

I Clarence, must write it for him. He proposed that we two go out and see if any help could be afforded the wounded. I was strenuous against the project. I said that if there were many, we could do but little for them; and it would not be wise for us to trust ourselves among them, anyway. But he could seldom be turned from a purpose once formed; so we shut off the electric current from the fences, took an escort along, climbed over the enclosing ramparts of dead knights, and moved out upon the field. The first wounded man who appealed for help, was sitting with his back against a dead comrade. When The Boss bent over him and spoke to him, the man recognized him and stabbed him. That knight was Sir Meliagraunce, as I found out by tearing off his helmet. He will not ask for help any more.

We carried The Boss to the cave and gave his wound, which was not very serious, the best care we could. In this service we had the help of Merlin, though we did not know it. He was disguised as a woman, and appeared to be a simple old peasant goodwife. In this disguise, with brown-stained face and smooth shaven, he had appeared a few days after Ths Boss was hurt, and offered to cook for us, saying her people had gone off to join certain new camps which the enemy were forming, and that she was starving. The Boss had been getting along very well, and had amused himself with finishing up his record.

We were glad to have this woman, for we were short handed. We were in a trap, you see—a trap of our own making. If we stayed where we were, our dead would kill us; it we moved out of our defences, we should no longer be invincible. We had conquered; in turn we were conquered. The Boss recognized this; we all recognized it. If we could go to one of those new camps and patch up some kind of terms with the enemy—yes, but The Boss could not go, and neither could I, for I was among the first that were made sick by the poisonous air bred by those dead thousands. Others were taken down, and still others. To-morrow—

To-morrow. It is here. And with it the end. About midnight I awoke, and saw that hag making curious passes in the air about The Boss's head and face, and wondered what it meant. Everybody but the dynamo-watch lay steeped in sleep; there was no sound. The woman ceased from her mysterious foolery, and started tip-toeing toward the door. I called out—

"Stop! What have you been doing?"

She halted, and said with an accent of malicious satisfaction:

"Ye were conquerors; ye are conquered! These others are perishing—you also. Ye shall all die in this place—every one— except *him.* He sleepeth, now—and shall sleep thirteen centuries.

I am Merlin!''

Then such a delirium of silly laughter overtook him that he reeled about like a drunken man, and presently fetched up against one of our wires. His mouth is spread open yet; apparently he is still laughing. I suppose the face will retain that petrified laugh until the corpse turns to dust.

The Boss has never stirred—sleeps like a stone. If he does not wake to-day we shall understand what kind of a sleep it is, and his body will then be borne to a place in one of the remote recesses of the cave where none will ever find it to desecrate it. As for the rest of us—well, it is agreed that if any one of us ever escapes alive from this place, he will write the fact here, and loyally hide this Manuscript with The Boss, our dear good chief, whose property it is, be he alive or dead.

END OF THE MANUSCRIPT

FINAL P. S. BY M. T.

The dawn was come when I laid the Manuscript aside. The rain had almost ceased, the world was gray and sad, the exhausted storm was sighing and sobbing itself to rest. I went to the stranger's room, and listened at his door, which was slightly ajar. I could hear his voice, and so I knocked. There was no answer, but I still heard the voice. I peeped in. The man lay on his back, in bed, talking brokenly but with spirit, and punctuating with his arms, which he thrashed about, restlessly, as sick people do in delirium. I slipped in softly and bent over him. His mutterings and ejaculations went on. I spoke—merely a word, to call his attention. His glassy eyes and his ashy face were alight in an instant with pleasure, gratitude, gladness, welcome:

"O, Sandy, you are come at last—how I have longed for you! Sit by me—do not leave me—never leave me again, Sandy, never again. Where is your hand?—give it me, dear, let me hold it—there—now all is well, all is peace, and I am happy again—*we* are happy again, isn't it so, Sandy? You are so dim, so vague, you are but a mist, a cloud, but you are *here*, and that is blessedness sufficient; and I have your hand; don't take it away—it is for only a little while, I shall not require it long. . . . . Was that the child? . . . .Hello-Central! . . . She doesn't answer. Asleep, perhaps? Bring her when she wakes, and let me touch her hands, her face, her hair, and tell her good-bye. . . . . . . Sandy! . . . . . Yes, you are there. I lost myself a moment, and I thought you were gone. . . Have I been sick long? it must be so; it seems months to me. And such dreams!

such strange and awful dreams, Sandy! Dreams that were as real as
reality—delirium, of course, but *so* real! Why, I thought the king
was dead, I thought you were in Gaul and couldn't get home, I
thought there was a revolution; in the fantastic frenzy of these
dreams, I thought that Clarence and I and a handful of my cadets
fought and exterminated the whole chivalry of England! But even
that was not the strangest. I seemed to be a creature out of a remote
unborn age, centuries hence, and even *that* was as real as the rest!
Yes, I seemed to have flown back out of that age into this of ours,
and then forward to it again, and was set down, a stranger and
forlorn in that strange England, with an abyss of thirteen centuries
yawning between me and you! between me and my home and my
friends! between me and all that is dear to me, all that could make
life worth the living! It was awful—awfuler than you can ever
imagine, Sandy. Ah, watch by me, Sandy—stay by me every
moment—*don't* let me go out of my mind again; death is nothing,
let it come, but not with those dreams, not with the torture of those
hideous dreams—I cannot endure *that* again. . . . .
Sandy? . . . . ."

He lay muttering incoherently some little time; then for a time he
lay silent, and apparently sinking away toward death. Presently his
fingers began to pick busily at the coverlet, and by that sign I knew
that his end was at hand. With the first suggestion of the
death-rattle in his throat he started up slightly, and seemed to listen;
then he said:

"A bugle? . . . . . It is the king! The drawbridge, there! Man the
battlements!—turn out the—"

He was getting up his last "effect;" but he never finished it.

"The Private History of a Campaign That Failed" was the basis of Twain's speech, *"An Author's Soldiering,"* given in Baltimore in 1900. It was printed as a story in Century Magazine *in 1885 and later appeared in the book* Merry Tales, *published in 1892 by C.L. Webster, New York.*

THE PRIVATE HISTORY OF A CAMPAIGN THAT FAILED

You have heard from a great many people who did something in the war; is it not fair and right that you listen a little moment to one who started out to do something in it, but didn't? Thousands entered the war, got just a taste of it, and then stepped out again permanently. These, by their very numbers, are respectable, and are therefore entitled to a sort of voice—not a loud one, but a modest one; not a boastful one, but an apologetic one. They ought not to be allowed much space among better people—people who did something. I grant that; but they ought at least to be allowed to state why they didn't do anything, and also to explain the process by which they didn't do anything. Surely this kind of light must have a sort of value.

Out West there was a good deal of confusion in men's minds during the first months of the great trouble—a good deal of unsettledness, of leaning first this way, then that, then the other way. It was hard for us to get our bearings. I call to mind an instance of this. I was piloting on the Mississippi when the news came that South Carolina had gone out of the Union on the 20th of December, 1860. My pilot mate was a New Yorker. He was strong for the Union; so was I. But he would not listen to me with any patience; my loyalty was smirched, to his eye, because my father had owned slaves. I said, in palliation of this dark fact, that I had heard my father say, some years before he died, that slavery was a great wrong, and that he would free the solitary negro he then owned if he could think it right to give away the property of the family when he was so straitened in means. My mate retorted that a mere impulse was nothing—anybody could pretend to a good impulse; and went on decrying my Unionism and libeling my ancestry. A month later the secession atmosphere had considerably thickened on the Lower

Mississippi, and I became a rebel; so did he. We were together in New Orleans the 26th of January, when Louisiana went out of the Union. He did his full share of the rebel shouting, but was bitterly opposed to letting me do mine. He said that I came of bad stock—of a father who had been willing to set slaves free. In the following summer he was piloting a Federal gunboat and shouting for the Union again, and I was in the Confederate army. I held his note for some borrowed money. He was one of the most upright men I ever knew, but he repudiated that note without hesitation because I was a rebel and the son of a man who owned slaves.

In that summer—of 1861—the first wash of the wave of war broke upon the shores of Missouri. Our State was invaded by the Union forces. They took possession of St. Louis, Jefferson Barracks, and some other points. The Governor, Claib Jackson, issued his proclamation calling out fifty thousand militia to repel the invader.

I was visiting in the small town where my boyhood had been spent —Hannibal, Marion County. Several of us got together in a secret place by night and formed ourselves into a military company. One Tom Lyman, a young fellow of a good deal of spirit but of no military experience, was made captain; I was made second lieutenant. We had no first lieutenant; I do not know why; it was long ago. There were fifteen of us. By the advice of an innocent connected with the organization we called ourselves the Marion Rangers. I do not remember that any one found fault with the name. I did not; I thought it sounded quite well. The young fellow who proposed this title was perhaps a fair sample of the kind of stuff we were made of. He was young, ignorant, good-natured, well-meaning, trivial, full of romance, and given to reading chivalric novels and singing forlorn love-ditties. He had some pathetic little nickel-plated aristocratic instincts, and detested his name, which was Dunlap; detested it, partly because it was nearly as common in that region as Smith, but mainly because it had a plebeian sound to his ear. So he tried to ennoble it by writing it in this way: d'Unlap. That contented his eye, but left his ear unsatisfied, for people gave the new name the same old pronunciation—emphasis on the front end of it. He then did the bravest thing that can be imagined—a thing to make one shiver when one remembers how the world is given to resenting shams and affectations; he began to write his name so: d'Un Lap. And he waited patiently through the long storm of mud that was flung at this work of art, and he had his reward at last; for he lived to see that name accepted, and the emphasis put where he wanted it by people who had known him all his life, and to whom the tribe of Dunlaps had been as familiar as the rain and the sunshine for forty years. So sure of victory at last is the courage that can wait. He said he had found, by consulting some ancient French chronicles, that the name was rightly and originally written d'Un Lap; and said that if it were translated into English it would mean Peterson: Lap,

Latin or Greek, he said, for stone or rock, same as the French *pierre,* that is to say, Peter; *d',* of or from; *un,* a or one; hence, d'Un Lap, of or from a stone or a Peter; that is to say, one who is the son of a stone, the son of a Peter—Peterson. Our militia company were not learned, and the explanation confused them; so they called him Peterson Dunlap. He proved useful to us in his way; he named our camps for us, and he generally struck a name that was "no slouch," as the boys said.

That is one sample of us. Another was Ed Stevens, son of the town jeweler—trim-built, handsome, graceful, neat as a cat; bright, educated, but given over entirely to fun. There was nothing serious in life to him. As far as he was concerned, this military expedition of ours was simply a holiday. I should say that about half of us looked upon it in the same way; not consciously perhaps, but unconsciously. We did not think; we were not capable of it. As for myself, I was full of unreasoning joy to be done with turning out of bed at midnight and four in the morning for a while; grateful to have a change, new scenes, new occupations, a new interest. In my thoughts that was as far as I went; I did not go into the details; as a rule, one doesn't at twenty-four.

Another sample was Smith, the blacksmith's apprentice. This vast donkey had some pluck, of a slow and sluggish nature, but a soft heart; at one time he would knock a horse down for some impropriety, and at another he would get homesick and cry. However, he had one ultimate credit to his account which some of us hadn't: he stuck to the war, and was killed in battle at last.

Jo Bowers, another sample, was a huge, good-natured, flax-headed lubber; lazy, sentimental, full of harmless brag, a grumbler by nature; an experienced, industrious, ambitious, and often quite picturesque liar, and yet not a successful one, for he had had no intelligent training, but was allowed to come up just any way. This life was serious enough to him, and seldom satisfactory. But he was a good fellow anyway, and the boys all liked him. He was made orderly sergeant; Stevens was made corporal.

These samples will answer—and they are quite fair ones. Well, this herd of cattle started for the war. What could you expect of them? They did as well as they knew how; but really what was justly to be expected of them? Nothing, I should say. That is what they did.

We waited for a dark night, for caution and secrecy were necessary; then, towards midnight, we stole in couples and from various directions to the Griffith place, beyond the town; from that point we set out together on foot. Hannibal lies at the extreme south-eastern corner of Marion County, on the Mississippi River; our objective point was the hamlet of New London, ten miles away, in Ralls County.

The first hour was all fun, all idle nonsense and laughter. But that could not be kept up. The steady trudging came to be like work;

the play had somehow oozed out of it; the stillness of the woods and the somberness of the night began to throw a depressing influence over the spirits of the boys, and presently the talking died out and each person shut himself up in his own thoughts. During the last half of the second hour nobody said a word.

Now we approached a log farmhouse where, according to report, there was a guard of five Union soldiers. Lyman called a halt; and there, in the deep gloom of the overhanging branches, he began to whisper a plan of assault upon that house, which made the gloom more depressing than it was before. It was a crucial moment; we realized, with a cold suddenness, that here was no jest—we were standing face to face with actual war. We were equal to the occasion. In our response there was no hesitation, no indecision: we said that if Lyman wanted to meddle with those soldiers, he could go ahead and do it; but if he waited for us to follow him, he would wait a long time.

Lyman urged, pleaded, tried to shame us, but it had no effect. Our course was plain, our minds were made up: we would flank the farmhouse—go out around. And that was what we did.

We struck into the woods and entered upon a rough time, stumbling over roots, getting tangled in vines, and torn by briers. At last we reached an open place in a safe region, and sat down, blown and hot, to cool off and nurse our scratches and bruises. Lyman was annoyed, but the rest of us were cheerful; we had flanked the farmhouse, we had made our first military movement, and it was a success; we had nothing to fret about, were feeling just the other way. Horse-play and laughing began again; the expedition was become a holiday frolic once more.

Then we had two more hours of dull trudging and ultimate silence and depression; then, about dawn, we straggled into New London, soiled, heel-blistered, fagged with our little march, and all of us except Stevens in a sour and raspy humor and privately down on the war. We stacked our shabby old shotguns in Colonel Ralls's barn, and then went in a body and breakfasted with that veteran of the Mexican War. Afterwards he took us to a distant meadow, and there in the shade of a tree we listened to an old-fashioned speech from him, full of gunpowder and glory, full of that adjective-piling, mixed metaphor, and windy declamation which were regarded as eloquence in that ancient time and that remote region; and then he swore us on the Bible to be faithful to the State of Missouri and drive all invaders from her soil, no matter whence they might come or under what flag they might march. This mixed us considerably, and we could not make out just what service we were embarked in; but Colonel Ralls, the practiced politician and phrase-juggler, was not similarly in doubt; he knew quite clearly that he had invested us in the cause of the Southern Confederacy. He closed the solemnities by belting around me the sword which his neighbor, Colonel Brown, had worn at Buena Vista and Molino del Rey; and he accompanied this act with another impressive blast.

Then we formed in line of battle and marched four miles to a shady and pleasant piece of woods on the border of the far-reaching expanses of a flowery prairie. It was an enchanting region for war—our kind of war.

We pierced the forest about half a mile, and took up a strong position, with some low, rocky, and wooded hills behind us, and a purling, limpid creek in front. Straightway half the command were in swimming and the other half fishing. The ass with the French name gave this position a romantic title, but it was too long, so the boys shortened and simplified it to Camp Ralls.

We occupied an old maple sugar camp, whose half-rotted troughs were still propped against the trees. A long corn-crib served for sleeping quarters for the battalion. On our left, half a mile away, were Mason's farm and house; and he was a friend to the cause. Shortly after noon the farmers began to arrive from several directions, with mules and horses for our use, and these they lent us for as long as the war might last, which they judged would be about three months. The animals were of all sizes, all colors, and all breeds. They were mainly young and frisky, and nobody in the command could stay on them long at a time; for we were town boys, and ignorant of horsemanship. The creature that fell to my share was a very small mule, and yet so quick and active that it could throw me without difficulty; and it did this whenever I got on it. Then it would bray—stretching its neck out, laying its ears back, and spreading its jaws till you could see down to its works. It was a disagreeable animal in every way. If I took it by the bridle and tried to lead it off the grounds, it would sit down and brace back, and no one could budge it. However, I was not entirely destitute of military resources, and I did presently manage to spoil this game; for I had seen many a steamboat aground in my time, and knew a trick or two which even a grounded mule would be obliged to respect. There was a well by the corn-crib; so I substituted thirty fathom of rope for the bridle, and fetched him home with the windlass.

I will anticipate here sufficiently to say that we did learn to ride, after some days' practice, but never well. We could not learn to like our animals; they were not choice ones, and most of them had annoying peculiarities of one kind or another. Stevens's horse would carry him, when he was not noticing, under the huge excrescences which form on the trunks of oak trees, and wipe him out of the saddle; in this way Stevens got several bad hurts. Sergeant Bowers's horse was very large and tall, with slim, long legs, and looked like a railroad bridge. His size enabled him to reach all about, and as far as he wanted to, with his head; so he was always biting Bowers's legs. On the march, in the sun, Bowers slept a good deal; and as soon as the horse recognized that he was asleep he would reach around and bite him on the leg. His legs were black and blue with bites. This was the only thing that could ever make him swear, but this always did; whenever his horse bit him he always swore, and of course Stevens, who laughed at everything, laughed at this, and would even get into such convulsions over it as to lose his balance and fall off his horse; and then Bowers, already irritated by the pain of the horse-bite, would resent the laughter with hard language, and there would be a quarrel; so that horse made no end of trouble and bad blood in the command.

However I will get back to where I was—our first afternoon in the sugar-camp. The sugar-troughs came very handy as horse-troughs, and we had plenty of corn to fill them with. I ordered Sergeant Bowers to feed my mule; but he said that if I reckoned he went to war to be a dry-nurse to a mule, it wouldn't take me very long to find out my mistake. I believed that this was insubordination, but I was full of uncertainties about everything military, and so I let the thing pass, and went and ordered Smith, the blacksmith's apprentice, to feed the mule; but he merely gave me a large, cold, sarcastic grin, such as an ostensibly seven-year-old horse gives you when you lift his lip and find he is fourteen, and turned his back on me. I then went to the captain, and asked if it was not right and proper and military for me to have an orderly. He said it was, but as there was only one orderly in the corps, it was but right that he himself should have Bowers on his **staff.** Bowers said he wouldn't serve on anybody's staff; and if anybody thought he could make him, let him try it. So, of course, the thing had to be dropped; there was no other way.

Next, nobody would cook; it was considered a degradation; so we had no dinner. We lazied the rest of the pleasant afternoon away, some dozing under the trees, some smoking cob-pipes and talking sweethearts and war, some playing games. By late supper-time all hands were famished; and to meet the difficulty all hands turned to, on an equal footing, and gathered wood, built fires, and cooked the meal. Afterwards everything was smooth for a while; then trouble broke out between the corporal and the sergeant, each claiming to rank the other. Nobody knew which was the higher office; so Lyman had to settle the matter by making the rank of both officers equal. The commander of an ignorant crew like that has many troubles and vexations which probably do not occur in the regular army at all. However, with the song-singing and yarn-spinning around the camp-fire, everything presently became serene again; and by and by we raked the corn down level in one end of the crib, and all went to bed on it, tying a horse to the door, so that he would neigh if any one tried to get in.[1]

We had some horsemanship drill every forenoon; then, afternoons, we rode off here and there in squads a few miles, and visited the farmers' girls, and had a youthful good time, and got an honest good dinner or supper, and then home again to camp, happy and content.

For a time life was idly delicious, it was perfect; there was nothing to mar it. Then came some farmers with an alarm one day. They said it was rumored that the enemy were advancing in our direction from over Hyde's prairie. The result was a sharp stir among us, and general consternation. It was a rude awakening from our pleasant trance. The rumor was but a rumor—nothing definite about it; so, in the confusion, we did not know which way to retreat. Lyman was for not retreating at all in these uncertain circumstances; but he found that if he tried to maintain that attitude he would fare badly, for the command were in no humor to put up with insubordination. So he yielded the point and called a council of war—to consist of himself and the three other officers; but the privates made such a fuss about being left out that we had to allow them to remain, for they were already present, and doing the most of the talking too. The question was, which way to retreat; but all were so flurried that nobody seemed to have even a guess to offer. Except Lyman. He explained in a few calm words that, inasmuch as the enemy were approaching from over Hyde's prairie, our course was simple: all we had to do was not to retreat *towards* him; any other direction would answer our needs perfectly. Everybody saw in a moment how true this was, and how wise; so Lyman got a great many compliments. It was now decided that we should fall back on Mason's farm.

It was after dark by this time, and as we could not know how soon the enemy might arrive, it did not seem best to try to take the horses and things with us; so we only took the guns and ammunition, and started at once. The route was very rough and hilly and rocky, and presently the night grew very black and rain began to fall; so we had a troublesome time of it, struggling and stumbling along in the dark; and soon some person slipped and fell, and then the next person behind stumbled over him and fell, and so did the rest, one after the other; and then Bowers came with the keg of powder in his arms, while the command were all mixed together, arms and legs, on the muddy slope; and so he fell, of course, with the keg, and this started the whole detachment down the hill in a body, and they landed in the brook at the bottom in a pile, and each that was undermost pulling the hair and scratching and biting those that were on top of him; and those that were being scratched and bitten scratching and biting the rest in their turn, and all saying they would die before they would ever go to war again if they ever got out of this brook this time, and the invader might rot for all they cared, and the country along with him—and all such talk as that, which was dismal to hear and take part in, in such smothered, low voices, and such a grisly dark place and so wet, and the enemy, maybe, coming any moment.

The keg of powder was lost, and the guns, too; so the growling and complaining continued straight along while the brigade pawed around the pasty hillside and slopped around in the brook hunting for these things; consequently we lost considerable time at this; and then we heard a sound, and held our breath and listened, and it seemed to be the enemy coming, though it could have been a cow, for it had a cough like a cow; but we did not wait, but left a couple of guns behind and struck out for Mason's again as briskly as we could scramble along in the dark. But we got lost presently among the rugged little ravines, and wasted a deal of time finding the way again, so it was after nine when we reached Mason's stile at last; and then before we could open our mouths to give the countersign several dogs came bounding over the fence, with great riot and noise, and each of them took a soldier by the slack of his trousers and began to back away with him. We could not shoot the dogs without endangering the persons they were attached to; so we had to look on helpless, at what was perhaps the most mortifying spectacle of the Civil War. There was light enough, and to spare, for the Masons had now run out on the porch with candles in their hands. The old man and his son came and undid the dogs without difficulty, all but Bowers's; but they couldn't undo his dog, they didn't know his combination; he was of the bull kind, and seemed to be set with a Yale time-lock; but they got him loose at last with some scalding water, of which Bowers got his share and returned thanks. Peterson Dunlap afterwards made up a fine name for this engagement, and also for the night march which preceded it, but both have long ago faded out of my memory.

We now went into the house, and they began to ask us a world of questions, whereby it presently came out that we did not know anything concerning who or what we were running from; so the old gentleman made himself very frank, and said we were a curious breed of soldiers, and guessed we could be depended on to end up the war in time, because no government could stand the expense of the shoe-leather we should cost it trying to follow us around. "Marion *Rangers!* good name, b'gosh!" said he. And wanted to know why we hadn't had a picket-guard at the place where the road entered the prairie, and why we hadn't sent out a scouting party to spy out the enemy and bring us an account of his strength, and so on, before jumping up and stampeding out of a strong position upon a mere rumor—and so on, and so forth, till he made us all feel shabbier than the dogs had done, not half so enthusiastically welcome. So we went to bed shamed and low-spirited; except Stevens. Soon Stevens began to devise a garment for Bowers which could be made to automatically display his battle-scars to the grateful, or conceal them from the envious, according to his occasions; but Bowers was in no humor for this, so there was a fight, and when it was over Stevens had some battle-scars of his own to think about.

Then we got a little sleep. But after all we had gone through, our activities were not over for the night; for about two o'clock in the morning we heard a shout of warning from down the lane, accompanied by a chorus from all the dogs, and in a moment everybody was up and flying around to find out what the alarm was about. The alarmist was a horseman who gave notice that a detachment of Union soldiers was on its way from Hannibal with orders to capture and hang any bands like ours which it could find, and said we had no time to lose. Farmer Mason was in a flurry this time himself. He hurried us out of the house with all haste, and sent one of his negroes with us to show us where to hide ourselves and our telltale guns among the ravines half a mile away. It was raining heavily.

We struck down the lane, then across some rocky pasture-land which offered good advantages for stumbling; consequently we were down in the mud most of the time, and every time a man went down he black-guarded the war, and the people that started it, and everybody connected with it, and gave himself the master dose of all for being so foolish as to go into it. At last we reached the wooded mouth of a ravine, and there we huddled ourselves under the streaming trees, and sent the negro back home. It was a dismal and heart-breaking time. We were like to be drowned with the rain, deafened with the howling wind and the booming thunder, and blinded by the lightning. It was, indeed, a wild night. The drenching we were getting was misery enough, but a deeper misery still was the reflection that the halter might end us before we were a day older. A death of this shameful sort had not occurred to us as being among the possibilities of war. It took the romance all out of the campaign, and turned our dreams of glory into a repulsive nightmare. As for doubting that so barbarous an order had been given, not one of us did that.

The long night wore itself out at last, and then the negro came to us with the news that the alarm had manifestly been a false one, and that breakfast would soon be ready. Straightway we were light-hearted again, and the world was bright, and life as full of hope and promise as ever—for we were young then. How long ago that was! Twenty-four years.

The mongrel child of philology named the night's refuge Camp Devastation, and no soul objected. The Masons gave us a Missouri country breakfast, in Missourian abundance, and we needed it: hot biscuits; hot "wheat bread," prettily criss-crossed in a lattice pattern on top; hot corn pone; fried chicken; bacon, coffee, eggs, milk, buttermilk, etc.; and the world may be confidently challenged to furnish the equal of such a breakfast, as it is cooked in the South.

We stayed several days at Mason's; and after all these years the memory of the dullness, and stillness, and lifelessness of that slumberous farmhouse still oppresses my spirit as with a sense of the presence of death and mourning. There was nothing to do, nothing to think about; there was no interest in life. The male part of the household were away in the fields all day, the women were busy and out of our sight; there was no sound but the plaintive wailing of a spinning-wheel, forever moaning out from some distant room—the most lonesome sound in nature, a sound steeped and sodden with homesickness and the emptiness of life. The family went to bed about dark every night, and as we were not invited to intrude any new customs we naturally followed theirs. Those nights were a hundred years long to youths accustomed to being up till twelve. We lay awake and miserable till that hour every time, and grew old and decrepit waiting through the still eternities for the clock-strikes. This was no place for town boys. So at last it was with something very like joy that we received news that the enemy were on our track again. With a new birth of the old warrior spirit we sprang to our places in line of battle and fell back on Camp Ralls.

Captain Lyman had take a hint from Mason's talk, and he now gave orders that our camp should be guarded against surprise by the posting of pickets. I was ordered to place a picket at the forks of the road in Hyde's prairie. Night shut down black and threatening. I told Sergeant Bowers to go out to that place and stay till midnight; and, just as I was expecting, he said he wouldn't do it. I tried to get others to go, but all refused. Some excused themselves on account of the weather; but the rest were frank enough to say they wouldn't go in any kind of weather. This kind of thing sounds odd now, and impossible, but there was no surprise in it at the time. On the contrary, it seemed a perfectly natural thing to do. There were scores of little camps scattered over Missouri where the same thing was happening. These camps were composed of young men who had been born and reared to a sturdy independence, and who did not know what it meant to be ordered around by Tom, Dick, and Harry, whom they had known familiarly all their lives, in the village or on the farm. It is quite within the probabilities that this same thing was happening all over the South. James Redpath recognized the justice of this assumption, and furnished the following instance in support of it. During a short stay in East Tennessee he was in a citizen colonel's tent one day talking, when a big private appeared at the door, and, without salute or other circumlocution, said to the colonel:

"Say, Jim, I'm a-goin' home for a few days."

"What for?"

"Well, I hain't b'en there for a right smart while, and I'd like to see how things is comin' on."

"How long are you going to be gone?"

" 'Bout two weeks."

"Well, don't be gone longer than that; and get back sooner if you can."

That was all, and the citizen officer resumed his conversation where the private had broken it off. This was in the first months of the war, of course. The camps in our part of Missouri were under Brigadier-General Thomas H. Harris. He was a townsman of ours, a first-rate fellow, and well liked; but we had all familiarly known him as the sole and modest-salaried operator in our telegraph office, where he had to send about one dispatch a week in ordinary times, and two when there was a rush of business; consequently, when he appeared in our midst one day, on the wing, and delivered a military command of some sort, in a large military fashion, nobody was surprised at the response which he got from the assembled soldiery:

"Oh, now, what'll you take to *don't,* Tom Harris?"

It was quite the natural thing. One might justly imagine that we were hopeless material for war. And so we seemed, in our ignorant state; but there were those among us who afterwards learned the grim trade; learned to obey like machines; became valuable soldiers; fought all through the war, and came out at the end with excellent records. One of the very boys who refused to go out on picket duty that night, and called me an ass for thinking he would expose himself to danger in such a foolhardy way, had become distinguished for intrepidity before he was a year older.

I did secure my picket that night—not by authority, but by diplomacy. I got Bowers to go by agreeing to exchange ranks with him for the time being, and go along and stand the watch with him as his subordinate. We stayed out there a couple of dreary hours in the pitchy darkness and the rain, with nothing to modify the dreariness but Bowers's monotonous growlings at the war and the weather; then we began to nod, and presently found it next to impossible to stay in the saddle; so we gave up the tedious job, and went back to the camp without waiting for the relief guard. We rode into camp without interruption or objection from anybody, and the enemy could have done the same, for there were no sentries. Everybody was asleep; at midnight there was nobody to send out another picket, so none was sent. We never tried to establish a watch at night again, as far as I remember, but we generally kept a picket out in the daytime.

In that camp the whole command slept on the corn in the big corn-crib; and there was usually a general row before morning, for the place was full of rats, and they would scramble over the boys' bodies and faces, annoying and irritating everybody; and now and then they would bite some one's toe, and the person who owned the toe would start up and magnify his English and begin to throw corn in the dark. The ears were half as heavy as bricks, and when they struck they hurt. The persons struck would respond, and inside of five minutes every man would be locked in a death-grip with his neighbor. There was a grievous deal of blood shed in the corn-crib, but this was all that was spilt while I was in the war.

No, that is not quite true. But for one circumstance it would
have been all. I will come to that now.

Our scares were frequent. Every few days rumors would come that
the enemy were approaching. In these cases we always fell back on
some other camp of ours; we never stayed where we were. But the
rumors always turned out to be false; so at last even we began to
grow indifferent to them. One night a negro was sent to our corn-
crib with the same old warning: the enemy was hovering in our
neighborhood. We all said let him hover. We resolved to stay still
and be comfortable. It was a fine warlike resolution, and no doubt
we all felt the stir of it in our veins—for a moment. We had been
having a very jolly time, that was full of horse-play and school-boy
hilarity; but that cooled down now, and presently the fast-waning
fire of forced jokes and forced laughs died out altogether, and the
company became silent. Silent and nervous. And soon uneasy—
worried—apprehensive. We had said we would stay, and we were
committed. We could have been persuaded to go, but there was
nobody brave enough to suggest it. An almost noiseless movement
presently began in the dark by a general but unvoiced impulse.
When the movement was completed each man knew that he was
not the only person who had crept to the front wall and had his eye
at a crack between the logs. No, we were all there; all there with
our hearts in our throats, and staring out towards the sugar-troughs
where the forest footpath came through. It was late, and there
was a deep woodsy stillness everywhere. There was a veiled
moonlight, which was only just strong enough to enable us to mark
the general shape of objects. Presently a muffled sound caught our
ears, and we recognized it as the hoof-beats of a horse or horses.
And right away a figure appeared in the forest path; it could have
been made of smoke, its mass had so little sharpness of outline. It
was a man on horseback, and it seemed to me that there were others
behind him. I got hold of a gun in the dark, and pushed it through
a crack between the logs, hardly knowing what I was doing, I was so
dazed with fright. Somebody said "Fire!" I pulled the trigger. I
seemed to see a hundred flashes and hear a hundred reports; then I
saw the man fall down out of the saddle. My first feeling was of
surprised gratification; my first impulse was an apprentice-
sportsman's impulse to run and pick up his game. Somebody said,
hardly audibly, "Good—we've got him!—wait for the rest." But
the rest did not come. We waited—listened—still no more came.
There was not a sound, not the whisper of a leaf; just perfect
stillness; an uncanny kind of stillness, which was all the more
uncanny on account of the damp, earthy, late-night smells now
rising and pervading it. Then, wondering, we crept stealthily out,
and approached the man. When we got to him the moon revealed
him distinctly. He was lying on his back, with his arms abroad;
his mouth was open and his chest heaving with long gasps, and his

white shirt-front was all splashed with blood. The thought shot through me that I was a murderer; that I had killed a man—a man who had never done me any harm. That was the coldest sensation that ever went through my marrow. I was down by him in a moment, helplessly stroking his forehead; and I would have given anything then—my own life freely—to make him again what he had been five minutes before. And all the boys seemed to be feeling in the same way; they hung over him, full of pitying interest, and tried all they could to help him, and said all sorts of regretful things. They had forgotten all about the enemy; they thought only of this one forlorn unit of the foe. Once my imagination persuaded me that the dying man gave me a reproachful look out of his shadowy eyes, and it seemed to me that I could rather he had stabbed me than done that. He muttered and mumbled like a dreamer in his sleep about his wife and his child; and I thought with a new despair, "This thing that I have done does not end with him; it falls upon *them* too, and they never did me any harm, any more than he."

In a little while the man was dead. He was killed in war; killed in fair and legitimate war; killed in battle, as you may say; and yet he was as sincerely mourned by the opposing force as if he had been their brother. The boys stood there a half-hour sorrowing over him, and recalling the details of the tragedy, and wondering who he might be, and if he were a spy, and saying that if it were to do over again they would not hurt him unless he attacked them first. It soon came out that mine was not the only shot fired; there were five others—a division of the guilt which was a great relief to me, since it in some degree lightened and diminished the burden I was carrying. There were six shots fired at once; but I was not in my right mind at the time, and my heated imagination had magnified my one shot into a volley.

The man was not in uniform, and was not armed. He was a stranger in the country; that was all we ever found out about him. The thought of him got to preying upon me every night; I could not get rid of it. I could not drive it away, the taking of that unoffending life seemed such a wanton thing. And it seemed an epitome of war; that all war must be just that—the killing of strangers against whom you feel no personal animosity; strangers whom, in other circumstances, you would help if you found them in trouble, and who would help you if you needed it. My campaign was spoiled. It seemed to me that I was not righty equipped for this awful business; that war was intended for men, and I for a child's nurse. I resolved to retire from this avocation of sham soldiership while I could save some remnant of my self-respect. These morbid thoughts clung to me against reason; for at bottom I did not believe I had touched that man. The law of probabilities decreed me guiltless of his blood; for in all my small experience with guns I had never hit anything I had tried to hit, and I knew I had done my best to hit him. Yet there was no solace in the thought. Against a diseased imagination demonstration goes for nothing.

The rest of my war experience was of a piece with what I have already told of it. We kept monotonously falling back upon one camp or another, and eating up the country. I marvel now at the patience of the farmers and their families. They ought to have shot us; on the contrary, they were as hospitably kind and courteous to us as if we had deserved it. In one of these camps we found Ab Grimes, an Upper Mississippi pilot, who afterwards became famous as a dare-devil rebel spy, whose career bristled with desperate adventures. The look and style of his comrades suggested that they had not come into the war to play, and their deeds made good the conjecture later. They were fine horsemen and good revolver shots; but their favorite arm was the lasso. Each had one at his pommel, and could snatch a man out of the saddle with it every time, on a full gallop, at any reasonable distance.

In another camp the chief was a fierce and profane old blacksmith of sixty, and he had furnished his twenty recruits with gigantic home-made bowie-knives, to be swung with two hands, like the *machetes* of the Isthmus. It was a grisly spectacle to see that earnest band practicing their murderous cuts and slashes under the eye of that remorseless old fanatic.

The last camp which we fell back upon was in a hollow near the village of Florida, where I was born—in Monroe County. Here we were warned one day that a Union colonel was sweeping down on us with a whole regiment at his heel. This looked decidedly serious. Our boys went apart and consulted; then we went back and told the other companies present that the war was a disappointment to us, and we were going to disband. They were getting ready themselves to fall back on some place or other, and were only waiting for General Tom Harris, who was expected to arrive at any moment; so they tried to persuade us to wait a little while, but the majority of us said no, we were accustomed to falling back, and didn't need any of Tom Harris's help; we could get along perfectly well without him—and save time, too. So about half of our fifteen, including myself, mounted and left on the instant; the others yielded to persuasion and stayed—stayed through the war.

An hour later we met General Harris on the road, with two or three people in his company—his staff, probably, but we could not tell; none of them were in uniform; uniforms had not come into vogue among us yet. Harris ordered us back; but we told him there was a Union colonel coming with a whole regiment in his wake, and it looked as if there was going to be a disturbance; so we had concluded to go home. He raged a little, but it was of no use; our minds were made up. We had done our share; had killed one man, exterminated one army, such as it was; let him go and kill the rest,

and that would end the war. I did not see that brisk young
general again until last year; then he was wearing white hair
and whiskers.

In time I came to know that Union colonel whose coming
frightened me out of the war and crippled the Southern cause to
that extent—General Grant. I came within a few hours of seeing
him when he was as unknown as I was myself; at a time when
anybody could have said, "Grant?—Ulysses S. Grant? I do not
remember hearing the name before." It seems difficult to realize
that there was once a time when such a remark could be rationally
made; but there *was,* and I was within a few miles of the place and
the occasion, too, though proceeding in the other direction.

The thoughtful will not throw this war paper of mine lightly aside
as being valueless. It has this value: it is a not unfair picture of what
went on in many and many a militia camp in the first months of the
rebellion, when the green recruits were without discipline, without
the steadying and heartening influence of trained leaders; when
all their circumstances were new and strange, and charged with
exaggerated terrors, and before the invaluable experience of actual
collision in the field had turned them from rabbits into soldiers.
If this side of the picture of that early day has not before been put
into history, then history has been to that degree incomplete, for
it had and has its rightful place there. There was more Bull Run
material scattered through the early camps of this country than
exhibited itself at Bull Run. And yet it learned its trade presently,
and helped to fight the great battles later. I could have become a
soldier myself if I had waited. I had got part of it learned; I knew
more about retreating than the man that invented retreating.

[1]It was always my impression that that was what the horse was there for, and I know that it
was also the impression of at least one other of the command, for we talked about it at the time,
and admired the military ingenuity of the device; but when I was out West, three years ago, I
was told by Mr. A. G. Fuqua, a member of our company, that the horse was his; that the leaving
him tied at the door was a matter of mere forgetfulness, and that to attribute it to intelligent
invention was to give him quite too much credit. In support of his position he called my attention
to the suggestive fact that the artifice was not employed again. I had not thought of that before.

"The £1,000,000 Bank Note" first appeared in Century Magazine *in January, 1893. It made its first appearance in book form in a collection called* The £1,000,000 Bank Note and Other New Stories, *published by C.L. Webster, New York, 1893.*

THE £1,000,000 BANK NOTE

When I was twenty-seven years old, I was a mining-broker's clerk in San Francisco, and an expert in all the details of stock traffic. I was alone in the world, and had nothing to depend upon but my wits and a clean reputation; but these were setting my feet in the road to eventual fortune, and I was content with the prospect.

My time was my own after the afternoon board, Saturdays, and I was accustomed to put it in on a little sail-boat on the bay. One day I ventured too far, and was carried out to sea. Just at nightfall, when hope was about gone, I was picked up by a small brig which was bound for London. It was a long and stormy voyage, and they made me work my passage without pay, as a common sailor. When I stepped ashore in London my clothes were ragged and shabby, and I had only a dollar in my pocket. This money fed and sheltered me twenty-four hours. During the next twenty-four I went without food and shelter.

About ten o'clock on the following morning, seedy and hungry, I was dragging myself along Portland Place, when a child that was passing, towed by a nurse-maid, tossed a luscious big pear—minus one bite—into the gutter. I stopped, of course, and fastened my desiring eye on that muddy treasure. My mouth watered for it, my stomach craved it, my whole being begged for it. But every time I made a move to get it some passing eye detected my purpose, and of course I straightened up then, and looked indifferent, and pretended that I hadn't been thinking about the pear at all. This same thing kept happening and happening, and I couldn't get the pear. I was just getting desperate enough to brave all the shame, and to seize it, when a window behind me was raised, and a gentleman spoke out of it, saying:

"Step in here, please."

I was admitted by a gorgeous flunkey, and shown into a sumptuous room where a couple of elderly gentlemen were sitting. They sent away the servant, and made me sit down. They had just finished their breakfast, and the sight of the remains of it almost overpowered me. I could hardly keep my wits together in the presence of that food, but as I was not asked to sample it, I had to bear my trouble as best I could.

Now, something had been happening there a little before, which I did not know anything about until a good many days afterwards, but I will tell you about it now. Those two old brothers had been having a pretty hot argument a couple of days before, and had ended by agreeing to decide it by a bet, which is the English way of settling everything.

You will remember that the Bank of England once issued two notes of a million pounds each, to be used for a special purpose connected with some public transaction with a foreign country. For some reason or other only one of these had been used and canceled; the other still lay in the vaults of the Bank. Well, the brothers, chatting along, happened to get to wondering what might be the fate of a perfectly honest and intelligent stranger who should be turned adrift in London without a friend, and with no money but that million-pound bank-note, and no way to account for his being in possession of it. Brother A said he would starve to death; Brother B said he wouldn't. Brother A said he couldn't offer it at a bank or anywhere else, because he would be arrested on the spot. So they went on disputing till Brother B said he would bet twenty thousand pounds that the man would live thirty days, *anyway,* on that million, and keep out of jail, too. Brother A took him up. Brother B went down to the Bank and bought that note. Just like an Englishman, you see; pluck to the backbone. Then he dictated a letter, which one of his clerks wrote out in a beautiful round hand, and then the two brothers sat at the window a whole day watching for the right man to give it to.

They saw many honest faces go by that were not intelligent enough; many that were intelligent, but not honest enough; many that were both, but the possessors were not poor enough, or, if poor enough, were not strangers. There was always a defect, until I came along; but they agreed that I filled the bill all around; so they elected me unanimously, and there I was now waiting to know why I was called in. They began to ask me questions about myself, and pretty soon they had my story. Finally they told me I would answer their purpose. I said I was sincerely glad, and asked what it was. Then one of them handed me an envelope, and said I would find the explanation inside. I was going to open it, but he said no; take it to my lodgings, and look it over carefully, and not be hasty or rash. I was puzzled, and wanted to discuss the matter a little further, but they didn't; so I took my leave, feeling hurt and insulted to be made the butt of what was apparently some kind of a practical joke, and yet obliged to put up with it, not being in circumstances to resent affronts from rich and strong folk.

I would have picked up the pear now and eaten it before all the world, but it was gone; so I had lost that by this unlucky business, and the thought of it did not soften my feeling towards those men. As soon as I was out of sight of that house I opened my envelope, and saw that it contained money! My opinion of those people changed, I can tell you! I lost not a moment, but shoved note and money into my vest pocket, and broke for the nearest cheap eating house. Well, how I did eat! When at last I couldn't hold any more, I took out my money and unfolded it, took one glimpse and nearly fainted. Five millions of dollars! Why, it made my head swim.

I must have sat there stunned and blinking at the note as much as a minute before I came rightly to myself again. The first thing I noticed, then, was the landlord. His eye was on the note, and he was petrified. He was worshipping, with all his body and soul, but he looked as if he couldn't stir hand or foot. I took my cue in a moment, and did the only rational thing there was to do. I reached the note towards him, and said, carelessly:

"Give me the change, please."

Then he was restored to his normal condition, and made a thousand apologies for not being able to break the bill, and I couldn't get him to touch it. He wanted to look at it, and keep on looking at it; he couldn't seem to get enough of it to quench the thirst of his eye, but he shrank from touching it as if it had been something too sacred for poor common clay to handle. I said:

"I am sorry if it is an inconvenience, but I must insist. Please change it; I haven't anything else."

But he said that wasn't any matter; he was quite willing to let the trifle stand over till another time. I said I might not be in his neighborhood again for a good while; but he said it was of no consequence, he could wait, and, moreover, I could have anything I wanted, any time I chose, and let the account run as long as I pleased. He said he hoped he wasn't afraid to trust as rich a gentleman as I was, merely because I was of a merry disposition, and chose to play larks on the public in the matter of dress. By this time another customer was entering, and the landlord hinted to me to put the monster out of sight; then he bowed me all the way to the door, and I started straight for that house and those brothers, to correct the mistake which had been made before the police should hunt me up, and help me do it. I was pretty nervous; in fact, pretty badly frightened, though, of course, I was no way in fault; but I knew men well enough to know that when they find they've given a tramp a million-pound bill when they thought it was a one-pounder, they are in a frantic rage against *him* instead of quarreling with their own near-sightedness, as they ought. As I approached the house my excitement began to abate, for all was quiet there, which made me feel pretty sure the blunder was not discovered yet. I rang. The same servant appeared. I asked for those gentlemen.

"They are gone." This in the lofty, cold way of that fellow's tribe.

"Gone? Gone where?"

"On a journey."

"But whereabouts?"

"To the Continent, I think."

"The Continent?"

"Yes, sir."

"Which way—by what route?"

"I can't say, sir."

"When will they be back?"

"In a month, they said."

"A month! Oh, this is awful! Give me *some* sort of idea of how to get a word to them. It's of the last importance."

"I can't, indeed. I've no idea where they've gone, sir."

"Then I must see some member of the family."

"Family's away, too; been abroad months—in Egypt and India, I think."

"Man, there's been an immense mistake made. They'll be back before night. Will you tell them I've been here, and that I will keep coming till it's all made right, and they needn't be afraid?"

"I'll tell them, if they come back, but I am not expecting them. They said you would be here in an hour to make inquiries, but I must tell you it's all right, they'll be here on time and expect you."

So I had to give it up and go away. What a riddle it all was! I was like to lose my mind. They would be here "on time." What could that mean? Oh, the letter would explain, maybe. I had forgotten the letter; I got it out and read it. This is what it said:

"You are an intelligent and honest man, as one may see by your face. We conceive you to be poor and a stranger. Enclosed you will find a sum of money. It is lent to you for thirty days, without interest. Report at this house at the end of that time. I have a bet on you. If I win it you shall have any situation that is in my gift—any, that is, that you shall be able to prove yourself familiar with and competent to fill."

No signature, no address, no date.

Well, here was a coil to be in! You are posted on what had preceded all this, but I was not. It was just a deep, dark puzzle to me. I hadn't the least idea what the game was, nor whether harm was meant me or a kindness. I went into a park, and sat down to try to think it out, and to consider what I had best do.

At the end of an hour my reasonings had crystallized into this verdict.

Maybe those men mean me well, maybe they mean me ill; no way to decide that—let it go. They've got a game, or a scheme, or an experiment, of some kind on hand; no way to determine what it is—

let it go. There's a bet on me; no way to find out what it is—let it go. That disposes of the indeterminable quantities; the remainder of the matter is tangible, solid, and may be classed and labeled with certainty. If I ask the Bank of England to place this bill to the credit of the man it belongs to, they'll do it, for they know him, although I don't; but they will ask me how I came in possession of it, and if I tell the truth, they'll put me in the asylum, naturally, and a lie will land me in jail. The same result would follow if I tried to bank the bill anywhere or to borrow money on it. I have got to carry this immense burden around until those men come back, whether I want to or not. It is useless to me, as useless as a handful of ashes, and yet I must take care of it, and watch over it, while I beg my living. I couldn't *give* it away, if I should try, for neither honest citizen nor highwayman would accept it or meddle with it for anything. Those brothers are safe, because they can stop payment, and the Bank will make them whole; but meantime I've got to do a month's suffering without wages or profit—unless I help win that bet, whatever it may be, and get that situation that I am promised. I *should* like to get that; men of their sort have situations in their gift that are worth having.

I got to thinking a good deal about that situation. My hopes began to rise high. Without doubt the salary would be large. It would begin in a month; after that I should be all right. Pretty soon I was feeling first-rate. By this time I was tramping the streets again. The sight of a tailor-shop gave me a sharp longing to shed my rags, and to clothe myself decently once more. Could I afford it? No; I had nothing in the world but a million pounds. So I forced myself to go on by. But soon I was drifting back again. The temptation persecuted me cruelly. I must have passed that shop back and forth six times during that manful struggle. At last I gave in; I had to. I asked if they had a misfit suit that had been thrown on their hands. The fellow I spoke to nodded his head towards another fellow, and gave me no answer. I went to the indicated fellow, and he indicated another fellow with *his* head, and no words. I went to him, and he said:

" 'Tend to you presently."

I waited till he was done with what he was at, then he took me into a back room, and overhauled a pile of rejected suits, and selected the rattiest one for me. I put it on. It didn't fit, and wasn't in any way attractive, but it was new, and I was anxious to have it; so I didn't find any fault, but said, with some diffidence:

"It would be an accommodation to me if you could wait some days for the money. I haven't any small change about me."

The fellow worked up a most sarcastic expression of countenance, and said:

"Oh, you haven't? Well, of course, I didn't expect it. I'd only expect gentlemen like you to carry large change."

I was nettled, and said:

"My friend, you shouldn't judge a stranger always by the clothes he wears. I am quite able to pay for this suit; I simply didn't wish to put you to the trouble of changing a large note."

He modified his style a little at that, and said, though still with something of an air:

"I didn't mean any particular harm, but as long as rebukes are going, I might say it wasn't quite your affair to jump to the conclusion that we couldn't change any note that you might happen to be carrying around. On the contrary, we *can.*"

I handed the note to him, and said:

"Oh, very well; I apologize."

He received it with a smile, one of those large smiles which goes all around over, and has folds in it, and wrinkles, and spirals, and looks like the place where you have thrown a brick in a pond; and then in the act of his taking a glimpse of the bill this smile froze solid, and turned yellow, and looked like those wavy, wormy spreads of lava which you find hardened on little levels on the side of Vesuvius. I never before saw a smile caught like that, and perpetuated. The man stood there holding the bill, and looking like that, and the proprietor hustled up to see what was the matter, and said, briskly:

"Well, what's up? what's the trouble? what's wanting?"

I said: "There isn't any trouble. I'm waiting for my change."

"Come, come; get him his change, Tod; get him his change."

Tod retorted: "Get him his change! It's easy to say, sir; but look at the bill yourself."

The proprietor took a look, gave a low, eloquent whistle, then made a dive for the pile of rejected clothing, and began to snatch it this way and that, talking all the time excitedly, and as if to himself:

"Sell an eccentric millionaire such an unspeakable suit as that! Tod's a fool—a born fool. Always doing something like this. Drives every millionaire away from this place, because he can't tell a millionaire from a tramp, and never could. Ah, here's the thing I am after. Please get those things off, sir, and throw them in the fire. Do me the favor to put on this shirt and this suit; it's just the thing, the very thing—plain, rich, modest, and just ducally nobby; made to order for a foreign prince—you may know him, sir, his Serene Highness the Hospodar of Halifax; had to leave it with us and take a mourning-suit because his mother was going to die— which she didn't. But that's all right; we can't always have things the way we—that is, the way they—there! trousers all right, they fit you to a charm, sir; now the waistcoat; aha, right again! now the coat—lord! look at that, now! Perfect—the whole thing! I never saw such a triumph in all my experience."

I expressed my satisfaction.

"Quite right, sir, quite right; it'll do for a make-shift, I'm bound to say. But wait till you see what we'll get up for you on your own measure. Come, Tod, book and pen; get at it. Length of leg, 32"— and so on. Before I could get in a word he had measured me, and was giving orders for dress-suits, morning suits, shirts, and all sorts of things. When I got a chance I said:

"But, my dear sir, I *can't* give these orders, unless you can wait indefinitely, or change the bill."

"Indefinitely! It's a weak word, sir, a weak word. Eternally— *that's* the word, sir. Tod, rush these things through, and send them to the gentleman's address without any waste of time. Let the minor customers wait. Set down the gentleman's address and—"

"I'm changing my quarters. I will drop in and leave the new address."

"Quite right, sir, quite right. One moment—let me show you out, sir. There—good day, sir, good day."

Well, don't you see what was bound to happen? I drifted naturally into buying whatever I wanted, and asking for change. Within a week I was sumptuously equipped with all needful comforts and luxuries, and was housed in an expensive private hotel in Hanover Square. I took my dinners there, but for breakfast I stuck by Harris's humble feeding house, where I had got my first meal on my million-pound bill. I was the making of Harris. The fact had gone all abroad that the foreign crank who carried million-pound bills in his vest pocket was the patron saint of the place. That was enough. From being a poor, struggling, little hand-to-mouth enterprise, it had become celebrated, and overcrowded with customers. Harris was so grateful that he forced loans upon me, and would not be denied; and so, pauper as I was, I had money to spend, and was living like the rich and the great. I judged that there was going to be a crash by and by, but I was in now and must swim across or drown. You see there was just that element of impending disaster to give a serious side, a sober side, yes, a tragic side, to a state of things which would otherwise have been purely ridiculous. In the night, in the dark, the tragedy part was always to the front, and always warning, always threatening; and so I moaned and tossed, and sleep was hard to find. But in the cheerful day-light the tragedy element faded out and disappeared, and I walked on air, and was happy to giddiness, to intoxication, you may say.

And it was natural; for I had become one of the notorieties of the metropolis of the world, and it turned my head, not just a little, but a good deal. You could not take up a newspaper, English, Scotch, or Irish, without finding in it one or more references to the "vest-pocket million-pounder" and his latest doings and sayings. At first, in these mentions, I was at the bottom of the personal-gossip column; next, I was listed above the knights, next above the baronets, next above the barons, and so on, and so on, climbing steadily, as my notoriety augmented, until I reached the highest altitude possible, and there I remained, taking precedence of all dukes not royal, and of all eccesiastics except the primate of all England. But mind, this was not fame; as yet I had achieved only notoriety. Then came the climaxing stroke—the accolade, so to speak—which in a single instant transmuted the perishable dross of notoriety into the enduring gold of fame: *Punch* caricatured me! Yes, I was a made man now; my place was established. I might be joked about still, but reverently, not hilariously, not rudely; I could be smiled at, but not laughed at. The time for that had gone by. *Punch* pictured me all a-flutter with rags, dickering with a beef-eater for the Tower of London. Well, you can imagine how it was with a young fellow who had never been taken notice of before, and now all of a sudden couldn't say a thing that wasn't taken up and repeated everywhere; couldn't stir abroad without constantly overhearing the remark flying from lip to lip, "There he goes; that's him!" couldn't take his breakfast without a crowd to look on; couldn't appear in an opera-box without concentrating there the fire of a thousand lorgnettes. Why, I just swam in glory all day long—that is the amount of it.

You know, I even kept my old suit of rags, and every now and then appeared in them, so as to have the old pleasure of buying trifles, and being insulted, and then shooting the scoffer dead with the million-pound bill. But I couldn't keep that up. The illustrated papers made the outfit so familiar that when I went out in it I was at once recognized and followed by a crowd, and if I attempted a purchase the man would offer me his whole shop on credit before I could pull my note on him.

About the tenth day of my fame I went to fulfil my duty to my flag by paying my respects to the American minister. He received me with the enthusiasm proper in my case, upbraided me for being so tardy in my duty, and said that there was only one way to get his forgiveness, and that was to take the seat at his dinner-party that night made vacant by the illness of one of his guests. I said I would, and we got to talking. It turned out that he and my father had been schoolmates in boyhood, Yale students together later, and always warm friends up to my father's death. So then he required me to put in at his house all the odd time I might have to spare, and I was very willing, of course.

In fact, I was more than willing; I was glad. When the crash should come, he might somehow be able to save me from total destruction; I didn't know how, but he might think of a way, maybe. I couldn't venture to unbosom myself to him at this late date, a thing which I would have been quick to do in the beginning of this awful career of mine in London. No, I couldn't venture it now; I was in too deep; that is, too deep for me to be risking revelations to so new a friend, though not clear beyond my depth, as *I* looked at it. Because, you see, with all my borrowing, I was carefully keeping within my means—I mean within my salary. Of course, I couldn't *know* what my salary was going to be, but I had a good enough basis for an estimate in the fact, that if I won the bet I was to have *choice* of any situation in that rich old gentleman's gift provided I was competent—and I should certainly prove competent; I hadn't any doubt about that. And as to the bet, I wasn't worrying about that; I had always been lucky. Now my estimate of the salary was six hundred to a thousand a year; say, six hundred for the first year, and so on up year by year, till I struck the upper figure by proved merit. At present I was only in debt for my first year's salary. Everybody had been trying to lend me money, but I had fought off the most of them on one pretext or another; so this indebtedness represented only £300 borrowed money, the other £300 represented my keep and my purchases. I believed my second year's salary would carry me through the rest of the month if I went on being cautious and economical, and I intended to look sharply out for that. My month ended, my employer back from his journey, I should be all right once more, for I should at once divide the two years' salary among my creditors by assignment, and get right down to my work.

It was a lovely dinner-party of fourteen. The Duke and Duchess of Shoreditch, and their daughter the Lady Anne-Grace-Eleanor-Celeste-and-so-forth-and-so-forth-de-Bohun, the Earl and Countess of Newgate, Viscount Cheapside, Lord and Lady Blatherskite, some untitled people of both sexes, the minister and his wife and daughter, and his daughter's visiting friend, an English girl of twenty-two, named Portia Langham, whom I fell in love with in two minutes, and she with me—I could see it without glasses. There was still another guest, an American—but I am a little ahead of my story. While the people were still in the drawing-room, whetting up for dinner, and coldly inspecting the late comers, the servant announced:

"Mr. Lloyd Hastings."

The moment the usual civilities were over, Hastings caught sight of me, and came straight with cordially outstretched hand; then stopped short when about to shake, and said, with an embarrassed look:

"I beg your pardon, sir, I thought I knew you."

"Why, you do know me, old fellow."

"No. Are *you* the—the—"

"Vest-pocket monster? I am, indeed. Don't be afraid to call me by my nickname; I'm used to it."

"Well, well, well, this is a surprise. Once or twice I've seen your own name coupled with the nickname, but it never occurred to me that *you* could be the Henry Adams referred to. Why, it isn't six months since you were clerking away for Blake Hopkins in Frisco on a salary, and sitting up nights on an extra allowance, helping me arrange and verify the Gould and Curry Extension papers and statistics. The idea of your being in London, and a vast millionaire, and a colossal celebrity! Why, it's the Arabian Nights come again. Man, I can't take it in at all; can't realize it; give me time to settle the whirl in my head."

"The fact is, Lloyd, you are no worse off than I am. I can't realize it myself."

"Dear me, it *is* stunning, now isn't it? Why, it's just three months to-day since we went to the Miners' restaurant—"

"No; the What Cheer."

"Right, it *was* the What Cheer; went there at two in the morning, and had a chop and coffee after a hard six-hours grind over those Extension papers, and I tried to persuade you to come to London with me, and offered to get leave of absence for you and pay all your expenses, and give you something over if I succeeded in making the sale; and you would not listen to me, said I wouldn't succeed, and you couldn't afford to lose the run of business and be no end of time getting the hang of things again when you got back home. And yet here you are. How odd it all is! How did you happen to come, and whatever *did* give you this incredible start?"

"Oh, just an accident. It's a long story—a romance, a body may say. I'll tell you all about it, but not now."

"When?"

"The end of this month."

"That's more than a fortnight yet. It's too much of a strain on a person's curiosity. Make it a week."

"I can't. You'll know why, by and by. But how's the trade getting along?"

His cheerfulness vanished like a breath, and he said with a sigh:

"You were a true prophet, Hal, a true prophet. I wish I hadn't come. I don't want to talk about it."

"But you must. You must come and stop with me to-night, when we leave here, and tell me all about it."

"Oh, may I? Are you in earnest?" and the water showed in his eyes.

"Yes; I want to hear the whole story, every word."

"I'm so grateful! Just to find a human interest once more, in some voice and in some eye, in me and affairs of mine, after what I've been through here—lord! I could go down on my knees for it!"

He gripped my hand hard, and braced up, and was all right and lively after that for the dinner—which didn't come off. No; the usual thing happened, the thing that is always happening under that vicious and aggravating English system—the matter of precedence couldn't be settled, and so there was no dinner. Englishmen always eat dinner before they go out to dinner, because *they* know the risks they are running; but nobody ever warns the stranger, and so he walks placidly into the trap. Of course, nobody was hurt this time, because we had all been to dinner, none of us being novices excepting Hastings, and he having been informed by the minister at the time that he invited him that in deference to the English custom he had not provided any dinner. Everybody took a lady and processioned down to the dining-room, because it is usual to go through the motions; but there the dispute began. The Duke of Shoreditch wanted to take precedence, and sit at the head of the table, holding that he outranked a minister who represented merely a nation and not a monarch; but I stood for my rights, and refused to yield. In the gossip column I ranked all dukes not royal, and said so, and claimed precedence of this one. It couldn't be settled, of course, struggle as we might and did, he finally (and injudiciously) trying to play birth and antiquity, and I "seeing" his Conqueror and "raising" him with Adam, whose direct posterity I was, as shown by my name, while *he* was of a collateral branch, as shown by *his*, and by his recent Norman origin; so we all processioned back to the drawing-room again and had a perpendicular lunch— plate of sardines and a strawberry, and you group yourself and stand up and eat it. Here the religion of precedence is not so strenuous; the two persons of highest rank chuck up a shilling, the one that wins has first go at his strawberry, and the loser gets the shilling. The next two chuck up, then the next two, and so on. After refreshment, tables were brought, and we all played cribbage, sixpence a game. The English never play any game for amusement. If they can't make something or lose something—they don't care which—they won't play.

We had a lovely time; certainly two of us had, Miss Langham and I. I was so bewitched with her that I couldn't count my hands if they went above a double sequence; and when I struck home I never discovered it, and started up the outside row again, and would have lost the game every time, only the girl did the same, she being in just my condition, you see; and consequently neither of us ever got out, or cared to wonder why we didn't; we only just knew we were happy, and didn't wish to know anything else, and didn't want to be interrupted. And I *told* her—I did, indeed—told her I loved her; and she—well, she blushed till her hair turned red, but she liked it; she *said* she did. Oh, there was never such an evening! Every time I pegged I put on a postscript; every time she pegged she acknowledged receipt of it, counting the hands the same. Why, I couldn't even say "Two for his heels" without adding, "*My*, how sweet you do look!" and she would say, "Fifteen two, fifteen four, fifteen six, and a pair are eight, and eight are sixteen— *do* you think so?"—peeping out aslant from under her lashes, you know, so sweet and cunning. Oh, it was just *too*-too!

Well, I was perfectly honest and square with her; told her I hadn't a cent in the world but just the million-pound note she'd heard so much talk about, and *it* didn't belong to me, and that started her curiosity; and then I talked low, and told her the whole history right from the start, and it nearly killed her laughing. What in the nation she could find to laugh about *I* couldn't see, but there it was; every half-minute some new detail would fetch her, and I would have to stop as much as a minute and a half to give her a chance to settle down again. Why, she laughed herself lame—she did, indeed; I never saw anything like it. I mean I never saw a painful story—a story of a person's troubles and worries and fears—produce just *that* kind of effect before. So I loved her all the more, seeing she could be so cheerful when there wasn't anything to be cheerful about; for I might soon need that kind of wife, you know, the way things looked. Of course, I told her we should have to wait a couple of years, till I could catch up on my salary; but she didn't mind that, only she hoped I would be as careful as possible in the matter of expenses, and not let them run the least risk of trenching on our third year's pay. Then she began to get a little worried, and wondered if we were making any mistake, and starting the salary on a higher figure for the first year than I would get. This was good sense, and it made me feel a little less confident than I had been feeling before; but it gave me a good business idea, and I brought it frankly out.

"Portia, dear, would you mind going with me that day, when I confront those old gentlemen?"

She shrank a little, but said:

"N-o; if my being with you would help hearten you. But—would it be quite proper, do you think?"

"No, I don't know that it would—in fact, I'm afraid it wouldn't; but, you see, there's so *much* dependent upon it that—"

"Then I'll go anyway, proper or improper," she said, with a beautiful and generous enthusiasm. "Oh, I shall be so happy to think I'm helping!"

"Helping, dear? Why, you'll be doing it all. You're so beautiful and so lovely and so winning, that with you there I can pile our salary up till I break those good old fellows, and they'll never have the heart to struggle."

Sho! you should have seen the rich blood mount, and her happy eyes shine!

"You wicked flatterer! There isn't a word of truth in what you say, but still I'll go with you. Maybe it will teach you not to expect other people to look with your eyes."

Were my doubts dissipated? Was my confidence restored? You may judge by this fact: privately I raised my salary to twelve hundred the first year on the spot. But I didn't tell her; I saved it for a surprise.

All the way home I was in the clouds, Hastings talking, I not hearing a word. When he and I entered my parlor, he brought me to myself with his fervent appreciations of my manifold comforts and luxuries.

"Let me just stand here a little and look my fill. Dear me! it's a palace—it's just a palace! And in it everything a body *could* desire, including cosey coal fire and supper standing ready. Henry, it doesn't merely make me realize how rich you are; it makes me realize, to the bone, to the marrow, how poor I am—how poor I am, and how miserable, how defeated, routed, annihilated!"

Plague take it! this language gave me the cold shudders. It scared me broad awake, and made me comprehend that I was standing on a half-inch crust, with a crater underneath. *I* didn't know I had been dreaming—that is, I hadn't been allowing myself to know it for a while back; but *now*—oh, dear! Deep in debt, not a cent in the world, a lovely girl's happiness or woe in my hands, and nothing in front of me but a salary which might never—oh, *would* never—materialize! Oh, oh, oh! I am ruined past hope! nothing can save me!

"Henry, the mere unconsidered drippings of your daily income would—"

"Oh, my daily income! Here, down with this hot Scotch, and cheer up your soul. Here's with you! Or, no—you're hungry; sit down and—"

"Not a bite for me; I'm past it. I can't eat, these days; but I'll drink with you till I drop. Come!"

"Barrel for barrel, I'm with you! Ready? Here we go! Now, then, Lloyd, unreel your story while I brew."

"Unreel it? What, again?"

"Again? What do you mean by that?"

"Why, I mean do you want to hear it *over* again?"

"Do I want to hear it *over* again? This *is* a puzzler. Wait; don't take any more of that liquid. You don't need it."

"Look here, Henry, you alarm me. Didn't I tell you the whole story on the way here?"

"You?"

"Yes, I."

"I'll be hanged if I heard a word of it."

"Henry, this is a serious thing. It troubles me. What did you take up yonder at the minister's?"

Then it all flashed on me, and I owned up like a man.

"I took the dearest girl in this world—prisoner!"

So then he came with a rush, and we shook, and shook, and shook till our hands ached; and he didn't blame me for not having heard a word of a story which had lasted while we walked three miles. He just sat down then, like the patient, good fellow he was, and told it all over again. Synopsized, it amounted to this: He had come to England with what he thought was a grand opportunity; he had an "option" to sell the Gould and Curry Extension for the "locators" of it, and keep all he could get over a million dollars. He had worked hard, had pulled every wire he knew of, had left no honest expedient untried, had spent nearly all the money he had in the world, had not been able to get a solitary capitalist to listen to him, and his option would run out at the end of the month. In a word, he was ruined. Then he jumped up and cried out:

"Henry, you can save me! You can save me, and you're the only man in the universe that can. Will you do it? *Won't* you do it?"

"Tell me how. Speak out, my boy."

"Give me a million and my passage home for my 'option'! Don't, *don't* refuse!"

I was in a kind of agony. I was right on the point of coming out with the words, "Lloyd, I'm a pauper myself—absolutely penniless, and in *debt!*" But a white-hot idea came flaming through my head, and I gripped my jaws together, and calmed myself down till I was as cold as a capitalist. Then I said, in a commercial and self-possessed way:

"I will save you, Lloyd—"

"Then I'm already saved! God be merciful to you forever! If ever I—"

"Let me finish, Lloyd. I will save you, but not in that way; for that would not be fair to you, after your hard work, and the risks you've run. I don't need to buy mines; I can keep my capital moving, in a commercial center like London, without that; it's what I'm at, all the time; but here is what I'll do. I know all about that mine, of course; I know its immense value, and can swear to it if anybody wishes it. You shall sell out inside of the fortnight for three millions cash, using my name freely, and we'll divide, share and share alike."

Do you know, he would have danced the furniture to kindling-wood in his insane joy, and broken everything on the place, if I hadn't tripped him up and tied him.

Then he lay there, perfectly happy, saying:

"I may use your name! Your name—think of it! Man, they'll flock in droves, these rich Londoners; they'll *fight* for that stock! I'm a made man, I'm a made man forever, and I'll never forget you as long as I live!"

In less than twenty-four hours London was abuzz! I hadn't anything to do, day after day, but sit at home, and say to all comers:

"Yes; I told him to refer to me. I know the man, and I know the mine. His character is above reproach, and the mine is worth far more than he asks for it."

Meantime I spent all my evenings at the minister's with Portia. I didn't say a word to her about the mine; I saved it for a surprise. We talked salary; never anything but salary and love; sometimes love, sometimes salary, sometimes love and salary together. And my! the interest the minister's wife and daughter took in our little affair, and the endless ingenuities they invented to save us from interruption, and to keep the minister in the dark and unsuspicious—well, it was just lovely of them!

When the month was up at last, I had a million dollars to my credit in the London and County Bank, and Hastings was fixed in the same way. Dressed at my level best, I drove by the house in Portland Place, judged by the look of things that my birds were home again, went on towards the minister's and got my precious, and we started back, talking salary with all our might. She was so excited and anxious that it made her just intolerably beautiful. I said:

"Dearie, the way you're looking it's a crime to strike for a salary a single penny under three thousand a year."

"Henry, Henry, you'll ruin us!"

"Don't you be afraid. Just keep up those looks, and trust to me. It'll all come out right."

So, as it turned out, I had to keep bolstering up *her* courage all the way. She kept pleading with me, and saying:

"Oh, please remember that if we ask for too much we may get no salary at all; and then what will become of us, with no way in the world to earn our living?"

We were ushered in by that same servant, and there they were, the two old gentlemen. Of course, they were surprised to see that wonderful creature with me, but I said:

"It's all right, gentlemen; she is my future stay and helpmate."

And I introduced them to her, and called them by name. It didn't surprise them; they knew I would know enough to consult the directory. They seated us, and were very polite to me, and very solicitous to relieve her from embarrassment, and put her as much at her ease as they could. Then I said:

"Gentlemen, I am ready to report."

"We are glad to hear it," said *my* man, "for now we can decide the bet which my brother Abel and I made. If you have won for me, you shall have any situation in my gift. Have you the million-pound note?"

"Here it is, sir," and I handed it to him.

"I've won!" he shouted, and slapped Abel on the back. "*Now* what do you say, brother?"

"I say he *did* survive, and I've lost twenty thousand pounds. I I never would have believed it."

"I've a further report to make," I said, "and a pretty long one. I want you to let me come soon, and detail my whole month's history; and I promise you it's worth hearing. Meantime, take a look at that."

"What, man! Certificate of deposit for £200,000. Is it yours?"

"Mine. I earned it by thirty days' judicious use of that little loan you let me have. And the only use I made of it was to buy trifles and offer the bill in change."

"Come, this is astonishing! It's incredible, man!"

"Never mind, I'll prove it. Don't take my word unsupported."

But now Portia's turn was come to be surprised. Her eyes were spread wide, and she said:

"Henry, is that really your money? Have you been fibbing to me?"

"I have, indeed, dearie. But you'll forgive me, *I* know."

She put up an arch pout, and said:

"Don't you be so sure. You are a naughty thing to deceive me so!"

"Oh, you'll get over it, sweetheart, you'll get over it; it was only fun, you know. Come, let's be going."

"But wait, wait! The situation, you know. I want to give you the situation," said my man.

"Well," I said, "I'm just as grateful as I can be, but really I don't want one."

"But you can have the very choicest one in my gift."

"Thanks again, with all my heart; but I don't even want *that* one."

"Henry, I'm ashamed of you. You don't half thank the good gentleman. May I do it for you?"

"Indeed, you shall, dear, if you can improve it. Let us see you try."

She walked to my man, got up in his lap, put her arm round his neck, and kissed him right on the mouth. Then the two old gentlemen shouted with laughter, but I was dumfounded, just pertified, as you may say. Portia said:

"Papa, he has said you haven't a situation in your gift that he'd take; and I feel just as hurt as—"

"My darling, is that your papa?"

"Yes; he's my step-papa, and the dearest one that ever was. You understand now, don't you, why I was able to laugh when you told me at the minister's, not knowing my relationships, what trouble and worry papa's and Uncle Abel's scheme was giving you?"

Of course, I spoke right up now, without any fooling, and went straight to the point.

"Oh, my dearest dear sir, I want to take back what I said. You *have* got a situation open that I want."

"Name it."

"Son-in-law."

"Well, well, well! But you know, if you haven't ever served in that capacity, you, of course, can't furnish recommendations of a sort to satisfy the conditions of the contract, and so—"

"Try me—oh, do, I beg of you! Only just try me thirty or forty years, and if—"

"Oh, well, all right; it's but a little thing to ask, take her along."

Happy, we two? There are not words enough in the unabridged to describe it. And when London got the whole history, a day or two later, of my month's adventures with that bank-note, and how they ended, did London talk, and have a good time? Yes.

My Portia's papa took that friendly and hospitable bill back to the Bank of England and cashed it; then the Bank canceled it and made him a present of it, and he gave it to us at our wedding, and it has always hung in its frame in the sacredest place in our home ever since. For it gave me my Portia. But for it I could not have remained in London, would not have appeared at the minister's, never should have met her. And so I always say, "Yes, it's a million-pounder, as you see; but it never made but one purchase in its life, and *then* got the article for only about a tenth part of its value."

An unusual aspect of "Playing Courier" is that it was first printed in the English periodical, The Illustrated London News, *December, 1881. One month later it appeared in* The New York Sun, *and eventually found its way into book form as part of* The £1,000,000 Bank Note and Other New Stories, *published in 1893 by C.L. Webster, New York.*

PLAYING COURIER

A time would come when we must go from Aixles-Bains to Geneva, and from thence, by a series of day-long and tangled journeys, to Bayreuth in Bavaria. I should have to have a courier, of course, to take care of so considerable a party as mine.

But I procrastinated. The time slipped along, and at last I woke up one day to the fact that we were ready to move and had no courier. I then resolved upon what I felt was a foolhardy thing, but I was in the humor of it. I said I would make the first stage without help—I did it.

I brought the party from Aix to Geneva by myself—four people. The distance was two hours and more, and there was one change of cars. There was not an accident of any kind, except leaving a valise and some other matters on the platform—a thing which can hardly be called an accident, it is so common. So I offered to conduct the party all the way to Bayreuth.

This was a blunder, though it did not seem so at the time. There was more detail than I thought there would be: 1, two persons whom we had left in a Genevan pension some weeks before must be collected and brought to the hotel; 2, I must notify the people on the Grand Quay who store trunks to bring seven of our stored trunks to the hotel and carry back seven which they would find piled in the lobby; 3, I must find out what part of Europe Bayreuth was in and buy seven railway tickets for that point; 4, I must send a telegram to a friend in the Netherlands; 5, it was now two in the afternoon, and we must look sharp and be ready for the first night train and make sure of sleeping-car tickets; 6, I must draw money at the bank.

It seemed to me that the sleeping-car tickets must be the most important thing, so I went to the station myself to make sure; hotel messengers are not always brisk people. It was a hot day and

I ought to have driven, but it seemed better economy to walk. It did not turn out so, because I lost my way and trebled the distance. I applied for the tickets, and they asked me which route I wanted to go by, and that embarrassed me and made me lose my head, there were so many people standing around, and I not knowing anything about the routes and not supposing there were going to be two; so I judged it best to go back and map out the road and come again.

I took a cab this time, but on my way upstairs at the hotel I remembered that I was out of cigars, so I thought it would be well to get some while the matter was in my mind. It was only round the corner and I didn't need the cab. I asked the cabman to wait where he was. Thinking of the telegram and trying to word it in my head, I forgot the cigars and the cab, and walked on indefinitely. I was going to have the hotel people send the telegram, but as I could not be far from the post-office by this time, I thought I would do it myself. But it was further than I had supposed. I found the place at last and wrote the telegram and handed it in. The clerk was a severe-looking, fidgety man, and he began to fire French questions at me in such a liquid form that I could not detect the joints between his words, and this made me lose my head again. But an Englishman stepped up and said the clerk wanted to know where he was to send the telegram. I could not tell him, because it was not my telegram, and I explained that I was merely sending it for a member of my party. But nothing would pacify the clerk but the address; so I said that if he was so particular I would go back and get it.

However, I thought I would go and collect those lacking two persons first, for it would be best to do everything systematically and in order, and one detail at a time. Then I remembered the cab was eating up my substances down at the hotel yonder; so I called another cab and told the man to go down and fetch it to the post office and wait till I came.

I had a long hot walk to collect those people, and when I got there they couldn't come with me because they had heavy satchels and must have a cab. I went away to find one, but before I ran across any I noticed that I had reached the neighborhood of the Grand Quay—at least I thought I had—so I judged I could save time by stepping around and arranging about the trunks. I stepped around about a mile, and although I did not find the Grand Quay, I found a cigar shop, and remembered about the cigars. I said I was going to Bayreuth, and wanted enough for the journey. The man asked me which route I was going to take. I said I did not know. He said he would recommend me to go by Zurich and various other places which he named, and offered to sell me seven second-class through tickets for $22 apiece, which would be throwing off the discount which the railroads allowed him. I was already tired of riding second-class on first-class tickets, so I took him up.

By and by I found Natural & Co.'s storage office, and told them to send seven of our trunks to the hotel and pile them up in the lobby. It seemed to me that I was not delivering the whole of the message, still it was all I could find in my head.

Next I found the bank and asked for some money, but I had left my letter of credit somewhere and was not able to draw. I remembered now that I must have left it lying on the table where I wrote my telegram; so I got a cab and drove to the post-office and went upstairs, and they said that a letter of credit had indeed been left on the table, but that it was now in the hands of the police authorities, and it would be necessary for me to go there and prove property. They sent a boy with me, and we went out the back way and walked a couple of miles and found the place; and then I remembered about my cabs, and asked the boy to send them to me when he got back to the post-office. It was nightfall now, and the Mayor had gone to dinner. I thought I would go to dinner myself, but the officer on duty thought differently, and I stayed. The Mayor dropped in a half-past ten, but said it was too late to do anything to-night—come at 9:30 in the morning. The officer wanted to keep me all night, and said I was a suspicious looking person, and probably did not own the letter of credit, and didn't know what a letter of credit was, but merely saw the real owner leave it lying on the table, and wanted to get it because I was probably a person that would want anything he could get, whether it was valuable or not. But the Mayor said he saw nothing suspicious about me, and that I seemed a harmless person and nothing the matter with me but a wandering mind, and not much of that. So I thanked him and he set me free, and I went home in my three cabs.

As I was dog-tired and in no condition to answer questions with discretion, I thought I would not disturb the Expedition at that time of night, as there was a vacant room I knew of at the other end of the hall; but I did not quite arrive there, as a watch had been set, the Expedition being anxious about me. I was placed in a galling situation. The Expedition sat stiff and forbidding on four chairs in a row, with shawls and things all on, satchels and guide-books in lap. They had been sitting like that for four hours, and the glass going down all the time. Yes, and they were waiting—waiting for me. It seemed to me that nothing but a sudden, happily contrived, and brilliant *tour de force* could break this iron front and make a diversion in my favor; so I shied my hat into the arena and followed it with a skip and a jump, shouting blithely:

"Ha, ha, here we all are, Mr. Merryman!"

Nothing could be deeper or stiller than the absence of applause which followed. But I kept on; there seemed no other way, though my confidence, poor enough before, had got a deadly check and was in effect gone.

I tried to be jocund out of a heavy heart, I tried to touch the other hearts there and soften the bitter resentment in those faces by throwing off bright and airy fun and making of the whole ghastly thing a joyously humorous incident, but this idea was not well conceived. It was not the right atmosphere for it. I got not one smile; not one line in those offended faces relaxed; I thawed nothing of the winter that looked out of those frosty eyes. I started one more breezy, poor effort, but the head of the Expedition cut into the center of it and said:

"Where have you been?"

I saw by the manner of this that the idea was to get down to cold business now. So I began my travels, but was cut short again.

"Where are the two others? We have been in frightful anxiety about them."

"Oh, they're all right. I was to fetch a cab. I will go straight off, and—"

"Sit down! Don't you know it is eleven o'clock? Where did you leave them?"

"At the pension."

"Why didn't you bring them?"

"Because we couldn't carry the satchels. And so I thought—"

"Thought! You should not try to think. One cannot think without the proper machinery. It is two miles to that pension. Did you go there without a cab?"

"I—well I didn't intend to; it only happened so."

"How did it happen so?"

"Because I was at the post-office and I remembered that I had left a cab waiting here, and so, to stop that expense, I sent another cab to—to—"

"To what?"

"Well. I don't remember now, but I think the new cab was to have the hotel pay the old cab, and send it away."

"What good would that do?"

"What good would it do? It would stop the expense, wouldn't it?"

"By putting the new cab in its place to continue the expense?"

I didn't say anything.

"Why didn't you have the new cab come back for you?"

"Oh, that is what I did. I remember now. Yes, that is what I did. Because I recollect that when I—"

"Well, then, why didn't it come back for you?"

"To the post-office? Why, it did."

"Very well, then, how did you come to walk to the pension?"

"I—I don't quite remember how that happened. Oh, yes, I do remember now. I wrote the dispatch to send to the Netherlands, and—"

"Oh, thank goodness, you did accomplish something! I wouldn't have had you fail to send—what makes you look like that! You are trying to avoid my eye. That dispatch is the most important thing that— You haven't sent that dispatch!"

"I haven't said I didn't send it."

"You don't need to. Oh, dear, I wouldn't have had that telegram fail for anything. Why didn't you send it?"

"Well, you see, with so many things to do and think of, I—they're very particular there, and after I had written the telegram—"

"Oh, never mind, let it go, explanations can't help the matter now—what will he think of us?"

"Oh, that's all right, that's all right, he'll think we gave the telegram to the hotel people, and that they—"

"Why, certainly! Why didn't you do that? There was no other rational way."

"Yes, I know, but then I had it on my mind that I must be sure and get to the bank and draw some money——"

"Well, you are entitled to some credit, after all, for thinking of that, and I don't wish to be too hard on you, though you must acknowledge yourself that you have cost us all a good deal of trouble, and some of it not necessary. How much did you draw?"

"Well, I—I had an idea that—that—"

"That what?"

"That—well, it seems to me that in the circumstances—so many of us, you know, and—and—"

"What are you mooning about? Do turn your face this way and let me—why, you haven't drawn any money!"

"Well, the banker said—"

"Never mind what the banker said. You must have had a reason of your own. Not a reason, exactly, but something which—"

"Well, then, the simple fact was that I hadn't my letter of credit."

"Hadn't your letter of credit?"

"Hadn't my letter of credit."

"Don't repeat me like that. Where was it?"

"At the post-office."

"What was it doing there?"

"Well, I forgot it and left it there."

"Upon my word, I've seen a good many couriers, but of all the couriers that ever I—"

"I've done the best I could."

"Well, so you have, poor thing, and I'm wrong to abuse you so when you've been working yourself to death while we've been sitting here only thinking of our vexations instead of feeling grateful for what you were trying to do for us. It will all come out right. We can take the 7:30 train in the morning just as well. You've bought the tickets?"

"I have—and it's a bargain, too. Second class."

"I'm glad of it. Everybody else travels second class, and we might just as well save that ruinous extra charge. What did you pay?"

"Twenty-two dollars apiece—through to Bayreuth."

"Why, I didn't know you could buy through tickets anywhere but in London and Paris."

"Some people can't, maybe; but some people can—of whom I am one of which, it appears."

"It seems a rather high price."

"On the contrary, the dealer knocked off his commission."

"Dealer?"

"Yes—I bought them at a cigar shop."

"That reminds me. We shall have to get up pretty early, and so there should be no packing to do. Your umbrella, your rubbers, your cigars—**what** is the matter?"

"Hang it, I've left the cigars at the bank."

"Just think of it! Well, your umbrella?"

"I'll have that all right. There's no hurry."

"**What** do you mean by that?"

"Oh, that's all right; I'll take care of—"

"Where is that umbrella?"

"It's just the merest step—it won't take me—"

"Where is it?"

"Well, I think I left it at the cigar shop; but anyway—"

"Take your feet out from under that thing. It's just as I expected! Where are your rubbers?"

"They—well—"

"Where are your rubbers?"

"It's got so dry now—well, everybody says there's not going to be another drop of—"

"Where—are—your—rubbers?"

"Well, you see—well, it was this way. First, the officer said—"

"What officer?"

"Police officer; but the Mayor, he—"

"What Mayor?"

"Mayor of Geneva; but I said—"

"Wait. What is the matter with you?"

"Who, me? Nothing. They both tried to persuade me to stay, and—"

"Stay where?"

"Well—the fact is—"

"Where have you been? What's kept you out till half-past ten at night?"

"Oh, you see, after I lost my letter of credit, I—"

"You are beating around the bush a good deal. Now, answer the question in just one straightforward word. Where are those rubbers?"

"They—well; they're in the county jail."

I started a placating smile, but it petrified. The climate was unsuitable. Spending three or four hours in jail did not seem to the Expedition humorous. Neither did it to me, at bottom.

I had to explain the whole thing, and, of course, it came out then that we couldn't take the early train, because that would leave my letter of credit in hock still. It did look as if we had all got to go to bed estranged and unhappy, but by good luck that was prevented. There happened to be mention of the trunks, and I was able to say I had attended to that feature.

"There, you are just as good and thoughtful and painstaking and intelligent as you can be, and it's a shame to find so much fault with you, and there sha'n't be another word of it. You've done beautifully, admirably, and I'm sorry I ever said one ungrateful word to you."

This hit deeper than some of the other things and made me uncomfortable, because I wasn't feeling as solid about that trunk errand as I wanted to. There seemed somehow to be a defect about it somewhere, though I couldn't put my finger on it, and didn't like to stir the matter just now, it being late and maybe well enough to let well enough alone.

Of course there was music in the morning, when it was found that we couldn't leave by the early train. But I had no time to wait; I got only the opening bars of the overture, and then started out to get my letter of credit.

It seemed a good time to look into the trunk business and rectify it if it needed it, and I had a suspicion that it did. I was too late. The concierge said he had shipped the trunks to Zurich the evening before. I asked him how he could do that without exhibiting passage tickets.

"Not necessary in Switzerland. You pay for your trunks and send them where you please. Nothing goes free but your hand baggage."

"How much did you pay on them?"

"A hundred and forty francs."

"Twenty-eight dollars. There's something wrong about that trunk business, sure."

Next I met the porter. He said:

"You have not slept well, is it not. You have the worn look. If you would like a courier, a good one has arrived last night, and is not engaged for five days already, by the name of Ludi. We recommend him; das heisst, the Grand Hotel Beau Rivage recommends him."

I declined with coldness. My spirit was not broken yet. And I did not like having my condition taken notice of in this way. I was at the country jail by nine o'clock hoping that the Mayor might chance to come before his regular hour; but he didn't. It was dull there. Every time I offered to touch anything, or look at anything, or do anything, or refrain from doing anything, the policeman said it was "defendu." I thought I would practice my French on him, but he wouldn't have that either. It seemed to make him particularly bitter to hear his own tongue.

The Mayor came at last, and then there was no trouble; for the minute he had convened the Supreme Court—they always do whenever there is valuable property in dispute—and got everything shipshape and sentries posted, and had prayer by the chaplain; my unsealed letter was brought and opened, and there wasn't anything in it but some photographs; because, as I remembered now, I had taken out the letter of credit so as to make room for the photographs, and had put the letter in my other pocket, which I proved to everybody's satisfaction by fetching it out and showing it with a good deal of exultation. So then the court looked at each other in a vacant kind of way, and then at me, and then at each other again, and finally let me go, but said it was imprudent for me to be at large, and asked me what my profession was. I said I was a courier. They lifted up their eyes in a kind of reverent way and said, "Du lieber Gott!" and I said a word of courteous thanks for their apparent admiration, and hurried off to the bank.

However, being a courier was already making me a great stickler for order and system and one thing at a time and each thing in its own proper turn; so I passed by the bank and branched off and started for the two lacking members of the Expedition. A cab lazied by, and I took it upon persuasion. I gained no speed by this, but it was a resposeful turnout and I liked reposefulness. The week-long jubilations over the six hundredth anniversary of the birth of Swiss liberty and the Signing of the Compact was at flood tide, and all the street were clothed in fluttering flags.

The horse and the driver had been drunk three days and nights, and had known no stall nor bed meantime. They looked as I felt—dreamy and seedy. But we arrived in course of time. I went in and rang, and asked a housemaid to rush out the lacking members. She said something which I did not understand, and I returned to the chariot. The girl had probably told me that those people did not belong on her floor, and that it would be judicious for me to go higher, and ring from floor to floor till I found them; for in those Swiss flats there does not seem to be any way to find the right family but to be patient and guess your way along up. I calculated that I must wait fifteen minutes, there being three details inseparable from an occasion of this sort: 1, put on hats and come down and climb in; 2, return of one to get "my other glove;" 3, presently, return of the other one to fetch "my *French Verbs at a Glance.*" I would muse during the fifteen minutes and take it easy.

A very still and blank interval ensued, and then I felt a hand on my shoulder and started. The intruder was a policeman. I glanced up and perceived that there was new scenery. There was a good deal of a crowd, and they had that pleased and interested look which such a crowd wears when they see that somebody is out of luck. The horse was asleep, and so was the driver, and some boys had hung them and me full of gaudy decorations stolen from the innumerable banner poles. It was a scandalous spectacle. The officer said:

"I'm sorry, but we can't have you sleeping here all day."

I was wounded and said with dignity:

"I beg your pardon, I was not sleeping; I was thinking."

"Well, you can think if you want to, but you've got to think to yourself; you disturb the whole neighborhood."

It was a poor joke, and it made the crowd laugh. I snore at night sometimes, but it is not likely that I would do such a thing in the daytime and in such a place. The officer undecorated us, and seemed sorry for our friendlessness, and really tried to be humane, but he said we mustn't stop there any longer or he would have to charge us rent—it was the law, he said, and he went on to say in a sociable way that I was looking pretty mouldy, and he wished he knew—

I shut him off pretty austerely, and said I hoped one might celebrate a little these days, especially when one was personally concerned.

"Personally?" he asked. "How?"

"Because 600 years ago an ancestor of mine signed the compact."

He reflected a moment, then looked me over and said:

"Ancestor! It's my opinion you signed it yourself. For of all the old ancient relics that ever I—but never mind about that. What is it you are waiting here for so long?"

I said:

"I'm not waiting here so long at all. I'm waiting fifteen minutes till they forget a glove and a book and go back and get them." Then I told him who they were that I had come for.

He was very obliging, and began to shout inquiries to the tiers of heads and shoulders projecting from the windows above us. Then a woman away up there sang out:

"Oh, they? Why I got them a cab and they left here long ago—half-past eight, I should say."

It was annoying. I glanced at my watch, but didn't say anything. The officer said:

"It is a quarter of twelve, you see. You should have inquired better. You have been asleep three-quarters of an hour, and in such a sun as this. You are baked—baked black. It is wonderful. And you will miss your train, perhaps. You interest me greatly. What is your occupation?"

I said I was a courier. It seemed to stun him, and before he could come to we were gone.

When I arrived in the third story of the hotel I found our quarters vacant. I was not surprised. The moment a courier takes his eye off his tribe they go shopping. The nearer it is to train time the surer they are to go. I sat down to try and think out what I had best do next, but presently the hall boy found me there, and said the Expedition had gone to the station half an hour before. It was the first time I had known them to do a rational thing, and it was very confusing. This is one of the things that make a courier's life so difficult and uncertain. Just as matters are going the smoothest, his people will strike a lucid interval, and down go all his arrangements to wreck and ruin.

The train was to leave at twelve noon sharp. It was now ten minutes after twelve. I could be at the station in ten minutes. I saw I had no great amount of leeway, for this was the lightning express, and on the Continent the lightning expresses are pretty fastidious about getting away some time during the advertised day. My people were the only ones remaining in the waiting-room; everybody else had passed through and "mounted the train," as they say in those regions. They were exhausted with nervousness and fret, but I comforted them and heartened them up, and we made our rush.

But no; we were out of luck again. The doorkeeper was not satisfied with the tickets. He examined them cautiously, deliberately, suspiciously; then glared at me a while, and after that he called another official. The two examined the tickets and called another official. These called others, and the convention discussed and discussed, and gesticulated and carried on, until I begged that they would consider how time was flying, and just pass a few resolutions and let us go. Then they said very courteously that there was a defect in the tickets, and asked me where I got them.

I judged I saw what the trouble was now. You see, I had bought the tickets in a cigar shop, and, of course, the tobacco smell was on them; without doubt, the thing they were up to was to work the tickets through the Custom House and to collect duty on that smell. So I resolved to be perfectly frank; it is sometimes the best way. I said:

"Gentlemen, I will not deceive you. These railway tickets—"

"Ah, pardon, monsieur! These are not railway tickets."

"Oh," I said, "is that the defect?"

"Ah, truly yes, monsieur. These are lottery tickets, yes; and it is a lottery which has been drawn two years ago."

I affected to be greatly amused; it is all one can do in such circumstances; it is all one can do, and yet there is no value in it; it deceives nobody, and you can see that everybody around pities you and is ashamed of you. One of the hardest situations in life, I think, is to be full of grief and a sense of defeat and shabbiness that way, and yet have to put on an outside of archness and gayety, while all the time you know that your own Expedition, the treasures of your heart, and whose love and reverence you are by the custom of our civilization entitled to, are being consumed with humiliation before strangers to see you earning and getting a compassion which is a stigma, a brand—a brand which certifies you to be—oh, anything and everything which is fatal to human respect.

I said, cheerily, it was all right, just one of those little accidents that was likely to happen to anybody—I would have the right tickets in two minutes, and we would catch the train yet, and, moreover, have something to laugh about all through the journey. I did get the tickets in time, all stamped and complete, but then it turned out that I couldn't take them, because in taking so much pains about the two missing members, I had skipped the bank and hadn't the money. So then the train left, and there didn't seem to be anything to do but go back to the hotel, which we did; but it was kind of melancholy and not much said. I tried to start a few subjects, like scenery and transubstantiation, and those sorts of things, but they didn't seem to hit the weather right.

We had lost our good rooms, but we got some others which were pretty scattering, but would answer. I judged things would brighten now, but the Head of the Expedition said, "Send up the trunks." It made me feel pretty cold. There was a doubtful something about the trunk business. I was almost sure of it. I was going to suggest—

But a wave of the hand sufficiently restrained me, and I was informed that we would now camp for three days and see if we could rest up.

I said all right, never mind ringing; I would go down and attend to the trunks myself. I got a cab and went straight to Mr. Charles Natural's place, and asked what order it was I had left there.

"To send seven trunks to the hotel."

"And were you to bring any back?"

"No."

"You are sure I didn't tell you to bring back seven that would be found piled in the lobby?"

"Absolutely sure you didn't."

"Then the whole fourteen are gone to Zurich or Jericho or somewhere, and there is going to be more debris around that hotel when the Expedition—"

I didn't finish, because my mind was getting to be in a good deal of a whirl, and when you are that way you think you have finished a sentence when you haven't, and you go mooning and dreaming away, and the first thing you know you get run over by a dray or a cow or something.

I left the cab there—I forgot it—and on my way back I thought it all out and concluded to resign, because otherwise I should be nearly sure to be discharged. But I didn't believe it would be a good idea to resign in person; I could do it by message. So I sent for Mr. Ludi and explained that there was a courier going to resign on account of incompatibility or fatigue or something, and as he had four or five vacant days, I would like to insert him into that vacancy if he thought he could fill it. When everything was arranged I got him to go up and say to the Expedition that, owing to an error made by Mr. Natural's people, we were out of trunks here, but would have plenty in Zurich, and we'd better take the first train, freight, gravel, or construction, and move right along.

He attended to that and came down with an invitation for me to go up—yes, certainly; and, while we walked along over to the bank to get money, and collect my cigars and tobacco, and to the cigar shop to trade back the lottery tickets and get my umbrella, and to Mr. Natural's to pay that cab and send it away, and to the county jail to get my rubbers and leave p. p. c. cards for the Mayor and Supreme Court, he described the weather to me that was prevailing on the upper levels there with the Expedition, and I saw that I was doing very well where I was.

I stayed out in the woods till four P.M., to let the weather moderate, and then turned up at the station just in time to take the three o'clock express for Zurich along with the Expedition, now in the hands of Ludi, who conducted its complex affairs with little apparent effort or inconvenience.

Well, I had worked like a slave while I was in office, and done the very best I knew how; yet all that these people dwelt upon or seemed to care to remember was the defects of my administration, not its creditable features. They would skip over a thousand creditable features to remark upon and reiterate and fuss about just one fact, till it seemed to me they would wear it out; and not much of a fact, either, taken by itself—the fact that I elected myself courier in Geneva, and put in work enough to carry a circus to Jerusalem, and yet never even got my gang out of the town. I finally said I didn't wish to hear any more about the subject, it made me tired. And I told them to their faces that I would never be a courier again to save anybody's life. And if I live long enough I'll prove it. I think it's a difficult, brain-racking, overworked, and thoroughly ungrateful office, and the main bulk of its wages is a sore heart and a bruised spirit.

FENIMORE COOPER'S LITERARY OFFENSES

"Fenimore Cooper's Literary Offenses," a superior satirical essay, was first published in The North American Review, *July, 1895. It eventually surfaced in the volume* How to Tell a Story and Other Essays, *published in 1897 by Harper and Brothers, New York.*

FENIMORE COOPER'S LITERARY OFFENSES

The Pathfinder and *The Deerslayer* stand at the head of Cooper's novels as artistic creations. There are others of his works which contain parts as perfect as are to be found in these, and scenes even more thrilling. Not one can be compared with either of them as a finished whole.

The defects in both of these tales are comparatively slight. They were pure works of art.—*Prof. Lounsbury.*

The five tales reveal an extraordinary fulness of invention.

...One of the very greatest characters in fiction, "Natty Bumppo."...

The craft of the woodsman, the tricks of the trapper, all the delicate art of the forest, were familiar to Cooper from his youth up.—*Prof. Brander Matthews.*

Cooper is the greatest artist in the domain of romantic fiction yet produced by America.—*Wilkie Collins.*

It seems to me that it was far from right for the Professor of English Literature in Yale, the Professor of English Literature in Columbia, and Wilkie Collins, to deliver opinions on Cooper's literature without having read some of it. It would have been much more decorous to keep silent and let persons talk who have read Cooper.

Cooper's art has some defects. In one place in *Deerslayer,* and in the restricted space of two-thirds of a page, Cooper has scored 114 offences against literary art out of a possible 115. It breaks the record.

There are nineteen rules governing literary art in the domain of romantic fiction—some say twenty-two. In *Deerslayer* Cooper violated eighteen of them. These eighteen require:

1. That a tale shall accomplish something and arrive somewhere. But the *Deerslayer* tale accomplishes nothing and arrives in the air.

2. They require that the episodes of a tale shall be necessary parts of the tale, and shall help to develop it. But as the *Deerslayer* tale is not a tale, and accomplishes nothing and arrives nowhere, the episodes have no rightful place in the work, since there was

nothing for them to develop.

3. They require that the personages in a tale shall be alive, except in the case of corpses, and that always the reader shall be able to tell the corpses from the others. But this detail has often been overlooked in the *Deerslayer* tale.

4. They require that the personages in a tale, both dead and alive, shall exhibit a sufficient excuse for being there. But this detail also has been overlooked in the *Deerslayer* tale.

5. They require that when the personages of a tale deal in conversation, the talk shall sound like human talk, and be talk such as human beings would be likely to talk in the given circumstances, and have a discoverable meaning, also a discoverable purpose, and a show of relevancy, and remain in the neighborhood of the subject in hand, and be interesting to the reader, and help out the tale, and stop when the people cannot think of anything more to say. But this requirement has been ignored from the beginning of the *Deerslayer* tale to the end of it.

6. They require that when the author describes the character of a personage in his tale, the conduct and conversation of that personage shall justify said description. But this law gets little or no attention in the *Deerslayer* tale, as "Natty Bumppo's" case will amply prove.

7. They require that when a personage talks like an illustrated, gilt-edged, tree-calf, hand tooled, seven-dollar Friendship's Offering in the beginning of a paragraph, he shall not talk like a negro minstrel in the end of it. But this rule is flung down and danced upon in the *Deerslayer* tale.

8. They require that crass stupidities shall not be played upon the reader as "the craft of the woodsman, the delicate art of the forest," by either the author or the people in the tale. But this rule is persistently violated in the *Deerslayer* tale.

9. They require that the personages of a tale shall confine themselves to possibilities and let miracles alone; or, if they venture a miracle, the author must so plausibly set it forth as to make it look possible and reasonable. But these rules are not respected in the *Deerslayer* tale.

10. They require that the author shall make the reader feel a deep interest in the personages of his tale and in their fate; and that he shall make the reader love the good people in the tale and hate the bad ones. But the reader of the *Deerslayer* tale dislikes the good people in it, is indifferent to the others, and wishes they would all get drowned together.

11. They require that the characters in a tale shall be so clearly defined that the reader can tell beforehand what each will do in a given emergency. But in the *Deerslayer* tale this rule is vacated.

In addition to these large rules there are some little ones. These require that the author shall

12. *Say* what he is proposing to say, not merely come near it.
13. Use the right word, not its second cousin.
14. Eschew surplusage.
15. Not omit necessary details.
16. Avoid slovenliness of form.
17. Use good grammar.
18. Employ a simple and straightforward style.

Even these seven are coldly and persistently violated in the *Deerslayer* tale.

Cooper's gift in the way of invention was not a rich endowment; but such as it was he liked to work it, he was pleased with the effects, and indeed he did some quite sweet things with it. In his little box of stage properties he kept six or eight cunning devices, tricks, artifices for his savages and woodsmen to deceive and circumvent each other with, and he was never so happy as when he was working these innocent things and seeing them go. A favorite one was to make a moccasined person tread in the tracks of the moccasined enemy, and thus hide his own trail. Cooper wore out barrels and barrels of moccasins in working that trick. Another stage-property that he pulled out of his box pretty frequently was his broken twig. He prized his broken twig above all the rest of his effects, and worked it the hardest. It is a restful chapter in any book of his when somebody doesn't step on a dry twig and alarm all the reds and whites for two hundred yards around. Every time a Cooper person is in peril, and absolute silence is worth four dollars a minute, he is sure to step on a dry twig. There may be a hundred handier things to step on, but that wouldn't satisfy Cooper. Cooper requires him to turn out and find a dry twig; and if he can't do it, go and borrow one. In fact the Leather Stocking Series ought to have been called the Broken Twig Series.

I am sorry there is not room to put in a few dozen instances of the delicate art of the forest, as practiced by Natty Bumppo and some of the other Cooperian experts. Perhaps we may venture two or three samples. Cooper was a sailor—a naval officer; yet he gravely tells us how a vessel, driving toward a lee shore in a gale, is steered for a particular spot by her skipper because he knows of an *undertow* there which will hold her back against the gale and save her. For just pure woodcraft, or sailorcraft, or whatever it is, isn't that neat? For several years Cooper was daily in the society of artillery, and he ought to have noticed that when a cannon ball strikes the ground it either buries itself or skips a hundred feet or so; skips again a hundred feet or so—and so on, till it finally gets tired and rolls. Now in one place he loses some "females"—as he always calls women—in the edge of a wood near a plain at night in a fog, on purpose to give Bumppo a chance to show off the delicate art of the forest before the reader. These mislaid people are hunting for a fort. They hear a cannon-blast, and a cannon-ball presently

comes rolling into the wood and stops at their feet. To the females
this suggests nothing. The case is very different with the admirable
Bumppo. I wish I may never know peace again if he doesn't strike
out promptly and *follow the track* of that cannon-ball across the
plain through the dense fog and find the fort. Isn't it a daisy? If
Cooper had any real knowledge of Nature's ways of doing things,
he had a most delicate art in concealing the fact. For instance:
one of his acute Indian experts, Chingachgook (pronounced
Chicago, I think), has lost the trail of a person he is tracking through
the forest. Apparently that trail is hopelessly lost. Neither you nor
I could ever have guessed out the way to find it. It was very different
with Chicago. Chicago was not stumped for long. He turned a
running stream out of its course, and there, in the slush in its old bed,
were that person's moccasin-tracks. The current did not wash them
away, as it would have done in all other like cases—no, even the
eternal laws of Nature have to vacate when Cooper wants to put up
a delicate job of woodcraft on the reader.

We must be a little wary when Brander Matthews tells us that
Cooper's books "reveal an extraordinary fulness of invention."
As a rule, I am quite willing to accept Brander Matthews's literary
judgments and applaud his lucid and graceful phrasing of them;
but that particular statement needs to be taken with a few tons
of salt. Bless your heart, Cooper hadn't any more invention than a
horse; and I don't mean a high-class horse, either; I mean a clothes-
horse. It would be very difficult to find a really clever "situation"
in Cooper's books; and still more difficult to find one of any kind
which he has failed to render absurd by his handling of it. Look
at the episodes of "the caves;" and at the celebrated scuffle between
Maqua and those others on the table-land a few days later; and
at Hurry Harry's queer water-transit from the castle to the ark;
and at Deerslayer's half hour with his first corpse; and at the quarrel
between Hurry Harry and Deerslayer later; and at—but choose for
yourself; you can't go amiss.

If Cooper had been an observer, his inventive faculty would
have worked better, not more interestingly, but more rationally,
more plausibly. Cooper's proudest creations in the way of
"situations" suffer noticeably from the absence of the observer's
protecting gift. Cooper's eye was splendidly inaccurate. Cooper
seldom saw anything correctly. He saw nearly all things as
through a glass eye, darkly. Of course a man who cannot see the
commonest little everyday matters accurately is working at a
disadvantage when he is constructing a "situation." In the
Deerslayer tale Cooper has a stream which is fifty feet wide, where
it flows out of a lake; it presently narrows to twenty as it meanders
along for no given reason, and yet, when a stream acts like that
it ought to be required to explain itself. Fourteen pages later the
width of the brook's outlet from the lake has suddenly shrunk thirty

feet, and become "the narrowest part of the stream." This shrinkage
is not accounted for. The stream has bends in it, a sure indication
that it has alluvial banks, and cuts them; yet these bends are only
thirty and fifty feet long. If Cooper had been a nice and punctilious
observer he would have noticed that the bends were oftener nine
hundred feet long than short of it.

Cooper made the exit of that stream fifty feet wide in the first
place, for no particular reason; in the second place, he narrowed
it to less than twenty to accommodate some Indians. He bends a
"sapling" to the form of an arch over this narrow passage, and
conceals six Indians in its foliage. They are "laying" for a settler's
scow or ark which is coming up the stream on its way to the lake;
it is being hauled against the stiff current by a rope whose stationary
end is anchored in the lake; its rate of progress cannot be more than
a mile an hour. Cooper describes the ark, but pretty obscurely.
In the matter of dimensions "it was little more than a modern canal
boat." Let us guess, then, that it was about 140 feet long. It was of
"greater breadth than common." Let us guess, then, that it was
about sixteen feet wide. This leviathan had been prowling down
bends which were but a third as long as itself, and scraping between
banks where it had only two feet of space to spare on each side.
We cannot too much admire this miracle. A low-roofed log dwelling
occupies "two-third's of the ark's length"—a dwelling ninety feet
long and sixteen feet wide, let us say—a kind of vestibule train.
The dwelling has two rooms—each forty-five feet long and sixteen
feet wide, let us guess. One of them is the bed-room of the Hutter
girls, Judith and Hetty; the other is the parlor, in the day time, at
night it is papa's bed chamber. The ark is arriving at the stream's
exit, now, whose width has been reduced to less than twenty feet to
accommodate the Indians—say to eighteen. There is a foot to spare
on each side of the boat. Did the Indians notice that there was going
to be a tight squeeze there? Did they notice that they could make
money by climbing down out of that arched sapling and just
stepping aboard when the ark scraped by? No; other Indians would
have noticed these things, but Cooper's Indians never notice
anything. Cooper thinks they are marvellous creatures for noticing,
but he was almost always in error about his Indians. There was
seldom a sane one among them.

The ark is 140 feet long; the dwelling is 90 feet long. The idea of
the Indians is to drop softly and secretly from the arched
sapling to the dwelling as the ark creeps along under it at the rate
of a mile an hour, and butcher the family. It will take the ark a
minute and a half to pass under. It will take the 90-foot dwelling a
minute to pass under. Now, then, what did the six Indians do? It
would take you thirty years to guess, and even then you would have
to give it up, I believe. Therefore, I will tell you what the Indians
did. Their chief, a person of quite extraordinary intellect for a

Cooper Indian, warily watched the canal boat as it squeezed along under him, and when he had got his calculations fined down to exactly the right shade, as he judged, he let go and dropped. And *missed the house!* That is actually what he did. He missed the house, and landed in the stern of the scow. It was not much of a fall, yet it knocked him silly. He lay there unconscious. If the house had been 97 feet long, he would have made the trip. The fault was Cooper's, not his. The error lay in the construction of the house. Cooper was no architect.

There still remained in the roost five Indians. The boat has passed under and is now out of their reach. Let me explain what the five did—you would not be able to reason it out for yourself. No. 1 jumped for the boat, but fell in the water astern of it. Then No. 2 jumped for the boat, but fell in the water still further astern of it. Then No. 3 jumped for the boat, and fell a good way astern of it. Then No. 4 jumped for the boat, and fell in the water *away* astern. Then even No. 5 made a jump for the boat—for he was a Cooper Indian. In the matter of intellect, the difference between a Cooper Indian and the Indian that stands in front of the cigar shop is not spacious. The scow episode is really a sublime burst of invention; but it does not thrill, because the inaccuracy of the details throws a sort of air of fictitiousness and general improbability over it. This comes of Cooper's inadequacy as an observer.

The reader will find some examples of Cooper's high talent for inaccurate observation in the account of the shooting match in *The Pathfinder.* "A common wrought nail was driven lightly into the target, its head having been first touched with paint." The color of the paint is not stated—an important omission, but Cooper deals freely in important omissions. No, after all, it was not an important omission; for this nail head is a *hundred yards* from the marksman and could not be seen by them at that distance no matter what its color might be. How far can the best eyes see a common house fly? A hundred yards? It is quite impossible. Very well, eyes that cannot see a house fly that is a hundred yards away cannot see an ordinary nail head at that distance, for the size of the two objects is the same. It takes a keen eye to see a fly or a nail head at fifty yards—one hundred and fifty feet. Can the reader do it?

The nail was lightly driven, its head painted, and game called. Then the Cooper miracles began. The bullet of the first marksman chipped an edge of the nail head; the next man's bullet drove the nail a little way into the target—and removed all the paint. Haven't the miracles gone far enough now? Not to suit Cooper; for the purpose of this whole scheme is to show off his prodigy, Deerslayer-Hawkeye-Long-Rifle-Leather-Stocking-Pathfinder-Bumppo before the ladies.

"Be all ready to clench it, boys!" cried out Pathfinder, stepping into his friend's tracks the instant they were vacant. "Never mind a new nail; I can see that, though the paint is gone, and what I can see, I can hit at a hundred yards, though it were only a mosquito's eye. Be ready to clench!"

The rifle cracked, the bullet sped its way and the head of the nail was buried in the wood, covered by the piece of flattened lead.

There, you see, is a man who could hunt flies with a rifle, and command a ducal salary in a Wild West show to-day, if we had him back with us.

The recorded feat is certainly surprising, just as it stands; but it is not surprising enough for Cooper. Cooper adds a touch. He has made Pathfinder do this miracle with another man's rifle, and not only that, but Pathfinder did not have even the advantage of loading it himself. He had everything against him, and yet he made that impossible shot, and not only made it, but did it with absolute confidence, saying, "Be ready to clench." Now a person like that would have undertaken that same feat with a brickbat, and with Cooper to help he would have achieved it, too.

Pathfinder showed off handsomely that day before the ladies. His very first feat was a thing which no Wild West show can touch. He was standing with the group of marksmen, observing—a hundred yards from the target, mind: one Jasper raised his rifle and drove the centre of the bull's-eye. Then the quartermaster fired. The target exhibited no result this time. There was a laugh. "It's a dead miss," said Major Lundie. Pathfinder waited an impressive moment or two, then said in that calm, indifferent, know-it-all way of his, "No, Major—he has covered Jasper's bullet, as will be seen if any one will take the trouble to examine the target."

Wasn't it remarkable! How *could* he see that little pellet fly through the air and enter that distant bullet-hole? Yet that is what he did; for nothing is impossible to a Cooper person. Did any of those people have any deep-seated doubts about this thing? No; for that would imply sanity, and these were all Cooper people.

The respect for Pathfinder's skill and for his *quickness and accuracy of sight* (the italics are mine) was so profound and general, that the instant he made this declaration the spectators began to distrust their own opinions, and a dozen rushed to the target in order to ascertain the fact. There, sure enough, it was found that the quartermaster's bullet had gone through the hole made by Jasper's, and that, too, so accurately as to require a minute examination to be certain of the circumstances, which, however, was soon established by discovering one bullet over the other in the stump against which the target was placed.

They made a "minute" examination; but never mind, how could they know that there were two bullets in that hole without digging the latest one out? for neither probe nor eyesight could prove the presence of any more than one bullet. Did they dig? No; as we shall see. It is the Pathfinder's turn now; he steps out before the ladies, takes aim, and fires.

But alas! here is a disappointment; an incredible, an unimaginable disappointment—for the target's aspect is unchanged; there is nothing there but that same old bullet hole!

"If one dared to hint at such a thing," cried Major Duncan, "I should say that the Pathfinder has also missed the target."

As nobody had missed it yet, the "also" was not necessary; but never mind about that, for the Pathfinder is going to speak.

"No, no, Major," said he, confidently, "that *would* be a risky declaration. I didn't load the piece, and can't say what was in it, but if it was lead, you will find the bullet driving down those of the Quartermaster and Jasper, else is not my name Pathfinder."

A shout from the target announced the truth of this assertion.

Is the miracle sufficient as it stands? Not for Cooper. The Pathfinder speaks again, as he "now slowly advances towards the stage occupied by the females:"

"That's not all, boys, that's not all; if you find the target touched at all, I'll own to a miss. The Quartermaster cut the wood, but you'll find no wood cut by that last messenger."

The miracle is at last complete. He knew—doubtless *saw*—at the distance of a hundred yards—that his bullet had passed into the hole *without fraying the edges.* There were now three bullets in that one hole—three bullets imbedded processionally in the body of the stump back of the target. Everybody knew this—somehow or other—and yet nobody had dug any of them out to make sure. Cooper is not a close observer, but he is interesting. He is certainly always that, no matter what happens. And he is more interesting when he is not noticing what he is about than when he is. This is a considerable merit.

The conversations in the Cooper books have a curious sound in our modern ears. To believe that such talk really ever came out of people's mouths would be to believe that there was a time when time was of no value to a person who thought he had something to say; when a man's mouth was a rolling-mill, and busied itself all day long in turning four-foot pigs of thought into thirty-foot bars of conversational railroad iron by attenuation; when subjects were seldom faithfully stuck to, but the talk wandered all around and arrived nowhere; when conversations consisted mainly of irrelevances, with here and there a relevancy, a relevancy with an embarrassed look, as not being able to explain how it got there.

Cooper was certainly not a master in the construction of dialogue. Inaccurate observation defeated him here as it defeated him in so many other enterprises of his. He even failed to notice that the man who talks corrupt English six days in the week must and will talk it on the seventh, and can't help himself. In the *Deerslayer* story he lets Deerslayer talk the showiest kind of book talk sometimes, and at other times the basest of base dialects. For instance, when some one asks him if he has a sweetheart, and if so, where she abides, this is his majestic answer:

"She's in the forest—hanging from the boughs of the trees, in a soft rain—in the dew on the open grass—the clouds that float about in the blue heavens—the birds that sing in the woods—the sweet springs where I slake my thirst—and in all the other glorious gifts that come from God's Providence!"

And he preceded that, a little before, with this:

"It consarns me as all things that touches a fri'nd consarns a fri'nd."

And this is another of his remarks:

"If I was Injin born, now, I might tell of this, or carry in the scalp and boast of the expl'ite afore the whole tribe; or if my inimy had only been a bear"—and so on.

We cannot imagine such a thing as a veteran Scotch Commander-in-Chief comporting himself in the field like a windy melodramatic actor, but Cooper could. On one occasion Alice and Cora were being chased by the French through a fog in the neighborhood of their father's fort:

"Point de quartier aux coquins!" cried an eager pursuer, who seemed to direct the operations of the enemy.

"Stand firm and be ready, my gallant 60ths!" suddenly exclaimed a voice above them; "wait to see the enemy; fire low, and sweep the glacis."

"Father! father!" exclaimed a piercing cry from out the mist; "it is I! Alice! thy own Elsie! spare, O! save your daughters!"

"Hold!" shouted the former speaker, in the awful tones of parental agony, the sound reaching even to the woods, and rolling back in solemn echo. " 'Tis she! God has restored me my children! Throw open the sally-port; to the field, 60ths, to the field; pull not a trigger, lest ye kill my lambs! Drive off these dogs of France with your steel."

Cooper's word-sense was singularly dull. When a person has a poor ear for music he will flat and sharp right along without knowing it. He keeps near the tune, but it is *not* the tune. When a person has a poor ear for words, the result is a literary flatting and sharping; you perceive what he is intending to say, but you also perceive that he doesn't *say* it. This is Cooper. He was not a word-musician. His ear was satisfied with the *approximate* word. I will furnish some circumstantial evidence in support of this charge. My instances are gathered from half a dozen pages of the tale called *Deerslayer.* He uses "verbal," for "oral"; "precision," for "facility"; "phenomena," for "marvels"; "necessary," for "predetermined"; "unsophisticated," for "primitive"; "preparation," for "expectancy"; "rebuked," for "subdued"; "dependent on," for "resulting from"; "fact," for "condition"; "fact," for "conjecture"; "precaution," for "caution"; "explain," for "determine"; "mortified," for "disappointed"; "meretricious," for "factitious"; "materially," for "considerably"; "decreasing," for "deepening"; "increasing," for "disappearing"; "embedded,"

for "enclosed"; "treacherous," for "hostile"; "stood," for
"stooped"; "softened," for "replaced"; "rejoined," for "remarked";
"situation," for "condition"; "different," for "differing";
"insensible," for "unsentient"; "brevity," for "celerity";
"distrusted," for "suspicious"; "mental imbecility," for
"imbecility"; "eyes," for "sight"; "counteracting," for "opposing";
"funeral obsequies," for "obsequies."

There have been daring people in the world who claimed that
Cooper could write English, but they are all dead now—all dead but
Lounsbury. I don't remember that Lounsbury makes the claim in
so many words, still he makes it, for he says that *Deerslayer* is a
"pure work of art." Pure, in that connection, means faultless—
faultless in all details—and language is a detail. If Mr. Lounsbury
had only compared Cooper's English with the English which he
writes himself—but it is plain that he didn't; and so it is likely that
he imagines until this day that Cooper's is as clean and compact as
his own. Now I feel sure, deep down in my heart, that Cooper wrote
about the poorest English that exists in our language, and that the
English of *Deerslayer* is the very worst than even Cooper ever wrote.

I may be mistaken, but it does seem to me that *Deerslayer* is not a
work of art in any sense; it does seem to me that it is destitute of
every detail that goes to the making of a work of art; in truth, it
seems to me that *Deerslayer* is just simply a literary *delirium
tremens*.

A work of art? It has no invention; it has no order, system,
sequence, or result; it has no lifelikeness, no thrill, no stir, no
seeming of reality; its characters are confusedly drawn, and by their
acts and words they prove that they are not the sort of people the
author claims that they are; its humor is pathetic; its pathos is
funny; its conversations are—oh! indescribable; its love-scenes
odious; its English a crime against the language.

Counting these out, what is left is Art. I think we must all
admit that.

THE MAN THAT CORRUPTED
HADLEYBURG

"The Man That Corrupted Hadleyburg" appeared first in Harper's Magazine, *December, 1899. This master-piece of American literature was published in book form under the title* The Man That Corrupted Hadleyburg and Other Stories and Essays, *Harper and Brothers, New York and London, in 1900. It has been said that the publishers added* Other Stories and Essays *to the title because they had difficulty in deciding whether it was a story or an essay.*

THE MAN THAT CORRUPTED HADLEYBURG

I

It was many years ago. Hadleyburg was the most honest and upright town in all the region round about. It had kept that reputation unsmirched during three generations, and was prouder of it than of any other of its possessions. It was so proud of it, and so anxious to insure its perpetuation, that it began to teach the principles of honest dealing to its babies in the cradle, and made the like teachings the staple of their culture thenceforward through all the years devoted to their education. Also, throughout the formative years temptations were kept out of the way of the young people, so that their honesty could have every chance to harden and solidify, and become a part of their very bone. The neighboring towns were jealous of this honorable supremacy, and affected to sneer at Hadleyburg's pride in it and call it vanity; but all the same they were obliged to acknowledge that Hadleyburg was in reality an incorruptible town; and if pressed they would also acknowledge that the mere fact that a young man hailed from Hadleyburg was all the recommendation he needed when he went forth from his natal town to seek for responsible employment.

But at last, in the drift of time, Hadleyburg had the ill luck to offend a passing stranger—possibly without knowing it, certainly without caring, for Hadleyburg was sufficient unto itself, and cared not a rap for strangers or their opinions. Still, it would have been well to make an exception in this one's case, for he was a bitter man and revengeful. All through his wanderings during a whole year he kept his injury in mind, and gave all his leisure moments to trying to invent a compensating satisfaction for it. He contrived many plans, and all of them were good, but none of them was quite sweeping enough; the poorest of them would hurt a great many individuals, but what he wanted was a plan which would comprehend the entire town, and not let so much as one person escape unhurt. At last he had a fortunate idea, and when it fell into his brain it lit up his whole head with an evil joy. He began to form a plan at once, saying to himself, "That is the thing to do—I will corrupt the town."

Six months later he went to Hadleyburg, and arrived in a buggy at the house of the old cashier of the bank about ten at night. He got a sack out of the buggy, shouldered it, and staggered with it through the cottage yard, and knocked at the door. A woman's voice said "Come in, " and he entered, and set his sack behind the stove in the parlor, saying politely to the old lady who sat reading the *Missionary Herald* by the lamp:

"Pray keep your seat, madam, I will not disturb you. There—now it is pretty well concealed; one would hardly know it was there. Can I see your husband a moment, madam?"

No, he was gone to Brixton, and might not return before morning.

"Very well, madam, it is no matter. I merely wanted to leave that sack in his care, to be delivered to the rightful owner when he shall be found. I am a stranger; he does not know me; I am merely passing through the town to-night to discharge a matter which has been long in my mind. My errand is now completed, and I go pleased and a little proud, and you will never see me again. There is a paper attached to the sack which will explain everything. Good-night, madam."

The old lady was afraid of the mysterious big stranger, and was glad to see him go. But her curiosity was roused, and she went straight to the sack and brought away the paper. It began as follows:

"TO BE PUBLISHED; or, the right man sought out by private inquiry—either will answer. This sack contains gold coin weighing a hundred and sixty pounds four ounces—"

"Mercy on us, and the door not locked!"

Mrs. Richards flew to it all in a tremble and locked it, then pulled down the window-shades and stood frightened, worried, and wondering if there was anything else she could do toward making herself and the money more safe. She listened awhile for burglars, then surrendered to curiosity and went back to the lamp and finished reading the paper:

"I am a foreigner, and am presently going back to my own country, to remain there permanently. I am grateful to America for what I have received at her hands during my long stay under her flag; and to one of her citizens—a citizen of Hadleyburg—I am especially grateful for a great kindness done me a year or two ago. Two great kindnesses, in fact. I will explain. I was a gambler. I say I WAS. I was a ruined gambler. I arrived in this village at night, hungry and without a penny. I asked for help—in the dark; I was ashamed to beg in the light. I begged of the right man. He gave me twenty dollars—that is to say, he gave me life, as I considered it. He also gave me fortune: for out of that money I have made myself rich at the gaming-table. And

finally, a remark which he made to me has remained with me to this day, and has at last conquered me; and in conquering has saved the remnant of my morals: I shall gamble no more. Now I have no idea who that man was, but I want him found, and I want him to have this money, to give away, throw away, or keep, as he pleases. It is merely my way of testifying my gratitude to him. If I could stay, I would find him myself; but no matter, he will be found. This is an honest town, an incorruptible town, and I know I can trust it without fear. This man can be identified by the remark which he made to me; I feel persuaded that he will remember it.

"And now my plan is this: If you prefer to conduct the inquiry privately, do so. Tell the contents of this present writing to any one who is likely to be the right man. If he shall answer, 'I am the man; the remark I made was so-and-so,' apply the test—to wit; open the sack, and in it you will find a sealed envelope containing that remark. If the remark mentioned by the candidate tallies with it, give him the money, and ask no further questions, for he is certainly the right man.

"But if you shall prefer a public inquiry, then publish this present writing in the local paper—with these instructions added, to wit: Thirty days from now, let the candidate appear at the town-hall at eight in the evening (Friday), and hand his remark, in a sealed envelope, to the Rev. Mr. Burgess (if he will be kind enough to act); and let Mr. Burgess there and then destroy the seals of the sack, open it, and see if the remark is correct; if correct, let the money be delivered, with my sincere gratitude, to my benefactor thus identified."

Mrs. Richards sat down, gently quivering with excitement, and was soon lost in things—after this pattern: "What a strange thing it is! . . .And what a fortune for that kind man who set his bread afloat upon the waters! . . .If it had only been my husband that did it!—for we are so poor, so old and poor! . . ." Then, with a sigh— "But it was not my Edward; no, it was not he that gave a stranger twenty dollars. It is a pity, too; I see it now. . ." Then, with a shudder— "But it is *gambler's* money! the wages of sin: we couldn't take it; we couldn't touch it. I don't like to be near it; it seems a defilement." She moved to a farther chair. . . ."I wish Edward would come, and take it to the bank; a burglar might come at any moment; it is dreadful to be here all alone with it."

At eleven Mr. Richards arrived, and while his wife was saying, "I am *so* glad you've come!" he was saying, "I'm so tired—tired clear out; it is dreadful to be poor, and have to make these dismal journeys at my time of life. Always at the grind, grind, grind, on a salary—another man's slave, and he sitting at home in his slippers, rich and comfortable."

"I am so sorry for you, Edward, you know that; but be comforted: we have our livelihood; we have our good name—"

"Yes, Mary, and that is everything. Don't mind my talk—it's just a moment's irritation and doesn't mean anything. Kiss me— there, it's all gone now, and I am not complaining any more. What have you been getting? What's in the sack?"

Then his wife told him the great secret. It dazed him for a moment; then he said:

"It weighs a hundred and sixty pounds? Why, Mary, it's for-ty thou-sand dollars—think of it—a whole fortune! Not ten men in this village are worth that much. Give me the paper."

He skimmed through it and said:

"Isn't it an adventure! Why, it's a romance; it's like the impossible things one reads about in books, and never sees in life." He was well stirred up now; cheerful, even gleeful. He tapped his old wife on the cheek, and said, humorously, "Why, we're rich, Mary, rich; all we've got to do is to bury the money and burn the papers. If the gambler ever comes to inquire, we'll merely look coldly upon him and say: 'What is this nonsense you are talking? We have never heard of you and your sack of gold before;' and then he would look foolish, and—"

"And in the meantime, while you are running on with your jokes, the money is still here, and it is fast getting along toward burglar-time."

"True. Very well, what shall we do—make the inquiry private? No, not that: it would spoil the romance. The public method is better. Think what a noise it will make! And it will make all the other towns jealous; for no stranger would trust such a thing to any town but Hadleyburg, and they know it. It's a great card for us. I must get to the printing-office now, or I shall be too late."

"But stop—stop—don't leave me here alone with it, Edward!"

But he was gone. For only a little while, however. Not far from his own house he met the editor-proprietor of the paper, and gave him the document, and said, "Here is a good thing for you, Cox—put it in."

"It may be too late, Mr. Richards, but I'll see."

At home again he and his wife sat down to talk the charming mystery over; they were in no condition for sleep. The first question was, Who could the citizen have been who gave the stranger the twenty dollars? It seemed a simple one; both answered it in the same breath—

"Barclay Goodson."

"Yes," said Richards, "he could have done it, and it would have been like him, but there's not another in the town."

"Everybody will grant that, Edward—grant it privately, anyway. For six months, now, the village has been its own proper self once more—honest, narrow, self-righteous, and stingy."

"It is what he always called it, to the day of his death—said it right out publicly, too."

"Yes, and he was hated for it."

"Oh, of course; but he didn't care. I reckon he was the best-hated man among us, except the Reverend Burgess."

"Well, Burgess deserves it—he will never get another congregation here. Mean as the town is, it knows how to estimate *him*. Edward, doesn't it seem odd that the stranger should appoint Burgess to deliver the money?"

"Well, yes—it does. That is—that is—"

"Why so much that-*is*-ing? Would *you* select him?"

"Mary, maybe the stranger knows him better than this village does."

"Much *that* would help Burgess!"

The husband seemed perplexed for an answer; the wife kept a steady eye upon him, and waited. Finally Richards said, with the hesitancy of one who is making a statement which is likely to encounter doubt,

"Mary, Burgess is not a bad man."

His wife was certainly surprised.

"Nonsense!" she exclaimed.

"He is not a bad man. I know. The whole of his unpopularity had its foundation in that one thing—the thing that made so much noise."

"That 'one thing,' indeed! As if that 'one thing' wasn't enough, all by itself."

"Plenty. Plenty. Only he wasn't guilty of it."

"How you talk! Not guilty of it! Everybody knows he *was* guilty."

"Mary, I give you my word—he was innocent."

"I can't believe it, and I don't. How do you know?"

"It is a confession. I am ashamed, but I will make it. I was the only man who knew he was innocent. I could have saved him, and— and—well, you know how the town was wrought up—I hadn't the pluck to do it. It would have turned everybody against me. I felt mean, ever so mean; but I didn't dare; I hadn't the manliness to face that."

Mary looked troubled, and for a while was silent. Then she said, stammeringly:

"I—I don't think it would have done for you to—to— One mustn't—er—public opinion—one has to be so careful—so—" It was a difficult road, and she got mired; but after a little she got started again. "It was a great pity, but— Why, we couldn't afford it, Edward—we couldn't indeed. Oh, I wouldn't have had you do it for anything!"

"It would have lost us the good-will of so many people, Mary; and then—and then—"

"What troubles me now is, what *he* thinks of us, Edward."

"He? *He* doesn'r suspect that I could have saved him."

"Oh," exclaimed the wife, in a tone of relief, "I am glad of that. As long as he doesn't know that you could have saved him, he—he— well, that makes it a great deal better. Why, I might have known he didn't know, because he is always trying to be friendly with us, as little encouragement as we give him. More than once people have twitted me with it. There's the Wilsons, and the Wilcoxes, and the Harknesses, they take a mean pleasure in saying, '*Your friend* Burgess,' because they know it pesters me. I wish he wouldn't persist in liking us so; I can't think why he keeps it up."

"I can explain it. It's another confession. When the thing was new

and hot, and the town made a plan to ride him on a rail, my
conscience hurt me so that I couldn't stand it, and I went privately
and gave him notice, and he got out of the town and staid out till
it was safe to come back."

"Edward! If the town had found it out—"

"*Don't!* It scares me yet, to think of it. I repented of if the minute
it was done; and I was even afraid to tell you, lest your face might
betray it to somebody. I didn't sleep any that night, for worrying.
But after a few days I saw that no one was going to suspect me, and
after that I got to feeling glad I did it. And I feel glad yet, Mary—
glad through and through."

"So do I, now, for it would have been a dreadful way to treat him.
Yes, I'm glad; for really you did owe him that, you know. But,
Edward, suppose it should come out yet, some day!"

"It won't."

"Why?"

"Because everybody thinks it was Goodson."

"Of course they would!"

"Certainly. And of course *he* didn't care. They persuaded poor
old Sawlsberry to go and charge it on him, and he went blustering
over there and did it. Goodson looked him over, like as if he was
hunting for a place on him that he could despise the most, then he
says, 'So you are the Committee of Inquiry, are you?' Sawlsberry
said that was about what he was. 'Hm. Do they require particulars,
or do you reckon a kind of a *general* answer will do?' 'If they require
particulars, I will come back, Mr. Goodson; I will take the general
answer first.' 'Very well, then, tell them to go to hell—I reckon that's
general enough. And I'll give you some advice, Sawlsberry; when you
come back for the particulars, fetch a basket to carry the relics of
yourself home in.' "

"Just like Goodson; it's got all the marks. He had only one vanity:
he thought he could give advice better than any other person."

"It settled the business, and saved us, Mary. The subject was
dropped."

"Bless you, I'm not doubting *that.*"

Then they took up the gold-sack mystery again, with strong
interest. Soon the conversation began to suffer breaks—
interruptions caused by absorbed thinkings. The breaks grew more
and more frequent. At last Richards lost himself wholly in thought.
He sat long, gazing vacantly at the floor, and by and by he began
to punctuate his thoughts with little nervous movements of his hands
that seemed to indicate vexation. Meantime his wife too had
relapsed into a thoughtful silence, and her movements were
beginning to show a troubled discomfort. Finally Richards got up
and strode aimlessly about the room, plowing his hands through
his hair, much as a somnambulist might do who was having a bad
dream. Then he seemed to arrive at a definte purpose; and without a

word he put on his hat and passed quickly out of the house. His wife sat brooding, with a drawn face, and did not seem to be aware that she was alone. Now and then she murmured, 'Lead us not into t— . . . but—but—we are so poor, so poor! . . . Lead us not into. . . . Ah, who would be hurt by it?—and no one would ever know. . . . Lead us. . . ." The voice died out in mumblings. After a little she glanced up and muttered in a half-frightened, half-glad way—

"He is gone! But, oh dear, he may be too late!too late. . . . Maybe not—maybe there is still time." She rose and stood thinking, nervously clasping and unclasping her hands. A slight shudder shook her frame, and she said, out of a dry throat. "God forgive me—it's awful to think such things—but . . . Lord, how we are made—how strangely we are made!"

She turned the light low, and slipped stealthily over and kneeled down by the sack and felt of its ridgy sides with her hands, and fondled them lovingly; and there was a gloating light in her poor old eyes. She fell into fits of absence; and came half out of them at times to mutter, "If we had only waited!—oh, if we had only waited a little, and not been in such a hurry!"

Meantime Cox had gone home from his office and told his wife all about the strange thing that had happened, and they had talked it over eagerly, and guessed that the late Goodson was the only man in the town who could have helped a suffering stranger with so noble a sum as twenty dollars. Then there was a pause, and the two became thoughtful and silent. And by and by nervous and fidgety. At last the wife said, as if to herself,

"Nobody knows this secret but the Richardses . . . and us . . . nobody."

The husband came out of his thinkings with a slight start, and gazed wistfully at his wife, whose face was become very pale; then he hesitatingly rose, and glanced furtively at his hat, then at his wife— a sort of mute inquiry. Mrs. Cox swallowed once or twice, with her hand at her throat, then in place of speech she nodded her head. In a moment she was alone, and mumbling to herself.

And now Richards and Cox were hurrying through the deserted streets, from opposite directions. They met, panting, at the foot of the printing-office stairs; by the night-light there they read each other's face. Cox whispered,

"Nobody knows about this but us?"

The whispered answer was,

"Not a soul—on honor, not a soul!"

"If it isn't too late to—"

The men were starting up-stairs; at this moment they were overtaken by a boy, and Cox asked,

"Is that you, Johnny?"

"Yes, sir."

"You needn't ship the early mail—nor *any* mail; wait till I tell you."

"It's already gone, sir."

"*Gone?*" It had the sound of an unspeakable disappointment in it.

"Yes, sir. Time-table for Brixton and all the towns beyond changed to-day, sir—had to get the papers in twenty minutes earlier than common. I had to rush; if I had been two minutes later—"

The men turned and walked slowly away, not waiting to hear the rest. Neither of them spoke during ten minutes; then Cox said, in a vexed tone,

"What possessed you to be in such a hurry, *I* can't make out."

The answer was humble enough:

"I see it now, but somehow I never thought, you know, until it was too late. But the next time—"

"Next time be hanged! It won't come in a thousand years."

Then the friends separated without a good-night, and dragged themselves home with the gait of mortally stricken men. At their homes their wives sprang up with an eager "Well?"—then saw the answer with their eyes and sank down sorrowing, without waiting for it to come in words. In both houses a discussion followed of a heated sort—a new thing; there had been discussions before, but not heated ones, not ungentle ones. The discussions to-night were a sort of seeming plagiarisms of each other. Mrs. Richards said,

"If you had only waited, Edward—if you had only stopped to think; but no, you must run straight to the printing-office and spread it all over the world."

"It *said* publish it."

"That is nothing; it also said do it privately, if you liked. There, now—is that true, or not?"

"Why, yes—yes, it is true; but when I thought what a stir it would make, and what a compliment it was to Hadleyburg that a stranger should trust it so—"

"Oh, certainly, I know all that; but if you had only stopped to think, you would have seen that you *couldn't* find the right man, because he is in his grave, and hasn't left chick nor child nor relation behind him; and as long as the money went to somebody that awfully needed it, and nobody would be hurt by it, and—and—"

She broke down, crying. Her husband tried to think of some comforting thing to say, and presently came out with this:

"But after all, Mary, it must be for the best—it *must* be; we know that. And we must remember that it was so ordered—"

"Ordered! Oh, everything's *ordered,* when a person has to find some way out when he has been stupid. Just the same, it was *ordered* that the money should come to us in this special way, and it was you that must take it on yourself to go meddling with the designs of Providence—and who gave you the right? It was wicked, that is what it was—just blasphemous presumption, and no more becoming to a meek and humble professor of—"

"But, Mary, you know how we have been trained all our lives long, like the whole village, till it is absolutely second nature to us to stop not a single moment to think when there's an honest thing to be done—"

"Oh, I know it, I know it—it's been one everlasting training and training and training in honesty—honesty shielded, from the very cradle, against every possible temptation, and so it's *artificial* honesty, and weak as water when temptation comes, as we have seen this night. God knows I never had shade nor shadow of a doubt of my petrified and indestructible honesty until now—and now, under the very first big and real temptation, I—Edward, it is my belief that this town's honesty is as rotten as mine is; as rotten as yours is. It is a mean town, a hard, stingy town, and hasn't a virtue in the world but this honesty it is so celebrated for and so conceited about; and so help me, I do believe that if ever the day comes that its honesty falls under great temptation, its grand reputation will go to ruin like a house of cards. There, now, I've made confession, and I feel better; I am a humbug, and I've been one all my life, without knowing it. Let no man call me honest again—I will not have it."

"I—well, Mary, I feel a good deal as you do; I certainly do. It seems strange, too, so strange. I never could have believed it—never."

A long silence followed; both were sunk in thought. At last the wife looked up and said,

"I know what you are thinking, Edward."

Richards had the embarrassed look of a person who is caught.

"I am ashamed to confess it, Mary, but—"

"It's no matter, Edward, I was thinking the same question myself."

"I hope so. State it."

"You were thinking, if a body could only guess out *what the remark was* that Goodson made to the stranger."

"It's perfectly true. I feel guilty and ashamed. And you?"

"I'm past it. Let us make a pallet here; we've got to stand watch till the bank vault opens in the morning and admits the sack. . . . Oh dear, oh dear—if we hadn't made the mistake!"

The pallet was made, and Mary said:

"The open sesame—what could it have been? I do wonder what that remark could have been? But come; we will get to bed now."

"And sleep?"

"No: think."

"Yes, think."

By this time the Coxes too had completed their spat and their reconciliation, and were turning in—to think, to think, and toss, and fret, and worry over what the remark could possibly have been which

Goodson made to the stranded derelict; that golden remark; that remark worth forty thousand dollars, cash.

The reason that the village telegraph office was open later than usual that night was this: The foreman of Cox's paper was the local representative of the Associated Press. One might say its honorary representative, for it wasn't four times a year that he could furnish thirty words that would be accepted. But this time it was different. His dispatch stating what he had caught got an instant answer:

"Send the whole thing—all the details—twelve hundred words."

A colossal order! The foreman filled the bill; and he was the proudest man in the State. By breakfast-time the next morning the name of Hadleyburg the Incorruptible was on every lip in America, from Montreal to the Gulf, from the glaciers of Alaska to the orange-groves of Florida; and millions and millions of people were discussing the stranger and his money-sack, and wondering if the right man would be found, and hoping some more news about the matter would come soon—right away.

II

Hadleyburg village woke up world-celebrated—astonished—happy—vain. Vain beyond imagination. Its nineteen principal citizens and their wives went about shaking hands with each other, and beaming, and smiling, and congratulating, and saying *this* thing adds a new word to the dictionary—*Hadleyburg,* synonym for *incorruptible*—destined to live in dictionaries forever! And the minor and unimportant citizens and their wives went around acting in much the same way. Everybody ran to the bank to see the gold-sack; and before noon grieved and envious crowds began to flock in from Brixton and all neighboring towns; and that afternoon and next day reporters began to arrive from everywhere to verify the sack and its history and write the whole thing up anew, and make dashing free-hand pictures of the sack, and of Richards's house, and the bank, and the Presbyterian church, and the Baptist church, and the public square, and the town-hall where the test would be applied and the money delivered; and damnable portraits of the Richardses, and Pinkerton the banker, and Cox, and the foreman, and Reverend Burgess, and the postmaster—and even of Jack Halliday, who was the loafing, good-natured, no-account, irreverent fisherman, hunter, boys' friend, stray-dogs' friend, typical "Sam Lawson" of the town. The little mean, smirking, oily Pinkerton showed the sack to all comers, and rubbed his sleek palms together pleasantly, and enlarged upon the town's fine old reputation for honesty and upon this wonderful endorsement of it, and hoped and believed that the example would now spread far and wide over the American world, and be epoch-making in the matter of moral regeneration. And so on, and so on.

By the end of a week things had quieted down again; the wild intoxication of pride and joy had sobered to a soft, sweet, silent delight—a sort of deep, nameless, unutterable content. All faces bore a look of peaceful, holy happiness.

Then a change came. It was a gradual change: so gradual that its beginnings were hardly noticed; maybe were not noticed at all, except by Jack Halliday, who always noticed everything; and always made fun of it, too, no matter what it was. He began to throw out chaffing remarks about people not looking quite so happy as they did a day or two ago; and next he claimed that the new aspect was deepening to positive sadness; next, that it was taking on a sick look; and finally he said that everybody was become so moody, thoughtful, and absent-minded that he could rob the meanest man in town of a cent out of the bottom of his breeches pocket and not disturb his revery.

At this stage—or at about this stage—a saying like this was dropped at bedtime—with a sigh, usually—by the head of each of the nineteen principal households— "Ah, what *could* have been the remark that Goodson made?"

And straightway—with a shudder—came this, from the man's wife:

"Oh, *don't!* What horrible thing are you mulling in your mind? Put it away from you, for God's sake!"

But that question was wrung from those men again the next night —and got the same retort. But weaker.

And the third night the men uttered the question yet again—with anguish, and absently. This time—and the following night—the wives fidgeted feebly, and tried to say something. But didn't.

And the night after that they found their tongues and responded— longingly,

"Oh, if we *could* only guess!"

Halliday's comments grew daily more and more sparklingly disagreeable and disparaging. He went diligently about, laughing at the town, individually and in mass. But his laugh was the only one left in the village: it fell upon a hollow and mournful vacancy and emptiness. Not even a smile was findable anywhere. Halliday carried a cigar-box around on a tripod, playing that it was a camera, and halted all passers and aimed the thing and said, "Ready!—now look pleasant, please," but not even this capital joke could surprise the dreary faces into any softening.

So three weeks passed—one week was left. It was Saturday evening—after supper. Instead of the aforetime Saturday-evening flutter and bustle and shopping and larking, the streets were empty and desolate. Richards and his old wife sat apart in their little parlor —miserable and thinking. This was become their evening habit now:

the lifelong habit which had preceded it, of reading, knitting, and contented chat, or receiving or paying neighborly calls, was dead and gone and forgotten, ages ago—two or three weeks ago; nobody talked now, nobody read, nobody visited—the whole village sat at home, sighing, worrying, silent. Trying to guess out that remark.

The postman left a letter. Richards glanced listlessly at the superscription and the postmark—unfamiliar, both—and tossed the letter on the table and resumed his might-have-beens and his hopeless dull miseries where he had left them off. Two or three hours later his wife got wearily up and was going away to bed without a good-night—custom now—but she stopped near the letter and eyed it awhile with a dead interest, then broke it open, and began to skim it over. Richards, sitting there with his chair tilted back against the wall and his chin between his knees, heard something fall. It was his wife. He sprang to her side, but she cried out:

"Leave me alone, I am too happy. Read the letter—read it!"

He did. He devoured it, his brain reeling. The letter was from a distant State, and it said:

"I am a stranger to you, but no matter: I have something to tell. I have just arrived home from Mexico, and learned about that episode. Of course you do not know who made that remark, but I know, and I am the only person living who does know. It was GOODSON. I knew him well, many years ago. I passed through your village that very night, and was his guest till the midnight train came along. I overheard him make that remark to the stranger in the dark—it was in Hale Alley. He and I talked of it the rest of the way home, and while smoking in his house. He mentioned many of your villagers in the course of his talk—most of them in a very uncomplimentary way, but two or three favorably; among these latter yourself. I say 'favorably'—nothing stronger. I remember his saying he did not actually LIKE any person in the town—not one; but that you—I THINK he said you—am almost sure—had done him a very great service once, possibly without knowing the full value of it, and he wished he had a fortune, he would leave it to you when he died, and a curse apiece for the rest of the citizens. Now, then, if it was you that did him that service, you are his legitimate heir, and entitled to the sack of gold. I know that I can trust to your honor and honesty, for in a citizen of Hadleyburg these virtues are an unfailing inheritance, and so I am going to reveal to you the remark well satisfied that if you are not the right man you will seek and find the right one and see that poor Goodson's debt of gratitude for the service referred to is paid. This is the remark: 'YOU ARE FAR FROM BEING A BAD MAN. GO, AND REFORM.'
"HOWARD L. STEPHENSON"

"Oh, Edward, the money is ours, and I am so grateful, *oh,* so grateful—kiss me, dear, it's forever since we kissed—and we needed it so—the money—and now you are free of Pinkerton and his bank, and nobody's slave any more; it seems to me I could fly for joy."

It was a happy half-hour that the couple spent there on the settee caressing each other; it was the old days come again—days that had began with their courtship and lasted without a break till the stranger brought the deadly money. By and by the wife said:

"Oh, Edward, how lucky it was you did him that grand service, poor Goodson! I never liked him, but I love him now. And it was fine and beautiful of you never to mention it or brag about it." Then, with a touch of reproach, "But you ought to have told *me,* Edward, you ought to have told your wife, you know."

"Well, I—er—well, Mary, you see—"

"Now stop hemming and hawing, and tell me about it, Edward. I
always loved you, and now I'm proud of you. Everybody believes
there was only one good generous soul in this village, and now it
turns out that you—Edward, why don't you tell me?"

"Well—er—er— Why, Mary, I can't!"

"You *can't? Why* can't you?"

"You see, he—well, he—he made me promise I wouldn't."

The wife looked him over, and said, very slowly,

"Made—you—promise? Edward, what do you tell me that for?"

"Mary, do you think I would lie?"

She was troubled and silent for a moment, then she laid her hand
within his and said:

"No . . . no. We have wandered far enough from our bearings—
God spare us that! In all your life you have never uttered a lie. But
now—now that the foundations of things seem to be crumbling from
under us, we—we—" She lost her voice for a moment, then said,
brokenly, "Lead us not into temptation. . . . I think you made the
promise, Edward. Let it rest so. Let us keep away from that ground.
Now—that is all gone by; let us be happy again; it is no time for
clouds."

Edward found it something of an effort to comply, for his mind
kept wandering—trying to remember what the service was that he
had done Goodson.

The couple lay awake the most of the night, Mary happy and busy,
Edward busy but not so happy. Mary was planning what she would
do with the money. Edward was trying to recall that service. At first
his conscience was sore on account of the lie he had told Mary—if it
was a lie. After much reflection—suppose it *was* a lie? What then?
Was it such a great matter? Aren't we always *acting* lies? Then why
not *tell* them? Look at Mary—look what she had done. While he was
hurrying off on his honest errand, what was she doing? Lamenting
because the papers hadn't been destroyed and the money kept! Is
theft better than lying?

That point lost its sting—the lie dropped into the background and
left comfort behind it. The next point came to the front: *Had* he
rendered that service? Well, here was Goodson's own evidence as
reported in Stephenson's letter; there could be no better evidence
than that—it was even *proof* that he had rendered it. Of course. So
that point was settled. . . . No, not quite. He recalled with a wince
that this unknown Mr. Stephenson was just a trifle unsure as to
whether the performer of it was Richards or some other—and, oh
dear, he had put Richards on his honor! He must himself decide
whither that money must go—and Mr. Stephenson was not doubting
that if he was the wrong man he would go honorably and find the
right one. Oh, it was odious to put a man in such a situation—ah,
why couldn't Stephenson have left out that doubt! What did he want
to intrude that for?

Further reflection. How did it happen that *Richards's* name remained in Stephenson's mind as indicating the right man, and not some other man's name? That looked good. Yes, that looked very good. In fact, it went on looking better and better, straight along—until by and by it grew into positive *proof.* And then Richards put the matter at once out of his mind, for he had a private instinct that a proof once established is better left so.

He was feeling reasonably comfortable now, but there was still one other detail that kept pushing itself on his notice: of course he had done that service—that was settled; but what *was* that service? He must recall it—he would not go to sleep till he had recalled it; it would make his peace of mind perfect. And so he thought and thought. He thought of a dozen things—possible services, even probable services—but none of them seemed adequate, none of them seemed large enough, none of them seemed worth the money—worth the fortune Goodson had wished he could leave in his will. And besides, he couldn't remember having done them, anyway, Now, then—now, then—what *kind* of a service would it be that would make a man so inordinately grateful? Ah—the saving of his soul! That must be it. Yes, he could remember, now, how he once set himself the task of converting Goodson, and labored at it as much as —he was going to say three months; but upon closer examination it shrunk to a month, then to a week, then to a day, then to nothing. Yes, he remembered now, and with unwelcome vividness, that Goodson had told him to go to thunder and mind his own business— *he* wasn't hankering to follow Hadleyburg to heaven!

So that solution was a failure—he hadn't saved Goodson's soul. Richards was discouraged. Then after a little came another idea: had he saved Goodson's property? No, that wouldn't do—he hadn't any. His life? That is it! Of course. Why, he might have thought of it before. This time he was on the right track, sure. His imagination-mill was hard at work in a minute, now.

Thereafter during a stretch of two exhausting hours he was busy saving Goodson's life. He saved it in all kinds of difficult and perilous ways. In every case he got it saved satisfactorily up to a certain point; then, just as he was beginning to get well persuaded that it had really happened, a troublesome detail would turn up which made the whole thing impossible. As in the matter of drowning, for instance. In that case he had swum out and tugged Goodson ashore in an unconscious state with a great crowd looking on and applauding, but when he had got it all thought out and was just beginning to remember all about it, a whole swarm of disqualifying details arrived on the ground: the town would have known of the circumstance, Mary would have known of it, it would glare like a limelight in his own memory instead of being an inconspicuous service which he had possibly rendered "without knowing its full value." And at this point he remembered that he couldn't swim, anyway.

Ah—*there* was a point which he had been overlooking from the start: it had to be a service which he had rendered "possibly without knowing the full value of it." Why, really, that ought to be an easy hunt—much easier than those others. And sure enough, by and by he found it. Goodson, years and years ago, came near marrying a very sweet and pretty girl, named Nancy Hewitt, but in some way or other the match had been broken off; the girl died, Goodson remained a bachelor, and by and by became a soured one and a frank despiser of the human species. Soon after the girl's death the village found out, or thought it had found out, that she carried a spoonful of negro blood in her veins. Richards worked at these details a good while, and in the end he thought he remembered things concerning them which must have gotten mislaid in his memory through long neglect. He seemed to dimly remember that it was *he* that found out about the negro blood; that it was he that told the village; that the village told Goodson where they got it; that he thus saved Goodson from marrying the tainted girl; that he had done him this great service "without knowing the full value of it," in fact without knowing that he *was* doing it; but that Goodson knew the value of it, and what a narrow escape he had had, and so went to his grave grateful to his benefactor and wishing he had a fortune to leave him. It was all clear and simple now, and the more he went over it the more luminous and certain it grew; and at last, when he nestled to sleep satisfied and happy, he remembered the whole thing just as if it had been yesterday. In fact, he dimly remembered Goodson's *telling* him his gratitude once. Meantime Mary had spent six thousand dollars on a new house for herself and a pair of slippers for her pastor, and then had fallen peacefully to rest.

That came Saturday evening the postman had delivered a letter to each of the other principal citizens—nineteen letters in all. No two of the envelopes were alike, and no two of the superscriptions were in the same hand, but the letters inside were just like each other in every detail but one. They were exact copies of the letter received by Richards—handwriting and all—and were all signed by Stephenson, but in place of Richards's name each receiver's own name appeared.

All night long eighteen principal citizens did what their caste-brother Richards was doing at the same time—they put in their energies trying to remember what notable service it was that they had unconsciously done Barclay Goodson. In no case was it a holiday job; still they succeeded.

And while they were at this work, which was difficult, their wives put in the night spending the money, which was easy. During that one night the nineteen wives spent an average of seven thousand dollars each out of the forty thousand in the sack—a hundred and thirty-three altogether.

Next day there was a surprise for Jack Halliday. He noticed that

the faces of the nineteen chief citizens and their wives bore that
expression of peaceful and holy happiness again. He could not
understand it, neither was he able to invent any remarks about it
that could damage it or disturb it. And so it was his turn to be
dissatisfied with life. His private guesses at the reasons for the
happiness failed in all instances, upon examination. When he met
Mrs. Wilcox and noticed the placid ecstasy in her face, he said to
himself, "Her cat has had kittens"—and went and asked the cook: it
was not so; the cook had detected the happiness, but did not know
the cause. When Halliday found the duplicate ecstasy in the face of
"Shadbelly" Billson (village nickname), he was sure some neighbor
of Billson's had broken his leg, but inquiry showed that this had not
happened. The subdued ecstasy in Gregory Yates's face could mean
but one thing—he was a mother-in-law short: it was another
mistake. "And Pinkerton—Pinkerton—he has collected ten cents
that he thought he was going to lose." And so on, and so on. In some
cases the guesses had to remain in doubt, in the others they proved
distinct errors. In the end Halliday said to himself, "Anyway it foots
up that there's nineteen Hadleyburg families temporarily in heaven:
I don't know how it happened; I only know Providence is off duty
to-day."

An architect and builder from the next State had lately ventured
to set up a small business in this unpromising village, and his sign
had not been hanging out a week. Not a customer yet; he was a
discouraged man, and sorry he had come. But his weather changed
suddenly now. First one and then another chief citizen's wife said to
him privately:

"Come to my house Monday week—but say nothing about it for
the present. We think of building."

He got eleven invitations that day. That night he wrote his
daughter and broke off her match with her student. He said she
could marry a mile higher than that.

Pinkerton the banker and two or three other well-to-do men
planned country-seats—but waited. That kind don't count their
chickens until they are hatched.

The Wilsons devised a grand new thing—a fancy-dress ball. They
made no actual promises, but told all their acquaintanceship in
confidence that they were thinking the matter over and thought they
should give it—"and if we do, you will be invited, of course." People
were surprised, and said, one to another, "Why, they are crazy, those
poor Wilsons, they can't afford it." Several among the nineteen said
privately to their husbands, "It is a good idea: we will keep still till
their cheap thing is over, then *we* will give one that will make it sick."

The days drifted along, and the bill of future squanderings rose
higher and higher, wilder and wilder, more and more foolish and
reckless. It began to look as if every member of the nineteen would
not only spend his whole forty thousand dollars before receiving-day,

but be actually in debt by the time he got the money. In some cases light-headed people did not stop with planning to spend, they really spent—on credit. They bought land, mortgages, farms, speculative stocks, fine clothes, horses, and various other things, paid down the bonus, and made themselves liable for the rest—at ten days.

Presently the sober second thought came, and Halliday noticed that a ghastly anxiety was beginning to show up in a good many faces. Again he was puzzled, and didn't know what to make of it. "The Wilcox kittens aren't dead, for they weren't born; nobody's broken a leg; there's no shrinkage in mother-in-laws; *nothing* has happened— it is an unsolvable mystery."

There was another puzzled man, too—the Rev. Mr. Burgess. For days, wherever he went, people seemed to follow him or to be watching out for him; and if he ever found himself in a retired spot, a member of the nineteen would be sure to appear, thrust an envelope privately into his hand, whisper "To be opened at the town-hall Friday evening," then vanish away like a guilty thing. He was expecting that there might be one claimant for the sack,—doubtful, however, Goodson being dead,—but it never occurred to him that all this crowd might be claimants. When the great Friday came at last, he found that he had nineteen envelopes.

III

The town-hall had never looked finer. The platform at the end of it was backed by a showy draping of flags; at intervals along the walls were festoons of flags; the gallery fronts were clothed in flags; the supporting columns were swathed in flags; all this was to impress the stranger, for he would be there in considerable force, and in a large degree he would be connected with the press. The house was full. The 412 fixed seats were occupied; also the 68 extra chairs which had been packed into the aisles; the steps of the platform were occupied; some distinguished strangers were given seats on the platform; at the horseshoe of tables which fenced the front and sides of the platform sat a strong force of special correspondents who had come from everywhere. It was the best-dressed house the town had ever produced. There were some tolerably expensive toilets there, and in several cases the ladies who wore them had the look of being unfamiliar with that kind of clothes. At least the town thought they had that look, but the notion could have arisen from the town's knowledge of the fact that these ladies had never inhabited such clothes before.

The gold-sack stood on a little table at the front of the platform where all the house could see it. The bulk of the house gazed at it with a burning interest, a mouth-watering interest, a wistful and pathetic interest; a minority of nineteen couples gazed at it tenderly, lovingly, proprietarily, and the male half of this minority kept saying

over to themselves the moving little impromptu speeches of
thankfulness for the audience's applause and congratulations which
they were presently going to get up and deliver. Every now and then
one of these got a piece of paper out of his vest pocket and privately
glanced at it to refresh his memory.

Of course there was a buzz of conversation going on—there always
is; but at last when the Rev. Mr. Burgess rose and laid his hand on
the sack he could hear his microbes gnaw, the place was so still. He
related the curious history of the sack, then went on to speak in
warm terms of Hadleyburg's old and well-earned reputation for
spotless honesty, and of the town's just pride in this reputation. He
said that this reputation was a treasure of priceless value; that under
Providence its value had now become inestimably enhanced, for the
recent episode had spread this fame far and wide, and thus had
focused the eyes of the American world upon this village, and made
its name for all time, as he hoped and believed, a synonym for
commercial incorruptibility. [*Applause.*] "And who is to be the
guardian of this noble treasure—the community as a whole? No! The
responsibility is individual, not communal. From this day forth each
and every one of you is in his own person its special guardian, and
individually responsible that no harm shall come to it. Do you—does
each of you—accept this great trust? [*Tummultuous assent.*] Then
all is well. Transmit it to your children and to your children's
children. To-day your purity is beyond reproach—see to it that it
shall remain so. To-day there is not a person in your community who
could be beguiled to touch a penny not his own—see to it that you
abide in this grace. [*"We will! we will!"*] This is not the place to make
comparisons between ourselves and other communities—some of
them ungracious toward us; they have their ways, we have ours; let
us be content. [*Applause.*] I am done. Under my hand, my friends,
rests a stranger's eloquent recognition of what we are; through him
the world will always henceforth know what we are. We do not know
who he is, but in your name I utter your gratitude, and ask you to
raise your voices in endorsement."

The house rose in a body and made the walls quake with the
thunders of its thankfulness for the space of a long minute. Then it
sat down, and Mr. Burgess took an envelope out of his pocket. The
house held its breath while he slit the envelope open and took from it
a slip of paper. He read its contents—slowly and impressively—the
audience listening with tranced attention to this magic document,
each of whose words stood for an ingot of gold:

"'*The remark which I made to the distressed stranger was this:
"You are very far from being a bad man; go, and reform."*'" "Then
he continued:

"We shall know in a moment now whether the remark here quoted
corresponds with the one concealed in the sack; and if that shall
prove to be so—and it undoubtedly will—this sack of gold belongs to

a fellow-citizen who will henceforth stand before the nation as the symbol of the special virtue which has made our town famous throughout the land—Mr. Billson!"

The house had gotten itself all ready to burst into the proper tornado of applause; but instead of doing it, it seemed stricken with a paralysis; there was a deep hush for a moment or two, then a wave of whispered murmurs swept the place—of about this tenor: *"Billson!* oh, come, this is *too* thin! Twenty dollars to a stranger—or *anybody—Billson!* tell it to the marines!" And now at this point the house caught its breath all of a sudden in a new access of astonishment, for it discovered that whereas in one part of the hall Deacon Billson was standing up with his head meekly bowed, in another part of it Lawyer Wilson was doing the same. There was a wondering silence now for a while.

Everybody was puzzled, and nineteen couples were surprised and indignant.

Billson and Wilson turned and stared at each other. Billson asked, bitingly,

"Why do *you* rise, Mr. Wilson?"

"Because I have a right to. Perhaps you will be good enough to explain to the house why *you* rise?"

"With great pleasure. Because I wrote that paper."

"It is an impudent falsity! I wrote it myself."

It was Burgess's turn to be paralyzed. He stood looking vacantly at first one of the men and then the other, and did not seem to know what to do. The house was stupefied. Lawyer Wilson spoke up, now, and said,

"I ask the Chair to read the name signed to that paper."

That brought the Chair to itself, and it read out the name,

" 'John Wharton *Billson.*' "

"There! shouted Billson, "what have you got to say for yourself, now? And what kind of apology are you going to make to me and to this insulted house for the imposture which you have attempted to play here?"

"No apologies are due, sir; and as for the rest of it, I publicly charge you with pilfering my note from Mr. Burgess and substituting a copy of it signed with your own name. There is no other way by which you could have gotten hold of the test-remark; I alone, of living men, possessed the secret of its wording."

There was likely to be a scandalous state of things if this went on; everybody noticed with distress that the short-hand scribes were scribbling like mad; many people were crying "Chair, Chair! Order! order!" Burgess rapped with his gavel, and said:

"Let us not forget the proprieties due. There has evidently been a mistake somewhere, but surely that is all. If Mr. Wilson gave me an envelope—and I remember now that he did—I still have it."

He took one out of his pocket, opened it, glanced at it, looked surprised and worried, and stood silent a few moments. Then he waved his hand in a wandering and mechanical way, and made an effort or two to say something, then gave it up, despondently. Several voices cried out:

"Read it! read it! What is it?"

So he began in a dazed and sleep-walker fashion:

" 'The remark which I made to the unhappy stranger was this: "You are far from being a bad man. [The house gazed at him, marveling.] Go, and reform." ' [Murmurs: "Amazing! what can this mean?"] This one," said the Chair, "is signed Thurlow G. Wilson."

"There!" cried Wilson, "I reckon that settles it! I knew perfectly well my note was purloined."

"Purloined!" retorted Billson. "I'll let you know that neither you nor any man of your kidney must venture to—"

The Chair. "Order, gentlemen, order! Take your seats, both of you, please."

They obeyed, shaking their heads and grumbling angrily. The house was profoundly puzzled; it did not know what to do with this curious emergency. Presently Thompson got up. Thompson was the hatter. He would have liked to be a Nineteener; but such was not for him: his stock of hats was not considerable enough for the position. He said:

"Mr. Chairman, if I may be permitted to make a suggestion, can both of these gentlemen be right? I put it to you, sir, can both have happened to say the very same words to the stranger? It seems to me—"

The tanner got up and interrupted him. The tanner was a disgruntled man; he believed himself entitled to be a Nineteener, but he couldn't get recognition. It made him a little unpleasant in his ways and speech. Said he:

"Sho, that's not the point! That could happen—twice in a hundred years—but not the other thing. Neither of them gave the twenty dollars!"

[A ripple of applause.]

Billson. "I did!"

Wilson. "I did!"

Then each accused the other of pilfering.

The Chair. "Order! Sit down, if you please—both of you. Neither of the notes has been out of my possession at any moment."

A Voice. "Good—that settles that!"

The Tanner. "Mr. Chairman, one thing is now plain: one of these men has been eavesdropping under the other one's bed, and filching family secrets. If it is not unparliamentary to suggest it, I will remark that both are equal to it. [The Chair. "Order! order!"] I withdraw the remark, sir, and will confine myself to suggesting that if one of them has overheard the other reveal the test-remark to this wife, we shall catch him now."

A Voice. "How?"

The Tanner. "Easily. The two have not quoted the remark in exactly the same words. You would have noticed that, if there hadn't been a considerable stretch of time and an exciting quarrel inserted between the two readings."

A Voice. "Name the difference."

The Tanner. "The word *very* is in Billson's note, and not in the other."

Many Voices. "That's so—he's right!"

The Tanner. "And so, if the Chair will examine the test-remark in the sack, we shall know which of these two frauds— [*The Chair.* "Order!"]—which of these two adventurers—[*The Chair.* "Order! order!"]—which of these two gentlemen—[*laughter and applause*]—is entitled to wear the belt as being the first dishonest blatherskite ever bred in this town—which he has dishonored, and which will be a sultry place for him from now out!" [*Vigorous applause.*]

Many Voices. "Open it!—open the sack!"

Mr. Burgess made a slit in the sack, slid his hand in and brought out an envelope. In it were a couple of folded notes. He said:

"One of these is marked, 'Not to be examined until all written communications which have been addressed to the Chair—if any—shall have been read.' The other is marked *'The Test.'* Allow me. It is worded—to wit:

" 'I do not require that the first half of the remark which was made to me by my benefactor shall be quoted with exactness, for it was not striking, and could be forgotten; but its closing fifteen words are quite striking, and I think easily rememberable; unless *these* shall be accurately reproduced, let the applicant be regarded as an impostor. My benefactor began by saying he seldom gave advice to any one, but that it always bore the hall-mark of high value when he did give it. Then he said this—and it has never faded from my memory: *"You are far from being a bad man—* " '"

Fifty Voices. "That settles it—the money's Wilson's! Wilson! Wilson! Speech! Speech!"

People jumped up and crowded around Wilson, wringing his hand and congratulating fervently—meantime the Chair was hammering with the gavel and shouting:

"Order, gentlemen! Order! Order! Let me finish reading, please." When quiet was restored, the reading was resumed—as follows:

" ' "*Go, and reform—or, mark my words—some day, for your sins, you will die and go to hell or Hadleyburg—* TRY AND MAKE IT THE FORMER." ' "

A ghastly silence followed. First an angry cloud began to settle darkly upon the faces of the citizenship; after a pause the cloud began to rise, and a tickled expression tried to take its place; tried so hard that it was only kept under with great and painful difficulty; the reporters, the Brixtonites, and other strangers bent their heads down and shielded their faces with their hands, and managed to hold in by main strength and heroic courtesy. At this most inopportune time burst upon the stillness the roar of a solitary voice —Jack Halliday's: "*That's* got the hall-mark on it!"

Then the house let go, strangers and all. Even Mr. Burgess's gravity broke down presently, then the audience considered itself officially absolved from all restraint, and it made the most of its privilege. It was a good long laugh, and a tempestuously whole-hearted one, but it ceased at last—long enough for Mr. Burgess to try to resume, and for the people to get their eyes partially wiped; then it broke out again; and afterward yet again; then at last Burgess was able to get out these serious words:

"It is useless to try to disguise the fact—we find ourselves in the presence of a matter of grave import. It involves the honor of your town, it strikes at the town's good name. The difference of a single word between the test-remarks offered by Mr. Wilson and Mr. Billson was itself a serious thing, since it indicated that one or the other of these gentlemen had committed a theft—"

The two men were sitting limp, nerveless, crushed; but at these words both were electrified into movement, and started to get up—

"Sit down!" said the Chair, sharply, and they obeyed. "That, as I have said, was a serious thing. And it was—but for only one of them. But the matter has become graver; for the honor of *both* is now in formidable peril. Shall I go even further, and say in inextricable peril? *Both* left out the crucial fifteen words." He paused. During several moments he allowed the pervading stillness to gather and deepen its impressive effects, then added: "There would seem to be but one way whereby this could happen. I ask these gentlemen—Was there *collusion?—agreement?*"

A low murmur sifted through the house; its import was, "He's got them both."

Billson was not used to emergencies; he sat in a helpless collapse. But Wilson was a lawyer. He struggled to his feet, pale and worried, and said:

"I ask the indulgence of the house while I explain this most painful matter. I am sorry to say what I am about to say, since it must inflict irreparable injury upon Mr. Billson, whom I have always esteemed and respected until now, and in whose invulnerability to temptation I entirely believed—as did you all. But for the preservation of my own honor I must speak—and with frankness. I confess with shame—and I now beseech your pardon for it—that I said to the ruined stranger all of the words contained in the test-remark, including the disparaging fifteen. [*Sensation.*] When the late publication was made I recalled them, and I resolved to claim the sack of coin, for by every right I was entitled to it. Now I will ask you to consider this point, and weigh it well: that stranger's gratitude to me that night knew no bounds; he said himself that he could find no words for it that were adequate, and that if he should ever be able he would repay me a thousand fold. Now, then, I ask you this: Could I expect—could I believe—could I even remotely imagine—that, feeling as he did, he would do so ungrateful a thing as to add those quite unnecessary fifteen words to his test?—set a trap for me?— expose me as a slanderer of my own town before my own people assembled in a public hall? It was preposterous; it was impossible. His test would contain only the kindly opening clause of my remark. Of that I had no shadow of doubt. You would have thought as I did. You would not have expected a base betrayal from one whom you had befriended and against whom you had committed no offense. And so, with perfect confidence, perfect trust, I wrote on a piece of paper the opening words—ending with 'Go, and reform,'—and signed it. When I was about to put it in an envelope I was called into my back office, and without thinking I left the paper lying open on my desk." He stopped, turned his head slowly toward Billson, waited a moment, then added: "I ask you to note this: when I returned, a little later, Mr. Billson was retiring by my street door." [*Sensation.*]

In a moment Billson was on his feet and shouting:

"It's a lie! It's an infamous lie!"

The Chair. "Be seated, sir! Mr. Wilson has the floor."

Billson's friends pulled him into his seat and quieted him, and Wilson went on:

"Those are the simple facts. My note was now lying in a different place on the table from where I had left it. I noticed that, but attached no importance to it, thinking a draught had blown it there. That Mr. Billson would read a private paper was a thing which could not occur to me; he was an honorable man, and he would be above that. If you will allow me to say it, I think his extra word *'very'* stands explained; it is attributable to a defect of memory. I was the only man in the world who could furnish here any detail of the test-remark—by *honorable* means. I have finished."

There is nothing in the world like a persuasive speech to fuddle the mental apparatus and upset the convictions and debauch the emotions of an audience not practiced in the tricks and delusions of oratory. Wilson sat down victorious. The house submerged him in tides of approving applause; friends swarmed to him and shook him by the hand and congratulated him, and Billson was shouted down and not allowed to say a word. The Chair hammered and hammered with its gavel, and kept shouting,

"But let us proceed, gentlemen, let us proceed!"

At last there was a measurable degree of quiet, and the hatter said:

"But what is there to proceed with, sir, but to deliver the money?"

Voices. "That's it! That's it! come forward, Wilson!"

The Hatter. "I move three cheers for Mr. Wilson, Symbol of the special virtue which—"

The cheers burst forth before he could finish; and in the midst of them—and in the midst of the clamor of the gavel also—some enthusiasts mounted Wilson on a big friend's shoulder and were going to fetch him in triumph to the platform. The Chair's voice now rose above the noise—

"Order! To your places! You forget that there is still a document to be read." When quiet had been restored he took up the document, and was going to read it, but laid it down again, saying, "I forgot; this is not to be read until all written communications received by me have first been read." He took an envelope out of his pocket, removed its enclosure, glanced at it—seemed astonished—held it out and gazed at it—stared at it.

Twenty or thirty voices cried out:

"What is it? Read it! read it!"

And he did—slowly, and wondering:

"'The remark which I made to the stranger—[*Voices*. "Hello! how's this?"]—was this: "You are far from being a bad man. [*Voices*. "Great Scott!"] Go, and reform."' [*Voice*. "Oh, saw my leg off!"] Signed by Mr. Pinkerton the banker.'"

The pandemonium of delight which turned itself loose now was of a sort to make the judicious weep. Those whose withers were unwrung laughed till the tears ran down; the reporters, in throes of laughter, set down disordered pot-hooks which would never in the world be decipherable; and a sleeping dog jumped up, scared out of its wits, and barked itself crazy at the turmoil. All manner of cries were scattered through the din: "We're getting rich—*two* Symbols of Incorruptibility!—without counting Billson!" "*Three!*—count Shadbelly in—we can't have too many!" "All right—Billson's elected!" "Alas, poor Wilson—victim of *two* thieves!"

A Powerful Voice. "Silence! The Chair's fished up something more out of its pocket."

Voices. "Hurrah! Is it something fresh? Read it! read! read!"

The Chair [*reading*.] "'The remark which I made,' etc.: "You are far from being a bad man. Go," etc. Signed, "Gregory Yates."'"

Tornado of Voices. "Four Symbols!" "'Rah for Yates!" "Fish again!"

The house was in a roaring humor now, and ready to get all the fun out of the occasion that might be in it. Several Nineteeners, looking pale and distressed, got up and began to work their way toward the aisles, but a score of shouts went up:

"The doors, the doors—close the doors; no Incorruptible shall leave this place! Sit down, everybody!"

The mandate was obeyed.

"Fish again! Read! read!"

The Chair fished again, and once more the familiar words began to fall from its lips— "'You are far from being a bad man—'"

"Name! name! What's his name?"

"'L. Ingoldsby Sargent.'"

"Five elected! Pile up the Symbols! Go on, go on!"

"'You are far from being a bad—'"

"Name! name!"

"'Nicholas Whitworth.'"

"Hooray! hooray! it's a symbolical day!"

Somebody wailed in, and began to sing this rhyme (leaving out "it's") to the lovely "Mikado" tune of "When a man's afraid, a beautiful maid—"; the audience joined in, with joy; then, just in time, somebody contributed another line—

"And don't you this forget—"

The house roared it out. A third line was at once furnished—

"Corruptibles far from Hadleyburg are—"

The house roared that one too. As the last note died, Jack Halliday's voice rose high and clear, freighted with a final line—

"But the Symbols are here, you bet!"

That was sung, with booming enthusiasm. Then the happy house started in at the beginning and sang the four lines through twice, with immense swing and dash, and finished up with a crashing three-times-three and a tiger for "Hadleyburg the Incorruptible and all Symbols of it which we shall find worthy to receive the hall-mark to-night."

Then the shoutings at the Chair began again, all over the place:

"Go on! go on! Read! read some more! Read all you've got!"

"That's it— go on! We are winning eternal celebrity!"

A dozen men got up now and began to protest. They said that this farce was the work of some abandoned joker, and was an insult to the whole community. Without a doubt these signatures were all forgeries—

"Sit down! sit down! Shut up! You are confessing. We'll find *your* names in the lot."

"Mr. Chairman, how many of those envelopes have you got?"

The Chair counted.

"Together with those that have been already examined, there are nineteen."

A storm of derisive applause broke out.

"Perhaps they all contain the secret. I move that you open them all and read every signature that is attached to a note of that sort—and read also the first eight words of the note."

"Second the motion!"

It was put and carried—uproariously. Then poor old Richards got up, and his wife rose and stood at his side. Her head was bent down, so that none might see that she was crying. Her husband gave her his arm, and so supporting her, he began to speak in a quavering voice:

"My friends, you have known us two—Mary and me—all our lives, and I think you have liked us and respected us—"

The Chair interrupted him:

"Allow me. It is quite true—that which you are saying, Mr. Richards— this town *does* know you two; it *does* like you; it *does* respect you; more—it honors you and *loves* you—"

Halliday's voice rang out:

"That's the hall-marked truth, too! If the Chair is right, let the house speak up and say it. Rise! Now, then—hip! hip! hip!—all together!"

The house rose in mass, faced toward the old couple eagerly, filled the air with a snowstorm of waving handkerchiefs, and delivered the cheers with all its affectionate heart.

The Chair then continued:

"What I was going to say is this: We know your good heart, Mr. Richards, but this is not a time for the exercise of charity toward offenders. [*Shouts of "Right! right!"*] I see your generous purpose in your face, but I cannot allow you to plead for these men—"

"But I was going to—"

"Please take your seat, Mr. Richards. We must examine the rest of these notes—simple fairness to the men who have already been exposed requires this. As soon as that has been done—I give you my word for this—you shall be heard."

Many Voices. "Right!—the Chair is right—no interruption can be permitted at this stage! Go on!—the names! the names!—according to the terms of the motion!"

The old couple sat reluctantly down, and the husband whispered to the wife, "It is pitifully hard to have to wait; the shame will be greater than ever when they find we were only going to plead for *ourselves.*"

Straightway the jollity broke loose again with the reading of the names.

"'You are far from being a bad man—' Signature, 'Robert J. Titmarsh.'

"'You are far from being a bad man—' Signature, 'Eliphalet Weeks.'

"'You are far from being a bad man—' Signature, 'Oscar B. Wilder.'"

At this point the house lit upon the idea of taking the eight words out of the Chairman's hands. He was not unthankful for that. Thenceforward he held up each note in its turn, and waited. The house droned out the eight words in a massed and measured and musical deep volume of sound (with a daringly close resemblance to a well-known church chant)—"'You are f-a-r from being a b-a-a-a-d man.'" Then the Chair said, "Signature, 'Archibald Wilcox.'" And so on, and so on, name after name, and everybody had an increasingly and gloriously good time except the wretched Nineteen. Now and then, when a particularly shining name was called, the house made the Chair wait while it chanted the whole of the test-remark from the beginning to the closing words, "And go to hell or Hadleyburg—try and make it the for-or-m-e-r!" and in these special cases they added a grand and agonized and imposing "A-a-a-a-*men!*"

The list dwindled, dwindled, dwindled, poor old Richards keeping tally of the count, wincing when a name resembling his own was pronounced, and waiting in miserable suspense for the time to come when it would be his humiliating privilege to rise with Mary and finish his plea, which he was intending to word thus: ". . . for until now we have never done any wrong thing, but have gone our humble way unreproached. We are very poor, we are old, and have no chick nor child to help us; we were sorely tempted, and we fell. It was my purpose when I got up before to make confession and beg that my name might not be read out in this public place, for it seemed to us that we could not bear it; but I was prevented. It was just; it was our place to suffer with the rest. It has been hard for us. It is the first time we have ever heard our name fall from any one's lips—sullied. Be merciful—for the sake of the better days; make our shame as light to bear as in your charity you can." At this point in his revery Mary nudged him, perceiving that his mind was absent. The house was chanting, "You are f-a-r," etc.

"Be ready," Mary whispered. "Your name comes now; he has read eighteen."

The chant ended.

"Next! next! next!" came volleying from all over the house.

Burgess put his hand into his pocket. The old couple, trembling, began to rise. Burgess fumbled a moment, then said,

"I find I have read them all."

Faint with joy and surprise, the couple sank into their seats, and Mary whispered,

"Oh, bless God, we are saved!—he has lost ours—I wouldn't give this for a hundred of those sacks!"

The house burst out with its "Mikado" travesty, and sang it three times with ever-increasing enthusiasm, rising to its feet when it reached for the third time the closing line—

> "But the Symbols are here, you bet!"

and finishing up with cheers and a tiger for "Hadleyburg purity and our eighteen immortal representatives of it."

Then Wingate, the saddler, got up and proposed cheers "for the cleanest man in town, the one solitary important citizen in it who didn't try to steal that money—Edward Richards."

They were given with great and moving heartiness; then somebody proposed that Richards be elected sole guardian and Symbol of the now Sacred Hadleyburg Tradition, with power and right to stand up and look the whole sarcastic world in the face.

Passed, by acclamation; then they sang the "Mikado" again, and ended it with,

> "And there's *one* Symbol left, you bet!"

There was a pause; then—

A Voice. "Now, then, who's to get the sack?"

The Tanner (with bitter sarcasm). "That's easy. The money has to be divided among the eighteen Incorruptibles. They gave the suffering stranger twenty dollars apiece—and that remark—each in his turn—it took twenty-two minutes for the procession to move past. Staked the stranger—total contribution, $360. All they want is just the loan back—and interest—forty thousand dollars altogether."

Many Voices [derisively.] "That's it! Divvy! divvy! Be kind to the poor—don't keep them waiting!"

The Chair. "Order! I now offer the stranger's remaining document. It says: 'If no claimant shall appear [*grand chorus of groans*], I desire that you open the sack and count out the money to the principal citizens of your town, they to take it in trust [*cries of "Oh! Oh! Oh!"*], and use it in such ways as to them shall seem best for the propagation and preservation of your community's noble reputation for incorruptible honesty [*more cries*]—a reputation to which their names and their efforts will add a new and far-reaching lustre.' [*Enthusiastic outburst of sarcastic applause.*] That seems to be all. No—here is a postscript:

"'P.S.—CITIZENS OF HADLEYBURG: There *is* no test-remark—nobody made one. [*Great sensation.*] There wasn't any pauper stranger, nor any twenty-dollar contribution, nor any accompanying benediction and compliment—these are all inventions. [*General buzz and hum of astonishment and delight.*] Allow me to tell my story—it will take but a word or two. I passed through your town at a certain time, and received a deep offense which I had not earned. Any other man would have been content to kill one or two of you and call it square, but to me that would have been a trivial revenge, and inadequate; for the dead do not *suffer.* Besides, I could not kill you all—and, anyway, made as I am, even that would not have satisfied me. I wanted to damage every man in the place, and every woman—and not in their bodies or in their estate, but in their vanity—the place where feeble and foolish people are most vulnerable. So I disguised myself and came back and studied you. You were easy game. You had an old and lofty reputation for honesty, and naturally you were proud of it—it was your treasure of treasures, the very apple of your eye. As soon as I found out that you carefully and vigilantly kept yourselves and your children *out of temptation,* I knew how to proceed. Why, you simple creatures, the weakest of all weak things is a virtue which has not been tested in the fire. I laid a plan, and gathered a list of names. My project was to corrupt Hadleyburg the Incorruptible. My idea was to make liars and thieves of nearly half a hundred smirchless men and women who had never in their lives uttered a lie or stolen a penny. I was afraid of Goodson. He was neither born nor reared in Hadleyburg. I was afraid that if I started to operate my scheme by getting my letter laid before you, you would say to yourselves, "Goodson is the only man among us who would give away twenty dollars to a poor devil"—and then you might not bite at my bait. But Heaven took Goodson; then I knew I was safe, and I set my trap and baited it. It may be that I shall not catch all the men to whom I mailed the pretended test secret, but I shall catch the most of them, if I knew Hadleyburg nature. [*Voices.* "Right—he got every last one of them."] I believe they will even steal ostensible *gamble*-money, rather than miss, poor, tempted, and mistrained fellows. I am hoping to eternally and everlastingly squelch your vanity and give Hadleyburg a new renown—one that will *stick*—and spread far. If I have succeeded, open the sack and summon the Committee on Propagation and Preservation of the Hadleyburg Reputation.'"

A Cyclone of Voices. "Open it! Open it! The Eighteen to the front! Committee on Propagation of the Tradition! Forward—the Incorruptibles!"

The Chair ripped the sack wide, and gathered up a handful of bright, broad, yellow coins, shook them together, then examined them—

"Friends, they are only gilded disks of lead!"

There was a crashing outbreak of delight over this news, and when the noise had subsided, the tanner called out:

"By right of apparent seniority in this business, Mr. Wilson is Chairman of the Committee on Propagation of the Tradition. I suggest that he step forward on behalf of his pals, and receive in trust the money."

A Hundred Voices. "Wilson! Wilson! Wilson! Speech! Speech!"

Wilson [*in a voice trembling with anger.*] "You will allow me to say, and without apologies for my language, *damn* the money!"

A Voice. "Oh, and him a Baptist!"

A Voice. "Seventeen Symbols left! Step up, gentlemen, and assume your trust!"

There was a pause—no response.

The Saddler. "Mr. Chairman, we've got *one* clean man left, anyway, out of the late aristocracy; and he needs money, and deserves it. I move that you appoint Jack Halliday to get up there and auction off that sack of gilt twenty-dollar pieces, and give the result to the right man—the man whom Hadleyburg delights to honor—Edward Richards."

This was received with great enthusiasm, the dog taking a hand again; the saddler started the bids at a dollar, the Brixton folk and Barnum's representative fought hard for it, the people cheered every jump that the bids made, the excitement climbed moment by moment higher and higher, the bidders got on their mettle and grew steadily more and more daring, more and more determined, the jumps went from a dollar up to five, then to ten, then to twenty, then fifty, then to a hundred, then—

At the beginning of the auction Richards whispered in distress to his wife: "O Mary, can we allow it? It—it—you see, it is an honor-reward, a testimonial to purity of character, and—and—can we allow it? Hadn't I better get up and—O Mary, what ought we to do? —what do you think we— [*Halliday's voice. "Fifteen I'm bid!—fifteen for the sack!—twenty!—ah, thanks!—thirty—thanks again! Thirty, thirty, thirty!—do I hear forty?—forty it is! Keep the ball rolling, gentlemen, keep it rolling!—fifty!—thanks, noble Roman! going at fifty, fifty, fifty!—seventy!—ninety!—splendid!—a hundred!—pile it up, pile it up!—hundred and twenty—forty!—just in time!—hundred and fifty!—TWO hundred!—superb! Do I hear two h—thanks!two hundred and fifty!—"*]

"It is another temptation, Edward—I'm all in a tremble—but, oh, we've escaped *one* temptation, and that ought to warn us to— [*"Six did I hear?—thanks!—six fifty, six f—*SEVEN *hundred!"*] And yet, Edward, when you think—nobody susp— [*"Eight hundred dollars!—hurrah!—make it nine!—Mr. Parsons, did I hear you say —thanks—nine!—this noble sack of virgin lead going at only nine hundred dollars, gilding and all—come! do I hear—a thousand!—gratefully yours!—did some one say eleven?—a sack which is going to be the most celebrated in the whole Uni—"*] O Edward" (beginning to sob), "we are *so* poor!—but—but—do as you think best—do as you think best."

Edward fell—that is, he sat still; sat with a conscience which was not satisfied, but which was overpowered by circumstances.

Meantime a stranger, who looked like an amateur detective gotten up as an impossible English earl, had been watching the evening's proceedings with manifest interest, and with a contented expression in his face; and he had been privately commenting to himself. He was now soliloquizing somewhat like this: "None of the Eighteen are bidding; that is not satisfactory; I must change that—the dramatic unities require it; they must buy the sack they tried to steal; they must pay a heavy price, too—some of them are rich. And another thing, when I make a mistake in Hadleyburg nature the man that puts that error upon me is entitled to a high honorarium, and some one must pay it. This poor old Richards has brought my judgment to shame; he is an honest man:—I don't understand it, but I acknowledge it. Yes, he saw my deuces *and* with a straight flush, and by rights the pot is his. And it shall be a jack-pot, too, if I can manage it. He disappointed me, but let that pass."

He was watching the bidding. At a thousand, the market broke; the prices tumbled swiftly. He waited—and still watched. One competitor dropped out; then another, and another. He put in a bid or two, now. When the bids had sunk to ten dollars, he added a five; some one raised him a three; he waited a moment, then flung in a fifty-dollar jump, and the sack was his—at $1,282. The house broke out in cheers—then stopped; for he was on his feet, and had lifted his hand. He began to speak.

"I desire to say a word, and ask a favor. I am a speculator in rarities, and I have dealings with persons interested in numismatics all over the world. I can make a profit on this purchase, just as it stands; but there is a way, if I can get your approval, whereby I can make every one of these leaden twenty-dollar pieces worth its face in gold, and perhaps more. Grant me that approval, and I will give part of my gains to your Mr. Richards, whose invulnerable probity you have so justly and so cordially recognized to-night; his share shall be ten thousand dollars, and I will hand him the money to-morrow. [*Great applause from the house.* But the "invulnerable probity" made the Richardses blush prettily; however, it went for modesty, and did no harm.] If you will pass my proposition by a good majority —I would like a two-thirds vote—I will regard that as the town's consent, and that is all I ask. Rarities are always helped by any device which will rouse curiosity and compel remark. Now if I may have your permission to stamp upon the faces of each of these ostensible coins the names of the eighteen gentlemen who—"

Nine-tenths of the audience were on their feet in a moment—dog and all—and the proposition was carried with a whirlwind of approving applause and laughter.

They sat down, and all the Symbols except "Dr." Clay Harkness got up, violently protesting against the proposed outrage, and threatening to—

"I beg you not to threaten me," said the stranger, calmly. "I know my legal rights, and am not accustomed to being frightened at bluster." [*Applause.*] He sat down. "Dr." Harkness saw an opportunity here. He was one of the two very rich men of the place, and Pinkerton was the other. Harkness was proprietor of a mint; that is to say, a popular patent medicine. He was running for the Legislature on one ticket, and Pinkerton on the other. It was a close race and a hot one, and getting hotter every day. Both had strong appetites for money; each had bought a great tract of land, with a purpose; there was going to be a new railway, and each wanted to be in the Legislature and help locate the route to his own advantage; a single vote might make the decision, and with it two or three fortunes. The stake was large, and Harkness was a daring speculator. He was sitting close to the stranger. He leaned over while one or another of the other Symbols was entertaining the house with protests and appeals, and asked, in a whisper,

"What is your price for the sack?"

"Forty thousand dollars."

"I'll give you twenty."

"No."

"Twenty-five."

"No."

"Say thirty."

"The price is forty thousand dollars; not a penny less."

"All right, I'll give it. I will come to the hotel at ten in the morning. I don't want it known; will see you privately."

"Very good." Then the stranger got up and said to the house:

"I find it late. The speeches of these gentlemen are not without merit, not without interest, not without grace; yet if I may be excused I will take my leave. I thank you for the great favor which you have shown me in granting my petition. I ask the Chair to keep the sack for me until to-morrow, and to hand these three five-hundred-dollar notes to Mr. Richards." They were passed up to the Chair. "At nine I will call for the sack, and at eleven will deliver the rest of the ten thousand to Mr. Richards in person, at his home. Good night."

Then he slipped out, and left the audience making a vast noise, which was composed of a mixture of cheers, the "Mikado" song, dog-disapproval, and the chant, "You are f-a-r-from being a b-a-a-d man—a-a-a-a-men!"

IV

At home the Richardses had to endure congratulations and compliments until midnight. Then they were left to themselves. They looked a little sad, and they sat silent and thinking. Finally Mary sighed and said,

"Do you think we are to blame, Edward—*much* to blame?" and her eyes wandered to the accusing triplet of big bank notes lying on the table, where the congratulators had been gloating over them and reverently fingering them. Edward did not answer at once; then he brought out a sigh and said, hesitatingly:

"We—we couldn't help it, Mary. It—well, it was ordered. *All* things are."

Mary glanced up and looked at him steadily, but he didn't return the look. Presently she said:

"I thought congratulations and praises always tasted good. But— it seems to me, now—Edward?"

"Well?"

"Are you going to stay in the bank?"

"N-no."

"Resign?"

"In the morning—by note."

"It does seem best."

Richards bowed his head in his hands and muttered:

"Before, I was not afraid to let oceans of people's money pour through my hands, but—Mary, I am so tired, so tired—"

"We will go to bed."

At nine in the morning the stranger called for the sack and took it to the hotel in a cab. At ten Harkness had a talk with him privately. The stranger asked for and got five checks on a metropolitan bank— drawn to "Bearer,"—four for $1,500 each, and one for $34,000. He put one of the former in his pocketbook, and the remainder, representing $38,500, he put in an envelope, and with these he added a note, which he wrote after Harkness was gone. At eleven he called at the Richards house and knocked. Mrs. Richards peeped through the shutters, then went and received the envelope, and the stranger disappeared without a word. She came back flushed and a little unsteady on her legs, and gasped out:

"I am sure I recognized him! Last night it seemed to me that maybe I had seen him somewhere before."

"He is the man that brought the sack here?"

"I am almost sure of it."

"Then he is the ostensible Stephenson, too, and sold every important citizen in this town with his bogus secret. Now if he has sent checks instead of money, we are sold, too, after we thought we had escaped. I was beginning to feel fairly comfortable once more, after my night's rest, but the look of that envelope makes me sick. It isn't fat enough; $8,500 in even the largest bank notes makes more bulk than that."

"Checks signed by Stephenson! I am resigned to take the $8,500 if it could come in bank notes—for it does seem that it was so ordered, Mary—but I have never had much courage, and I have not the pluck to try to market a check signed with that disastrous name. It would be a trap. That man tried to catch me; we escaped somehow or other; and now he is trying a new way. If it is checks—"

"Oh, Edward, it is *too* bad!" and she held up the checks and began to cry.

"Put them in the fire! quick! we mustn't be tempted. It is a trick to make the world laugh at *us*, along with the rest, and— Give them to *me*, since you can't do it!" He snatched them and tried to hold his grip till he could get to the stove; but he was human, he was a cashier, and he stopped a moment to make sure of the signature. Then he came near to fainting.

"Fan me, Mary, fan me! They are the same as gold!"

"Oh, how lovely, Edward! Why?"

"Signed by Harkness. What can the mystery of that be, Mary?"

"Edward, do you think—"

"Look here—look at this! Fifteen—fifteen—fifteen—thirty-four. Thirty-eight thousand five hundred! Mary, the sack isn't worth twelve dollars, and Harkness—apparently—has paid about par for it."

"And does it all come to us, do you think—instead of the ten thousand?"

"Why, it looks like it. And the checks are made to 'Bearer,' too."

"Is that good, Edward? What is it for?"

"A hint to collect them at some distant bank, I reckon. Perhaps Harkness doesn't want the matter known. What is that—a note?"

"Yes. It was with the checks."

It was in the "Stephenson" handwriting, but there was no signature. It said:

"I am a disappointed man. Your honesty is beyond the reach of temptation. I had a different idea about it, but I wronged you in that, and I beg pardon, and do it sincerely. I honor you—and that is sincere too. This town is not worthy to kiss the hem of your garment. Dear sir, I made a square bet with myself that there were nineteen debauchable men in your self-righteous community. I have lost. Take the whole pot, you are entitled to it."

Richards drew a deep sigh, and said:

"It seems written with fire—it burns so. Mary—I am miserable again."

"I, too. Ah, dear, I wish—"

"To think, Mary—he *believes* in me."

"Oh, don't, Edward—I can't bear it."

"If those beautiful words were deserved, Mary—and God knows I believed I deserved them once—I think I could give the forty thousand dollars for them. And I would put that paper away, as representing more than gold and jewels, and keep it always. But now —We could not live in the shadow of its accusing presence, Mary."

He put it in the fire.

A messenger arrived and delivered an envelope.

Richards took from it a note and read it; it was from Burgess.

"You saved me, in a difficult time. I saved you last night. It was at cost of a lie, but I made the sacrifice freely, and out of a grateful heart. None in this village knows so well as I know how brave and good and noble you are. At bottom you cannot respect me, knowing as you do of that matter of which I am accused, and by the general voice condemned; but I beg that you will at least believe that I am a grateful man; it will help me to bear my burden.
[*Signed*] "BURGESS."

"Saved, once more. And on such terms!" He put the note in the fire. "I—I wish I were dead, Mary, I wish I were out of it all."

"Oh, these are bitter, bitter days, Edward. The stabs, through their very generosity, are so deep—and they come so fast!"

Three days before the election each of two thousand voters suddenly found himself in possession of a prized memento—one of the renowned bogus double-eagles. Around one of its faces was stamped these words: "THE REMARK I MADE TO THE POOR STRANGER WAS—" Around the other face was stamped these: "GO, AND REFORM. [SIGNED] PINKERTON." Thus the entire remaining refuse of the renowned joke was emptied upon a single head, and with calamitous effect. It revived the recent vast laugh and concentrated it upon Pinkerton; and Harkness's election was a walkover.

Within twenty-four hours after the Richardses had received their checks their consciences were quieting down, discouraged; the old couple were learning to reconcile themselves to the sin which they had now committed. But they were to learn, now, that a sin takes on new and real terrors when there seems a chance that it is going to be found out. This gives it a fresh and most substantial and important aspect. At church the morning sermon was of the usual pattern; it was the same old things said in the same old way; they had heard them a thousand times and found them innocuous, next to meaningless, and easy to sleep under; but now it was different: the sermon seemed to bristle with accusation; it seemed aimed straight and specially at people who were concealing deadly sins. After church they got away from the mob of congratulators as soon as they could, and hurried homeward, chilled to the bone at they did not know what—vague, shadowy, indefinite fears. And by chance they caught a glimpse of attention to their nod of recognition! He hadn't seen it; but they did not know that. What could his conduct mean? It might mean—it might mean—oh, a dozen dreadful things. Was it possible that he knew that Richards could have cleared him of guilt in that bygone time, and had been silently waiting for a chance to even up accounts? At home, in their distress they got to imagining that their servant might have been in the next room listening when Richards revealed the secret to his wife that he knew of Burgess's innocence; next, Richards began to imagine that he had heard the swish of a gown in there at that time; next, he was sure he *had* heard it. They would call Sarah in, on a pretext, and watch her face; if she had been betraying them to Mr. Burgess, it would show in her manner. They asked her some questions—questions which were so random and incoherent and seemingly purposeless that the girl felt sure that the old people's minds had been affected by their sudden good fortune; the sharp and watchful gaze which they bent upon her frightened her, and that completed the business. She blushed, she became nervous and confused, and to the old people these were plain signs of guilt—guilt of some fearful sort or other—without doubt she was a spy and a traitor. When they were alone again they began to piece many unrelated things together and get horrible results out of the combination. When things had got about to the worst, Richards was delivered of a sudden gasp, and his wife asked,

"Oh, what is it?—what is it?"

"The note—Burgess's note! Its language was sarcastic, I see it now." He quoted: "'At bottom you cannot respect me, *knowing,* as you do, of *that matter* of which I am accused'—oh, it is perfectly plain, now, God help me! He knows that I know! You see the ingenuity of the phrasing. It was a trap—and like a fool, I walked into it. And Mary—?"

"Oh, it is dreadful—I know what you are going to say—he didn't return your transcript of the pretended test-remark."

"No—kept it to destroy us with. Mary, he has exposed us to some already. I know it—I know it well. I saw it in a dozen faces after church. Ah, he wouldn't answer our nod of recognition—*he* knew what he had been doing!"

In the night the doctor was called. The news went around in the morning that the old couple were rather seriously ill—prostrated by the exhausting excitement growing out of their great windfall, the congratulations, and the late hours, the doctor said. The town was sincerely distressed; for these old people were about all it had left to be proud of, now.

Two days later the news was worse. The old couple were delirious, and were doing strange things. By witness of the nurses, Richards had exhibited checks—for $8,500? No—for an amazing sum— $38,500! What could be the explanation of this gigantic piece of luck?

The following day the nurses had more news—and wonderful. They had concluded to hide the checks, lest harm come to them; but when they searched they were gone from under the patient's pillow— vanished away. The patient said:

"Let the pillow alone; what do you want?"

"We thought it best that the checks—"

"You will never see them again—they are destroyed. They came from Satan. I saw the hell-brand on them, and I knew they were sent to betray me to sin." Then he fell to gabbling strange and dreadful things which were not clearly understandable, and which the doctor admonished them to keep to themselves.

Richards was right; the checks were never seen again.

A nurse must have talked in her sleep, for within two days the forbidden gabblings were the property of the town; and they were of a surprising sort. They seemed to indicate that Richards had been a claimant for the sack himself, and that Burgess had concealed that fact and then maliciously betrayed it.

Burgess was taxed with this and stoutly denied it. And he said it was not fair to attach weight to the chatter of a sick old man who was out of his mind. Still, suspicion was in the air, and there was much talk.

After a day or two it was reported that Mrs. Richards's delirious deliveries were getting to be duplicates of her husband's. Suspicion flamed up into conviction, now, and the town's pride in the purity of its one undiscredited important citizen began to dim down and flicker toward extinction.

Six days passed, then came more news. The old couple were dying. Richards's mind cleared in his latest hour, and he sent for Burgess. Burgess said:

"Let the room be cleared. I think he wishes to say something in privacy."

"No!" said Richards: "I want witnesses. I want you all to hear my confession, so that I may die a man, and not a dog. I was clean—artificially—like the rest; and like the rest I fell when temptation came. I signed a lie, and claimed the miserable sack. Mr. Burgess remembered that I had done him a service, and in gratitude (and ignorance) he suppressed my claim and saved me. You know the thing that was charged against Burgess years ago. My testimony, and mine alone, could have cleared him, and I was a coward, and left him to suffer disgrace—"

"No—no—Mr. Richards, you—"

"My servant betrayed my secret to him—"

"No one has betrayed anything to me—"

—"and then he did a natural and justifiable thing, he repented of the saving kindness which he had done me, and he *exposed* me—as I deserved—"

"Never!—I make oath—"

"Out of my heart I forgive him."

Burgess's impassioned protestation fell upon deaf ears; the dying man passed away without knowing that once more he had done poor Burgess a wrong. The old wife died that night.

The last of the sacred Nineteen had fallen a prey to the fiendish sack; the town was stripped of the last rag of its ancient glory. Its mourning was not showy, but it was deep.

By act of the Legislature—upon prayer and petition—Hadleyburg was allowed to change its name to (never mind what—I will not give it away), and leave one word out of the motto that for many generations had graced the town's official seal.

It is an honest town once more, and the man will have to rise early that catches it napping again.

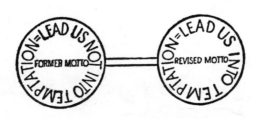